BARNABY RUDGE

Editor's Note

Barnaby Rudge *is a tale of the "Gordon" or "No Popery" riots of 1780 in London. It was the first important work in which Dickens described life and characters not of his own time; and the riot scenes, which make such vivid reading, follow closely the historical records except in one respect: Dennis the hangman was really condemned to death; but he is missing from the lists of those actually hanged, and is believed to have been reprieved. In the story, he is dragged to the scaffold, a very poltroon. Perhaps the only character identifiable as having close personal association with Dickens is that important one— Grip. He was drawn from two ravens that the author successively owned, the first of which—as he was dying—uttered his favourite expression: "Hulloa, old girl!" For biographical details (additional to those in the novel) about this raven and his successor-in-sin, the reader should on no account miss Dickens's Preface. Edgar Allan Poe, the Master of mysteries, unravelled the plot of* Barnaby Rudge *from the earliest numbers published serially in 1841 before the full development of the story was known. Wilkie Collins considered it the weakest book that Dickens ever wrote. Bulwer-Lytton thought that the author had done nothing finer in point of art. And the public has always gratefully accepted the novel as being between these two extremes of critical valuation. This edition is printed from the one carefully corrected by Dickens in 1867-1868.*

Barnaby Arrives upon the Scene.

BARNABY RUDGE

A TALE OF THE RIOTS OF 'EIGHTY

BY

CHARLES DICKENS

ILLUSTRATED BY
HABLOT K. BROWNE
(PHIZ)

LONDON:
HAZELL, WATSON & VINEY, LTD.

PREFACE

THE late Mr. Waterton having, some time ago, expressed his opinion that ravens are gradually becoming extinct in England, I offered the few following words about my experience of these birds.

The raven in this story is a compound of two great originals, of whom I was, at different times, the proud possessor. The first was in the bloom of his youth, when he was discovered in a modest retirement in London, by a friend of mine, and given to me. He had from the first, as Sir Hugh Evans says of Anne Page, "good gifts," which he improved by study and attention in a most exemplary manner. He slept in a stable—generally on horseback—and so terrified a Newfoundland dog by his preternatural sagacity, that he has been known, by the mere superiority of his genius, to walk off unmolested with the dog's dinner, from before his face. He was rapidly rising in acquirements and virtues, when, in an evil hour, his stable was newly painted. He observed the workmen closely, saw that they were careful of the paint, and immediately burned to possess it. On their going to dinner, he ate up all they had left behind, consisting of a pound or two of white lead; and this youthful indiscretion terminated in death.

While I was yet inconsolable for his loss, another friend of mine in Yorkshire discovered an older and more gifted raven at a village public-house, which he prevailed upon the landlord to part with for a consideration, and sent up to me. The first act of this Sage, was, to administer to the effects of his predecessor, by disinterring all the cheese and halfpence he had buried in the garden—a work of immense labour and research, to which he devoted all the energies of his mind. When he had achieved his task, he applied himself to the acquisition of stable language, in which he soon became such an adept, that he

would perch outside my window and drive imaginary horses with
great skill, all day. Perhaps even I never saw him at his best, for his
former master sent his duty with him, "and if I wished the bird to
come out very strong, would I be so good as to show him a drunken
man"—which I never did, having (unfortunately) none but sober
people at hand. But I could hardly have respected him more, whatever the stimulating influences of this sight might have been. He
had not the least respect, I am sorry to say, for me in return, or for
anybody but the cook; to whom he was attached—but only, I fear,
as a Policeman might have been. Once, I met him unexpectedly,
about half-a-mile from my house, walking down the middle of a
public street, attended by a pretty large crowd, and spontaneously
exhibiting the whole of his accomplishments. His gravity under
those trying circumstances, I can never forget, nor the extraordinary gallantry with which, refusing to be brought home, he
defended himself behind a pump, until overpowered by numbers.
It may have been that he was too bright a genius to live long, or
it may have been that he took some pernicious substance into his bill,
and thence into his maw—which is not improbable, seeing that he
new-pointed the greater part of the garden-wall by digging out the
mortar, broke countless squares of glass by scraping away the putty
all round the frames, and tore up and swallowed, in splinters, the
greater part of a wooden staircase of six steps and a landing—but
after some three years he too was taken ill, and died before the
kitchen fire. He kept his eye to the last upon the meat as it roasted,
and suddenly turned over on his back with a sepulchral cry of
"Cuckoo!" Since then I have been ravenless.

No account of the Gordon Riots having been to my knowledge
introduced into any Work of Fiction, and the subject presenting
very extraordinary and remarkable features, I was led to project
this Tale.

It is unnecessary to say, that those shameful tumults, while they
reflect indelible disgrace upon the time in which they occurred, and
all who had act or part in them, teach a good lesson. That what we
falsely call a religious cry is easily raised by men who have no

religion, and who in their daily practice set at nought the commonest principles of right and wrong; that it is begotten of intolerance and persecution; that it is senseless, besotted, inveterate and unmerciful; all History teaches us. But perhaps we do not know it in our hearts too well, to profit by even so humble an example as the "No Popery" riots of Seventeen Hundred and Eighty.

However imperfectly those disturbances are set forth in the following pages, they are impartially painted by one who has no sympathy with the Romish Church, though he acknowledges, as most men do, some esteemed friends among the followers of its creed.

In the description of the principal outrages, reference has been had to the best authorities of that time, such as they are; the account given in this Tale, of all the main features of the Riots, is substantially correct.

Mr. Dennis's allusions to the flourishing condition of his trade in those days, have their foundation in Truth, and not in the Author's fancy. Any file of old Newspapers, or odd volume of the Annual Register, will prove this with terrible ease.

Even the case of Mary Jones, dwelt upon with so much pleasure by the same character, is no effort of invention. The facts were stated, exactly as they are stated here, in the House of Commons. Whether they afforded as much entertainment to the merry gentlemen assembled there, as some other most affecting circumstances of a similar nature mentioned by Sir Samuel Romilly, is not recorded.

That the case of Mary Jones may speak the more emphatically for itself, I subjoin it, as related by SIR WILLIAM MEREDITH in a speech in Parliament, "on Frequent Executions," made in 1777.

"Under this act," the Shop-lifting Act, "one Mary Jones was executed, whose case I shall just mention; it was at the time when press warrants were issued, on the alarm about Falkland Islands. The woman's husband was pressed, their goods seized for some debts of his, and she, with two small children, turned into the streets a-begging. It is a circumstance not to be forgotten, that she was very young (under nineteen), and most remarkably handsome. She went to a linen-draper's shop, took some coarse linen off the counter, and slipped it under her cloak; the shopman saw her, and she laid it down: for this she was hanged. Her defence was (I have the trial in my pocket), 'that she had lived in credit, and wanted for nothing, till a press-gang came and stole her husband from her; but since then, she had no bed to lie on; nothing to give her children to eat; and they were almost naked; and perhaps she might have done something wrong, for she hardly knew what she did.' The parish officers testified the truth of this story; but it seems, there had been a good deal of shop-lifting about Ludgate; an example was thought necessary; and this woman was hanged for the comfort and satisfaction of shopkeepers in Ludgate Street. When brought to receive sentence, she behaved in such a frantic manner, as proved her mind to be in a distracted and desponding state; and the child was suckling at her breast when she set out for Tyburn."

BARNABY RUDGE

CHAPTER I

In the year 1775, there stood upon the borders of Epping Forest, at a distance of about twelve miles from London—measuring from the Standard in Cornhill, or rather from the spot on or near to which the Standard used to be in the days of yore—a house of public entertainment called the Maypole; which fact was demonstrated to all such travellers as could neither read nor write (and at that time a vast number both of travellers and stay-at-homes were in this condition) by the emblem reared on the roadside over against the house, which, if not of those goodly proportions that Maypoles were wont to present in olden times, was a fair young ash, thirty feet in height, and straight as any arrow that ever English yeoman drew.

The Maypole—by which term from henceforth is meant the house, and not its sign—the Maypole was an old building, with more gable ends than a lazy man would care to count on a sunny day; huge zig-zag chimneys, out of which it seemed as though even smoke could not choose but come in more than naturally fantastic shapes, imparted to it in its tortuous progress; and vast stables, gloomy, ruinous, and empty. The place was said to have been built in the days of King Henry the Eighth; and there was a legend, not only that Queen Elizabeth had slept there one night while upon a hunting excursion, to wit, in a certain oak-panelled room with a deep bay window, but that next morning, while standing on a mounting-block before the door with one foot in the stirrup, the virgin monarch had then and there boxed and cuffed an unlucky page for some neglect of duty. The matter-of-fact and doubtful folks, of whom there were a few among the Maypole customers, as unluckily there always are in every little community, were inclined to look upon this tradition as rather apocryphal; but, whenever the landlord of that ancient hostelry appealed to the mounting-block itself as evidence, and triumphantly pointed out that there it stood in the same place to that very day, the doubters never failed to be put down by a large majority, and all true believers exulted as in a victory.

Whether these, and many other stories of the like nature, were true or untrue, the Maypole was really an old house, a very old house, perhaps as old as it claimed to be, and perhaps older, which will sometimes happen with houses of an uncertain, as with ladies of a certain, age. Its windows were old diamond-pane lattices, its floors were sunken and uneven, its ceilings blackened by the hand of time, and heavy with massive beams. Over the doorway was an ancient porch, quaintly and grotesquely carved; and here on summer evenings the more favoured customers smoked and drank—ay, and sang many a good song too, sometimes—reposing on two grim-looking high-backed settles, which, like the twin dragons of some fairy tale, guarded the entrance to the mansion.

In the chimneys of the disused rooms, swallows had built their nests for many a long year, and from earliest spring to latest autumn whole colonies of sparrows chirped and twittered in the eaves. There were more pigeons about the dreary stable yard and out-buildings than anybody but the landlord could reckon up. The wheeling and circling flights of runts, fantails, tumblers, and pouters, were perhaps not quite consistent with the grave and sober character of the building, but the monotonous cooing, which never ceased to be raised by some among them all day long, suited it exactly, and seemed to lull it to rest. With its overhanging stories, drowsy little panes of glass, and front bulging out and projecting over the pathway, the old house looked as if it were nodding in its sleep. Indeed, it needed no very great stretch of fancy to detect in it other resemblances to humanity. The bricks of which it was built had originally been a deep dark red, but had grown yellow and discoloured like an old man's skin; the sturdy timbers had decayed like teeth; and here and there the ivy, like a warm garment to comfort it in its age, wrapt its green leaves closely round the time-worn walls.

It was a hale and hearty age though, still: and in the summer or autumn evenings, when the glow of the setting sun fell upon the oak and chestnut trees of the adjacent forest, the old house, partaking of its lustre, seemed their fit companion, and to have many good years of life in him yet.

The evening with which we have to do, was neither a summer nor an autumn one, but the twilight of a day in March, when the wind howled dismally among the bare branches of the trees, and rumbling in the wide chimneys and driving the rain against the windows of the Maypole Inn, gave such of its frequenters as chanced to be there at the moment an undeniable reason for prolonging their stay, and caused the landlord to prophesy that the night would certainly clear at eleven o'clock precisely,—which by a remarkable coincidence was the hour at which he always closed his house.

The name of him upon whom the spirit of prophecy thus descended was John Willet, a burly, large-headed man with a fat face, which betokened profound obstinacy and slowness of apprehension, combined with a very strong reliance upon his own merits. It was John Willet's ordinary boast in his more placid moods that if he were slow he was sure; which assertion could, in one sense at least, be by no means gainsaid, seeing that he was in everything unquestionably the reverse of fast, and withal one of the most dogged and positive fellows in existence—always sure that what he thought or said or did was right, and holding it as a thing quite settled and ordained by the laws of nature and Providence, that anybody who said or did or thought otherwise must be inevitably and of necessity wrong.

Mr. Willet walked slowly up to the window, flattened his fat nose against the cold glass, and shading his eyes that his sight might not be affected by the ruddy glow of the fire, looked abroad. Then he walked slowly back to his old seat in the chimney-corner, and, composing himself in it with a slight shiver, such as a man might give way to and so acquire an additional relish for the warm blaze, said, looking round upon his guests:

"It'll clear at eleven o'clock. No sooner and no later. Not before and not arterwards."

"How do you make out that?" said a little man in the opposite corner. "The moon is past the full, and she rises at nine."

John looked sedately and solemnly at his questioner until he had brought his mind to bear upon the whole of his observation, and then made answer, in a tone which seemed to imply that the moon was peculiarly his business and nobody else's:

"Never you mind about the moon. Don't you trouble yourself about her. You let the moon alone, and I'll let you alone."

"No offence I hope?" said the little man.

Again John waited leisurely until the observation had thoroughly penetrated to his brain, and then replying, "No offence *as yet*," applied a light to his pipe and smoked in placid silence; now and then casting a sidelong look at a man wrapped in a loose riding-coat with huge cuffs ornamented with tarnished silver lace and large metal buttons, who sat apart from the regular frequenters of the house, and wearing a hat flapped over his face, which was still further shaded by the hand on which his forehead rested, looked unsociable enough.

There was another guest, who sat, booted and spurred, at some distance from the fire also, and whose thoughts—to judge from his folded arms and knitted brows, and from the untasted liquor before him—were occupied with other matters than the topics under discussion or the persons who discussed them. This was a young man of about eight-and-twenty, rather above the middle height, and though of a somewhat slight figure, gracefully and strongly made. He wore his own dark hair, and was accoutred in a riding-dress, which, together with his large boots (resembling in shape and fashion those worn by our Life Guardsmen at the present day), showed indisputable traces of the bad condition of the roads. But travel-stained though he was, he was well and even richly attired, and without being over-dressed looked a gallant gentleman.

Lying upon the table beside him, as he had carelessly thrown them down, were a heavy riding-whip and a slouched hat, the latter worn no doubt as being best suited to the inclemency of the weather. There, too, were a pair of pistols in a holster-case, and a short riding-cloak. Little of his face was visible, except the long dark lashes which concealed his downcast eyes, but an air of careless ease and natural gracefulness of demeanour pervaded the figure, and seemed to comprehend even those slight accessories, which were all handsome and in good keeping.

Towards this young gentleman the eyes of Mr. Willet wandered but once, and then as if in mute inquiry whether he had observed his silent neighbour. It was plain that John and the young gentleman had often met before. Finding that his look was not returned, or indeed observed by the person to whom it was addressed, John gradually concentrated the whole power of his eyes into one focus, and brought it to bear upon the man in the flapped hat, at whom he came to stare in course of time with an intensity so remarkable, that it affected his fireside cronies, who all, as with one accord, took their pipes from their lips, and stared with open mouths at the stranger likewise.

The sturdy landlord had a large pair of dull fish-like eyes, and the little man who had hazarded the remark about the moon (and who was the parish-clerk and bell-ringer of Chigwell; a village hard by) had little round black shiny eyes like beads; moreover this little man wore at the knees of his rusty black breeches, and on his rusty black coat, and all down his long flapped waistcoat, little queer buttons like nothing except his eyes; but so like them, that as they twinkled and glistened in the light of the fire, which shone too in his bright shoe-buckles, he seemed all eyes from head to foot, and to be gazing with every one of them at the unknown customer. No wonder that a man should grow restless under such an inspection as this, to say nothing of the eyes belonging to short Tom Cobb the general chandler and post-office keeper, and long Phil Parkes the ranger, both of whom, infected by the example of their companions, regarded him of the flapped hat no less attentively.

The stranger became restless; perhaps from being exposed to this raking fire of eyes, perhaps from the nature of his previous meditations—most probably from the latter cause, for as he changed his position and looked hastily round, he started to find himself the object of such keen regard, and darted an angry and suspicious glance at the fireside group. It had the effect of immediately diverting all eyes to the chimney, except those of John Willet, who finding himself, as it were, caught in the fact, and not being (as has been already observed) of a very ready nature, remained staring at his guest in a particularly awkward and disconcerted manner.

"Well?" said the stranger.

Well. There was not much in well. It was not a long speech. "I thought you gave an order," said the landlord, after a pause of two or three minutes for consideration.

The stranger took off his hat, and disclosed the hard features of a man of sixty or thereabouts, much weather-beaten and worn by time, and the naturally harsh expression of which was not improved by a dark handkerchief which was bound tightly round his head, and, while it served the purpose of a wig, shaded his forehead, and almost hid his eyebrows. If it were intended to conceal or divert attention from a deep gash, now healed into an ugly seam, which when it was first inflicted must have laid bare his cheekbone, the object was but indifferently attained, for it could scarcely fail to be noted at a glance. His complexion was of a cadaverous hue, and he had a grizzly jagged beard of some three weeks' date. Such was the figure (very meanly and poorly clad) that now rose from the seat, and stalking across the room sat down in a corner of the chimney, which the politeness or fears of the little clerk very readily assigned to him.

"A highwayman!" whispered Tom Cobb to Parkes the ranger.

"Do you suppose highwaymen don't dress handsomer than that?" replied Parkes. "It's a better business than you think for, Tom, and highwaymen don't need or use to be shabby, take my word for it."

Meanwhile the subject of their speculations had done due honour to the house by calling for some drink, which was promptly supplied by the landlord's son Joe, a broad-shouldered strapping young fellow of twenty, whom it pleased his father still to consider a little boy, and to treat accordingly. Stretching out his hands to warm them by the blazing fire, the man turned his head towards the company, and after running his eye sharply over them, said in a voice well suited to his appearance:

"What house is that which stands a mile or so from here?"

"Public-house?" said the landlord, with his usual deliberation.

"Public-house, father!" exclaimed Joe, "where's the public house within a mile or so of the Maypole? He means the great house—the Warren—naturally and of course. The old red brick house, sir, that stands in its own grounds——?"

"Ay," said the stranger.

"And that fifteen or twenty years ago stood in a park five times as broad, which with other and richer property has bit by bit changed hands and dwindled away—more's the pity!" pursued the young man.

"Maybe," was the reply. "But my question related to the owner. What it has been I don't care to know, and what it is I can see for myself."

The heir-apparent to the Maypole pressed his finger on his lips, and glancing at the young gentleman already noticed, who had changed his attitude when the house was first mentioned, replied in a lower tone,

"The owner's name is Haredale, Mr. Geoffrey Haredale, and"— again he glanced in the same direction as before—"and a worthy gentleman too—hem!"

Paying as little regard to this admonitory cough, as to the significant gesture that had preceded it, the stranger pursued his questioning.

"I turned out of my way coming here, and took the footpath that crosses the grounds. Who was the young lady that I saw entering a carriage? His daughter?"

"Why, how should I know, honest man?" replied Joe, contriving in the course of some arrangements about the hearth, to advance close to his questioner and pluck him by the sleeve, "*I* didn't see the young lady you know. Whew! There's the wind again—*and* rain— well it *is* a night!"

"Rough weather indeed!" observed the strange man.

"You're used to it?" said Joe, catching at anything which seemed to promise a diversion of the subject.

"Pretty well," returned the other. "About the young lady—has Mr. Haredale a daughter?"

"No, no," said the young fellow fretfully, "he's a single gentleman
—he's—be quiet, can't you, man? Don't you see this talk is not
relished yonder?"

Regardless of this whispered remonstrance, and affecting not to
hear it, his tormentor provokingly continued:

"Single men have had daughters before now. Perhaps she may be
his daughter, though he is not married."

"What do you mean?" said Joe, adding in an under tone as he
approached him again, "You'll come in for it presently, I know you
will!"

"I mean no harm"—returned the traveller boldly, "and have said
none that I know of. I ask a few questions—as any stranger may, and
not unnaturally—about the inmates of a remarkable house in a
neighbourhood which is new to me, and you are as aghast and disturbed as if I were talking treason against King George. Perhaps you
can tell me why, sir, for (as I say) I am a stranger, and this is Greek
to me?"

The latter observation was addressed to the obvious cause of Joe
Willet's discomposure, who had risen and was adjusting his riding-
cloak preparatory to sallying abroad. Briefly replying that he could
give him no information, the young man beckoned to Joe, and handing him a piece of money in payment of his reckoning, hurried out
attended by young Willet himself, who taking up a candle followed
to light him to the house door.

While Joe was absent on this errand, the elder Willet and his
three companions continued to smoke with profound gravity, and in
a deep silence, each having his eyes fixed on a huge copper boiler that
was suspended over the fire. After some time John Willet slowly
shook his head, and thereupon his friends slowly shook theirs; but
no man withdrew his eyes from the boiler, or altered the solemn
expression of his countenance in the slightest degree.

At length Joe returned—very talkative and conciliatory, as though
with a strong presentiment that he was going to be found fault with.

"Such a thing as love is!" he said, drawing a chair near the fire, and
looking round for sympathy. "He has set off to walk to London,—
all the way to London. His nag gone lame in riding out here this
blessed afternoon, and comfortably littered down in our stable at this
minute; and he giving up a good hot supper and our best bed, because Miss Haredale has gone to a masquerade up in town, and he
has set his heart upon seeing her! I don't think I could persuade
myself to do that, beautiful as she is,—but then I'm not in love (at
least I don't think I am,) and that's the whole difference."

"He is in love then?" said the stranger.

"Rather," replied Joe. "He'll never be more in love, and may very
easily be less."

"Silence, sir!" cried his father.

"What a chap you are, Joe!" said Long Parkes.

"Such a inconsiderate lad!" murmured Tom Cobb.

"Putting himself forward and wringing the very nose off his own father's face!" exclaimed the parish-clerk, metaphorically.

"What *have* I done?" reasoned poor Joe.

"Silence, sir!" returned his father, "what do you mean by talking, when you see people that are more than two or three times your age, sitting still and silent and not dreaming of saying a word?"

"Why that's the proper time for me to talk, isn't it?" said Joe rebelliously.

"The proper time, sir!" retorted his father, "the proper time's no time."

"Ah to be sure!" muttered Parkes, nodding gravely to the other two who nodded likewise, observing under their breaths that that was the point.

"The proper time's no time, sir," repeated John Willet; "when I was your age I never talked, I never wanted to talk. I listened and improved myself, that's what *I* did."

"And you'd find your father rather a tough customer in argeyment, Joe, if anybody was to try and tackle him," said Parkes.

"For the matter o' that, Phil!" observed Mr. Willet, blowing a long, thin, spiral cloud of smoke out of the corner of his mouth, and staring at it abstractedly as it floated away; "For the matter o' that, Phil, argeyment is a gift of Natur. If Natur has gifted a man with powers of argeyment, a man has a right to make the best of 'em, and has not a right to stand on false delicacy, and deny that he is so gifted; for that is a turning of his back on Natur, a flouting of her, a slighting of her precious caskets, and a proving of one's self to be a swine that isn't worth her scattering pearls before."

The landlord pausing here for a very long time, Mr. Parkes naturally concluded that he had brought his discourse to an end; and therefore, turning to the young man with some austerity, exclaimed:

"You hear what your father says, Joe? You wouldn't much like to tackle him in argeyment, I'm thinking, sir."

"IF," said John Willet, turning his eyes from the ceiling to the face of his interrupter, and uttering the monosyllable in capitals, to apprise him that he had put in his oar, as the vulgar say, with unbecoming and irreverent haste; "IF, sir, Natur has fixed upon me the gift of argeyment, why should I not own to it, and rather glory in the same? Yes, sir, I *am* a tough customer that way. You are right, sir. My toughness has been proved, sir, in this room many and many a time, as I think you know; and if you don't know," added John, putting his pipe in his mouth again, "so much the better, for I an't proud and am not a going to tell you."

A general murmur from his three cronies, and a general shaking of heads at the copper boiler, assured John Willet that they had had good experience of his powers and needed no further evidence to assure them of his superiority. John smoked with a little more dignity and surveyed them in silence.

"It's all very fine talking," muttered Joe, who had been fidgeting in his chair with divers uneasy gestures. "But if you mean to tell me that I'm never to open my lips——"

"Silence, sir!" roared his father. "No, you never are. When your opinion's wanted, you give it. When you're spoke to, you speak. When your opinion's not wanted and you're not spoke to, don't give an opinion and don't you speak. The world's undergone a nice alteration since my time, certainly. My belief is that there an't any boys left—that there isn't such a thing as a boy—that there's nothing now between a male baby and a man—and that all the boys went out with his blessed Majesty King George the Second."

"That's a very true observation, always excepting the young princes," said the parish-clerk, who, as the representative of church and state in that company, held himself bound to the nicest loyalty. "If it's godly and righteous for boys, being of the ages of boys, to behave themselves like boys, then the young princes must be boys and cannot be otherwise."

"Did you ever hear tell of mermaids, sir?" said Mr. Willet.

"Certainly I have," replied the clerk.

"Very good," said Mr. Willet. "According to the constitution of mermaids, so much of a mermaid as is not a woman must be a fish. According to the constitution of young princes, so much of a young prince (if anything) as is not actually an angel, must be godly and righteous. Therefore if it's becoming and godly and righteous in the young princes (as it is at their ages) that they should be boys, they are and must be boys, and cannot by possibility be anything else."

This elucidation of a knotty point being received with such marks of approval as to put John Willet into a good humour, he contented himself with repeating to his son his command of silence, and addressing the stranger, said:

"If you had asked your questions of a grown-up person—of me or any of these gentlemen—you'd have had some satisfaction, and wouldn't have wasted breath. Miss Haredale is Mr. Geoffrey Haredale's niece."

"Is her father alive?" said the man, carelessly.

"No," rejoined the landlord, "he is not alive, and he is not dead——"

"Not dead!" cried the other.

"Not dead in a common sort of way," said the landlord.

The cronies nodded to each other, and Mr. Parkes remarked in an under tone, shaking his head meanwhile as who should say, "let no man contradict me, for I won't believe him," that John Willet was in amazing force to-night, and fit to tackle a Chief Justice.

The stranger suffered a short pause to elapse, and then asked abruptly, "What do you mean?"

"More than you think for, friend," returned John Willet. "Perhaps there's more meaning in them words than you suspect."

"Perhaps there is," said the strange man, gruffly; "but what the devil do you speak in such mysteries for? You tell me, first, that a man is not alive, nor yet dead—then, that he's not dead in a common sort of way—then, that you mean a great deal more than I think for. To tell you the truth, you may do that easily; for so far as I can make out, you mean nothing. What *do* you mean, I ask again?"

"That," returned the landlord, a little brought down from his dignity by the stranger's surliness, "is a Maypole story, and has been any time these four-and-twenty years. That story is Solomon Daisy's story. It belongs to the house; and nobody but Solomon Daisy has ever told it under this roof, or ever shall—that's more."

The man glanced at the parish-clerk, whose air of consciousness and importance plainly betokened him to be the person referred to, and, observing that he had taken his pipe from his lips, after a very long whiff to keep it alight, and was evidently about to tell his story without further solicitation, gathered his large coat about him, and shrinking further back was almost lost in the gloom of the spacious chimney-corner, except when the flame, struggling from under a great faggot, whose weight almost crushed it for the time, shot upward with a strong and sudden glare, and illumining his figure for a moment, seemed afterwards to cast it into deeper obscurity than before.

By this flickering light, which made the old room, with its heavy timbers and panelled walls, look as if it were built of polished ebony —the wind roaring and howling without, now rattling the latch and creaking the hinges of the stout oaken door, and now driving at the casement as though it would beat it in—by this light, and under circumstances so auspicious, Solomon Daisy began his tale:

"It was Mr. Reuben Haredale, Mr. Geoffrey's elder brother——"

Here he came to a dead stop, and made so long a pause that even John Willet grew impatient and asked why he did not proceed.

"Cobb," said Solomon Daisy, dropping his voice and appealing to the post-office keeper; "what day of the month is this?"

"The nineteenth."

"Of March," said the clerk, bending forward, "the nineteenth of March; that's very strange."

In a low voice they all acquiesced, and Solomon went on:

"It was Mr. Reuben Haredale, Mr. Geoffrey's elder brother, that twenty-two years ago was the owner of the Warren, which, as Joe has said—not that you remember it, Joe, for a boy like you can't do that, but because you have often heard me say so—was then a much larger and better place, and a much more valuable property than it is now. His lady was lately dead, and he was left with one child—the Miss Haredale you have been inquiring about—who was then scarcely a year old."

Although the speaker addressed himself to the man who had shown so much curiosity about this same family, and made a pause here as if expecting some exclamation of surprise or encouragement, the latter made no remark, nor gave any indication that he heard or was interested in what was said. Solomon therefore turned to his old companions, whose noses were brightly illuminated by the deep red glow from the bowls of their pipes; assured, by long experience, of their attention, and resolved to show his sense of such indecent behaviour.

"Mr. Haredale," said Solomon, turning his back upon the strange man, "left this place when his lady died, feeling it lonely like, and went up to London, where he stopped some months; but finding that place as lonely as this—as I suppose and have always heard say—he suddenly came back again, with his little girl to the Warren, bringing with him besides, that day, only two women servants, and his steward, and a gardener."

Mr. Daisy stopped to take a whiff at his pipe, which was going out, and then proceeded—at first in a snuffling tone, occasioned by keen enjoyment of the tobacco and strong pulling at the pipe, and afterwards with increasing distinctness:

"—Bringing with him two women servants, and his steward, and a gardener. The rest stopped behind up in London, and were to follow next day. It happened that that night, an old gentleman who lived at Chigwell-row, and had long been poorly, deceased, and an order came to me at half after twelve o'clock at night to go and toll the passing-bell."

There was a movement in the little group of listeners, sufficiently indicative of the strong repugnance any one of them would have felt to have turned out at such a time upon such an errand. The clerk felt and understood it, and pursued his theme accordingly.

"It *was* a dreary thing, especially as the grave-digger was laid up in his bed, from long working in a damp soil and sitting down to take his dinner on cold tombstones, and I was consequently under obligation to go alone, for it was too late to hope to get any other companion. However, I wasn't unprepared for it; as the old gentleman had often made it a request that the bell should be tolled as soon as possible after the breath was out of his body, and he had been expected to go for some days. I put as good a face upon it as I could, and muffling myself up (for it was mortal cold), started out with a lighted lantern in one hand and the key of the church in the other."

At this point of the narrative, the dress of the strange man rustled as if he had turned himself to hear more distinctly. Slightly pointing over his shoulder, Solomon elevated his eyebrows and nodded a silent inquiry to Joe whether this was the case. Joe shaded his eyes with his hand and peered into the corner, but could make out nothing, and so shook his head.

"It was just such a night as this; blowing a hurricane, raining heavily, and very dark—I often think now, darker than I ever saw it before or since; that may be my fancy, but the houses were all close shut and the folks in doors, and perhaps there is only one other man who knows how dark it really was. I got into the church, chained the door back so that it should keep ajar—for, to tell the truth, I didn't like to be shut in there alone—and putting my lantern on the stone seat in the little corner where the bell-rope is, sat down beside it to trim the candle.

"I sat down to trim the candle, and when I had done so I could not persuade myself to get up again, and go about my work. I don't know how it was, but I thought of all the ghost stories I had ever heard, even those that I had heard when I was a boy at school, and had forgotten long ago; and they didn't come into my head one after another, but all crowding at once, like. I recollected one story there was in the village, how that on a certain night in the year (it might be that very night for anything I knew), all the dead people came out of the ground and sat at the heads of their own graves till morning. This made me think how many people I had known, were buried between the church door and the churchyard gate, and what a dreadful thing it would be to have to pass among them and know them again, so earthy and unlike themselves. I had known all the niches and arches in the church from a child; still, I couldn't persuade myself that those were their natural shadows which I saw on the pavement, but felt sure there were some ugly figures hiding among 'em and peeping out. Thinking on in this way, I began to think of the old gentleman who was just dead, and I could have sworn, as I looked up the dark chancel, that I saw him in his usual place, wrapping his shroud about him and shivering as if he felt it cold. All this time I sat listening and listening, and hardly dared to breathe. At length I started up and took the bell-rope in my hands. At that minute there rang—not that bell, for I had hardly touched the rope—but another!

"I heard the ringing of another bell, and a deep bell too, plainly. It was only for an instant, and even then the wind carried the sound away, but I heard it. I listened for a long time, but it rang no more. I had heard of the corpse candles, and at last I persuaded myself that this must be a corpse bell tolling of itself at midnight for the dead. I tolled my bell—how, or how long, I don't know—and ran home to bed as fast as I could touch the ground.

"I was up early next morning after a restless night, and told the story to my neighbours. Some were serious and some made light of it; I don't think anybody believed it real. But, that morning, Mr. Reuben Haredale was found murdered in his bed-chamber; and in his hand was a piece of the cord attached to an alarm-bell outside the roof, which hung in his room and had been cut asunder, no doubt by the murderer, when he seized it.

"That was the bell I heard.

"A bureau was found opened, and a cash-box, which Mr. Haredale had brought down that day, and was supposed to contain a large sum of money, was gone. The steward and gardener were both missing and both suspected for a long time, but they were never found, though hunted far and wide. And far enough they might have looked for poor Mr. Rudge the steward, whose body—scarcely to be recognised by his clothes and the watch and ring he wore—was found, months afterwards, at the bottom of a piece of water in the grounds, with a deep gash in the breast where he had been stabbed with a knife. He was only partly dressed; and people all agreed that he had been sitting up reading in his own room, where there were many traces of blood, and was suddenly fallen upon and killed before his master.

"Everybody now knew that the gardener must be the murderer,

and though he has never been heard of from that day to this, he will be, mark my words. The crime was committed this day two-and-twenty years—on the nineteenth of March, one thousand seven hundred and fifty-three. On the nineteenth of March in some year—no matter when—I know it, I am sure of it, for we have always, in some strange way or other, been brought back to the subject on that day ever since—on the nineteenth of March in some year, sooner or later, that man will be discovered."

CHAPTER II

"A STRANGE story!" said the man who had been the cause of the narration.—"Stranger still if it comes about as you predict. Is that all?"

A question so unexpected, nettled Solomon Daisy not a little. By dint of relating the story very often, and ornamenting it (according to village report) with a few flourishes suggested by the various hearers from time to time, he had come by degrees to tell it with great effect; and "is that all?" after the climax, was not what he was accustomed to.

"Is that all?" he repeated, "yes, that's all, sir. And enough too, I think."

"I think so too. My horse, young man! He is but a hack hired from a roadside posting house, but he must carry me to London to-night."

"To-night!" said Joe.

"To-night," returned the other. "What do you stare at? This tavern would seem to be a house of call for all the gaping idlers of the neighbourhood!"

At this remark, which evidently had reference to the scrutiny he had undergone, as mentioned in the foregoing chapter, the eyes of John Willet and his friends were diverted with marvellous rapidity to the copper boiler again. Not so with Joe, who, being a mettlesome fellow, returned the stranger's angry glance with a steady look, and rejoined:

"It is not a very bold thing to wonder at your going on to-night. Surely you have been asked such a harmless question in an inn before, and in better weather than this. I thought you mightn't know the way, as you seem strange to this part."

"The way—" repeated the other, irritably.

"Yes. *Do* you know it?"

"I'll—humph!—I'll find it," replied the man, waving his hand and turning on his heel. "Landlord, take the reckoning here."

John Willet did as he was desired; for on that point he was seldom slow, except in the particulars of giving change, and testing the goodness of any piece of coin that was proffered to him, by the application of his teeth or his tongue, or some other test, or in doubtful cases, by a long series of tests terminating in its rejection. The guest then wrapped his garments about him so as to shelter himself as effectually as he could from the rough weather, and without any word or sign of farewell betook himself to the stable-yard. Here Joe (who had left the room on the conclusion of their short dialogue) was protecting himself and the horse from the rain under the shelter of an old pent-house roof.

"He's pretty much of my opinion," said Joe, patting the horse upon the neck. "I'll wager that your stopping here to-night would please him better than it would please me."

"He and I are of different opinions, as we have been more than once on our way here," was the short reply.

"So I was thinking before you came out, for he has felt your spurs, poor beast."

The stranger adjusted his coat-collar about his face, and made no answer.

"You'll know me again, I see," he said, marking the young fellow's earnest gaze, when he had sprung into the saddle.

"The man's worth knowing, master, who travels a road he don't know, mounted on a jaded horse, and leaves good quarters to do it on such a night as this."

"You have sharp eyes and a sharp tongue I find."

"Both I hope by nature, but the last grows rusty sometimes for want of using."

"Use the first less too, and keep their sharpness for your sweet-hearts, boy," said the man.

So saying he shook his hand from the bridle, struck him roughly on the head with the butt end of his whip, and galloped away; dashing through the mud and darkness with a headlong speed, which few badly mounted horsemen would have cared to venture, even had they been thoroughly acquainted with the country; and which, to one who knew nothing of the way he rode, was attended at every step with great hazard and danger.

The roads, even within twelve miles of London, were at that time ill paved, seldom repaired, and very badly made. The way this rider traversed had been ploughed up by the wheels of heavy waggons, and rendered rotten by the frosts and thaws of the preceding winter, or possibly of many winters. Great holes and gaps had been worn into the soil, which, being now filled with water from the late rains, were not easily distinguishable even by day; and a plunge into any one of them might have brought down a surer-footed horse than the poor beast now urged forward to the utmost extent of his powers. Sharp flints and stones rolled from under his hoofs continually; the rider could scarcely see beyond the animal's head, or farther on either side than his own arm would have extended. At that time, too, all the roads in the neighbourhood of the metropolis were infested by foot-pads or highwaymen, and it was a night, of all others, in which any evil-disposed person of this class might have pursued his unlawful calling with little fear of detection.

Still, the traveller dashed forward at the same reckless pace, regardless alike of the dirt and wet which flew about his head, the profound darkness of the night, and the probability of encountering

some desperate characters abroad. At every turn and angle, even
where a deviation from the direct course might have been least
expected, and could not possibly be seen until he was close upon it,
he guided the bridle with an unerring hand, and kept the middle of
the road. Thus he sped onward, raising himself in the stirrups, leaning his body forward until it almost touched the horse's neck, and
flourishing his heavy whip above his head with the fervour of a
madman.

There are times when, the elements being in unusual commotion,
those who are bent on daring enterprises, or agitated by great
thoughts, whether of good or evil, feel a mysterious sympathy with
the tumult of nature, and are roused into corresponding violence.
In the midst of thunder, lightning, and storm, many tremendous
deeds have been committed; men, self-possessed before, have given
a sudden loose to passions they could no longer control. The demons
of wrath and despair have striven to emulate those who ride the
whirlwind and direct the storm; and man, lashed into madness with
the roaring winds and boiling waters, has become for the time as
wild and merciless as the elements themselves.

Whether the traveller was possessed by thoughts which the fury
of the night had heated and stimulated into a quicker current, or
was merely impelled by some strong motive to reach his journey's
end, on he swept more like a hunted phantom than a man, nor
checked his pace until, arriving at some cross roads, one of which
led by a longer route to the place whence he had lately started, he
bore down so suddenly upon a vehicle which was coming towards
him, that in the effort to avoid it he well-nigh pulled his horse upon
his haunches, and narrowly escaped being thrown.

"Yoho!" cried the voice of a man. "What's that? who goes there?"

"A friend!" replied the traveller.

"A friend!" repeated the voice. "Who calls himself a friend and
rides like that, abusing Heaven's gifts in the shape of horseflesh, and
endangering, not only his own neck (which might be no great matter)
but the necks of other people?"

"You have a lantern there, I see," said the traveller dismounting,
"lend it me for a moment. You have wounded my horse, I think, with
your shaft or wheel."

"Wounded him!" cried the other, "if I haven't killed him, it's no
fault of yours. What do you mean by galloping along the king's highway like that, eh?"

"Give me the light," returned the traveller, snatching it from his
hand, "and don't ask idle questions of a man who is in no mood for
talking."

"If you had said you were in no mood for talking before, I should
perhaps have been in no mood for lighting," said the voice.
"Hows'ever as it's the poor horse that's damaged and not you, one
of you is welcome to the light at all events—but it's not the crusty
one."

The traveller returned no answer to this speech, but holding the light near to his panting and reeking beast, examined him in limb and carcass. Meanwhile, the other man sat very composedly in his vehicle, which was a kind of chaise with a depository for a large bag of tools, and watched his proceedings with a careful eye.

The looker-on was a round, red-faced, sturdy yeoman, with a double chin, and a voice husky with good living, good sleeping, good humour, and good health. He was past the prime of life, but Father Time is not always a hard parent, and, though he tarries for none of his children, often lays his hand lightly upon those who have used him well; making them old men and women inexorably enough, but leaving their hearts and spirits young and in full vigour. With such people the grey head is but the impression of the old fellow's hand in giving them his blessing, and every wrinkle but a notch in the quiet calendar of a well-spent life.

The person whom the traveller had so abruptly encountered was of this kind bluff, hale, hearty, and in a green old age: at peace with himself, and evidently disposed to be so with all the world. Although muffled up in divers coats and handkerchiefs—one of which, passed over his crown, and tied in a convenient crease of his double chin, secured his three-cornered hat and bob-wig from blowing off his head —there was no disguising his plump and comfortable figure; neither did certain dirty finger-marks upon his face give it any other than an odd and comical expression, through which its natural good humour shone with undiminished lustre.

"He is not hurt," said the traveller at length, raising his head and the lantern together.

"You have found that out at last, have you?" rejoined the old man. "My eyes have seen more light than yours, but I wouldn't change with you."

"What do you mean?"

"Mean! I could have told you he wasn't hurt, five minutes ago. Give me the light, friend; ride forward at a gentler pace; and good night."

In handing up the lantern, the man necessarily cast its rays full on the speaker's face. Their eyes met at the instant. He suddenly dropped it and crushed it with his foot.

"Did you never see a locksmith before, that you start as if you had come upon a ghost?" cried the old man in the chaise, "or is this," he added hastily, thrusting his hand into the tool basket and drawing out a hammer, "a scheme for robbing me? I know these roads, friend. When I travel them, I carry nothing but a few shillings, and not a crown's worth of them. I tell you plainly, to save us both trouble, that there's nothing to be got from me but a pretty stout arm considering my years, and this tool, which, mayhap from long acquaint-ance with, I can use pretty briskly. You shall not have it all your own way, I promise you, if you play at that game." With these words he stood upon the defensive.

"I am not what you take me for, Gabriel Varden," replied the other.

"Then what and who are you?" returned the locksmith. "You know my name it seems. Let me know yours."

"I have not gained the information from any confidence of yours, but from the inscription on your cart which tells it to all the town," replied the traveller.

"You have better eyes for that than you had for your horse, then," said Varden, descending nimbly from his chaise; "who are you? Let me see your face."

While the locksmith alighted, the traveller had regained his saddle, from which he now confronted the old man, who, moving as the horse moved in chafing under the tightened rein, kept close beside him.

"Let me see your face, I say."

"Stand off!"

"No masquerading tricks," said the locksmith, "and tales at the club to-morrow, how Gabriel Varden was frightened by a surly voice and a dark night. Stand—let me see your face."

Finding that further resistance would only involve him in a personal struggle with an antagonist by no means to be despised, the traveller threw back his coat, and stooping down looked steadily at the locksmith.

Perhaps two men more powerfully contrasted, never opposed each other face to face. The ruddy features of the locksmith so set off and heightened the excessive paleness of the man on horseback, that he looked like a bloodless ghost, while the moisture, which hard riding had brought out upon his skin, hung there in dark and heavy drops, like dews of agony and death. The countenance of the old locksmith lighted up with the smile of one expecting to detect in this unpromising stranger some latent roguery of eye or lip, which should reveal a familiar person in that arch disguise, and spoil his jest. The face of the other, sullen and fierce, but shrinking too, was that of a man who stood at bay; while his firmly closed jaws, his puckered mouth, and more than all a certain stealthy motion of the hand within his breast, seemed to announce a desperate purpose very foreign to acting, or child's play.

Thus they regarded each other for some time, in silence.

"Humph!" he said when he had scanned his features; "I don't know you."

"Don't desire to?"—returned the other, muffling himself as before.

"I don't," said Gabriel; "to be plain with you, friend, you don't carry in your countenance a letter of recommendation."

"It's not my wish," said the traveller. "My humour is to be avoided."

"Well," said the locksmith bluntly, "I think you'll have your humour."

"I will, at any cost," rejoined the traveller. "In proof of it, lay this to heart—that you were never in such peril of your life as you have been within these few moments; when you are within five minutes of breathing your last, you will not be nearer death than you have been to-night!"

"Aye!" said the sturdy locksmith.

"Aye! and a violent death."

"From whose hand?"

"From mine," replied the traveller.

With that he put spurs to his horse, and rode away; at first plashing heavily through the mire at a smart trot, but gradually increasing in speed until the last sound of his horse's hoofs died away upon the wind; when he was again hurrying on at the same furious gallop, which had been his pace when the locksmith first encountered him.

Gabriel Varden remained standing in the road with the broken lantern in his hand, listening in stupefied silence until no sound reached his ear but the moaning of the wind, and the fast-falling rain; when he struck himself one or two smart blows in the breast by way of rousing himself, and broke into an exclamation of surprise.

"What in the name of wonder can this fellow be! a madman? a highwayman? a cut-throat? If he had not scoured off so fast, we'd have seen who was in most danger, he or I. I never nearer death than I have been to-night! I hope I may be no nearer to it for a score of years to come—if so, I'll be content to be no farther from it. My stars!—a pretty brag this to a stout man—pooh, pooh!"

Gabriel resumed his seat, and looked wistfully up the road by which the traveller had come; murmuring in a half whisper:

"The Maypole—two miles to the Maypole. I came the other road from the Warren after a long day's work at locks and bells, on purpose that I should not come by the Maypole and break my promise to Martha by looking in—there's resolution! It would be dangerous to go on to London without a light; and it's four miles, and a good half-mile besides, to the Halfway-House; and between this and that is the very place where one needs a light most. Two miles to the Maypole! I told Martha I wouldn't; I said I wouldn't, and I didn't—there's resolution!"

Repeating these two last words very often, as if to compensate for the little resolution he was going to show by piquing himself on the great resolution he had shown, Gabriel Varden quietly turned back, determining to get a light at the Maypole, and to take nothing but a light.

When he got to the Maypole, however, and Joe, responding to his well-known hail, came running out to the horse's head, leaving the door open behind him, and disclosing a delicious perspective of warmth and brightness—when the ruddy gleam of the fire, streaming through the old red curtains of the common room, seemed to bring with it, as part of itself, a pleasant hum of voices, and a fragrant odour of steaming grog and rare tobacco, all steeped as it were in the cheerful glow—when the shadows, flitting across the curtain, showed that those inside had risen from their snug seats, and were making room in the snuggest corner (how well he knew that corner!) for the honest locksmith, and a broad glare, suddenly streaming up, bespoke the goodness of the crackling log from which a brilliant train of

sparks was doubtless at that moment whirling up the chimney in
honour of his coming—when, superadded to these enticements, there
stole upon him from the distant kitchen a gentle sound of frying,
with a musical clatter of plates and dishes, and a savoury smell that
made even the boisterous wind a perfume—Gabriel felt his firmness
oozing rapidly away. He tried to look stoically at the tavern, but
his features would relax into a look of fondness. He turned his
head the other way, and the cold black country seemed to frown him
off, and drive him for a refuge into its hospitable arms.

"The merciful man, Joe," said the locksmith, "is merciful to his
beast. I'll get out for a little while."

And how natural it was to get out! And how unnatural it seemed
for a sober man to be plodding wearily along through miry roads,
encountering the rude buffets of the wind and pelting of the rain,
when there was a clean floor covered with crisp white sand, a well-
swept hearth, a blazing fire, a table decorated with white cloth,
bright pewter flagons, and other tempting preparations for a well-
cooked meal—when there were these things, and company disposed
to make the most of them, all ready to his hand, and entreating him
to enjoyment!

CHAPTER III

SUCH were the locksmith's thoughts when first seated in the snug
corner, and slowly recovering from a pleasant defect of vision—
pleasant, because occasioned by the wind blowing in his eyes—which
made it a matter of sound policy and duty to himself, that he should
take refuge from the weather, and tempted him, for the same reason,
to aggravate a slight cough, and declare he felt but poorly. Such were
still his thoughts more than a full hour afterwards, when, supper
over, he still sat with shining jovial face in the same warm nook,
listening to the cricket-like chirrup of little Solomon Daisy, and bearing no unimportant or slightly respected part in the social gossip
round the Maypole fire.

"I wish he may be an honest man, that's all," said Solomon, winding up a variety of speculations relative to the stranger, concerning
whom Gabriel had compared notes with the company, and so raised
a grave discussion; "*I* wish he may be an honest man."

"So we all do, I suppose, don't we?" observed the locksmith.

"I don't," said Joe.

"No!" cried Gabriel.

"No. He struck me with his whip, the coward, when he was
mounted and I afoot, and I should be better pleased that he turned
out what I think him."

"And what may that be, Joe?"

"No good, Mr. Varden. You may shake your head, father, but I
say no good, and will say no good, and I would say no good a hundred
times over, if that would bring him back to have the drubbing he
deserves."

"Hold your tongue, sir," said John Willet.

"I won't, father. It's all along of you that he ventured to do what he did. Seeing me treated like a child, and put down like a fool, *he* plucks up a heart and has a fling at a fellow that he thinks—and may well think too—hasn't a grain of spirit. But he's mistaken, as I'll show him, and as I'll show all of you before long."

"Does the boy know what he's a saying of!" cried the astonished John Willet.

"Father," returned Joe, "I know what I say and mean, well—better than you do when you hear me. I can bear with you, but I cannot bear the contempt that your treating me in the way you do, brings upon me from others every day. Look at other young men of my age. Have they no liberty, no will, no right to speak? Are they obliged to sit mum-chance, and to be ordered about till they are the laughing-stock of young and old? I am a bye-word all over Chigwell, and I say—and it's fairer my saying so now, than waiting till you are dead, and I have got your money—I say, that before long I shall be driven to break such bounds, and that when I do, it won't be me that you'll have to blame, but your own self, and no other."

John Willet was so amazed by the exasperation and boldness of his hopeful son, that he sat as one bewildered, staring in a ludicrous manner at the boiler, and endeavouring, but quite ineffectually, to collect his tardy thoughts, and invent an answer. The guests, scarcely less disturbed, were equally at a loss; and at length, with a variety of muttered, half-expressed condolences, and pieces of advice, rose to depart; being at the same time slightly muddled with liquor.

The honest locksmith alone addressed a few words of coherent and sensible advice to both parties, urging John Willet to remember that Joe was nearly arrived at man's estate, and should not be ruled with too tight a hand, and exhorting Joe himself to bear with his father's caprices, and rather endeavour to turn them aside by temperate remonstrance than by ill-timed rebellion. This advice was received as such advice usually is. On John Willet it made almost as much impression as on the sign outside the door, while Joe, who took it in the best part, avowed himself more obliged than he could well express, but politely intimated his intention nevertheless of taking his own course uninfluenced by anybody.

"You have always been a very good friend to me, Mr. Varden," he said, as they stood without, in the porch, and the locksmith was equipping himself for his journey home; "I take it very kind of you to say all this, but the time's nearly come when the Maypole and I must part company."

"Roving stones gather no moss, Joe," said Gabriel.

"Nor mile-stones much," replied Joe. "I'm little better than one here, and see as much of the world."

"Then, what would you do, Joe?" pursued the locksmith, stroking his chin reflectively. "What could you be? where could you go, you see?"

"I must trust to chance, Mr. Varden."

"A bad thing to trust to, Joe. I don't like it. I always tell my girl when we talk about a husband for her, never to trust to chance, but to make sure beforehand that she has a good man and true, and then chance will neither make her nor break her. What are you fidgeting about there, Joe? Nothing gone in the harness I hope?"

"No, no," said Joe—finding, however, something very engrossing to do in the way of strapping and buckling—"Miss Dolly quite well?"

"Hearty, thankye. She looks pretty enough to be well, and good too."

"She's always both, sir—"

"So she is, thank God!"

"I hope," said Joe after some hesitation, "that you won't tell this story against me—this of my having been beat like the boy they'd make of me—at all events, till I have met this man again and settled the account. It'll be a better story then."

"Why who should I tell it to?" returned Gabriel. "They know it here, and I'm not likely to come across anybody else who would care about it."

"That's true enough," said the young fellow with a sigh. "I quite forgot that. Yes, that's true!"

So saying, he raised his face, which was very red,—no doubt from the exertion of strapping and buckling as aforesaid,—and giving the reins to the old man, who had by this time taken his seat, sighed again and bade him good night.

"Good night!" cried Gabriel. "Now think better of what we have just been speaking of, and don't be rash, there's a good fellow! I have an interest in you, and wouldn't have you cast yourself away. Good night!"

Returning his cheery farewell with cordial good-will, Joe Willet lingered until the sound of wheels ceased to vibrate in his ears, and then, shaking his head mournfully, re-entered the house.

Gabriel Varden went his way towards London, thinking of a great many things, and most of all of flaming terms in which to relate his adventure, and so account satisfactorily to Mrs. Varden for visiting the Maypole, despite certain solemn covenants between himself and that lady. Thinking begets, not only thought, but drowsiness occasionally, and the more the locksmith thought, the more sleepy he became.

A man may be very sober—or at least firmly set upon his legs on that neutral ground which lies between the confines of perfect sobriety and slight tipsiness—and yet feel a strong tendency to mingle up present circumstances with others which have no manner of connection with them; to confound all consideration of persons, things, times, and places; and to jumble his disjointed thoughts together in a kind of mental kaleidoscope, producing combinations as unexpected as they are transitory. This was Gabriel Varden's state, as, nodding in his dog sleep, and leaving his horse to pursue a road with which he was well acquainted, he got over the ground unconsciously, and drew nearer and nearer home. He had roused himself once, when the horse stopped until the turnpike gate was opened, and had cried a lusty "good night!" to the toll-keeper; but then he awoke out of a dream about picking a lock in the stomach of the Great Mogul, and even when he did wake, mixed up the turnpike man with his mother-in-law who had been dead twenty years. It is not surprising, therefore, that he soon relapsed, and jogged heavily along, quite insensible to his progress.

And, now, he approached the great city, which lay out-stretched before him like a dark shadow on the ground, reddening the sluggish air with a deep dull light, that told of labyrinths of public ways and shops, and swarms of busy people. Approaching nearer and nearer yet, this halo began to fade, and the causes which produced it slowly to develop themselves. Long lines of poorly lighted streets might be faintly traced, with here and there a lighter spot, where lamps were clustered round a square or market, or round some great building; after a time these grew more distinct, and the lamps themselves were visible; slight yellow specks, that seemed to be rapidly snuffed out, one by one, as intervening obstacles hid them from the sight. Then, sounds arose—the striking of church clocks, the distant bark of dogs, the hum of traffic in the streets; then outlines might be traced—tall steeples looming in the air, and piles of unequal roofs oppressed by chimneys; then, the noise swelled into a louder sound, and forms grew more distinct and numerous still, and London—visible in the darkness by its own faint light, and not by that of Heaven—was at hand.

The locksmith, however, all unconscious of its near vicinity, still jogged on, half sleeping and half waking, when a loud cry at no great distance ahead, roused him with a start.

For a moment or two he looked about him like a man who had been transported to some strange country in his sleep, but soon recognising familiar objects, rubbed his eyes lazily and might have relapsed again, but that the cry was repeated—not once or twice or thrice, but many times, and each time, if possible, with increased vehemence. Thoroughly aroused, Gabriel, who was a bold man and not easily daunted, made straight to the spot, urging on his stout little horse as if for life or death.

The matter indeed looked sufficiently serious, for, coming to the place whence the cries had proceeded, he descried the figure of a man extended in an apparently lifeless state upon the pathway, and, hovering round him, another person with a torch in his hand, which he waved in the air with a wild impatience, redoubling meanwhile those cries for help which had brought the locksmith to the spot.

"What's here to do?" said the old man, alighting. "How's this—what—Barnaby?"

The bearer of the torch shook his long loose hair back from his eyes, and thrusting his face eagerly into that of the locksmith, fixed upon him a look which told his history at once.

"You know me, Barnaby?" said Varden.

He nodded—not once or twice, but a score of times, and that with a fantastic exaggeration which would have kept his head in motion

for an hour, but that the locksmith held up his finger, and fixing his
eye sternly upon him caused him to desist; then pointed to the body
with an inquiring look.

"There's blood upon him," said Barnaby with a shudder. "It
makes me sick!"

"How came it there?" demanded Varden.

"Steel, steel, steel!" he replied fiercely, imitating with his hand
the thrust of a sword.

"Is he robbed?" said the locksmith.

Barnaby caught him by the arm, and nodded "Yes;" then pointed
towards the city.

"Oh!" said the old man, bending over the body and looking round
as he spoke into Barnaby's pale face, strangely lighted up by something that was *not* intellect. "The robber made off that way, did he?
Well, well, never mind that just now. Hold your torch this way—a
little farther off—so. Now stand quiet, while I try to see what harm
is done."

With these words, he applied himself to a closer examination of
the prostrate form, while Barnaby, holding the torch as he had been
directed, looked on in silence, fascinated by interest or curiosity, but
repelled nevertheless by some strong and secret horror which convulsed him in every nerve.

As he stood, at that moment, half shrinking back and half bending
forward, both his face and figure were full in the strong glare of the
link, and as distinctly revealed as though it had been broad day.
He was about three-and-twenty years old, and though rather spare,
of a fair height and strong make. His hair, of which he had a great
profusion, was red, and hanging in disorder about his face and
shoulders, gave to his restless looks an expression quite unearthly—
enhanced by the paleness of his complexion, and the glassy lustre of
his large protruding eyes. Startling as his aspect was, the features
were good, and there was something even plaintive in his wan and
haggard aspect. But, the absence of the soul is far more terrible in a
living man than in a dead one; and in this unfortunate being its
noblest powers were wanting.

His dress was of green, clumsily trimmed here and there—
apparently by his own hands—with gaudy lace; brightest where the
cloth was most worn and soiled, and poorest where it was at the best.
A pair of tawdry ruffles dangled at his wrists, while his throat was
nearly bare. He had ornamented his hat with a cluster of peacock's
feathers, but they were limp and broken, and now trailed negligently
down his back. Girt to his side was the steel hilt of an old sword without blade or scabbard; and some parti-coloured ends of ribands and
poor glass toys completed the ornamental portion of his attire. The
fluttered and confused disposition of all the motley scraps that
formed his dress, bespoke, in a scarcely less degree than his eager
and unsettled manner, the disorder of his mind, and by a grotesque
contrast set off and heightened the more impressive wildness of
his face.

"Barnaby," said the locksmith, after a hasty but careful inspection, "this man is not dead, but he has a wound in his side, and is in a fainting-fit."

"I know him, I know him!" cried Barnaby, clapping his hands.

"Know him?" repeated the locksmith.

"Hush!" said Barnaby, laying his fingers upon his lips. "He went out to-day a wooing. I wouldn't for a light guinea that he should never go a wooing again, for, if he did, some eyes would grow dim that are now as bright as—see, when I talk of eyes, the stars come out! Whose eyes are they? If they are angels' eyes, why do they look down here and see good men hurt, and only wink and sparkle all the night?"

"Now Heaven help this silly fellow," murmured the perplexed locksmith; "can he know this gentleman? His mother's house is not far off; I had better see if she can tell me who he is. Barnaby, my man, help me to put him in the chaise, and we'll ride home together."

"I can't touch him!" cried the idiot falling back, and shuddering as with a strong spasm; "he's bloody!"

"It's in his nature I know," muttered the locksmith, "it's cruel to ask him, but I must have help. Barnaby—good Barnaby—dear Barnaby—if you know this gentleman, for the sake of his life and everybody's life that loves him, help me to raise him and lay him down."

"Cover him then, wrap him close—don't let me see it—smell it—hear the word. Don't speak the word—don't!"

"No, no, I'll not. There, you see he's covered now. Gently. Well done, well done!"

They placed him in the carriage with great ease, for Barnaby was strong and active, but all the time they were so occupied he shivered from head to foot, and evidently experienced an ecstasy of terror.

This accomplished, and the wounded man being covered with Varden's own great-coat which he took off for the purpose, they proceeded onward at a brisk pace: Barnaby gaily counting the stars upon his fingers, and Gabriel inwardly congratulating himself upon having an adventure now, which would silence Mrs. Varden on the subject of the Maypole, for that night, or there was no faith in woman.

CHAPTER IV

IN the venerable suburb—it was a suburb once—of Clerkenwell, towards that part of its confines which is nearest to the Charter House, and in one of those cool, shady streets, of which a few, widely scattered and dispersed, yet remain in such old parts of the metropolis,—each tenement quietly vegetating like an ancient citizen who long ago retired from business, and dozing on in its infirmity until in course of time it tumbles down, and is replaced by some extravagant young heir, flaunting in stucco and ornamental work, and all the vanities of modern days,—in this quarter, and in a street of this description, the business of the present chapter lies.

At the time of which it treats, though only six-and-sixty years ago, a very large part of what is London now had no existence. Even in the brains of the wildest speculators, there had sprung up no long rows of streets connecting Highgate with Whitechapel, no assemblages of palaces in the swampy levels, nor little cities in the open fields. Although this part of town was then, as now, parcelled out in streets, and plentifully peopled, it wore a different aspect. There were gardens to many of the houses, and trees by the pavement side; with an air of freshness breathing up and down, which in these days would be sought in vain. Fields were nigh at hand, through which the New River took its winding course, and where there was merry hay-making in the summer time. Nature was not so far removed, or hard to get at, as in these days; and although there were busy trades in Clerkenwell, and working jewellers by scores, it was a purer place, with farmhouses nearer to it than many modern Londoners would readily believe, and lovers' walks at no great distance, which turned into squalid courts, long before the lovers of this age were born, or, as the phrase goes, thought of.

In one of these streets, the cleanest of them all, and on the shady side of the way—for good housewives know that sunlight damages their cherished furniture, and so choose the shade rather than its intrusive glare—there stood the house with which we have to deal. It was a modest building, not very straight, not large, not tall; not bold-faced, with great staring windows, but a shy, blinking house, with a conical roof going up into a peak over its garret window of four small panes of glass, like a cocked hat on the head of an elderly gentleman with one eye. It was not built of brick or lofty stone, but of wood and plaster; it was not planned with a dull and wearisome regard to regularity, for no one window matched the other, or seemed to have the slightest reference to anything besides itself.

The shop—for it had a shop—was, with reference to the first floor, where shops usually are; and there all resemblance between it and any other shop stopped short and ceased. People who went in and out didn't go up a flight of steps to it, or walk easily in upon a level with the street, but dived down three steep stairs, as into a cellar. Its floor was paved with stone and brick, as that of any other cellar might be; and in lieu of window framed and glazed it had a great black wooden flap or shutter, nearly breast high from the ground, which turned back in the day-time, admitting as much cold air as light, and very often more. Behind this shop was a wainscoted parlour, looking first into a paved yard, and beyond that again into a little terrace garden, raised some feet above it. Any stranger would have supposed that this wainscoted parlour, saving for the door of communication by which he had entered, was cut off and detached from all the world; and indeed most strangers on their first entrance were observed to grow extremely thoughtful, as weighing and pondering in their minds whether the upper rooms were only approachable by ladders from without; never suspecting that two of the most unassuming and unlikely doors in existence, which the most ingenious mechanician on earth must of necessity have supposed to be the doors of closets, opened out of this room—each without the smallest preparation, or so much as a quarter of an inch of passage—upon two dark winding flights of stairs, the one upward, the other downward, which were the sole means of communication between that chamber and the other portions of the house.

With all these oddities, there was not a neater, more scrupulously tidy, or more punctiliously ordered house, in Clerkenwell, in London, in all England. There were not cleaner windows, or whiter floors, or brighter stoves, or more highly shining articles of furniture in old mahogany; there was not more rubbing, scrubbing, burnishing and polishing, in the whole street put together. Nor was this excellence attained without some cost and trouble and great expenditure of voice, as the neighbours were frequently reminded when the good lady of the house overlooked and assisted in its being put to rights on cleaning days—which were usually from Monday morning till Saturday night, both days inclusive.

Leaning against the door-post of this, his dwelling, the locksmith stood early on the morning after he had met with the wounded man, gazing disconsolately at a great wooden emblem of a key, painted in vivid yellow to resemble gold, which dangled from the house-front, and swung to and fro with a mournful creaking noise, as if complaining that it had nothing to unlock. Sometimes, he looked over his shoulder into the shop, which was so dark and dingy with numerous tokens of his trade, and so blackened by the smoke of a little forge, near which his 'prentice was at work, that it would have been difficult for one unused to such espials to have distinguished anything but various tools of uncouth make and shape, great bunches of rusty keys, fragments of iron, half-finished locks, and such-like things, which garnished the walls and hung in clusters from the ceiling.

After a long and patient contemplation of the golden key, and many such backward glances, Gabriel stepped into the road, and stole a look at the upper windows. One of them chanced to be thrown open at the moment, and a roguish face met his; a face lighted up by the loveliest pair of sparkling eyes that ever locksmith looked upon; the face of a pretty, laughing, girl; dimpled and fresh, and healthful —the very impersonation of good-humour and blooming beauty.

"Hush!" she whispered, bending forward and pointing archly to the window underneath. "Mother is still asleep."

"Still, my dear," returned the locksmith in the same tone. "You talk as if she had been asleep all night, instead of little more than half an hour. But I'm very thankful. Sleep's a blessing—no doubt about it." The last few words he muttered to himself.

"How cruel of you to keep us up so late this morning, and never tell us where you were, or send us word!" said the girl.

"Ah, Dolly, Dolly!" returned the locksmith, shaking his head, and smiling, "how cruel of you to run up-stairs to bed! Come down to breakfast, madcap, and come down lightly, or you'll wake your mother. She must be tired, I am sure—*I* am."

Keeping these latter words to himself, and returning his daughter's nod, he was passing into the workshop, with the smile she had awakened still beaming on his face, when he just caught sight of his 'prentice's brown paper cap ducking down to avoid observation, and shrinking from the window back to its former place, which the wearer no sooner reached than he began to hammer lustily.

"Listening again, Simon!" said Gabriel to himself. "That's bad. What in the name of wonder does he expect the girl to say, that I always catch him listening when *she* speaks, and never at any other time! A bad habit, Sim, a sneaking, underhanded way. Ah! you may hammer, but you won't beat that out of me, if you work at it till your time's up!"

So saying, and shaking his head gravely, he re-entered the workshop, and confronted the subject of these remarks.

"There's enough of that just now," said the locksmith. "You needn't make any more of that confounded clatter. Breakfast's ready."

"Sir," said Sim, looking up with amazing politeness, and a peculiar little bow cut short off at the neck. "I shall attend you immediately."

"I suppose," muttered Gabriel, "that's out of the 'Prentice's Garland, or the 'Prentice's Delight, or the 'Prentice's Warbler, or the 'Prentice's Guide to the Gallows, or some such improving text-book. Now he's going to beautify himself—here's a precious locksmith!"

Quite unconscious that his master was looking on from the dark corner by the parlour door, Sim threw off the paper cap, sprang from his seat, and in two extraordinary steps, something between skating and minuet dancing, bounded to a washing place at the other end of the shop, and there removed from his face and hands all traces of his previous work—practising the same step all the time with the utmost gravity. This done, he drew from some concealed place a little scrap of looking-glass, and with its assistance arranged his hair, and ascertained the exact state of a little carbuncle on his nose. Having now completed his toilet, he placed the fragment of mirror on a low bench, and looked over his shoulder at so much of his legs as could be reflected in that small compass, with the greatest possible complacency and satisfaction.

Sim, as he was called in the locksmith's family, or Mr. Simon Tappertit, as he called himself, and required all men to style him out of doors, on holidays, and Sundays out,—was an old-fashioned, thin-faced, sleek-haired, sharp-nosed, small-eyed little fellow, very little more than five feet high, and thoroughly convinced in his own mind that he was above the middle size; rather tall, in fact, than otherwise. Of his figure, which was well enough formed, though somewhat of the leanest, he entertained the highest admiration; and with his legs, which, in knee-breeches, were perfect curiosities of littleness, he was enraptured to a degree amounting to enthusiasm. He also had some majestic, shadowy ideas, which had never been quite fathomed by his intimate friends, concerning the power of his eye. Indeed he had

been known to go so far as to boast that he could utterly quell and
subdue the haughtiest beauty by a simple process, which he termed
"eyeing her over;" but it must be added, that neither of this faculty,
nor of the power he claimed to have, through the same gift, of van-
quishing and heaving down dumb animals, even in a rabid state, had
he ever furnished evidence which could be deemed quite satisfactory
and conclusive.

It may be inferred from these premises, that in the small body of
Mr. Tappertit there was locked up an ambitious and aspiring soul.
As certain liquors, confined in casks too cramped in their dimensions,
will ferment, and fret, and chafe in their imprisonment, so the
spiritual essence or soul of Mr. Tappertit would sometimes fume within that precious cask, his body, until, with great foam and froth and
splutter, it would force a vent, and carry all before it. It was his
custom to remark, in reference to any one of these occasions, that his
soul had got into his head; and in this novel kind of intoxication
many scrapes and mishaps befell him which he had frequently concealed with no small difficulty from his worthy master.

Sim Tappertit, among the other fancies upon which his before-
mentioned soul was for ever feasting and regaling itself (and which
fancies, like the liver of Prometheus, grew as they were fed upon),
had a mighty notion of his order; and had been heard by the servant-
maid openly expressing his regret that the 'prentices no longer carried
clubs wherewith to mace the citizens: that was his strong expression.
He was likewise reported to have said that in former times a stigma
had been cast upon the body by the execution of George Barnwell, to
which they should not have basely submitted, but should have
demanded him of the legislature—temperately at first; then by an
appeal to arms, if necessary—to be dealt with as they in their
wisdom might think fit. These thoughts always led him to consider
what a glorious engine the 'prentices might yet become if they had
but a master spirit at their head; and then he would darkly, and to
the terror of his hearers, hint at certain reckless fellows that he knew
of, and at a certain Lion Heart ready to become their captain, who,
once afoot, would make the Lord Mayor tremble on his throne.

In respect of dress and personal decoration, Sim Tappertit was no
less of an adventurous and enterprising character. He had been seen,
beyond dispute, to pull off ruffles of the finest quality at the corner
of the street on Sunday nights, and to put them carefully in his
pocket before returning home; and it was quite notorious that on all
great holiday occasions it was his habit to exchange his plain steel
knee-buckles for a pair of glittering paste, under cover of a friendly
post, planted most conveniently in that same spot. Add to this that
he was in years just twenty, in his looks much older, and in conceit
at least two hundred; that he had no objection to be jested with,
touching his admiration of his master's daughter; and had even, when
called upon at a certain obscure tavern to pledge the lady whom he
honoured with his love, toasted, with many winks and leers, a fair
creature whose Christian name, he said, began with a D—;—and

as much is known of Sim Tappertit, who has by this time followed the locksmith in to breakfast, as is necessary to be known in making his acquaintance.

It was a substantial meal; for, over and above the ordinary tea equipage, the board creaked beneath the weight of a jolly round of beef, a ham of the first magnitude, and sundry towers of buttered Yorkshire cake, piled slice upon slice in most alluring order. There was also a goodly jug of well-browned clay, fashioned into the form of an old gentleman, not by any means unlike the locksmith, atop of whose bald head was a fine white froth answering to his wig, indicative, beyond dispute, of sparkling home-brewed ale. But, better far than fair home-brewed, or Yorkshire cake, or ham, or beef, or anything to eat or drink that earth or air or water can supply, there sat, presiding over all, the locksmith's rosy daughter, before whose dark eyes even beef grew insignificant, and malt became as nothing.

Fathers should never kiss their daughters when young men are by. It's too much. There are bounds to human endurance. So thought Sim Tappertit when Gabriel drew those rosy lips to his—those lips within Sim's reach from day to day, and yet so far off. He had a respect for his master, but he wished the Yorkshire cake might choke him.

"Father," said the locksmith's daughter, when this salute was over, and they took their seats at table, "what is this I hear about last night?"

"All true, my dear; true as the Gospel, Doll."

"Young Mr. Chester robbed, and lying wounded in the road, when you came up!"

"Ay—Mr. Edward. And beside him, Barnaby, calling for help with all his might. It was well it happened as it did; for the road's a lonely one, the hour was late, and, the night being cold, and poor Barnaby even less sensible than usual from surprise and fright, the young gentleman might have met his death in a very short time."

"I dread to think of it!" cried his daughter with a shudder. "How did you know him?"

"Know him!" returned the locksmith. "I didn't know him—how could I? I had never seen him, often as I had heard and spoken of him. I took him to Mrs. Rudge's; and she no sooner saw him than the truth came out."

"Miss Emma, father—If this news should reach her, enlarged upon as it is sure to be, she will go distracted."

"Why, lookye there again, how a man suffers for being good-natured," said the locksmith. "Miss Emma was with her uncle at the masquerade at Carlisle House, where she had gone, as the people at the Warren told me, sorely against her will. What does your blockhead father when he and Mrs. Rudge have laid their heads together, but goes there when he ought to be abed, makes interest with his friend the doorkeeper, slips him on a mask and domino, and mixes with the masquers."

"And like himself to do so!" cried the girl, putting her fair arm round his neck, and giving him a most enthusiastic kiss.

"Like himself!" repeated Gabriel, affecting to grumble, but evidently delighted with the part he had taken, and with her praise. "Very like himself—so your mother said. However, he mingled with the crowd, and prettily worried and badgered he was, I warrant you, with people squeaking, 'Don't you know me?' and 'I've found you out,' and all that kind of nonsense in his ears. He might have wandered on till now, but in a little room there was a young lady who had taken off her mask, on account of the place being very warm, and was sitting there alone."

"And that was she?" said his daughter hastily.

"And that was she," replied the locksmith; "and I no sooner whispered her what the matter was—as softly, Doll, and with nearly as much art as you could have used yourself—than she gives a kind of scream and faints away."

"What did you do—what happened next?" asked his daughter.

"Why, the masks came flocking round, with a general noise and hubbub, and I thought myself in luck to get clear off, that's all," rejoined the locksmith. "What happened when I reached home you may guess, if you didn't hear it. Ah! Well, it's a poor heart that never rejoices.—Put Toby this way, my dear."

This Toby was the brown jug of which previous mention has been made. Applying his lips to the worthy old gentleman's benevolent forehead, the locksmith, who had all this time been ravaging among the eatables, kept them there so long, at the same time raising the vessel slowly in the air, that at length Toby stood on his head upon his nose, when he smacked his lips, and set him on the table again with fond reluctance.

Although Sim Tappertit had taken no share in this conversation, no part of it being addressed to him, he had not been wanting in such silent manifestations of astonishment, as he deemed most compatible with the favourable display of his eyes. Regarding the pause which now ensued, as a particularly advantageous opportunity for doing great execution with them upon the locksmith's daughter (who he had no doubt was looking at him in mute admiration), he began to screw and twist his face, and especially those features, into such extraordinary, hideous, and unparalleled contortions, that Gabriel, who happened to look towards him, was stricken with amazement.

"Why, what the devil's the matter with the lad?" cried the locksmith. "Is he choking?"

"Who?" demanded Sim, with some disdain.

"Who? why, you," returned his master. "What do you mean by making those horrible faces over your breakfast?"

"Faces are matters of taste, sir," said Mr. Tappertit, rather discomfited; not the less so because he saw the locksmith's daughter smiling.

"Sim," rejoined Gabriel, laughing heartily. "Don't be a fool, for I'd rather see you in your senses. These young fellows," he added, turning to his daughter, "are always committing some folly or another.

There was a quarrel between Joe Willet and old John last night—
though I can't say Joe was much in fault either. He'll be missing one
of these mornings, and will have gone away upon some wild-goose
errand, seeking his fortune.—What, what's the matter, Doll? *You*
are making faces now. The girls are as bad as the boys every bit!"

"It's the tea," said Dolly, turning alternately very red and very
white, which is no doubt the effect of a slight scald—"so very hot."

Mr. Tappertit looked immensely big at a quartern loaf on the
table, and breathed hard.

"Is that all?" returned the locksmith. "Put some more milk in it.—
Yes, I am sorry for Joe, because he is a likely young fellow, and gains
upon one every time one sees him. But he'll start off, you'll find.
Indeed he told me as much himself!"

"Indeed!" cried Dolly in a faint voice. "In—deed!"

"Is the tea tickling your throat still, my dear?" said the locksmith.

But, before his daughter could make him any answer, she was
taken with a troublesome cough, and it was such a very unpleasant
cough, that, when she left off, the tears were starting in her bright
eyes. The good-natured locksmith was still patting her on the back
and applying such gentle restoratives, when a message arrived from
Mrs. Varden, making known to all whom it might concern, that she
felt too much indisposed to rise after her great agitation and anxiety
of the previous night; and therefore desired to be immediately
accommodated with the little black tea-pot of strong mixed tea, a
couple of rounds of buttered toast, a middling-sized dish of beef and
ham cut thin, and the Protestant Manual in two volumes post
octavo. Like some other ladies who in remote ages flourished upon
this globe, Mrs. Varden was most devout when most ill-tempered.
Whenever she and her husband were at unusual variance, then the
Protestant Manual was in high feather.

Knowing from experience what these requests portended, the
triumvirate broke up; Dolly to see the orders executed with all despatch; Gabriel, to some out-of-door work in his little chaise; and Sim,
to his daily duty in the workshop, to which retreat he carried the big
look, although the loaf remained behind.

Indeed the big look increased immensely, and when he had tied his
apron on, became quite gigantic. It was not until he had several
times walked up and down with folded arms, and the longest strides
he could take, and had kicked a great many small articles out of his
way, that his lip began to curl. At length, a gloomy derision came
upon his features, and he smiled; uttering meanwhile with supreme
contempt the monosyllable "Joe!"

"I eyed her over, while he talked about the fellow," he said, "and
that was of course the reason of her being confused. Joe!"

He walked up and down again much quicker than before, and if
possible with longer strides; sometimes stopping to take a glance at
his legs, and sometimes to jerk out, and cast from him, another
"Joe!" In the course of a quarter of an hour or so he again assumed
the paper cap and tried to work. No, It could not be done.

"I'll do nothing to-day," said Mr. Tappertit, dashing it down again, "but grind. I'll grind up all the tools. Grinding will suit my present humour well. Joe!"

Whirr-r-r-r. The grindstone was soon in motion; the sparks were flying off in showers. This was the occupation for his heated spirit.

Whirr-r-r-r-r-r.

"Something will come of this!" said Mr. Tappertit, pausing as if in triumph, and wiping his heated face upon his sleeve. "Something will come of this. I hope it mayn't be human gore!"

Whirr-r-r-r-r-r-r.

CHAPTER V

As soon as the business of the day was over, the locksmith sallied forth, alone, to visit the wounded gentleman and ascertain the progress of his recovery. The house where he had left him was in a by-street in Southwark, not far from London Bridge; and thither he hied with all speed, bent upon returning with as little delay as might be, and getting to bed betimes.

The evening was boisterous—scarcely better than the previous night had been. It was not easy for a stout man like Gabriel to keep his legs at the street corners, or to make head against the high wind, which often fairly got the better of him, and drove him back some paces, or, in defiance of all his energy, forced him to take shelter in an arch or doorway until the fury of the gust was spent. Occasionally a hat or wig, or both, came spinning and trundling past him, like a mad thing; while the more serious spectacle of falling tiles and slates, or of masses of brick and mortar or fragments of stone-coping rattling upon the pavement near at hand, and splitting into fragments, did not increase the pleasure of the journey, or make the way less dreary.

"A trying night for a man like me to walk in!" said the locksmith, as he knocked softly at the widow's door. "I'd rather be in old John's chimney-corner, faith!"

"Who's there?" demanded a woman's voice from within. Being answered, it added a hasty word of welcome, and the door was quickly opened.

She was about forty—perhaps two or three years older—with a cheerful aspect, and a face that had once been pretty. It bore traces of affliction and care, but they were of an old date, and Time had smoothed them. Any one who had bestowed but a casual glance on Barnaby might have known that this was his mother, from the strong resemblance between them; but where in his face there was wildness and vacancy, in hers there was the patient composure of long effort and quiet resignation.

One thing about his face was very strange and startling. You could not look upon it in its most cheerful mood without feeling that it had some extraordinary capacity of expressing terror. It was not on the surface. It was in no one feature that it lingered. You could not take the eyes or mouth, or lines upon the cheek, and say, if this or that were otherwise, it would not be so. Yet there it always lurked—something for ever dimly seen, but ever there, and never absent for a moment. It was the faintest, palest shadow of some look, to which an instant of intense and most unutterable horror only could have given birth; but indistinct and feeble as it was, it did suggest what that look must have been, and fixed it in the mind as if it had had existence in a dream.

More faintly imaged, and wanting force and purpose, as it were, because of his darkened intellect, there was this same stamp upon the son. Seen in a picture, it must have had some legend with it, and would have haunted those who looked upon the canvas. They who knew the Maypole story, and could remember what the widow was, before her husband's and his master's murder, understood it well. They recollected how the change had come, and could call to mind that when her son was born, upon the very day the deed was known, he bore upon his wrist what seemed a smear of blood but half washed out.

"God save you, neighbour!" said the locksmith, as he followed her, with the air of an old friend, into a little parlour where a cheerful fire was burning.

"And you," she answered smiling. "Your kind heart has brought you here again. Nothing will keep you at home, I know of old, if there are friends to serve or comfort, out of doors."

"Tut, tut," returned the locksmith, rubbing his hands and warming them. "You women are such talkers. What of the patient, neighbour?"

"He is sleeping now. He was very restless towards daylight, and for some hours tossed and tumbled sadly. But the fever has left him, and the doctor says he will soon mend. He must not be removed until to-morrow."

"He has had visitors to-day—humph?" said Gabriel, slyly.

"Yes. Old Mr. Chester has been here ever since we sent for him, and had not been gone many minutes when you knocked."

"No ladies?" said Gabriel, elevating his eyebrows and looking disappointed.

"A letter," replied the widow.

"Come. That's better than nothing!" replied the locksmith. "Who was the bearer?"

"Barnaby, of course."

"Barnaby's a jewel!" said Varden; "and comes and goes with ease where we who think ourselves much wiser would make but a poor hand of it. He is not out wandering, again, I hope?"

"Thank Heaven he is in his bed; having been up all night, as you know, and on his feet all day. He was quite tired out. Ah, neighbour, if I could but see him oftener so—if I could but tame down that terrible restlessness——"

"In good time," said the locksmith, kindly, "in good time—don't be down-hearted. To my mind he grows wiser every day."

The widow shook her head. And yet, though she knew the locksmith sought to cheer her, and spoke from no conviction of his own, she was glad to hear even this praise of her poor benighted son.

"He will be a 'cute man yet," resumed the locksmith. "Take care, when we are growing old and foolish, Barnaby doesn't put us to the blush, that's all. But our other friend," he added, looking under the table and about the floor—"sharpest and cunningest of all the sharp and cunning ones—where's he?"

"In Barnaby's room," rejoined the widow, with a faint smile.

"Ah! He's a knowing blade!" said Varden, shaking his head. "I should be sorry to talk secrets before him. Oh! He's a deep customer. I've no doubt he can read, and write, and cast accounts if he chooses. What was that? Him tapping at the door?"

"No," returned the widow. "It was in the street, I think. Hark! Yes. There again! 'Tis some one knocking softly at the shutter. Who can it be!"

They had been speaking in a low tone, for the invalid lay overhead, and the walls and ceilings being thin and poorly built, the sound of their voices might otherwise have disturbed his slumber. The party without, whoever it was, could have stood close to the shutter without hearing anything spoken; and, seeing the light through the chinks and finding all so quiet, might have been persuaded that only one person was there.

"Some thief or ruffian maybe," said the locksmith. "Give me the light."

"No, no," she returned hastily. "Such visitors have never come to this poor dwelling. Do you stay here. You're within call, at the worst. I would rather go myself—alone."

"Why?" said the locksmith, unwillingly relinquishing the candle he had caught up from the table.

"Because—I don't know why—because the wish is so strong upon me," she rejoined. "There again—do not detain me, I beg of you!"

Gabriel looked at her, in great surprise to see one who was usually so mild and quiet thus agitated, and with so little cause. She left the room and closed the door behind her. She stood for a moment as if hesitating, with her hand upon the lock. In this short interval the knocking came again, and a voice close to the window—a voice the locksmith seemed to recollect, and to have some disagreeable association with—whispered "Make haste."

The words were uttered in that low distinct voice which finds its way so readily to sleepers' ears, and wakes them in a fright. For a moment it startled even the locksmith; who involuntarily drew back from the window, and listened.

The wind rumbling in the chimney made it difficult to hear what passed, but he could tell that the door was opened, that there was the tread of a man upon the creaking boards, and then a moment's silence—broken by a suppressed something which was not a shriek, or groan, or cry for help, and yet might have been either or all three; and the words "My God!" uttered in a voice it chilled him to hear.

He rushed out upon the instant. There, at last, was that dreadful look—the very one he seemed to know so well and yet had never seen before—upon her face. There she stood, frozen to the ground, gazing with starting eyes, and livid cheeks, and every feature fixed and ghastly, upon the man he had encountered in the dark last night. His eyes met those of the locksmith. It was but a flash, an instant, a breath upon the polished glass, and he was gone.

The locksmith was upon him—had the skirts of his streaming garment almost in his grasp—when his arms were tightly clutched, and the widow flung herself upon the ground before him.

"The other way—the other way," she cried. "He went the other way. Turn—turn!"

"The other way! I see him now," rejoined the locksmith, pointing —"yonder—there—there is his shadow passing by that light. What —who is this? Let me go."

"Come back, come back!" exclaimed the woman, clasping him. "Do not touch him on your life. I charge you, come back. He carries other lives besides his own. Come back!"

"What does this mean?" cried the locksmith.

"No matter what it means, don't ask, don't speak, don't think about it. He is not to be followed, checked, or stopped. Come back!"

The old man looked at her in wonder, as she writhed and clung about him; and, borne down by her passion, suffered her to drag him into the house. It was not until she had chained and double-locked the door, fastened every bolt and bar with the heat and fury of a maniac, and drawn him back into the room, that she turned upon him, once again, that stony look of horror, and, sinking down into a chair, covered her face, and shuddered, as though the hand of death were on her.

CHAPTER VI

BEYOND all measure astonished by the strange occurrences which had passed with so much violence and rapidity, the locksmith gazed upon the shuddering figure in the chair like one half stupefied, and would have gazed much longer, had not his tongue been loosened by compassion and humanity.

"You are ill," said Gabriel. "Let me call some neighbour in."

"Not for the world," she rejoined, motioning to him with her trembling hand, and holding her face averted. "It is enough that you have been by, to see this."

"Nay, more than enough—or less," said Gabriel.

"Be it so," she returned. "As you like. Ask me no questions, I entreat you."

"Neighbour," said the locksmith, after a pause. "Is this fair, or reasonable, or just to yourself? Is it like you, who have known me so long and sought my advice in all matters—like you, who from a girl have had a strong mind and a staunch heart?"

"I have need of them," she replied. "I am growing old, both in years and care. Perhaps that, and too much trial, have made them weaker than they used to be. Do not speak to me."

"How can I see what I have seen, and hold my peace!" returned the locksmith. "Who was that man, and why has his coming made this change in you?"

She was silent, but held to the chair as though to save herself from falling on the ground.

"I take the licence of an old acquaintance, Mary," said the locksmith, "who has ever had a warm regard for you, and maybe has tried to prove it when he could. Who is this ill-favoured man, and what has he to do with you? Who is this ghost, that is only seen in the black nights and bad weather? How does he know, and why does he haunt this house, whispering through chinks and crevices, as if there was that between him and you, which neither durst so much as speak aloud of. Who is he?"

"You do well to say he haunts this house," returned the widow, faintly. "His shadow has been upon it and me, in light and darkness, at noonday and midnight. And now, at last, he has come in the body!"

"But he wouldn't have gone in the body," returned the locksmith with some irritation, "if you had left my arms and legs at liberty. What riddle is it?"

"It is one," she answered, rising as she spoke, "that must remain for ever as it is. I dare not say more than that."

"Dare not!" repeated the wondering locksmith.

"Do not press me," she replied. "I am sick and faint, and every faculty of life seems dead within me.—No!—Do not touch me, either."

Gabriel, who had stepped forward to render her assistance, fell back as she made this hasty exclamation, and regarded her in silent wonder.

"Let me go my way home," she said in a low voice, "and let the hands of no honest man touch mine to-night." When she had tottered to the door, she turned, and added with a stronger effort, "This is a secret, which, of necessity, I trust to you. You are a true man. As you have ever been good and kind to me,—keep it. If any noise was heard above, make some excuse—say anything but what you really saw, and never let a word or look between us, recall this circumstance. I trust to you. Mind, I trust to you. How much I trust, you never can conceive."

Casting her eyes upon him for an instant, she withdrew, and left him there alone.

Gabriel, not knowing what to think, stood staring at the door with a countenance full of surprise and dismay. The more he pondered on what had passed, the less able he was to give it any favourable interpretation. To find this widow woman, whose life for so many years had been supposed to be one of solitude and retirement, and who, in her quiet suffering character, had gained the good opinion and respect of all who knew her—to find her linked mysteriously with an ill-omened man, alarmed at his appearance, and yet favouring his escape, was a discovery that pained as much as startled him. Her reliance on his secrecy, and his tacit acquiescence, increased his distress of mind. If he had spoken boldly, persisted in questioning her, detained her when she rose to leave the room, made any kind of protest, instead of silently compromising himself, as he felt he had done, he would have been more at ease.

"Why did I let her say it was a secret, and she trusted it to me!" said Gabriel, putting his wig on one side to scratch his head with greater ease, and looking ruefully at the fire. "I have no more readiness than old John himself. Why didn't I say firmly, 'You have no right to such secrets, and I demand of you to tell me what this means,' instead of standing gaping at her, like an old mooncalf as I am! But there's my weakness. I can be obstinate enough with men if need be, but women may twist me round their fingers at their pleasure."

He took his wig off outright as he made this reflection, and, warming his handkerchief at the fire, began to rub and polish his bald head with it, until it glistened again.

"And yet," said the locksmith, softening under this soothing process, and stopping to smile, "it *may* be nothing. Any drunken brawler trying to make his way into the house, would have alarmed a quiet soul like her. But then"—and here was the vexation—"how came it to be that man; how comes he to have this influence over her; how came she to favour his getting away from me; and, more than all, how came she not to say it was a sudden fright, and nothing more? It's a sad thing to have, in one minute, reason to mistrust a person I have known so long, and an old sweetheart into the bargain; but what else can I do, with all this upon my mind!—Is that Barnaby outside there?"

"Ay!" he cried, looking in and nodding. "Sure enough it's Barnaby —how did you guess?"

"By your shadow," said the locksmith.

"Oho!" cried Barnaby, glancing over his shoulder. "He's a merry fellow, that shadow, and keeps close to me, though I *am* silly. We have such pranks, such walks, such runs, such gambols on the grass! Sometimes he'll be half as tall as a church steeple, and sometimes no bigger than a dwarf. Now, he goes on before, and now behind, and anon he'll be stealing on, on this side, or on that, stopping whenever I stop, and thinking I can't see him, though I have my eye on him sharp enough. Oh! he's a merry fellow. Tell me—is he silly too! I think he is."

"Why?" asked Gabriel.

"Because he never tires of mocking me, but does it all day long.— Why don't you come?"

"Where?"

"Up-stairs. He wants you. Stay—where's *his* shadow? Come. You're a wise man; tell me that."

"Beside him, Barnaby; beside him, I suppose," returned the locksmith.

"No!" he replied, shaking his head. "Guess again."

"Gone out a walking, maybe?"

"He has changed shadows with a woman," the idiot whispered in his ear, and then fell back with a look of triumph. "Her shadow's always with him, and his with her. That's sport I think, eh?"

"Barnaby," said the locksmith, with a grave look; "come hither, lad."

"I know what you want to say. I know!" he replied, keeping away from him. "But I'm cunning, I'm silent. I only say so much to you— are you ready?" As he spoke, he caught up the light and waved it with a wild laugh above his head.

"Softly—gently," said the locksmith, exerting all his influence to keep him calm and quiet. "I thought you had been asleep."

"So I *have* been asleep," he rejoined, with widely-opened eyes. "There have been great faces coming and going—close to my face, and then a mile away—low places to creep through, whether I would or no—high churches to fall down from—strange creatures crowded up together neck and heels, to sit upon the bed—that's sleep, eh?"

"Dreams, Barnaby, dreams," said the locksmith.

"Dreams!" he echoed softly, drawing closer to him. "Those are not dreams."

"What are," replied the locksmith, "if they are not?"

"I dreamed," said Barnaby, passing his arm through Varden's, and peering close into his face as he answered in a whisper, "I dreamed just now that something—it was in the shape of a man— followed me—came softly after me—wouldn't let me be—but was always hiding and crouching, like a cat in dark corners, waiting till I should pass; when it crept out and came softly after me.—Did you ever see me run?"

"Many a time, you know."

"You never saw me run as I did in this dream. Still it came creeping on to worry me. Nearer, nearer, nearer—I ran faster—leaped— sprung out of bed, and to the window—and there, in the street below —but he is waiting for us. Are you coming?"

"What in the street below, Barnaby?" said Varden, imagining that he traced some connection between this vision and what had actually occurred.

Barnaby looked into his face, muttered incoherently, waved the light above his head again, laughed, and drawing the locksmith's arm more tightly through his own, led him up the stairs in silence.

They entered a homely bedchamber, garnished in a scanty way with chairs, whose spindle-shanks bespoke their age, and other furniture of very little worth; but clean and neatly kept. Reclining in an easy-chair before the fire, pale and weak from waste of blood, was Edward Chester, the young gentleman who had been the first to quit the Maypole on the previous night, and who, extending his hand to the locksmith, welcomed him as his preserver and friend.

"Say no more, sir, say no more," said Gabriel. "I hope I would have done at least as much for any man in such a strait, and most of all, for you, sir. A certain young lady," he added, with some hesitation, "has done us many a kind turn, and we naturally feel—I hope I give you no offence in saying this, sir?"

The young man smiled and shook his head; at the same time moving in his chair as if in pain.

"It's no great matter," he said, in answer to the locksmith's sympathising look, "a mere uneasiness arising at least as much from being cooped up here, as from the slight wound I have, or from the loss of blood. Be seated, Mr. Varden."

"If I may make so bold, Mr. Edward, as to lean upon your chair," returned the locksmith, accommodating his action to his speech, and bending over him, "I'll stand here for the convenience of speaking low. Barnaby is not in his quietest humour to-night, and at such times talking never does him good."

They both glanced at the subject of this remark, who had taken a seat on the other side of the fire, and, smiling vacantly, was making puzzles on his fingers with a skein of string.

"Pray, tell me, sir," said Varden, dropping his voice still lower, "exactly what happened last night. I have my reason for inquiring. You left the Maypole, alone?"

"And walked homeward alone, until I had nearly reached the place where you found me, when I heard the gallop of a horse."

"Behind you?" said the locksmith.

"Indeed, yes—behind me. It was a single rider, who soon overtook me, and checking his horse, inquired the way to London."

"You were on the alert, sir, knowing how many highwaymen there are, scouring the roads in all directions?" said Varden.

"I was, but I had only a stick, having imprudently left my pistols in their holster-case with the landlord's son. I directed him as he desired. Before the words had passed my lips, he rode upon me furiously, as if bent on trampling me down beneath his horse's hoofs. In starting aside, I slipped and fell. You found me with this stab and an ugly bruise or two, and without my purse—in which he found little enough for his pains. And now, Mr. Varden," he added, shaking the locksmith by the hand, "saving the extent of my gratitude to you, you know as much as I."

"Except," said Gabriel, bending down yet more, and looking cautiously towards their silent neighbour, "except in respect of the robber himself. What like was he, sir? Speak low, if you please. Barnaby means no harm, but I have watched him oftener than you, and I know, little as you would think it, that he's listening now."

It required a strong confidence in the locksmith's veracity to lead any one to this belief, for every sense and faculty that Barnaby possessed, seemed to be fixed upon his game, to the exclusion of all other things. Something in the young man's face expressed this opinion, for Gabriel repeated what he had just said, more earnestly than before, and with another glance towards Barnaby, again asked what like the man was.

"The night was so dark," said Edward, "the attack so sudden, and he so wrapped and muffled up, that I can hardly say. It seems that—"

"Don't mention his name, sir," returned the locksmith, following his look towards Barnaby; "I know *he* saw him. I want to know what *you* saw."

"All I remember is," said Edward, "that as he checked his horse his hat was blown off. He caught it, and replaced it on his head, which I observed was bound with a dark handkerchief. A stranger entered the Maypole while I was there, whom I had not seen—for I had sat apart for reasons of my own—and when I rose to leave the room and glanced round, he was in the shadow of the chimney and hidden from my sight. But, if he and the robber were two different persons their voices were strangely and most remarkably alike; for directly the man addressed me in the road, I recognised his speech again."

"It is as I feared. The very man was here to-night," thought the locksmith, changing colour. "What dark history is this!"

"Halloa!" cried a hoarse voice in his ear. "Halloa, halloa, halloa! Bow wow wow. What's the matter here! Hal-loa!"

The speaker—who made the locksmith start as if he had seen some supernatural agent—was a large raven, who had perched upon the top of the easy-chair, unseen by him and Edward, and listened with a polite attention and a most extraordinary appearance of comprehending every word, to all they had said up to this point; turning his head from one to the other, as if his office were to judge between them, and it were of the very last importance that he should not lose a word.

"Look at him!" said Varden, divided between admiration of the bird and a kind of fear of him. "Was there ever such a knowing imp as that! Oh he's a dreadful fellow!"

The raven, with his head very much on one side, and his bright eye shining like a diamond, preserved a thoughtful silence for a few seconds, and then replied in a voice so hoarse and distant, that it seemed to come through his thick feathers rather than out of his mouth.

"Halloa, halloa, halloa! What's the matter here! Keep up your spirits. Never say die. Bow wow wow. I'm a devil, I'm a devil, I'm a devil. Hurrah!"—And then, as if exulting in his infernal character, he began to whistle.

"I more than half believe he speaks the truth. Upon my word I do," said Varden. "Do you see how he looks at me, as if he knew what I was saying?"

To which the bird, balancing himself on tiptoe, as it were, and moving his body up and down in a sort of grave dance, rejoined, "I'm a devil, I'm a devil, I'm a devil," and flapped his wings against his sides as if he were bursting with laughter. Barnaby clapped his hands, and fairly rolled upon the ground in an ecstasy of delight.

"Strange companions, sir," said the locksmith, shaking his head, and looking from one to the other. "The bird has all the wit."

"Strange indeed!" said Edward, holding out his forefinger to the raven, who, in acknowledgment of the attention, made a dive at it immediately with his iron bill. "Is he old?"

"A mere boy, sir," replied the locksmith. "A hundred and twenty, or thereabouts. Call him down, Barnaby, my man."

"Call him!" echoed Barnaby, sitting upright upon the floor, and staring vacantly at Gabriel, as he thrust his hair back from his face. "But who can make him come! He calls me, and makes me go where he will. He goes on before, and I follow. He's the master, and I'm the man. Is that the truth, Grip?"

The raven gave a short, comfortable, confidential kind of croak;— a most expressive croak, which seemed to say, "You needn't let these fellows into our secrets. We understand each other. It's all right."

"*I* make *him* come?" cried Barnaby, pointing to the bird. "Him, who never goes to sleep, or so much as winks!—Why, any time of night, you may see his eyes in my dark room, shining like two sparks. And every night, and all night too, he's broad awake, talking to himself, thinking what he shall do to-morrow, where we shall go, and what he shall steal, and hide, and bury. *I* make *him* come. Ha ha ha!"

On second thoughts, the bird appeared disposed to come of himself. After a short survey of the ground, and a few sidelong looks at the ceiling and at everybody present in turn, he fluttered to the floor, and went to Barnaby—not in a hop, or walk, or run, but in a pace like that of a very particular gentleman with exceedingly tight boots on, trying to walk fast over loose pebbles. Then, stepping into his extended hand, and condescending to be held out at arm's length, he gave vent to a succession of sounds, not unlike the drawing of some eight or ten dozen of long corks, and again asserted his brimstone birth and parentage with great distinctness.

The locksmith shook his head—perhaps in some doubt of the creature's being really nothing but a bird—perhaps in pity for Barnaby, who by this time had him in his arms, and was rolling about, with him, on the ground. As he raised his eyes from the poor fellow he encountered those of his mother, who had entered the room, and was looking on in silence.

She was quite white in the face, even to her lips, but had wholly subdued her emotion, and wore her usual quiet look. Varden fancied as he glanced at her that she shrunk from his eye; and that she busied herself about the wounded gentleman to avoid him the better.

It was time he went to bed, she said. He was to be removed to his own home on the morrow, and he had already exceeded his time for sitting up, by a full hour. Acting on this hint, the locksmith prepared to take his leave.

"By the bye," said Edward, as he shook him by the hand, and looked from him to Mrs. Rudge and back again, "what noise was that below? I heard your voice in the midst of it, and should have inquired before, but our other conversation drove it from my memory. What was it?"

The locksmith looked towards her, and bit his lip. She leant against the chair, and bent her eyes upon the ground. Barnaby too—he was listening.

—"Some mad or drunken fellow, sir," Varden at length made answer, looking steadily at the widow as he spoke. "He mistook the house, and tried to force an entrance."

She breathed more freely, but stood quite motionless. As the locksmith said "Good night," and Barnaby caught up the candle to light him down the stairs, she took it from him, and charged him—with more haste and earnestness than so slight an occasion appeared to warrant—not to stir. The raven followed them to satisfy himself that all was right below, and when they reached the street-door, stood on the bottom stair drawing corks out of number.

With a trembling hand she unfastened the chain and bolts, and turned the key. As she had her hand upon the latch, the locksmith said in a low voice.

"I have told a lie to-night, for your sake, Mary, and for the sake of bygone times and old acquaintance, when I would scorn to do so for my own. I hope I may have done no harm, or led to none. I can't help the suspicions you have forced upon me, and I am loth, I tell you plainly, to leave Mr. Edward here. Take care he comes to no hurt. I doubt the safety of this roof, and am glad he leaves it so soon. Now, let me go."

For a moment she hid her face in her hands and wept; but resisting the strong impulse which evidently moved her to reply, opened the door—no wider than was sufficient for the passage of his body—and motioned him away. As the locksmith stood upon the step, it was chained and locked behind him, and the raven, in furtherance of these precautions, barked like a lusty house-dog.

"In league with that ill-looking figure that might have fallen from a gibbet—he listening and hiding here—Barnaby first upon the spot last night—can she who has always borne so fair a name be guilty of such crimes in secret!" said the locksmith, musing. "Heaven forgive me if I am wrong, and send me just thoughts; but she is poor, the temptation may be great, and we daily hear of things as strange.— Ay, bark away, my friend. If there's any wickedness going on, that raven's in it, I'll be sworn."

CHAPTER VII

MRS. VARDEN was a lady of what is commonly called an uncertain temper—a phrase which being interpreted signifies a temper tolerably certain to make everybody more or less uncomfortable. Thus it generally happened, that when other people were merry, Mrs. Varden was dull; and that when other people were dull, Mrs. Varden was disposed to be amazingly cheerful. Indeed the worthy housewife was of such a capricious nature, that she not only attained a higher pitch of genius than Macbeth, in respect of her ability to be wise, amazed, temperate and furious, loyal and neutral in an instant, but would sometimes ring the changes backwards and forwards on all possible moods and flights in one short quarter of an hour; performing, as it were, a kind of triple bob major on the peal of instruments in the female belfry, with a skilfulness and rapidity of execution that astonished all who heard her.

It had been observed in this good lady (who did not want for personal attractions, being plump and buxom to look at, though like her fair daughter, somewhat short in stature) that this uncertainty of disposition strengthened and increased with her temporal prosperity; and divers wise men and matrons, on friendly terms with the locksmith and his family, even went so far as to assert, that a tumble down some half-dozen rounds in the world's ladder—such as the breaking of the bank in which her husband kept his money, or some little fall of that kind—would be the making of her, and could hardly fail to render her one of the most agreeable companions in existence. Whether they were right or wrong in this conjecture, certain it is that minds, like bodies, will often fall into a pimpled ill-conditioned state from mere excess of comfort, and like them, are often successfully cured by remedies in themselves very nauseous and unpalatable.

Mrs. Varden's chief aider and abettor, and at the same time her principal victim and object of wrath, was her single domestic servant, one Miss Miggs; or as she was called, in conformity with those prejudices of society which lop and top from poor handmaidens all such genteel excrescences—Miggs. This Miggs was a tall young lady, very much addicted to patterns in private life; slender and shrewish, of a rather uncomfortable figure, and though not absolutely ill-looking, of a sharp and acid visage. As a general principle and abstract proposition, Miggs held the male sex to be utterly contemptible and unworthy of notice; to be fickle, false, base, sottish, inclined to perjury, and wholly undeserving. When particularly exasperated against them (which, scandal said, was when Sim Tappertit slighted her most) she was accustomed to wish with great emphasis that the whole race of women could but die off, in order that the men might be brought to know the real value of the blessings by which they set so little store; nay, her feeling for her order ran so high, that she sometimes declared, if she could have only good security for a fair, round number—say ten thousand—of young virgins following her example, she would, to spite mankind, hang, drown, stab, or poison herself, with a joy past all expression.

It was the voice of Miggs that greeted the locksmith, when he knocked at his own house, with a shrill cry of "Who's there?"

"Me, girl, me," returned Gabriel.

"What, already, sir!" said Miggs, opening the door with a look of surprise. "We were just getting on our nightcaps to sit up,—me and mistress. Oh, she has been so bad!"

Miggs said this with an air of uncommon candour and concern; but the parlour-door was standing open, and as Gabriel very well knew for whose ears it was designed, he regarded her with anything but an approving look as he passed in.

"Master's come home, mim," cried Miggs, running before him into the parlour. "You was wrong, mim, and I was right. I thought he wouldn't keep us up so late, two nights running, mim. Master's always considerate so far. I'm so glad, mim, on your account. I'm a little"—here Miggs simpered—"a little sleepy myself; I'll own it now, mim, though I said I wasn't when you asked me. It ain't of no consequence, mim, of course."

"You had better," said the locksmith, who most devoutly wished that Barnaby's raven was at Miggs's ankles, "you had better get to bed at once then."

"Thanking you kindly, sir," returned Miggs, "I couldn't take my rest in peace, nor fix my thoughts upon my prayers, otherways than that I knew mistress was comfortable in her bed this night; by rights she ought to have been there, hours ago."

"You're talkative, mistress," said Varden, pulling off his great-coat, and looking at her askew.

"Taking the hint, sir," cried Miggs, with a flushed face, "and thanking you for it most kindly, I will make bold to say, that if I give offence by having consideration for my mistress, I do not ask your pardon, but am content to get myself into trouble and to be in suffering."

Here Mrs. Varden, who, with her countenance shrouded in a large nightcap, had been all this time intent upon the Protestant Manual, looked round, and acknowledged Miggs's championship by com-manding her to hold her tongue.

Every little bone in Miggs's throat and neck developed itself with a spitefulness quite alarming, as she replied, "Yes, mim, I will."

"How do you find yourself now, my dear?" said the locksmith, taking a chair near his wife (who had resumed her book), and rubbing his knees hard as he made the inquiry.

"You're very anxious to know, an't you?" returned Mrs. Varden, with her eyes upon the print. "You, that have not been near me all day, and wouldn't have been if I was dying!"

"My dear Martha—" said Gabriel.

Mrs. Varden turned over to the next page; then went back again to the bottom line over leaf to be quite sure of the last words; and then went on reading with an appearance of the deepest interest and study.

"My dear Martha," said the locksmith, "how can you say such things, when you know you don't mean them? If you were dying! Why, if there was anything serious the matter with you, Martha, shouldn't I be in constant attendance upon you?"

"Yes!" cried Mrs. Varden, bursting into tears, "yes, you would. I don't doubt it, Varden. Certainly you would. That's as much as to tell me that you would be hovering round me like a vulture, waiting till the breath was out of my body, that you might go and marry somebody else."

Miggs groaned in sympathy—a little short groan, checked in its birth, and changed into a cough. It seemed to say, "I can't help it. It's wrung from me by the dreadful brutality of that monster master."

"But you'll break my heart one of these days," added Mrs. Varden,

with more resignation, "and then we shall both be happy. My only
desire is to see Dolly comfortably settled, and when she is, you may
settle *me* as soon as you like."

"Ah!" cried Miggs—and coughed again.

Poor Gabriel twisted his wig about in silence for a long time, and
then said mildly, "Has Dolly gone to bed?"

"Your master speaks to you," said Mrs. Varden, looking sternly
over her shoulder at Miss Miggs in waiting.

"No, my dear, I spoke to you," suggested the locksmith.

"Did you hear me, Miggs?" cried the obdurate lady, stamping her
foot upon the ground. "*You* are beginning to despise me now, are
you? But this is example!"

At this cruel rebuke, Miggs, whose tears were always ready, for
large or small parties, on the shortest notice and the most reasonable
terms, fell a crying violently; holding both her hands tight upon her
heart meanwhile, as if nothing less would prevent its splitting into
small fragments. Mrs. Varden, who likewise possessed that faculty
in high perfection, wept too, against Miggs; and with such effect that
Miggs gave in after a time, and, except for an occasional sob, which
seemed to threaten some remote intention of breaking out again,
left her mistress in possession of the field. Her superiority being
thoroughly asserted, that lady soon desisted likewise, and fell into a
quiet melancholy.

The relief was so great, and the fatiguing occurrences of last night
so completely overpowered the locksmith, that he nodded in his
chair, and would doubtless have slept there all night, but for the
voice of Mrs. Varden, which, after a pause of some five minutes,
awoke him with a start.

"If I am ever," said Mrs. V.—not scolding, but in a sort of monotonous remonstrance—"in spirits, if I am ever cheerful, if I am ever
more than usually disposed to be talkative and comfortable, this is
the way I am treated."

"Such spirits as you was in too, mim, but half an hour ago!" cried
Miggs. "I never see such company!"

"Because," said Mrs. Varden, "because I never interfere or interrupt; because I never question where anybody comes or goes; because
my whole mind and soul is bent on saving where I can save, and
labouring in this house;—therefore, they try me as they do."

"Martha," urged the locksmith, endeavouring to look as wakeful
as possible, "what is it you complain of? I really came home with
every wish and desire to be happy. I did, indeed."

"What do I complain of!" retorted his wife. "Is it a chilling thing
to have one's husband sulking and falling asleep directly he comes
home—to have him freezing all one's warm-heartedness, and throwing cold water over the fireside? Is it natural, when I know he went
out upon a matter in which I am as much interested as anybody can
be, that I shou'd wish to know all that has happened, or that he
should tell me without my begging and praying him to do it? Is that
natural, or is it not?"

"I am very sorry, Martha," said the good-natured locksmith. "I was really afraid you were not disposed to talk pleasantly; I'll tell you everything; I shall only be too glad, my dear."

"No, Varden," returned his wife, rising with dignity. "I dare say—thank you! I'm not a child to be corrected one minute and petted the next—I'm a little too old for that, Varden. Miggs, carry the light. *You* can be cheerful, Miggs, at least."

Miggs, who, to this moment, had been in the very depths of compassionate despondency, passed instantly into the liveliest state conceivable, and tossing her head as she glanced towards the locksmith, bore off her mistress and the light together.

"Now, who would think," thought Varden, shrugging his shoulders and drawing his chair nearer to the fire, "that that woman could ever be pleasant and agreeable? And yet she can be. Well, well, all of us have our faults. I'll not be hard upon hers. We have been man and wife too long for that."

He dozed again—not the less pleasantly, perhaps, for his hearty temper. While his eyes were closed, the door leading to the upper stairs was partially opened; and a head appeared, which, at sight of him, hastily drew back again.

"I wish," murmured Gabriel, waking at the noise, and looking round the room, "I wish somebody would marry Miggs. But that's impossible! I wonder whether there's any madman alive, who would marry Miggs!"

This was such a vast speculation that he fell into a doze again, and slept until the fire was quite burnt out. At last he roused himself; and having double-locked the street-door according to custom, and put the key in his pocket, went off to bed.

He had not left the room in darkness many minutes, when the head again appeared, and Sim Tappertit entered, bearing in his hand a little lamp.

"What the devil business has he to stop up so late!" muttered Sim, passing into the workshop, and setting it down upon the forge "Here's half the night gone already. There's only one good that has ever come to me out of this cursed old rusty mechanical trade, and that's this piece of ironmongery, upon my soul!"

As he spoke, he drew from the right hand, or rather right leg pocket of his smalls, a clumsy large-sized key, which he inserted cautiously in the lock his master had secured, and softly opened the door. That done, he replaced his piece of secret workmanship in his pocket; and leaving the lamp burning, and closing the door carefully and without noise, stole out into the street—as little suspected by the locksmith in his sound deep sleep, as by Barnaby himself in his phantom-haunted dreams.

CHAPTER VIII

CLEAR of the locksmith's house, Sim Tappertit laid aside his cautious manner, and assuming in its stead that of a ruffling, swaggering,

roving blade, who would rather kill a man than otherwise, and eat
him too if needful, made the best of his way along the darkened
streets.

Half pausing for an instant now and then to smite his pocket and
assure himself of the safety of his master key, he hurried on to Barbican, and turning into one of the narrowest of the narrow streets
which diverged from that centre, slackened his pace and wiped his
heated brow, as if the termination of his walk were near at hand.

It was not a very choice spot for midnight expeditions, being in
truth one of more than questionable character, and of an appearance
by no means inviting. From the main street he had entered, itself
little better than an alley, a low-browed doorway led into a blind
court, or yard, profoundly dark, unpaved, and reeking with stagnant
odours. Into this ill-favoured pit the locksmith's vagrant 'prentice
groped his way; and stopping at a house from whose defaced and
rotten front the rude effigy of a bottle swung to and fro like some
gibbeted malefactor, struck thrice upon an iron grating with his foot.
After listening in vain for some response to his signal, Mr. Tappertit
became impatient and struck the grating thrice again.

A further delay ensued, but it was not of long duration. The ground
seemed to open at his feet, and a ragged head appeared.

"Is that the captain?" said a voice as ragged as the head.

"Yes," replied Mr. Tappertit haughtily, descending as he spoke,
"who should it be?"

"It's so late, we gave you up," returned the voice, as its owner
stopped to shut and fasten the grating. "You're late, sir."

"Lead on," said Mr. Tappertit, with a gloomy majesty, "and make
remarks when I require you. Forward!"

This latter word of command was perhaps somewhat theatrical
and unnecessary, inasmuch as the descent was by a very narrow,
steep, and slippery flight of steps, and any rashness or departure from
the beaten track must have ended in a yawning water-butt. But Mr.
Tappertit being, like some other great commanders, favourable to
strong effects, and personal display, cried "Forward!" again, in the
hoarsest voice he could assume; and led the way, with folded arms
and knitted brows, to the cellar down below, where there was a small
copper fixed in one corner, a chair or two, a form and table, a glimmering fire, and a truckle-bed, covered with a ragged patchwork rug.

"Welcome, noble captain!" cried a lanky figure, rising as from a
nap.

The captain nodded. Then, throwing off his outer coat, he stood
composed in all his dignity, and eyed his follower over.

"What news to-night?" he asked, when he had looked into his
very soul.

"Nothing particular," replied the other, stretching himself—and
he was so long already that it was quite alarming to see him do it—
"how come you to be so late?"

"No matter," was all the captain deigned to say in answer. "Is the
room prepared?"

"It is," replied the follower.

"The comrade—is he here?"

"Yes. And a sprinkling of the others—you hear 'em?"

"Playing skittles!" said the captain moodily. "Light-hearted revellers!"

There was no doubt respecting the particular amusement in which these heedless spirits were indulging, for even in the close and stifling atmosphere of the vault, the noise sounded like distant thunder. It certainly appeared, at first sight, a singular spot to choose, for that or any other purpose of relaxation, if the other cellars answered to the one in which this brief colloquy took place; for the floors were of sodden earth, the walls and roof of damp bare brick tapestried with the tracks of snails and slugs; the air was sickening, tainted, and offensive. It seemed, from one strong flavour which was uppermost among the various odours of the place, that it had, at no very distant period, been used as a storehouse for cheeses; a circumstance which, while it accounted for the greasy moisture that hung about it, was aggreeably suggestive of rats. It was naturally damp besides, and little trees of fungus sprung from every mouldering corner.

The proprietor of this charming retreat, and owner of the ragged head before mentioned—for he wore an old tie-wig as bare and frouzy as a stunted hearth-broom—had by this time joined them; and stood a little apart, rubbing his hands, wagging his hoary bristled chin, and smiling in silence. His eyes were closed; but had they been wide open, it would have been easy to tell, from the attentive expression of the face he turned towards them—pale and unwholesome as might be expected in one of his underground existence—and from a certain anxious raising and quivering of the lids, that he was blind.

"Even Stagg hath been asleep," said the long comrade, nodding towards this person.

"Sound, captain, sound!" cried the blind man; "what does my noble captain drink—is it brandy, rum, usquebaugh? Is it soaked gunpowder, or blazing oil? Give it a name, heart of oak, and we'd get it for you, if it was wine from a bishop's cellar, or melted gold from King George's mint."

"See," said Mr. Tappertit haughtily, "that it's something strong, and comes quick; and so long as you take care of that, you may bring it from the devil's cellar, if you like."

"Boldly said, noble captain!" rejoined the blind man. "Spoken like the 'Prentices' Glory. Ha, ha! From the devil's cellar! A brave joke! The captain joketh. Ha, ha, ha!"

"I'll tell you what, my fine feller," said Mr. Tappertit, eyeing the host over as he walked to a closet, and took out a bottle and glass as carelessly as if he had been in full possession of his sight, "if you make that row, you'll find that the captain's very far from joking, and so I tell you."

"He's got his eyes on me!" cried Stagg, stopping short on his way back, and affecting to screen his face with the bottle. "I feel 'em though I can't see 'em. Take 'em off, noble captain. Remove 'em, for they pierce like gimlets."

Mr. Tappertit smiled grimly at his comrade; and twisting out one more look—a kind of ocular screw—under the influence of which the blind man feigned to undergo great anguish and torture, bade him, in a softened tone, approach, and hold his peace.

"I obey you, captain," cried Stagg, drawing close to him and filling out a bumper without spilling a drop, by reason that he held his little finger at the brim of the glass, and stopped at the instant the liquor touched it, "drink, noble governor. Death to all masters, life to all 'prentices, and love to all fair damsels. Drink, brave general, and warm your gallant heart!"

Mr. Tappertit condescended to take the glass from his outstretched hand. Stagg then dropped on one knee, and gently smoothed the calves of his legs, with an air of humble admiration.

"That I had but eyes!" he cried, "to behold my captain's symmetrical proportions! That I had but eyes, to look upon these twin invaders of domestic peace!"

"Get out!" said Mr. Tappertit, glancing downward at his favourite limbs. "Go along, will you, Stagg!"

"When I touch my own afterwards," cried the host, smiting them reproachfully, "I hate 'em. Comparatively speaking, they've no more shape than wooden legs, beside these models of my noble captain's."

"Yours!" exclaimed Mr. Tappertit. "No, I should think not. Don't talk about those precious old toothpicks in the same breath with mine; that's rather too much. Here. Take the glass. Benjamin. Lead on. To business!"

With these words, he folded his arms again; and frowning with a sullen majesty, passed with his companion through a little door at the upper end of the cellar, and disappeared; leaving Stagg to his private meditations.

The vault they entered, strewn with sawdust and dimly lighted, was between the outer one from which they had just come, and that in which the skittle-players were diverting themselves; as was manifested by the increased noise and clamour of tongues, which was suddenly stopped, however, and replaced by a dead silence, at a signal from the long comrade. Then, this young gentleman, going to a little cupboard, returned with a thigh-bone, which in former times must have been part and parcel of some individual at least as long as himself, and placed the same in the hands of Mr. Tappertit; who, receiving it as a sceptre and staff of authority, cocked his three-cornered hat fiercely on the top of his head, and mounted a large table, whereupon a chair of state, cheerfully ornamented with a couple of skulls, was placed ready for his reception.

He had no sooner assumed this position, than another young gentleman appeared, bearing in his arms a huge clasped book, who made him a profound obeisance, and delivering it to the long comrade, advanced to the table, and turning his back upon it, stood there Atlas-wise. Then, the long comrade got upon the table too;

Barnaby Rudge 59

and seating himself in a lower chair than Mr. Tappertit's, with much state and ceremony, placed the large book on the shoulders of their mute companion as deliberately as if he had been a wooden desk, and prepared to make entries therein with a pen of corresponding size.

When the long comrade had made these preparations, he looked towards Mr. Tappertit; and Mr. Tappertit, flourishing the bone, knocked nine times therewith upon one of the skulls. At the ninth stroke, a third young gentleman emerged from the door leading to the skittle-ground, and bowing low, awaited his commands.

" 'Prentice!" said the mighty captain, "who waits without?"

The 'prentice made answer that a stranger was in attendance, who claimed admission into that secret society of 'Prentice Knights, and a free participation in their rights, privileges, and immunities. Thereupon Mr. Tappertit flourished the bone again, and giving the other skull a prodigious rap on the nose, exclaimed "Admit him!" At these dread words the 'prentice bowed once more, and so withdrew as he had come.

There soon appeared at the same door, two other 'prentices, having between them a third, whose eyes were bandaged, and who was attired in a bag-wig, and a broad-skirted coat, trimmed with tarnished lace; and who was girded with a sword, in compliance with the laws of the Institution regulating the introduction of candidates, which required them to assume this courtly dress, and kept it constantly in lavender, for their convenience. One of the conductors of this novice held a rusty blunderbuss pointed towards his ear, and the other a very ancient sabre, with which he carved imaginary offenders as he came along in a sanguinary and anatomical manner.

As this silent group advanced, Mr. Tappertit fixed his hat upon his head. The novice then laid his hand upon his breast and bent before him. When he had humbled himself sufficiently, the captain ordered the bandage to be removed, and proceeded to eye him over.

"Ha!" said the captain, thoughtfully, when he had concluded this ordeal. "Proceed."

The long comrade read aloud as follows:—"Mark Gilbert. Age nineteen. Bound to Thomas Curzon, hosier, Golden Fleece, Aldgate. Loves Curzon's daughter. Cannot say that Curzon's daughter loves him. Should think it probable. Curzon pulled his ears last Tuesday week."

"How!" cried the captain, starting.

"For looking at his daughter, please you," said the novice.

"Write Curzon down, Denounced," said the captain. "Put a black cross against the name of Curzon."

"So please you," said the novice, "that's not the worst—he calls his 'prentice idle dog, and stops his beer unless he works to his liking. He gives Dutch cheese, too, eating Cheshire, sir, himself; and Sundays out, are only once a month."

"This," said Mr. Tappertit gravely, "is a flagrant case. Put two black crosses to the name of Curzon."

"If the society," said the novice, who was an ill-looking, one-sided, shambling lad, with sunken eyes set close together in his head —"if the society would burn his house down—for he's not insured— or beat him as he comes home from his club at night, or help me to carry off his daughter, and marry her at the Fleet, whether she gave consent or no—"

Mr. Tappertit waved his grizzly truncheon as an admonition to him not to interrupt, and ordered three black crosses to the name of Curzon.

"Which means," he said in gracious explanation, "vengeance, complete and terrible. 'Prentice, do you love the Constitution?"

To which the novice (being to that end instructed by his attendant sponsors) replied "I do!"

"The Church, the State, and everything established—but the masters?" quoth the captain.

Again the novice said "I do."

Having said it, he listened meekly to the captain, who in an address prepared for such occasions, told him how that under that same Constitution (which was kept in a strong box somewhere, but where exactly he could not find out, or he would have endeavoured to procure a copy of it), the 'prentices had, in times gone by, had frequent holidays of right, broken people's heads by scores, defied their masters, nay, even achieved some glorious murders in the streets, which privileges had gradually been wrested from them, and in all which noble aspirations they were now restrained; how the degrading checks imposed upon them were unquestionably attribut-able to the innovating spirit of the times, and how they united therefore to resist all change, except such change as would restore those good old English customs, by which they would stand for all. After illustrating the wisdom of going backward, by reference to that sagacious fish, the crab, and the not unfrequent practice of the mule and donkey, he described their general objects; which were briefly vengeance on their Tyrant Masters (of whose grievous and insupportable oppression no 'prentice could entertain a moment's doubt) and the restoration, as aforesaid, of their ancient rights and holidays; for neither of which objects were they now quite ripe, being barely twenty strong, but which they pledged themselves to pursue with fire and sword when needful. Then he described the oath which every member of that small remnant of a noble body took, and which was of a dreadful and impressive kind; binding him, at the bidding of his chief, to resist and obstruct the Lord Mayor, sword-bearer, and chaplain; to despise the authority of the sheriffs; and to hold the court of aldermen as nought; but not an any account, in case the fulness of time should bring a general rising of 'prentices, to damage or in any way disfigure Temple Bar, which was strictly constitutional and always to be approached with reverence. Having gone over these several heads with great eloquence and force, and having further informed the novice that this society had its origin in his own teeming brain, stimulated by a swelling sense of wrong and outrage,

Mr. Tappertit demanded whether he had strength of heart to take the mightly pledge required, or whether he would withdraw while retreat was yet in his power.

To this the novice made rejoinder, that he would take the vow, though it should choke him; and it was accordingly administered with many impressive circumstances, among which the lighting up of the two skulls with a candle-end inside of each, and a great many flourishes with the bone, were chiefly conspicuous; not to mention a variety of grave exercises with the blunderbuss and sabre, and some dismal groaning by unseen 'prentices without. All these dark and direful ceremonies, being at length completed, the table was put aside, the chair of state removed, the sceptre locked up in its usual cupboard, the doors of communication between the three cellars thrown freely open, and the 'Prentice Knights resigned themselves to merriment.

But Mr. Tappertit, who had a soul above the vulgar herd, and who on account of his greatness, could only afford to be merry now and then, threw himself on a bench with the air of a man who was faint with dignity. He looked with an indifferent eye, alike on skittles, cards, and dice, thinking only of the locksmith's daughter, and the base degenerate days on which he had fallen.

"My noble captain neither games, nor sings, nor dances," said his host, taking a seat beside him. "Drink, gallant general!"

Mr. Tappertit drained the proffered goblet to the dregs; then thrust his hands into his pockets, and with a lowering visage walked among the skittles, while his followers (such is the influence of superior genius) restrained the ardent ball, and held his little shins in dumb respect.

"If I had been born a corsair or a pirate, a brigand, genteel highwayman or patriot—and they're the same thing," thought Mr. Tappertit, musing among the nine-pins, "I should have been all right. But to drag out a ignoble existence unbeknown to mankind in general—patience! I will be famous yet. A voice within me keeps on whispering Greatness. I shall burst out one of these days, and when I do, what power can keep me down? I feel my soul getting into my head at the idea. More drink here!"

"The novice," pursued Mr. Tapperitt, not exactly in a voice of thunder, for his tones, to say the truth, were rather cracked and shrill—but very impressively, notwithstanding—"where is he?"

"Here, noble captain!" cried Stagg. "One stands beside me who I feel is a stranger."

"Have you," said Mr. Tappertit, letting his gaze fall on the party indicated, who was indeed the new knight, by this time restored to his own apparel; "have you the impression of your street-door key in wax?"

The long comrade anticipated the reply, by producing it from the shelf on which it had been deposited.

"Good," said Mr. Tappertit, scrutinising it attentively, while a breathless silence reigned around; for he had constructed secret door

keys for the whole society, and perhaps owed something of his
influence to that mean and trivial circumstance—on such slight
accidents do even men of mind depend!—"This is easily made.
Come hither, friend."

With that, he beckoned the new knight apart, and putting the
pattern in his pocket, motioned to him to walk by his side.

"And so," he said, when they had taken a few turns up and down,
"you—you love your master's daughter?"

"I do," said the 'prentice. "Honour bright. No chaff, you know."

"Have you," rejoined Mr. Tappertit, catching him by the wrist,
and giving him a look which would have been expressive of the most
deadly malevolence, but for an accidental hiccup that rather
interfered with it; "have you a—a rival?"

"Not as I know on," replied the 'prentice.

"If you had now—" said Mr. Tappertit—"what would you—
eh?—"

The 'prentice looked fierce and clenched his fists.

"It is enough," cried Mr. Tappertit hastily, "we understand each
other. We are observed. I thank you."

So saying, he cast him off again; and calling the long comrade aside
after taking a few hasty turns by himself, bade him immediately
write and post against the wall, a notice, proscribing one Joseph
Willet (commonly known as Joe) of Chigwell; forbidding all 'Prentice
Knights to succour, comfort, or hold communion with him; and
requiring them, on pain of excommunication, to molest, hurt,
wrong, annoy, and pick quarrels with the said Joseph, whensoever
and wheresoever they, or any of them, should happen to encounter
him.

Having relieved his mind by this energetic proceeding, he condescended to approach the festive board, and warming by degrees, at
length deigned to preside, and even to enchant the company with a
song. After this, he rose to such a pitch as to consent to regale the
society with a hornpipe, which he actually performed to the music
of a fiddle (played by an ingenious member) with such surpassing
agility and brilliancy of execution, that the spectators could not be
sufficiently enthusiastic in their admiration; and their host protested,
with tears in his eyes, that he had never truly felt his blindness until
that moment.

But the host withdrawing—probably to weep in secret—soon
returned with the information that it wanted little more than an
hour of day, and that all the cocks in Barbican had already begun to
crow, as if their lives depended on it. At this intelligence, the 'Prentice
Knights arose in haste, and marshalling into a line, filed off one by
one and dispersed with all speed to their several homes, leaving their
leader to pass the grating last.

"Good night, noble captain," whispered the blind man as he held
it open for his passage out. "Farewell, brave general. Bye, bye,
illustrious commander. Good luck go with you for a—conceited,
bragging, empty-headed, duck-legged idiot."

With which parting words, coolly added as he listened to his receding footsteps and locked the gate upon himself, he descended the steps, and lighting the fire below the little copper, prepared, without any assistance, for his daily occupation; which was to retail at the area-head above pennyworths of broth and soup, and savoury puddings, compounded of such scraps as were to be bought in the heap for the least money at Fleet Market in the evening time; and for the sale of which he had need to have depended chiefly on his private connection, for the court had no thoroughfare, and was not that kind of place in which many people were likely to take the air, or to frequent as an agreeable promenade.

CHAPTER IX

CHRONICLERS are privileged to enter where they list, to come and go through keyholes, to ride upon the wind, to overcome, in their soarings up and down, all obstacles of distance, time, and place. Thrice blessed be this last consideration, since it enables us to follow the disdainful Miggs even into the sanctity of her chamber, and to hold her in sweet companionship through the dreary watches of the night!

Miss Miggs, having undone her mistress, as she phrased it (which means, assisted to undress her), and having seen her comfortably to bed in the back room on the first floor, withdrew to her own apartment, in the attic story. Notwithstanding her declaration in the locksmith's presence, she was in no mood for sleep; so, putting her light upon the table and withdrawing the little window curtain, she gazed out pensively at the wild night sky.

Perhaps she wondered what star was destined for her habitation when she had run her little course below; perhaps speculated which of those glimmering spheres might be the natal orb of Mr. Tappertit; perhaps marvelled how they could gaze down on that perfidious creature, man, and not sicken and turn green as chemists' lamps; perhaps thought of nothing in particular. Whatever she thought about, there she sat, until her attention, alive to anything connected with the insinuating 'prentice, was attracted by a noise in the next room to her own—his room; the room in which he slept, and dreamed —it might be, sometimes dreamed of her.

That he was not dreaming now, unless he was taking a walk in his sleep, was clear, for every now and then there came a shuffling noise, as though he were engaged in polishing the whitewashed wall; then a gentle creaking of his door; then the faintest indication of his stealthy footsteps on the landing-place outside. Noting this latter circumstance, Miss Miggs turned pale and shuddered, as mistrusting his intentions; and more than once exclaimed, below her breath, "Oh! what a Providence it is, as I am bolted in!"—which, owing doubtless to her alarm, was a confusion of ideas on her part between a bolt and its use; for though there was one on the door, it was not fastened.

Miss Miggs's sense of hearing, however, having as sharp an edge as her temper, and being of the same snappish and suspicious kind, very soon informed her that the footsteps passed her door, and appeared to have some object quite separate and disconnected from herself. At this discovery she became more alarmed than ever, and was about to give utterance to those cries of "Thieves!" and " Murder!" which she had hitherto restrained, when it occurred to her to look softly out, and see that her fears had some good palpable foundation.

Looking out accordingly, and stretching her neck over the hand-rail, she descried, to her great amazement, Mr. Tappertit completely dressed, stealing down-stairs, one step at a time, with his shoes in one hand and a lamp in the other. Following him with her eyes, and going down a little way herself to get the better of an intervening angle, she beheld him thrust his head in at the parlour-door, draw it back again with great swiftness, and immediately begin a retreat up-stairs with all possible expedition.

"Here's mysteries!" said the damsel, when she was safe in her own room again, quite out of breath. "Oh gracious, here's mysteries!"

The prospect of finding anybody out in anything, would have kept Miss Miggs awake under the influence of henbane. Presently, she heard the step again, as she would have done if it had been that of a feather endowed with motion and walking down on tiptoe. Then gliding out as before, she again beheld the retreating figure of the 'prentice; again he looked cautiously in at the parlour-door, but this time instead of retreating, he passed in and disappeared.

Miggs was back in her room, and had her head out of the window, before an elderly gentleman could have winked and recovered from it. Out he came at the street-door, shut it carefully behind him, tried it with his knee and swaggered off, putting something in his pocket as he went along. At this spectacle Miggs cried "Gracious!" again, and then "Goodness gracious!" and then "Goodness gracious me!" and then, candle in hand, went down-stairs as he had done. Coming to the workshop, she saw the lamp burning on the forge, and everything as Sim had left it.

"Why I wish I may only have a walking funeral, and never be buried decent with a mourning-coach and feathers, if the boy hasn't been and made a key for his own self!" cried Miggs. "Oh the little villain!"

This conclusion was not arrived at without consideration, and much peeping and peering about; nor was it unassisted by the recollection that she had on several occasions come upon the 'prentice suddenly, and found him busy at some mysterious occupation. Lest the fact of Miss Miggs calling him, on whom she stooped to cast a favourable eye, a boy, should create surprise in any breast, it may be observed that she invariably affected to regard all male bipeds under thirty as mere chits and infants; which phenomenon is not unusual in ladies of Miss Miggs's temper, and is indeed generally found to be the associate of such indomitable and savage virtue.

Miss Miggs deliberated within herself for some little time, looking hard at the shop-door while she did so, as though her eyes and thoughts were both upon it; and then, taking a sheet of paper from a drawer, twisted it into a long thin spiral tube. Having filled this instrument with a quantity of small coal-dust from the forge, she approached the door, and dropping on one knee before it, dexterously blew into the keyhole as much of these fine ashes as the lock would hold. When she had filled it to the brim in a very workmanlike and skilful manner she crept up-stairs again, and chuckled as she went.

"There!" cried Miggs, rubbing her hands, "now let's see whether you won't be glad to take some notice of me, mister. He, he, he! You'll have eyes for somebody besides Miss Dolly now, I think. A fat-faced puss she is, as ever *I* come across!"

As she uttered this criticism, she glanced approvingly at her small mirror, as who should say, I thank my stars that can't be said of me! —as it certainly could not; for Miss Miggs's style of beauty was of that kind which Mr. Tappertit himself had not inaptly termed, in private, "scraggy."

"I don't go to bed this night!" said Miggs, wrapping herself in a shawl, and drawing a couple of chairs near the window, flouncing down upon one, and putting her feet upon the other, "till you come home, my lad. I wouldn't," said Miggs viciously, "no, not for five-and-forty pound!"

With that, and with an expression of face in which a great number of opposite ingredients, such as mischief, cunning, malice, triumph, and patient expectation, were all mixed up together in a kind of physiognomical punch, Miss Miggs composed herself to wait and listen, like some fair ogress who had set a trap and was watching for a nibble from a plump young traveller.

She sat there, with perfect composure, all night. At length, just upon break of day, there was a footstep in the street, and presently she could hear Mr. Tappertit stop at the door. Then she could make out that he tried his key—that he was blowing into it—that he knocked it on the nearest post to beat the dust out—that he took it under a lamp to look at it—that he poked bits of stick into the lock to clear it—that he peeped into the keyhole, first with one eye, and then with the other—that he tried the key again—that he couldn't turn it, and what was worse, couldn't get it out—that he bent it— that then it was much less disposed to come out than before—that he gave it a mighty twist and a great pull, and then it came out so suddenly that he staggered backwards—that he kicked the door— that he shook it—finally, that he smote his forehead, and sat down on the step in despair.

When this crisis had arrived, Miss Miggs, affecting to be exhausted with terror, and to cling to the window-sill for support, put out her nightcap, and demanded in a faint voice who was there.

Mr. Tappertit cried "Hush!" and, backing into the road, exhorted her in frenzied pantomine to secrecy and silence.

"Tell me one thing," said Miggs "Is it thieves?"

"No—no—no!" cried Mr. Tappertit.

"Then," said Miggs, more faintly than before, "it's fire. Where is it, sir? It's near this room, I know. I've a good conscience, sir, and would much rather die than go down a ladder. All I wish is, respecting my love to my married sister, Golden Lion Court, number twenty-sivin, second bell-handle on the right-hand door-post."

"Miggs!" cried Mr. Tappertit, "don't you know me? Sim, you know —Sim—"

"Oh! what about him!" cried Miggs, clasping her hands. "Is he in any danger? Is he in the midst of flames and blazes! Oh gracious, gracious!"

"Why I'm here, an't I?" rejoined Mr. Tappertit, knocking himself on the breast. "Don't you see me? What a fool you are, Miggs!"

"There!" cried Miggs, unmindful of this compliment. "Why—so it—Goodness, what is the meaning of—If you please, mim, here's—"

"No, no!" cried Mr. Tappertit, standing on tiptoe, as if by that means he, in the street, were any nearer being able to stop the mouth of Miggs in the garret. "Don't!—I've been out without leave and something or another's the matter with the lock. Come down, and undo the shop window, that I may get in that way."

"I dursn't do it, Simmun," cried Miggs—for that was her pronunciation of his Christian name. "I dursn't do it, indeed. You know as well as anybody, how particular I am. And to come down in the dead of night, when the house is wrapped in slumbers and weiled in obscurity." And there she stopped and shivered, for her modesty caught cold at the very thought.

"But, Miggs," cried Mr. Tappertit, getting under the lamp, that she might see his eyes. "My darling Miggs—"

Miggs screamed slightly.

"—That I love so much, and never can help thinking of," and it is impossible to describe the use he made of his eyes when he said this— "do—for my sake, do."

"Oh Simmun," cried Miggs, "this is worse than all. I know if I come down, you'll go, and—"

"And what, my precious!" said Mr. Tappertit.

"And try," said Miggs, hysterically, "to kiss me, or some such dreadfulness; I know you will!"

"I swear I won't," said Mr. Tappertit, with remarkable earnestness. "Upon my soul I won't. It's getting broad day, and the watchman's waking up. Angelic Miggs! If you'll only come and let me in, I promise you faithfully and truly I won't."

Miss Miggs, whose gentle heart was touched, did not wait for the oath (knowing how strong the temptation was, and fearing he might forswear himself), but tripped lightly down the stairs, and with her own fair hands drew back the rough fastenings of the workshop window. Having helped the wayward 'prentice in, she faintly articulated the words "Simmun is safe!" and yielding to her woman's nature, immediately became insensible.

"I knew I should quench her," said Sim, rather embarrassed by this circumstance. "Of course I was certain it would come to this, but there was nothing else to be done—if I hadn't eyed her over, she

Miss Miggs..

wouldn't have come down. Here. Keep up a minute, Miggs. What a slippery figure she is! There's no holding her, comfortably. Do keep up a minute, Miggs, will you?"

As Miggs, however, was deaf to all entreaties, Mr. Tappertit leant her against the wall as one might dispose of a walking-stick or umbrella, until he had secured the window, when he took her in his arms again, and, in short stages and with great difficulty—arising from her being tall, and his being short, and perhaps in some degree from that peculiar physical conformation on which he had already remarked—carried her up-stairs, and planting her in the same umbrella and walking-stick fashion, just inside her own door, left her to her repose.

"He may be as cool as he likes," said Miss Miggs, recovering as soon as she was left alone; "but I'm in his confidence and he can't help himself, nor couldn't if he was twenty Simmunses!"

CHAPTER X

IT was one of those mornings, common in early spring, when the year, fickle and changeable in its youth like all other created things, is undecided whether to step backward into winter or forward into summer, and its uncertainty inclines now to the one and now to the other, and now to both at once—wooing summer in the sunshine, and lingering still with winter in the shade—it was, in short, one of those mornings, when it is hot and cold, wet and dry, bright and lowering, sad and cheerful, withering and genial, in the compass of one short hour, that old John Willet, who was dropping asleep over the copper boiler, was roused by the sound of a horse's feet, and glancing out at window, beheld a traveller of goodly promise, checking his bridle at the Maypole door.

He was none of your flippant young fellows, who would call for a tankard of mulled ale, and make themselves as much at home as if they had ordered a hogshead of wine; none of your audacious young swaggerers, who would even penetrate into the bar—that solemn sanctuary—and, smiting old John upon the back, inquire if there was never a pretty girl in the house, and where he hid his little chamber-maids, with a hundred other impertinences of that nature; none of your free-and-easy companions, who would scrape their boots upon the fire-dogs in the common room, and be not at all particular on the subject of spittoons; none of your unconscionable blades, requiring impossible chops, and taking unheard of pickles for granted. He was a staid, grave, placid gentleman, something past the prime of life, yet upright in his carriage, for all that, and slim as a greyhound. He was well mounted upon a sturdy chestnut cob, and had the graceful seat of an experienced horseman; while his riding gear, though free from such fopperies as were then in vogue, was handsome and well chosen. He wore a riding-coat of a somewhat brighter green than might have been expected to suit the taste of a gentleman of his years, with a short, black velvet cape, and laced pocket-holes and cuffs, all of a jaunty fashion; his linen, too, was of the finest kind, worked in a rich pattern at the wrists and throat, and scrupulously white. Although he seemed, judging from the mud he had picked up on the way, to have come from London, his horse was as smooth and cool as his own iron-grey periwig and pigtail. Neither man nor beast had turned a single hair; and saving for his soiled skirts and spatterdashes, this gentleman with his blooming face, white teeth, exactly-ordered dress, and perfect calmness, might have come from making an elaborate and leisurely toilet, to sit for an equestrian portrait at old John Willet's gate.

It must not be supposed that John observed these several characteristics by other than very slow degrees, or that he took in more than half a one at a time, or that he even made up his mind upon that, without a great deal of very serious consideration. Indeed, if he had been distracted in the first instance by questionings and orders, it would have taken him at the least a fortnight to have noted what is here set down; but it happened that the gentleman, being struck with the old house, or with the plump pigeons which were skimming and curtseying about it, or with the tall maypole, on the top of which a weathercock, which had been out of order for fifteen years, performed a perpetual walk to the music of its own creaking, sat for some little time looking round in silence. Hence John, standing with his hand upon the horse's bridle, and his great eyes on the rider, and with nothing passing to divert his thoughts, had really got some of these little circumstances into his brain by the time he was called upon to speak.

"A quaint place this," said the gentleman—and his voice was as rich as his dress. "Are you the landlord?"

"At your service, sir," replied John Willet.

"You can give my horse good stabling, can you, and me an early dinner (I am not particular what, so that it be cleanly served), and a decent room—of which there seems to be no lack in this great mansion," said the stranger, again running his eyes over the exterior.

"You can have, sir," returned John with a readiness quite surprising, "anything you please."

"It's well I am easily satisfied," returned the other with a smile, "or that might prove a hardy pledge, my friend." And so saying, he dismounted, with the aid of the block before the door, in a twinkling.

"Halloa there! Hugh!" roared John. "I ask your pardon, sir, for keeping you standing in the porch; but my son has gone to town on business, and the boy being, as I may say, of a kind of use to me, I'm put out when he's away. Hugh!—a dreadful idle vagrant fellow, sir, half a gipsy, as I think—always sleeping in the sun in summer, and in the straw in winter time, sir—Hugh! Dear Lord, to keep a gentleman a waiting here through him!—Hugh! I wish that chap was dead, I do indeed."

"Possibly he is," returned the other. "I should think if he were living, he would have heard you by this time."

"In his fits of laziness, he sleeps so desperate hard," said the distracted host, "that if you were to fire off cannon-balls into his ears, it wouldn't wake him, sir."

The guest made no remark upon this novel cure for drowsiness, and recipe for making people lively, but, with his hands clasped behind him, stood in the porch very much amused to see old John, with the bridle in his hand, wavering between a strong impulse to abandon the animal to his fate, and half a disposition to lead him into the house, and shut him up in the parlour, while he waited on his master.

"Pillory the fellow, here is he at last!" cried John, in the very height and zenith of his distress. "Did you hear me a calling, villain?"

The figure he addressed made no answer, but putting his hand upon the saddle, sprung into it at a bound, turned the horse's head towards the stable, and was gone in an instant.

"Brisk enough when he is awake," said the guest.

"Brisk enough, sir!" replied John, looking at the place where the horse had been, as if not yet understanding quite, what had become of him. "He melts, I think. He goes like a drop of froth. You look at him, and there he is. You look at him again, and—there he isn't."

Having, in the absence of any more words, put this sudden climax to what he had faintly intended should be a long explanation of the whole life and character of his man, the oracular John Willet led the gentleman up his wide dismantled staircase into the Maypole's best apartment.

It was spacious enough in all conscience, occupying the whole depth of the house, and having at either end a great bay window, as large as many modern rooms; in which some few panes of stained glass, emblazoned with fragments of armorial bearings, though cracked, and patched, and shattered, yet remained; attesting, by their presence, that the former owner had made the very light subservient to his state, and pressed the sun itself into his list of flatterers; bidding it, when it shone into his chamber, reflect the badges of his ancient family, and take new hues and colours from their pride.

But those were old days, and now every little ray came and went as it would; telling the plain, bare, searching truth. Although the best room of the inn, it had the melancholy aspect of grandeur in decay, and was much too vast for comfort. Rich rustling hangings, waving on the walls; and, better far, the rustling of youth and beauty's dress; the light of women's eyes, outshining the tapers and their own rich jewels; the sound of gentle tongues, and music, and the tread of maiden feet, had once been there, and filled it with delight. But they were gone, and with them all its gladness. It was no longer a home; children were never born and bred there; the fireside had become mercenary—a something to be bought and sold—a very courtezan; let who would die, or sit beside, or leave it, it was still the same— it missed nobody, cared for nobody, had equal smiles and warmth for all. God help the man whose heart ever changes with the world, as an old mansion when it becomes an inn!

No effort had been made to furnish this chilly waste, but before the broad chimney a colony of chairs and tables had been planted on a square of carpet, flanked by a ghostly screen, enriched with figures, grinning and grotesque. After lighting with his own hands the faggots which were heaped upon the hearth, old John withdrew to hold grave council with his cook, touching the stranger's entertainment; while the guest himself, seeing small comfort in the yet unkindled wood, opened a lattice in the distant window, and basked in a sickly gleam of cold March sun.

Leaving the window now and then, to rake the crackling logs together, or pace the echoing room from end to end, he closed it when the fire was quite burnt up, and having wheeled the easiest chair into the warmest corner, summoned John Willet.

"Sir," said John.

He wanted pen, ink, and paper. There was an old standish on the high mantel-shelf containing a dusty apology for all three. Having set this before him, the landlord was retiring, when he motioned him to stay.

"There's a house not far from here," said the guest when he had written a few lines, "which you call the Warren, I believe?"

As this was said in the tone of one who knew the fact, and asked the question as a thing of course, John contented himself with nodding his head in the affirmative; at the same time taking one hand out of his pockets to cough behind, and then putting it in again.

"I want this note"—said the guest, glancing on what he had written, and folding it, "conveyed there without loss of time, and an answer brought back here. Have you a messenger at hand?"

John was thoughtful for a minute or thereabouts, and then said Yes.

"Let me see him," said the guest.

This was disconcerting; for Joe being out, and Hugh engaged in rubbing down the chestnut cob, he designed sending on the errand, Barnaby, who had just then arrived in one of his rambles, and who, so that he thought himself employed on a grave and serious business, would go anywhere.

"Why the truth is," said John after a long pause, "that the person who'd go quickest, is a sort of natural, as one may say, sir; and though quick of foot, and as much to be trusted as the post itself, he's not good at talking, being touched and flighty, sir."

"You don't," said the guest, raising his eyes to John's fat face, "you don't mean—what's the fellow's name—you don't mean Barnaby?"

"Yes, I do," returned the landlord, his features turning quite expressive with surprise.

"How comes he to be here?" inquired the guest, leaning back in his chair; speaking in the bland, even tone, from which he never varied; and with the same soft, courteous, never-changing smile upon his face. "I saw him in London last night."

"He's, for ever, here one hour, and there the next," returned old John, after the usual pause to get the question in his mind. "Sometimes he walks, and sometimes runs. He's known along the road by everybody, and sometimes comes here in a cart or chaise, and sometimes riding double. He comes and goes, through wind, rain, snow, and hail, and on the darkest nights. Nothing hurts *him*."

"He goes often to the Warren, does he not?" said the guest carelessly. "I seem to remember his mother telling me something to that effect yesterday. But I was not attending to the good woman much."

"You're right, sir," John made answer, "he does. His father, sir, was murdered in that house."

"So I have heard," returned the guest, taking a gold toothpick from his pocket with the same sweet smile. "A very disagreeable circumstance for the family."

"Very," said John with a puzzled look, as if it occurred to him, dimly and afar off, that this might by possibility be a cool way of treating the subject.

"All the circumstances after a murder," said the guest soliloquising, "must be dreadfully unpleasant—so much bustle and disturbance—no repose—a constant dwelling upon one subject—and the running in and out, and up and down stairs, intolerable. I wouldn't have such a thing happen to anybody I was nearly interested in, on any account. 'Twould be enough to wear one's life out.—You were going to say, friend—" he added, turning to John again.

"Only that Mrs. Rudge lives on a little pension from the family, and that Barnaby's as free of the house as any cat or dog about it," answered John. "Shall he do your errand, sir?"

"Oh yes," replied the guest. "Oh certainly. Let him do it by all means. Please to bring him here that I may charge him to be quick. If he objects to come you may tell him it's Mr. Chester. He will remember my name, I dare say."

John was so very much astonished to find who his visitor was, that he could express no astonishment at all, by looks or otherwise, but left the room as if he were in the most placid and imperturbable of all possible conditions. It has been reported that when he got down-stairs, he looked steadily at the boiler for ten minutes by the clock, and all that time never once left off shaking his head; for which statement there would seem to be some ground of truth and feasibility, inasmuch as that interval of time did certainly elapse, before he returned with Barnaby to the guest's apartment.

"Come hither, lad," said Mr. Chester. "You know Mr. Geoffrey Haredale?"

Barnaby laughed, and looked at the landlord as though he would say, "You hear him?" John, who was greatly shocked at this breach of decorum, clapped his finger to his nose, and shook his head in mute remonstrance.

"He knows him, sir," said John, frowning aside at Barnaby, "as well as you or I do."

"I haven't the pleasure of much acquaintance with the gentleman," returned the guest. "*You* may have. Limit the comparison to yourself, my friend."

Although this was said with the same easy affability, and the same smile, John felt himself put down, and laying the indignity at Barnaby's door, determined to kick his raven, on the very first opportunity.

"Give that," said the guest, who had by this time sealed the note, and who beckoned his messenger towards him as he spoke, "into Mr. Haredale's own hands. Wait for an answer, and bring it back to me—here. If you should find that Mr. Haredale is engaged just now, tell him—can he remember a message, landlord?"

"When he chooses, sir," replied John. "He won't forget this one."

"How are you sure of that?"

John merely pointed to him as he stood with his head bent forward, and his earnest gaze fixed closely on his questioner's face; and nodded sagely.

"Tell him then, Barnaby, should he be engaged," said Mr. Chester, "that I shall be glad to wait his convenience here, and to see him (if he will call) at any time this evening.—At the worst I can have a bed here, Willet, I suppose?"

Old John, immensely flattered by the personal notoriety implied in this familiar form of address, answered, with something like a knowing look, "I should believe you could, sir," and was turning over in his mind various forms of eulogium, with the view of selecting one appropriate to the qualities of his best bed, when his ideas were put to flight by Mr. Chester giving Barnaby the letter, and bidding him make all speed away.

"Speed!" said Barnaby, folding the little packet in his breast. "Speed! If you want to see hurry and mystery, come here. Here!"

With that, he put his hand, very much to John Willet's horror, on the guest's fine broadcloth sleeve, and led him stealthily to the back window.

"Look down there," he said softly; "do you mark how they whisper in each other's ears; then dance and leap, to make believe they are in sport? Do you see how they stop for a moment, when they think there is no one looking, and mutter among themselves again; and then how they roll and gambol, delighted with the mischief they've been plotting? Look at 'em now. See how they whirl and plunge. And now they stop again, and whisper, cautiously, together—little thinking, mind, how often I have lain upon the grass and watched them. I say—what is it that they plot and hatch? Do you know?"

"They are only clothes," returned the guest, "such as we wear; hanging on those lines to dry, and fluttering in the wind."

"Clothes!" echoed Barnaby, looking close into his face, and falling quickly back. "Ha ha! Why, how much better to be silly, than as wise as you! You don't see shadowy people there, like those that live in sleep—not you. Nor eyes in the knotted panes of glass, nor swift ghosts when it blows hard, nor do you hear voices in the air, nor see men stalking in the sky—not you! I lead a merrier life than you, with all your cleverness. You're the dull men. We're the bright ones. Ha! ha! I'll not change with you, clever as you are,—not I!"

With that, he waved his hat above his head, and darted off.

"A strange creature, upon my word!" said the guest, pulling out a handsome box, and taking a pinch of snuff.

"He wants imagination," said Mr. Willet, very slowly, and after a long silence; "that's what he wants. I've tried to instil it into him, many and many's the time; but"—John added this in confidence—"he an't made for it; that's the fact."

To record that Mr. Chester smiled at John's remark would be little to the purpose, for he preserved the same conciliatory and pleasant look at all times. He drew his chair nearer to the fire though, as a kind of hint that he would prefer to be alone, and John, having no reasonable excuse for remaining, left him to himself.

Very thoughtful old John Willet was, while the dinner was preparing; and if his brain were ever less clear at one time than another, it is but reasonable to suppose that he addled it in no slight degree by shaking his head so much that day. That Mr. Chester, between whom and Mr. Haredale, it was notorious to all the neighbourhood, a deep and bitter animosity existed, should come down there for the sole purpose, as it seemed, of seeing him, and should choose the Maypole for their place of meeting, and should send to him express, were stumbling-blocks John could not overcome. The only resource he had, was to consult the boiler, and wait impatiently for Barnaby's return.

But Barnaby delayed beyond all precedent. The visitor's dinner was served, removed, his wine was set, the fire replenished, the hearth clean swept; the light waned without, it grew dusk, became quite dark, and still no Barnaby appeared. Yet, though John Willet was full of wonder and misgiving, his guest sat cross-legged in the easy-chair, to all appearance as little ruffled in his thoughts as in his dress—the same calm, easy, cool gentleman, without a care or thought beyond his golden toothpick.

"Barnaby's late," John ventured to observe, as he placed a pair of tarnished candlesticks, some three feet high, upon the table, and snuffed the lights they held.

"He is rather so," replied the guest, sipping his wine. "He will not be much longer, I dare say."

John coughed and raked the fire together.

"As your roads bear no very good character, if I may judge from my son's mishap, though," said Mr. Chester, "and as I have no fancy to be knocked on the head—which is not only disconcerting at the moment, but places one, besides, in a ridiculous position with respect to the people who chance to pick one up—I shall stop here to-night. I think you said you had a bed to spare."

"Such a bed, sir," returned John Willet; "ay, such a bed as few, even of the gentry's houses, own. A fixter here, sir. I've heard say that bedstead is nigh two hundred years of age. Your noble son—a fine young gentleman—slept in it last, sir, half a year ago."

"Upon my life, a recommendation!" said the guest, shrugging his shoulders and wheeling his chair nearer to the fire. "See that it be well aired, Mr. Willet, and let a blazing fire be lighted there at once. This house is something damp and chilly."

John raked the faggots up again, more from habit than presence of mind, or any reference to this remark, and was about to withdraw, when a bounding step was heard upon the stair, and Barnaby came panting in.

"He'll have his foot in the stirrup in an hour's time," he cried, advancing. "He has been riding hard all day—has just come home—but will be in the saddle again as soon as he has eat and drink, to meet his loving friend."

"Was that his message?" asked the visitor, looking up, but without the smallest discomposure—or at least without the show of any.

"All but the last words," Barnaby rejoined. "He meant those. I saw that, in his face."

"This for your pains," said the other, putting money in his hand, and glancing at him steadfastly. "This for your pains, sharp Barnaby."

"For Grip, and me, and Hugh, to share among us," he rejoined, putting it up, and nodding, as he counted it off his fingers. "Grip one, me two, Hugh three; the dog, the goat, the cats—well, we shall spend it pretty soon, I warn you. Stay.—Look. Do you wise men see nothing there, now?"

He bent eagerly down on one knee, and gazed intently at the smoke, which was rolling up the chimney in a thick black cloud. John Willet, who appeared to consider himself particularly and chiefly referred to under the term wise men, looked that way likewise, and with great solidity of feature.

"Now, where do they go to, when they spring so fast up there," asked Barnaby; "eh? Why do they tread so closely on each other's heels, and why are they always in a hurry—which is what you blame me for, when I only take pattern by these busy folk about me. More of 'em! catching to each other's skirts; and as fast as they go, others come! What a merry dance it is! I would that Grip and I could frisk like that!"

"What has he in that basket at his back?" asked the guest after a few moments, during which Barnaby was still bending down to look higher up the chimney, and earnestly watching the smoke.

"In this?" he answered, jumping up, before John Willet could reply—shaking it as he spoke, and stooping his head to listen. "In this? What is there here? Tell him!"

"A devil, a devil, a devil!" cried a hoarse voice.

"Here's money?" said Barnaby, chinking it in his hand, "money for a treat, Grip!"

"Hurrah! Hurrah! Hurrah!" replied the raven, "keep up your spirits. Never say die. Bow, wow, wow!"

Mr. Willet, who appeared to entertain strong doubts whether a customer in a laced coat and fine linen could be supposed to have any acquaintance even with the existence of such unpolite gentry as the bird claimed to belong to, took Barnaby off at this juncture, with the view of preventing any other improper declarations, and quitted the room with his very best bow.

CHAPTER XI

THERE was great news that night for the regular Maypole customers, to each of whom, as he straggled in to occupy his allotted seat in the chimney-corner, John, with a most impressive slowness of delivery, and in an apoplectic whisper, communicated the fact that Mr. Chester was alone in the large room up-stairs, and was waiting the arrival of Mr. Geoffrey Haredale, to whom he had sent a letter (doubtless of a threatening nature) by the hands of Barnaby, then and there present.

For a little knot of smokers and solemn gossips, who had seldom any new topics of discussion, this was a perfect God-send. Here was a good, dark-looking mystery progressing under that very roof—brought home to the fireside, as it were, and enjoyable without the smallest pains or trouble. It is extraordinary what a zest and relish it gave to the drink, and how it heightened the flavour of the tobacco. Every man smoked his pipe with a face of grave and serious delight, and looked at his neighbour with a sort of quiet congratulation. Nay, it was felt to be such a holiday and special night, that, on the motion of little Solomon Daisy, every man (including John himself) put down his sixpence for a can of flip, which grateful beverage was brewed with all despatch, and set down in the midst of them on the brick floor; both that it might simmer and stew before the fire, and that its fragrant steam, rising up among them, and mixing with the wreaths of vapour from their pipes, might shroud them in a delicious atmosphere of their own, and shut out all the world. The very furniture of the room seemed to mellow and deepen in its tone; the ceiling and walls looked blacker and more highly polished, the curtains of a ruddier red; the fire burnt clear and high, and the crickets in the hearth-stone chirped with a more than wonted satisfaction.

There were present two, however, who showed but little interest in the general contentment. Of these, one was Barnaby himself, who slept, or, to avoid being beset with questions, feigned to sleep, in the chimney-corner; the other, Hugh, who, sleeping too, lay stretched upon the bench on the opposite side, in the full glare of the blazing fire.

The light that fell upon this slumbering form, showed it in all its muscular and handsome proportions. It was that of a young man, of a hale athletic figure, and a giant's strength, whose sunburnt face and swarthy throat, overgrown with jet black hair, might have served a painter for a model. Loosely attired, in the coarsest and roughest garb, with scraps of straw and hay—his usual bed—clinging here and there, and mingling with his uncombed locks, he had fallen asleep in a posture as careless as his dress. The negligence and disorder of the whole man, with something fierce and sullen in his features, gave him a picturesque appearance, that attracted the regards even of the Maypole customers who knew him well, and caused Long Parkes to say that Hugh looked more like a poaching rascal to-night than ever he had seen him yet.

"He's waiting here, I suppose," said Solomon, "to take Mr. Haredale's horse."

"That's it, sir," replied John Willet. "He's not often in the house, you know. He's more at his ease among horses then men. I look upon him as a animal himself."

Following up this opinion with a shrug that seemed meant to say, "we can't expect everybody to be like us," John put his pipe into his mouth again, and smoked like one who felt his superiority over the general run of mankind.

"That chap, sir," said John, taking it out again after a time, and pointing at him with the stem, "though he's got all his faculties about him—bottled up and corked down, if I may say so, somewhere or another—"

"Very good!" said Parkes, nodding his head. "A very good expression, Johnny. You'll be a tackling somebody presently. You're in twig to-night, I see."

"Take care," said Mr. Willet, not at all grateful for the compliment, "that I don't tackle you, sir, which I shall certainly endeavour to do, if you interrupt me when I'm making observations.—That chap, I was a saying, though he has all his faculties about him, somewhere or another, bottled up and corked down, has no more imagination than Barnaby has. And why hasn't he?"

The three friends shook their heads at each other; saying by that action, without the trouble of opening their lips, "Do you observe what a philosophical mind our friend has?"

"Why hasn't he?" said John, gently striking the table with his open hand. "Because they was never drawed out of him when he was a boy. That's why. What would any of us have been, if our fathers hadn't drawed our faculties out of us? What would my boy Joe have been, if I hadn't drawed his faculties out of him?—Do you mind what I'm a saying of, gentlemen?"

"Ah! we mind you," cried Parkes. "Go on improving of us, Johnny."

"Consequently, then," said Mr. Willet, "that chap, whose mother was hung when he was a little boy, along with six others, for passing bad notes—and it's a blessed thing to think how many people are hung in batches every six weeks for that, and such-like offences, as showing how wide awake our government is—that chap was then turned loose, and had to mind cows, and frighten birds away, and what not, for a few pence to live on, and so got on by degrees to mind horses, and to sleep in course of time in lofts and litter, instead of under haystacks and hedges, till at last he come to be hostler at the Maypole for his board and lodging and a annual trifle—that chap that can't read nor write, and has never had much to do with anything but animals, and has never lived in any way but like the animals he has lived among, *is* a animal. And," said Mr. Willet, arriving at his logical conclusion, "is to be treated accordingly."

"Willet," said Solomon Daisy, who had exhibited some impatience at the intrusion of so unworthy a subject on their more interesting theme, "when Mr. Chester come this morning, did he order the large room?"

"He signified, sir," said John, "that he wanted a large apartment. Yes. Certainly."

"Why then, I'll tell you what," said Solomon, speaking softly and with an earnest look. "He and Mr. Haredale are going to fight a duel in it."

Everybody looked at Mr. Willet, after this alarming suggestion. Mr. Willet looked at the fire, weighing in his own mind the effect which such an occurrence would be likely to have on the establishment. "Well," said John, "I don't know—I am sure—I remember that when I went up last, he *had* put the lights upon the mantel-shelf."

"It's as plain," returned Solomon, "as the nose on Parkes's face"— Mr. Parkes, who had a large nose, rubbed it, and looked as if he considered this a personal allusion—"they'll fight in that room. You know by the newspapers what a common thing it is for gentlemen to fight in coffee-houses without seconds. One of 'em will be wounded or perhaps killed in this house."

"That was a challenge that Barnaby took then, eh?" said John.

"—Inclosing a slip of paper with the measure of his sword upon it, I'll bet a guinea," answered the little man. "We know what sort of gentleman Mr. Haredale is. You have told us what Barnaby said about his looks, when he came back. Depend upon it, I'm right. Now, mind."

The flip had had no flavour till now. The tobacco had been of mere English growth, compared with its present taste. A duel in that great old rambling room up-stairs, and the best bed ordered already for the wounded man!

"Would it be swords or pistols, now?" said John.

"Heaven knows. Perhaps both," returned Solomon. "The gentlemen wear swords, and may easily have pistols in their pockets—most likely have, indeed. If they fire at each other without effect, then they'll draw, and go to work in earnest."

A shade passed over Mr. Willet's face as he thought of broken windows and disabled furniture, but bethinking himself that one of the parties would probably be left alive to pay the damage, he brightened up again.

"And then," said Solomon, looking from face to face, "then we shall have one of those stains upon the floor that never come out. If Mr. Haredale wins, depend upon it, it'll be a deep one; or if he loses, it will perhaps be deeper still, for he'll never give in unless he's beaten down. We know him better, eh?"

"Better indeed!" they whispered all together.

"As to its ever being got out again," said Solomon, "I tell you it never will, or can be. Why, do you know that it has been tried, at a certain house we are acquainted with?"

"The Warren!" cried John. "No, sure!"

"Yes, sure—yes. It's only known by very few. It has been whispered about though for all that. They planed the board away, but there it was. They went deep, but it went deeper. They put new boards down, but there was one great spot that came through still, and showed itself in the old place. And—harkye—draw nearer—Mr. Geoffrey made that room his study, and sits there, always, with his foot (as I have heard) upon it; and he believes, through thinking of it long and very much, that it will never fade until he finds the man who did the deed."

As this recital ended, and they all drew closer round the fire, the tramp of a horse was heard without.

"The very man!" cried John, starting up. "Hugh! Hugh!"

The sleeper staggered to his feet, and hurried after him. John quickly returned, ushering in with great attention and deference (for Mr. Haredale was his landlord) the long-expected visitor, who strode into the room clanking his heavy boots upon the floor; and looking keenly round upon the bowing group, raised his hat in acknowledgment of their profound respect.

"You have a stranger here, Willet, who sent to me," he said, in a voice which sounded naturally stern and deep. "Where is he?"

"In the great room up-stairs, sir," answered John.

"Show the way. Your staircase is dark, I know. Gentlemen, good night."

With that, he signed to the landlord to go on before; and went clanking out, and up the stairs; old John, in his agitation, ingeniously lighting everything but the way, and making a stumble at every second step.

"Stop!" he said, when they reached the landing. "I can announce myself. Don't wait."

He laid his hand upon the door, entered, and shut it heavily. Mr. Willet was by no means disposed to stand there listening by himself, especially as the walls were very thick; so descended, with much greater alacrity than he had come up, and joined his friends below.

CHAPTER XII

THERE was a brief pause in the state-room of the Maypole, as Mr. Haredale tried the lock to satisfy himself that he had shut the door securely, and, striding up the dark chamber to where the screen inclosed a little patch of light and warmth, presented himself, abruptly and in silence, before the smiling guest.

If the two had no greater sympathy in their inward thoughts than in their outward bearing and appearance, the meeting did not seem likely to prove a very calm or pleasant one. With no great disparity between them in point of years, they were, in every other respect, as unlike and far removed from each other as two men could well be. The one was soft-spoken, delicately made, precise, and elegant; the other, a burly square-built man, negligently dressed, rough and abrupt in manner, stern, and, in his present mood, forbidding both in look and speech. The one preserved a calm and placid smile; the other, a distrustful frown. The new-comer, indeed, appeared bent on showing by his every tone and gesture his determined opposition and hostility to the man he had come to meet. The guest who received him, on the other hand, seemed to feel that the contrast between them was all in his favour, and to derive a quiet exultation from it which put him more at his ease than ever.

"Haredale," said this gentleman, without the least appearance of embarrassment or reserve, "I am very glad to see you."

"Let us dispense with compliments. They are misplaced between us," returned the other, waving his hand, "and say plainly what we have to say. You have asked me to meet you. I am here. Why do we stand face to face again?"

"Still the same frank and sturdy character, I see!"

"Good or bad, sir, I am," returned the other, leaning his arm upon the chimney-piece, and turning a haughty look upon the occupant of the easy-chair, "the man I used to be. I have lost no old likings or dislikings; my memory has not failed me by a hair's-breadth. You ask me to give you a meeting. I say, I am here."

"Our meeting, Haredale," said Mr. Chester, tapping his snuff-box, and following with a smile the impatient gesture he had made—perhaps unconsciously—towards his sword, "is one of conference and peace, I hope?"

"I have come here," returned the other, "at your desire, holding myself bound to meet you, when and where you would. I have not come to bandy pleasant speeches, or hollow professions. You are a smooth man of the world, sir, and at such play have me at a disadvantage. The very last man on this earth with whom I would enter the lists to combat with gentle compliments and masked faces, is Mr. Chester, I do assure you. I am not his match at such weapons, and have reason to believe that few men are."

"You do me a great deal of honour, Haredale," returned the other, most composedly, "and I thank you. I will be frank with you—"

"I beg your pardon—will be what?"

"Frank—open—perfectly candid."

"Hah!" cried Mr. Haredale, drawing his breath. "But don't let me interrupt you."

"So resolved am I to hold this course," returned the other, tasting his wine with great deliberation, "that I have determined not to quarrel with you, and not to be betrayed into a warm expression or hasty word."

"There again," said Mr. Haredale, "you have me at a great advantage. Your self-command—"

"Is not to be disturbed, when it will serve my purpose, you would say"—rejoined the other, interrupting him with the same complacency. "Granted. I allow it. And I have a purpose to serve now. So have you. I am sure our object is the same. Let us attain it like sensible men, who have ceased to be boys some time.—Do you drink?"

"With my friends," returned the other.

"At least," said Mr. Chester, "you will be seated?"

"I will stand," returned Mr. Haredale impatiently, "on this dis-

mantled beggared hearth, and not pollute it, fallen as it is, with
mockeries. Go on.''

"You are wrong, Haredale," said the other, crossing his legs, and
smiling as he held his glass up in the bright glow of the fire. "You are
really very wrong. The world is a lively place enough, in which we
must accommodate ourselves to circumstances, sail with the stream
as glibly as we can, be content to take froth for substance, the surface
for the depth, the counterfeit for the real coin. I wonder no philosopher has ever established that our globe itself is hollow. It should
be, if Nature is consistent in her works."

"*You* think it is, perhaps?"

"I should say," he returned, sipping his wine, "there could be no
doubt about it. Well; we, in trifling with this jingling toy, have had
the ill-luck to jostle and fall out. We are not what the world calls
friends; but we are as good and true and loving friends for all that,
as nine out of every ten of those on whom it bestows the title. You
have a niece, and I a son—a fine lad, Haredale, but foolish. They fall
in love with each other, and form what this same world calls an
attachment; meaning a something fanciful and false like the rest,
which, if it took its own free time, would break like any other bubble.
But it may not have its own free time—will not, if they are left alone
—and the question is, shall we two, because society calls us enemies,
stand aloof, and let them rush into each other's arms, when, by
approaching each other sensibly, as we do now, we can prevent it,
and part them?"

"I love my niece," said Mr. Haredale, after a short silence. "It
may sound strangely in your ears; but I love her."

"Strangely, my good fellow!" cried Mr. Chester, lazily filling his
glass again, and pulling out his toothpick. "Not at all. I like Ned too
—or, as you say, love him—that's the word among such near relations.
I'm very fond of Ned. He's an amazingly good fellow, and a handsome
fellow—foolish and weak as yet; that's all. But the thing is, Haredale
—for I'll be very frank, as I told you I would at first—independently
of any dislike that you and I might have to being related to each
other, and independently of the religious differences between us—
and damn it, that's important—I couldn't afford a match of this
description. Ned and I couldn't do it. It's impossible."

"Curb your tongue, in God's name, if this conversation is to last,"
retorted Mr. Haredale fiercely. "I have said I love my niece. Do you
think that, loving her, I would have her fling her heart away on any
man who had your blood in his veins?"

"You see," said the other, not at all disturbed, "the advantage of
being so frank and open. Just what I was about to add, upon my
honour! I am amazingly attached to Ned—quite doat upon him,
indeed—and even if we could afford to throw ourselves away, that
very objection would be quite insuperable.—I wish you'd take some
wine?"

"Mark me," said Mr. Haredale, striding to the table, and laying
his hand upon it heavily. "If any man believes—presumes to think—

that I, in word or deed, or in the wildest dream, ever entertained remotely the idea of Emma Haredale's favouring the suit of any one who was akin to you—in any way—I care not what—he lies. He lies, and does me grievous wrong, in the mere thought."

"Haredale," returned the other, rocking himself to and fro as in assent, and nodding at the fire, "it's extremely manly, and really very generous in you, to meet me in this unreserved and handsome way. Upon my word, those are exactly my sentiments, only expressed with much more force and power than I could use—you know my sluggish nature, and will forgive me, I am sure."

"While I would restrain her from all correspondence with your son, and sever their intercourse here, though it should cause her death," said Mr. Haredale, who had been pacing to and fro, "I would do it kindly and tenderly if I can. I have a trust to discharge, which my nature is not formed to understand, and, for this reason, the bare fact of there being any love between them comes upon me to-night, almost for the first time."

"I am more delighted than I can possibly tell you," rejoined Mr. Chester with the utmost blandness, "to find my own impression so confirmed. You see the advantage of our having met. We understand each other. We quite agree. We have a most complete and thorough explanation, and we know what course to take.—Why don't you taste your tenant's wine? It's really very good."

"Pray who," said Mr. Haredale, "have aided Emma, or your son? Who are their go-betweens, and agents—do you know?"

"All the good people hereabouts—the neighbourhood in general, I think," returned the other, with his most affable smile. "The messenger I sent to you to-day, foremost among them all."

"The idiot? Barnaby?"

"You are surprised? I am glad of that, for I was rather so myself. Yes. I wrung that from his mother—a very decent sort of woman—from whom, indeed, I chiefly learnt how serious the matter had become, and so determined to ride out here to-day, and hold a parley with you on this neutral ground.—You're stouter than you used to be, Haredale, but you look extremely well."

"Our business, I presume, is nearly at an end," said Mr. Haredale, with an expression of impatience he was at no pains to conceal. "Trust me, Mr. Chester, my niece shall change from this time. I will appeal," he added in a lower tone, "to her woman's heart, her dignity, her pride, her duty—"

"I shall do the same by Ned," said Mr. Chester, restoring some errant faggots to their places in the grate with the toe of his boot. "If there is anything real in this world, it is those amazingly fine feelings and those natural obligations which must subsist between father and son. I shall put it to him on every ground of moral and religious feeling. I shall represent to him that we cannot possibly afford it—that I have always looked forward to his marrying well, for a genteel provision for myself in the autumn of life—that there are a great many clamorous dogs to pay, whose claims are perfectly just and right, and who must be paid out of his wife's fortune. In short, that the very highest and most honourable feelings of our nature, with every consideration of filial duty and affection, and all that sort of thing, imperatively demand that he should run away with an heiress."

"And break her heart as speedily as possible?" said Mr. Haredale, drawing on his glove.

"There Ned will act exactly as he pleases," returned the other, sipping his wine; "that's entirely his affair. I wouldn't for the world interfere with my son, Haredale, beyond a certain point. The relationship between father and son, you know, is positively quite a holy kind of bond.—*Won't* you let me persuade you to take one glass of wine? Well! as you please, as you please," he added, helping himself again.

"Chester," said Mr. Haredale, after a short silence, during which he had eyed his smiling face from time to time intently, "you have the head and heart of an evil spirit in all matters of deception."

"Your health!" said the other, with a nod. "But I have interrupted you—"

"If now," pursued Mr. Haredale, "we should find it difficult to separate these young people, and break off their intercourse—if, for instance, you find it difficult on your side, what course do you intend to take?"

"Nothing plainer, my good fellow, nothing easier," returned the other, shrugging his shoulders and stretching himself more comfortably before the fire. "I shall then exert those powers on which you flatter me so highly—though, upon my word, I don't deserve your compliments to their full extent—and resort to a few little trivial subterfuges for rousing jealousy and resentment. You see?"

"In short, justifying the means by the end, we are, as a last resource for tearing them asunder, to resort to treachery and—and lying," said Mr. Haredale.

"Oh dear no. Fie, fie!" returned the other, relishing a pinch of snuff extremely. "Not lying. Only a little management, a little diplomacy, a little—intriguing, that's the word."

"I wish," said Mr. Haredale, moving to and fro, and stopping, and moving on again, like one who was ill at ease, "that this could have been foreseen or prevented. But as it has gone so far, and it is necessary for us to act, it is of no use shrinking or regretting. Well! I shall second your endeavours to the utmost of my power. There is one topic in the whole wide range of human thoughts on which we both agree. We shall act in concert, but apart. There will be no need, I hope, for us to meet again."

"Are you going?" said Mr. Chester, rising with a graceful indolence. "Let me light you down the stairs."

"Pray keep your seat," returned the other drily, "I know the way." So, waving his hand slightly, and putting on his hat as he turned upon his heel, he went clanking out as he had come, shut the door behind him, and tramped down the echoing stairs.

"Pah! A very coarse animal, indeed!" said Mr. Chester, composing himself in the easy-chair again. "A rough brute. Quite a human badger!"

John Willet and his friends, who had been listening intently for the clash of swords, or firing of pistols in the great room, and had indeed settled the order in which they should rush in when summoned —in which procession old John had carefully arranged that he should bring up the rear—were very much astonished to see Mr. Haredale come down without a scratch, call for his horse, and ride away thoughtfully at a foot-pace. After some consideration, it was decided that he had left the gentleman above, for dead, and had adopted this stratagem to divert suspicion or pursuit.

As this conclusion involved the necessity of their going up-stairs forthwith, they were about to ascend in the order they had agreed upon, when a smart ringing at the guest's bell, as if he had pulled it vigorously, overthrew all their speculations, and involved them in great uncertainty and doubt. At length Mr. Willet agreed to go up-stairs himself, escorted by Hugh and Barnaby, as the strongest and stoutest fellows on the premises, who were to make their appearance under pretence of clearing away the glasses.

Under this protection, the brave and broad-faced John boldly entered the room, half a foot in advance, and received an order for a boot-jack without trembling. But when it was brought, and he leant his sturdy shoulder to the guest, Mr. Willet was observed to look very hard into his boots as he pulled them off, and, by opening his eyes much wider than usual, to appear to express some surprise and disappointment at not finding them full of blood. He took occasion, too, to examine the gentleman as closely as he could, expecting to discover sundry loopholes in his person, pierced by his adversary's sword. Finding none, however, and observing in course of time that his guest was as cool and unruffled, both in his dress and temper, as he had been all day, old John at last heaved a deep sigh, and began to think no duel had been fought that night.

"And now, Willet," said Mr. Chester, "if the room's well aired, I'll try the merits of that famous bed."

"The room, sir," returned John, taking up a candle, and nudging Barnaby and Hugh to accompany them, in case the gentleman should unexpectedly drop down faint or dead from some internal wound, "the room's as warm as any toast in a tankard. Barnaby, take you that other candle, and go on before. Hugh! Follow up, sir, with the easy-chair."

In this order—and still, in his earnest inspection, holding his candle very close to the guest; now making him feel extremely warm about the legs, now threatening to set his wig on fire, and constantly begging his pardon with great awkwardness and embarrassment—John led the party to the best bedroom, which was nearly as large as the chamber from which they had come, and held, drawn out near the fire for warmth, a great old spectral bedstead, hung with faded brocade, and ornamented, at the top of each carved post, with a plume of feathers that had once been white, but with dust and age had now grown hearse-like and funereal.

"Good night, my friends," said Mr. Chester with a sweet smile,
seating himself, when he had surveyed the room from end to end, in
the easy-chair which his attendants wheeled before the fire. "Good-
night! Barnaby, my good fellow, you say some prayers before you go
to bed, I hope?"

Barnaby nodded. "He has some nonsense that he calls his prayers,
sir," returned old John, officiously. "I'm afraid there an't much good
in 'em."

"And Hugh?" said Mr. Chester, turning to him.

"Not I," he answered. "I know his"—pointing to Barnaby—
"they're well enough. He sings 'em sometimes in the straw. I listen."

"He's quite a animal, sir," John whispered in his ear with dignity.
"You'll excuse him, I'm sure. If he has any soul at all, sir, it must be
such a very small one that it don't signify what he does or doesn't in
that way. Good night, sir!"

The guest rejoined "God bless you!" with a fervour that was quite
affecting; and John, beckoning his guards to go before, bowed himself out of the room, and left him to his rest in the Maypole's ancient
bed.

CHAPTER XIII

If Joseph Willet, the denounced and proscribed of 'prentices, had
happened to be at home when his father's courtly guest presented
himself before the Maypole door—that is, if it had not perversely
chanced to be one of the half-dozen days in the whole year on which
he was at liberty to absent himself for as many hours without question or reproach—he would have contrived, by hook or crook, to
dive to the very bottom of Mr. Chester's mystery and to come at his
purpose with as much certainty as though he had been his confidential adviser. In that fortunate case, the lovers would have had quick
warning of the ills that threatened them, and the aid of various
timely and wise suggestions to boot; for all Joe's readiness of thought
and action, and all his sympathies and good wishes, were enlisted in
favour of the young people, and were staunch in devotion to their
cause. Whether this disposition arose out of his old prepossessions in
favour of the young lady, whose history had surrounded her in his
mind, almost from his cradle, with circumstances of unusual interest;
or from his attachment towards the young gentleman, into whose
confidence he had, through his shrewdness and alacrity, and the
tendering of sundry important services as a spy and messenger, almost imperceptibly glided; whether they had their origin in either
of these sources, or in the habit natural to youth, or in the constant
badgering and worrying of his venerable parent, or in any hidden
little love affair of his own which gave him something of a fellow-
feeling in the matter, it is needless to inquire—especially as Joe was
out of the way, and had no opportunity on that particular occasion
of testifying to his sentiments either on one side or the other.

It was, in fact, the twenty-fifth of March, which, as most people know to their cost, is, and has been time out of mind, one of those unpleasant epochs termed quarter-days. On this twenty-fifth of March, it was John Willet's pride annually to settle, in hard cash, his account with a certain vintner and distiller in the city of London; to give into whose hands a canvas bag containing its exact amount, and not a penny more or less, was the end and object of a journey for Joe, so surely as the year and day came round.

This journey was performed upon an old grey mare, concerning whom John had an indistinct set of ideas hovering about him, to the effect that she could win a plate or cup if she tried. She never had tried, and probably never would now, being some fourteen or fifteen years of age, short in wind, long in body, and rather the worse for wear in respect of her mane and tail. Notwithstanding these slight defects, John perfectly gloried in the animal; and when she was brought round to the door by Hugh, actually retired into the bar, and there, in a secret grove of lemons, laughed with pride.

"There's a bit of horseflesh, Hugh!" said John, when he had recovered enough self-command to appear at the door again, "There's a comely creature! There's high mettle! There's bone!"

There was bone enough beyond all doubt; and so Hugh seemed to think, as he sat sideways in the saddle, lazily doubled up with his chin nearly touching his knees; and heedless of the dangling stirrups and loose bridle-rein, sauntered up and down on the little green before the door.

"Mind you take good care of her, sir," said John, appealing from this insensible person to his son and heir, who now appeared, fully equipped and ready. "Don't you ride hard."

"I should be puzzled to do that, I think, father," Joe replied, casting a disconsolate look at the animal.

"None of your impudence, sir, if you please," retorted old John. "What would you ride, sir? A wild ass or zebra would be too tame for you, wouldn't he, eh, sir? You'd like to ride a roaring lion, wouldn't you, sir, eh, sir? Hold your tongue, sir." When Mr. Willet, in his differences with his son, had exhausted all the questions that occurred to him, and Joe had said nothing at all in answer, he generally wound up by bidding him hold his tongue.

"And what does the boy mean," added Mr. Willet, after he had stared at him for a little time, in a species of stupefaction, "by cocking his hat, to such an extent! Are you going to kill the wintner, sir?"

"No," said Joe, tartly; "I'm not. Now your mind's at ease, father."

"With a milintary air, too!" said Mr. Willet, surveying him from top to toe; "with a swaggering, fire-eating, biling-water drinking sort of way with him. And what do you mean by pulling up the crocuses and snowdrops, eh, sir?"

"It's only a little nosegay," said Joe, reddening. "There's no harm in that, I hope?"

"You're a boy of business, you are, sir!" said Mr. Willet, disdainfully, "to go supposing that wintners care for nosegays."

"I don't suppose anything of the kind," returned Joe. "Let them keep their red noses for bottles and tankards. These are going to Mr. Varden's house."

"And do you suppose *he* minds such things as crocuses?" demanded John.

"I don't know, and to say the truth, I don't care," said Joe. "Come father, give me the money, and in the name of patience let me go."

"There it is, sir," replied John; "and take care of it; and mind you don't make too much haste back, but give the mare a long rest.—Do you mind?"

"Ay, I mind," returned Joe. "She'll need it, Heaven knows."

"And don't you score up too much at the Black Lion," said John. "Mind that too."

"Then why don't you let me have some money of my own?" retorted Joe, sorrowfully; "why don't you, father? What do you send me into London for, giving me only the right to call for my dinner at the Black Lion, which you're to pay for next time you go, as if I was not to be trusted with a few shillings? Why do you use me like this? It's not right of you. You can't expect me to be quiet under it."

"Let him have money!" cried John, in a drowsy reverie. "What does he call money—guineas? Hasn't he got money? Over and above the tolls, hasn't he one and sixpence?"

"One and sixpence!" repeated his son contemptuously.

"Yes, sir," returned John, "one and sixpence. When I was your age, I had never seen so much money, in a heap. A shilling of it is in case of accidents—the mare casting a shoe, or the like of that. The other sixpence is to spend in the diversions of London; and the diversion I recommend is to go to the top of the Monument, and sitting there. There's no temptation there, sir—no drink—no young women—no bad characters of any sort—nothing but imagination. That's the way I enjoyed myself when I was your age, sir."

To this, Joe made no answer, but beckoning Hugh, leaped into the saddle and rode away; and a very stalwart, manly horseman he looked, deserving a better charger than it was his fortune to bestride. John stood staring after him, or rather after the grey mare (for he had no eyes for her rider), until man and beast had been out of sight some twenty minutes, when he began to think they were gone, and slowly re-entering the house, fell into a gentle doze.

The unfortunate grey mare, who was the agony of Joe's life, floundered along at her own will and pleasure until the Maypole was no longer visible, and then contracting her legs into what a puppet would have been looked upon as a clumsy and awkward imitation of a canter, mended her pace all at once, and did it of her own accord. The acquaintance with her rider's usual mode of proceeding, which suggested this improvement in hers, impelled her likewise to turn up a bye-way, leading—not to London, but through lanes running parallel with the road they had come, and passing within a few hundred yards of the Maypole, which led finally to an inclosure surrounding a large, old, red-brick mansion—the same of which mention was made as the Warren in the first chapter of this history. Coming to a dead stop in a little copse thereabout, she suffered her rider to dismount with right good-will, and to tie her to the trunk of a tree.

"Stay there, old girl," said Joe, "and let us see whether there's any little commission for me to-day." So saying, he left her to browse upon such stunted grass and weeds as happened to grow within the length of her tether, and passing through a wicket gate, entered the grounds on foot.

The pathway, after a very few minutes' walking, brought him close to the house, towards which, and especially towards one particular window, he directed many covert glances. It was a dreary, silent building, with echoing courtyards, desolated turret-chambers, and whole suites of rooms shut up and mouldering to ruin.

The terrace-garden, dark with the shade of overhanging trees, had an air of melancholy that was quite oppressive. Great iron gates, disused for many years, and red with rust, drooping on their hinges and overgrown with long rank grass, seemed as though they tried to sink into the ground, and hide their fallen state among the friendly weeds. The fantastic monsters on the walls, green with age and damp, and covered here and there with moss, looked grim and desolate. There was a sombre aspect even on that part of the mansion which was inhabited and kept in good repair, that struck the beholder with a sense of sadness; of something forlorn and failing, whence cheerfulness was banished. It would have been difficult to imagine a bright fire blazing in the dull and darkened rooms, or to picture any gaiety of heart or revelry that the frowning walls shut in. It seemed a place where such things had been, but could be no more—the very ghost of a house, haunting the old spot in its old outward form, and that was all.

Much of this decayed and sombre look was attributable, no doubt, to the death of its former master, and the temper of its present occupant; but remembering the tale connected with the mansion, it seemed the very place for such a deed, and one that might have been its predestined theatre years upon years ago. Viewed with reference to this legend, the sheet of water where the steward's body had been found appeared to wear a black and sullen character, such as no other pool might own; the bell upon the roof that had told the tale of murder to the midnight wind, became a very phantom whose voice would raise the listener's hair on end; and every leafless bough that nodded to another, had its stealthy whispering of the crime.

Joe paced up and down the path, sometimes stopping in affected contemplation of the building or the prospect, sometimes leaning against a tree with an assumed air of idleness and indifference, but always keeping an eye upon the window he had singled out at first. After some quarter of an hour's delay, a small white hand was waved to him for an instant from this casement, and the young man, with a respectful bow, departed; saying under his breath as he crossed his horse again, "No errand for me to-day!"

But the air of smartness, the cock of the hat to which John Willet

had objected, and the spring nosegay, all betokened some little
errand of his own, having a more interesting object than a vintner or
even a locksmith. So, indeed, it turned out; for when he had settled
with the vintner—whose place of business was down in some deep
cellars hard by Thames-street, and who was as purple-faced an old
gentleman as if he had all his life supported their arched roof on his
head—when he had settled the account, and taken the receipt, and
declined tasting more than three glasses of old sherry, to the unbounded astonishment of the purple-faced vintner, who, gimlet in
hand, had projected an attack upon at least a score of dusty casks,
and who stood transfixed, or morally gimleted as it were, to his own
wall—when he had done all this, and disposed besides of a frugal
dinner at the Black Lion in Whitechapel; spurning the Monument
and John's advice, he turned his steps towards the locksmith's
house, attracted by the eyes of blooming Dolly Varden.

Joe was by no means a sheepish fellow, but, for all that, when he
got to the corner of the street in which the locksmith lived, he could
by no means make up his mind to walk straight to the house. First,
he resolved to stroll up another street for five minutes, then up
another street for five minutes more, and so on until he had lost full
half an hour, when he made a bold plunge and found himself with
a red face and a beating heart in the smoky workshop.

"Joe Willet, or his ghost?" said Varden, rising from the desk at
which he was busy with his books, and looking at him under his
spectacles. "Which is it? Joe in the flesh, eh? That's hearty. And how
are all the Chigwell company, Joe?"

"Much as usual, sir—they and I agree as well as ever."

"Well, well!" said the locksmith. "We must be patient, Joe, and
bear with old folks' foibles. How's the mare, Joe? Does she do the
four miles an hour as easily as ever? Ha, ha, ha! Does she, Joe?
Eh!—What have we there, Joe—a nosegay!"

"A very poor one, sir—I thought Miss Dolly—"

"No, no," said Gabriel, dropping his voice, and shaking his head,
"not Dolly. Give 'em to her mother, Joe. A great deal better give
'em to her mother. Would you mind giving 'em to Mrs. Varden,
Joe?"

"Oh no, sir," Joe replied, and endeavouring, but not with the
greatest possible success, to hide his disappointment. "I shall be
very glad, I'm sure."

"That's right," said the locksmith, patting him on the back. "It
don't matter who has 'em, Joe?"

"Not a bit, sir."—Dear heart, how the words stuck in his throat!

"Come in," said Gabriel. "I have just been called to tea. She's in
the parlour."

"She," thought Joe. "Which of 'em I wonder—Mrs. or Miss?" The
locksmith settled the doubt as neatly as if it had been expressed
aloud, by leading him to the door, and saying, "Martha, my dear,
here's young Mr. Willet."

Now, Mrs. Varden, regarding the Maypole as a sort of human man-trap, or decoy for husbands; viewing its proprietor, and all who aided and abetted him, in the light of so many poachers among Christian men; and believing, moreover, that the publicans coupled with sinners in Holy Writ were veritable licensed victuallers; was far from being favourably disposed towards her visitor. Wherefore she was taken faint directly; and being duly presented with the crocuses and snowdrops, divined on further consideration that they were the occasion of the languor which had seized upon her spirits. "I'm afraid I couldn't bear the room another minute," said the good lady, "if they remain here. *Would* you excuse my putting them out of window?"

Joe begged she wouldn't mention it on any account, and smiled feebly as he saw them deposited on the sill outside. If anybody could have known the pains he had taken to make up that despised and misused bunch of flowers!—

"I feel it quite a relief to get rid of them, I assure you." said Mrs. Varden. "I'm better already." And indeed she did appear to have plucked up her spirits.

Joe expressed his gratitude to Providence for this favourable dispensation, and tried to look as if he didn't wonder where Dolly was.

"You're sad people at Chigwell, Mr. Joseph," said Mrs. V.

"I hope not, ma'am," returned Joe.

"You're the cruellest and most inconsiderate people in the world," said Mrs. Varden, bridling. "I wonder old Mr. Willet, having been a married man himself, doesn't know better than to conduct himself as he does. His doing it for profit is no excuse. I would rather pay the money twenty times over, and have Varden come home like a respectable and sober tradesman. If there is one character," said Mrs. Varden with great emphasis, "that offends and disgusts me more than another, it is a sot."

"Come, Martha, my dear," said the locksmith cheerily, "let us have tea, and don't let us talk about sots. There are none here, and Joe don't want to hear about them, I dare say."

At this crisis, Miggs appeared with toast.

"I dare say he does not," said Mrs. Varden; "and I dare say you do not, Varden. It's a very unpleasant subject I have no doubt, though I won't say it's personal"—Miggs coughed—"whatever I may be forced to think," Miggs sneezed expressively. "You never will know, Varden, and nobody at young Mr. Willet's age—you'll excuse me, sir —can be expected to know what a woman suffers when she is waiting at home under such circumstances. If you don't believe me, as I know you don't, here's Miggs, who is only too often a witness of it— ask her."

"Oh! she were very bad the other night, sir, indeed she were," said Miggs. "If you hadn't the sweetness of an angel in you, mim, I don't think you could abear it, I raly don't."

"Miggs," said Mrs. Varden, "you're profane."

"Begging your pardon, mim," returned Miggs, with a shrill rapidity, "such was not my intentions, and such I hope is not my character, though I am but a servant."

"Answering me, Miggs, and providing yourself," retorted her mistress, looking round with dignity, "is one and the same thing. How dare you speak of angels in connection with your sinful fellow-beings—mere"—said Mrs. Varden, glancing at herself in a neighbouring mirror, and arranging the ribbon of her cap in a more becoming fashion—"mere worms and grovellers as we are!"

"I did not intend, mim, if you please, to give offence," said Miggs, confident in the strength of her compliment, and developing strongly in the throat as usual, "and I did not expect it would be took as such. I hope I know my own unworthiness, and that I hate and despise myself and all my fellow-creatures as every practicable Christian should."

"You'll have the goodness, if you please," said Mrs. Varden, loftily, "to step up-stairs and see if Dolly has finished dressing, and to tell her that the chair that was ordered for her will be here in a minute, and that if she keeps it waiting, I shall send it away that instant—I'm sorry to see that you don't take your tea, Varden, and that you don't take yours, Mr. Joseph; though of course it would be foolish of me to expect that anything that can be had at home, and in the company of females, would please *you*."

This pronoun was understood in the plural sense, and included both gentlemen, upon both of whom it was rather hard and undeserved, for Gabriel had applied himself to the meal with a very promising appetite, until it was spoilt by Mrs. Varden herself, and Joe had as great a liking for the female society of the locksmith's house—or for a part of it at all events—as man could well entertain.

But he had no opportunity to say anything in his own defence, for at that moment Dolly herself appeared, and struck him quite dumb with her beauty. Never had Dolly looked so handsome as she did then, in all the glow and grace of youth, with all her charms increased a hundredfold by a most becoming dress, by a thousand little coquettish ways which nobody could assume with a better grace, and all the sparkling expectation of that accursed party. It is impossible to tell how Joe hated that party wherever it was, and all the other people who were going to it, whoever they were.

And she hardly looked at him—no, hardly looked at him. And when the chair was seen through the open door coming blundering into the workshop, she actually clapped her hands and seemed glad to go. But Joe gave her his arm—there was some comfort in that—and handed her into it. To see her seat herself inside, with her laughing eyes brighter than diamonds, and her hand—surely she had the prettiest hand in the world—on the ledge of the open window, and her little finger provokingly and pertly tilted up, as if it wondered why Joe didn't squeeze or kiss it! To think how well one or two of the modest snowdrops would have become that delicate bodice, and how they were lying neglected outside the parlour window! To see how Miggs looked on with a face expressive of knowing how all this loveliness was got up, and of being in the secret of every string and pin and hook and eye, and of saying it ain't half as real as you think, and I could look quite as well myself if I took the pains! To hear that provoking precious little scream when the chair was hoisted on its poles, and to catch that transient but not-to-be-forgotten vision of the happy face within—what torments and aggravations, and yet what delights were these! The very chairmen seemed favoured rivals as they bore her down the street.

There never was such an alteration in a small room in a small time as in that parlour when they went back to finish tea. So dark, so deserted, so perfectly disenchanted. It seemed such sheer nonsense to be sitting tamely there, when she was at a dance with more lovers than man could calculate fluttering about her—with the whole party doting on and adoring her, and wanting to marry her. Miggs was hovering about too; and the fact of her existence, the mere circumstance of her ever having been born, appeared, after Dolly, such an unaccountable practical joke. It was impossible to talk. It couldn't be done. He had nothing left for it but to stir his tea round, and round and round, and ruminate on all the fascinations of the locksmith's lovely daughter.

Gabriel was dull too. It was a part of the certain uncertainty of Mrs. Varden's temper, that when they were in this condition, she should be gay and sprightly.

"I need have a cheerful disposition, I am sure," said the smiling housewife, "to preserve many spirits at all; and how I do it I can scarcely tell."

"Ah, mim," sighed Miggs, "begging your pardon for the interruption, there an't a many like you."

"Take away, Miggs," said Mrs. Varden, rising, "take away, pray. I know I'm a restraint here, and as I wish everybody to enjoy themselves as they best can, I feel I had better go."

"No, no, Martha," cried the locksmith. "Stop here. I'm sure we shall be very sorry to lose you, eh, Joe!" Joe started, and said "Certainly."

"Thank you, Varden, my dear," returned his wife; "but I know your wishes better. Tobacco and beer, or spirits, have much greater attractions than any *I* can boast of, and therefore I shall go and sit up-stairs and look out of window, my love. Good night, Mr. Joseph, I'm very glad to have seen you, and I only wish I could have provided something more suitable to your taste. Remember me very kindly if you please to old Mr. Willet, and tell him that whenever he comes here I have a crow to pluck with him. Good night!"

Having uttered these words with great sweetness of manner, the good lady dropped a curtsey remarkable for its condescension, and serenely withdrew.

And it was for this Joe had looked forward to the twenty-fifth of March for weeks and weeks, and had gathered the flowers with so much care, and had cocked his hat, and made himself so smart! This was the end of all his bold determination, resolved upon for the

hundredth time, to speak out to Dolly and tell her how he loved her!
To see her for a minute—for but a minute—to find her going out to
a party and glad to go; to be looked upon as a common pipe-smoker,
beer-bibber, spirit-guzzler, and tosspot! He bade farewell to his
friend the locksmith, and hastened to take horse at the Black Lion
thinking as he turned towards home, as many another Joe had
thought before and since, that there was an end to all his hopes—that
the thing was impossible and never could be—that she didn't care
for him—that he was wretched for life—and that the only congenial
prospect left him, was to go for a soldier or a sailor, and get some
obliging enemy to knock his brains out as soon as possible.

CHAPTER XIV

JOE WILLET rode leisurely along in his desponding mood, picturing
the locksmith's daughter going down long country-dances, and
poussetting dreadfully with bold strangers—which was almost too
much to bear—when he heard the tramp of a horse's feet behind
him, and looking back, saw a well-mounted gentleman advancing at
a smart canter. As this rider passed, he checked his steed, and called
him of the Maypole by his name. Joe set spurs to the grey mare, and
was at his side directly.

"I thought it was you, sir," he said, touching his hat. "A fair
evening, sir. Glad to see you out of doors again."

The gentleman smiled and nodded. "What gay doings have been
going on to-day, Joe? Is she as pretty as ever? Nay, don't blush,
man."

"If I had coloured at all, Mr. Edward," said Joe, "which I didn't
know I did, it was to think I should have been such a fool as ever to
have any hope of her. She's as far out of my reach as—as Heaven is."

"Well, Joe, I hope that's not altogether beyond it," said Edward,
good-humouredly. "Eh?"

"Ah!" sighed Joe. "It's all very fine talking, sir. Proverbs are
easily made in cold blood. But it can't be helped. Are you bound for
our house, sir?"

"Yes. As I am not quite strong yet, I shall stay there to-night, and
ride home coolly in the morning."

"If you're in no particular hurry," said Joe after a short silence,
"and will bear with the pace of this poor jade, I shall be glad to ride
on with you to the Warren, sir, and hold your horse when you dismount. It'll save you having to walk from the Maypole, there and
back again. I can spare the time well, sir, for I am too soon."

"And so am I," returned Edward, "though I was unconsciously
riding fast just now, in compliment I suppose to the pace of my
thoughts, which were travelling post. We will keep together, Joe,
willingly, and be as good company as may be. And cheer up, cheer
up, think of the locksmith's daughter with a stout heart, and you
shall win her yet."

Joe shook his head; but there was something so cheery in the buoyant hopeful manner of this speech, that his spirits rose under its influence, and communicated as it would seem some new impulse even to the grey mare, who, breaking from her sober amble into a gentle trot, emulated the pace of Edward Chester's horse, and appeared to flatter herself that he was doing his very best.

It was a fine dry night, and the light of a young moon, which was then just rising, shed around that peace and tranquillity which gives to evening time its most delicious charm. The lengthened shadows of the trees, softened as if reflected in still water, threw their carpet on the path the travellers pursued, and the light wind stirred yet more softly than before, as though it were soothing Nature in her sleep. By little and little they ceased talking, and rode on side by side in a pleasant silence.

"The Maypole lights are brilliant to-night," said Edward, as they rode along the lane from which, while the intervening trees were bare of leaves, that hostelry was visible.

"Brilliant indeed, sir," returned Joe, rising in his stirrups to get a better view. "Lights in the large room, and a fire glimmering in the best bed-chamber? Why, what company can this be for, I wonder!"

"Some benighted horseman wending towards London and deterred from going on to-night by the marvellous tales of my frined the highwayman, I suppose," said Edward.

"He must be a horseman of good quality to have such accommodations. Your bed too, sir——!"

"No matter, Joe. Any other room will do for me. But come— there's nine striking. We may push on."

They cantered forward at as brisk a pace as Joe's charger could attain, and presently stopped in the little copse where he had left her in the morning. Edward dismounted, gave his bridle to his companion, and walked with a light step towards the house.

A female servant was waiting at a side gate in the garden-wall, and admitted him without delay. He hurried along the terrace-walk, and darted up a flight of broad steps leading into an old and gloomy hall, whose walls were ornamented with rusty suits of armour, antlers, weapons of the chase, and such-like garniture. Here he paused, but not long; for as he looked round, as if expecting the attendant to have followed, and wondering she had not done so, a lovely girl appeared, whose dark hair next moment rested on his breast. Almost at the same instant a heavy hand was laid upon her arm, Edward felt himself thrust away, and Mr. Haredale stood between them.

He regarded the young man sternly without removing his hat; with one hand clasped his niece, and with the other, in which he held his riding-whip, motioned him towards the door. The young man drew himself up, and returned his gaze.

"This is well done of you sir, to corrupt my servants, and enter my house unbidden and in secret, like a thief!" said Mr. Haredale. "Leave it, sir, and return no more."

"Miss Haredale's presence," returned the young man, " and your relationship to her, give you a licence which, if you are a brave man, you will not abuse. You have compelled me to this course, and the fault is yours—not mine."

"It is neither generous, nor honourable, nor the act of a true man, sir," retorted the other, "to tamper with the affections of a weak, trusting girl, while you shrink, in your unworthiness, from her guardian and protector, and dare not meet the light of day. More than this I will not say to you, save that I forbid you in this house, and require you to be gone."

"It is neither generous, nor honourable, nor the act of a true man to play the spy," said Edward. "Your words simply dishonour, and I reject them with the scorn they merit."

"You will find," said Mr. Haredale, calmly, "your trusty go-between in waiting at the gate by which you entered. I have played no spy's part, sir. I chanced to see you pass the gate, and followed. You might have heard me knocking for admission, had you been less swift of foot, or lingered in the garden. Please to withdraw. Your presence here is offensive to me and distressful to my niece." As he said these words, he passed his arm about the waist of the terrified and weeping girl, and drew her closer to him; and though the habitual severity of his manner was scarcely changed, there was yet apparent in the action an air of kindness and sympathy for her distress.

"Mr. Haredale," said Edward, "your arm encircles her on whom I have set my every hope and thought, and to purchase one minute's happiness for whom I would gladly lay down my life; this house is the casket that holds the precious jewel of my existence. Your niece has plighted her faith to me, and I have plighted mine to her. What have I done that you should hold me in this light esteem, and give me these discourteous words?"

"You have done that, sir," answered Mr. Haredale, "which must be undone. You have tied a lover's-knot here which must be cut asunder. Take good heed of what I say. Must I cancel the bond between ye. I reject you, and all of your kith and kin—all the false, hollow, heartless stock."

"High words, sir," said Edward, scornfully.

"Words of purpose and meaning, as you will find," replied the other. "Lay them to heart."

"Lay you then, these," said Edward. "Your cold and sullen temper, which chills every breast about you, which turns affection into fear, and changes duty into dread, has forced us on this secret course, repugnant to our nature and our wish, and far more foreign, sir, to us than you. I am not a false, a hollow, or a heartless man; the character is yours, who poorly venture on these injurious terms, against the truth, and under the shelter whereof I reminded you just now. You shall not cancel the bond between us. I will not abandon this pursuit. I rely upon your niece's truth and honour, and set your influence at nought. I leave her with a confidence in her pure faith, which you will never weaken, and with no concern but that I do not leave her in some gentler care."

With that, he pressed her cold hand to his lips, and once more encountering and returning Mr. Haredale's steady look, withdrew.

A few words to Joe as he mounted his horse sufficiently explained what had passed, and renewed all that young gentleman's despondency with tenfold aggravation. They rode back to the Maypole without exchanging a syllable, and arrived at the door with heavy hearts.

Old John, who had peeped from behind the red curtain as they rode up shouting for Hugh, was out directly, and said with great importance as he held the young man's stirrup,

"He's comfortable in bed—the best bed. A thorough gentleman; the smilingest, affablest gentleman I ever had to do with."

"Who, Willet?" said Edward carelessly, as he dismounted.

"Your worthy father, sir," replied John. "Your honourable, venerable father."

"What does he mean?" said Edward, looking, with a mixture of alarm and doubt, at Joe.

"What *do* you mean?" said Joe. "Don't you see Mr. Edward doesn't understand, father?"

"Why, didn't you know of it, sir?" said John, opening his eyes wide. "How very singular! Bless you, he's been here ever since noon to-day, and Mr. Haredale has been having a long talk with him, and hasn't been gone an hour."

"My father, Willet!"

"Yes, sir, he told me so—a handsome, slim, upright gentleman, in green-and-gold. In your old room up yonder, sir. No doubt you can go in, sir," said John, walking backwards into the road and looking up at the window. "He hasn't put out his candles yet, I see."

Edward glanced at the window also, and hastily murmuring that he had changed his mind—forgotten something—and must return to London, mounted his horse again and rode away; leaving the Willets, father and son, looking at each other in mute astonishment.

CHAPTER XV

AT noon next day, John Willet's guest sat lingering over his breakfast in his own home, surrounded by a variety of comforts, which left the Maypole's highest flight and utmost stretch of accommodation at an infinite distance behind, and suggested comparisons very much to the disadvantage and disfavour of that venerable tavern.

In the broad old-fashioned window-seat—as capacious as many modern sofas, and cushioned to serve the purpose of a luxurious settee—in the broad old-fashioned window-seat of a roomy chamber, Mr. Chester lounged, very much at his ease, over a well-furnished breakfast-table. He had exchanged his riding-coat for a handsome morning-gown, his boots for slippers; had been at great pains to atone for the having been obliged to make his toilet when he rose without the aid of dressing-case and tiring equipage; and, having gradually forgotten through these means the discomforts of an indifferent night and an early ride, was in a state of perfect complacency, indolence and satisfaction.

The situation in which he found himself, indeed, was particularly favourable to the growth of these feelings; for, not to mention the lazy influence of a late and lonely breakfast, with the additional sedative of a newspaper, there was an air of repose about his place of residence peculiar to itself, and which hangs about it, even in these times, when it is more bustling and busy than it was in days of yore.

There are, still, worse places than the Temple, on a sultry day, for basking in the sun, or resting idly in the shade. There is yet a drowsiness in its courts, and a dreamy dulness in its streets and gardens; those who pace its lanes and squares may yet hear the echoes of their footsteps on the sounding stones, and read upon its gates, in passing from the tumult of the Strand or Fleet Street, "Who enters here leaves noise behind." There is still the plash of falling water in fair Fountain Court, and there are yet nooks and corners where dun-haunted students may look down from their dusty garrets, on a vagrant ray of sunlight patching the shade of the tall houses, and seldom troubled to reflect a passing stranger's form. There is yet, in the Temple, something of a clerkly monkish atmosphere, which public offices of law have not disturbed, and even legal firms have failed to scare away. In summer time, its pumps suggest to thirsty idlers, springs cooler, and more sparkling, and deeper than other wells; and as they trace the spillings of full pitchers on the heated ground, they snuff the freshness, and, sighing, cast sad looks towards the Thames, and think of baths and boats, and saunter on, despondent.

It was in a room in Paper Buildings—a row of goodly tenements, shaded in front by ancient trees, and looking, at the back, upon the Temple Gardens—that this, our idler, lounged; now taking up again the paper he had laid down a hundred times; now trifling with the fragments of his meal; now pulling forth his golden toothpick, and glancing leisurely about the room, or out at window into the trim garden walks, where a few early loiterers were already pacing to and fro. Here a pair of lovers met to quarrel and make up; there a dark-eyed nursery-maid had better eyes for Templars than her charge; on this hand an ancient spinster, with her lapdog in a string, regarded both enormities with scornful sidelong looks; on that a weazen old gentleman, ogling the nursery-maid, looked with like scorn upon the spinster, and wondered she didn't know she was no longer young. Apart from all these, on the river's margin two or three couple of business-talkers walked slowly up and down in earnest conversation; and one young man sat thoughtfully on a bench, alone.

"Ned is amazingly patient!" said Mr. Chester, glancing at this last-named person as he set down his tea-cup and plied the golden toothpick, "immensely patient! He was sitting yonder when I began to dress, and has scarcely changed his posture since. A most eccentric dog!"

As he spoke, the figure rose, and came towards him with a rapid pace.

"Really, as if he had heard me," said the father, resuming his newspaper with a yawn. "Dear Ned!"

Presently the room-door opened, and the young man entered; to whom his father gently waved his hand, and smiled.

"Are you at leisure for a little conversation, sir?" said Edward.

"Surely, Ned. I am always at leisure. You know my constitution. —Have you breakfasted?"

"Three hours ago."

"What a very early dog!" cried his father, contemplating him from behind the toothpick, with a languid smile.

"The truth is," said Edward, bringing a chair forward, and seating himself near the table, "that I slept but ill last night, and was glad to rise. The cause of my uneasiness cannot but be known to you, sir; and it is upon that I wish to speak."

"My dear boy," returned his father, "confide in me, I beg. But you know my constitution—don't be prosy, Ned."

"I will be plain, and brief," said Edward.

"Don't say you will, my good fellow," returned his father, crossing his legs, "or you certainly will not. You are going to tell me—"

"Plainly this, then," said the son, with an air of great concern, "that I know where you were last night—from being on the spot, indeed—and whom you saw, and what your purpose was."

"You don't say so!" cried his father. "I am delighted to hear it. It saves us the worry, and terrible wear and tear of a long explanation, and is a great relief for both. At the very house! Why didn't you come up? I should have been charmed to see you."

"I knew that what I had to say would be better said after a night's reflection, when both of us were cool," returned the son.

"'Fore Gad, Ned," rejoined the father, "I was cool enough last night. That detestable Maypole! By some infernal contrivance of the builder, it holds the wind and keeps it fresh. You remember the sharp east wind that blew so hard five weeks ago? I give you my honour it was rampant in that old house last night, though out of doors there was a dead calm. But you were saying—"

"I was about to say, Heaven knows how seriously and earnestly, that you have made me wretched, sir. Will you hear me gravely for a moment?"

"My dear Ned," said his father, "I will hear you with the patience of an anchorite. Oblige me with the milk."

"I saw Miss Haredale last night," Edward resumed, when he had complied with this request; "her uncle, in her presence, immediately after your interview, and, as of course I know, in consequence of it, forbade me the house, and, with circumstances of indignity which are of your creation I am sure, commanded me to leave it on the instant."

"For his manner of doing so, I give you my honour, Ned, I am not accountable," said his father. "That you must excuse. He is a mere boor, a log, a brute, with no address in life.—Positively a fly in the jug. The first I have seen this year."

Edward rose, and paced the room. His imperturbable parent sipped his tea.

"Father," said the young man, stopping at length before him, "we must not trifle in this matter. We must not deceive each other, or ourselves. Let me pursue the manly open part I wish to take, and do not repel me by this unkind indifference."

"Whether I am indifferent or no," returned the other, "I leave you, my dear boy, to judge. A ride of twenty-five or thirty miles, through miry roads—a Maypole dinner—a tête-à-tête with Haredale, which, vanity apart, was quite a Valentine and Orson business—a Maypole bed—Maypole landlord, and a Maypole retinue of idiots and centaurs; —whether the voluntary endurance of these things looks like indifference, dear Ned, or like the excessive anxiety, and devotion and all that sort of thing, of a parent, you shall determine for yourself."

"I wish you to consider, sir," said Edward, "in what a cruel situation I am placed. Loving Miss Haredale as I do—"

"My dear fellow," interrupted his father with a compassionate smile, "you do nothing of the kind. You don't know anything about it. There's no such thing, I assure you. Now, do take my word for it. You have good sense, Ned,—great good sense. I wonder you should be guilty of such amazing absurdities. You really surprise me."

"I repeat," said his son firmly, "that I love her. You have interposed to part us, and have, to the extent I have just now told you of, succeeded. May I induce you, sir, in time, to think more favourably of our attachment, or is it your intention and your fixed design to hold us asunder if you can?"

"My dear Ned," returned his father, taking a pinch of snuff and pushing his box towards him, "that *is* my purpose most undoubtedly."

"The time that has elapsed," rejoined his son, "since I began to know her worth, has flown in such a dream that until now I have hardly paused to reflect upon my true position. What is it? From my childhood I have been accustomed to luxury and idleness, and have been bred as though my fortune were large, and my expectations almost without a limit. The idea of wealth has been familiarised to me from my cradle. I have been taught to look upon those means, by which men raise themselves to riches and distinction, as being beyond my breeding, and beneath my care. I have been, as the phrase is, liberally educated, and am fit for nothing. I find myself at last wholly dependent upon you, with no resource but in your favour. In this momentous question of my life we do not, and it would seem we never can, agree. I have shrunk instinctively alike from those to whom you have urged me to pay court, and from the motives of interest and gain which have rendered them in your eyes visible objects for my suit. If there never has been thus much plain-speaking between us before, sir, the fault has not been mine, indeed. If I seem to speak too plainly now, it is, believe me, father, in the hope that there may be a franker spirit, a worthier reliance, and a kinder confidence between us in time to come."

"My good fellow," said his smiling father, "you quite affect me. Go on, dear Edward, I beg. But remember your promise. There is great earnestness, vast candour, a manifest sincerity in all you say, but I fear I observe the faintest indications of a tendency to prose."

"I am very sorry, sir."

"I am very sorry, too, Ned, but you know that I cannot fix my mind for any long period upon one subject. If you'll come to the point at once, I'll imagine all that ought to go before, and conclude it said. Oblige me with the milk again. Listening invariably makes me feverish."

"What I would say then, tends to this," said Edward. "I cannot bear this absolute dependence, sir, even upon you. Time has been lost and opportunity thrown away, but I am yet a young man, and may retrieve it. Will you give me the means of devoting such abilities and energies as I possess, to some worthy pursuit? Will you let me try to make for myself an honourable path in life? For any term you please to name—say for five years if you will—I will pledge myself to move no further in the matter of our difference without your full concurrence. During that period, I will endeavour earnestly and patiently if ever man did, to open some prospect for myself, and free you from the burden you fear I should become if I married one whose worth and beauty are her chief endowments. Will you do this, sir? At the expiration of the term we agree upon, let us discuss this subject again. Till then, unless it is revived by you, let it never be renewed between us."

"My dear Ned," returned his father, laying down the newspaper at which he had been glancing carelessly, and throwing himself back in the window-seat, "I believe you know how very much I dislike what are called family affairs, which are only fit for plebeian Christmas days, and have no manner of business with people of our condition. But as you are proceeding upon a mistake, Ned—altogether upon a mistake—I will conquer my repugnance to entering on such matters, and give you a perfectly plain and candid answer, if you will do me the favour to shut the door."

Edward having obeyed him, he took an elegant little knife from his pocket, and paring his nails, continued:

"You have to thank me, Ned, for being of good family; for your mother, charming person as she was, and almost broken-hearted, and so forth, as she left me, when she was prematurely compelled to become immortal—had nothing to boast of in that respect."

"Her father was at least an eminent lawyer, sir," said Edward.

"Quite right, Ned; perfectly so. He stood high at the bar, had a great name and great wealth, but having risen from nothing—I have always closed my eyes to the circumstance and steadily resisted its contemplation, but I fear his father dealt in pork, and that his business did once involve cow-heel and sausage—he wished to marry his daughter into a good family. He had his heart's desire, Ned. I was a younger son's younger son, and I married her. We each had our object, and gained it. She stepped at once into the politest and best circles, and I stepped into a fortune which I assure you was very necessary to my comfort—quite indispensable. Now, my good fellow, that fortune is among the things that have been. It is gone, Ned, and has been gone—how old are you? I always forget."

"Seven-and-twenty, sir."

"Are you indeed?" cried his father, raising his eyelids in a languishing surprise. "So much! Then I should say, Ned, that as nearly as I remember, its skirts vanished from human knowledge, about eighteen or nineteen years ago. It was about that time when I came to live in these chambers (once your grandfather's, and bequeathed by that extremely respectable person to me), and commenced to live upon an inconsiderable annuity and my past reputation."

"You are jesting with me, sir," said Edward.

"Not in the slightest degree, I assure you," returned his father with great composure. "These family topics are so extremely dry, that I am sorry to say they don't admit of any such relief. It is for that reason, and because they have an appearance of business, that I dislike them so very much. Well! You know the rest. A son, Ned, unless he is old enough to be a companion—that is to say, unless he is some two or three and twenty—is not the kind of thing to have about one. He is a restraint upon his father, his father is a restraint upon him, and they make each other mutually uncomfortable. Therefore, until within the last four years or so—I have a poor memory for dates, and if I mistake, you will correct me in your own mind—you pursued your studies at a distance, and picked up a great variety of accomplishments. Occasionally we passed a week or two together here, and disconcerted each other as only such near relations can. At last you came home, I candidly tell you, my dear boy, that if you had been awkward and overgrown, I should have exported you to some distant part of the world."

"I wish with all my soul you had, sir," said Edward.

"No you don't, Ned," said his father coolly; "you are mistaken, I assure you. I found you a handsome, prepossessing, elegant fellow, and I threw you into the society I can still command. Having done that, my dear fellow, I consider that I have provided for you in life, and rely upon your doing something to provide for me in return."

"I do not understand your meaning, sir."

"My meaning, Ned, is obvious—I observe another fly in the cream-jug, but have the goodness not to take it out as you did the first, for their walk when their legs are milky, is extremely ungraceful and disagreeable—my meaning is, that you must do as I did; that you must marry well and make the most of yourself."

"A mere fortune-hunter!" cried the son, indignantly.

"What in the devil's name, Ned, would you be!" returned the father. "All men are fortune-hunters, are they not? The law, the church, the court, the camp—see how they are all crowded with fortune-hunters, jostling, each other in the pursuit. The Stock-exchange, the pulpit, the counting-house, the royal drawing-room, the senate,—what but fortune-hunters are they filled with? A fortune hunter! Yes, You *are* one; and you would be nothing else, my dear Ned, if you were the greatest courtier, lawyer, legislator, prelate, or merchant, in existence. If you are squeamish and moral, Ned, console yourself with the reflection that at the very worst your fortune-hunting can make but one person miserable or unhappy. How many people do you suppose these other kinds of huntsmen crush in following their sport—hundreds at a step? Or thousands?"

The young man leant his head upon his hand, and made no answer.

"I am quite charmed," said the father rising, and walking slowly to and fro—stopping now and then to glance at himself in the mirror, or survey a picture through his glass, with the air of a connoisseur, "that we have had this conversation, Ned, unpromising as it was. It establishes a confidence between us which is quite delightful, and was certainly necessary, though how you can ever have mistaken our positions and designs, I confess I cannot understand. I conceived, until I found your fancy for this girl, that all these points were tacitly agreed upon between us."

"I knew you were embarrassed, sir," returned the son, raising his head for a moment, and then falling into his former attitude, "but I had no idea we were the beggared wretches you describe. How could I suppose it, bred as I have been; witnessing the life you have always led; and the appearance you have always made?"

"My dear child," said the father—"for you really talk so like a child that I must call you one—you were bred upon a careful principle; the very manner of your education, I assure you, maintained my credit surprisingly. As to the life I lead, I must lead it, Ned. I must have these little refinements about me. I have always been used to them, and I cannot exist without them. They must surround me, you observe, and therefore they are here. With regard to our circumstances, Ned, you may set your mind at rest upon that score. They are desperate. Your own appearance is by no means despicable, and our joint pocket-money alone devours our income. That's the truth."

"Why have I never known this before? Why have you encouraged me, sir, to an expenditure and mode of life to which we have no right or title?"

"My good fellow," returned his father more compassionately than ever, "if you made no appearance, how could you possibly succeed in the pursuit for which I destined you? As to our mode of life, every man has a right to live in the best way he can; and to make himself as comfortable as he can, or he is an unnatural scoundrel. Our debts, I grant, are very great, and therefore it the more behoves you, as a young man of principle and honour, to pay them off as speedily as possible."

"The villain's part," muttered Edward, "that I have unconsciously played! I to win the heart of Emma Haredale! I would, for her sake, I had died first!"

"I am glad you see, Ned," returned his father, "how perfectly self-evident it is, that nothing can be done in that quarter. But apart from this, and the necessity of your speedily bestowing yourself on another (as you know you could to-morrow, if you chose), I wish you'd look upon it pleasantly. In a religious point of view alone, how could you ever think of uniting yourself to a Catholic, unless she was amazingly rich? You ought to be so very Protestant, coming of such a Protestant family as you do. Let us be moral, Ned, or we are nothing. Even if one could set that objection aside, which is impossible, we come to another which is quite conclusive. The very idea of marrying a girl whose father was killed, like meat! Good God, Ned, how disagreeable! Consider the impossibility of having any respect for your father-in-law under such unpleasant circumstances—think of his having been 'viewed' by jurors, and 'sat upon' by coroners, and of his very doubtful position in the family ever afterwards. It seems to me such an indelicate sort of thing that I really think the girl ought to have been put to death by the state to prevent its happening. But I tease you perhaps. You would rather be alone? My dear Ned, most willingly. God bless you. I shall be going out presently, but we shall meet to-night, or if not to-night, certainly to-morrow. Take care of yourself in the mean time, for both our sakes. You are a person of great consequence to me, Ned—of vast consequence indeed. God bless you!"

With these words, the father, who had been arranging his cravat in the glass, while he uttered them in a disconnected careless manner, withdrew, humming a tune as he went. The son, who had appeared so lost in thought as not to hear or understand them, remained quite still and silent. After the lapse of half an hour or so, the elder Chester, gaily dressed, went out. The younger still sat with his head resting on his hands, in what appeared to be a kind of stupor.

CHAPTER XVI

A SERIES of pictures representing the streets of London in the night, even at the comparatively recent date of this tale, would present to the eye something so very different in character from the reality which is witnessed in these times, that it would be difficult for the beholder to recognise his most familiar walks in the altered aspect of little more than half a century ago.

They were, one and all, from the broadest and best to the narrowest and least frequented, very dark. The oil and cotton lamps, though regularly trimmed twice or thrice in the long winter nights, burnt feebly at the best; and at a late hour, when they were unassisted by the lamps and candles in the shops, cast but a narrow track of doubtful light upon the footway, leaving the projecting doors and housefronts in the deepest gloom. Many of the courts and lanes were left in total darkness; those of the meaner sort, where one glimmering light twinkled for a score of houses, being favoured in no slight degree. Even in these places, the inhabitants had often good reason for extinguishing their lamp as soon as it was lighted; and the watch being utterly inefficient and powerless to prevent them, they did so at their pleasure. Thus, in the lightest thoroughfares, there was at every turn some obscure and dangerous spot whither a thief might fly for shelter, and few would care to follow; and the city being belted round by fields, green lanes, waste grounds, and lonely roads, dividing it at that time from the suburbs that have joined it since, escape, even where the pursuit was hot, was rendered easy.

It is no wonder that with these favouring circumstances in full and constant operation, street robberies, often accompanied by cruel wounds, and not unfrequently by loss of life, should have been of nightly occurrence in the very heart of London, or that quiet folks should have had great dread of traversing its streets after the shops were closed. It was not unusual for those who wended home alone at midnight, to keep the middle of the road, the better to guard against surprise from lurking footpads; few would venture to repair at a late hour to Kentish Town or Hampstead, or even to Kensington or Chelsea, unarmed and unattended; while he who had been loudest and most valiant at the supper-table or the tavern, and had but a mile or so to go, was glad to fee a link-boy to escort him home.

There were many other characteristics—not quite so disagreeable —about the thoroughfares of London then, with which they had been long familiar. Some of the shops, especially those to the eastward of Temple Bar, still adhered to the old practice of hanging out a sign; and the creaking and swinging of these boards in their iron frames on windy nights, formed a strange and mournful concert for the ears of those who lay awake in bed or hurried through the streets. Long stands of hackney-chairs and groups of chairmen, compared with whom the coachmen of our day are gentle and polite, obstructed the way and filled the air with clamour; night-cellars, indicated by a little stream of light crossing the pavement, and stretching out half-way into the road, and by the stifled roar of voices from below, yawned for the reception and entertainment of the most abandoned of both sexes; under every shed and bulk small groups of link-boys gamed away the earnings of the day; or one more weary than the rest, gave way to sleep, and let the fragment of his torch fall hissing on the puddled ground.

Then there was the watch with staff and lantern crying the hour, and the kind of weather; and those who woke up at his voice and turned them round in bed, were glad to hear it rained, or snowed, or blew, or froze, for very comfort's sake. The solitary passenger was startled by the chairmen's cry of "By your leave there!" as two came trotting past him with their empty vehicle—carried backwards to show its being disengaged—and hurried to the nearest stand. Many a private chair, too, inclosing some fine lady, monstrously hooped and furbelowed, and preceded by running-footmen bearing flambeaux— for which extinguishers are yet suspended before the doors of a few houses of the better sort—made the way gay and light as it danced along, and darker and more dismal when it had passed. It was not unusual for these running gentry, who carried it with a very high hand, to quarrel in the servants' hall while waiting for their masters and mistresses; and, falling to blows either there or in the street without, to strew the place of skirmish with hair-powder, fragments of bag-wigs, and scattered nosegays. Gaming, the vice which ran so high among all classes (the fashion being of course set by the upper), was generally the cause of these disputes; for cards and dice were as openly used, and worked as much mischief, and yielded as much excitement below stairs, as above. While incidents like these, arising out of drums and masquerades and parties at quadrille, were passing at the west end of the town, heavy stage-coaches and scarce heavier waggons were lumbering slowly towards the city, the coachmen, guard, and passengers, armed to the teeth, and the coach—a day or so perhaps behind its time, but that was nothing—despoiled by highwaymen; who made no scruple to attack, alone and single-handed, a whole caravan of goods and men, and sometimes shot a passenger or two, and were sometimes shot themselves, as the case might be. On the morrow, rumours of this new act of daring on the road yielded matter for a few hours' conversation through the town, and a Public Progress of some fine gentleman (half drunk) to Tyburn, dressed in the newest fashion, and damning the ordinary with unspeakable gallantry and grace, furnished to the populace, at once a pleasant excitement and a wholesome and profound example.

Among all the dangerous characters who, in such a state of society, prowled and skulked in the metropolis at night, there was one man from whom many as uncouth and fierce as he, shrunk with an involuntary dread. Who he was, or whence he came, was a question often asked, but which none could answer. His name was unknown, he had never been seen until within about eight days or thereabouts, and was equally a stranger to the old ruffians, upon whose haunts he ventured fearlessly, as to the young. He could be no spy, for he never removed his slouched hat to look about him, entered into conversation with no man, heeded nothing that passed, listened to no discourse, regarded nobody that came or went. But so surely as the dead of night set in, so surely this man was in the midst of the loose concourse in the night-cellar where outcasts of every grade resorted; and there he sat till morning.

He was not only a spectre at their licentious feasts; a something in the midst of their revelry and riot that chilled and haunted them; but out of doors he was the same. Directly it was dark, he was abroad —never in company with any one, but always alone; never lingering or loitering, but always walking swiftly; and looking (so they said who had seen him) over his shoulder from time to time, and as he did so quickening his pace. In the fields, the lanes, the roads, in all quarters of the town—east, west, north, and south—that man was seen gliding on like a shadow. He was always hurrying away. Those who encountered him, saw him steal past, caught sight of the backward glance, and so lost him in the darkness.

This constant restlessness, and flitting to and fro, gave rise to strange stories. He was seen in such distant and remote places, at times so nearly tallying with each other, that some doubted whether there were not two of them, or more—some, whether he had not unearthly means of travelling from spot to spot. The footpad hiding in a ditch had marked him passing like a ghost along its brink; the vagrant had met him on the dark high-road; the beggar had seen him pause upon the bridge to look down at the water, and then sweep on again; they who dealt in bodies with the surgeons could swear he slept in churchyards, and that they had beheld him glide away among the tombs on their approach. And as they told these stories to each other, one who had looked about him would pull his neighbour by the sleeve, and there he would be among them.

At last, one man—he was one of those whose commerce lay among the graves—resolved to question this strange companion. Next night, when he had eat his poor meal voraciously (he was accustomed to do that, they had observed, as though he had no other in the day), this fellow sat down at his elbow.

"A black night, master!"

"It is a black night."

"Blacker than last, though that was pitchy too. Didn't I pass you near the turnpike in the Oxford-road?"

"It's like you may. I don't know."

"Come, come, master," cried the fellow, urged on by the looks of his comrades, and slapping him on the shoulder; "be more companionable and communicative. Be more the gentleman in this good company. There are tales among us that you have sold yourself to the devil, and I know not what."

"We all have, have we not?" returned the stranger, looking up. "If we were fewer in number, perhaps he would give better wages."

"It goes rather hard with you, indeed," said the fellow, as the stranger disclosed his haggard unwashed face, and torn clothes. "What of that? Be merry, master. A stave of a roaring song now—"

"Sing you, if you desire to hear one," replied the other, shaking him roughly off; "and don't touch me if you're a prudent man; I carry arms which go off easily—they have done so, before now—and make it dangerous for strangers who don't know the trick of them, to lay hands upon me."

"Do you threaten?" said the fellow.

"Yes," returned the other, rising and turning upon him, and looking fiercely round as if in apprehension of a general attack.

His voice, and look, and bearing—all expressive of the wildest recklessness and desperation—daunted while they repelled the bystanders. Although in a very different sphere of action now, they were not without much of the effect they had wrought at the Maypole Inn.

"I am what you all are, and live as you all do," said the man sternly, after a short silence. "I am in hiding here like the rest, and if we were surprised would perhaps do my part with the best of ye. If it's my humour to be left to myself, let me have it. Otherwise,"— and here he swore a tremendous oath—"there'll be mischief done in this place, though there *are* odds of a score against me."

A low murmur, having its origin perhaps in a dread of the man and the mystery that surrounded him, or perhaps in a sincere opinion on the part of some of those present, that it would be an inconvenient precedent to meddle too curiously with a gentleman's private affairs if he saw reason to conceal them, warned the fellow who had occasioned this discussion that he had best pursue it no farther. After a short time the strange man lay down upon a bench to sleep, and when they thought of him again, they found he was gone.

Next night, as soon as it was dark, he was abroad again and traversing the streets; he was before the locksmith's house more than once, but the family were out, and it was close shut. This night he crossed London Bridge and passed into Southwark. As he glided down a bye-street, a woman with a little basket on her arm, turned into it at the other end. Directly he observed her, he sought the shelter of an archway, and stood aside until she had passed. Then he emerged cautiously from his hiding-place, and followed.

She went into several shops to purchase various kinds of household necessaries, and round every place at which she stopped he hovered like her evil spirit; following her when she reappeared. It was nigh eleven o'clock, and the passengers in the streets were thinning fast, when she turned, doubtless to go home. The phantom still followed her.

She turned into the same bye-street in which he had seen her first, which, being free from shops, and narrow, was extremely dark. She quickened her pace here, as though distrustful of being stopped, and robbed of such trifling property as she carried with her. He crept along on the other side of the road. Had she been gifted with the speed of wind, it seemed as if his terrible shadow would have tracked her down.

At length the widow—for she it was—reached her own door, and, panting for breath, paused to take the key from her basket. In a flush and glow, with the haste she had made, and the pleasure of being safe at home, she stooped to draw it out, when, raising her head, she saw him standing silently beside her: the apparition of a dream.

His hand was on her mouth, but that was needless, for her tongue clove to its roof, and her power of utterance was gone. "I have been looking for you many nights. Is the house empty? Answer me. Is any one inside?"

She could only answer by a rattle in her throat.

"Make me a sign."

She seemed to indicate that there was no one there. He took the key, unlocked the door, carried her in, and secured it carefully behind them.

CHAPTER XVII

IT was a chilly night, and the fire in the widow's parlour had burnt low. Her strange companion placed her in a chair, and stooping down before the half-extinguished ashes, raked them together and fanned them with his hat. From time to time he glanced at her over his shoulder, as though to assure himself of her remaining quiet and making no effort to depart; and that done, busied himself about the fire again.

It was not without reason that he took these pains, for his dress was dank and drenched with wet, his jaws rattled with cold, and he shivered from head to foot. It had rained hard during the previous night and for some hours in the morning, but since noon it had been fine. Wheresoever he had passed the hours of darkness, his condition sufficiently betokened that many of them had been spent beneath the open sky. Besmeared with mire; his saturated clothes clinging with a damp embrace about his limbs; his beard unshaven, his face unwashed, his meagre cheeks worn into deep hollows,—a more miserable wretch could hardly be, than this man who now cowered down upon the widow's hearth, and watched the struggling flame with bloodshot eyes.

She had covered her face with her hands, fearing, as it seemed, to look towards him. So they remained for some short time in silence. Glancing round again, he asked at length:

"Is this your house?"

"It is. Why, in the name of Heaven, do you darken it?"

"Give me meat and drink," he answered sullenly, "or I dare do more than that. The very marrow in my bones is cold with wet and hunger. I must have warmth and food, and I will have them here."

"You were the robber on the Chigwell-road."

"I was."

"And nearly a murderer then."

"The will was not wanting. There was one came upon me and raised the hue-and-cry, that it would have gone hard with, but for his nimbleness. I made a thrust at him."

"You thrust your sword at *him!*" cried the widow, looking upwards. "You hear this man! you hear and saw!"

He looked at her, as, with her head thrown back, and her hands tight clenched together, she uttered these words in an agony of appeal. Then, starting to his feet as she had done, he advanced towards her.

"Beware!" she cried in a suppressed voice, whose firmness stopped him midway. "Do not so much as touch me with a finger, or you are lost; body and soul, you are lost."

"Hear me," he replied, menacing her with his hand. "I, that in the form of a man live the life of a hunted beast! that in the body am a spirit, a ghost upon the earth, a thing from which all creatures shrink, save those curst beings of another world, who will not leave me;—I am, in my desperation of this night, past all fear but that of the hell in which I exist from day to day. Give the alarm, cry out, refuse to shelter me. I will not hurt you. But I will not be taken alive; and so surely as you threaten me above your breath, I fall a dead man on this floor. The blood with which I sprinkle it, be on you and yours, in the name of the Evil Spirit that tempts men to their ruin!"

As he spoke, he took a pistol from his breast, and firmly clutched it in his hand.

"Remove this man from me, good Heaven!" cried the widow. "In thy grace and mercy, give him one minute's penitence, and strike him dead!"

"It has no such purpose," he said, confronting her. "It is deaf. Give me to eat and drink, lest I do that it cannot help my doing, and will not do for you."

"Will you leave me, if I do thus much? Will you leave me and return no more?"

"I will promise nothing," he rejoined, seating himself at the table, "nothing but this—I will execute my threat if you betray me."

She rose at length, and going to a closet or pantry in the room, brought out some fragments of cold meat and bread and put them on the table. He asked for brandy, and for water. These she produced likewise; and he ate and drank with the voracity of a famished hound. All the time he was so engaged she kept at the uttermost distance of the chamber, and sat there shuddering, but with her face towards him. She never turned her back upon him once; and although when she passed him (as she was obliged to do in going to and from the cupboard) she gathered the skirts of her garment about her, as if even its touching his by chance were horrible to think of, still, in the midst of all this dread and terror, she kept her face towards his own, and watched his every movement.

His repast ended—if that can be called one, which was a mere ravenous satisfying of the calls of hunger—he moved his chair towards the fire again, and warming himself before the blaze which had now sprung brightly up, accosted her once more.

"I am an outcast, to whom a roof above his head is often an uncommon luxury, and the food a beggar would reject is delicate fare. You live here at your ease. Do you live alone?"

"I do not," she made answer with an effort.

"Who dwells here besides?"

"One—it is no matter who. You had best begone, or he may find you here. Why do you linger?"

"For warmth," he replied, spreading out his hands before the fire. "For warmth. You are rich, perhaps?"

"Very," she said faintly. "Very rich. No doubt I am very rich."

"At least you are not penniless. You have some money. You were making purchases to-night."

"I have a little left. It is but a few shillings."

"Give me your purse. You had it in your hand at the door. Give it to me!"

She stepped to the table and laid it down. He reached across, took it up, and told the contents into his hand. As he was counting them, she listened for a moment, and sprung towards him.

"Take what there is, take all, take more if more were there, but go before it is too late. I have heard a wayward step without, I know full well. It will return directly. Begone."

"What do you mean?"

"Do not stop to ask. I will not answer. Much as I dread to touch you, I would drag you to the door if I possessed the strength, rather than you should lose an instant. Miserable wretch! fly from this place."

"If there are spies without, I am safer here," replied the man, standing aghast. "I will remain here, and will not fly till the danger is past."

"It is too late!" cried the widow, who had listened for the step, and not to him. "Hark to that foot upon the ground. Do you tremble to hear it! It is my son, my idiot son!"

As she said this wildly, there came a heavy knocking at the door. He looked at her, and she at him.

"Let him come in," said the man, hoarsely. "I fear him less than the dark, houseless night. He knocks again. Let him come in!"

"The dread of this hour," returned the widow, "has been upon me all my life, and I will not. Evil will fall upon him, if you stand eye to eye. My blighted boy! Oh! all good angels who know the truth—hear a poor mother's prayer, and spare my boy from knowledge of this man!"

"He rattles at the shutters!" cried the man. "He calls you. That voice and cry! It was he who grappled with me in the road. Was it he?"

She had sunk upon her knees, and so knelt down, moving her lips, but uttering no sound. As he gazed upon her, uncertain what to do or where to turn, the shutters flew open. He had barely time to catch a knife from the table, sheathe it in the loose sleeve of his coat, hide in the closet, and do all with the lightning's speed, when Barnaby tapped at the bare glass, and raised the sash exultingly.

"Why, who can keep out Grip and me!" he cried, thrusting in his head, and staring round the room. "Are you there, mother? How long you keep us from the fire and light!"

She stammered some excuse and tendered him her hand. But Barnaby sprung lightly in without assistance, and putting his arms about her neck, kissed her a hundred times.

"We have been afield, mother—leaping ditches, scrambling through hedges, running down steep banks, up and away, and hurrying on. The wind has been blowing, and the rushes and young plants bowing and bending to it, lest it should do them harm, the cowards—and Grip—ha ha ha!—brave Grip, who cares for nothing, and when the wind rolls him over in the dust, turns manfully to bite it—Grip, bold Grip, has quarrelled with every little bowing twig—thinking, he told me, that it mocked him—and has worried it like a bull-dog. Ha ha ha!"

The raven, in his little basket at his master's back, hearing this frequent mention of his name in a tone of exultation, expressed his sympathy by crowing like a cock, and afterwards running over his various phrases of speech with such rapidity, and in so many varieties of hoarseness, that they sounded like the murmurs of a crowd of people.

"He takes such care of me besides!" said Barnaby. "Such care, mother! He watches all the time I sleep, and when I shut my eyes and make-believe to slumber, he practises new learning softly; but he keeps his eye on me the while, and if he sees me laugh, though never so little, stops directly. He won't surprise me till he's perfect."

The raven crowed again in a rapturous manner which plainly said, "Those are certainly some of my characteristics, and I glory in them." In the meantime, Barnaby closed the window and secured it, and coming to the fireplace, prepared to sit down with his face to the closet. But his mother prevented this, by hastily taking that side herself, and motioning him towards the other.

"How pale you are to-night!" said Barnaby, leaning on his stick. "We have been cruel, Grip, and made her anxious!"

Anxious in good truth, and sick at heart! The listener held the door of his hiding-place open with his hand, and closely watched her son. Grip—alive to everything his master was unconscious of—had his head out of the basket, and in return was watching him intently with his glistening eye.

"He flaps his wings," said Barnaby, turning almost quickly enough to catch the retreating form and closing door, "as if there were strangers here, but Grip is wiser than to fancy that. Jump then!"

Accepting this invitation with a dignity peculiar to himself, the bird hopped up on his master's shoulder, from that to his extended hand, and so to the ground. Barnaby unstrapping the basket and putting it down in a corner with the lid open, Grip's first care was to shut it down with all possible despatch, and then to stand upon it. Believing, no doubt, that he had now rendered it utterly impossible and beyond the power of mortal man, to shut him up in it any more, he drew a great many corks in triumph, and uttered a corresponding number of hurrahs.

"Mother!" said Barnaby, laying aside his hat and stick, and returning to the chair from which he had risen, "I'll tell you where we have been to-day, and what we have been doing,—shall I?"

She took his hand in hers, and holding it, nodded the word she could not speak.

"You mustn't tell," said Barnaby, holding up his finger, "for it's a secret, mind, and only known to me, and Grip, and Hugh. We had the dog with us, but he's not like Grip, clever as he is, and doesn't guess it yet, I'll wager.—Why do you look behind me so?"

"Did I?" she answered faintly. "I didn't know I did. Come nearer me."

"You are frightened!" said Barnaby, changing colour. "Mother—you don't see—"

"See what?"

"There's—there's none of this about, is there?" he answered in a whisper, drawing closer to her and clasping the mark upon his wrist. "I am afraid there is, somewhere. You make my hair stand on end, and my flesh creep. Why do you look like that? Is it in the room as I have seen it in my dreams, dashing the ceiling and the walls with red? Tell me. Is it?"

He fell into a shivering fit as he put the question, and shutting out the light with his hands, sat shaking in every limb until it had passed away. After a time, he raised his head and looked about him.

"Is it gone?"

"There has been nothing here," rejoined his mother, soothing him. "Nothing indeed, dear Barnaby. Look! You see there are but you and me."

He gazed at her vacantly, and, becoming reassured by degrees, burst into a wild laugh.

"But let us see," he said, thoughtfully. "We were talking? Was it you and me? Where have we been?"

"Nowhere but here."

"Aye, but Hugh, and I," said Barnaby,—"that's it. Maypole Hugh, and I, you know, and Grip—we have been lying in the forest, and among the trees by the roadside, with a dark lantern after night came on, and the dog in a noose ready to slip him when the man came by."

"What man?"

"The robber; him that the stars winked at. We have waited for him after dark these many nights, and we shall have him. I'd know him in a thousand. Mother, see here! This is the man. Look!"

He twisted his handkerchief round his head, pulled his hat upon his brow, wrapped his coat about him, and stood up before her: so like the original he counterfeited, that the dark figure peering out behind him might have passed for his own shadow.

"Ha ha ha! We shall have him," he cried, ridding himself of the semblance as hastily as he had assumed it. "You shall see him, mother, bound hand and foot, and brought to London at a saddle-girth; and you shall hear of him at Tyburn Tree if we have luck. So Hugh says. You're pale again, and trembling. And why *do* you look behind me so?"

"It is nothing," she answered. "I am not quite well. Go you to bed dear, and leave me here."

"To bed!" he answered. "I don't like bed. I like to lie before the fire, watching the prospects in the burning coals—the rivers, hills, and dells, in the deep, red sunset, and the wild faces. I am hungry too, and Grip has eaten nothing since broad noon. Let us to supper. Grip! To supper, lad!"

The raven flapped his wings, and, croaking his satisfaction, hopped to the feet of his master, and there held his bill open, ready for snapping up such lumps of meat as he should throw him. Of these he received about a score in rapid succession, without the smallest discomposure.

"That's all," said Barnaby.

"More!" cried Grip. "More!"

But it appearing for a certainty that no more was to be had, he retreated with his store; and disgorging the morsels one by one from his pouch, hid them in various corners—taking particular care, however, to avoid the closet, as being doubtful of the hidden man's propensities and power of resisting temptation. When he had concluded these arrangements, he took a turn or two across the room with an elaborate assumption of having nothing on his mind (but with one eye hard upon his treasure all the time), and then, and not till then, began to drag it out, piece by piece, and eat it with the utmost relish.

Barnaby, for his part, having pressed his mother to eat, in vain, made a hearty supper too. Once during the progress of his meal, he wanted more bread from the closet and rose to get it. She hurriedly interposed to prevent him, and summoning her utmost fortitude, passed into the recess, and brought it out herself.

"Mother," said Barnaby, looking at her steadfastly as she sat down beside him after doing so; "is to-day my birthday?"

"To-day!" she answered. "Don't you recollect it was but a week or so ago, and that summer, autumn, and winter have to pass before it comes again?"

"I remember that it has been so till now," said Barnaby. "But I think to-day must be my birthday too, for all that."

She asked him why? "I'll tell you why," he said. "I have always seen you—I didn't let you know it, but I have—on the evening of that day grow very sad. I have seen you cry when Grip and I were most glad; and look frightened with no reason; and I have touched your hand, and felt that it was cold—as it is now. Once, mother (on a birthday that was, also), Grip and I thought of this after we went up-stairs to bed, and when it was midnight, striking one o'clock, we came down to your door to see if you were well. You were on your knees. I forget what it was you said. Grip, what was it we heard her say that night?"

"I'm a devil!" rejoined the raven promptly.

"No, no," said Barnaby. "But you said something in a prayer; and when you rose and walked about, you looked (as you have done ever since, mother, towards night on my birthday) just as you do now. I have found that out, you see, though I am silly. So I say you're wrong; and this must be my birthday—my birthday, Grip!"

The bird received this information with a crow of such duration as a cock, gifted with intelligence beyond all others of his kind, might usher in the longest day with. Then, as if he had well considered the sentiment, and regarded it as apposite to birthdays, he cried, "Never say die!" a great many times, and flapped his wings for emphasis.

The widow tried to make light of Barnaby's remark, and endeavoured to divert his attention to some new subject; too easy a task at all times, as she knew. His supper done, Barnaby, regardless of her entreaties, stretched himself on the mat before the fire; Grip perched upon his leg, and divided his time between dozing in the grateful warmth, and endeavouring (as it presently appeared) to recall a new accomplishment he had been studying all day.

A long and profound silence ensued, broken only by some change of position on the part of Barnaby, whose eyes were still wide open and intently fixed upon the fire; or by an effort of recollection on the part of Grip, who would cry in a low voice from time to time, "Polly put the ket—" and there stop short, forgetting the remainder, and go off in a doze again.

After a long interval, Barnaby's breathing grew more deep and regular, and his eyes were closed. But even then the unquiet spirit of the raven interposed. "Polly put the ket—" cried Grip, and his master was broad awake again.

At length Barnaby slept soundly, and the bird with his bill sunk upon his breast, his breast itself puffed out into a comfortable alderman-like form, and his bright eye growing smaller and smaller, really seemed to be subsiding into a state of repose. Now and then he muttered in a sepulchral voice, "Polly put the ket—" but very drowsily, and more like a drunken man than a reflecting raven.

The widow, scarcely venturing to breathe, rose from her seat. The man glided from the closet, and extinguished the candle.

"—tle on," cried Grip, suddenly struck with an idea and very much excited. "—tle on. Hurrah! Polly put the ket-tle on, we'll all have tea; Polly put the ket-tle on, we'll all have tea. Hurrah, hurrah, hurrah! I'm a devil, I'm a devil, I'm a ket-tle on, Keep up your spirits, Never say die, Bow, wow, wow, I'm a devil, I'm a ket-tle, I'm a—Polly put the ket-tle on, we'll all have tea."

They stood rooted to the ground, as though it had been a voice from the grave.

But even this failed to awaken the sleeper. He turned over towards the fire, his arm fell to the ground, and his head drooped heavily upon it. The widow and her unwelcome visitor gazed at him and at each other for a moment, and then she motioned him towards the door.

"Stay," he whispered. "You teach your son well."

"I have taught him nothing that you heard to-night. Depart instantly, or I will rouse him."

"You are free to do so. Shall I rouse him?"

"You dare not do that."

"I dare do anything, I have told you. He knows me well, it seems. At least I will know him."

"Would you kill him in his sleep?" cried the widow, throwing herself between them.

"Woman," he returned between his teeth, as he motioned her aside, "I would see him nearer, and I will. If you want one of us to kill the other, wake him."

With that he advanced, and bending down over the prostrate form, softly turned back the head and looked into the face. The light of the fire was upon it, and its every lineament was revealed distinctly. He contemplated it for a brief space, and hastily uprose.

"Observe," he whispered in the widow's ear: "In him, of whose existence I was ignorant until to-night, I have you in my power. Be careful how you use me. Be careful how you use me. I am destitute and starving, and a wanderer upon the earth. I may take a sure and slow revenge."

"There is some dreadful meaning in your words. I do not fathom it."

"There is a meaning in them, and I see you fathom it to its very depth. You have anticipated it for years; you have told me as much. I leave you to digest it. Do not forget my warning."

He pointed, as he left her, to the slumbering form, and stealthily withdrawing, made his way into the street. She fell on her knees beside the sleeper, and remained like one stricken into stone, until the tears which fear had frozen so long, came tenderly to her relief.

"Oh Thou," she cried, "who hast taught me such deep love for this one remnant of the promise of a happy life, out of whose affliction, even perhaps the comfort springs that he is ever a relying, loving child to me—never growing old or cold at heart, but needing my care and duty in his manly strength as in his cradle-time—help him, in his darkened walk through this sad world, or he is doomed, and my poor heart is broken!"

CHAPTER XVIII

GLIDING along the silent streets, and holding his course where they were darkest and most gloomy, the man who had left the widow's house crossed London Bridge, and arriving in the City, plunged into the backways, lanes, and courts, between Cornhill and Smithfield; with no more fixedness of purpose than to lose himself among their windings, and baffle pursuit, if any one were dogging his steps.

It was the dead time of the night, and all was quiet. Now and then a drowsy watchman's footsteps sounded on the pavement, or the lamp-lighter on his rounds went flashing past, leaving behind a little track of smoke mingled with glowing morsels of his red-hot link. He hid himself even from these partakers of his lonely walk, and, shrinking in some arch or doorway while they passed, issued forth again when they were gone and so pursued his solitary way.

To be shelterless and alone in the open country, hearing the wind moan and watching for day through the whole long weary night; to listen to the falling rain, and crouch for warmth beneath the lee of some old barn or rick, or in the hollow of a tree; are dismal things— but not so dismal as the wandering up and down where shelter is, and beds and sleepers are by thousands; a houseless rejected creature. To pace the echoing stones from hour to hour, counting the dull chimes of the clocks; to watch the lights twinkling in chamber windows, to think what happy forgetfulness each house shuts in; that here are children coiled together in their beds, here youth, here age, here poverty, here wealth, all equal in their sleep, and all at rest; to have nothing in common with the slumbering world around, not even sleep, Heaven's gift to all its creatures, and be akin to nothing but despair; to feel, by the wretched contrast with everything on every hand, more utterly alone and cast away than in a trackless desert; this is a kind of suffering, on which the rivers of great cities close full many a time, and which the solitude in crowds alone awakens.

The miserable man paced up and down the streets—so long, so wearisome, so like each other—and often cast a wistful look towards the east, hoping to see the first faint streaks of day. But obdurate night had yet possession of the sky, and his disturbed and restless walk found no relief.

One house in a back street was bright with the cheerful glare of lights; there was the sound of music in it too, and the tread of dancers, and there were cheerful voices, and many a burst of laughter. To this place—to be near something that was awake and glad—he returned again and again; and more than one of those who left it when the merriment was at its height, felt it a check upon their mirthful mood to see him flitting to and fro like an uneasy ghost. At last the guests departed, one and all; and then the house was close shut up, and became as dull and silent as the rest.

His wanderings brought him at one time to the city jail. Instead of hastening from it as a place of ill omen, and one he had cause to shun, he sat down on some steps hard by, and resting his chin upon his hand, gazed upon its rough and frowning walls as though even they became a refuge in his jaded eyes. He paced it round and round, came back to the same spot, and sat down again. He did this often, and once, with a hasty movement, crossed to where some men were watching in the prison lodge, and had his foot upon the steps as though determined to accost them. But looking round, he saw that the day began to break, and failing in his purpose, turned and fled.

He was soon in the quarter he had lately traversed, and pacing to and fro again as he had done before. He was passing down a mean street, when from an alley close at hand some shouts of revelry arose, and there came straggling forth a dozen madcaps, whooping and calling to each other, who, parting noisily, took different ways and dispersed in smaller groups.

Hoping that some low place of entertainment which would afford him a safe refuge might be near at hand, he turned into this court when they were all gone, and looked about for a half-opened door, or lighted window, or other indication of the place whence they had come. It was so profoundly dark, however, and so ill-favoured, that he concluded they had but turned up there, missing their way, and were pouring out again when he observed them. With this impression, and finding there was no outlet but that by which he had entered, he was about to turn, when from a grating near his feet a sudden stream of light appeared, and the sound of talking came. He retreated into a doorway to see who these talkers were, and to listen to them.

The light came to the level of the pavement as he did this, and a man ascended, bearing in his hand a torch. This figure unlocked and held open the grating as for the passage of another, who presently appeared, in the form of a young man of small stature and uncommon self-importance, dressed in an obsolete and very gaudy fashion.

"Good night, noble captain," said he with the torch. "Farewell, commander. Good luck, illustrious general!"

In return to these compliments the other bade him hold his tongue, and keep his noise to himself; and laid upon him many similar injunctions, with great fluency of speech and sternness of manner.

"Commend me, captain, to the stricken Miggs," returned the torch-bearer in a lower voice. "My captain flies at higher game than Miggses. Ha, ha, ha! My captain is an eagle, both as respects his eye and soaring wings. My captain breaketh hearts as other bachelors break eggs at breakfast."

"What a fool you are, Stagg!" said Mr. Tappertit, stepping on the pavement of the court, and brushing from his legs the dust he had contracted in his passage upward.

"His precious limbs!" cried Stagg, clasping one of his ankles. "Shall a Miggs aspire to these proportions! No, no, my captain. We will inveigle ladies fair, and wed them in our secret cavern. We will unite ourselves with blooming beauties, captain."

"I'll tell you what, my buck," said Mr. Tappertit, releasing his leg; "I'll trouble you not to take liberties, and not to broach certain questions unless certain questions are broached to you. Speak when you're spoke to on particular subjects, and not otherways. Hold the torch up till I've got to the end of the court, and then kennel yourself, do you hear?"

"I hear you, noble captain."

"Obey then," said Mr. Tappertit haughtily. "Gentlemen, lead on!" With which word of command (addressed to an imaginary staff or retinue) he folded his arms, and walked with surpassing dignity down the court.

His obsequious follower stood holding the torch above his head, and then the observer saw for the first time, from his place of concealment, that he was blind. Some involuntary motion on his part caught the quick ear of the blind man, before he was conscious of having moved an inch towards him, for he turned suddenly and cried, "Who's there?"

"A man," said the other, advancing. "A friend."

"A stranger!" rejoined the blind man. "Strangers are not my friends. What do you there?"

"I saw your company come out, and waited here till they were gone. I want a lodging."

"A lodging at this time!" returned Stagg, pointing towards the dawn as though he saw it. "Do you know the day is breaking?"

"I know it," rejoined the other, "to my cost. I have been traversing this iron-hearted town all night."

"You had better traverse it again," said the blind man, preparing to descend, "till you find some lodgings suitable to your taste. I don't let any."

"Stay!" cried the other, holding him by the arm.

"I'll beat this light about that hangdog face of yours (for hangdog it is, if it answers to your voice), and rouse the neighbourhood besides, if you detain me," said the blind man. "Let me go. Do you hear?"

"Do *you* hear!" returned the other, chinking a few shillings together, and hurriedly pressing them into his hand. "I beg nothing of you. I will pay for the shelter you give me. Death! Is it much to ask of such as you! I have come from the country, and desire to rest where there are none to question me. I am faint, exhausted, worn out, almost dead. Let me lie down, like a dog, before your fire. I ask no more than that. If you would be rid of me, I will depart to-morrow."

"If a gentleman has been unfortunate on the road," muttered Stagg, yielding to the other, who, pressing on him, had already

gained a footing on the steps—"and can pay for his accommodation—"

"I will pay you with all I have. I am just now past the want of
food, God knows, and wish but to purchase shelter. What companion
have you below?"

"None."

"Then fasten your grate there, and show me the way. Quick!"

The blind man complied after a moment's hesitation, and they
descended together. The dialogue had passed as hurriedly as the
words could be spoken, and they stood in his wretched room before
he had had time to recover from his first surprise.

"May I see where that door leads to, and what is beyond?" said
the man, glancing keenly round. "You will not mind that?"

"I will show you myself. Follow me, or go before. Take your
choice."

He bade him lead the way, and, by the light of the torch which his
conductor held up for the purpose, inspected all three cellars narrowly. Assured that the blind man had spoken truth, and that he
lived there alone, the visitor returned with him to the first, in which
a fire was burning, and flung himself with a deep groan upon the
ground before it.

His host pursued his usual occupation without seeming to heed
him any further. But directly he fell asleep—and he noted his falling
into a slumber, as readily as the keenest-sighted man could have
done—he knelt down beside him, and passed his hand lightly but
carefully over his face and person.

His sleep was checkered with starts and moans, and sometimes
with a muttered word or two. His hands were clenched, his brow
bent, and his mouth firmly set. All this, the blind man accurately
marked; and as if his curiosity were strongly awakened, and he had
already some inkling of his mystery, he sat watching him, if the
expression may be used, and listening, until it was broad day

CHAPTER XIX

DOLLY VARDEN's pretty little head was yet bewildered by various
recollections of the party, and her bright eyes were yet dazzled by a
crowd of images, dancing before them like motes in the sunbeams,
among which the effigy of one partner in particular did especially
figure, the same being a young coachmaker (a master in his own right)
who had given her to understand, when he handed her into the chair
at parting, that it was his fixed resolve to neglect his business from
that time, and die slowly for the love of her—Dolly's head, and eyes,
and thoughts, and seven senses, were all in a state of flutter and
confusion for which the party was accountable, although it was now
three days old, when, as she was sitting listlessly at breakfast,
reading all manner of fortunes (that is to say, of married and
flourishing fortunes) in the grounds of her tea-cup, a step was heard
in the workshop, and Mr. Edward Chester was descried through the

glass door, standing among the rusty locks and keys, like love among the roses—for which apt comparison the historian may by no means take any credit to himself, the same being the invention, in a sentimental mood, of the chaste and modest Miggs, who, beholding him from the doorsteps she was then cleaning, did, in her maiden meditation, give utterance to the simile.

The locksmith, who happened at the moment to have his eyes thrown upward and his head backward, in an intense communing with Toby, did not see his visitor, until Mrs. Varden, more watchful than the rest, had desired Sim Tappertit to open the glass door and give him admission—from which untoward circumstance the good lady argued (for she could deduce a precious moral from the most trifling event) that to take a draught of small ale in the morning was to observe a pernicious, irreligious, and Pagan custom, the relish whereof should be left to swine, and Satan, or at least to Popish persons, and should be shunned by the righteous as a work of sin and evil. She would no doubt have pursued her admonition much further, and would have founded on it a long list of precious precepts of inestimable value, but that the young gentleman standing by in a somewhat uncomfortable and discomfited manner while she read her spouse this lecture, occasioned her to bring it to a premature conclusion.

"I'm sure you'll excuse me, sir," said Mrs. Varden, rising and curtseying. "Varden is so very thoughtless, and needs so much reminding—Sim, bring a chair here."

Mr. Tappertit obeyed, with a flourish implying that he did so, under protest.

"And you can go, Sim," said the locksmith.

Mr. Tappertit obeyed again, still under protest; and betaking himself to the workshop, began seriously to fear that he might find it necessary to poison his master, before his time was out.

In the meantime, Edward returned suitable replies to Mrs. Varden's courtesies, and that lady brightened up very much; so that when he accepted a dish of tea from the fair hands of Dolly, she was perfectly agreeable.

"I am sure if there's anything we can do,—Varden, or I, or Dolly either,—to serve you, sir, at any time, you have only to say it, and it shall be done," said Mrs. V.

"I am much obliged to you, I am sure," returned Edward. "You encourage me to say that I have come here now, to beg your good offices."

Mrs. Varden was delighted beyond measure.

"It occurred to me that probably your fair daughter might be going to the Warren either to-day or to-morrow," said Edward, glancing at Dolly; "and if so, and you will allow her to take charge of this letter, ma'am, you will oblige me more than I can tell you. The truth is, that while I am very anxious it should reach its destination, I have particular reasons for not trusting it to any other conveyance; so that without your help, I am wholly at a loss."

"She was not going that way, sir, either to-day, or to-morrow, nor indeed all the week," the lady graciously rejoined, "but we shall be very glad to put ourselves out of the way on your account, and if you wish it, you may depend upon its going to-day. You might suppose," said Mrs. Varden, frowning at her husband, "from Varden's sitting there so glum and silent, that he objected to this arrangement; but you must not mind that, sir, if you please. It's his way at home. Out of doors, he can be cheerful and talkative enough."

Now, the fact was, that the unfortunate locksmith, blessing his stars to find his helpmate in such good humour, had been sitting with a beaming face, hearing this discourse with a joy past all expression. Wherefore this sudden attack quite took him by surprise.

"My dear Martha—" he said.

"Oh yes, I dare say," interrupted Mrs. Varden, with a smile of mingled scorn and pleasantry. "Very dear! We all know that."

"No, but, my good soul," said Gabriel, "you are quite mistaken. You are indeed. I was delighted to find you so kind and ready. I waited, my dear, anxiously, I assure you, to hear what you would say."

"You waited anxiously," repeated Mrs. V. "Yes! Thank you, Varden. You waited, as you always do, that I might bear the blame, if any came of it. But I am used to it," said the lady with a kind of solemn titter, "and that's my comfort!"

"I give you my word, Martha—" said Gabriel.

"Let me give you *my* word, my dear," interposed his wife with a Christian smile, "that such discussions as these between married people, are much better left alone. Therefore, if you please, Varden, we'll drop the subject. I have no wish to pursue it. I could. I might say a great deal. But I would rather not. Pray don't say any more."

"I don't want to say any more," rejoined the goaded locksmith.

"Well then, don't," said Mrs. Varden.

"Nor did I begin it, Martha," added the locksmith, good humouredly, "I must say that."

"You did not begin it, Varden!" exclaimed his wife, opening her eyes very wide and looking round upon the company, as though she would say, You hear this man! "You did not begin it, Varden! But you shall not say I was out of temper. No, you did not begin it, oh dear no, not you, my dear!"

"Well, well," said the locksmith. "That's settled then."

"Oh yes," rejoined his wife, "quite. If you like to say Dolly began it, my dear, I shall not contradict you. I know my duty. I need know it, I am sure. I am often obliged to bear it in mind, when my inclination perhaps would be for the moment to forget it. Thank you, Varden." And so, with a mighty show of humility and forgiveness, she folded her hands, and looked round again, with a smile which plainly said, "If you desire to see the first and foremost among female martyrs, here she is, on view!"

This little incident, illustrative though it was of Mrs. Varden's extraordinary sweetness and amiability, had so strong a tendency to

check the conversation and to disconcert all parties but that excellent
lady, that only a few monosyllables were uttered until Edward
withdrew; which he presently did, thanking the lady of the house a
great many times for her condescension, and whispering in Dolly's
ear that he would call on the morrow, in case there should happen
to be an answer to the note—which, indeed, she knew without
his telling, as Barnaby and his friend Grip had dropped in on
the previous night to prepare her for the visit which was then
terminating.

Gabriel, who had attended Edward to the door, came back with his
hands in his pockets; and, after fidgeting about the room in a very
uneasy manner, and casting a great many sidelong looks at Mrs.
Varden (who with the calmest countenance in the world was five
fathoms deep in the Protestant Manual), inquired of Dolly how she
meant to go. Dolly supposed by the stage-coach, and looked at her
lady mother, who finding herself silently appealed to, dived down at
least another fathom into the Manual, and became unconscious of all
earthly things.

"Martha—" said the locksmith.

"I hear you, Varden," said his wife, without rising to the surface.

"I am sorry, my dear, you have such an objection to the Maypole
and old John, for otherways as it's a very fine morning, and Saturday's not a busy day with us, we might have all three gone to
Chigwell in the chaise, and had quite a happy day of it."

Mrs. Varden immediately closed the Manual, and bursting into
tears, requested to be led up-stairs.

"What is the matter now, Martha?" inquired the locksmith.

To which Martha rejoined, "Oh! don't speak to me," and protested
in agony that if anybody had told her so, she wouldn't have believed
it.

"But, Martha," said Gabriel, putting himself in the way as she
was moving off with the aid of Dolly's shoulder, "wouldn't have
believed what? Tell me what's wrong now. Do tell me. Upon my soul
I don't know. Do *you* know, child? Damme!" cried the locksmith,
plucking at his wig in a kind of frenzy, "nobody does know, I verily
believe, but Miggs!"

"Miggs," said Mrs. Varden faintly, and with symptoms of approaching incoherence, "is attached to me, and that is sufficient to
draw down hatred upon her in this house. She is a comfort to me,
whatever she may be to others."

"She's no comfort to me," cried Gabriel, made bold by despair.
"She's the misery of my life. She's all the plagues of Egypt in one."

"She's considered so, I have no doubt," said Mrs. Varden. "I
was prepared for that; it's natural; it's of a piece with the rest. When
you taunt me as you do to my face, how can I wonder that you
taunt her behind her back!" And here the incoherence coming on
very strong, Mrs. Varden wept, and laughed, and sobbed, and
shivered, and hiccoughed, and choked; and said she knew it was very
foolish but she couldn't help it; and that when she was dead and

gone, perhaps they would be sorry for it—which really under the circumstances did not appear quite so probable as she seemed to think—with a great deal more to the same effect. In a word, she passed with great decency through all the ceremonies incidental to such occasions; and being supported up-stairs, was deposited in a highly spasmodic state on her own bed, where Miss Miggs shortly afterwards flung herself upon the body.

The philosophy of all this was, that Mrs. Varden wanted to go to Chigwell; that she did not want to make any concession or explanation; that she would only go on being implored and entreated so to do; and that she would accept no other terms. Accordingly, after a vast amount of moaning and crying up-stairs, and much damping of foreheads, and vinegaring of temples, and hartshorning of noses, and so forth; and after most pathetic adjurations from Miggs, assisted by warm brandy-and-water not over-weak, and divers other cordials, also of a stimulating quality, administered at first in teaspoonfuls and afterwards in increasing doses, and of which Miss Miggs herself partook as a preventive measure (for fainting is infectious); after all these remedies, and many more too numerous to mention, but not to take, had been applied; and many verbal consolations, moral, religious, and miscellaneous, had been superadded thereto; the locksmith humbled himself, and the end was gained.

"If it's only for the sake of peace and quietness, father," said Dolly, urging him to go up-stairs.

"Oh, Doll, Doll," said her good-natured father. "If you ever have a husband of your own—"

Dolly glanced at the glass.

"—Well, *when* you have," said the locksmith, "never faint, my darling. More domestic unhappiness has come of easy fainting, Doll, than from all the greater passions put together. Remember that, my dear, if you would be really happy, which you never can be, if your husband isn't. And a word in your ear, my precious. Never have a Miggs about you!"

With this advice he kissed his blooming daughter on the cheek, and slowly repaired to Mrs. Varden's room; where that lady, lying all pale and languid on her couch, was refreshing herself with a sight of her last new bonnet, which Miggs, as a means of calming her scattered spirits, displayed to the best advantage at her bedside.

"Here's master, mim," said Miggs. "Oh, what a happiness it is when man and wife come round again! Oh gracious, to think that him and her should ever have a word together!" In the energy of these sentiments, which were uttered as an apostrophe to the Heavens in general, Miss Miggs perched the bonnet on the top of her own head, and folding her hands, turned on her tears.

"I can't help it," cried Miggs. "I couldn't, if I was to be drowned in 'em. She has such a forgiving spirit! She'll forget all that has passed, and go along with you, sir—Oh, if it were to the world's end, she'd go along with you."

Mrs. Varden with a faint smile gently reproved her attendant for this enthusiasm, and reminded her at the same time that she was far too unwell to venture out that day.

"Oh no, you're not, mim, indeed you're not," said Miggs; "I repeal to master; master knows you're not, mim. The hair, and motion of the shay, will do you good, mim, and you must not give way, you must not raly. She must keep up, mustn't she, sir, for all our sakes? I was a telling her that, just now. She must remember us, even if she forgets herself. Master will persuade you, mim, I'm sure. There's Miss Dolly's a-going you know, and master, and you, and all so happy and so comfortable. Oh!" cried Miggs, turning on the tears again, previous to quitting the room in great emotion, "I never see such a blessed one as she is for the forgiveness of her spirit, I never, never, never did. Nor more did master neither; no, nor no one—never!"

For five minutes or thereabouts, Mrs. Varden remained mildly opposed to all her husband's prayers that she would oblige him by taking a day's pleasure, but relenting at length, she suffered herself to be persuaded, and granting him her free forgiveness (the merit whereof, she meekly said, rested with the Manual and not with her), desired that Miggs might come and help her dress. The handmaid attended promptly, and it is but justice to their joint exertion to record that, when the good lady came down-stairs in course of time completely decked out for the journey, she really looked as if nothing had happened, and appeared in the very best health imaginable.

As to Dolly, there she was again, the very pink and pattern of good looks, in a smart little cherry-coloured mantle, with a hood of the same drawn over her head, and upon the top of that hood, a little straw hat trimmed with cherry-coloured ribbons, and worn the merest trifle on one side—just enough in short to make it the wicked-est and most provoking head-dress that ever malicious milliner devised. And not to speak of the manner in which these cherry-coloured decorations brightened her eyes, or vied with her lips, or shed a new bloom on her face, she wore such a cruel little muff, and such a heart-rending pair of shoes, and was so surrounded and hemmed in, as it were, by aggravations of all kinds, that when Mr. Tappertit, holding the horse's head, saw her come out of the house alone, such impulses came over him to decoy her into the chaise and drive off like mad, that he would unquestionably have done it, but for certain uneasy doubts besetting him as to the shortest way to Gretna Green; whether it was up the street or down, or up the right-hand turning or the left; and whether, supposing all the turnpikes to be carried by storm, the blacksmith in the end would marry them on credit; which by reason of his clerical office appeared, even to his excited imagination, so unlikely, that he hesitated. And while he stood hesitating, and looking post-chaises-and-six at Dolly, out came his master and his mistress, and the constant Miggs, and the opportunity was gone for ever. For now the chaise creaked upon its springs, and Mrs. Varden was inside; and now it creaked again, and more than ever, and the locksmith was inside; and now it bounded once, as if its heart beat lightly, and Dolly was inside; and now it was gone and its place was empty, and he and that dreary Miggs were standing in the street together.

The hearty locksmith was in as good a humour as if nothing had occurred for the last twelve months to put him out of his way, Dolly was all smiles and graces, and Mrs. Varden was agreeable beyond all precedent. As they jogged through the streets talking of this thing and of that, who should be descried upon the pavement but that very coachmaker, looking so genteel that nobody would have believed he had ever had anything to do with a coach but riding in it, and bowing like any nobleman. To be sure Dolly was confused when she bowed again, and to be sure the cherry-coloured ribbons trembled a little when she met his mournful eye, which seemed to say, "I have kept my word, I have begun, the business is going to the devil, and you're the cause of it." There he stood, rooted to the ground: as Dolly said, like a statue; and as Mrs. Varden said, like a pump; till they turned the corner: and when her father thought it was like his impudence, and her mother wondered what he meant by it, Dolly blushed again till her very hood was pale.

But on they went, not the less merrily for this, and there was the locksmith in the incautious fulness of his heart "pulling-up" at all manner of places, and evincing a most intimate acquaintance with all the taverns on the road, and all the landlords and all the landladies, with whom, indeed, the little horse was on equally friendly terms, for he kept on stopping of his own accord. Never were people so glad to see other people as these landlords and landladies were to behold Mr. Varden and Mrs. Varden and Miss Varden; and wouldn't they get out, said one; and they really must walk up-stairs, said another; and she would take it ill and be quite certain they were proud if they wouldn't have a little taste of something, said a third; and so on, that it was really quite a Progress rather than a ride, and one continued scene of hospitality from beginning to end. It was pleasant enough to be held in such esteem, not to mention the refreshments; so Mrs. Varden said nothing at the time, and was all affability and delight—but such a body of evidence as she collected against the unfortunate locksmith that day, to be used thereafter as occasion might require, never was got together for matrimonial purposes.

In course of time—and in course of a pretty long time too, for these agreeable interruptions delayed them not a little,—they arrived upon the skirts of the Forest, and riding pleasantly on among the trees, came at last to the Maypole, where the locksmith's cheerful "Yoho!" speedily brought to the porch old John, and after him young Joe, both of whom were so transfixed at sight of the ladies, that for a moment they were perfectly unable to give them any welcome, and could do nothing but stare.

It was only for a moment, however, that Joe forgot himself, for speedily reviving he thrust his drowsy father aside—to Mr. Willet's mighty and inexpressible indignation—and darting out, stood ready to help them to alight. It was necessary for Dolly to get out first. Joe

had her in his arms;—yes, though for a space of time no longer than
you could count one in, Joe had her in his arms. Here was a glimpse
of happiness!

It would be difficult to describe what a flat and commonplace
affair the helping of Mrs. Varden out afterwards was, but Joe did it,
and did it too with the best grace in the world. Then old John, who,
entertaining a dull and foggy sort of idea that Mrs. Varden wasn't
fond of him, had been in some doubt whether she might not have
come for purposes of assault and battery, took courage, hoped she was
well, and offered to conduct her into the house. This tender being
amicably received, they marched in together; Joe and Dolly followed,
arm-in-arm, (happiness again!) and Varden brought up the rear.

Old John would have it that they must sit in the bar, and nobody
objecting, into the bar they went. All bars are snug places, but the
Maypole's was the very snuggest, cosiest, and completest bar, that
ever the wit of man devised. Such amazing bottles in old oaken
pigeon-holes; such gleaming tankards dangling from pegs at about
the same inclination as thirsty men would hold them to their lips;
such sturdy little Dutch kegs ranged in rows on shelves; so many
lemons hanging in separate nets, and forming the fragrant grove
already mentioned in this chronicle, suggestive, with goodly loaves
of snowy sugar stowed away hard by, of punch, idealised beyond all
mortal knowledge; such closets, such presses, such drawers full of
pipes, such places for putting things away in hollow window-seats, all
crammed to the throat with eatables, drinkables, or savoury condiments; lastly, and to crown all, as typical of the immense resources
of the establishment, and its defiances to all visitors to cut and come
again, such a stupendous cheese!

It is a poor heart that never rejoices—it must have been the poorest,
weakest, and most watery heart that ever beat, which would not
have warmed towards the Maypole bar. Mrs. Varden's did directly.
She could no more have reproached John Willet among those household gods, the kegs and bottles, lemons, pipes, and cheese, than she
could have stabbed him with his own bright carving-knife. The order
for dinner too—it might have soothed a savage. "A bit of fish," said
John to the cook, "and some lamb chops (breaded, with plenty of
ketchup), and a good salad, and a roast spring chicken, with a dish
of sausages and mashed potatoes, or something of that sort." Something of that sort! The resources of these inns! To talk carelessly
about dishes, which in themselves were a first-rate holiday kind of
dinner, suitable to one's wedding-day, as something of that sort.
meaning, if you can't get a spring chicken, any other trifle in the way
of poultry will do—such as a peacock, perhaps! The kitchen too, with
its great broad cavernous chimney; the kitchen, where nothing in
the way of cookery seemed impossible; where you could believe in
anything to eat, they chose to tell you of. Mrs. Varden returned
from the contemplation of these wonders to the bar again, with a
head quite dizzy and bewildered. Her housekeeping capacity was
not large enough to comprehend them. She was obliged to go to

sleep. Waking was pain, in the midst of such immensity.

Dolly in the meanwhile, whose gay heart and head ran upon other matters, passed out at the garden door, and glancing back now and then (but of course not wondering whether Joe saw her), tripped away by a path across the fields with which she was well acquainted, to discharge her mission at the Warren; and this deponent hath been informed and verily believes, that you might have seen many less pleasant objects than the cherry-coloured mantle and ribbons as they went fluttering along the green meadows in the bright light of the day, like giddy things as they were.

CHAPTER XX

THE proud consciousness of her trust, and the great importance she derived from it, might have advertised it to all the house if she had had to run the gauntlet of its inhabitants; but as Dolly had played in every dull room and passage many and many a time, when a child, and had ever since been the humble friend of Miss Haredale, whose foster sister she was, she was as free of the building as the young lady herself. So, using no greater precaution than holding her breath and walking on tiptoe as she passed the library door, she went straight to Emma's room as a privileged visitor.

It was the liveliest room in the building. The chamber was sombre like the rest for the matter of that, but the presence of youth and beauty would make a prison cheerful (saving alas! that confinement withers them), and lend some charms of their own to the gloomiest scene. Birds, flowers, books, drawing, music, and a hundred such graceful tokens of feminine loves and cares, filled it with more of life and human sympathy than the whole house besides seemed made to hold. There was heart in the room; and who that has a heart, ever fails to recognise the silent presence of another!

Dolly had one undoubtedly, and it was not a tough one either, though there was a little mist of coquettishness about it, such as sometimes surrounds that sun of life in its morning, and slightly dims its lustre. Thus, when Emma rose to greet her, and kissing her affectionately on the cheek told her, in her quiet way, that she had been very unhappy, the tears stood in Dolly's eyes, and she felt more sorry than she could tell; but the next moment she had happened to raise them to the glass, and there really was something there so exceedingly agreeable, that as she sighed, she smiled, and felt surprisingly consoled.

"I have heard about it, Miss," said Dolly, "and it's very sad indeed, but when things are at the worst they are sure to mend."

"But are you sure they are at the worst?" asked Emma with a smile.

"Why, I don't see how they can very well be more unpromising than they are; I really don't," said Dolly. "And I bring something to begin with."

"Not from Edward?"

Dolly nodded and smiled, and feeling in her pockets (there were pockets in those days) with an affectation of not being able to find what she wanted, which greatly enhanced her importance, at length produced the letter. As Emma hastily broke the seal and became absorbed in its contents, Dolly's eyes, by one of those strange accidents for which there is no accounting, wandered to the glass again. She could not help wondering whether the coachmaker suffered very much, and quite pitied the poor man.

It was a long letter—a very long letter, written close on all four sides of the sheet of paper, and crossed afterwards; but it was not a consolatory letter, for as Emma read it she stopped from time to time to put her handkerchief to her eyes. To be sure Dolly marvelled greatly to see her in so much distress, for to her thinking a love affair ought to be one of the best jokes, and the slyest, merriest kind of thing in life. But she set it down in her own mind that all this came from Miss Haredale's being so constant, and that if she would only take on with some other young gentleman—just in the most innocent way possible, to keep her first lover up to the mark—she would find herself inexpressibly comforted.

"I am sure that's what I should do if it was me," thought Dolly. "To make one's sweetheart miserable is well enough and quite right, but to be made miserable one's self is a little too much!"

However it wouldn't do to say so, and therefore she sat looking on in silence. She needed a pretty considerable stretch of patience, for when the long letter had been read once all through it was read again, and when it had been read twice all through it was read again. During this tedious process, Dolly beguiled the time in the most improving manner that occurred to her, by curling her hair on her fingers, with the aid of the looking-glass before mentioned, and giving it some killing twists.

Everything has an end. Even young ladies in love cannot read their letters for ever. In the course of time the packet was folded up, and it only remained to write the answer.

But as this promised to be a work of time likewise, Emma said she would put it off until after dinner, and that Dolly must dine with her. As Dolly had made up her mind to do so beforehand, she required very little pressing; and when they had settled this point, they went to walk in the garden.

They strolled up and down the terrace walks, talking incessantly— at least, Dolly never left off once—and making that quarter of the sad and mournful house quite gay. Not that they talked loudly or laughed much, but they were both so very handsome, and it was such a breezy day, and their light dresses and dark curls appeared so free and joyous in their abandonment, and Emma was so fair, and Dolly so rosy, and Emma so delicately shaped, and Dolly so plump, and—in short, there are no flowers for any garden like such flowers, let horticulturists say what they may, and both house and garden seemed to know it, and to brighten up sensibly.

After this, came the dinner and the letter writing, and some more talking, in the course of which Miss Haredale took occasion to charge upon Dolly certain flirtish and inconstant propensities, which accusations Dolly seemed to think very complimentary indeed, and to be mightily amused with. Finding her quite incorrigible in this respect, Emma suffered her to depart; but not before she had confided to her that important and never-sufficiently-to-be-taken-care-of answer, and endowed her moreover with a pretty little bracelet as a keepsake. Having clasped it on her arm, and again advised her half in jest and half in earnest to amend her roguish ways, for she knew she was fond of Joe at heart (which Dolly stoutly denied, with a great many haughty protestations that she hoped she could do better than that indeed! and so forth), she bade her farewell; and after calling her back to give her more supplementary messages for Edward, than anybody with tenfold the gravity of Dolly Varden could be reasonably expected to remember, at length dismissed her.

Dolly bade her good-bye, and tripping lightly down the stairs arrived at the dreaded library door, and was about to pass it again on tiptoe, when it opened, and behold! there stood Mr. Haredale. Now Dolly had from her childhood associated with this gentleman the idea of something grim and ghostly, and being at the moment conscience-stricken besides, the sight of him threw her into such a flurry that she could neither acknowledge his presence nor run away, so she gave a great start, and then with downcast eyes stood still and trembled.

"Come here, girl," said Mr. Haredale, taking her by the hand. "I want to speak to you."

"If you please, sir, I'm in a hurry," faltered Dolly, "and—you have frightened me by coming so suddenly upon me, sir—I would rather go, sir, if you'll be so good as to let me."

"Immediately," said Mr. Haredale, who had by this time led her into the room and closed the door. "You shall go directly. You have just left Emma?"

"Yes, sir, just this minute.—Father's waiting for me, sir, if you'll please to have the goodness—"

"I know. I know," said Mr. Haredale. "Answer me a question. What did you bring here to-day?"

"Bring here, sir?" faltered Dolly.

"You will tell me the truth, I am sure. Yes."

Dolly hesitated for a little while, and somewhat emboldened by his manner, said at last, "Well then, sir. It was a letter."

"From Mr. Edward Chester, of course. And you are the bearer of the answer?"

Dolly hesitated again, and not being able to decide upon any other course of action, burst into tears.

"You alarm yourself without cause," said Mr. Haredale. "Why are you so foolish? Surely you can answer me. You know that I have but to put the question to Emma and learn the truth directly. Have you the answer with you?"

Dolly had what is popularly called a spirit of her own, and being now fairly at bay, made the best of it.

"Yes, sir," she rejoined, trembling and frightened as she was. "Yes, sir, I have. You may kill me if you please, sir, but I won't give it up. I'm very sorry,—but I won't. There, sir."

"I commend your firmness and your plain-speaking," said Mr. Haredale. "Rest assured that I have as little desire to take your letter as your life. You are a very discreet messenger and a good girl."

Not feeling quite certain, as she afterwards said, whether he might not be "coming over her" with these compliments, Dolly kept as far from him as she could, cried again, and resolved to defend her pocket (for the letter was there) to the last extremity.

"I have some design," said Mr. Haredale after a short silence, during which a smile, as he regarded her, had struggled through the gloom and melancholy, that was natural to his face, "of providing a companion for my niece; for her life is a very lonely one. Would you like the office? You are the oldest friend she has, and the best entitled to it."

"I don't know, sir," answered Dolly, not sure but he was bantering her; "I can't say. I don't know what they might wish at home. I couldn't give an opinion, sir."

"If your friends had no objection, would you have any?" said Mr. Haredale. "Come. There's a plain question, and easy to answer."

"None at all that I know of, sir," replied Dolly. "I should be very glad to be near Miss Emma of course, and always am."

"That's well," said Mr. Haredale. "That is all I had to say. You are anxious to go. Don't let me detain you."

Dolly didn't let him, nor did she wait for him to try, for the words had no sooner passed his lips than she was out of the room, out of the house, and in the fields again.

The first thing to be done, of course, when she came to herself, and considered what a flurry she had been in, was to cry afresh; and the next thing, when she reflected how well she had got over it, was to laugh heartily. The tears once banished gave place to smiles, and at last Dolly laughed so much that she was fain to lean against a tree, and give vent to her exultation. When she could laugh no longer, and was quite tired, she put her head-dress to rights, dried her eyes, looked very merrily and triumphantly at the Warren chimneys, which were just visible, and resumed her walk.

The twilight had come on, and it was quickly growing dusk, but the path was so familiar to her from frequent traversing that she hardly thought of this, and certainly felt no uneasiness at being left alone. Moreover, there was the bracelet to admire; and when she had given it a good rub, and held it out at arm's length, it sparkled and glittered so beautifully on her wrist, that to look at it in every point of view and with every possible turn of the arm, was quite an absorbing business. There was the letter too, and it looked so mysterious and knowing, when she took it out of her pocket, and it held, as she knew, so much inside, that to turn it over and over, and think about it, and wonder how it began, and how it ended, and what it said all through, was another matter of constant occupation. Between the bracelet and the letter, there was quite enough to do without thinking of anything else; and admiring each by turns, Dolly went on gaily.

As she passed through a wicket-gate to where the path was narrow, and lay between two hedges garnished here and there with trees, she heard a rustling close at hand, which brought her to a sudden stop. She listened. All was very quiet, and she went on again—not absolutely frightened, but a little quicker than before perhaps, and possibly not quite so much at her ease, for a check of that kind is startling.

She had no sooner moved on again, than she was conscious of the same sound, which was like that of a person tramping stealthily among bushes and brushwood. Looking towards the spot whence it appeared to come, she almost fancied she could make out a crouching figure. She stopped again. All was quiet as before. On she went once more—decidedly faster now—and tried to sing softly to herself. It must be the wind.

But how came the wind to blow only when she walked, and cease when she stood still? She stopped involuntarily as she made the reflection, and the rustling noise stopped likewise. She was really frightened now, and was yet hesitating what to do, when the bushes crackled and snapped, and a man came plunging through them, close before her.

CHAPTER XXI

IT was for the moment an inexpressible relief to Dolly, to recognise in the person who forced himself into the path so abruptly, and now stood directly in her way, Hugh of the Maypole, whose name she uttered in a tone of delighted surprise that came from her heart.

"Was it you?" she said. "How glad I am to see you! and how could you terrify me so!"

In answer to which, he said nothing at all, but stood quite still, looking at her.

"Did you come to meet me?" asked Dolly.

Hugh nodded, and muttered something to the effect that he had been waiting for her, and had expected her sooner.

"I thought it likely they would send," said Dolly, greatly reassured by this.

"Nobody sent me," was his sullen answer. "I came of my own accord."

The rough bearing of this fellow, and his wild, uncouth appearance, had often filled the girl with a vague apprehension even when other people were by, and had occasioned her to shrink from him involuntarily. The having him for an unbidden companion in so solitary a place, with the darkness fast gathering about them, renewed and even increased the alarm she had felt at first.

If his manner had been merely dogged and passively fierce, as usual, she would have had no greater dislike to his company than she always felt—perhaps, indeed, would have been rather glad to have had him at hand. But there was something of coarse bold admiration in his look, which terrified her very much. She glanced timidly towards him, uncertain whether to go forward or retreat, and he stood gazing at her like a handsome satyr; and so they remained for some short time without stirring or breaking silence. At length Dolly took courage, shot past him, and hurried on.

"Why do you spend so much breath in avoiding me?" said Hugh, accommodating his pace to hers, and keeping close at her side.

"I wish to get back as quickly as I can, and you walk too near me," answered Dolly.

"Too near!" said Hugh, stooping over her so that she could feel his breath upon her forehead. "Why too near? You're always proud to *me*, mistress."

"I am proud to no one. You mistake me," answered Dolly. "Fall back, if you please, or go on."

"Nay, mistress," he rejoined, endeavouring to draw her arm through his, "I'll walk with you."

She released herself, and clenching her little hand, struck him with right good will. At this, Maypole Hugh burst into a roar of laughter, and passing his arm about her waist, held her in his strong grasp as easily as if she had been a bird.

"Ha ha ha! Well done, mistress! Strike again. You shall beat my face, and tear my hair, and pluck my beard up by the roots, and welcome, for the sake of your bright eyes. Strike again, mistress. Do. Ha ha ha! I like it."

"Let me go," she cried, endeavouring with both her hands to push him off. "Let me go this moment."

"You had as good be kinder to me, Sweetlips," said Hugh. "You had, indeed! Come. Tell me now. Why are you always so proud? I don't quarrel with you for it. I love you when you're proud. Ha ha ha! You can't hide your beauty from a poor fellow; that's a comfort!"

She gave him no answer, but as he had not yet checked her progress, continued to press forward as rapidly as she could. At length, between the hurry she had made, her terror, and the tightness of his embrace, her strength failed her, and she could go no further.

"Hugh," cried the panting girl, "good Hugh; if you will leave me I will give you anything—everything I have—and never tell one word of this to any living creature."

"You had best not," he answered. "Harkye, little dove, ye had best not. All about here know me, and what I dare do if I have a mind. If ever you are going to tell, stop when the words are on your lips, and think of the mischief you'll bring, if you do, upon some innocent heads that you wouldn't wish to hurt a hair of. Bring trouble on me, and I'll bring trouble and something more on them in return. I care no more for them than for so many dogs; not so much— why should I? I'd sooner kill a man than a dog any day. I've never been sorry for a man's death in all my life, and I have for a dog's."

There was something so thoroughly savage in the manner of these expressions, and the looks and gestures by which they were accom-

Hugh Surprises Dolly.

panied, that her great fear of him gave her new strength, and enabled her by a sudden effort to extricate herself and run fleetly from him. But Hugh was as nimble, strong, and swift of foot, as any man in broad England, and it was but a fruitless expenditure of energy, for he had her in his encircling arms again before she had gone a hundred yards.

"Softly, darling—gently—would you fly from rough Hugh, that loves you as well as any drawing-room gallant?"

"I would," she answered, struggling to free herself again. "I will. Help!"

"A fine for crying out," said Hugh. "Ha ha ha! A fine, pretty one, from your lips. I pay myself! Ha ha ha!"

"Help! help! help!" As she shrieked with the utmost violence she could exert, a shout was heard in answer, and another, and another.

"Thank Heaven!" cried the girl in an ecstasy. "Joe, dear Joe, this way. Help!"

Her assailant paused, and stood irresolute for a moment, but the shouts drawing nearer and coming quick upon them, forced him to a speedy decision. He released her, whispered with a menacing look, "Tell *him:* and see what follows!" and leaping the hedge, was gone in an instant. Dolly darted off, and fairly ran into Joe Willet's open arms.

"What is the matter? are you hurt? what was it? who was it? where is he? what was he like?" with a great many encouraging expressions and assurances of safety, were the first words Joe poured forth. But poor little Dolly was so breathless and terrified that for some time she was quite unable to answer him, and hung upon his shoulder, sobbing and crying as if her heart would break.

Joe had not the smallest objection to have her hanging on his shoulder; no, not the least, though it crushed the cherry-coloured ribbons sadly, and put the smart little hat out of all shape. But he couldn't bear to see her cry; it went to his very heart. He tried to console her, bent over her, whispered to her—some say kissed her, but that's a fable. At any rate he said all the kind and tender things he could think of, and Dolly let him go on and didn't interrupt him once, and it was a good ten minutes before she was able to raise her head and thank him.

"What was it that frightened you?" said Joe.

A man whose person was unknown to her had followed her, she answered; he began by begging, and went on to threats of robbery, which he was on the point of carrying into execution, and would have executed, but for Joe's timely aid. The hesitation and confusion with which she said this, Joe attributed to the fright she had sustained, and no suspicion of the truth occurred to him for a moment.

"Stop when the words are on your lips." A hundred times that night, and very often afterwards, when the disclosure was rising to her tongue, Dolly thought of that, and repressed it. A deeply rooted dread of the man; the conviction that his ferocious nature, once roused, would stop at nothing; and the strong assurance that if she

impeached him, the full measure of his wrath and vengeance would
be wreaked on Joe, who had preserved her; these were considerations
she had not the courage to overcome, and inducements to secrecy
too powerful for her to surmount.

Joe, for his part, was a great deal too happy to inquire very curiously into the matter; and Dolly being yet too tremulous to walk
without assistance, they went forward very slowly, and in his mind
very pleasantly, until the Maypole lights were near at hand, twinkling
their cheerful welcome, when Dolly stopped suddenly and with a
half scream exclaimed,

"The letter!"

"What letter?" cried Joe.

"That I was carrying—I had it in my hand. My bracelet too," she
said, clasping her wrist. "I have lost them both."

"Do you mean just now?" said Joe.

"Either I dropped them then, or they were taken from me,"
answered Dolly, vainly searching her pocket and rustling her dress.
"They are gone, both gone. What an unhappy girl I am!" With these
words poor Dolly, who to do her justice was quite as sorry for the loss
of the letter as for her bracelet, fell a crying again, and bemoaned her
fate most movingly.

Joe tried to comfort her with the assurance that directly he had
housed her in the Maypole, he would return to the spot with a lantern
(for it was now quite dark) and make strict search for the missing
articles, which there was great probability of his finding, as it was
not likely that anybody had passed that way since, and she was not
conscious that they had been forcibly taken from her. Dolly thanked
him very heartily for this offer, though with no great hope of his
quest being successful; and so with many lamentations on her side,
and many hopeful words on his, and much weakness on the part of
Dolly and much tender supporting on the part of Joe, they reached
the Maypole bar at last, where the locksmith and his wife and old
John were yet keeping high festival.

Mr. Willet received the intelligence of Dolly's trouble with that surprising presence of mind and readiness of speech for which he was so
eminently distinguished above all other men. Mrs. Varden expressed
her sympathy for her daughter's distress by scolding her roundly for
being so late ; and the honest locksmith divided himself between con-
doling with and kissing Dolly, and shaking hands heartily with Joe,
whom he could not sufficiently praise or thank.

In reference to this latter point, old John was far from agreeing
with his friend; for besides that he by no means approved of an
adventurous spirit in the abstract, it occurred to him that if his son
and heir had been seriously damaged in a scuffle, the consequences
would assuredly have been expensive and inconvenient, and might
perhaps have proved detrimental to the Maypole business. Wherefore
and because he looked with no favourable eye upon young girls, but
rather considered that they and the whole female sex were a kind of
nonsensical mistake on the part of Nature, he took occasion to retire

and shake his head in private at the boiler; inspired by which silent oracle, he was moved to give Joe various stealthy nudges with his elbow, as a parental reproof and gentle admonition to mind his own business and not make a fool of himself.

Joe, however, took down the lantern and lighted it; and arming himself with a stout stick, asked whether Hugh was in the stable.

"He's lying asleep before the kitchen fire, sir," said Mr. Willet. "What do you want him for?"

"I want him to come with me to look after this bracelet and letter," answered Joe. "Halloa there! Hugh!"

Dolly turned pale as death, and felt as if she must faint forthwith. After a few moments, Hugh came staggering in, stretching himself and yawning according to custom, and presenting every appearance of having been roused from a sound nap.

"Here, sleepy-head," said Joe, giving him the lantern. "Carry this, and bring the dog, and that small cudgel of yours. And woe betide the fellow if we come upon him."

"What fellow?" growled Hugh, rubbing his eyes and shaking himself.

"What fellow?" returned Joe, who was in a state of great valour and bustle; "a fellow you ought to know of, and be more alive about. It's well for the like of you, lazy giant that you are, to be snoring your time away in chimney-corners, when honest men's daughters can't cross even our quiet meadows at nightfall without being set upon by footpads, and frightened out of their precious lives."

"They never rob me," cried Hugh with a laugh. "I have got nothing to lose. But I'd as lief knock them at head as any other man. How many are there?"

"Only one," said Dolly faintly, for everybody looked at her.

"And what was he like, mistress?" said Hugh with a glance at young Willet, so slight and momentary that the scowl it conveyed was lost on all but her. "About my height?"

"Not—not so tall," Dolly replied, scarce knowing what she said.

"His dress," said Hugh, looking at her keenly, "like—like any of ours now? I know all the people hereabouts, and maybe could give a guess at the man, if I had anything to guide me."

Dolly faltered and turned paler yet; then answered that he was wrapped in a loose coat and had his face hidden by a handkerchief, and that she could give no other description of him.

"You wouldn't know him if you saw him then, belike?" said Hugh with a malicious grin.

"I should not," answered Dolly, bursting into tears again. "I don't wish to see him. I can't bear to think of him. I can't talk about him any more. Don't go to look for these things, Mr. Joe, pray don't. I entreat you not to go with that man."

"Not to go with me!" cried Hugh. "I'm too rough for them all. They're all afraid of me. Why, bless you, mistress, I've the tenderest heart alive. I love all the ladies, ma'am," said Hugh, turning to the locksmith's wife.

273*

Mrs. Varden opined that if he did, he ought to be ashamed of himself; such sentiments being more consistent (so she argued) with a benighted Mussulman or wild Islander than with a staunch Protestant. Arguing from this imperfect state of his morals, Mrs. Varden further opined that he had never studied the Manual. Hugh admitting that he never had, and moreover that he couldn't read, Mrs. Varden declared with much severity, that he ought to be even more ashamed of himself than before, and strongly recommended him to save up his pocket-money for the purchase of one, and further to teach himself the contents with all convenient diligence. She was still pursuing this train of discourse, when Hugh, somewhat unceremoniously and irreverently, followed his young master out, and left her to edify the rest of the company. This she proceeded to do, and finding that Mr. Willet's eyes were fixed upon her with an appearance of deep attention, gradually addressed the whole of her discourse to him, whom she entertained with a moral and theological lecture of considerable length, in the conviction that great workings were taking place in his spirit. The simple truth was, however, that Mr. Willet, although his eyes were wide open and he saw a woman before him whose head by long and steady looking at seemed to grow bigger and bigger until it filled the whole bar, was to all other intents and purposes fast asleep and so sat leaning back in his chair with his hands in his pockets until his son's return caused him to wake up with a deep sigh, and a faint impression that he had been dreaming about pickled pork and greens —a vision of his slumbers which was no doubt referable to the circumstance of Mrs. Varden's having frequently pronounced the word "Grace" with much emphasis; which word, entering the portals of Mr. Willet's brain as they stood ajar, and coupling itself with the words "before meat," which were there ranging about, did in time suggest a particular kind of meat together with that description of vegetable which is usually its companion.

The search was wholly unsuccessful. Joe had groped along the path a dozen times, and among the grass, and in the dry ditch, and in the hedge, but all in vain. Dolly, who was quite inconsolable for her loss, wrote a note to Miss Haredale giving her the same account of it that she had given at the Maypole, which Joe undertook to deliver as soon as the family were stirring next day. That done, they sat down to tea in the bar, where there was an uncommon display of buttered toast, and—in order that they might not grow faint for want of sustenance, and might have a decent halting-place or half-way house between dinner and supper—a few savoury trifles in the shape of great rashers of broiled ham, which being well cured, done to a turn, and smoking hot, sent forth a tempting and delicious fragrance.

Mrs. Varden was seldom very Protestant at meals, unless it happened that they were under-done, or over-done, or indeed that anything occurred to put her out of humour. Her spirits rose considerably on beholding these goodly preparations, and from the nothingness of good works, she passed to the somethingness of ham and toast with great cheerfulness. Nay, under the influence of these wholesome stimulants, she sharply reproved her daughter for being low and despondent (which she considered an unacceptable frame of mind), and remarked, as she held her own plate for a fresh supply, that it would be well for Dolly, who pined over the loss of a toy and a sheet of paper, if she would reflect upon the voluntary sacrifices of the missionaries in foreign parts who lived chiefly on salads.

The proceedings of such a day occasion various fluctuations in the human thermometer, and especially in instruments so sensitively and delicately constructed as Mrs. Varden. Thus, at dinner Mrs. V. stood at summer heat; genial, smiling, and delightful. After dinner, in the sunshine of the wine, she went up at least half-a-dozen degrees, and was perfectly enchanting. As its effect subsided, she fell rapidly, went to sleep for an hour or so at temperate, and woke at something below freezing. Now she was at summer heat again, in the shade; and when tea was over, and old John, producing a bottle of cordial from one of the oaken cases, insisted on her sipping two glasses thereof in slow succession, she stood steadily at ninety for one hour and a quarter. Profiting by experience, the locksmith took advantage of this genial weather to smoke his pipe in the porch, and in consequence of this prudent management, he was fully prepared, when the glass went down again, to start homewards directly.

The horse was accordingly put in, and the chaise brought round to the door. Joe, who would on no account be dissuaded from escorting them until they had passed the most dreary and solitary part of the road, led out the grey mare at the same time; and having helped Dolly into her seat (more happiness!) sprung gaily into the saddle. Then, after many good nights, and admonitions to wrap up, and glancing of lights, and handing in of cloaks and shawls, the chaise rolled away, and Joe trotted beside it—on Dolly's side, no doubt, and pretty close to the wheel too.

CHAPTER XXII

IT was a fine bright night, and for all her lowness of spirits Dolly kept looking up at the stars in a manner so bewitching (and *she* knew it!) that Joe was clean out of his senses, and plainly showed that if ever a man were—not to say over head and ears, but over the Monument and the top of Saint Paul's in love, that man was himself. The road was a very good one; not at all a jolting road, or an uneven one; and yet Dolly held the side of the chaise with one little hand, all the way. If there had been an executioner behind him with an uplifted axe ready to chop off his head if he touched that hand, Joe couldn't have helped doing it. From putting his own hand upon it as if by chance, and taking it away again after a minute or so, he got to riding along without taking it off at all; as if he, the escort, were bound to do that as an important part of his duty, and had come out for the purpose. The most curious circumstances about this little incident was, that Dolly didn't seem to know of it. She looked so innocent and uncon-scious when she turned her eyes on Joe, that it was quite provoking.

She talked though; talked about her fright, and about Joe's coming up to rescue her, and about her gratitude, and about her fear that she might not have thanked him enough, and about their always being friends from that time forth—and about all that sort of thing. And when Joe said, not friends he hoped, Dolly was quite surprised, and said not enemies she hoped; and when Joe said, couldn't they be something much better than either, Dolly all of a sudden found out a star which was brighter than all the other stars, and begged to call his attention to the same, and was ten thousand times more innocent and unconscious than ever.

In this manner they travelled along, talking very little above a whisper, and wishing the road could be stretched out to some dozen times its natural length—at least that was Joe's desire—when, as they were getting clear of the forest and emerging on the more frequented road, they heard behind them the sound of a horse's feet at a round trot, which growing rapidly louder as it drew nearer, elicited a scream from Mrs. Varden, and the cry "A friend!" from the rider, who now came panting up, and checked his horse beside them.

"This man again!" cried Dolly, shuddering.

"Hugh!" said Joe. "What errand are you upon?"

"I come to ride back with you," he answered, glancing covertly at the locksmith's daughter. "*He* sent me."

"My father!" said poor Joe; adding under his breath, with a very unfilial apostrophe, "Will he never think me man enough to take care of myself!"

"Aye!" returned Hugh to the first part of the inquiry. "The roads are not safe just now, he says, and you'd better have a companion."

"Ride on then," said Joe. "I'm not going to turn yet."

Hugh complied, and they went on again. It was his whim or humour to ride immediately before the chaise, and from this position he constantly turned his head, and looked back. Dolly felt that he looked at her, but she averted her eyes and feared to raise them once, so great was the dread with which he had inspired her.

This interruption, and the consequent wakefulness of Mrs. Varden, who had been nodding in her sleep up to this point, except for a minute or two at a time, when she roused herself to scold the locksmith for audaciously taking hold of her to prevent her nodding herself out of the chaise, put a restraint upon the whispered conversation, and made it difficult of resumption. Indeed, before they had gone another mile, Gabriel stopped at his wife's desire, and that good lady protested she would not hear of Joe's going a step further on any account whatever. It was in vain for Joe to protest on the other hand that he was by no means tired, and would turn back presently, and would see them safely past such a point, and so forth. Mrs. Varden was obdurate, and being so was not to be overcome by mortal agency.

"Good night—if I must say it," said Joe, sorrowfully.

"Good night," said Dolly. She would have added, "Take care of that man, and pray don't trust him," but he had turned his horse's head, and was standing close to them. She had therefore nothing for it but to suffer Joe to give her hand a gentle squeeze, and when the chaise had gone on for some distance, to look back and wave it, as he still lingered on the spot where they had parted, with the tall dark figure of Hugh beside him.

What she thought about, going home; and whether the coachmaker held as favourable a place in her meditations as he had occupied in the morning, is unknown. They reached home at last—at last, for it was a long way, made none the shorter by Mrs. Varden's grumbling. Miggs hearing the sound of wheels was at the door immediately.

"Here they are, Simmun! Here they are!" cried Miggs, clapping her hands, and issuing forth to help her mistress to alight. "Bring a chair, Simmun. Now, an't you the better for it, mim? Don't you feel more yourself than you would have done if you'd have stopped at home? Oh, gracious! how cold you are! Goodness me, sir, she's a perfect heap of ice."

"I can't help it, my good girl. You had better take her in to the fire," said the locksmith.

"Master sounds unfeeling, mim," said Miggs, in a tone of commiseration, "but such is not his intentions, I'm sure. After what he has seen of you this day, I never will believe but that he has a deal more affection in his heart than to speak unkind. Come in and sit yourself down by the fire ; there's a good dear—do."

Mrs. Varden complied. The locksmith followed with his hands in his pockets, and Mr. Tappertit trundled off with the chaise to a neighbouring stable.

"Martha, my dear," said the locksmith, when they reached the parlour, "if you'll look to Dolly yourself, or let somebody else do it, perhaps it will be only kind and reasonable. She has been frightened, you know, and is not at all well to-night."

In fact, Dolly had thrown herself upon the sofa, quite regardless of all the little finery of which she had been so proud in the morning, and with her face buried in her hands was crying very much.

At first sight of this phenomenon (for Dolly was by no means accustomed to displays of this sort, rather learning from her mother's example to avoid them as much as possible) Mrs. Varden expressed her belief that never was any woman so beset as she; that her life was a continued scene of trial; that whenever she was disposed to be well and cheerful, so sure were the people around her to throw, by some means or other, a damp upon her spirits; and that, as she had enjoyed herself that day, and Heaven knew it was very seldom she did enjoy herself, so she was now to pay the penalty. To all such propositions Miggs assented freely. Poor Dolly, however, grew none the better for these restoratives, but rather worse, indeed; and seeing that she was really ill, both Mrs. Varden and Miggs were moved to compassion, and tended her in earnest.

But even then, their very kindness shaped itself into their usual course of policy, and though Dolly was in a swoon, it was rendered clear to the meanest capacity, that Mrs. Varden was the sufferer. Thus when Dolly began to get a little better, and passed into that

stage in which matrons hold that remonstrance and argument may
be successfully applied, her mother represented to her, with tears in
her eyes, that if she had been flurried and worried that day, she must
remember it was the common lot of humanity, and in especial of
womankind, who through the whole of their existence must expect
no less, and were bound to make up their minds to meek endurance
and patient resignation. Mrs. Varden entreated her to remember that
one of these days she would, in all probability, have to do violence
to her feelings so far as to be married; and that marriage, as she might
see every day of her life (and truly she did) was a state requiring great
fortitude and forbearance. She represented to her in lively colours,
that if she (Mrs. V.) had not, in steering her course through this vale
of tears, been supported by a strong principle of duty which alone
upheld and prevented her from drooping, she must have been in her
grave many years ago; in which case she desired to know what would
have become of that errant spirit (meaning the locksmith), of whose
eye she was the very apple, and in whose path she was, as it were, a
shining light and guiding star?

Miss Miggs also put in her word to the same effect. She said that
indeed and indeed Miss Dolly might take pattern by her blessed
mother, who, she always had said, and always would say, though she
were to be hanged , drawn, and quartered for it next minute, was the
mildest, amiablest, forgivingest-spirited, longest-sufferingest female
as ever she could have believed; the mere narration of whose excellen-
cies had worked such a wholesome change in the mind of her own
sister-in-law, that, whereas, before, she and her busband lived like
cat and dog, and were in the habit of exchanging brass candlesticks,
pot-lids, flat-irons, and other such strong resentments, they were now
the happiest and affectionatest couple upon earth; as could be proved
any day on application at Golden Lion Court, number twenty-sivin,
second bell-handle on the right-hand door-post. After glancing at
herself as a comparatively worthless vessel, but still as one of some
desert, she besought her to bear in mind that her aforesaid dear and
only mother was of a weakly constitution and excitable temperament, who had constantly to sustain afflictions in domestic life,
compared with which thieves and robbers were as nothing, and yet
never sunk down or gave way to despair or wrath, but, in prize-
fighting phraseology, always came up to time with a cheerful countenance, and went in to win as if nothing had happened. When Miggs
finished her solo, her mistress struck in again, and the two together
performed a duet to the same purpose; the burden being, that Mrs.
Varden was persecuted perfection, and Mr. Varden, as the representative of mankind in that apartment, a creature of vicious and brutal
habits, utterly insensible to the blessings he enjoyed. Of so refined a
character, indeed, was their talent of assault under the mask of
sympathy, that when Dolly, recovering, embraced her father tenderly,
as in vindication of his goodness, Mrs. Varden expressed her solemn
hope that this would be a lesson to him for the remainder of his life,
and that he would do some little justice to a woman's nature ever

afterwards—in which aspiration Miss Miggs, by divers sniffs and coughs, more significant than the longest oration, expressed her entire concurrence.

But the great joy of Migg's heart was, that she not only picked up a full account of what had happened, but had the exquisite delight of conveying it to Mr. Tappertit for his jealousy and torture. For that gentleman, on account of Dolly's indisposition, had been requested to take his supper in the workshop, and it was conveyed thither by Miss Migg's own fair hands.

"Oh, Simmun!" said the young lady, "such goings on to-day! Oh, gracious me, Simmun!"

Mr. Tappertit, who was not in the best of humours, and who disliked Miss Miggs more when she laid her hand on her heart and panted for breath than at any other time, as her deficiency of outline was most apparent under such circumstances, eyed her over in his loftiest style, and deigned to express no curiosity whatever.

"I never heard the like, nor nobody else," pursued Miggs. "The idea of interfering with *her*. What people can see in her to make it worth their while to do so, that's the joke—he he he!"

Finding there was a lady in the case, Mr. Tappertit haughtily requested his fair friend to be more explicit, and demanded to know what she meant by "her."

"Why, that Dolly," said Miggs, with an extremely sharp emphasis on the name. "But, oh upon my word and honour, young Joseph Willet is a brave one; and he do deserve her, that he do."

"Woman!" said Mr. Tappertit, jumping off the counter on which he was seated; "beware!"

"My stars, Simmun!" cried Miggs, in affected astonishment. "You frighten me to death! What's the matter?"

"There are strings," said Mr. Tappertit, flourishing his bread-and-cheese knife in the air, "in the human heart that had better not be wibrated. That's what's the matter."

"Oh, very well—if you're in a huff," cried Miggs, turning away.

"Huff or no huff," said Mr. Tappertit, detaining her by the wrist. "What do you mean, Jezebel? What were you going to say? Answer me!"

Notwithstanding this uncivil exhortation, Miggs gladly did as she was required; and told him how that their young mistress, being alone in the meadows after dark, had been attacked by three or four tall men, who would have certainly borne her away and perhaps murdered her, but for the timely arrival of Joseph Willet, who with his own single hand put them all to flight, and rescued her; to the lasting admiration of his fellow-creatures generally, and to the eternal love and gratitude of Dolly Varden.

"Very good," said Mr. Tappertit, fetching a long breath when the tale was told, and rubbing his hair up till it stood stiff and straight on end all over his head. "His days are numbered."

"Oh, Simmun!"

"I tell you," said the 'prentice, "his days are numbered. Leave me.

Get along with you."

Miggs departed at his bidding, but less because of his bidding than because she desired to chuckle in secret. When she had given vent to her satisfaction, she returned to the parlour; where the locksmith, stimulated by quietness and Toby, had become talkative, and was disposed to take a cheerful review of the occurrences of the day. But Mrs. Varden, whose practical religion (as is not uncommon) was usually of the retrospective order, cut him short by declaiming on the sinfulness of such junketings, and holding that it was high time to go to bed. To bed therefore she withdrew, with an aspect as grim and gloomy as that of the Maypole's own state coach; and to bed the rest of the establishment soon afterwards repaired.

CHAPTER XXIII

TWILIGHT had given place to night some hours, and it was high noon in those quarters of the town in which "the world" conde-scended to dwell—the world being then, as now, of very limited dimensions and easily lodged—when Mr. Chester reclined upon a sofa in his dressing-room in the Temple, entertaining himself with a book.

He was dressing, as it seemed, by easy stages, and having per-formed half the journey was taking a long rest. Completely attired as to his legs and feet in the trimmest fashion of the day, he had yet the remainder of his toilet to perform. The coat was stretched, like a refined scarecrow, on its separate horse; the waistcoat was displayed to the best advantage; the various ornamental articles of dress were severally set out in most alluring order; and yet he lay dangling his legs between the sofa and the ground, as intent upon his book as if there were nothing but bed before him.

"Upon my honour," he said, at length raising his eyes to the ceiling with the air of a man who was reflecting seriously on what he had read; "upon my honour, the most masterly composition, the most delicate thoughts, the finest code of morality, and the most gentle-manly sentiments in the universe! Ah, Ned, Ned, if you would but form your mind by such precepts, we should have but one common feeling on every subject that could possibly arise between us!"

This apostrophe was addressed, like the rest of his remarks, to empty air: for Edward was not present, and the father was quite alone.

"My Lord Chesterfield," he said, pressing his hand tenderly upon the book as he laid it down, "if I could but have profited by your genius soon enough to have formed my son on the model you have left to all wise fathers, both he and I would have been rich men. Shakespeare was undoubtedly very fine in his way; Milton good, though prosy; Lord Bacon deep, and decidedly knowing; but the writer who should be his country's pride, is my Lord Chesterfield."

He became thoughtful again, and the toothpick was in requisition.

"I thought I was tolerably accomplished as a man of the world," he continued, "I flattered myself that I was pretty well versed in all those little arts and graces which distinguish men of the world from boors and peasants, and separate their character from those intensely vulgar sentiments which are called the national character. Apart from any natural prepossession in my own favour, I believed I was. Still, in every page of this enlightened writer, I find some captivating hypocrisy which has never occurred to me before, or some superlative piece of selfishness to which I was utterly a stranger. I should quite blush for myself before this stupendous creature, if, remembering his precepts, one might blush at anything. An amazing man! a nobleman indeed! any King or Queen may make a Lord, but only the Devil himself—and the Graces—can make a Chesterfield."

Men who are thoroughly false and hollow, seldom try to hide those vices from themselves; and yet in the very act of avowing them, they lay claim to the virtues they feign most to despise. "For," say they, "this is honesty, this is truth. All mankind are like us, but they have not the candour to avow it." The more they affect to deny the existence of any sincerity in the world, the more they would be thought to possess it in its boldest shape; and this an unconscious compliment to Truth on the part of these philosophers, which will turn the laugh against them to the Day of Judgment.

Mr. Chester, having extolled his favourite author, as above recited, took up the book again in the excess of his admiration and was composing himself for a further perusal of its sublime morality, when he was disturbed by a noise at the outer door; occasioned as it seemed by the endeavours of his servant to obstruct the entrance of some unwelcome visitor.

"A late hour for an importunate creditor," he said, raising his eyebrows with as indolent an expression of wonder as if the noise were in the street, and one with which he had not the smallest possible concern. "Much after their accustomed time. The usual pretence I suppose. No doubt a heavy payment to make up to-morrow. Poor fellow, he loses time, and time is money as the good proverb says—I never found it out though. Well. What now? You know I am not at home."

"A man, sir," replied the servant, who was to the full as cool and negligent in his way as his master, "has brought home the riding-whip you lost the other day. I told him you were out, but he said he was to wait while I brought it in, and wouldn't go till I did."

"He was quite right," returned his master, "and you're a blockhead, possessing no judgment or discretion whatever. Tell him to come in, and see that he rubs his shoes for exactly five minutes first."

The man laid the whip on a chair, and withdrew. The master, who had only heard his foot upon the ground and had not taken the trouble to turn round and look at him, shut his book, and pursued the train of ideas his entrance had disturbed.

"If time were money," he said, handling his snuff-box, "I would compound with my creditors, and give them—let me see—how much a day? There's my nap after dinner—an hour—they're extremely welcome to that, and to make the most of it. In the morning, between my breakfast and the paper, I could spare them another hour; in the evening before dinner say another. Three hours a day. They might pay themselves in calls, with interest, in twelve months. I think I shall propose it to them. Ah, my centaur, are you there?"

"Here I am," replied Hugh, striding in, followed by a dog, as rough and sullen as himself; "and trouble enough I've had to get here. What do you ask me to come for, and keep me out when I *do* come?"

"My good fellow," returned the other, raising his head a little from the cushion and carelessly surveying him from top to toe, "I am delighted to see you, and to have, in your being here, the very best proof that you are not kept out. How are you?"

"I'm well enough," said Hugh impatiently.

"You look a perfect marvel of health. Sit down."

"I'd rather stand," said Hugh.

"Please yourself, my good fellow," returned Mr. Chester rising, slowly pulling off the loose robe he wore, and sitting down before the dressing-glass. "Please yourself by all means."

Having said this in the politest and blandest tone possible, he went on dressing, and took no further notice of his guest, who stood in the same spot as uncertain what to do next, eyeing him sulkily from time to time.

"Are you going to speak to me, master?" he said, after a long silence.

"My worthy creature," returned Mr. Chester, "you are a little ruffled and out of humour. I'll wait till you're quite yourself again. I am in no hurry."

This behaviour had its intended effect. It humbled and abashed the man, and made him still more irresolute and uncertain. Hard words he could have returned, violence he would have repaid with interest; but this cool, complacent, contemptuous, self-possessed reception, caused him to feel his inferiority more completely than the most elaborate arguments. Everything contributed to this effect. His own rough speech, contrasted with the soft persuasive accents of the other; his rude bearing, and Mr. Chester's polished manner; the disorder and negligence of his ragged dress, and the elegant attire he saw before him; with all the unaccustomed luxuries and comforts of the room, and the silence that gave him leisure to observe these things, and feel how ill at ease they made him; all these influences, which have too often some effect on tortured minds and become of almost resistless power when brought to bear on such a mind as his, quelled Hugh completely. He moved by little and little nearer to Mr. Chester's chair, and glancing over his shoulder at the reflection of his face in the glass, as if seeking for some encouragement in its expression, said at length, with a rough attempt at conciliation.

"*Are* you going to speak to me, master, or am I to go away?"

"Speak you," said Mr. Chester, "speak you, good fellow. I have spoken, have I not? I am waiting for you."

"Why, look'ee, sir," returned Hugh with increased embarrassment, "am I the man that you privately left your whip with before you rode away from the Maypole, and told to bring it back whenever he might want to see you on a certain subject?"

"No doubt the same, or you have a twin brother," said Mr. Chester, glancing at the reflection of his anxious face; "which is not probable, I should say."

"Then I have come, sir," said Hugh, "and I have brought it back, and something else along with it. A letter, sir, it is, that I took from the person who had charge of it." As he spoke, he laid upon the dressing-table, Dolly's lost epistle. The very letter that had cost her so much trouble.

"Did you obtain this by force, my good fellow?" said Mr. Chester, casting his eye upon it without the least perceptible surprise or pleasure.

"Not quite," said Hugh. "Partly."

"Who was the messenger from whom you took it?"

"A woman. One Varden's daughter."

"Oh indeed!" said Mr. Chester gaily. "What else did you take from her?"

"What else?"

"Yes," said the other, in a drawling manner, for he was fixing a very small patch of sticking plaster on a very small pimple near the corner of his mouth. "What else?"

"Well—a kiss," replied Hugh, after some hesitation.

"And what else?"

"Nothing."

"I think," said Mr. Chester, in the same easy tone, and smiling twice or thrice to try if the patch adhered—"I think there was something else. I have heard a trifle of jewellery spoken of—a mere trifle—a thing of such little value, indeed, that you may have forgotten it. Do you remember anything of the kind—such as a bracelet now, for instance?"

Hugh with a muttered oath thrust his hand into his breast, and drawing the bracelet forth, wrapped in a scrap of hay, was about to lay it on the table likewise, when his patron stopped his hand and bade him put it up again.

"You took that for yourself, my excellent friend," he said, "and may keep it. I am neither a thief, nor a receiver. Don't show it to me. You had better hide it again, and lose no time. Don't let me see where you put it either," he added, turning away his head.

"You're not a receiver!" said Hugh bluntly, despite the increasing awe in which he held him. "What do you call *that*, master?" striking the letter with his heavy hand.

"I call that quite another thing," said Mr. Chester coolly. "I shall prove it presently, as you will see. You are thirsty, I suppose?"

Hugh drew his sleeve across his lips, and gruffly answered yes.

"Step to that closet and bring me a bottle you will see there, and a glass."

He obeyed. His patron followed him with his eyes, and when his back was turned, smiled as he had never done when he stood beside the mirror. On his return he filled the glass, and bade him drink. That dram despatched, he poured him out another, and another.

"How many can you bear?" he said, filling the glass again.

"As many as you like to give me. Pour on. Fill high. A bumper with a bead in the middle! Give me enough of this," he added, as he tossed it down his hairy throat, "and I'll do murder if you ask me!"

"As I don't mean to ask you, and you might possibly do it without being invited if you went on much further," said Mr. Chester with great composure, "we will stop, if agreeable to you, my good friend, at the next glass. You were drinking before you came here."

"I always am when I can get it," cried Hugh boisterously, waving the empty glass above his head, and throwing himself into a rude dancing attitude. "I always am. Why not? Ha ha ha! What's so good to me as this? What ever has been? What else has kept away the cold on bitter nights, and driven hunger off in starving times? What else has given me the strength and courage of a man, when men would have left me to die, a puny child? I should never have had a man's heart but for this. I should have died in a ditch. Where's he who when I was a weak and sickly wretch, with trembling legs and fading sight, bade me cheer up, as this did? I never knew him; not I. I drink to the drink, master. Ha ha ha!"

"You are an exceedingly cheerful young man," said Mr. Chester, putting on his cravat with great deliberation, and slightly moving his head from side to side to settle his chin in its proper place. "Quite a boon companion."

"Do you see this hand, master," said Hugh, "and this arm?" baring the brawny limb to the elbow. "It was once mere skin and bone, and would have been dust in some poor churchyard by this time, but for the drink."

"You may cover it," said Mr. Chester, "it's sufficiently real in your sleeve."

"I should never have been spirited up to take a kiss from the proud little beauty, master, but for the drink," cried Hugh. "Ha ha ha! It was a good one. As sweet as honey-suckle I warrant you. I thank the drink for it. I'll drink to the drink again, master. Fill me one more. Come. One more!"

"You are such a promising fellow," said his patron, putting on his waistcoat with great nicety, and taking no heed of this request, "that I must caution you against having too many impulses from the drink, and getting hung before your time. What's your age?"

"I don't know."

"At any rate," said Mr. Chester, "you are young enough to escape what I may call a natural death for some years to come. How can you trust yourself in my hands on so short an acquaintance, with a halter round your neck? What a confiding nature yours must be!"

Hugh fell back a pace or two and surveyed him with a look of mingled terror, indignation, and surprise. Regarding himself in the glass with the same complacency as before, and speaking as smoothly as if he were discussing some pleasant chit-chat of the town, his patron went on:

"Robbery on the king's highway, my young friend, is a very dangerous and ticklish occupation. It is pleasant, I have no doubt, while it lasts; but like many other pleasures in this transitory world, it seldom lasts long. And really if, in the ingenuousness of youth, you open your heart so readily on the subject, I am afraid your career will be an extremely short one."

"How's this?" said Hugh. "What do you talk of, master? Who was it set me on?"

"Who?" said Mr. Chester, wheeling sharply round, and looking at him for the first time. "I didn't hear you. Who was it?"

Hugh faltered, and muttered something which was not audible.

"Who was it? I am curious to know," said Mr. Chester, with surpassing affability. "Some rustic beauty perhaps? But be cautious, my good friend. They are not always to be trusted. Do take my advice now, and be careful of yourself." With these words he turned to the glass again, and went on with his toilet.

Hugh would have answered him that he, the questioner himself, had set him on, but the words stuck in his throat. The consummate art with which his patron had led him to this point, and managed the whole conversation, perfectly baffled him. He did not doubt that if he had made the retort which was on his lips when Mr. Chester turned round and questioned him so keenly, he would straightway have given him into custody and had him dragged before a justice with the stolen property upon him; in which case it was as certain he would have been hung as it was that he had been born. The ascendency which it was the purpose of the man of the world to establish over this savage instrument, was gained from that time. Hugh's submission was complete. He dreaded him beyond description; and felt that accident and artifice had spun a web about him, which at a touch from such a master-hand as he, would bind him to the gallows.

With these thoughts passing through his mind, and yet wondering at the very same time how he who came there rioting in the confidence of this man (as he thought), should be so soon and so thoroughly subdued, Hugh stood cowering before him, regarding him uneasily from time to time, while he finished dressing. When he had done so, he took up the letter, broke the seal, and throwing himself back in his chair, read it leisurely through.

"Very neatly worded upon my life! Quite a woman's letter, full of what people call tenderness, and disinterestedness, and heart, and all that sort of thing!"

As he spoke, he twisted it up, and glancing lazily round at Hugh as though he would say "You see this?" held it in the flame of the candle. When it was in a full blaze, he tossed it into the grate, and there it smouldered away.

"It was directed to my son," he said, turning to Hugh, "and you did quite right to bring it here. I opened it on my own responsibility, and you see what I have done with it. Take this, for your trouble."

Hugh stepped forward to receive the piece of money he held out to him. As he put it in his hand, he added:

"If you should happen to find anything else of this sort, or to pick up any kind of information you may think I would like to have, bring it here, will you, my good fellow?"

This was said with a smile which implied—or Hugh thought it did —"fail to do so at your peril!" He answered that he would.

"And don't," said his patron, with an air of the very kindest patronage, "don't be at all downcast or uneasy respecting that little rashness we have been speaking of. Your neck is as safe in my hands, my good fellow, as though a baby's fingers clasped it, I assure you.— Take another glass. You are quieter now."

Hugh accepted it from his hand, and looking stealthily at his smiling face, drank the contents in silence.

"Don't you—ha, ha!—don't you drink to the drink any more?" said Mr. Chester, in his most winning manner.

"To you, sir," was the sullen answer, with something approaching to a bow. "I drink to you."

"Thank you. God bless you. By the bye, what is your name, my good soul? You are called Hugh, I know, of course—your other name?"

"I have no other name."

"A very strange fellow! Do you mean that you never knew one, or that you don't choose to tell it? Which?"

"I'd tell it if I could," said Hugh, quickly. "I can't. I have been always called Hugh; nothing more. I never knew, nor saw, nor thought about a father; and I was a boy of six—that's not very old —when they hung my mother up at Tyburn for a couple of thousand men to stare at. They might have let her live. She was poor enough."

"How very sad!" exclaimed his patron, with a condescending smile. "I have no doubt she was an exceedingly fine woman."

"You see that dog of mine?" said Hugh, abruptly.

"Faithful, I dare say?" rejoined his patron, looking at him through his glass; "and immensely clever? Virtuous and gifted animals, whether man or beast, always are so very hideous."

"Such a dog as that, and one of the same breed, was the only living thing except me that howled that day," said Hugh. "Out of the two thousand odd—there was a larger crowd for its being a woman—the dog and I alone had any pity. If he'd have been a man, he'd have been glad to be quit of her, for she had been forced to keep him lean and half-starved; but being a dog, and not having a man's sense, he was sorry."

"It was dull of the brute, certainly," said Mr. Chester, "and very like a brute."

Hugh made no rejoinder, but whistling to his dog, who sprung up at the sound and came jumping and sporting about him, bade his sympathising friend good night.

"Good night," he returned. "Remember; you're safe with me— quite safe. So long as you deserve it, my good fellow, as I hope you always will, you have a friend in me, on whose silence you may rely. Now do be careful of yourself, pray do, and consider what jeopardy you might have stood in. Good night! bless you."

Hugh truckled before the hidden meaning of these words as much as such a being could, and crept out of the door so submissively and subserviently—with an air, in short, so different from that with which he had entered—that his patron on being left alone, smiled more than ever.

"And yet," he said, as he took a pinch of snuff, "I do not like their having hanged his mother. The fellow has a fine eye, and I am sure she was handsome. But very probably she was coarse—red-nosed, perhaps, and had clumsy feet. Aye, it was all for the best, no doubt."

With this comforting reflection, he put on his coat, took a farewell glance at the glass, and summoned his man, who promptly attended, followed by a chair and its two bearers.

"Foh!" said Mr. Chester. "The very atmosphere that centaur has breathed, seems tainted with the cart and ladder. Here, Peak. Bring some scent and sprinkle the floor; and take away the chair he sat upon, and air it; and dash a little of that mixture upon me. I am stifled!"

The man obeyed; and the room and its master being both purified, nothing remained for Mr. Chester but to demand his hat, to fold it jauntily under his arm, to take his seat in the chair and be carried off; humming a fashionable tune.

CHAPTER XXIV

How the accomplished gentleman spent the evening in the midst of a dazzling and brilliant circle; how he enchanted all those with whom he mingled by the grace of his deportment, the politeness of his manner, the vivacity of his conversation, and the sweetness of his voice; how it was observed in every corner, that Chester was a man of that happy disposition that nothing ruffled him, that he was one on whom the world's cares and errors sat lightly as his dress, and in whose smiling face a calm and tranquil mind was constantly reflected; how honest men, who by instinct knew him better, bowed down before him nevertheless, deferred to his every word, and courted his favourable notice; how people, who really had good in them, went with the stream, and fawned and flattered, and approved, and despised themselves while they did so, and yet had not the courage to resist; how, in short, he was one of those who are received and cherished in society (as the phrase is) by scores who individually would shrink from and be repelled by the object of their lavish regard; are things of course, which will suggest themselves. Matter so common-place needs but a passing glance, and there an end.

The despisers of mankind—apart from the mere fools and mimics, of that creed—are of two sorts. They who believe their merit neglected and unappreciated, make up one class; they who receive adulation and flattery, knowing their own worthlessness, compose the other. Be sure that the coldest-hearted misanthropes are ever of this last order.

Mr. Chester sat up in bed next morning, sipping his coffee, and remembering with a kind of contemptuous satisfaction how he had shone last night, and how he had been caressed and courted, when his servant brought in a very small scrap of dirty paper, tightly sealed in two places, on the inside whereof was inscribed in pretty large text these words. "A friend. Desiring of a conference. Immediate. Private. Burn it when you've read it."

"Where in the name of the Gunpowder Plot did you pick up this?" said his master.

It was given him by a person then waiting at the door, the man replied.

"With a cloak and dagger?" said Mr. Chester.

With nothing more threatening about him, it appeared, than a leather apron and a dirty face. "Let him come in." In he came—Mr. Tappertit; with his hair still on end, and a great lock in his hand, which he put down on the floor in the middle of the chamber as if he were about to go through some performances in which it was a necessary agent.

"Sir," said Mr. Tappertit with a low bow, "I thank you for this condescension, and am glad to see you. Pardon the menial office in which I am engaged, sir, and extend your sympathies to one, who, humble as his appearance is, has inn'ard workings far above his station."

Mr. Chester held the bed-curtain farther back, and looked at him with a vague impression that he was some maniac, who had not only broken open the door of his place of confinement, but had brought away the lock. Mr. Tappertit bowed again, and displayed his legs to the best advantage.

"You have heard, sir," said Mr. Tappertit, laying his hand upon his breast, "of G. Varden Locksmith and bell-hanger and repairs neatly executed in town and country, Clerkenwell, London?"

"What then?" asked Mr. Chester.

"I'm his 'prentice, sir."

"What *then?*"

"Ahem!" said Mr. Tappertit. "Would you permit me to shut the door, sir, and will you further, sir, give me your honour bright, that what passes between us is in the strictest confidence?"

Mr. Chester laid himself calmly down in bed again, and turning a perfectly undisturbed face towards the strange apparition, which had by this time closed the door, begged him to speak out, and to be as rational as he could, without putting himself to any very great personal inconvenience.

"In the first place, sir," said Mr. Tappertit, producing a small pocket-handkerchief, and shaking it out of the folds, "as I have not a card about me (for the envy of masters debases us below that level) allow me to offer the best substitute that circumstances will admit of.

If you will take that in your own hand, sir, and cast your eye on the right-hand corner," said Mr. Tappertit, offering it with a graceful air, "you will meet with my credentials."

"Thank you," answered Mr. Chester, politely accepting, and turning to some blood-red characters at one end. " 'Four. Simon Tappertit. One.' Is that the——"

"Without the numbers, sir, that is my name," replied the 'prentice. "They are merely intended as directions to the washerwoman, and have no connection with myself or family. *Your* name, sir," said Mr. Tappertit, looking very hard at his nightcap, "is Chester, I suppose? You needn't pull it off, sir, thank you. I observe E. C. from here. We will take the rest for granted."

"Pray, Mr. Tappertit," said Mr. Chester, "has that complicated piece of ironmongery which you have done me the favour to bring with you, any immediate connection with the business we are to discuss?"

"It has not, sir," rejoined the 'prentice. "It's going to be fitted on a ware'us-door in Thames-street."

"Perhaps, as that is the case," said Mr. Chester, "and as it has a stronger flavour of oil than I usually refresh my bedroom with, you will oblige me so far as to put it outside the door?"

"By all means, sir," said Mr. Tappertit, suiting the action to the word.

"You'll excuse my mentioning it, I hope?"

"Don't apologise, sir, I beg. And now, if you please, to business."

During the whole of this dialogue, Mr. Chester had suffered nothing but his smile of unvarying serenity and politeness to appear upon his face. Sim Tappertit, who had far too good an opinion of himself to suspect that anybody could be playing upon him, thought within himself that this was something like the respect to which he was entitled, and drew a comparison from this courteous demeanour of a stranger, by no means favourable to the worthy locksmith.

"From what passes in our house," said Mr. Tappertit, "I am aware, sir, that your son keeps company with a young lady against your inclinations. Sir, your son has not used me well."

"Mr. Tappertit," said the other, "you grieve me beyond description."

"Thank you, sir," replied the 'prentice. "I'm glad to hear you say so. He's very proud, sir, is your son; very haughty."

"I am afraid he *is* haughty," said Mr. Chester. "Do you know I was really afraid of that before; and you confirm me?"

"To recount the menial offices I've had to do for your son, sir," said Mr. Tappertit; "the chairs I've had to hand him, the coaches I've had to call for him, the numerous degrading duties, wholly unconnected with my indenters, that I've had to do for him, would fill a family Bible. Besides which, sir, he is but a young man himself, and I do not consider 'thank'ee, Sim,' a proper form of address on those occasions."

"Mr. Tappertit, your wisdom is beyond your years. Pray go on."

"I thank you for your good opinion, sir," said Sim, much gratified, "and will endeavour so to do. Now, sir, on this account (and perhaps for another reason or two which I needn't go into) I am on your side. And what I tell you is this—that as long as our people go backwards and forwards, to and fro, up and down, to that there jolly old Maypole, lettering, and messaging, and fetching and carrying, you couldn't help your son keeping company with that young lady by deputy,—not if he was minded night and day by all the Horse Guards, and every man of 'em in the very fullest uniform."

Mr. Tappertit stopped to take breath after this, and then started fresh again.

"Now, sir, I am a coming to the point. You will inquire of me, 'how is this to be prevented?' I'll tell you how. If an honest, civil, smiling gentleman like you—"

"Mr. Tappertit—really—"

"No, no, I'm serious," rejoined the 'prentice, "I am, upon my soul. If an honest, civil, smiling gentleman like you, was to talk but ten minutes to our old woman—that's Mrs. Varden—and flatter her up a bit, you'd gain her over for ever. Then there's this point got—that her daughter Dolly,"—here a flush came over Mr. Tappertit's face— "wouldn't be allowed to be a go-between from that time forward; and till that point's got, there's nothing ever will prevent her. Mind that."

"Mr. Tappertit, your knowledge of human nature—"

"Wait a minute," said Sim, folding his arms with a dreadful calmness. "Now I come to THE point. Sir, there is a villain at that Maypole, a monster in human shape, a vagabond of the deepest dye, that unless you get rid of, and have kidnapped and carried off at the very least—nothing less will do—will marry your son to that young woman, as certainly and as surely as if he was the Archbishop of Canterbury himself. He will, sir, for the hatred and malice that he bears to you; let alone the pleasure of doing a bad action, which to him is its own reward. If you knew how this chap, this Joseph Willet—that's his name—comes backwards and forwards to our house, libelling, and denouncing, and threatening you, and how I shudder when I hear him, you'd hate him worse than I do,—worse than I do, sir," said Mr. Tappertit wildly, putting his hair up straighter, and making a crunching noise with his teeth; "if such a thing be possible."

"A little private vengeance in this, Mr. Tappertit?"

"Private vengeance, sir, or public sentiment, or both combined— destroy him," said Mr. Tappertit. "Miggs says so too. Miggs and me both say so. We can't bear the plotting and undermining that takes place. Our souls recoil from it. Barnaby Rudge and Mrs. Rudge are in it likewise; but the villain, Joseph Willet, is the ringleader. Their plottings and schemes are known to me and Miggs. If you want information of 'em, apply to us. Put Joseph Willet down, sir. Destroy him. Crush him. And be happy."

With these words, Mr. Tappertit, who seemed to expect no reply,

and to hold it as a necessary consequence of his eloquence that his
hearer should be utterly stunned, dumbfoundered, and overwhelmed,
folded his arms so that the palm of each hand rested on the opposite
shoulder, and disappeared after the manner of those mysterious
warners of whom he had read in cheap story-books.

"That fellow," said Mr. Chester, relaxing his face when he was
fairly gone, "is good practice. I *have* some command of my features,
beyond all doubt. He fully confirms what I suspected, though;
and blunt tools are sometimes found of use, where sharper instruments would fail. I fear I may be obliged to make great havoc
among these worthy people. A troublesome necessity! I quite feel for
them."

With that he fell into a quiet slumber:—subsided into such a gentle,
pleasant sleep, that it was quite infantine.

CHAPTER XXV

LEAVING the favoured, and well-received, and flattered of the
world; him of the world most worldly, who never compromised himself by an ungentlemanly action, and never was guilty of a manly
one; to lie smilingly asleep—for even sleep, working but little change
in his dissembling face, became with him a piece of cold, conventional
hypocrisy—we follow in the steps of two slow travellers on foot,
making towards Chigwell.

Barnaby and his mother. Grip in their company, of course.

The widow, to whom each painful mile seemed longer than the
last, toiled wearily along; while Barnaby, yielding to every inconstant
impulse, fluttered here and there, now leaving her far behind, now
lingering far behind himself, now darting into some by-lane or path
and leaving her to pursue her way alone, until he stealthily emerged
again and came upon her with a wild shout of merriment, as his wayward and capricious nature prompted. Now he would call to her
from the topmost branch of some high tree by the roadside; now
using his tall staff as a leaping-pole, come flying over ditch or hedge
or five-barred gate; now run with surprising swiftness for a mile or
more on the straight road, and halting, sport upon a patch of grass
with Grip till she came up. These were his delights; and when his
patient mother heard his merry voice, or looked into his flushed and
healthy face, she would not have abated them by one sad word or
murmur, though each had been to her a source of suffering in the
same degree as it was to him of pleasure.

It is something to look upon enjoyment, so that it be free and wild
and in the face of nature, though it is but the enjoyment of an idiot.
It is something to know that Heaven has left the capacity of gladness
in such a creature's breast; it is something to be assured that, however lightly men may crush that faculty in their fellows, the Great
Creator of mankind imparts it even to his despised and slighted
work. Who would not rather see a poor idiot happy in the sunlight,
than a wise man pining in a darkened jail!

Ye men of gloom and austerity, who paint the face of Infinite Benevolence with an eternal frown; read in the Everlasting Book, wide open to your view, the lesson it would teach. Its pictures are not in black and sombre hues, but bright and glowing tints; its music—save when ye drown it—is not in sighs and groans, but songs and cheerful sounds. Listen to the million voices in the summer air, and find one dismal as your own. Remember, if ye can, the sense of hope and pleasure which every glad return of day awakens in the breast of all your kind who have not changed their nature; and learn some wisdom even from the witless, when their hearts are lifted up they know not why, by all the mirth and happiness it brings.

The widow's breast was full of care, was laden heavily with secret dread and sorrow; but her boy's gaiety of heart gladdened her, and beguiled the long journey. Sometimes he would bid her lean upon his arm, and would keep beside her steadily for a short distance; but it was more his nature to be rambling to and fro, and she better liked to see him free and happy, even than to have him near her, because she loved him better than herself.

She had quitted the place to which they were travelling, directly after the event which had changed her whole existence; and for two-and-twenty years had never had courage to revisit it. It was her native village. How many recollections crowded on her mind when it appeared in sight!

Two-and-twenty years. Her boy's whole life and history. The last time she looked back upon those roofs among the trees, she carried him in her arms, an infant. How often since that time had she sat beside him night and day watching for the dawn of mind that never came; how had she feared, and doubted, and yet hoped, long after conviction forced itself upon her! The little stratagems she had devised to try him, the little tokens he had given in his childish way—not of dulness but of something infinitely worse, so ghastly and unchild-like in its cunning—came back as vividly as if but yesterday had intervened. The room in which they used to be; the spot in which his cradle stood; he, old and elfin-like in face, but ever dear to her, gazing at her with a wild and vacant eye, and crooning some uncouth song as she sat by and rocked him; every circumstance of his infancy came thronging back, and the most trivial, perhaps, the most distinctly.

His older childhood, too; the strange imaginings he had; his terror of certain senseless things—familiar objects he endowed with life; the slow and gradual breaking out of that one horror, in which, before his birth, his darkened intellect began; how, in the midst of all, she had found some hope and comfort in his being unlike another child, and had gone on almost believing in the slow development of his mind until he grew a man, and then his childhood was complete and lasting; one after another, all these old thoughts sprung up within her, strong after their long slumber and bitterer than ever.

She took his arm and they hurried through the village street. It was the same as it was wont to be in old times, yet different too, and wore another air. The change was in herself, not it; but she never thought of that, and wondered at its alteration, and where it lay, and what it was.

The people all knew Barnaby, and the children of the place came flocking round him—as she remembered to have done with their fathers and mothers round some silly beggarman, when a child herself. None of them knew her; they passed each well-remembered house, and yard, and homestead; and striking into the fields, were soon alone again.

The Warren was the end of their journey. Mr. Haredale was walking in the garden, and seeing them as they passed the iron gate, unlocked it, and bade them enter that way.

"At length you have mustered heart to visit the old place," he said to the widow. "I am glad you have."

"For the first time, and the last, sir," she replied.

"The first for many years, but not the last?"

"The very last."

"You mean," said Mr. Haredale, regarding her with some surprise, "that having made this effort, you are resolved not to persevere and are determined to relapse? This is unworthy of you. I have often told you, you should return here. You would be happier here than elsewhere, I know. As to Barnaby, it's quite his home."

"And Grip's," said Barnaby, holding the basket open. The raven hopped gravely out, and perching on his shoulder and addressing himself to Mr. Haredale, cried—as a hint, perhaps, that some temperate refreshment would be acceptable—"Polly put the ket-tle on, we'll all have tea!"

"Hear me, Mary," said Mr. Haredale kindly, as he motioned her to walk with him towards the house. "Your life has been an example of patience and fortitude, except in this one particular which has often given me great pain. It is enough to know that you were cruelly involved in the calamity which deprived me of an only brother, and Emma of her father, without being obliged to suppose (as I sometimes am) that you associate us with the author of our joint misfortunes."

"Associate *you* with him, sir!" she cried.

"Indeed," said Mr. Haredale, "I think you do. I almost believe that because your husband was bound by so many ties to our relation, and died in his service and defence, you have come in some sort to connect us with his murder."

"Alas!" she answered. "You little know my heart, sir. You little know the truth!"

"It is natural you should do so; it is very probable you may, without being conscious of it," said Mr. Haredale, speaking more to himself than her. "We are a fallen house. Money, dispensed with the most lavish hand, would be a poor recompense for sufferings like yours; and thinly scattered by hands so pinched and tied as ours, it becomes a miserable mockery. I feel it so, God knows," he added, hastily. "Why should I wonder if she does!"

"You do me wrong, dear sir, indeed," she rejoined with great earnestness; "and yet when you come to hear what I desire your leave to say—"

"I shall find my doubts confirmed?" he said, observing that she faltered and became confused. "Well!"

He quickened his pace for a few steps, but fell back again to her side, and said:

"And you come all this way at last, solely to speak to me?"

She answered, "Yes."

"A curse," he muttered, "upon the wretched state of us proud beggars, from whom the poor and rich are equally at a distance; the one being forced to treat us with a show of cold respect; the other condescending to us in their every deed and word, and keeping more aloof, the nearer they approach us.—Why, if it were pain to you (as it must have been) to break for this slight purpose the chain of habit forged through two-and-twenty years, could you not let me know your wish, and beg me to come to you?"

"There was not time, sir," she rejoined. "I took my resolution but last night, and taking it, felt that I must not lose a day—a day! an hour—in having speech with you."

They had by this time reached the house. Mr. Haredale paused for a moment and looked at her as if surprised by the energy of her manner. Observing, however, that she took no heed of him, but glanced up, shuddering, at the old walls with which such horrors were connected in her mind, he led her by a private stair into his library, where Emma was seated in a window, reading.

The young lady, seeing who approached, hastily rose and laid aside her book, and with many kind words, and not without tears, gave her a warm and earnest welcome. But the widow shrunk from her embrace, as though she feared her, and sunk down trembling on a chair.

"It is the return to this place after so long an absence," said Emma gently. "Pray ring, dear uncle—or stay—Barnaby will run himself and ask for wine—"

"Not for the world," she cried. "It would have another taste—I could not touch it. I want but a minute's rest. Nothing but that."

Miss Haredale stood beside her chair, regarding her with silent pity. She remained for a little time quite still; then rose and turned to Mr. Haredale, who had sat down in his easy chair, and was contemplating her with fixed attention.

The tale connected with the mansion borne in mind, it seemed, as has been already said, the chosen theatre for such a deed as it had known. The room in which this group were now assembled— hard by the very chamber where the act was done—dull, dark, and sombre; heavy with worm-eaten books; deadened and shut in by faded hangings, muffling every sound; shadowed mournfully by trees whose rustling boughs gave ever and anon a spectral knocking at the glass; wore, beyond all others in the house, a ghostly, gloomy air. Nor were the group assembled there, unfitting tenants of the spot. The widow, with her marked and startling face and downcast eyes; Mr. Haredale stern and despondent ever; his niece beside him, like, yet most unlike, the picture of her father, which gazed reproachfully down upon them from the blackened wall; Barnaby, with his vacant look and restless eye; were all in keeping with the place, and actors in the legend. Nay, the very raven, who had hopped upon the table and with the air of some old necromancer appeared to be profoundly studying a great folio volume that lay open on a desk, was strictly in unison with the rest, and looked like the embodied spirit of evil biding his time of mischief.

"I scarcely know," said the widow, breaking silence, "how to begin. You will think my mind disordered."

"The whole tenor of your quiet and reproachless life since you were last here," returned Mr. Haredale, mildly, "shall bear witness for you. Why do you fear to awaken such a suspicion? You do not speak to strangers. You have not to claim our interest or consideration for the first time. Be more yourself. Take heart. Any advice or assistance that I can give you, you know is yours of right, and freely yours."

"What if I came, sir," she rejoined, "I who have but one other friend on earth, to reject your aid from this moment, and to say that henceforth I launch myself upon the world, alone and unassisted, to sink or swim as Heaven may decree!"

"You would have, if you came to me for such a purpose," said Mr. Haredale calmly, "some reason to assign for conduct so extraordinary, which—if one may entertain the possibility of anything so wild and strange—would have its weight of course."

"That, sir," she answered, "is the misery of my distress. I can give no reason whatever. My own bare word is all that I can offer. It is my duty, my imperative and bounden duty. If I did not discharge it, I should be a base and guilty wretch. Having said that, my lips are sealed, and I can say no more."

As though she felt relieved at having said so much, and had nerved herself to the remainder of her task, she spoke from this time with a firmer voice and heightened courage.

"Heaven is my witness, as my own heart is—and yours, dear young lady, will speak for me, I know—that I have lived, since that time we all have bitter reason to remember, in unchanging devotion and gratitude to this family. Heaven is my witness that go where I may, I shall preserve those feelings unimpaired. And it is my witness, too, that they alone impel me to the course I must take, and from which nothing now shall turn me, as I hope for mercy."

"These are strange riddles," said Mr. Haredale.

"In this world, sir," she replied, "they may, perhaps, never be explained. In another, the Truth will be discovered in its own good time. And may that time," she added in a low voice, "be far distant!"

"Let me be sure," said Mr. Haredale, "that I understand you, for I am doubtful of my own senses. Do you mean that you are resolved voluntarily to deprive yourself of those means of support you have received from us so long—that you are determined to resign the annuity we settled on you twenty years ago—to leave house, and home, and goods, and begin life anew—and this, for some secret reason or monstrous fancy which is incapable of explanation, which only now exists, and has been dormant all this time? In the name of God, under what delusion are you labouring?"

"As I am deeply thankful," she made answer, "for the kindness of those, alive and dead, who have owned this house; and as I would not have its roof fall down and crush me, or its very walls drip blood, my name being spoken in their hearing; I never will again subsist upon their bounty, or let it help me to subsistence. You do not know," she added, suddenly, "to what uses it may be applied; into what hands it may pass. I do, and I renounce it."

"Surely," said Mr. Haredale, "its uses rest with you."

"They did. They rest with me no longer. It may be—it *is*—devoted to purposes that mock the dead in their graves. It never can prosper with me. It will bring some other heavy judgment on the head of my dear son, whose innocence will suffer for his mother's guilt."

"What words are these!" cried Mr. Haredale, regarding her with wonder. "Among what associates have you fallen? Into what guilt have you ever been betrayed?"

"I am guilty, and yet innocent; wrong, yet right; good in intention, though constrained to shield and aid the bad. Ask me no more questions, sir; but believe that I am rather to be pitied than condemned. I must leave my house tomorrow, for while I stay there, it is haunted. My future dwelling, if I am to live in peace, must be a secret. If my poor boy should ever stray this way, do not tempt him to disclose it or have him watched when he returns; for if we are hunted, we must fly again. And now this load is off my mind I beseech you—and you, dear Miss Haredale, too—to trust me if you can, and think of me kindly as you have been used to do. If I die and cannot tell my secret even then (for that may come to pass), it will sit the lighter on my breast in that hour for this day's work; and on that day, and every day until it comes, I will pray for and thank you both, and trouble you no more."

With that, she would have left them, but they detained her, and with many soothing words and kind entreaties, besought her to consider what she did, and above all to repose more freely upon them, and say what weighed so sorely on her mind. Finding her deaf to their persuasions, Mr. Haredale suggested, as a last resource, that she should confide in Emma, of whom, as a young person and one of her own sex, she might stand in less dread than of himself. From this proposal, however, she recoiled with the same indescribable repugnance she had manifested when they met. The utmost that could be wrung from her was, a promise that she would receive Mr. Haredale at her own house next evening, and in the mean time reconsider her determination and their dissuasions—though any change on her part, as she told them, was quite hopeless. This condition made at last, they reluctantly suffered her to depart, since she would neither eat nor drink within the house; and she, and Barnaby, and Grip, accordingly went out as they had come, by the private stair and garden-gate; seeing and being seen of no one by the way.

It was remarkable in the raven that during the whole interview he had kept his eye on his book with exactly the air of a very sly human rascal, who, under the mask of pretending to read hard, was listening to everything. He still appeared to have the conversation very strongly in his mind, for although, when they were alone again, he issued orders for the instant preparation of innumerable kettles for purposes of tea, he was thoughtful, and rather seemed to do so from an abstract sense of duty, than with any regard to making himself agreeable, or being what is commonly called good company.

They were to return by the coach. As there was an interval of full two hours before it started, and they needed rest and some refreshment, Barnaby begged hard for a visit to the Maypole. But his mother, who had no wish to be recognised by any of those who had known her long ago, and who feared besides that Mr. Haredale might, on second thoughts, despatch some messenger to that place of entertainment in quest of her, proposed to wait in the churchyard instead. As it was easy for Barnaby to buy and carry thither such humble viands as they required, he cheerfully assented, and in the churchyard they sat down to take their frugal dinner.

Here again, the raven was in a highly reflective state; walking up and down when he had dined, with an air of elderly complacency which was strongly suggestive of his having his hands under his coat-tails; and appearing to read the tombstones with a very critical taste. Sometimes, after a long inspection of an epitaph, he would strop his beak upon the grave to which it referred, and cry in his hoarse tones, "I'm a devil, I'm a devil, I'm a devil!" but whether he addressed his observations to any supposed person below, or merely threw them off as a general remark, is matter of uncertainty.

It was a quiet pretty spot, but a sad one for Barnaby's mother; for Mr. Reuben Haredale lay there, and near the vault in which his ashes rested, was a stone to the memory of her own husband, with a brief inscription recording how and when he had lost his life. She sat here, thoughtful and apart, until their time was out, and the distant horn told that the coach was coming.

Barnaby, who had been sleeping on the grass, sprung up quickly at the sound; and Grip, who appeared to understand it equally well, walked into his basket straightway, entreating society in general (as though he intended a kind of satire upon them in connection with churchyards) never to say die on any terms. They were soon on the coach-top and rolling along the road.

It went round by the Maypole, and stopped at the door. Joe was from home, and Hugh came sluggishly out to hand up the parcel that it called for. There was no fear of old John coming out. They could see him from the coach-roof fast asleep in his cosy bar. It was a part of John's character. He made a point of going to sleep at the coach's time. He despised gadding about; he looked upon coaches as things that ought to be indicted; as disturbers of the peace of mankind; as restless, bustling, busy, horn-blowing contrivances, quite beneath the dignity of men, and only suited to giddy girls that did nothing but chatter and go a-shopping. "We know nothing about coaches here, sir," John would say, if any unlucky stranger made inquiry touching the offensive vehicles; "we don't book for 'em; we'd rather not; they're more trouble than they're worth, with their noise and rattle. If you like to wait for 'em you can; but we don't know anything about 'em; they may call and they may not— there's a carrier—he was looked upon as quite good enough for us, when *I* was a boy."

She dropped her veil as Hugh climbed up, and while he hung behind, and talked to Barnaby in whispers. But neither he nor any other person spoke to her, or noticed her, or had any curiosity about her; and so, an alien, she visited and left the village where she had been born, and had lived a merry child, a comely girl, a happy wife— where she had known all her enjoyment of life, and had entered on its hardest sorrows.

CHAPTER XXVI

"AND you're not surprised to hear this, Varden?" said Mr. Haredale. "Well! You and she have always been the best friends, and you should understand her if anybody does."

"I ask your pardon, sir," rejoined the locksmith. "I didn't say I understood her. I wouldn't have the presumption to say that of any woman. It's not so easily done. But I am not so much surprised, sir, as you expected me to be, certainly."

"May I ask why not, my good friend?"

"I have seen, sir," returned the locksmith with evident reluctance, "I have seen in connection with her, something that has filled me with distrust and uneasiness. She has made bad friends, how, or when, I don't know; but that her house is a refuge for one robber and cut-throat at least I am certain. There sir! Now it's out."

"Varden!"

"My own eyes, sir, are my witnesses, and for her sake I would be willingly half-blind, if I could but have the pleasure of mistrusting 'em. I have kept the secret till now, and it will go no further than yourself, I know; but I tell you that with my own eyes—broad awake—I saw, in the passage of her house one evening after dark, the highwayman who robbed and wounded Mr. Edward Chester, and on the same night threatened me."

"And you made no effort to detain him?" said Mr. Haredale quickly.

"Sir," returned the locksmith, "she herself prevented me—held me, with all her strength, and hung about me until he had got clear off." And having gone so far, he related circumstantially all that had passed upon the night in question.

This dialogue was held in a low tone in the locksmith's little parlour, into which honest Gabriel had shown his visitor on his arrival. Mr. Haredale had called upon him to entreat his company to the widow's, that he might have the assistance of his persuasion and influence; and out of this circumstance the conversation had arisen.

"I forebore," said Gabriel, "from repeating one word of this to anybody, as it could do her no good and might do her great harm. I thought and hoped, to say the truth, that she would come to me, and talk to me about it, and tell me how it was; but though I have purposely put myself in her way more than once or twice, she has never touched upon the subject—except by a look. And indeed," said the good-natured locksmith, "there was a good deal in the look, more than could have been put into a great many words. It said among other matters 'Don't ask me anything' so imploringly, that I didn't ask her anything. You'll think me an old fool, I know, sir. If it's any relief to call me one, pray do."

"I am greatly disturbed by what you tell me," said Mr. Haredale, after a silence. "What meaning do you attach to it?"

The locksmith shook his head, and looked doubtfully out of window at the failing light.

"She cannot have married again," said Mr. Haredale.

"Not without our knowledge surely, sir."

"She may have done so, in the fear that it would lead, if known, to some objection or estrangement. Suppose she married incautiously —it is not improbable, for her existence has been a lonely and monotonous one for many years—and the man turned out a ruffian, she would be anxious to screen him, and yet would revolt from his crimes. This might be. It bears strongly on the whole drift of her discourse yesterday, and would quite explain her conduct. Do you suppose Barnaby is privy to these circumstances?"

"Quite impossible to say, sir," returned the locksmith, shaking his head again: "and next to impossible to find out from him. If what you suppose is really the case, I tremble for the lad—a notable person, sir, to put to bad uses—"

"It is not possible, Varden," said Mr. Haredale, in a still lower tone of voice than he had spoken yet, "that we have been blinded and deceived by this woman from the beginning? It is not possible that this connection was formed in her husband's lifetime, and led to his and my brother's—"

"Good God, sir," cried Gabriel, interrupting him, "don't entertain such dark thoughts for a moment. Five-and-twenty years ago, where was there a girl like her? A gay, handsome, laughing, bright-eyed damsel! Think what she was, sir. It makes my heart ache now, even now, though I'm an old man, with a woman for a daughter, to think what she was and what she is. We all change, but that's with Time; Time does his work honestly, and I don't mind him. A fig for Time, sir. Use him well, and he's a hearty fellow, and scorns to have you at a disadvantage. But care and suffering (and those have changed her) are devils, sir—secret, stealthy, undermining devils—who tread down the brightest flowers in Eden, and do more havoc in a month than Time does in a year. Picture to yourself for one minute what Mary was before they went to work with her fresh heart and face—do her that justice—and say whether such a thing is possible."

"You're a good fellow, Varden," said Mr. Haredale, "and are quite right. I have brooded on that subject so long, that every breath of suspicion carries me back to it. You are quite right."

"It isn't, sir," cried the locksmith with brightened eyes, and sturdy honest voice; "it isn't because I courted her before Rudge, and failed, that I say she was too good for him. She would have been as much too good for me. But she *was* too good for him; he wasn't free and frank enough for her. I don't reproach his memory with it, poor fellow; I only want to put her before you as she really was. For myself, I'll keep her old picture in my mind; and thinking of that, and what has altered her, I'll stand her friend, and try to win her back to peace. And damme, sir," cried Gabriel, "with your pardon for the word, I'd do the same if she had married fifty highwaymen in a twelvemonth; and think it in the Protestant Manual too, though Martha said it wasn't, tooth and nail, till doomsday!"

If the dark little parlour had been filled with a dense fog, which, clearing away in an instant, left it all radiance and brightness, it could not have been more suddenly cheered than by this outbreak on the part of the hearty locksmith. In a voice nearly as full and round as his own, Mr. Haredale cried "Well said!" and bade him come away without more parley; the locksmith complied right willingly; and both getting into a hackney coach which was waiting at the door, drove off straightway.

They alighted at the street corner, and dismissing their conveyance, walked to the house. To their first knock at the door there was no response. A second met with the like result. But in answer to the third, which was of a more vigorous kind, the parlour window-sash was gently raised, and a musical voice cried:

"Haredale, my dear fellow, I am extremely glad to see you. How very much you have improved in your appearance since our last meeting! I never saw you looking better. *How* do you do?"

Mr. Haredale turned his eyes towards the casement whence the voice proceeded, though there was no need to do so, to recognise the speaker, and Mr. Chester waved his hand, and smiled a courteous welcome.

"The door will be opened immediately," he said. "There is nobody but a very dilapidated female to perform such offices. You will excuse her infirmities? If she were in a more elevated station of society, she would be gouty. Being but a hewer of wood and drawer of water, she is rheumatic. My dear Haredale, these are natural class distinctions, depend upon it."

Mr. Haredale, whose face resumed its lowering and distrustful look the moment he heard the voice, inclined his head stiffly, and turned his back upon the speaker.

"Not opened yet," said Mr. Chester. "Dear me! I hope the aged soul has not caught her foot in some unlucky cobweb by the way. She is there at last! Come in, I beg!"

Mr. Haredale entered, followed by the locksmith. Turning with a look of great astonishment to the old woman who had opened the door, he inquired for Mrs. Rudge—for Barnaby. They were both gone, she replied, wagging her ancient head, for good. There was a gentleman in the parlour, who perhaps could tell them more. That was all *she* knew.

"Pray, sir," said Mr. Haredale, presenting himself before this new tenant, "where is the person whom I came here to see?"

"My dear friend," he returned, "I have not the least idea."

"Your trifling is ill-timed," retorted the other in a suppressed tone and voice, "and its subject ill-chosen. Reserve it for those who are your friends, and do not expend it on me. I lay no claim to the distinction, and have the self-denial to reject it."

"My dear, good sir," said Mr. Chester, "you are heated with walking. Sit down, I beg. Our friend is—"

"Is but a plain honest man," returned Mr. Haredale, "and quite unworthy of your notice."

"Gabriel Varden by name, sir," said the locksmith bluntly.

"A worthy English yeoman!" said Mr. Chester. "A most worthy yeoman, of whom I have frequently heard my son Ned—darling fellow—speak, and have often wished to see. Varden, my good friend, I am glad to know you. You wonder now," he said, turning languidly to Mr. Haredale, "to see me here. Now, I am sure you do."

Mr. Haredale glanced at him—not fondly or admiringly—smiled, and held his peace.

"The mystery is solved in a moment," said Mr. Chester; "in a moment. Will you step aside with me one instant? You remember our little compact in reference to Ned, and your dear niece, Haredale? You remember the list of assistants in their innocent intrigue? You remember these two people being among them? My dear fellow, congratulate yourself, and me. I have bought them off."

"You have done what?" said Mr. Haredale.

"Bought them of," returned his smiling friend. "I have found it necessary to take some active steps towards setting this boy and girl attachment quite at rest, and have begun by removing these two agents. You are surprised? Who *can* withstand the influence of a little money! They wanted it, and have been bought off. We have nothing more to fear from them. They are gone."

"Gone!" echoed Mr. Haredale. "Where?"

"My dear fellow—and you must permit me to say again, that you never looked so young; so positively boyish as you do to-night—the Lord knows where; I believe Columbus himself wouldn't find them. Between you and me they have their hidden reasons, but upon that point I have pledged myself to secrecy. She appointed to see you here to-night I know, but found it inconvenient, and couldn't wait.

Here is the key of the door. I am afraid you'll find it inconveniently large; but as the tenement is yours, your good-nature will excuse that, Haredale, I am certain!''

CHAPTER XXVII

MR. HAREDALE stood in the widow's parlour with the door-key in his hand, gazing by turns at Mr. Chester and at Gabriel Varden, and occasionally glancing downward at the key as in the hope that of its own accord it would unlock the mystery; until Mr. Chester, putting on his hat and gloves, and sweetly inquiring whether they were walking in the same direction, recalled him to himself.

"No," he said. "Our roads diverge—widely, as you know. For the present, I shall remain here."

"You will be hipped, Haredale; you will be miserable, melancholy, utterly wretched," returned the other. "It's a place of the very last description for a man of your temper. I know it will make you very miserable."

"Let it," said Mr. Haredale, sitting down; "and thrive upon the thought. Good night!"

Feigning to be wholly unconscious of the abrupt wave of the hand which rendered this farewell tantamount to a dismissal, Mr. Chester retorted with a bland and heartfelt benediction, and inquired of Gabriel in what direction *he* was going.

"Yours, sir, would be too much honour for the like of me," replied the locksmith, hesitating.

"I wish you to remain here a little while, Varden," said Mr. Haredale, without looking towards them. "I have a word or two to say to you."

"I will not intrude upon your conference another moment," said Mr. Chester with inconceivable politeness. "May it be satisfactory to you both! God bless you!" So saying, and bestowing upon the locksmith a most refulgent smile, he left them.

"A deplorably constituted creature, that rugged person," he said, as he walked along the street; "he is an atrocity that carries its own punishment along with it—a bear that gnaws himself. And here is one of the inestimable advantages of having a perfect command over one's inclinations. I have been tempted in these two short interviews, to draw upon that fellow, fifty times. Five men in six would have yielded to the impulse. By suppressing mine, I wound him deeper and more keenly than if I were the best swordsman in all Europe, and he the worst. You are the wise man's very last resource," he said, tapping the hilt of his weapon; "we can but appeal to you when all else is said and done. To come to you before, and thereby spare our adversaries so much, is a barbarian mode of warfare, quite unworthy of any man with the remotest pretensions to delicacy of feeling, or refinement."

He smiled so very pleasantly as he communed with himself after this manner, that a beggar was emboldened to follow for alms, and to dog his footsteps for some distance. He was gratified by the circumstance, feeling it complimentary to his power of feature, and as a reward suffered the man to follow him until he called a chair, when he graciously dismissed him with a fervent blessing.

"Which is as easy as cursing," he wisely added, as he took his seat, "and more becoming to the face.—To Clerkenwell, my good creatures, if you please!" The chairmen were rendered quite vivacious by having such a courteous burden, and to Clerkenwell they went at a fair round trot.

Alighting at a certain point he had indicated to them upon the road, and paying them something less than they expected from a fare of such gentle speech, he turned into the street in which the locksmith dwelt, and presently stood beneath the shadow of the Golden Key. Mr. Tappertit, who was hard at work by lamp-light, in a corner of the workshop, remained unconscious of his presence until a hand upon his shoulder made him start and turn his head.

"Industry," said Mr. Chester, "is the soul of business, and the keystone of prosperity. Mr. Tappertit, I shall expect you to invite me to dinner when you are Lord Mayor of London."

"Sir," returned the 'prentice, laying down his hammer, and rubbing his nose on the back of a very sooty hand, "I scorn the Lord Mayor and everything that belongs to him. We must have another state of society, sir, before you catch me being Lord Mayor. How de do, sir?"

"The better, Mr. Tappertit, for looking into your ingenuous face once more. I hope you are well."

"I am as well, sir," said Sim, standing up to get nearer to his ear, and whispering hoarsely, "as any man can be under the aggravations to which I am exposed. My life's a burden to me. If it wasn't for wengeance, I'd play at pitch and toss with it on the losing hazard."

"Is Mrs. Varden at home?" said Mr. Chester.

"Sir," returned Sim, eyeing him over with a look of concentrated expression—"she is. Did you wish to see her?"

Mr. Chester nodded.

"Then come this way, sir," said Sim, wiping his face upon his apron. "Follow me, sir.—Would you permit me to whisper in your ear, one half a second?"

"By all means."

Mr. Tappertit raised himself on tiptoe, applied his lips to Mr. Chester's ear, drew back his head without saying anything, looked hard at him, applied them to his ear again, again drew back, and finally whispered—"The name is Joseph Willet. Hush! I say no more."

Having said that much, he beckoned the visitor with a mysterious aspect to follow him to the parlour door, where he announced him in the voice of a gentleman usher. "Mr. Chester."

"And not Mr. Ed'dard, mind," said Sim, looking into the door again, and adding this by way of postscript in his own person; "it's his father."

"But do not let his father," said Mr. Chester, advancing hat in hand, as he observed the effect of this last explanatory announce-

ment, "do not let his father be any check or restraint on your
domestic occupation, Miss Varden."

"Oh! Now! There! An't I always a-saying it!" exclaimed Miggs,
clapping her hands. "If he an't been and took Missis for her own
daughter. Well, she *do* look like it, that she do. Only think of that,
mim!"

"Is it possible," said Mr. Chester in his softest tones, "that this is
Mrs. Varden! I am amazed. That is not your daughter, Mrs. Varden?
No, no. Your sister."

"My daughter, indeed, sir," returned Mrs. V., blushing with great
juvenility.

"Ah, Mrs. Varden!" cried the visitor. "Ah, ma'am—humanity is
indeed a happy lot, when we can repeat ourselves in others, and still
be young as they. You must allow me to salute you—the custom of
the country, my dear madam—your daughter too."

Dolly showed some reluctance to perform this ceremony, but was
sharply reproved by Mrs. Varden, who insisted on her undergoing it
that minute. For pride, she said with great severity, was one of the
seven deadly sins, and humility and lowliness of heart were virtues.
Wherefore she desired that Dolly would be kissed immediately, on
pain of her just displeasure; at the same time giving her to understand that whatever she saw her mother do, she might safely do herself, without being at the trouble of any reasoning or reflection on the
subject—which, indeed, was offensive and undutiful, and in direct
contravention of the church catechism.

Thus admonished, Dolly complied, though by no means willingly;
for there was a broad, bold look of admiration in Mr. Chester's face,
refined and polished though it sought to be, which distressed her very
much. As she stood with downcast eyes, not liking to look up and
meet his, he gazed upon her with an approving air, and then turned to
her mother.

"My friend Gabriel (whose acquaintance I only made this very
evening) should be a happy man, Mrs. Varden."

"Ah!" sighed Mrs. V., shaking her head.

"Ah!" echoed Miggs.

"Is that the case?" said Mr. Chester, compassionately. "Dear me!"

"Master has no intentions, sir," murmured Miggs as she sidled up
to him, "but to be as grateful as his natur will let him, for everythink
he owns which it is in his powers to appreciate. But we never, sir"—
said Miggs, looking sideways at Mrs. Varden, and interlarding her
discourse with a sigh—"we never know the full value of *some* wines
and fig-trees till we lose 'em. So much the worse, sir, for them as has
the slighting of 'em on their consciences when they're gone to be in
full blow elsewhere." And Miss Miggs cast up her eyes to signify where
that might be.

As Mrs. Varden distinctly heard, and was intended to hear, all
that Miggs said, and as these words appeared to convey in meta-
phorical terms a presage or foreboding that she would at some early
period droop beneath her trials and take an easy flight towards the

stars, she immediately began to languish, and taking a volume of the Manual from a neighbouring table, leant her arm upon it as though she were Hope and that her Anchor. Mr. Chester perceiving this, and seeing how the volume was lettered on the back, took it gently from her hand, and turned the fluttering leaves.

"My favourite book, dear madam. How often, how very often in his early life—before he can remember"—(this clause was strictly true)—"have I deduced little easy moral lessons from its pages, for my dear son Ned! You know Ned?"

Mrs. Varden had that honour, and a fine affable young gentleman he was.

"You're a mother, Mrs. Varden," said Mr. Chester, taking a pinch of snuff, "and you know what I, as a father, feel, when he is praised. He gives me some uneasiness—much uneasiness—he's of a roving nature, ma'am—from flower to flower—from sweet to sweet—but his is the butterfly time of life, and we must not be hard upon such trifling."

He glanced at Dolly. She was attending evidently to what he said. Just what he desired!

"The only thing I object to in this little trait of Ned's is," said Mr. Chester, "—and the mention of his name reminds me, by the way, that I am about to beg the favour of a minute's talk with you alone —the only thing I object to in it, is, that it *does* partake of insincerity. Now, however I may attempt to disguise the fact from myself in my affection for Ned, still I always revert to this—that if we are not sincere, we are nothing. Nothing upon earth. Let us be sincere, my dear madam—"

"—and Protestant," murmured Mrs. Varden.

"—and Protestant above all things. Let us be sincere and Protestant, strictly moral, strictly just (though always with a leaning towards mercy), strictly honest, and strictly true, and we gain—it is a slight point, certainly, but still it is something tangible; we throw up a groundwork and foundation, so to speak, of goodness, on which we may afterwards erect some worthy superstructure."

Now, to be sure, Mrs. Varden thought, here is a perfect character. Here is a meek, righteous, thoroughgoing Christian, who, having mastered all these qualities, so difficult of attainment; who, having dropped a pinch of salt on the tails of all the cardinal virtues, and caught them every one; makes light of their possession, and pants for more morality. For the good woman never doubted (as many good men and women never do), that this slighting kind of profession, this setting so little store by great matters, this seeming to say, "I am not proud, I am what you hear, but I consider myself no better than other people; let us change the subject, pray"—was perfectly genuine and true. He so contrived it, and said it in that way that it appeared to have been forced from him, and its effect was marvellous.

Aware of the impression he had made—few men were quicker than he at such discoveries—Mr. Chester followed up the blow by propounding certain virtuous maxims, somewhat vague and general in their nature, doubtless, and occasionally partaking of the character of truisms, worn a little out at elbow, but delivered in so charming a voice and with such uncommon serenity and peace of mind, that they answered as well as the best. Nor is this to be wondered at; for as hollow vessels produce a far more musical sound in falling than those which are substantial, so it will oftentimes be found that sentiments which have nothing in them make the loudest ringing in the world, and are the most relished.

Mr. Chester, with the volume gently extended in one hand, and with the other planted lightly on his breast, talked to them in the most delicious manner possible; and quite enchanted all his hearers, notwithstanding their conflicting interests and thoughts. Even Dolly, who, between his keen regards and her eyeing over by Mr. Tappertit, was put quite out of countenance, could not help owning within herself that he was the sweetest-spoken gentleman she had ever seen. Even Miss Miggs, who was divided between admiration of Mr. Chester and a mortal jealousy of her young mistress, had sufficient leisure to be propitiated. Even Mr. Tappertit, though occupied as we have seen in gazing at his heart's delight, could not wholly divert his thoughts from the voice of the other charmer. Mrs. Varden, to her own private thinking, had never been so improved in all her life; and when Mr. Chester, rising and craving permission to speak with her apart, took her by the hand and led her at arm's length up-stairs to the best sitting-room, she almost deemed him something more than human.

"Dear madam," he said, pressing her hand delicately to his lips; "be seated."

Mrs. Varden called up quite a courtly air, and became seated.

"You guess my object?" said Mr. Chester, drawing a chair towards her. "You divine my purpose? I am an affectionate parent, my dear Mrs. Varden."

"That I am sure you are, sir," said Mrs. V.

"Thank you," returned Mr. Chester, tapping his snuff-box lid. "Heavy moral responsibilities rest with parents, Mrs. Varden."

Mrs. Varden slightly raised her hands, shook her head, and looked at the ground as though she saw straight through the globe, out at the other end, and into the immensity of space beyond.

"I may confide in you," said Mr. Chester, "without reserve. I love my son, ma'am, dearly; and loving him as I do, I would save him from working certain misery. You know of his attachment to Miss Haredale. You have abetted him in it, and very kind of you it was to do so. I am deeply obliged to you—most deeply obliged to you—for your interest in his behalf; but, my dear ma'am, it is a mistaken one, I do assure you."

Mrs. Varden stammered that she was sorry—

"Sorry, my dear ma'am," he interposed. "Never be sorry for what is so very amiable, so very good in intention, so perfectly like yourself. But there are grave and weighty reasons, pressing family considerations, and apart even from these, points of religious difference, which interpose themselves, and render their union impossible; utterly im-possible. I should have mentioned these circumstances to your husband; but he has—you will excuse my saying this so freely—he has *not* your quickness of apprehension or depth of moral sense. What an extremely airy house this is, and how beautifully kept! For one like myself—a widower so long—these tokens of female care and superintendence have inexpressible charms.''

Mrs. Varden began to think (she scarcely knew why) that the young Mr. Chester must be in the wrong and the old Mr. Chester must be in the right.

"My son Ned," resumed her tempter with his utmost winning air, "has had, I am told, your lovely daughter's aid, and your open-hearted husband's.''

"—Much more than mine, sir," said Mrs. Varden; "a great deal more. I have often had my doubts. It's a—''

"A bad example," suggested Mr. Chester. "It is. No doubt it is. Your daughter is at that age when to set before her an encouragement for young persons to rebel against their parents on this most important point, is particularly injudicious. You are quite right. I ought to have thought of that myself, but it escaped me, I confess—so far superior are your sex to ours, dear madam, in point of penetration and sagacity.''

Mrs. Varden looked as wise as if she had really said something to deserve this compliment—firmly believed she had, in short—and her faith in her own shrewdness increased considerably.

"My dear ma'am," said Mr. Chester, "you embolden me to be plain with you. My son and I are at variance on this point. The young lady and her natural guardian differ upon it, also. And the closing point is, that my son is bound by his duty to me, by his honour, by every solemn tie and obligation, to marry some one else.''

"Engaged to marry another lady!" quoth Mrs. Varden, holding up her hands.

"My dear madam, brought up, educated, and trained, expressly for that purpose. Expressly for that purpose.—Miss Haredale, I am told, is a very charming creature.''

"I am her foster-mother, and should know—the best young lady in the world," said Mrs. Varden.

"I have not the smallest doubt of it. I am sure she is. And you, who have stood in that tender relation towards her, are bound to consult her happiness. Now, can I—as I have said to Haredale, who quite agrees—can I possibly stand by, and suffer her to throw herself away (although she *is* of a Catholic family) upon a young fellow who, as yet, has no heart at all? It is no imputation upon him to say he has not, because young men who have plunged deeply into the frivolities and conventionalities of society, very seldom have. Their hearts never grow, my dear ma'am, till after thirty. I don't believe, no, I do *not* believe, that I had any heart myself when I was Ned's age.''

"Oh, sir," said Mrs. Varden, "I think you must have had. It's

impossible that you, who have so much now, can ever have been
without any."

"I hope," he answered, shrugging his shoulders meekly, "I have a
little; I hope, a very little—Heaven knows! But to return to Ned;
I have no doubt you thought, and therefore interfered benevolently
in his behalf, that I objected to Miss Haredale. How very natural!
My dear madam, I object to him—to him—emphatically to Ned
himself."

Mrs. Varden was perfectly aghast at the disclosure.

"He has, if he honourably fulfils this solemn obligation of which
I have told you—and he must be honourable, dear Mrs. Varden, or
he is no son of mine—a fortune within his reach. He is of most
expensive, ruinously expensive habits; and if, in a moment of caprice
and wilfulness, he were to marry this young lady, and so deprive
himself of the means of gratifying the tastes to which he had been
so long accustomed, he would—my dear madam, he would break
the gentle creature's heart. Mrs. Varden, my good lady, my dear soul,
I put it to you—is such a sacrifice to be endured? Is the female heart
a thing to be trifled with in this way? Ask your own, my dear madam.
Ask your own, I beseech you."

"Truly," thought Mrs. Varden, "this gentleman is a saint. But,"
she added aloud, and not unnaturally, "if you take Miss Emma's
lover away, sir, what becomes of the poor thing's heart then?"

"The very point," said Mr. Chester, not at all abashed, "to which
I wished to lead you. A marriage with my son, whom I should be
compelled to disown, would be followed by years of misery; they
would be separated, my dear madam, in a twelvemonth. To break
off this attachment, which is more fancied than real, as you and I
know very well, will cost the dear girl but a few tears, and she is
happy again. Take the case of your own daughter, the young lady
down-stairs, who is your breathing image"—Mrs. Varden coughed
and simpered—"there is a young man, (I am sorry to say, a dissolute
fellow, of very indifferent character,) of whom I have heard Ned
speak—Bullet was it—Pullet—Mullet—"

"There is a young man of the name of Joseph Willet, sir," said
Mrs. Varden, folding her hands loftily.

"That's he," cried Mr. Chester. "Suppose this Joseph Willet now,
were to aspire to the affections of your charming daughter, and were
to engage them."

"It would be like his impudence," interposed Mrs. Varden, bridling,
"to dare to think of such a thing!"

"My dear madam, that's the whole case. I know it would be like
his impudence. It is like Ned's impudence to do as he has done; but
you would not on that account, or because of a few tears from your
beautiful daughter, refrain from checking their inclinations in their
birth. I meant to have reasoned thus with your husband when I saw
him at Mrs. Rudge's this evening—"

"My husband," said Mrs. Varden, interposing with emotion,
"would be a great deal better at home than going to Mrs. Rudge's so

often. I don't know what he does there. I don't see what occasion
he has to busy himself in her affairs at all, sir."

"If I don't appear to express my concurrence in those last sentiments of yours," returned Mr. Chester, "quite so strongly as you
might desire, it is because his being there, my dear madam, and not
proving conversational, led me hither, and procured me the happiness
of this interview with one, in whom the whole management, conduct,
and prosperity of her family are centred, I perceive."

With that he took Mrs. Varden's hand again, and having pressed
it to his lips with the high-flown gallantry of the day—a little
burlesqued to render it the more striking in the good lady's unaccustomed eyes—proceeded in the same strain of mingled sophistry,
cajolery, and flattery, to entreat that her utmost influence might be
exerted to restrain her husband and daughter from any further
promotion of Edward's suit to Miss Haredale, and from aiding or
abetting either party in any way. Mrs. Varden was but a woman, and
had her share of vanity, obstinacy, and love of power. She entered
into a secret treaty of alliance, offensive and defensive, with her
insinuating visitor; and really did believe, as many others would
have done who saw and heard him, that in so doing she furthered
the ends of truth, justice, and morality, in a very uncommon degree.

Overjoyed by the success of his negotiation, and mightily amused
within himself, Mr. Chester conducted her down-stairs in the same
state as before; and having repeated the previous ceremony of salutation, which also as before comprehended Dolly, took his leave; first
completing the conquest of Miss Miggs's heart, by inquiring if "this
young lady" would light him to the door.

"Oh, mim," said Miggs, returning with the candle. "Oh gracious
me, mim, there's a gentleman! Was there ever such an angel to talk
as he is—and such a sweet-looking man! So upright and noble, that
he seems to despise the very ground he walks on! and yet so mild and
condescending, that he seems to say 'but I will take notice on it too.'
And to think of his taking you for Miss Dolly, and Miss Dolly for
your sister—Oh, my goodness me, if I was master wouldn't I be
jealous of him!"

Mrs. Varden reproved her handmaid for this vain-speaking; but
very gently and mildly—quite smilingly indeed—remarking that
she was a foolish, giddy, light-headed girl, whose spirits carried her
beyond all bounds, and who didn't mean half she said, or she would
be quite angry with her.

"For my part," said Dolly, in a thoughtful manner, "I half believe
Mr. Chester is something like Miggs in that respect. For all his politeness and pleasant speaking, I am pretty sure he was making game
of us, more than once."

"If you venture to say such a thing again, and to speak ill of people
behind their backs in my presence, Miss," said Mrs. Varden, "I shall
insist upon your taking a candle and going to bed directly. How dare
you, Dolly? I'm astonished at you. The rudeness of your whole
behaviour this evening has been disgraceful. Did anybody ever hear,"

cried the enraged matron, bursting into tears, "of a daughter telling her own mother she has been made game of!"

What a very uncertain temper Mrs. Varden's was!

CHAPTER XXVIII

REPAIRING to a noted coffee-house in Covent Garden when he left the locksmith's, Mr. Chester sat long over a late dinner, entertaining himself exceedingly with the whimsical recollection of his recent proceedings, and congratulating himself very much on his great cleverness. Influenced by these thoughts, his face wore an expression so benign and tranquil, that the waiter in immediate attendance upon him felt he could almost have died in his defence, and settled in his own mind (until the receipt of the bill, and a very small fee for very great trouble disabused it of the idea) that such an apostolic customer was worth half-a-dozen of the ordinary run of visitors, at least.

A visit to the gaming-table—not as a heated, anxious venturer, but one whom it was quite a treat to see staking his two or three pieces in deference to the follies of society, and smiling with equal benevolence on winners and losers—made it late before he reached home. It was his custom to bid his servant go to bed at his own time unless he had orders to the contrary, and to leave a candle on the common stair. There was a lamp on the landing by which he could always light it when he came home late, and having a key of the door about him he could enter and go to bed at his pleasure.

He opened the glass of the dull lamp, whose wick, burnt up and swollen like a drunkard's nose, came flying off in little carbuncles at the candle's touch, and scattering hot sparks about, rendered it matter of some difficulty to kindle the lazy taper; when a noise, as of a man snoring deeply some steps higher up, caused him to pause and listen. It was the heavy breathing of a sleeper, close at hand. Some fellow had laid down on the open staircase, and was slumbering soundly. Having lighted the candle at length and opened his own door, he softly ascended, holding the taper high above his head, and peering cautiously about; curious to see what kind of man had chosen so comfortless a shelter for his lodging.

With his head upon the landing and his great limbs flung over half-a-dozen stairs, as careless as though he were a dead man whom drunken bearers had thrown down by chance, there lay Hugh, face uppermost, his long hair drooping like some wild weed upon his wooden pillow, and his huge chest heaving with the sounds which so unwontedly disturbed the place and hour.

He who came upon him so unexpectedly was about to break his rest by thrusting him with his foot, when, glancing at his upturned face, he arrested himself in the very action, and stooping down and shading the candle with his hand, examined his features closely. Close as his first inspection was, it did not suffice, for he passed the light, still carefully shaded as before, across and across his face, and yet observed him with a searching eye.

While he was thus engaged, the sleeper without any starting or turning round, awoke. There was a kind of fascination in meeting his steady gaze so suddenly, which took from the other the presence of mind to withdraw his eyes, and forced him, as it were, to meet his look. So they remained staring at each other, until Mr. Chester at last broke silence, and asked him in a low voice, why he lay sleeping there.

"I thought," said Hugh, struggling into a sitting posture and gazing at him intently still, "that you were a part of my dream. It was a curious one. I hope it may never come true, master."

"What makes you shiver?"

"The—the cold, I suppose," he growled, as he shook himself and rose. "I hardly know where I am yet."

"Do you know me?" said Mr. Chester.

"Ay, I know you," he answered. "I was dreaming of you—we're not where I thought we were. That's a comfort."

He looked round him as he spoke, and in particular looked above his head, as though he half expected to be standing under some object which had had existence in his dream. Then he rubbed his eyes and shook himself again, and followed his conductor into his own rooms.

Mr. Chester lighted the candles which stood upon his dressing-table, and wheeling an easy chair towards the fire, which was yet burning, stirred up a cheerful blaze, sat down before it, and bade his uncouth visitor "Come here," and draw his boots off.

"You have been drinking again, my fine fellow," he said, as Hugh went down on one knee, and did as he was told.

"As I'm alive, master, I've walked the twelve long miles, and waited here I don't know how long, and had no drink between my lips since dinner-time at noon."

"And can you do nothing better, my pleasant friend, than fall asleep, and shake the very building with your snores?" said Mr. Chester. "Can't you dream in your straw at home, dull dog as you are, that you need come here to do it?—Reach me those slippers, and tread softly."

Hugh obeyed in silence.

"And harkee, my dear young gentleman," said Mr. Chester, as he put them on, "the next time you dream, don't let it be of me, but of some dog or horse with whom you are better acquainted. Fill the glass once—you'll find it and the bottle in the same place—and empty it to keep yourself awake."

Hugh obeyed again—even more zealously—and having done so, presented himself before his patron.

"Now," said Mr. Chester, "what do you want with me?"

"There was news to-day," returned Hugh. "Your son was at our house—came down on horseback. He tried to see the young woman, but couldn't get sight of her. He left some letter or some message which our Joe had charge of, but he and the old one quarrelled about it when your son had gone, and the old one wouldn't let it be delivered. He says (that's the old one does) that none of his people shall interfere and get him into trouble. He's a landlord, he says, and lives on everybody's custom."

"He's a jewel," smiled Mr. Chester, "and the better for being a dull one.—Well?"

"Varden's daughter—that's the girl I kissed—"

"—and stole the bracelet from upon the king's highway," said Mr. Chester, composedly. "Yes; what of her?"

"She wrote a note at our house to the young woman, saying she lost the letter I brought to you, and you burnt. Our Joe was to carry it, but the old one kept him at home all next day, on purpose that he shouldn't. Next morning he gave it to me to take; and here it is."

"You didn't deliver it then, my good friend?" said Mr. Chester, twirling Dolly's note between his finger and thumb, and feigning to be surprised.

"I supposed you'd want to have it," retorted Hugh. "Burn one, burn all, I thought."

"My devil-may-care acquaintance," said Mr. Chester—"really if you do not draw some nicer distinctions, your career will be cut short with most surprising suddenness. Don't you know that the letter you brought to me, was directed to my son who resides in this very place? And can you descry no difference between his letters and those addressed to other people?"

"If you don't want it," said Hugh, disconcerted by this reproof, for he had expected high praise, "give it me back, and I'll deliver it. I don't know how to please you, master."

"I shall deliver it," returned his patron, putting it away after a moment's consideration, "myself. Does the young lady walk out, on fine mornings?"

"Mostly—about noon is her usual time."

"Alone?"

"Yes, alone."

"Where?"

"In the grounds before the house.—Them that the foot-path crosses."

"If the weather should be fine, I may throw myself in her way to-morrow, perhaps," said Mr. Chester, as coolly as if she were one of his ordinary acquaintance. "Mr. Hugh, if I should ride up to the Maypole door, you will do me the favour only to have seen me once. You must suppress your gratitude, and endeavour to forget my forbearance in the matter of the bracelet. It is natural it should break out, and it does you honour; but when other folks are by, you must, for your own sake and safety, be as like your usual self as though you owed me no obligation whatever, and had never stood within these walls. You comprehend me?"

Hugh understood him perfectly. After a pause he muttered that he hoped his patron would involve him in no trouble about this last letter; for he had kept it back solely with the view of pleasing him. He was continuing in this strain, when Mr. Chester with a most beneficent and patronising air cut him short by saying:

"My good fellow, you have my promise, my word, my sealed bond, (for a verbal pledge with me is quite as good), that I will always protect you so long as you deserve it. Now, do set your mind at rest. Keep it at ease, I beg of you. When a man puts himself in my power so thoroughly as you have done, I really feel as though he had a kind of claim upon me. I am more disposed to mercy and forbearance under such circumstances than I can tell you, Hugh. Do look upon me as your protector, and rest assured, I entreat you, that on the subject of that indiscretion, you may preserve, as long as you and I are friends, the lightest heart that ever beat within a human breast. Fill that glass once more to cheer you on your road homewards—I am really quite ashamed to think how far you have to go—and then God bless you for the night."

"They think," said Hugh, when he had tossed the liquor down, "that I am sleeping soundly in the stable. Ha ha ha! The stable door is shut, but the steed's gone, master."

"You are a most convivial fellow," returned his friend, "and I love your humour of all things. Good night! Take the greatest possible care of yourself, for my sake!"

It was remarkable that during the whole interview, each had endeavoured to catch stolen glances of the other's face, and had never looked full at it. They interchanged one brief and hasty glance as Hugh went out, averted their eyes directly, and so separated. Hugh closed the double doors behind him, carefully and without noise; and Mr. Chester remained in his easy chair, with his gaze intently fixed upon the fire.

"Well!" he said, after meditating for a long time—and said with a deep sigh and an uneasy shifting of his attitude, as though he dismissed some other subject from his thoughts, and returned to that which had held possession of them all the day—"the plot thickens; I have thrown the shell; it will explode, I think, in eight-and-forty hours, and should scatter these good folks amazingly. We shall see!"

He went to bed and fell asleep, but had not slept long when he started up and thought that Hugh was at the outer door, calling in a strange voice, very different from his own, to be admitted. The delusion was so strange upon him, and was so full of that vague terror of the night in which such visions have their being, that he rose, and taking his sheathed sword in his hand, opened the door, and looked out upon the staircase, and towards the spot where Hugh had lain asleep; and even spoke to him by name. But all was dark and quiet, and creeping back to bed again, he fell, after an hour's uneasy watching, into a second sleep, and woke no more till morning.

CHAPTER XXIX

THE thoughts of worldly men are for ever regulated by a moral law of gravitation, which, like the physical one, holds them down to

earth. The bright glory of day, and the silent wonders of a starlit
night, appeal to their minds in vain. There are no signs in the sun,
or in the moon, or in the stars, for their reading. They are like some
wise men, who, learning to know each planet by its Latin name, have
quite forgotten such small heavenly constellations as Charity, Forbearance, Universal Love, and Mercy, although they shine by night
and day so brightly that the blind may see them; and who, looking
upward at the spangled sky, see nothing there but the reflection of
their own great wisdom and book-learning.

It is curious to imagine these people of the world, busy in thought,
turning their eyes towards the countless spheres that shine above us,
and making them reflect the only images their minds contain. The
man who lives but in the breath of princes, has nothing in his sight
but stars for courtiers' breasts. The envious man beholds his neighbours' honours even in the sky; to the money-hoarded, and the mass
of worldly folk, the whole great universe above glitters with sterling
coin—fresh from the mint—stamped with the sovereign's head
coming always between them and heaven, turn where they may. So
do the shadows of our own desires stand between us and our better
angels, and thus their brightness is eclipsed.

Everything was fresh and gay, as though the world were but that
morning made, when Mr. Chester rode at a tranquil pace along the
Forest road. Though early in the season, it was warm and genial
weather; the trees were budding into leaf, the hedges and the grass
were green, the air was musical with songs of birds, and high above
them all the lark poured out her richest melody. In shady spots the
morning dew sparkled on each young leaf and blade of grass; and
where the sun was shining, some diamond drops yet glistened brightly,
as in unwillingness to leave so fair a world, and have such brief existence. Even the light wind, whose rustling was as gentle to the ear as
softly-falling water, had its hope and promise; and, leaving a pleasant
fragrance in its track as it went fluttering by, whispered of its intercourse with Summer, and of his happy coming.

The solitary rider went glancing on among the trees, from sunlight
into shade and back again, at the same even pace—looking about
him, certainly, from time to time, but with no greater thought of the
day or the scene through which he moved, than that he was fortunate
(being choicely dressed) to have such favourable weather. He smiled
very complacently at such times, but rather as if he were satisfied
with himself than with anything else: and so went riding on, upon
his chestnut cob, as pleasant to look upon as his own horse, and
probably far less sensitive to the many cheerful influences by which
he was surrounded.

In the course of time, the Maypole's massive chimneys rose upon
his view: but he quickened not his pace one jot, and with the same
cool gravity rode up to the tavern porch. John Willet, who was toasting his red face before a great fire in the bar, and who, with surpassing
foresight and quickness of apprehension, had been thinking, as he
looked at the blue sky, that if that state of things lasted much longer

it might ultimately become necessary to leave off fires and throw the windows open, issued forth to hold his stirrup; calling lustily for Hugh.

"Oh, you're here, are you, sir?" said John, rather surprised by the quickness with which he appeared. "Take this here valuable animal into the stable, and have more than particular care of him if you want to keep your place. A mortal lazy fellow, sir: he needs a deal of looking after."

"But you have a son," returned Mr. Chester, giving his bridle to Hugh as he dismounted, and acknowledging his salute by a careless motion of his hand towards his hat. "Why don't you make *him* useful?"

"Why, the truth is, sir," replied John with great importance, "that my son—what, you're a-listening are you, villain?"

"Who's listening?" returned Hugh angrily. "A treat, indeed, to hear *you* speak! Would you have me take him in till he's cool?"

"Walk him up and down further off then, sir," cried old John, "and when you see me and a noble gentleman entertaining ourselves with talk, keep your distance. If you don't know your distance, sir," added Mr. Willet, after an enormously long pause, during which he fixed his great dull eyes on Hugh, and waited with exemplary patience for any little property in the way of ideas that might come to him, "we'll find a way to teach you, pretty soon."

Hugh shrugged his shoulders scornfully, and in his reckless swaggering way, crossed to the other side of the little green, and there, with the bridle slung loosely over his shoulder, led the horse to and fro, glancing at his master every now and then from under his bushy eyebrows, with as sinister an aspect as one would desire to see.

Mr. Chester, who, without appearing to do so, had eyed him attentively during this brief dispute, stepped into the porch, and turning abruptly to Mr. Willet, said,

"You keep strange servants, John."

"Strange enough to look at, sir, certainly," answered the host; "but out of doors; for horses, dogs, and the likes of that; there an't a better man in England than is that Maypole Hugh yonder. He an't fit for indoors," added Mr. Willet, with the confidential air of a man who felt his own superior nature. "*I* do that; but if that chap had only a little imagination, sir—"

"He's an active fellow now, I dare swear," said Mr. Chester, in a musing tone, which seemed to suggest that he would have said the same had there been nobody to hear him.

"Active, sir!" retorted John, with quite an expression in his face; "that chap! Hallo there! You, sir! Bring that horse here, and go and hang my wig on the weathercock, to show this gentleman whether you're one of the lively sort or not."

Hugh made no answer, but throwing the bridle to his master, and snatching his wig from his head, in a manner so unceremonious and hasty that the action discomposed Mr. Willet not a little, though performed at his own special desire, climbed nimbly to the very

summit of the maypole before the house, and hanging the wig upon
the weathercock, sent it twirling round like a roasting jack. Having
achieved this performance, he cast it on the ground, and sliding down
the pole with inconceivable rapidity, alighted on his feet almost as
soon as it had touched the earth.

"There, sir," said John, relapsing into his stolid state, "you won't
see that at many houses, besides the Maypole, where there's good
accommodation for man and beast—nor that neither, though that
with him is nothing."

This last remark bore reference to his vaulting on horse-back, as
upon Mr. Chester's first visit, and quickly disappearing by the stable
gate.

"That with him is nothing," repeated Mr. Willet, brushing his wig
with his wrist, and inwardly resolving to distribute a small charge for
dust and damage to that article of dress, through the various items
of his guest's bill; "he'll get out of a'most any winder in the house.
There never was such a chap for flinging himself about and never
hurting his bones. It's my opinion, sir, that it's pretty nearly all
owing to his not having any imagination and if that imagination
could be (which it can't) knocked into him, he'd never be able to do
it any more. But we was a-talking, sir, about my son."

" True, Willet, true," said his visitor, turning again towards the
landlord with that serenity of face. "My good friend, what about
him?"

It has been reported that Mr. Willet, previously to making answer,
winked. But as he was never known to be guilty of such lightness of
conduct either before or afterwards, this may be looked upon as a
malicious invention of his enemies—founded, perhaps, upon the
undisputed circumstance of his taking his guest by the third breast
button of his coat, counting downwards from the chin, and pouring
his reply into his ear:

"Sir," whispered John, with dignity, "I know my duty. We want
no love-making here, sir, unbeknown to parents. I respect a certain
young gentleman, taking him in the light of a young gentleman; I
respect a certain young lady, taking her in the light of a young lady;
but of the two as a couple, I have no knowledge, sir, none whatever.
My son, sir, is upon his patrole."

"I thought I saw him looking through the corner window but this
moment," said Mr. Chester, who naturally thought that being on
patrole, implied walking about somewhere.

"No doubt you did, sir," returned John. "He is upon his patrole of
honour, sir, not to leave the premises. Me and some friends of mine
that use the Maypole of an evening, sir, considered what was best
to be done with him, to prevent his doing anything unpleasant in
opposing your desires; and we've put him on his patrole. And what's
more, sir, he won't be off his patrole for a pretty long time to come, I
can tell you that."

When he had communicated this bright idea, which had its origin
in the perusal by the village cronies of a newspaper, containing

among other matters, an account of how some officer pending the
sentence of some court-martial had been enlarged on parole, Mr.
Willet drew back from his guest's ear, and without any visible
alteration of feature, chuckled thrice audibly This nearest approach
to a laugh in which he ever indulged (and that but seldom and only on
extreme occasions), never even curled his lip or effected the smallest
change in—no, not so much as a slight wagging of—his great, fat,
double chin, which at these times, as at all others, remained a perfect
desert in the broad map of his face; one changeless, dull, tremendous
blank.

Lest it should be matter of surprise to any, that Mr. Willet adopted
this bold course in opposition to one whom he had often entertained,
and who had always paid his way at the Maypole gallantly, it may
be remarked that it was his very penetration and sagacity in this
respect, which occasioned him to indulge in those unusual demonstrations of jocularity, just now recorded. For Mr. Willet, after carefully balancing father and son in his mental scales, had arrived at the
distinct conclusion that the old gentleman was a better sort of a
customer than the young one. Throwing his landlord into the same
scale, which was already turned by this consideration, and heaping
upon him, again, his strong desires to run counter to the unfortunate
Joe, and his opposition as a general principle to all matters of love and
matrimony, it went down to the very ground straightway, and sent
the light cause of the younger gentleman flying upwards to the
ceiling. Mr. Chester was not the kind of man to be by any means dim-
sighted to Mr. Willet's motives, but he thanked him as graciously as
if he had been one of the most disinterested marytrs that ever shone
on earth; and leaving him, with many complimentary reliances on his
great taste and judgment, to prepare whatever dinner he might deem
most fitting the occasion, bent his steps towards the Warren.

Dressed with more than his usual elegance; assuming a gracefulness of manner, which, though it was the result of long study, sat
easily upon him and became him well; composing his features into
their most serene and prepossessing expression; and setting in short
that guard upon himself, at every point, which denoted that he
attached no slight importance to the impression he was about to
make; he entered the bounds of Miss Haredale's usual walk. He had
not gone far, or looked about him long, when he descried coming towards him, a female figure. A glimpse of the form and dress as she
crossed a little wooden bridge which lay between them, satisfied him
that he had found her whom he desired to see. He threw himself in
her way, and a very few paces brought them close together.

He raised his hat from his head, and yielding the path, suffered her
to pass him. Then, as if the idea had but that moment occurred to him,
he turned hastily back and said in an agitated voice:

"I beg pardon—do I address Miss Haredale?"

She stopped in some confusion at being so unexpectedly accosted
by a stranger; and answered "Yes."

"Something told me," he said, *looking* a compliment to her beauty.

"that it could be no other. Miss Haredale, I bear a name which is not unknown to you—which it is a pride, and yet a pain to me to know, sounds pleasantly in your ears. I am a man advanced in life, as you see. I am the father of him whom you honour and distinguish above all other men. May I for weighty reasons which fill me with distress, beg but a minute's conversation with you here?"

Who that was inexperienced in deceit, and had a frank and youthful heart, could doubt the speaker's truth—could doubt it too, when the voice that spoke, was like the faint echo of one she knew so well, and so much loved to hear? She inclined her head, and stopping, cast her eyes upon the ground.

"A little more apart—among these trees. It is an old man's hand, Miss Haredale; an honest one, believe me."

She put hers in it as he said these words, and suffered him to lead her to a neighbouring seat.

"You alarm me, sir," she said in a low voice. "You are not the bearer of any ill news, I hope?"

"Of none that you anticipate," he answered, sitting down beside her. "Edward is well—quite well. It is of him I wish to speak, certainly; but I have no misfortune to communicate."

She bowed her head again, and made as though she would have begged him to proceed; but said nothing.

"I am sensible that I speak to you at a disadvantage, dear Miss Haredale. Believe me that I am not so forgetful of the feelings of my younger days as not to know that you are little disposed to view me with favour. You have heard me described as cold-hearted, calculating, selfish—"

"I have never, sir,"—she interposed with an altered manner and a firmer voice; "I have never heard you spoken of in harsh or disrespectful terms. You do a great wrong to Edward's nature if you believe him capable of any mean or base proceeding."

"Pardon me, my sweet young lady, but your uncle—"

"Nor is it my uncle's nature either," she replied, with a heightened colour in her cheek. "It is not his nature to stab in the dark, nor is it mine to love such deeds."

She rose as she spoke, and would have left him; but he detained her with a gentle hand, and besought her in such persuasive accents to hear him but another minute, that she was easily prevailed upon to comply, and so sat down again.

"And it is," said Mr. Chester, looking upward, and apostrophising the air; "It is this frank, ingenuous, noble nature, Ned, that you can wound so lightly. Shame—shame upon you, boy!"

She turned towards him quickly, and with a scornful look and flashing eyes. There were tears in Mr. Chester's eyes, but he dashed them hurriedly away, as though unwilling that his weakness should be known, and regarded her with mingled admiration and compassion.

"I never until now," he said, "believed, that the frivolous actions of a young man could move me like these of my own son. I never knew till now, the worth of a woman's heart, which boys so lightly win, and lightly fling away. Trust me, dear young lady, that I never until now did know your worth; and though an abhorrence of deceit and falsehood has impelled me to seek you out, and would have done so had you been the poorest and least gifted of your sex, I should have lacked the fortitude to sustain this interview could I have pictured you to my imagination as you really are."

Oh! If Mrs. Varden could have seen the virtuous gentleman as he said these words, with indignation sparkling from his eyes—if she could have heard his broken, quavering voice—if she could have beheld him as he stood bareheaded in the sunlight, and with unwonted energy poured forth his eloquence!

With a haughty face, but pale and trembling too, Emma regarded him in silence. She neither spoke nor moved, but gazed upon him as though she would look into his heart.

"I throw off," said Mr. Chester, "the restraint which natural affection would impose on some men, and reject all bonds but those of truth and duty. Miss Haredale, you are deceived; you are deceived by your unworthy lover, and my unworthy son."

Still she looked at him steadily, and still said not one word.

"I have ever opposed his professions of love for you; you will do me the justice, dear Miss Haredale, to remember that. Your uncle and myself were enemies in early life, and if I had sought retaliation, I might have found it here. But as we grow older, we grow wiser—better, I would fain hope—and from the first, I have opposed him in this attempt. I foresaw the end, and would have spared you, if I could."

"Speak plainly, sir," she faltered. "You deceive me, or are deceived yourself. I do not believe you—I cannot—I should not."

"First," said Mr. Chester, soothingly, "for there may be in your mind some latent angry feeling to which I would not appeal, pray, take this letter. It reached my hand by chance, and by mistake, and should have accounted to you (as I am told) for my son's not answering some other note of yours. God forbid, Miss Haredale," said the good gentleman, with great emotion, "that there should be in your gentle breast one causeless ground of quarrel with him. You should know, and you will see, that he was in no fault here."

There appeared something so very candid, so scrupulously honourable, so very truthful and just in this course—something which rendered the upright person who resorted to it, so worthy of belief—that Emma's heart, for the first time, sunk within her. She turned away and burst into tears.

"I would," said Mr. Chester, leaning over her, and speaking in mild and quite venerable accents; "I would, dear girl, it were my task to banish, not increase, those tokens of your grief. My son, my erring son,—I will not call him deliberately criminal in this, for men so young, who have been inconstant twice or thrice before, act without reflection, almost without a knowledge of the wrong they do, —will break his plighted faith to you; has broken it even now. Shall I stop here, and having given you this warning, leave it to be fulfilled; or shall I go on?"

"You will go on, sir," she answered, "and speak more plainly yet, in justice both to him and me."

"My dear girl," said Mr. Chester, bending over her more affectionately still; "whom I would call my daughter, but the Fates forbid, Edward seeks to break with you upon a false and most unwarrantable pretence. I have it on his own showing; in his own hand. Forgive me, if I have had a watch upon his conduct; I am his father; I had a regard for your peace and his honour, and no better resource was left me. There lies on his desk at this present moment, ready for transmission to you, a letter, in which he tells you that our poverty— our poverty; his and mine, Miss Haredale—forbids him to pursue his claim upon your hand; in which he offers, involuntarily proposes, to free you from your pledge; and talks magnanimously (men do so very commonly, in such cases) of being in time more worthy of your regard—and so forth. A letter, to be plain, in which he not only jilts you—pardon the word; I would summon to your aid your pride and dignity—not only jilts you, I fear, in favour of the object whose slighting treatment first inspired his brief passion for yourself and gave it birth in wounded vanity, but affects to make a merit and a virtue of the act."

She glanced proudly at him once more, as by an involuntary impulse, and with a swelling breast rejoined, "If what you say be true, he takes much needless trouble, sir, to compass his design. He is very tender of my peace of mind. I quite thank him."

"The truth of what I tell you, dear young lady," he replied, "you will test by the receipt or non-receipt of the letter of which I speak.— Haredale, my dear fellow, I am delighted to see you, although we meet under singular circumstances, and upon a melancholy occasion. I hope you are very well."

At these words the young lady raised her eyes, which were filled with tears; and seeing that her uncle indeed stood before them, and being quite unequal to the trial of hearing or of speaking one word more, hurriedly withdrew, and left them. They stood looking at each other, and at her retreating figure, and for a long time neither of them spoke.

"What does this mean? Explain it," said Mr. Haredale at length. "Why are you here, and why with her?"

"My dear friend," rejoined the other, resuming his accustomed manner with infinite readiness, and throwing himself upon the bench with a weary air, "you told me not very long ago, at that delightful old tavern of which you are the esteemed proprietor (and a most charming establishment it is for persons of rural pursuits and in robust health, who are not liable to take cold), that I had the head and heart of an evil spirit in all matters of deception. I thought at the time; I really did think; you flattered me. But now I begin to wonder at your discernment, and vanity apart, do honestly believe you spoke the truth. Did you ever counterfeit extreme ingenuousness and honest indignation? My dear fellow, you have no conception, if you never did, how faint the effort makes one."

Mr. Haredale surveyed him with a look of cold contempt. "You may evade an explanation, I know," he said, folding his arms. "But I must have it. I can wait."

"Not at all. Not at all, my good fellow. You shall not wait a moment," returned his friend, as he lazily crossed his legs. "The simplest thing in the world. It lies in a nutshell. Ned has written her a letter—a boyish, honest, sentimental composition, which remains as yet in his desk, because he hasn't had the heart to send it. I have taken a liberty, for which my parental affection and anxiety are a sufficient excuse, and possessed myself of the contents. I have described them to your niece (a most enchanting person, Haredale; quite an angelic creature), with a little colouring and description adapted to our purpose. It's done. You may be quite easy. It's all over. Deprived of their adherents and mediators; her pride and jealousy roused to the utmost; with nobody to undeceive her, and you to confirm me; you will find that their intercourse will close with her answer. If she receives Ned's letter by to-morrow noon, you may date their parting from to-morrow night. No thanks, I beg; you owe me none. I have acted for myself; and if I have forwarded our compact with all the ardour even you could have desired, I have done so selfishly, indeed."

"I curse the compact, as you call it, with my whole heart and soul," returned the other. "It was made in an evil hour. I have bound myself to a lie; I have leagued myself with you; and though I did so with a righteous motive, and though it cost me such an effort as haply few men know, I hate and despise myself for the deed."

"You are very warm," said Mr. Chester with a languid smile.

"I *am* warm. I am maddened by your coldness. 'Death, Chester, if your blood ran warmer in your veins, and there were no restraints upon me, such as those that hold and drag me back—well; it is done; you tell me so, and on such a point I may believe you. When I am most remorseful for this treachery, I will think of you and your marriage, and try to justify myself in such remembrances, for having torn asunder Emma and your son, at any cost. Our bond is cancelled now, and we may part."

Mr. Chester kissed his hand gracefully; and with the same tranquil face he had preserved throughout—even when he had seen his companion so tortured and transported by his passion that his whole frame was shaken—lay in his lounging posture on the seat and watched him as he walked away.

"My scape-goat and my drudge at school," he said, raising his head to look after him; "my friend of later days, who could not keep his mistress when he had won her, and threw me in her way to carry off the prize; I triumph in the present and the past. Bark on, ill-favoured, ill-conditioned cur; fortune has ever been with me—I like to hear you."

The spot where they had met, was in an avenue of trees. Mr. Haredale not passing out on either hand, had walked straight on. He chanced to turn his head when at some considerable distance, and seeing that his late companion had by that time risen and was looking after him, stood still as though he half expected him to follow and waited for his coming up.

"It *may* come to that one day, but not yet," said Mr. Chester, waving his hand, as though they were the best of friends, and turning away. "Not yet, Haredale. Life is pleasant enough to me; dull and full of heaviness to you. No. To cross swords with such a man —to indulge his humour unless upon extremity—would be weak indeed."

For all that, he drew his sword as he walked along, and in an absent humour ran his eye from hilt to point full twenty times. But thoughtfulness begets wrinkles; remembering this, he soon put it up, smoothed his contracted brow, hummed a gay tune with greater gaiety of manner, and was his unruffled self again.

CHAPTER XXX

A HOMELY proverb recognises the existence of a troublesome class of persons, who, having an inch conceded them, will take an ell. Not to quote the illustrious examples of those heroic scourges of mankind, whose amiable path in life has been from birth to death through blood, and fire, and ruin, and who would seem to have existed for no better purpose than to teach mankind that as the absence of pain is pleasure, so the earth, purged of their presence, may be deemed a blessed place—not to quote such mighty instances, it will be sufficient to refer to old John Willet.

Old John having long encroached a good standard inch, full measure, on the liberty of Joe, and having snipped off a Flemish ell in the matter of the parole, grew so despotic and so great, that his thirst for conquest knew no bounds. The more young Joe submitted, the more absolute old John became. The ell soon faded into nothing. Yards, furlongs, miles arose; and on went old John in the pleasantest manner possible, trimming off an exuberance in this place, shearing away some liberty of speech or action in that, and conducting himself in his small way with as much high mightiness and majesty, as the most glorious tyrant that ever had his statue reared in the public ways, of ancient or of modern times.

As great men are urged on to the abuse of power (when they need urging, which is not often), by their flatterers and dependents, so old John was impelled to these exercises of authority by the applause and admiration of his Maypole cronies, who, in the intervals of their nightly pipes and pots, would shake their heads and say that Mr. Willet was a father of the good old English sort; that there were no new-fangled notions or modern ways in him; that he put them in mind of what their fathers were when they were boys; that there was no mistake about him; that it would be well for the country if there were more like him, and more was the pity that there were not; with many other original remarks of that nature. Then they would condescendingly give Joe to understand that it was all for his good, and he would be thankful for it one day; and in particular, Mr. Cobb would acquaint him, that when he was his age, his father thought no more of giving him a parental kick, or a box on the ears, or a cuff on the head, or some little admonition of that sort, than he did of any other ordinary duty of life; and he would further remark, with looks of great significance, that but for this judicious bringing up, he might have never been the man he was at that present speaking; which was probable enough, as he was, beyond all question, the dullest dog of the party. In short, between old John and old John's friends, there never was an unfortunate young fellow so bullied, badgered, worried, fretted, and brow-beaten; so constantly beset, or made so tired of his life, as poor Joe Willet.

This had come to be the recognised and established state of things; but as John was very anxious to flourish his supremacy before the eyes of Mr. Chester, he did that day exceed himself, and did so goad and chafe his son and heir, that but for Joe's having made a solemn vow to keep his hands in his pockets when they were not otherwise engaged, it is impossible to say what he might have done with them. But the longest day has an end, and at length Mr. Chester came down-stairs to mount his horse, which was ready at the door.

As old John was not in the way at the moment, Joe, who was sitting in the bar ruminating on his dismal fate and the manifold perfections of Dolly Varden, ran out to hold the guest's stirrup and assist him to mount. Mr. Chester was scarcely in the saddle, and Joe was in the very act of making him a graceful bow, when old John came diving out of the porch, and collared him.

"None of that, sir," said John, "none of that, sir. No breaking of patroles. How dare you come out of the door, sir, without leave? You're trying to get away, sir, are you, and to make a traitor of yourself again? What do you mean, sir?"

"Let me go, father," said Joe, imploringly, as he marked the smile upon their visitor's face, and observed the pleasure his disgrace afforded him. "This is too bad. Who wants to get away?"

"Who wants to get away!" cried John, shaking him. "Why you do, sir, you do. You're the boy, sir," added John, collaring with one hand, and aiding the effect of a farewell bow to the visitor with the other, "that wants to sneak into houses, and stir up differences between noble gentlemen and their sons, are you, eh? Hold your tongue, sir."

Joe made no effort to reply. It was the crowning circumstance of his degradation. He extricated himself from his father's grasp, darted an angry look at the departing guest, and returned into the house.

"But for her," thought Joe, as he threw his arms upon a table in the common room, and laid his head upon them, "but for Dolly, who couldn't bear should think me the rascal they would make me out to be if I ran away, this house and I should part to-night."

It being evening by this time, Solomon Daisy, Tom Cobb, and Long Parkes, were all in the common room too, and had from the window been witnesses of what had just occurred. Mr. Willet joining them soon afterwards, received the compliments of the company with great composure, and lighting his pipe, sat down among them.

"We'll see, gentlemen," said John, after a long pause, "who's the master of this house, and who isn't. We'll see whether boys are to govern men, or men are to govern boys."

"And quite right too," assented Solomon Daisy with some approving nods; "quite right, Johnny. Very good, Johnny. Well said, Mr. Willet. Brayvo, sir."

John slowly brought his eyes to bear upon him, looked at him for a long time, and finally made answer to the unspeakable consternation of his hearers, "When I want encouragement from you, sir, I'll ask you for it. You let me alone, sir. I can get on without you, I hope. Don't you tackle me, sir, if you please."

"Don't take it ill, Johnny; I didn't mean any harm," pleaded the little man.

"Very good, sir," said John, more than usually obstinate after his late success. "Never mind, sir. I can stand pretty firm of myself, sir, I believe, without being shored up by you." And having given utterance to this retort, Mr. Willet fixed his eyes upon the boiler, and fell into a kind of tobacco-trance.

The spirits of the company being somewhat damped by this embarrassing line of conduct on the part of their host, nothing more was said for a long time; but at length Mr. Cobb took upon himself to remark, as he rose to knock the ashes out of his pipe, that he hoped Joe would thenceforth learn to obey his father in all things; that he had found, that day, he was not one of the sort of men who were to be trifled with; and that he would recommend him, poetically speaking, to mind his eye for the future.

"I'd recommend you, in return," said Joe, looking up with a flushed face, "not to talk to me."

"Hold your tongue, sir," cried Mr. Willet, suddenly rousing himself, and turning round.

"I won't, father," cried Joe, smiting the table with his fist, so that the jugs and glasses rung again; "these things are hard enough to bear from you; from anybody else I never will endure them any more. Therefore I say, Mr. Cobb, don't talk to me."

"Why, who are you," said Mr. Cobb, sneeringly, "that you're not to be talked to, eh, Joe?"

To which Joe returned no answer, but with a very ominous shake of the head, resumed his old position, which he would have peacefully preserved until the house shut up at night, but that Mr. Cobb, stimulated by the wonder of the company at the young man's presumption, retorted with sundry taunts, which proved too much for flesh and blood to bear. Crowding into one moment the vexation and the wrath of years, Joe started up, overturned the table, fell upon his long enemy, pummelled him with all his might and main, and finished by driving him with surprising swiftness against a heap of spittoons in one corner; plunging into which, head foremost, with a

Mr. Chester's Departure.

tremendous crash, he lay at full length among the ruins, stunned and motionless. Then, without waiting to receive the compliments of the bystanders on the victory he had won, he retreated to his own bed-chamber, and considering himself in a state of siege, piled all the portable furniture against the door by way of barricade.

"I have done it now," said Joe, as he sat down upon his bedstead and wiped his heated face. "I knew it would come at last. The May-pole and I must part company. I'm a roving vagabond—she hates me for evermore—it's all over!"

CHAPTER XXXI

PONDERING on his unhappy lot, Joe sat and listened for a long time, expecting every moment to hear their creaking footsteps on the stairs, or to be greeted by his worthy father with a summons to capitulate unconditionally, and deliver himself up straightway. But neither voice nor footstep came; and though some distant echoes, as of closing doors and people hurrying in and out of rooms, resounding from time to time through the great passages, and penetrating to his remote seclusion, gave note of unusual commotion down-stairs, no nearer sound disturbed his place of retreat, which seemed the quieter for these far-off noises, and was as dull and full of gloom as any hermit's cell.

It came on darker and darker. The old-fashioned furniture of the chamber, which was a kind of hospital for all the invalided movables in the house, grew indistinct and shadowy in its many shapes; chairs and tables, which by day were as honest cripples as need be, assumed a doubtful and mysterious character; and one old leprous screen of faded Indian leather and gold binding, which had kept out many a cold breath of air in days of yore and shut in many a jolly face, frowned on him with a spectral aspect, and stood at full height in its allotted corner, like some gaunt ghost who waited to be questioned. A portrait opposite the window—a queer, old grey-eyed general, in an oval frame—seemed to wink and doze as the light decayed, and at length, when the last faint glimmering speck of day went out, to shut its eyes in good earnest, and fall sound asleep. There was such a hush and mystery about everything, that Joe could not help following its example; and so went off into a slumber likewise, and dreamed of Dolly, till the clock of Chigwell church struck two.

Still nobody came. The distant noises in the house had ceased, and out of doors all was quiet too; save for the occasional barking of some deep-mouthed dog, and the shaking of the branches by the night wind. He gazed mournfully out of window at each well-known object as it lay sleeping in the dim light of the moon; and creeping back to his former seat, thought about the late uproar, until, with long thinking of, it seemed to have occurred a month ago. Thus between dozing, and thinking, and walking to the window and looking out, the night wore away; the grim old screen, and the kindred chairs and tables, began slowly to reveal themselves in their accus-

tomed forms; the grey-eyed general seemed to wink and yawn and
rouse himself; and at last he was broad awake again, and very uncomfortable and cold and haggard he looked, in the dull grey light of
morning.

The sun had begun to peep above the forest trees, and already
flung across the curling mist bright bars of gold, when Joe dropped
from his window on the ground below, a little bundle and his trusty
stick, and prepared to descend himself.

It was not a very difficult task; for there were so many projections
and gable ends in the way, that they formed a series of clumsy steps,
with no greater obstacle than a jump of some few feet at last. Joe,
with his stick and bundle on his shoulder, quickly stood on the firm
earth, and looked up at the old Maypole, it might be for the last
time.

He didn't apostrophise it, for he was no great scholar. He didn't
curse it, for he had little ill-will to give to anything on earth. He felt
more affectionate and kind to it than ever he had done in all his life
before, so said with all his heart, "God bless you!" as a parting wish,
and turned away.

He walked along at a brisk pace, big with great thoughts of going
for a soldier and dying in some foreign country where it was very hot
and sandy, and leaving God knows what unheard-of wealth in prize-
money to Dolly, who would be very much affected when she came
to know of it; and full of such youthful visions, which were sometimes sanguine and sometimes melancholy, but always had her for
their main point and centre, pushed on vigorously until the noise of
London sounded in his ears, and the Black Lion hove in sight.

It was only eight o'clock then, and very much astonished the
Black Lion was, to see him come walking in with dust upon his feet
at that early hour, with no grey mare to bear him company. But as
he ordered breakfast to be got ready with all speed, and on its being
set before him gave indisputable tokens of a hearty appetite, the
Lion received him, as usual, with a hospitable welcome; and treated
him with those marks of distinction, which, as a regular customer,
and one within the freemasonry of the trade, he had a right to claim.

This Lion or landlord,—for he was called both man and beast, by
reason of his having instructed the artist who painted his sign, to
convey into the features of the lordly brute whose effigy it bore, as
near a counterpart of his own face as his skill could compass and
devise,—was a gentleman almost as quick of apprehension, and of
almost as subtle a wit, as the mighty John himself. But the difference
between them lay in this; that whereas Mr. Willet's extreme sagacity
and acuteness were the efforts of unassisted nature, the Lion stood
indebted, in no small amount, to beer; of which he swiggered such
copious draughts, that most of his faculties were utterly drowned and
washed away, except the one great faculty of sleep, which he retained
in surprising perfection. The creaking Lion over the house-door was,
therefore, to say the truth, rather a drowsy, tame, and feeble lion;
and as these social representatives of a savage class are usually of a

conventional character (being depicted, for the most part, in impossible attitudes and of unearthly colours), he was frequently supposed by the more ignorant and uninformed among the neighbours, to be the veritable portrait of the host as he appeared on the occasion of some great funeral ceremony or public mourning.

"What noisy fellow is that in the next room?" said Joe, when he had disposed of his breakfast, and had washed and brushed himself.

"A recruiting serjeant," replied the Lion.

Joe started involuntarily. Here was the very thing he had been dreaming of, all the way along.

"And I wish," said the Lion, "he was anywhere else but here. The party make noise enough, but don't call for much. There's great cry there, Mr. Willet, but very little wool. Your father wouldn't like 'em, I know."

Perhaps not much under any circumstances. Perhaps if he could have known what was passing at that moment in Joe's mind, he would have liked them still less.

"Is he recruiting for a—for a fine regiment?" said Joe, glancing at a little round mirror that hung in the bar.

"I believe he is," replied the host. "It's much the same thing, whatever regiment he's recruiting for. I'm told there an't a deal of difference between a fine man and another one, when they're shot through and through."

"They're not all shot," said Joe.

"No," the Lion answered, "not all. Those that are—supposing it's done easy—are the best off in my opinion."

"Ah!" retorted Joe, "but you don't care for glory."

"For what?" said the Lion.

"Glory."

"No," returned the Lion, with supreme indifference. "I don't. You're right in that, Mr. Willet. When Glory comes here, and calls for anything to drink and changes a guinea to pay for it, I'll give it him for nothing. It's my belief, sir, that the Glory's Arms wouldn't do a very strong business."

These remarks were not at all comforting. Joe walked out, stopped at the door of the next room, and listened. The serjeant was describing military life. It was all drinking, he said, except that there were frequent intervals of eating and love-making. A battle was the finest thing in the world—when your side won it—and Englishmen always did that. "Supposing you should be killed, sir?" said a timid voice in one corner. "Well, sir, supposing you should be," said the serjeant, "what then? Your country loves you, sir; his Majesty King George the Third loves you; your memory is honoured, revered, respected; everybody's fond of you, and grateful to you; your name's wrote down at full length in a book in the War-office. Damme, gentlemen, we must all die some time, or another, eh?"

The voice coughed, and said no more.

Joe walked into the room. A group of half-a-dozen fellows had gathered together in the tap-room, and were listening with greedy

ears. One of them, a carter in a smock frock, seemed wavering and
disposed to enlist. The rest, who were by no means disposed, strongly
urged him to do so (according to the custom of mankind), backed
the serjeant's arguments, and grinned among themselves. "I say
nothing, boys," said the serjeant, who sat a little apart, drinking his
liquor. "For lads of spirit"—here he cast an eye on Joe—"this is the
time. I don't want to inveigle you. The king's not come to that, I
hope. Brisk young blood is what we want; not milk and water. We
won't take five men out of six. We want top-sawyers, we do. I'm not
a-going to tell tales out of school, but, damme, if every gentleman's
son that carries arms in our corps, through being under a cloud and
having little differences with his relations, was counted up"—here
his eye fell on Joe again, and so good-naturedly, that Joe beckoned
him out. He came directly.

"You're a gentleman, by G—!" was his first remark, as he slapped
him on the back. "You're a gentleman in disguise. So am I. Let's
swear a friendship."

Joe didn't exactly do that, but he shook hands with him, and
thanked him for his good opinion.

"You want to serve," said his new friend. "You shall. You were
made for it. You're one of us by nature. What'll you take to drink?"

"Nothing just now," replied Joe, smiling faintly. "I haven't quite
made up my mind."

"A mettlesome fellow like you, and not made up his mind!" cried
the serjeant. "Here—let me give the bell a pull, and you'll make up
your mind in half a minute, I know."

"You're right so far"—answered Joe, "for if you pull the bell here,
where I'm known, there'll be an end of my soldiering inclinations in
no time. Look in my face. You see me, do you?"

"I do," replied the serjeant with an oath, "and a finer young fellow
or one better qualified to serve his king and country I never set my"
—he used an adjective in this place—"eyes on."

"Thank you," said Joe, "I didn't ask you for want of a compliment, but thank you all the same. Do I look like a sneaking fellow
or a liar?"

The serjeant rejoined with many choice asseverations that he
didn't; and that if his (the serjeant's) own father were to say he did,
he would run the old gentlemen through the body cheerfully, and
consider it a meritorious action.

Joe expressed his obligations, and continued, "You can trust me
then, and credit what I say. I believe I shall enlist in your regiment
to-night. The reason I don't do so now is because I don't want
until to-night, to do what I can't recall. Where shall I find you, this
evening?"

His friend replied with some unwillingness, and after much ineffectual entreaty having for its object the immediate settlement of
the business, that his quarters would be at the Crooked Billet in
Tower-street; where he would be found waking until midnight, and
sleeping until breakfast time to-morrow.

"And if I do come—which it's a million to one, I shall—when will you take me out of London?" demanded Joe.

"To-morrow morning, at half after eight o'clock," replied the serjeant. "You'll go abroad—a country where it's all sunshine and plunder—the finest climate in the world."

"To go abroad," said Joe, shaking hands with him, "is the very thing I want. You may expect me."

"You're the kind of lad for us," cried the serjeant, holding Joe's hand in his, in the excess of his admiration. "You're the boy to push your fortune. I don't say it because I bear you any envy, or would take away from the credit of the rise you'll make, but if I had been bred and taught like you, I'd have been a colonel by this time."

"Tush, man," said Joe, "I'm not so young as that. Needs must when the devil drives; and the devil that drives me is an empty pocket and an unhappy home. For the present, good-bye."

"For king and country!" cried the serjeant, flourishing his cap.

"For bread and meat!" cried Joe, snapping his fingers. And so they parted.

He had very little money in his pocket; so little, indeed, that after paying for his breakfast (which he was too honest and perhaps too proud to score up to his father's charge) he had but a penny left. He had courage, notwithstanding, to resist all the affectionate importunities of the serjeant, who waylaid him at the door with many protestations of eternal friendship, and did in particular request that he would do him the favour to accept of only one shilling as a temporary accommodation. Rejecting his offers both of cash and credit, Joe walked away with stick and bundle as before, bent upon getting through the day as he best could, and going down to the locksmith's in the dusk of the evening; for it should go hard, he had resolved, but he would have a parting word with charming Dolly Varden.

He went out by Islington and so on to Highgate, and sat on many stones and gates, but there were no voices in the bells to bid him turn. Since the time of noble Whittington, fair flower of merchants, bells have come to have less sympathy with humankind. They only ring for money and on state occasions. Wanderers have increased in number; ships leave the Thames for distant regions, carrying from stem to stern no other cargo; the bells are silent; they ring out no entreaties or regrets; they are used to it and have grown worldly.

Joe bought a roll, and reduced his purse to the condition (with a difference) of that celebrated purse of Fortunatus, which, whatever were its favoured owner's necessities, had one unvarying amount in it. In these real times, when all the Fairies are dead and buried, there are still a great many purses which possess that quality. The sum-total they contain is expressed in arithmetic by a circle, and whether it be added to or multiplied by its own amount, the result of the problem is more easily stated than any known in figures.

Evening drew on at last. With the desolate and solitary feeling of one who had no home or shelter, and was alone utterly in the world for the first time, he bent his steps towards the locksmith's house.

He had delayed till now, knowing that Mrs. Varden sometimes went out alone, or with Miggs for her sole attendant, to lectures in the evening; and devoutly hoping that this might be one of her nights of moral culture.

He had walked up and down before the house, on the opposite side of the way, two or three times, when as he returned to it again, he caught a glimpse of a fluttering skirt at the door. It was Dolly's—to whom else could it belong? no dress but hers had such a flow as that. He plucked up his spirits, and followed it into the workshop of the Golden Key.

His darkening the door caused her to look round. Oh that face! "If it hadn't been for that," thought Joe, "I should never have walked into poor Tom Cobb. She's twenty times handsomer than ever. She might marry a Lord!"

He didn't say this. He only thought it—perhaps looked it also. Dolly was glad to see him, and was *so* sorry her father and mother were away from home. Joe begged she wouldn't mention it on any account.

Dolly hesitated to lead the way into the parlour, for there it was nearly dark; at the same time she hesitated to stand talking in the workshop, which was yet light and open to the street. They had got by some means, too, before the little forge; and Joe having her hand in his (which he had no right to have, for Dolly only gave it him to shake), it was so like standing before some homely altar being married that it was the most embarrassing state of things in the world.

"I have come," said Joe," to say good-bye—to say good-bye for I don't know how many years; perhaps for ever. I am going abroad."

Now this was exactly what he should not have said. Here he was, talking like a gentleman at large who was free to come and go and roam about the world at pleasure, when that gallant coachmaker had vowed but the night before that Miss Varden held him bound in adamantine chains; and had positively stated in so many words that she was killing him by inches, and that in a fortnight more or thereabouts he expected to make a decent end and leave the business to his mother.

Dolly released her hand and said "Indeed!" She remarked in the same breath that it was a fine night, and in short, betrayed no more emotion than the forge itself.

"I couldn't go," said Joe, "without coming to see you. I hadn't the heart to."

Dolly was more sorry than she could tell, that he should have taken so much trouble. It was such a long way, and he must have such a deal to do. And how *was* Mr. Willet—that dear old gentleman—"

"Is this all you say!" cried Joe.

All! Good gracious, what did the man expect! She was obliged to take her apron in her hand and run her eyes along the hem from corner to corner, to keep herself from laughing in his face;—not because his gaze confused her—not at all.

Joe had small experience in love affairs, and had no notion how

different young ladies are at different times; he had expected to take
Dolly up again at the very point where he had left her after that
delicious evening ride, and was no more prepared for such an alteration than to see the sun and moon change places. He had buoyed
himself up all day with an indistinct idea that she would certainly say
"Don't go," or "Don't leave us," or "Why do you go?" or "Why do
you leave us?" or would give him some little encouragement of that
sort; he had even entertained the possibility of her bursting into tears,
of her throwing herself into his arms, of her falling down in a fainting
fit without previous word or sign; but any approach to such a line of
conduct as this, had been so far from his thoughts that he could only
look at her in silent wonder.

Dolly in the meanwhile, turned to the corners of her apron, and
measured the sides, and smoothed out the wrinkles, and was as
silent as he. At last after a long pause, Joe said good-bye. "Good-bye"
—said Dolly—with as pleasant a smile as if he were going into the
next street, and were coming back to supper; "good-bye."

"Come," said Joe, putting out both hands, "Dolly, dear Dolly,
don't let us part like this. I love you dearly, with all my heart and
soul; with as much truth and earnestness as ever man loved woman
in this world, I do believe. I am a poor fellow, as you know—poorer
now than ever, for I have fled from home, not being able to bear it any
longer, and must fight my own way without help. You are beautiful,
admired, are loved by everybody, are well off and happy; and may
you ever be so! Heaven forbid I should ever make you otherwise; but
give me a word of comfort. Say something kind to me. I have no
right to expect it of you, I know, but I ask it because I love you, and
shall treasure the slightest word from you all through my life. Dolly,
dearest, have you nothing to say to me?"

No. Nothing. Dolly was a coquette by nature, and a spoilt child.
She had no notion of being carried by storm in this way. The coachmaker would have been dissolved in tears, and would have knelt
down, and called himself names, and clasped his hands, and beat his
breast, and tugged wildly at his cravat, and done all kinds of poetry.
Joe had no business to be going abroad. He had no right to be able
to do it. If he was in adamantine chains, he couldn't.

"I have said good-bye," said Dolly, "twice. Take your arm away
directly, Mr. Joseph, or I'll call Miggs."

"I'll not reproach you," answered Joe, "it's my fault, no doubt.
I have thought sometimes that you didn't quite despise me, but I was
a fool to think so. Every one must, who has seen the life I have led—
you most of all. God bless you!"

He was gone, actually gone. Dolly waited a little while, thinking
he would return, peeped out at the door, looked up the street and
down as well as the increasing darkness would allow, came in again,
waited a little longer, went up-stairs humming a tune, bolted herself
in, laid her head down on her bed, and cried as if her heart would
break. And yet such natures are made up of so many contradictions,
that if Joe Willet had come back that night, next day, next week,

next month, the odds are a hundred to one she would have treated him in the very same manner, and have wept for it afterwards with the very same distress.

She had no sooner left the workshop than there cautiously peered out from behind the chimney of the forge, a face which had already emerged from the same concealment twice or thrice, unseen, and which, after satisfying itself that it was now alone, was followed by a leg, a shoulder, and so on by degrees, until the form of Mr. Tappertit stood confessed, with a brown-paper cap stuck negligently on one side of its head, and its arms very much akimbo.

"Have my ears deceived me," said the 'prentice, "or do I dream! am I to thank thee, Fortun', or to cus thee—which?"

He gravely descended from his elevation, took down his piece of looking-glass, planted it against the wall upon the usual bench, twisted his head round, and looked closely at his legs.

"If they're a dream," said Sim, "let sculptures have such wisions, and chisel 'em out when they wake. This is reality. Sleep has no such limbs as them. Tremble, Willet, and despair. She's mine! She's mine!"

With these triumphant expressions, he seized a hammer and dealt a heavy blow at a vice, which in his mind's eye represented the sconce or head of Joseph Willet. That done, he burst into a peal of laughter which startled Miss Miggs even in her distant kitchen, and dipping his head into a bowl of water, had recourse to a jack-towel inside the closet door, which served the double purpose of smothering his feelings and drying his face.

Joe, disconsolate and down-hearted, but full of courage too, on leaving the locksmith's house made the best of his way to the Crooked Billet, and there inquired for his friend the serjeant, who, expecting no man less, received him with open arms. In the course of five minutes after his arrival at that house of entertainment, he was enrolled among the gallant defenders of his native land; and within half an hour, was regaled with a steaming supper of boiled tripe and onions, prepared, as his friend assured him more than once, at the express command of his most Sacred Majesty the King. To this meal, which tasted very savoury after his long fasting, he did ample justice; and when he had followed it up, or down, with a variety of loyal and patriotic toasts, he was conducted to a straw mattress in a loft over the stable, and locked in there for the night.

The next morning, he found that the obliging care of his martial friend had decorated his hat with sundry parti-coloured streamers, which made a very lively appearance; and in company with that officer, and three other military gentlemen newly enrolled, who were under a cloud so dense that it only left three shoes, a boot, and a coat and a half visible among them, repaired to the river-side. Here they were joined by a corporal and four more heroes, of whom two were drunk and daring, and two sober and penitent, but each of whom, like Joe, had his dusty stick and bundle. The party embarked in a passage-boat bound for Gravesend, whence they were to proceed on foot to Chatham; the wind was in their favour, and they soon left London behind them, a mere dark mist—a giant phantom in the air.

CHAPTER XXXII

MISFORTUNES, saith the adage, never come singly. There is little doubt that troubles are exceedingly gregarious in their nature, and flying in flocks, are apt to perch capriciously; crowding on the heads of some poor wights until there is not an inch of room left on their unlucky crowns, and taking no more notice of others who offer as good resting-places for the soles of their feet, than if they had no existence. It may have happened that a flight of troubles brooding over London, and looking out for Joseph Willet, whom they couldn't find, darted down haphazard on the first young man that caught their fancy, and settled on him instead. However this may be, certain it is that on the very day of Joe's departure they swarmed about the ears of Edward Chester, and did so buzz and flap their wings, and persecute him, that he was most profoundly wretched.

It was evening, and just eight o'clock, when he and his father, having wine and dessert set before them, were left to themselves for the first time that day. They had dined together, but a third person had been present during the meal, and until they met at table they had not seen each other since the previous night.

Edward was reserved and silent, Mr. Chester was more than usually gay; but not caring, as it seemed, to open a conversation with one whose humour was so different, he vented the lightness of his spirit in smiles and sparkling looks, and made no effort to awaken his attention. So they remained for some time: the father lying on a sofa with his accustomed air of negligence; the son seated opposite to him with downcast eyes, busied, it was plain, with painful and uneasy thoughts.

"My dear Edward," said Mr. Chester at length, with a most engaging laugh, "do not extend your drowsy influence to the decanter. Suffer *that* to circulate, let your spirits be never so stagnant."

Edward begged his pardon, passed it, and relapsed into his former state.

"You do wrong not to fill your glass," said Mr. Chester, holding up his own before the light. "Wine in moderation—not in excess, for that makes men ugly—has a thousand pleasant influences. It brightens the eye, improves the voice, imparts a new vivacity to one's thoughts and conversation: you should try it, Ned."

"Ah, father!" cried his son, "if—"

"My good fellow," interposed the parent hastily, as he set down his glass, and raised his eyebrows with a startled and horrified expression, "for Heaven's sake don't call me by that obsolete and ancient name. Have some regard for delicacy. Am I grey, or wrinkled, do I go on crutches, have I lost my teeth, that you adopt such a mode of address? Good God, how very coarse!"

"I was about to speak to you from my heart, sir," returned Edward, "in the confidence which should subsist between us; and you check me in the outset."

"Now *do*, Ned, *do* not," said Mr. Chester, raising his delicate hand imploringly, "talk in that monstrous manner. About to speak from your heart. Don't you know that the heart is an ingenious part of our formation—the centre of the blood-vessels and all that sort of thing—which has no more to do with what you say or think, than your knees have? How can you be so very vulgar and absurd? These anatomical allusions should be left to gentlemen of the medical profession. They are really not agreeable in society. You quite surprise me, Ned."

"Well! there are no such things to wound, or heal, or have regard for. I know your creed, sir, and will say no more," returned his son.

"There again," said Mr. Chester, sipping his wine, "you are wrong. I distinctly say there are such things. We know there are. The hearts of animals—of bullocks, sheep, and so forth—are cooked and devoured, as I am told, by the lower classes, with a vast deal of relish. Men are sometimes stabbed to the heart, shot to the heart; but as to speaking from the heart, or to the heart, or being warm-hearted, or cold-hearted, or broken-hearted, or being all heart, or having no heart—pah! these things are nonsense, Ned."

"No doubt, sir," returned his son, seeing that he paused for him to speak. "No doubt."

"There's Haredale's niece, your late flame," said Mr. Chester, as a careless illustration of his meaning. "No doubt in your mind she was all heart once. Now she has none at all. Yet she is the same person, Ned, exactly."

"She is a changed person, sir," cried Edward, reddening; "and changed by vile means, I believe."

"You have had a cool dismissal, have you?" said his father. "Poor Ned! I told you last night what would happen.—May I ask you for the nut-crackers?"

"She has been tampered with, and most treacherously deceived," cried Edward, rising from his seat. "I never will believe that the knowledge of my real position, given her by myself, has worked this change. I know she is beset and tortured. But though our contract is at an end, and broken past all redemption; though I charge upon her want of firmness and want of truth, both to herself and me; I do not now, and never will believe, that any sordid motive, or her own unbiassed will, has led her to this course—never!"

"You make me blush," returned his father gaily, "for the folly of your nature, in which—but we never know ourselves—I devoutly hope there is no reflection of my own. With regard to the young lady herself, she has done what is very natural and proper, my dear fellow; what you yourself proposed, as I learn from Haredale; and what I predicted—with no great exercise of sagacity—she would do. She supposed you to be rich, or at least quite rich enough; and found you poor. Marriage is a civil contract; people marry to better their worldly condition and improve appearances; it is an affair of house and furniture, of liveries, servants, equipage, and so forth. The lady being poor and you poor also, there is an end of the matter. You cannot enter upon these considerations, and have no manner of business with the ceremony. I drink her health in this glass, and respect and honour her for her extreme good sense. It is a lesson to you. Fill yours, Ned."

"It is a lesson," returned his son, "by which I hope I may never profit, and if years and experience impress it on—"

"Don't say on the heart," interposed his father.

"On men whom the world and its hypocrisy have spoiled," said Edward warmly; "Heaven keep me from its knowledge."

"Come, sir," returned his father, raising himself a little on the sofa, and looking straight towards him; "we have had enough of this. Remember, if you please, your interest, your duty, your moral obligations, your filial affections, and all that sort of thing which it is so very delightful and charming to reflect upon; or you will repent it."

"I shall never repent the preservation of my self-respect, sir," said Edward. "Forgive me if I say that I will not sacrifice it at your bidding, and that I will not pursue the track which you would have me take, and to which the secret share you have had in this late separation tends."

His father rose a little higher still, and looking at him as though curious to know if he were quite resolved and earnest, dropped gently down again, and said in the calmest voice—eating his nuts meanwhile,

"Edward, my father had a son, who being a fool like you, and, like you, entertaining low and disobedient sentiments, he disinherited and cursed one morning after breakfast. The circumstance occurs to me with a singular clearness of recollection this evening. I remember eating muffins at the time, with marmalade. He led a miserable life (the son I mean) and died early; it was a happy release on all accounts; he degraded the family very much. It is a sad circumstance, Edward, when a father finds it necessary to resort to such strong measures."

"It is," replied Edward, "and it is sad when a son, proffering him his love and duty in their best and truest sense, finds himself repelled at every turn, and forced to disobey. Dear father," he added, more earnestly though in a gentler tone, "I have reflected many times on what occured between us when we first discussed this subject. Let there be a confidence between us; not in terms, but truth. Hear what I have to say."

"As I anticipate what it is, and cannot fail to do so, Edward," returned his father coldly, "I decline. I couldn't possibly. I am sure it would put me out of temper, which is a state of mind I can't endure. If you intend to mar my plans for your establishment in life, and the preservation of that gentility and becoming pride, which our family have so long sustained—if, in short you are resolved to take your own course, you must take it, and my curse with it. I am very sorry, but there's really no alternative."

"The curse may pass your lips," said Edward, "but it will be but empty breath. I do not believe that any man on earth has greater power to call one down upon his fellow—least of all, upon his own child—than he has to make one drop of rain or flake of snow fall from the clouds above us at his impious bidding. Beware, sir, what you do."

"You are so very irreligious, so exceedingly undutiful, so horribly profane," rejoined his father, turning his face lazily towards him, and cracking another nut, "that I positively must interrupt you here. It is quite impossible we can continue to go on, upon such terms as these. If you will do me the favour to ring the bell, the servant will show you to the door. Return to this roof no more, I beg you. Go, sir, since you have no moral sense remaining; and go to the Devil, at my express desire. Good day."

Edward left the room without another word or look and turned his back upon the house for ever.

The father's face was slightly flushed and heated, but his manner was quite unchanged, as he rang the bell again, and addressed the servant on his entrance.

"Peak—if that gentleman who has just gone out—"

"I beg your pardon, sir, Mr. Edward?"

"Were there more than one, dolt, that you ask the question?—If that gentleman should send here for his wardrobe, let him have it, do you hear? If he should call himself at any time, I'm not at home. You'll tell him so, and shut the door."

So, it soon got whispered about, that Mr. Chester was very unfortunate in his son, who had occasioned him great grief and sorrow. And the good people who heard this and told it again, marvelled the more at his equanimity and even temper, and said what an amiable nature that man must have, who, having undergone so much, could be so placid and so calm. And when Edward's name was spoken, Society shook its head, and laid its finger on its lip, and sighed, and looked very grave; and those who had sons about his age, waxed wrathful and indignant, and hoped, for Virtue's sake, that he was dead. And the world went on turning round as usual for five years, concerning which this Narrative is silent.

CHAPTER XXXIII

ONE wintry evening, early in the year of our Lord one thousand seven hundred and eighty, a keen north wind arose as it grew dark, and night came on with black and dismal looks. A bitter storm of sleet, sharp, dense, and icy-cold, swept the wet streets, and rattled on the trembling windows. Sign-boards, shaken past endurance in their creaking frames, fell crashing on the pavement; old tottering chimneys reeled and staggered in the blast; and many a steeple rocked again that night, as though the earth were troubled.

It was not a time for those who could by any means get light and warmth, to brave the fury of the weather. In coffee-houses of the better sort, guests crowded round the fire, forgot to be political, and told each other with a secret gladness that the blast grew fiercer every minute. Each humble tavern by the water-side, had its group of un-couth figures round the hearth, who talked of vessels foundering at sea, and all hands lost; related many a dismal tale of shipwreck and drowned men, and hoped that some they knew were safe, and shook their heads in doubt. In private dwellings, children clustered near the blaze; listening with timid pleasure to tales of ghosts and goblins, and tall figures clad in white standing by bedsides, and people who had gone to sleep in old churches and being over-looked had found themselves alone there at the dead hour of the night: until they shuddered at the thought of the dark rooms up-stairs, yet loved to hear the wind moan too, and hoped it would continue bravely. From time to time these happy in-door people stopped to listen, or one held up his finger and cried "Hark!" and then above the rumbling in the chimney, and the fast pattering on the glass, was heard, a wailing, rushing sound, which shook the walls as though a giant's hand were on them; then a hoarse roar as if the sea had risen; then such a whirl and tumult that the air seemed mad; and then, with a lengthened howl, the waves of wind swept on, and left a moment's interval of rest.

Cheerily, though there were none abroad to see it, shone the May-pole light that evening. Blessings on the red—deep, ruby, glowing red—old curtain of the window; blending into one rich stream of bright-ness, fire and candle, meat, drink, and company, and gleaming like a jovial eye upon the bleak waste out of doors! Within, what carpet like its crunching sand, what music merry as its crackling logs, what perfume like its kitchen's dainty breath, what weather genial as its hearty warmth! Blessings on the old house, how sturdily it stood! How did the vexed wind chafe and roar about its stalwart roof; how did it pant and strive with its wide chimneys, which still poured forth from their hospitable throats, great clouds of smoke, and puffed defiance in its face; how, above all, did it drive and rattle at the case-ment, emulous to extinguish that cheerful glow, which would not be put down and seemed the brighter for the conflict!

The profusion too, the rich and lavish bounty, of that goodly tavern! It was not enough that one fire roared and sparkled on its spacious hearth; in the tiles which paved and compassed it, five hundred flickering fires burnt brightly also. It was not enough that one red curtain shut the wild night out, and shed its cheerful influence on the room. In every saucepan lid, and candlestick, and vessel of copper, brass, or tin that hung upon the walls, were countless ruddy hangings, flashing and gleaming with every motion of the blaze, and offering, let the eye wander where it might, interminable vistas of the same rich colour. The old oak wainscoting, the beams, the chairs, the seats, reflected it in a deep dull glimmer. There were fires and red curtains in the very eyes of the drinkers, in their buttons, in their liquor, in the pipes they smoked.

Mr. Willet sat in what had been his accustomed place five years before, with his eyes on the eternal boiler; and had sat there since the clock struck eight, giving no other signs of life than breathing with a loud and constant snore (though he was wide awake), and from time to time putting his glass to his lips, or knocking the ashes out of his pipe, and filling it anew. It was now half-past ten. Mr. Cobb and long Phil Parkes were his companions, as of old, and for two mortal hours and a half, none of the company had pronounced one word.

Whether people, by dint of sitting together in the same place and the same relative positions, and doing exactly the same things for a great many years, acquire a sixth sense, or some unknown power of influencing each other which serves them in its stead, is a question for philosophy to settle. But certain it is that old John Willet, Mr. Parkes, and Mr. Cobb, were one and all firmly of opinion that they were very jolly companions—rather choice spirits than otherwise; that they looked at each other every now and then as if there were a perpetual interchange of ideas going on among them; that no man considered himself or his neighbour by any means silent; and that each of them nodded occasionally when he caught the eye of another, as if he would say "You have expressed yourself extremely well, sir, in relation to that sentiment, and I quite agree with you."

The room was so very warm, the tobacco so very good, and the fire so very soothing, that Mr. Willet by degrees began to doze; but as he had perfectly acquired, by dint of long habit, the art of smoking in his sleep, and as his breathing was pretty much the same, awake or asleep, saving that in the latter case he sometimes experienced a slight difficulty in respiration (such as a carpenter meets with when he is planing and comes to a knot), neither of his companions was aware of the circumstance, until he met with one of these impediments and was obliged to try again.

"Johnny's dropped off," said Mr. Parkes in a whisper.

"Fast as a top," said Mr. Cobb.

Neither of them said any more until Mr. Willet came to another knot—one of surpassing obduracy—which bade fair to throw him into convulsions, but which he got over at last without waking, by an effort quite superhuman.

"He sleeps uncommon hard," said Mr. Cobb.

Mr. Parkes, who was possibly a hard sleeper himself, replied with some disdain "Not a bit on it;" and directed his eyes towards a hand-bill pasted over the chimney-piece, which was decorated at the top with a woodcut representing a youth of tender years running away very fast, with a bundle over his shoulder at the end of a stick, and —to carry out the idea—a finger-post and a mile-stone beside him. Mr. Cobb likewise turned his eyes in the same direction, and surveyed the placard as if that were the first time he had ever beheld it. Now, this was a document which Mr. Willet had himself indited on the disappearance of his son Joseph, acquainting the nobility and gentry and the public in general with the circumstances of his having left his home; describing his dress and appearance; and offering a reward of five pounds to any person or persons who would pack him up and return him safely to the Maypole at Chigwell, or lodge him in any of his Majesty's jails until such time as his father should come and claim him. In this advertisement Mr. Willet had obstinately persisted,

despite the advice and entreaties of his friends, in describing his son
as a "young boy;" and furthermore as being from eighteen inches to a
couple of feet shorter than he really was; two circumstances which
perhaps acounted, in some degree, for its never having been produc-
tive of any other effect than the transmission to Chigwell at various
times and at a vast expense, of some five-and-forty runaways varying
from six years old to twelve.

Mr. Cobb and Mr. Parkes looked mysteriously at this composition,
at each other, and at old John. From the time he had pasted it up
with his own hands, Mr. Willet had never by word or sign alluded to
the subject, or encouraged any one else to do so. Nobody had the least
notion what his thoughts or opinions were, connected with it; whether
he remembered it or forgot it; whether he had any idea that such
an event had ever taken place. Therefore, even while he slept, no
one ventured to refer to it in his presence; and for such sufficient
reasons, these his chosen friends were silent now.

Mr. Willet had got by this time into such a complication of knots,
that it was perfectly clear he must wake or die. He chose the former
alternative, and opened his eyes.

"If he don't come in five minutes," said John, "I shall have supper
without him."

The antecedent of this pronoun had been mentioned for the last
time at eight o'clock. Messrs. Parkes and Cobb being used to this
style of conversation, replied without difficulty that to be sure
Solomon was very late, and they wondered what had happened to
detain him.

"He an't blown away, I suppose," said Parkes. "It's enough to
carry a man of his figure off his legs, and easy too. Do you hear it? It
blows great guns, indeed. There'll be many a crash in the Forest
to-night, I reckon, and many a broken branch upon the ground
to-morrow."

"It won't break anything in the Maypole, I take it, sir," returned
old John. "Let it try. I give it leave—what's that?"

"The wind," cried Parkes. "It's howling like a Christian, and has
been all night long."

"Did you ever, sir," asked John, after a minute's contemplation,
"hear the wind say 'Maypole?'"

"Why, what man ever did?" said Parkes.

"Nor 'ahoy,' perhaps?" added John.

"No. Nor that either."

"Very good, sir," said Mr. Willet, perfectly unmoved; "then if
that was the wind just now, and you'll wait a little time without
speaking, you'll hear it say both words very plain."

Mr. Willet was right. After listening for a few moments, they
could clearly hear, above the roar and tumult out of doors, this
shout repeated; and that with a shrillness and energy, which denoted
that it came from some person in great distress or terror. They
looked at each other, turned pale, and held their breath. No man
stirred.

It was in this emergency that Mr. Willet displayed something of that strength of mind and plenitude of mental resource, which rendered him the admiration of all his friends and neighbours. After looking at Messrs. Parkes and Cobb for some time in silence, he clapped his two hands to his cheeks, and sent forth a roar which made the glasses dance and rafters ring—a long-sustained, discordant bellow, that rolled onward with the wind, and startling every echo, made the night a hundred times more boisterous—a deep, loud, dismal bray, that sounded like a human gong. Then, with every vein in his head and face swoln with the great exertion, and his countenance suffused with a lively purple, he drew a little nearer to the fire, and turning his back upon it, said with dignity:

"If that's any comfort to anybody, they're welcome to it. If it an't, I'm sorry for 'em. If either of you two gentlemen likes to go out and see what's the matter, you can. I'm not curious, myself."

While he spoke the cry drew nearer and nearer, footsteps passed the window, the latch of the door was raised, it opened, was violently shut again, and Solomon Daisy, with a lighted lantern in his hand, and the rain streaming from his disordered dress, dashed into the room.

A more complete picture of terror than the little man presented, it would be difficult to imagine. The perspiration stood in beads upon his face, his knees knocked together, his every limb trembled, the power of articulation was quite gone; and there he stood, panting for breath, gazing on them with such livid ashy looks, that they were infected with his fear, though ignorant of its occasion, and, reflecting his dismayed and horror-stricken visage, stared back again without venturing to question him; until old John Willet, in a fit of temporary insanity, made a dive at his cravat, and, seizing him by that portion of his dress, shook him to and fro until his very teeth appeared to rattle in his head.

"Tell us what's the matter, sir," said John, "or I'll kill you. Tell us what's the matter, sir, or in another second I'll have your head under the biler. How dare you look like that? Is anybody a-following of you? What do you mean? Say something, or I'll be the death of you, I will."

Mr. Willet, in his frenzy, was so near keeping his word to the very letter (Solomon Daisy's eyes already beginning to roll in an alarming manner, and certain guttural sounds, as of a choking man, to issue from his throat) that the two bystanders, recovering in some degree, plucked him off his victim by main force, and placed the little clerk of Chigwell in a chair. Directing a fearful gaze all round the room, he implored them in a faint voice to give him some drink; and above all to lock the house-door and close and bar the shutters of the room, without a moment's loss of time. The latter request did not tend to reassure his hearers, or to fill them with the most comfortable sensations; they complied with it, however, with the greatest expedition; and having handed him a bumper of brandy-and-water, nearly boiling hot, waited to hear what he might have to tell them.

"Oh, Johnny," said Solomon, shaking him by the hand. "Oh, Parkes. Oh, Tommy Cobb. Why did I leave this house to-night! On the nineteenth of March—of all nights in the year, on the nineteenth of March!"

They all drew closer to the fire. Parkes, who was nearest to the door, started and looked over his shoulder. Mr. Willet, with great indignation, inquired what the devil he meant by that—and then said, "God forgive me," and glanced over his own shoulder, and came a little nearer.

"When I left here to-night," said Solomon Daisy, "I little thought what day of the month it was. I have never gone alone into the church after dark on this day, for seven-and-twenty years. I have heard it said that as we keep our birthdays when we are alive, so the ghosts of dead people, who are not easy in their graves, keep the day they died upon.—How the wind roars!"

Nobody spoke. All eyes were fastened on Solomon.

"I might have known," he said, "what night it was, by the foul weather. There's no such night in the whole year round as this is, always. I never sleep quietly in my bed on the nineteenth of March."

"Go on," said Tom Cobb, in a low voice. "Nor I neither."

Solomon raised his glass to his lips; put it down upon the floor with such a trembling hand that the spoon tinkled in it like a little bell; and continued thus:

"Have I ever said that we are always brought back to this subject in some strange way, when the nineteenth of this month comes round? Do you suppose it was by accident, I forgot to wind up the church-clock? I never forgot it at any other time, though it's such a clumsy thing that it has to be wound up every day. Why should it escape my memory on this day of all others?

"I made as much haste down there as I could when I went from here, but I had to go home first for the keys; and the wind and rain being dead against me all the way, it was pretty well as much as I could do at times to keep my legs. I got there at last, opened the church-door, and went in. I had not met a soul all the way, and you may judge whether it was dull or not. Neither of you would bear me company. If you could have known what was to come, you'd have been in the right.

"The wind was so strong, that it was as much as I could do to shut the church-door by putting my whole weight against it; and even as it was, it burst wide open twice, with such strength that any of you would have sworn, if you had been leaning against it, as I was, that somebody was pushing on the other side. However, I got the key turned, went into the belfry, and wound up the clock—which was very near run down, and would have stood stock-still in half an hour.

"As I took up my lantern again to leave the church, it came upon me all at once that this was the nineteenth of March. It came upon me with a kind of shock, as if a hand had struck the thought upon my forehead; at the very same moment, I heard a voice outside the tower—rising from among the graves."

Here old John precipitately interrupted the speaker, and begged
that if Mr. Parkes (who was seated opposite to him and was staring
directly over his head) saw anything, he would have the goodness to
mention it. Mr. Parkes apologised, and remarked that he was only
listening; to which Mr. Willet angrily retorted, that his listening with
that kind of expression in his face was not agreeable, and that if he
couldn't look like other people, he had better put his pocket-handkerchief over his head. Mr. Parkes with great submission pledged himself to do so, if again required, and John Willet turning to Solomon
desired him to proceed. After waiting until a violent gust of wind
and rain, which seemed to shake even that sturdy house to its
foundation, had passed away, the little man complied:

"Never tell me that it was my fancy, or that it was any other
sound which I mistook for that I tell you of. I heard the wind whistle
through the arches of the church. I heard the steeple strain and
creak. I heard the rain as it came driving against the walls. I felt the
bells shake. I saw the ropes sway to and fro. And I heard that voice."

"What did it say?" asked Tom Cobb.

"I don't know what; I don't know that it spoke. It gave a kind of
cry, as any one of us might do, if something dreadful followed us in a
dream, and came upon us unawares; and then it died off: seeming to
pass quite round the church."

"I don't see much in that," said John drawing a long breath, and
looking round him like a man who felt relieved.

"Perhaps not," returned his friend, "but that's not all."

"What more do you mean to say, sir, is to come?" asked John,
pausing in the act of wiping his face upon his apron.

"What are you a-going to tell us of next?"

"What I saw."

"What I saw."

"Saw!" echoed all three, bending forward.

"When I opened the church-door to come out," said the little man,
with an expression of face which bore ample testimony to the
sincerity of his conviction, "when I opened the church door to come
out, which I did suddenly, for I wanted to get it shut again before
another gust of wind came up, there crossed me—so close, that by
stretching out my finger I could have touched it—something in the
likeness of a man. It was bareheaded to the storm. It turned its
face without stopping, and fixed its eyes on mine. It was a ghost—
a spirit."

"Whose?" they all three cried together.

In the excess of his emotion (for he fell back trembling in his chair,
and waved his hand as if entreating them to question him no further),
his answer was lost on all but old John Willet, who happened to be
seated close beside him.

"Who!" cried Parkes and Tom Cobb, looking eagerly by turns at
Solomon Daisy and at Mr. Willet. "Who was it?"

"Gentlemen," said Mr. Willet after a long pause, "you needn't ask.
The likeness of a murdered man. This is the nineteenth of March."

A profound silence ensued.

"If you'll take my advice," said John, "we had better, one and all, keep this a secret. Such tales would not be liked at the Warren. Let us keep it to ourselves for the present time at all events, or we may get into trouble, and Solomon may lose his place. Whether it was really as he says, or whether it wasn't, is no matter. Right or wrong, nobody would believe him. As to the probabilities, I don't myself think," said Mr. Willet, eyeing the corners of the room in a manner which showed that, like some other philosophers, he was not quite easy in his theory, "that a ghost as had been a man of sense in his lifetime, would be out a-walking in such weather—I only know that *I* wouldn't, if I was one."

But this heretical doctrine was strongly opposed by the other three, who quoted a great many precedents to show that bad weather was the very time for such appearances; and Mr. Parkes (who had had a ghost in his family, by the mother's side) argued the matter with so much ingenuity and force of illustration, that John was only saved from having to retract his opinion by the opportune appearance of supper, to which they applied themselves with a dreadful relish. Even Solomon Daisy himself, by dint of the elevating influences of fire, lights, brandy, and good company, so far recovered as to handle his knife and fork in a highly creditable manner and to display a capacity both of eating and drinking, such as banished all fear of his having sustained any lasting injury from his fright.

Supper done, they crowded round the fire again, and, as is common on such occasions, propounded all manner of leading questions calculated to surround the story with new horrors and surprises. But Solomon Daisy, notwithstanding these temptations, adhered so steadily to his original account, and repeated it so often, with such slight variations, and with such solemn asseverations of its truth and reality, that his hearers were (with good reason) more astonished than at first. As he took John Willet's view of the matter in regard to the propriety of not bruiting the tale abroad, unless the spirit should appear to him again, in which case it would be necessary to take immediate counsel with the clergyman, it was solemnly resolved that it should be hushed up and kept quiet. And as most men like to have a secret to tell which may exalt their own importance, they arrived at this conclusion with perfect unanimity.

As it was by this time growing late, and was long past their usual hour of separating, the cronies parted for the night. Solomon Daisy, with a fresh candle in his lantern, repaired homewards under the escort of long Phil Parkes and Mr. Cobb, who were rather more nervous than himself. Mr. Willet, after seeing them to the door, returned to collect his thoughts with the assistance of the boiler, and to listen to the storm of wind and rain, which had not yet abated one jot of its fury.

CHAPTER XXXIV

BEFORE old John had looked at the boiler quite twenty minutes, he got his ideas into a focus, and brought them to bear upon Solomon Daisy's story. The more he thought of it the more impressed he became with a sense of his own wisdom, and a desire that Mr. Haredale should be impressed with it likewise. At length, to the end that he might sustain a principal and important character in the affair; and might have the start of Solomon and his two friends, through whose means he knew the adventure, with a variety of exaggerations, would be known to at least a score of people, and most likely to Mr. Haredale himself, by breakfast-time to-morrow; he determined to repair to the Warren before going to bed.

"He's my landlord," thought John, as he took a candle in his hand, and setting it down in a corner out of the wind's way, opened a casement in the rear of the house, looking towards the stables. "We haven't met of late years so often as we used to do—changes are taking place in the family—it's desirable that I should stand as well with them, in point of dignity, as possible—the whispering about of this here tale will anger him—it's good to have confidences with a gentleman of his natur', and set one's-self right besides. Halloa there! Hugh—Hugh. Hal-loa!"

When he had repeated this shout a dozen times, and started every pigeon from its slumbers, a door in one of the ruinous old buildings opened, and a rough voice demanded what was amiss now, that a man couldn't even have his sleep in quiet.

"What! Haven't you sleep enough, growler, that you're not to be knocked up for once?" said John.

"No," replied the voice, as the speaker yawned and shook himself. "Not half enough."

"I don't know how you *can* sleep, with the wind a bellowsing and roaring about you, making the tiles fly like a pack of cards," said John; "but no matter for that. Wrap yourself up in something or another, and come here, for you must go as far as the Warren with me. And look sharp about it."

Hugh, with much low growling and muttering, went back into his lair; and presently reappeared, carrying a lantern and a cudgel, and enveloped from head to foot in an old, frowzy, slouching horse-cloth. Mr. Willet received this figure at the back-door, and ushered him into the bar, while he wrapped himself in sundry great-coats and capes, and so tied and knotted his face in shawls and handkerchiefs, that how he breathed was a mystery.

"You don't take a man out of doors at near midnight in such weather, without putting some heart into him, do you, master?" said Hugh.

"Yes I do, sir," returned Mr. Willet. "I put the heart (as you call it) into him when he has brought me safe home again, and his standing steady on his legs an't of so much consequence. So hold that

light up, if you please, and go on a step or two before, to show the
way."

Hugh obeyed with a very indifferent grace, and a longing glance
at the bottles. Old John, laying strict injunctions on his cook to
keep the doors locked in his absence, and to open to nobody but
himself on pain of dismissal, followed him into the blustering darkness out of doors.

The way was wet and dismal, and the night so black, that if Mr.
Willet had been his own pilot, he would have walked into a deep
horse-pond within a few hundred yards of his own house, and would
certainly have terminated his career in that ignoble sphere of action.
But Hugh, who had a sight as keen as any hawk's, and, apart from
that endowment, could have found his way blindfold to any place
within a dozen miles, dragged old John along, quite deaf to his
remonstrances, and took his own course without the slightest
reference to, or notice of, his master. So they made head against the
wind as they best could; Hugh crushing the wet grass beneath his
heavy tread, and stalking on after his ordinary savage fashion; John
Willet following at arm's length, picking his steps, and now looking
about him, now for bogs and ditches, and now for such stray ghosts
as might be wandering abroad, with looks of as much dismay and
uneasiness as his immovable face was capable of expressing.

At length he stood upon the broad gravel-walk before the Warren-
house. The building was profoundly dark, and none were moving
near it save themselves. From one solitary turret-chamber, however,
there shone a ray of light; and towards this peak of comfort in the
cold, cheerless, silent scene, Mr. Willet bade his pilot lead him.

"The old room," said John, looking timidly upward; "Mr. Reuben's own apartment, God be with us! I wonder his brother likes to
sit there, so late at night—on this night too."

"Why, where else should he sit?" asked Hugh, holding the lantern
to his breast, to keep the candle from the wind, while he trimmed it
with his fingers. "It's snug enough, an't it?"

"Snug!" said John indignantly. "You have a comfortable idea of
snugness, you have, sir. Do you know what was done in that room,
you ruffian?"

"Why, what is it the worse for that!" cried Hugh, looking into
John's fat face. "Does it keep out the rain, and snow, and wind, the
less for that? Is it less warm or dry, because a man was killed there?
Ha, ha, ha! Never believe it, master. One man's no such matter as
that comes to."

Mr. Willet fixed his dull eyes on his follower, and began—by a
species of inspiration—to think it just barely possible that he was
something of a dangerous character, and that it might be advisable
to get rid of him one of these days. He was too prudent to say anything, with the journey home before him; and therefore turned to the
iron gate before which this brief dialogue had passed, and pulled the
handle of the bell that hung beside it. The turret at which the light
appeared being at one corner of the building, and only divided from

the path by one of the garden-walks, upon which this gate opened, Mr. Haredale threw up the window directly, and demanded who was there.

"Begging pardon, sir," said John, "I knew you sat up late, and made bold to come round, having a word to say to you."

"Willet—is it not?"

"Of the Maypole—at your service, sir."

Mr. Haredale closed the window, and withdrew. He presently appeared at a door in the bottom of the turret, and coming across the garden-walk, unlocked the gate and let them in.

"You are a late visitor, Willet. What is the matter?"

"Nothing to speak of, sir," said John; "an idle tale, I thought you ought to know of; nothing more."

"Let your man go forward with the lantern, and give me your hand. The stairs are crooked and narrow. Gently with your light, friend. You swing it like a censer."

Hugh, who had already reached the turret, held it more steadily and ascended first, turning round from time to time to shed his light downwards on the step. Mr. Haredale following next, eyed his lowering face with no great favour; and Hugh, looking down on him, returned his glances with interest, as they climbed the winding stairs.

It terminated in a little ante-room adjoining that from which they had seen the light. Mr. Haredale entered first, and led the way through it into the latter chamber, where he seated himself at a writing-table from which he had risen when they had rung the bell.

"Come in," he said, beckoning to old John, who remained bowing at the door. "Not you, friend," he added hastily to Hugh, who entered also. "Willet, why do you bring that fellow here?"

"Why, sir," returned John, elevating his eyebrows, and lowering his voice to the tone in which the question had been asked him, 'he's a good guard, you see."

"Don't be too sure of that," said Mr. Haredale, looking towards him as he spoke. "I doubt it. He has an evil eye."

"There's no imagination in his eye," returned Mr. Willet, glancing over his shoulder at the organ in question, "certainly."

"There is no good there, be assured," said Mr. Haredale. "Wait in that little room, friend, and close the door between us."

Hugh shrugged his shoulders, and with a disdainful look, which showed, either that he had overheard, or that he guessed the purport of their whispering, did as he was told. When he was shut out, Mr. Haredale turned to John, and bade him go on with what he had to say, but not to speak too loud, for there were quick ears yonder.

Thus cautioned, Mr. Willet, in an oily whisper, recited all that he had heard and said that night; laying particular stress upon his own sagacity, upon his great regard for the family, and upon his solicitude for their peace of mind and happiness. The story moved his auditor much more than he had expected. Mr. Haredale often changed his attitude, rose and paced the room, returned again, desired him to repeat, as nearly as he could, the very words that Solomon had used, and gave so many other signs of being disturbed and ill at ease, that even Mr. Willet was surprised.

"You did quite right," he said, at the end of a long conversation, "to bid them keep this story secret. It is a foolish fancy on the part of this weak-brained man, bred in his fears and superstition. But Miss Haredale, though she would know it to be so, would be disturbed by it if it reached her ears; it is too nearly connected with a subject very painful to us all, to be heard with indifference. You were most prudent, and have laid me under a great obligation. I thank you very much."

This was equal to John's most sanguine expectations; but he would have preferred Mr. Haredale's looking at him when he spoke, as if he really did thank him, to his walking up and down, speaking by fits and starts, often stopping with his eyes fixed on the ground, moving hurriedly on again, like one distracted, and seeming almost unconscious of what he said or did.

This, however, was his manner; and it was so embarrassing to John that he sat quite passive for a long time, not knowing what to do. At length he rose. Mr. Haredale stared at him for a moment as though he had quite forgotten his being present, then shook hands with him, and opened the door. Hugh, who was, or feigned to be, fast asleep on the antechamber floor, sprang up on their entrance, and throwing his cloak about him, grasped his stick and lantern, and prepared to descend the stairs.

"Stay," said Mr. Haredale. "Will this man drink?"

"Drink! He'd drink the Thames up, if it was strong enough, sir," replied John Willet. "He'll have something when he gets home. He's better without it, now, sir."

"Nay. Half the distance is done," said Hugh. "What a hard master you are! I shall go home the better for one glassful, half-way. Come!"

As John made no reply, Mr. Haredale brought out a glass of liquor and gave it to Hugh, who, as he took it in his hand, threw part of it upon the floor.

"What do you mean by splashing your drink about a gentleman's house, sir?" said John.

"I'm drinking a toast," Hugh rejoined, holding the glass above his head, and fixing his eyes on Mr. Haredale's face; "a toast to this house and its master." With that he muttered something to himself, and drank the rest, and setting down the glass, preceded them without another word.

John was a good deal scandalised by this observance, but seeing that Mr. Haredale took little heed of what Hugh said or did, and that his thoughts were otherwise employed, he offered no apology, and went in silence down the stairs, across the walk, and through the garden-gate. They stopped upon the outer side for Hugh to hold the light while Mr. Haredale locked it on the inner; and then John saw with wonder (as he often afterwards related), that he was very pale, and that his face had changed so much and grown so haggard since their entrance, that he almost seemed another man.

They were in the open road again, and John Willet was walking on behind his escort, as he had come, thinking very steadily of what he had just now seen, when Hugh drew him suddenly aside, and almost at the same instant three horsemen swept past—the nearest brushed his shoulder even then—who, checking their steeds as suddenly as they could, stood still, and waited for their coming up.

CHAPTER XXXV

WHEN John Willet saw that the horsemen wheeled smartly round, and drew up three abreast in the narrow road, waiting for him and his man to join them, it occurred to him with unusual precipitation that they must be highwaymen; and had Hugh been armed with a blunderbuss, in place of his stout cudgel, he would certainly have ordered him to fire it off at a venture, and would, while the word of command was obeyed, have consulted his own personal safety in immediate flight. Under the circumstances of disadvantage, however, in which he and his guard were placed, he deemed it prudent to adopt a different style of generalship, and therefore whispered his attendant to address them in the most peaceable and courteous terms. By way of acting up to the spirit and letter of this instruction, Hugh stepped forward, and flourishing his staff before the very eyes of the rider nearest to him, demanded roughly what he and his fellows meant by so nearly galloping over them, and why they scoured the king's highway at that late hour of night.

The man whom he addressed was beginning an angry reply in the same strain, when he was checked by the horseman in the centre, who, interposing with an air of authority, inquired in a somewhat loud but not harsh or unpleasant voice:

"Pray, is this the London road?"

"If you follow it right, it is," replied Hugh roughly.

"Nay, brother," said the same person, "you're but a churlish Englishman, if Englishman you be—which I should much doubt but for your tongue. Your companion, I am sure, will answer me more civilly. How say you, friend?"

"I say it is the London road, sir," answered John. "And I wish," he added in a subdued voice, as he turned to Hugh, "that you was in any other road, you vagabond. Are you tired of your life, sir, that you go a-trying to provoke three great neck-or-nothing chaps, that could keep on running over us, back'ards and for'ards, till we was dead, and then take our bodies up behind 'em, and drown us ten miles off?"

"How far is it to London?" inquired the same speaker.

"Why, from here, sir," answered John, persuasively, "it's thirteen very easy mile."

The adjective was thrown in, as an inducement to the travellers to ride away with all speed; but instead of having the desired effect, it elicited from the same person, the remark, "Thirteen miles! That's a long distance!" which was followed by a short pause of indecision.

"Pray," said the gentleman, "are there any inns hereabouts?"

At the word "inns," John plucked up his spirit in a surprising manner; his fears rolled off like smoke; all the landlord stirred within him.

"There are no inns," rejoined Mr. Willet, with a strong emphasis on the plural number; "but there's a Inn—one Inn—the Maypole Inn. That's a Inn indeed. You won't see the like of that Inn often."

"You keep it, perhaps?" said the horseman, smiling.

"I do, sir," replied John, greatly wondering how he had found this out.

"And how far is the Maypole from here?"

"About a mile"—John was going to add that it was the easiest mile in all the world, when the third rider, who had hitherto kept a little in the rear, suddenly interposed:

"And have you one excellent bed, landlord? Hem! A bed that you can recommend—a bed that you are sure is well aired—a bed that has been slept in by some perfectly respectable and unexceptionable person?"

"We don't take in no tagrag and bobtail at our house, sir," answered John. "And as to the bed itself—"

"Say, as to three beds," interposed the gentleman who had spoken before; "for we shall want three if we stay, though my friend only speaks of one."

"No, no, my lord; you are too good, you are too kind; but your life is of far too much importance to the nation in these portentous times, to be placed upon a level with one so useless and so poor as mine. A great cause, my lord, a mighty cause, depends on you. You are its leader and its champion, its advanced guard and its van. It is the cause of our altars and our homes, our country and our faith. Let *me* sleep on a chair—the carpet—anywhere. No one will repine if *I* take cold or fever. Let John Grueby pass the night beneath the open sky —no one will pine for *him*. But forty thousand men of this our island in the wave (exclusive of women and children) rivet their eyes and thoughts on Lord George Gordon; and every day, from the rising up of the sun to the going down of the same, pray for his health and vigour. My lord," said the speaker, rising in his stirrups, "it is a glorious cause, and must not be forgotten. My lord, it is a mighty cause, and must not be endangered. My lord, it is a holy cause, and must not be deserted."

"It *is* a holy cause," exclaimed his lordship, lifting up his hat with great solemnity. "Amen."

"John Grueby," said the long-winded gentleman, in a tone of mild reproof, "his lordship said Amen."

"I heard my lord, sir," said the man, sitting like a statue on his horse.

"And do not *you* say Amen, likewise?"

To which John Grueby made no reply at all, but sat looking straight before him.

"You surprise me, Grueby," said the gentleman. "At a crisis like

the present, when Queen Elizabeth, that maiden monarch, weeps
within her tomb, and Bloody Mary, with a brow of gloom and shadow
stalks triumphant—"

"Oh, sir," cried the man, gruffly, "where's the use of talking of
Bloody Mary, under such circumstances as the present, when my
lord's wet through, and tired with hard riding? Let's either go on to
London, sir, or put up at once; or that unfort'nate Bloody Mary will
have more to answer for—and she's done a deal more harm in her
grave than she ever did in her lifetime, I believe."

By this time Mr. Willet, who had never heard so many words
spoken together at one time, or delivered with such volubility and
emphasis as by the long-winded gentleman; and whose brain, being
wholly unable to sustain or compass them, had quite given itself up
for lost; recovered so far as to observe that there was ample accommodation at the Maypole for all the party: good beds; neat wines;
excellent entertainment for man and beast; private rooms for large
and small parties; dinners dressed upon the shortest notice; choice
stabling, and a lock-up coach-house; and, in short, to run over such
recommendatory scraps of language as were painted up on various
portions of the building, and which in the course of some forty years
he had learnt to repeat with tolerable correctness. He was considering whether it was at all possible to insert any novel sentences to the
same purpose, when the gentleman who had spoken first, turning to
him of the long wind, exclaimed, "What say you, Gashford? Shall
we tarry at this house he speaks of, or press forward? You shall
decide."

"I would submit, my lord, then," returned the person he appealed
to, in a silky tone, "that your health and spirits—so important, under
Providence, to our great cause, our pure and truthful cause"—here
his lordship pulled off his hat again, though it was raining hard—
"require refreshment and repose."

"Go on before, landlord, and show the way," said Lord George
Gordon; "we will follow at a footpace."

"If you'll give me leave, my lord," said John Grueby, in a low
voice, "I'll change my proper place, and ride before you. The looks
of the landlord's friend are not over honest, and it may be as well to
be cautious with him."

"John Grueby is quite right," interposed Mr. Gashford, falling
back hastily. "My lord, a life so precious as yours must not be put in
peril. Go forward, John, by all means. If you have any reason to suspect the fellow, blow his brains out."

John made no answer, but looking straight before him, as his
custom seemed to be when the secretary spoke, bade Hugh push on,
and followed close behind him. Then came his lordship, with Mr.
Willet at his bridle rein; and, last of all, his lordship's secretary—
for that, it seemed, was Gashford's office.

Hugh strode briskly on, often looking back at the servant, whose
horse was close upon his heels, and glancing with a leer at his holster
case of pistols, by which he seemed to set great store. He was a square

built, strong-made, bull-necked fellow, of the true English breed; and as Hugh measured him with his eye, he measured Hugh, regarding him meanwhile with a look of bluff disdain. He was much older than the Maypole man, being to all appearance five and-forty; but was one of those self-possessed, hard-headed, imperturbable fellows, who, if they are ever beaten at fisticuffs, or other kind of warfare, never know it, and go on coolly till they win.

"If I led you wrong now," said Hugh, tauntingly, "you'd —ha ha ha!—you'd shoot me through the head, I suppose."

John Grueby took no more notice of this remark than if he had been deaf and Hugh dumb; but kept riding on quite comfortably, with his eyes fixed on the horizon.

"Did you ever try a fall with a man when you were young, master?" said Hugh. "Can you make any play at single-stick?"

John Grueby looked at him sideways with the same contented air, but deigned not a word in answer.

"—Like this?" said Hugh, giving his cudgel one of those skilful flourishes, in which the rustic of that time delighted. "Whoop!"

"—Or that," returned John Grueby, beating down his guard with his whip, and striking him on the head with its butt end. "Yes, I played a little once. You wear your hair too long; I should have cracked your crown if it had been a little shorter."

It was a pretty smart, loud-sounding rap, as it was, and evidently astonished Hugh; who, for the moment, seemed disposed to drag his new acquaintance from his saddle. But his face betokening neither malice, triumph, rage, nor any lingering idea that he had given him offence; his eyes gazing steadily in the old direction, and his manner being as careless and composed as if he had merely brushed away a fly; Hugh was so puzzled, and so disposed to look upon him as a customer of almost supernatural toughness, that he merely laughed, and cried "Well done!" then, sheering off a little, led the way in silence.

Before the lapse of many minutes the party halted at the Maypole door. Lord George and his secretary quickly dismounting, gave their horses to their servant, who, under the guidance of Hugh, repaired to the stables. Right glad to escape from the inclemency of the night, they followed Mr. Willet into the common room, and stood warming themselves and drying their clothes before the cheerful fire, while he busied himself with such orders and preparations as his guest's high quality required.

As he bustled in and out of the room intent on these arrangements, he had an opportunity of observing the two travellers, of whom, as yet, he knew nothing but the voice. The lord, the great personage who did the Maypole so much honour, was about the middle height, of a slender make, and sallow complexion, with an aquiline nose, and long hair of a reddish brown, combed perfectly straight and smooth about his ears, and slightly powdered, but without the faintest vestige of a curl. He was attired, under his great-coat, in a full suit of black, quite free from any ornament, and of the most precise and sober

cut. The gravity of his dress, together with a certain lankness of cheek
and stiffness of deportment, added nearly ten years to his age, but
his figure was that of one not yet past thirty. As he stood musing
in the red glow of the fire, it was striking to observe his very bright
large eye, which betrayed a restlessness of thought and purpose,
singularly at variance with the studied composure and sobriety of
his mien, and with his quaint and sad apparel. It had nothing harsh
or cruel in its expression; neither had his face, which was thin and
mild, and wore an air of melancholy; but it was suggestive of an air
of indefinable uneasiness, which infected those who looked upon him,
and filled them with a kind of pity for the man: though why it did so,
they would have some trouble to explain.

Gashford, the secretary, was taller, angularly made, high-shouldered, bony, and ungraceful. His dress, in imitation of his superior,
was demure and staid in the extreme; his manner, formal and constrained. This gentleman had an overhanging brow, great hands and
feet and ears, and a pair of eyes that seemed to have made an unnatural retreat into his head, and to have dug themselves a cave to
hide in. His manner was smooth and humble, but very sly and slinking. He wore the aspect of a man who was always lying in wait for
something that *wouldn't* come to pass; but he looked patient—very
patient—and fawned like a spaniel dog. Even now, while he warmed
and rubbed his hands before the blaze, he had the air of one who only
presumed to enjoy it in his degree as a commoner; and though he
knew his lord was not regarding him, he looked into his face from
time to time, and with a meek and deferential manner, smiled as if
for practice.

Such were the guests whom old John Willet, with a fixed and
leaden eye, surveyed a hundred times, and to whom he now advanced
with a state candlestick in each hand, beseeching them to follow
him into a worthier chamber. "For my lord," said John—it is odd
enough, but certain people seem to have as great a pleasure in pronouncing titles as their owners have in wearing them—"this room,
my lord, isn't at all the sort of place for your lordship, and I have to
beg your lordship's pardon for keeping you here, my lord, one
minute."

With this address, John ushered them up-stairs into the state
apartment, which, like many other things of state, was cold and
comfortless. Their own footsteps, reverberating through the spacious
room, struck upon their hearing with a hollow sound; and its damp
and chilly atmosphere was rendered doubly cheerless by contrast
with the homely warmth they had deserted.

It was of no use, however, to propose a return to the place they
had quitted, for the preparations went on so briskly that there was
no time to stop them. John, with the tall candlesticks in his hands,
bowed them up to the fire-place; Hugh, striding in with a lighted
brand and pile of fire-wood, cast it down upon the hearth, and set it
in a blaze; John Grueby (who had a great blue cockade in his hat,
which he appeared to despise mightily) brought in the portmanteau

he had carried on his horse, and placed it on the floor; and presently all three were busily engaged in drawing out the screen, laying the cloth, inspecting the beds, lighting fires in the bedrooms, expediting the supper, and making everything as cosy and as snug as might be, on so short a notice. In less than an hour's time, supper had been served, and ate, and cleared away; and Lord George and his secretary, with slippered feet, and legs stretched out before the fire, sat over some hot mulled wine together.

"So ends, my lord," said Gashford, filling his glass with great complacency, "the blessed work of a most blessed day."

"And of a blessed yesterday," said his lordship, raising his head.

"Ah!"—and here the secretary clasped his hands—"a blessed yesterday indeed! The Protestants of Suffolk are godly men and true. Though others of our countrymen have lost their way in darkness, even as we, my lord, did lose our road to night, theirs is the light and glory."

"Did I move them, Gashford?" said Lord George.

"Move them, my lord! Move them! They cried to be led on against the Papists, they vowed a dreadful vengeance on their heads, they roared like men possessed—"

"But not by devils," said his lord.

"By devils! my lord! By angels."

"Yes—oh surely—by angels, no doubt," said Lord George, thrusting his hands into his pockets, taking them out again to bite his nails, and looking uncomfortably at the fire. "Of course by angels—eh, Gashford?"

"You do not doubt it, my lord?" said the secretary.

"No—no," returned his lord. "No. Why should I? I suppose it would be decidedly irreligious to doubt it—wouldn't it, Gashford? Though there certainly were," he added, without waiting for an answer, "some plaguy ill-looking characters among them."

"When you warmed," said the secretary, looking sharply at the other's downcast eyes, which brightened slowly as he spoke; "when you warmed into that noble outbreak; when you told them that you were never of the lukewarm or the timid tribe, and bade them take heed that they were prepared to follow one who would lead them on, though to the very death; when you spoke of a hundred and twenty thousand men across the Scottish border who would take their own redress at any time, if it were not conceded; when you cried 'Perish the Pope and all his base adherents; the penal laws against them shall never be repealed while Englishmen have hearts and hands'— and waved your own and touched your sword; and when they cried 'No Popery!' and you cried 'No; not even if we wade in blood,' and they threw up their hats and cried 'Hurrah! not even if we wade in blood; No Popery! Lord George! Down with the Papists—Vengeance on their heads.' when this was said and done, and a word from you, my lord, could raise or still the tumult—ah! then I felt what greatness was indeed, and thought, When was there ever power like this of Lord George Gordon's!"

"It's a great power. You're right. It is a great power!" he cried with sparkling eyes. "But—dear Gashford—did I really say all that?"

"And how much more!" cried the secretary, looking upwards. "Ah! how much more!"

"And I told them what you say, about the one hundred and forty thousand men in Scotland, did I!" he asked with evident delight. "That was bold."

"Our cause is boldness. Truth is always bold."

"Certainly. So is religion. She's bold, Gashford?"

"The true religion is, my lord."

"And that's ours," he rejoined, moving uneasily in his seat, and biting his nails as though he would pare them to the quick. "There can be no doubt of ours being the true one. You feel as certain of that as I do, Gashford, don't you?"

"Does my lord ask *me*," whined Gashford, drawing his chair nearer with an injured air, and laying his broad flat hand upon the table; "*me*," he repeated, bending the dark hollows of his eyes upon him with an unwholesome smile, "who, stricken by the magic of his eloquence in Scotland but a year ago, abjured the errors of the Romish church, and clung to him as one whose timely hand had plucked me from a pit?"

"True. No—no. I—I didn't mean it," replied the other, shaking him by the hand, rising from his seat, and pacing restlessly about the room. "It's a proud thing to lead the people, Gashford," he added as he made a sudden halt.

"By force of reason too," returned the pliant secretary.

"Ay, to be sure. They may cough and jeer, and groan in Parliament, and call me fool and madman, but which of them can raise this human sea and make it swell and roar at pleasure? Not one."

"Not one," repeated Gashford.

"Which of them can say for his honesty, what I can say for mine; which of them has refused a minister's bribe of one thousand pounds a year, to resign his seat in favour of another? Not one."

"Not one," repeated Gashford again—taking the lion's share of the mulled wine between whiles.

"And as we are honest, true, and in a sacred cause, Gashford," said Lord George with a heightened colour and in a louder voice, as he laid his fevered hand upon his shoulder, "and are the only men who regard the mass of people out of doors, or are regarded by them, we will uphold them to the last; and will raise a cry against these un-English Papists which shall re-echo through the country, and roll with a noise like thunder. I will be worthy of the motto on my coat of arms, 'Called and chosen and faithful.' "

"Called," said the secretary, "by Heaven."

"I am."

"Chosen by the people."

"Yes."

"Faithful to both."

"To the block!"

It would be difficult to convey an adequate idea of the excited manner in which he gave these answers to the secretary's promptings; of the rapidity of his utterance, or the violence of his tone and gesture in which, struggling through his Puritan's demeanour, was something wild and ungovernable which broke through all restraint. For some minutes he walked rapidly up and down the room, then stopping suddenly, exclaimed,

"Gashford—*You* moved them yesterday too. Oh yes! You did."

"I shone with a reflected light, my lord," replied the humble secretary, laying his hand upon his heart. "I did my best."

"You did well," said his master, "and are a great and worthy instrument. If you will ring for John Grueby to carry the portmanteau into my room, and will wait here while I undress, we will dispose of business as usual, if you're not too tired."

"Too tired, my lord!—But this is his consideration! Christian from head to foot." With which soliloquy, the secretary tilted the jug, and looked very hard into the mulled wine, to see how much remained.

John Willet and John Grueby appeared together. The one bearing the great candlesticks, and the other the portmanteau, showed the deluded lord into his chamber; and left the secretary alone, to yawn and shake himself, and finally to fall asleep before the fire.

"Now, Mr. Gashford sir," said John Grueby in his ear, after what appeared to him a moment of unconsciousness; "my lord's abed."

"Oh. Very good, John," was his mild reply. "Thank you, John. Nobody need sit up. I know my room."

"I hope you're not a-going to trouble your head to-night, or my lord's head neither, with anything more about Bloody Mary," said John. "I wish the blessed old creetur had never been born."

"I said you might go to bed, John," returned the secretary. You didn't hear me, I think."

"Between Bloody Marys, and blue cockades, and glorious Queen Besses, and no Poperys, and Protestant associations, and making of speeches," pursued John Grueby, looking, as usual, a long way off, and taking no notice of this hint, "my lord's half off his head. When we go out o' doors, such a set of ragamuffins comes a-shouting after us, 'Gordon for ever!' that I'm ashamed of myself and don't know where to look. When we're in-doors they come a-roaring and screaming about the house like so many devils; and my lord instead of ordering them to be drove away, goes out into the balcony and demeans himself by making speeches to 'em, and calls 'em 'Men of England,' and 'Fellow-countrymen,' as if he was fond of 'em and thanked 'em for coming. I can't make it out, but they're all mixed up somehow or another with that unfort'nate Bloody Mary, and call her name out till they're hoarse. They're all Protestants too—every man and boy among 'em: and Protestants are very fond of spoons I find, and silver-plate in general, whenever area-gates is left open accidentally. I wish that was the worst of it, and that no more harm might be to come; but if you don't stop these ugly customers in time, Mr. Gashford (and I know you; you're the man that blows the fire), you'll find 'em grow a little bit too strong for you. One of these evenings, when the weather gets warmer and Protestants are thirsty, they'll be pulling London down,—and I never heard that Bloody Mary went as far as *that*."

Gashford had vanished long ago, and these remarks had been bestowed on empty air. Not at all discomposed by the discovery, John Grueby fixed his hat on, wrong side foremost that he might be unconscious of the shadow of the obnoxious cockade, and withdrew to bed; shaking his head in a very gloomy and pathetic manner until he reached his chamber.

CHAPTER XXXVI

GASHFORD, with a smiling face, but still with looks of profound deference and humility, betook himself towards his master's room, smoothing his hair down as he went, and humming a psalm tune. As he approached Lord George's door, he cleared his throat and hummed more vigorously.

There was a remarkable contrast between this man's occupation at the moment, and the expression of his countenance, which was singularly repulsive and malicious. His beetling brow almost obscured his eyes; his lip was curled contemptuously; his very shoulders seemed to sneer in stealthy whisperings with his great flapped ears.

"Hush!" he muttered softly, as he peeped in at the chamber-door. "He seems to be asleep. Pray Heaven he is! Too much watching, too much care, too much thought—ah! Lord preserve him for a martyr! He is a saint, if ever saint drew breath on this bad earth."

Placing his light upon a table, he walked on tiptoe to the fire, and sitting in a chair before it with his back towards the bed, went on communing with himself like one who thought aloud:

"The saviour of his country and his country's religion, the friend of his poor countrymen, the enemy of the proud and harsh; beloved of the rejected and oppressed, adored by forty thousand bold and loyal English hearts—what happy slumbers his should be!" And here he sighed, and warmed his hands, and shook his head as men do when their hearts are full, and heaved another sigh, and warmed his hands again.

"Why, Gashford?" said Lord George, who was lying broad awake, upon his side, and had been staring at him from his entrance.

"My—my lord," said Gashford, starting and looking round as though in great surprise. "I have disturbed you!"

"I have not been sleeping."

"Not sleeping!" he repeated, with assumed confusion. "What can I say for having in your presence given utterance to thoughts—but they were sincere—they were sincere!" exclaimed the secretary, drawing his sleeve in a hasty way across his eyes; "and why should I regret your having heard them?"

"Gashford," said the poor lord, stretching out his hand with manifest emotion. "Do not regret it. You love me well, I know—too well. I don't deserve such homage."

Gashford made no reply, but grasped the hand and pressed it to his lips. Then rising, and taking from the trunk a little desk, he placed it on the table near the fire, unlocked it with a key he carried in his pocket, sat down before it, took out a pen, and, before dipping it in the inkstand, sucked it—to compose the fashion of his mouth perhaps, on which a smile was hovering yet.

"How do our numbers stand since last enrolling-night?" inquired Lord George. "Are we really forty thousand strong, or do we still speak in round numbers when we take the Association at that amount?"

"Our total now exceeds that number by a score and three," Gashford replied, casting his eyes upon his papers.

"The funds?"

"Not *very* improving; but there is some manna in the wilderness, my lord. Hem! On Friday night the widows' mites dropped in. 'Forty scavengers, three and fourpence. An aged pew-opener of St. Martin's parish, sixpence. A bell-ringer of the established church, sixpence. A Protestant infant, newly born, one halfpenny. The United Link Boys, three shillings—one bad. The anti-popish prisoners in Newgate, five and fourpence. A friend in Bedlam, half-a-crown. Dennis the hangman, one shilling.' "

"That Dennis," said his lordship, "is an earnest man. I marked him in the crowd in Welbeck-street, last Friday."

"A good man," rejoined the secretary, "a staunch, sincere, and truly zealous man."

"He should be encouraged," said Lord George. "Make a note of Dennis. I'll talk with him."

Gashford obeyed, and went on reading from his list:

" 'The Friends of Reason, half-a-guinea. The Friends of Liberty, half-a-guinea. The Friends of Peace, half-a-guinea. The Friends of Charity, half-a guinea. The Friends of Mercy, half-a-guinea. The Associated Rememberers of Bloody Mary, half-a-guinea. The United Bull-dogs, half-a-guinea.' "

"The United Bull-dogs," said Lord George, biting his nails most horribly, "are a new society, are they not?"

"Formerly the 'Prentice Knights, my lord. The indentures of the old members expiring by degrees, they changed their name, it seems, though they still have 'prentices among them, as well as workmen."

"What is their president's name?" inquired Lord George.

"President," said Gashford, reading, "Mr. Simon Tappertit."

"I remember him. The little man, who sometimes brings an elderly sister to our meetings, and sometimes another female too, who is conscientious, I have no doubt, but not well-favoured?"

"The very same, my lord."

"Tappertit is an earnest man," said Lord George, thoughtfully. "Eh, Gashford?"

"One of the foremost among them all, my lord. He snuffs the battle from afar, like a war-horse. He throws his hat up in the street as if he were inspired, and makes most stirring speeches from the shoulders of his friends."

"Make a note of Tappertit," said Lord George Gordon. "We may advance him to a place of trust."

"That," rejoined the secretary, doing as he was told, "is all—except Mrs. Varden's box (fourteenth time of opening), seven shillings and sixpence in silver and copper, and half-a-guinea in gold; and Miggs (being the saving of a quarter's wages), one-and-threepence."

"Miggs," said Lord George. "Is that a man?"

"The name is entered on the list as a woman," replied the secretary. "I think she is the tall spare female of whom you spoke just now, my lord, as not being well-favoured, who sometimes comes to hear the speeches—along with Tappertit and Mrs. Varden."

"Mrs. Varden is the elderly lady then, is she?"

The secretary nodded, and rubbed the bridge of his nose with the feather of his pen.

"She is a zealous sister," said Lord George. "Her collection goes on prosperously, and is pursued with fervour. Has her husband joined?"

"A malignant," returned the secretary, folding up his papers. "Unworthy such a wife. He remains in outer darkness and steadily refuses."

"The consequences be upon his own head!—Gashford!"

"My lord!"

"You don't think," he turned restlessly in his bed as he spoke, "these people will desert me, when the hour arrives? I have spoken boldly for them, ventured much, suppressed nothing. They'll not fall off, will they?"

"No fear of that, my lord," said Gashford, with a meaning look, which was rather the involuntary expression of his own thoughts than intended as any confirmation of his words, for the other's face was turned away. "Be sure there is no fear of that."

"Nor," he said with a more restless motion than before, "of their—but they *can* sustain no harm from leaguing for this purpose. Right is on our side, though Might may be against us. You feel as sure of that as I—honestly, you do?"

The secretary was beginning with "You do not doubt," when the other interrupted him, and impatiently rejoined:

"Doubt. No. Who says I doubt? If I doubted should I cast away relatives, friends, everything, for this unhappy country's sake; this unhappy country," he cried, springing up in bed, after repeating the phrase "unhappy country's sake," to himself, at least a dozen times, "forsaken of God and man, delivered over to a dangerous confederacy of Popish powers; the prey of corruption, idolatry, and despotism! Who says I doubt? Am I called, and chosen, and faithful? Tell me. Am I, or am I not?"

"To God, the country, and yourself," cried Gashford.

"I am. I will be. I say again, I will be: to the block. Who says as much! Do you? Does any man alive?"

The secretary drooped his head with an expression of perfect acquiescence in anything that had been said or might be; and Lord George gradually sinking down upon his pillow, fell asleep.

Although there was something very ludicrous in his vehement manner, taken in conjunction with his meagre aspect and ungraceful presence, it would scarcely have provoked a smile in any man of kindly feeling; or even if it had, he would have felt sorry and almost angry with himself next moment, for yielding to the impulse. This lord was sincere in his violence and in his wavering. A nature prone to false enthusiasm, and the vanity of being a leader, were the worst qualities apparent in his composition. All the rest was weakness—sheer weakness; and it is the unhappy lot of thoroughly weak men, that their very sympathies, affections, confidences—all the qualities which in better constituted minds are virtues—dwindle into foibles, or turn into downright vices.

Gashford, with many a sly look towards the bed, sat chuckling at his master's folly, until his deep and heavy breathing warned him that he might retire. Locking his desk, and replacing it within the trunk (but not before he had taken from a secret lining two printed handbills), he cautiously withdrew; looking back, as he went, at the pale face of the slumbering man, above whose head the dusty plumes that crowned the Maypole couch, waved drearily and sadly as though it were a bier.

Stopping on the staircase to listen that all was quiet, and to take off his shoes lest his footsteps should alarm any light sleeper who might be near at hand, he descended to the ground floor, and thrust one of his bills beneath the great door of the house. That done, he crept softly back to his own chamber, and from the window let another fall—carefully wrapt round a stone to save it from the wind—into the yard below.

They were addressed on the back "To every Protestant into whose hands this shall come," and bore within what follows:

"Men and Brethren. Whoever shall find this letter, will take it as a warning to join, without delay, the friends of Lord George Gordon. There are great events at hand; and the times are dangerous and troubled. Read this carefully, keep it clean, and drop it somewhere else. For King and Country. Union."

"More seed, more seed," said Gashford as he closed the window. "When will the harvest come!"

CHAPTER XXXVII

To surround anything, however monstrous or ridiculous, with an air of mystery, is to invest it with a secret charm, and power of attraction which to the crowd is irresistible. False priests, false prophets, false doctors, false patriots, false prodigies of every kind, veiling their proceedings in mystery, have always addressed themselves at an immense advantage to the popular credulity, and have been, perhaps, more indebted to that resource in gaining and keeping for a time the upper hand of Truth and Common Sense, than to any half-dozen items in the whole catalogue of imposture. Curiosity is, and has been from the creation of the world, a master-passion. To awaken it, to gratify it by slight degrees, and yet leave something always in suspense, is to establish the surest hold that can be had, in wrong, on the unthinking portion of mankind.

If a man had stood on London Bridge, calling till he was hoarse, upon the passers-by, to join with Lord George Gordon, although for an object which no man understood, and which in that very incident had a charm of its own,—the probability is, that he might have influenced a score of people in a month. If all zealous Protestants had been publicly urged to join an association for the avowed purpose of singing a hymn or two occasionally, and hearing some indifferent speeches made, and ultimately of petitioning Parliament not to pass an act for abolishing the penal laws against Roman Catholic priests, the penalty of perpetual imprisonment denounced against those who educated children in that persuasion, and the disqualification of all members of the Romish church to inherit real property in the United Kingdom by right of purchase or descent,—matters so far removed from the business and bosoms of the mass, might perhaps have called together a hundred people. But when vague rumours got abroad, that in this Protestant association a secret power was mustering against the government for undefined and mighty purposes; when the air was filled with whispers of a confederacy among the Popish powers to degrade and enslave England, establish an inquisition in London, and turn the pens of Smithfield market into stakes and cauldrons; when terrors and alarms which no man understood were perpetually broached, both in and out of Parliament, by one enthusiast who did not understand himself, and bygone bugbears which had lain quietly in their graves for centuries, were raised again to haunt the ignorant and credulous; when all this was done, as it were, in the dark, the secret invitations to join the Great Protestant Association in defence of religion, life, and liberty, were dropped in the public ways, thrust under the house-doors, tossed in at windows, and pressed into the hands of those who trod the streets by night; when they glared from every wall, and shone on every post and pillar, so that stocks and stones appeared infected with the common fear, urging all men to join together blindfold in resistance of they knew not what, they knew not why;—then the mania spread indeed, and the body, still increasing every day, grew forty thousand strong.

So said, at least, in this month of March, 1780, Lord George Gordon, the Association's president. Whether it was the fact or otherwise, few men knew or cared to ascertain. It had never made any public demonstration; had scarcely ever been heard of, save through him; had never been seen; and was supposed by many to be the mere creature of his disordered brain. He was accustomed to talk largely about numbers of men—stimulated, as it was inferred, by certain successful disturbances, arising out of the same subject, which had occurred in Scotland in the previous year; was looked upon as a cracked-brained member of the lower house, who attacked all parties and sided with none, and was very little regarded. It was known that there was discontent abroad—there always is; he had been accustomed to address the people by placard, speech, and pamphlet, upon other questions; nothing had come, in England, of his past exertions, and nothing was apprehended from his present. Just as he has come upon the reader, he had come, from time to time, upon the public, and been forgotten in a day; as suddenly as he appears in these pages, after a blank of five long years, did he and his proceedings begin to force themselves, about this period, upon the notice of thousands of people, who had mingled in active life during the whole interval, and who, without being deaf or blind to passing events, had scarcely ever thought of him before.

"My lord," said Gashford in his ear, as he drew the curtains of his bed betimes; "my lord!"

"Yes—who's that? What is it?"

"The clock has struck nine," returned the secretary with meekly folded hands. "You have slept well? I hope you have slept well? If my prayers are heard, you are refreshed indeed."

"To say the truth, I have slept so soundly," said Lord George, rubbing his eyes and looking round the room, "that I don't remember quite—what place is this?"

"My lord!" cried Gashford, with a smile.

"Oh!" returned his superior. "Yes. You're not a Jew then?"

"A Jew!" exclaimed the pious secretary, recoiling.

"I dreamed that we were Jews, Gashford. You and I—both of us—Jews with long beards."

"Heaven forbid, my lord! We might as well be Papists."

"I suppose we might," returned the other, very quickly. "Eh? You really think so, Gashford?"

"Surely I do," the secretary cried, with looks of great surprise.

"Humph!" he muttered. "Yes, that seems reasonable."

"I hope, my lord—" the secretary began.

"Hope!" he echoed, interrupting him. "Why do you say, you hope? There's no harm in thinking of such things."

"Not in dreams," returned the secretary.

"In dreams! No, nor waking either."

—"'Called, and chosen, and faithful,'" said Gashford, taking up Lord George's watch which lay upon a chair, and seeming to read the inscription on the seal, abstractedly.

It was the slightest action possible, not obtruded on his notice, and apparently the result of a moment's absence of mind, not worth remark. But as the words were uttered, Lord George, who had been going on impetuously, stopped short, reddened, and was silent. Apparently quite unconscious of this change in his demeanour, the wily secretary stepped a little apart, under pretence of pulling up the window-blind, and returning when the other had had time to recover, said:

"The holy cause goes bravely on, my lord. I was not idle, even last night. I dropped two of the handbills before I went to bed, and both are gone this morning. Nobody in the house has mentioned the circumstance of finding them, though I have been down-stairs full half-an-hour. One or two recruits will be their first fruit, I predict; and who shall say how many more, with Heaven's blessing on your inspired exertions!"

"It was a famous device in the beginning," replied Lord George; "an excellent device, and did good service in Scotland. It was quite worthy of you. You remind me not to be a sluggard, Gashford, when the vineyard is menaced with destruction, and may be trodden down by Papist feet. Let the horses be saddled in half-an-hour. We must be up and doing!"

He said this with a heightened colour, and in a tone of such enthusiasm, that the secretary deemed all further prompting needless, and withdrew.

"—Dreamed he was a Jew," he said thoughtfully, as he closed the bedroom door. "He may come to that before he dies. It's like enough. Well! After a time, and provided I lost nothing by it, I don't see why that religion shouldn't suit me as well as any other. There are rich men among the Jews; shaving is very troublesome;—yes, it would suit me well enough. For the present, though, we must be Christian to the core. Our prophetic motto will suit all creeds in their turn, that's a comfort." Reflecting on this source of consolation, he reached the sitting-room, and rang the bell for breakfast.

Lord George was quickly dressed (for his plain toilet was easily made), and as he was no less frugal in his repasts than in his Puritan attire, his share of the meal was soon dispatched. The secretary, however, more devoted to the good things of this world, or more intent on sustaining his strength and spirits for the sake of the Protestant cause, ate and drank to the last minute, and required indeed some three or four reminders from John Grueby, before he could resolve to tear himself away from Mr. Willet's plentiful providing.

At length he came down-stairs, wiping his greasy mouth, and having paid John Willet's bill, climbed into his saddle. Lord George, who had been walking up and down before the house talking to himself with earnest gestures, mounted his horse; and returning old John Willet's stately bow, as well as the parting salutation of a dozen idlers whom the rumour of a live lord being about to leave the Maypole had gathered round the porch, they rode away, with stout John Grueby in the rear.

If Lord George Gordon had appeared in the eyes of Mr. Willet, overnight, a nobleman of somewhat quaint and odd exterior, the impression was confirmed this morning, and increased a hundredfold. Sitting bolt upright upon his bony steed, with his long, straight hair, dangling about his face and fluttering in the wind; his limbs all angular and rigid, his elbows stuck out on either side ungracefully, and his whole frame jogged and shaken at every motion of his horse's feet; a more grotesque or more ungainly figure can hardly be conceived. In lieu of whip, he carried in his hand a great gold-headed cane, as large as any footman carries in these days; and his various modes of holding this unwieldy weapon—now upright before his face like the sabre of a horse-soldier, now over his shoulder like a musket, now between his finger and thumb, but always in some uncouth and awkward fashion—contributed in no small degree to the absurdity of his appearance. Stiff, lank, and solemn, dressed in an unusual manner, and ostentatiously exhibiting—whether by design or accident—all his peculiarities of carriage, gesture, and conduct, all the qualities, natural and artificial, in which he differed from other men; he might have moved the sternest looker-on to laughter, and fully provoked the smiles and whispered jests which greeted his departure from the Maypole inn.

Quite unconscious, however, of the effect he produced, he trotted on beside his secretary, talking to himself nearly all the way, until they came within a mile or two of London, when now and then some passenger went by who knew him by sight, and pointed him out to some one else, and perhaps stood looking after him, or cried in jest or earnest as it might be, "Hurrah, Geordie! No Popery!" at which he would gravely pull off his hat, and bow. When they reached the town and rode along the streets, these notices became more frequent; some laughed, some hissed, some turned their heads and smiled, some wondered who he was, some ran along the pavement by his side and cheered. When this happened in a crush of carts and chairs and coaches, he would make a dead stop, and pulling off his hat, cry, "Gentlemen, No Popery!" to which the gentlemen would respond with lusty voices, and with three times three; and then, on he would go again with a score or so of the raggedest, following at his horse's heels, and shouting till their throats were parched.

The old ladies too—there were a great many old ladies in the streets, and these all knew him. Some of them—not those of the highest rank, but such as sold fruit from baskets and carried burdens —clapped their shrivelled hands, and raised a weazen, piping, shrill "Hurrah, my lord." Others waved their hands or handkerchiefs, or shook their fans or parasols, or threw up windows and called in haste to those within, to come and see. All these marks of popular esteem, he received with profound gravity and respect; bowing very low, and so frequently that his hat was more off his head than on; and looking up at the houses as he passed along, with the air of one who was making a public entry, and yet was not puffed up or proud.

So they rode (to the deep and unspeakable disgust of John Grueby) the whole length of Whitechapel, Leadenhall-street, and Cheapside, and into St. Paul's Churchyard. Arriving close to the cathedral, he halted; spoke to Gashford; and looking upward at its lofty dome, shook his head, as though he said "The Church in Danger!" Then to be sure, the bystanders stretched their throats indeed; and he went on again with mighty acclamations from the mob, and lower bows than ever.

So along the Strand, up Swallow-street, into the Oxford-road, and thence to his house in Welbeck-street, near Cavendish-square, whither he was attended by a few dozen idlers; of whom he took leave on the steps with this brief parting, "Gentlemen, No Popery. Good day. God bless you." This being rather a shorter address than they expected, was received with some displeasure, and cries of "A speech! a speech!" which might have been complied with, but that John Grueby, making a mad charge upon them with all three horses, on his way to the stables, caused them to disperse into the adjoining fields, where they presently fell to pitch and toss, chuck-farthing, odd or even, dog-fighting, and other Protestant recreations.

In the afternoon Lord George came forth again, dressed in a black velvet coat, and trousers and waistcoat of the Gordon plaid, all of the same Quaker cut; and in this costume, which made him look a dozen times more strange and singular than before, went down on foot to Westminster. Gashford, meanwhile, bestirred himself in business matters; with which he was still engaged when, shortly after dusk, John Grueby entered and announced a visitor.

"Let him come in," said Gashford.

"Here! come in!" growled John to somebody without. "You're a Protestant, an't you?"

"*I* should think so," replied a deep gruff voice.

"You've the looks of it," said John Grueby. "I'd have known you for one, anywhere." With which remark he gave the visitor admission, retired, and shut the door.

The man who now confronted Gashford, was a squat, thickset personage, with a low, retreating forehead, a coarse shock head of hair, and eyes so small and near together, that his broken nose alone seemed to prevent their meeting and fusing into one of the usual size. A dingy handkerchief twisted like a cord about his neck, left its great veins exposed to view, and they were swoln and starting, as though with gulping down strong passions, malice, and ill-will. His dress was of threadbare velveteen—a faded, rusty, whitened black, like the ashes of a pipe or a coal fire after a day's extinction; discoloured with the soils of many a stale debauch, and reeking yet with pot-house odours. In lieu of buckles at his knees, he wore unequal loops of packthread; and in his grimy hands he held a knotted stick, the knob of which was carved into a rough likeness of his own vile face. Such was the visitor who doffed his three-cornered hat in Gashford's presence, and waited, leering, for his notice.

"Ah! Dennis!" cried the secretary. "Sit down."

"I see my lord down yonder—" cried the man, with a jerk of his thumb towards the quarter that he spoke of, "and he says to me, says my lord, 'If you've nothing to do, Dennis, go up to my house and talk with Muster Gashford.' Of course I'd nothing to do, you know. These an't my working hours. Ha ha! I was a-taking the air when I see my lord, that's what I was doing. I takes the air by night, as the howls does, Muster Gashford."

"And sometimes in the day-time, eh?" said the secretary—"when you go out in state you know."

"Ha ha!" roared the fellow, smiting his leg; "for a gentleman as 'ull say a pleasant thing in a pleasant way, give me Muster Gashford agin' all London and Westminster! My lord an't a bad 'un at that, but he's a fool to you. Ah to be sure,—when I go out in state."

"And have your carriage," said the secretary; "and your chaplain, eh? and all the rest of it?"

"You'll be the death of me," cried Dennis, with another roar, "you will. But what's in the wind now, Muster Gashford," he asked hoarsely, "eh? Are we to be under orders to pull down one of them Popish chapels—or what?"

"Hush!" said the secretary, suffering the faintest smile to play upon his face. "Hush! God bless me, Dennis! We associate, you know, for strictly peaceable and lawful purposes."

"*I* know, bless you," returned the man, thrusting his tongue into his cheek; "I entered a' purpose, didn't I!"

"No doubt," said Gashford, smiling as before. And when he said so, Dennis roared again, and smote his leg still harder, and falling into fits of laughter, wiped his eyes with the corner of his neckerchief, and cried "Muster Gashford agin' all England hollow!"

"Lord George and I were talking of you last night," said Gashford, after a pause. "He says you are a very earnest fellow."

"So I am," returned the hangman.

"And that you truly hate the Papists."

"So I do," and he confirmed it with a good round oath. "Lookye here, Muster Gashford," said the fellow, laying his hat and stick upon the floor, and slowly beating the palm of one hand with the fingers of the other; "Ob-serve. I'm a constitutional officer that works for my living, and does my work creditable. Do I, or do I not?"

"Unquestionably."

"Very good. Stop a minute. My work is sound, Protestant, constitutional, English work. Is it, or is it not?"

"No man alive can doubt it."

"Nor dead neither. Parliament says this here—says Parliament, 'If any man, woman, or child, does anything which goes again a certain number of our acts'—how many hanging laws may there be at this present time, Muster Gashford? Fifty?"

"I don't exactly know how many," replied Gashford, leaning back in his chair and yawning; "a great number though."

"Well, say fifty. Parliament says 'If any man, woman, or child, does anything again any one of them fifty acts, that man, woman, or child, shall be worked off by Dennis.' George the Third steps in when they number very strong at the end of a sessions, and says 'These are too many for Dennis. I'll have half for *my*self and Dennis shall have half for *him*self;' and sometimes he throws me in one over that I don't expect, as he did three year ago, when I got Mary Jones, a young woman of nineteen who come up to Tyburn with a infant at her breast, and was worked off for taking a piece of cloth off the counter of a shop in Ludgate-hill, and putting it down again when the shopman see her; and who had never done any harm before, and only tried to do that, in consequence of her husband having been pressed three weeks previous, and she being left to beg, with two young children—as was proved upon the trial. Ha ha!—Well! That being the law and the practice of England, is the glory of England, an't it, Muster Gashford?"

"Certainly," said the secretary.

"And in times to come," pursued the hangman, "if our grandsons should think of their grandfathers' times, and find these things altered, they'll say 'Those were days indeed, and we've been going down hill ever since.'—Won't they, Muster Gashford?"

"I have no doubt they will," said the secretary.

"Well then, look here," said the hangman. "If these Papists gets into power, and begins to boil and roast instead of hang, what becomes of my work! If they touch my work that's a part of so many laws, what becomes of the laws in general, what becomes of the religion, what becomes of the country!—Did you ever go to church, Muster Gashford?"

"Ever!" repeated the secretary with some indignation; "of course."

"Well," said the ruffian, "I've been once—twice, counting the time I was christened—and when I heard the Parliament prayed for, and thought how many new hanging laws they made every sessions, I considered that *I* was prayed for. Now mind, Muster Gashford," said the fellow, taking up his stick and shaking it with a ferocious air, "I mustn't have my Protestant work touched, nor this here Protestant state of things altered in no degree, if I can help it; I mustn't have no Papists interfering with me, unless they come to be worked off in course of law; I mustn't have no biling, no roasting, no frying—nothing but hanging. My lord may well call me an earnest fellow. In support of the great Protestant principle of having plenty of that, I'll," and here he beat his club upon the ground, "burn, fight, kill—do anything you bid me, so that it's bold and devilish—though the end of it was, that I got hung myself.—There, Muster Gashford!"

He appropriately followed up this frequent prostitution of a noble word to the vilest purposes, by pouring out in a kind of ecstasy at least a score of most tremendous oaths; then wiped his heated face upon his neckerchief, and cried, "No Popery! I'm a religious man, by G—!"

Gashford had leant back in his chair, regarded him with eyes so sunken, and so shadowed by his heavy brows, that for aught the hangman saw of them, he might have been stone blind. He remained smiling in silence for a short time longer, and then said, slowly and distinctly:

"You are indeed an earnest fellow, Dennis—a most valuable fellow—the staunchest man I know of in our ranks. But you must calm yourself; you must be peaceful, lawful, mild as any lamb. I am sure you will be though."

"Ay, ay, we shall see, Muster Gashford, we shall see. You won't have to complain of me," returned the other, shaking his head.

"I am sure I shall not," said the secretary in the same mild tone, and with the same emphasis. "We shall have, we think, about next month, or May, when this Papist relief bill comes before the house, to convene our whole body for the first time. My lord has thoughts of our walking in procession through the streets—just as an innocent display of strength—and accompanying our petition down to the door of the House of Commons."

" The sooner the better," said Dennis, with another oath.

"We shall have to draw up in divisions, our numbers being so large; and, I believe I may venture to say," resumed Gashford, affecting not to hear the interruption, "though I have no direct instructions to that effect—that Lord George has thought of you as an excellent leader for one of these parties. I have no doubt you would be an admirable one."

"Try me," said the fellow, with an ugly wink.

"You would be cool, I know," pursued the secretary, still smiling, and still managing his eyes so that he could watch him closely, and really not be seen in turn, "obedient to orders, and perfectly temperate. You would lead your party into no danger, I am certain."

"I'd lead them, Muster Gashford,"—the hangman was beginning in a reckless way, when Gashford started forward, laid his finger on his lips, and feigned to write, just as the door was opened by John Grueby.

"Oh!" said John, looking in; "here's another Protestant."

"Some other room, John," cried Gashford in his blandest voice. "I am engaged just now."

But John had brought this new visitor to the door, and he walked in unbidden, as the words were uttered; giving to view the form and features, rough attire, and reckless air, of Hugh.

CHAPTER XXXVIII

THE secretary put his hand before his eyes to shade them from the glare of the lamp, and for some moments looked at Hugh with a frowning brow, as if he remembered to have seen him lately, but could not call to mind where, or on what occasion. His uncertainty was very brief, for before Hugh had spoken a word, he said, as his countenance cleared up:

"Ay, ay, I recollect. It's quite right, John, you needn't wait. Don't go, Dennis."

"Your servant, master," said Hugh, as Grueby disappeared.

"Yours, friend," returned the secretary in his smoothest manner. "What brings *you* here? We left nothing behind us, I hope?"

Hugh gave a short laugh, and thrusting his hand into his breast, produced one of the handbills, soiled and dirty from lying out of doors all night, which he laid upon the secretary's desk after flattening it upon his knee, and smoothing out the wrinkles with his heavy palm.

"Nothing but that, master. It fell into good hands, you see."

"What is this!" said Gashford, turning it over with an air of perfectly natural surprise. "Where did you get it from, my good fellow; what does it mean? I don't understand this at all."

A little disconcerted by this reception, Hugh looked from the secretary to Dennis, who had risen and was standing at the table too, observing the stranger by stealth, and seeming to derive the utmost satisfaction from his manners and appearance. Considering himself silently appealed to by this action, Mr. Dennis shook his head thrice, as if to say of Gashford, "No. He don't know anything at all about it. I know he don't. I'll take my oath he don't;" and hiding his profile from Hugh with one long end of his frowzy neckerchief, nodded and chuckled behind this screen in extreme approval of the secretary's proceedings.

"It tells the man that finds it, to come here, don't it?" asked Hugh. "I'm no scholar, myself, but I showed it to a friend, and he said it did."

"It certainly does," said Gashford, opening his eyes to their utmost width; "really this is the most remarkable circumstance I have ever known. How did you come by this piece of paper, my good friend?"

"Muster Gashford," wheezed the hangman under his breath, "agin' all Newgate!"

Whether Hugh heard him, or saw by his manner that he was being played upon, or perceived the secretary's drift of himself, he came in his blunt way to the point at once.

"Here!" he said, stretching out his hand and taking it back; "never mind the bill, or what it says, or what it don't say. You don't know anything about it, master,—no more do I,—no more does he," glancing at Dennis. "None of us know what it means, or where it comes from: there's an end of that. Now I want to make one against the Catholics. I'm a No-Popery man, and ready to be sworn in. That's what I've come here for."

"Put him down on the roll, Muster Gashford," said Dennis approvingly. "That's the way to go to work—right to the end at once, and no palaver."

"What's the use of shooting wide of the mark, eh, old boy!" cried Hugh.

"My sentiments all over!" rejoined the hangman. "This is the sort of chap for my division, Muster Gashford. Down with him, sir. Put him on the roll. I'd stand godfather to him, if he was to be christened in a bonfire, made of the ruins of the Bank of England."

With these and other expressions of confidence of the like flattering kind, Mr. Dennis gave him a hearty slap on the back, which Hugh was not slow to return.

"No Popery, brother!" cried the hangman.

"No Property, brother!" responded Hugh.

"Popery, Popery," said the secretary with his usual mildness.

"It's all the same!" cried Dennis. "It's all right. Down with him, Muster Gashford. Down with everybody, down with everything!

Hurrah for the Protestant religion! That's the time of day, Muster Gashford!"

The secretary regarded them both with a very favourable expression of countenance, while they gave loose to these and other demonstrations of their patriotic purpose; and was about to make some remark aloud, when Dennis, stepping up to him, and shading his mouth with his hand, said, in a hoarse whisper, as he nudged him with his elbow:

"Don't split upon a constitutional officer's profession, Muster Gashford. There are popular prejudices, you know, and he mightn't like it. Wait till he comes to be more intimate with me. He's a fine-built chap, an't he?"

"A powerful fellow indeed!"

"Did you ever, Muster Gashford," whispered Dennis, with a horrible kind of admiration, such as that with which a cannibal might regard his intimate friend, when hungry,—"did you ever"—and here he drew still closer to his ear, and fenced his mouth with both his open hands—"see such a throat as his? Do but cast your eye upon it. There's a neck for stretching, Muster Gashford!"

The secretary assented to this proposition with the best grace he could assume—it is difficult to feign a true professional relish: which is eccentric sometimes—and after asking the candidate a few unimportant questions, proceeded to enrol him a member of the Great Protestant Association of England. If anything could have exceeded Mr. Dennis's joy on the happy conclusion of this ceremony, it would have been the rapture with which he received the announcement that the new member could neither read nor write: those two arts being (as Mr. Dennis swore) the greatest possible curse a civilised community could know, and militating more against the professional emoluments and usefulness of the great constitutional office he had the honour to hold, than any adverse circumstances that could present themselves to his imagination.

The enrolment being completed, and Hugh having been informed by Gashford, in his peculiar manner, of the peaceful and strictly lawful objects contemplated by the body to which he now belonged —during which recital Mr. Dennis nudged him very much with his elbow, and made divers remarkable faces—the secretary gave them both to understand that he desired to be alone. Therefore they took their leaves without delay, and came out of the house together.

"Are you walking, brother?" said Dennis.

"Ay!" returned Hugh. "Where you will."

"That's social," said his new friend. "Which way shall we take? Shall we go and have a look at doors that we shall make a pretty good clattering at, before long—eh, brother?"

Hugh answering in the affirmative, they went slowly down to Westminster, where both houses of Parliament were then sitting. Mingling in the crowd of carriages, horses, servants, chairmen, link-boys, porters, and idlers of all kinds, they lounged about; while Hugh's new friend pointed out to him significantly the weak parts of the

building, how easy it was to get into the lobby, and so to the very
door of the House of Commons; and how plainly, when they marched
down there in grand array, their roars and shouts would be heard by
the members inside; with a great deal more to the same purpose, all
of which Hugh received with manifest delight.

He told him, too, who some of the Lords and Commons were, by
name, as they came in and out; whether they were friendly to the
Papists or otherwise; and bade him take notice of their liveries and
equipages, that he might be sure of them, in case of need. Sometimes
he drew him close to the windows of a passing carriage, that he might
see its master's face by the light of the lamps; and, both in respect
of people and localities, he showed so much acquaintance with everything around, that it was plain he had often studied there before;
as indeed, when they grew a little more confidential, he confessed
he had.

Perhaps the most striking part of all this was, the number of
people—never in groups of more than two or three together—who
seemed to be skulking about the crowd for the same purpose. To the
greater part of these, a slight nod or a look from Hugh's companion
was sufficient greeting; but, now and then, some man would come and
stand beside him in the throng, and, without turning his head or
appearing to communicate with him, would say a word or two in a low
voice, which he would answer in the same cautious manner. Then
they would part, like strangers. Some of these men often reappeared
again unexpectedly in the crowd close to Hugh, and, as they passed
by, pressed his hand, or looked him sternly in the face; but they never
spoke to him, nor he to them: no, not a word.

It was remarkable, too, that whenever they happened to stand
where there was any press of people, and Hugh chanced to be looking
downward, he was sure to see an arm stretched out—under his own
perhaps, or perhaps across him—which thrust some paper into the
hand or pocket of a bystander, and was so suddenly withdrawn that
it was impossible to tell from whom it came; nor could he see in any
face, on glancing quickly round, the least confusion or surprise. They
often trod upon a paper like the one he carried in his breast, but his
companion whispered him not to touch it or to take it up,—not even
to look towards it,—so there they let them lie, and passed on.

When they had paraded the street and all the avenues of the building in this manner for near two hours, they turned away, and his
friend asked him what he thought of what he had seen, and whether
he was prepared for a good hot piece of work if it should come to that.
"The hotter the better," said Hugh, "I'm prepared for anything."—
"So am I," said his friend, "and so are many of us;" and they shook
hands upon it with a great oath, and with many terrible imprecations on the Papists.

As they were thirsty by this time, Dennis proposed that they
should repair together to The Boot, where there was good company
and strong liquor. Hugh yielding a ready assent, they bent their
steps that way with no loss of time.

This Boot was a lone house of public entertainment, situated in the fields at the back of the Foundling Hospital; a very solitary spot at that period, and quite deserted after dark. The tavern stood at some distance from any high road, and was approachable only by a dark and narrow lane; so that Hugh was much surprised to find several people drinking there, and great merriment going on. He was still more surprised to find among them almost every face that had caught his attention in the crowd; but his companion having whispered him outside the door, that it was not considered good manners at The Boot to appear at all curious about the company, he kept his own counsel, and made no show of recognition.

Before putting his lips to the liquor which was brought for them, Dennis drank in a loud voice the health of Lord George Gordon, President of the Great Protestant Association; which toast Hugh pledged likewise, with corresponding enthusiasm. A fiddler who was present, and who appeared to act as the appointed minstrel of the company, forthwith struck up a Scotch reel; and that in tones so invigorating, that Hugh and his friend (who had both been drinking before) rose from their seats as by previous concert, and, to the great admiration of the assembled guests, performed an extemporaneous No-Popery Dance.

CHAPTER XXXIX

THE applause which the performance of Hugh and his new friend elicited from the company at The Boot, had not yet subsided, and the two dancers were still panting from their exertions, which had been of a rather extreme and violent character, when the party was reinforced by the arrival of some more guests, who, being a detachment of United Bull-dogs, were received with very flattering marks of distinction and respect.

The leader of this small party—for, including himself, they were but three in number—was our old acquaintance, Mr. Tappertit, who seemed, physically speaking, to have grown smaller with years (particularly as to his legs, which were stupendously little), but who, in a moral point of view, in personal dignity and self-esteem, had swelled into a giant. Nor was it by any means difficult for the most unobservant person to detect this state of feeling in the quondam 'prentice, for it not only proclaimed itself impressively and beyond mistake in his majestic walk and kindling eye, but found a striking means of revelation in his turned-up nose, which scouted all things of earth with deep disdain, and sought communion with its kindred skies.

Mr. Tappertit, as chief or captain of the Bull-dogs, was attended by his two lieutenants; one, the tall comrade of his younger life; the other, a 'Prentice Knight in days of yore—Mark Gilbert, bound in the olden time to Thomas Curzon of the Golden Fleece. These gentlemen, like himself, were now emancipated from their 'prentice thraldom, and served as journeymen; but they were, in humble emulation of his great example, bold and daring spirits, and aspired to a distinguished state in great political events. Hence their connection with the Protestant Association of England, sanctioned by the name of Lord George Gordon; and hence their present visit to The Boot.

"Gentlemen!" said Mr. Tappertit, taking off his hat as a great general might in addressing his troops. "Well met. My lord does me and you the honour to send his compliments per self."

"You've seen my lord too, have you?" asked Dennis. "*I* see him this afternoon."

"My duty called me to the Lobby when our shop shut up; and I saw him there, sir," Mr. Tappertit replied, as he and his lieutenants took their seats. "How do *you* do?"

"Lively, master, lively," said the fellow. "Here's a new brother, regularly put down in black and white by Muster Gashford; a credit to the cause; one of the stick-at-nothing sort; one arter my own heart. D'ye see him? Has he got the looks of a man that'll do, do you think?" he cried, as he slapped Hugh on the back.

"Looks or no looks," said Hugh, with a drunken flourish of his arm, "I'm the man you want. I hate the Papists, every one of 'em. They hate me and I hate them. They do me all the harm they can, and I'll do them all the harm *I* can. Hurrah!"

"Was there ever," said Dennis, looking round the room, when the echo of his boisterous voice had died away; "was there ever such a game boy! Why, I mean to say, brothers, that if Muster Gashford had gone a hundred mile and got together fifty men of the common run, they wouldn't have been worth this one."

The greater part of the company implicitly subscribed to this opinion, and testified their faith in Hugh by nods and looks of great significance. Mr. Tappertit sat and contemplated him for a long time in silence, as if he suspended his judgment; then drew a little nearer to him, and eyed him over more carefully; then went close up to him, and took him apart into a dark corner.

"I say," he began, with a thoughtful brow, "haven't I seen you before?"

"It's like you may," said Hugh, in his careless way. "I don't know; shouldn't wonder."

"No, but it's very easily settled," returned Sim. "Look at me. Did you ever see *me* before? You wouldn't be likely to forget it, you know, if you ever did. Look at me. Don't be afraid; I won't do you any harm. Take a good look—steady now."

The encouraging way in which Mr. Tappertit made this request, and coupled it with an assurance that he needn't be frightened, amused Hugh mightily—so much indeed, that he saw nothing at all of the small man before him, through closing his eyes in a fit of hearty laughter, which shook his great broad sides until they ached again.

"Come!" said Mr. Tappertit, growing a little impatient under this disrespectful treatment. "Do you know me, feller?"

"Not I," cried Hugh. "Ha ha ha! Not I! But I should like to."

"And yet I'd have wagered a seven-shilling piece," said Mr. Tappertit, folding his arms, and confronting him with his legs wide apart and firmly planted on the ground, "that you once were hostler at the Maypole."

Hugh opened his eyes on hearing this, and looked at him in great surprise.

"—And so you were, too," said Mr. Tappertit, pushing him away with a condescending playfulness. "When did *my* eyes ever deceive—unless it was a young woman! Don't you know me now?"

"Why it an't—" Hugh faltered.

"An't it?" said Mr. Tappertit. "Are you sure of that? You remember G. Varden, don't you?"

Certainly Hugh did, and he remembered D. Varden too; but that he didn't tell him.

"You remember coming down there, before I was out of my time, to ask after a vagabond that had bolted off, and left his disconsolate father a prey to the bitterest emotions, and all the rest of it—don't you?" said Mr. Tappertit.

"Of course I do!" cried Hugh. "And I saw you there."

"Saw me there!" said Mr. Tappertit. "Yes, I should think you did see me there. The place would be troubled to go on without me. Don't you remember my thinking you liked the vagabond, and on that account going to quarrel with you; and then finding you detested him worse than poison, going to drink with you? Don't you remember that?"

"To be sure!" cried Hugh.

"Well! and are you in the same mind now?" said Mr. Tappertit.

"Yes!" roared Hugh.

"You speak like a man," said Mr. Tappertit, "and I'll shake hands with you." With these conciliatory expressions he suited the action to the word; and Hugh meeting his advances readily, they performed the ceremony with a show of great heartiness.

"I find," said Mr. Tappertit, looking round on the assembled guests, "that brother What's-his-name and I are old acquaintance.—You never heard anything more of that rascal, I suppose, eh?"

"Not a syllable," replied Hugh. "I never want to. I don't believe I ever shall. He's dead long ago, I hope."

"It's to be hoped, for the sake of mankind in general and the happiness of society, that he is," said Mr. Tappertit, rubbing his palm upon his legs, and looking at it between whiles. "Is your other hand at all cleaner? Much the same. Well, I'll owe you another shake. We'll suppose it done, if you've no objection."

Hugh laughed again, and with such thorough abandonment to his mad humour, that his limbs seemed dislocated, and his whole frame in danger of tumbling to pieces; but Mr. Tappertit, so far from receiving this extreme merriment with any irritation, was pleased to regard it with the utmost favour, and even to join in it, so far as one of his gravity and station could, with any regard to that decency and decorum which men in high places are expected to maintain.

Mr. Tappertit did not stop here, as many public characters might

have done, but calling up his brace of lieutenants, introduced Hugh
to them with high commendation; declaring him to be a man who,
at such times as those in which they lived, could not be too much
cherished. Further, he did him the honour to remark, that he would
be an acquisition of which even the United Bull-dogs might be proud;
and finding, upon sounding him, that he was quite ready and willing
to enter the society (for he was not at all particular, and would have
leagued himself that night with anything, or anybody, for any purpose whatsoever), caused the necessary preliminaries to be gone into
upon the spot. This tribute to his great merit delighted no man more
than Mr. Dennis, as he himself proclaimed with several rare and surprising oaths; and indeed it gave unmingled satisfaction to the whole
assembly.

"Make anything you like of me!" cried Hugh, flourishing the can
he had emptied more than once. "Put me on any duty you please.
I'm your man. I'll do it. Here's my captain—here's my leader. Ha ha
ha! Let him give me the word of command, and I'll fight the whole
parliament House single-handed, or set a lighted torch to the King's
Throne itself!" With that, he smote Mr. Tappertit on the back, with
such violence that his little body seemed to shrink into a mere nothing; and roared again until the very foundlings near at hand were
startled in their beds.

In fact, a sense of something whimsical in their companionship
seemed to have taken entire possession of his rude brain. The bare
fact of being patronised by a great man whom he could have crushed
with one hand, appeared in his eyes so eccentric and humorous, that
a kind of ferocious merriment gained the mastery over him, and
quite subdued his brutal nature. He roared and roared again; toasted
Mr. Tappertit a hundred times; declared himself a Bull-dog to the
core; and vowed to be faithful to him to the last drop of blood in his
veins.

All these compliments Mr. Tappertit received as matters of course
—flattering enough in their way, but entirely attributable to his vast
superiority. His dignified self-possession only delighted Hugh the
more; and in a word, this giant and the dwarf struck up a friendship
which bade fair to be of long continuance, as the one held it to be his
right to command, and the other considered it an exquisite pleasantry to obey. Nor was Hugh by any means a passive follower, who
scrupled to act without precise and definite orders; for when Mr.
Tappertit mounted on an empty case which stood by way of rostrum
in the room, and volunteered a speech upon the alarming crisis then
at hand, he placed himself beside the orator, and though he grinned
from ear to ear at every word he said, threw out such expressive hints
to scoffers in the management of his cudgel, that those who were at
first the most disposed to interrupt, became remarkably attentive,
and were the loudest in their approbation.

It was not all noise and jest, however, at The Boot, nor were the
whole party listeners to the speech. There were some men at the other
end of the room (which was a long, low-roofed chamber) in earnest

Mr. Tapperit Makes a Speech.

conversation all the time; and when any of this group went out, fresh people were sure to come in soon afterwards and sit down in their places, as though the others had relieved them on some watch or duty; which it was pretty clear they did, for these changes took place by the clock, at intervals of half an hour. These persons whispered very much among themselves, and kept aloof, and often looked round as jealous of their speech being overheard; some two or three among them entered in books what seemed to be reports from the others; when they were not thus employed, one of them would turn to the newspapers which were strewn upon the table, and from the St. James's Chronicle, the Herald, Chronicle, or Public Advertiser, would read to the rest in a low voice some passage having reference to the topic in which they were all so deeply interested. But the great attraction was a pamphlet called The Thunderer, which espoused their own opinions, and was supposed at that time to emanate directly from the Association. This was always in request; and whether read aloud, to an eager knot of listeners, or by some solitary man, was certain to be followed by stormy talking and excited looks.

In the midst of all this merriment, and admiration of his captain, Hugh was made sensible by these and other tokens, of the presence of an air of mystery, akin to that which so much impressed him out of doors. It was impossible to discard a sense that something serious was going on, and that under the noisy revel of the public-house, there lurked unseen and dangerous matter. Little affected by this, however, he was perfectly satisfied with his quarters and would have remained there till morning, but that his conductor rose soon after midnight, to go home; Mr. Tappertit following his example, left him no excuse to stay. So they all three left the house together: roaring a No-Popery song until the fields resounded with the dismal noise.

"Cheer up, captain!" cried Hugh, when they had roared themselves out of breath. "Another stave!"

Mr. Tappertit, nothing loath, began again; and so the three went staggering on, arm-in-arm, shouting like madmen, and defying the watch with great valour. Indeed this did not require any unusual bravery or boldness, as the watchmen of that time, being selected for the office on account of excessive age and extraordinary infirmity, had a custom of shutting themselves up tight in their boxes on the first symptoms of disturbance, and remaining there until they disappeared. In these proceedings, Mr. Dennis, who had a gruff voice and lungs of considerable power, distinguished himself very much, and acquired great credit with his two companions.

"What a queer fellow you are!" said Mr. Tappertit. "You're so precious sly and close. Why don't you ever tell what trade you're of?"

"Answer the captain instantly," cried Hugh, beating his hat down on his head; "why don't you ever tell what trade you're of?"

"I'm of as gen-teel a calling, brother, as any man in England—as light a business as any gentleman could desire."

"Was you 'prenticed to it?" asked Mr. Tappertit.

"No. Natural genius," said Mr. Dennis. "No 'prenticing. It comes by natur'. Muster Gashford knows my calling. Look at that hand of mine—many and many a job that hand has done, with a neatness and dex-terity, never known afore. When I look at that hand," said Mr. Dennis, shaking it in the air, "and remember the helegant bits of work it has turned off, I feel quite molloncholy to think it should ever grow old and feeble. But sich is life!"

He heaved a deep sigh as he indulged in these reflections, and putting his fingers with an absent air on Hugh's throat, and par-ticularly under his left ear, as if he were studying the anatomical development of that part of his frame, shook his head in a despondent manner and actually shed tears.

"You're a kind of artist, I suppose—eh!" said Mr. Tappertit.

"Yes," rejoined Dennis; "yes—I may call myself a artist—a fancy workman—art improves natur'—that's my motto."

"And what do you call this?" said Mr. Tappertit, taking his stick out of his hand.

"That's my portrait atop," Dennis replied; "d'ye think it's like?"

"Why—it's a little too handsome," said Mr. Tappertit. "Who did it? You?"

"I!" repeated Dennis, gazing fondly on his image. "I wish I had the talent. That was carved by a friend of mine, as is now no more. The very day afore he died, he cut that with his pocket-knife from memory! 'I'll die game,' says my friend, 'and my last moments shall be dewoted to making Dennis's pictur'.' That's it."

"That was a queer fancy, wasn't it?" said Mr. Tappertit.

"It *was* a queer fancy," rejoined the other, breathing on his fictitious nose, and polishing it with the cuff of his coat, "but he was a queer subject altogether—a kind of gipsy—one of the finest, stand-up men, you ever see. Ah! He told me some things that would startle you a bit, did that friend of mine, on the morning when he died."

"You were with him at the time, were you?" said Mr. Tappertit.

"Yes," he answered with a curious look, "I was there. Oh! yes certainly, I was there. He wouldn't have gone off half as comfortable without me. I had been with three or four of his family under the same circumstances. They were all fine fellows."

"They must have been fond of you," remarked Mr. Tappertit, looking at him sideways.

"I don't know that they was exactly fond of me," said Dennis, with a little hesitation, "but they all had me near 'em when they departed. I come in for their wardrobes too. This very handkecher that you see round my neck, belonged to him that I've been speaking of—him as did that likeness."

Mr. Tappertit glanced at the article referred to, and appeared to think that the deceased's ideas of dress were of a peculiar and by no means an expensive kind. He made no remark upon the point, however, and suffered his mysterious companion to proceed without interruption.

"These smalls," said Dennis, rubbing his legs; "these very smalls—they belonged to a friend of mine that's left off sich incumbrances for ever: this coat too—I've often walked behind this coat, in the street, and wondered whether it would ever come to me: this pair of shoes have danced a hornpipe for another man, afore my eyes, full half-a-dozen times at least: and as to my hat," he said, taking it off, and whirling it round upon his fist—"Lord! I've seen this hat go up Holborn on the box of a hackney-coach—ah, many and many a day!"

"You don't mean to say their old wearers are *all* dead, I hope?" said Mr. Tappertit, falling a little distance from him as he spoke.

"Every one of 'em," replied Dennis. "Every man Jack!"

There was something so very ghastly in this circumstance, and it appeared to account, in such a very strange and dismal manner, for his faded dress—which, in this new aspect, seemed discoloured by the earth from graves—that Mr. Tappertit abruptly found he was going another way, and, stopping short, bade him good night with the utmost heartiness. As they happened to be near the Old Bailey, and Mr. Dennis knew there were turnkeys in the lodge with whom he could pass the night, and discuss professional subjects of common interest among them before a rousing fire, and over a social glass, he separated from his companions without any great regret, and warmly shaking hands with Hugh, and making an early appointment for their meeting at The Boot, left them to pursue their road.

"That's a strange sort of man," said Mr. Tappertit, watching the hackney-coachman's hat as it went bobbing down the street. "I don't know what to make of him. Why can't he have his smalls made to order, or wear live clothes at any rate?"

"He's a lucky man, captain," cried Hugh. "I should like to have such friends as his."

"I hope he don't get 'em to make their wills, and then knock 'em on the head," said Mr. Tappertit, musing. "But come. The United B.'s expect me. On!—What's the matter?"

"I quite forgot," said Hugh, who had started at the striking of a neighbouring clock. "I have somebody to see to-night—I must turn back directly. The drinking and singing put it out of my head. It's well I remembered it!"

Mr. Tappertit looked at him as though he were about to give utterance to some very majestic sentiments in reference to this act of desertion, but as it was clear, from Hugh's hasty manner, that the engagement was one of a pressing nature, he graciously forbore, and gave him his permission to depart immediately, which Hugh acknowledged with a roar of laughter.

"Good night, captain!" he cried. "I am yours to the death, remember!"

"Farewell!" said Mr. Tappertit, waving his hand. "Be bold and vigilant!"

"No Popery, captain!" roared Hugh.

"England in blood first!" cried his desperate leader. Whereat

Hugh cheered and laughed, and ran off like a greyhound.

"That man will prove a credit to my corps," said Simon, turning thoughtfully upon his heel. "And let me see. In an altered state of society—which must ensue if we break out and are victorious—when the locksmith's child is mine, Miggs must be got rid of somehow, or she'll poison the tea-kettle one evening when I'm out. He might marry Miggs, if he was drunk enough. It shall be done. I'll make a note of it."

CHAPTER XL

LITTLE thinking of the plan for his happy settlement in life which had suggested itself to the teeming brain of his provident commander, Hugh made no pause until Saint Dunstan's giants struck the hour above him, when he worked the handle of a pump which stood hard by, with great vigour, and thrusting his head under the spout, let the water gush upon him until a little stream ran down from every uncombed hair, and he was wet to the waist. Considerably refreshed by this ablution, both in mind and body, and almost sobered for the time, he dried himself as he best could; then crossed the road, and plied the knocker of the Middle Temple gate.

The night-porter looked through a small grating in the portal with a surly eye, and cried "Halloa!" which greeting Hugh returned in kind, and bade him open quickly.

"We don't sell beer here," cried the man; "what else do you want?"

"To come in," Hugh replied, with a kick at the door.

"Where to go?"

"Paper Buildings."

"Whose chambers?"

"Sir John Chester's." Each of which answers, he emphasised with another kick.

After a little growling on the other side, the gate was opened, and he passed in: undergoing a close inspection from the porter as he did so.

"You wanting Sir John, at this time of night!" said the man.

"Ay!" said Hugh. "I! What of that?"

"Why, I must go with you and see that you do, for I don't believe it."

"Come along then."

Eyeing him with suspicious looks, the man, with key and lantern, walked on at his side, and attended him to Sir John Chester's door, at which Hugh gave one knock, that echoed through the dark staircase like a ghostly summons, and made the dull light tremble in the drowsy lamp.

"Do you think he wants me now?" said Hugh.

Before the man had time to answer, a footstep was heard within, a light appeared, and Sir John, in his dressing-gown and slippers, opened the door.

"I ask your pardon, Sir John," said the porter, pulling off his hat.

"Here's a young man says he wants to speak to you. It's late for strangers. I thought it best to see that all was right."

"Aha!" cried Sir John, raising his eyebrows. "It's you, messenger, is it? Go in. Quite right, friend, I commend your prudence highly. Thank you. God bless you. Good night."

To be commended, thanked, God-blessed, and bade good night by one who carried "Sir" before his name, and wrote himself M.P. to boot, was something for a porter. He withdrew with much humility and reverence. Sir John followed his late visitor into the dressing-room, and sitting in his easy-chair before the fire, and moving it so that he could see him as he stood, hat in hand, beside the door, looked at him from head to foot.

The old face, calm and pleasant as ever; the complexion, quite juvenile in its bloom and clearness; the same smile; the wonted precision and elegance of dress; the white, well-ordered teeth, the delicate hands; the composed and quiet manner; everything as it used to be: no mark of age or passion, envy, hate, or discontent: all unruffled and serene, and quite delightful to behold.

He wrote himself M.P.—but how? Why, thus. It was a proud family—more proud, indeed, than wealthy. He had stood in danger of arrest; of bailiffs, and a jail—a vulgar jail, to which the common people with small incomes went. Gentlemen of ancient houses have no privilege of exemption from such cruel laws—unless they are of one great house, and then they have. A proud man of his stock and kindred had the means of sending him there. He offered—not indeed to pay his debts, but to let him sit for a close borough until his own son came of age, which, if he lived, would come to pass in twenty years. It was quite as good as an Insolvent Act, and infinitely more genteel. So Sir John Chester was a member of Parliament.

But how Sir John? Nothing so simple, or so easy. One touch with a sword of state, and the transformation was effected. John Chester, Esquire, M.P., attended court—went up with an address—headed a deputation. Such elegance of manner, so many graces of deportment, such powers of conversation, could never pass unnoticed. Mr. was too common for such merit. A man so gentlemanly should have been—but Fortune is capricious—born a Duke: just as some dukes should have been born labourers. He caught the fancy of the king, knelt down a grub, and rose a butterfly. John Chester, Esquire, was knighted and became Sir John.

"I thought when you left me this evening, my esteemed acquaintance," said Sir John after a pretty long silence, "that you intended to return with all despatch?"

"So I did, master."

"And so you have?" he retorted, glancing at his watch. "Is that what you would say?"

Instead of replying, Hugh changed the leg on which he leant, shuffled his cap from one hand to the other, looked at the ground, the wall, the ceiling, and finally at Sir John himself; before whose pleasant face he lowered his eyes again, and fixed them on the floor.

"And how have you been employing yourself in the meanwhile?"
quoth Sir John, lazily crossing his legs. "Where have you been? what
harm have you been doing?"

"No harm at all, master," growled Hugh, with humility. "I have
only done as you ordered."

"As I *what?*" returned Sir John.

"Well then," said Hugh uneasily, "as you advised, or said I
ought, or said I might, or said that you would do, if you was me.
Don't be so hard upon me, master."

Something like an expression of triumph in the perfect control he
had established over this rough instrument appeared in the knight's
face for an instant; but it vanished directly, as he said—paring his
nails while speaking:

"When you say I ordered you, my good fellow, you imply that I
directed you to do something for me—something I wanted done—
something for my own ends and purposes—you see? Now I am sure I
needn't enlarge upon the extreme absurdity if such an idea, however
unintentional; so please"—and here he turned his eyes upon him—
"to be more guarded. Will you?"

"I meant to give you no offence," said Hugh. "I don't know what
to say. You catch me up so very short."

"You will be caught up much shorter, my good friend—infinitely
shorter—one of these days, depend upon it," replied his patron
calmly. "By-the-bye, instead of wondering why you have been so
long, my wonder should be why you came at all. Why did you?"

"You know, master," said Hugh, "that I couldn't read the bill I
found, and that supposing it to be something particular from the
way it was wrapped up, I brought it here."

"And could you ask no one else to read it, Bruin?" said Sir John.

"No one that I could trust with secrets, master. Since Barnaby
Rudge was lost sight of for good and all—and that's five years ago—
I haven't talked with any one but you."

"You have done me honour I am sure."

"I have come to and fro, master, all through that time, when three
was anything to tell, because I knew that you'd be angry with me if I
stayed away," said Hugh, blurting the words out, after an embarrassed silence; "and because I wished to please you if I could, and
not to have you go against me. There. That's the true reason why I
came to-night. You know that, master, I am sure."

"You are a specious fellow," returned Sir John, fixing his eyes
upon him, "and carry two faces under your hood, as well as the best.
Didn't you give me in this room, this evening, any other reason; no
dislike of anybody who has slighted you lately, on all occasions,
abused you, treated you with rudeness; acted towards you, more as if
you were a mongrel dog than a man like himself?"

"To be sure I did!" cried Hugh, his passion rising, as the other
meant it should; "and I say it all over now, again. I'd do anything to
have some revenge on him—anything. And when you told me that he
and all the Catholics would suffer from those who joined together

under that handbill, I said I'd make one of 'em, if their master was the devil himself. I *am* one of 'em. See whether I am as good as my word and turn out to be among the foremost, or no. I mayn't have much head, master, but I've head enough to remember those that use me ill. You shall see, and so shall he, and so shall hundreds more, how my spirit backs me when the time comes. My bark is nothing to my bite. Some that I know had better have a wild lion among them than me, when I am fairly loose—they had!"

The knight looked at him with a smile of far deeper meaning than ordinary; and pointing to the old cupboard, followed him with his eyes while he filled and drank a glass of liquor; and smiled when his back was turned, with deeper meaning yet.

"You are in a blustering mood, my friend," he said, when Hugh confronted him again.

"Not I, master!" cried Hugh. "I don't say half I mean. I can't. I haven't got the gift. There are talkers enough among us; I'll be one of the doers."

"Oh! you have joined those fellows then?" said Sir John, with an air of most profound indifference.

"Yes. I went up to the house you told me of, and got put down upon the muster. There was another man there named Dennis—"

"Dennis, eh!" cried Sir John, laughing. "Ay, ay! a pleasant fellow, I believe?"

"A roaring dog, master—one after my own heart—hot upon the matter too—red hot."

"So I have heard," replied Sir John, carelessly. "You don't happen to know his trade, do you?"

"He wouldn't say," cried Hugh. "He keeps it secret."

"Ha ha!" laughed Sir John. "A strange fancy—a weakness with some persons—you'll know it one day, I dare swear."

"We're intimate already," said Hugh.

"Quite natural! And have been drinking together, eh?" pursued Sir John. "Did you say what place you went to in company, when you left Lord George's?"

Hugh had not said or thought of saying, but he told him; and this inquiry being followed by a long train of questions, he related all that had passed both in and out of doors, the kind of people he had seen, their numbers, state of feeling, mode of conversation, apparent expectations and intentions. His questioning was so artfully contrived, that he seemed even in his own eyes to volunteer all this information rather than to have it wrested from him; and he was brought to this state of feeling so naturally, that when Mr. Chester yawned at length and declared himself quite wearied out, he made a rough kind of excuse for having talked so much.

"There—get you gone," said Sir John, holding the door open in his hand. "You have made a pretty evening's work. I told you not to do this. You may get into trouble. You'll have an opportunity of revenging yourself on your proud friend Haredale, though, and for that, you'd hazard anything I suppose?"

"I would," retorted Hugh, stopping in his passage out and looking back; "but what do *I* risk! What do I stand a chance of losing, master? Friends, home? A fig for 'em all; I have none; they are nothing to me. Give me a good scuffle; let me pay off old scores in a bold riot where there are men to stand by me; and then use me as you like—it don't matter much to me what the end is!"

"What have you done with that paper?" said Sir John.

"I have it here, master."

"Drop it again as you go along; it's as well not to keep such things about you."

Hugh nodded, and touching his cap with an air of as much respect as he could summon up, departed.

Sir John, fastening the doors behind him, went back to his dressing-room, and sat down once again before the fire, at which he gazed for a long time, in earnest meditation.

"This happens fortunately," he said, breaking into a smile, "and promises well. Let me see. My relative and I, who are the most Protestant fellows in the world, give our worst wishes to the Roman Catholic cause; and to Saville, who introduces their bill, I have a personal objection besides; but as each of us has himself for the first article in his creed, we cannot commit ourselves by joining with a very extravagant madman, such as this Gordon most undoubtedly is. Now really, to foment his disturbances in secret, through the medium of such a very apt instrument as my savage friend here, may further our real ends; and to express at all becoming seasons, in moderate and polite terms, a disapprobation of his proceedings, though we agree with him in principle, will certainly be to gain a character for honesty and uprightness of purpose, which cannot fail to do us infinite service, and to raise us into some importance. Good! So much for public grounds. As to private considerations, I confess that if these vagabonds *would* make some riotous demonstration (which does not appear impossible), and *would* inflict some little chastisement on Haredale as a not inactive man among his sect, it would be extremely agreeable to my feelings, and would amuse me beyond measure. Good again! Perhaps better!"

When he came to this point, he took a pinch of snuff; then beginning slowly to undress, he resumed his meditations, by saying with a smile:

"I fear, I *do* fear exceedingly, that my friend is following fast in the footsteps of his mother. His intimacy with Mr. Dennis is very ominous. But I have no doubt he must have come to that end any way. If I lend him a helping hand, the only difference is, that he may, upon the whole, possibly drink a few gallons, or puncheons, or hogsheads, less in this life than he otherwise would. It's no business of mine. It's a matter of very small importance!"

So he took another pinch of snuff, and went to bed.

CHAPTER XLI

FROM the workshop of the Golden Key, there issued forth a tinkling sound, so merry and good-humoured, that it suggested the idea of some one working blithely, and made quite pleasant music. No man who hammered on at a dull monotonous duty, could have brought such cheerful notes from steel and iron; none but a chirping, healthy, honest-hearted fellow, who made the best of everything, and felt kindly towards everybody, could have done it for an instant. He might have been a coppersmith, and still been musical. If he had sat in a jolting waggon, full of rods of iron, it seemed as if he would have brought some harmony out of it.

Tink, tink, tink—clear as a silver bell, and audible at every pause of the streets' harsher noises, as though it said, "I don't care; nothing puts me out; I am resolved to be happy." Women scolded, children squalled, heavy carts went rumbling by, horrible cries proceeded from the lungs of hawkers; still it struck in again, no higher, no lower, no louder, no softer; not thrusting itself on people's notice a bit the more for having been outdone by louder sounds—tink, tink, tink, tink, tink.

It was a perfect embodiment of the still small voice, free from all cold, hoarseness, huskiness, or unhealthiness of any kind; foot-passengers slackened their pace, and were disposed to linger near it; neighbours who had got up splenetic that morning, felt good-humour stealing on them as they heard it, and by degrees became quite sprightly; mothers danced their babies to its ringing; still the same magical tink, tink, tink, came gaily from the workshop of the Golden Key.

Who but the locksmith could have made such music! A gleam of sun shining through the unsashed window, and chequering the dark workshop with a broad patch of light, fell full upon him, as though attracted by his sunny heart. There he stood working at his anvil, his face all radiant with exercise and gladness, his sleeves turned up, his wig pushed off his shining forehead—the easiest, freest, happiest man in all the world. Beside him sat a sleek cat, purring and winking in the light, and falling every now and then into an idle doze, as from excess of comfort. Toby looked on from a tall bench hard by; one beaming smile, from his broad nut-brown face down to the slack-baked buckles in his shoes. The very locks that hung around had something jovial in their rust, and seemed like gouty gentlemen of hearty natures, disposed to joke on their infirmities. There was nothing surly or severe in the whole scene. It seemed impossible that any one of the innumerable keys could fit a churlish strong-box or a prison-door. Cellars of beer and wine, rooms where there were fires, books, gossip, and cheering laughter—these were their proper sphere of action. Places of distrust and cruelty, and restraint, they would have left quadruple-locked for ever.

Tink, tink, tink. The locksmith paused at last, and wiped his brow. The silence roused the cat, who, jumping softly down, crept to the door, and watched with tiger eyes a bird-cage in an opposite window. Gabriel lifted Toby to his mouth, and took a hearty draught.

Then, as he stood upright, with his head flung back, and his portly chest thrown out, you would have seen that Gabriel's lower man was clothed in military gear. Glancing at the wall beyond, there might have been espied, hanging on their several pegs, a cap and feather, broad-sword, sash, and coat of scarlet; which any man learned in such matters would have known from their make and pattern to be the uniform of a serjeant in the Royal East London Volunteers.

As the locksmith put his mug down empty, on the bench whence it had smiled on him before, he glanced at these articles with a laughing eye, and looking at them with his head a little on one side, as though he would get them all into a focus, said, leaning on his hammer:

"Time was, now, I remember, when I was like to run mad with the desire to wear a coat of that colour. If any one (except my father) had called me a fool for my pains, how I should have fired and fumed! But what a fool I must have been, sure-ly!"

"Ah!" sighed Mrs. Varden, who had entered unobserved. "A fool indeed. A man at your time of life, Varden, should know better now."

"Why, what a ridiculous woman you are, Martha," said the locksmith, turning round with a smile.

"Certainly," replied Mrs. V. with great demureness. "Of course I am. I know that, Varden. Thank you."

"I mean—" began the locksmith.

"Yes," said his wife, "I know what you mean. You speak quite plain enough to be understood, Varden. It's very kind of you to adapt yourself to my capacity, I am sure."

"Tut, tut, Martha," rejoined the locksmith; "don't take offence at nothing. I mean, how strange it is of you to run down volunteering, when it's done to defend you and all the other women, and our own fireside and everybody else's, in case of need."

"It's unchristian," cried Mrs. Varden, shaking her head.

"Unchristian!" said the locksmith. "Why, what the devil—"

Mrs. Varden looked at the ceiling, as in expectation that the consequence of this profanity would be the immediate descent of the four-post bedstead on the second floor, together with the best sitting-room on the first; but no visible judgment occurring, she heaved a deep sigh, and begged her husband, in a tone of resignation, to go on, and by all means to blaspheme as much as possible, because he knew she liked it.

The locksmith did for a moment seem disposed to gratify her, but he gave a great gulp, and mildly rejoined:

"I was going to say, what on earth do you call it unchristian for? Which would be most unchristian, Martha—to sit quietly down and let our houses be sacked by a foreign army, or to turn out like men and drive em off? Shouldn't I be a nice sort of a Christian, if I crept into a corner of my own chimney and looked on while a parcel of whiskered savages bore off Dolly—or you?''

When he said "or you," Mrs. Varden, despite herself, relaxed into a smile. There was something complimentary in the idea. "In such a state of things as that, indeed—'' she simpered.

"As that!" repeated the locksmith. "Well, that would be the state of things directly. Even Miggs would go. Some black tambourine-player, with a great turban on, would be bearing *her* off, and, unless the tambourine-player was proof against kicking and scratching, it's my belief he'd have the worst of it. Ha ha ha! I'd forgive the tambourine-player. I wouldn't have him interfered with on any account, poor fellow." And here the locksmith laughed again so heartily, that tears came into his eyes—much to Mrs. Varden's indignation, who thought the capture of so sound a Protestant and estimable a private character as Miggs by a pagan negro, a circumstance too shocking and awful for contemplation.

The picture Gabriel had drawn, indeed, threatened serious consequences, and would indubitably have led to them, but luckily at that moment a light footstep crossed the threshold, and Dolly, running in, threw her arms round her old father's neck and hugged him tight.

"Here she is at last!" cried Gabriel. "And how well you look, Doll, and how late you are, my darling!"

How well she looked? Well? Why, if he had exhausted every laudatory adjective in the dictionary, it wouldn't have been praise enough. When and where was there ever such a plump, roguish, comely, bright-eyed, enticing, bewitching, captivating, maddening little puss in all this world, as Dolly! What was the Dolly of five years ago, to the Dolly of that day! How many coachmakers, saddlers, cabinetmakers, and professors of other useful arts, had deserted their fathers, mothers, sisters, brothers, and, most of all, their cousins, for the love of her! How many unknown gentlemen—supposed to be of mighty fortunes, if not titles—had waited round the corner after dark, and tempted Miggs the incorruptible, with golden guineas, to deliver offers of marriage folded up in love-letters! How many disconsolate fathers and substantial tradesmen had waited on the locksmith for the same purpose, with dismal tales of how their sons had lost their appetites, and taken to shut themselves up in dark bedrooms, and wandering in desolate suburbs with pale faces, and all because of Dolly Varden's loveliness and cruelty! How many young men, in all previous times of unprecedented steadiness, had turned suddenly wild and wicked for the same reason, and, in an ecstasy of unrequited love, taken to wrench off door-knockers, and invert the boxes of rheumatic watchmen! How had she recruited the king's service, both by sea and land, through rendering desperate his loving subjects between the ages of eighteen and twenty-five! How many young ladies had publicly professed, with tears in their eyes, that for their tastes she was much too short, too tall, too bold, too cold, too stout, too thin, too fair, too dark—too everything but handsome! How many old ladies, taking counsel together, had thanked Heaven their daughters were not like her, and had hoped she might come to no harm, and had thought she would come to no good, and had wondered what people saw in her, and had arrived at the conclusion that she was "going off" in her looks, or had never come on in them, and that she was a thorough imposition and a popular mistake!"

And yet here was this same Dolly Varden, so whimsical and hard to please that she was Dolly Varden still, all smiles and dimples and pleasant looks, and caring no more for the fifty or sixty young fellows who at that very moment were breaking their hearts to marry her, than if so many oysters had been crossed in love and opened afterwards.

Dolly hugged her father as has been already stated, and having hugged her mother also, accompanied both into the little parlour where the cloth was already laid for dinner, and where Miss Miggs— a trifle more rigid and bony than of yore—received her with a sort of hysterical gasp, intended for a smile. Into the hands of that young virgin, she delivered her bonnet and walking dress (all of a dreadful, artful, and designing kind), and then said with a laugh, which rivalled the locksmith's music, "How glad I always am to be at home again!"

"And how glad we always are, Doll," said her father, putting back the dark hair from her sparkling eyes, "to have you at home. Give me a kiss."

If there had been anybody of the male kind there to see her do it— but there was not—it was a mercy.

"I don't like your being at the Warren," said the locksmith, "I can't bear to have you out of my sight. And what is the news over yonder, Doll?"

"What news there is, I think you know already," replied his daughter. "I am sure you do though."

"Ay?" cried the locksmith. "What's that?"

"Come, come," said Dolly, "you know very well. I want you to tell me why Mr. Haredale—eh, how gruff he is again, to be sure!—has been away from home for some days past, and why he is travelling about (we know he *is* travelling, because of his letters) without telling his own niece why or wherefore."

"Miss Emma doesn't want to know, I'll swear," returned the locksmith.

"I don't know that," said Dolly; "but *I* do, at any rate. Do tell me. Why is he so secret, and what is this ghost story, which nobody is to tell Miss Emma, and which seems to be mixed up with his going away? Now I see you know by your colouring so."

"What the story means, or is, or has to do with it, I know no more than you, my dear," returned the locksmith, "except that it's some foolish fear of little Solomon's—which has, indeed, no meaning in it, I suppose. As to Mr. Haredale's journey, he goes, as I believe—"

"Yes," said Dolly.

"As I believe," resumed the locksmith, pinching her cheek, "on business, Doll. What it may be, is quite another matter. Read Blue Beard, and don't be too curious, pet; it's no business of yours or mine, depend upon that; and here's dinner, which is much more to the purpose."

Dolly might have remonstrated against this summary dismissal of the subject, notwithstanding the appearance of dinner, but at the mention of Blue Beard Mrs. Varden interposed, protesting she could not find it in her conscience to sit tamely by, and hear her child recommended to peruse the adventures of a Turk and Mussulman—far less of a fabulous Turk, which she considered that potentate to be. She held that, in such stirring and tremendous times as those in which they lived, it would be much more to the purpose if Dolly became a regular subscriber to the Thunderer, where she would have an opportunity of reading Lord George Gordon's speeches word for word, which would be a greater comfort and solace to her than a hundred and fifty Blue Beards ever could impart. She appealed in support of this proposition to Miss Miggs, then in waiting, who said that indeed the peace of mind she had derived from the perusal of that paper generally, but especially of one article of the very last week as ever was, entitled "Great Britain drenched in gore," exceeded all belief; the same composition, she added, had also wrought such a comforting effect on the mind of a married sister of hers, then resident at Golden Lion Court, number twenty-sivin, second bell-handle on the right-hand door-post, that, being in a delicate state of health, and in fact expecting an addition to her family, she had been seized with fits directly after its perusal, and had raved of the Inquisition ever since; to the great improvement of her husband and friends. Miss Miggs went on to say that she would recommend all those whose hearts were hardened to hear Lord George themselves, whom she commended first, in respect of his steady Protestantism, then of his oratory, then of his eyes, then of his nose, then of his legs, and lastly of his figure generally, which she looked upon as fit for any statue, prince, or angel, to which sentiment Mrs. Varden fully subscribed.

Mrs. Varden having cut in, looked at a box upon the mantel-shelf, painted in imitation of a very red-brick dwelling-house, with a yellow roof; having at top a real chimney, down which voluntary subscribers dropped their silver, gold, or pence, into the parlour, and on the door the counterfeit presentment of a brass plate, whereon was legibly inscribed "Protestant Association:"—and looking at it, said that it was to her a source of poignant misery to think that Varden never had, of all his substance, dropped anything into that temple, save one in secret—as she afterwards discovered—two fragments of tobacco-pipe, which she hoped would not be put down to his last account. That Dolly, she was grieved so say, was no less backward in her contributions, better loving, as it seemed, to purchase ribbons and such gauds, than to encourage the great cause, then in such heavy tribulation; and that she did entreat her (her father she much feared could not be moved) not to despise, but imitate, the bright example of Miss Miggs, who flung her wages, as it were, into the very countenance of the Pope, and bruised his features with her quarter's money.

"Oh, mim," said Miggs, "don't relude to that. I had no intentions, mim, that nobody should know. Such sacrifices as I can make, are quite a widder's mite. It's all I have," cried Miggs with a great burst of tears—for with her they never came on by degrees—"but it's made up to me in other ways; it's well made up."

This was quite true, though not perhaps in the sense that Miggs intended. As she never failed to keep her self-denial full in Mrs. Varden's view, it drew forth so many gifts of caps and gowns and other articles of dress, that upon the whole the red-brick house was perhaps the best investment for her small capital she could possibly have hit upon; returning her interest, at the rate of seven or eight per cent. in money, and fifty at least in personal repute and credit.

"You needn't cry, Miggs," said Mrs. Varden, herself in tears; "you needn't be ashamed of it, though your poor mistress *is* on the same side."

Miggs howled at this remark, in a peculiarly dismal way, and said she knowed that master hated her. That it was a dreadful thing to live in families and have dislikes, and not give satisfactions. That to make divisions was a thing she could not abear to think of, neither could her feelings let her do it. That if it was master's wishes as she and him should part, it was best they should part, and she hoped he might be the happier for it, and always wishes him well, and that he might find somebody as would meet his dispositions. It would be a hard trial, she said, to part from such a missis, but she could meet any suffering when her conscience told her she was in the rights, and therefore she was willing even to go that lengths. She did not think, she added, that she could long survive the separations, but, as she was hated and looked upon unpleasant, perhaps her dying as soon as possible would be the best endings for all parties. With this affecting conclusion, Miss Miggs shed more tears, and sobbed abundantly.

"Can you bear this, Varden?" said his wife in a solemn voice, laying down her knife and fork.

"Why, not very well, my dear," rejoined the locksmith, "but I try to keep my temper."

"Don't let there be words on my account, mim," sobbed Miggs. "It's much the best that we should part. I wouldn't stay—oh, gracious me!—and make dissensions, not for a annual gold mine, and found in tea and sugar."

Lest the reader should be at any loss to discover the cause of Miss Miggs's deep emotion, it may be whispered apart that, happening to be listening, as her custom sometimes was, when Gabriel and his wife conversed together, she had heard the locksmith's joke relative to the foreign black who played the tambourine, and bursting with the spiteful feelings which the taunt awoke in her fair breast, exploded in the manner we have witnessed. Matters having now arrived at a crisis, the locksmith, as usual, and for the sake of peace and quietness, gave in.

"What are you crying for, girl?" he said. "What's the matter with you? What are you talking about hatred for? *I* don't hate you; I don't hate anybody. Dry your eyes and make yourself agreeable, in Heaven's name, and let us all be happy while we can."

The allied powers deeming it good generalship to consider this a sufficient apology on the part of the enemy, and confession of having been in the wrong, did dry their eyes and take it in good part. Miss Miggs observed that she bore no malice, no not to her greatest foe, whom she rather loved the more indeed, the greater persecution she sustained. Mrs. Varden approved of this meek and forgiving spirit in high terms, and incidentally declared as a closing article of agreement, that Dolly should accompany her to the Clerkenwell branch of the association, that very night. This was an extraordinary instance of her great prudence and policy; having had this end in view from the first, and entertaining a secret misgiving that the locksmith (who was bold when Dolly was in question) would object, she had backed Miss Miggs up to this point, in order that she might have him at a disadvantage. The manœuvre succeeded so well that Gabriel only made a wry face, and with the warning he had just had, fresh in his mind, did not dare to say one word.

The difference ended, therefore, in Miggs being presented with a gown by Mrs. Varden and half-a-crown by Dolly, as if she had eminently distinguished herself in the paths of morality and goodness. Mrs. V., according to custom, expressed her hope that Varden would take a lesson from what had passed and learn more generous conduct for the time to come; and the dinner being now cold and nobody's appetite very much improved by what had passed, they went on with it, as Mrs. Varden said, "like Christians."

As there was to be a grand parade of the Royal East London Volunteers that afternoon, the locksmith did no more work; but sat down comfortably with his pipe in his mouth, and his arm round his pretty daughter's waist, looking lovingly on Mrs. V., from time to time, and exhibiting from the crown of his head to the sole of his foot, one smiling surface of good humour. And to be sure, when it was time to dress him in his regimentals, and Dolly, hanging about him in all kinds of graceful winning ways, helped to button and buckle and brush him up and get him into one of the tightest coats that ever was made by mortal tailor, he was the proudest father in all England.

"What a handy jade it is!" said the locksmith to Mrs. Varden, who stood by with folded hands—rather proud of her husband too—while Miggs held his cap and sword at arm's length, as if mistrusting that the latter might run some one through the body of its own accord; "but never marry a soldier, Doll, my dear."

Dolly didn't ask why not, or say a word, indeed, but stooped her head down very low to tie his sash.

"I never wear this dress," said honest Gabriel, "but I think of poor Joe Willet. I love Joe; he was always a favourite of mine. Poor Joe!— Dear heart, my girl, don't tie me in so tight."

Dolly laughed—not like herself at all—the strangest little laugh that could be—and held her head down lower still.

"Poor Joe!" resumed the locksmith, muttering to himself; "I always wish he had come to me. I might have made it up between them, if he had. Ah! old John made a great mistake in his way of acting by that lad—a great mistake.—Have you nearly tied that sash, my dear?''

What an ill-made sash it was! There it was, loose again and trailing on the ground. Dolly was obliged to kneel down, and recommence at the beginning.

"Never mind young Willet, Varden," said his wife, frowning; "you might find some one more deserving to talk about, I think."

Miss Miggs gave a great sniff to the same effect.

"Nay, Martha," cried the locksmith, "don't let us bear too hard upon him. If the lad is dead indeed, we'll deal kindly by his memory."

"A runaway and a vagabond!" said Mrs. Varden.

Miss Miggs expressed her concurrence as before.

"A runaway, my dear, but not a vagabond," returned the locksmith in a gentle tone. "He behaved himself well, did Joe—always—and was a handsome manly fellow. Don't call him a vagabond, Martha."

Mrs. Varden coughed—and so did Miggs.

"He tried hard to gain your good opinion, Martha, I can tell you," said the locksmith smiling, and stroking his chin. "Ah! that he did. It seems but yesterday that he followed me out to the Maypole door one night, and begged me not to say how like a boy they used him—say here, at home, he meant, though at the time, I recollect, I didn't understand. 'And how's Miss Dolly, sir?' says Joe," pursued the locksmith, musing sorrowfully. "Ah! Poor Joe!"

"Well, I declare," cried Miggs. "Oh! Goodness gracious me!"

"What's the matter now?" said Gabriel, turning sharply to her.

"Why, if here an't Miss Dolly," said the handmaid, stooping down to look into her face, "a-giving way to floods of tears. Oh, mim! oh, sir. Raly it's give me such a turn," cried the susceptible damsel, pressing her hand upon her side to quell the palpitation of her heart, "that you might knock me down with a feather."

The locksmith, after glancing at Miss Miggs as if he could have wished to have a feather brought straightway, looked on with a broad stare while Dolly hurried away, followed by that sympathising young woman: then turning to his wife, stammered out, "Is Dolly ill? Have I done anything? Is it my fault?"

"Your fault!" cried Mrs. V. reproachfully. "There—you had better make haste out."

"What have I done?" said poor Gabriel. "It was agreed that Mr. Edward's name was never to be mentioned, and I have not spoken of him, have I?"

Mrs. Varden merely replied that she had no patience with him, and bounced off after the other two. The unfortunate locksmith wound his sash about him, girded on his sword, put on his cap, and walked out.

"I am not much of a dab at my exercise," he said under his breath, "but I shall get into fewer scrapes at that work than at this. Every man came into the world for something; my department seems to be to make every woman cry without meaning it. It's rather hard!''

But he forgot it before he reached the end of the street, and went on with a shining face, nodding to the neighbours, and showering about his friendly greetings like mild spring rain.

CHAPTER XLII

THE Royal East London Volunteers made a brilliant sight that day: formed into lines, squares, circles, triangles, and what not, to the beating of drums, and the streaming of flags; and performed a vast number of complex evolutions, in all of which Serjeant Varden bore a conspicuous share. Having displayed their military prowess to the utmost in these warlike shows they marched in glittering order to the Chelsea Bun-house, and regaled in the adjacent taverns until dark. Then at sound of drum they fell in again, and returned amidst the shouting of His Majesty's lieges to the place from whence they came.

The homeward march being somewhat tardy,—owing to the un-soldierlike behaviour of certain corporals, who, being gentlemen of sedentary pursuits in private life and excitable out of doors, broke several windows with their bayonets, and rendered it imperative on the commanding officer to deliver them over to a strong guard, with whom they fought at intervals as they came along,—it was nine o'clock when the locksmith reached home. A hackney-coach was waiting near his door; and as he passed it, Mr. Haredale looked from the window and called him by his name.

"The sight of you is good for sore eyes, sir,'' said the locksmith, stepping up to him. "I wish you had walked in though, rather than waited here.''

"There is nobody at home, I find,'' Mr. Haredale answered; "besides, I desired to be as private as I could.''

"Humph!'' muttered the locksmith, looking round at his house. "Gone with Simon Tappertit to that precious Branch, no doubt.''

Mr. Haredale invited him to come into the coach, and, if he were not tired or anxious to go home, to ride with him a little way that they might have some talk together. Gabriel cheerfully complied, and the coachman mounting his box drove off.

"Varden,'' said Mr. Haredale, after a minute's pause, "you will be amazed to hear what errand I am on; it will seem a very strange one.''

"I have no doubt it's a reasonable one, sir, and has a meaning in it,'' replied the locksmith; "or it would not be yours at all. Have you just come back to town, sir?''

"But half an hour ago.''

"Bringing no news of Barnaby, or his mother?'' said the locksmith dubiously. "Ah! you needn't shake your head, sir. It was a wild-goose chase. I feared that, from the first. You exhausted all reasonable means of discovery when they went away. To begin again after so long a time has passed is hopeless, sir—quite hopeless.''

"Why, where are they?'' he returned impatiently. "Where can they be? Above ground?''

"God knows," rejoined the locksmith, "many that I knew above it five years ago, have their beds under the grass now. And the world is a wide place. It's a hopeless attempt, sir, believe me. We must leave the discovery of this mystery, like all others, to time, and accident, and Heaven's pleasure."

"Varden, my good fellow," said Mr. Haredale, "I have a deeper meaning in my present anxiety to find them out, than you can fathom. It is not a mere whim; it is not the casual revival of my old wishes and desires; but an earnest, solemn purpose. My thoughts and dreams all tend to it, and fix it in my mind. I have no rest by day or night; I have no peace or quiet; I am haunted."

His voice was so altered from its usual tones, and his manner bespoke so much emotion, that Gabriel, in his wonder, could only sit and look towards him in the darkness, and fancy the expression of his face.

"Do not ask me," continued Mr. Haredale, "to explain myself. If I were to do so, you would think me the victim of some hideous fancy. It is enough that this is so, and that I cannot—no, I cannot—lie quietly in my bed, without doing what will seem to you incomprehensible."

"Since when, sir," said the locksmith after a pause, "has this uneasy feeling been upon you?"

Mr. Haredale hesitated for some moments, and then replied: "Since the night of the storm. In short, since the last nineteenth of March."

As though he feared that Varden might express surprise, or reason with him, he hastily went on:

"You will think, I know, I labour under some delusion. Perhaps I do. But it is not a morbid one; it is a wholesome action of the mind, reasoning on actual occurrences. You know the furniture remains in Mrs. Rudge's house and that it has been shut up, by my orders, since she went away, save once a-week or so, when an old neighbour visits it to scare away the rats. I am on my way there now."

"For what purpose?" asked the locksmith.

"To pass the night there," he replied; "and not to-night alone, but many nights. This is a secret which I trust to you in case of any unexpected emergency. You will not come, unless in case of strong necessity, to me; from dusk to broad day I shall be there. Emma, your daughter, and the rest, suppose me out of London, as I have been until within this hour. Do not undeceive them. This is the errand I am bound upon. I know I may confide it to you, and I rely upon your questioning me no more at this time."

With that, as if to change the theme, he led the astounded locksmith back to the night of the Maypole highwayman, to the robbery of Edward Chester, to the reappearance of the man at Mrs. Rudge's house, and to all the strange circumstances which afterwards occurred. He even asked him carelessly about the man's height, his face, his figure, whether he was like any one he had ever seen—like Hugh, for instance, or any man he had known at any time—and put many questions of that sort, which the locksmith, considering them as mere

devices to engage his attention and prevent his expressing the
astonishment he felt, answered pretty much at random.

At length, they arrived at the corner of the street in which the
house stood, where Mr. Haredale, alighting, dismissed the coach. "If
you desire to see me safely lodged," he said, turning to the locksmith
with a gloomy smile, "you can."

Gabriel, to whom all former marvels had been nothing in comparison with this, followed him along the narrow pavement in silence.
When they reached the door, Mr. Haredale softly opened it with a key
he had about him, and closing it when Varden entered, they were
left in thorough darkness.

They groped their way into the ground-floor room. Here Mr.
Haredale struck a light, and kindled a pocket taper he had brought
with him for the purpose. It was then, when the flame was full upon
him, that the locksmith saw for the first time how haggard, pale, and
changed he looked; how worn and thin he was; how perfectly his whole
appearance coincided with all that he had said so strangely as they
rode along. It was not an unnatural impulse in Gabriel, after what he
had heard, to note curiously the expression of his eyes. It was
perfectly collected and rational;—so much so, indeed, that he felt
ashamed of his momentary suspicion, and drooped his own when Mr.
Haredale looked towards him, as if he feared they would betray his
thoughts.

"Will you walk through the house?" said Mr. Haredale, with a
glance towards the window, the crazy shutters of which were closed
and fastened. "Speak low."

There was a kind of awe about the place, which would have rendered it difficult to speak in any other manner. Gabriel whispered
"Yes," and followed him up-stairs.

Everything was just as they had seen it last. There was a sense of
closeness from the exclusion of fresh air, and a gloom and heaviness
around, as though long imprisonment had made the very silence sad.
The homely hangings of the beds and windows had begun to droop;
the dust lay thick upon their dwindling folds; and damps had made
their way through ceiling, wall, and floor. The boards creaked beneath
their tread, as if resenting the unaccustomed intrusion; nimble
spiders, paralysed by the taper's glare, checked the motion of their
hundred legs upon the wall or dropped like lifeless things upon the
ground; the death-watch ticked; and the scampering feet of rats and
mice rattled behind the wainscot.

As they looked about them on the decaying furniture, it was
strange to find how vividly it presented those to whom it had belonged,
and with whom it was once familiar. Grip seemed to perch again upon
his high-backed chair; Barnaby to crouch in his old favourite corner
by the fire; the mother to resume her usual seat, and watch him as of
old. Even when they could separate these objects from the phantom
of the mind which they invoked, the latter only glided out of sight,
but lingered near them still; for then they seemed to lurk in closets
and behind the doors, ready to start out and suddenly accost them in

well-remembered tones.

They went down-stairs, and again into the room they had just now left. Mr. Haredale unbuckled his sword and laid it on the table, with a pair of pocket pistols; then told the locksmith he would light him to the door.

"But this is a dull place, sir," said Gabriel, lingering; "may no one share your watch?"

He shook his head, and so plainly evinced his wish to be alone, that Gabriel could say no more. In another moment the locksmith was standing in the street, whence he could see that the light once more travelled up-stairs, and soon returning to the room below, shone brightly through the chinks of the shutters.

If ever man were sorely puzzled and perplexed, the locksmith was, that night. Even when snugly seated by his own fireside, with Mrs. Varden opposite in a night-cap and night-jacket, and Dolly beside him (in a most distracting dishabille) curling her hair, and smiling as if she had never cried in all her life and never could—even then, with Toby at his elbow and his pipe in his mouth, and Miggs (but that perhaps was not much) falling asleep in the background, he could not quite discard his wonder and uneasiness. So in his dreams—still there was Mr. Haredale, haggard and careworn, listening in the solitary house to every sound that stirred, with the taper shining through the chinks until the day should turn it pale and end his nightly watching.

CHAPTER XLIII

NEXT morning brought no satisfaction to the locksmith's thoughts, nor next day, nor the next, nor many others. Often after nightfall he entered the street, and turned his eyes towards the well-known house; and as surely as he did so, there was the solitary light, still gleaming through the crevices of the window-shutter, while all within was motionless, noiseless, cheerless, as a grave. Unwilling to hazard Mr. Haredale's favour by disobeying his strict injunction, he never ventured to knock at the door or to make his presence known in any way. But whenever strong interest and curiosity attracted him to the spot —which was not seldom—the light was always there.

If he could have known what passed within, the knowledge would have yielded him no clue to this mysterious vigil. At twilight, Mr. Haredale shut himself up, and at daybreak he came forth. He never missed a night, always came and went alone, and never varied his proceedings in the least degree.

The manner of his watch was this. At dusk, he entered the house in the same way as when the locksmith bore him company, kindled a light, went through the rooms, and narrowly examined them. That done, he returned to the chamber on the ground-floor, and laying his sword and pistols on the table, sat by it until morning.

He usually had a book with him, and often tried to read, but never fixed his eyes or thoughts upon it for five minutes together. The slightest noise without doors, caught his ear; a step upon the pavement seemed to make his heart leap.

He was not without some refreshment during the long lonely hours; generally carrying in his pocket a sandwich of bread and meat, and a small flask of wine. The latter diluted with large quantities of water, he drank in a heated, feverish way, as though his throat were dried; but he scarcely ever broke his fast, by so much as a crumb of bread.

If this voluntary sacrifice of sleep and comfort had its origin, as the locksmith on consideration was disposed to think, in any superstitious expectation of the fulfilment of a dream or vision connected with the event on which he had brooded for so many years, and if he waited for some ghostly visitor who walked abroad when men lay sleeping in their beds, he showed no trace of fear or wavering. His stern features expressed inflexible resolution; his brows were puckered and his lips compressed, with deep and settled purpose; and when he started at a noise and listened, it was not with the start of fear but hope, and catching up his sword as though the hour had come at last he would clutch it in his tight-clenched hand, and listen with sparkling eyes and eager looks, until it died away.

These disappointments were numerous, for they ensued on almost every sound, but his constancy was not shaken. Still, every night he was at his post, the same stern, sleepless, sentinel; and still night passed, and morning dawned, and he must watch again.

This went on for weeks; he had taken a lodging at Vauxhall in which to pass the day and rest himself; and from this place, when the tide served, he usually came to London Bridge from Westminster by water, in order that he might avoid the busy streets.

One evening, shortly before twilight, he came his accustomed road upon the river's bank, intending to pass through Westminster Hall into Palace Yard, and there take boat to London Bridge as usual. There was a pretty large concourse of people assembled round the Houses of Parliament, looking at the members as they entered and departed, and giving vent to rather noisy demonstrations of approval or dislike, according to their known opinions. As he made his way among the throng, he heard once or twice the No-Popery cry, which was then becoming pretty familiar to the ears of most men; but holding it in very slight regard, and observing that the idlers were of the lowest grade, he neither thought nor cared about it, but made his way along, with perfect indifference.

There were many little knots and groups of persons in Westminster Hall: some few looking upward at its noble ceiling, and at the rays of evening light, tinted by the setting sun, which streamed in aslant through its small windows, and growing dimmer by degrees, were quenched in the gathering gloom below; some, noisy passengers, mechanics going home from work, and otherwise, who hurried quickly through, waking the echoes with their voices, and soon darkening the small door in the distance, as they passed into the street beyond; some, in busy conference together on political or private matters, pacing slowly up and down with eyes that sought the ground, and seeming, by their attitudes, to listen earnestly from head to foot.

Here, a dozen squabbling urchins made a very Babel in the air; there, a solitary man, half clerk, half mendicant, paced up and down with hungry dejection in his look and gait; at his elbow passed an errand-lad, swinging his basket round and round, and with his shrill whistle riving the very timbers of the roof; while a more observant schoolboy, half-way through, pocketed his ball, and eyed the distant beadle as he came looming on. It was that time of evening when, if you shut your eyes and open them again, the darkness of an hour appears to have gathered in a second. The smooth-worn pavement, dusty with foot-steps, still called upon the lofty walls to reiterate the shuffle and the tread of feet unceasingly, save when the closing of some heavy door resounded through the building like a clap of thunder, and drowned all other noises in its rolling sound.

Mr. Haredale, glancing only at such of these groups as he passed nearest to, and then in a manner betokening that his thoughts were elsewhere, had nearly traversed the Hall, when two persons before him caught his attention. One of these, a gentleman in elegant attire, carried in his hand a cane, which he twirled in a jaunty manner as he loitered on; the other, an obsequious, crouching, fawning figure, list-ened to what he said—at times throwing in a humble word himself—and, with his shoulders shrugged up to his ears, rubbed his hands sub-missively, or answered at intervals by an inclination of the head, half-way between a nod of acquiescence, and a bow of most profound respect.

In the abstract there was nothing very remarkable in this pair, for servility waiting on a handsome suit of clothes and a cane—not to speak of gold and silver sticks, or wands of office—is common enough. But there was that about the well-dressed man, yes, and about the other likewise, which struck Mr. Haredale with no pleasant feeling. He hesitated, stopped, and would have stepped aside and turned out of his path, but at the moment, the other two faced about quickly, and stumbled upon him before he could avoid them.

The gentleman with the cane lifted his hat and had begun to tender an apology, which Mr. Haredale had begun as hastily to acknowledge and walk away, when he stopped short and cried, "Haredale! Gad bless me, this is strange indeed!"

"It is," he returned impatiently; "yes—a—"

"My dear friend," cried the other, detaining him, "why such great speed? One minute, Haredale, for the sake of old acquaintance.'

"I am in haste," he said. "Neither of us has sought this meeting. Let it be a brief one. Good night!"

"Fie, fie!" replied Sir John (for it was he), "how very churlish! We were speaking of you. Your name was on my lips—perhaps you heard me mention it? No? I am sorry for that. I am really sorry.—You know our friend here, Haredale? This is really a most remarkable meeting!"

The friend, plainly very ill at ease, had made bold to press Sir John's arm, and to give him other significant hints that he was desirous of avoiding this introduction. As it did not suit Sir John's purpose, however, that it should be evaded, he appeared quite unconscious of these silent remonstrances, and inclined his hand towards him, as he spoke, to call attention to him more particularly.

The friend, therefore, had nothing for it, but to muster up the pleasantest smile he could, and to make a conciliatory bow, as Mr. Haredale turned his eyes upon him. Seeing that he was recognised, he put out his hand in an awkward and embarrassed manner, which was not mended by its contemptuous rejection.

"Mr. Gashford!" said Haredale, coldly. "It is as I have heard then. You have left the darkness for the light, sir, and hate those whose opinions you formerly held, with all the bitterness of a renegade. You are an honour, sir, to any cause. I wish the one you espouse at present much joy of the acquisition it has made."

The secretary rubbed his hands and bowed, as though he would disarm his adversary by humbling himself before him, Sir John Chester again exclaimed, with an air of great gaiety, "Now, really, this is a most remarkable meeting!" and took a pinch of snuff with his usual self-possession.

"Mr. Haredale," said Gashford, stealthily raising his eyes, and letting them drop again when they met the other's steady gaze, "is too conscientious, too honourable, too manly, I am sure, to attach unworthy motives to an honest change of opinions, even though it implies a doubt of those he holds himself. Mr. Haredale is too just, too generous, too clear-sighted in his moral vision, to—"

"Yes, sir!" he rejoined with a sarcastic smile, finding the secretary stopped. "You were saying—"

Gashford meekly shrugged his shoulders, and looking on the ground again, was silent.

"No, but let us really," interposed Sir John at this juncture, "let us really, for a moment, contemplate the very remarkable character of this meeting. Haredale, my dear friend, pardon me if I think you are not sufficiently impressed with its singularity. Here we stand, by no previous appointment or arrangement, three old schoolfellows, in Westminster Hall; three old boarders in a remarkably dull and shady seminary at Saint Omer's, where you, being Catholics and of necessity educated out of England, were brought up; and where I, being a promising young Protestant at that time, was sent to learn the French tongue from a native of Paris!"

"Add to the singularity, Sir John," said Mr. Haredale, "that some of your Protestants of promise are at this moment leagued in yonder building, to prevent our having the surpassing and unheard-of privilege of teaching our children to read and write—here—in this land, where thousands of us enter your service every year, and to preserve the freedom of which, we die in bloody battles abroad, in heaps; and that others of you, to the number of some thousands as I learn, are led on to look on all men of my creed as wolves and beasts of prey, by this man Gashford. Add to it besides, the bare fact that this man lives in society, walks the streets in broad day—I was about to say, holds up his head, but that he does not—and it will be strange, and very strange, I grant you."

"Oh! you are hard upon our friend," replied Sir John, with an engaging smile. "You are really very hard upon our friend!"

"Let him go on, Sir John," said Gashford, fumbling with his gloves. "Let him go on. I can make allowances, Sir John. I am honoured with your good opinion, and I can dispense with Mr. Haredale's. Mr. Haredale is a sufferer from the penal laws, and I can't expect his favour."

"You have so much of my favour, sir," retorted Mr. Haredale, with a bitter glance at the third party in their conversation, "that I am glad to see you in such good company. You are the essence of your great Association, in yourselves."

"Now, there you mistake," said Sir John, in his most benignant way. "There—which is a most remarkable circumstance for a man of your punctuality and exactness, Haredale—you fall into error. I don't belong to the body; I have an immense respect for its members, but I don't belong to it; although I am, it is certainly true, the conscientious opponent of your being relieved. I feel it my duty to be so; it is a most unfortunate necessity; and cost me a bitter struggle.— Will you try this box? If you don't object to a trifling infusion of a very chaste scent, you'll find its flavour exquisite."

"I ask your pardon, Sir John," said Mr. Haredale, declining the proffer with a motion of his hand, "for having ranked you among the humble instruments who are obvious and in all men's sight. I should have done more justice to your genius. Men of your capacity plot in secrecy and safety, and leave exposed posts to the duller wits."

"Don't apologise, for the world," replied Sir John sweetly; "old friends like you and I may be allowed some freedom, or the deuce is in it."

Gashford, who had been very restless all this time, but had not once looked up, now turned to Sir John, and ventured to mutter something to the effect that he must go, or my lord would perhaps be waiting.

"Don't distress yourself, good sir," said Mr. Haredale, "I'll take my leave, and put you at your ease—" which he was about to do without ceremony, when he was stayed by a buzz and murmur at the upper end of the hall, and, looking in that direction, saw Lord George Gordon coming in, with a crowd of people round him.

There was a lurking look of triumph, though very differently expressed, in the faces of his two companions, which made it a natural impulse on Mr. Haredale's part not to give way before this leader, but to stand there while he passed. He drew himself up and, clasping his hands behind him, looked on with a proud and scornful aspect, while Lord George slowly advanced (for the press was great about him) towards the spot where they were standing.

He had left the House of Commons but that moment and had come straight down into the Hall, bringing with him, as his custom was, intelligence of what has been said that night in reference to the Papists, and what petitions had been presented in their favour, and who had supported them, and when the bill was to be brought in.

and when it would be advisable to present their own Great Protestant petition. All this he told the persons about him in a loud voice, and with great abundance of ungainly gesture. Those who were nearest him made comments to each other, and vented threats and murmurings; those who were outside the crowd cried, "Silence," and "Stand back," or closed in upon the rest, endeavouring to make a forcible exchange of places: and so they came driving on in a very disorderly and irregular way, as it is the manner of a crowd to do.

When they were very near to where the secretary, Sir John, and Mr. Haredale stood, Lord George turned round and, making a few remarks of a sufficiently violent and incoherent kind, concluded with the usual sentiment, and called for three cheers to back it. While these were in the act of being given with great energy, he extricated himself from the press, and stepped up to Gashford's side. Both he and Sir John being well known to the populace, they fell back a little and left the four standing together.

"Mr. Haredale, Lord George," said Sir John Chester, seeing that the nobleman regarded him with an inquisitive look. "A Catholic gentleman unfortunately—most unhappily a Catholic—but an esteemed acquaintance of mine, and once of Mr. Gashford's. My dear Haredale, this is Lord George Gordon."

"I should have known that, had I been ignorant of his lordship's person," said Mr. Haredale. "I hope there is but one gentleman in England, who addressing an ignorant and excited throng, would speak of a large body of his fellow-subjects in such injurious language as I heard this moment. For shame, my lord, for shame!"

"I cannot talk to you, sir," replied Lord George in a loud voice, and waving his hand in a disturbed and agitated manner; "we have nothing in common."

"We have much in common—many things—all that the Almighty gave us," said Mr. Haredale; "and common charity, not to say common sense and common decency, should teach you to refrain from these proceedings. If every one of those men had arms in their hands at this moment, as they have them in their heads, I would not leave this place without telling you that you disgrace your station."

"I don't hear you, sir," he replied in the same manner as before; "I can't hear you. It is indifferent to me what you say. Don't retort, Gashford," for the secretary had made a show of wishing to do so; "I can hold no communion with the worshippers of idols."

As he said this, he glanced at Sir John, who lifted his hands and eyebrows, as if deploring the intemperate conduct of Mr. Haredale, and smiled in admiration of the crowd and of their leader.

"*He* retort!" cried Haredale. "Look you here, my lord. Do you know this man?"

Lord George replied by laying his hand upon the shoulder of his cringing secretary, and viewing him with a smile of confidence.

"This man," said Mr. Haredale, eyeing him from top to toe, "who in his boyhood was a thief, and has been from that time to this, a servile, false, and truckling knave: this man, who has crawled and crept through life, wounding the hands he licked, and biting those he fawned upon: this sycophant, who never knew what honour, truth, or courage meant; who robbed his benefactor's daughter of her virtue, and married her to break her heart, and did it, with stripes and cruelty: this creature, who has whined at kitchen windows for the broken food, and begged for halfpence at our chapel doors: this apostle of the faith, whose tender conscience cannot bear the altars where his vicious life was publicly denounced—Do you know this man?"

"Oh, really—you are very, very hard upon our friend!" exclaimed Sir John.

"Let Mr. Haredale go on," said Gashford, upon whose unwholesome face the perspiration had broken out during this speech, in blotches of wet; "I don't mind him, Sir John; it's quite as indifferent to me what he says, as it is to my lord. If he reviles my lord, as you have heard, Sir John, how can *I* hope to escape?"

"It is not enough, my lord," Mr. Haredale continued, "that I, as good a gentleman as you, must hold my property, such as it is, by a trick at which the state connives because of these hard laws; and that we may not teach our youth in schools the common principles of right and wrong; but must we be denounced and ridden by such men as this! Here is a man to head your No-Popery cry! For shame! For shame!"

The infatuated nobleman had glanced more than once at Sir John Chester, as if to inquire whether there was any truth in these statements concerning Gashford, and Sir John had as often plainly answered by a shrug or look, "Oh, dear me! no." He now said, in the same loud key, and in the same strange manner as before:

"I have nothing to say, sir, in reply, and no desire to hear anything more. I beg you won't obtrude your conversation, or these personal attacks, upon me. I shall not be deterred from doing my duty to my country and my countrymen, by any such attempts, whether they proceed from emissaries of the Pope or not, I assure you. Come, Gashford!"

They had walked on a few paces while speaking, and were now at the Hall-door, through which they passed together. Mr. Haredale, without any leave-taking, turned away to the river stairs, which were close at hand, and hailed the only boatman who remained there.

But the throng of people—the foremost of whom had heard every word that Lord George Gordon said, and among all of whom the rumour had been rapidly dispersed that the stranger was a Papist who was bearding him for his advocacy of the popular cause—came pouring out pell-mell, and, forcing the nobleman, his secretary, and Sir John Chester on before them, so that they appeared to be at their head, crowded to the top of the stairs where Mr. Haredale waited until the boat was ready, and there stood still, leaving him on a little clear space by himself.

They were not silent, however, though inactive. At first some indistinct mutterings arose among them, which were followed by a hiss or two, and these swelled by degrees into a perfect storm. Then one voice said, "Down with the Papists!" and there was a pretty general cheer, but nothing more. After a lull of a few moments, one man cried out, "Stone him;" another, "Duck him;" another, in a stentorian voice, "No Popery!" This favourite cry the rest re-echoed, and the mob, which might have been two hundred strong, joined in a general shout.

Mr. Haredale had stood calmly on the brink of the steps, until they made this demonstration, when he looked round contemptuously, and walked at a slow pace down the stairs. He was pretty near the boat, when Gashford, as if without intention, turned about, and directly afterwards a great stone was thrown by some hand, in the crowd, which struck him on the head, and made him stagger like a drunken man.

The blood sprung freely from the wound, and trickled down his coat. He turned directly, and rushing up the steps with a boldness and passion which made them all fall back, demanded:

"Who did that? Show me the man who hit me."

Not a soul moved; except some in the rear who slunk off, and, escaping to the other side of the way, looked on like indifferent spectators.

"Who did that?" he repeated. "Show me the man who did it. Dog, was it you? It was your deed, if not your hand—I know you."

He threw himself on Gashford as he said the words, and hurled him to the ground. There was a sudden motion in the crowd, and some laid hands upon him, but his sword was out, and they fell off again.

"My lord—Sir John,"—he cried, "draw one of you—you are responsible for this outrage, and I look to you. Draw, if you are gentlemen." With that he struck Sir John upon the breast with the flat of his weapon, and with a burning face and flashing eyes stood upon his guard; alone, before them all.

For an instant, for the briefest space of time the mind can readily conceive, there was a change in Sir John's smooth face, such as no man ever saw there. The next moment, he stepped forward, and laid one hand on Mr. Haredale's arm, while with the other he endeavoured to appease the crowd.

"My dear friend, my good Haredale, you are blinded with passion —it's very natural, extremely natural—but you don't know friends from foes."

"I know them all, sir, I can distinguish well—" he retorted, almost mad with rage. "Sir John, Lord George—do you hear me? Are you cowards?"

"Never mind, sir," said a man, forcing his way between and pushing him towards the stairs, with friendly violence, "never mind asking that. For God's sake get away. What *can* you do against this number? And there are as many more in the next street, who'll be round directly,"—indeed they began to pour in as he said the words —"you'd be giddy from that cut, in the first heat of a scuffle. Now do retire, sir, or take my word for it you'll be worse used than you would be if every man in the crowd was a woman, and that woman Bloody Mary. Come, sir, make haste—as quick as you can."

Mr. Haredale, who began to turn faint and sick, felt how sensible this advice was, and descended the steps with his unknown friend's assistance. John Grueby (for John it was) helped him into the boat, and giving him a shove off, which sent her thirty feet into the tide, bade the waterman pull away like a Briton; and walked up again as composedly as if he had just landed.

There was at first a slight disposition on the part of the mob to resent this interference; but John looking particularly strong and cool, and wearing besides Lord George's livery, they thought better of it, and contented themselves with sending a shower of small missiles after the boat, which plashed harmlessly in the water; for she had by this time cleared the bridge, and was darting swiftly down the centre of the stream.

From this amusement, they proceeded to giving Protestant knocks at the doors of private houses, breaking a few lamps, and assaulting some stray constables. But, it being whispered that a detachment of Life Guards had been sent for, they took to their heels with great expedition, and left the street quite clear.

CHAPTER XLIV

WHEN the concourse separated, and, dividing into chance clusters, drew off in various directions, there still remained upon the scene of the late disturbance, one man. This man was Gashford, who, bruised by his late fall and hurt in a much greater degree by the indignity he had undergone, and the exposure of which he had been the victim, limped up and down, breathing curses and threats of vengeance.

It was not the secretary's nature to waste his wrath in words. While he vented the froth of his malevolence in those effusions, he kept a steady eye on two men, who, having disappeared with the rest when the alarm was spread, and since returned, and were now visible in the moonlight at no great distance, as they walked to and fro, and talked together.

He made no move towards them, but waited patiently on the dark side of the street, until they were tired of strolling backwards and forwards and walked away in company. Then he followed, but at some distance: keeping them in view, without appearing to have that object, or being seen by them.

They went up Parliament-street, past Saint Martin's church, and away by Saint Giles's to Tottenham Court Road, at the back of which upon the western side, was then a place called the Green Lanes. This was a retired spot, not of the choicest kind, leading into the fields. Great heaps of ashes; stagnant pools, overgrown with rank grass and duckweed; broken turnstiles; and the upright posts of palings long since carried off for firewood, which menaced all heedless walkers with their jagged and rusty nails; were the leading features of the landscape: while here and there a donkey, or a ragged horse, tethered to a stake, and cropping off a wretched meal from the coarse stunted turf, were quite in keeping with the scene, and would have suggested (if the houses had not done so, sufficiently, of themselves) how very poor the people were who lived in the crazy huts adjacent, and how fool-hardy it might prove for one who carried money, or wore decent clothes, to walk that way alone, unless by daylight.

Poverty has its whims and shows of taste, as wealth has. Some of these cabins were turreted, some had false windows painted on their rotten walls; one had a mimic clock, upon a crazy tower of four feet high, which screened the chimney; each in its little patch of ground had a rude seat or arbour. The population dealt in bones, in rags, in broken glass, in old wheels, in birds, and dogs. These, in their several ways of stowage, filled the gardens; and shedding a perfume, not of the most delicious nature, in the air, filled it besides with yelps, and screams, and howlings.

Into this retreat, the secretary followed the two men whom he had held in sight; and here he saw them safely lodged, in one of the mean-est houses, which was but a room, and that of small dimensions. He waited without, until the sound of their voices, joined in a discordant song, assured him they were making merry; and then approaching the door by means of a tottering plank which crossed the ditch in front, knocked at it with his hand.

"Muster Gashford!" said the man who opened it, taking his pipe from his mouth, in evident surprise. "Why, who'd have thought of this here honour! Walk in, Muster Gashford—walk in, sir."

Gashford required no second invitation, and entered with a gracious air. There was a fire in the rusty grate (for though the spring was pretty far advanced, the nights were cold), and on a stool beside it Hugh sat smoking. Dennis placed a chair, his only one, for the secretary, in front of the hearth; and took his seat again upon the stool he had left when he rose to give the visitor admission.

"What's in the wind now, Muster Gashford?" he said, as he resumed his pipe, and looked at him askew. "Any orders from head-quarters? Are we going to begin? What is it, Muster Gashford?"

"Oh, nothing, nothing," rejoined the secretary, with a friendly nod to Hugh. "We have broken the ice though. We had a little spurt to-day—eh, Dennis?"

"A very little one," growled the hangman. "Not half enough for me."

"Nor me neither!" cried Hugh. "Give us something to do with life in it—with life in it, master. Ha, ha!"

"Why, you wouldn't," said the secretary, with his worst expression of face, and in his mildest tones, "have anything to do, with—with death in it?"

"I don't know that," replied Hugh. "I'm open to orders. I don't care; not I."

"Nor I!" vociferated Dennis.

"Brave fellows!" said the secretary, in as pastor-like a voice as if he were commending them for some uncommon act of valour and generosity. "By the bye"—and here he stopped and warmed his hands: then suddenly looked up—"who threw that stone to-day?"

Mr. Dennis coughed and shook his head, as who should say, "A mystery indeed!" Hugh sat and smoked in silence.

"It was well done!" said the secretary, warming his hands again. "I should like to know that man."

"Would you?" said Dennis, after looking at his face to assure himself that he was serious. "Would you like to know that man, Muster Gashford?"

"I should, indeed," replied the secretary.

"Why then, Lord love you," said the hangman, in his hoarsest chuckle, as he pointed with his pipe to Hugh, "there he sits. That's the man. My stars and halters, Muster Gashford," he added in a whisper, as he drew his stool close to him and jogged him with his elbow, "what a interesting blade he is! He wants as much holding in as a thorough-bred bull-dog. If it hadn't been for me to-day, he'd have had that 'ere Roman down, and made a riot of it, in another minute."

"And why not?" cried Hugh in a surly voice, as he overheard this last remark. "Where's the good of putting things off? Strike while the iron's hot; that's what I say."

"Ah!" retorted Dennis, shaking his head, with a kind of pity for his friend's ingenuous youth; "but suppose the iron an't hot, brother! You must get people's blood up afore you strike, and have 'em in the humour. There wasn't quite enough to provoke 'em to-day, I tell you. If you'd had your way, you'd have spoilt the fun to come, and ruined us."

"Dennis is quite right," said Gashford, smoothly. "He is perfectly correct. Dennis has great knowledge of the world."

"I ought to have, Muster Gashford, seeing what a many people I've helped out of it, eh?" grinned the hangman, whispering the words behind his hand.

The secretary laughed at this, just as much as Dennis could desire, and when he had done, said, turning to Hugh:

"Dennis's policy was mine, as you may have observed. You saw, for instance, how I fell when I was set upon. I made no resistance. I did nothing to provoke an outbreak. Oh, dear no!"

"No, by the Lord Harry!" cried Dennis with a noisy laugh, "you went down very quiet, Muster Gashford—and very flat besides. I thinks to myself at the time 'it's all up with Muster Gashford!' I never see a man lay flatter not more still—with the life in him—than you did to-day. He's a rough 'un to play with, is that 'ere Papist, and that's the fact."

The secretary's face, as Dennis roared with laughter, and turned his wrinkled eyes on Hugh who did the like, might have furnished a study for the Devil's picture. He sat quite silent until they were serious again, and then said, looking round:

"We are very pleasant here; so very pleasant, Dennis, that but for my lord's particular desire that I should sup with him, and the time

being very near at hand, I should be inclined to stay, until it would be
hardly safe to go homeward. I come upon a little business—yes, I do
—as you supposed. It's very flattering to you; being this. If we ever
should be obliged—and we can't tell, you know—this is a very uncertain world—"

"I believe you, Muster Gashford," interposed the hangman with a
grave nod. "The uncertainties as I've seen in reference to this here
state of existence, the unexpected contingencies as have come about!
—Oh my eye!" Feeling the subject much too vast for expression, he
puffed at his pipe again, and looked the rest.

"I say," resumed the secretary, in a slow, impressive way; "we
can't tell what may come to pass; and if we should be obliged, against
our wills, to have recourse to violence, my lord (who has suffered
terribly to-day, as far as words can go) consigns to you two—bearing
in mind my recommendation of you both, as good staunch men,
beyond all doubt and suspicion—the pleasant task of punishing this
Haredale. You may do as you please with him, or his, provided that
you show no mercy, and no quarter, and leave no two beams of his
house standing where the builder placed them. You may sack it,
burn it, do with it as you like, but it must come down; it must be
razed to the ground; and he, and all belonging to him, left as shelterless as new-born infants whom their mothers have exposed. Do you
understand me?" said Gashford, pausing, and pressing his hands
together gently.

"Understand you, master!" cried Hugh. "You speak plain now.
Why this *is* hearty!"

"I knew you would like it," said Gashford, shaking him by the
hand; "I thought you would. Good night! Don't rise, Dennis: I would
rather find my way alone. I may have to make other visits here, and
it's pleasant to come and go without disturbing you. I can find my
way perfectly well. Good night!"

He was gone, and had shut the door behind him. They looked at
each other, and nodded approvingly: Dennis stirred up the fire.

"This looks a little more like business!" he said.

"Ay, indeed!" cried Hugh; "this suits me!"

"I've heerd it said of Muster Gashford," said the hangman, "that
he'd a surprising memory and wonderful firmness—that he never
forgot, and never forgave.—Let's drink his health!"

Hugh readily complied—pouring no liquor on the floor when he
drank this toast—and they pledged the secretary as a man after
their own hearts, in a bumper.

CHAPTER XLV

WHILE the worst passions of the worst men were thus working in the
dark, and the mantle of religion, assumed to cover the ugliest de-
formities, threatened to become the shroud of all that was good and
peaceful in society, a circumstance occurred which once more altered
the position of two persons from whom this history has long been

separated, and to whom it must now return.

In a small English country town, the inhabitants of which supported themselves by the labour of their hands in plaiting and preparing straw for those who made bonnets and other articles of dress and ornament from that material,—concealed under an assumed name, and living in a quiet poverty which knew no change, no pleasures, and few cares but that of struggling on from day to day in one great toil for bread,—dwelt Barnaby and his mother. Their poor cottage had known no stranger's foot since they sought the shelter of its roof five years before; nor had they in all that time held any commerce or communication with the old world from which they had fled. To labour in peace, and devote her labour and her life to her poor son, was all the widow sought. If happiness can be said at any time to be the lot of one on whom a secret sorrow preys, she was happy now. Tranquillity, resignation, and her strong love of him who needed it so much, formed the small circle of her quiet joys; and while that remained unbroken, she was contented.

For Barnaby himself, the time which had flown by, had passed him like the wind. The daily suns of years had shed no brighter gleam of reason on his mind; no dawn had broken on his long, dark night. He would sit sometimes—often for days together—on a low seat by the fire or by the cottage door, busy at work (for he had learnt the art his mother plied), and listening, God help him, to the tales she would repeat, as a lure to keep him in her sight. He had no recollection of these little narratives; the tale of yesterday was new to him upon the morrow; but he liked them at the moment; and when the humour held him, would remain patiently within doors, hearing her stories like a little child, and working cheerfully from sunrise until it was too dark to see.

At other times,—and then their scanty earnings were barely sufficient to furnish them with food, though of the coarsest sort,—he would wander abroad from dawn of day until the twilight deepened into night. Few in that place, even of the children, could be idle, and he had no companions of his own kind. Indeed there were not many who could have kept up with him in his rambles, had there been a legion. But there were a score of vagabond dogs belonging to the neighbours, who served his purpose quite as well. With two or three of these, or sometimes with a full half-dozen barking at his heels, he would sally forth on some long expedition that consumed the day; and though, on their return at nightfall, the dogs would come home limping and sore-footed, and almost spent with their fatigue, Barnaby was up and off again at sunrise with some new attendants of the same class, with whom he would return in like manner. On all these travels, Grip, in his little basket at his master's back, was a constant member of the party, and when they set off in fine weather and in high spirits, no dog barked louder than the raven.

Their pleasures on these excursions were simple enough. A crust of bread and scrap of meat, with water from the brook or spring, sufficed for their repast. Barnaby's enjoyments were, to walk, and run, and leap, till he was tired; then to lie down in the long grass, or by the growing corn, or in the shade of some tall tree, looking upward at the light clouds as they floated over the blue surface of the sky, and listening to the lark as she poured out her brilliant song. There were wild-flowers to pluck—the bright red poppy, the gentle harebell, the cowslip, and the rose. There were birds to watch; fish; ants; worms; hares or rabbits, as they darted across the distant pathway in the wood and so were gone: millions of living things to have an interest in, and lie in wait for, and clap hands and shout in memory of, when they had disappeared. In default of these, or when they wearied, there was the merry sunlight to hunt out, as it crept in aslant through leaves and boughs of trees, and hid far down—deep, deep, in hollow places—like a silver pool, where nodding branches seemed to bathe and sport; sweet scents of summer air breathing over fields of beans or clover; the perfume of wet leaves or moss; the life of waving trees, and shadows always changing. When these or any of them tired, or in excess of pleasing tempted him to shut his eyes, there was slumber in the midst of all these soft delights, with the gentle wind murmuring like music in his ears, and everything around melting into one delicious dream.

Their hut—for it was little more—stood on the outskirts of the town, at a short distance from the high road, but in a secluded place, where few chance passengers strayed at any season of the year. It had a plot of garden-ground attached, which Barnaby, in fits and starts of working trimmed, and kept in order. Within doors and without, his mother laboured for their common good; and hail, rain, snow, or sunshine, found no difference in her.

Though so far removed from the scenes of her past life, and with so little thought or hope of ever visiting them again, she seemed to have a strange desire to know what happened in the busy world. Any old newspaper, or scrap of intelligence from London, she caught at with avidity. The excitement it produced was not of a pleasurable kind, for her manner at such times expressed the keenest anxiety and dread; but it never faded in the least degree. Then, and in stormy winter nights, when the wind blew loud and strong, the old expression came into her face, and she would be seized with a fit of trembling, like one who had an ague. But Barnaby noted little of this; and putting a great constraint upon herself, she usually recovered her accustomed manner before the change had caught his observation.

Grip was by no means an idle or unprofitable member of the humble household. Partly by dint of Barnaby's tuition, and partly by pursuing a species of self-instruction common to his tribe, and exerting his powers of observation to the utmost, he had acquired a degree of sagacity which rendered him famous for miles round. His conversational powers and surprising performances were the universal theme: and as many persons came to see the wonderful raven, and none left his exertions unrewarded—when he condescended to exhibit, which was not always, for genius is capricious—his earnings formed an important item in the common stock. Indeed, the bird himself appeared to know his value well; for though he was perfectly free and unrestrained in the presence of Barnaby and his mother, he maintained in public an amazing gravity, and never stooped to any other gratuitous performances than biting the ankles of vagabond boys (an exercise in which he much delighted), killing a fowl or two occasionally, and swallowing the dinners of various neighbouring dogs, of whom the boldest held him in great awe and dread.

Time had glided on in this way, and nothing had happened to disturb or change their mode of life, when, one summer's night in June, they were in their little garden, resting from the labours of the day. The widow's work was yet upon her knee and strewn upon the ground about her; and Barnaby stood leaning on his spade, gazing at the brightness in the west, and singing softly to himself.

"A brave evening, mother! If we had, chinking in our pockets, but a few specks of that gold which is piled up yonder in the sky, we should be rich for life."

"We are better as we are," returned the widow with a quiet smile. "Let us be contented, and we do not want and need not care to have it, though it lay shining at our feet."

"Ay!" said Barnaby, resting with crossed arms on his spade, and looking wistfully at the sunset, "that's well enough, mother; but gold's a good thing to have. I wish that I knew where to find it. Grip and I could do much with gold, be sure of that."

"What would you do?" she asked.

"What! A world of things. We'd dress finely—you and I, I mean; not Grip—keep horses, dogs, wear bright colours and feathers, do no more work, live delicately and at our ease. Oh, we'd find uses for it, mother, and uses that would do us good. I would I knew where gold was buried. How hard I'd work to dig it up!"

"You do not know," said his mother, rising from her seat and laying her hand upon his shoulder, "what men have done to win it, and how they have found, too late, that it glitters brightest at a distance, and turns quite dim and dull when handled."

"Ah, ay; so you say; so you think," he answered, still looking eagerly in the same direction. "For all that, mother, I should like to try."

"Do you not see," she said, "how red it is? Nothing bears so many stains of blood as gold. Avoid it. None have such cause to hate its name as we have. Do not so much as think of it, dear love. It has brought such misery and suffering on your head and mine as few have known, and God grant few may have to undergo. I would rather we were dead and laid down in our graves, than you should ever come to love it."

For a moment Barnaby withdrew his eyes and looked at her with wonder. Then, glancing from the redness in the sky to the mark upon his wrist as if he would compare the two, he seemed about to question her with earnestness, when a new object caught his wandering attention, and made him quite forgetful of his purpose.

This was a man with dusty feet and garments, who stood, bareheaded, behind the hedge that divided their patch of garden from the pathway, and leant meekly forward as if he sought to mingle with their conversation, and waited for his time to speak. His face was turned towards the brightness, too, but the light that fell upon it showed that he was blind and saw it not.

"A blessing on those voices!" said the wayfarer. "I feel the beauty of the night more keenly, when I hear them. They are like eyes to me. Will they speak again, and cheer the heart of a poor traveller?"

"Have you no guide?" asked the widow, after a moment's pause.

"None but that," he answered, pointing with his staff towards the sun; "and sometimes a milder one at night, but she is idle now."

"Have you travelled far?"

"A weary way and long," rejoined the traveller as he shook his head. "A weary, weary, way. I struck my stick just now upon the bucket of your well—be pleased to let me have a draught of water, lady."

"Why do you call me lady?" she returned. "I am as poor as you."

"Your speech is soft and gentle, and I judge by that," replied the man. "The coarsest stuffs and finest silks are—apart from the sense of touch—alike to me. I cannot judge you by your dress."

"Come round this way," said Barnaby, who had passed out at the garden-gate and now stood close beside him. "Put your hand in mine. You're blind and always in the dark, eh? Are you frightened in the dark? Do you see great crowds of faces, now? Do they grin and chatter?"

"Alas!" returned the other, "I see nothing. Waking or sleeping, nothing."

Barnaby looked curiously at his eyes, and touching them with his fingers, as an inquisitive child might, led him towards the house.

"You have come a long distance," said the widow, meeting him at the door. "How have you found your way so far?"

"Use and necessity are good teachers, as I have heard—the best of any," said the blind man, sitting down upon the chair to which Barnaby had led him, and putting his hat and stick upon the red-tiled floor. "May neither you nor your son ever learn under them. They are rough masters."

"You have wandered from the road, too," said the widow, in a tone of pity.

"Maybe, maybe," returned the blind man with a sigh, and yet with something of a smile upon his face, "that's likely. Handposts and milestones are dumb, indeed, to me. Thank you the more for this rest, and this refreshing drink!"

As he spoke, he raised the mug of water to his mouth. It was clear, and cold, and sparkling, but not to his taste nevertheless, or his thirst was not very great, for he only wetted his lips and put it down again.

He wore, hanging with a long strap round his neck, a kind of scrip or wallet, in which to carry food. The widow set some bread and cheese before him, but he thanked her, and said that through the kindness of the charitable he had broken his fast once since morning, and was not hungry. When he had made her this reply, he opened his wallet, and took out a few pence, which was all it appeared to contain.

"Might I make bold to ask," he said, turning towards where Barnaby stood looking on, "that one who has the gift of sight, would lay this out for me in bread to keep me on my way? Heaven's blessing on the young feet that will bestir themselves in aid of one so helpless as a sightless man?"

Barnaby looked at his mother, who nodded assent; in another moment he was gone upon his charitable errand. The blind man sat listening with an attentive face, until long after the sound of his retreating footsteps was inaudible to the widow, and then said suddenly, and in a very altered tone:

"There are various degrees and kinds of blindness, widow. There is the connubial blindness, ma'am, which perhaps you may have observed in the course of your own experience, and which is a kind of wilful and self-bandaging blindness. There is the blindness of party, ma'am, and public men, which is the blindness of a mad bull in the midst of a regiment of soldiers clothed in red. There is the blind confidence of youth, which is the blindness of young kittens, whose eyes have not yet opened on the world; and there is that physical blindness, ma'am, of which I am, contrary to my own desire, a most illustrious example. Added to these, ma'am, is that blindness of the intellect, of which we have a specimen in your interesting son, and which, having sometimes glimmerings and dawnings of the light, is scarcely to be trusted as a total darkness. Therefore, ma'am, I have taken the liberty to get him out of the way for a short time, while you and I confer together, and this precaution arising out of the delicacy of my sentiments towards yourself, you will excuse me, ma'am, I know."

Having delivered himself of this speech with many flourishes of manner, he drew from beneath his coat a flat stone bottle, and holding the cork between his teeth, qualified his mug of water with a plentiful infusion of the liquor it contained. He politely drained the bumper to her health, and the ladies, and setting it down empty, smacked his lips with infinite relish.

"I am a citizen of the world, ma'am," said the blind man, corking his bottle, "and if I seem to conduct myself with freedom, it is therefore. You wonder who I am, ma'am, and what has brought me here. Such experiences of human nature as I have, leads me to that conclusion, without the aid of eyes by which to read the movements of your soul as depicted in your feminine features. I will satisfy your curiosity immediately, ma'am; im-mediately." With that he slapped his bottle on its broad back, and having put it under his garment as before, crossed his legs and folded his hands, and settled himself in his chair, previous to proceeding any further.

The change in his manner was so unexpected, the craft and wickedness of his deportment were so much aggravated by his condition—for we are accustomed to see in those who have lost a human sense, something in its place almost divine—and this alteration

bred so many fears in her whom he addressed, that she could not
pronounce one word. After waiting, as it seemed, for some remark or
answer, and awaiting in vain, the visitor resumed:

"Madam, my name is Stagg. A friend of mine who has desired the
honour of meeting with you any time these five years past, has
commissioned me to call upon you. I should be glad to whisper that
gentleman's name in your ears.—Zounds, ma'am, are you deaf? Do
you hear me say that I should be glad to whisper my friend's name in
your ear?"

"You need not repeat it," said the widow, with a stifled groan; "I
see too well from whom you come."

"But as a man of honour, ma'am," said the blind man, striking
himself on the breast, "whose credentials must not be disputed, I
take leave to say that I *will* mention that gentleman's name. Ay, ay,"
he added, seeming to catch with his quick ear the very motion of her
hand, "but not aloud. With your leave, ma'am, I desire the favour of
a whisper."

She moved towards him, and stooped down. He muttered a word
in her ear, and, wringing her hands, she paced up and down the room
like one distracted. The blind man, with perfect composure, produced
his bottle again, mixed another glass-full; put it up as before; and,
drinking from time to time, followed her with his face in silence.

"You are slow in conversation, widow," he said after a time,
pausing in his draught. "We shall have to talk before your son."

"What would you have me do?" she answered. "What do you
want?"

"We are poor, widow, we are poor," he retorted, stretching out
his right hand, and rubbing his thumb upon its palm.

"Poor!" she cried. "And what am I?"

"Comparisons are odious," said the blind man. "I don't know, I
don't care. I say that we are poor. My friend's circumstances are
indifferent, and so are mine. We must have our rights, widow, or we
must be bought off. But you know that, as well as I, so where is the
use of talking?"

She still walked wildly to and fro. At length, stopping abruptly
before him, she said:

"Is he near here?"

"He is. Close at hand."

"Then I am lost!"

"Not lost, widow," said the blind man, calmly; "only found. Shall
I call him?"

"Not for the world," she answered, with a shudder.

"Very good," he replied, crossing his legs again, for he had made as
though he would rise and walk to the door. "As you please, widow.
His presence is not necessary that I know of. But both he and I
must live; to live, we must eat and drink; to eat and drink, we must
have money:—I say no more."

"Do you know how pinched and destitute I am?" she retorted. "I
do not think you do, or can. If you had eyes, and could look around

you on this poor place, you would have pity on me. Oh! let your heart be softened by your own affliction, friend, and have some sympathy with mine."

The blind man snapped his fingers as he answered:

"—Beside the question, ma'am, beside the question. I have the softest heart in the world, but I can't live upon it. Many a gentleman lives well upon a soft head, who would find a heart of the same quality a very great drawback. Listen to me. This is a matter of business, with which sympathies and sentiments have nothing to do. As a mutual friend, I wish to arrange it in a satisfactory manner, if possible; and thus the case stands.—If you are very poor now, it's your own choice. You have friends who, in case of need, are always ready to help you. My friend is in a more destitute and desolate situation than most men, and, you and he being linked together in a common cause, he naturally looks to you to assist him. He has boarded and lodged with me a long time (for as I said just now, I am very soft-hearted), and I quite approve of his entertaining this opinion. You have always had a roof over your head; he has always been an outcast. You have your son to comfort and assist you; he has nobody at all. The advantages must not be all one side. You are in the same boat, and we must divide the ballast a little more equally."

She was about to speak, but he checked her, and went on.

"The only way of doing this, is by making up a little purse now and then for my friend; and that's what I advise. He bears you no malice that I know of, ma'am: so little, that although you have treated him harshly more than once, and driven him, I may say, out of doors, he has that regard for you that I believe even if you disappointed him now, he would consent to take charge of your son, and to make a man of him."

He laid a great stress on these latter words, and paused as if to find out what effect they had produced. She only answered by her tears.

"He is a likely lad," said the blind man, thoughtfully, "for many purposes, and not ill-disposed to try his fortune in a little change and bustle, if I may judge from what I heard of his talk with you tonight.—Come. In a word, my friend has pressing necessity for twenty pounds. You, who can give up an annuity, can get that sum for him. It's a pity you should be troubled. You seem very comfortable here, and it's worth that much to remain so. Twenty pounds, widow, is a moderate demand. You know where to apply for it; a post will bring it you.—Twenty pounds!"

She was about to answer him again, but again he stopped her.

"Don't say anything hastily; you might be sorry for it. Think of it a little while. Twenty pounds—of other people's money—how easy! Turn it over in your mind. I'm in no hurry. Night's coming on, and if I don't sleep here, I shall not go far. Twenty pounds! Consider of it, ma'am, for twenty minutes; give each pound a minute; that's a fair allowance. I'll enjoy the air the while, which is very mild and pleasant in these parts."

With these words he groped his way to the door, carrying his chair with him. Then seating himself, under a spreading honeysuckle, and stretching his legs across the threshold so that no person could pass in or out without his knowledge, he took from his pocket a pipe, flint, steel and tinder-box, and began to smoke. It was a lovely evening, of that gentle kind, and at that time of year, when the twilight is most beautiful. Pausing now and then to let his smoke curl slowly off, and to sniff the grateful fragrance of the flowers, he sat there at his ease—as though the cottage were his proper dwelling, and he had held undisputed possession of it all his life—waiting for the widow's answer and for Barnaby's return.

CHAPTER XLVI

When Barnaby returned with the bread, the sight of the pious old pilgrim smoking his pipe and making himself so thoroughly at home, appeared to surprise even him; the more so, as that worthy person instead of putting up the loaf in his wallet as a scarce and precious article, tossed it carelessly on the table, and producing his bottle, bade him sit down and drink.

"For I carry some comfort you see," he said. "Taste that. Is it good?"

The water stood in Barnaby's eyes as he coughed from the strength of that draught, and answered in the affirmative.

"Drink some more," said the blind man: "don't be afraid of it. You don't taste anything like that, often, eh?"

"Often!" cried Barnaby. "Never!"

"Too poor?" returned the blind man with a sigh. "Ay. That's bad. Your mother, poor soul, would be happier if she was richer, Barnaby."

"Why, so I tell her—the very thing I told her just before you came to-night, when all that gold was in the sky," said Barnaby, drawing his chair nearer to him, and looking eagerly in his face. "Tell me. Is there any way of being rich, that I could find out?"

"Any way! A hundred ways."

"Ay, ay?" he returned. "Do you say so? What are they?—Nay, mother, it's for your sake I ask; not mine;—for yours, indeed. What are they?"

The blind man turned his face, on which there was a smile of triumph, to where the widow stood in great distress; and answered,

"Why, they are not to be found out by stay-at-homes, my good friend."

"By stay-at-homes!" cried Barnaby, plucking at his sleeve. "But I am not one. Now, there you mistake. I am often out before the sun, and travel home when he has gone to rest. I am away in the woods before the day has reached the shady places, and am often there when the bright moon is peeping through the boughs, and looking down upon the other moon that lives in the water. As I walk along, I try to find, among the grass and moss, some of that small money for which she works so hard and used to shed so many tears. As I lie asleep in the shade, I dream of it—dream of digging it up in heaps; and spying it out, hidden under bushes; and seeing it sparkle, as the dew-drops do, among the leaves. But I never find it. Tell me where it is. I'd go there, if the journey were a whole year long, because I know she would be happier when I came home and brought some with me. Speak again. I'll listen to you if you talk all night."

The blind man passed his hand lightly over the poor fellow's face, and finding that his elbows were planted on the table, that his chin rested on his two hands, that he leaned eagerly forward, and that his whole manner expressed the utmost interest and anxiety, paused for a minute as though he desired the widow to observe this fully, and then made answer:

"It's in the world, bold Barnaby, the merry world; not in solitary places like those you pass your time in, but in crowds, and where there's noise and rattle."

"Good! Good!" cried Barnaby, rubbing his hands. "Yes! I love that. Grip loves it too. It suits us both. That's brave!"

"—The kind of places," said the blind man, "that a young fellow likes, and in which a good son may do more for his mother, and himself to boot, in a month, than he could here in all his life—that is, if he had a friend, you know, and some one to advise with."

"You hear this, mother?" cried Barnaby, turning to her with delight. "Never tell me we shouldn't heed it, if it lay shining at our feet. Why do we heed it so much now? Who do you toil from morning until night?"

"Surely," said the blind man, "surely. Have you no answer, widow? Is your mind," he slowly added, "not made up yet?"

"Let me speak with you," she answered, "apart."

"Lay your hand upon my sleeve," said Stagg, arising from the table; "and lead me where you will. Courage, bold Barnaby. We'll talk more of this: I've a fancy for you. Wait there till I come back. Now, widow."

She led him out at the door, and into the little garden, where they stopped.

"You are a fit agent," she said, in a half breathless manner, "and well represent the man who sent you here."

"I'll tell him that you said so," Stagg retorted. "He has a regard for you, and will respect me the more (if possible) for your praise. We must have our rights, widow."

"Rights! Do you know," she said, "that a word from me—"

"Why do you stop?" returned the blind man calmly, after a long pause. "Do I know that a word from you would place my friend in the last position of the dance of life? Yes, I do. What of that? It will never be spoken, widow."

"You are sure of that?"

"Quite—so sure, that I don't come here to discuss the question. I say we must have our rights, or we must be bought off. Keep to that point, or let me return to my young friend, for I have an interest in the lad, and desire to put him in the way of making his fortune.

Bah! you needn't speak," he added hastily; "I know what you would say: you have hinted at it once already. Have I no feeling for you, because I am blind? No, I have not. Why do you expect me, being in darkness, to be better than men who have their sight—why should you? Is the hand of Heaven more manifest in my having no eyes, than in your having two? It's the cant of you folks to be horrified if a blind man robs, or lies, or steals; oh yes, it's far worse in him, who can barely live on the few halfpence that are thrown to him in streets, than in you, who can see, and work, and are not dependent on the mercies of the world. A curse on you! You who have five senses may be wicked at your pleasure; we who have four, and want the most important, are to live and be moral on our affliction. The true charity and justice of rich to poor, all the world over!"

He paused a moment when he had said these words, and caught the sound of money, jingling in her hand.

"Well?" he cried, quickly resuming his former manner. "That should lead to something. The point, widow?"

"First answer me one question," she replied. "You say he is close at hand. Has he left London?"

"Being close at hand, widow, it would seem he has," returned the blind man.

"I mean, for good? You know that."

"Yes, for good. The truth is, widow, that his making a longer stay there might have had disagreeable consequences. He has come away for that reason."

"Listen," said the widow, telling some money out, upon a bench beside them. "Count."

"Six," said the blind man, listening attentively. "Any more?"

"They are the savings," she answered, "of five years. Six guineas."

He put out his hand for one of the coins; felt it carefully, put it between his teeth, rung it on the bench; and nodded to her to proceed.

"These have been scraped together and laid by, lest sickness or death should separate my son and me. They have been purchased at the price of much hunger, hard labour, and want of rest. If you *can* take them—do—on condition that you leave this place upon the instant, and enter no more into that room, where he sits now, expecting your return."

"Six guineas," said the blind man, shaking his head, "though of the fullest weight that were ever coined, fall very far short of twenty pounds, widow."

"For such a sum, as you know, I must write to a distant part of the country. To do that, and receive an answer, I must have time."

"Two days?" said Stagg.

"More."

"Four days?"

"A week. Return on this day week, at the same hour, but not to the house. Wait at the corner of the lane."

"Of course," said the blind man, with a crafty look, "I shall find you there?"

"Where else can I take refuge? Is it not enough that you have made a beggar of me, and that I have sacrificed my whole store, so hardly earned, to preserve this home?"

"Humph!" said the blind man, after some consideration. "Set me with my face towards the point you speak of, and in the middle of the road. Is this the spot?"

"It is."

"On this day week at sunset. And think of him within doors.—For the present, good night."

She made no answer, nor did he stop for any. He went slowly away, turning his head from time to time, and stopping to listen, as if he were curious to know whether he was watched by any one. The shadows of night were closing fast around, and he was soon lost in the gloom. It was not, however, until she had traversed the lane from end to end, and made sure that he was gone, that she re-entered the cottage, and hurriedly barred the door and window.

"Mother!" said Barnaby. "What is the matter? Where is the blind man?"

"He is gone."

"Gone!" he cried, starting up. "I must have more talk with him. Which way did he take?"

"I don't know," she answered, folding her arms about him. "You must not go out to-night. There are ghosts and dreams abroad."

"Ay?" said Barnaby, in a frightened whisper.

"It is not safe to stir. We must leave this place to-morrow."

"This place! This cottage—and the little garden, mother!"

"Yes. To-morrow morning at sunrise. We must travel to London; lose ourselves in that wide place—there would be some trace of us in any other town—then travel on again, and find some new abode."

Little persuasion was required to reconcile Barnaby to anything that promised change. In another minute, he was wild with delight; in another, full of grief at the prospect of parting with his friends the dogs; in another, wild again; then he was fearful of what she had said to prevent his wandering abroad that night, and full of terrors and strange questions. His light-heartedness in the end surmounted all his other feelings, and lying down in his clothes to the end that he might be ready on the morrow, he soon fell fast asleep before the poor turf fire.

His mother did not close her eyes, but sat beside him, watching. Every breath of wind sounded in her ears like that dreaded footstep at the door, or like that hand upon the latch, and made the calm summer night, a night of horror. At length the welcome day appeared. When she had made the little preparations which were needful for their journey, and had prayed upon her knees with many tears, she roused Barnaby, who jumped up gaily at her summons.

His clothes were few enough, and to carry Grip was a labour of love. As the sun shed his earliest beams upon the earth, they closed the door of their deserted home, and turned away. The sky was blue and bright. The air was fresh and filled with a thousand perfumes.

Barnaby looked upward, and laughed with all his heart.

But it was a day he usually devoted to a long ramble, and one of the dogs—the ugliest of them all—came bounding up, and jumping round him in the fulness of his joy. He had to bid him go back in a surly tone, and his heart smote him while he did so. The dog retreated; turned with a half-incredulous, half-imploring look; came a little back; and stopped.

It was the last appeal of an old companion and a faithful friend—cast off. Barnaby could bear no more, and as he shook his head and waved his playmate home, he burst into tears.

"Oh mother, mother, how mournful he will be when he scratches at the door, and finds it always shut!"

There was such a sense of home in the thought, that though her own eyes overflowed she would not have obliterated the recollection of it, either from her own mind or from his, for the wealth of the whole wide world.

CHAPTER XLVII

In the exhaustless catalogue of Heaven's mercies to mankind, the power we have of finding some germs of comfort in the hardest trials must ever occupy the foremost place; not only because it supports and upholds us when we most require to be sustained, but because in this source of consolation there is something, we have reason to believe, of the divine spirit; something of that goodness which detects amidst our own evil doings, a redeeming quality; something which, even in our fallen nature, we possess in common with the angels; which had its being in the old time when they trod the earth, and lingers on it, yet, in pity.

How often, on their journey, did the widow remember with a grateful heart, that out of his deprivation Barnaby's cheerfulness and affection sprung! How often did she call to mind that but for that, he might have been sullen, morose, unkind, far removed from her—vicious, perhaps, and cruel! How often had she cause for comfort, in his strength, and hope, and in his simple nature! Those feeble powers of mind which rendered him so soon forgetful of the past, save in brief gleams and flashes,—even they were a comfort now. The world to him was full of happiness; in every tree, and plant, and flower, in every bird, and beast, and tiny insect whom a breath of summer wind laid low upon the ground, he had delight. His delight was hers; and where many a wise son would have made her sorrowful, this poor light-hearted idiot filled her breast with thankfulness and love.

Their stock of money was low, but from the hoard she had told into the blind man's hand, the widow had withheld one guinea. This, with the few pence she possessed besides, was to two persons of their frugal habits, a goodly sum in bank. Moreover they had Grip in company; and when they must otherwise have changed the guinea, it was but to make him exhibit outside an alehouse door, or in a village street, or in the grounds or gardens of a mansion of the better sort, and scores who would have given nothing in charity, were ready to bargain for more amusement from the talking bird.

One day—for they moved slowly, and although they had many rides in carts and waggons, were on the road a week—Barnaby, with Grip upon his shoulder and his mother following, begged permission at a trim lodge to go up to the great house, at the other end of the avenue, and show his raven. The man within was inclined to give them admittance, and was indeed about to do so, when a stout gentleman with a long whip in his hand, and a flushed faced which seemed to indicate that he had had his morning's draught, rode up to the gate, and called in a loud voice and with more oaths than the occasion seemed to warrant to have it opened directly.

"Who hast thou got here?" said the gentleman angrily, as the man threw the gate wide open, and pulled off his hat, "who are these? Eh? art a beggar, woman?"

The widow answered with a curtsey, that they were poor travellers.

"Vagrants," said the gentleman, "vagrants and vagabonds. Thee wish to be made acquainted with the cage, dost thee—the cage, the stocks, and the whipping-post? Where dost come from?"

She told him in a timid manner,—for he was very loud, hoarse, and red-faced,—and besought him not to be angry, for they meant no harm, and would go upon their way that moment.

"Don't be too sure of that," replied the gentleman, "we don't allow vagrants to roam about this place. I know what thou want'st—stray linen drying on hedges, and stray poultry, eh? What hast got in that basket, lazy hound?"

"Grip, Grip, Grip—Grip, the clever, Grip the wicked, Grip the knowing—Grip, Grip, Grip," cried the raven, whom Barnaby had shut up on the approach of this stern personage. "I'm a devil I'm a devil I'm a devil, Never say die Hurrah Bow wow wow, Polly put the kettle on we'll all have tea."

"Take the vermin out, scoundrel," said the gentleman, "and let me see him."

Barnaby, thus condescendingly addressed, produced his bird, but not without much fear and trembling, and set him down upon the ground; which he had no sooner done than Grip drew fifty corks at least, and then began to dance; at the same time eyeing the gentleman with surprising insolence of manner, and screwing his head so much on one side that he appeared desirous of screwing it off upon the spot.

The cork-drawing seemed to make a greater impression on the gentleman's mind, than the raven's power of speech, and was indeed particularly adapted to his habits and capacity. He desired to have that done again, but despite his being very peremptory, and notwithstanding that Barnaby coaxed to the utmost, Grip turned a deaf ear to the request, and preserved a dead silence.

"Bring him along," said the gentleman, pointing to the house. But Grip, who had watched the action, anticipated his master, by

hopping on before them;—constantly flapping his wings, and screaming "cook!" meanwhile, as a hint perhaps that there was company
coming, and a small collation would be acceptable.

Barnaby and his mother walked on, on either side of the gentleman on horseback, who surveyed each of them from time to time in
a proud and coarse manner, and occasionally thundered out some
question, the tone of which alarmed Barnaby so much that he could
find no answer, and, as a matter of course, could make him no reply.
On one of these occasions, when the gentleman appeared disposed to
exercise his horsewhip, the widow ventured to inform him in a low
voice and with tears in her eyes, that her son was of weak mind.

"An idiot, eh?" said the gentleman, looking at Barnaby as he spoke.
"And how long hast thou been an idiot?"

"She knows," was Barnaby's timid answer, pointing to his mother
—"I—always, I believe."

"From his birth," said the widow.

"I don't believe it," cried the gentleman, "not a bit of it. It's an
excuse not to work. There's nothing like flogging to cure that disorder.
I'd make a difference in him in ten minutes, I'll be bound."

"Heaven has made none in more than twice ten years, sir," said
the widow mildly.

"Then why don't you shut him up? we pay enough for county
institutions, damn 'em. But thou'd rather drag him about to excite
charity—of course. Ay, I know thee."

Now, this gentleman had various endearing appellations among
his intimate friends. By some he was called "a country gentleman of
the true school," by some "a fine old country gentleman," by some "a
sporting gentleman," by some "a thorough-bred Englishman," by
some "a genuine John Bull;" but they all agreed in one respect, and
that was, that it was a pity there were not more like him, and that
because there were not, the country was going to rack and ruin every
day. He was in the commission of the peace, and could write his name
almost legibly; but his greatest qualifications were, that he was more
severe with poachers, was a better shot, a harder rider, had better
horses, kept better dogs, could eat more solid food, drink more strong
wine, go to bed every night more drunk and get up every morning
more sober, than any man in the county. In knowledge of horseflesh
he was almost equal to a farrier, in stable learning he surpassed his
own head groom, and in gluttony not a pig on his estate was a match
for him. He had no seat in Parliament himself, but he was extremely
patriotic, and usually drove his voters up to the poll with his own
hands. He was warmly attached to church and state, and never
appointed to the living in his gift any but a three-bottle man and a
first-rate fox-hunter. He mistrusted the honesty of all poor people
who could read and write, and had a secret jealousy of his own wife
(a young lady whom he had married for what his friends called "the
good old English reason," that her father's property adjoined his
own) for possessing those accomplishments in a greater degree than
himself. In short, Barnaby being an idiot, and Grip a creature of mere

brute instinct, it would be very hard to say what this gentleman was.

He rode up to the door of a handsome house approached by a great flight of steps, where a man was waiting to take his horse, and led the way into a large hall, which, spacious as it was, was tainted with the fumes of last night's stale debauch. Great-coats, riding-whips, bridles, top-boots, spurs, and such gear, were strewn about on all sides, and formed, with some huge stag's antlers, and a few portraits of dogs and horses, its principal embellishments.

Throwing himself into a great chair (in which, by the bye, he often snored away the night, when he had been, according to his admirers, a finer gentleman than usual) he bade the man to tell his mistress to come down: and presently there appeared, a little flurried, as it seemed, by the unwonted summons, a lady much younger than himself, who had the appearance of being in delicate health, and not too happy.

"Here! Thou'st no delight in following the hounds as an English-woman should have," said the gentleman. "See to this here. That'll please thee perhaps."

The lady smiled, sat down at a little distance from him, and glanced at Barnaby with a look of pity.

"He's an idiot, the woman says," observed the gentleman, shaking his head; "I don't believe it."

"Are you his mother?" asked the lady.

She answered yes.

"What's the use of asking *her?*" said the gentleman, thrusting his hands into his breeches pockets. "She'll tell thee so, of course. Most likely he's hired, at so much a day. There. Get on. Make him do something."

Grip having by this time recovered his urbanity, condescended, at Barnaby's solicitation, to repeat his various phrases of speech, and to go through the whole of his performances with the utmost success. The corks, and the never say die, afforded the gentleman so much delight that he demanded the repetition of this part of the entertainment, until Grip got into his basket, and positively refused to say another word, good or bad. The lady too, was much amused with him; and the closing point of his obstinacy so delighted her husband that he burst into a roar of laughter, and demanded his price.

Barnaby looked as though he didn't understand his meaning. Probably he did not.

"His price," said the gentleman, rattling the money in his pockets, "what dost want for him? How much?"

"He's not to be sold," replied Barnaby, shutting up the basket in a great hurry, and throwing the strap over his shoulder, "Mother, come away."

"Thou seest how much of an idiot he is, book-learner," said the gentleman, looking scornfully at his wife. "He can make a bargain. What dost want for him, old woman?"

"He is my son's constant companion," said the widow. "He is not to be sold, sir, indeed."

"Not to be sold!" cried the gentleman, growing ten times redder, hoarser, and louder than before. "Not to be sold!"

"Indeed no," she answered. "We have never thought of parting with him, sir, I do assure you."

He was evidently about to make a very passionate retort, when a few murmured words from his wife happening to catch his ear, he turned sharply round, and said, "Eh? What?"

"We can hardly expect them to sell the bird, against their own desire," she faltered. "If they prefer to keep him—"

"Prefer to keep him!" he echoed. "These people who go tramping about the country a-pilfering and vagabondising on all hands, prefer to keep a bird, when a landed proprietor and a justice asks his price! That old woman's been to school. I know she has. Don't tell me no," he roared to the widow, "I say, yes."

Barnaby's mother pleaded guilty to the accusation, and hoped there was no harm in it.

"No harm!" said the gentleman. "No. No harm. No harm, ye old rebel, not a bit of harm. If my clerk was here, I'd set ye in the stocks, I would, or lay ye in jail for prowling up and down, on the look-out for petty larcenies, ye limb of a gipsy. Here, Simon, put these pilferers out, shove 'em into the road, out with 'em! Ye don't want to sell the bird, ye that come here to beg, don't ye? If they an't out in double-quick, set the dogs upon 'em!"

They waited for no further dismissal, but fled precipitately, leaving the gentleman to storm away by himself (for the poor lady had already retreated), and making a great many vain attempts to silence Grip, who, excited by the noise, drew corks enough for a city feast as they hurried down the avenue, and appeared to congratulate himself beyond measure on having been the cause of the disturbance. When they had nearly reached the lodge, another servant, emerging from the shrubbery, feigned to be very active in ordering them off, but this man put a crown into the widow's hand, and whispering that his lady sent it, thrust them gently from the gate.

This incident only suggested to the widow's mind, when they halted at an alehouse some miles further on, and heard the justice's character as given by his friends, that perhaps something more than capacity of stomach and tastes for the kennel and the stable, were required to form either a perfect country gentleman, a thorough-bred Englishman, or a genuine John Bull; and that possibly the terms were sometimes misappropriated, not to say disgraced. She little thought then, that a circumstance so slight would ever influence their future fortunes; but time and experience enlightened her in this respect.

"Mother," said Barnaby, as they were sitting next day in a waggon which was to take them within ten miles of the capital, "we're going to London first, you said. Shall we see that blind man there?"

She was about to answer "Heaven forbid!" but checked herself, and told him No, she thought not; why did he ask?

"He's a wise man," said Barnaby, with a thoughtful countenance.

"I wish that we may meet with him again. What was it that he said of crowds? That gold was to be found where people crowded, and not among the trees and in such quiet places? He spoke as if he loved it; London is a crowded place; I think we shall meet him there."

"But why do you desire to see him, love?" she asked.

"Because," said Barnaby, looking wistfully at her, "he talked to me about gold, which is a rare thing, and say what you will a thing you would like to have, I know. And because he came and went away so strangely—just as white-headed old men come sometimes to my bed's foot in the night, and say what I can't remember when the bright day returns. He told me he'd come back. I wonder why he broke his word!"

"But you never thought of being rich or gay, before, dear Barnaby. You have always been contented."

He laughed and bade her say that again, then cried, "Ay ay—oh yes," and laughed once more. Then something passed that caught his fancy, and the topic wandered from his mind, and was succeeded by another just as fleeting.

But it was plain from what he had said, and from his returning to the point more than once that day, and on the next, that the blind man's visit, and indeed his words, had taken strong possession of his mind. Whether the idea of wealth had occurred to him for the first time on looking at the golden clouds that evening—and images were often presented to his thoughts by outward objects quite as remote and distant; or whether their poor and humble way of life had suggested it, by contrast, long ago; or whether the accident (as he would deem it) of the blind man's pursuing the current of his own remarks, had done so at the moment; or he had been impressed by the mere circumstance of the man being blind, and, therefore, unlike any one with whom he had talked before; it was impossible to tell. She tried every means to discover, but in vain; and the probability is that Barnaby himself was equally in the dark.

It filled her with uneasiness to find him harping on this string, but all that she could do was to lead him quickly to some other subject, and to dismiss it from his brain. To caution him against their visitor, to show any fear or suspicion in reference to him, would only be, she feared, to increase that interest with which Barnaby regarded him, and to strengthen his desire to meet him once again. She hoped, by plunging into the crowd, to rid herself of her terrible pursuer, and then, by journeying to a distance and observing increased caution, if that were possible, to live again unknown, in secrecy and peace.

They reached, in course of time, their halting-place within ten miles of London, and lay there for the night, after bargaining to be carried on for a trifle next day, in a light van which was returning empty, and was to start at five o'clock in the morning. The driver was punctual, the road good—save for the dust, the weather being very hot and dry—and at seven in the forenoon of Friday the second of June, one thousand seven hundred and eighty, they alighted at the foot of Westminster Bridge, bade their conductor farewell, and stood alone, together, on the scorching pavement. For the freshness which night sheds upon such busy thoroughfares had already departed, and the sun was shining with uncommon lustre.

CHAPTER XLVIII

UNCERTAIN where to go next, and bewildered by the crowd of people who were already astir, they sat down in one of the recesses on the bridge, to rest. They soon became aware that the stream of life was all pouring one way, and that a vast throng of persons were crossing the river from the Middlesex to the Surrey shore, in unusual haste and evident excitement. They were, for the most part, in knots of two or three, or sometimes half-a-dozen; they spoke little together—many of them were quite silent; and hurried on as if they had one absorbing object in view, which was common to them all.

They were surprised to see that nearly every man in this great concourse, which still came pouring past, without slackening in the least, wore in his hat a blue cockade; and that the chance passengers who were not so decorated, appeared timidly anxious to escape observation or attack, and gave them the wall as if they would conciliate them. This, however, was natural enough, considering their inferiority in point of numbers; for the proportion of those who were blue cockades, to those who were dressed as usual, was at least forty or fifty to one. There was no quarrelling, however: the blue cockades went swarming on, passing each other when they could, and making all the speed that was possible in such a multitude; and exchanged nothing more than looks, and very often not even those, with such of the passers-by as were not of their number.

At first, the current of people had been confined to the two pathways, and but a few more eager stragglers kept the road. But after half an hour or so, the passage was completely blocked up by the great press, which, being now closely wedged together, and impeded by the carts and coaches it encountered, moved but slowly, and was sometimes at a stand for five or ten minutes together.

After the lapse of nearly two hours, the numbers began to diminish visibly, and gradually dwindling away, by little and little, left the bridge quite clear, save that, now and then, some hot and dusty man, with the cockade in his hat, and his coat thrown over his shoulder, went panting by, fearful of being too late, or stopped to ask which way his friends had taken, and being directed, hastened on again like one refreshed. In this comparative solitude, which seemed quite strange and novel after the late crowd, the widow had for the first time an opportunity of inquiring of an old man who came and sat beside them, what was the meaning of that great assemblage.

"Why, where have you come from," he returned, "that you haven't heard of Lord George Gordon's great association? This is the day that he presents the petition against the Catholics, God bless him!"

"What have all these men to do with that?" she said.

"What have they to do with it!" the old man replied. "Why, how

you talk! Don't you know his lordship has declared he won't present
it to the house at all, unless it is attended to the door by forty
thousand good and true men at least? There's a crowd for you!''

"A crowd indeed!" said Barnaby. "Do you hear that, mother!"

"And they're mustering yonder, as I am told," resumed the old
man, "nigh upon a hundred thousand strong. Ah! Let Lord George
alone. He knows his power. There'll be a good many faces inside them
three windows over there," and he pointed to where the House of
Commons overlooked the river, "that'll turn pale when good Lord
George gets up this afternoon, and with reason too! Ay, ay. Let his
lordship alone. Let him alone. *He* knows!" And so, with much
mumbling and chuckling and shaking of his forefinger, he rose, with
the assistance of his stick, and tottered off.

"Mother!" said Barnaby, "that's a brave crowd he talks of.
Come!"

"Not to join it!" cried his mother.

"Yes, yes," he answered, plucking at her sleeve. "Why not?
Come!"

"You don't know," she urged, "what mischief they may do, where
they may lead you, what their meaning. Dear Barnaby, for my
sake—"

"For your sake!" he cried, patting her hand. "Well! It *is* for your
sake, mother. You remember what the blind man said, about the
gold. Here's a brave crowd! Come! Or wait till I come back—yes,
yes, wait here."

She tried with all the earnestness her fears engendered, to turn him
from his purpose, but in vain. He was stooping down to buckle on his
shoe, when a hackney-coach passed them rather quickly, and a voice
inside called to the driver to stop.

"Young man," said a voice within.

"Who's that?" cried Barnaby, looking up.

"Do you wear this ornament?" returned the stranger, holding out
a blue cockade.

"In Heaven's name, no. Pray do not give it him!" exclaimed the
widow.

"Speak for yourself, woman," said the man within the coach,
coldly. "Leave the young man to his choice; he's old enough to make
it, and to snap your apron-strings. He knows, without your telling,
whether he wears the sign of a loyal Englishman or not."

Barnaby, trembling with impatience, cried "Yes! yes, yes, I do,"
as he had cried a dozen times already. The man threw him a cockade,
and crying "Make haste to St. George's Fields," ordered the coachman to drive on fast; and left them.

With hands that trembled with his eagerness to fix the bauble in
his hat, Barnaby was adjusting it as he best could, and hurriedly
replying to the tears and entreaties of his mother, when two gentlemen passed on the opposite side of the way. Observing them, and
seeing how Barnaby was occupied, they stopped, whispered together
for an instant, turned back, and came over to them.

"Why are you sitting here?" said one of them, who was dressed in a plain suit of black, wore long lank hair, and carried a great cane. "Why have you not gone with the rest?"

"I am going, sir," replied Barnaby, finishing his task, and putting his hat on with an air of pride. "I shall be there directly."

"Say 'my lord,' young man, when his lordship does you the honour of speaking to you," said the second gentleman mildly. "If you don't know Lord George Gordon when you see him, it's high time you should."

"Nay, Gashford," said Lord George, as Barnaby pulled off his hat again and made him a low bow, "it's no great matter on a day like this, which every Englishman will remember with delight and pride. Put on your hat, friend, and follow us, for you lag behind and are late. It's past ten now. Didn't you know that the hour for assembling was ten o'clock?"

Barnaby shook his head and looked vacantly from one to the other.

"You might have known it, friend," said Gashford, "it was perfectly understood. How came you to be so ill informed!"

"He cannot tell you, sir," the widow interposed. "It's of no use to ask him. We are but this morning come from a long distance in the country, and know nothing of these matters."

"The cause has taken a deep root, and has spread its branches far and wide," said Lord George to his secretary. "This is a pleasant hearing. I thank Heaven for it!"

"Amen!" cried Gashford with a solemn face.

"You do not understand me, my lord," said the widow. "Pardon me, but you cruelly mistake my meaning. We know nothing of these matters. We have no desire or right to join in what you are about to do. This is my son, my poor afflicted son, dearer to me than my own life. In mercy's name, my lord, go your way alone, and do not tempt him into danger!"

"My good woman," said Gashford, "how can you!—Dear me!— What do you mean by tempting, and by danger? Do you think his lordship is a roaring lion, going about and seeking whom he may devour? God bless me!"

"No, no, my lord, forgive me," implored the widow, laying both her hands upon his breast, and scarcely knowing what she did, or said, in the earnestness of her supplication, "but there are reasons why you should hear my earnest, mother's prayer, and leave my son with me. Oh do. He is not in his right senses, he is not, indeed!"

"It is a bad sign of the wickedness of these times," said Lord George, evading her touch, and colouring deeply, "that those who cling to the truth and support the right cause, are set down as mad. Have you the heart to say this of your own son, unnatural mother!"

"I am astonished at you!" said Gashford, with a kind of meek severity. "This is a very sad picture of female depravity."

"He has surely no appearance," said Lord George, glancing at Barnaby, and whispering in his secretary's ear, "of being deranged? And even if he had, we must not construe any trifling peculiarity into madness. Which of us"—and here he turned red again—"would be safe, if that were made the law!"

"Not one," replied the secretary; "in that case, the greater the zeal, the truth, and talent; the more direct the call from above; the clearer would be the madness. With regard to this young man, my lord," he added, with a lip that slightly curled as he looked at Barnaby, who stood twirling his hat, and stealthily beckoning them to come away, "he is as sensible and self-possessed as any one I ever saw."

"And you desire to make one of this great body?" said Lord George, addressing him; "and intended to make one, did you?"

"Yes—yes," said Barnaby, with sparkling eyes. "To be sure I did! I told her so myself."

"I see," replied Lord George, with a reproachful glance at the unhappy mother. "I thought so. Follow me and this gentleman, and you shall have your wish."

Barnaby kissed his mother tenderly on the cheek, and bidding her be of good cheer, for their fortunes were both made now, did as he was desired. She, poor woman, followed too—with how much fear and grief it would be hard to tell.

They passed quickly through the Bridge-road, where the shops were all shut up (for the passage of the great crowd and the expectation of their return had alarmed the tradesmen for their goods and windows), and where, in the upper stories, all the inhabitants were congregated, looking down into the street below, with faces variously expressive of alarm, of interest, expectancy, and indignation. Some of these applauded, and some hissed; but regardless of these interruptions—for the noise of a vast congregation of people at a little distance, sounded in his ears, like the roaring of the sea—Lord George Gordon quickened his pace, and presently arrived before St. George's Fields.

They were really fields at that time, and of considerable extent. Here an immense multitude was collected, bearing flags of various kinds and sizes, but all of the same colour—blue, like the cockades—some sections marching to and fro in military array, and others drawn up in circles, squares, and lines. A large portion, both of the bodies which paraded the ground, and of those which remained stationary, were occupied in singing hymns or psalms. With whomsoever this originated, it was well done; for the sound of so many thousand voices in the air must have stirred the heart of any man within him, and could not fail to have a wonderful effect upon enthusiasts, however mistaken.

Scouts had been posted in advance of the great body, to give notice of their leader's coming. These falling back, the word was quickly passed through the whole host, and for a short interval there ensued a profound and deathlike silence, during which the mass was so still and quiet, that the fluttering of a banner caught the eye, and became a circumstance of note. Then they burst into a tremendous shout, into another, and another; and the air seemed rent and shaken, as if by the discharge of cannon.

"Gashford!" cried Lord George, pressing his secretary's arm tight within his own, and speaking with as much emotion in his voice, as in his altered face, "I am called indeed, now. I feel and know it. I am the leader of a host. If they summoned me at this moment with one voice to lead them on to death, I'd do it—Yes, and fall first myself!"

"It is a proud sight," said the secretary. "It is a noble day for England, and for the great cause throughout the world. Such homage, my lord, as I, an humble but devoted man, can render—"

"What are you doing?" cried his master, catching him by both hands; for he had made a show of kneeling at his feet. "Do not unfit me, dear Gashford, for the solemn duty of this glorious day—" the tears stood in the eyes of the poor gentleman as he said the words.— "Let us go among them; we have to find a place in some division for this new recruit—give me your hand."

Gashford slid his cold insidious palm into his master's grasp, and so, hand in hand, and followed still by Barnaby and by his mother too, they mingled with the concourse.

They had by this time taken to their singing again, and as their leader passed between their ranks, they raised their voices to their utmost. Many of those who were banded together to support the religion of their country, even unto death, had never heard a hymn or psalm in all their lives. But these fellows having for the most part strong lungs, and being naturally fond of singing, chanted any ribaldry or nonsense that occurred to them, feeling pretty certain that it would not be detected in the general chorus, and not caring much if it were. Many of these voluntaries were sung under the very nose of Lord George Gordon, who, quite unconscious of their burden, passed on with his usual stiff and solemn deportment, very much edified and delighted by the pious conduct of his followers.

So they went on and on, up this line, down that, round the exterior of this circle, and on every side of that hollow square; and still there were lines, and squares, and circles out of number to review. The day being now intensely hot, and the sun striking down his fiercest rays upon the field, those who carried heavy banners began to grow faint and weary; most of the number assembled were fain to pull off their neckcloths, and throw their coats and waistcoats open; and some, towards the centre, quite overpowered by the excessive heat, which was of course rendered more unendurable by the multitude around them, lay down upon the grass, and offered all they had about them for a drink of water. Still, no man left the ground, not even of those who were so distressed; still Lord George, streaming from every pore, went on with Gashford; and still Barnaby and his mother followed close behind them.

They had arrived at the top of a long line of some eight hundred men in single file, and Lord George had turned his head to look back, when a loud cry of recognition—in that peculiar and half-stifled tone which a voice has, when it is raised in the open air and in the midst of a great concourse of persons—was heard, and a man stepped with a shout of laughter from the rank, and smote Barnaby on the shoulders with his heavy hand.

"How now!" he cried. "Barnaby Rudge! Why, where have you been hiding for these hundred years?"

Barnaby had been thinking within himself that the smell of the trodden grass brought back his old days at cricket, when he was a young boy and played on Chigwell Green. Confused by this sudden and boisterous address, he stared in a bewildered manner at the man, and could scarcely say "What! Hugh!"

"Hugh!" echoed the other; "ay Hugh—Maypole Hugh! You remember my dog? He's alive now, and will know you, I warrant. What, you wear the colour, do you? Well done! Ha ha ha!"

"You know this young man, I see," said Lord George.

"Know him, my lord! as well as I know my own right hand. My captain knows him. We all know him."

"Will you take him into your division?"

"It hasn't in it a better, nor a nimbler, nor a more active man, than Barnaby Rudge," said Hugh. "Show me the man who says it has! Fall in, Barnaby. He shall march, my lord between me and Dennis; and he shall carry," he added, taking a flag from the hand of a tired man who tendered it, "the gayest silken streamer in this valiant army."

"In the name of God, no!" shrieked the widow, darting forward. "Barnaby—my lord—see—he'll come back—Barnaby—Barnaby!"

"Women in the field!" cried Hugh, stepping between them, and holding her off. "Holloa! My captain there!"

"What's the matter here?" cried Simon Tappertit, bustling up in a great heat. "Do you call this order?"

"Nothing like it, captain," answered Hugh, still holding her back with his outstretched hand. "It's against all orders. Ladies are carrying off our gallant soldiers from their duty. The word of command, captain! They're filing off the ground. Quick!"

"Close!" cried Simon, with the whole power of his lungs. "Form! March!"

She was thrown to the ground; the whole field was in motion; Barnaby was whirled away into the heart of a dense mass of men, and she saw him no more.

CHAPTER XLIX

THE mob had been divided from its first assemblage into four divisions; the London, the Westminster, the Southwark, and the Scotch. Each of these divisions being subdivided into various bodies, and these bodies being drawn up in various forms and figures, the general arrangement was, except to the few chiefs and leaders, as unintelligible as the plan of a great battle to the meanest soldier in the field. It was not without its method, however; for, in a very short space of time after being put in motion, the crowd had resolved itself into three great parties, and were prepared, as had been arranged, to cross the river by different bridges, and make for the House of Commons in separate detachments.

At the head of that division which had Westminster Bridge for its approach to the scene of action, Lord George Gordon took his post; with Gashford at his right hand, and sundry ruffians, of most unpromising appearance, forming a kind of staff about him. The conduct of a second party, whose route lay by Blackfriars, was entrusted to a committee of management, including perhaps a dozen men: while the third, which was to go by London Bridge, and through the main streets, in order that their numbers and their serious intentions might be the better known and appreciated by the citizens, were led by Simon Tappertit (assisted by a few subalterns, selected from the Brotherhood of United Bulldogs), Dennis the hangman, Hugh, and some others.

The word of command being given, each of these great bodies took the road assigned to it, and departed on its way, in perfect order and profound silence. That which went through the City greatly exceeded the others in number, and was of such prodigious extent that when the rear began to move, the front was nearly four miles in advance, notwithstanding that the men marched three abreast and followed very close upon each other.

At the head of this party, in the place where Hugh, in the madness of his humour, had stationed him, and walking between that dangerous companion and the hangman, went Barnaby; as many a man among the thousands who looked on that day afterwards remembered well. Forgetful of all other things in the ecstasy of the moment, his face flushed and his eyes sparkling with delight, heedless of the weight of the great banner he carried, and mindful only of its flashing in the sun and rustling in the summer breeze, on he went, proud, happy, elated past all telling:—the only light-hearted undesigning creature, in the whole assembly.

"What do you think of this?" asked Hugh, as they passed through the crowded streets, and looked up at the windows which were thronged with spectators. "They have all turned out to see our flags and streamers? Eh, Barnaby? Why, Barnaby's the greatest man of all the pack! His flag's the largest of the lot, the brightest too. There's nothing in the show like Barnaby. All eyes are turned on him. Ha ha ha!"

"Don't make that din, brother," growled the hangman, glancing with no very approving eyes at Barnaby as he spoke: "I hope he don't think there's nothing to be done but carrying that there piece of blue rag, like a boy at a breaking up. You're ready for action I hope, eh? You I mean," he added, nudging Barnaby roughly with his elbow. "What are you staring at? Why don't you speak?"

Barnaby had been gazing at his flag, and looked vacantly from his questioner to Hugh.

"He don't understand your way," said the latter. "Here, I'll explain it to him. Barnaby old boy, attend to me."

"I'll attend," said Barnaby, looking anxiously round; "but I wish I could see her somewhere."

"See who?" demanded Dennis in a gruff tone. "You an't in love I hope, brother? That an't the sort of thing for us, you know. We mustn't have no love here."

"She would be proud indeed to see me now, eh, Hugh?" said Barnaby. "Wouldn't it make her glad to see me at the head of this large show? She'd cry for joy, I know she would. Where *can* she be? She never sees me at my best, and what do I care to be gay and fine if *she's* not by?"

"Why, what palaver's this?" asked Mr. Dennis with supreme disdain. "We an't got no sentimental members among us, I hope."

"Don't be uneasy, brother," cried Hugh, "he's only talking of his mother."

"Of his what?" said Mr. Dennis with a strong oath.

"His mother."

"And I have combined myself with this here section, and turned out on this here memorable day, to hear men talk about their mothers!" growled Mr. Dennis with extreme disgust. "The notion of a man's sweetheart's bad enough, but a man's mother!"—and here his disgust was so extreme that he spat upon the ground, and could say no more.

"Barnaby's right," cried Hugh with a grin, "and I say it. Lookee, bold lad. If she's not here to see, it's because I've provided for her, and sent half-a-dozen gentlemen, every one of 'em with a blue flag (but not half as fine as yours), to take her, in state, to a grand house all hung round with gold and silver banners, and everything else you please, where she'll wait till you come, and want for nothing."

"Ay!" said Barnaby, his face beaming with delight: "have you indeed? That's a good hearing. That's fine! Kind Hugh!"

"But nothing to what will come, bless you," retorted Hugh, with a wink at Dennis, who regarded his new companion in arms with great astonishment.

"No, indeed?" cried Barnaby.

"Nothing at all," said Hugh. "Money, cocked hats and feathers, red coats and gold lace; all the fine things there are, ever were, or will be; will belong to us if we are true to that noble gentleman—the best man in the world—carry our flags for a few days, and keep 'em safe. That's all we've got to do."

"Is that all?" cried Barnaby with glistening eyes, as he clutched his pole the tighter; "I warrant you I keep this one safe, then. You have put it in good hands. You know me, Hugh. Nobody shall wrest this flag away."

"Well said!" cried Hugh. "Ha ha! Nobly said! That's the old stout Barnaby, that I have climbed and leaped with, many and many a day —I knew I was not mistaken in Barnaby.—Don't you see, man," he added in a whisper, as he slipped to the other side of Dennis, "that the lad's a natural, and can be got to do anything, if you take him in the right way. Letting alone the fun he is, he's worth a dozen men, in earnest, as you'd find if you tried a fall with him. Leave him to me. You shall soon see whether he's of use or not."

Mr. Dennis received these explanatory remarks with many nods and winks, and softened his behaviour towards Barnaby from that moment. Hugh, laying his finger on his nose, stepped back into his former place, and they proceeded in silence.

It was between two and three o'clock in the afternoon when the three great parties met at Westminster, and, uniting into one huge mass, raised a tremendous shout. This was not only done in token of their presence, but as a signal to those on whom the task devolved, that it was time to take possession of the lobbies of both Houses, and of the various avenues of approach, and of the gallery stairs. To the last-named place, Hugh and Dennis, still with their pupil between them, rushed straightway; Barnaby having given his flag into the hands of one of their own party, who kept them at the outer door. Their followers pressing on behind, they were borne as on a great wave to the very doors of the gallery, whence it was impossible to retreat, even if they had been so inclined, by reason of the throng which choked up the passages. It is a familiar expression in describing a great crowd, that a person might have walked upon the people's heads. In this case it was actually done; for a boy who had by some means got among the concourse, and was in imminent danger of suffocation, climbed to the shoulders of a man beside him and walked upon the people's hats and heads into the open street; traversing in his passage the whole length of two staircases and a long gallery. Nor was the swarm without less dense; for a basket which had been tossed into the crowd, was jerked from head to head, and shoulder to shoulder, and went spinning and whirling on above them, until it was lost to view, without ever once falling in among them or coming near the ground.

Through this vast throng, sprinkled doubtless here and there with honest zealots, but composed for the most part of the very scum and refuse of London, whose growth was fostered by bad criminal laws, bad prison regulations, and the worst conceivable police, such of the members of both Houses of Parliament as had not taken the precaution to be already at their posts, were compelled to fight and force their way. Their carriages were stopped and broken; the wheels wrenched off, the glasses shivered to atoms; the panels beaten in; drivers, footmen and masters, pulled from their seats and rolled in the mud. Lords, commoners, and reverend bishops, with little distinction of person or party, were kicked and pinched and hustled; passed from hand to hand through various stages of ill-usage; and sent to their fellow-senators at last with their clothes hanging in ribands about them, their bagwigs torn off, themselves speechless and breathless, and their persons covered with the powder which had been cuffed and beaten out of their hair. One lord was so long in the hands of the populace, that the Peers as a body resolved to sally forth and rescue him, and were in the act of doing so, when he happily appeared among them covered with dirt and bruises, and hardly to be recognised by those who knew him best. The noise and uproar were on the increase every moment. The air was filled with execrations, hoots and howlings. The mob raged and roared, like a mad monster as it was, unceasingly, and each new outrage served to swell its fury.

Within doors, matters were even yet more threatening. Lord George—preceded by a man who carried the immense petition on a porter's knot through the lobby to the door of the House of Commons, where it was received by two officers of the House who rolled it up to the table ready for presentation—had taken his seat at an early hour, before the Speaker went to prayers. His followers pouring in at the same time, the lobby and all the avenues were immediately filled, as we have seen. Thus the members were not only attacked in their passage through the streets, but were set upon within the very walls of Parliament; while the tumult, both within and without, was so great, that those who attempted to speak could scarcely hear their own voices: far less, consult upon the course it would be wise to take in such extremity, or animate each other to dignified and firm resistance. So sure as any member, just arrived, with dress disordered and dishevelled hair, came struggling through the crowd in the lobby, it yelled and screamed in triumph; and when the door of the House, partially and cautiously opened by those within for his admission, gave them a momentary glimpse of the interior, they grew more wild and savage, like beasts at the sight of prey, and made a rush against the portal which strained its locks and bolts in their staples, and shook the very beams.

The strangers' gallery, which was immediately above the door of the House, had been ordered to be closed on the first rumour of disturbance, and was empty; save that now and then Lord George took his seat there, for the convenience of coming to the head of the stairs which led to it, and repeating to the people what had passed within. It was on these stairs that Barnaby, Hugh, and Dennis were posted. There were two flights, short, steep, and narrow, running parallel to each other, and leading to two little doors communicating with a low passage which opened on the gallery. Between them was a kind of well, or unglazed skylight, for the admission of light and air into the lobby, which might be some eighteen or twenty feet below.

Upon one of these little staircases—not that at the head of which Lord George appeared from time to time, but the other—Gashford stood with his elbow on the banister, and his cheek resting on his hand, with his usual crafty aspect. Whenever he varied this attitude in the slightest degree—so much as by the gentlest motion of his arm—the uproar was certain to increase, not merely there, but in the lobby below; from which place no doubt, some man who acted as fugleman to the rest, was constantly looking up and watching him.

"Order!" cried Hugh, in a voice which made itself heard even above the roar and tumult, as Lord George appeared at the top of the staircase. "News! News from my lord!"

The noise continued notwithstanding his appearance, until Gashford looked round. There was silence immediately—even among the people in the passages without, and on the other staircases, who could neither see nor hear, but to whom, notwithstanding, the signal was conveyed with marvellous rapidity.

"Gentlemen," said Lord George, who was very pale and agitated, "we must be firm. They talk of delays, but we must have no delays. They talk of taking your petition into consideration next Tuesday, but we must have it considered now. Present appearances look bad for our success, but we must succeed and will!"

"We must succeed and will!" echoed the crowd. And so among their shouts and cheers and other cries, he bowed to them and retired, and presently came back again. There was another gesture from Gashford, and a dead silence directly.

"I am afraid," he said, this time, "that we have little reason, gentlemen, to hope for any redress from the proceedings of Parliament. But we must redress our own grievances, we must meet again, we must put our trust in Providence, and it will bless our endeavours."

This speech being a little more temperate than the last, was not so favourably received. When the noise and exasperation were at their height, he came back once more, and told them that the alarm had gone forth for many miles round; that when the King heard of their assembling together in that great body, he had no doubt, His Majesty would send down private orders to have their wishes complied with; and—with the manner of his speech as childish, irresolute, and uncertain as his matter—was proceeding in this strain, when two gentlemen suddenly appeared at the door where he stood, and pressing past him and coming a step or two lower down upon the stairs, confronted the people.

The boldness of this action quite took them by surprise. They were not the less disconcerted, when one of the gentlemen, turning to Lord George, spoke thus—in a loud voice that they might hear him well, but quite coolly and collectedly.

"You may tell these people, if you please, my lord, that I am General Conway of whom they have heard; and that I oppose this petition, and all their proceedings, and yours. I am a soldier, you may tell them, and I will protect the freedom of this place with my sword. You see, my lord, that the members of this House are all in arms to-day; you know that the entrance to it is a narrow one; you cannot be ignorant that there are men within these walls who are determined to defend that pass to the last, and before whom many lives must fall if your adherents persevere. Have a care what you do."

"And, my Lord George," said the other gentleman, addressing him in like manner, "I desire them to hear this, from me—Colonel Gordon—your near relation. If a man among this crowd, whose uproar strikes us deaf, crosses the threshold of the House of Commons, I swear to run my sword that moment—not into his, but into your body!"

With that, they stepped back again, keeping their faces towards the crowd; took each an arm of the misguided nobleman; drew him into the passage, and shut the door; which they directly locked and fastened on the inside.

This was so quickly done, and the demeanour of both gentlemen—who were not young men either—was so gallant and resolute, that the crowd faltered and stared at each other with irresolute and timid looks. Many tried to turn towards the door; some of the faintest-hearted cried they had best go back, and called to those behind to give way; and the panic and confusion were increasing rapidly, when Gashford whispered Hugh.

"What now!" Hugh roared aloud, turning towards them. "Why go back? Where can you do better than here, boys! One good rush against these doors and one below at the same time, will do the business. Rush on, then! As to the door below, let those stand back who are afraid. Let those who are not afraid, try who shall be the first to pass it. Here goes! Look out down there!"

Without the delay of an instant, he threw himself headlong over the banisters into the lobby below. He had hardly touched the ground when Barnaby was at his side. The chaplain's assistant, and some members who were imploring the people to retire, immediately withdrew; and then, with a great shout, both crowds threw themselves against the doors pell-mell, and besieged the House in earnest.

At that moment, when a second onset must have brought them into collision with those who stood on the defensive within, in which case great loss of life and bloodshed would inevitably have ensued,—the hindmost portion of the crowd gave way, and the rumour spread from mouth to mouth that a messenger had been despatched by water for the military, who were forming in the street. Fearful of sustaining a charge in the narrow passages in which they were so closely wedged together, the throng poured out as impetuously as they had flocked in. As the whole stream turned at once, Barnaby and Hugh went with it: and so, fighting and struggling and trampling on fallen men, and being trampled on in turn themselves, they and the whole mass floated by degrees into the open street, where a large detachment of the Guards, both horse and foot, came hurrying up; clearing the ground before them so rapidly that the people seemed to melt away as they advanced.

The word of command to halt being given, the soldiers formed across the street; the rioters, breathless and exhausted with their late exertions, formed likewise, though in a very irregular and disorderly manner. The commanding officer rode hastily into the open space between the two bodies, accompanied by a magistrate and an officer of the House of Commons, for whose accommodation a couple of troopers had hastily dismounted. The Riot Act was read, but not a man stirred.

In the first rank of the insurgents, Barnaby and Hugh stood side by side. Somebody had thrust into Barnaby's hands when he came out into the street, his precious flag; which, being now rolled up and tied round the pole, looked like a giant quarter-staff as he grasped it firmly and stood upon his guard. If ever man believed with his whole heart and soul that he was engaged in a just cause, and that he was bound to stand by his leader to the last, poor Barnaby believed it of himself and Lord George Gordon.

After an ineffectual attempt to make himself heard, the magistrate gave the word and the Horse Guards came riding in among the crowd. But, even then, he galloped here and there, exhorting the people to disperse; and, although heavy stones were thrown at the men, and some were desperately cut and bruised, they had no orders but to make prisoners of such of the rioters as were the most active, and to drive the people back with the flat of their sabres. As the horses came in among them, the throng gave way at many points, and the Guards, following up their advantage, were rapidly clearing the ground, when two or three of the foremost, who were in a manner cut off from the rest by the people closing round them, made straight towards Barnaby and Hugh, who had no doubt been pointed out as the two men who dropped into the lobby: laying about them now with some effect, and inflicting on the more turbulent of their opponents, a few slight flesh wounds, under the influence of which a man dropped, here and there, into the arms of his fellows, amid much groaning and confusion.

At the sight of gashed and bloody faces, seen for a moment in the crowd, then hidden by the press around them, Barnaby turned pale and sick. But he stood his ground, and grasping his pole more firmly yet, kept his eyes fixed upon the nearest soldier—nodding his head meanwhile, as Hugh, with a scowling visage, whispered in his ear.

The soldier came spurring on, making his horse rear as the people pressed about him, cutting at the hands of those who would have grasped his rein and forced his charger back, and waving to his comrades to follow—and still Barnaby, without retreating an inch, waited for his coming. Some called to him to fly, and some were in the very act of closing round him, to prevent his being taken, when the pole swept into the air above the people's heads, and the man's saddle was empty in an instant.

Then, he and Hugh turned and fled, the crowd opening to let them pass, and closing up again so quickly that there was no clue to the course they had taken. Panting for breath, hot, dusty, and exhausted with fatigue, they reached the river-side in safety, and getting into a boat with all despatch were soon out of any immediate danger.

As they glided down the river, they plainly heard the people cheering; and supposing they might have forced the soldiers to retreat, lay upon their oars for a few minutes, uncertain whether to return or not. But the crowd passing along Westminster Bridge, soon assured them that the populace were dispersing; and Hugh rightly guessed from this, that they had cheered the magistrate for offering to dismiss the military on condition of their immediate departure to their several homes, and that he and Barnaby were better where they were. He advised, therefore, that they should proceed to Black-friars, and, going ashore at the bridge, make the best of their way to The Boot; where there was not only good entertainment and safe lodging, but where they would certainly be joined by many of their late companions. Barnaby assenting, they decided on this course of action, and pulled for Blackfriars accordingly.

They landed at a critical time, and fortunately for themselves at the right moment. For, coming into Fleet-street, they found it in an unusual stir; and inquiring the cause, were told that a body of Horse Guards had just galloped past, and that they were escorting some rioters whom they had made prisoners, to Newgate for safety. Not at all ill-pleased to have so narrowly escaped the calvacade, they lost no more time in asking questions, but hurried to The Boot with as much speed as Hugh considered it prudent to make, without appearing singular or attracting an inconvenient share of public notice.

CHAPTER L

THEY were among the first to reach the tavern, but they had not been there many minutes, when several groups of men who had formed part of the crowd, came straggling in. Among them were Simon Tappertit and Mr. Dennis; both of whom, but especially the latter, greeted Barnaby with the utmost warmth, and paid him many compliments on the prowess he had shown.

"Which," said Dennis, with an oath, as he rested his bludgeon in a corner with his hat upon it, and took his seat at the same table with them, "it does me good to think of. There was a opportunity! But it led to nothing. For my part, I don't know what would. There's no spirit among the people in these here times. Bring something to eat and drink here. I'm disgusted with humanity."

"On what account?" asked Mr. Tappertit, who had been quenching his fiery face in a half-gallon can. "Don't you consider this a good beginning, mister?"

"Give me security that it an't a ending," rejoined the hangman. "When that soldier went down, we might have made London ours; but no;—we stand, and gape, and look on—the justice (I wish he had had a bullet in each eye, as he would have had, if we'd gone to work my way) says 'My lads, if you'll give me your word to disperse, I'll order off the military,'—our people sets up a hurrah, throws up the game with the winning cards in their hands, and skulks away like a pack of tame curs as they are. Ah," said the hangman, in a tone of deep disgust, "it makes me blush for my feller creeturs. I wish I had been born a ox, I do!"

"You'd have been quite as agreeable a character if you had been, I think," returned Simon Tappertit, going out in a lofty manner.

"Don't be too sure of that," rejoined the hangman, calling after him; "if I was a horned animal at the present moment, with the smallest grain of sense, I'd toss every man in this company, excepting them two," meaning Hugh and Barnaby, "for his manner of conducting himself this day."

With which mournful review of their proceedings, Mr. Dennis sought consolation in cold boiled beef and beer; but without at all relaxing the grim and dissatisfied expression of his face, the gloom of which was rather deepened than dissipated by their grateful influence.

The company who were thus libelled might have retaliated by

strong words, if not by blows, but they were dispirited and worn out. The greater part of them had fasted since morning; all had suffered extremely from the excessive heat; and between the day's shouting, exertion, and excitement, many had quite lost their voices, and so much of their strength that they could hardly stand. Then they were uncertain what to do next, fearful of the consequences of what they had done already, and sensible that after all they had carried no point, but had indeed left matters worse than they had found them. Of those who had come to The Boot, many dropped off within an hour; such of them as were really honest and sincere, never, after the morning's experience, to return, or to hold any communication with their late companions. Others remained but to refresh themselves, and then went home desponding; others who had theretofore been regular in their attendance, avoided the place altogether. The half-dozen prisoners whom the Guards had taken, were magnified by report into half-a-hundred at least; and their friends, being faint and sober, so slackened in their energy, and so drooped beneath these dispiriting influences, that by eight o'clock in the evening, Dennis, Hugh, and Barnaby, were left alone. Even they were fast asleep upon the benches, when Gashford's entrance roused them.

"Oh! you *are* here then?" said the secretary. "Dear me!"

"Why, where should we be, Muster Gashford!" Dennis rejoined as he rose into a sitting posture.

"Oh nowhere, nowhere," he returned with excessive mildness. "The streets are filled with blue cockades. I rather thought you might have been among them. I am glad you are not."

"You have orders for us, master, then?" said Hugh.

"Oh dear, no. Not I. No orders, my good fellow. What orders should I have? You are not in my service."

"Muster Gashford," remonstrated Dennis, "we belong to the cause, don't we?"

"The cause!" repeated the secretary, looking at him in a sort of abstraction. "There is no cause. The cause is lost."

"Lost!"

"Oh yes. You have heard, I suppose? The petition is rejected by a hundred and ninety-two, to six. It's quite final. We might have spared ourselves some trouble. That, and my lord's vexation, are the only circumstances I regret. I am quite satisfied in all other respects."

As he said this, he took a penknife from his pocket, and putting his hat upon his knee, began to busy himself in ripping off the blue cockade which he had worn all day; at the same time humming a psalm tune which had been very popular in the morning, and dwelling on it with a gentle regret.

His two adherents looked at each other, and at him, as if they were at a loss how to pursue the subject. At length Hugh, after some elbowing and winking between himself and Mr. Dennis, ventured to stay his hand, and to ask him why he meddled with that riband in his hat.

"Because," said the secretary, looking up with something between a snarl and a smile, "because to sit still and wear it, or to fall asleep and wear it, is a mockery. That's all, friend."

"What would you have us do, master!" cried Hugh.

"Nothing," returned Gashford, shrugging his shoulders, "nothing. When my lord was reproached and threatened for standing by you, I, as a prudent man, would have had you do nothing. When the soldiers were trampling you under their horses' feet, I would have had you do nothing. When one of them was struck down by a daring hand, and I saw confusion and dismay in all their faces, I would have had you do nothing—just what you did, in short. This is the young man who had so little prudence and so much boldness. Ah! I am sorry for him."

"Sorry, master!" cried Hugh.

"Sorry, Muster Gashford!" echoed Dennis.

"In case there should be a proclamation out to-morrow, offering five hundred pounds, or some such trifle, for his apprehension; and in case it should include another man who dropped into the lobby from the stairs above," said Gashford, coldly; "still, do nothing."

"Fire and fury, master!" cried Hugh, starting up. "What have we done, that you should talk to us like this!"

"Nothing," returned Gashford with a sneer. "If you are cast into prison; if the young man"—here he looked hard at Barnaby's attentive face—"is dragged from us and from his friends; perhaps from people whom he loves, and whom his death would kill; is thrown into jail, brought out and hanged before their eyes; still, do nothing. You'll find it your best policy, I have no doubt."

"Come on!" cried Hugh, striding towards the door. "Dennis—Barnaby—come on!"

"Where? To do what?" said Gashford, slipping past him, and standing with his back against it.

"Anywhere! Anything!" cried Hugh. "Stand aside, master, or the window will serve our turn as well. Let us out!"

"Ha ha ha! You are of such—of such an impetuous nature," said Gashford, changing his manner for one of the utmost good fellowship and the pleasantest raillery; "you are such an excitable creature—but you'll drink with me before you go?"

"Oh, yes—certainly," growled Dennis, drawing his sleeve across his thirsty lips. "No malice, brother. Drink with Muster Gashford!"

Hugh wiped his heated brow, and relaxed into a smile. The artful secretary laughed outright.

"Some liquor here! Be quick, or he'll not stop, even for that. He is a man of such desperate ardour!" said the smooth secretary, whom Mr. Dennis corroborated with sundry nods and muttered oaths. "Once roused, he is a fellow of such fierce determination!"

Hugh poised his sturdy arm aloft, and clapping Barnaby on the back, bade him fear nothing. They shook hands together—poor Barnaby evidently possessed with the idea that he was among the most virtuous and disinterested heroes in the world—and Gashford laughed again.

"I hear," he said smoothly, as he stood among them with a great measure of liquor in his hand, and filled their glasses as quickly and as often as they chose, "I hear—but I cannot say whether it be true or false—that the men who are loitering in the streets to-night are half disposed to pull down a Romish chapel or two, and that they only want leaders. I even heard mention of those in Duke-street, Lincoln's-Inn Fields, and in Warwick-street, Golden-square; but common report, you know—You are not going?"

"—To do nothing, master, eh?" cried Hugh. "No jails and halter for Barnaby and me. They must be frightened out of that. Leaders are wanted, are they? Now, boys!"

"A most impetuous fellow!" cried the secretary. "Ha ha! A courageous, boisterous, most vehement fellow! A man who—"

There was no need to finish the sentence, for they had rushed out of the house, and were far beyond hearing. He stopped in the middle of a laugh, listened, drew on his gloves, and, clasping his hands behind him, paced the deserted room for a long time, then bent his steps towards the busy town, and walked into the streets.

They were filled with people, for the rumour of that day's proceedings had made a great noise. Those persons who did not care to leave home, were at their doors or windows, and one topic of discourse prevailed on every side. Some reported that the riots were effectually put down; others that they had broken out again: some that Lord George Gordon had been sent under a strong guard to the Tower; others that an attempt had been made upon the King's life, that the soldiers had been again called out, and that the noise of musketry in a distant part of the town had been plainly heard within an hour. As it grew darker, these stories became more direful and mysterious; and often, when some frightened passenger ran past with tidings that the rioters were not far off, and were coming up, the doors were shut and barred, lower windows made secure, and as much consternation engendered, as if the city were invaded by a foreign army.

Gashford walked stealthily about, listening to all he heard, and diffusing or confirming, whenever he had an opportunity, such false intelligence as suited his own purpose; and, busily occupied in this way, turned into Holborn for the twentieth time, when a great many women and children came flying along the street—often panting and looking back—and the confused murmur of numerous voices struck upon his ear. Assured by these tokens, and by the red light which began to flash upon the houses on either side, that some of his friends were indeed approaching, he begged a moment's shelter at a door which opened as he passed, and running with some other persons to an upper window, looked out upon the crowd.

They had torches among them, and the chief faces were distinctly visible. That they had been engaged in the destruction of some building was sufficiently apparent, and that it was a Catholic place of worship was evident from the spoils they bore as trophies, which were easily recognisable for the vestments of priests, and rich fragments of altar furniture. Covered with soot, and dirt, and dust, and lime; their garments torn to rags; their hair hanging wildly about them; their hands and faces jagged and bleeding with the wounds of rusty nails; Barnaby, Hugh, and Dennis hurried on before them all, like hideous madmen. After them the dense throng came fighting on: some singing; some shouting in triumph; some quarrelling among themselves; some menacing the spectators as they passed; some with great wooden fragments, on which they spent their rage as if they had been alive, rending them limb from limb, and hurling the scattered morsels high into the air; some in a drunken state, unconscious of the hurts they had received from falling bricks, and stones, and beams; one borne upon a shutter, in the very midst, covered with a dingy cloth, a senseless, ghastly heap. Thus—a vision of coarse faces, with here and there a blot of flaring, smoky light; a dream of demon heads and savage eyes, and sticks and iron bars uplifted in the air, and whirled about; a bewildering horror, in which so much was seen, and yet so little, which seemed so long, and yet so short, in which there were so many phantoms, not to be forgotten all through life, and yet so many things that could not be observed in one distracting glimpse—it flitted onward, and was gone.

As it passed away upon its work of wrath and ruin, a piercing scream was heard. A knot of persons ran towards the spot; Gashford, who just then emerged into the street, among them. He was on the outskirts of the little concourse. and could not see or hear what passed within; but one who had a better place, informed him that a widow woman had descried her son among the rioters.

"Is that all?" said the secretary, turning his face homewards. "Well! I think this looks a little more like business!"

CHAPTER LI

PROMISING as these outrages were to Gashford's view, and much like business as they looked, they extended that night no farther. The soldiers were again called out, again they took half-a-dozen prisoners, and again the crowd dispersed after a short and bloodless scuffle. Hot and drunken though they were, they had not yet broken all bounds and set all law and government at defiance. Something of their habitual deference to the authority erected by society for its own preservation yet remained among them, and had its majesty been vindicated in time, the secretary would have had to digest a bitter disappointment.

By midnight, the streets were clear and quiet, and, save that there stood in two parts of the town a heap of nodding walls and piles of rubbish, where there had been at sunset a rich and handsome building, everything wore its usual aspect. Even the Catholic gentry and tradesmen, of whom there were many resident in different parts of the City and its suburbs, had no fear for their lives or property, and but little indignation for the wrong they had already sustained in the plunder and destruction of their temples of worship. An honest confidence in the government under whose protection they had lived for many years, and a well-founded reliance on the good feeling and right thinking of the great mass of the community, with whom, notwithstanding their religious differences, they were every day in habits of confidential, affectionate, and friendly intercourse, reassured them, even under the excesses that had been committed; and convinced them that they were Protestants in anything but the name, were no more to be considered as abettors of these disgraceful occurrences than they themselves were chargeable with the uses of the block, the rack, the gibbet, and the stake in cruel Mary's reign.

The clock was on the stroke of one, when Gabriel Varden, with his lady and Miss Miggs, sat waiting in the little parlour. This fact; the toppling wicks of the dull, wasted candles; the silence that prevailed; and, above all, the nightcaps of both maid and matron, were sufficient evidence that they had been prepared for bed some time ago, and had some reason for sitting up so far beyond their usual hour.

If any other corroborative testimony had been required, it would have been abundantly furnished in the actions of Miss Miggs, who, having arrived at that restless state and sensitive condition of the nervous system which are the result of long watching, did, by a constant rubbing and tweaking of her nose, a perpetual change of position (arising from sudden growth of imaginary knots and knobs in her chair), a frequent friction of her eyebrows, the incessant recurrence of a small cough, a small groan, a gasp, a sign, a sniff, a spasmodic start, and by other demonstrations of that nature, so file down and rasp, as it were, the patience of the locksmith, that after looking at her in silence for some time, he at last broke out into this apostrophe:—

"Miggs, my good girl, go to bed—do go to bed. You're really worse than the dripping of a hundred water-butts outside the window, or the scratching of as many mice behind the wainscot. I can't bear it. Do go to bed, Miggs. To oblige me—do."

"You haven't got nothing to untie, sir," returned Miss Miggs, "and therefore your requests does not surprise me. But missis has—and while you sit up, mim"—she added, turning to the locksmith's wife, "I couldn't, no, not if twenty times the quantity of cold water was aperiently running down my back at this moment, go to bed with a quiet spirit."

Having spoken these words, Miss Miggs made divers efforts to rub her shoulders in an impossible place, and shivered from head to foot; thereby giving the beholders to understand that the imaginery cascade was still in full flow, but that a sense of duty upheld her under that and all other sufferings, and nerved her to endurance.

Mrs. Varden being too sleepy to speak, and Miss Miggs having, as the phrase is, said her say, the locksmith had nothing for it but to sigh and be as quiet as he could.

But to be quiet with such a basilisk before him was impossible. If he looked another way, it was worse to feel that she was rubbing her cheek, or twitching her ear, or winking her eye, or making all kinds of extraordinary shapes with her nose, than to see her do it. If she was for a moment free from any of these complaints, it was only because of her foot being asleep, or of her arm having got the fidgets, or of her leg being doubled up with the cramp, or of some other horrible disorder which racked her whole frame. If she did enjoy a moment's ease, then with her eyes shut and her mouth wide open, she would be seen to sit very stiff and upright in her chair; then to nod a little way forward, and stop with a jerk; then to nod a little farther forward, and stop with another jerk; then to recover herself; then to come forward again—lower—lower—lower—by very slow degrees, until, just as it seemed impossible that she could preserve her balance for another instant, and the locksmith was about to call out in an agony, to save her from dashing down upon her forehead and fracturing her skull, then all of a sudden and without the smallest notice, she would come upright and rigid again with her eyes open, and in her countenance an expression of defiance, sleepy but yet most obstinate, which plainly said "I've never once closed 'em since I looked at you last, and I'll take my oath of it!"

At length, after the clock had struck two, there was a sound at the street door, as if somebody had fallen against the knocker by accident. Miss Miggs immediately jumping up and clapping her hands, cried with a drowsy mingling of the sacred and profane, "Ally Looyer, mim! there's Simmun's knock!"

"Who's there?" said Gabriel.

"Me!" cried the well-known voice of Mr. Tappertit. Gabriel opened the door, and gave him admission.

He did not cut a very insinuating figure, for a man of his stature suffers in a crowd; and having been active in yesterday morning's work, his dress was literally crushed from head to foot: his hat being beaten out of all shape, and his shoes trodden down at heel like slippers. His coat fluttered in strips about him, the buckles were torn away both from his knees and feet, half his neckerchief was gone, and the bosom of his shirt was rent to tatters. Yet notwithstanding all these personal disadvantages; despite his being very weak from heat and fatigue; and so begrimed with mud and dust that he might have been in a case, for anything of the real texture (either of his skin or apparel) that the eye could discern; he stalked haughtily into the parlour, and throwing himself into a chair, and endeavouring to thrust his hands into the pockets of his small-clothes, which were turned inside out and displayed upon his legs, like tassels, surveyed the household with a gloomy dignity.

"Simon," said the locksmith gravely, "how comes it that you return home at this time of night, and in this condition? Give me an assurance that you have not been among the rioters, and I am satisfied."

"Sir," replied Mr. Tappertit, with a contemptuous look, "I wonder at *your* assurance in making such demands."

"You have been drinking," said the locksmith.

"As a general principle, and in the most offensive sense of the words, sir," returned his journeyman with great self-possession, "I consider you a liar. In that last observation you have unintentionally —unintentionally, sir,—struck upon the truth."

"Martha," said the locksmith, turning to his wife, and shaking his head sorrowfully, while a smile at the absurd figure before him still played upon his open face, "I trust it may turn out that this poor lad is not the victim of the knaves and fools we have so often had words about, and who have done so much harm to-day. If he has been at Warwick-street or Duke-street to-night—"

"He has been at neither, sir," cried Mr. Tappertit in a loud voice, which he suddenly dropped into a whisper as he repeated, with eyes fixed upon the locksmith, "he has been at neither."

"I am glad of it, with all my heart," said the locksmith in a serious tone; "for if he had been, and it could be proved against him, Martha, your Great Association would have been to him the cart that draws men to the gallows and leaves them hanging in the air. It would, as sure as we're alive!"

Mrs. Varden was too much scared by Simon's altered manner and appearance, and by the accounts of the rioters which had reached her ears that night, to offer any retort, or to have recourse to her usual matrimonial policy. Miss Miggs wrung her hands, and wept.

"He was not at Duke-street, or at Warwick-street, G. Varden," said Simon, sternly; "but he *was* at Westminster. Perhaps, sir, he kicked a county member, perhaps, sir, he tapped a lord—you may stare, sir, I repeat it—blood flowed from noses, and perhaps he tapped a lord. Who knows? This," he added, putting his hand into his waistcoat-pocket, and taking out a large tooth, at the sight of which both Miggs and Mrs. Varden screamed, "this was a bishop's. Beware, G. Varden!"

"Now, I would rather," said the locksmith hastily, "have paid five hundred pounds, than had this come to pass. You idiot, do you know what peril you stand in?"

"I know it, sir," replied his journeyman, "and it is my glory. I was there, everybody saw me there. I was conspicuous, and prominent. I will abide the consequences."

The locksmith, really disturbed and agitated, paced to and fro in silence—glancing at his former 'prentice every now and then— and at length stopping before him, said:

"Get to bed, and sleep for a couple of hours that you make wake penitent, and with some of your senses about you. Be sorry for what you have done, and we will try to save you. If I call him by five o'clock," said Varden, turning hurriedly to his wife, "and he washes himself clean and changes his dress, he may get to the Tower Stairs, and away by the Gravesend tide-boat, before any search is made for him. From there he can easily get on to Canterbury, where your cousin will give him work till this storm has blown over. I am not sure that I do right in screening him from the punishment he deserves, but he has lived in this house, man and boy, for a dozen years, and I should be sorry if for this one day's work he made a miserable end.

Lock the front-door, Miggs, and show no light towards the street when you go up-stairs. Quick, Simon! Get to bed!"

"And do you suppose, sir," retorted Mr. Tappertit, with a thickness and slowness of speech which contrasted forcibly with the rapidity and earnestness of his kind-hearted master—"and do you suppose, sir, that I am base and mean enough to accept your servile proposition?—Miscreant!"

"Whatever you please, Sim, but get to bed. Every minute is of consequence. The light here, Miggs!"

"Yes, yes, oh do! Go to bed directly," cried the two women together.

Mr. Tappertit stood upon his feet, and pushing his chair away to show that he needed no assistance, answered, swaying himself to and fro, and managing his head as if it had no connection whatever with his body:

"You spoke of Miggs, sir—Miggs may be smothered!"

"Oh Simmun!" ejaculated that young lady in a faint voice. "Oh mim! Oh sir! Oh goodness gracious, what a turn he has given me!"

"This family may all be smothered, sir," returned Mr. Tappertit, after glancing at her with a smile of ineffable disdain, "excepting Mrs. V. I have come here, sir, for her sake, this night. Mrs. Varden, take this piece of paper. It's a protection, ma'am. You may need it."

With these words he held out at arm's length, a dirty crumpled scrap of writing. The locksmith took it from him, opened it, and read as follows:

"All good friends to our cause I hope will be particular, and do no injury to the property of any true Protestant. I am well asssured that the proprietor of this house is a staunch and worthy friend to the cause.

"GEORGE GORDON."

"What's this!" said the locksmith, with an altered face.

"Something that'll do you good service, young feller," replied his journeyman, "as you'll find. Keep that safe, and where you can lay your hand upon it in an instant. And chalk 'No Popery' on your door to-morrow night, and for a week to come—that's all."

"This is a genuine document," said the locksmith, "I know, for I have seen the hand before. What threat does it imply? What devil is abroad?"

"A fiery devil," retorted Sim; "a flaming, furious devil. Don't you put yourself in its way, or you're done for, my buck. Be warned in time, G. Varden. Farewell!"

But here the two women threw themselves in his way—especially Miss Miggs, who fell upon him with such fervour that she pinned him against the wall—and conjured him in moving words not to go forth till he was sober; to listen to reason; to think of it; to take some rest, and then determine.

"I tell you," said Mr. Tappertit, "that my mind is made up. My bleeding country calls me and I go! Miggs, if you don't get out of the way, I'll pinch you."

Miss Miggs, still clinging to the rebel, screamed once vociferously —but whether in the distraction of her mind, or because of his having executed his threat, is uncertain.

"Release me," said Simon, struggling to free himself from her chaste, but spider-like embrace. "Let me go! I have made arrangements for you in an altered state of society, and mean to provide for you comfortably in life—there! Will that satisfy you?"

"Oh Simmun!" cried Miss Miggs. "Oh my blessed Simmun! Oh mim! what are my feelings at this conflicting moment!"

Of a rather turbulent description, it would seem; for her nightcap had been knocked off in the scuffle, and she was on her knees upon the floor, making a strange revelation of blue and yellow curl-papers, straggling locks of hair, tags of staylaces, and strings of it's impossible to say what; panting for breath, clasping her hands, turning her eyes upwards, shedding abundance of tears, and exhibiting various other symptoms of the acutest mental suffering.

"I leave," said Simon, turning to his master, with an utter disregard of Miggs's maidenly affliction, "a box of things up-stairs. Do what you like with 'em. *I* don't want 'em. I'm never coming back here, any more. Provide yourself, sir, with a journeyman; I'm my country's journeyman; henceforward that's *my* line of business."

"Be what you like in two hours' time, but now go up to bed," returned the locksmith, planting himself in the doorway. "Do you hear me? Go to bed!"

"I hear you, and defy you, Varden," rejoined Simon Tappertit. "This night, sir, I have been in the country, planning an expedition which shall fill your bell-hanging soul with wonder and dismay. The plot demands my utmost energy. Let me pass!"

"I'll knock you down if you come near the door," replied the locksmith. "You had better go to bed!"

Simon made no answer, but gathering himself up as straight as he could, plunged head foremost at his old master, and the two went driving out into the workshop together, plying their hands and feet so briskly that they looked like half-a-dozen, while Miggs and Mrs. Varden screamed for twelve.

It would have been easy for Varden to knock his old 'prentice down, and bind him hand and foot; but as he was loth to hurt him in his then defenceless state, he contented himself with parrying his blows when he could, taking them in perfect good part when he could not, and keeping between him and the door, until a favourable opportunity should present itself for forcing him to retreat up-stairs, and shutting him up in his own room. But, in the goodness of his heart, he calculated too much upon his adversary's weakness, and forgot that drunken men who have lost the power of walking steadily, can often run. Watching his time, Simon Tappertit made a cunning show of falling back, staggered unexpectedly forward, brushed past him, opened the door (he knew the trick of that lock well), and darted down the street like a mad dog. The locksmith paused for a moment in the excess of his astonishment, and then gave chase.

It was an excellent season for a run, for at that silent hour the streets were deserted, the air was cool, and the flying figure before him distinctly visible at a great distance, as it sped away, with a long gaunt shadow following at its heels. But the short-winded locksmith had no chance against a man of Sim's youth and spare figure, though the day had been when he could have run him down in no time. The space between them rapidly increased, and as the rays of the rising sun streamed upon Simon in the act of turning a distant corner, Gabriel Varden was fain to give up, and sit down on a door-step to fetch his breath. Simon meanwhile, without once stopping, fled at the same degree of swiftness to The Boot, where, as he well knew, some of his company were lying, and at which respectable hostelry— for he had already acquired the distinction of being in great peril of the law—a friendly watch had been expecting him all night, and was even now on the look-out for his coming.

"Go thy ways, Sim, go thy ways," said the locksmith, as soon as he could speak. "I have done my best for thee, poor lad, and would have saved thee, but the rope is round thy neck, I fear."

So saying, and shaking his head in a very sorrowful and disconsolate manner, he turned back, and soon re-entered his own house, where Mrs. Varden and the faithful Miggs had been anxiously expecting his return.

Now Mrs. Varden (and by consequence Miss Miggs likewise) was impressed with a secret misgiving that she had done wrong; that she had, to the utmost of her small means, aided and abetted the growth of disturbances, the end of which it was impossible to foresee; that she had led remotely to the scene which had just passed; and that the locksmith's time for triumph and reproach had now arrived indeed. And so strongly did Mrs. Varden feel this, and so crestfallen was she in consequence, that while her husband was pursuing their lost journeyman, she secreted under her chair the little red-brick dwelling-house with the yellow roof, lest it should furnish new occasion for reference to the painful theme; and now hid the same still more, with the skirts of her dress.

But it happened that the locksmith had been thinking of this very article on his way home, and that, coming into the room and not seeing it, he at once demanded where it was.

Mrs. Varden had no resource but to produce it, which she did with many tears, and broken protestations that if she could have known—

"Yes, yes," said Varden, "of course—I know that. I don't mean to reproach you, my dear. But recollect from this time that all good things perverted to evil purposes, are worse than those which are naturally bad. A thoroughly wicked woman, is wicked indeed. When religion goes wrong, she is very wrong, for the same reason. Let us say no more about it, my dear."

So he dropped the red-brick dwelling-house on the floor, and setting his heel upon it, crushed it into pieces. The halfpence, and sixpences and other voluntary contributions, rolled about in all directions, but nobody offered to touch them, or to take them up.

"That," said the locksmith, "is easily disposed of, and I would to Heaven that everything growing out of the same society could be settled as easily."

"It happens very fortunately, Varden," said his wife, with her handkerchief to her eyes, "that in case any more disturbances should happen—which I hope not; I sincerely hope not—"

"I hope so too, my dear."

"—That in case any should occur, we have the piece of paper which that poor misguided young man brought."

"Ay, to be sure," said the locksmith, turning quickly round. "Where is that piece of paper?"

Mrs. Varden stood aghast as he took it from her out-stretched hand, tore it into fragments, and threw them under the grate.

"Not use it!" she said.

"Use it!" cried the locksmith. "No! Let them come and pull the roof about our ears; let them burn us out of house and home; I'd neither have the protection of their leader, nor chalk their howl upon my door, though, for not doing it, they shot me on my own threshold. Use it! Let them come and do their worst. The first man who crosses my door-step on such an errand as theirs, had better be a hundred miles away. Let him look to it. The others may have their will. I wouldn't beg or buy them off, if, instead of every pound of iron in the place, there was a hundred-weight of gold. Get you to bed, Martha. I shall take down the shutters and go to work."

"So early!" said his wife.

"Ay," replied the locksmith cheerily, "so early. Come when they may, they shall not find us skulking and hiding, as if we feared to take our portion of the light of day, and left it all to them. So pleasant dreams to you, my dear, and cheerful sleep!"

With that he gave his wife a hearty kiss, and bade her delay no longer, or it would be time to rise before she lay down to rest. Mrs. Varden quite amiably and meekly walked up-stairs, followed by Miggs, who, although a good deal subdued, could not refrain from sundry stimulative coughs and sniffs by the way, or from holding up her hands in astonishment at the daring conduct of master.

CHAPTER LII

A MOB is usually a creature of very mysterious existence, particularly in a large city. Where it comes from or whither it goes, few men can tell. Assembling and dispersing with equal suddenness, it is as difficult to follow to its various sources as the sea itself; nor does the parallel stop here, for the ocean is not more fickle and uncertain, more terrible when roused, more unreasonable, or more cruel.

The people who were boisterous at Westminster upon the Friday morning, and were eagerly bent upon the work of devastation in Duke-street and Warwick-street at night, were, in the mass, the same. Allowing for the chance accessions of which any crowd is morally sure in a town where there must always be a large number of idle and profligate persons, one and the same mob was at both places. Yet they spread themselves in various directions when they dispersed in the afternoon, made no appointment for re-assembling, had no definite purpose or design, and indeed, for anything they knew, were scattered beyond the hope of future union.

At The Boot, which, as has been shown, was in a manner the headquarters of the rioters, there were not, upon this Friday night, a dozen people. Some slept in the stable and outhouses, some in the common room, some two or three in beds. The rest were in their usual homes or haunts. Perhaps not a score in all lay in the adjacent fields and lanes, and under haystacks, or near the warmth of brick-kilns, who had not their accustomed place of rest beneath the open sky. As to the public ways within the town, they had their ordinary nightly occupants, and no others; the usual amount of vice and wretchedness, but no more.

The experience of one evening, however, had taught the reckless leaders of disturbance, that they had but to show themselves in the streets, to be immediately surrounded by materials which they could only have kept together when their aid was not required, at great risk, expense, and trouble. Once possessed of this secret, they were as confident as if twenty thousand men, devoted to their will, had been encamped about them, and assumed a confidence which could not have been surpassed, though that had really been the case. All day, Saturday, they remained quiet. On Sunday, they rather studied how to keep their men within call, and in full hope, than to follow out, by any fierce measure, their first day's proceedings.

"I hope," said Dennis, as, with a loud yawn, he raised his body from a heap of straw on which he had been sleeping, and supporting his head upon his hand, appealed to Hugh on Sunday morning, "that Muster Gashford allows some rest? Perhaps he'd have us at work again already, eh?"

"It's not his way to let matters drop, you may be sure of that," growled Hugh in answer. "I'm in no humour to stir yet, though. I'm as stiff as a dead body, and as full of ugly scratches as if I had been fighting all day yesterday with wild cats."

"You've so much enthusiasm, that's it," said Dennis, looking with great admiration at the uncombed head, matted beard, and torn hands and face of the wild figure before him; "you're such a devil of a fellow. You hurt yourself a hundred times more than you need, because you will be foremost in everything and will do more than the rest."

"For the matter of that," returned Hugh, shaking back his ragged hair and glancing towards the door of the stable in which they lay; "there's one yonder as good as me. What did I tell you about him? Did I say he was worth a dozen, when you doubted him?"

Mr. Dennis rolled lazily over upon his breast, and resting his chin upon his hand in imitation of the attitude in which Hugh lay, said, as he too looked towards the door:

"Ay, ay, you knew him, brother, you knew him. But who'd suppose to look at that chap now, that he could be the man he is! Isn't it a thousand cruel pities, brother, that instead of taking his nat'ral rest and qualifying himself for further exertions in this here *honourable* cause, he should be playing at soldiers like a boy? And his cleanliness too!" said Mr. Dennis, who certainly had no reason to entertain a fellow feeling with anybody who was particular on that score; "what weakness he's guilty of, with respect to his cleanliness. At five o'clock this morning, there he was at the pump, though any one would think he had gone through enough, the day before yesterday, to be pretty fast asleep at that time. But no—when I woke for a minute or two, there he was at the pump, and if you'd seen him sticking them peacock's feathers into his hat when he'd done washing —ah! I'm sorry he's such a imperfect character, but the best on us is incomplete in some pint of view or another."

The subject of this dialogue and of these concluding remarks, which were uttered in a tone of philosophical meditation, was, as the reader will have divined, no other than Barnaby, who, with his flag in his hand, stood sentry in the little patch of sunlight at the distant door, or walked to and fro outside, singing softly to himself, and keeping time to the music of some clear church bells. Whether he stood still, leaning with both hands on the flag-staff, or, bearing it upon his shoulder, paced slowly up and down, the careful arrangement of his poor dress, and his erect and lofty bearing, showed how high a sense he had of the great importance of his trust, and how happy and how proud it made him. To Hugh and his companion, who lay in a dark corner of the gloomy shed, he, and the sunlight, and the peaceful Sabbath sound to which he made response, seemed like a bright picture framed by the door, and set off by the stable's blackness. The whole formed such a contrast to themselves, as they lay wallowing, like some obscene animals, in their squalor and wickedness on the two heaps of straw, that for a few moments they looked on without speaking, and felt almost ashamed.

"Ah!" said Hugh at length, carrying it off with a laugh: "he's a rare fellow is Barnaby, and can do more, with less rest, or meat, or drink, than any of us. As to his soldiering, *I* put him on duty there."

"Then there was a object in it, and a proper good one too, I'll be sworn," retorted Dennis with a broad grin, and an oath of the same quality. "What's was it, brother?"

"Why, you see," said Hugh, crawling a little nearer to him, "that our noble captain yonder, came in yesterday morning rather the worse for liquor, and was—like you and me—ditto last night."

Dennis looked to where Simon Tappertit lay coiled upon a truss of hay, snoring profoundly, and nodded.

"And our noble captain," continued Hugh with another laugh, "our noble captain and I have planned for to-morrow a roaring expedition, with good profit in it."

"Again the Papists?" asked Dennis, rubbing his hands.

"Ay, against the Papists—against one of 'em at least, that some of us, and I for one, owe a good heavy grudge to."

"Not Muster Gashford's friend that he spoke to us about in my house, eh?" said Dennis, brimful of pleasant expectation.

"The same man," said Hugh.

"That's your sort," cried Mr. Dennis, gaily shaking hands with him, "that's the kind of game. Let's have revenges and injuries, and all that, and we shall get on twice as fast. Now you talk, indeed!"

"Ha ha ha! The captain," added Hugh, "has thoughts of carrying off a woman in the bustle, and—ha ha ha!—and so have I!"

Mr. Dennis received this part of the scheme with a wry face, observing that as a general principle he objected to women altogether, as being unsafe and slippery persons on whom there was no calculating with any certainty, and who were never in the same mind for four-and-twenty hours at a stretch. He might have expatiated on this suggestive theme at much greater length, but that it occurred to him to ask what connection existed between the proposed expedition and Barnaby's being posted at the stable-door as sentry; to which Hugh cautiously replied in these words:

"Why, the people we mean to visit, were friends of his, once upon a time, and I know that much of him to feel pretty sure that if he thought we were going to do them any harm, he'd be no friend to our side, but would lend a ready hand to the other. So I've persuaded him (for I know him of old) that Lord George has picked him out to guard this place to-morrow while we're away, and that it's a great honour—and so he's on duty now, and as proud of it as if he was a general. Ha ha! What do you say to me for a careful man as well as a devil of a one?"

Mr. Dennis exhausted himself in compliments, and then added, "But about the expedition itself—"

"About that," said Hugh, "you shall hear all particulars from me and the great captain conjointly and both together—for see, he's waking up. Rouse yourself, lion-heart. Ha ha! Put a good face upon it, and drink again. Another hair of the dog that bit you, captain! Call for drink! There's enough of gold and silver cups and candlesticks buried underneath my bed," he added, rolling back the straw, and pointing to where the ground was newly turned, "to pay for it, if it was a score of casks full. Drink, captain!"

Mr. Tappertit received these jovial promptings with a very bad grace, being much the worse, both in mind and body, for his two nights of debauch, and but indifferently able to stand upon his legs. With Hugh's assistance, however, he contrived to stagger to the pump; and having refreshed himself with an abundant draught of cold water, and a copious shower of the same refreshing liquid on his head and face, he ordered some rum and milk to be served; and upon that innocent beverage and some biscuits and cheese made a pretty hearty meal. That done, he disposed himself in an easy attitude on the ground beside his two companions (who were carousing after their own tastes), and proceeded to enlighten Mr. Dennis in reference to to-morrow's project.

That their conversation was an interesting one, was rendered manifest by its length, and by the close attention of all three. That it was
not of an oppressively grave character, but was enlivened by various
pleasantries arising out of the subject, was clear from their loud and
frequent roars of laughter, which startled Barnaby on his post, and
made him wonder at their levity. But he was not summoned to join
them, until they had eaten, and drunk, and slept, and talked together for some hours; not, indeed, until the twilight; when they informed him that they were about to make a slight demonstration in
the streets—just to keep the people's hands in, as it was Sunday
night, and the public might otherwise be disappointed—and that he
was free to accompany them if he would.

Without the slightest preparation, saving that they carried clubs
and wore blue cockade, they sallied out into the streets; and, with no
more settled design than that of doing as much mischief as they could,
paraded them at random. Their numbers rapidly increasing, they
soon divided into parties; and agreeing to meet by-and-by, in the
fields near Welbeck-street, scoured the town in various directions.
The largest body, and that which augmented with the greatest
rapidity, was the one to which Hugh and Barnaby belonged. This
took its way towards Moorfields, where there was a rich chapel, and in
which neighbourhood several Catholic families were known to reside.

Beginning with the private houses so occupied they broke open the
doors and windows; and while they destroyed the furniture and left
but the bare walls, made a sharp search for tools and engines of
destruction, such as hammers, pokers, axes, saws, and such-like
instruments. Many of the rioters made belts of cord, of handkerchiefs,
or any material they found at hand, and wore these weapons as
openly as pioneers upon a field-day. There was not the least disguise
or concealment—indeed, on this night, very little excitement or hurry.
From the chapels, they tore down and took away the very altars,
benches, pulpits, pews, and flooring; from the dwelling-houses, the
very wainscoting and stairs. This Sunday evening's recreation they
pursued like mere workmen who had a certain task to do, and did it.
Fifty resolute men might have turned them at any moment; a single
company of soldiers could have scattered them like dust; but no man
interposed, no authority restrained them, and, except by the terrified
persons who fled from their approach, they were as little heeded as if
they were pursuing their lawful occupations with the utmost sobriety
and good conduct.

In the same manner, they marched to the place of rendezvous
agreed upon, made great fires in the fields, and reserving the most
valuable of their spoils, burnt the rest. Priestly garments, images of
saints, rich stuffs and ornaments, altar-furniture and household goods,
were cast into the flames, and shed a glare on the whole country round;
but they danced and howled, and roared about these fires till they
were tired, and were never for an instant checked.

As the main body filed off from this scene of action and passed down Welbeck-street, they came upon Gashford, who had been a witness of their proceedings, and was walking stealthily along the pavement. Keeping up with him, and yet not seeming to speak, Hugh muttered in his ear:

"Is this better, master?"

"No," said Gashford. "It is not."

"What would you have?" said Hugh. "Fevers are never at their height at once. They must get on by degrees."

"I would have you," said Gashford, pinching his arm with such malevolence that his nails seemed to meet in the skin: "I would have you put some meaning into your work. Fools! Can you make no better bonfires than of rags and scraps! Can you burn nothing whole?"

"A little patience, master," said Hugh. "Wait but a few hours, and you shall see. Look for a redness in the sky to-morrow night."

With that, he fell back into his place beside Barnaby; and when the secretary looked after him, both were lost in the crowd.

CHAPTER LIII

THE next day was ushered in by merry peals of bells, and by the firing of the Tower guns; flags were hoisted on many of the church-steeples; the usual demonstrations were made in honour of the anniversary of the King's birthday; and every man went about his pleasure or business as if the city were in perfect order, and there were no half-smouldering embers in its secret places, which, on the approach of night, would kindle up again and scatter ruin and dismay abroad. The leaders of the riot, rendered still more daring by the success of last night and by the booty they had acquired, kept steadily together, and only thought of implicating the mass of their followers so deeply that no hope of pardon or reward might tempt them to betray their more notorious confederates into the hands of justice.

Indeed, the sense of having gone too far to be forgiven, held the timid together no less than the bold. Many who would readily have pointed out the foremost rioters and given evidence against them, felt that excape by that means was hopeless, when their every act had been observed by scores of people who had taken no part in the disturbances; who had suffered in their persons, peace, or property, by the outrages of the mob; who would be most willing witnesses; and whom the government would, no doubt, prefer to any King's evidence that might be offered. Many of this class had deserted their usual occupations on the Saturday morning; some had been seen by their employers active in the tumult; others knew they must be suspected, and that they would be discharged if they returned; others had been desperate from the beginning and comforted themselves with the homely proverb, that, being hanged at all, they might as well be hanged for a sheep as a lamb. They all hoped and believed, in a greater or less degree, that the government they seemed to have paralysed, would, in its terror, come to terms with them in the end, and suffer them to make their own conditions. The least sanguine among them reasoned with himself that, at the worst, they were too many all to be punished, and that he had as good a chance of escape as any other man. The great mass never reasoned or thought at all, but were stimulated by their own headlong passions, by poverty, by ignorance, by the love of mischief, and the hope of plunder.

One other circumstance is worthy of remark; and that is, that from the moment of their first outbreak at Westminster, every symptom of order or preconcerted arrangement among them vanished. When they divided into parties and ran to different quarters of the town, it was on the spontaneous suggestion of the moment. Each party swelled as it went along, like rivers as they roll towards the sea; new leaders sprang up as they were wanted, disappeared when the necessity was over, and reappeared at the next crisis. Each tumult took shape and form from the circumstances of the moment; sober workmen, going home from their day's labour, were seen to cast down their baskets of tools and become rioters in an instant; mere boys on errands did the like. In a word, a moral plague ran through the city. The noise, and hurry, and excitement, had for hundreds and hundreds an attraction they had no firmness to resist. The contagion spread like a dread fever; an infectious madness, as yet not near its height, seized on new victims every hour, and society began to tremble at their ravings.

It was between two and three o'clock in the afternoon when Gashford looked into the lair described in the last chapter, and seeing only Barnaby and Dennis there, inquired for Hugh.

He was out, Barnaby told him; had gone out more than an hour ago; and had not yet returned.

"Dennis!" said the smiling secretary, in his smoothest voice, as he sat down cross-legged on a barrel, "Dennis!"

The hangman struggled into a sitting posture directly, and with his eyes wide open, looked towards him.

"How do you do, Dennis?" said Gashford, nodding. "I hope you have suffered no inconvenience from your late exertions, Dennis?"

"I always will say of you, Muster Gashford," returned the hangman, staring at him, "that that 'ere quiet way of yours might almost wake a dead man. It is," he added, with a muttered oath—still staring at him in a thoughtful manner—"so awful sly!"

"So distinct, eh, Dennis?"

"Distinct!" he answered, scratching his head, and keeping his eyes upon the secretary's face; "I seem to hear it, Muster Gashford, in my wery bones."

"I am very glad your sense of hearing is so sharp, and that I succeed in making myself so intelligible," said Gashford, in his unvarying, even tone. "Where is your friend?"

Mr. Dennis looked round as in expectation of beholding him asleep upon his bed of straw; then remembering he had seen him go out, replied:

"I can't say where he is, Muster Gashford; I expected him back afore now. I hope it isn't time that we was busy, Muster Gashford?"

"Nay," said the secretary, "who should know that as well as you?

How can *I* tell you, Dennis? You are perfect master of your own actions, you know, and accountable to nobody—except sometimes to the law, eh?"

Dennis, who was very much baffled by the cool matter-of-course manner of this reply, recovered his self-possession on his professional pursuits being referred to, and pointing towards Barnaby, shook his head and frowned.

"Hush!" cried Barnaby.

"Ah! Do hush about that, Muster Gashford," said the hangman in a low voice, "pop'lar prejudices—you always forget—well, Barnaby, my lad, what's the matter."

"I hear him coming," he answered. "Hark! Do you mark that? That's his foot! Bless you, I know his step, and his dog's too. Tramp, tramp, pit-pat, on they come together, and, ha ha ha!—and here they are!" he cried, joyfully welcoming Hugh with both hands, and then patting him fondly on the back, as if instead of being the rough companion he was, he had been one of the most prepossessing of men. "Here he is, and safe too! I am glad to see him back again, old Hugh!"

"I'm a Turk if he don't give me a warmer welcome always than any man of sense," said Hugh, shaking hands with him with a kind of ferocious friendship, strange enough to see. "How are you, boy?"

"Hearty!" cried Barnaby, waving his hat. "Ha ha ha! And merry too, Hugh! And ready to do anything for the good cause, and the right, and to help the kind, mild, pale-faced gentleman—the lord they used so ill—eh, Hugh?"

"Ay!" returned his friend, dropping his hand and looking at Gashford for an instant with a changed expression before he spoke to him. "Good day, master!"

"And good day to you," replied the secretary, nursing his leg. "And many good days—whole years of them, I hope. You are heated."

"So would you have been, master," said Hugh, wiping his face, "if you'd been running here as fast as I have."

"You know the news, then? Yes, I supposed you would have heard it."

"News! what news?"

"You don't?" cried Gashford, raising his eyebrows with an exclamation of surprise. "Dear me! Come; then I *am* the first to make you acquainted with your distinguished position, after all. Do you see the King's Arms a-top?" he smilingly asked, as he took a large paper from his pocket, unfolded it, and held it out for Hugh's inspection.

"Well!" said Hugh. "What's that to me?"

"Much. A great deal," replied the secretary. "Read it."

"I told you, the first time I saw you, that I couldn't read," said Hugh, impatiently. "What in the Devil's name's inside of it?"

"It is a proclamation from the King in Council," said Gashford "dated to-day, and offering a reward of five hundred pounds—five hundred pounds is a great deal of money, and a large temptation to some people—to any one who will discover the person or persons most active in demolishing those chapels on Saturday night."

"Is that all?" cried Hugh, with an indifferent air. "I knew of that."

"Truly I might have known you did," said Gashford, smiling, and folding up the document again. "Your friend, I might have guessed—indeed I did guess—was sure to tell you."

"My friend!" stammered Hugh, with an unsuccessful effort to appear surprised. "What friend?"

"Tut tut—do you suppose I don't know where you have been?" retorted Gashford, rubbing his hands, and beating the back of one on the palm of the other, and looking at him with a cunning eye. "How dull you think me! Shall I say his name?"

"No," said Hugh, with a hasty glance towards Dennis.

"You have also heard from him, no doubt," resumed the secretary, after a moment's pause, "that the rioters who have been taken (poor fellows) are committed for trial, and that some very active witnesses have had the temerity to appear against them. Among others—" and here he clenched his teeth, as if he would suppress by force some violent words that rose upon his tongue; and spoke very slowly. "Among others, a gentleman who saw the work going on in Warwick-street; a Catholic gentleman; one Haredale."

Hugh would have prevented his uttering the word, but it was out already. Hearing the name, Barnaby turned swiftly round.

"Duty, duty, bold Barnaby!" cried Hugh, assuming his wildest and most rapid manner, and thrusting into his hand his staff and flag which leant against the wall. "Mount guard without loss of time, for we are off upon our expedition. Up, Dennis, and get ready! Take care that no one turns the straw upon my bed, brave Barnaby; we know what's underneath it—eh? Now, master, quick! What you have to say, say speedily, for the little captain and a cluster of 'em are in the fields, and only waiting for us. Sharp's the word, and strike's the action. Quick!"

Barnaby was not proof against this bustle and despatch. The look of mingled astonishment and anger which had appeared in his face when he turned towards them, faded from it as the words passed from his memory, like breath from a polished mirror; and grasping the weapon which Hugh forced upon him, he proudly took his station at the door, beyond their hearing.

"You might have spoiled our plans, master," said Hugh. "*You*, too, of all men!"

"Who would have supposed that *he* would be so quick?" urged Gashford.

"He's as quick sometimes—I don't mean with his hands, for that you know, but with his head—as you or any man," said Hugh. "Dennis, it's time we were going; they're waiting for us; I came to tell you. Reach me my stick and belt. Here! Lend a hand, master. Fling this over my shoulder, and buckle it behind, will you?"

"Brisk as ever!" said the secretary, adjusting it for him as he desired.

"A man need be brisk to-day; there's brisk work afoot."

"There is, is there?" said Gashford. He said it with such a provoking assumption of ignorance, that Hugh, looking over his shoulder and angrily down upon him, replied:

"Is there! You know there is! Who knows better than you, master, that the first great step to be taken is to make examples of these witnesses, and frighten all men from appearing against us or any of our body, any more?"

"There's one we know of," returned Gashford, with an expressive smile, "who is at least as well informed upon that subject as you or I."

"If we mean the same gentleman, as I suppose we do," Hugh rejoined softly, "I tell you this—he's as good and quick information about everything as"—here he paused and looked round, as if to make quite sure that the person in question was not within hearing—"as Old Nick himself. Have you done that, master? How slow you are!"

"It's quite fast now," said Gashford, rising. "I say—you didn't find that your friend disapproved of to-day's little expedition? Ha ha ha! It is fortunate it jumps so well with the witness's policy; for, once planned, it must have been carried out. And now you are going, eh?"

"Now we are going, master!" Hugh replied. "Any parting words?"

"Oh dear, no," said Gashford sweetly. "None!"

"You're sure?" cried Hugh, nudging the grinning Dennis.

"Quite sure, eh, Muster Gashford?" chuckled the hangman.

Gashford paused a moment, struggling with his caution and his malice; then putting himself between the two men, and laying a hand upon the arm of each, said, in a cramped whisper:

"Do not, my good friends—I am sure you will not—forget our talk one night—in your house, Dennis—about this person. No mercy, no quarter, no two beams of his house to be left standing where the builder placed them! Fire, the saying goes, is a good servant, but a bad master. Make it *his* master; he deserves no better. But I am sure you will be firm, I am sure you will be very resolute, I am sure you will remember that he thirsts for your lives, and those of all your brave companions. If you ever acted like staunch fellows, you will do so to-day. Won't you, Dennis—won't you, Hugh?"

The two looked at him, and at each other; then bursting into a roar of laughter, brandished their staves above their heads, shook hands, and hurried out.

When they had been gone a little time, Gashford followed. They were yet in sight, and hastening to that part of the adjacent fields in which their fellows had already mustered; Hugh was looking back, and flourishing his hat to Barnaby, who, delighted with his trust, replied in the same way, and then resumed his pacing up and down before the stable-door, where his feet had worn a path already. And when Gashford himself was far distant, and looked back for the last time, he was still walking to and fro, with the same measured tread; the most devoted and the blithest champion that ever maintained a post, and felt his heart lifted up with a brave sense of duty, and determination to defend it to the last.

Smiling at the simplicity of the poor idiot, Gashford betook himself to Welbeck-street by a different path from that which he knew the rioters would take, and sitting down behind a curtain in one of the upper windows of Lord George Gordon's house, waited impatiently for their coming. They were so long, that although he knew it had been settled they should come that way, he had a misgiving they must have changed their plans and taken some other route. But at length the roar of voices was heard in the neighbouring fields, and soon afterwards they came thronging past, in a great body.

However, they were not all, nor nearly all, in one body, but were, as he soon found, divided into four parties, each of which stopped before the house to give three cheers, and then went on; the leaders crying out in what direction they were going, and calling on the spectators to join them. The first detachment, carrying, by way of banners, some relics of the havoc they had made in Moorfields, proclaimed that they were on their way to Chelsea, whence they would return in the same order, to make of the spoil they bore, a great bonfire, near at hand. The second gave out that they were bound for Wapping, to destroy a chapel; the third, that their place of destination was East Smithfield, and their object the same. All this was done in broad, bright, summer day. Gay carriages and chairs stopped to let them pass, or turned back to avoid them; people on foot stood aside in doorways, or perhaps knocked and begged permission to stand at a window, or in the hall, until the rioters had passed: but nobody interfered with them; and when they had gone by, everything went on as usual.

There still remained the fourth body, and for that the secretary looked with a most intense eagerness. At last it came up. It was numerous, and composed of picked men; for as he gazed down among them, he recognised many upturned faces which he knew well—those of Simon Tappertit, Hugh, and Dennis in the front, of course. They halted and cheered, as the others had done; but when they moved again, they did not, like them, proclaim what design they had. Hugh merely raised his hat upon the bludgeon he carried, and glancing at a spectator on the opposite side of the way, was gone.

Gashford followed the direction of his glance instinctively, and saw, standing on the pavement, and wearing the blue cockade, Sir John Chester. He held his hat an inch or two above his head, to propitiate the mob; and, resting gracefully on his cane, smiling pleasantly, and displaying his dress and person to the very best advantage, looked on in the most tranquil state imaginable. For all that, and quick and dexterous as he was, Gashford had seen him recognise Hugh with the air of a patron. He had no longer any eyes for the crowd, but fixed his keen regards upon Sir John.

He stood in the same place and posture until the last man in the concourse had turned the corner of the street; then very deliberately took the blue cockade out of his hat; put it carefully in his pocket, ready for the next emergency; refreshed himself with a pinch of snuff; put up his box; and was walking slowly off, when a passing carriage stopped, and a lady's hand let down the glass. Sir John's hat was off again immediately. After a minute's conversation at the carriage-window, in which it was apparent that he was vastly entertaining on the subject of the mob, he stepped lightly in, and was driven away.

The secretary smiled, but he had other thoughts to dwell upon, and soon dismissed the topic. Dinner was brought him, but he sent it down untasted; and, in restless pacings up and down the room, and constant glances at the clock, and many futile efforts to sit down and read, or to go to sleep, or look out of the window, consumed four weary hours. When the dial told him thus much time had crept away, he stole up-stairs to the top of the house, and coming out upon the roof sat down, with his face towards the east.

Heedless of the fresh air that blew upon his heated brow, of the pleasant meadows from which he turned, of the piles of roofs and chimneys upon which he looked, of the smoke and rising mist he vainly sought to pierce, of the shrill cries of children at their evening sports, the distant hum and turmoil of the town, the cheerful country breath that rustled past to meet it, and to droop, and die; he watched, and watched, till it was dark—save for the specks of light that twinkled in the streets below and far away—and, as the darkness deepened, strained his gaze and grew more eager yet.

"Nothing but gloom in that direction, still!" he muttered restlessly. "Dog! where is the redness in the sky, you promised me!"

CHAPTER LIV

RUMOURS of the prevailing disturbances had, by this time, begun to be pretty generally circulated through the towns and villages round London, and the tidings were everywhere received with that appetite for the marvellous and love of the terrible which have probably been among the natural characteristics of mankind since the creation of the world. These accounts, however, appeared, to many persons at that day—as they would to us at the present, but that we know them to be a matter of history—so monstrous and improbable, that a great number of those who were resident at a distance, and who were credulous enough on the other points, were really unable to bring their minds to believe that such things could be; and rejected the intelligence they received on all hands, as wholly fabulous and absurd.

Mr. Willet—not so much, perhaps, on account of his having argued and settled the matter with himself, as by reason of his constitutional obstinacy—was one of those who positively refused to entertain the current topic for a moment. On this very evening, and perhaps at the very time when Gashford kept his solitary watch, old John was so red in the face with perpetually shaking his head in contradiction of his three ancient cronies and pot companions, that he was quite a phenomenon to behold, and lighted up the Maypole Porch wherein they sat together, like a monstrous carbuncle in a fairy tale.

"Do you think, sir," said Mr. Willet, looking hard at Solomon
Daisy—for it was his custom in cases of personal altercation to
fasten upon the smallest man in the party—"do you think, sir, that
I'm a born fool?"

"No, no, Johnny," returned Solomon, looking round upon the
little circle of which he formed a part: "we all know better than that.
You're no fool, Johnny. No, no!"

Mr. Cobb and Mr. Parkes shook their heads in unison, muttering,
"No, no, Johnny, not you!" But as such compliments had usually
the effect of making Mr. Willet rather more dogged than before, he
surveyed them with a look of deep disdain, and returned for answer:

"Then what do you mean by coming here, and telling me that this
evening you're a-going to walk up to London together—you three—
you—and have the evidence of your own senses? An't," said Mr.
Willet, putting his pipe in his mouth with an air of solemn disgust,
"an't the evidence of *my* senses enough for you?"

"But we haven't got it, Johnny," pleaded Parkes, humbly.

"You haven't got it, sir?" repeated Mr. Willet, eyeing him from
top to toe. "You haven't got it, sir? You *have* got it, sir. Don't I tell
you that His blessed Majesty King George the Third would no more
stand a rioting and rollicking in his streets, than he'd stand being
crowed over by his own Parliament?"

"Yes, Johnny, but that's your sense—not your senses," said the
adventurous Mr. Parkes.

"How do *you* know?" retorted John with great dignity. "You're a
contradicting pretty free, you are, sir. How do *you* know which it is?
I'm not aware I ever told you, sir."

Mr. Parkes finding himself in the position of having got into
metaphysics without exactly seeing his way out of them, stammered
forth an apology and retreated from the argument. There then
ensued a silence of some ten minutes or a quarter of an hour, at the
expiration of which period Mr. Willet was observed to rumble and
shake with laughter, and presently remarked, in reference to his late
adversary, "that he hoped he had tackled him enough." Thereupon
Messrs. Cobb and Daisy laughed, and nodded, and Parkes was
looked upon as thoroughly and effectually put down.

"Do you suppose if all this was true, that Mr. Haredale would be
constantly away from home, as he is?" said John, after another
silence. "Do you think he wouldn't be afraid to leave his house with
them two young women in it, and only a couple of men, or so?"

"Ay, but then you know," returned Solomon Daisy, "his house is
a goodish way out of London, and they do say that the rioters won't
go more than two mile, or three at the farthest, off the stones.
Besides, you know, some of the Catholic gentlefolks have actually
sent trinkets and such-like down here for safety—at least, so the
story goes."

"The story goes!" said Mr. Willet testily. "Yes, sir. The story goes
that you saw a ghost last March. But nobody believes it."

"Well!" said Solomon, rising, to divert the attention of his two friends, who tittered at this retort: "believed or disbelieved, it's true; and true or not, if we mean to go to London, we must be going at once. So shake hands, Johnny, and good night."

"I shall shake hands," returned the landlord, putting his into his pockets, "with no man as goes to London on such nonsensical errands."

The three cronies were therefore reduced to the necessity of shaking his elbows; having performed that ceremony, and brought from the house their hats, and sticks, and great-coats, they bade him good night and departed; promising to bring him on the morrow full and true accounts of the real state of the city, and if it were quiet, to give him the full merit of his victory.

John Willet looked after them, as they plodded along the road in the rich glow of a summer evening; and knocking the ashes out of his pipe, laughed inwardly at their folly, until his sides were sore. When he had quite exhausted himself—which took some time, for he laughed as slowly as he thought and spoke—he sat himself comfortably with his back to the house, put his legs upon the bench, then his apron over his face, and fell sound asleep.

How long he slept, matters not; but it was for no brief space, for when he awoke, the rich light had faded, the sombre hues of night were falling fast upon the landscape, and a few bright stars were already twinkling overhead. The birds were all at roost, the daisies on the green had closed their fairy hoods, the honeysuckle twining round the porch exhaled its perfume in a twofold degree, as though it lost its coyness at that silent time and loved to shed its fragrance on the night; the ivy scarcely stirred its deep green leaves. How tranquil, and how beautiful it was!

Was there no sound in the air, besides the gentle rustling of the trees and the grasshopper's merry chirp? Hark! Something very faint and distant, not unlike the murmuring in a sea-shell. Now it grew louder, fainter now, and now it altogether died away. Presently, it came again, subsided, came once more, grew louder, fainter—swelled into a roar. It was on the road, and varied with its windings. All at once it burst into a distinct sound—the voices, and the tramping feet of many men.

It is questionable whether old John Willet, even then, would have thought of the rioters but for the cries of his cook and housemaid, who ran screaming up-stairs and locked themselves into one of the old garrets,—shrieking dismally when they had done so, by way of rendering their place of refuge perfectly secret and secure. These two females did afterwards depone that Mr. Willet in his consternation uttered but one word, and called that up the stairs in a stentorian voice, six distinct times. But as this word was a monosyllable, which, however inoffensive when applied to the quadruped it denotes, is highly reprehensible when used in connection with females of unimpeachable character, many persons were inclined to believe that the young women laboured under some hallucination caused by excessive fear; and that their ears deceived them.

Be this as it may, John Willet, in whom the very uttermost extent of dull-headed perplexity supplied the place of courage, stationed himself in the porch, and waited for their coming up. Once, it dimly occurred to him that there was a kind of door to the house, which had a lock and bolts; and at the same time some shadowy ideas of shutters to the lower windows, flitted through his brain. But he stood stock still, looking down the road in the direction in which the noise was rapidly advancing, and did not so much as take his hands out of his pockets.

He had not to wait long. A dark mass, looming through a cloud of dust, soon became visible; the mob quickened their pace; shouting and whooping like savages, they came rushing on pell-mell; and in a few seconds he was bandied from hand to hand, in the heart of a crowd of men.

"Halloa!" cried a voice he knew, as the man who spoke came cleaving through the throng. "Where is he? Give him to me. Don't hurt him. How now, old Jack! Ha ha ha!"

Mr. Willet looked at him, and saw it was Hugh; but he said nothing, and thought nothing.

"These lads are thirsty and must drink!" cried Hugh, thrusting him back towards the house. "Bustle, Jack, bustle. Show us the best—the very best—the over-proof that you keep for your own drinking, Jack!"

John faintly articulated the words, "Who's to pay?"

"He says 'Who's to pay?'" cried Hugh, with a roar of laughter which was loudly echoed by the crowd. Then turning to John, he added, "Pay! Why, nobody."

John stared round at the mass of faces—some grinning, some fierce, some lighted up by torches, some indistinct, some dusky and shadowy: some looking at him, some at his house, some at each other —and while he was, as he thought, in the very act of doing so, found himself, without any consciousness of having moved, in the bar; sitting down in an arm-chair, and watching the destruction of his property, as if it were some queer play or entertainment, of an astonishing and stupefying nature, but having no reference to himself—that he could make out—at all.

Yes. Here was the bar—the bar that the boldest never entered without special invitation—the sanctuary, the mystery, the hallowed ground: here it was, crammed with men, clubs, sticks, torches, pistols; filled with a deafening noise, oaths, shouts, screams, hootings; changed all at once into a bear-garden, a madhouse, an infernal temple: men darting in and out, by door and window, smashing the glass, turning the taps, drinking liquor out of China punchbowls, sitting astride of casks, smoking private and personal pipes, cutting down the sacred grove of lemons, hacking and hewing at the cele- brated cheese, breaking open inviolable drawers, putting things in their pockets which didn't belong to them, dividing his own money before his own eyes, wantonly wasting, breaking, pulling down and tearing up: nothing quiet, nothing private: men everywhere—above, below, overhead, in the bedrooms, in the kitchen, in the yard, in the stables—clambering in at windows when there were doors wide open; dropping out of windows when the stairs were handy; leaping over the banisters into chasms of passages: new faces and figures presenting themselves every instant—some yelling, some singing, some fighting, some breaking glass and crockery, some laying the dust with the liquor they couldn't drink, some ringing the bells till they pulled them down, others beating them with pokers till they beat them into fragments: more men still—more, more, more— swarming on like insects: noise, smoke, light, darkness, frolic, anger, laughter, groans, plunder, fear, and ruin!

Nearly all the time while John looked on at this bewildering scene, Hugh kept near him; and though he was the loudest, wildest, most destructive villain there, he saved his old master's bones a score of times. Nay, even when Mr. Tappertit, excited by liquor, came up, and in assertion of his prerogative politely kicked John Willet on the shins, Hugh bade him return the compliment; and if old John had had sufficient presence of mind to understand this whispered direction, and to profit by it, he might no doubt, under Hugh's protection, have done so with impunity.

At length the band began to re-assemble outside the house, and to call to those within, to join them, for they were losing time. These murmurs increasing, and attaining a high pitch, Hugh, and some of those who yet lingered in the bar, and who plainly were the leaders of the troop, took counsel together, apart, as to what was to be done with John, to keep him quiet until their Chigwell work was over. Some proposed to set the house on fire and leave him in it; others, that he should be reduced to a state of temporary insensibility, by knocking on the head; others, that he should be sworn to sit where he was until to-morrow at the same hour; others again, that he should be gagged and taken off with them, under a sufficient guard. All these propositions being overruled, it was concluded, at last, to bind him in his chair, and the word was passed for Dennis.

"Look'ee here, Jack!" said Hugh, striding up to him: "We are going to tie you, hand and foot, but otherwise you won't be hurt. D'ye hear?"

John Willet looked at another man, as if he didn't know which was the speaker, and muttered something about an ordinary every Sunday at two o'clock.

"You won't be hurt I tell you, Jack—do you hear me?" roared Hugh, impressing the assurance upon him by means of a heavy blow on the back. "He's so dead scared, he's woolgathering, I think. Give him a drop of something to drink here. Hand over, one of you."

A glass of liquor being passed forward, Hugh poured the contents down old John's throat. Mr. Willet feebly smacked his lips, thrust his hand into his pocket, and inquired what was to pay; adding, as he looked vacantly round, that he believed there was a trifle of broken glass—

"He's out of his senses for the time, it's my belief," said Hugh, after shaking him, without any visible effect upon his system, until his keys rattled in his pocket.

"Where's that Dennis?"

The word was again passed, and presently Mr. Dennis, with a long cord bound about his middle, something after the manner of a friar, came hurrying in, attended by a body-guard of half-a-dozen of his men.

"Come! Be alive here!" cried Hugh, stamping his foot upon the ground. "Make haste!"

Dennis, with a wink and a nod, unwound the cord from about his person, and raising his eyes to the ceiling, looked all over it, and round the walls and cornice, with a curious eye; then shook his head.

"Move, man, can't you!" cried Hugh, with another impatient stamp of his foot. "Are we to wait here, till the cry has gone for ten miles round, and our work's interrupted?"

"It's all very fine talking, brother," answered Dennis, stepping towards him; "but unless"—and here he whispered in his ear—"unless we do it over the door, it can't be done at all in this here room."

"What can't?" Hugh demanded.

"What can't!" retorted Dennis. "Why, the old man can't."

"Why, you weren't going to hang him!" cried Hugh.

"No, brother?" returned the hangman with a stare. "What else?"

Hugh made no answer, but snatching the rope from his companion's hand, proceeded to bind old John himself; but his very first move was so bungling and unskilful, that Mr. Dennis entreated, almost with tears in his eyes, that he might be permitted to perform the duty. Hugh consenting, he achieved it in a twinkling.

"There," he said, looking mournfully at John Willet, who displayed no more emotion in his bonds than he had shown out of them. "That's what I call pretty and workmanlike. He's quite a picter now. But, brother, just a word with you—now that he's ready trussed, as one may say, wouldn't it be better for all parties if we was to work him off? It would read uncommon well in the newspapers, it would indeed. The public would think a great deal more on us!"

Hugh, inferring what his companion meant, rather from his gestures than his technical mode of expressing himself (to which, as he was ignorant of his calling, he wanted the clue), rejected this proposition for the second time, and gave the word "Forward!" which was echoed by a hundred voices from without.

"To the Warren!" shouted Dennis as he ran out, followed by the rest. "A witness's house, my lads!"

A loud yell followed, and the whole throng hurried off, mad for pillage and destruction. Hugh lingered behind for a few moments to stimulate himself with more drink, and to set all the taps running, a few of which had accidentally been spared; then, glancing round the despoiled and plundered room, through whose shattered window the rioters had thrust the Maypole itself,—for even that had been sawn down,—lighted a torch, clapped the mute and motionless John Willet on the back, and waving his light above his head, and uttering a fierce shout, hastened after his companions.

CHAPTER LV

JOHN WILLET, left alone in his dismantled bar, continued to sit staring about him; awake as to his eyes, certainly, but with all his powers of reason and reflection in a sound and dreamless sleep. He looked round upon the room which had been for years, and was within an hour ago, the pride of his heart; and not a muscle of his face was moved. The night, without, looked black and cold through the dreary gaps in the casement; the precious liquids, now nearly leaked away, dripped with a hollow sound upon the floor; the Maypole peered ruefully in through the broken window, like the bowsprit of a wrecked ship; the ground might have been the bottom of the sea, it was so strewn with precious fragments. Currents of air rushed in, as the old doors jarred and creaked upon their hinges; the candles flickered and guttered down, and made long winding-sheets; the cheery deep-red curtains flapped and fluttered idly in the wind; even the stout Dutch kegs, overthrown and lying empty in dark corners, seemed the mere husks of good fellows whose jollity had departed, and who could kindle with a friendly glow no more. John saw this desolation, and yet saw it not. He was perfectly contented to sit there, staring at it, and felt no more indignation or discomfort in his bonds than if they had been robes of honour. So far as he was personally concerned, old Time lay snoring, and the world stood still.

Save for the dripping from the barrels, the rustling of such light fragments of destruction as the wind affected, and the dull creaking of the open doors, all was profoundly quiet: indeed, these sounds, like the ticking of the death-watch in the night, only made the silence they invaded deeper and more apparent. But quiet or noisy, it was all one to John. If a train of heavy artillery could have come up and commenced ball practice outside the window, it would have been all the same to him. He was a long way beyond surprise. A ghost couldn't have overtaken him.

By and by he heard a footstep—a hurried, and yet cautious footstep—coming on towards the house. It stopped, advanced again, then seemed to go quite round it. Having done that, it came beneath the window, and a head looked in.

It was strongly relieved against the darkness outside by the glare of the guttering candles. A pale, worn, withered face; the eyes—but that was owing to its gaunt condition—unnaturally large and bright; the hair, a grizzled black. It gave a searching glance all round the room, and a deep voice said:

"Are you alone in this house?"

John made no sign, though the question was repeated twice, and he heard it distinctly. After a moment's pause, the man got in at the window. John was not at all surprised at this, either. There had been so much getting in and out of window in the course of the last hour or so, that he had quite forgotten the door, and seemed to have lived among such exercises from infancy.

The man wore a large, dark, faded cloak, and a slouched hat; he walked up close to John, and looked at him. John returned the compliment with interest.

"How long have you been sitting thus?" said the man.

John considered, but nothing came of it.

"Which way have the party gone?"

Some wandering speculations relative to the fashion of the stranger's boots, got into Mr. Willet's mind by some accident or other, but they got out again in a hurry, and left him in his former state.

"You would do well to speak," said the man: "you may keep a whole skin, though you have nothing else left that can be hurt. Which way have the party gone?"

"That!" said John, finding his voice all at once, and nodding with perfect good faith—he couldn't point; he was so tightly bound—in exactly the opposite direction to the right one.

"You lie!" said the man angrily, and with a threatening gesture. "I came that way. You would betray me."

It was so evident that John's imperturbability was not assumed, but was the result of the late proceedings under his roof, that the man stayed his hand in the very act of striking him, and turned away.

John looked after him without so much as a twitch in a single nerve of his face. He seized a glass, and holding it under one of the little casks until a few drops were collected, drank them greedily off; then throwing it down upon the floor impatiently, he took the vessel in his hands and drained it into his throat. Some scraps of bread and meat were scattered about, and on these he fell next; eating them with voracity, and pausing every now and then to listen for some fancied noise outside. When he had refreshed himself in this manner with violent haste, and raised another barrel to his lips, he pulled his hat upon his brow as though he were about to leave the house, and turned to John.

"Where are your servants?"

Mr. Willet indistinctly remembered to have heard the rioters calling to them to throw the key of the room in which they were, out of window, for their keeping. He therefore replied, "Locked up."

"Well for them if they remain quiet, and well for you if you do the like," said the man. "Now show me the way the party went."

This time Mr. Willet indicated it correctly. The man was hurrying to the door, when suddenly there came towards them on the wind, the loud and rapid tolling of an alarm-bell, and then a bright and vivid glare streamed up, which illumined, not only the whole chamber, but all the country.

It was not the sudden change from darkness to this dreadful light, it was not the sound of distant shrieks and shouts of triumph, it was not this dread invasion of the serenity and peace of night, that drove the man back as though a thunderbolt had struck him. It was the Bell. If the ghastliest shape the human mind has ever pictured in its wildest dreams had risen up before him, he could not have staggered backward from its touch, as he did from the first sound of that loud iron voice. With eyes that started from his head, his limbs convulsed, his face most horrible to see, he raised one arm high up into the air, and holding something visionary back and down, with his other hand, drove at it as though he held a knife and stabbed it to the heart. He clutched his hair, and stopped his ears, and travelled madly round and round; then gave a frightful cry, and with it rushed away: still, still, the Bell tolled on and seemed to follow him—louder and louder, hotter and hotter yet. The glare grew brighter, the roar of voices deeper; the crash of heavy bodies falling, shook the air; bright streams of sparks rose up into the sky; but louder than them all—rising faster far, to Heaven—a million times more fierce and furious—pouring forth dreadful secrets after its long silence—speaking the language of the dead—the Bell—the Bell!

What hunt of spectres could surpass that dread pursuit and flight! Had there been a legion of them on his track, he could have better borne it. They would have had a beginning and an end, but here all space was full. The one pursuing voice was everywhere: it sounded in the earth, the air; shook the long grass, and howled among the trembling trees. The echoes caught it up, the owls hooted as it flew upon the breeze; the nightingale was silent and hid herself among the thickest boughs: it seemed to goad and urge the angry fire, and lash it into madness; everything was steeped in one prevailing red; the glow was everywhere; nature was drenched in blood: still the remorseless crying of that awful voice—the Bell, the Bell!

It ceased; but not in his ears. The knell was at his heart. No work of man had ever voice like that which sounded there, and warned him that it cried unceasingly to Heaven. Who could hear that bell, and not know what it said! There was murder in its every note—cruel, relentless, savage murder—the murder of a confiding man, by one who held his every trust. Its ringing summoned phantoms from their graves. What face was that, in which a friendly smile changed to a look of half incredulous horror, which stiffened for a moment into one of pain, then changed again into an imploring glance at Heaven, and so fell idly down with upturned eyes, like the dead stags' he had often peeped at when a little child: shrinking and shuddering—there was a dreadful thing to think of now!—and clinging to an apron as he looked! He sank upon the ground, and grovelling down as if he would dig himself a place to hide in, covered his face and ears; but no, no, no,—a hundred walls and roofs of brass would not shut out that bell, for in it spoke the wrathful voice of God, and from that voice, the whole wide universe could not afford a refuge!

While he rushed up and down, not knowing where to turn, and while he lay crouching there, the work went briskly on indeed. When they left the Maypole, the rioters formed into a solid body, and advanced at a quick pace towards the Warren. Rumour of their approach having gone before, they found the garden-doors fast closed, the windows made secure, and the house profoundly dark: not a light being visible in any portion of the building. After some fruitless ringing at the bells, and beating at the iron gates, they drew off a few paces to reconnoitre, and confer upon the course it would be best to take.

Very little conference was needed, when all were bent upon one desperate purpose infuriated with liquor, and flushed with successful riot. The word being given to surround the house, some climbed the gates, or dropped into the shallow trench and scaled the garden wall, while others pulled down the solid iron fence, and while they made a breach to enter by, made deadly weapons of the bars. The house being completely encircled, a small number of men were despatched to break open a tool-shed in the garden; and during their absence on this errand, the remainder contented themselves with knocking violently at the doors, and calling to those within, to come down and open them on peril of their lives.

No answer being returned to this repeated summons, and the detachment who had been sent away, coming back with an accession of pickaxes, spades, and hoes, they,—together with those who had such arms already, or carried (as many did) axes, poles, and crow-bars,—struggled into the foremost rank, ready to beset the doors and windows. They had not at this time more than a dozen lighted torches among them; but when these preparations were completed, flaming links were distributed and passed from hand to hand with such rapidity, that, in a minute's time, at least two-thirds of the whole roaring mass bore, each man in his hand, a blazing brand. Whirling these about their heads they raised a loud shout, and fell to work upon the doors and windows.

Amidst the clattering of heavy blows, the rattling of broken glass, the cries and execrations of the mob, and all the din and turmoil of the scene, Hugh and his friends kept together at the turret-door where Mr. Haredale had last admitted him and old John Willet; and spent their united force on that. It was a strong old oaken door, guarded by good bolts and a heavy bar, but it soon went crashing in upon the narrow stairs behind, and made, as it were, a platform to facilitate their tearing up into the rooms above. Almost at the same moment, a dozen other points were forced, and at every one the crowd poured in like water.

A few armed servant-men were posted in the hall, and when the rioters forced an entrance there, they fired some half-a-dozen shots. But these taking no effect, and the concourse coming on like an army of devils, they only thought of consulting their own safety, and retreated, echoing their assailants' cries, and hoping in the confusion to be taken for rioters themselves; in which stratagem they succeeded, with the exception of one old man who was never heard of again, and was said to have had his brains beaten out with an iron bar (one of his fellows reported that he had seen the old man fall), and to have been afterwards burnt in the flames.

The besiegers being now in complete possession of the house, spread themselves over it from garret to cellar, and plied their demon labours fiercely. While some small parties kindled bonfires under-neath the windows, others broke up the furniture and cast the frag-ments down to feed the flames below; where the apertures in the wall (windows no longer) were large enough, they threw out tables, chests of drawers, beds, mirrors, pictures, and flung them whole into the fire; while every fresh addition to the blazing masses was received with shouts, and howls, and yells, which added new and dismal terrors to the conflagration. Those who had axes and had spent their fury on the movables, chopped and tore down the doors and window frames, broke up the flooring, hewed away the rafters, and buried men who lingered in the upper rooms, in heaps of ruins. Some searched the drawers, the chests, the boxes, writing-desks, and closets, for jewels, plate, and money; while others, less mindful of gain and more mad for destruction, cast their whole contents into the court-yard without examination, and called to those below, to heap them on the blaze. Men who had been into the cellars, and had staved the casks, rushed to and fro stark mad, setting fire to all they saw—often to the dresses of their own friends—and kindling the building in so many parts that some had no time for escape, and were seen, with drooping hands and blackened faces, hanging senseless on the window-sills to which they had crawled, until they were sucked and drawn into the burning gulf. The more the fire crackled and raged, the wilder and more cruel the men grew; as though moving in that element they became fiends, and changed their earthly nature for the qualities that give delight in hell.

The burning pile, revealing rooms and passages red hot, through gaps made in the crumbling walls; the tributary fires that licked the outer bricks and stones, with their long forked tongues, and ran up to meet the glowing mass within; the shining of the flames upon the villains who looked on and fed them; the roaring of the angry blaze, so bright and high that it seemed in its rapacity to have swallowed up the very smoke; the living flakes the wind bore rapidly away and hurried on with, like a storm of fiery snow; the noiseless breaking of great beams of wood, which fell like feathers on the heap of ashes, and crumbled in the very act to sparks and powder; the lurid tinge that overspread the sky, and the darkness, very deep by contrast, which prevailed around; the exposure to the coarse, common gaze, of every little nook which usages of home had made a sacred place, and the destruction by rude hands of every little household favourite which old associations made a dear and precious thing: all this taking place—not among pitying looks and friendly murmurs of compassion, but brutal shouts and exultations, which seemed to make the very rats who stood by the old house too long, creatures with some claim upon the pity and regard of those its roof had sheltered:—combined to form a scene never to be forgotten by those who saw it and were not actors in the work, so long as life endured.

And who were they? The alarm-bell rang—and it was pulled by no faint or hesitating hands—for a long time; but not a soul was seen. Some of the insurgents said that when it ceased, they heard the shrieks of women, and saw some garments fluttering in the air, as a party of men bore away no unresisting burdens. No one could say that this was true or false, in such an uproar; but where was Hugh? Who among them had seen him, since the forcing of the doors? The cry spread through the body. Where was Hugh!

"Here!" he hoarsely cried, appearing from the darkness; out of breath, and blackened with the smoke. "We have done all we can; the fire is burning itself out; and even the corners where it hasn't spread, are nothing but heaps of ruins. Disperse, my lads, while the coast's clear; get back by different ways; and meet as usual!" With that, he disappeared again,—contrary to his wont, for he was always first to advance, and last to go away,—leaving them to follow homewards as they would.

It was not an easy task to draw off such a throng. If Bedlam gates had been flung open wide, there would not have issued forth such maniacs as the frenzy of that night had made. There were men there, who danced and trampled on the beds of flowers as though they trod down human enemies, and wrenched them from the stalks, like savages who twisted human necks. There were men who cast their lighted torches in the air, and suffered them to fall upon their heads and faces, blistering the skin with deep unseemly burns. There were men who rushed up to the fire, and paddled in it with their hands as if in water; and others who were restrained by force from plunging in, to gratify their deadly longing. On the skull of one drunken lad— not twenty, by his looks—who lay upon the ground with a bottle to his mouth, the lead from the roof came streaming down in a shower of liquid fire, white hot; melting his head like wax. When the scattered parties were collected, men—living yet, but singed as with hot irons —were plucked out of the cellars, and carried off upon the shoulders of others, who strove to wake them as they went along, with ribald jokes, and left them, dead, in the passages of hospitals. But of all the howling throng not one learnt mercy from, nor sickened at, these sights; nor was the fierce, besotted, senseless rage of one man glutted.

Slowly, and in small clusters, with hoarse hurrahs and repetitions of their usual cry, the assembly dropped away. The last few red-eyed stragglers reeled after those who had gone before; the distant noise of men calling to each other, and whistling for others whom they missed, grew fainter and fainter; at length even these sounds died away, and silence reigned alone.

Silence indeed! The glare of the flames had sunk into a fitful, flashing light; and the gentle stars, invisible till now, looked down upon the blackening heap. A dull smoke hung upon the ruin, as though to hide it from those eyes of Heaven; and the wind forbore to move it. Bare walls, roof open to the sky—chambers, where the beloved dead had, many and many a fair day, risen to new life and energy; where so many dear ones had been sad and merry; which were connected with so many thoughts and hopes, regrets and changes—all gone. Nothing left but a dull and dreary blank—a smouldering heap of dust and ashes—the silence and solitude of utter desolation.

CHAPTER LVI

THE Maypole cronies, little dreaming of the change so soon to come upon their favourite haunt, struck through the Forest path upon their way to London; and avoiding the main road, which was hot and dusty, kept to the by-paths and the fields. As they drew nearer to their destination, they began to make inquiries of the people whom they passed, concerning the riots, and the truth or falsehood of the stories they had heard. The answers went far beyond any intelligence that had spread to quiet Chigwell. One man told them that that afternoon the Guards, conveying to Newgate some rioters who had been re-examined, had been set upon by the mob and compelled to retreat; another, that the houses of two witnesses near Clare Market were about to be pulled down when he came away; another, that Sir George Saville's house in Leicester Fields was to be burned that night, and that it would go hard with Sir George if he fell into the people's hands, as it was he who had brought in the Catholic bill. All accounts agreed that the mob were out in stronger numbers and more numerous parties than had yet appeared; that the streets were unsafe; that no man's house or life was worth an hour's purchase; that the public consternation was increasing every moment; and that many families had already fled the city. One fellow who wore the popular colour, damned them for not having cockades in their hats, and bade them set a good watch to-morrow night upon their prison doors, for the locks would have a straining; another asked if they were fire-proof, that they walked abroad without the distinguishing mark of all good and true men; and a third who rode on horseback, and was quite alone, ordered them to throw each man a shilling, in his hat, towards the support of the rioters. Although they were afraid to refuse compliance with this demand, and were much alarmed by these reports, they agreed, having come so far, to go forward, and see the real state of things with their own eyes. So they pushed on quicker, as men do who are excited by portentous news; and ruminating on what they had heard, spoke little to each other.

It was now night, and as they came nearer to the city they had dismal confirmation of this intelligence in three great fires, all close together, which burnt fiercely and were gloomily reflected in the sky. Arriving in the immediate suburbs, they found that almost every house had chalked upon its door in large characters "No Popery," that the shops were shut, and that alarm and anxiety were depicted in every face they passed.

Noting these things with a degree of apprehension which neither of the three cared to impart, in its full extent, to his companions, they came to a turnpike-gate, which was shut. They were passing through the turnstile on the path, when a horseman rode up from London at a hard gallop, and called to the toll-keeper in a voice of great agitation, to open quickly in the name of God.

The adjuration was so earnest and vehement, that the man, with a lantern in his hand, came running out—toll-keeper though he was—and was about to throw the gate open, when happening to look behind him, he exclaimed, "Good Heaven, what's that! Another fire!"

At this, the three turned their heads, and saw in the distance—straight in the direction whence they had come—a broad sheet of flame, casting a threatening light upon the clouds, which glimmered as though the conflagration were behind them, and showed like a wrathful sunset.

"My mind misgives me," said the horseman, "or I know from what far building those flames come. Don't stand aghast, my good fellow. Open the gate!"

"Sir," cried the man, laying his hand upon his horse's bridle as he let him through: "I know you now, sir; be advised by me; do not go on. I saw them pass, and know what kind of men they are. You will be murdered."

"So be it!" said the horseman, looking intently towards the fire, and not at him who spoke.

"But, sir—sir," cried the man, grasping at his rein more tightly yet, "if you do go on, wear the blue riband. Here, sir," he added, taking one from his own hat, "it's necessity, not choice, that makes me wear it; it's love of life and home, sir. Wear it for this one night, sir; only for this one night."

"Do!" cried the three friends, pressing round his horse. "Mr. Haredale—worthy sir—good gentleman—pray be persuaded."

"Who's that?" cried Mr. Haredale, stooping down to look. "Did I hear Daisy's voice?"

"You did, sir," cried the little man. "Do be persuaded, sir. This gentleman says very true. Your life may hang upon it."

"Are you," said Mr. Haredale abruptly, "afraid to come with me?"

"I, sir?—N-n-no."

"Put that riband in your hat. If we meet the rioters, swear that I took you prisoner for wearing it. I will tell them so with my own lips; for as I hope for mercy when I die, I will take no quarter from them, nor shall they have quarter from me, if we come hand to hand to-night. Up here—behind me—quick! Clasp me tight round the body, and fear nothing."

In an instant they were riding away, at full gallop, in a dense cloud of dust, and speeding on, like hunters in a dream.

It was well the good horse knew the road he traversed, for never once—no, never once in all the journey—did Mr. Haredale cast his eyes upon the ground, or turn them, for an instant, from the light towards which they sped so madly. Once he said in a low voice "It *is* my house," but that was the only time he spoke. When they came to dark and doubtful places, he never forgot to put his hand upon the little man to hold him more securely in his seat, but he kept his head erect and his eyes fixed on the fire, then, and always.

The road was dangerous enough, for they went the nearest way—headlong—far from the highway—by lonely lanes and paths, where waggon-wheels had worn deep ruts; where hedge and ditch hemmed in the narrow strip of ground; and tall trees, arching over head, made it profoundly dark. But on, on, on, with neither stop nor stumble, till they reached the Maypole door, and could plainly see that the fire began to fade, as if for want of fuel.

"Down—for one moment—for but one moment," said Mr. Haredale, helping Daisy to the ground, and following himself. "Willet—Willet—where are my niece and servants—Willet!"

Crying to him distractedly, he rushed into the bar.—The landlord bound and fastened to his chair; the place dismantled, stripped, and pulled about his ears;—nobody could have taken shelter here.

He was a strong man, accustomed to restrain himself, and suppress his strong emotions; but this preparation for what was to follow—though he had seen that fire burning, and knew that his house must be razed to the ground—was more than he could bear. He covered his face with his hands for a moment, and turned away his head.

"Johnny, Johnny," said Solomon—and the simple-hearted fellow cried outright, and wrung his hands—"Oh dear old Johnny, here's a change! That the Maypole bar should come to this, and we should live to see it! The old Warren too, Johnny—Mr. Haredale—oh, Johnny, what a piteous sight this is!"

Pointing to Mr. Haredale as he said these words, little Solomon Daisy put his elbows on the back of Mr. Willet's chair, and fairly blubbered on his shoulder.

While Solomon was speaking, old John sat, mute as a stock-fish, staring at him with an unearthly glare, and displaying, by every possible symptom, entire and complete unconsciousness. But when Solomon was silent again, John followed, with his great round eyes, the direction of his looks, and did appear to have some dawning distant notion that somebody had come to see him.

"You know us, don't you, Johnny?" said the little clerk, rapping himself on the breast. "Daisy, you know—Chigwell Church—bell-ringer—little desk on Sundays—eh, Johnny?"

Mr. Willet reflected for a few moments, and then muttered, as it were mechanically: "Let us sing to the praise and glory of—"

"Yes, to be sure," cried the little man, hastily; "that's it—that's me, Johnny. You're all right now, an't you? Say you're all right, Johnny."

"All right?" pondered Mr. Willet, as if that were a matter entirely between himself and his conscience. "All right? Ah!"

"They haven't been misusing you with sticks, or pokers, or any other blunt instruments—have they, Johnny?" asked Solomon, with a very anxious glance at Mr. Willet's head. "They didn't beat you, did they?"

John knitted his brow; looked downwards, as if he were mentally engaged in some arithmetical calculation; then upwards, as if the total would not come at his call; then at Solomon Daisy, from his eyebrow to his shoe-buckle; then very slowly round the bar. And then a great, round, leaden-looking, and not at all transparent tear, came rolling out of each eye, and he said, as he shook his head:

"If they'd only had the goodness to murder me, I'd have thanked 'em kindly."

"No, no, no, don't say that, Johnny," whimpered his little friend. "It's very, very bad, but not quite so bad as that. No, no!"

"Look'ee here, sir!" cried John, turning his rueful eyes on Mr. Haredale, who had dropped on one knee, and was hastily beginning to untie his bonds. "Look'ee here, sir! The very Maypole—the old dumb Maypole—stares in at the winder, as if it said, 'John Willet, John Willet, let's go and pitch ourselves in the nighest pool of water as is deep enough to hold us; for our day is over!'"

"Don't, Johnny, don't," cried his friend: no less affected with this mournful effort of Mr. Willet's imagination, than by the sepulchral tone in which he had spoken of the Maypole. "Please don't, Johnny!"

"Your loss is great, and your misfortune a heavy one," said Mr. Haredale, looking restlessly towards the door: "and this is not a time to comfort you. If it were, I am in no condition to do so. Before I leave you, tell me one thing, and try to tell me plainly. I implore you. Have you seen, or heard of Emma?"

"No!" said Mr. Willet.

"Nor any one but these bloodhounds?"

"No!"

"They rode away, I trust in Heaven, before these dreadful scenes began," said Mr. Haredale, who, between his agitation, his eagerness to mount his horse again, and the dexterity with which the cords were tied, had scarcely yet undone one knot. "A knife, Daisy!"

"You didn't," said John, looking about, as though he had lost his pocket-handkerchief, or some such slight article—"either of you gentlemen—see a—a coffin anywheres, did you?"

"Willet!" cried Mr. Haredale. Solomon dropped the knife, and instantly becoming limp from head to foot, exclaimed "Good gracious!"

"—Because," said John, not at all regarding them, "a dead man called a little time ago, on his way yonder. I could have told you what name was on the plate, if he had brought his coffin with him, and left it behind. If he didn't, it don't signify."

His landlord, who had listened to these words with breathless attention, started that moment to his feet; and, without a word, drew Solomon Daisy to the door, mounted his horse, took him up behind again, and flew rather than galloped towards the pile of ruins, which that day's sun had shone upon, a stately house. Mr. Willet stared after them, listened, looked down upon himself to make quite sure that he was still unbound, and, without any manifestation of impatience, disappointment, or surprise, gently relapsed into the condition from which he had so imperfectly recovered.

Mr. Haredale tied his horse to the trunk of a tree, and grasping his companion's arm, stole softly along the footpath, and into what had been the garden of his house. He stopped for an instant to look upon its smoking walls, and at the stars that shone through roof and floor upon the heap of crumbling ashes. Solomon glanced timidly in his face, but his lips were tightly pressed together, a resolute and stern expression sat upon his brow, and not a tear, a look, or gesture indicating grief, escaped him.

He drew his sword; felt for a moment in his breast, as though he carried other arms about him; then grasping Solomon by the wrist again, went with a cautious step all round the house. He looked into every doorway and gap in the wall; retraced his steps at every rustling of the air among the leaves; and searched in every shadowed nook with outstretched hands. Thus they made the circuit of the building: but they returned to the spot from which they had set out, without encountering any human being, or finding the least trace of any concealed straggler.

After a short pause, Mr. Haredale shouted twice or thrice. Then cried aloud, "Is there any one in hiding here, who knows my voice! There is nothing to fear now. If any of my people are near, I entreat them to answer!" He called them all by name; his voice was echoed in many mournful tones; then all was silent as before.

They were standing near the foot of the turret, where the alarm-bell hung. The fire had raged there, and the floors had been sawn, and hewn, and beaten down, besides. It was open to the night; but a part of the staircase still remained, winding upward from a great mound of dust and cinders. Fragments of the jagged and broken steps offered an insecure and giddy footing here and there, and then were lost again, behind protruding angles of the wall, or in the deep shadows cast upon it by other portions of the ruin; for by this time the moon had risen, and shone brightly.

As they stood here, listening to the echoes as they died away, and hoping in vain to hear a voice they knew, some of the ashes in this turret slipped and rolled down. Startled by the least noise in that melancholy place, Solomon looked up in his companion's face, and saw that he had turned towards the spot, and that he watched and listened keenly.

He covered the little man's mouth with his hand, and looked again. Instantly, with kindling eyes, he bade him on his life keep still, and neither speak nor move. Then holding his breath, and stooping down, he stole into the turret, with his drawn sword in his hand, and disappeared.

Terrified to be left there by himself, under such desolate circumstances, and after all he had seen and heard that night, Solomon would have followed, but there had been something in Mr. Haredale's manner and his look, the recollection of which held him spell-bound. He stood rooted to the spot; and scarcely venturing to breathe, looked up with mingled fear and wonder.

Again the ashes slipped and rolled—very, very softly—again—and then again, as though they crumbled underneath the tread of a stealthy foot. And now a figure was dimly visible; climbing very softly; and often stopping to look down; now it pursued its difficult way; and now it was hidden from the view again.

Barnaby Rudge

It emerged once more, into the shadowy and uncertain light—higher now, but not much, for the way was steep and toilsome, and its progress very slow. What phantom of the brain did he pursue; and why did he look down so constantly. He knew he was alone? Surely his mind was not affected by that night's loss and agony. He was not about to throw himself headlong from the summit of the tottering wall. Solomon turned sick, and clasped his hands. His limbs trembled beneath him, and a cold sweat broke out upon his pallid face.

If he complied with Mr. Haredale's last injunction now, it was because he had not the power to speak or move. He strained his gaze, and fixed it on a patch of moonlight, into which, if he continued to ascend, he must soon emerge. When he appeared there, he would try to call to him.

Again the ashes slipped and crumbled; some stones rolled down, and fell with a dull, heavy sound upon the ground below. He kept his eyes upon the piece of moonlight. The figure was coming on, for its shadow was already thrown upon the wall. Now it appeared—and now looked round at him—and now—

The horror-stricken clerk uttered a scream that pierced the air, and cried "The ghost! The ghost!"

Long before the echo of his cry had died away, another form rushed out into the light, flung itself upon the foremost one, knelt down upon its breast, and clutched its throat with both hands.

"Villain!" cried Mr. Haredale, in a terrible voice—for it was he. "Dead and buried, as all men supposed through your infernal arts, but reserved by Heaven for this—at last—at last—I have you. You, whose hands are red with my brother's blood, and that of his faithful servant, shed to conceal your own atrocious guilt.—You, Rudge, double murderer and monster, I arrest you in the name of God, who has delivered you into my hands. No. Though you had the strength of twenty men," he added, as the murderer writhed and struggled, "you could not escape me or loosen my grasp to-night!"

CHAPTER LVII

BARNABY, armed as we have seen, continued to pace up and down before the stable-door; glad to be alone again, and heartily rejoicing in the unaccustomed silence and tranquillity. After the whirl of noise and riot in which the last two days had been passed, the pleasures of solitude and peace were enhanced a thousandfold. He felt quite happy; and as he leaned upon his staff and mused, a bright smile overspread his face, and none but cheerful visions floated into his brain.

Had he no thought of her, whose sole delight he was, and whom he had unconsciously plunged in such bitter sorrow and such deep affliction? Oh, yes. She was at the heart of all his cheerful hopes and proud reflections. It was she whom all this honour and distinction were to gladden; the joy and profit were for her. What delight it gave her to hear of the bravery of her poor boy! Ah! He would have known that, without Hugh's telling him. And what a precious thing it was to know she lived so happily, and heard with so much pride (he pictured to himself her look when they told her) that he was in such high esteem: bold among the boldest, and trusted before them all. And when these frays were over, and the good lord had conquered his enemies, and they were all at peace again, and he and she were rich, what happiness they would have in talking of these troubled times when he was a great soldier: and when they sat alone together in the tranquil twilight, and she had no longer reason to be anxious for the morrow, what pleasure would he have in the reflection that this was his doing—his—poor foolish Barnaby's; and in patting her on the cheek, and saying with a merry laugh, "Am I silly now, mother—am I silly now?"

With a lighter heart and step, and eyes the brighter for the happy tear that dimmed them for a moment, Barnaby resumed his walk; and singing gaily to himself, kept guard upon his quiet post.

His comrade Grip, the partner of his watch, though fond of basking in the sunshine, preferred to-day to walk about the stable; having a great deal to do in the way of scattering the straw, hiding under it such small articles as had been casually left about, and haunting Hugh's bed, to which he seemed to have taken a particular attachment. Sometimes Barnaby looked in and called him, and then he came hopping out; but he merely did this as a concession to his master's weakness, and soon returned again to his own grave pursuits: peering into the straw with his bill, and rapidly covering up the place, as if, Midas-like, he were whispering secrets to the earth and burying them; constantly busying himself upon the sly; and affecting, whenever Barnaby came past, to look up in the clouds and have nothing whatever on his mind: in short, conducting himself, in many respects, in a more than usually thoughtful, deep, and mysterious manner.

As the day crept on, Barnaby, who had no directions forbidding him to eat and drink upon his post, but had been, on the contrary, supplied with a bottle of beer and a basket of provisions, determined to break his fast, which he had not done since morning. To this end, he sat down on the ground before the door, and putting his staff across his knees in case of alarm or surprise, summoned Grip to dinner.

This call, the bird obeyed with great alacrity; crying, as he sidled up to his master, "I'm a devil, I'm a Polly, I'm a kettle, I'm a Protestant, No Popery!" Having learnt this latter sentiment from the gentry among whom he had lived of late, he delivered it with uncommon emphasis.

"Well said, Grip!" cried his master, as he fed him with the daintiest bits. "Well said, old boy!"

"Never say die, bow wow wow, keep up your spirits, Grip Grip Grip, Holloa! We'll all have tea, I'm a Protestant kettle, No Popery!" cried the raven.

"Gordon for ever, Grip!" cried Barnaby.

The raven, placing his head upon the ground, looked at his master sideways, as though he would have said, "Say that again!" Perfectly understanding his desire, Barnaby repeated the phrase a great many times. The bird listened with profound attention; sometimes repeating the popular cry in a low voice, as if to compare the two, and try if it would at all help him to this new accomplishment; sometimes flapping his wings, or barking; and sometimes in a kind of desperation drawing a multitude of corks, with extraordinary viciousness.

Barnaby was so intent upon his favourite, that he was not at first aware of the approach of two persons on horseback, who were riding at a foot-pace, and coming straight towards his post. When he perceived them, however, which he did when they were within some fifty yards of him, he jumped hastily up, and ordering Grip within doors, stood with both hands on his staff, waiting until he should know whether they were friends or foes.

He had hardly done so, when he observed that those who advanced were a gentleman and his servant; almost at the same moment he recognised Lord George Gordon, before whom he stood uncovered, with his eyes turned towards the ground.

"Good day!" said Lord George, not reining in his horse until he was close beside him. "Well!"

"All quiet, sir, all safe!" cried Barnaby. "The rest are away—they went by that path—that one. A grand party!"

"Ay?" said Lord George, looking thoughtfully at him. "And you?"

"Oh! They left me here to watch—to mount guard—to keep everything secure till they come back. I'll do it, sir, for your sake. You're a good gentleman; a kind gentleman—ay, you are. There are many against you, but we'll be a match for them, never fear!"

"What's that?" said Lord George—pointing to the raven who was peeping out of the stable-door—but still looking thoughtfully, and in some perplexity, it seemed, at Barnaby.

"Why, don't you know!" retorted Barnaby, with a wondering laugh. "Not know what *he* is! A bird, to be sure. My bird—my friend—Grip."

"A devil, a kettle, a Grip, a Polly, a Protestant, no Popery!" cried the raven.

"Though, indeed," added Barnaby, laying his hand upon the neck of Lord George's horse, and speaking softly; "you had good reason to ask me what he is, for sometimes it puzzles me—and I am used to him—to think he's only a bird. He's my brother, Grip is—always with me—always talking—always merry—eh, Grip?"

The raven answered by an affectionate croak, and hopping on his master's arm, which he held downward for that purpose, submitted with an air of perfect indifference to be fondled, and turned his restless, curious eye, now upon Lord George, and now upon his man.

Lord George, biting his nails in a discomfited manner, regarded Barnaby for some time in silence; then beckoning to his servant, said:

"Come hither, John."

John Grueby touched his hat, and came.

"Have you ever seen this young man before?" his master asked in a low voice.

"Twice, my lord," said John. "I see him in the crowd last night and Saturday."

"Did—did it seem to you that his manner was at all wild or strange?" Lord George demanded, faltering.

"Mad," said John, with emphatic brevity.

"And why do you think him mad, sir?" said his master, speaking in a peevish tone. "Don't use that word too freely. Why do you think him mad?"

"My lord," John Grueby answered, "look at his dress, look at his eyes, look at his restless way, hear him cry 'No Popery!' Mad, my lord."

"So because one man dresses unlike another," returned his angry master, glancing at himself, "and happens to differ from other men in his carriage and manner, and to advocate a great cause which the corrupt and irreligious desert, he is to be accounted mad, is he?"

"Stark, staring, raving, roaring mad, my lord," returned the unmoved John.

"Do you say this to my face?" cried his master, turning sharply upon him.

"To any man, my lord, who asks me," answered John.

"Mr. Gashford, I find, was right," said Lord George; "I thought him prejudiced, though I ought to have known a man like him better than to have supposed it possible!"

"I shall never have Mr. Gashford's good word, my lord," replied John, touching his hat respectfully, "and I don't covet it."

"You are an ill-conditioned, most ungrateful fellow," said Lord George: "a spy, for anything I know. Mr. Gashford is perfectly correct, as I might have felt convinced he was. I have done wrong to retain you in my service. It is a tacit insult to him as my choice and confidential friend to do so, remembering the cause you sided with, on the day he was maligned at Westminster. You will leave me to-night—nay, as soon as we reach home. The sooner the better."

"If it comes to that, I say so too, my lord. Let Mr. Gashford have his will. As to my being a spy, my lord, you know me better than to believe it, I am sure. I don't know much about causes. My cause is the cause of one man against two hundred; and I hope it always will be."

"You have said quite enough," returned Lord George, motioning him to go back. "I desire to hear no more."

"If you'll let me have another word, my lord," returned John Grueby, "I'd give this silly fellow a caution not to stay here by himself. The proclamation is in a good many hands already, and it's well known that he was concerned in the business it relates to. He had better get to a place of safety if he can, poor creature."

"You hear what this man says?" cried Lord George, addressing Barnaby, who had looked on and wondered while this dialogue passed. "He thinks you may be afraid to remain upon your post, and are kept here perhaps against your will. What do you say?"

"I think, young man," said John, in explanation, "that the soldiers may turn out and take you; and that if they do, you will certainly be hung by the neck till you're dead—dead—dead. And I think you had better go from here, as fast as you can. That's what *I* think."

"He's a coward, Grip, a coward!" cried Barnaby, putting the raven on the ground, and shouldering his staff. "Let them come! Gordon for ever! Let them come!"

"Ay!" said Lord George, "let them! Let us see who will venture to attack a power like ours; the solemn league of a whole people. *This* a madman! You have said well, very well. I am proud to be the leader of such men as you."

Barnaby's heart swelled within his bosom as he heard these words. He took Lord George's hand and carried to his lips; patted his horse's crest, as if the affection and admiration he had conceived for the man extended to the animal he rode; then unfurling his flag, and proudly waving it, resumed his pacing up and down.

Lord George, with a kindling eye and glowing cheek, took off his hat, and flourishing it above his head, bade him exultingly Farewell!—then cantered off at a brisk pace; after glancing angrily round to see that his servant followed. Honest John set spurs to his horse and rode after his master, but not before he had again warned Barnaby to retreat, with many significant gestures, which indeed he continued to make, and Barnaby to resist until the windings of the road concealed them from each other's view.

Left to himself again with a still higher sense of the importance of his post, and stimulated to enthusiasm by the special notice and encouragement of his leader, Barnaby walked to and fro in a delicious trance rather than as a waking man. The sunshine which prevailed around was in his mind. He had but one desire ungratified. If she could only see him now!

The day wore on; its heat was gently giving place to the cool of evening; a light wind sprung up, fanning his long hair, and making the banner rustle pleasantly above his head. There was a freedom and freshness in the sound and in the time, which chimed exactly with his mood. He was happier than ever.

He was leaning on his staff looking towards the declining sun, and reflecting with a smile that he stood sentinel at that moment over buried gold, when two or three figures appeared in the distance, making towards the house at a rapid pace, and motioning with their hands as though they urged its inmates to retreat from some approaching danger. As they drew nearer, they became more earnest in their gestures; and they were no sooner within hearing, than the foremost among them cried that the soldiers were coming up.

At these words, Barnaby furled his flag, and tied it round the pole. His heart beat high while he did so, but he had no more fear or thought of retreating than the pole itself. The friendly stragglers hurried past him, after giving him notice of his danger, and quickly passed into the house, where the utmost confusion immediately prevailed. As those within hastily closed the windows and the doors, they urged him by looks and signs to fly without loss of time, and called to him many times to do so; but he only shook his head indignantly in answer, and stood the firmer on his post. Finding that he was not to be persuaded, they took care of themselves; and leaving the place with only one old woman in it, speedily withdrew.

As yet there had been no symptom of the news having any better foundation than in the fears of those who brought it, but The Boot had not been deserted five minutes, when there appeared, coming across the fields, a body of men who, it was easy to see, by the glitter of their arms and ornaments in the sun, and by their orderly and regular mode of advancing—for they came on as one man—were soldiers. In a very little time, Barnaby knew that they were a strong detachment of the Foot Guards, having along with them two gentlemen in private clothes, and a small party of Horse; the latter brought up the rear, and were not in number more than six or eight.

They advanced steadily; neither quickening their pace as they came nearer, nor raising any cry, nor showing the least emotion or anxiety. Though this was a matter of course in the case of regular troops, even to Barnaby, there was something particularly impressive and disconcerting in it to one accustomed to the noise and tumult of an undisciplined mob. For all that, he stood his ground not a whit the less resolutely, and looked on undismayed.

Presently, they marched into the yard, and halted. The commanding-officer despatched a messenger to the horsemen, one of whom came riding back. Some words passed between them, and they glanced at Barnaby; who well remembered the man he had unhorsed at Westminster, and saw him now before his eyes. The man being speedily dismissed, saluted, and rode back to his comrades, who were drawn up apart at a short distance.

The officer then gave the word to prime and load. The heavy ringing of the musket-stocks upon the ground, and the sharp and rapid rattling of the ramrods in their barrels, were a kind of relief to Barnaby, deadly though he knew the purport of such sounds to be. When this was done, other commands were given, and the soldiers instantaneously formed in single file all round the house and stables; completely encircling them in every part, at a distance, perhaps, of some half-dozen yards; at least that seemed in Barnaby's eyes to be about the space left between himself and those who confronted him. The horsemen remained drawn up by themselves as before.

The two gentlemen in private clothes who had kept aloof, now rode forward, one on either side the officer. The proclamation having been produced and read by one of them, the officer called on Barnaby to surrender.

He made no answer, but stepping within the door, before which he had kept guard, held his pole crosswise to protect it. In the midst of a profound silence, he was again called upon to yield.

Still he offered no reply. Indeed he had enough to do, to run his eye backward and forward along the half-dozen men who immediately fronted him, and settle hurriedly within himself at which of them he would strike first, when they pressed on him. He caught the eye of one in the centre, and resolved to hew that fellow down, though he died for it.

Again there was a dead silence, and again the same voice called upon him to deliver himself up.

Next moment he was back in the stable, dealing blows about him like a madman. Two of the men lay stretched at his feet: the one he had marked, dropped first—he had a thought for that, even in the hot blood and hurry of the struggle. Another blow—another! Down, mastered, wounded in the breast by a heavy blow from the butt-end of a gun (he saw the weapon in the act of falling)—breathless—and a prisoner.

An exclamation of surprise from the officer recalled him, in some degree, to himself. He looked round. Grip, after working in secret all the afternoon, and with redoubled vigour while everybody's attention was distracted, had plucked away the straw from Hugh's bed, and turned up the loose ground with his iron bill. The hole had been recklessly filled to the brim, and was merely sprinkled with earth. Golden cups, spoons, candlesticks, coined guineas—all the riches were revealed.

They brought spades and a sack; dug up everything that was hidden there; and carried away more than two men could lift. They handcuffed him and bound his arms, searched him, and took away all he had. Nobody questioned or reproached him, or seemed to have much curiosity about him. The two men he had stunned were carried off by their companions in the same business-like way in which everything else was done. Finally, he was left under a guard of four soldiers with fixed bayonets, while the officer directed in person the search of the house and the other buildings connected with it.

This was soon completed. The soldiers formed again in the yard; he was marched out, with his guard about him; and ordered to fall in, where a space was left. The others closed up all round, and so they moved away, with the prisoner in the centre.

When they came into the streets, he felt he was a sight; and looking up as they passed quickly along, could see people running to the windows a little too late, and throwing up the sashes to look after him. Sometimes he met a staring face beyond the heads about him, or under the arms of his conductors, or peering down upon him from a waggon-top or coach-box; but this was all he saw, being surrounded by so many men. The very noises of the streets seemed muffled and subdued; and the air came stale and hot upon him, like the sickly breath of an oven.

Tramp, tramp. Tramp, tramp. Heads erect, shoulders square, every man stepping in exact time—all so orderly and regular—nobody looking at him—nobody seeming conscious of his presence,—he could hardly believe he was a Prisoner. But at the word, though only thought, not spoken, he felt the handcuffs galling his wrists, the cord pressing his arms to his sides: the loaded guns levelled at his head: and those cold, bright, sharp, shining points turned towards him: the mere looking down at which, now that he was bound and helpless, made the warm current of his life run cold.

CHAPTER LVIII

THEY were not long in reaching the barracks, for the officer who commanded the party was desirous to avoid rousing the people by the display of military force in the streets, and was humanely anxious to give as little opportunity as possible for any attempt at rescue; knowing that it must lead to bloodshed and loss of life, and that if the civil authorities by whom he was accompanied, empowered him to order his men to fire, many innocent persons would probably fall, whom curiosity or idleness had attracted to the spot. He therefore led the party briskly on, avoiding with a merciful prudence the more public and crowded thoroughfares, and pursuing those which he deemed least likely to be infested by disorderly persons. This wise proceeding not only enabled them to gain their quarters without any interruption, but completely baffled a body of rioters who had assembled in one of the main streets, through which it was considered certain they would pass, and who remained gathered together for the purpose of releasing the prisoner from their hands, long after they had deposited him in a place of security, closed the barrack-gates, and set a double guard at every entrance for its better protection.

Arrived at this place, poor Barnaby was marched into a stone-floored room, where there was a very powerful smell of tobacco, a strong thorough draught of air, and a great wooden bedstead, large enough for a score of men. Several soldiers in undress were lounging about, or eating from tin cans; military accoutrements dangled on rows of pegs along the whitewashed wall; and some half-dozen men lay fast asleep upon their backs, snoring in concert. After remaining here just long enough to note these things, he was marched out again, and conveyed across the parade-ground to another portion of the building.

Perhaps a man never sees so much at a glance as when he is in a situation of extremity. The chances are a hundred to one, that if Barnaby had lounged in at the gate to look about him, he would have lounged out again with a very imperfect idea of the place, and would have remembered very little about it. But as he was taken handcuffed across the gravelled area, nothing escaped his notice. The dry, arid look of the dusty square, and of the bare brick building; the clothes hanging at some of the windows; and the men in their shirt-sleeves and braces, lolling with half their bodies out of the others; the green sun-blinds at the officers' quarters, and the little scanty trees in front; the drummer-boys practising in a distant court-yard; the men at drill on the parade; the two soldiers carrying a basket between them, who winked to each other as he went by, and slily pointed to their throats; the spruce Serjeant who hurried past with a cane in his hand, and under his arm a clasped book with a vellum cover; the fellows in the ground-floor rooms, furbishing and brushing up their different articles

Barnaby in Prison.

of dress, who stopped to look at him, and whose voices as they spoke together echoed loudly through the empty galleries and passages;— everything, down to the stand of muskets before the guard-house, and the drum with a pipe-clayed belt attached, in one corner, impressed itself upon his observation, as though he had noticed them in the same place a hundred times, or had been a whole day among them, in place of one brief hurried minute.

He was taken into a small paved back yard, and there they opened a great door, plated with iron, and pierced some five feet above the ground with a few holes to let in air and light. Into this dungeon he was walked straightway; and having locked him up there, and placed a sentry over him, they left him to his meditations.

The cell, or black hole, for it had those words painted on the door, was very dark, and having recently accommodated a drunken deserter, by no means clean. Barnaby felt his way to some straw at the farther end, and looking towards the door, tried to accustom himself to the gloom, which, coming from the bright sunshine out of doors, was not an easy task.

There was a kind of portico or colonnade outside, and this obstructed even the little light that at the best could have found its way through the small apertures in the door. The footsteps of the sentinel echoed monotonously as he paced its stone pavement to and fro (reminding Barnaby of the watch he had so lately kept himself); and as he passed and repassed the door, he made the cell for an instant so black by the interposition of his body, that his going away again seemed like the appearance of a new ray of light, and was quite a circumstance to look for.

When the prisoner had sat some time upon the ground, gazing at the chinks, and listening to the advancing and receding footsteps of his guard, the man stood still upon his post. Barnaby, quite unable to think, or to speculate on what would be done with him, had been lulled into a kind of doze by his regular pace; but his stopping roused him; and then he became aware that two men were in conversation under the colonnade, and very near the door of his cell.

How long they had been talking there, he could not tell, for he had fallen into an unconsciousness of his real position, and when the footsteps ceased, was answering aloud some question which seemed to have been put to him by Hugh in the stable, though of the fancied purport, either of question or reply, notwithstanding that he awoke with the latter on his lips, he had no recollection whatever. The first words that reached his ears, were these:

"Why is he brought here then, if he has to be taken away again so soon?"

"Why where would you have him go! Damme, he's not as safe anywhere as among the king's troops, is he? What *would* you do with him? Would you hand him over to a pack of cowardly civilians, that shake in their shoes till they wear the soles out, with trembling at the threats of the ragamuffins he belongs to?"

"That's true enough."

"True enough!—I'll tell you what. I wish, Tom Green, that I was a commissioned instead of a non-commissioned officer, and that I had the command of two companies—only two companies—of my own regiment. Call me out to stop these riots—give me the needful authority, and half-a-dozen rounds of ball cartridge—"

"Ay!" said the other voice. "That's all very well, but they won't give the needful authority. If the magistrate won't give the word, what's the officer to do?"

Not very well knowing, as it seemed, how to overcome this difficulty, the other man contented himself with damning the magistrates.

"With all my heart," said his friend.

"Where's the use of a magistrate?" returned the other voice. "What's a magistrate in this case, but an impertinent, unnecessary, unconstitutional sort of interference? Here's a proclamation. Here's a man referred to in that proclamation. Here's proof against him, and a witness on the spot. Damme! Take him out and shoot him, sir. Who wants a magistrate?"

"When does he go before Sir John Fielding?" asked the man who had spoken first.

"To-night at eight o'clock," returned the other. "Mark what follows. The magistrate commits him to Newgate. Our people take him to Newgate. The rioters pelt our people. Our people retire before the rioters. Stones are thrown, insults are offered, not a shot's fired. Why? Because of the magistrates. Damn the magistrates!"

When he had in some degree relieved his mind by cursing the magistrates in various other forms of speech, the man was silent, save for a low growling, still having reference to those authorities, which from time to time escaped him.

Barnaby, who had wit enough to know that this conversation concerned, and very nearly concerned, himself, remained perfectly quiet until they ceased to speak, when he groped his way to the door, and peeping through the air-holes, tried to make out what kind of men they were, to whom he had been listening.

The one who condemned the civil power in such strong terms, was a serjeant—engaged just then, as the streaming ribands in his cap announced, on the recruiting service. He stood leaning sideways against a pillar nearly opposite the door, and as he growled to himself, drew figures on the pavement with his cane. The other man had his back towards the dungeon, and Barnaby could only see his form. To judge from that, he was a gallant, manly, handsome fellow, but he had lost his left arm. It had been taken off between the elbow and the shoulder, and his empty coat-sleeve hung across his breast.

It was probably this circumstance which gave him an interest beyond any that his companion could boast of, and attracted Barnaby's attention. There was something soldierly in his bearing, and he wore a jaunty cap and jacket. Perhaps he had been in the service at one time or other. If he had, it could not have been very long ago, for he was but a young fellow now.

"Well, well," he said thoughtfully; "let the fault be where it may, it makes a man sorrowful to come back to old England, and see her in this condition."

"I suppose the pigs will join 'em next," said the serjeant, with an imprecation on the rioters, "now that the birds have set 'em the example."

"The birds!" repeated Tom Green.

"Ah—birds," said the serjeant testily; "that's English, an't it?"

"I don't know what you mean."

"Go to the guard-house, and see. You'll find a bird there, that's got their cry as pat as any of 'em, and bawls 'No Popery,' like a man —or like a devil, as he says he is. I shouldn't wonder. The devil's loose in London somewhere. Damme if I wouldn't twist his neck round, on the chance, if I had *my* way."

The young man had taken two or three steps away, as if to go and see this creature, when he was arrested by the voice of Barnaby.

"It's mine," he called out, half laughing and half weeping—"my pet, my friend Grip. Ha ha ha! Don't hurt him, he has done no harm. I taught him; it's my fault. Let me have him, if you please. He's the only friend I have left now. He'll not dance, or talk, or whistle for you, I know; but he will for me, because he knows me and loves me— though you wouldn't think it—very well. You wouldn't hurt a bird, I'm sure. You're a brave soldier, sir, and wouldn't harm a woman or a child—no, no, nor a poor bird, I'm certain."

This latter adjuration was addressed to the serjeant, whom Barnaby judged from his red coat to be high in office, and able to seal Grip's destiny by a word. But that gentleman, in reply, surlily damned him for a thief and rebel as he was, and with many disinterested imprecations on his own eyes, liver, blood, and body, assured him that if it rested with him to decide, he would put a final stopper on the bird, and his master too.

"You talk boldly to a caged man," said Barnaby, in anger. "If I was on the other side of the door and there were none to part us, you'd change your note—ay, you may toss your head—you would! Kill the bird—do. Kill anything you can, and so revenge yourself on those who with their bare hands untied could do as much to you!"

Having vented his defiance, he flung himself into the furthest corner of his prison, and muttering, "Good-bye, Grip—good-bye, dear old Grip!" shed tears for the first time since he had been taken captive; and hid his face in the straw.

He had had some fancy at first, that the one-armed man would help him, or would give him a kind word in answer. He hardly knew why, but he hoped and thought so. The young fellow had stopped when he called out, and checking himself in the very act of turning round, stood listening to every word he said. Perhaps he built his feeble trust on this; perhaps on his being young, and having a frank and honest manner. However that might be, he built on sand. The other went away directly he had finished speaking, and neither answered him, nor returned. No matter. They were all against him here: he might have known as much. "Good-bye, old Grip, good-bye!"

After some time, they came and unlocked the door, and called to him to come out. He rose directly, and complied, for he would not have *them* think he was subdued or frightened. He walked out like a man, and looked from face to face.

None of them returned his gaze or seemed to notice it. They marched him back to the parade by the way they had brought him, and there they halted, among a body of soldiers, at least twice as numerous as that which had taken him prisoner in the afternoon. The officer he had seen before, bade him in a few brief words take notice that if he attempted to escape, no matter how favourable a chance he might suppose he had, certain of the men had orders to fire upon him, that moment. They then closed round him as before, and marched him off again.

In the same unbroken order they arrived at Bow-street, followed and beset on all sides by a crowd which was continually increasing. Here he was placed before a blind gentleman, and asked if he wished to say anything. Not he. What had he got to tell them? After a very little talking, which he was careless of and quite indifferent to, they told him he was to go to Newgate, and took him away.

He went out into the street, so surrounded and hemmed in on every side by soldiers, that he could see nothing; but he knew there was a great crowd of people, by the murmur; and that they were not friendly to the soldiers, was soon rendered evident by their yells and hisses. How often and how eagerly he listened for the voice of Hugh! No. There was not a voice he knew among them all. Was Hugh a prisoner too? Was there no hope!

As they came nearer and nearer to the prison, the hootings of the people grew more violent; stones were thrown; and every now and then, a rush was made against the soldiers, which they staggered under. One of them, close before him, smarting under a blow upon the temple, levelled his musket, but the officer struck it upwards with his sword, and ordered him on peril of his life to desist. This was the last thing he saw with any distinctness, for directly afterwards he was tossed about, and beaten to and fro, as though in a tempestuous sea. But go where he would, there were the same guards about him. Twice or thrice he was thrown down, and so were they; but even then, he could not elude their vigilance for a moment. They were up again, and had closed about him, before he, with his wrists so tightly bound, could scramble to his feet. Fenced in, thus, he felt himself hoisted to the top of a low flight of steps, and then for a moment he caught a glimpse of the fighting in the crowd, and of a few red coats sprinkled together, here and there, struggling to rejoin their fellows. Next moment, everything was dark and gloomy, and he was standing in the prison lobby; the centre of a group of men.

A smith was speedily in attendance, who riveted upon him a set of heavy irons. Stumbling on as well as he could, beneath the unusual burden of these fetters, he was conducted to a strong stone cell, where, fastening the door with locks, and bolts, and chains, they left him, well secured; having first, unseen by him, thrust in Grip, who, with his head drooping and his deep black plumes rough and rumpled, appeared to comprehend and to partake, his master's fallen fortunes.

CHAPTER LIX

IT is necessary at this juncture to return to Hugh, who, having, as we have seen, called to the rioters to disperse from about the Warren, and meet again as usual, glided back into the darkness from which he had emerged, and reappeared no more that night.

He paused in the copse which sheltered him from the observation of his mad companions, and waited to ascertain whether they drew off at his bidding, or still lingered and called to him to join them. Some few, he saw, were indisposed to go away without him, and made towards the spot where he stood concealed as though they were about to follow in his footsteps, and urge him to come back; but these men, being in their turn called to by their friends, and in truth not greatly caring to venture into the dark parts of the grounds, where they might be easily surprised and taken, if any of the neighbours or retainers of the family were watching them from among the trees, soon abandoned the idea, and hastily assembling such men as they found of their mind at the moment, straggled off.

When he was satisfied that the great mass of the insurgents were imitating this example, and that the ground was rapidly clearing, he plunged into the thickest portion of the little wood; and, crashing the branches as he went, made straight towards a distant light: guided by that, and by the sullen glow of the fire behind him.

As he drew nearer and nearer to the twinkling beacon towards which he bent his course, the red glare of a few torches began to reveal itself, and the voices of men speaking together in a subdued tone broke the silence which, save for a distant shouting now and then, already prevailed. At length he cleared the wood, and, springing across a ditch, stood in a dark lane, where a small body of ill-looking vagabonds, whom he had left there some twenty minutes before, waited his coming with impatience.

They were gathered round an old post-chaise or chariot, driven by one of themselves, who sat postilion-wise upon the near horse. The blinds were drawn up, and Mr. Tappertit and Dennis kept guard at the two windows. The former assumed the command of the party, for he challenged Hugh as he advanced towards them; and when he did so, those who were resting on the ground about the carriage rose to their feet and clustered round him.

"Well!" said Simon, in a low voice; "is all right?"

"Right enough," replied Hugh, in the same tone. "They're dispersing now—had begun before I came away."

"And is the coast clear?"

"Clear enough before our men, I take it," said Hugh. "There are not many who, knowing of their word over yonder, will want to meddle with 'em to-night.—Who's got some drink here?"

Everybody had some plunder from the cellar; half-a-dozen flasks and bottles were offered directly. He selected the largest, and putting it to his mouth, sent the wine gurgling down his throat. Having emptied it, he threw it down, and stretched out his hand for another, which he emptied likewise, at a draught. Another was given him, and this he half emptied too. Reserving what remained to finish with, he asked:

"Have you got anything to eat, any of you? I'm as ravenous as a hungry wolf. Which of you was in the larder—come?"

"I was, brother," said Dennis, pulling off his hat, and fumbling in the crown. "There's a matter of cold venison pastry somewhere or another here, if that'll do."

"Do!" cried Hugh, seating himself on the pathway. "Bring it out! Quick! Show a light here, and gather round! Let me sup in state, my lads! Ha ha ha!"

Entering into his boisterous humour, for they all had drunk deeply, and were as wild as he, they crowded about him, while two of their number who had torches, held them up, one on either side of him, that his banquet might not be despatched in the dark. Mr. Dennis, having by this time succeeded in extricating from his hat a great mass of pastry, which had been wedged in so tightly that it was not easily got out, put in before him; and Hugh, having borrowed a notched and jagged knife from one of the company, fell to work upon it vigorously.

"I should recommend you to swallow a little fire every day, about an hour afore dinner, brother," said Dennis, after a pause. "It seems to agree with you, and to stimulate your appetite."

Hugh looked at him, and at the blackened faces by which he was surrounded, and, stopping for a moment to flourish his knife above his head, answered with a roar of laughter.

"Keep order, there, will you?" said Simon Tappertit.

"Why isn't a man allowed to regale himself, noble captain," retorted his lieutenant, parting the men who stood between them, with his knife, that he might see him,—"to regale himself a little bit after such work as mine? What a hard captain! What a strict captain! What a tyrannical captain! Ha ha ha!"

"I wish one of you fellers would hold a bottle to his mouth to keep him quiet," said Simon, "unless you want the military to be down upon us."

"And what if they are down upon us!" retorted Hugh. "Who cares? Who's afraid? Let 'em come, *I* say, let 'em come. The more, the merrier. Give me bold Barnaby at my side, and we two will settle the military, without troubling any of you. Barnaby's the man for the military. Barnaby's health."

But as the majority of those present were by no means anxious for a second engagement that night, being already weary and exhausted, they sided with Mr. Tappertit, and pressed him to make haste with his supper, for they had already delayed too long. Knowing, even in the height of his frenzy, that they incurred great danger by lingering so near the scene of the late outrages, Hugh made an end of his meal without more remonstrance, and rising, stepped up to Mr. Tappertit, and smote him on the back.

"Now then," he cried, "I'm ready. There are brave birds inside this cage, eh? Delicate birds,—tender, loving, little doves. I caged 'em—I caged 'em—one more peep!"

He thrust the little man aside as he spoke, and mounting on the steps, which were half let down, pulled down the blind by force, and stared into the chaise like an ogre into his larder.

"Ha ha ha! and did you scratch, and pinch, and struggle, pretty mistress?" he cried, as he grasped a little hand that sought in vain to free itself from his grip: "you, so bright-eyed, and cherry-lipped, and daintily made? But I love you better for it, mistress. Ay, I do. You should stab me and welcome, so that it pleased you, and you had to cure me afterwards. I love to see you proud and scornful. It makes you handsomer than ever; and who so handsome as you at any time, my pretty one!"

"Come!" said Mr. Tappertit, who had waited during this speech with considerable impatience. "There's enough of that. Come down."

The little hand seconded this admonition by thrusting Hugh's great head away with all its force, and drawing up the blind, amidst his noisy laughter, and vows that he must have another look, for the last glimpse of that sweet face had provoked him past all bearing. However, as the suppressed impatience of the party now broke out into open murmurs, he abandoned this design, and taking his seat upon the bar, contented himself with tapping at the front windows of the carriage, and trying to steal a glance inside; Mr. Tappertit, mounting the steps and hanging on by the door, issued his directions to the driver with a commanding voice and attitude; the rest got up behind, or ran by the side of the carriage, as they could; some, in imitation of Hugh, endeavoured to see the face he had praised so highly, and were reminded of their impertinence by hints from the cudgel of Mr. Tappertit. Thus they pursued their journey by circuitous and winding roads; preserving, except when they halted to take breath, or to quarrel about the best way of reaching London, pretty good order and tolerable silence.

In the mean time, Dolly—beautiful, bewitching, captivating little Dolly—her hair dishevelled, her dress torn, her dark eyelashes wet with tears, her bosom heaving—her face, now pale with fear, now crimsoned with indignation—her whole self a hundred times more beautiful in this heightened aspect than ever she had been before— vainly strove to comfort Emma Haredale, and to impart to her the consolation of which she stood in so much need herself. The soldiers were sure to come; they must be rescued; it would be impossible to convey them through the streets of London when they set the threats of their guards at defiance, and shrieked to the passengers for help. If they did this when they came into the more frequented ways, she was certain—she was quite certain—they must be released. So poor Dolly said, and so poor Dolly tried to think; but the invariable conclusion of all such arguments was, that Dolly burst into tears;

cried, as she wrung her hands, what would they do or think, or who would comfort them, at home, at the Golden Key; and sobbed most piteously.

Miss Haredale, whose feelings were usually of a quieter kind than Dolly's, and not so much upon the surface, was dreadfully alarmed, and indeed had only just recovered from a swoon. She was very pale, and the hand which Dolly held was quite cold; but she bade her, nevertheless, remember that, under Providence, much must depend upon their own discretion; that if they remained quiet and lulled the vigilance of the ruffians into whose hands they had fallen, the chances of their being able to procure assistance when they reached the town, were very much increased; that unless society were quite unhinged, that pursuit must be immediately commenced; and that her uncle, she might be sure, would never rest until he had found them out and rescued them. But as she said these latter words, the idea that he had fallen in a general massacre of the Catholics that night—no very wild or improbable supposition after what they had seen and undergone—struck her dumb; and, lost in the horrors they had witnessed, and those they might be yet reserved for, she sat incapable of thought, or speech, or outward show of grief: as rigid, and almost as white and cold, as marble.

Oh, how many, many times, in that long ride, did Dolly think of her old lover,—poor, fond, slighted Joe! How many, many times, did she recall that night when she ran into his arms from the very man now projecting his hateful gaze into the darkness where she sat, and leering through the glass in monstrous admiration! And when she thought of Joe, and what a brave fellow he was, and how he would have rode boldly up, and dashed in among these villains now, yes, though they were double the number—and here she clenched her little hand, and pressed her foot upon the ground—the pride she felt for a moment in having won his heart, faded in a burst of tears, and she sobbed more bitterly than ever.

As the night wore on, and they proceeded by ways which were quite unknown to them—for they could recognise none of the objects of which they sometimes caught a hurried glimpse—their fears increased; nor were they without good foundation; it was not difficult for two beautiful young women to find, in their being borne they knew not whither by a band of daring villains who eyed them as some among these fellows did, reasons for the worst alarm. When they at last entered London, by a suburb with which they were wholly unacquainted, it was past midnight, and the streets were dark and empty. Nor was this the worst, for the carriage stopping in a lonely spot, Hugh suddenly opened the door, jumped in, and took his seat between them.

It was in vain they cried for help. He put his arm about the neck of each, and swore to stifle them with kisses if they were not as silent as the grave.

"I come here to keep you quiet," he said, "and that's the means I shall take. So don't be quiet, pretty mistresses—make a noise—do

—and I shall like it all the better."

They were proceeding at a rapid pace, and apparently with fewer attendants than before, though it was so dark (the torches being extinguished) that this was mere conjecture. They shrunk from his touch, each into the farthest corner of the carriage; but shrink as Dolly would, his arm encircled her waist, and held her fast. She neither cried nor spoke, for terror and disgust deprived her of the power; but she plucked at his hand as though she would die in the effort to disengage herself; and crouching on the ground, with her head averted and held down, repelled him with a strength she wondered at as much as he. The carriage stopped again.

"Lift this one out," said Hugh to the man who opened the door, as he took Miss Haredale's hand, and felt how heavily it fell. "She's fainted."

"So much the better," growled Dennis—it was that amiable gentleman. "She's quiet. I always like 'em to faint, unless they're very tender and composed."

"Can you take her by yourself?" asked Hugh.

"I don't know till I try. I ought to be able to; I've lifted up a good many in my time," said the hangman. "Up then! She's no small weight, brother; none of these here fine gals are. Up again! Now we have her."

Having by this time hoisted the young lady into his arms, he staggered off with his burden.

"Look ye, pretty bird," said Hugh, drawing Dolly towards him. "Remember what I told you—a kiss for every cry. Scream, if you love me, darling. Scream once, mistress. Pretty mistress, only once, if you love me."

Thrusting his face away with all her force, and holding down her head, Dolly submitted to be carried out of the chaise, and borne after Miss Haredale into a miserable cottage, where Hugh, after hugging her to his breast, set her gently down upon the floor.

Poor Dolly! Do what she would, she only looked the better for it, and tempted them the more. When her eyes flashed angrily, and her ripe lips slightly parted, to give her rapid breathing vent, who could resist it? When she wept and sobbed as though her heart would break, and bemoaned her miseries in the sweetest voice that ever fell upon a listener's ear, who could be insensible to the little winning pettishness which now and then displayed itself, even in the sincerity and earnestness of her grief? When, forgetful for a moment of herself, as she was now, she fell on her knees beside her friend, and bent over her, and laid her cheek to hers, and put her arms about her, what mortal eyes could have avoided wandering to the delicate bodice, the streaming hair, the neglected dress, the perfect abandonment and unconsciousness of the blooming little beauty? Who could look on and see her lavish caresses and endearments, and not desire to be in Emma Haredale's place; to be either her or Dolly; either the hugging or the hugged? Not Hugh. Not Dennis.

"I tell you what it is, young women," said Mr. Dennis, "I an't much of a lady's man myself, nor am I a party in the present business further than lending a willing hand to my friends; but if I see much more of this here sort of thing, I shall become a principal instead of a accessory. I tell you candid."

"Why have you brought us here?" said Emma. "Are we to be murdered?"

"Murdered!" cried Dennis, sitting down upon a stool, and regarding her with great favour. "Why, my dear, who'd murder sich chickabiddies as you? If you was to ask me, now, whether you was brought here to be married, there might be something in it."

And here he exchanged a grin with Hugh, who removed his eyes from Dolly for the purpose.

"No, no," said Dennis, "there'll be no murdering, my pets. Nothing of that sort. Quite the contrary."

"You are an older man than your companion, sir," said Emma, trembling. "Have you no pity for us? Do you not consider that we are women?"

"I do indeed, my dear," retorted Dennis. "It would be very hard not to, with two such specimens afore my eyes. Ha ha! Oh yes, I consider that. We all consider that, miss."

He shook his head waggishly, leered at Hugh again, and laughed very much, as if he had said a noble thing, and rather thought he was coming out.

"There'll be no murdering, my dear. Not a bit on it. I tell you what though, brother," said Dennis, cocking his hat for the convenience of scratching his head, and looking gravely at Hugh, "it's worthy of notice, as a proof of the amazing equalness and dignity of our law, that it don't make no distinction between men and women. I've heerd the judge say, sometimes, to a highwayman or housebreaker as had tied the ladies neck and heels—you'll excuse me making mention of it, my darlings—and put 'em in a cellar, that he showed no consideration to women. Now, I say that there judge didn't know his business, brother; and that if I had been that there highwayman or housebreaker, I should have made answer: 'What are you talking of, my lord? I showed the women as much consideration as the law does, and what more would you have me do?' If you was to count up in the newspapers the number of females as have been worked off in this here city alone, in the last ten year," said Mr. Dennis thoughtfully, "you'd be surprised at the total—quite amazed, you would. There's a dignified and equal thing; a beautiful thing! But we've no security for its lasting. Now that they've begun to favour these here Papists, I shouldn't wonder if they went and altered even *that*, one of these days. Upon my soul, I shouldn't."

The subject, perhaps from being of too exclusive and professional a nature, failed to interest Hugh as much as his friend had anticipated. But he had no time to pursue it, for at this crisis Mr. Tappertit entered precipitately; at sight of whom Dolly uttered a scream of joy, and fairly threw herself into his arms.

"I knew it, I was sure of it!" cried Dolly, "My dear father's at the door. Thank God, thank God! Bless you, Sim. Heaven bless you for this!"

Simon Tappertit, who had at first implicitly believed that the locksmith's daughter, unable any longer to suppress her secret passion for himself, was about to give it full vent in its intensity, and to declare that she was his for ever, looked extremely foolish when she said these words;—the more so, as they were received by Hugh and Dennis with a loud laugh, which made her draw back, and regard him with a fixed and earnest look.

"Miss Haredale," said Sim, after a very awkward silence, "I hope you're as comfortable as circumstances will permit of. Dolly Varden, my darling—my own, my lovely one—I hope *you're* pretty comfortable likewise."

Poor little Dolly! She saw how it was; hid her face in her hands; and sobbed more bitterly than ever.

"You meet in me, Miss V.," said Simon, laying his hand upon his breast, "not a 'prentice, not a workman, not a slave, not the wictim of your father's tyrannical behaviour, but the leader of a great people, the captain of a noble band, in which these gentlemen are, as I may say, corporals and serjeants. You behold in me, not a private individual, but a public character; not a mender of locks, but a healer of the wounds of his unhappy country. Dolly V., sweet Dolly V., for how many years have I looked forward to this present meeting! For how many years has it been my intention to exalt and ennoble you! I redeem it. Behold in me, your husband. Yes, beautiful Dolly— charmer—enslaver—S. Tappertit is all your own!"

As he said these words he advanced towards her. Dolly retreated till she could go no farther, and then sank down upon the floor. Thinking it very possible that this might be maiden modesty, Simon essayed to raise her; on which Dolly, goaded to desperation, wound her hands in his hair, and crying out amidst her tears that he was a dreadful little wretch, and always had been, shook, and pulled, and beat him, until he was fain to call for help most lustily. Hugh had never admired her half so much as at that moment.

"She's in an excited state to-night," said Simon, as he smoothed his rumpled feathers, "and don't know when she's well off. Let her be by herself till to-morrow, and that'll bring her down a little. Carry her into the next house!"

Hugh had her in his arms directly. It might be that Mr. Tappertit's heart was really softened by her distress, or it might be that he felt it in some degree indecorous that his intended bride should be struggling in the grasp of another man. He commanded him, on second thoughts, to put her down again, and looked moodily on as she flew to Miss Haredale's side, and clinging to her dress, hid her flushed face in its folds.

"They shall remain here together till to-morrow," said Simon, who had now quite recovered his dignity—"till to-morrow. Come away!"

"Ay!" cried Hugh. "Come away, captain. Ha ha ha!"

"What are you laughing at?" demanded Simon sternly.

"Nothing, captain, nothing," Hugh rejoined; and as he spoke, and clapped his hand upon the shoulder of the little man, he laughed again, for some unknown reason, with tenfold violence.

Mr. Tappertit surveyed him from head to foot with lofty scorn (this only made him laugh the more), and turning to the prisoners, said:

"You'll take notice, ladies, that this place is well watched on every side, and that the least noise is certain to be attended with unpleasant consequences. You'll hear—both of you—more of our intentions tomorrow. In the mean time, don't show yourselves at the window, or appeal to any of the people you may see pass it; for if you do, it'll be known directly that you come from a Catholic house, and all the exertions our men can make, may not be able to save your lives."

With this last caution, which was true enough, he turned to the door, followed by Hugh and Dennis. They paused for a moment, going out, to look at them clasped in each other's arms, and then left the cottage; fastening the door, and setting a good watch upon it, and indeed all round the house.

"I say," growled Dennis, as they walked in company, "that's a dainty pair. Muster Gashford's one is as handsome as the other, eh?"

"Hush!" said Hugh, hastily. "Don't you mention names. It's a bad habit."

"I wouldn't like to be *him*, then (as you don't like names), when he breaks it out to her; that's all," said Dennis. She's one of them fine, black-eyed, proud gals, as I wouldn't trust at such times with a knife too near 'em. I've seen some of that sort, afore now. I recollect one that was worked off, many year ago—and there was a gentleman in that case too—that says to me, with her lip a trembling, but her hand as steady as ever I see one; 'Dennis, I'm near my end, but if I had a dagger in these fingers, and he was within my reach, I'd strike him dead afore me;'—ah, she did—and she'd have done it too!"

"Strike who dead?" demanded Hugh.

"How should I know, brother?" answered Dennis. "*She* never said; not she."

Hugh looked, for a moment, as though he would have made some further inquiry into this incoherent recollection; but Simon Tappertit, who had been meditating deeply, gave his thoughts a new direction.

"Hugh!" said Sim. "You have done well to-day. You shall be rewarded. So have you, Dennis.—There's no young woman *you* want to carry off, is there?"

"N—no," returned that gentleman, stroking his grizzly beard, which was some two inches long. "None in partikler, I think."

"Very good," said Sim; "then we'll find some other way of making it up to you. As to you, old boy"—he turned to Hugh—"you shall have Miggs (her that I promised you, you know) within three days. Mind. I pass my word for it."

Hugh thanked him heartily; and as he did so, his laughing fit returned with such violence that he was obliged to hold his side with one hand, and to lean with the other on the shoulder of his small captain, without whose support he would certainly have rolled upon the ground.

CHAPTER LX

THE three worthies turned their faces towards The Boot, with the intention of passing the night in that place of rendezvous, and of seeking the repose they so much needed in the shelter of their old den; for now that the mischief and destruction they had purposed were achieved, and their prisoners were safely bestowed for the night, they began to be conscious of exhaustion, and to feel the wasting effects of the madness which had led to such deplorable results.

Notwithstanding the lassitude and fatigue which oppressed him now, in common with his two companions, and indeed with all who had taken an active share in that night's work, Hugh's boisterous merriment broke out afresh whenever he looked at Simon Tappertit, and vented itself—much to that gentleman's indignation—in such shouts of laughter as bade fair to bring the watch upon them, and involve them in a skirmish, to which in their present worn-out condition they might prove by no means equal. Even Mr. Dennis, who was not at all particular on the score of gravity or dignity, and who had a great relish for his young friend's eccentric humours, took occasion to remonstrate with him on this imprudent behaviour, which he held to be a species of suicide, tantamount to a man's working himself off without being overtaken by the law, than which he could imagine nothing more ridiculous or impertinent.

Not abating one jot of his noisy mirth for these remonstrances, Hugh reeled along between them, having an arm of each, until they hove in sight of The Boot, and were within a field or two of that convenient tavern. He happened by great good luck to have roared and shouted himself into silence by this time. They were proceeding onward without noise, when a scout who had been creeping about the ditches all night, to warn any stragglers from encroaching further on what was now such dangerous ground, peeped cautiously from his hiding-place, and called to them to stop.

"Stop! and why?" said Hugh.

Because (the scout replied) the house was filled with constables and soldiers; having been surprised that afternoon. The inmates had fled or been taken into custody, he could not say which. He had prevented a great many people from approaching nearer, and he believed they had gone to the markets and such places to pass the night. He had seen the distant fires, but they were all out now. He had heard the people who passed and repassed, speaking of them too, and could report that the prevailing opinion was one of apprehension and dismay. He had not heard a word of Barnaby—didn't even know his name—but it had been said in his hearing that some man had been taken and carried off to Newgate. Whether this was true or false, he could not affirm.

The three took counsel together, on hearing this, and debated what it might be best to do. Hugh, deeming it possible that Barnaby was in the hands of the soldiers, and at that moment under detention at The Boot, was for advancing stealthily, and firing the house; but his companions, who objected to such rash measures unless they had a crowd at their backs, represented that if Barnaby were taken he had assuredly been removed to a stronger prison; they would never have dreamed, he said, of keeping him all night in a place so weak and open to attack. Yielding to this reasoning, and to their persuasions, Hugh consented to turn back and to repair to Fleet Market; for which place, it seemed, a few of their boldest associates had shaped their course, on receiving the same intelligence.

Feeling their strength recruited and their spirits roused, now that there was a new necessity for action, they hurried away quite forgetful of the fatigue under which they had been sinking but a few minutes before; and soon arrived at their new place of destination.

Fleet Market, at that time, was a long irregular row of wooden sheds and pent-houses, occupying the centre of what is now called Farringdon-street. They were jumbled together in a most unsightly fashion, in the middle of the road; to the great obstruction of the thoroughfare and the annoyance of passengers, who were fain to make their way, as they best could, among carts, baskets, barrows, trucks, casks, bulks, and benches, and to jostle with porters, hucksters, waggoners, and a motley crowd of buyers, sellers, pickpockets, vagrants, and idlers. The air was perfumed with the stench of rotten leaves and faded fruit; the refuse of the butchers' stalls, and offal and garbage of a hundred kinds. It was indispensable to most public conveniences in those days, that they should be public nuisances likewise; and Fleet Market maintained the principle to admiration.

To this place, perhaps because its sheds and baskets were a tolerable substitute for beds, or perhaps because it afforded the means of a hasty barricade in case of need, many of the rioters had straggled, not only that night, but for two or three nights before. It was now broad day, but the morning being cold, a group of them were gathered round a fire in a public house, drinking hot purl, and smoking pipes, and planning new schemes for to-morrow.

Hugh and his two friends being known to most of these men, were received with signal marks of approbation, and inducted into the most honourable seats. The room-door was closed and fastened to keep intruders at a distance, and then they proceeded to exchange news.

"The soldiers have taken possession of The Boot, I hear," said Hugh. "Who knows anything about it?"

Several cried that they did; but the majority of the company having been engaged in the assault upon the Warren, and all present having been concerned in one or other of the night's expeditions, it proved that they knew no more than Hugh himself; having been merely warned by each other, or by the scout, and knowing nothing of their own knowledge.

"We left a man on guard there to-day," said Hugh, looking round him, "who is not here. You know who it is—Barnaby, who brought the soldier down, at Westminster. Has any man seen or heard of him?"

They shook their heads, and murmured an answer in the negative, as each man looked round and appealed to his fellow; when a noise was heard without, and a man was heard to say that he wanted Hugh —that he must see Hugh.

"He is but one man," cried Hugh to those who kept the door; "let him come in."

"Ay, ay!" muttered the others. "Let him come in. Let him come in."

The door was accordingly unlocked and opened. A one-armed man, with his head and face tied up with a bloody cloth, as though he had been severely beaten, his clothes torn, and his remaining hand grasping a thick stick, rushed in among them, and panting for breath, demanded which was Hugh.

"Here he is," replied the person he inquired for. "I am Hugh. What do you want with me?"

"I have a message for you," said the man. "You know one Barnaby."

"What of him? Did he send the message?"

"Yes. He's taken. He's in one of the strong cells in Newgate. He defended himself as well as he could, but was overpowered by numbers. That's his message."

"When did you see him?" asked Hugh hastily.

"On his way to prison, where he was taken by a party of soldiers. They took a by-road, and not the one we expected. I was one of the few who tried to rescue him, and he called to me, and told me to tell Hugh where he was. We made a good struggle, though it failed. Look here!"

He pointed to his dress and to his bandaged head, and still panting for breath, glanced round the room; then faced towards Hugh again.

"I know you by sight," he said, "for I was in the crowd on Friday, and on Saturday, and yesterday, but I didn't know your name. You're a bold fellow, I know. So is he. He fought like a lion to-night, but it was of no use. *I* did my best, considering that I want this limb."

Again he glanced inquisitively round the room—or seemed to do so, for his face was nearly hidden by the bandage—and again facing sharply towards Hugh, grasped his stick as if he half expected to be set upon, and stood on the defensive.

If he had any such apprehension, however, he was speedily reassured by the demeanour of all present. None thought of the bearer of the tidings. He was lost in the news he brought. Oaths, threats, and execrations, were vented on all sides. Some cried that if they bore this tamely, another day would see them all in jail; some, that they should have rescued the other prisoners, and this would not have happened. One man cried in a loud voice, "Who'll follow me to Newgate!" and there was a loud shout and general rush towards the door.

But Hugh and Dennis stood with their backs against it, and kept them back, until the clamour had so far subsided that their voices could be heard, when they called to them together that to go now, in broad day, would be madness; and that if they waited until night and arranged a plan of attack, they might release, not only their own companions, but all the prisoners, and burn down the jail.

"Not that jail alone," cried Hugh, "but every jail in London. They shall have no place to put their prisoners in. We'll burn them all down; make bonfires of them every one! Here!" he cried, catching at the hangman's hand. "Let all who're men here, join with us. Shake hands upon it. Barnaby out of jail, and not a jail left standing! Who joins?"

Every man there. And they swore a great oath to release their friends from Newgate next night; to force the doors and burn the jail; or perish in the fire themselves.

CHAPTER LXI

On that same night—events so crowd upon each other in convulsed and distracted times, that more than the stirring incidents of a whole life often become compressed into the compass of four-and-twenty hours—on that same night, Mr. Haredale, having strongly bound his prisoner, with the assistance of the sexton, and forced him to mount his horse, conducted him to Chigwell; bent upon procuring a conveyance to London from that place, and carrying him at once before a justice. The disturbed state of the town would be, he knew, a sufficient reason for demanding the murderer's committal to prison before daybreak, as no man could answer for the security of any of the watch-houses or ordinary places of detention; and to convey a prisoner through the streets when the mob were again abroad, would not only be a task of great danger and hazard, but would be to challenge an attempt at rescue. Directing the sexton to lead the horse, he walked close by the murderer's side, and in this order they reached the village about the middle of the night.

The people were all awake and up, for they were fearful of being burnt in their beds, and sought to comfort and assure each other by watching in company. A few of the stoutest-hearted were armed and gathered in a body on the green. To these, who knew him well, Mr. Haredale addressed himself, briefly narrating what had happened, and beseeching them to aid in conveying the criminal to London before the dawn of day.

But not a man among them dared to help him by so much as the motion of a finger. The rioters, in their passage through the village, had menaced with their fiercest vengeance, any person who should aid in extinguishing the fire, or render the least assistance to him, or any Catholic whomsoever. Their threats extended to their lives and all they possessed. They were assembled for their own protection, and could not endanger themselves by lending any aid to him. This they told him, not without hesitation and regret, as they kept aloof in the moonlight and glanced fearfully at the ghostly rider, who, with his head drooping on his breast and his hat slouched down upon his brow, neither moved nor spoke.

Finding it impossible to persuade them, and indeed hardly knowing how to do so after what they had seen of the fury of the crowd, Mr. Haredale besought them that at least they would leave him free to act for himself, and would suffer him to take the only chaise and pair of horses that the place afforded. This was not acceded to without some difficulty, but in the end they told him to do what he could, and go away from them in Heaven's name.

Leaving the sexton at the horses' bridle, he drew out the chaise with his own hands, and would have harnessed the horses, but that the post-boy of the village—a soft-hearted, good-for-nothing, vaga- bond kind of fellow—was moved by his earnestness and passion, throwing down a pitchfork with which he was armed, swore that the rioters might cut him into mince-meat if they liked, but he would not stand by and see an honest gentleman who had done no wrong, reduced to such extremity, without doing what he could to help him. Mr. Haredale shook him warmly by the hand, and thanked him from his heart. In five minutes' time the chaise was ready, and this good scape-grace in his saddle. The murderer was put inside, the blinds were drawn up, the sexton took his seat upon the bar, Mr. Haredale mounted his horse and rode close beside the door; and so they started in the dead of night, and in profound silence, for London.

The consternation was so extreme that even the horses which had escaped the flames at the Warren, could find no friends to shelter them. They passed them on the road, browsing on the stunted grass; and the driver told them, that the poor beasts had wandered to the village first, but had been driven away, lest they should bring the vengeance of the crowd on any of the inhabitants.

Nor was this feeling confined to such small places, where the people were timid, ignorant, and unprotected. When they came near Lon- don they met, in the grey light of morning, more than one poor Catholic family who, terrified by the threats and warnings of their neighbours, were quitting the city on foot, and who told them they could hire no cart or horse for the removal of their goods, and had been compelled to leave them behind, at the mercy of the crowd. Near Mile-end they passed a house, the master of which, a Catholic gentleman of small means, having hired a waggon to remove his furniture by midnight, had had it all brought down into the street, to wait the vehicle's arrival, and save time in the packing. But the man with whom he made the bargain, alarmed by the fires that night, and by the sight of the rioters passing his door, had refused to keep it: and the poor gentleman, with his wife and servant and their little children, were sitting trembling among their goods in the open street, dreading the arrival of day and not knowing where to turn or what to do.

It was the same, they heard, with the public conveyances. The panic was so great that the mails and stage-coaches were afraid to

carry passengers who professed the obnoxious religion. If the drivers
knew them, or they admitted that they held that creed, they would
not take them, no, though they offered large sums; and yesterday,
people had been afraid to recognise Catholic acquaintance in the
streets, lest they should be marked by spies, and burnt out, as it was
called, in consequence. One mild old man—a priest, whose chapel
was destroyed; a very feeble, patient, inoffensive creature—who was
trudging away, alone, designing to walk some distance from town,
and then try his fortune with the coaches, told Mr. Haredale that he
feared he might not find a magistrate who would have the hardihood
to commit a prisoner to jail, on his complaint. But notwithstanding
these discouraging accounts they went on, and reached the Mansion
House soon after sunrise.

Mr. Haredale threw himself from his horse, but he had no need to
knock at the door, for it was already open, and there stood upon the
step a portly old man, with a very red, or rather purple face, who with
an anxious expression of countenance, was remonstrating with some
unseen personage upstairs, while the porter essayed to close the door
by degrees and get rid of him. With the intense impatience and
excitement natural to one in his condition, Mr. Haredale thrust himself forward and was about to speak, when the fat old gentleman
interposed:

"My good sir," said he, "pray let me get an answer. This is the
sixth time I have been here. I was here five times yesterday. My
house is threatened with destruction. It is to be burned down to-
night, and was to have been last night, but they had other business
on their hands. Pray let me get an answer."

"My good sir," returned Mr. Haredale, shaking his head, "my
house is burned to the ground. But Heaven forbid that yours should
be. Get your answer. Be brief, in mercy to me."

"Now, you hear this, my lord?"—said the old gentleman, calling
up the stairs, to where the skirt of a dressing-gown fluttered on the
landing-place. "Here is a gentleman here, whose house was actually
burnt down last night."

"Dear me, dear me," replied a testy voice, "I am very sorry for it,
but what am I to do? I can't build it up again. The chief magistrate
of the city can't go and be a rebuilding of people's houses, my good
sir. Stuff and nonsense!"

"But the chief magistrate of the city can prevent people's houses
from having any need to be rebuilt, if the chief magistrate's a man,
and not a dummy—can't he, my lord?" cried the old gentleman in a
choleric manner.

"You are disrespectable, sir," said the Lord Mayor—"leastways,
disrespectful I mean."

"Disrespectful, my lord!" returned the old gentleman. "I was
respectful five times yesterday. I can't be respectful for ever. Men
can't stand on being respectful when their houses are going to be
burnt over their heads, with them in 'em. What am I to do, my lord?
Am I to have any protection!"

"I told you yesterday, sir," said the Lord Mayor, "that you might have an alderman in your house, if you could get one to come."

"What the devil's the good of an alderman?" returned the choleric old gentleman.

"—To awe the crowd, sir," said the Lord Mayor.

"Oh Lord ha' mercy!" whimpered the old gentleman, as he wiped his forehead in a state of ludicrous distress, "to think of sending an alderman to awe a crowd! Why, my lord, if they were even so many babies, fed on mother's milk, what do you think they'd care for an alderman! Will *you* come?"

"I!" said the Lord Mayor, most emphatically. "Certainly not."

"Then what," returned the old gentleman, "what am I to do? Am I a citizen of England? Am I to have the benefit of the laws? Am I to have any return for the King's taxes?"

"I don't know, I am sure," said the Lord Mayor; "what a pity it is you're a Catholic! Why couldn't you be a Protestant, and then you wouldn't have got yourself into such a mess? I'm sure I don't know what's to be done.—There are great people at the bottom of these riots.—Oh dear me, what a thing it is to be a public character!—You must look in again in the course of the day.—Would a javelin-man do?—Or there's Phillips the constable,—*he's* disengaged,—he's not very old for a man at his time of life, except in his legs, and if you put him up at a window he'd look quite young by candle-light, and might frighten 'em very much—Oh dear!—well!—we'll see about it."

"Stop!" cried Mr. Haredale, pressing the door open as the porter strove to shut it, and speaking rapidly. "My Lord Mayor, I beg you not to go away. I have a man here, who committed a murder eight-and-twenty years ago. Half-a-dozen words from me, on oath, will justify you in committing him to prison for re-examination. I only seek, just now, to have him consigned to a place of safety. The least delay may involve his being rescued by the rioters."

"Oh dear me!" cried the Lord Mayor. "God bless my soul—and body—oh Lor!—well I!—there are great people at the bottom of these riots, you know.—You really mustn't."

"My lord," said Mr. Haredale, "the murdered gentleman was my brother; I succeeded to his inheritance; there were not wanting slanderous tongues at that time, to whisper that the guilt of this most foul and cruel deed was mine—mine, who loved him, as he knows in Heaven, dearly. The time has come, after all these years of gloom and misery, for avenging him, and bringing to light a crime so artful and so devilish that it has no parallel. Every second's delay on your part loosens this man's bloody hands again, and leads to his escape. My lord, I charge you hear me, and despatch this matter on the instant."

"Oh dear me!" cried the chief magistrate; "these an't business hours, you know—I wonder at you—how ungentlemanly it is of you —you mustn't—you really mustn't.—And I suppose *you* are a Catholic too?"

"I am," said Mr. Haredale.

"God bless my soul, I believe people turn Catholics a' purpose to vex and worrit me," cried the Lord Mayor. "I wish you wouldn't come here; they'll be setting the Mansion House afire next, and we shall have you to thank for it. You must lock your prisoner up, sir—give him to a watchman—and—and call again at a proper time. Then we'll see about it!"

Before Mr. Haredale could answer, the sharp closing of a door and drawing of its bolts gave notice that the Lord Mayor had retreated to his bedroom, and that further remonstrance would be unavailing. The two clients retreated likewise, and the porter shut them out into the street.

"That's the way he puts me off," said the old gentleman. "I can get no redress and no help. What are you going to do, sir?"

"To try elsewhere," answered Mr. Haredale, who was by this time on horseback.

"I feel for you, I assure you—and well I may, for we are in a common cause," said the old gentleman. "I may not have a house to offer you to-night; let me tender it while I can. On second thoughts though," he added, putting up a pocket-book he had produced while speaking, "I'll not give you a card, for if it was found upon you, it might get you into trouble. Langdale—that's my name—vintner and distiller—Holborn Hill—you're heartily welcome, if you'll come."

Mr. Haredale bowed, and rode off, close beside the chaise as before; determining to repair to the house of Sir John Fielding, who had the reputation of being a bold and active magistrate, and fully resolved, in case the rioters should come upon them, to do execution on the murderer with his own hands, rather than suffer him to be released.

They arrived at the magistrate's dwelling, however, without molestation (for the mob, as we have seen, were then intent on deeper schemes), and knocked at the door. As it had been pretty generally rumoured that Sir John was proscribed by the rioters, a body of thief-takers had been keeping watch in the house all night. To one of them Mr. Haredale stated his business, which appearing to the man of sufficient moment to warrant his arousing the justice, procured him an immediate audience.

No time was lost in committing the murderer to Newgate; then a new building, recently completed at a vast expense, and considered to be of enormous strength. The warrant being made out, three of the thief-takers bound him afresh (he had been struggling, it seemed, in the chaise, and had loosened his manacles); gagged him lest they should meet with any of the mob, and he should call to them for help; and seated themselves, along with him in the carriage. These men being all well armed, made a formidable escort; but they drew up the blinds again, as though the carriage were empty, and directed Mr. Haredale to ride forward, that he might not attract attention by seeming to belong to it.

The wisdom of this proceeding was sufficiently obvious, for as they hurried through the city they passed among several groups of men, who, if they had not supposed the chaise to be quite empty, would certainly have stopped it. But those within keeping quite close, and the driver tarrying to be asked no questions, they reached the prison without interruption, and, once there, had him out safe, and within its gloomy walls, in a twinkling.

With eager eyes and strained attention, Mr. Haredale saw him chained, and locked and barred up in his cell. Nay, when he had left the jail, and stood in the free street, without, he felt the iron plates upon the doors with his hands, and drew them over the stone wall, to assure himself that it was real; and to exult in its being so strong, and rough, and cold. It was not until he turned his back upon the jail and glanced along the empty streets, so lifeless and quiet in the bright morning, that he felt the weight upon his heart; that he knew he was tortured by anxiety for those he had left at home; and that home itself was but another bead in the long rosary of his regrets.

CHAPTER LXII

THE prisoner, left to himself, sat down upon his bedstead: and resting his elbows on his knees, and his chin upon his hands, remained in that attitude for hours. It would be hard to say, of what nature his reflections were. They had no distinctness, and, saving for some flashes now and then, no reference to his condition or the train of circumstances by which it had been brought. The cracks in the pavement of his cell, the chinks in the wall where stone was joined to stone, the bars in the window, the iron ring upon the floor,—such things as these, subsiding strangely into one another, and awakening an indescribable kind of interest and amusement, engrossed his whole mind; and although at the bottom of his every thought there was an uneasy sense of guilt, and dread of death, he felt no more than that vague consciousness of it, which a sleeper has of pain. It pursues him through his dreams, gnaws at the heart of all his fancied pleasures, robs the banquet of its taste, music of its sweetness, makes happiness itself unhappy, and yet is no bodily sensation, but a phantom without shape, or form, or visible presence; pervading everything, but having no existence; recognisable everywhere, but nowhere seen, or touched, or met with face to face, until the sleep is past, and waking agony returns.

After a long time the door of his cell opened. He looked up; saw the blind man enter; and relapsed into his former position.

Guided by his breathing, the visitor advanced to where he sat; and stopping beside him, and stretching out his hand to assure himself that he was right, remained, for a good space, silent.

"This is bad, Rudge. This is bad," he said at length.

The prisoner shuffled with his feet upon the ground in turning his body from him, but made no other answer.

"How were you taken?" he asked. "And where? You never told me more than half your secret. No matter; I know it now. How was it, and where, eh?" he asked again, coming still nearer to him.

"At Chigwell," said the other.

"At Chigwell! How came you there?"

"Because I went there to avoid the man I stumbled on," he answered. "Because I was chased and driven there, by him and Fate. Because I was urged to go there, by something stronger than my own will. When I found him watching in the house she used to live in, night after night, I knew I never could escape him—never! and when I heard the Bell—"

He shivered; muttered that it was very cold; paced quickly up and down the narrow cell; and sitting down again, fell into his old posture.

"You were saying," said the blind man, after another pause, "that when you heard the Bell—"

"Let it be, will you?" he retorted in a hurried voice. "It hangs there yet."

The blind man turned a wistful and inquisitive face towards him, but he continued to speak, without noticing him.

"I went to Chigwell in search of the mob. I have been so hunted and beset by this man, that I knew my only hope of safety lay in joining them. They had gone on before; I followed them when it left off."

"When what left off?"

"The Bell. They had quitted the place. I hoped that some of them might be still lingering among the ruins, and was searching for them when I heard"—he drew a long breath, and wiped his forehead with his sleeve—"his voice."

"Saying what?"

"No matter what. I don't know. I was then at the foot of the turret, where I did the—"

"Ay," said the blind man, nodding his head with perfect composure, "I understand."

"I climbed the stair, or so much of it as was left; meaning to hide till he had gone. But he heard me; and followed almost as soon as I set foot upon the ashes."

"You might have hidden in the wall, and thrown him down, or stabbed him," said the blind man.

"Might I? Between that man and me, was one who led him on—I saw it, though he did not—and raised above his head a bloody hand. It was in the room above that _he_ and I stood glaring at each other on the night of the murder, and before he fell he raised his hand like that, and fixed his eyes on me. I knew the chase would end there."

"You have a strong fancy," said the blind man, with a smile.

"Strengthen yours with blood, and see what it will come to."

He groaned, and rocked himself, and looking up, for the first time, said, in a low, hollow voice:

"Eight-and-twenty years! Eight-and-twenty years! He has never changed in all that time, never grown older, nor altered in the least degree. He has been before me in the dark night, and the broad sunny day; in the twilight, the moonlight, the sunlight, the light of fire, and lamp, and candle; and in the deepest gloom. Always the same! In company, in solitude, on land, on ship-board; sometimes leaving me alone for months, and sometimes always with me. I have seen him, at sea, come gliding in the dead of night along the bright reflection of the moon in the calm water; and I have seen him, on quays and market-places, with his hand uplifted, towering, the centre of a busy crowd, unconscious of the terrible form that had its silent stand among them. Fancy! Are you real? Am I? Are these iron fetters, riveted on me by the smith's hammer, or are they fancies I can shatter at a blow?"

The blind man listened in silence.

"Fancy! Do I fancy that I killed him? Do I fancy that as I left the chamber where he lay, I saw the face of a man peeping from a dark door, who plainly showed me by his fearful looks that he suspected what I had done? Do I remember that I spoke fairly to him—that I drew nearer—nearer yet—with the hot knife in my sleeve? Do I fancy how *he* died? Did he stagger back into the angle of the wall into which I had hemmed him, and, bleeding inwardly, stand, not fall, a corpse before me? Did I see him, for an instant, as I see you now, erect and on his feet—but dead!"

The blind man, who knew that he had risen, motioned him to sit down again upon his bedstead; but he took no notice of the gesture.

"It was then I thought, for the first time, of fastening the murder upon him. It was then I dressed him in my clothes, and dragged him down the back-stairs to the piece of water. Do I remember listening to the bubbles that came rising up when I had rolled him in? Do I remember wiping the water from my face, and because the body splashed it there, in its descent, feeling as if it *must* be blood?

"Did I go home when I had done? And oh, my God! how long it took to do! Did I stand before my wife, and tell her? Did I see her fall upon the ground; and, when I stooped to raise her, did she thrust me back with a force that cast me off as if I had been a child, staining the hand with which she clasped my wrist? Is *that* fancy?

"Did she go down upon her knees, and call on Heaven to witness that she and her unborn child renounced me from that hour; and did she, in words so solemn that they turned me cold—me, fresh from the horrors my own hands had made—warn me to fly while there was time; for though she would be silent, being my wretched wife, she would not shelter me? Did I go forth that night, abjured of God and man, and anchored deep in hell, to wander at my cable's length about the earth, and surely be drawn down at last?"

"Why did you return?" said the blind man.

"Why is blood red? I could no more help it, than I could live without breath. I struggled against the impulse, but I was drawn back, through every difficult and adverse circumstance, as by a mighty engine. Nothing could stop me. The day and hour were none of my choice. Sleeping and waking, I had been among the old haunts for years—had visited my own grave. Why did I come back? Because this jail was gaping for me, and he stood beckoning at the door."

"You were not known?" said the blind man.

"I was a man who had been twenty-two years dead. No I was not known."

"You should have kept your secret better."

"*My* secret? *Mine*? It was a secret any breath of air could whisper at its will. The stars had it in their twinkling, the water in its flowing, the leaves in their rustling, the seasons in their return. It lurked in stranger's faces, and their voices. Everything had lips on which it always trembled.—*My* secret!"

"It was revealed by your own act at any rate," said the blind man.

"The act was not mine. I did it, but it was not mine. I was forced at times to wander round, and round, and round that spot. If you had chained me up when the fit was on me, I should have broken away, and gone there. As truly as the loadstone draws iron towards it, so he, lying at the bottom of his grave, could draw me near him when he would. Was that fancy? Did I like to go there, or did I strive and wrestle with the power that forced me?"

The blind man shrugged his shoulders, and smiled incredulously. The prisoner again resumed his old attitude, and for a long time both were mute.

"I suppose then," said his visitor, at length breaking silence, "that you are penitent and resigned; that you desire to make peace with everybody (in particular, with your wife who has brought you to this); and that you ask no greater favour than to be carried to Tyburn as soon as possible? That being the case, I had better take my leave. I am not good enough to be company for you."

"Have I not told you," said the other fiercely, "that I have striven and wrestled with the power that brought me here? Has my whole life for eight-and-twenty years, been one perpetual struggle and resistance, and do you think I want to lie down and die? Do all men shrink from death—I most of all!"

"That's better said. That's better spoken, Rudge—but I'll not call you that again—than anything you have said yet," returned the blind man, speaking more familiarly, and laying his hands upon his arm. "Lookye,—I never killed a man myself, for I have never been placed in a position that made it worth my while. Farther, I am not an advocate for killing men, and I don't think I should recommend it or like it—for it's very hazardous—under any circumstances. But as you had the misfortune to get into this trouble before I made your acquaintance, and as you have been my companion, and have been of use to me for a long time now, I overlook that part of the matter, and am only anxious that you shouldn't die unnecessarily. Now, I do not consider that, at present, it is at all necessary."

"What else is left me?" returned the prisoner. "To eat my way through these walls with my teeth!"

"Something easier than that," returned his friend. "Promise me that you will talk no more of these fancies of yours—idle, foolish things, quite beneath a man—and I'll tell you what I mean."

"Tell me," said the other.

"Your worthy lady with the tender conscience; your scrupulous, virtuous, punctilious, but not blindly affectionate wife—"

"What of her?"

"Is now in London."

"A curse upon her, be she where she may!"

"That's natural enough. If she had taken her annuity as usual, you would not have been here, and we should have been better off. But that's apart from the business. She's in London. Scared, as I suppose, and have no doubt, by my representation when I waited upon her, that you were close at hand (which I, of course, urged only as an inducement to compliance, knowing that she was not pining to see you), she left that place, and travelled up to London."

"How do you know?"

"From my friend the noble captain—the illustrious general—the bladder, Mr. Tappertit. I learnt from him the last time I saw him, which was yesterday, that your son who is called Barnaby—not after his father I suppose—"

"Death! does that matter now!"

"—You are impatient," said the blind man, calmly; "it's a good sign, and looks like life—that your son Barnaby had been lured away from her by one of his companions who knew him of old, at Chigwell; and that he is now among the rioters."

"And what is that to me? If father and son be hanged together, what comfort shall I find in that?"

"Stay—stay, my friend," returned the blind man, with a cunning look, "you travel fast to journeys' ends. Suppose I track my lady out, and say thus much: 'You want your son, ma'am—good. I, knowing those who tempt him to remain among them, can restore him to you, ma'am—good. You must pay a price, ma'am, for his restoration—good again. The price is small, and easy to be paid—dear ma'am, that's best of all.'"

"What mockery is this?"

"Very likely, she may reply in those words. 'No mockery at all,' I answer: 'Madam, a person said to be your husband (identity is difficult of proof after the lapse of many years) is in prison, his life in peril—the charge against him, murder. Now, ma'am, your husband has been dead a long, long time. The gentleman never can be confounded with him, if you will have the goodness to say a few words, on oath, as to when he died, and how; and that this person (who I am told resembles him in some degree) is no more he than I am. Such testimony will set the question quite at rest. Pledge yourself to me to give it, ma'am, and I will undertake to keep your son (a fine lad) out of harm's way until you have done this trifling service, when he shall be delivered up to you, safe and sound. On the other hand, if you decline to do so, I fear he will be betrayed, and handed over to the law, which will assuredly sentence him to suffer death. It is, in fact, a choice between his life and death. If you refuse, he swings. If you comply, the timber is not grown, nor the hemp sown, that shall do him any harm.'"

"There is a gleam of hope in this!" cried the prisoner.

"A gleam!" returned his friend, "a noon-blaze; a full and glorious daylight. Hush! I hear the tread of distant feet. Rely on me."

"When shall I hear more?"

"As soon as I do. I shall hope, to-morrow. They are coming to say that our time for talk is over. I hear the jingling of the keys. Not another word of this just now, or they may overhear us."

As he said these words, the lock was turned, and one of the prison turnkeys appearing at the door, announced that it was time for visitors to leave the jail.

"So soon!" said Stagg, meekly. "But it can't be helped. Cheer up, friend. This mistake will soon be set at rest, and then you are a man again! If this charitable gentleman will lead a blind man (who has nothing in return but prayers) to the prison-porch, and set him with his face towards the west, he will do a worthy deed. Thank you, good sir. I thank you very kindly."

So saying, and pausing for an instant at the door to turn his grinning face towards his friend, he departed.

When the officer had seen him to the porch, he returned, and again unlocking and unbarring the door of the cell, set it wide open, informing its inmate that he was at liberty to walk in the adjacent yard, if he thought proper, for an hour.

The prisoner answered with a sullen nod; and being left alone again, sat brooding over what he had heard, and pondering upon the hopes the recent conversation had awakened; gazing abstractedly, the while he did so, on the light without, and watching the shadows thrown by one wall on another, and on the stone-paved ground.

It was a dull, square yard, made cold and gloomy by high walls, and seeming to chill the very sunlight. The stone, so bare, and rough, and obdurate, filled even him with longing thoughts of meadow-land and trees; and with a burning wish to be at liberty. As he looked, he rose, and leaning against the door-post, gazed up at the bright blue sky, smiling even on the dreary home of crime. He seemed, for a moment, to remember lying on his back in some sweet-scented place, and gazing at it through moving branches, long ago.

His attention was suddenly attracted by a clanking sound—he knew what it was, for he had startled himself by making the same noise in walking to the door. Presently a voice began to sing, and he saw the shadow of a figure on the pavement. It stopped—was silent all at once, as though the person for a moment had forgotten where he was, but soon remembered—and so, with the same clanking noise, the shadow disappeared.

He walked out into the court and paced it to and fro; startling the echoes, as he went, with the harsh jangling of his fetters. There was a door near his, which, like his, stood ajar.

He had not taken half-a-dozen turns up and down the yard, when, standing still to observe this door, he heard the clanking sound again. A face looked out of the grated window—he saw it very dimly, for the cell was dark and the bars were heavy—and directly afterwards, a man appeared, and came towards him.

For the sense of loneliness he had, he might have been in jail a year. Made eager by the hope of companionship, he quickened his pace, and hastened to meet the man halfway—

What was this! His son!

They stood face to face, staring at each other. He shrinking and cowed, despite himself; Barnaby struggling with his imperfect memory, and wondering where he had seen that face before. He was not uncertain long, for suddenly he laid hands upon him, and striving to bear him to the ground, cried:

"Ah! I know! You are the robber!"

He said nothing in reply at first, but held down his head, and struggled with him silently. Finding the younger man too strong for him, he raised his face, looking close into his eyes, and said,

"I am your father."

God knows what magic the name had for his ears; but Barnaby released his hold, fell back, and looked at him aghast. Suddenly he sprung towards him, put his arms about his neck, and pressed his head against his cheek.

Yes, yes, he was; he was sure he was. But where had he been so long, and why had he left his mother by herself, or worse than by herself, with her poor foolish boy? And had she really been as happy as they said. And where was she? Was she near there? She was not happy now, and he in jail? Ah, no.

Not a word was said in answer; but Grip croaked loudly, and hopped about them, round and round, as if enclosing them in a magic circle, and invoking all the powers of mischief.

CHAPTER LXIII

DURING the whole of this day, every regiment in or near the metropolis was on duty in one or other part of the town; and the regulars and militia, in obedience to the orders which were sent to every barrack and station within twenty-four hours' journey, began to pour in by all the roads. But the disturbance had attained to such a formidable height, and the rioters had grown, with impunity, to be so audacious, that the sight of this great force, continually augmented by new arrivals, instead of operating as a check, stimulated them to outrages of greater hardihood than any they had yet committed; and helped to kindle a flame in London, the like of which had never been beheld, even in its ancient and rebellious times.

All yesterday, and on this day likewise, the commander-in-chief endeavoured to arouse the magistrates to a sense of their duty, and in particular the Lord Mayor, who was the faintest-hearted and most timid of them all. With this object, large bodies of the soldiery were several times despatched to the Mansion House to await his orders: but as he could, by no threats or persuasions, be induced to give any, and as the men remained in the open street, fruitlessly for any good purpose, and thrivingly for a very bad one; these laudable attempts did harm rather than good. For the crowd, becoming speedily

acquainted with the Lord Mayor's temper, did not fail to take
advantage of it by boasting that even the civil authorities were
opposed to the Papists, and could not find it in their hearts to molest
those who were guilty of no other offence. These vaunts they took
care to make within the hearing of the soldiers; and they, being
naturally loth to quarrel with the people, received their advances
kindly enough: answering, when they were asked if they desired to
fire upon their countrymen, "No, they would be damned if they did;"
and showing much honest simplicity and good nature. The feeling
that the military were No-Popery men, and were ripe for disobeying
orders and joining the mob, soon became very prevalent in consequence. Rumours of their disaffection, and of their leaning
towards the popular cause, spread from mouth to mouth with
astonishing rapidity; and whenever they were drawn up idly in the
streets or squares, there was sure to be a crowd about them, cheering
and shaking hands, and treating them with a great show of confidence and affection.

By this time the crowd was everywhere; all concealment and
disguise were laid aside, and they pervaded the whole town. If any
man among them wanted money, he had but to knock at the door of a
dwelling-house, or walk into a shop, and demand it in the rioters'
name; and his demand was instantly complied with. The peaceable
citizens being afraid to lay hands upon them, singly and alone, it may
be easily supposed that when gathered together in bodies, they were
perfectly secure from interruption. They assembled in the streets,
traversed them at their will and pleasure, and publicly concerted
their plans. Business was quite suspended; the greater part of the
shops were closed; most of the houses displayed a blue flag in token
of their adherence to the popular side; and even the Jews in Houndsditch, Whitechapel, and those quarters, wrote upon their doors or
window-shutters "This House is a True Protestant." The crowd was
the law, and never was the law held in greater dread, or more
implicitly obeyed.

It was about six o'clock in the evening, when a vast mob poured
into Lincoln's Inn Fields by every avenue, and divided—evidently in
pursuance of a previous design—into several parties. It must not be
understood that this arrangement was known to the whole crowd,
but that it was the work of a few leaders; who, mingling with the men
as they came upon the ground, and calling to them to fall into this or
that party, effected it as rapidly as if it had been determined on by a
council of the whole number, and every man had known his place.

It was perfectly notorious to the assemblage that the largest body,
which comprehended about two-thirds of the whole, was designed for
the attack on Newgate. It comprehended all the rioters who had been
conspicuous in any of their former proceedings; all those whom they
recommended as daring hands and fit for the work; all those whose
companions had been taken in the riots; and a great number of
people who were relatives or friends of felons in the jail. This last
class included, not only the most desperate and utterly abandoned

villains in London, but some who were comparatively innocent. There was more than one woman there, disguised in man's attire and bent upon the rescue of a child or brother. There were the two sons of a man who lay under sentence of death, and who was to be executed along with three others, on the next day but one. There was a great party of boys whose fellow-pickpockets were in the prison; and at the skirts of all, a score of miserable women, outcasts from the world seeking to release some other fallen creature as miserable as themselves, or moved by a general sympathy perhaps—God knows—with all who were without hope, and wretched.

Old swords, and pistols without ball or powder; sledge-hammers, knives, axes, saws, and weapons pillaged from the butchers' shops; a forest of iron bars and wooden clubs; long ladders for scaling the walls, each carried on the shoulders of a dozen men; lighted torches; tow smeared with pitch, and tar, and brimstone; staves roughly plucked from fence and paling; and even crutches taken from crippled beggars in the streets; composed their arms. When all was ready, Hugh and Dennis, with Simon Tappertit between them, led the way. Roaring and chafing like an angry sea, the crowd pressed after them.

Instead of going straight down Holborn to the jail, as all expected, their leaders took the way to Clerkenwell, and pouring down a quiet street, halted before a locksmith's house—the Golden Key.

"Beat at the door," cried Hugh to the men about him. "We want one of his craft to-night. Beat it in, if no one answers."

The shop was shut. Both door and shutters were of a strong and sturdy kind, and they knocked without effect. But the impatient crowd raising a cry of "Set fire to the house!" and torches being passed to the front, an upper window was thrown open, and the stout old locksmith stood before them.

"What now, you villains!" he demanded. "Where is my daughter?"

"Ask no questions of us, old man," retorted Hugh, waving his comrades to be silent, "but come down, and bring the tools of your trade. We want you."

"Want me!" cried the locksmith, glancing at the regimental dress he wore. "Ay, and if some that I could name possessed the hearts of mice, ye should have had me long ago. Mark me, my lad—and you about him do the same. There are a score among ye whom I see now and know, who are dead men from this hour. Begone! and rob an undertaker's while you can! You'll want some coffins before long."

"Will you come down?" cried Hugh.

"Will you give me my daughter, ruffian?" cried the locksmith.

"I know nothing of her," Hugh rejoined. "Burn the door!"

"Stop!" cried the locksmith, in a voice that made them falter—presenting, as he spoke, a gun. "Let an old man do that. You can spare him better."

The young fellow who held the light, and who was stooping down before the door, rose hastily at these words, and fell back. The locksmith ran his eye along the upturned faces, and kept the weapon levelled at the threshold of his house. It had no other rest than his shoulder, but was as steady as the house itself.

"Let the man who does it, take heed to his prayers," he said firmly; "I warn him."

Snatching a torch from one who stood near him, Hugh was stepping forward with an oath, when he was arrested by a shrill and piercing shriek, and, looking upward, saw a fluttering garment on the house-top.

There was another shriek, and another, and then a shrill voice cried, "Is Simmun below!" At the same moment a lean neck was stretched over the parapet, and Miss Miggs, indistinctly seen in the gathering gloom of evening, screeched in a frenzied manner, "Oh! dear gentlemen, let me hear Simmuns's answer from his own lips. Speak to me, Simmun. Speak to me!"

Mr. Tappertit, who was not at all flattered by this compliment, looked up, and bidding her hold her peace, ordered her to come down and open the door, for they wanted her master, and would take no denial.

"Oh good gentlemen!" cried Miss Miggs. "Oh my own precious, precious Simmun—"

"Hold your nonsense, will you!" retorted Mr. Tappertit; "and come down and open the door.—G. Varden, drop that gun, or it will be worse for you."

"Don't mind his gun," screamed Miss Miggs. "Simmun and gentlemen, I poured a mug of table-beer right down the barrel."

The crowd gave a loud shout, which was followed by a roar of laughter.

"It wouldn't go off, not if you was to load it up to the muzzle," screamed Miggs. "Simmun and gentlemen, I'm locked up in the front attic, through the little door on the right hand when you think you've got to the very top of the stairs—and up the flight of corner steps, being careful not to knock your heads against the rafters, and not to tread on one side in case you should fall into the two-pair bedroom through the lath and plaster, which do not bear, but the contrairy. Simmun and gentlemen, I've been locked up here for safety, but my endeavours has always been, and always will be, to be on the right side—the blessed side—and to prenounce the Pope of Babylon, and all her inward and her outward workings, which is Pagin. My sentiments is of little consequence, I know," cried Miggs, with additional shrillness, "for my positions is but a servant, and as sich, of humilities, still I gives expressions to my feelings, and places my reliances on them which entertains my own opinions!"

Without taking much notice of these outpourings of Miss Miggs after she had made her first announcement in relation to the gun, the crowd raised a ladder against the window where the locksmith stood, and notwithstanding that he closed, and fastened, and defended it manfully, soon forced an entrance by shivering the glass and breaking in the frames. After dealing a few stout blows about him, he found

himself defenceless, in the midst of a furious crowd, which overflowed
the room and softened off in a confused heap of faces at the door and
window.

They were very wrathful with him (for he had wounded two men),
and even called out to those in front, to bring him forth and hang
him on a lamp-post. But Gabriel was quite undaunted, and looked
from Hugh and Dennis, who held him by either arm, to Simon
Tappertit, who confronted him.

"You have robbed me of my daughter," said the locksmith, "who
is far dearer to me than my life; and you may take my life, if you
will. I bless God that I have been enabled to keep my wife free of
this scene; and that He has made me a man who will not ask mercy
at such hands as yours."

"And a wery game old gentleman you are," said Mr. Dennis,
approvingly; "and you express yourself like a man. What's the odds,
brother, whether it's a lamp-post to-night, or a feather-bed ten year
to come, eh?"

The locksmith glanced at him disdainfully, but returned no other
answer.

"For my part," said the hangman, who particularly favoured the
lamp-post suggestion, "I honour your principles. They're mine
exactly. In such sentiments as them," and here he emphasised his discourse with an oath, "I'm ready to meet you or any man half-way.—
Have you got a bit of cord anywheres handy? Don't put yourself out
of the way, if you haven't. A handkecher will do."

"Don't be a fool, master," whispered Hugh, seizing Varden roughly
by the shoulder; "but do as you're bid. You'll soon hear what you're
wanted for. Do it!"

"I'll do nothing at your request, or that of any scoundrel here,"
returned the locksmith. "If you want any service from me, you may
spare yourselves the pains of telling me what it is. I tell you, beforehand, I'll do nothing for you."

Mr. Dennis was so affected by this constancy on the part of the
staunch old man, that he protested—almost with tears in his eyes—
that to baulk his inclinations would be an act of cruelty and hard
dealing to which he, for one, never could reconcile his conscience.
The gentleman, he said, had avowed in so many words that he was
ready for working off; such being the case, he considered it their duty
as a civilised and enlightened crowd, to work him off. It was not often,
he observed, that they had it in their power to accommodate themselves to the wishes of those from whom they had the misfortune to
differ. Having now found an individual who expressed a desire which
they could reasonably indulge (and for himself he was free to confess
that in his opinion that desire did honour to his feelings), he hoped
they would decide to accede to his proposition before going any
further. It was an experiment which, skilfully and dexterously performed, would be over in five minutes, with great comfort and satisfaction to all parties; and though it did not become him (Mr. Dennis)
to speak well of himself, he trusted he might be allowed to say that he

had a practical knowledge of the subject, and, being naturally of an obliging and friendly disposition, would work the gentleman off with a deal of pleasure.

These remarks, which were addressed in the midst of a frightful din and turmoil to those immediately about him, were received with great favour; not so much, perhaps, because of the hangman's eloquence, as on account of the locksmith's obstinacy. Gabriel was in imminent peril, and he knew it; but he preserved a steady silence; and would have done so, if they had been debating whether they should roast him at a slow fire.

As the hangman spoke, there was some stir and confusion on the ladder; and directly he was silent—so immediately upon his holding his peace, that the crowd below had no time to learn what he had been saying, or to shout in response—some one at the window cried:

"He has a grey head. He is an old man. Don't hurt him!"

The locksmith turned, with a start, towards the place from which the words had come, and looked hurriedly at the people who were hanging on the ladder and clinging to each other.

"Pay no respect to my grey hair, young man," he said, answering the voice and not any one he saw. "I don't ask it. My heart is green enough to scorn and despise every man among you, band of robbers that you are!"

This incautious speech by no means tended to appease the ferocity of the crowd. They cried again to have him brought out; and it would have gone hard with the honest locksmith, but that Hugh reminded them, in answer, that they wanted his services, and must have them.

"So, tell him what we want," he said to Simon Tappertit, "and quickly. And open your ears, master, if you would ever use them after to-night."

Gabriel folded his arms, which were now at liberty, and eyed his old 'prentice in silence.

"Lookye, Varden," said Sim, "we're bound for Newgate."

"I know you are," returned the locksmith. "You never said a truer word than that."

"To burn it down, I mean," said Simon, "and force the gates, and set the prisoners at liberty. You helped to make the lock of the great door."

"I did," said the locksmith. "You owe me no thanks for that—as you'll find before long."

"Maybe," returned his journeyman, "but you must show us how to force it."

"Must I!"

"Yes; for you know, and I don't. You must come along with us, and pick it with your own hands."

"When I do," said the locksmith quietly, "my hands shall drop off at the wrists, and you shall wear them, Simon Tappertit, on your shoulders for epaulettes."

"We'll see that," cried Hugh, interposing, as the indignation of the crowd again burst forth. "You fill a basket with the tools he'll want, while I bring him downstairs. Open the doors below, some of you. and light the great captain, others! Is there no business afoot, my lads, that you can do nothing but stand and grumble?"

They looked at one another, and quickly dispersing, swarmed over the house, plundering and breaking, according to their custom, and carrying off such articles of value as happened to please their fancy. They had no great length of time for these proceedings, for the basket of tools was soon prepared and slung over a man's shoulders. The preparations being now completed, and everything ready for the attack, those who were pillaging and destroying in the other rooms were called down to the workshop. They were about to issue forth, when the man who had been last up-stairs, stepped forward, and asked if the young woman in the garret (who was making a terrible noise, he said, and kept on screaming without the least cessation) was to be released?

For his own part, Simon Tappertit would certainly have replied in the negative, but the mass of his companions, mindful of the good service she had done in the matter of the gun, being of a different opinion, he had nothing for it but to answer, Yes. The man, accordingly, went back again to the rescue, and presently returned with Miss Miggs, limp and doubled up, and very damp from much weeping.

As the young lady had given no tokens of consciousness on their way down-stairs, the bearer reported her either dead or dying; and being at some loss what to do with her, was looking round for a convenient bench or heap of ashes on which to place her senseless form, when she suddenly came upon her feet by some mysterious means, thrust back her hair, stared wildly at Mr. Tappertit, cried "My Simmuns's life is not a wictim!" and dropped into his arms with such promptitude that he staggered and reeled some paces back, beneath his lovely burden.

"Oh bother!" said Mr. Tappertit. "Here. Catch hold of her, somebody. Lock her up again; she never ought to have been let out."

"My Simmun!" cried Miss Miggs, in tears, and faintly. "My for ever, ever blessed Simmun!"

"Hold up, will you?" said Mr. Tappertit, in a very unresponsive tone. "I'll let you fall if you don't. What are you sliding your feet off the ground for?"

"My angel Simmuns!" murmured Miggs—"he promised—"

"Promised! Well, and I'll keep my promise," answered Simon, testily. "I mean to provide for you, don't I? Stand up!"

"Where am I to go? What is to become of me after my actions of this night!" cried Miggs. "What resting-places now remains but in the silent tombses!"

"I wish you was in the silent tombses, I do," cried Mr. Tappertit, "and boxed up tight, in a good strong one. Here," he cried to one of the bystanders, in whose ear he whispered for a moment: "Take her off, will you? You understand where?"

The fellow nodded; and taking her in his arms, notwithstanding her broken protestations, and her struggles (which latter species of opposition, involving scratches, was much more difficult of resistance), carried her away. They who were in the house poured out into the street; the locksmith was taken to the head of the crowd, and required to walk between his two conductors; the whole body was put in rapid motion; and without any shouting or noise they bore down straight on Newgate, and halted in a dense mass before the prison-gate.

CHAPTER LXIV

BREAKING the silence they had hitherto preserved, they raised a great cry as soon as they were ranged before the jail, and demanded to speak to the governor. This visit was not wholly unexpected, for his house, which fronted the street, was strongly barricaded, the wicket-gate of the prison was closed up, and at no loophole or grating was any person to be seen. Before they had repeated their summons many times, a man appeared upon the roof of the governor's house, and asked what it was they wanted.

Some said one thing, some another, and some only groaned and hissed. It being now nearly dark, and the house high, many persons in the throng were not aware that any had come to answer them, and continued their clamour until the intelligence was gradually diffused through the whole concourse. Ten minutes or more elapsed before any one voice could be heard with tolerable distinctness; during which interval the figure remained perched alone, against the summer-evening sky, looking down into the troubled street.

"Are you," said Hugh at length, "Mr. Akerman, the head jailer here?"

"Of course he is, brother," whispered Dennis. But Hugh, without minding him, took his answer from the man himself.

"Yes," he said. "I am."

"You have got some friends of ours in your custody, master."

"I have a good many people in my custody." He glanced downward, as he spoke, into the jail: and the feeling that he could see into the different yards, and that he overlooked everything which was hidden from their view by the rugged walls, so lashed and goaded the mob, that they howled like wolves.

"Deliver up our friends," said Hugh, "and you may keep the rest."

"It's my duty to keep them all. I shall do my duty."

"If you don't throw the doors open, we shall break 'em down," said Hugh; "for we will have the rioters out."

"All I can do, good people," Akerman replied, "is to exhort you to disperse; and to remind you that the consequences of any disturbances in this place, will be very severe, and bitterly repented by most of you when it is too late."

He made as though he would retire when he had said these words, but he was checked by the voice of the locksmith.

"Mr. Akerman," cried Gabriel, "Mr. Akerman."

"I will hear no more from any of you," replied the governor, turning towards the speaker, and waving his hand.

"But I am not one of them," said Gabriel. "I am an honest man, Mr. Akerman; a respectable tradesman—Gabriel Varden, the locksmith. You know me?"

"You among the crowd!" cried the governor in an altered voice.

"Brought here by force—brought here to pick the lock of the great door for them," rejoined the locksmith. "Bear witness for me, Mr. Akerman, that I refuse to do it; and that I will not do it, come what may of my refusal. If any violence is done to me, please to remember this."

"Is there no way of helping you?" said the governor.

"None, Mr. Akerman. You'll do your duty, and I'll do mine. Once again, you robbers and cut-throats," said the locksmith, turning round upon them, "I refuse. Ah! Howl till you're hoarse. I refuse."

"Stay—stay!" said the jailer, hastily. "Mr. Varden, I know you for a worthy man, and one who would do no unlawful act except upon compulsion—"

"Upon compulsion, sir," interposed the locksmith, who felt that the tone in which this was said, conveyed the speaker's impression that he had ample excuse for yielding to the furious multitude who beset and hemmed him in, on every side, and among whom he stood, an old man, quite alone; "upon compulsion, sir, I'll do nothing."

"Where is that man," said the keeper, anxiously, "who spoke to me just now?"

"Here!" Hugh replied.

"Do you know what the guilt of murder is, and that by keeping that honest tradesman at your side you endanger his life!"

"We know it very well," he answered, "for what else did we bring him here? Let's have our friends, master, and you shall have your friend. Is that fair, lads?"

The mob replied to him with a loud Hurrah!

"You see how it is, sir?" cried Varden. "Keep 'em out, in King George's name. Remember what I have said. Good night!"

There was no more parley. A shower of stones and other missiles compelled the keeper of the jail to retire; and the mob, pressing on, and swarming round the walls, forced Gabriel Varden close up to the door.

In vain the basket of tools was laid upon the ground before him, and he was urged in turn by promises, by blows, by offers of reward, and threats of instant death, to do the office for which they had brought him there. "No," cried the sturdy locksmith, "I will not!"

He had never loved his life so well as then, but nothing could move him. The savage faces that glared upon him, look where he would; the cries of those who thirsted, like wild animals, for his blood; the sight of men pressing forward, and trampling down their fellows, as they strove to reach him, and struck at him above the heads of other men, with axes and with iron bars; all failed to daunt him. He looked from man to man, and face to face, and still, with quickened breath and lessening colour, cried firmly, "I will not!"

Dennis dealt him a blow upon the face which felled him to the ground. He sprung up again like a man in the prime of life, and with blood upon his forehead, caught him by the throat.

"You cowardly dog!" he said: "Give me my daughter. Give me my daughter."

They struggled together. Some cried "Kill him," and some (but they were not near enough) strove to trample him to death. Tug as he would at the old man's wrists, the hangman could not force him to unclench his hands.

"Is this all the return you make me, you ungrateful monster?" he articulated with great difficulty, and with many oaths.

"Give me my daughter!" cried the locksmith, who was now as fierce as those who gathered round him: "Give me my daughter!"

He was down again, and up, and down once more, and buffeting with a score of them, who bandied him from hand to hand, when one tall fellow, fresh from a slaughter-house, whose dress and great thigh-boots smoked hot with grease and blood, raised a pole-axe, and swearing a horrible oath, aimed it at the old man's uncovered head. At that instant, and in the very act, he fell himself, as if struck by lightning, and over his body a one-armed man came darting to the locksmith's side. Another man was with him, and both caught the locksmith roughly in their grasp.

"Leave him to us," they cried to Hugh—struggling, as they spoke, to force a passage backward through the crowd. "Leave him to us. Why do you waste your whole strength on such as he, when a couple of men can finish him in as many minutes! You lose time. Remember the prisoners! remember Barnaby!"

The cry ran through the mob. Hammers began to rattle on the walls; and every man strove to reach the prison, and be among the foremost rank. Fighting their way through the press and struggle, as desperately as if they were in the midst of enemies rather than their own friends, the two men retreated with the locksmith between them, and dragged him through the very heart of the concourse.

And now the strokes began to fall like hail upon the gate, and on the strong building; for those who could not reach the door, spent their fierce rage on anything—even on the great blocks of stone, which shivered their weapons into fragments, and made their hands and arms to tingle as if the walls were active in their stout resistance, and dealt them back their blows. The clash of iron ringing upon iron, mingled with the deafening tumult and sounded high above it, as the great sledge-hammers rattled on the nailed and plated door: the sparks flew off in showers; men worked in gangs, and at short intervals relieved each other, that all their strength might be devoted to the work; but there stood the portal still, as grim and dark and strong as ever, and, saving for the dints upon its battered surface, quite unchanged.

While some brought all their energies to bear upon this toilsome task; and some, rearing ladders against the prison, tried to clamber to the summit of the walls they were too short to scale; and some again engaged a body of police a hundred strong, and beat them back and trod them under foot for force of numbers; others besieged the house on which the jailers had appeared, and driving in the door, brought out his furniture, and piled it up against the prison-gate, to make a bonfire which should burn it down. As soon as this device was understood, all those who had laboured hitherto, cast down their tools and helped to swell the heap; which reached half-way across the street, and was so high, that those who threw more fuel on the top, got up by ladders. When all the keeper's goods were flung upon this costly pile, to the last fragment, they smeared it with the pitch, and tar, and rosin they had brought, and sprinkled it with turpentine. To all the woodwork round the prison-doors they did the like, leaving not a joist or beam untouched. This infernal christening performed, they fired the pile with lighted matches and with blazing tow, and then stood by, awaiting the result.

The furniture being very dry, and rendered more combustible by wax and oil, besides the arts they had used, took fire at once. The flames roared high and fiercely, blackening the prison-wall, and twining up its lofty front like burning serpents. At first they crowded round the blaze, and vented their exultation only in their looks: but when it grew hotter and fiercer—when it crackled, leaped, and roared like a great furnace—when it shone upon the opposite houses, and lighted up not only the pale and wondering faces at the windows, but the inmost corners of each habitation—when through the deep red heat and glow, the fire was seen sporting and toying with the door, now clinging to its obdurate surface, now gliding off with fierce inconstancy and soaring high into the sky, anon returning to fold it in its burning grasp and lure it to its ruin—when it shone and gleamed so brightly that the church clock of St. Sepulchre's so often pointing to the hour of death, was legible in broad day, and the vane upon its steeple-top glittered in the unwonted light like something richly jewelled—when blackened stone and sombre brick grew ruddy in the deep reflection, and windows shone like burnished gold, dotting the longest distance in the fiery vista with their specks of brightness—when wall and tower, and roof and chimney-stack, seemed drunk, and in the flickering glare appeared to reel and stagger—when scores of objects, never seen before, burst out upon the view, and things the most familiar put on some new aspect—then the mob began to join the whirl, and with loud yells, and shouts, and clamour, such as happily is seldom heard, bestirred themselves to feed the fire, and keep it at its height.

Although the heat was so intense that the paint on the houses over against the prison, parched and crackled up, and swelling into boils, as it were from excess of torture, broke and crumbled away; although the glass fell from the window-sashes, and the lead and iron on the roofs blistered the incautious hand that touched them, and the sparrows in the eaves took wing, and rendered giddy by the smoke, fell fluttering down upon the blazing pile; still the fire was tended unceasingly by busy hands, and round it, men were going always.

They never slackened in their zeal, or kept aloof, but pressed upon the flames so hard, that those in front had much ado to save themselves from being thrust in; if one man swooned or dropped, a dozen struggled for his place, and that although they knew the pain, and thirst, and pressure to be unendurable. Those who fell down in fainting-fits, and were not crushed or burnt, were carried to an inn-yard close at hand, and dashed with water from a pump; of which buckets full were passed from man to man among the crowd; but such was the strong desire of all to drink, and such the fighting to be first, that, for the most part, the whole contents were spilled upon the ground, without the lips of one man being moistened.

Meanwhile, and in the midst of all the roar and outcry, those who were nearest to the pile, heaped up again the burning fragments that came toppling down, and raked the fire about the door, which, although a sheet of flame, was still a door fast locked and barred, and kept them out. Great pieces of blazing wood were passed, besides, above the people's heads to such as stood about the ladders, and some of these, climbing up to the topmost stave, and holding on with one hand by the prison wall, exerted all their skill and force to cast these fire-brands on the roof, or down into the yards within. In many instances their efforts were successful; which occasioned a new and appalling addition to the horrors of the scene: for the prisoners within, seeing from between their bars that the fire caught in many places and thrived fiercely, and being all locked up in strong cells for the night, began to know that they were in danger of being burnt alive. This terrible fear, spreading from cell to cell, and from yard to yard, vented itself is such dismal cries and wailings, and in such dreadful shrieks for help, that the whole jail resounded with the noise; which was loudly heard even above the shouting of the mob and roaring of the flames, and was so full of agony and despair, that it made the boldest tremble.

It was remarkable that these cries began in that quarter of the jail which fronted Newgate-street, where it was well known, the men who were to suffer death on Thursday were confined. And not only were these four who had so short a time to live, the first to whom the dread of being burnt occurred, but they were, throughout, the most important of all: for they could be plainly heard, notwithstanding the great thickness of the walls, crying that the wind set that way, and that the flames would shortly reach them; and calling to the officers of the jail to come and quench the fire from a cistern which was in their yard, and full of water. Judging from what the crowd outside the walls could hear from time to time, these four doomed wretches never ceased to call for help; and that with as much distraction, and in as great a frenzy of attachment to existence, as though each had an honoured, happy life before him, instead of eight-and-forty hours of miserable imprisonment, and then a violent and shameful death.

But the anguish and suffering of the two sons of one of these men, when they heard, or fancied that they heard, their father's voice, is past description. After wringing their hands and rushing to and fro as if they were stark mad, one mounted on the shoulders of his brother, and tried to clamber up the face of the high wall, guarded at the top with spikes and points of iron. And when he fell among the crowd, he was not deterred by his bruises, but mounted up again, and fell again, and, when he found the feat impossible, began to beat the stones and tear them with his hands, as if he could that way make a breach in the strong building, and force a passage in. At last, they cleft their way among the mob about the door, though many men, a dozen times their match, had tried in vain to do so, and were seen, in—yes, in—the fire, striving to prize it down, with crowbars.

Nor were they alone affected by the outcry from within the prison. The women who were looking on, shrieked loudly, beat their hands together, stopped their ears; and many fainted: the men who were not near the walls and active in the siege, rather than do nothing, tore up the pavement of the street, and did so with a haste and fury they could not have surpassed if that had been the jail, and they were near their object. Not one living creature in the throng was for an instant still. The whole great mass was mad.

A shout! Another! Another yet, though few knew why, or what it meant. But those around the gate had seen it slowly yield, and drop from its topmost hinge. It hung on that side by but one, but it was upright still, because of the bar, and its having sunk, of its own weight, into the heap of ashes at its foot. There was now a gap at the top of the doorway, through which could be descried a gloomy passage, cavernous and dark. Pile up the fire!

It burnt fiercely. The door was red-hot, and the gap wider. They vainly tried to shield their faces with their hands, and standing as if in readiness for a spring, watched the place. Dark figures, some crawling on their hands and knees, some carried in the arms of others, were seen to pass along the roof. It was plain the jail could hold out no longer. The keeper, and his officers, and their wives and children, were escaping. Pile up the fire!

The door sank down again: it settled deeper in the cinders— tottered—yielded—was down!

As they shouted again, they fell back, for a moment, and left a clear space about the fire that lay between them and the jail entry. Hugh leapt upon the blazing heap, and scattering a train of sparks into the air, and making the dark lobby glitter with those that hung upon his dress, dashed into the jail.

The hangman followed. And then so many rushed upon their track, that the fire got trodden down and thinly strewn about the street; but there was no need of it now, for, inside and out, the prison was in flames.

CHAPTER LXV

DURING the whole course of the terrible scene which was now at its height, one man in the jail suffered a degree of fear and mental torment which had no parallel in the endurance, even of those who lay under sentence of death.

When the rioters first assembled before the building, the murderer was roused from sleep—if such slumbers as his may have that blessed name—by the roar of voices, and the struggling of a great crowd. He started up as these sounds met his ear, and, sitting on his bedstead, listened.

After a short interval of silence the noise burst out again. Still listening attentively, he made out, in course of time, that the jail was besieged by a furious multitude. His guilty conscience instantly arrayed these men against himself, and brought the fear upon him that he would be singled out, and torn to pieces.

Once impressed with the terror of this conceit, everything tended to confirm and strengthen it. His double crime, the circumstances under which it had been committed, the length of time that had elapsed, and its discovery in spite of all, made him, as it were, the visible object of the Almighty's wrath. In all the crime and vice and moral gloom of the great pest-house of the capital, he stood alone, marked and singled out by his great guilt, a Lucifer among the devils. The other prisoners were a host, hiding and sheltering each other—a crowd like that without the walls. He was one man against the whole united concourse; a single, solitary, lonely man, from whom the very captives in the jail fell off and shrunk appalled.

It might be that the intelligence of his capture having been bruited abroad, they had come there purposely to drag him out and kill him in the street; or it might be that they were the rioters, and, in pursuance of an old design, had come to sack the prison. But in either case he had no belief or hope that they would spare him. Every shout they raised, and every sound they made, was a blow upon his heart. As the attack went on, he grew more wild and frantic in his terror: tried to pull away the bars that guarded the chimney and prevented him from climbing up: called loudly on the turnkeys to cluster round the cell and save him from the fury of the rabble; or put him in some dungeon underground, no matter of what depth, how dark it was, or loathsome, or beset with rats and creeping things, so that it hid him and was hard to find.

But no one came, or answered him. Fearful, even while he cried to them, of attracting attention, he was silent. By and bye, he saw, as he looked from his grated window, a strange glimmering on the stone walls and pavements of the yard. It was feeble at first, and came and went, as though some officers with torches were passing to and fro upon the roof of the prison. Soon it reddened, and lighted brands came whirling down, spattering the ground with fire, and burning sullenly in corners. One rolled beneath a wooden bench, and set it in a blaze; another caught a water-spout, and so went climbing up the wall, leaving a long straight track of fire behind it. After a time, a slow thick shower of burning fragments, from some upper portion of the prison which was blazing nigh, began to fall before his door. Remembering that it opened outwards, he knew that every spark which fell upon the heap, and in the act lost its bright life, and died an ugly speck of dust and rubbish, helped to entomb him in a living grave. Still, though the jail resounded with shrieks and cries for help, —though the fire bounded up as if each separate flame had had a tiger's life, and roared as though, in every one, there were a hungry voice—though the heat began to grow intense, and the air suffocating, and the clamour without increased, and the danger of his situation even from one merciless element was every moment more extreme,—still he was afraid to raise his voice again, lest the crowd should break in, and should, of their own ears or from the information given them by the other prisoners, get the clue to his place of confinement. Thus fearful alike of those within the prison and of those without; of noise and silence; light and darkness; of being released, and being left there to die; he was so tortured and tormented, that nothing man has ever done to man in the horrible caprice of power and cruelty, exceeds his self-inflicted punishment.

Now, now, the door was down. Now they came rushing through the jail, calling to each other in the vaulted passages; clashing the iron gates dividing yard from yard; beating at the doors of cells and wards; wrenching off bolts and locks and bars; tearing down the doorposts to get men out; endeavouring to drag them by main force through gaps and windows where a child could scarcely pass; whooping and yelling without a moment's rest; and running through the heat and flames as if they were cased in metal. By their legs, their arms, the hair upon their heads, they dragged the prisoners out. Some threw themselves upon their captives as they got towards the door, and tried to file away their irons; some danced about them with a frenzied joy, and rent their clothes, and were ready, as it seemed, to tear them limb from limb. Now a party of a dozen men came darting through the yard into which the murderer cast fearful glances from his darkened window; dragging a prisoner along the ground whose dress they had nearly torn from his body in their mad eagerness to set him free, and who was bleeding and senseless in their hands. Now a score of prisoners ran to and fro, who had lost themselves in the intricacies of the prison, and were so bewildered with the noise and glare that they knew not where to turn or what to do, and still cried out for help, as loudly as before. Anon some famished wretch whose theft had been a loaf of bread, or scrap of butcher's meat, came skulking past, barefooted—going slowly away because that jail, his house, was burning; not because he had any other, or had friends to meet, or old haunts to revisit, or any liberty to gain but liberty to starve and die. And then a knot of highwaymen went trooping by, conducted by the friends they had among the crowd, who muffled their fetters as they went along, with handkerchiefs and bands of hay, and wrapped them in coats and cloaks, and gave them drink from bottles, and held it to their lips, because of their handcuffs which there was no time to remove. All this, and Heaven knows how much more, was done amidst a noise, a hurry, and distraction, like nothing that we know of, even in our dreams; which seemed for ever on the rise, and never to decrease for the space of a single instant.

He was still looking down from his window upon these things, when a band of men with torches, ladders, axes, and many kinds of weapons, poured into the yard, and hammering at his door, inquired if there were any prisoner within. He left the window when he saw them coming, and drew back into the remotest corner of the cell; but although he returned them no answer, they had a fancy that some one was inside, for they presently set ladders against it, and began to tear away the bars at the casement; not only that, indeed, but with pickaxes to hew down the very stones in the wall.

As soon as they had made a breach at the window, large enough for the admission of a man's head, one of them thrust in a torch and looked all round the room. He followed this man's gaze until it rested on himself, and heard him demand why he had not answered, but made him no reply.

In the general surprise and wonder, they were used to this; without saying anything more, they enlarged the breach until it was large enough to admit the body of a man, and then came dropping down upon the floor, one after another, until the cell was full. They caught him up among them, handed him to the window, and those who stood upon the ladders passed him down upon the pavement of the yard. Then the rest came out, one after another, and, bidding him fly, and lose no time, or the way would be choked up, hurried away to rescue others.

It seemed not a minute's work from first to last. He staggered to his feet, incredulous of what had happened, when the yard was filled again, and a crowd rushed on, hurrying Barnaby among them. In another minute—not so much: another minute! the same instant, with no lapse or interval between!—he and his son were being passed from hand to hand, through the dense crowd in the street, and were glancing backward at a burning pile which some one said was Newgate.

From the moment of their first entrance into the prison, the crowd dispersed themselves about it, and swarmed into every chink and crevice, as if they had a perfect acquaintance with its innermost parts and bore in their minds an exact plan of the whole. For this immediate knowledge of the place, they were, no doubt, in a great degree, indebted to the hangman, who stood in the lobby, directing some to go this way, some that, and some the other; and who materially assisted in bringing about the wonderful rapidity with which the release of the prisoners was effected.

But this functionary of the law reserved one important piece of intelligence, and kept it snugly to himself. When he had issued his instructions relative to every other part of the building, and the mob were dispersed from end to end, and busy at their work, he took a bundle of keys from a kind of cupboard in the wall, and going by a kind of passage near the chapel (it joined the governor's house, and was then on fire), betook himself to the condemned cells, which were a series of small, strong, dismal rooms, opening on a low gallery, guarded, at the end at which he entered, by a strong iron wicket, and at its opposite extremity by two doors and a thick gate. Having double locked the wicket, and assured himself that the other entrances were well secured, he sat down on a bench in the gallery, and sucked the head of his stick with the utmost complacency, tranquillity, and contentment.

It would have been strange enough, a man's enjoying himself in this quiet manner, while the prison was burning, and such a tumult was cleaving the air, though he had been outside the walls. But here, in the very heart of the building, and moreover with the prayers and cries of the four men under sentence sounding in his ears, and their hands, stretched out through the gratings in their cell-doors, clasped in frantic entreaty before his very eyes, it was particularly remarkable. Indeed, Mr. Dennis appeared to think it an uncommon circumstance, and to banter himself upon it; for he thrust his hat on one side as some men do when they are in a waggish humour, sucked the head of his stick with a higher relish, and smiled as though he would say, "Dennis, you're a rum dog; you're a queer fellow; you're capital company, Dennis, and quite a character!"

He sat in this way for some minutes, while the four men in the cells, certain that somebody had entered the gallery, but could not see who, gave vent to such piteous entreaties as wretches in their miserable condition may be supposed to have been inspired with: urging, whoever it was, to set them at liberty, for the love of Heaven; and protesting, with great fervour, and truly enough, perhaps, for the time, that if they escaped, they would amend their ways, and would never, never, never again do wrong before God or man, but would lead penitent and sober lives, and sorrowfully repent the crimes they had committed. The terrible energy with which they spoke, would have moved any person, no matter how good or just (if any good or just person could have strayed into that sad place that night), to have set them at liberty; and, while he would have left any other punishment to its free course, to have saved them from this last dreadful and repulsive penalty; which never turned a man inclined to evil, and has hardened thousands who were half inclined to good.

Mr. Dennis, who had been bred and matured in the good old school, and had administered the good old laws on the good old plan, always once and sometimes twice every six weeks, for a long time, bore these appeals with a deal of philosophy. Being at last, however, rather disturbed in his pleasant reflection by their repetition, he rapped at one of the doors with his stick, and cried:

"Hold your noise there, will you?"

At this they all cried together that they were to be hanged on the next day but one; and again implored his aid.

"Aid! For what!" said Mr. Dennis, playfully rapping the knuckles of the hand nearest him.

"To save us!" they cried.

"Oh, certainly," said Mr. Dennis, winking at the wall in the absence of any friend with whom he could humour the joke. "And so you're to be worked off, are you, brothers?"

"Unless we are released to-night," one of them cried, "we are dead men!"

"I tell you what it is," said the hangman, gravely; "I'm afraid, my friend, that you're not in that 'ere state of mind that's suitable to your condition, then; you're not a-going to be released: don't think it—Will you leave off that 'ere indecent row? I wonder you an't ashamed of yourselves, I do."

He followed up this reproof by rapping every set of knuckles one after the other, and having done so, resumed his seat again with a cheerful countenance.

"You've had law," he said, crossing his legs and elevating his eyebrows: "laws have been made a' purpose for you; a wery handsome prison's been made a' purpose for you; a parson's kept a' purpose for you; a constitootional officer's appointed a' purpose for you; carts is maintained a' purpose for you—and yet you're not contented!—*Will* you hold that noise, you sir in the furthest?"

A groan was the only answer.

"So well as I can make out," said Mr. Dennis, in a tone of mingled badinage and remonstrance, "there's not a man among you. I begin to think I'm on the opposite side, and among the ladies; though for the matter of that, I've seen a many ladies face it out, in a manner that did honour to the sex.—You in number two, don't grind them teeth of yours. Worse manners," said the hangman, rapping at the door with his stick, "I never see in this place, afore. I'm ashamed of you. You're a disgrace to the Bailey."

After pausing for a moment to hear if anything could be pleaded in justification, Mr. Dennis resumed in a sort of coaxing tone:

"Now look'ee here, you four. I'm come here to take care of you, and see that you an't burnt, instead of the other thing. It's no use your making any noise, for you won't be found out by them as has broken in, and you'll only be hoarse when you come to the speeches, —which is a pity. What I say in respect to the speeches always is, 'Give it mouth.' That's my maxim. Give it mouth. I've heerd," said the hangman, pulling off his hat to take his handkerchief from the crown and wipe his face, and then putting it on again a little more on one side than before, "I've heerd a eloquence on them boards—you know what boards I mean—and have heerd a degree of mouth given to them speeches, that they was so clear as a bell, and as good as a play. There's a pattern! And always, when a thing of this nature's to come off, what I stand up for, is, a proper frame of mind. Let's have a proper frame of mind, and we can go through with it, creditable—pleasant—sociable. Whatever you do (and I address myself, in particular, to you in the furthest), never snivel. I'd sooner by half, though I lose by it, see a man tear his clothes a' purpose to spile 'em before they come to me, than find him snivelling. It's ten to one a better frame of mind, every way!"

While the hangman addressed them to this effect, in the tone and with the air of a pastor in familiar conversation with his flock, the noise had been in some degree subdued; for the rioters were busy in conveying the prisoners to the Sessions House, which was beyond the main walls of the prison, though connected with it, and the crowd were busy too, in passing them from thence along the street. But when he had got thus far in his discourse, the sound of voices in the yard showed plainly that the mob had returned and were coming that way; and directly afterwards a violent crashing at the gate below, gave note of their attack upon the cells (as they were called) at last.

It was in vain the hangman ran from door to door, and covered the grates, one after another, with his hat, in futile efforts to stifle the cries of the four men within; it was in vain he dogged their outstretched hands, and beat them with his stick, or menaced them with new and lingering pains in the execution of his office; the place resounded with their cries. These, together with the feeling that they were now the last men in the jail, so worked upon and stimulated the besiegers, that in an incredibly short space of time they forced the strong grate down below, which was formed of iron rods two inches square, drove in the two other doors, as if they had been but deal partitions, and stood at the end of the gallery with only a bar or two between them and the cell.

"Halloa!" cried Hugh, who was the first to look into the dusky passage: "Dennis before us! Well done, old boy. Be quick, and open here, for we shall be suffocated in the smoke, going out."

"Go out at once, then," said Dennis. "What do you want here?"

"Want!" echoed Hugh. "The four men."

"Four devils!" cried the hangman. "Don't you know they're left for death on Thursday? Don't you respect the law—the constitootion—nothing? Let the four men be."

"Is this a time for joking?" cried Hugh. "Do you hear 'em? Pull away these bars that have got fixed between the door and the ground; and let us in."

"Brother," said the hangman, in a low voice, as he stooped under pretence of doing what Hugh desired, but only looked up in his face, "can't you leave these here four men to me, if I've the whim! You do what you like, and have what you like of everything for your share,—give me my share. I want these four men left alone, I tell you!"

"Pull the bars down, or stand out of the way," was Hugh's reply.

"You can turn the crowd if you like, you know that well enough, brother," said the hangman, slowly. "What! You *will* come in, will you?"

"Yes."

"You won't let these men alone, and leave 'em to me? You've no respect for nothing—haven't you?" said the hangman, retreating to the door by which he had entered, and regarding his companion with a scowl. "You *will* come in, will you, brother?"

"I tell you, yes. What the devil ails you? Where are you going?"

"No matter where I'm going," rejoined the hangman, looking in again at the iron wicket, which he had nearly shut upon himself, and held ajar. "Remember where you're coming. That's all!"

With that, he shook his likeness at Hugh, and giving him a grin, compared with which his usual smile was amiable, disappeared, and shut the door.

Hugh paused no longer, but goaded alike by the cries of the convicts, and by the impatience of the crowd, warned the man immediately behind him—the way was only wide enough for one abreast—to stand back, and wielded a sledge-hammer with such strength, that after a few blows the iron bent and broke, and gave them free admittance.

If the two sons of one of these men, of whom mention has been made, were furious in their zeal before, they had now the wrath and vigour of lions. Calling to the man within each cell, to keep as far back as he could, lest the axes crashing through the door should wound him, a party went to work upon each one, to beat it in by sheer strength, and force the bolts and staples from their hold. But although these two lads had the weakest party, and the worst armed, and did not begin until after the others, having stopped to whisper to him through the grate, that door was the first open, and that man was the first out. As they dragged him into the gallery to knock off his irons, he fell down among them, a mere heap of chains, and was carried out in that state on men's shoulders, with no sign of life.

The release of these four wretched creatures, and conveying them, astounded and bewildered, into the streets so full of life—a spectacle they had never thought to see again, until they emerged from solitude and silence upon that last journey, when the air should be heavy with the pent-up breath of thousands, and the streets and houses should be built and roofed with human faces, not with bricks and tiles and stones—was the crowning horror of the scene. Their pale and haggard looks and hollow eyes; their staggering feet, and hands stretched out as if to save themselves from falling; their wandering and uncertain air; the way they heaved and gasped for breath, as though in water, when they were first plunged into the crowd; all marked them for the men. No need to say "this one was doomed to die;" for there were the words broadly stamped and branded on his face. The crowd fell off, as if they had been laid out for burial, and had risen in their shrouds; and many were seen to shudder, as though they had been actually dead men, when they chanced to touch or brush against their garments.

At the bidding of the mob, the houses were all illuminated that night—lighted up from top to bottom as at a time of public gaiety and joy. Many years afterwards, old people who lived in their youth near this part of the city, remembered being in a great glare of light, within doors and without, and as they looked, timid and frightened children, from the windows, seeing *a face* go by. Though the whole great crowd and all its other terrors had faded from their recollection, this one object remained; alone, distinct, and well remembered. Even in the unpractised minds of infants, one of these doomed men darting past, and but an instant seen, was an image of force enough to dim the whole concourse; to find itself an all-absorbing place, and hold it ever after.

When the last task had been achieved, the shouts and cries grew fainter; the clank of fetters, which had resounded on all sides as the prisoners escaped; was heard no more; all the noises of the crowd subsided into a hoarse and sullen murmur as it passed into the distance; and when the human tide had rolled away, a melancholy heap of smoking ruins marked the spot where it had lately chafed and roared.

CHAPTER LXVI

ALTHOUGH he had had no rest upon the previous night, and had watched with little intermission for some weeks past, sleeping only in the day by starts and snatches, Mr. Haredale, from the dawn of morning until sunset, sought his niece in every place where he deemed it possible she could have taken refuge. All day long, nothing, save a draught of water, passed his lips; though he prosecuted his inquiries far and wide, and never so much as sat down, once.

In every quarter he could think of; at Chigwell and in London; at the houses of the tradespeople with whom he dealt, and of the friends he knew; he pursued his search. A prey to the most harrowing anxieties and apprehensions, he went from magistrate to magistrate, and finally to the Secretary of State. The only comfort he received was from the minister, who assured him that the Government, being now driven to the exercise of the extreme prerogatives of the Crown, were determined to exert them; that a proclamation would probably be out upon the morrow, giving to the military, discretionary and unlimited power in the suppression of the riots; that the sympathies of the King, the Administration, and both Houses of Parliament, and indeed of all good men of every religious persuasion, were strongly with the injured Catholics; and that justice should be done them at any cost or hazard. He told him, moreover, that other persons whose houses had been burnt, had for a time lost sight of their children or their relatives, but had, in every case, within his knowledge, succeeded in discovering them; that his complaint should be remembered and fully stated in the instructions given to the officers in command, and to all the inferior myrmidons of justice; and that everything that could be done to help him, should be done, with a good-will and in good faith.

Grateful for this consolation, feeble as it was in its reference to the past, and little hope as it afforded him in connection with the subject of distress which lay nearest to his heart; and really thankful for the interest the minister expressed, and seemed to feel, in his condition; Mr. Haredale withdrew. He found himself, with the night coming on, alone in the streets; and destitute of any place in which to lay his head.

He entered an hotel near Charing Cross, and ordered some refreshment and a bed. He saw that his faint and worn appearance attracted the attention of the landlord and his waiters; and thinking that they might suppose him to be penniless, took out his purse, and laid it on the table. It was not that, the landlord said, in a faltering voice. If he were one of those who had suffered by the rioters, he durst not give him entertainment. He had a family of children, and had been twice warned to be careful in receiving guests. He heartily prayed his forgiveness, but what could he do?

Nothing. No man felt that more sincerely than Mr. Haredale. He told the man as much, and left the house.

Feeling that he might have anticipated this occurrence, after what he had seen at Chigwell in the morning, where no man dared to touch a spade, though he offered a large reward to all who would come and dig among the ruins of his house, he walked along the Strand; too proud to expose himself to another refusal, and of too generous a spirit to involve in distress or ruin any honest tradesman who might be weak enough to give him shelter. He wandered into one of the streets by the side of the river, and was pacing in a thoughtful manner up and down, thinking of things that had happened long ago, when he heard a servant-man at an upper window call to another at the opposite side of the street, that the mob were setting fire to Newgate.

To Newgate! where that man was! His failing strength returned, his energies came back with tenfold vigour, on the instant. If it were possible—if they should set the murderer free—was he, after all he had undergone, to die with the suspicion of having slain his own brother, dimly gathering about him—

He had no consciousness of going to the jail; but there he stood, before it. There was the crowd wedged and pressed together in a dense, dark, moving mass; and there were the flames soaring up into the air. His head turned round and round, lights flashed before his eyes, and he struggled hard with two men.

"Nay, nay," said one. "Be more yourself, my good sir. We attract attention here. Come away. What can you do among so many men?"

"The gentleman's always for doing something," said the other, forcing him along as he spoke. "I like him for that. I do like him for that."

They had by this time got him into a court, hard by the prison. He looked from one to the other, and as he tried to release himself, felt that he tottered on his feet. He who had spoken first, was the old gentleman whom he had seen at the Lord Mayor's. The other was John Grueby, who had stood by him so manfully at Westminster.

"What does this mean?" he asked them faintly. "How came we together?"

"On the skirts of the crowd," returned the distiller; "but come with us. Pray come with us. You seem to know my friend here?"

"Surely," said Mr. Haredale, looking in a kind of stupor at John.

"He'll tell you then," returned the old gentleman, "that I am a man to be trusted. He's my servant. He was lately (as you know, I, have no doubt) in Lord George Gordon's service; but he left it, and brought, in pure good-will to me and others, who are marked by the rioters, such intelligence as he had picked up, of their designs."

"—On one condition, please, sir," said John, touching his hat. "No evidence against my lord—a misled man—a kind-hearted man, sir. My lord never intended this."

"The condition will be observed, of course," rejoined the old distiller. "It's a point of honour. But come with us, sir; pray come with us."

John Grueby added no entreaties, but he adopted a different kind of persuasion, by putting his arm through one of Mr. Haredale's, while his master took the other, and leading him away with all speed.

Sensible, from a strange lightness in his head, and a difficulty in fixing his thoughts on anything, even to the extent of bearing his companions in his mind for a minute together without looking at them, that his brain was affected by the agitation and suffering through which he had passed, and to which he was still a prey, Mr. Haredale let them lead him where they would. As they went along, he was conscious of having no command over what he said or thought and that he had a fear of going mad.

The distiller lived, as he had told him when they first met, on Holborn Hill, where he had great storehouses and drove a large trade. They approached his house by a back entrance, lest they should attract the notice of the crowd, and went into an upper room which faced towards the street; the windows, however, in common with those of every other room in the house, were boarded up inside, in order that, out of doors, all might appear quite dark.

They laid him on a sofa in this chamber, perfectly insensible; but John immediately fetching a surgeon, who took from him a large quantity of blood, he gradually came to himself. As he was, for the time, too weak to walk, they had no difficulty in persuading him to remain there all night, and got him to bed without loss of a minute. That done, they gave him a cordial and some toast, and presently a pretty strong composing-draught, under the influence of which he soon fell into a lethargy, and, for a time, forgot his troubles.

The vintner, who was a very hearty old fellow and a worthy man, had no thoughts of going to bed himself, for he had received several threatening warnings from the rioters, and had indeed gone out that evening to try and gather from the conversation of the mob whether his house was to be the next attacked. He sat all night in an easy-chair in the same room—dozing a little now and then—and received from time to time the reports of John Grueby and two or three other trustworthy persons in his employ, who went out into the streets as scouts; and for whose entertainment an ample allowance of good cheer (which the old vintner, despite his anxiety, now and then attacked himself) was set forth in an adjoining chamber.

These accounts were of a sufficiently alarming nature from the first; but as the night wore on, they grew so much worse, and involved such a fearful amount of riot and destruction, that in com-

parison with these new tidings all the previous disturbances sunk
to nothing.

The first intelligence that came, was of the taking of Newgate, and
the escape of all the prisoners, whose track, as they made up Holborn and into the adjacent streets, was proclaimed to those citizens
who were shut up in their houses, by the rattling of their chains,
which formed a dismal concert, and was heard in every direction,
as though so many forges were at work. The flames, too, shone so
brightly through the vintner's skylights, that the rooms and staircases below were nearly as light as in broad day; while the distant
shouting of the mob seemed to shake the very walls and ceilings.

At length they were heard approaching the house, and some
minutes of terrible anxiety ensued. They came close up, and stopped
before it; but after giving three loud yells, went on. And although
they returned several times that night, creating new alarms each
time, they did nothing there; having their hands full. Shortly after
they had gone away for the first time, one of the scouts came running
in with the news that they had stopped before Lord Mansfield's
house in Bloomsbury Square.

Soon afterwards, there came another, and another, and then the
first returned again, and so, by little and little, their tale was this:—
That the mob gathering round Lord Mansfield's house, had called
on those within to open the door, and receiving no reply (for Lord and
Lady Mansfield were at that moment escaping by the backway),
forced an entrance according to their usual custom. That they then
began to demolish the house with great fury, and setting fire to it in
several parts, involved in a common ruin the whole of the costly
furniture, the plate and jewels, a beautiful gallery of pictures, the
rarest collection of manuscripts ever possessed by any one private
person in the world, and worse than all, because nothing could
replace this loss, the great Law Library, on almost every page of
which were notes in the Judge's own hand, of inestimable value,—
being the results of the study and experience of his whole life. That
while they were howling and exulting round the fire, a troop of
soldiers, with a magistrate among them, came up, and being too late
(for the mischief was by that time done), began to disperse the crowd.
That the Riot Act being read, and the crowd still resisting, the
soldiers received orders to fire, and levelling their muskets shot dead
at the first discharge six men and a woman, and wounded many
persons; and loading again directly, fired another volley, but over the
people's heads it was supposed, as none were seen to fall. That thereupon, and daunted by the shrieks and tumult, the crowd began to
disperse, and the soldiers went away, leaving the killed and wounded
on the ground: which they had no sooner done than the rioters came
back again, and taking up the dead bodies, and the wounded people,
formed into a rude procession, having the bodies in the front. That in
this order they paraded off with a horrible merriment; fixing weapons
in the dead men's hands to make them look as if alive; and preceded
by a fellow ringing Lord Mansfield's dinner-bell with all his might.

The Riots at their Height.

The scouts reported further, that this party meeting with some others who had been at similar work elsewhere, they all united into one, and drafting off a few men with the killed and wounded, marched away to Lord Mansfield's country seat at Caen Wood, between Hampstead and Highgate; bent upon destroying that house likewise, and lighting up a great fire there, which from that height should be seen all over London. But in this, they were disappointed, for a party of horse having arrived before them, they retreated faster than they went, and came straight back to town.

There being now a great many parties in the streets, each went to work according to its humour, and a dozen houses were quickly blazing, including those of Sir John Fielding and two other Justices, and four in Holborn—one of the greatest thoroughfares in London—which were all burning at the same time, and burned until they went out of themselves, for the people cut the engine hose, and would not suffer the firemen to play upon the flames. At one house near Moorfields, they found in one of the rooms some canary birds in cages, and these they cast into the fire alive. The poor little creatures screamed, it was said, like infants, when they were flung upon the blaze; and one man was so touched that he tried in vain to save them, which roused the indignation of the crowd, and nearly cost him his life.

At the same house, one of the fellows who went through the rooms, breaking the furniture and helping to destroy the building, found a child's doll—a poor toy—which he exhibited at the window to the mob below, as the image of some unholy saint which the late occupants had worshipped. While he was doing this, another man with an equally tender conscience (they had both been foremost in throwing down the canary birds for roasting alive), took his seat on the parapet of the house, and harangued the crowd from a pamphlet circulated by the Association, relative to the true principles of Christianity! Meanwhile the Lord Mayor, with his hands in his pockets, looked on as an idle man might look at any other show, and seem mightily satisfied to have got a good place.

Such were the accounts brought to the old vintner by his servants as he sat at the side of Mr. Haredale's bed, having been unable even to doze, after the first part of the night; too much disturbed by his own fears; by the cries of the mob, the light of the fires, and the firing of the soldiers. Such, with the addition of the release of all the prisoners in the New Jail at Clerkenwell, and as many robberies of passengers in the streets as the crowd had leisure to indulge in, were the scenes of which Mr. Haredale was happily unconscious, and which were all enacted before midnight.

CHAPTER LXVII

WHEN darkness broke away, and morning began to dawn, the town wore a strange aspect indeed.

Sleep had hardly been thought of all night. The general alarm was so apparent in the faces of the inhabitants, and its expression was so aggravated by want of rest (few persons, with any property to lose, having dared to go to bed since Monday), that a stranger coming into the streets would have supposed some mortal pest or plague to have been raging. In place of the usual cheerfulness and animation of morning, everything was dead and silent. The shops remained unopened, offices and warehouses were shut, the coach and chair stands were deserted, no carts or waggons rumbled through the slowly waking streets, the early cries were all hushed; a universal gloom prevailed. Great numbers of people were out, even at daybreak, but they flitted to and fro as though they shrank from the sound of their own footsteps; the public ways were haunted rather than frequented; and round the smoking ruins people stood apart from one another and in silence, not venturing to condemn the rioters, or to be supposed to do so, even in whispers.

At the Lord President's in Piccadilly, at Lambeth Palace, at the Lord Chancellor's in Great Ormond Street, in the Royal Exchange, the Bank, the Guildhall, the Inns of Court, the Courts of Law, and every chamber fronting the streets, near Westminster Hall and the Houses of Parliament, parties of soldiers were posted before daylight. A body of Horse Guards paraded Palace-yard; an encampment was formed in the Park, where fifteen hundred men and five battalions of Militia were under arms; the Tower was fortified, the drawbridges were raised, the cannon loaded and pointed, and two regiments of artillery busied in strengthening the fortress and preparing it for defence. A numerous detachment of soldiers were stationed to keep guard at the New River Head, which the people had threatened to attack, and where, it was said, they meant to cut off the main-pipes, so that there might be no water for the extinction of the flames. In the Poultry, and on Cornhill, and at several other leading points, iron chains were drawn across the street; parties of soldiers were distributed in some of the old city churches while it was yet dark; and in several private houses (among them, Lord Rockingham's in Grosvenor Square); which were blockaded as though to sustain a siege, and had guns pointed from the windows. When the sun rose, it shone into handsome apartments filled with armed men; the furniture hastily heaped away in corners, and made of little or no account, in the terror of the time—on arms glittering in city chambers, among desks and stools, and dusty books—into little smoky churchyards in odd lanes and by-ways, with soldiers lying down among the tombs, or lounging under the shade of the one old tree, and their pile of muskets sparkling in the light—on solitary sentries pacing up and down in courtyards, silent now, but yesterday resounding with the din and hum of business—everywhere on guard-rooms, garrisons, and threatening preparations.

As the day crept on, still more unusual sights were witnessed in the streets. The gates of the King's Bench and Fleet Prisons being opened at the usual hour, were found to have notices fixed to them, announcing that the rioters would come that night to burn them down. The wardens, too well knowing the likelihood there was of this promise being fulfilled, were fain to set their prisoners at liberty, and give them leave to move their goods; so, all day, such of them as had any furniture were occupied in conveying it, some to this place, some to that, and not a few to the broker's shops, where they gladly sold it, for any wretched price those gentry chose to give. There were some broken men among these debtors who had been in jail so long, and were so miserable and destitute of friends, so dead to the world, and utterly forgotten and uncared for, that they implored their jailers not to set them free, and to send them, if need were, to some other place of custody. But they, refusing to comply, lest they should incur the anger of the mob, turned them into the streets, where they wandered up and down, hardly remembering the ways untrodden by their feet so long, and crying—such abject things those rotten-hearted jails had made them—as they slunk off in their rags, and dragged their slipshod feet along the pavement.

Even of the three hundred prisoners who had escaped from New-gate, there were some—a few, but there were some—who sought their jailers out and delivered themselves up; preferring imprisonment and punishment to the horrors of such another night as the last. Many of the convicts, drawn back to their own place of captivity by some indescribable attraction, or by a desire to exult over it in its downfall and glut their revenge by seeing it in ashes, actually went back in broad noon, and loitered about the cells. Fifty were retaken at one time on this next day, within the prison walls; but their fate did not deter others, for there they went in spite of everything, and there they were taken in twos and threes, twice or thrice a day, all through the week. Of the fifty just mentioned, some were occupied in endeavouring to rekindle the fire; but in general they seemed to have no object in view but to prowl and lounge about the old place: being often found asleep in the ruins, or sitting talking there, or even eating and drinking, as in a choice retreat.

Besides the notices on the gates of the Fleet and the King's Bench, many similar announcements were left, before one o'clock at noon, at the houses of private individuals; and further, the mob proclaimed their intention of seizing on the Bank, the Mint, the Arsenal at Wool-wich, and the Royal Palaces. The notices were seldom delivered by more than one man, who, if it were at a shop, went in, and laid it, with a bloody threat perhaps, upon the counter; or if it were at a private house, knocked at the door, and thrust it in the servant's hand. Notwithstanding the presence of the military in every quarter of the town, and the great force in the Park, these messengers did their errands with impunity all through the day. So did two boys who went down Holborn alone, armed with bars taken from the railings of Lord Mansfield's house, and demanded money for the rioters. So did a tall man on horseback who made a collection for the same purpose in Fleet street, and refused to take anything but gold.

A rumour had now got into circulation, too, which diffused a greater dread all through London, even than these publicly announced intentions of the rioters, though all men knew that if they were successfully effected, there must ensue a national bankruptcy and general ruin. It was said that they meant to throw the gates of Bedlam open, and let all the madmen loose. This suggested such dreadful images to the people's minds, and was indeed an act so fraught with new and unimaginable horrors in the contemplation, that it beset them more than any loss or cruelty of which they could foresee the worst, and drove many sane men nearly mad themselves.

So the day passed on: the prisoners moving their goods; people running to and fro in the streets, carrying away their property; groups standing in silence round the ruins; all business suspended; and the soldiers disposed as has been already mentioned, remaining quite inactive. So the day passed on, and dreaded night drew near again.

At last, at seven o'clock in the evening, the Privy Council issued a solemn proclamation that it was now necessary to employ the military, and that the officers had most direct and effectual orders, by an immediate exertion of their utmost force, to repress the disturbances; and warning all good subjects of the King to keep themselves, their servants, and apprentices, within doors that night. There was then delivered out to every soldier on duty, thirty-six rounds of powder and ball; the drums beat; and the whole force was under arms at sunset.

The City authorities, stimulated by these vigorous measures, held a Common Council; passing a vote thanking the military associations who had tendered their aid to the civil authorities; accepted it; and placed them under the direction of the two sheriffs. At the Queen's palace, a double guard, the yeomen on duty, the groom-porters, and all other attendants, were stationed in the passages and on the staircases at seven o'clock, with strict instructions to be watchful on their posts all night; and all the doors were locked. The gentlemen of the Temple, and the other Inns, mounted guard within their gates, and strengthened them with the great stones of the pavement, which they took up for the purpose. In Lincoln's Inn, they gave up the hall and commons to the Northumberland Militia, under the command of Lord Algernon Percy; in some few of the city wards, the burgesses turned out, and without making a very fierce show, looked brave enough. Some hundreds of stout gentlemen threw themselves, armed to the teeth, into the halls of the different companies, double-locked and bolted all the gates, and dared the rioters (among themselves) to come on at their peril. These arrangements being all made simultaneously, or nearly so, were completed by the time it got dark; and then the streets were comparatively clear, and were guarded at all the great corners and chief avenues by the troops: while parties of the officers rode up and down in all directions, ordering chance stragglers home, and admonishing the residents to keep within their houses, and, if any firing ensued, not to approach the windows. More chains were drawn across such of the thoroughfares as were of a nature to favour the approach of a great crowd, and at each of these points a considerable force was stationed. All these precautions having been taken, and it being now quite dark, those in command awaited the result in some anxiety: and not without hope that such vigilant demonstrations might of themselves dishearten the populace, and prevent any new outrages.

But in this reckoning they were cruelly mistaken, for in half an hour, or less, as though the setting in of night had been their pre-concerted signal, the rioters having previously, in small parties, prevented the lighting of the street lamps, rose like a great sea; and that in so many places at once, and with such inconceivable fury, that those who had the direction of the troops knew not, at first, where to turn or what to do. One after another, new fires blazed up in every quarter of the town, as though it were the intention of the insurgents to wrap the city in a circle of flames, which, contracting by degrees, should burn the whole to ashes; the crowd swarmed and roared in every street; and none but rioters and soldiers being out of doors, it seemed to the latter as if all London were arrayed against them, and they stood alone against the town.

In two hours, six-and-thirty fires were raging—six-and-thirty great conflagrations. Among them the Borough Clink in Tooley-street, the King's Bench, the Fleet, and the New Bridewell. In almost every street, there was a battle; and in every quarter the muskets of the troops were heard above the shouts and tumult of the mob. The firing began in the Poultry, where the chain was drawn across the road, where nearly a score of people were killed on the first discharge. Their bodies having been hastily carried into St. Mildred's Church by the soldiers, the latter fired again, and following fast upon the crowd, who began to give way when they saw the execution that was done, formed across Cheapside and charged them at the point of the bayonet.

The streets were now a dreadful spectacle. The shouts of the rabble, the shrieks of women, the cries of the wounded, and the constant firing, formed a deafening and an awful accompaniment to the sights which every corner presented. Wherever the road was obstructed by the chains, there the fighting and the loss of life were greatest; but there was hot work and bloodshed in almost every leading thoroughfare.

At Holborn Bridge, and on Holborn Hill, the confusion was greater than in any other part; for the crowd that poured out of the city in two great streams, one by Ludgate Hill, and one by Newgate-street, united at that spot, and formed a mass so dense, that at every volley the people seemed to fall in heaps. At this place, a large detachment of soldiery were posted, who fired, now up Fleet Market, now up Holborn, now up Snow Hill—constantly raking the streets in each direction. At this place, too, several large fires were burning, so that all the terrors of that terrible night seemed to be concentrated in one spot.

Full twenty times, the rioters, headed by one man who wielded an axe in his right hand, and bestrode a brewer's horse of great size and strength, caparisoned with fetters taken out of Newgate, which clanked and jingled as he went, made an attempt to force a passage at this point, and fire the vintner's house. Full twenty times they were repulsed with loss of life, and still came back again; and though the fellow at their head was marked and singled out by all, and was a conspicuous object as the only rioter on horseback, not a man could hit him. So surely as the smoke cleared away, so surely there was he; calling hoarsely to his companions, brandishing his axe above his head, and dashing on as though he bore a charmed life, and was proof against ball and powder.

This man was Hugh; and in every part of the riot, he was seen. He headed two attacks upon the Bank, helped to break open the Toll-houses on Blackfriars Bridge, and cast the money into the street; fired two of the prisons with his own hand: was here, and there, and everywhere—always foremost—always active—striking at the soldiers, cheering on the crowd, making his horse's iron music heard through all the yell and uproar: but never hurt or stopped. Turn him at one place, and he made a new struggle in another; force him to retreat at this point, and he advanced on that, directly. Driven from Holborn for the twentieth time, he rode at the head of a great crowd straight upon Saint Paul's, attacked a guard of soldiers who kept watch over a body of prisoners within the iron railings, forced them to retreat, rescued the men they had in custody, and with this accession to his party, came back again, mad with liquor and excitement and hallooing them on like a demon.

It would have been no easy task for the most careful rider to sit a horse in the midst of such a throng and tumult; but though this madman rolled upon his back (he had no saddle) like a boat upon the sea, he never for an instant lost his seat, or failed to guide him where he would. Through the very thickest of the press, over dead bodies and burning fragments, now on the pavement, now in the road, now riding up a flight of steps to make himself the more conspicuous to his party, and now forcing a passage through a mass of human beings, so closely squeezed together that it seemed as if the edge of a knife would scarcely part them,—on he went, as though he could surmount all obstacles by the mere exercise of his will. And perhaps his not being shot was in some degree attributable to this very circumstance; for his extreme audacity, and the conviction that he must be one of those to whom the proclamation referred, inspired the soldiers with a desire to take him alive, and diverted many an aim which otherwise might have been more near the mark.

The vintner and Mr. Haredale, unable to sit quietly listening to the noise without seeing what went on, had climbed to the roof of the house, and hiding behind a stack of chimneys, were looking cautiously down into the street, almost hoping that after so many repulses the rioters would be foiled, when a great shout proclaimed that a party were coming round the other way; and the dismal jingling of those accursed fetters warned them next moment that they too were led by Hugh. The soldiers had advanced into Fleet Market and were dispersing the people there; so that they came on with hardly any check, and were soon before the house.

"All's over now," said the vintner. "Fifty thousand pounds will be scattered in a minute. We must save ourselves. We can do no more, and shall have reason to be thankful if we do as much."

Their first impulse was, to clamber along the roofs of the houses, and, knocking at some garret window for admission, pass down that way into the street, and so escape. But another fierce cry from below, and a general upturning of the faces of the crowd, apprised them that they were discovered, and even that Mr. Haredale was recognised; for Hugh, seeing him plainly in the bright glare of the fire, which in that part made it as light as day, called to him by his name, and swore to have his life.

"Leave me here," said Mr. Haredale, "and in Heaven's name, my good friend, save yourself! Come on!" he muttered, as he turned towards Hugh and faced him without any further effort at concealment: "This roof is high, and if we close, we will die together!"

"Madness," said the honest vintner, pulling him back, "sheer madness. Hear reason, sir. My good sir, hear reason. I could never make myself heard by knocking at a window now; and even if I could, no one would be bold enough to connive at my escape. Through the cellars, there's a kind of passage into the back street by which we roll casks in and out. We shall have time to get down there before they can force an entry. Do not delay an instant, but come with me—for both our sakes—for mine—my dear good sir!"

As he spoke, and drew Mr. Haredale back, they had both a glimpse of the street. It was but a glimpse, but it showed them the crowd, gathering and clustering round the house: some of the armed men pressing to the front to break down the doors and windows, some bringing brands from the nearest fire, some with lifted faces following their course upon the roof and pointing them out to their companions: all raging and roaring like the flames they lighted up. They saw some men thirsting for the treasures of strong liquor which they knew were stored within; they saw others, who had been wounded, sinking down into the opposite doorways and dying, solitary wretches in the midst of all the vast assemblage; here, a frightened woman trying to escape; and there a lost child; and there a drunken ruffian, unconscious of the death-wound on his head, raving and fighting to the last. All these things, and even such trivial incidents as a man with his hat off, or turning round, or stooping down, or shaking hands with another, they marked distinctly; yet in a glance so brief, that, in the act of stepping back, they lost the whole, and saw but the pale faces of each other, and the red sky above them.

Mr. Haredale yielded to the entreaties of his companion—more because he was resolved to defend him, than for any thought he had of his own life, or any care he entertained for his own safety—and quickly re-entering the house, they descended the stairs together. Loud blows were thundering on the shutters, crowbars were already thrust beneath the door, the glass fell from the sashes, a deep light shone through every crevice, and they heard the voices of the foremost in the crowd so closely to every chink and keyhole, that they seemed to be hoarsely whispering their threats into their very ears. They had but a moment reached the bottom of the cellar-steps and shut the door behind them, when the mob broke in.

The vaults were profoundly dark, and having no torch or candle— for they had been afraid to carry one, lest it should betray their place of refuge—they were obliged to grope with their hands. But they were not long without light, for they had not gone far when they heard the crowd forcing the door; and, looking back among the low-arched passages, could see them in the distance, hurrying to and fro with flashing links, broaching the casks, staving the great vats, turning off upon the right hand and the left, into the different cellars, and lying down to drink at the channels of strong spirits which were already flowing on the ground.

They hurried on, not the less quickly for this; and had reached the only vault which lay between them and the passage out, when suddenly from the direction in which they were going, a strong light gleamed upon their faces; and before they could slip aside, or turn back, or hide themselves, two men (one bearing a torch) came upon them, and cried in an astonished whisper, "Here they are!"

At the same instant they pulled off what they wore upon their heads. Mr. Haredale saw before him Edward Chester, and then saw, when the vintner gasped his name, Joe Willet.

Ay, the same Joe, though with an arm the less, who used to make the quarterly journey on the grey mare to pay the bill to the purple-faced vintner; and that very same purple-faced vintner, formerly of Thames-street, now looked him in the face, and challenged him by name.

"Give me your hand," said Joe softly, taking it whether the astonished vintner would or no. "Don't fear to shake it; it's a friendly one and a hearty one, though it has no fellow. Why, how well you look and how bluff you are! And you—God bless you, sir. Take heart, take heart. We'll find them. Be of good cheer; we have not been idle."

There was something so honest and frank in Joe's speech, that Mr. Haredale put his hand in his involuntarily, though their meeting was suspicious enough. But his glance at Edward Chester, and that gentleman's keeping aloof, were not lost upon Joe, who said bluntly, glancing at Edward while he spoke:

"Times are changed, Mr. Haredale, and times have come when we ought to know friends from enemies, and make no confusion of names. Let me tell you that but for this gentleman, you would most likely have been dead by this time, or badly wounded at the best."

"What do you say?" cried Mr. Haredale.

"I say," said Joe, "first, that it was a bold thing to be in the crowd at all disguised as one of them; though I won't say much about that, on second thoughts, for that's my case too. Secondly, that it was a brave and glorious action—that's what I call it—to strike that fellow off his horse before their eyes!"

"What fellow! Whose eyes!"

"What fellow, sir!" cried Joe: "a fellow who has no good-will to you, and who has the daring and devilry in him of twenty fellows. I know him of old. Once in the house *he* would have found you, here or anywhere. The rest owe you no particular grudge, and, unless they see you, will only think of drinking themselves dead. But we lose time. Are you ready?"

"Quite," said Edward. "Put out the torch, Joe, and go on. And be silent, there's a good fellow."

"Silent or not silent," murmured Joe, as he dropped the flaring link upon the ground, crushed it with his foot, and gave his hand to Mr. Haredale, "it was a brave and glorious action;—no man can alter that."

Both Mr. Haredale and the worthy vintner were too amazed and too much hurried to ask any further questions, so followed their conductors in silence. It seemed, from a short whispering which presently ensued between them and the vintner relative to the best way of escape, that they had entered by the back-door, with the connivance of John Grueby, who watched outside with the key in his pocket, and whom they had taken into their confidence. A party of the crowd coming up that way, just as they entered, John had double-locked the door again, and made off for the soldiers, so that means of retreat was cut off from under them.

However, as the front-door had been forced, and this minor crowd, being anxious to get at the liquor, had no fancy for losing time in breaking down another, but had gone round and got in from Holborn with the rest, the narrow lane in the rear was quite free of people. So, when they had crawled through the passage indicated by the vintner (which was a mere shelving-trap for the admission of casks), and had managed with some difficulty to unchain and raise the door at the upper end, they emerged into the street without being observed or interrupted. Joe still holding Mr. Haredale tight, and Edward taking the same care of the vintner, they hurried through the streets at a rapid pace; occasionally standing aside to let some fugitives go by, or to keep out of the way of the soldiers who followed them, and whose questions, when they halted to put any, were speedily stopped by one whispered word from Joe.

CHAPTER LXVIII

WHILE Newgate was burning on the previous night, Barnaby and his father, having been passed among the crowd from hand to hand, stood in Smithfield, on the outskirts of the mob, gazing at the flames like men who had been suddenly roused from sleep. Some moments elapsed before they could distinctly remember where they were, or how they got there; or recollected that while they were standing idle and listless spectators of the fire, they had tools in their hands which had been hurriedly given them that they might free themselves from their fetters.

Barnaby, heavily ironed as he was, if he had obeyed his first impulse, or if he had been alone, would have made his way back to the side of Hugh, who to his clouded intellect now shone forth with the new lustre of being his preserver and truest friend. But his father's terror of remaining in the streets, communicated itself to him when he comprehended the full extent of his fears, and impressed him with the same eagerness to fly to a place of safety.

In a corner of the market among the pens for cattle, Barnaby knelt down, and pausing every now and then to pass his hand over his father's face, or look up to him with a smile, knocked off his irons. When he had seen him spring, a free man, to his feet, and had given vent to the transport of delight which the sight awakened, he went to work upon his own, which soon fell rattling down upon the ground, and left his limbs unfettered.

Gliding away together when this task was accomplished, and passing several groups of men, each gathered round a stooping figure to hide him from those who passed, but unable to repress the clanking sound of hammers, which told that they too were busy at the same work,—the two fugitives made towards Clerkenwell, and passing thence to Islington, as the nearest point of egress, were quickly in the fields. After wandering about for a long time, they found in a pasture near Finchley a poor shed, with walls of mud, and roof of grass and brambles, built for some cow-herd, but now deserted. Here, they lay down for the rest of the night.

They wandered to and fro when it was day, and once Barnaby went off alone to a cluster of little cottages two or three miles away, to purchase some bread and milk. But finding no better shelter, they returned to the same place, and lay down again to wait for night.

Heaven alone can tell, with what vague hopes of duty, and affection; with what strange promptings of nature, intelligible to him as to a man of radiant mind and most enlarged capacity; with what dim memories of children he had played with when a child himself, who had prattled of their fathers, and of loving them, and being loved; with how many half-remembered, dreamy associations of his mother's grief and tears and widowhood; he watched and tended this man. But that a vague and shadowy crowd of such ideas came slowly on him; that they taught him to be sorry when he looked upon his haggard face, that they overflowed his eyes when he stooped to kiss him, that they kept him waking in a tearful gladness, shading him from the sun, fanning him with leaves, soothing him when he started to sleep—ah! what a troubled sleep it was—and wondering when *she* would come to join them and be happy, is the truth. He sat beside him all that day; listening for her footsteps in every breath of air, looking for her shadow on the gentle-waving grass, twining the hedge flowers for her pleasure when she came, and his when he awoke; and stooping down from time to time to listen to his mutterings, and wonder why he was so restless in that quiet place. The sun went down, and night came on, and he was still quite tranquil; busied with these thoughts, as if there were no other people in the world, and the dull cloud of smoke hanging on the immense city in the distance, hid no vices, no crimes, no life or death, or cause of disquiet—nothing but clear air.

But the hour had come now when he must go alone to find out the blind man (a task that filled him with delight,) and bring him to that place; taking especial care that he was not watched or followed on his way back. He listened to the directions he must observe, repeated them again and again, and after twice or thrice returning to surprise his father with a light-hearted laugh, went forth, at last, upon his errand: leaving Grip, whom he had carried from the jail in his arms, to his care.

Fleet of foot, and anxious to return, he sped swiftly on towards the city, but could not reach it before the fires began, and made the night angry with their dismal lustre. When he entered the town—it might be that he was changed by going there without his late companions, and on no violent errand; or by the beautiful solitude in which he had passed the day, or by the thoughts that had come upon him, but it seemed peopled by a legion of devils. This flight and pursuit, this cruel burning and destroying, these dreadful cries and stunning noises, were *they* the good lord's noble cause!

Though almost stupefied by the bewildering scene, still he found the blind man's house. It was shut up and tenantless.

He waited for a long while, but no one came. At last he withdrew; and as he knew by this time that the soldiers were firing, and many people must have been killed, he went down into Holborn, where he heard the great crowd was, to try if he could find Hugh, and persuade him to avoid the danger, and return with him.

If he had been stunned and shocked before, his horror was increased a thousandfold when he got into this vortex of the riot, and not being an actor in the terrible spectacle, had it all before his eyes. But there, in the midst, towering above them all, close before the house they were attacking now, was Hugh on horseback, calling to the rest!

Sickened by the sights surrounding him on every side, and by the heat and roar, and crash, he forced his way among the crowd (where many recognised him, and with shouts pressed back to let him pass), and in time was nearly up with Hugh, who was savagely threatening some one, but whom, or what he said, he could not, in the great confusion, understand. At that moment the crowd forced their way into the house, and Hugh—it was impossible to see by what means, in such a concourse—fell headlong down.

Barnaby was beside him when he staggered to his feet. It was well he made him hear his voice, or Hugh, with his uplifted axe, would have cleft his skull in twain.

"Barnaby—you! Whose hand was that, that struck me down?"

"Not mine."

"Whose!—I say, whose!" he cried, reeling back, and looking wildly round. "What are you doing? Where is he? Show me!"

"You are hurt," said Barnaby—as indeed he was, in the head,

both by the blow he had received, and by his horse's hoof. "Come away with me."

As he spoke, he took the horse's bridle in his hand, turned him, and dragged Hugh several paces. This brought them out of the crowd, which was pouring from the street into the vintner's cellars.

"Where's—where's Dennis?" said Hugh, coming to a stop, and checking Barnaby with his strong arm. "Where has he been all day ? What did he mean by leaving me as he did, in the jail, last night? Tell me, you—d'ye hear!"

With a flourish of his dangerous weapon, he fell down upon the ground like a log. After a minute, though already frantic with drinking and with the wound in his head, he crawled to a stream of burning spirit which was pouring down the kennel, and began to drink at it as if it were a brook of water.

Barnaby drew him away, and forced him to rise. Though he could neither stand nor walk, he involuntarily staggered to his horse, climbed upon his back, and clung there. After vainly attempting to divest the animal of his clanking trappings, Barnaby sprung up behind him, snatched the bridle, turned into Leather Lane, which was close at hand, and urged the frightened horse into a heavy trot.

He looked back, once, before he left the street; and looked upon a sight not easily to be erased, even from his remembrance, so long as he had life.

The vintner's house with half-a-dozen others near at hand, was one great, glowing blaze. All night, no one had essayed to quench the flames, or stop their progress; but now a body of soldiers were actively engaged in pulling down two old wooden houses, which were every moment in danger of taking fire, and which could scarcely fail, if they were left to burn, to extend the conflagration immensely. The tumbling down of nodding walls and heavy blocks of wood, the hooting and the execrations of the crowd, the distant firing of other military detachments, the distracted looks and cries of those whose habitations were in danger, the hurrying to and fro of frightened people with their goods; the reflections in every quarter of the sky, of deep, red, soaring flames, as though the last day had come and the whole universe were burning; the dust, and smoke, and drift of fiery particles, scorching and kindling all it fell upon; the hot unwholesome vapour, the blight on everything; the stars, and moon, and very sky, obliterated;—made up such a sum of dreariness and ruin, that it seemed as if the face of Heaven were blotted out, and night, in its rest and quiet, and softened light, never could look upon the earth again.

But there was a worse spectacle than this—worse by far than fire and smoke, or even the rabble's unappeasable and maniac rage. The gutters of the street, and every crack and fissure in the stones, ran with a scorching spirit, which being dammed up by busy hands, over-flowed the road and pavement, and formed a great pool, into which the people dropped down dead by dozens. They lay in heaps all round this fearful pond, husbands and wives, fathers and sons, mothers and daughters, women with children in their arms and babies at their breasts, and drank until they died. While some stooped with their lips to the brink and never raised their heads again, others sprang up from their fiery draught, and danced, half in a mad triumph, and half in the agony of suffocation, until they fell, and steeped their corpses in the liquor that had killed them. Nor was even this the worst or most appalling kind of death that happened on this fatal night. From the burning cellars, where they drank out of hats, pails, buckets, tubs, and shoes, some men were drawn, alive, but all alight from head to foot; who, in their unendurable anguish and suffering, making for anything that had the look of water, rolled, hissing, in this hideous lake, and splashed up liquid fire which lapped in all it met with as it ran along the surface, and neither spared the living nor the dead. On this last night of the great riots—for the last night it was—the wretched victims of a senseless outcry, became themselves the dust and ashes of the flames they had kindled, and strewed the public streets of London

With all he saw in this last glance fixed indelibly upon his mind, Barnaby hurried from the city which enclosed such horrors; and holding down his head that he might not even see the glare of the fires upon the quiet landscape, was soon in the still country roads.

He stopped at about half-a-mile from the shed where his father lay, and with some difficulty making Hugh sensible that he must dismount, sunk the horse's furniture in a pool of stagnant water, and turned the animal loose. That done, he supported his companion as well as he could, and led him slowly forward.

CHAPTER LXIX

IT was the dead of night, and very dark, when Barnaby, with his stumbling comrade, approached the place where he had left his father; but he could see him stealing away into the gloom, distrustful even of him, and rapidly retreating. After calling to him twice or thrice that there was nothing to fear, but without effect, he suffered Hugh to sink upon the ground, and followed to bring him back.

He continued to creep away, until Barnaby was close upon him; then turned, and said in a terrible, though suppressed voice:

"Let me go. Do not lay hands upon me. You have told her; and you and she together have betrayed me!"

Barnaby looked at him, in silence.

"You have seen your mother!"

"No," cried Barnaby, eagerly. "Not for a long time—longer than I can tell. A whole year, I think. Is she here?"

His father looked upon him steadfastly for a few moments, and then said—drawing nearer to him as he spoke, for, seeing his face, and hearing his words, it was impossible to doubt his truth:

"What man is that?"

"Hugh—Hugh. Only Hugh. You know him. *He* will not harm you. Why, you're afraid of Hugh! Ha ha ha! Afraid of gruff, old, noisy Hugh!"

"What man is he, I ask you?" he rejoined so fiercely, that Barnaby stopped in his laugh, and shrinking back, surveyed him with a look of terrified amazement.

"Why, how stern you are! You make me fear you, though you are my father. Why do you speak to me so?"

"—I want," he answered, putting away the hand which his son with a timid desire to propitiate him, laid upon his sleeve,—"I want an answer, and you give me only jeers and questions. Who have you brought with you to this hiding-place, poor fool; and where is the blind man?"

"I don't know where. His house was close shut. I waited, but no person came; that was no fault of mine. This is Hugh—brave Hugh, who broke into that ugly jail, and set us free. Aha! You like him now, do you? You like him now!"

"Why does he lie upon the ground?"

"He has had a fall, and has been drinking. The fields and trees go round, and round, and round with him, and the ground heaves under his feet. You know him? You remember? See!"

They had by this time returned to where he lay, and both stooped over him to look into his face.

"I recollect the man," his father murmured. "Why did you bring him here?"

"Because he would have been killed if I had left him over yonder. They were firing guns and shedding blood. Does the sight of blood turn you sick, father? I see it does, by your face. That's like me— What are you looking at!"

"At nothing!" said the murderer softly, as he started back a pace or two, and gazed with sunken jaw and staring eyes above his son's head. "At nothing!"

He remained in the same attitude and with the same expression on his face for a minute or more; then glanced slowly round as if he had lost something; and went shivering back, towards the shed.

"Shall I bring him in, father?" asked Barnaby, who had looked on, wondering.

He only answered with a suppressed groan, and lying down upon the ground, wrapped his cloak about his head, and shrunk into the darkest corner.

Finding that nothing would rouse Hugh now, or make him sensible for a moment, Barnaby dragged him along the grass, and laid him on a little heap of refuse hay and straw which had been his own bed; first having brought some water from a running stream hard by, and washed his wound, and laved his hands and face. Then he lay down himself, between the two, to pass the night; and looking at the stars, fell fast asleep.

Awakened early in the morning, by the sunshine and the songs of birds, and hum of insects, he left them sleeping in the hut, and walked into the sweet and pleasant air. But he felt that on his jaded senses, oppressed and burdened with the dreadful scenes of last night, and many nights before, all the beauties of opening day, which

he had so often tasted, and in which he had had such deep delight,
fell heavily. He thought of the blithe mornings when he and the dogs
went bounding on together through the woods and fields; and the
recollection filled his eyes with tears. He had no consciousness, God
help him, of having done wrong, nor had he any new perception of
the merits of the cause in which he had been engaged, or those of the
men who advocated it; but he was full of cares now, and regrets, and
dismal recollections, and wishes (quite unknown to him before) that
this or that event had never happened, and that the sorrow and
suffering of so many people had been spared. And now he began to
think how happy they would be—his father, mother, he, and Hugh—
if they rambled away together, and lived in some lonely place, where
there were none of these troubles; and that perhaps the blind man,
who had talked so wisely about gold, and told him of the great
secrets he knew, could teach them how to live without being pinched
by want. As this occurred to him, he was the more sorry that he had
not seen him last night; and he was still brooding over this regret,
when his father came, and touched him on the shoulder.

"Ah!" cried Barnaby, starting from his fit of thoughtfulness. "Is it
only you?"

"Who should it be?"

"I almost thought," he answered, "it was the blind man. I must
have some talk with him, father."

"And so must I, for without seeing him, I don't know where to fly
or what to do, and lingering here, is death. You must go to him
again, and bring him here."

"Must I," cried Barnaby delighted; "that's brave, father. That's
what I want to do."

"But you must bring only him, and none other. And though you
wait at his door a whole day and night, still you must wait, and not
come back without him."

"Don't you fear that," he cried gaily. "He shall come, he shall
come."

"Trim off these gewgaws," said his father, plucking the scraps of
ribbon and the feathers from his hat, "and over your own dress wear
my cloak. Take heed how you go, and they will be too busy in the
streets to notice you. Of your coming back you need take no account,
for he'll manage that, safely."

"To be sure!" said Barnaby. "To be sure he will! A wise man,
father, and one who can teach us to be rich. Oh! I know him, I know
him."

He was speedily dressed, and as well disguised as he could be. With
a lighter heart he then set off upon his second journey, leaving Hugh,
who was still in a drunken stupor, stretched upon the ground within
the shed, and his father walking to and fro before it.

The murderer, full of anxious thoughts, looked after him, and
paced up and down, disquieted by every breath of air that whispered
among the boughs, and by every light shadow thrown by the passing
clouds, upon the daisied ground. He was anxious for his safe return,

and yet, though his own life and safety hung upon it, felt a relief while he was gone. In the intense selfishness which the constant presence before him of his great crimes, and their consequences here and hereafter, engendered, every thought of Barnaby, as his son, was swallowed up and lost. Still, his presence was a torture and reproach; in his wild eyes, there were terrible images of that guilty night; with his unearthly aspect, and his half-formed mind, he seemed to the murderer a creature who had sprung into existence from his victim's blood. He could not bear his look, his voice, his touch; and yet he was forced, by his own desperate condition and his only hope of cheating the gibbet, to have him by his side, and to know that he was inseparable from his single chance of escape.

He walked to and fro, with little rest, all day, revolving these things in his mind; and still Hugh lay, unconscious, in the shed. At length, when the sun was setting, Barnaby returned, leading the blind man, and talking earnestly to him as they came along together.

The murderer advanced to meet them, and bidding his son go on and speak to Hugh, who had just then staggered to his feet, took his place at the blind man's elbow, and slowly followed, towards the shed.

"Why did you send *him?*" said Stagg. "Don't you know it was the way to have him lost, as soon as found?"

"Would you have had me come myself?" returned the other.

"Humph! Perhaps not. I was before the jail on Tuesday night, but missed you in the crowd. I was out last night, too. There was good work last night—gay work—profitable work"—he added, rattling the money in his pockets.

"Have you—"

"—Seen your good lady? Yes."

"Do you mean to tell me more, or not?"

"I'll tell you all," returned the blind man, with a laugh. "Excuse me—but I love to see you so impatient. There's energy in it."

"Does she consent to say the word that may save me?"

"No," returned the blind man emphatically, as he turned his face towards him. "No. Thus it is. She has been at death's door since she lost her darling—has been insensible, and I know not what. I tracked her to a hospital, and presented myself (with your leave) at her bedside. Our talk was not a long one, for she was weak, and there being people near, I was not quite easy. But I told her all that you and I agreed upon, and pointed out the young gentleman's position, in strong terms. She tried to soften me, but that, of course (as I told her), was lost time. She cried and moaned, you may be sure; all women do. Then, of a sudden, she found her voice and strength, and said that Heaven would help her and her innocent son; and that to Heaven she appealed against us—which she did; in really very pretty language, I assure you. I advised her, as a friend, not to count too much on assistance from any such distant quarter—recommended her to think of it—told her where I lived—said I knew she would send to me before noon, next day—and left her, either in a faint, or shamming."

When he had concluded this narration, during which he had made several pauses, for the convenience of cracking and eating nuts, of which he seemed to have a pocketful, the blind man pulled a flask from his pocket, took a draught himself, and offered it to his companion. "You won't, won't you?" he said, feeling that he pushed it from him. "Well! Then the gallant gentleman who's lodging with you, will. Hallo, bully!"

"Death!" said the other, holding him back. "Will you tell me what I am to do!"

"Do! Nothing easier. Make a moonlight flitting in two hours' time with the young gentleman (he's quite ready to go; I have been giving him good advice as we came along), and get as far from London as you can. Let me know where you are, and leave the rest to me. She *must* come round; she can't hold out long; and as to the chances of your being retaken in the meanwhile, why it wasn't one man who got out of Newgate, but three hundred. Think of that, for your comfort."

"We must support life. How?"

"How!" repeated the blind man. "By eating and drinking. And how get meat and drink, but by paying for it! Money!" he cried, slapping his pocket. "Is money the word? Why, the streets have been running money. Devil send that the sport's not over yet, for these are jolly times; golden, rare, roaring, scrambling times. Hallo, bully! Hallo! Hallo! Drink, bully, drink. Where are ye there! Hallo!"

With such vociferations, and with a boisterous manner which bespoke his perfect abandonment to the general licence and disorder, he groped his way towards the shed, where Hugh and Barnaby were sitting on the ground.

"Put it about!" he cried, handing his flask to Hugh. "The kennels run with wine and gold. Guineas and strong water flow from the very pumps. About with it, don't spare it!"

Exhausted, unwashed, unshorn, begrimed with smoke and dust, his hair clotted with blood, his voice quite gone, so that he spoke in whispers; his skin parched up by fever, his whole body bruised and cut, and beaten about, Hugh still took the flask, and raised it to his lips. He was in the act of drinking, when the front of the shed was suddenly darkened, and Dennis stood before them.

"No offence, no offence," said that personage in a conciliatory tone, as Hugh stopped in his draught, and eyed him, with no pleasant look, from head to foot. "No offence, brother. Barnaby here too, eh! How are you, Barnaby? And two other gentlemen! Your humble servant, gentlemen. No offence to *you* either, I hope. Eh, brothers?"

Notwithstanding that he spoke in this very friendly and confident manner, he seemed to have considerable hesitation about entering, and remained outside the roof. He was rather better dressed than usual: wearing the same suit of threadbare black, it is true, but having round his neck an unwholesome-looking cravat of a yellowish white; and, on his hands great leather gloves, such as a gardener might wear in following his trade. His shoes were newly greased, and ornamented with a pair of rusty iron buckles; the pack-thread at his knees had been renewed; and where he wanted buttons, he wore pins. Altogether, he had something the look of a tipstaff, or a bailiff's follower, desperately faded, but who had a notion of keeping up the appearance of a professional character, and making the best of the worst means.

"You're very snug here," said Mr. Dennis, pulling out a mouldy pocket-handkerchief, which looked like a decomposed halter, and wiping his forehead in a nervous manner.

"Not snug enough to prevent your finding us, it seems," Hugh answered, sulkily.

"Why, I'll tell you what, brother," said Dennis, with a friendly smile, "when you don't want me to know which way you're riding, you must wear another sort of bells on your horse. Ah! I know the sound of them you wore last night, and have got quick ears for 'em; that's the truth. Well, but how are you, brother?"

He had by this time approached, and now ventured to sit down by him.

"How am I?" answered Hugh. "Where were you yesterday? Where did you go when you left me in the jail? Why did you leave me? And what did you mean by rolling your eyes and shaking your fist at me, eh?"

"I shake my fist?—at you, brother!" said Dennis, gently checking Hugh's uplifted hand, which looked threatening.

"Your stick, then; it's all one."

"Lord love you, brother, I meant nothing. You don't understand me by half. I shouldn't wonder now," he added, in the tone of a desponding and an injured man, "but you thought, because I wanted them chaps left in the prison, that I was a going to desert the banners?"

Hugh told him, with an oath, that he had thought so.

"Well!" said Mr. Dennis, mournfully, "if you an't enough to make a man mistrust his feller-creeturs, I don't know what is. Desert the banners! Me! Ned Dennis, as was so christened by his own father!— Is this axe your'n, brother!"

"Yes, it's mine," said Hugh, in the same sullen manner as before; "it might have hurt you, if you had come in its way once or twice last night. Put it down."

"Might have hurt me!" said Mr. Dennis, still keeping it in his hand, and feeling the edge with an air of abstraction. "Might have hurt me! and me exerting myself all the time to the wery best advantage. Here's a world! And you're not a-going to ask me to take a sup out of that 'ere bottle, eh?"

Hugh passed it towards him. As he raised it to his lips, Barnaby jumped up, and motioning them to be silent, looked eagerly out.

"What's the matter, Barnaby?" said Dennis, glancing at Hugh and dropping the flask, but still holding the axe in his hand.

"Hush!" he answered softly. "What do I see glittering behind the hedge?"

"What!" cried the hangman, raising his voice to its highest pitch, and laying hold of him and Hugh. "Not SOLDIERS, surely!"

That moment, the shed was filled with armed men; and a body of horse, galloping into the field, drew up before it.

"There!" said Dennis, who remained untouched among them when they had seized their prisoners; "it's them two young ones, gentlemen, that the proclamation puts a price on. This other's an escaped felon.—I'm sorry for it, brother," he added, in a tone of resignation, addressing himself to Hugh; "but you've brought it on yourself; you forced me to do it; you wouldn't respect the soundest constitootional principles, you know; you went and wiolated the wery framework of society. I had sooner have given away a trifle in charity than done this, I would upon my soul.—If you'll keep fast hold on 'em, gentlemen, I think I can make a shift to tie 'em better than you can."

But this operation was postponed for a few moments by a new occurrence. The blind man, whose ears were quicker than most people's sight, had been alarmed, before Barnaby, by a rustling in the bushes, under cover of which the soldiers had advanced. He retreated instantly—had hidden somewhere for a minute—and probably in his confusion mistaking the point at which he had emerged, was now running across the open meadow.

An officer cried directly that he had helped to plunder a house last night. He was loudly called on, to surrender. He ran the harder, and in a few seconds would have been out of gunshot. The word was given, and the men fired.

There was a breathless pause and a profound silence, during which all eyes were fixed upon him. He had been seen to start at the discharge, as if the report had frightened him. But he neither stopped nor slackened his pace in the least, and ran on full forty yards further. Then, without one reel or stagger, or sign of faintness, or quivering of any limb, he dropped.

Some of them hurried up to where he lay;—the hangman with them. Everything had passed so quickly, that the smoke had not yet scattered, but curled slowly off in a little cloud, which seemed like the dead man's spirit moving solemnly away. There were a few drops of blood upon the grass—more, when they turned him over— that was all.

"Look here! Look here!" said the hangman, stooping one knee beside the body, and gazing up with a disconcolate face at the officer and men. "Here's a pretty sight!"

"Stand out of the way," replied the officer. "Serjeant! see what he had about him."

The man turned his pockets out upon the grass, and counted, besides some foreign coins and two rings, five-and-forty guineas in gold. These were bundled up in a handkerchief and carried away; the body remained there for the present, but six men and the serjeant were left to take it to the nearest public-house.

"Now then, if you're going," said the serjeant, clapping Dennis on the back, and pointing after the officer who was walking towards the shed.

To which Mr. Dennis only replied, "Don't talk to me!" and then repeated what he had said before, namely, "Here's a pretty sight!"

"It's not one that you care for much, I should think," observed the serjeant coolly.

"Why, who," said Mr. Dennis rising, "should care for it, if I don't?"

"Oh! I didn't know you was so tender-hearted," said the serjeant. "That's all!"

"Tender-hearted!" echoed Dennis. "Tender-hearted! Look at this man. Do you call *this* constitootional? Do you see him shot through and through instead of being worked off like a Briton? Damme, if I know which party to side with. You're as bad as the other. What's to become of the country if the military power's to go a superseding the civilians in this way? Where's this poor feller-creetur's rights as a citizen, that he didn't have *me* in his last moments! I was here. I was willing. I was ready. These are nice times, brother, to have the dead crying out against us in this way, and sleep comfortably in our beds arterwards; wery nice!"

Whether he derived any material consolation from binding the prisoners, is uncertain; most probably he did. At all events his being summoned to that work, diverted him, for the time, from these painful reflections, and gave his thoughts a more congenial occupation.

They were not all three carried off together, but in two parties: Barnaby and his father, going by one road in the centre of a body of foot; and Hugh, fast bound upon a horse, and strongly guarded by a troop of calvary, being taken by another.

They had no opportunity for the least communication, in the short interval which preceded their departure; being kept strictly apart. Hugh only observed that Barnaby walked with a drooping head among his guard, and, without raising his eyes, that he tried to wave his fettered hand when he passed. For himself, he buoyed up his courage as he rode along, with the assurance that the mob would force his jail wherever it might be, and set him at liberty. But when they got into London, and more especially into Fleet Market, lately the stronghold of the rioters, where the military were rooting out the last remnant of the crowd, he saw that this hope was gone, and felt that he was riding to his death.

CHAPTER LXX

Mr. Dennis having despatched this piece of business without any personal hurt or inconvenience, and having now retired into the tranquil respectability of private life, resolved to solace himself with half an hour or so of female society. With this amiable purpose in his mind, he bent his steps towards the house where Dolly and Miss Haredale were still confined, and whither Miss Miggs had also been removed by order of Mr. Simon Tappertit.

As he walked along the streets with his leather gloves clasped behind him, and his face indicative of cheerful thought and pleasant calculation, Mr. Dennis might have been likened unto a farmer ruminating among his crops, and enjoying by anticipation the bountiful gifts of Providence. Look where he would, some heap of ruins afforded him rich promise of a working off; the whole town appeared to have been ploughed and sown, and nurtured by most genial weather; and a goodly harvest was at hand.

Having taken up arms and resorted to deeds of violence, with the great main object of preserving the Old Bailey in all its purity, and the gallows in all its pristine usefulness and moral grandeur, it would perhaps be going too far to assert that Mr. Dennis had ever distinctly contemplated and foreseen this happy state of things. He rather looked upon it as one of those beautiful dispensations which are inscrutably brought about for the behoof and advantage of good men. He felt, as it were, personally referred to, in this prosperous ripening for the gibbet; and had never considered himself so much the pet and favourite child of Destiny, or loved that lady so well or with such a calm and virtuous reliance, in all his life.

As to being taken up, himself, for a rioter, and punished with the rest, Mr. Dennis dismissed that possibility from his thoughts as an idle chimera; arguing that the line of conduct he had adopted at Newgate, and the service he had rendered that day, would be more than a set-off against any evidence which might identify him as a member of the crowd. That any charge of companionship which might be made against him by those who were themselves in danger, would certainly go for nought. And that if any trivial indiscretion on his part should unluckily come out, the uncommon usefulness of his office, at present, and the great demand for the excercise of its functions, would certainly cause it to be winked at, and passed over. In a word, he had played his cards throughout, with great care; had changed sides at the very nick of time; had delivered up two of the most notorious rioters, and a distinguished felon to boot; and was quite at his ease.

Saving—for there is a reservation; and even Mr. Dennis was not perfectly happy—saving for one circumstance; to wit, the forcible detention of Dolly and Miss Haredale, in a house almost adjoining his own. This was a stumbling-block; for if they were discovered and released, they could, by the testimony they had it in their power to give, place him in a situation of great jeopardy; and to set them at liberty, first extorting from them an oath of secrecy and silence, was a thing not to be thought of. It was more, perhaps, with an eye to the danger which lurked in this quarter, than from his abstract love of conversation with the sex, that the hangman, quickening his steps, now hastened into their society, cursing the amorous natures of Hugh and Mr. Tappertit with great heartiness, at every step he took.

When he entered the miserable room in which they were confined, Dolly and Miss Haredale withdrew in silence to the remotest corner. But Miss Miggs, who was particularly tender of her reputation, immediately fell upon her knees and began to scream very loud, crying, "What will become of me!"—"Where is Mr. Simmuns!"—"Have mercy, good gentleman, on my sex's weaknesses!"—with other doleful lamentations of that nature, which she delivered with great propriety and decorum.

"Miss, miss," whispered Dennis, beckoning to her with his fore-finger, "come here—I won't hurt you. Come here, my lamb, will you?"

On hearing this tender epithet, Miss Miggs, who had left off scream-ing when he opened his lips, and had listened to him attentively, began again: crying "Oh I'm his lamb! He says I'm his lamb! Oh gracious, why wasn't I born old and ugly! Why was I ever made to be the youngest of six, and all of 'em dead and in their blessed graves, excepting one married sister, which is settled in Golden Lion Court, number twenty-sivin, second bell-handle on the—!"

"Don't I say I an't a-going to hurt you?" said Dennis, pointing to a chair. "Why, miss, what's the matter!"

"I don't know what mayn't be the matter!" cried Miss Miggs, clasping her hands distractedly. "Anything may be the matter!"

"But nothing is, I tell you," said the hangman. "First, stop that noise and come and sit down here, will you, chuckey?"

The coaxing tone in which he said these latter words might have failed in its object, if he had not accompanied them with sundry sharp jerks of his thumb over one shoulder, and with divers winks and thrustings of his tongue into his cheek, from which signals the damsel gathered that he sought to speak to her apart, concerning Miss Haredale and Dolly. Her curiosity being very powerful, and her jealousy by no means inactive, she arose, and with a great deal of shivering and starting back, and much muscular action among all the small bones in her throat, gradually approached him.

"Sit down," said the hangman.

Suiting the action to the word, he thrust her rather suddenly and prematurely into a chair, and designing to reassure her by a little harmless jocularity, such as is adapted to please and fascinate the sex, converted his right forefinger into an ideal bradawl or gimlet, and made as though he would screw the same into her side—whereat Miss Miggs shrieked again, and evinced symptoms of faintness.

"Lovey, my dear," whispered Dennis, drawing his chair close to hers. "When was your young man here last, eh?"

"*My* young man, good gentleman!" answered Miggs in a tone of exquisite distress.

"Ah! Simmuns, you know—him?" said Dennis.

"Mine indeed!" cried Miggs, with a burst of bitterness—and as she said it, she glanced towards Dolly. "*Mine*, good gentleman!"

This was just what Mr. Dennis wanted, and expected.

"Ah!" he said, looking so soothingly, not to say amorously on Miggs, that she sat, as she afterwards remarked, on pins and needles, of the sharpest Whitechapel kind, not knowing what intentions might be suggesting that expression to his features: "I was afraid of that. *I* saw as much myself. It's her fault. She *will* entice 'em."

"I wouldn't," cried Miggs, folding her hands and looking upwards with a kind of devout blankness, "I wouldn't lay myself out as she does; I wouldn't be as bold as her; I wouldn't seem to say to all male creeturs 'Come and kiss me' "—and here a shudder quite convulsed

her frame—"for any earthly crowns as might be offered. Worlds,"
Miggs added solemnly, "should not reduce me. No. Not if I was Wenis."

"Well, but you *are* Wenus you know," said Mr. Dennis, confidentially.

"No, I am not, good gentleman," answered Miggs, shaking her
head with an air of self-denial which seemed to imply that she might
be if she chose, but she hoped she knew better. "No, I am not, good
gentleman. Don't charge me with it."

Up to this time she had turned round, every now and then, to
where Dolly and Miss Haredale had retired, and uttered a scream, or
groan, or laid her hand upon her heart and trembled excessively,
with a view of keeping up appearances, and giving them to understand that she conversed with the visitor, under protest and on compulsion, and at a great personal sacrifice, for their common good.
But at this point, Mr. Dennis looked so very full of meaning, and gave
such a singularly expressive twitch to his face as a request to her to
come still nearer to him, that she abandoned these little arts, and
gave him her whole and undivided attention.

"When was Simmuns here, I say?" quoth Dennis, in her ear.

"Not since yesterday morning; and then only for a few minutes.
Not all day, the day before."

"You know he meant all along to carry off that one!" said Dennis,
indicating Dolly by the slightest possible jerk of his head:—"and
to hand you over to somebody else."

Miss Miggs, who had fallen into a terrible state of grief when the
first part of this sentence was spoken, recovered a little at the second,
and seemed by the sudden check she put upon her tears, to intimate
that possibly this arrangement might meet her views; and that it
might, perhaps, remain an open question.

"—But unfort'nately," pursued Dennis, who observed this: "somebody else was fond of her too, you see; and even if he wasn't, somebody else is took for a rioter, and it's all over with him."

Miss Miggs relapsed.

"Now I want," said Dennis, "to clear this house, and to see you
righted. What if I was to get her off, out of the way, eh?"

Miss Miggs, brightening again, rejoined, with many breaks and
pauses from excess of feeling, that temptations had been Simmun's
bane. That it was not his faults, but hers (meaning Dolly's). That
men did not see through these dreadful arts as women did, and therefore was caged and trapped, as Simmun had been. That she had no
personal motives to serve—far from it—on the contrary, her intentions was good towards all parties. But forasmuch as she knowed
that Simmun, if united to any designing and artful minxes (she would
name no names, for that was not her dispositions)—to *any* designing
and artful minxes—must be made miserable and unhappy for life,
she *did* incline towards prewentions. Such, she added, was her free
confessions. But as this was private feelings, and might perhaps be
looked upon as wengeance, she begged the gentleman would say no
more. Whatever he said, wishing to do her duty by all mankind, even

by them as had ever been her bitterest enemies, she would not listen
to him. With that she stopped her ears, and shook her head from
side to side, to intimate to Mr. Dennis that though he talked until he
had no breath left, she was as deaf as any adder.

"Lookee here, my sugar-stick," said Mr. Dennis, "if your view's
the same as mine, and you'll only be quiet and slip away at the right
time, I can have the house clear to-morrow, and be out of this trouble.
—Stop though! there's the other."

"Which other, sir?" asked Miggs—still with her fingers in her ears
and her head shaking obstinately.

"Why, the tallest, one, yonder," said Dennis, as he stroked his
chin, and added, in an undertone to himself, something about not
crossing Muster Gashford.

Miss Miggs replied (still being profoundly deaf) that if Miss Haredale stood in the way at all, he might make himself quite easy on that
score; as she had gathered, from what passed between Hugh and Mr.
Tappertit when they were last there, that she was to be removed
alone (not by them, but by somebody else), to-morrow night.

Mr. Dennis opened his eyes very wide at this piece of information,
whistled once, considered once, and finally slapped his head once and
nodded once, as if he had got the clue to this mysterious removal,
and so dismissed it. Then he imparted his design concerning Dolly to
Miss Miggs, who was taken more deaf than before, when he began;
and so remained, all through.

The notable scheme was this. Mr. Dennis was immediately to seek
out from among the rioters, some daring young fellow (and he had
one in his eye, he said), who, terrified by the threats he could hold out to
him, and alarmed by the capture of so many who were no better and
no worse than he, would gladly avail himself of any help to get abroad,
and out of harm's way, with his plunder, even though his journey
were incumbered by an unwilling companion; indeed, the unwilling
companion being a beautiful girl, would probably be an additional
inducement and temptation. Such a person found, he proposed to
bring him there on the ensuing night, when the tall one was taken
off, and Miss Miggs had purposely retired; and then that Dolly should
be gagged, muffled in a cloak, and carried in any handy conveyance
down to the river's side; where there were abundant means of getting
her smuggled snugly off in any small craft of doubtful character, and
no questions asked. With regard to the expense of this removal, he
would say, at a rough calculation, that two or three silver tea or
coffee pots, with something additional for drink (such as a muffineer,
or toast-rack), would more than cover it. Articles of plate of every
kind having been buried by the rioters in several lonely parts of
London, and particularly, as he knew, in St. James's Square, which,
though easy of access, was little frequented after dark, and had a
convenient piece of water in the midst, the needful funds were close
at hand, and could be had upon the shortest notice. With regard to
Dolly, the gentleman would exercise his own discretion. He would be
bound to do nothing but to take her away, and keep her away. All

other arrangements and dispositions would rest entirely with himself.

If Miss Miggs had had her hearing, no doubt she would have been greatly shocked by the indelicacy of a young female's going away with a stranger by night (for her moral feelings, as we have said, were of the tenderest kind); but directly Mr. Dennis ceased to speak, she reminded him that he had only wasted breath. She then went on to say (still with her fingers to her ears) that nothing less than a severe practical lesson would save the locksmith's daughter from utter ruin; and that she felt it, as it were, a moral obligation and a sacred duty to the family, to wish that some one would devise one for her reformation. Miss Miggs remarked, and very justly, as an abstract sentiment which happened to occur to her at the moment, that she dared to say the locksmith and his wife would murmur, and repine, if they were ever, by forcible abduction, or otherwise, to lose their child; but that we seldom knew, in this world, what was best for us: such being our sinful and imperfect natures, that very few arrived at that clear understanding.

Having brought their conversation to this satisfactory end, they parted: Dennis, to pursue his design, and take another walk about his farm: Miss Miggs, to launch, when he left her, into such a burst of mental anguish (which she gave them to understand was occasioned by certain tender things he had had the presumption and audacity to say), that little Dolly's heart was quite melted. Indeed, she said and did so much to soothe the outraged feeling of Miss Miggs, and looked so beautiful while doing so, that if that young maid had not had ample vent for her surpassing spite, in a knowledge of the mischief that was brewing, she must have scratched her features, on the spot.

CHAPTER LXXI

ALL next day, Emma Haredale, Dolly, and Miggs, remained cooped up together in what had now been their prison for so many days, without seeing any person, or hearing any sound but the murmured conversation, in an outer room, of the men who kept watch over them. There appeared to be more of these fellows than there had been hitherto; and they could no longer hear the voices of women, which they had before plainly distinguished. Some new excitement, too, seemed to prevail among them; for there was much stealthy going in and out, and a constant questioning of those who were newly arrived. They had previously been quite reckless in their behaviour; often making a great uproar; quarrelling among themselves, fighting, dancing and singing. They were now very subdued and silent, conversing almost in whispers, and stealing in and out with a soft and stealthy tread, very different from the boisterous trampling in which their arrivals and departures had hitherto been announced to the trembling captives.

Whether this change was occasioned by the presence among them of some person of authority in their ranks, or by any other cause, they were unable to decide. Sometimes they thought it was in part attributable to there being a sick man in the chamber, for last night there had been a shuffling of feet, as though a burden were brought in, and afterwards a moaning noise. But they had no means of ascertaining the truth: for any question or entreaty on their parts only provoked a storm of execrations, or something worse; and they were too happy to be left alone, unassailed by threats or admiration, to risk even that comfort, by any voluntary communication with those who held them in durance.

It was sufficiently evident, both to Emma and to the locksmith's little daughter herself, that she, Dolly, was the great object of attraction; and that so soon as they should have leisure to indulge in the softer passion, Hugh and Mr. Tappertit would certainly fall to blows for her sake; in which latter case, it was not very difficult to see whose prize she would become. With all her old horror of that man revived, and deepened into a degree of aversion and abhorrence which no language can describe; with a thousand old recollections and regrets, and causes of distress, anxiety, and fear, besetting her on all sides; poor Dolly Varden—sweet, blooming, buxom Dolly— began to hang her head, and fade, and droop, like a beautiful flower. The colour fled from her cheeks, her courage forsook her, her gentle heart failed. Unmindful of all her provoking caprices, forget- ful of all her conquests and inconstancy, with all her winning little vanities quite gone, she nestled all the livelong day in Emma Hare- dale's bosom; and, sometimes calling on her dear old grey-haired father, sometimes on her mother, and sometimes even on her old home, pined slowly away, like a poor bird in its cage.

Light hearts, light hearts, that float so gaily on a smooth stream, that are so sparkling and buoyant in the sunshine—down upon fruit, bloom upon flowers, blush in summer air, life of the winged insect, whose whole existence is a day—how soon ye sink in troubled water! Poor Dolly's heart—a little, gentle, idle, fickle thing; giddy, restless, fluttering; constant to nothing but bright looks, and smiles and laughter—Dolly's heart was breaking.

Emma had known grief, and could bear it better. She had little comfort to impart, but she could soothe and tend her, and she did so; and Dolly clung to her like a child to its nurse. In endeavouring to inspire her with some fortitude, she increased her own; and though the nights were long and the days dismal, and she felt the wasting influence of watching and fatigue, and had perhaps a more defined and clear perception of their destitute condition and its worse dan- gers, she uttered no complaint. Before the ruffians, in whose power they were, she bore herself so calmly, and with such an appearance, in the midst of all her terror, of a secret conviction that they dared not harm her, that there was not a man among them but held her in some degree of dread; and more than one believed she had a weapon hidden in her dress, and was prepared to use it.

Such was their condition when they were joined by Miss Miggs, who gave them to understand that she too had been taken prisoner

because of her charms, and detailed such feats of resistance she had
performed (her virtue having given her supernatural strength), that
they felt it quite a happiness to have her for a champion. Nor was
this the only comfort they derived at first from Miggs's presence and
society: for that young lady displayed such resignation and long-
suffering, and so much meek endurance, under her trials, and breathed
in all her chaste discourse a spirit of such holy confidence and resignation, and devout belief that all would happen for the best, that
Emma felt her courage strengthened by the bright example; never
doubting but that everything she said was true, and that she, like
them, was torn from all she loved, and agonised by doubt and apprehension. As to poor Dolly, she was roused, at first, by seeing one who
came from home; but when she heard under what circumstances she
had left it, and into whose hands her father had fallen, she wept more
bitterly than ever, and refused all comfort.

Miss Miggs was at some trouble to reprove her for this state of
mind, and to entreat her to take example by herself, who, she said,
was now receiving back, with interest, tenfold the amount of her
subscriptions to the red-brick dwelling-house, in the articles of peace
of mind and a quiet conscience. And while on serious topics, Miss
Miggs considered it her duty to try her hand at the conversion of Miss
Haredale; for whose improvement she launched into a polemical
address of some length, in the course whereof, she likened herself
unto a chosen missionary, and that young lady to a cannibal in
darkness. Indeed, she returned so often to these subjects and so
frequently called upon them to take a lesson from her,—at the same
time vaunting and, as it were, rioting in, her huge unworthiness, and
abundant excess of sin,—that, in the course of a short time, she
became, in that small chamber, rather a nuisance than a comfort, and
rendered them, if possible, even more unhappy than they had been
before.

The night had now come; and for the first time (for their jailers had
been regular in bringing food and candles), they were left in darkness.
Any change in their condition in such a place inspired new fears;
and when some hours had passed, and the gloom was still unbroken,
Emma could no longer repress her alarm.

They listened attentively. There was the same murmuring in the
outer room, and now and then a moan which seemed to be wrung
from a person in great pain, who made an effort to subdue it, but
could not. Even these men seemed to be in darkness too; for no light
shone through the chinks in the door, nor were they moving, as their
custom was, but quite still: the silence being unbroken by so much as
the creaking of a board.

At first, Miss Miggs wondered greatly in her own mind who this
sick person might be; but arriving, on second thoughts, at the conclusion that he was a part of the schemes on foot, and an artful
device soon to be employed with great success, she opined, for Miss
Haredale's comfort, that it must be some misguided Papist who had
been wounded: and this happy supposition encouraged her to say,

under her breath, "Ally Looyer!" several times.

"Is it possible," said Emma, with some indignation, "that you who have seen these men committing the outrages you have told us of, and who have fallen into their hands, like us, can exult in their cruelties!"

"Personal considerations, miss," rejoined Miggs, "sinks into nothing, afore a noble cause. Ally Looyer! Ally Looyer! Ally Looyer, good gentlemen!"

It seemed from the shrill pertinacity with which Miss Miggs repeated this form of acclamation, that she was calling the same through the keyhole of the door; but in the profound darkness she could not be seen.

"If the time has come—Heaven knows it may come at any moment —when they are bent on prosecuting the designs, whatever they may be, with which they have brought us here, can you still encourage, and take part with them?" demanded Emma.

"I thank my goodness-gracious-blessed-stars I can, miss," returned Miggs, with increased energy.—"Ally Looyer, good gentlemen!"

Even Dolly, cast down and disappointed as she was, revived at this, and bade Miggs hold her tongue directly.

"*Which*, was you pleased to observe, Miss Varden?" said Miggs, with a strong emphasis on the irrelative pronoun.

Dolly repeated her request.

"Ho, gracious me!" cried Miggs, with hysterical derision. "Ho, gracious me! Yes, to be sure I will. Ho yes! I am a abject slave, and a toiling, moiling, constant-working, always-being-found-fault-with, never-giving-satisfactions, nor-having-no-time-to-clean-oneself, potters' wessel—an't I, miss! Ho yes! My situations is lowly, and my capacities is limited, and my duties is to humble myself afore the base degenerating daughters of their blessed mothers as is fit to keep companies with holy saints but is born to persecutions from wicked relations—and to demean myself before them as is no better than Infidels—an't it, miss! Ho yes! My only becoming occupations is to help young flaunting pagins to brush and comb and titiwate theirselves into whitening and suppulchres, and leave the young men to think there an't a bit of padding in it nor no pinching ins nor fillings out nor pomatums nor deceits nor earthly wanities—an't it, miss!" Yes, to be sure it is—ho yes!"

Having delivered these ironical passages with a most wonderful volubility, and with a shrillness perfectly deafening (especially when she jerked out the interjections), Miss Miggs, from mere habit, and not because weeping was at all appropriate to the occasion, which was one of triumph, concluded by bursting into a flood of tears, and calling in an impassioned manner on the name of Simmuns.

What Emma Haredale and Dolly would have done, or how long Miss Miggs, now that she had hoisted her true colours, would have gone on waving them before their astonished senses, it is impossible to say. Nor is it necessary to speculate on these matters, for a startling interruption occurred at that moment, which took their whole attention by storm.

This was a violent knocking at the door of the house, and then its sudden bursting open; which was immediately succeeded by a scuffle in the room without, and the clash of weapons. Transported with the hope that rescue had at length arrived, Emma and Dolly shrieked aloud for help; nor were their shrieks unanswered; for after a hurried interval, a man, bearing in one hand a drawn sword, and in the other a taper, rushed into the chamber where they were confined.

It was some check upon their transport to find in this person an entire stranger, but they appealed to him, nevertheless, and besought him, in impassioned language, to restore them to their friends.

"For what other purpose am I here?" he answered, closing the door, and standing with his back against it. "With what object have I made my way to this place, through difficulty and danger, but to preserve you?"

With a joy for which it was impossible to find adequate expression, they embraced each other, and thanked Heaven for this most timely aid. Their deliverer stepped forward for a moment to put the light upon the table, and immediately returning to his former position against the door, bared his head, and looked on smilingly.

"You have news of my uncle, sir?" said Emma, turning hastily towards him.

"And of my father and mother?" added Dolly.

"Yes," he said. "Good news."

"They are alive and unhurt?" they both cried at once.

"Yes, and unhurt," he rejoined.

"And close at hand?"

"I did not say close at hand," he answered smoothly; "they are at no great distance. *Your* friends, sweet one," he added, addressing Dolly, "are within a few hours' journey. You will be restored to them, I hope, to-night."

"My uncle, sir—" faltered Emma.

"Your uncle, dear Miss Haredale, happily—I say happily, because he has succeeded where many of our creed have failed, and is safe— has crossed the sea, and is out of Britain."

"I thank God for it," said Emma, faintly.

"You say well. You have reason to be thankful: greater reason than it is possible for you, who have seen but one night of these cruel outrages, to imagine."

"Does he desire," said Emma, "'that I should follow him?"

"Do you ask if he desires it?" cried the stranger in surprise. "*If* he desires it! But you do not know the danger of remaining in England, the difficulty of escape, or the price hundreds would pay to secure the means, when you make that inquiry. Pardon me. I had forgotten that you could not, being a prisoner here."

"I gather, sir," said Emma, after a moment's pause, "from what you hint at, but fear to tell me, that I have witnessed but the beginning, and the least, of the violence to which we are exposed, and that it has not yet slackened in its fury?"

He shrugged his shoulders, shook his head, lifted up his hands; and with the same smooth smile, which was not a pleasant one to see, cast his eyes upon the ground, and remained silent.

"You may venture, sir, to speak plain," said Emma, "and to tell me the worst. We have undergone some preparation for it."

But here Dolly interposed, and entreated her not to hear the worst, but the best; and besought the gentleman to tell them the best, and to keep the remainder of his news until they were safe among their friends again.

"It is told in three words," he said, glancing at the locksmith's daughter with a look of some displeasure. "The people have risen, to a man against us; the streets are filled with soldiers, who support them and do their bidding. We have no protection but from above, and no safety but in flight; and that is a poor resource; for we are watched on every hand, and detained here, both by force and fraud. Miss Haredale, I cannot bear — believe me, that I cannot bear— by speaking of myself, or what I have done, or am prepared to do, to seem to vaunt my services before you. But, having powerful Protestant connections, and having my whole wealth embarked with theirs in shipping and commerce, I happily possessed the means of saving your uncle. I have the means of saving you; and in redemption of my sacred promise, made to him, I am here; pledged not to leave you until I have placed you in his arms. The treachery or penitence of one of the men about you, led to the discovery of your place of confinement; and that I have forced my way here, sword in hand, you see."

"You bring," said Emma, faltering, "some note or token from my uncle?"

"No, he doesn't," cried Dolly, pointing at him earnestly; "now I am sure he doesn't. Don't go with him for the world!"

"Hush, pretty fool — be silent," he replied, frowning angrily upon her. "No, Miss Haredale, I have no letter, nor any token of any kind; for while I sympathise with you, and such as you, on whom misfortune so heavy and so undeserved has fallen, I value my life. I carry, therefore, no writing which, found upon me, would lead to its certain loss. I never thought of bringing any other token, nor did Mr. Haredale think of entrusting me with one — possibly because he had good experience of my faith and honesty, and owed his life to me."

There was a reproof conveyed in these words, which to a nature like Emma Haredale's was well addressed. But Dolly, who was differently constituted, was by no means touched by it, and still conjured her, in all the terms of affection and attachment she could think of, not to be lured away.

"Time presses," said their visitor, who, although he sought to express the deepest interest, had something cold and even in his speech, that grated on the ear; "and danger surrounds us. If I have exposed myself to it, in vain, let it be so; but if you and he should ever meet again, do me justice. If you decide to remain (as I think you do), remember, Miss Haredale, that I left with a solemn caution, and acquitting myself of all the consequences to which you expose yourself."

"Stay, sir!" cried Emma—one moment, I beg you. Cannot we"—and she drew Dolly closer to her—"cannot we go together?"

"The task of conveying one female in safety through such scenes as we must encounter, to say nothing of attracting the attention of those who crowd the streets," he answered, "is enough. I have said that she will be restored to her friends to-night. If you accept the service I tender, Miss Haredale, she shall be instantly placed in safe conduct, and that promise redeemed. Do you decide to remain? People of all ranks and creeds are flying from the town, which is sacked from end to end. Let me be of use in some quarter. Do you stay, or go?"

"Dolly," said Emma, in a hurried manner, "my dear girl, this is our last hope. If we part now, it is only that we may meet again in happiness and honour. I will trust to this gentleman."

"No—no—no!" cried Dolly, clinging to her. "Pray, pray, do not!"

"You hear," said Emma, "that to-night—only to-night—within a few hours—think of that!—you will be among those who would die of grief to lose you, and who are now plunged in the deepest misery for your sake. Pray for me, dear girl, as I will for you; and never forget the many quiet hours we have passed together. Say one 'God bless you!' Say that at parting!"

But Dolly could say nothing; no, not when Emma kissed her cheek a hundred times, and covered it with tears, could she do more than hang upon her neck, and sob, and clasp, and hold her tight.

"We have time for no more of this," cried the man, unclenching her hands, and pushing her roughly off, as he drew Emma Haredale towards the door: "Now! Quick, outside there! are you ready?"

"Ay!" cried a loud voice, which made him start. "Quite ready! Stand back here, for your lives!"

And in an instant he was felled like an ox in the butcher's shambles—struck down as though a block of marble had fallen from the roof and crushed him—and cheerful light, and beaming faces came pouring in—and Emma was clasped in her uncle's embrace, and Dolly, with a shriek that pierced the air, fell into the arms of her father and mother.

What fainting there was, what laughing, what crying, what sobbing, what smiling, how much questioning, no answering, all talking together, all beside themselves with joy; what kissing, congratulating, embracing, shaking of hands, and falling into all these raptures, over and over again; no language can describe.

At length, and after a long time, the old locksmith went up and fairly hugged two strangers, who had stood apart and left them to themselves; and then they saw—whom? Yes, Edward Chester and Joseph Willet.

"See here!" cried the locksmith. "See here! where would any of us have been without these two? Oh, Mr. Edward, Mr. Edward—oh, Joe, Joe, how light, and yet how full, you have made my old heart to-night!"

"It was Mr. Edward that knocked him down, sir," said Joe: "I longed to do it, but I gave it up to him. Come, you brave and honest gentleman! Get your senses together, for you haven't long to lie here."

He had his foot upon the breast of their sham deliverer, in the absence of a spare arm; and gave him a gentle roll as he spoke. Gashford, for it was no other, crouching yet malignant, raised his scowling face, like sin subdued, and pleaded to be gently used.

"I have access to all my lord's papers, Mr. Haredale," he said, in a submissive voice: Mr. Haredale keeping his back towards him, and not once looking round: "there are very important documents among them. There are a great many in secret drawers, and distributed in various places, known only to my lord and me. I can give some very valuable information, and render important assistance to any inquiry. You will have to answer it, if I receive ill usage."

"Pah!" cried Joe, in deep disgust. "Get up, man; you're waited for, outside. Get up, do you hear?"

Gashford slowly rose; and picking up his hat, and looking with a baffled malevolence, yet with an air of despicable humility, all round the room, crawled out.

"And now, gentlemen," said Joe, who seemed to be the spokesman of the party, for all the rest were silent; "the sooner we get back to the Black Lion, the better, perhaps."

Mr. Haredale nodded assent, and drawing his niece's arm through his, and taking one of her hands between his own, passed out straightway; followed by the locksmith, Mrs. Varden, and Dolly—who would scarcely have presented a sufficient surface for all the hugs and caresses they bestowed upon her though she had been a dozen Dollys. Edward Chester and Joe followed.

And did Dolly never once look behind—not once? Was there not one little fleeting glimpse of the dark eye-lash, almost resting on her flushed cheek, and of the downcast sparkling eye it shaded? Joe thought there was—and he is not likely to have been mistaken; for there were not many eyes like Dolly's, that's the truth.

The outer room through which they had to pass, was full of men; among them, Mr. Dennis in safe keeping; and there had been, since yesterday, lying in hiding behind a wooden screen which was now thrown down, Simon Tappertit, the recreant 'prentice, burnt and bruised, and with a gun-shot wound in his body; and his legs—his perfect legs, the pride and glory of his life, the comfort of his existence—crushed into shapeless ugliness. Wondering no longer at the moans they had heard, Dolly kept closer to her father, and shuddered at the sight; but neither bruises, burns, nor gun-shot wound, nor all the torture of his shattered limbs, sent half so keen a pang to Simon's breast, as Dolly passing out, with Joe for her preserver.

A coach was ready at the door, and Dolly found herself safe and whole inside, between her father and mother, with Emma Haredale and her uncle, quite real, sitting opposite. But there was no Joe, no Edward; and they had said nothing. They had only bowed once, and kept at a distance. Dear heart! what a long way it was to the Black Lion.

CHAPTER LXXII

THE Black Lion was so far off, and occupied such a length of time in the getting at, that notwithstanding the strong presumptive evidence she had about her of the late events being real and of actual occurrence, Dolly could not divest herself of the belief that she must be in a dream which was lasting all night. Nor was she quite certain that she saw and heard with her own proper senses, even when the coach, in the fulness of time, stopped at the Black Lion, and the host of that tavern approached in a gush of cheerful light to help them to dismount, and give them hearty welcome.

There too, at the coach door, one on one side, one upon the other, were already Edward Chester and Joe Willet, who must have followed in another coach: and this was such a strange and unaccountable proceeding, that Dolly was the more inclined to favour the idea of her being fast asleep. But when Mr. Willet appeared—old John himself—so heavy-headed and obstinate, and with such a double chin as the liveliest imagination could never in its boldest flights have conjured up in all its vast proportions—then she stood corrected, and unwillingly admitted to herself that she was broad awake.

And Joe had lost an arm—he—that well-made, handsome, gallant fellow! As Dolly glanced towards him, and thought of the pain he must have suffered, and the far-off places in which he had been wandering, and wondered who had been his nurse, and hoped that whoever it was, she had been as kind and gentle and considerate as she would have been, the tears came rising to her bright eyes, one by one, little by little, until she could keep them back no longer, and so before them all, wept bitterly.

"We are all safe now, Dolly," said her father, kindly. "We shall not be separated any more. Cheer up, my love, cheer up!"

The locksmith's wife knew better perhaps, than he, what ailed her daughter. But Mrs. Varden being quite an altered woman—for the riots had done that good—added her word to his, and comforted her with similar representations.

"Mayhap," said Mr. Willet, senior, looking round upon the company, "she's hungry. That's what it is, depend upon it—I am, myself."

The Black Lion, who, like old John, had been waiting supper past all reasonable and conscionable hours, hailed this as a philosophical discovery of the profoundest and most penetrating kind; and the table being already spread, they sat down to supper straightway.

The conversation was not of the liveliest nature, nor were the appetites of some among them very keen. But, in both these respects, old John more than atoned for any deficiency on the part of the rest, and very much distinguished himself.

It was not in point of actual conversation that Mr. Willet shone so brilliantly, for he had none of his old cronies to "tackle," and was

rather timorous of venturing on Joe; having certain vague mis-
givings within him, that he was ready on the shortest notice, and on
receipt of the slightest offence, to fell the Black Lion to the floor of
his own parlour, and immediately to withdraw to China or some
other remote and unknown region, there to dwell for evermore, or at
least until he had got rid of his remaining arm and both legs, and
perhaps an eye or so, into the bargain. It was with a peculiar kind of
pantomime that Mr. Willet filled up every pause; and in this he was
considered by the Black Lion, who had been his familiar for some
years, quite to surpass and go beyond himself, and outrun the expectations of his most admiring friends.

The subject that worked in Mr. Willet's mind, and occasioned
these demonstrations, was no other than his son's bodily disfigurement, which he had never yet got himself thoroughly to believe, or
comprehend. Shortly after their first meeting, he had been observed
to wander, in a state of great perplexity, to the kitchen, and to direct
his gaze towards the fire, as if in search of his usual adviser in all
matters of doubt and difficulty. But there being no boiler at the
Black Lion, and the rioters having so beaten and battered his own
that it was quite unfit for further service, he wandered out again, in a
perfect bog of uncertainty and mental confusion, and in that state
took the strangest means of resolving his doubts: such as feeling the
sleeve of his son's great-coat, as deeming it possible that his arm
might be there; looking at his own arms and those of everybody else,
as if to assure himself that two and not one was the usual allowance;
sitting by the hour together in a brown study, as if he were endeavouring to recall Joe's image in his younger days, and to remember
whether he really had in those times one arm or a pair; and employing
himself in many other speculations of the same kind.

Finding himself at this supper, surrounded by faces with which he
had been so well acquainted in old times, Mr. Willet recurred to the
subject with uncommon vigour; apparently resolved to understand
it now or never. Sometimes, after every two or three mouthfuls, he
laid down his knife and fork, and stared at his son with all his might
—particularly at his maimed side; then, he looked slowly round the
table until he caught some person's eye, when he shook his head with
great solemnity, patted his shoulder, winked, or as one may say—for
winking was a very slow process with him—went to sleep with one
eye for a minute or two; and so, with another solemn shaking of his
head, took up his knife and fork again, and went on eating. Sometimes, he put his food into his mouth abstractedly, and, with all his
faculties concentrated on Joe, gazed at him in a fit of stupefaction as
he cut his meat with one hand, until he was recalled to himself by
symptoms of choking on his own part, and was by that means
restored to consciousness. At other times, he resorted to such small
devices as asking him for the salt, the pepper, the vinegar, the
mustard—anything that was on his maimed side—and watching
him as he handed it. By dint of these experiments, he did at last so
satisfy and convince himself, that, after a longer silence than he had

yet maintained, he laid down his knife and fork on either side his plate, drank a long draught from a tankard beside him (still keeping his eyes on Joe), and leaning backward in his chair and fetching a long breath, said, as he looked all round the board:

"It's been took off!"

"By George!" said the Black Lion, striking the table with his hand, "he's got it!"

"Yes, sir," said Mr. Willet, with the look of a man who felt that he had earned a compliment, and deserved it. "That's where it is. It's been took off."

"Tell him where it was done," said the Black Lion to Joe.

"At the defence of the Savannah, father."

"At the defence of the Salwanners," repeated Mr. Willet, softly; again looking round the table.

"In America, where the war is," said Joe.

"In America, where the war is," repeated Mr. Willet. "It was took off in the defence of the Salwanners in America where the war is." Continuing to repeat these words to himself in a low tone of voice (the same information had been conveyed to him in the same terms, at least fifty times before), Mr. Willet arose from table, walked round to Joe, felt his empty sleeve all the way up, from the cuff, to where the stump of his arm remained; shook his hand ; lighted his pipe at the fire, took a long whiff, walked to the door, turned round once when he had reached it, wiped his left eye with the back of his forefinger, and said, in a faltering voice: "My son's arm—was took off—at the defence of the—Salwanners—in America—where the war is"—with which words he withdrew, and returned no more that night.

Indeed, on various pretences, they all withdrew, one after another, save Dolly, who was left sitting there alone. It was a great relief to be alone, and she was crying to her heart's content, when she heard Joe's voice at the end of the passage, bidding somebody good night.

Good night! Then he was going elsewhere—to some distance, perhaps. To what kind of home *could* he be going, now that it was so late!

She heard him walk along the passage, and pass the door. But there was a hesitation in his footsteps. He turned back—Dolly's heart beat high—he looked in.

"Good night!"—he didn't say Dolly, but there was comfort in his not saying Miss Varden.

"Good night!" sobbed Dolly.

"I am sorry you take on so much, for what is past and gone," said Joe kindly. "Don't. I can't bear to see you do it. Think of it no longer. You are safe and happy now."

Dolly cried the more.

"You must have suffered very much within these few days—and yet you're not changed, unless it's for the better. They said you were, but I don't see it. You were—you were always very beautiful," said Joe, "but you are more beautiful than ever, now. You are indeed. There can be no harm in my saying so, for you must know it. You are told so very often, I am sure."

As a general principle, Dolly *did* know it, and *was* told so, very often. But the coachmaker had turned out, years ago, to be a special donkey; and whether she had been afraid of making similar discoveries in others, or had grown by dint of long custom to be careless of compliments generally, certain it is that although she cried so much, she was better pleased to be told so now, than ever she had been in her life.

"I shall bless your name," sobbed the locksmith's little daughter, "as long as I live. I shall never hear it spoken without feeling as if my heart would burst. I shall remember it in my prayers, every night and morning till I die!"

"Will you?" said Joe, eagerly. "Will you indeed? It makes me—well, it makes me very glad and proud to hear you say so."

Dolly still sobbed, and held her handkerchief to her eyes. Joe still stood, looking at her.

"Your voice," said Joe, "brings up old times so pleasantly, that, for the moment, I feel as if that night—there can be no harm in talking of that night now—had come back, and nothing had happened in the meantime. I feel as if I hadn't suffered any hardships, but had knocked down poor Tom Cobb only yesterday, and had come to see you with my bundle on my shoulder before running away—You remember?"

"Remember! But she said nothing. She raised her eyes for an instant. It was but a glance; a little, tearful, timid glance. It kept Joe silent though, for a long time.

"Well!" he said stoutly, "it was to be otherwise, and was. I have been abroad, fighting all the summer and frozen up all the winter, ever since. I have come back as poor in purse as I went, and crippled for life besides. But, Dolly, I would rather have lost this other arm—ay, I would rather have lost my head—than have come back to find you dead, or anything but what I always pictured you to myself, and what I always hoped and wished to find you. Thank God for all!"

Oh how much, and how keenly, the little coquette of five years ago, felt now! She had found her heart at last. Never having known its worth till now, she had never known the worth of his. How priceless it appeared!

"I did hope once," said Joe, in his homely way, "that I might come back a rich man, and marry you. But I was a boy then, and have long known better than that. I am a poor, maimed, discharged soldier, and must be content to rub through life as I can. I can't say even now, that I shall be glad to see you married, Dolly; but I *am* glad—yes, I am, and glad to think I can say so—to know that you are admired and courted, and can pick and choose for a happy life. It's a comfort to me to know that you'll talk to your husband about me; and I hope the time will come when I may be able to like him, and to shake hands with him, and to come and see you as a poor friend who knew you when you were a girl. God bless you!"

His hand *did* tremble; but for all that, he took it away again and left her.

CHAPTER LXXIII

By this Friday night—for it was on Friday in the riot week, that Emma and Dolly were rescued, by the timely aid of Joe and Edward Chester—the disturbances were entirely quelled, and peace and order were restored to the affrighted city. True, after what had happened, it was impossible for any man to say how long this better state of things might last, or how suddenly new outrages, exceeding even those so lately witnessed, might burst forth and fill its streets with ruin and bloodshed; for this reason, those who had fled from the recent tumults still kept at a distance, and many families, hitherto unable to procure the means of flight, now availed themselves of the calm, and withdrew into the country. The shops, too, from Tyburn to Whitechapel, were still shut; and very little business was transacted in any of the places of great commercial resort. But, notwithstanding, and in spite of the melancholy forebodings of that numerous class of society who see with the greatest clearness into the darkest perspectives, the town remained perfectly quiet. The strong military force disposed in every advantageous quarter, and stationed at every commanding point, held the scattered fragments of the mob in check; the search after rioters was prosecuted with unrelenting vigour; and if there were any among them so desperate and reckless as to be inclined, after the terrible scenes they had beheld, to venture forth again, they were so daunted by these resolute measures, that they quickly shrunk into their hiding-places, and had no thought but for their safety.

In a word, the crowd was utterly routed. Upwards of two hundred had been shot dead in the streets. Two hundred and fifty more were lying, badly wounded, in the hospitals; of whom seventy or eighty died within a short time afterwards. A hundred were already in custody, and more were taken every hour. How many perished in the conflagrations, or by their own excesses, is unknown; but that numbers found a terrible grave in the hot ashes of the flames they had kindled, or crept into vaults and cellars to drink in secret or to nurse their sores, and never saw the light again, is certain. When the embers of the fires had been black and cold for many weeks, the labourers' spades proved this, beyond a doubt.

Seventy-two private houses and four strong jails were destroyed in the four great days of these riots. The total loss of property, as estimated by the sufferers, was one hundred and fifty-five thousand pounds; at the lowest and least partial estimate of disinterested persons, it exceeded one hundred and twenty-five thousand pounds. For this immense loss, compensation was soon afterwards made out of the public purse, in pursuance of a vote of the House of Commons; the sum being levied on the various wards in the city, on the county, and the borough of Southwark. Both Lord Mansfield and Lord

Saville, however, who had been great sufferers, refused to accept of any compensation whatever.

The House of Commons, sitting on Tuesday with locked and guarded doors, had passed a resolution to the effect that, as soon as the tumults subsided, it would immediately proceed to consider the petitions presented from many of his Majesty's Protestant subjects, and would take the same into its serious consideration. While this question was under debate, Mr. Herbert, one of the members present, indignantly rose and called upon the House to observe that Lord George Gordon was then sitting under the gallery with the blue cockade, the signal of rebellion, in his hat. He was not only obliged, by those who sat near, to take it out; but offering to go into the street to pacify the mob with the somewhat indefinite assurance that the House was prepared to give them "the satisfaction they sought," was actually held down in his seat by the combined force of several members. In short, the disorder and violence which reigned triumphant out of doors, penetrated into the senate, and there, as elsewhere, terror and alarm prevailed, and ordinary forms were for the time forgotten.

On the Thursday, both Houses had adjourned until the following Monday se'nnight, declaring it impossible to pursue their deliberations with the necessary gravity and freedom, while they were surrounded by armed troops. And now that the rioters were dispersed, the citizens were beset with a new fear; for, finding the public thoroughfares and all their usual places of resort filled with soldiers entrusted with the free use of fire and sword, they began to lend a greedy ear to the rumours which were afloat of martial law being declared, and to dismal stories of prisoners having been seen hanging on lamp-posts in Cheapside and Fleet-street. These terrors being promptly dispelled by a Proclamation declaring all the rioters in custody would be tried by a special commission in due course of law, a fresh alarm was engendered by its being whispered abroad that French money had been found on some of the rioters, and that the disturbances had been fomented by foreign powers who sought to compass the overthrow and ruin of England. This report, which was strengthened by the diffusion of anonymous hand-bills, but which, if it had any foundation at all, probably owed its origin to the circumstance of some few coins which were not English money having been swept into the pockets of the insurgents with other miscellaneous booty, and afterwards discovered on the prisoners or the dead bodies,—caused a great sensation; and men's minds being in that excited state when they are most apt to catch at any shadow of apprehension, was bruited about with much industry.

All remaining quiet, however, during the whole of this Friday, and on this Friday night, and no new discoveries being made, confidence began to be restored, and the most timid and desponding breathed again. In Southwark, no fewer than three thousand of the inhabitants formed themselves into a watch, and patrolled the streets every hour. Nor were the citizens slow to follow so good an example: and it being the manner of peaceful men to be very bold when the danger is over, they were abundantly fierce and daring; not scrupling to question the stoutest passenger with great severity, and carrying it with a very high hand over all errand-boys, servant-girls, and 'prentices.

As day deepened into evening, and darkness crept into the nooks and corners of the town as if it were mustering in secret and gathering strength to venture into the open ways, Barnaby sat in his dungeon, wondering at the silence, and listening in vain for the noise and out-cry which had ushered in the night of late. Beside him, with his hand in hers, sat one in whose companionship he felt at peace. She was worn, and altered, full of grief, and heavy-hearted; but the same to him.

"Mother," he said, after a long silence: "how long,—how many days and nights,—shall I be kept here?"

"Not many, dear. I hope not many."

"You hope! Ay, but your hoping will not undo these chains. I hope, but they don't mind that. Grip hopes, but who cares for Grip?"

The raven gave a short, dull, melancholy croak. It said "Nobody," as plainly as a croak could speak.

"Who cares for Grip, except you and me?" said Barnaby, smooth-ing the bird's rumpled feathers with his hand. "He never speaks in this place: he never says a word in jail; he sits and mopes all day in his dark corner, dozing sometimes, and sometimes looking at the light that creeps in through the bars, and shines in his bright eye as if a spark from those great fires had fallen into the room and was burning yet. But who cares for Grip?"

The raven croaked again—Nobody.

"And by the way," said Barnaby, withdrawing his hand from the bird, and laying it upon his mother's arm, as he looked eagerly in her face; "if they kill me—they may: I heard it said they would—what will become of Grip when I am dead?"

The sound of the word, or the current of his own thoughts, sug-gested to Grip his old phrase "Never say die!" But he stopped short in the middle of it, drew a dismal cork, and subsided into a faint croak, as if he lacked the heart to get through the shortest sentence.

"Will they take *his* life as well as mine?" said Barnaby. "I wish they would. If you and I and he could die together, there would be none to feel sorry, or to grieve for us. But do what they will, I don't fear them, mother!"

"They will not harm you," she said, her tears choking her utter-ance. "They never will harm you, when they know all. I am sure they never will."

"Oh! Don't be too sure of that," cried Barnaby with pleasure in the belief that she was self-deceived, and in his own sagacity. "They have marked me from the first. I heard them say so to each other when they brought me to this place last night; and I believe them. Don't you cry for me. They said that I was bold, and so I am, and so I will be. You may think that I am silly, but I can die as well as another.—I have done no harm, have I?" he added quickly.

"None before Heaven," she answered.

"Why then," said Barnaby, "let them do their worst. You told me once—you—when I asked you what death meant, that it was nothing to be feared, if we did no harm.—Aha! mother, you thought I had forgotten that!"

His merry laugh and playful manner smote her to the heart. She drew him closer to her, and besought him to talk to her in whispers and to be very quiet, for it was getting dark, and their time was short, and she would soon have to leave him for the night.

"You will come to-morrow?" said Barnaby.

Yes. And every day. And they would never part again.

He joyfully replied that this was well, and what he wished, and what he had felt quite certain she would tell him; and then he asked her where she had been so long, and why she had not come to see him when he had been a great soldier, and ran through the wild schemes he had had for their being rich and living prosperously, and with some faint notion in his mind that she was sad and he had made her so, tried to console and comfort her, and talked of their former life and his old sports and freedom: little dreaming that every word he uttered only increased her sorrow, and that her tears fell faster at the freshened recollection of their lost tranquillity.

"Mother," said Barnaby, as they heard the man approaching to close the cells for the night, "when I spoke to you just now about my father you cried 'Hush!' and turned away your head. Why did you do so? Tell me why, in a word. You thought *he* was dead. You are not sorry that he is alive and has come back to us. Where is he? Here?"

"Do not ask any one where he is, or speak about him," she made answer.

"Why not?" said Barnaby. "Because he is a stern man, and talks roughly? Well! I don't like him, or want to be with him by myself; but why not speak about him?"

"Because I am sorry that he is alive; sorry that he has come back, and sorry that he and you have ever met. Because, dear Barnaby, the endeavour of my life has been to keep you two asunder."

"Father and son asunder! Why?"

"He has," she whispered in his ear, "he has shed blood. The time has come when you must know it. He has shed the blood of one who loved him well, and trusted him, and never did him wrong in word or deed."

Barnaby recoiled in horror, and glancing at his stained wrist for an instant, wrapped it, shuddering, in his dress.

"But," she added hastily as the key turned in the lock, "although we shun him, he is your father, dearest, and I am his wretched wife. They seek his life, and he will lose it. It must not be by our means; nay, if we could win him back to penitence, we should be bound to love him yet. Do not seem to know him, except as one who fled with you from the jail, and if they question you about him, do not answer them. God be with you through the night, dear boy! God be with you!"

She tore herself away, and in a few seconds Barnaby was alone. He stood for a long time rooted to the spot, with his face hidden in his hands; then flung himself, sobbing, on his miserable bed.

But the moon came slowly up in all her gentle glory, and the stars looked out, and through the small compass of the grated window, as through the narrow crevice of one good deed in a murky life of guilt, the face of Heaven shone bright and merciful. He raised his head; gazed upward at the quiet sky, which seemed to smile upon the earth in sadness, as if the night, more thoughtful than the day, looked down in sorrow on the sufferings and evil deeds of men; and felt its peace sink deep into his heart. He, a poor idiot, caged in his narrow cell, was as much lifted up to God, while gazing on the mild light, as the freest and most favoured man in all the spacious city; and in his ill-remembered prayer, and in the fragment of the childish hymn, with which he sung and crooned himself asleep, there breathed as true a spirit as ever studied homily expressed, or old cathedral arches echoed.

As his mother crossed a yard on her way out, she saw, through a grated door which separated it from another court, her husband, walking round and round, with his hands folded on his breast, and his head hung down. She asked the man who conducted her, if she might speak a word with this prisoner. Yes, but she must be quick, for he was locking up for the night, and there was but a minute or so to spare. Saying this, he unlocked the door, and bade her go in.

It grated harshly as it turned upon its hinges, but he was deaf to the noise, and still walked round and round the little court, without raising his head or changing his attitude in the least. She spoke to him, but her voice was weak, and failed her. At length she put herself in his track, and when he came near, stretched out her hand and touched him.

He started backward, trembling from head to foot; but seeing who it was, demanded why she came there. Before she could reply, he spoke again.

"Am I to live or die? Do you murder too, or spare?"

"My son—our son," she answered, "is in this prison."

"What is that to me?" he cried, stamping impatiently on the stone pavement. "I know it. He can no more aid me than I can aid him. If you are come to talk of him, begone!"

As he spoke he resumed his walk, and hurried round the court as before. When he came again to where she stood, he stopped, and said,

"Am I to live or die? Do you repent?"

"Oh!—do *you?*" she answered. "Will you, while time remains? Do not believe that I could save you, if I dared."

"Say if you would," he answered with an oath, as he tried to disengage himself and pass on. "Say if you would."

"Listen to me for one moment," she returned; "for but a moment. I am but newly risen from a sick-bed, from which I never hoped to rise again. The best among us think, at such a time, of good intentions half-performed and duties left undone. If I have ever, since that fatal night, omitted to pray for your repentance before death—if I omitted even then, anything which might tend to urge it on you when the horror of your crime was fresh—if, in our later meeting, I yielded to the dread that was upon me, and forgot to fall upon my knees and solemnly adjure you, in the name of him you sent to his account with Heaven, to prepare for the retribution which must come, and which is stealing on you now—I humbly before you, and in the agony of supplication in which you see me, beseech that you will let me make atonement."

"What is the meaning of your canting words?" he answered roughly. "Speak so that I may understand you."

"I will," she answered, "I desire to. Bear with me for a moment more. The hand of Him who set His curse on murder, is heavy on us now. You cannot doubt it. Our son, our innocent boy, on whom His anger fell before his birth, is in this place on peril of his life—brought here by your guilt; yes, by that alone, as Heaven sees and knows, for he has been led astray in the darkness of his intellect, and that is the terrible consequence of your crime."

"If you come, woman-like, to load me with reproaches—" he muttered, again endeavouring to break away.

"I do not. I have a different purpose. You must hear it. If not to-night, to-morrow; if not to-morrow, at another time. You *must* hear it. Husband, escape is hopeless—impossible."

"You tell me so, do you?" he said, raising his manacled hand, and shaking it. "You!"

"Yes," she said, with indescribable earnestness. "But why?"

"To make me easy in this jail. To make the time 'twixt this and death, pass pleasantly. For my good—yes, for my good, of course," he said, grinding his teeth, and smiling at her with a livid face.

"Not to load you with reproaches," she replied; "not to aggravate the tortures and miseries of your condition, not to give you one hard word, but to restore you to peace and hope. Husband, dear husband, if you will but confess this dreadful crime; if you will but implore forgiveness of Heaven and of those whom you have wronged on earth; if you will dismiss these vain uneasy thoughts, which never can be realised, and will rely on Penitence and on the Truth, I promise you, in the great name of the Creator, whose image you have defaced, that He will comfort and console you. And for myself," she cried, clasping her hands, and looking upward, "I swear before Him, as He knows my heart and reads it now, that from that hour I will love and cherish you as I did of old, and watch you night and day in the short interval that will remain to us, and soothe you with my truest love and duty, and pray with you, that one threatening judgment may be arrested, and that our boy may be spared to bless God, in his poor way, in the free air and light!"

He fell back and gazed at her while she poured out these words, as though he were for a moment awed by her manner, and knew not what to do. But anger and fear soon got the mastery of him, and he spurned her from him.

Lord George Gordon in the Tower.

"Begone!" he cried. "Leave me! You plot, do you! You plot to get speech with me, and let them know I am the man they say I am. A curse on you and on your boy."

"On him the curse has already fallen," she replied, wringing her hands.

"Let if fall heavier. Let it fall on one and all. I hate you both. The worst has come to me. The only comfort that I seek or I can have, will be the knowledge that it comes to you. Now go!"

She would have urged him gently, even then, but he menaced her with his chain.

"I say go—I say it for the last time. The gallows has me in its grasp, and it is a black phantom that may urge me on to something more. Begone! I curse the hour that I was born, the man I slew, and all the living world!"

In a paroxysm of wrath, and terror, and the fear of death, he broke from her, and rushed into the darkness of his cell, where he cast himself jangling down upon the stone floor, and smote it with his iron hands. The man returned to lock the dungeon door, and having done so, carried her away.

On that warm, balmy night in June, there were glad faces and light hearts in all quarters of the town, and sleep, banished by the late horrors, was doubly welcomed. On that night, families made merry in their houses, and greeted each other on the common danger they had escaped; and those who had been denounced, ventured into the streets; and they who had been plundered, got good shelter. Even the timorous Lord Mayor, who was summoned that night before the Privy Council to answer for his conduct, came back contented; observing to all his friends that he had got off very well with a reprimand, and repeating with huge satisfaction his memorable defence before the Council, "that such was his temerity, he thought death would have been his portion."

On that night, too, more of the scattered remnants of the mob were traced to their lurking-places, and taken; and in the hospitals, and deep among the ruins they had made, and in the ditches, and fields, many unshrouded wretches lay dead: envied by those who had been active in the disturbances, and who pillowed their doomed heads in the temporary jails.

And in the Tower, in a dreary room whose thick stone walls shut out the hum of life, and made a stillness which the records left by former prisoners with those silent witnesses seemed to deepen and intensify; remorseful for every act that had been done by every man among the cruel crowd; feeling for the time their guilt his own, and their lives put in peril by himself; and finding, amidst such reflections, little comfort in fanaticism, or in his fancied call; sat the unhappy author of all—Lord George Gordon.

He had been made prisoner that evening. "If you are sure it's me you want," he said to the officers, who waited outside with the warrant for his arrest on a charge of High Treason, "I am ready to accompany you"—which he did without resistance. He was conducted first before the Privy Council, and afterwards to the Horse Guards, and then was taken by way of Westminster Bridge and back over London Bridge (for the purpose of avoiding the main streets), to the Tower, under the strongest guard ever known to enter its gates with a single prisoner.

Of all his forty thousand men, not one remained to bear him company. Friends, dependents, followers,—none were there. His fawning secretary had played the traitor; and he whose weakness had been goaded and urged on by so many for their own purposes, was desolate and alone.

CHAPTER LXXIV

MR. DENNIS, having been made prisoner late in the evening, was removed to a neighbouring round-house for that night, and carried before a justice for examination on the next day, Saturday. The charges against him being numerous and weighty, and it being in particular proved, by the testimony of Gabriel Varden, that he had shown a special desire to take his life, he was committed for trial. Moreover he was honoured with the distinction of being considered a chief among the insurgents, and received from the magistrate's lips the complimentary assurance that he was in a position of imminent danger, and would do well to prepare himself for the worst.

To say that Mr. Dennis's modesty was not somewhat startled by these honours, or that he was altogether prepared for so flattering a reception, would be to claim for him a greater amount of stoical philosophy than even he possessed. Indeed this gentleman's stoicism was of that not uncommon kind, which enables a man to bear with exemplary fortitude the afflictions of his friends, but renders him, by way of counterpoise, rather selfish and sensitive in respect of any that happen to befall himself. It is therefore no disparagement to the great officer in question to state, without disguise or concealment, that he was at first very much alarmed, and that he betrayed divers emotions of fear, until his reasoning powers came to his relief, and set before him a more hopeful prospect.

In proportion as Mr. Dennis exercised these intellectual qualities with which he was gifted, in reviewing his best chances of coming off handsomely and with small personal inconvenience, his spirits rose, and his confidence increased. When he remembered the great estimation in which his office was held, and the constant demand for his services; when he bethought himself, how the Statute Book regarded him as a kind of Universal Medicine applicable to men, women, and children, of every age and variety of criminal constitution; and how high he stood, in his official capacity, in the favour of the Crown, and both Houses of Parliament, the Mint, the Bank of England and the Judges of the land; when he recollected that whatever Ministry was in or out, he remained their peculiar pet and panacea, and that for his sake England stood single and conspicuous among the civilised nations of the earth: when he called these things

to mind and dwelt upon them, he felt certain that the national gratitude *must* relieve him from the consequences of his late proceedings,
and would certainly restore him to his old place in the happy social
system.

With these crumbs, or as one may say, with these whole loaves of
comfort to regale upon, Mr. Dennis took his place among the escort
that awaited him, and repaired to jail with a manly indifference.
Arriving at Newgate, where some of the ruined cells had been hastily
fitted up for the safe keeping of rioters, he was warmly received by
the turnkeys, as an unusual and interesting case, which agreeably
relieved their monotonous duties. In this spirit, he was fettered with
great care, and conveyed into the interior of the prison.

"Brother," cried the hangman, as, following an officer, he traversed
under these novel circumstances the remains of passages with which
he was well acquainted, "am I going to be along with anybody?"

"If you'd have left more walls standing, you'd have been alone,"
was the reply. "As it is, we're cramped for room, and you'll have
company."

"Well," returned Dennis, "I don't object to company, brother. I
rather like company. I was formed for society, I was."

"That's rather a pity, an't it?" said the man.

"No," answered Dennis, "I'm not aware that it is. Why should it
be a pity, brother?"

"Oh! I don't know," said the man carelessly. "I thought that was
what you meant. Being formed for society, and being cut off in your
flower, you know—"

"I say," interposed the other quickly, "what are you talking of?
Don't. Who's a-going to be cut off in their flowers?"

"Oh, nobody particular. I thought you was, perhaps," said the man.

Mr. Dennis wiped his face, which had suddenly grown very hot,
and remarking in a tremulous voice to his conductor that he had
always been fond of his joke, followed him in silence until he stopped
at a door.

"This is my quarters, is it?" he asked facetiously.

"This is the shop, sir," replied his friend.

He was walking in, but not with the best possible grace, when he
suddenly stopped, and started back.

"Halloa!" said the officer. "You're nervous."

"Nervous!" whispered Dennis in great alarm. "Well I may be.
Shut the door."

"I will, when you're in," returned the man.

"But I can't go in there," whispered Dennis. "I can't be shut up
with that man. Do you want me to be throttled, brother?"

The officer seemed to entertain no particular desire on the subject
one way or other, but briefly remarking that he had his orders, and
intended to obey them, pushed him in, turned the key, and retired.

Dennis stood trembling with his back against the door, and
involuntarily raising his arm to defend himself, stared at a man, the
only other tenant of the cell, who lay, stretched at his full length,

upon a stone bench, and who paused in his deep breathing as if he were about to wake. But he rolled over on one side, let his arm fall negligently down, drew a long sigh, and murmuring indistinctly, fell fast asleep again.

Relieved in some degree by this, the hangman took his eyes for an instant from the slumbering figure, and glanced round the cell in search of some 'vantage-ground or weapon of defence. There was nothing moveable within it, but a clumsy table which could not be displaced without noise, and a heavy chair. Stealing on tiptoe towards this latter piece of furniture, he retired with it into the remotest corner, and intrenching himself behind it, watched the enemy with the utmost vigilance and caution.

The sleeping man was Hugh; and perhaps it was not unnatural for Dennis to feel in a state of very uncomfortable suspense, and to wish with his whole soul that he might never wake again. Tired of standing, he crouched down in his corner after some time, and rested on the cold pavement; but although Hugh's breathing still proclaimed that he was sleeping soundly, he could not trust him out of his sight for an instant. He was so afraid of him, and of some sudden onslaught, that he was not content to see his closed eyes through the chair-back, but every now and then, rose stealthily to his feet, and peered at him with outstretched neck, to assure himself that he really was still asleep, and was not about to spring upon him when he was off his guard.

He slept so long and so soundly, that Mr. Dennis began to think he might sleep on until the turnkey visited them. He was congratulating himself upon these promising appearances, and blessing his stars with much fervour, when one or two unpleasant symptoms manifested themselves: such as another motion of the arm, another sigh, a restless tossing of the head. Then, just as it seemed that he was about to fall heavily to the ground from his narrow bed, Hugh's eyes opened.

It happened that his face was turned directly towards his unexpected visitor. He looked lazily at him for some half-dozen seconds without any aspect of surprise or recognition; then suddenly jumped up, and with a great oath pronounced his name.

"Keep off, brother, keep off!" cried Dennis, dodging behind the chair. "Don't do me a mischief. I'm a prisoner like you. I haven't the free use of my limbs. I'm quite an old man. Don't hurt me!"

He whined out the last three words in such piteous accents, that Hugh, who had dragged away the chair, and aimed a blow at him with it, checked himself, and bade him get up.

"I'll get up certainly, brother," cried Dennis, anxious to propitiate him by any means in his power. "I'll comply with any request of yours, I'm sure. There—I'm up now. What can I do for you? Only say the word, and I'll do it."

"What can you do for me!" cried Hugh, clutching him by the collar with both hands, and shaking him as though he were bent on stopping his breath by that means. "What have you done for me?"

"The best. The best that could be done," returned the hangman.

Hugh made him no answer, but shaking him in his strong grip

until his teeth chattered in his head, cast him down upon the floor, and flung himself on the bench again.

"If it wasn't for the comfort it is to me, to see you here," he muttered, "I'd have crushed your head against it; I would."

It was some time before Dennis had breath enough to speak, but as soon as he could resume his propitiatory strain, he did so.

"I did the best that could be done, brother," he whined; "I did indeed. I was forced with two bayonets and I don't know how many bullets on each side of me, to point you out. If you hadn't been taken, you'd have been shot; and what a sight that would have been —a fine young man like you!"

"Will it be a better sight now?" asked Hugh, raising his head, with such a fierce expression, that the other durst not answer him just then.

"A deal better," said Dennis meekly, after a pause. "First, there's all the chances of the law, and they're five hundred strong. We may get off scot-free. Unlikelier things than that have come to pass. Even if we shouldn't, and the chances fail, we can but be worked off once: and when it's well done, it's so neat, so skilful, so captivating, if that don't seem too strong a word, that you'd hardly believe it could be brought to sich perfection. Kill one's fellow-creeturs off, with muskets!—Pah!" and his nature so revolted at the bare idea, that he spat upon the dungeon pavement.

His warming on this topic, which to one unacquainted with his pursuits and tastes appeared like courage; together with his artful suppression of his own secret hopes, and mention of himself as being in the same condition with Hugh; did more to soothe that ruffian than the most elaborate arguments could have done, or the most abject submission. He rested his arms upon his knees, and stooping forward, looked from beneath his shaggy hair at Dennis, with something of a smile upon his face.

"The fact is, brother," said the hangman, in a tone of greater confidence, "that you have got into bad company. The man that was with you was looked after more than you, and it was him I wanted. As to me, what have I got by it? Here we are, in one and the same plight."

"Lookee, rascal," said Hugh, contracting his brows, "I'm not altogether such a shallow blade but I know you expected to get something by it, or you wouldn't have done it. But it's done, and you're here, and it will soon be all over with you and me; and I'd as soon die as live, or live as die. Why should I trouble myself to have revenge on you? To eat, and drink, and go to sleep, as long as I stay here, is all I care for. If there was but a little more sun to bask in than can find its way into this cursed place, I'd lie in it all day, and not trouble myself to sit or stand up once. That's all the care I have for myself. Why should I care for *you?*"

Finishing this speech with a growl like the yawn of a wild beast, he stretched himself upon the bench again, and closed his eyes once more.

After looking at him in silence for some moments, Dennis, who was greatly relieved to find him in this mood, drew the chair towards his rough couch and sat down near him—taking the precaution, however, to keep out of the range of his brawny arm.

"Well said, brother; nothing could be better said," he ventured to observe. "We'll eat and drink of the best, and sleep our best, and make the best of it every way. Anything can be got for money. Let's spend it merrily."

"Ay," said Hugh, coiling himself into a new position.—"Where is it?"

"Why, they took mine from me at the lodge," said Mr. Dennis; "but mine's a peculiar case."

"Is it? They took mine too."

"Why then, I tell you what, brother," Dennis began. "You must look up your friends—"

"My friends!" cried Hugh, starting up and resting on his hands. "Where are my friends?"

"Your relations then," said Dennis.

"Ha ha ha!" laughed Hugh, waving one arm above his head. "He talks of friends to me—talks of relations to a man whose mother died the death in store for her son, and left him, a hungry brat, without a face he knew in all the world! He talks of this to me!"

"Brother," cried the hangman, whose features underwent a sudden change, "you don't mean to say—"

"I mean to say," Hugh interposed, "that they hung her up at Tyburn. What was good enough for her, is good enough for me. Let them do the like by me as soon as they please—the sooner the better. Say no more to me. I'm going to sleep."

"But I want to speak to you; I want to hear more about that," said Dennis, changing colour.

"If you're a wise man," growled Hugh, raising his head to look at him with a frown, "you'll hold your tongue. I tell you I'm going to sleep."

Dennis venturing to say something more in spite of this caution, the desperate fellow struck at him with all his force, and missing him, lay down again with many muttered oaths and imprecations, and turned his face towards the wall. After two or three ineffectual twitches at his dress, which he was hardy enough to venture upon, notwithstanding his dangerous humour, Mr. Dennis, who burnt, for reasons of his own, to pursue the conversation, had no alternative but to sit as patiently as he could: waiting his further pleasure.

CHAPTER LXXV

A MONTH has elapsed,—and we stand in the bed-chamber of Sir John Chester. Through the half-opened window, the Temple Garden looks green and pleasant; the placid river, gay with boat and barge, and dimpled with the plash of many an oar, sparkles in the distance; the sky is blue and clear; and the summer air steals gently in, filling

the room with perfume. The very town, the smoky town, is radiant.
High roofs and steeple tops, wont to look black and sullen, smile a
cheerful grey; every old gilded vane, and ball, and cross, glitters
anew in the bright morning sun; and, high among them all, St. Paul's
towers up, showing its lofty crest in burnished gold.

Sir John was breakfasting in bed. His chocolate and toast stood
upon a little table at his elbow; books and newspapers lay ready to
his hand, upon the coverlet; and, sometimes pausing to glance with
an air of tranquil satisfaction round the well-ordered room, and
sometimes to gaze indolently at the summer sky, he ate, and drank,
and read the news luxuriously.

The cheerful influence of the morning seemed to have some effect,
even upon his equable temper. His manner was unusually gay;
his smile more placid and agreeable than usual; his voice more clear
and pleasant. He laid down the newspaper he had been reading;
leaned back upon his pillow with the air of one who resigned himself
to a train of charming recollections; and after a pause, soliloquised as
follows:

"And my friend the centaur, goes the way of his mamma! I am
not surprised. And his mysterious friend Mr. Dennis, likewise! I am
not surprised. And my old postman, the exceedingly free-and-easy
young madman of Chigwell! I am quite rejoiced. It's the very best
thing that could possibly happen to him."

After delivering himself of these remarks, he fell again into his
smiling train of reflection; from which he roused himself at length to
finish his chocolate, which was getting cold, and ring the bell for more.

The new supply arriving, he took the cup from his servant's hand;
and saying, with a charming affability, "I am obliged to you, Peak,"
dismissed him.

"It is a remarkable circumstance," he mused, dallying lazily with
the teaspoon, "that my friend the madman should have been within
an ace of escaping, on his trial; and it was a good stroke of chance (or,
as the world would say, a providential occurrence) that the brother of
my Lord Mayor should have been in court, with other country justices, into whose very dense heads curiosity had penetrated. For
though the brother of my Lord Mayor was decidedly wrong; and
established his near relationship to that amusing person beyond all
doubt, in stating that my friend was sane, and had, to his knowledge, wandered about the country with a vagabond parent, avowing
revolutionary and rebellious sentiments; I am not the less obliged
to him for volunteering that evidence. These insane creatures make
such very odd and embarrassing remarks, that they really ought to be
hanged for the comfort of society."

The country justice had indeed turned the wavering scale against
poor Barnaby, and solved the doubt that trembled in his favour.
Grip little thought how much he had to answer for.

"They will be a singular party," said Sir John, leaning his head upon
his hand, and sipping his chocolate; "a very curious party. The
hangman himself; the centaur; and the madman. The centaur would

make a very handsome preparation in Surgeons' Hall, and would benefit science extremely. I hope they have taken care to bespeak him.—Peak, I am not at home, of course, to anybody but the hair-dresser."

This reminder to his servant was called forth by a knock at the door, which the man hastened to open. After a prolonged murmur of question and answer, he returned; and as he cautiously closed the room-door behind him, a man was heard to cough in the passage.

"Now, it is of no use, Peak," said Sir John, raising his hand in depreciation of his delivering any message; "I am not at home. I cannot possibly hear you. I told you I was not at home, and my word is sacred. Will you never do as you are desired?"

Having nothing to oppose to this reproof, the man was about to withdraw, when the visitor who had given occasion to it, probably rendered impatient by delay, knocked with his knuckles at the chamber-door, and called out that he had urgent business with Sir John Chester, which admitted of no delay.

"Let him in," said Sir John. "My good fellow," he added, when the door was opened, "how come you to intrude yourself in this extraordinary manner upon the privacy of a gentleman? How can you be so wholly destitute of self-respect as to be guilty of such remarkable ill-breeding?"

"My business, Sir John, is not of a common kind, I do assure you," returned the person he addressed. "If I have taken any uncommon course to get admission to you, I hope I shall be pardoned on that account."

"Well! we shall see!" returned Sir John, whose face cleared up when he saw who it was, and whose prepossessing smile was now restored. "I am sure we have met before," he added in his winning tone, "but really I forget your name?"

"My name is Gabriel Varden, sir."

"Varden, of course, Varden," returned Sir John, tapping his forehead. "Dear me, how very defective my memory becomes! Varden to be sure—Mr. Varden the locksmith. You have a charming wife, Mr. Varden, and a most beautiful daughter. They are well?"

Gabriel thanked him, and said they were.

"I rejoice to hear it," said Sir John. "Commend me to them when you return, and say that I wished I were fortunate enough to convey myself, the salute which I entrust you to deliver. And what," he asked very sweetly, after a moment's pause, "can I do for you? You may command me freely."

"I thank you, Sir John," said Gabriel, with some pride in his manner, "but I have come to ask no favour of you, though I come on business.—Private," he added, with a glance at the man who stood looking on, "and very pressing business."

"I cannot say you are the more welcome for being independent, and have nothing to ask of me," returned Sir John, graciously, "for I should have been happy to render you a service; still, you are welcome on any terms. Oblige me with some more chocolate, Peak, and don't wait."

The man retired, and left them alone.

"Sir John," said Gabriel, "I am a working-man, and have been so, all my life. If I don't prepare you enough for what I have to tell; if I come to the point too abruptly; and give you a shock, which a gentleman could have spared you, or at all events lessened very much; I hope you will give me credit for meaning well. I wish to be careful and considerate, and I trust that in a straightforward person like me, you'll take the will for the deed."

"Mr. Varden," returned the other, perfectly composed under this exordium; "I beg you'll take a chair. Chocolate, perhaps, you don't relish? Well! it *is* an acquired taste, no doubt."

"Sir John," said Gabriel, who had acknowledged with a bow the invitation to be seated, but had not availed himself of it; "Sir John" —he dropped his voice and drew nearer to the bed—"I am just now come from Newgate—"

"Good Gad!" cried Sir John, hastily sitting up in bed; "from Newgate, Mr. Varden! How could you be so very imprudent as to come from Newgate! Newgate, where there are jail-fevers, and ragged people, and bare-footed men and women, and a thousand horrors! Peak, bring the camphor, quick! Heaven and earth, Mr. Varden, my dear, good soul, how could you come from Newgate?"

Gabriel returned no answer, but looked on in silence while Peak (who had entered with the hot chocolate) ran to a drawer, and returning with a bottle, sprinkled his master's dressing-gown and the bedding; and besides moistening the locksmith himself, plentifully, described a circle round about him on the carpet. When he had done this, he again retired; and Sir John, reclining in an easy attitude upon his pillow, once more turned a smiling face towards his visitor.

"You will forgive me, Mr. Varden, I am sure, for being at first a little sensitive both on your account and my own. I confess I was startled, notwithstanding your delicate exordium. Might I ask you to do me the favour not to approach any nearer?—You have really come from Newgate!"

The locksmith inclined his head.

"In-deed! And now, Mr. Varden, all exaggeration and embellishment apart," said Sir John Chester, confidentially, as he sipped his chocolate, "what kind of place *is* Newgate?"

"A strange place, Sir John," returned the locksmith, "of a sad and doleful kind. A strange place, where many strange things are heard and seen; but few more strange than that I come to tell you of. The case is urgent. I am sent here."

"Not—no, no—not from the jail?"

"Yes, Sir John; from the jail."

"And my good, credulous, open-hearted friend," said Sir John, setting down his cup, and laughing,—"by whom?"

"By a man called Dennis—for many years the hangman, and to-morrow morning the hanged," returned the locksmith.

Sir John had expected—had been quite certain from the first— that he would say he had come from Hugh, and was prepared to meet him on that point. But this answer occasioned him a degree of astonishment, which, for the moment, he could not, with all his command of feature, prevent his face from expressing. He quickly subdued it, however, and said in the same light tone:

"And what does the gentleman require of me? My memory may be at fault again, but I don't recollect that I ever had the pleasure of an introduction to him, or that I ever numbered him among my personal friends, I do assure you, Mr. Varden."

"Sir John," returned the locksmith, gravely, "I will tell you, as nearly as I can, in the words he used to me, what he desires that you should know, and what you ought to know without a moment's loss of time."

Sir John Chester settled himself in a position of greater repose, and looked at his visitor with an expression of face which seemed to say, "This is an amusing fellow! I'll hear him out."

"You may have seen in the newspapers, sir," said Gabriel, pointing to the one which lay by his side, "that I was a witness against this man upon his trial some days since; and that it was not his fault I was alive, and able to speak to what I knew."

"*May* have seen!" cried Sir John. "My dear Mr. Varden, you are quite a public character, and live in all men's thoughts most deservedly. Nothing can exceed the interest with which I read your testimony, and remembered that I had the pleasure of a slight acquaintance with you.—I hope we shall have your portrait published?"

"This morning, sir," said the locksmith, taking no notice of these compliments, "early this morning, a message was brought to me from Newgate, at this man's request, desiring that I would go and see him, for he had something particular to communicate. I needn't tell you that he is no friend of mine, and that I had never seen him, until the rioters beset my house."

Sir John fanned himself gently with the newspaper, and nodded.

"I knew, however, from the general report," resumed Gabriel, "that the order for his execution to-morrow, went down to the prison last night; and looking upon him as a dying man, I complied with his request."

"You are quite a Christian, Mr. Varden," said Sir John; "and in that amiable capacity, you increase my desire that you should take a chair."

"He said," continued Gabriel, looking steadily at the knight, "that he had sent to me, because he had no friend or companion in the whole world (being the common hangman), and because he believed from the way in which I had given my evidence, that I was an honest man, and would act truly by him. He said that, being shunned by every one who knew his calling, even by people of the lowest and most wretched grade, and finding, when he joined the rioters, that the men he acted with had no suspicion of it (which I believe is true enough, for a poor fool of an old 'prentice of mine was one of them), he had kept his own counsel, up to the time of his being taken and put in jail."

"Very discreet of Mr. Dennis," observed Sir John with a slight yawn, though still with the utmost affability, "but—except for your admirable and lucid manner of telling it, which is perfect—not very interesting to me."

"When," pursued the locksmith, quite unabashed and wholly regardless of these interruptions, "when he was taken to the jail, he found that his fellow-prisoner, in the same room, was a young man, Hugh by name, a leader in the riots, who had been betrayed and given up by himself. From something which fell from this unhappy creature in the course of the angry words they had at meeting, he discovered that his mother had suffered the death to which they both are now condemned.—The time is very short, Sir John."

The knight laid down his paper fan, replaced his cup upon the table at his side, and, saving for the smile that lurked about his mouth, looked at the locksmith with as much steadiness as the locksmith looked at him.

"They have been in prison now, a month. One conversation led to many more; and the hangman soon found, from a comparison of time, and place, and dates, that he had executed the sentence of the law upon this woman, himself. She had been tempted by want—as so many people are—into the easy crime of passing forged notes. She was young and handsome; and the traders who employ men, women, and children in this traffic, looked upon her as one who was well adapted for their business, and who would probably go on without suspicion for a long time. But they were mistaken; for she was stopped in the commission of her very first offence, and died for it. She was of gipsy blood, Sir John—"

It might have been the effect of a passing cloud which obscured the sun, and cast a shadow on his face; but the knight turned deadly pale. Still he met the locksmith's eye, as before.

"She was of gipsy blood, Sir John," repeated Gabriel, "and had a high, free spirit. This, and her good looks, and her lofty manner, interested some gentlemen who were easily moved by dark eyes; and efforts were made to save her. They might have been successful, if she would have given them any clue to her history. But she never would, or did. There was reason to suspect that she would make an attempt upon her life. A watch was set upon her night and day; and from that time she never spoke again—"

Sir John stretched out his hand towards his cup. The locksmith going on, arrested it half-way.

"—Until she had but a minute to live. Then she broke silence, and said, in a low firm voice which no one heard but this executioner, for all other living creatures had retired and left her to her fate, 'If I had a dagger within these fingers and he was within my reach, I would strike him dead before me, even now!' The man asked 'Who?' She said, 'The father of her boy.'"

Sir John drew back his outstretched hand, and seeing that the locksmith paused, signed to him with easy politeness and without any new appearance of emotion, to proceed.

"It was the first word she had ever spoken, from which it could be understood that she had any relative on earth. 'Was the child alive?' he asked. 'Yes. He asked her where it was, its name, and whether she had any wish respecting it. She had but one, she said. It was that the boy might live and grow in utter ignorance of his father, so that no arts might teach him to be gentle and forgiving. When he became a man she trusted to the God of their tribe to bring the father and the son together, and revenge her through her child. He asked her other questions, but she spoke no more. Indeed, he says, she scarcely said this much to him, but stood with her face turned upwards to the sky, and never looked towards him once."

Sir John took a pinch of snuff; glanced approvingly at an elegant little sketch, entitled "Nature," on the wall; and raising his eyes to the locksmith's face again, said, with an air of courtesy and patronage, "You were observing, Mr. Varden—"

"That she never," returned the locksmith, who was not to be diverted by any artifice from his firm manner, and his steady gaze, "that she never looked towards him once, Sir John; and so she died, and he forgot her. But, some years afterwards, a man was sentenced to die the same death, who was a gipsy too; a sunburnt swarthy fellow, almost a wild man; and while he lay in prison, under sentence, he, who had seen the hangman more than once while he was free, cut an image of him on his stick, by way of braving death, and showing those who attended on him, how little he cared or thought about it. He gave this stick into his hands at Tyburn, and told him then, that the woman I had spoken of had left her own people to join a fine gentleman, and that, being deserted by him, and cast off by her old friends, she had sworn within her own proud breast, that whatever her misery might be, she would ask no help of any human being. He told him that she had kept her word to the last; and that, meeting even him in the streets—he had been fond of her once, it seems—she had slipped from him by a trick, and he never saw her again, until, being in one of the frequent crowds at Tyburn, with some of his rough companions, he had been driven almost mad by seeing, in the criminal under another name, whose death he had come to witness, herself. Standing in the same place in which she had stood, he told the hangman this, and told him, too, her real name, which only her own people and the gentleman for whose sake she had left them, knew.—That name he will tell again, Sir John, to none but you."

"To none but me!" exclaimed the knight, pausing in the act of raising his cup to his lips with a perfectly steady hand, and curling up his little finger for the better display of a brilliant ring with which it was ornamented: "but me!—My dear Mr. Varden, how very preposterous, to elect me for his confidence! With you at his elbow, too, who are so perfectly trustworthy!"

"Sir John, Sir John," returned the locksmith, "at twelve tomorrow, these men die. Hear the words I have to add, and do not hope to deceive me; for though I am a plain man of humble station,

and you are a gentleman of rank and learning, the truth raises me to
your level, and I KNOW that you anticipate the disclosure with which
I am about to end, and that you believe this doomed man, Hugh, to
be your son."

"Nay," said Sir John, bantering him with a gay air; "the wild
gentleman, who died so suddenly, scarcely went as far as that, I
think?"

"He did not," returned the locksmith, "for she had bound him by
some pledge, known only to these people, and which the worst among
them respect, not to tell your name: but, in a fantastic pattern on the
stick, he had carved some letters, and when the hangman asked it,
he bade him, especially if he should ever meet with her son in after
life, remember that place well."

"What place?"

"Chester."

The knight finished his cup of chocolate with an appearance of
infinite relish, and carefully wiped his lips upon his handkerchief.

"Sir John," said the locksmith, "this is all that has been told to me;
but since these two men have been left for death, they have conferred
together closely. See them, and hear what they can add. See this
Dennis, and learn from him what he has not trusted to me. If you,
who hold the clue to all, want corroboration (which you do not), the
means are easy."

"And to what," said Sir John Chester, rising on his elbow, after
smoothing the pillow for its reception; "my dear, good-natured,
estimable Mr. Varden—with whom I cannot be angry if I would—to
what does all this tend?"

"I take you for a man, Sir John, and I suppose it tends to some
pleading of natural affection in your breast," returned the locksmith.
"I suppose to the straining of every nerve, and the exertion of all the
influence you have, or can make, in behalf of your miserable son, and
the man who has disclosed his existence to you. At the worst, I
suppose to your seeing your son, and awakening him to a sense of his
crime and danger. He has no such sense now. Think what his life
must have been, when he said in my hearing, that if I moved you to
anything, it would be to hastening his death, and ensuring his silence,
if you had it in your power!"

"And have you, my good Mr. Varden," said Sir John in a tone of
mild reproof, "have you really lived to your present age, and
remained so very simple and credulous, as to approach a gentleman
of established character with such credentials as these, from desperate men in their last extremity, catching at any straw? Oh dear! Oh
fie, fie!"

The locksmith was going to interpose, but he stopped him:

"On any other subject, Mr. Varden, I shall be delighted—I shall
be charmed—to converse with you, but I owe it to my own character
not to pursue this topic for another moment."

"Think better of it sir, when I am gone," returned the locksmith;
"think better of it, sir. Although you have, thrice within as many

weeks, turned your lawful son, Mr. Edward, from your door, you may
have time, you may have years to make your peace with *him*, Sir
John: but that twelve o'clock will soon be here, and soon be past for
ever."

"I thank you very much," returned the knight, kissing his delicate
hand to the locksmith, "for your guileless advice; and I only wish,
my good soul, although your simplicity is quite captivating, that you
had a little more worldly wisdom. I never so much regretted the
arrival of my hair-dresser as I do at this moment. God bless you!
Good morning! You'll not forget my message to the ladies, Mr.
Varden? Peak, show Mr. Varden to the door."

Gabriel said no more, but gave the knight a parting look, and left
him. As he quitted the room, Sir John's face changed; and the smile
gave place to a haggard and anxious expression, like that of a weary
actor jaded by the performance of a difficult part. He rose from his
bed with a heavy sigh, and wrapped himself in his morning-gown.

"So she kept her word," he said, "and was constant to her threat!
I would I had never seen that dark face of hers,—I might have read
these consequences in it, from the first. This affair would make a
noise abroad, if it rested on better evidence; but, as it is, and by not
joining the scattered links of the chain, I can afford to slight it.—
Extremely distressing to be the parent of such an uncouth creature!
Still, I gave him very good advice. I told him he would certainly be
hanged. I could have done no more if I had known of our relationship;
and there are a great many fathers who have never done as much
for *their* natural children.—The hair-dresser may come in, Peak!"

The hair-dresser came in; and saw in Sir John Chester (whose
accommodating conscience was soon quieted by the numerous
precedents that occurred to him in support of his last observation)
the same imperturbable, fascinating, elegant gentleman he had seen
yesterday, and many yesterdays before.

CHAPTER LXXVI

As the locksmith walked slowly away from Sir John Chester's chambers, he lingered under the trees which shaded the path, almost
hoping that he might be summoned to return. He had turned back
thrice, and still loitered at the corner, when the clock struck twelve.

It was a solemn sound, and not merely for its reference to to-
morrow; for he knew that in that chime the murderer's knell was rung.
He had seen him pass along the crowded street, amidst the execra-
tion of the throng; and marked his quivering lip and trembling limbs;
the ashy hue upon his face, his clammy brow, the wild distraction of
his eye—the fear of death that swallowed up all other thoughts, and
gnawed without cessation at his heart and brain. He had marked the
wandering look, seeking for hope, and finding, turn where it would,
despair. He had seen the remorseful, pitiful, desolate creature, riding,
with his coffin by his side, to the gibbet. He knew that, to the last, he
had been an unyielding, obdurate man; that in the savage terror of

his condition he had hardened, rather than relented, to his wife and child; and that the last words which had passed his white lips were curses on them as his enemies.

Mr. Haredale had determined to be there, and see it done. Nothing but the evidence of his own senses could satisfy that gloomy thirst for retribution which had been gathering upon him for so many years. The locksmith knew this, and when the chimes had ceased to vibrate, hurried away to meet him.

"For these two men," he said, as he went, "I can do no more. Heaven have mercy on them!—alas! I say I can do no more for them, but whom *can* I help? Mary Rudge will have a home, and a firm friend when she most wants one; but Barnaby—poor Barnaby— willing Barnaby—what aid can I render him? There are many, many men of sense, God forgive me," cried the honest locksmith, stopping in a narrow court to pass his hand across his eyes, "I could better afford to lose than Barnaby. We have always been good friends but I never knew, till now, how much I loved the lad."

There were not many in the great city who thought of Barnaby that day, otherwise than as an actor in a show which was to take place to-morrow. But if the whole population had had him in their minds, and had wished his life to be spared, not one among them could have done so with a purer zeal or greater singleness of heart than the good locksmith.

Barnaby was to die. There was no hope. It is not the least evil attendant upon the frequent exhibition of this last dread punishment, of Death, that it hardens the minds of those who deal it out, and makes them, though they be amiable men in other respects, indifferent to, or unconscious of, their great responsibility. The word had gone forth that Barnaby was to die. It went forth, every month, for lighter crimes. It was a thing so common, that very few were startled by the awful sentence, or cared to question its propriety. Just then, too, when the law had been so flagrantly outraged, its dignity must be asserted. The symbol of its dignity,—stamped upon every page of the criminal statute book,—was the gallows; and Barnaby was to die.

They had tried to save him. The locksmith had carried petitions and memorials to the fountain-head, with his own hands. But the well was not one of mercy, and Barnaby was to die.

From the first his mother had never left him, save at night; and with her beside him, he was as usual contented. On this last day, he was more elated and more proud than he had been yet; and when she dropped the book she had been reading to him aloud, and fell upon his neck, he stopped in his busy task of folding a piece of crape about his hat, and wondered at her anguish. Grip uttered a feeble croak, half in encouragement, it seemed, and half in remonstrance, but he wanted heart to sustain it, and lapsed abruptly into silence.

With them who stood upon the brink of the great gulf which none can see beyond, Time, so soon to lose itself in vast Eternity, rolled on like a mighty river, swoln and rapid as it nears the sea. It was morning but now; they had sat and talked together in a dream; and here was evening. The dreadful hour of separation, which even yesterday had seemed so distant, was at hand.

They walked out into the court-yard, clinging to each other, but not speaking. Barnaby knew that the jail was a dull, sad, miserable place, and looked forward to to-morrow, as to a passage from it to something bright and beautiful. He had a vague impression too, that he was expected to be brave—that he was a man of great consequence, and that the prison people would be glad to make him weep. He trod the ground more firmly as he thought of this, and bade her take heart and cry no more, and feel how steady his hand was. "They call me silly, mother. They shall see to-morrow!"

Dennis and Hugh were in the court-yard. Hugh came forth from his cell as they did, stretching himself as though he had been sleeping. Dennis sat upon a bench in a corner, with his knees and chin huddled together, and rocked himself to and fro like a person in severe pain.

The mother and son remained on one side of the court, and these two men upon the other. Hugh strode up and down, glancing fiercely every now and then at the bright summer sky, and looking round, when he had done so, at the walls.

"No reprieve, no reprieve! Nobody comes near us. There's only the night left now!" moaned Dennis faintly, as he wrung his hands. "Do you think they'll reprieve me in the night, brother? I've known reprieves come in the night, afore now. I've known 'em come as late as five, six, and seven o'clock in the morning. Don't you think there's a good chance yet,—don't you? Say you do. Say *you* do, young man," whined the miserable creature, with an imploring gesture towards Barnaby, "or I shall go mad!"

"Better be mad than sane, here," said Hugh. "*Go* mad."

"But tell me what you think. Somebody tell me what he thinks!" cried the wretched object,—so mean, and wretched, and despicable, that even pity's self might have turned away, at sight of such a being in the likeness of a man —"isn't there a chance for me,—isn't there a good chance for me? Isn't it likely they may be doing this to frighten me? Don't you think it is? Oh!" he almost shrieked, as he wrung his hands, "won't anybody give me comfort!"

"You ought to be the best, instead of the worst," said Hugh, stopping before him. "Ha, ha, ha! See the hangman, when it comes home to him."

"You don't know what it is," cried Dennis, actually writhing as he spoke: "I do. That I should come to be worked off! I! I! That *I* should come!"

"And why not?" said Hugh, as he thrust back his matted hair to get a better view of his late associate. "How often, before I knew your trade, did I hear you talking of this as if it was a treat?"

"I an't unconsistent," screamed the miserable creature; "I'd talk so again, if I was hangman. Some other man has got my old opinions at this minute. That makes it worse. Somebody's longing to work me off. I know by myself that somebody must be!"

"He'll soon have his longing," said Hugh, resuming his walk.

"Think of that, and be quiet."

Although one of these men displayed, in his speech and bearing, the most reckless hardihood; and the other, in his every word and action, testified such an extreme of abject cowardice that it was humiliating to see him; it would be difficult to say which of them would most have repelled and shocked an observer. Hugh's was the dogged desperation of a savage at the stake; the hangman was reduced to a condition little better, if any, than that of a hound with the halter round his neck. Yet, as Mr. Dennis knew and could have told them, these were the two commonest states of mind in persons brought to their pass. Such was the wholesale growth of the seed sown by the law, that this kind of harvest was usually looked for, as a matter of course.

In one respect they all agreed. The wandering and uncontrollable train of thought, suggesting sudden recollections of things distant and long forgotten and remote from each other—the vague restless craving for something undefined, which nothing could satisfy—the swift flight of the minutes, fusing themselves into hours, as if by enchantment—the rapid coming of the solemn night—the shadow of death always upon them, and yet so dim and faint, that objects the meanest and most trivial started from the gloom beyond, and forced themselves upon the view—the impossibility of holding the mind, even if they had been so disposed, to penitence and preparation, or of keeping it to any point while one hideous fascination tempted it away—these things were common to them all, and varied only in their outward tokens.

"Fetch me the book I left within—upon your bed," she said to Barnaby, as the clock struck. "Kiss me first."

He looked in her face, and saw there, that the time was come. After a long embrace, he tore himself away, and ran to bring it to her; bidding her not stir till he came back. He soon returned, for a shriek recalled him,—but she was gone.

He ran to the yard-gate, and looked through. They were carrying her away. She had said her heart would break. It was better so.

"Don't you think," whimpered Dennis, creeping up to him, as he stood with his feet rooted to the ground, gazing at the blank walls—"don't you think there's still a chance? It's a dreadful end; it's a terrible end for a man like me. Don't you think there's a chance? I don't mean for you, I mean for me. Don't let *him* hear us" (meaning Hugh); "he's so desperate."

"Now then," said the officer, who had been lounging in and out with his hands in his pockets, and yawning as if he were in the last extremity for some subject of interest: "it's time to turn in, boys."

"Not yet," cried Dennis, "not yet. Not for an hour yet."

"I say,—your watch goes different from what it used to," returned the man. "Once upon a time it was always too fast. It's got the other fault now."

"My friend," cried the wretched creature, falling on his knees, "my dear friend—you always were my dear friend—there's some mistake.

Some letter has been mislaid, or some messenger has been stopped upon the way. He may have fallen dead. I saw a man once, fall down dead in the street, myself, and he had papers in his pocket. Send to inquire. Let somebody go to inquire. They never will hang me. They never can.—Yes, they will," he cried, starting to his feet with a terrible scream. "They'll hang me by a trick, and keep the pardon back. It's a plot against me. I shall lose my life!" And uttering another yell, he fell in a fit upon the ground.

"See the hangman when it comes home to him!" cried Hugh again, as they bore him away—"Ha ha ha! Courage, bold Barnaby, what care we? Your hand! They do well to put us out of the world, for if we got loose a second time, we wouldn't let them off so easy, eh? Another shake! A man can die but once. If you wake in the night, sing that out lustily, and fall asleep again. Ha ha ha!"

Barnaby glanced once more through the grate into the empty yard; and then watched Hugh as he strode to the steps leading to his sleeping-cell. He heard him shout, and burst into a roar of laughter, and saw him flourish his hat. Then he turned away himself, like one who walked in his sleep; and, without any sense of fear or sorrow, lay down on his pallet, listening for the clock to strike again.

CHAPTER LXXVII

The time wore on. The noises in the streets became less frequent by degrees, until silence was scarcely broken save by the bells in the church towers, marking the progress—softer and more stealthy while the city slumbered—of that Great Watcher with the hoary head, who never sleeps or rests. In the brief interval of darkness and repose which feverish towns enjoy, all busy sounds were hushed; and those who awoke from dreams lay listening in their beds, and longed for dawn, and wished the dead of the night were past.

Into the street outside the jail's main wall, workmen came straggling at this solemn hour, in groups of two or three, and meeting in the centre, cast their tools upon the ground and spoke in whispers. Others soon issued from the jail itself, bearing on their shoulders planks and beams; these materials being all brought forth, the rest bestirred themselves, and the dull sound of hammers began to echo through the stillness.

Here and there among this knot of labourers, one, with a lantern or a smoky link, stood by to light his fellows at their work; and by its doubtful aid, some might be dimly seen taking up the pavement of the road, while others held great upright posts, or fixed them in the holes thus made for their reception. Some dragged slowly on, towards the rest, an empty cart, which they brought rumbling from the prison-yard; while others erected strong barriers across the street. All were busily engaged. Their dusky figures moving to and fro, at that unusual hour, so active and so silent, might have been taken for those of shadowy creatures toiling at midnight on some ghostly unsubstantial work, which, like themselves, would vanish with the first gleam of day, and leave but morning mist and vapour.

While it was yet dark, a few lookers-on collected, who had plainly come there for the purpose and intended to remain: even those who had to pass the spot on their way to some other place, lingered, and lingered yet, as though the attraction of that were irresistible. Meanwhile the noise of saw and mallet went on briskly, mingled with the clattering of boards on the stone pavement of the road, and sometimes with the workmen's voices as they called to one another. Whenever the chimes of the neighbouring church were heard—and that was every quarter of an hour—a strange sensation, instantaneous and indescribable, but perfectly obvious, seemed to pervade them all.

Gradually, a faint brightness appeared in the east, and the air, which had been very warm all through the night, felt cool and chilly. Though there was no daylight yet, the darkness was diminished, and the stars looked pale. The prison, which had been a mere black mass with little shape or form, put on its usual aspect; and ever and anon a solitary watchman could be seen upon its roof, stopping to look down upon the preparations in the street. This man, from forming, as it were, a part of the jail, and knowing or being supposed to know all that was passing within, became an object of as much interest, and was as eagerly looked for, and as awfully pointed out, as if he had been a spirit.

By and by, the feeble light grew stronger, and the houses, with their sign-boards and inscriptions, stood plainly out, in the dull grey morning. Heavy stage waggons crawled from the inn-yard opposite; and travellers peeped out; and as they rolled sluggishly away, cast many a backward look towards the jail. And now, the sun's first beams came glancing into the street; and the night's work, which, in its various stages and in the varied fancies of the lookers-on, had taken a hundred shapes, wore its own proper form—a scaffold, and a gibbet.

As the warmth of the cheerful day began to shed itself upon the scanty crowd, the murmur of tongues was heard, shutters were thrown open, and blinds drawn up, and those who had slept in rooms over against the prison, where places to see the execution were let at high prices, rose hastily from their beds. In some of the houses, people were busy taking out the window sashes for the better accommodation of spectators; in others, the spectators were already seated, and beguiling the time with cards, or drink, or jokes among themselves. Some had purchased seats upon the house-tops, and were already crawling to their stations from parapet and garret-window. Some were yet bargaining for good places, and stood in them in a state of indecision: gazing at the slowly-swelling crowd, and at the workmen as they rested listlessly against the scaffold—affecting to listen with indifference to the proprietor's eulogy of the commanding view his house afforded, and the surpassing cheapness of his terms.

A fairer morning never shone. From the roofs and upper stories of these buildings, the spires of city churches and the great cathedral dome were visible, rising up beyond the prison into the blue sky, and clad in the colour of light summer clouds, and showing in the clear atmosphere their every scrap of tracery and fret-work, and every niche and loophole. All was brightness and promise, excepting in the street below, into which (for it yet lay in shadow) the eye looked down as into a dark trench, where, in the midst of so much life, and hope, and renewal of existence, stood the terrible instrument of death. It seemed as if the very sun forbore to look upon it.

But it was better, grim and sombre in the shade, than when, the day being advanced, it stood confessed in the full glare and glory of the sun, with its black paint blistering, and its nooses dangling in the light like loathsome garlands. It was better in the solitude and gloom of midnight with a few forms clustering about it, than in the freshness and the stir of morning: the centre of an eager crowd. It was better haunting the street like a spectre, when men were in their beds, and influencing perchance the city's dreams, than braving the broad day, and thrusting its obscene presence upon their waking senses.

Five o'clock had struck—six—seven—and eight. Along the two main streets at either end of the cross-way, a living stream had now set in, rolling towards the marts of gain and business. Carts, coaches, waggons, trucks, and barrows, forced a passage through the outskirts of the throng, and clattered onward in the same direction. Some of these which were public conveyances and had come from a short distance in the country, stopped; and the driver pointed to the gibbet with his whip, though he might have spared himself the pains, for the heads of all the passengers were turned that way without his help, and the coach-windows were stuck full of staring eyes. In some of the carts and waggons, women might be seen, glancing fearfully at the same unsightly thing; and even little children were held up above the people's heads to see what kind of a toy a gallows was, and learn how men were hanged.

Two rioters were to die before the prison, who had been concerned in the attack upon it; and one directly afterwards in Bloomsbury Square. At nine o'clock, a strong body of military marched into the street, and formed and lined a narrow passage into Holborn, which had been indifferently kept all night by constables. Through this, another cart was brought (the one already mentioned had been employed in the construction of the scaffold), and wheeled up to the prison-gate. These preparations made, the soldiers stood at ease; the officers lounged to and fro, in the alley they had made, or talked together at the scaffold's foot; and the concourse, which had been rapidly augmenting for some hours, and still received additions every minute, waited with an impatience which increased with every chime of St. Sepulchre's clock, for twelve at noon.

Up to this time they had been very quiet, comparatively silent, save when the arrival of some new party at a window, hitherto unoccupied, gave them something new to look at or to talk of. But, as the hour approached, a buzz and hum arose, which, deepening every moment, soon swelled into a roar, and seemed to fill the air. No words or even voices could be distinguished in this clamour, nor did they speak much to each other; though such as were better informed upon the topic than the rest, would tell their neighbours, perhaps, that they might know the hangman when he came out, by his being the shorter one: and that the man who was to suffer with him was named Hugh: and that it was Barnaby Rudge who would be hanged in Bloomsbury Square.

The hum grew, as the time drew near, so loud, that those who were at the windows could not hear the church-clock strike, though it was close at hand. Nor had they any need to hear it, either, for they could see it in the people's faces. So surely as another quarter chimed, there was a movement in the crowd—as if something had passed over it—as if the light upon them had been changed—in which the fact was readable as on a brazen dial, figured by a giant's hand.

Three quarters past eleven! The murmur now was deafening, yet every man seemed mute. Look where you would among the crowd, you saw strained eyes and lips compressed; it would have been difficult for the most vigilant observer to point this way or that, and say that yonder man had cried out. It were as easy to detect the motion of lips in a sea-shell.

Three quarters past eleven! Many spectators who had retired from the windows, came back refreshed, as though their watch had just begun. Those who had fallen asleep, roused themselves; and every person in the crowd made one last effort to better his position—which caused a press against the sturdy barriers that made them bend and yield like twigs. The officers, who until now had kept together, fell into their several positions, and gave the words of command. Swords were drawn, muskets shouldered, and the bright steel winding its way among the crowd, gleamed and glittered in the sun like a river. Along this shining path, two men came hurrying on, leading a horse, which was speedily harnessed to the cart at the prison door. Then, a profound silence replaced the tumult that had so long been gathering, and a breathless pause ensued. Every window was now choked up with heads; the house-tops teemed with people—clinging to chimneys, peering over gable-ends, and holding on where the sudden loosening of any brick or stone would dash them down into the street. The church tower, the church roof, the church yard, the prison leads, the very water-spouts and lamp-posts—every inch of room—swarmed with human life.

At the first stroke of twelve the prison-bell began to toll. Then the roar—mingled now with cries of "Hats off!" and "Poor fellows!" and, from some specks in the great concourse, with a shriek or groan—burst forth again. It was terrible to see—if any one in that distraction of excitement could have seen—the world of eager eyes, all strained upon the scaffold and the beam.

The hollow murmuring was heard within the jail as plainly as without. The three were brought forth into the yard, together, as it resounded through the air. They knew its import well.

"D'ye hear?" cried Hugh, undaunted by the sound. "They expect us! I heard them gathering when I woke in the night, and turned over on t'other side and fell asleep again. We shall see how they welcome the hangman, now that it comes home to him Ha, ha, ha!"

The Ordinary coming up at this moment, reproved him for his indecent mirth, and advised him to alter his demeanour.

"And why, master?" said Hugh. "Can I do better than bear it easily? *You* bear it easily enough. Oh! never tell me," he cried, as the other would have spoken, "for all your sad look and your solemn air, you think little enough of it! They say you're the best maker of lobster salads in London. Ha, ha! I've heard that, you see, before now. Is it a good one, this morning—is your hand in? How does the breakfast look? I hope there's enough, and to spare, for all this hungry company that'll sit down to it, when the sight's over."

"I fear," observed the clergyman, shaking his head, "that you are incorrigible."

"You're right. I am," rejoined Hugh sternly. "Be no hypocrite, master! You make a merry-making of this, every month; let me be merry, too. If you want a frightened fellow there's one that'll suit you. Try your hand upon him."

He pointed, as he spoke, to Dennis, who, with his legs trailing on the ground, was held between two men; and who trembled so, that all his joints and limbs seemed racked by spasms. Turning from this wretched spectacle, he called to Barnaby, who stood apart.

"What cheer, Barnaby? Don't be downcast, lad. Leave that to *him*."

"Bless you," cried Barnaby, stepping lightly towards him, "I'm not frightened, Hugh. I'm quite happy. I wouldn't desire to live now, if they'd let me. Look at me! Am I afraid to die? Will they see *me* tremble?"

Hugh gazed for a moment at his face, on which there was a strange, unearthly smile; and at his eye, which sparkled brightly; and interposing between him and the Ordinary, gruffly whispered to the latter:

"I wouldn't say much to him, master, if I was you. He may spoil your appetite for breakfast, though you *are* used to it."

He was the only one of the three who had washed or trimmed himself that morning. Neither of the others had done so, since their doom was pronounced. He still wore the broken peacock's feathers in his hat; and all his usual scraps of finery were carefully disposed about his person. His kindling eye, his firm step, his proud and resolute bearing, might have graced some lofty act of heroism; some voluntary sacrifice, born of a noble cause and pure enthusiasm; rather than that felon's death.

But all these things increased his guilt. They were mere assumptions. The law had declared it so, and so it must be. The good minister had been greatly shocked, not a quarter of an hour before, at his parting with Grip. For one in his condition, to fondle a bird!——

The yard was filled with people; bluff civic functionaries, officers of justice, soldiers, the curious in such matters, and guests who had been bidden as to a wedding. Hugh looked about him, nodded gloomily to some person in authority, who indicated with his hand in what direction he was to proceed; and clapping Barnaby on the shoulder, passed out with the gait of a lion.

They entered a large room, so near to the scaffold that the voices of those who stood about it, could be plainly heard: some beseeching the javelin-men to take them out of the crowd: others crying to those behind, to stand back, for they were pressed to death, and suffocating for want of air.

In the middle of this chamber, two smiths, with hammers, stood beside an anvil. Hugh walked straight up to them, and set his foot upon it with a sound as though it had been struck by a heavy weapon. Then, with folded arms, he stood to have his irons knocked off: scowling haughtily round, as those who were present eyed him narrowly and whispered to each other.

It took so much time to drag Dennis in, that this ceremony was over with Hugh, and nearly over with Barnaby, before he appeared. He no sooner came into the place he knew so well, however, and among faces with which he was so familiar, than he recovered strength and sense enough to clasp his hands and make a last appeal.

"Gentlemen, good gentlemen," cried the abject creature, grovelling down upon his knees, and actually prostrating himself upon the stone floor: "Governor, dear governor—honourable sheriffs—worthy gentlemen—have mercy upon a wretched man that has served His Majesty, and the Law, and Parliament, for so many years, and don't —don't let me die—because of a mistake."

"Dennis," said the governor of the jail, "you know what the course is, and that the order came with the rest. You know that we could do nothing, even if we would."

"All I ask, sir,—all I want and beg, is time, to make it sure," cried the trembling wretch, looking wildly round for sympathy. "The King and Government can't know it's me; I'm sure they can't know it's me; or they never would bring me to this dreadful slaughter-house. They know my name, but they don't know it's the same man. Stop my execution—for charity's sake stop my execution, gentle-men—till they can be told that I've been hangman here, nigh thirty year. Will no one go and tell them!" he implored, clenching his hands and glaring round, and round, and round again—"will no charitable person go and tell them!"

"Mr. Akerman," said a gentleman who stood by, after a moment's pause, "since it may possibly produce in this unhappy man a better frame of mind, even at this last minute, let me assure him that he was well known to have been the hangman, when his sentence was considered."

"—But perhaps they think on that account that the punishment's not so great," cried the criminal, shuffling towards this speaker on his knees, and holding up his folded hands; "whereas it's worse, it's worse a hundred times, to me than any man. Let them know that, sir. Let them know that. They've made it worse to me by giving me so much to do. Stop my execution till they know that!"

The governor beckoned with his hand, and the two men, who had supported him before, approached. He uttered a piercing cry:

"Wait! Wait! Only a moment—only one moment more! Give me a last chance of reprieve. One of us three is to go to Bloomsbury Square. Let me be the one. It may come in that time; it's sure to come. In the Lord's name let me be sent to Bloomsbury Square. Don't hang me here. It's murder."

They took him to the anvil; but even then he could be heard above the clinking of the smith's hammers, and the hoarse raging of the crowd, crying that he knew of Hugh's birth—that his father was living, and was a gentleman of influence and rank—that he had family secrets in his possession—that he could tell nothing unless they gave him time, but must die with them on his mind; and he continued to rave in this sort until his voice failed him, and he sank down a mere heap of clothes between the two attendants.

It was at this moment that the clock struck the first stroke of twelve, and the bell began to toll. The various officers, with the two sheriffs at their head, moved towards the door. All was ready when the last chime came upon the ear.

They told Hugh this, and asked if he had anything to say.

"To say!" he cried. "Not I. I'm ready.—Yes," he added, as his eye fell upon Barnaby, "I have a word to say, too. Come hither, lad."

There was, for the moment, something kind, and even tender, struggling in his fierce aspect, as he wrung his poor companion by the hand.

"I'll say this," he cried, looking firmly round, "that if I had ten lives to lose, and the loss of each would give me ten times the agony of the hardest death, I'd lay them all down—ay, I would, though you gentlemen may not believe it—to save this one. This one," he added, wringing his hand again, "that will be lost through me."

"Not through you," said the idiot, mildly. "Don't say that. You were not to blame. You have always been very good to me.—Hugh, we shall know what makes the stars shine, *now!*"

"I took him from her in a reckless mood, and didn't think what harm would come of it," said Hugh, laying his hand upon his head, and speaking in a lower voice. "I ask her pardon, and his—Look here," he added roughly, in his former tone. "You see this lad?"

They murmured "Yes," and seemed to wonder why he asked.

"That gentleman yonder"—pointing to the clergyman—"has often in the last few days spoken to me of faith, and strong belief. You see what I am—more brute than man, as I have been often told—but I had faith enough to believe, and did believe as strongly as any of you gentlemen can believe anything, that this one life would be spared. See what he is!—Look at him!"

Barnaby had moved towards the door, and stood beckoning him to follow.

"If this was not faith, and strong belief!" cried Hugh, raising his right arm aloft, and looking upward like a savage prophet whom the

near approach of Death had filled with inspiration, "where are they!
What else should teach me—me, born as I was born, and reared as
I have been reared—to hope for any mercy in this hardened, cruel,
unrelenting place! Upon these human shambles, I, who never raised
my hand in prayer till now, call down the wrath of God! On that
black tree, of which I am the ripened fruit, I do invoke the curse of
all its victims, past, and present, and to come. On the head of that
man, who, in his conscience, owns me for his son, I leave the wish
that he may never sicken on his bed of down, but die a violent death
as I do now, and have the night-wind for his only mourner. To this
I say, Amen, amen!"

His arm fell downward by his side; he turned; and moved towards
them with a steady step, the man he had been before.

"There is nothing more?" said the governor.

Hugh motioned Barnaby not to come near him (though without
looking in the direction where he stood) and answered, "There is
nothing more."

"Move forward!"

"—Unless," said Hugh, glancing hurriedly back,—"unless any
person here has a fancy for a dog; and not then, unless he means to
use him well. There's one, belongs to me, at the house I came from,
and it wouldn't be easy to find a better. He'll whine at first, but he'll
soon get over that.—You wonder that I think about a dog just now,"
he added, with a kind of laugh. "If any man deserved it of me half as
well, I'd think of *him*."

He spoke no more, but moved onward in his place, with a careless
air, though listening at the same time to the Service for the Dead,
with something between sullen attention and quickened curiosity.
As soon as he had passed the door, his miserable associate was carried
out; and the crowd beheld the rest.

Barnaby would have mounted the steps at the same time—indeed
he would have gone before them, but in both attempts he was restrained, as he was to undergo the sentence elsewhere. In a few
minutes the sheriffs re-appeared, the same procession was again
formed, and they passed through various rooms and passages to another door—that at which the cart was waiting. He held down his
head to avoid seeing what he knew his eyes must otherwise encounter,
and took his seat sorrowfully,—and yet with something of a childish
pride and pleasure,—in the vehicle. The officers fell into their places
at the sides, in front and in the rear; the sheriffs' carriages rolled on;
a guard of soldiers surrounded the whole; and they moved slowly
forward through the throng and pressure towards Lord Mansfield's
ruined house.

It was a sad sight—all the show, and strength, and glitter, assembled round one helpless creature—and sadder yet to note, as he
rode along, how his wandering thoughts found strange encouragement in the crowded windows and the concourse in the streets;
and how, even then, he felt the influence of the bright sky, and
looked up, smiling, into its deep unfathomable blue. But there had

been many such sights, since the riots were over—some so moving in their nature, and so repulsive too, that they were far more calculated to awaken pity for the sufferers, than respect for that law whose strong arm seemed in more than one case to be as wantonly stretched forth now that all was safe, as it had been basely paralysed in time of danger.

Two cripples—both mere boys—one with a leg of wood, one who dragged his twisted limbs along by the help of a crutch, were hanged in this same Bloomsbury Square. As the cart was about to glide from under them, it was observed that they stood with their faces from, not to, the house they had assisted to despoil; and their misery was protracted that this omission might be remedied. Another boy was hanged in Bow-street; other young lads in various quarters of the town. Four wretched women, too, were put to death. In a word, those who suffered as rioters were, for the most part, the weakest, meanest, and most miserable among them. It was a most exquisite satire upon the false religious cry which had led to so much misery, that some of these people owned themselves to be Catholics, and begged to be attended by their own priests.

One young man was hanged in Bishopsgate-street, whose aged grey-headed father waited for him at the gallows, kissed him at its foot when he arrived, and sat there, on the ground, till they took him down. They would have given him the body of his child; but he had no hearse, no coffin, nothing to remove it in, being too poor—and walked meekly away beside the cart that took it back to prison, trying, as he went, to touch its lifeless hand.

But the crowd had forgotten these matters, or cared little about them if they lived in their memory: and while one great multitude fought and hustled to get near the gibbet before Newgate, for a parting look, another followed in the train of poor lost Barnaby, to swell the throng that waited for him on the spot.

CHAPTER LXXVIII

ON this same day, and about this very hour, Mr. Willet the elder sat smoking his pipe in a chamber at the Black Lion. Although it was hot summer weather, Mr. Willet sat close to the fire. He was in a state of profound cogitation, with his own thoughts, and it was his custom at such times to stew himself slowly, under the impression that that process of cookery was favourable to the melting out of his ideas, which, when he began to simmer, sometimes oozed forth so copiously as to astonish even himself.

Mr. Willet had been several thousand times comforted by his friends and acquaintance, with the assurance that for the loss he had sustained in the damage done to the Maypole, he could "come upon the county." But as this phrase happened to bear an unfortunate resemblance to the popular expression of "coming on the parish," it suggested to Mr. Willet's mind no more consolatory visions than pauperism on an extensive scale, and ruin in a capacious aspect.

Consequently, he had never failed to receive the intelligence with a rueful shake of the head, or a dreary stare, and had been always observed to appear much more melancholy after a visit of condolence than at any other time in the whole four-and-twenty hours.

It chanced, however, that sitting over the fire on this particular occasion—perhaps because he was, as it were, done to a turn; perhaps because he was in an unusually bright state of mind; perhaps because he had considered the subject so long; perhaps because of all these favouring circumstances, taken together—it chanced that, sitting over the fire on this particular occasion, Mr. Willet did, afar off and in the remotest depths of his intellect, perceive a kind of lurking hint or faint suggestion, that out of the public purse there might issue funds for the restoration of the Maypole to its former high place among the taverns of the earth. And this dim ray of light did so diffuse itself within him, and did so kindle up and shine, that at last he had it as plainly and visibly before him as the blaze by which he sat; and, fully persuaded that he was the first to make the discovery, and that he had started, hunted down, fallen upon, and knocked on the head, a perfectly original idea which had never presented itself to any other man, alive or dead, he laid down his pipe, rubbed his hands, and chuckled audibly.

"Why, father!" cried Joe, entering at the moment, "you're in spirits to-day!"

"It's nothing partickler," said Mr. Willet, chuckling again. "It's nothing at all partickler, Joseph. Tell me something about the Salwanners." Having preferred this request, Mr. Willet chuckled a third time, and after these unusual demonstrations of levity, he put his pipe in his mouth again.

"What shall I tell you, father?" asked Joe, laying his hand upon his sire's shoulder, and looking down into his face. "That I have come back, poorer than a church mouse? You know that. That I have come back, maimed and crippled? You know that."

"It was took off," muttered Mr. Willet, with his eyes upon the fire, "at the defence of the Salwanners, in America, where the war is."

"Quite right," returned Joe, smiling, and leaning with his remaining elbow on the back of his father's chair; "the very subject I came to speak to you about. A man with one arm, father, is not of much use in the busy world."

This was one of those vast propositions which Mr. Willet had never considered for an instant, and required time to "tackle." Wherefore he made no answer.

"At all events," said Joe, "he can't pick and choose his means of earning a livelihood, as another man may. He can't say 'I will turn my hand to this,' or 'I won't turn my hand to that,' but must take what he can do, and be thankful it's no worse.—What did you say?"

Mr. Willet had been softly repeating to himself, in a musing tone, the words "defence of the Salwanners:" but he seemed embarrassed at having been overheard, and answered "Nothing."

"Now look here, father.—Mr. Edward has come to England from

the West Indies. When he was lost sight of (I ran away on the same day, father), he made a voyage to one of the islands, where a school-friend of his had settled; and, finding him, wasn't too proud to be employed on his estate, and—and in short, got on well, and is prospering, and has come over here on business of his own, and is going back again speedily. Our returning nearly at the same time, and meeting in the course of the late troubles, has been a good thing every way; for it has not only enabled us to do old friends some service, but has opened a path in life for me which I may tread without being a burden upon you. To be plain, father, he can employ me; I have satisfied myself that I can be of real use to him; and I'm going to carry my one arm away with him, and to make the most of it."

In the mind's eye of Mr. Willet, the West Indies, and indeed all foreign countries, were inhabited by savage nations, who were perpetually burying pipes of peace, flourishing tomahawks, and puncturing strange patterns in their bodies. He no sooner heard this announcement, therefore, than he leaned back in his chair, took his pipe from his lips, and stared at his son with as much dismay as if he already beheld him tied to a stake, and tortured for the entertainment of a lively population. In what form of expression his feelings would have found a vent, it is impossible to say. Nor is it necessary: for, before a syllable occurred to him, Dolly Varden came running into the room, in tears, threw herself on Joe's breast without a word of explanation, and clasped her white arms round his neck.

"Dolly!" cried Joe. "Dolly!"

"Ay, call me that; call me that always," exclaimed the locksmith's little daughter; "never speak coldly to me, never be distant, never again reprove me for the follies I have long repented, or I shall die, Joe."

"*I* reprove you!" said Joe.

"Yes—for every kind and honest word you uttered, went to my heart. For you, who have borne so much from me—for you, who owe your sufferings and pain to my caprice—for you to be so kind—so noble to me, Joe—"

He could say nothing to her. Not a syllable. There was an odd sort of eloquence in his one arm, which had crept round her waist: but his lips were mute.

"If you had reminded me by a word—only by one short word," sobbed Dolly, clinging yet closer to him, "how little I deserved that you should treat me with so much forbearance; if you had exulted only for one moment in your triumph, I could have borne it better."

"Triumph!" repeated Joe, with a smile which seemed to say, "I am a pretty figure for that."

"Yes, triumph," she cried, with her whole heart and soul in her earnest voice, and gushing tears; "for it *is* one. I am glad to think and know it is. I wouldn't be less humbled, dear—I wouldn't be without the recollection of that last time we spoke together in this place—no, not if I could recall the past, and make our parting, yesterday."

Did ever lover look as Joe looked now!

"Dear Joe," said Dolly, "I always loved you—in my own heart I always did, although I was so vain and giddy. I hoped you would come back that night. I made quite sure you would. I prayed for it on my knees. Through all these long, long years, I have never once forgotten you, or left off hoping that this happy time might come."

The eloquence of Joe's arm surpassed the most impassioned language; and so did that of his lips—yet he said nothing, either.

"And now, at last," cried Dolly, trembling with the fervour of her speech, "if you were sick, and shattered in your every limb; if you were ailing, weak, and sorrowful; if, instead of being what you are, you were in everybody's eyes but mine the wreck and ruin of a man; I would be your wife, dear love, with greater pride and joy, than if you were the stateliest lord in England!"

"What have I done," cried Joe, "what have I done to meet with this reward?"

"You have taught me," said Dolly, raising her pretty face to his, "to know myself, and your worth; to be something better than I was; to be more deserving of your true and manly nature. In years to come, dear Joe, you shall find that you have done so; for I will be, not only now, when we are young and full of hope, but when we have grown old and weary, your patient, gentle, never-tiring wife. I will never know a wish or care beyond our home and you, and I will always study how to please you with my best affection and my most devoted love. I will: indeed I will!"

Joe could only repeat his former eloquence—but it was very much to the purpose.

"They know of this, at home," said Dolly. "For your sake, I would leave even them; but they know it, and are glad of it, and are as proud of you as I am, and as full of gratitude.—You'll not come and see me as a poor friend who knew me when I was a girl, will you, dear Joe?"

Well, well! It don't matter what Joe said in answer, but he said a great deal; and Dolly said a great deal too: and he folded Dolly in his one arm pretty tight, considering that it was but one; and Dolly made no resistance: and if ever two people were happy in this world—which is not an utterly miserable one, with all its faults—we may, with some appearance of certainty, conclude that they were.

To say that during these proceedings Mr. Willet the elder underwent the greatest emotions of astonishment of which our common nature is susceptible—to say that he was in a perfect paralysis of surprise, and that he wandered into the most stupendous and theretofore unattainable heights of complicated amazement—would be to shadow forth his state of mind in the feeblest and lamest terms. If a roc, an eagle, a griffin, a flying elephant, a winged sea-horse, had suddenly appeared, and, taking him on its back, carried him bodily into the heart of the "Salwanners," it would have been to him as an every-day occurrence, in comparison with what he now beheld. To be sitting quietly by, seeing and hearing these things; to be completely overlooked, unnoticed, and disregarded, while his son and a young

lady were talking to each other in the most impassioned manner,
kissing each other, and making themselves in all respects perfectly
at home; was a position so tremendous, so inexplicable, so utterly
beyond the widest range of his capacity of comprehension, that he
fell into a lethargy of wonder, and could no more rouse himself than
an enchanted sleeper in the first year of his fairy lease, a century long.

"Father," said Joe, presenting Dolly. "You know who this is?"

Mr. Willet looked first at her, then at his son, then back again at
Dolly, and then made an ineffectual effort to extract a whiff from his
pipe, which had gone out long ago.

"Say a word, father, if it's only 'how d'ye do?' " urged Joe.

"Certainly, Joseph," answered Mr. Willet. "Oh yes! Why not?"

"To be sure," said Joe. "Why not?"

"Ah!" replied his father. "Why not?" and with this remark, which
he uttered in a low voice as though he were discussing some grave
question with himself, he used the little finger—if any of his fingers
can be said to have come under that denomination—of his right
hand as a tobacco-stopper, and was silent again.

And so he sat for half an hour at least, although Dolly, in the most
endearing of manners, hoped, a dozen times, that he was not angry
with her. So he sat for half an hour, quite motionless, and looking all
the while like nothing so much as a great Dutch Pin or Skittle. At
the expiration of that period, he suddenly, and without the least
notice, burst (to the great consternation of the young people) into a
very loud and very short laugh; and repeating "Certainly, Joseph.
Oh yes! Why not?" went out for a walk.

CHAPTER LXXIX

OLD JOHN did not walk near the Golden Key, for between the Golden
Key and the Black Lion there lay a wilderness of streets—as everybody knows who is acquainted with the relative bearings of Clerkenwell and Whitechapel—and he was by no means famous for pedestrian
exercises. But the Golden Key lies in our way, though it was out of
his; so to the Golden Key this chapter goes.

The Golden Key itself, fair emblem of the locksmith's trade, had
been pulled down by the rioters, and roughly trampled under foot.
But, now, it was hoisted up again in all the glory of a new coat of
paint, and showed more bravely even than in days of yore. Indeed
the whole housefront was spruce and trim, and so freshened up
throughout, that if there yet remained at large any of the rioters who
had been concerned in the attack upon it, the sight of the old, goodly,
prosperous dwelling, so revived, must have been to them as gall and
wormwood.

The shutters of the shop were closed, however, and the window-
blinds above were all pulled down, and in place of its usual cheerful
appearance, the house had a look of sadness and an air of mourning;
which the neighbours, who in old days had often seen poor Barnaby
go in and out, were at no loss to understand. The door stood partly

open; but the locksmith's hammer was unheard; the cat sat moping on the ashy forge; all was deserted, dark, and silent.

On the threshold of this door, Mr. Haredale and Edward Chester met. The younger man gave place; and both passing in with a familiar air, which seemed to denote that they were tarrying there, or were well accustomed to go to and fro unquestioned, shut it behind them.

Entering the old back-parlour, and ascending the flight of stairs, abrupt and steep, and quaintly fashioned as of old, they turned into the best room; the pride of Mrs. Varden's heart, and erst the scene of Miggs's household labours.

"Varden brought the mother here last evening, he told me?" said Mr. Haredale.

"She is above-stairs now—in the room over here," Edward rejoined. "Her grief, they say, is past all telling. I needn't add—for that you know beforehand, sir—that the care, humanity, and sympathy of these good people have no bounds."

" I am sure of that. Heaven repay them for it, and for much more. Varden is out?"

"He returned with your messenger, who arrived almost at the moment of his coming home himself. He was out the whole night—but that of course you know. He was with you the greater part of it?"

"He was. Without him, I should have lacked my right hand. He is an older man than I; but nothing can conquer him."

"The cheeriest, stoutest-hearted fellow in the world."

"He has a right to be. He has a right to be. A better creature never lived. He reaps what he has sown—no more."

"It is not all men," said Edward, after a moment's hesitation, "who have the happiness to do that."

"More than you imagine," returned Mr. Haredale. "We note the harvest more than the seed-time. You do so in me."

In truth his pale and haggard face, and gloomy bearing, had so far influenced the remark, that Edward was, for the moment, at a loss to answer him.

"Tut, tut," said Mr. Haredale, "'twas not very difficult to read a thought so natural. But you are mistaken nevertheless. I have had my share of sorrows—more than the common lot, perhaps, but I have borne them ill. I have broken where I should have bent; and have mused and brooded, when my spirit should have mixed with all God's great creation. The men who learn endurance, are they who call the whole world, brother. I have turned *from* the world, and I pay the penalty."

Edward would have interposed, but he went on without giving him time.

"It is too late to evade it now. I sometimes think, that if I had to live my life once more, I might amend this fault—not so much, I discover when I search my mind, for the love of what is right, as for my own sake. But even when I make these better resolutions, I instinctively recoil from the idea of suffering again what I have undergone; and in this circumstance I find the unwelcome assurance that I should still be the same man, though I could cancel the past, and begin anew, with its experience to guide me."

"Nay, you make too sure of that," said Edward.

"You think so," Mr. Haredale answered, "and I am glad you do. I know myself better, and therefore distrust myself more. Let us leave this subject for another—not so far removed from it as it might, at first sight, seem to be. Sir, you still love my niece, and she is still attached to you."

"I have that assurance from her own lips," said Edward, "and you know—I am sure you know—that I would not exchange it for any blessing life could yield me."

"You are frank, honourable, and disinterested," said Mr. Haredale; "you have forced the conviction that you are so, even on my once-jaundiced mind, and I believe you. Wait here till I come back."

He left the room as he spoke; but soon returned with his niece.

"On that first and only time," he said, looking from the one to the other, "when we three stood together under her father's roof, I told you to quit it, and charged you never to return."

"It is the only circumstance arising out of our love," observed Edward, "that I have forgotten."

"You own a name," said Mr. Haredale, "I had deep reason to remember. I was moved and goaded by recollections of personal wrong and injury, I know, but, even now I cannot charge myself with having, then, or ever, lost sight of a heartfelt desire for her true happiness; or with having acted—however much I was mistaken—with any other impulse than the one pure, single, earnest wish to be to her, as far as in my inferior nature lay, the father she had lost."

"Dear uncle," cried Emma, "I have known no parent but you. I have loved the memory of others, but I have loved you all my life. Never was father kinder to his child than you have been to me, without the interval of one harsh hour, since I can first remember."

"You speak too fondly," he answered, "and yet I cannot wish you were less partial; for I have a pleasure in hearing those words, and shall have in calling them to mind when we are far asunder, which nothing else could give me. Bear with me for a moment longer, Edward, for she and I have been together many years; and although I believe that in resigning her to you I put the seal upon her future happiness, I find it needs an effort."

He pressed her tenderly to his bosom, and after a minute's pause, resumed:

"I have done you wrong, sir, and I ask your forgiveness—in no common phrase, or show of sorrow; but with earnestness and sincerity. In the same spirit, I acknowledge to you both that the time has been when I connived at treachery and falsehood—which if I did not perpetrate myself, I still permitted—to rend you two asunder."

"You judge yourself too harshly," said Edward. "Let these things rest."

"They rise in judgment against me when I look back, and not now for the first time," he answered. "I cannot part from you without your full forgiveness; for busy life and I have little left in common now, and I have regrets enough to carry into solitude, without addition to the stock."

"You bear a blessing from us both," said Emma. "Never mingle thoughts of me—of me who owe you so much love and duty—with anything but undying affection and gratitude for the past, and bright hopes for the future."

"The future," returned her uncle, with a melancholy smile, "is a bright word for you, and its image should be wreathed with cheerful hopes. Mine is of another kind, but it will be one of peace, and free, I trust, from care or passion. When you quit England I shall leave it too. There are cloisters abroad; and now that the two great objects of my life are set at rest, I know no better home. You droop at that, forgetting that I am growing old, and that my course is nearly run. Well, we will speak of it again—not once or twice, but many times; and you shall give me cheerful counsel, Emma."

"And you will take it?" asked his niece.

"I'll listen to it," he answered, with a kiss, "and it will have its weight, be certain. What have I left to say? You have, of late, been much together. It is better and more fitting that the circumstances attendant on the past, which wrought your separation, and sowed between you suspicion and distrust, should not be entered on by me."

"Much, much better," whispered Emma.

"I avow my share in them," said Mr. Haredale, "though I held it, at the time, in detestation. Let no man turn aside, ever so slightly, from the broad path of honour, on the plausible pretence that he is justified by the goodness of his end. All good ends can be worked out by good means. Those that cannot, are bad; and may be counted so at once, and left alone."

He looked from her to Edward, and said in a gentler tone:

"In goods and fortune you are now nearly equal. I have been her faithful steward, and to that remnant of a richer property which my brother left her, I desire to add, in token of my love, a poor pittance, scarcely worth the mention, for which I have no longer any need. I am glad you go abroad. Let our ill-fated house remain the ruin it is. When you return, after a few thriving years, you will command a better, and a more fortunate one. We are friends?"

Edward took his extended hand, and grasped it heartily.

"You are neither slow nor cold in your response," said Mr. Haredale, doing the like by him, "and when I look upon you now, and know you, I feel that I would choose you for her husband. Her father had a generous nature, and you would have pleased him well. I give her to you in his name, and with his blessing. If the world and I part in this act, we part on happier terms than we have lived for many a day."

He placed her in his arms, and would have left the room, but that he was stopped in his passage to the door by a great noise at a distance, which made them start and pause.

It was a loud shouting, mingled with boisterous acclamations, that

rent the very air. It drew nearer and nearer every moment, and
approached so rapidly, that, even while they listened, it burst into
a deafening confusion of sounds at the street corner.

"This must be stopped—quieted," said Mr. Haredale, hastily.
"We should have foreseen this, and provided against it. I will go out
to them at once."

But, before he could reach the door, and before Edward could
catch up his hat and follow him, they were again arrested by a loud
shriek from above-stairs: and the locksmith's wife, bursting in, and
fairly running in Mr. Haredale's arms, cried out:

"She knows it all, dear sir!—she knows it all! We broke it out to
her by degrees, and she is quite prepared." Having made this
communication, and furthermore thanked Heaven with great fervour
and heartiness, the good lady, according to the custom of matrons,
on all occasions of excitement, fainted away directly.

They ran to the window, drew up the sash, and looked into the
crowded street. Among a dense mob of persons, of whom not one was
for an instant still, the locksmith's ruddy face and burly form could
be descried, beating about as though he was struggling with a rough
sea. Now, he was carried back a score of yards, now onward nearly to
the door, now back again, now forced against the opposite houses,
now against those adjoining his own: now carried up a flight of steps
and greeted by the outstretched hands of half a hundred men, while
the whole tumultuous concourse stretched their throats, and cheered
with all their might. Though he was really in a fair way to be torn to
pieces in the general enthusiasm, the locksmith, nothing discomposed,
echoed their shouts till he was as hoarse as they, and in a glow of joy
and right good-humour, waved his hat until the daylight shone
between its brim and crown.

But in all the bandyings from hand to hand, and strivings to and
fro, and sweepings here and there, which—saving that he looked more
jolly and more radiant after every struggle—troubled his peace of
mind no more than if he had been a straw upon the water's surface,
he never once released his firm grasp of an arm, drawn tight through
his. He sometimes turned to clap this friend upon the back, or
whisper in his ear a word of staunch encouragement, or cheer him
with a smile; but his great care was to shield him from the pressure,
and force a passage for him to the Golden Key. Passive and timid,
scared, pale, and wondering, and gazing at the throng as if he were
newly risen from the dead, and felt himself a ghost among the living,
Barnaby—not Barnaby in the spirit, but in flesh and blood, with
pulses, sinews, nerves, and beating heart, and strong affections—
clung to his stout old friend, and followed where he led.

And thus, in course of time, they reached the door, held ready for
their entrance by no unwilling hands. Then slipping in, and shutting
out the crowd by main force, Gabriel stood between Mr. Haredale and
Edward Chester, and Barnaby, rushing up the stairs, fell upon his
knees beside his mother's bed.

"Such is the blessed end, sir," cried the panting locksmith, to Mr.

Haredale, "of the best day's work we ever did. The rogues! it's been hard fighting to get away from 'em. I almost thought, once or twice, they'd have been too much for us with their kindness!"

They had striven, all the previous day, to rescue Barnaby from his impending fate. Failing in their attempts, in the first quarter to which they addressed themselves, they renewed them in another. Failing there, likewise, they began afresh at midnight; and made their way, not only to the judge and jury who had tried him, but to men of influence at court, to the young Prince of Wales, and even to the ante-chamber of the King himself. Successful, at last, in awakening an interest in his favour, and an inclination to inquire more dispassion-ately into his case, they had had an interview with the minister, in his bed, so late as eight o'clock that morning. The result of a search-ing inquiry (in which they, who had known the poor fellow from his childhood, did other good service, besides bringing it about) was, that between eleven and twelve o'clock, a free pardon to Barnaby Rudge was made out and signed, and entrusted to a horse-soldier for instant conveyance to the place of execution. This courier reached the spot just as the cart appeared in sight; and Barnaby being carried back to jail, Mr. Haredale, assured that all was safe, had gone straight from Bloomsbury Square to the Golden Key, leaving to Gabriel the grateful task of bringing him home in triumph.

"I needn't say," observed the locksmith, when he had shaken hands with all the males in the house, and hugged all the females, five-and-forty times, at least, "that except among ourselves, *I* didn't want to make a triumph of it. But, directly we got into the street we were known, and this hubbub began. Of the two," he added, as he wiped his crimson face, "and after experience of both, I think I'd rather be taken out of my house by a crowd of enemies, than escorted home by a mob of friends!"

It was plain enough, however, that this was mere talk on Gabriel's part, and that the whole proceeding afforded him the keenest delight; for the people continuing to make a great noise without, and to cheer as if their voices were in the freshest order, and good for a fortnight, he sent up-stairs for Grip (who had come home at his master's back, and had acknowledged the favours of the multitude by drawing blood from every finger that came within his reach), and with the bird upon his arm presented himself at the first-floor window, and waved his hat again until it dangled by a shred, between his finger and thumb. This demonstration having been received with appro-priate shouts, and silence being in some degree restored, he thanked them for their sympathy; and taking the liberty to inform them that there was a sick person in the house, proposed that they should give three cheers for King George, three more for Old England, and three more for nothing particular, as a closing ceremony. The crowd assent-ing, substituted Gabriel Varden for the nothing particular; and giving him one over, for good measure, dispersed in high good-humour.

What congratulations were exchanged among the inmates at the Golden Key, when they were left alone; what an overflowing of joy and happiness there was among them; how incapable it was of expression in Barnaby's own person; and how he went wildly from one to another, until he became so far tranquillised, as to stretch himself on the ground beside his mother's couch and fall into a deep sleep; are matters that need not be told. And it is well they happened to be of this class, for they would be very hard to tell, were their narration ever so indispensable.

Before leaving this bright picture, it may be well to glance at a dark and very different one which was presented to only a few eyes, that same night.

The scene was a churchyard; the time, midnight; the persons, Edward Chester, a clergyman, a grave-digger, and the four bearers of a homely coffin. They stood about a grave which had been newly dug, and one of the bearers held up a dim lantern,—the only light there—which shed its feeble ray upon the book of prayer. He placed it for a moment on the coffin, when he and his companions were about to lower it down. There was no inscription on the lid.

The mould fell solemnly upon the last house of this nameless man; and the rattling dust left a dismal echo even in the accustomed ears of those who had borne it to its resting-place. The grave was filled in to the top, and trodden down. They all left the spot together.

"You never saw him, living?" asked the clergyman, of Edward.

"Often, years ago; not knowing him for my brother."

"Never since?"

"Never. Yesterday, he steadily refused to see me. It was urged upon him, many times, at my desire."

"Still he refused? That was hardened and unnatural."

"Do you think so?"

"I infer that you do not?"

"You are right. We hear the world wonder, every day, at monsters of ingratitude. Did it never occur to you that it often looks for monsters of affection, as though they were things of course?"

They had reached the gate by this time, and bidding each other good night, departed on their separate ways.

CHAPTER LXXX

THAT afternoon, when he had slept off his fatigue; had shaved, and washed, and dressed, and freshened himself from top to toe; when he had dined, comforted himself with a pipe, an extra Toby, a nap in the great arm-chair, and a quiet chat with Mrs. Varden on everything that had happened, was happening, or about to happen, within the sphere of their domestic concern; the locksmith sat himself down at the tea-table in the little back-parlour: the rosiest, cosiest, merriest, heartiest, best-contented old buck, in Great Britain or out of it.

There he sat, with his beaming eye on Mrs. V., and his shining face suffused with gladness, and his capacious waistcoat smiling in every wrinkle, and his jovial humour peeping from under the table in the

very plumpness of his legs; a sight to turn the vinegar of misanthropy
into purest milk of human kindness. There he sat, watching his wife
as she decorated the room with flowers for the greater honour of Dolly
and Joseph Willet, who had gone out walking, and for whom the tea-
kettle had been singing gaily on the hob full twenty minutes, chirping
as never kettle chirped before; for whom the best service of real
undoubted china, patterned with divers round-faced mandarins
holding up broad umbrellas, was now displayed in all its glory; to
tempt whose appetites a clear, transparent, juicy ham, garnished
with cool green lettuce-leaves and fragrant cucumber, reposed upon a
shady table, covered with a snow-white cloth; for whose delight,
preserves and jams, crisp cakes and other pastry, short to eat, with
cunning twists, and cottage loaves, and rolls of bread both white and
brown, were all set forth in rich profusion; in whose youth Mrs. V.
herself had grown quite young, and stood there in a gown of red and
white: symmetrical in figure, buxom in bodice, ruddy in cheek and
lip, faultless in ankle, laughing in face and mood, in all respects delicious to behold—there sat the locksmith among all and every these
delights, the sun that shone upon them all: the centre of the system:
the source of light, heat, life, and frank enjoyment in the bright
household world.

And when had Dolly ever been the Dolly of that afternoon? To see
how she came in, arm-in-arm with Joe; and how she made an effort
not to blush or seem at all confused; and how she made believe she
didn't care to sit on his side of the table; and how she coaxed the
locksmith in a whisper not to joke; and how her colour came and went
in a little restless flutter of happiness, which made her do everything
wrong, and yet so charmingly wrong that it was better than right!—
why, the locksmith could have looked on at this (as he mentioned to
Mrs. Varden when they retired for the night) for four-and-twenty
hours at a stretch, and never wished it done.

The recollections, too, with which they made merry over that long
protracted tea! The glee with which the locksmith asked Joe if he
remembered that stormy night at the Maypole when he first asked
after Dolly—the laugh they all had, about that night when she was
going out to the party in the sedan-chair—the unmerciful manner in
which they rallied Mrs. Varden about putting those flowers outside
that very window—the difficulty Mrs. Varden found in joining the
laugh against herself, at first, and the extraordinary perception she
had of the joke when she overcame it—the confidential statements of
Joe concerning the precise day and hour when he was first conscious
of being fond of Dolly, and Dolly's blushing admissions, half volunteered and half extorted, as to the time from which she dated the
discovery that she "didn't mind" Joe—here was an exhaustless fund
of mirth and conversation.

Then, there was a great deal to be said regarding Mrs. Varden's
doubts, and motherly alarms, and shrewd suspicions; and it appeared
that from Mrs. Varden's penetration and extreme sagacity nothing
had ever been hidden. She had known it all along. She had seen it

from the first. She had always predicted it. She had been aware of it
before the principals. She had said within herself (for she remembered
the exact words) "that young Willet is certainly looking after our
Dolly, and *I* must look after *him*." Accordingly, she had looked after
him, and had observed many little circumstances (all of which she
named) so exceedingly minute that nobody else could make anything
out of them even now; and had, it seemed, from first to last, displayed
the most unbounded tact and most consummate generalship.

Of course the night when Joe *would* ride homeward by the side of
the chaise, and when Mrs. Varden *would* insist upon his going back
again, was not forgotten—nor the night when Dolly fainted on his
name being mentioned—nor the times upon times when Mrs. Varden,
ever watchful and prudent, had found her pining in her own chamber.
In short, nothing was forgotten; and everything by some means or
other brought them back to the conclusion, that that was the happiest
hour in all their lives; consequently, that everything must have
occurred for the best, and nothing could be suggested which would
have made it better.

While they were in the full glow of such discourse as this, there
came a startling knock at the door, opening from the street into the
workshop, which had been kept closed all day that the house might
be more quiet. Joe, as in duty bound, would hear of nobody but
himself going to open it; and accordingly left the room for that
purpose.

It would have been odd enough, certainly, if Joe had forgotten the
way to this door; and even if he had, as it was a pretty large one and
stood straight before him, he could not easily have missed it. But
Dolly, perhaps because she was in the flutter of spirits before mentioned, or perhaps because she thought he would not be able to open
it with his one arm—she could have no other reason—hurried out
after him; and they stopped so long in the passage—no doubt owing
to Joe's entreaties that she would not expose herself to the draught
of July air which must infallibly come rushing in on this same door
being opened—that the knock was repeated, in a yet more startling
manner than before.

"Is anybody going to open that door?" cried the locksmith. "Or
shall I come?"

Upon that, Dolly went running back into the parlour, all dimples
and blushes; and Joe opened it with a mighty noise, and other superfluous demonstrations of being in a violent hurry.

"Well," said the locksmith, when he reappeared: "what is it? eh,
Joe? what are you laughing at?"

"Nothing, sir. It's coming in."

"Who's coming in? what's coming in?" Mrs. Varden, as much at a
loss as her husband, could only shake her head in answer to his inquiring look: so, the locksmith wheeled his chair round to command a
better view of the room-door, and stared at it with his eyes wide
open, and a mingled expression of curiosity and wonder shining in his
jolly face.

Instead of some person or persons straightway appearing, divers remarkable sounds were heard, first in the workshop and afterwards in the little dark passage between it and the parlour, as though some unwieldy chest or heavy piece of furniture were being brought in, by an amount of human strength inadequate to the task. At length, after much struggling and bumping, and bruising of the wall on both sides, the door was forced open as by a battering-ram; and the locksmith, steadily regarding what appeared beyond, smote his thigh, elevated his eyebrows, opened his mouth, and cried in a loud voice expressive of the utmost consternation:

"Damme, if it an't Miggs come back!"

The young damsel whom he named no sooner heard these words, than deserting a small boy and a very large box by which she was accompanied, and advancing with such precipitation that her bonnet flew off her head, burst into the room, clasped her hands (in which she held a pair of pattens, one in each), raised her eyes devotedly to the ceiling, and shed a flood of tears.

"The old story!" cried the locksmith, looking at her in inexpressible desperation. "She was born to be a damper, this young woman! nothing can prevent it!"

"Ho master, ho mim!" cried Miggs, "can I constrain my feelings in these here once agin united moments! Ho Mr. Warden, here's blessedness among relations, sir! Here's forgivenesses of injuries, here's amicablenesses!"

The locksmith looked from his wife to Dolly, and from Dolly to Joe, and from Joe to Miggs, with his eyebrows still elevated and his mouth still open. When his eyes got back to Miggs, they rested on her; fascinated.

"To think," cried Miggs with hysterical joy, "that Mr. Joe, and dear Miss Dolly, has raly come together after all as has been said and done contrairy! To see them two a-settin' along with him and her, so pleasant and in all respects so affable and mild; and me not knowing of it, and not being in the ways to make no preparations for their teas. Ho what a cutting thing it is, and yet what sweet sensations is awoke within me!"

Either in clasping her hands again, or in an ecstasy of pious joy, Miss Miggs clinked her pattens after the manner of a pair of cymbals, at this juncture; and then resumed, in the softest accents:

"And did my missis think—ho goodness, did she think—as her own Miggs, which supported her under so many trials, and understood her natur' when them as intended well but acted rough, went so deep into her feelings—did she think as her own Miggs would ever leave her? Did she think as Miggs, though she was but a servant, and knowed that servitudes was no inheritances, would forgit that she was the humble instruments as always made it comfortable between them two when they fell out, and always told master of the meekness and forgiveness of her blessed dispositions! Did she think as Miggs had no attachments! Did she think that wages was her only object!"

To none of these interrogatories, whereof every one was more pathetically delivered than the last, did Mrs. Varden answer one word: but Miggs, not at all abashed by this circumstance, turned to the small boy in attendance—her eldest nephew—son of her own married sister—born in Golden Lion Court, number twenty-sivin, and bred in the very shadow of the second bell-handle on the right-hand door-post—and with a plentiful use of her pocket-handkerchief, addressed herself to him: requesting that on his return home he would console his parents for the loss of her, his aunt, by delivering to them a faithful statement of his having left her in the bosom of that family, with which, as his aforesaid parents well knew, her best affections were incorporated; that he would remind them that nothing less than her imperious sense of duty, and devoted attachment to her old master and missis, likewise Miss Dolly and young Mr. Joe, should ever have induced her to decline that pressing invitation which they, his parents, had, as he could testify, given her, to lodge and board with them, free of all cost and charge, for evermore; lastly, that he would help her with her box up-stairs, and then repair straight home, bearing her blessing and her strong injunctions to mingle in his prayers a supplication that he might in course of time grow up a locksmith, or a Mr. Joe, and have Mrs. Vardens and Miss Dollys for his relations and friends.

Having brought this admonition to an end—upon which, to say the truth, the young gentleman for whose benefit it was designed, bestowed little or no heed, having to all appearance his faculties absorbed in the contemplation of the sweetmeats,—Miss Miggs signified to the company in general that they were not to be uneasy, for she would soon return; and, with her nephew's aid, prepared to bear her wardrobe up the staircase.

"My dear," said the locksmith to his wife. "Do you desire this?"

"I desire it!" she answered. "I am astonished—I am amazed—at her audacity. Let her leave the house this moment."

Miggs, hearing this, let her end of the box fall heavily to the floor, gave a very loud sniff, crossed her arms, screwed down the corners of her mouth, and cried, in an ascending scale, "Ho, good gracious!" three distinct times.

"You hear what your mistress says, my love," remarked the locksmith. "You had better go, I think. Stay; take this with you, for the sake of old service."

Miss Miggs clutched the bank-note he took from his pocket-book and held out to her; deposited it in a small, red leather purse; put the purse in her pocket (displaying, as she did so, a considerable portion of some under-garment, made of flannel, and more black cotton stocking than is commonly seen in public); and, tossing her head, as she looked at Mrs. Varden, repeated—

"Ho, good gracious!"

"I think you said that once before, my dear," observed the locksmith.

"Times is changed, is they, mim!" cried Miggs, bridling; "you can spare me now, can you? You can keep 'em down without me? You're not in wants of any one to scold, or throw the blame upon, no longer, an't you, mim? I'm glad to find you've grown so independent. I wish you joy, I'm sure!"

With that she dropped a curtsey, and keeping her head erect, her ear towards Mrs. Varden, and her eye on the rest of the company, as she alluded to them in her remarks, proceeded:

"I'm quite delighted, I'm sure, to find sich independency, feeling sorry though, at the same time, mim, that you should have been forced into submissions when you couldn't help yourself—he he he! It must be great vexations, 'specially considering how ill you always spoke of Mr. Joe—to have him for a son-in-law at last; and I wonder Miss Dolly can put up with him, either, after being off and on for so many years with a coachmaker. But I *have* heerd say, that the coachmaker thought twice about it—he he he!—and that he told a young man as was a friend of his, that he hoped he knowed better than to be drawed into that; though she and all the family *did* pull uncommon strong!"

Here she paused for a reply, and receiving none, went on as before.

"I *have* heerd say, mim, that the illnesses of some ladies was all pretensions, and that they could faint away, stone dead, whenever they had the inclinations so to do. Of course I never see sich cases with my own eyes—ho no! He he he! Nor master neither—ho no! He he he! I *have* heerd the neighbours make remark as some one as they was acquainted with, was a poor good-natur'd mean-spirited creetur, as went out fishing for a wife one day, and caught a Tartar. Of course I never to my knowledge see the poor person himself. Nor did you neither, mim—ho no. I wonder who it can be—don't you, mim? No doubt you do, mim. Ho yes. He he he!"

Again Miggs paused for a reply; and none being offered, was so oppressed with teeming spite and spleen, that she seemed like to burst.

"I'm glad Miss Dolly can laugh," cried Miggs with a feeble titter. "I like to see folks a-laughing—so do you, mim, don't you? You was always glad to see people in spirits, wasn't you, mim? And you always did your best to keep 'em cheerful, didn't you, mim? Though there an't such a great deal to laugh at now either; is there, mim? It an't so much of a catch, after looking out sharp ever since she was a little chit, and costing such a deal in dress and show, to get a poor, common soldier, with one arm, is it, mim? He he! I wouldn't have a husband with one arm, anyways. I would have two arms. I would have two arms, if it was me, though instead of hands they'd only got hooks at the end, like our dustman!"

Miss Miggs was about to add, and had, indeed, begun to add, that, taking them in the abstract, dustmen were far more eligible matches than soldiers, though, to be sure, when people were past choosing they must take the best they could get, and think themselves well off too; but her vexation and chagrin being of that internally bitter sort which finds no relief in words, and is aggravated to madness by want of contradiction, she could hold out no longer, and burst into a storm of sobs and tears.

In this extremity she fell on the unlucky nephew, tooth and nail, and plucking a handful of hair from his head, demanded to know how long she was to stand there to be insulted, and whether or no he meant to help her to carry out the box again, and if he took a pleasure in hearing his family reviled: with other inquiries of that nature; at which disgrace and provocation, the small boy, who had been all this time gradually lashed into rebellion by the sight of unattainable pastry, walked off indignant, leaving his aunt and the box to follow at their leisure. Somehow or other, by dint of pushing and pulling, they did attain the street at last; where Miss Miggs, all blowzed with the exertion of getting there, and with her sobs and tears, sat down upon her property to rest and grieve, until she could ensnare some other youth to help her home.

"It's a thing to laugh at, Martha, not to care for," whispered the locksmith, as he followed his wife to the window, and good-humouredly dried her eyes. "What does it matter? You had seen your fault before. Come! Bring up Toby again, my dear; Dolly shall sing us a song; and we'll be all the merrier for this interruption!"

CHAPTER LXXXI

ANOTHER month had passed, and the end of August had nearly come, when Mr. Haredale stood alone in the mail-coach office at Bristol. Although but a few weeks had intervened since his conversation with Edward Chester and his niece, in the locksmith's house, and he had made no change, in the mean time, in his accustomed style of dress, his appearance was greatly altered. He looked much older, and more care-worn. Agitation and anxiety of mind scattered wrinkles and grey hairs with no unsparing hand; but deeper traces follow on the silent uprooting of old habits, and severing of dear, familiar ties. The affections may not be so easily wounded as the passions, but their hurts are deeper, and more lasting. He was now a solitary man, and the heart within him was dreary and lonesome.

He was not the less alone for having spent so many years in seclusion and retirement. This was no better preparation than a round of social cheerfulness: perhaps it even increased the keenness of his sensibility. He had been so dependent upon her for companionship and love; she had come to be so much a part and parcel of his existence; they had had so many cares and thoughts in common, which no one else had shared; that losing her was beginning life anew, and being required to summon up the hope and elasticity of youth, amid the doubts, distrusts, and weakened energies of age.

The effort he had made to part from her with seeming cheerfulness and hope—and they had parted only yesterday—left him the more depressed. With these feelings, he was about to revisit London for the last time, and look once more upon the walls of their old home, before turning his back upon it, for ever.

The journey was a very difficult one, in those days, from what the present generation find it; but it came to an end, as the longest journey will, and he stood again in the streets of the metropolis. He lay at the inn where the coach stopped, and resolved, before he went to bed, that he would make his arrival known to no one; would spend another night in London; and would spare himself the pang of parting, even with the honest locksmith.

Such conditions of the mind as that to which he was a prey when he lay down to rest, are favourable to the growth of disordered fancies, and uneasy visions. He knew this, even in the horror with which he started from his first sleep, and threw up the window to dispel it by the presence of some object, beyond the room, which had not been, as it were, the witness of his dream. But it was not a new terror of the night; it had been present to him before, in many shapes; it had haunted him in bygone times, and visited his pillow again and again. If it had been but an ugly object, a childish spectre, haunting his sleep, its return, in its old form, might have awakened a momentary sensation of fear, which, almost in the act of waking, would have passed away. This disquiet, however, lingered about him, and would yield to nothing. When he closed his eyes again, he felt it hovering near; as he slowly sunk into a slumber, he was conscious of its gathering strength and purpose, and gradually assuming its recent shape; when he sprang up from his bed, the same phantom vanished from his heated brain, and left him filled with a dread against which reason and waking thought were powerless.

The sun was up, before he could shake it off. He rose late, but not refreshed, and remained within doors all that day. He had a fancy for paying his last visit to the old spot in the evening, for he had been accustomed to walk there at that season, and desired to see it under the aspect that was most familiar to him. At such an hour as would afford him time to reach it a little before sunset, he left the inn, and turned into the busy street.

He had not gone far, and was thoughtfully making his way among the noisy crowd, when he felt a hand upon his shoulder, and, turning, recognised one of the waiters from the inn, who begged his pardon, but he had left his sword behind him.

"Why have you brought it to me?" he asked, stretching out his hand, and yet not taking it from the man, but looking at him in a disturbed and agitated manner.

The man was sorry to have disobliged him, and would carry it back again. The gentleman had said that he was going a little way into the country, and that he might not return until late. The roads were not very safe for single travellers after dark; and, since the riots, gentlemen had been more careful than ever, not to trust themselves unarmed in lonely places. "We thought you were a stranger, sir," he added, "and that you might believe our roads to be better than they are; but perhaps you know them well, and carry fire-arms—"

He took the sword, and putting it up at his side, thanked the man, and resumed his walk.

It was long remembered that he did this in a manner so strange, and with such a trembling hand, that the messenger stood looking after his retreating figure, doubtful whether he ought not to follow, and watch him. It was long remembered that he had been heard pacing his bedroom in the dead of the night; and the attendants had mentioned to each other in the morning, how fevered and how pale he looked; and that when this man went back to the inn, he told a fellow-servant that what he had observed in this short interview lay very heavy on his mind, and that he feared the gentleman intended to destroy himself, and would never come back alive.

With a half-consciousness that his manner had attracted the man's attention (remembering the expression of his face when they parted), Mr. Haredale quickened his steps; and arriving at a stand of coaches, bargained with the driver of the best to carry him so far on his road as the point where the footway struck across the fields, and to await his return at a house of entertainment which was within a stone's-throw of that place. Arriving there in due course, he alighted and pursued his way on foot.

He passed so near the Maypole, that he could see its smoke rising from among the trees, while a flock of pigeons—some of its old inhabitants, doubtless—sailed gaily home to roost, between him and the unclouded sky. "The old house will brighten up now," he said, as he looked towards it, "and there will be a merry fireside beneath its ivied roof. It is some comfort to know that everything will not be blighted hereabouts. I shall be glad to have one picture of life and cheerfulness to turn to, in my mind!"

He resumed his walk, and bent his steps towards the Warren. It was a clear, calm, silent evening, with hardly a breath of wind to stir the leaves, or any sound to break the stillness of the time, but drowsy sheep-bells tinkling in the distance, and, at intervals, the far-off lowing of cattle, or bark of village dogs. The sky was radiant with the softened glory of sunset; and on the earth, and in the air, a deep repose prevailed. At such an hour, he arrived at the deserted mansion which had been his home so long, and looked for the last time upon its blackened walls.

The ashes of the commonest fire are melancholy things, for in them there is an image of death and ruin,—of something that has been bright, and is but dull, cold, dreary dust,—with which our nature forces us to sympathise. How much more sad the crumbled embers of a home: the casting down of that great altar, where the worst among us sometimes perform the worship of the heart; and where the best have offered up such sacrifices, and done such deeds of heroism, as, chronicled, would put the proudest temples of old Time, with all their vaunting annals, to the blush!

He roused himself from a long train of meditation, and walked slowly round the house. It was by this time almost dark.

He had nearly made the circuit of the building, when he uttered a half-suppressed exclamation, started, and stood still. Reclining, in an

easy attitude, with his back against a tree, and contemplating the
ruin with an expression of pleasure,—a pleasure so keen that it
overcame his habitual indolence and command of feature, and
displayed itself utterly free from all restraint or reserve,—before
him, on his own ground, and triumphing then, as he had triumphed
in every misfortune and disappointment of his life, stood the man
whose presence, of all mankind, in any place, and least of all in that,
he could the least endure.

Although his blood so rose against this man, and his wrath so
stirred within him, that he could have struck him dead, he put such
fierce constraint upon himself that he passed him without a word or
look. Yes, and he would have gone on, and not turned, though to
resist the Devil who poured such hot temptation in his brain,
required an effort scarcely to be achieved, if this man had not
himself summoned him to stop: and that, with an assumed compassion in his voice which drove him well-nigh mad, and in an instant
routed all the self-command it had been anguish—acute, poignant
anguish—to sustain.

All consideration, reflection, mercy, forbearance; everything by
which a goaded man can curb his rage and passion; fled from him as
he turned back. And yet he said, slowly and quite calmly—far more
calmly than he had ever spoken to him before:

"Why have you called to me?"

"To remark," said Sir John Chester with his wonted composure,
"what an odd chance it is, that we should meet here!"

"It *is* a strange chance."

"Strange? The most remarkable and singular thing in the world. I
never ride in the evening; I have not done so for years. The whim
seized me, quite unaccountably, in the middle of last night.—How
very picturesque this is!"—He pointed, as he spoke, to the dismantled house, and raised his glass to his eye.

"You praise your own work very freely."

Sir John let fall his glass; inclined his face towards him with an
air of the most courteous inquiry; and slightly shook his head
as though he were remarking to himself, "I fear this animal is going
mad!"

"I say you praise your own work very freely," repeated Mr. Haredale.

"Work!" echoed Sir John, looking smilingly round. "Mine!—I
beg your pardon, I really beg your pardon—"

"Why, you see," said Mr. Haredale, "those walls. You see those
tottering gables. You see on every side where fire and smoke have
raged. You see the destruction that has been wanton here. Do you
not?"

"My good friend," returned the knight, gently checking his
impatience with his hand, "of course I do. I see everything you speak
of, when you stand aside, and do not interpose yourself between the
view and me. I am very sorry for you. If I had not had the pleasure to
meet you here, I think I should have written to tell you so. But you

don't bear it as well as I had expected—excuse me—no, you don't indeed."

He pulled out his snuff-box, and addressing him with the superior air of a man who, by reason of his higher nature, has a right to read a moral lesson to another, continued:

"For you are a philosopher, you know—one of that stern and rigid school who are far above the weaknesses of mankind in general. You are removed, a long way, from the frailties of the crowd. You contemplate them from a height, and rail at them with a most impressive bitterness. I have heard you."

"—And shall again," said Mr. Haredale.

"Thank you," returned the other. "Shall we walk as we talk? The damp falls rather heavily. Well,—as you please. But I grieve to say that I can spare you only a very few moments."

"I would," said Mr. Haredale, "you had spared me none. I would, with all my soul, you had been in Paradise (if such a monstrous lie could be enacted), rather than here to-night."

"Nay," returned the other—"really—you do yourself injustice. You are a rough companion, but I would not go so far to avoid you."

"Listen to me," said Mr. Haredale. "Listen to me."

"While you rail?" inquired Sir John.

"While I deliver your infamy. You urged and stimulated to do your work a fit agent, but one who in his nature—in the very essence of his being—is a traitor, and who has been false to you (despite the sympathy you two should have together) as he has been to all others. With hints, and looks, and crafty words, which told again are nothing, you set on Gashford to this work—this work before us now. With these same hints, and looks, and crafty words, which told again are nothing, you urged him on to gratify the deadly hate he owes me—I have earned it, I thank Heaven—by the abduction and dishonour of my niece. You did. I see denial in your looks," he cried, abruptly pointing in his face, and stepping back, "and denial is a lie!"

He had his hand upon his sword; but the knight, with a contemptuous smile, replied to him as coldly as before.

"You will take notice, sir—if you can discriminate sufficiently— that I have taken the trouble to deny nothing. Your discernment is hardly fine enough for the perusal of faces, not of a kind as coarse as your speech; nor has it ever been, that I remember; or, in one face that I could name, you would have read indifference, not to say disgust, somewhat sooner than you did. I speak of a long time ago,— but you understand me."

"Disguise it as you will, you mean denial. Denial explicit or reserved, expressed or left to be inferred, is still a lie. You say you don't deny. Do you admit?"

"You yourself," returned Sir John, suffering the current of his speech to flow as smoothly as if it had been stemmed by no one word of interruption, "publicly proclaimed the character of the gentleman in question (I think it was in Westminster Hall) in terms which relieve me from the necessity of making any further allusion to him. You may have been warranted; you may not have been; I can't say. Assuming the gentleman to be what you described, and to have made to you or any other person any statements that may have happened to suggest themselves to him, for the sake of his own security, or for the sake of money, or for his own amusement, or for any other consideration,—I have nothing to say of him, except that his extremely degrading situation appears to me to be shared with his employers. You are so very plain yourself, that you will excuse a little freedom in me, I am sure."

"Attend to me again, Sir John—but once," cried Mr. Haredale; "in your every look, and word, and gesture, you tell me this was not your act. I tell you that it was, and that you tampered with the man I speak of, and with your wretched son (whom God forgive!) to do this deed. You talk of degradation and character. You told me once that you had purchased the absence of the poor idiot and his mother, when (as I have discovered since, and then suspected) you had gone to tempt them, and had found them flown. To you I traced the insinuation that I alone reaped any harvest from my brother's death; and all the foul attacks and whispered calumnies that followed in its train. In every action of my life, from that first hope which you converted into grief and desolation, you have stood, like an adverse fate, between me and peace. In all, you have ever been the same cold blooded, hollow, false, unworthy villain. For the second time, and for the last, I cast these charges in your teeth, and spurn you from me as I would a faithless dog!"

With that he raised his arm, and struck him on the breast so that he staggered. Sir John, the instant he recovered, drew his sword, threw away the scabbard and his hat, and running on his adversary made a desperate lunge at his heart, which, but that his guard was quick and true, would have stretched him dead upon the grass.

In the act of striking him, the torrent of his opponent's rage had reached a stop. He parried his rapid thrusts, without returning them, and called to him, with a frantic kind of terror in his face, to keep back.

"Not to-night! not to-night!" he cried. "In God's name, not to-night!"

Seeing that he lowered his weapon, and that he would not thrust in turn, Sir John lowered his.

"Not to-night!" his adversary cried. "Be warned in time!"

"You told me—it must have been in a sort of inspiration—" said Sir John, quite deliberately, though now he dropped his mask, and showed his hatred in his face, "that this was the last time. Be assured it is! Did you believe our last meeting was forgotten? Did you believe that your every word and look was not to be accounted for, and was not well remembered? Do you believe that I have waited your time, or you mine? What kind of man is he who entered, with all his sickening cant of honesty and truth, into a bond with me to prevent a marriage he affected to dislike, and when I had redeemed my part to the spirit and the letter, skulked from his, and brought the match about in his own time, to rid himself of a burden he had grown tired of, and cast a spurious lustre on his house?''

"I have acted,'' cried Mr. Haredale, "with honour and in good faith. I do so now. Do not force me to renew this duel to-night!''

"You said my 'wretched' son, I think?'' said Sir John, with a smile. "Poor fool! The dupe of such a shallow knave—trapped into marriage by such an uncle and by such a niece—he well deserves your pity. But he is no longer a son of mine: you are welcome to the prize your craft has made, sir.''

"Once more,'' cried his opponent, wildly stamping on the ground, "although you tear me from my better angel, I implore you not to come within the reach of my sword to-night. Oh! why were you here at all! Why have we met! To-morrow would have cast us apart for ever!''

"That being the case,'' returned Sir John, without the least emotion, "it is very fortunate we have met to-night. Haredale, I have always despised you, as you know, but I have given you credit for a species of brute courage. For the honour of my judgment, which I had thought a good one, I am sorry to find you a coward.''

Not another word was spoken on either side. They crossed swords, though it was now quite dusk, and attacked each other fiercely. They were well matched, and each was thoroughly skilled in the management of his weapon.

After a few seconds they grew hotter and more furious, and pressing on each other inflicted and received several slight wounds. It was directly after receiving one of these in his arm, that Mr. Haredale, making a keener thrust as he felt the warm blood spirting out, plunged his sword through his opponent's body to the hilt.

Their eyes met, and were on each other as he drew it out. He put his arm about the dying man, who repulsed him, feebly, and dropped upon the turf. Raising himself upon his hands, he gazed at him for an instant, with scorn and hatred in his look; but, seeming to remember, even then, that this expression would distort his features after death, he tried to smile, and, faintly moving his right hand, as if to hide his bloody linen in his vest, fell back dead—the phantom of last night.

CHAPTER THE LAST

A PARTING glance at such of the actors in this little history as it has not, in the course of its events, dismissed, will bring it to an end.

Mr. Haredale fled that night. Before pursuit could be begun, indeed before Sir John was traced or missed, he had left the kingdom. Repairing straight to a religious establishment, known throughout Europe for the rigour and severity of its discipline, and for the merciless penitence it exacted from those who sought its shelter as a refuge from the world, he took the vows which thenceforth shut him out from nature and its kind, and after a few remorseful years was buried in its gloomy cloisters.

Two days elapsed before the body of Sir John was found. As soon as it was recognised and carried home, the faithful valet, true to his master's creed, eloped with all the cash and movables he could lay his hands on, and started as a finished gentleman upon his own account. In this career he met with great success, and would certainly have married an heiress in the end, but for an unlucky check which led to his premature decease. He sank under a contagious disorder, very prevalent at that time, and vulgarly termed the jail fever.

Lord George Gordon, remaining in his prison in the Tower until Monday the Fifth of February in the following year, was on that day solemnly tried at Westminster for High Treason. Of this crime he was, after a patient investigation, declared Not Guilty; upon the ground that there was no proof of his having called the multitude together with any traitorous or unlawful intentions. Yet so many people were there, still, to whom those riots taught no lesson of reproof or moderation, that a public subscription was set on foot in Scotland to defray the cost of his defence.

For seven years afterwards he remained, at the strong intercession of his friends, comparatively quiet; saving that he, every now and then, took occasion to display his zeal for the Protestant faith in some extravagant proceeding which was the delight of its enemies; and saving, besides, that he was formally excommunicated by the Archbishop of Canterbury, for refusing to appear as a witness in the Ecclesiastical Court when cited for that purpose. In the year 1788 he was stimulated by some new insanity to write and publish an injurious pamphlet, reflecting on the Queen of France, in very violent terms. Being indicted for the libel, and (after various strange demonstrations in court) found guilty, he fled into Holland in place of appearing to receive sentence: from whence, as the quiet burgomasters of Amsterdam had no relish for his company, he was sent home again with all speed. Arriving in the month of July at Harwich, and going thence to Birmingham, he made in the latter place, in August, a public profession of the Jewish religion; and figured there as a Jew until he was arrested, and brought back to London to receive the sentence he had evaded. By virtue of this sentence he was, in the month of December, cast into Newgate for five years and ten months, and required besides to pay a large fine, and to furnish heavy securities for his future good behaviour.

After addressing, in the midsummer of the following year, an appeal to the commiseration of the National Assembly of France, which the English minister refused to sanction, he composed himself to undergo his full term of punishment; and suffering his beard to grow nearly to his waist, and conforming in all respects to the ceremonies of his new religion, he applied himself to the study of history, and occasionally to the art of painting, in which, in his younger days, he had shown some skill. Deserted by his former friends, and treated in all respects like the worst criminal in the jail, he lingered on, quite cheerful and resigned, until the 1st of November, 1793, when he died in his cell, being then only three-and-forty years of age.

Many men with fewer sympathies for the distressed and needy, with less abilities and harder hearts, have made a shining figure and left a brilliant fame. He had his mourners. The prisoners bemoaned his loss, and missed him; for though his means were not large, his charity was great, and in bestowing alms among them he considered the necessities of all alike, and knew no distinction of sect or creed. There are wise men in the highways of the world who may learn something, even from this poor crazy lord who died in Newgate.

To the last, he was truly served by bluff John Grueby. John was at his side before he had been four-and-twenty hours in the Tower, and never left him until he died. He had one other constant attendant, in the person of a beautiful Jewish girl; who attached herself to him from feelings half religious, half romantic, but whose virtuous and disinterested character appears to have been beyond the censure even of the most censorious.

Gashford deserted him, of course. He subsisted for a time upon his traffic in his master's secrets; and, this trade failing when the stock was quite exhausted, procured an appointment in the honourable corps of spies and eaves-droppers employed by the government. As one of these wretched underlings, he did his drudgery, sometimes abroad, sometimes at home, and long endured the various miseries of such a station. Ten or a dozen years ago—not more—a meagre, wan old man, diseased and miserably poor, was found dead in his bed at an obscure inn in the Borough, where he was quite unknown. He had taken poison. There was no clue to his name; but it was discovered from certain entries in a pocket-book he carried, that he had been secretary to Lord George Gordon in the time of the famous riots.

Many months after the re-establishment of peace and order, and even when it had ceased to be the town-talk, that every military officer, kept at free quarters by the City during the late alarms, had cost for his board and lodging four pounds four per day, and every private soldier two and twopence half-penny; many months after even this engrossing topic was forgotten, and the United Bull-dogs were to a man all killed, imprisoned, or transported, Mr. Simon Tappertit, being removed from a hospital to prison, and thence to his place of trial, was discharged by proclamation, on two wooden legs. Shorn of his graceful limbs, and brought down from his high estate to circumstances of utter destitution, and the deepest misery, he made shift to stump back to his old master, and beg for some relief. By the locksmith's advice and aid, he was established in business as a shoe-black, and opened shop under an archway near the Horse Guards. This being a central quarter, he quickly made a very large connection; and on levee days, was sometimes known to have as many as twenty half-pay officers waiting their turn for polishing. Indeed his trade increased to that extent, that in course of time he entertained no less than two apprentices, besides taking for his wife the widow of an eminent bone and rag collector, formerly of Millbank. With this lady (who assisted in the business) he lived in great domestic happiness, only chequered by those little storms which serve to clear the atmosphere of wedlock, and brighten its horizon. In some of these gusts of bad weather, Mr. Tappertit would, in the assertion of his prerogative, so far forget himself, as to correct his lady with a brush, or boot, or shoe; while she (but only in extreme cases) would retaliate by taking off his legs, and leaving him exposed to the derision of those urchins who delight in mischief.

Miss Miggs, baffled in all her schemes, matrimonial and otherwise, and cast upon a thankless, undeserving world, turned very sharp and sour; and did at length become so acid, and did so pinch and slap and tweak the hair and noses of the youth of Golden Lion Court, that she was by one consent expelled that sanctuary, and desired to bless some other spot of earth, in preference. It chanced at that moment, that the justices of the peace for Middlesex proclaimed by public placard that they stood in need of a female turnkey for the County Bridewell, and appointed a day and hour for the inspection of candidates. Miss Miggs, attending at the time appointed, was instantly chosen and selected from one hundred and twenty-four competitors, and at once promoted to the office; which she held until her decease, more than thirty years afterwards, remaining single all that time. It was observed of this lady that while she was inflexible and grim to all her female flock, she was particularly so to those who could establish any claim to beauty: and it was often remarked as a proof of her indomitable virtue and severe chastity, that to such as had been frail she showed no mercy; always falling upon them on the slightest occasion, or on no occasion at all, with the fullest measure of her wrath. Among other useful inventions which she practised upon this class of offenders and bequeathed to posterity, was the art of inflicting an exquisitely vicious poke or dig with the wards of a key in the small of the back, near the spine. She likewise originated a mode of treading by accident (in pattens) on such as had small feet; also very remarkable for its ingenuity, and previously quite unknown.

It was not very long, you may be sure, before Joe Willet and Dolly Varden were made husband and wife, and with a handsome sum in bank (for the locksmith could afford to give his daughter a good dowry), reopened the Maypole. It was not very long, you may be sure, before a red-faced little boy was seen staggering about the Maypole passage, and kicking up his heels on the green before the door. It was not very long, counting by years, before there was a red-faced little girl, another red-faced little boy, and a whole troop of girls and boys: so that, go to Chigwell when you would, there would surely be seen, either in the village street, or on the green, or frolicking in the farm-yard—for it was a farm now, as well as a tavern— more small Joes and small Dollys than could be easily counted. It was not a very long time before these appearances ensued; but it *was a very* long time before Joe looked five years older, or Dolly either, or the locksmith either, or his wife either: for cheerfulness and content are great beautifiers, and are famous preservers of youthful looks, depend upon it.

It was a long time, too, before there was such a country inn as the

Maypole, in all England: indeed it is a great question whether there has ever been such another to this hour, or ever will be. It was a long time too—for Never, as the proverb says, is a long day—before they forgot to have an interest in wounded soldiers at the Maypole, or before Joe omitted to refresh them, for the sake of his old campaign; or before the serjeant left off looking in there, now and then; or before they fatigued themselves, or each other, by talking on these occasions of battles and sieges, and hard weather and hard service, and a thousand things belonging to a soldier's life. As to the great silver snuff-box which the King sent Joe with his own hand, because of his conduct in the Riots, what guest ever went to the Maypole without putting finger and thumb into that box, and taking a great pinch, though he had never taken a pinch of snuff before, and almost sneezed himself into convulsions even then? As to the purple-faced vintner, where is the man who lived in those times and never saw *him* at the Maypole: to all appearance as much at home in the best room, as if he lived there? And as to the feastings and christenings, and revellings at Christmas, and celebrations of birthdays, wedding-days, and all manner of days, both at the Maypole and the Golden Key,—if they are not notorious, what facts are?

Mr. Willet the elder, having been by some extraordinary means possessed with the idea that Joe wanted to be married, and that it would be well for him, his father, to retire into private life, and enable him to live in comfort, took up his abode in a small cottage at Chigwell; where they widened and enlarged the fireplace for him, hung up the boiler, and furthermore planted in the little garden outside the front-door, a fictitious Maypole; so that he was quite at home directly. To this, his new habitation, Tom Cobb, Phil Parkes, and Solomon Daisy went regularly every night: and in the chimney-corner, they all four quaffed, and smoked, and prosed, and dozed, as they had done of old. It being accidentally discovered after a short time that Mr. Willet still appeared to consider himself a landlord by profession, Joe provided him with a slate, upon which the old man regularly scored up vast accounts for meat, drink, and tobacco. As he grew older this passion increased upon him; and it became his delight to chalk against the name of each of his cronies a sum of enormous magnitude, and impossible to be paid: and such was his secret joy in these entries, that he would be perpetually seen going behind the door to look at them, and coming forth again, suffused with the liveliest satisfaction.

He never recovered the surprise the Rioters had given him, and remained in the same mental condition down to the last moment of his life. It was like to have been brought to a speedy termination by the first sight of his first grandchild, which appeared to fill him with the belief that some alarming miracle had happened to Joe. Being promptly blooded, however, by a skilful surgeon, he rallied; and although the doctors all agreed, on his being attacked with symptoms of apoplexy six months afterwards, that he ought to die, and took it very ill that he did not, he remained alive—possibly on account of his constitutional slowness—for nearly seven years more, when he was one morning found speechless in his bed. He lay in this state, free from all tokens of uneasiness, for a whole week, when he was suddenly restored to consciousness by hearing the nurse whisper in his son's ears that he was going. "I'm a-going, Joseph," said Mr. Willet, turning round upon the instant, "to the Salwanners"—and immediately gave up the ghost.

He left a large sum of money behind him; even more than he was supposed to have been worth, although the neighbours, according to the custom of mankind in calculating the wealth that other people ought to have saved, had estimated his property in good round numbers. Joe inherited the whole; so that he became a man of great consequence in those parts, and was perfectly independent.

Some time elapsed before Barnaby got the better of the shock he had sustained, or regained his old health and gaiety. But he recovered by degrees: and although he could never separate his condemnation and escape from the idea of a terrific dream, he became, in other respects, more rational. Dating from the time of his recovery, he had a better memory and greater steadiness of purpose; but a dark cloud overhung his whole previous existence, and never cleared away.

He was not the less happy for this; for his love of freedom and interest in all that moved or grew, or had its being in the elements, remained to him unimpaired. He lived with his mother on the May-pole farm, tending the poultry and the cattle, working in a garden of his own, and helping everywhere. He was known to every bird and beast about the place, and had a name for every one. Never was there a lighter-hearted husbandman, a creature more popular with young and old, a blither or more happy soul than Barnaby; and though he was free to ramble where he would, he never quitted Her, but was for evermore her stay and comfort.

It was remarkable that although he had that dim sense of the past, he sought out Hugh's dog, and took him under his care; and that he never could be tempted into London. When the Riots were many years old, and Edward and his wife came back to England with a family almost as numerous as Dolly's, and one day appeared at the Maypole porch, he knew them instantly, and wept and leaped for joy. But neither to visit them, nor on any other pretence, no matter how full of promise and enjoyment, could he be persuaded to set foot in the streets: nor did he ever conquer his repugnance or look upon the town again.

Grip soon recovered his looks, and became as glossy and sleek as ever. But he was profoundly silent. Whether he had forgotten the art of Polite Conversation in Newgate, or had made a vow in those troubled times to forego, for a period, the display of his accomplishments, is matter of uncertainty; but certain it is that for a whole year he never indulged in any other sound than a grave, decorous croak. At the expiration of that term, the morning being very bright and sunny, he was heard to address himself to the horses in the stable, upon the subject of the Kettle, so often mentioned in these pages;

and before the witness who overheard him could run into the house with the intelligence, and add to it upon his solemn affirmation the statement that he had heard him laugh, the bird himself advanced with fantastic steps to the very door of the bar, and there cried "I'm a devil, I'm a devil, *I*'m a devil!" with extraordinary rapture.

From that period (although he was supposed to be much affected by the death of Mr. Willet senior), he constantly practised and improved himself in the vulgar tongue, and, as he was a mere infant for a raven when Barnaby was grey, he has very probably gone on talking to the present time.

THE UNCOMMERCIAL TRAVELLER

Editor's Note

*"Figuratively speaking, I travel for the great house
of Human-interest Brothers, and have rather a large
connection in the fancy-goods way. Literally speaking, I am always wandering here and there from my
rooms in Covent Garden . . . seeing many little
things, and some great things, which, because they
interest me, I think may interest others."*——This,
in Dickens's own words, was the idea behind the
writing of the papers comprising The Uncommercial
Traveller. *They began in his periodical "All the
Year Round" in* 1860, *and continued occasionally
until "the autumn of his life." Sometimes they are
autobiographical : as when, in "Travelling Abroad,"
he is the small boy whose father pointed out Gadshill
Place as the house to get. Thirty-six years were to
pass before Dickens bought it out of wealth so
brilliantly and hardly earned. "Dullborough Town" is
Rochester ; and many of the "tramps" and "night-
walks" may even now be retraced along the roads of
Kent and among the streets of London. The present
edition is printed from the one carefully corrected by
the author in* 1867 *and* 1868.

A Cheap Theatre.

THE UNCOMMERCIAL TRAVELLER

BY

CHARLES DICKENS

FRONTISPIECE BY
HARRY FURNISS

LONDON:
HAZELL, WATSON & VINEY, LTD.

THE UNCOMMERCIAL TRAVELLER

CHARLES DICKENS

LONDON
HAZELL, WATSON & VINEY, LTD.

THE UNCOMMERCIAL
TRAVELLER

I

HIS GENERAL LINE OF BUSINESS

ALLOW me to introduce myself—first negatively.

No landlord is my friend and brother, no chambermaid loves me, no waiter worships me, no boots admires and envies me. No round of beef or tongue or ham is expressly cooked for me, no pigeon-pie is especially made for me, no hotel-advertisement is personally addressed to me, no hotel-room tapestried with great-coats and railway wrappers is set apart for me, no house of public entertainment in the United Kingdom greatly cares for my opinion of its brandy or sherry. When I go upon my journeys, I am not usually rated at a low figure in the bill ; when I come home from my journeys, I never get any commission. I know nothing about prices, and should have no idea, if I were put to it, how to wheedle a man into ordering something he doesn't want. As a town traveller, I am never to be seen driving a vehicle externally like a young and volatile pianoforte van, and internally like an oven in which a number of flat boxes are baking in layers. As a country traveller, I am rarely to be found in a gig, and am never to be encountered by a pleasure train, waiting on the platform of a branch station, quite a Druid in the midst of a light Stonehenge of samples.

And yet—proceeding now, to introduce myself positively—I am both a town traveller and a country traveller, and am always on the road. Figuratively speaking, I travel for the great house of Human Interest Brothers, and have rather a large connection in the fancy goods way. Literally speaking, I am always wandering here and there from my rooms in Covent-garden, London—now about the city streets : now, about the country by-roads—seeing many little things, and some great things, which, because they interest me, I think may interest others.

These are my brief credentials as the Uncommercial Traveller.

II

THE SHIPWRECK

NEVER had I seen a year going out, or going on, under quieter circumstances. Eighteen hundred and fifty-nine had but another day to live, and truly its end was Peace on that sea-shore that morning.

So settled and orderly was everything seaward, in the bright light of the sun and under the transparent shadows of the clouds, that it was hard to imagine the bay otherwise, for years past or to come, than it was that very day. The Tug-steamer lying a little off the shore, the Lighter lying still nearer to the shore, the boat alongside the Lighter, the regularly-turning windlass aboard the Lighter, the methodical figures at work, all slowly and regularly heaving up and down with the breathing of the sea, all seemed as much a part of the nature of the place as the tide itself. The tide was on the flow, and had been for some two hours and a half; there was a slight obstruction in the sea within a few yards of my feet: as if the stump of a tree with earth enough about it to keep it from lying horizontally on the water, had slipped a little from the land—and as I stood upon the beach and observed it dimpling the light swell that was coming in, I cast a stone over it.

So orderly, so quiet, so regular—the rising and falling of the Tug-steamer, the Lighter, and the boat—the turning of the windlass—the coming of the tide—that I myself seemed, to my own thinking, anything but new to the spot. Yet, I had never seen it in my life, a minute before, and had traversed two hundred miles to get at it. That very morning I had come bowling down, and struggling up, hill-country roads; looking back at snowy summits; meeting courteous peasants well to do, driving fat pigs and cattle to market: noting the neat and thrifty dwellings, with their unusual quantity of clean white linen, drying on the bushes; having windy weather suggested by every cotter's little rick, with its thatch straw-ridged and extra straw-ridged into overlapping compartments like the back of a rhinoceros. Had I not given a lift of fourteen miles to the Coast-guardsman (kit and all), who was coming to his spell of duty there, and had we not just now parted company? So it was; but the journey seemed to glide down into the placid sea, with other chafe and trouble, and for the moment nothing was so calmly and monotonously real under the sunlight as the gentle rising and falling of the water with its freight, the regular turning of the windlass aboard the Lighter, and the slight obstruction so very near my feet.

O reader, haply turning this page by the fireside at Home, and hearing the night wind rumble in the chimney, that slight obstruction was the uppermost fragment of the Wreck of the Royal Charter, Australian trader and passenger ship, Homeward bound, that struck here on the terrible morning of the twenty-sixth of this October, broke into three parts, went down with her treasure of at least five hundred human lives, and has never stirred since!

From which point, or from which, she drove ashore, stern foremost; on which side, or on which, she passed the little Island in the bay, for ages henceforth to be aground certain yards outside her; these are rendered bootless questions by the darkness of that night and the darkness of death. Here she went down.

Even as I stood on the beach with the words "Here she went down!" in my ears, a diver in his grotesque dress, dipped heavily over the side of the boat alongside the Lighter, and dropped to the bottom.

On the shore by the water's edge, was a rough tent, made of fragments of wreck, where other divers and workmen sheltered themselves, and where they had kept Christmas-day with rum and roast beef, to the destruction of their frail chimney. Cast up among the stones and boulders of the beach, were great spars of the lost vessel, and masses of iron twisted by the fury of the sea into the strangest forms. The timber was already bleached and iron rusted, and even these objects did no violence to the prevailing air the whole scene wore, of having been exactly the same for years and years.

Yet, only two short months had gone, since a man, living on the nearest hill-top overlooking the sea, being blown out of bed at about daybreak by the wind that had begun to strip his roof off, and getting upon a ladder with his nearest neighbour to construct some temporary device for keeping his house over his head, saw from the ladder's elevation as he looked down by chance towards the shore, some dark troubled object close in with the land. And he and the other, descending to the beach, and finding the sea mercilessly beating over a great broken ship, had clambered up the stony ways, like staircases without stairs, on which the wild village hangs in little clusters, as fruit hangs on boughs, and had given the alarm. And so, over the hill-slopes, and past the waterfall, and down the gullies where the land drains off into the ocean, the scattered quarrymen and fishermen inhabiting that part of Wales had come running to the dismal sight—their clergyman among them. And as they stood in the leaden morning, stricken with pity, leaning hard against the wind, their breath and vision often failing as the sleet and spray rushed at them from the ever forming and dissolving mountains of sea, and as the wool which was a part of the vessel's cargo blew in with the salt foam and remained upon the land when the foam melted, they saw the ship's life-boat put off from one of the heaps of wreck; and first, there were three men in her, and in a moment she capsized, and there were but two; and again, she was struck by a vast mass of water, and there was but one; and again, she was thrown bottom upward, and that one, with his arm struck through the broken planks and waving as if for the help that could never reach him, went down into the deep.

It was the clergyman himself from whom I heard this, while I stood on the shore, looking in his kind wholesome face as it turned to the spot where the boat had been. The divers were down then, and busy. They were "lifting" to-day the gold found yesterday—some five-and-twenty thousand pounds. Of three hundred and fifty thousand pounds' worth of gold, three hundred thousand pounds' worth, in round numbers, was at that time recovered. The great bulk of the remainder was surely and steadily coming up. Some loss of sovereigns there would be, of course; indeed, at first sovereigns had drifted in with the sand, and been scattered far and wide over the beach, like sea-shells; but most other golden treasure would be found. As it was brought up, it went aboard the Tug-steamer, where good account was taken of it. So tremendous had the force of the sea been when it broke the ship, that it had beaten one great ingot of gold, deep into a strong and heavy piece of her solid iron-work: in which, also, several loose sovereigns that the ingot had swept in before it, had been found, as firmly embedded as though the iron had been liquid when they were forced there. It had been remarked of such bodies come ashore, too, as had been seen by scientific men, that they had been stunned to death, and not suffocated. Observation, both of the internal change that had been wrought in them, and of their external expression, showed death to have been thus merciful and easy. The report was brought, while I was holding such discourse on the beach, that no more bodies had come ashore since last night. It began to be very doubtful whether many more would be thrown up, until the north-east winds of the early spring set in. Moreover, a great number of the passengers, and particularly the second-class women-passengers, were known to have been in the middle of the ship when she parted, and thus the collapsing wreck would have fallen upon them after yawning open, and would keep them down. A diver made known, even then, that he had come upon the body of a man, and had sought to release it from a great superincumbent weight; but that, finding he could not do so without mutilating the remains, he had left it where it was.

It was the kind and wholesome face I have made mention of as being then beside me, that I had purposed to myself to see, when I left home for Wales. I had heard of that clergyman, as having buried many scores of the shipwrecked people; of his having opened his house and heart to their agonised friends; of his having used a most sweet and patient diligence for weeks and weeks, in the performance of the forlornest offices that Man can render to his kind; of his having most tenderly and thoroughly devoted himself to the dead, and to those who were sorrowing for the dead. I had said to myself, "In the Christmas season of the year, I should like to see that man!" And he had swung the gate of his little garden in coming out to meet me, not half an hour ago.

So cheerful of spirit and guiltless of affectation, as true practical Christianity ever is! I read more of the New Testament in the fresh frank face going up the village beside me, in five minutes, than I have read in anathematising discourses (albeit put to press with enormous flourishing of trumpets), in all my life. I heard more of the Sacred Book in the cordial voice that had nothing to say about its owner, than in all the would-be celestial pairs of bellows that have ever blown conceit at me.

We climbed towards the little church, at a cheery pace, among the loose stones, the deep mud, the wet coarse grass, the outlying water, and other obstructions from which frost and snow had lately thawed. It was a mistake (my friend was glad to tell me, on the way) to suppose that the peasantry had shown any superstitious avoidance of the drowned; on the whole, they had done very well, and had assisted readily. Ten shillings had been paid for the bringing of each body up to the church, but the way was steep, and a horse and cart (in which it was wrapped in a sheet) were necessary, and three or four men, and, all things considered, it was not a great price. The people were none the richer for the wreck, for it was the season of the herring-shoal—and who could cast nets for fish, and find dead men and women in the draught?

He had the church keys in his hand, and opened the churchyard gate, and opened the church door; and we went in.

It is a little church of great antiquity; there is reason to believe that some church has occupied the spot, these thousand years or more. The pulpit was gone, and other things usually belonging to the church were gone, owing to its living congregation having deserted it for the neighbouring school-room, and yielded it up to the dead. The very Commandments had been shouldered out of their places, in the bringing in of the dead; the black wooden tables on which they were painted, were askew, and on the stone pavement below them, and on the stone pavement all over the church, were the marks and stains where the drowned had been laid down. The eye, with little or no aid from the imagination, could yet see how the bodies had been turned, and where the head had been and where the feet. Some faded traces of the wreck of the Australian ship may be discernible on the stone pavement of this little church, hundreds of years hence, when the digging for gold in Australia shall have long and long ceased out of the land.

Forty-four shipwrecked men and women lay here at one time, awaiting burial. Here, with weeping and wailing in every room of his house, my companion worked alone for hours, solemnly surrounded by eyes that could not see him, and by lips that could not speak to him, patiently examining the tattered clothing, cutting off buttons, hair, marks from linen, anything that might lead to subsequent identification, studying faces, looking for a scar, a bent finger, a crooked toe, comparing letters sent to him with the ruin about him. "My dearest brother had bright grey eyes and a pleasant smile," one sister wrote. O poor sister! well for you to be far from here, and keep that as your last remembrance of him!

The ladies of the clergyman's family, his wife and two sisters-in-law, came in among the bodies often. It grew to be the business of their lives to do so. Any new arrival of a bereaved woman would stimulate their pity to compare the description brought, with the dread realities. Sometimes, they would go back able to say, "I have found him," or, "I think she lies there." Perhaps, the mourner, unable to bear the sight of all that lay in the church, would be led in blindfold. Conducted to the spot with many compassionate words, and encouraged to look, she would say, with a piercing cry, "This is my boy!" and drop insensible on the insensible figure.

He soon observed that in some cases of women, the identification of persons, though complete, was quite at variance with the marks upon the linen ; this led him to notice that even the marks upon the linen were sometimes inconsistent with one another; and thus he came to understand that they had dressed in great haste and agitation, and that their clothes had become mixed together. The identification of men by their dress, was rendered extremely difficult, in consequence of a large proportion of them being dressed alike—in clothes of one kind, that is to say, supplied by slopsellers and outfitters, and not made by single garments but by hundreds. Many of the men were bringing over parrots, and had receipts upon them for the price of the birds; others had bills of exchange in their pockets, or in belts. Some of these documents, carefully unwrinkled and dried were little less fresh in appearance that day, than the present page will be under ordinary circumstances, after having been opened three or four times.

In that lonely place, it had not been easy to obtain even such common commodities in towns, as ordinary disinfectants. Pitch had been burnt in the church, as the readiest thing at hand, and the frying-pan in which it had bubbled over a brazier of coals was still there, with its ashes. Hard by the Communion-Table, were some boots that had been taken off the drowned and preserved—a gold-digger's boot, cut down the leg for its removal—a trodden-down man's ankle-boot with a buff cloth top—and others—soaked and sandy, weedy and salt.

From the church, we passed out into the churchyard. Here, there lay, at that time, one hundred and forty-five bodies, that had come ashore from the wreck. He had buried them, when not identified, in graves containing four each. He had numbered each body in a register describing it, and had placed a corresponding number on each coffin, and over each grave. Identified bodies he had buried singly, in private graves, in another part of the churchyard. Several bodies had been exhumed from the graves of four, as relatives had come from a distance and seen his register; and, when recognised, these have been reburied in private graves, so that the mourners might erect separate headstones over the remains. In all such cases he had performed the funeral service a second time, and the ladies of his house had attended. There had been no offence in the poor ashes when they were brought again to the light of day; the beneficent Earth had already absorbed it. The drowned were buried in their clothes. To supply the great sudden demand for coffins, he had got all the neighbouring people handy at tools, to work the livelong day, and Sunday likewise. The coffins were neatly formed;—I had seen two, waiting for occupants, under the lee of the ruined walls of a stone hut on the beach, within call of the tent where the Christmas Feast was held. Similarly, one of the graves for four was lying open and ready, here, in the churchyard. So much of the scanty space was already devoted to the wrecked people, that the villagers had begun to express uneasy doubts whether they themselves could lie in their own ground, with their forefathers and descendants, by-and-by. The churchyard being but a step from the clergyman's dwelling-house, we crossed to the latter; the white surplice was hanging up near the door ready to be put on at any time, for a funeral service.

The cheerful earnestness of this good Christian minister was as consolatory, as the circumstances out of which it shone were sad. I never have seen anything more delightfully genuine than the calm dismissal by himself and his household of all they had undergone, as a simple duty that was quietly done and ended. In speaking of it, they spoke of it with great compassion for the bereaved; but laid no stress upon their own hard share in those weary weeks, except as it had attached many people to them as friends, and elicited many touching expressions of gratitude. This clergyman's brother—himself the clergyman of two adjoining parishes, who had buried thirty-four of the bodies in his own churchyard, and who had done to them all that his brother had done as to the larger number—must be understood as included in the family. He was there, with his neatly arranged papers, and made no more account of his trouble than anybody else did. Down to yesterday's post outward, my clergyman alone had written one thousand and seventy-five letters to relatives and friends of the lost people. In the absence of self-assertion, it was only through my now and then delicately putting a question as the occasion arose, that I became informed of these things. It was only when I had remarked again and again, in the church, on the awful nature of the scene of death he had been required so closely to familiarise himself with for the soothing of the living, that he had casually said, without the least abatement of his cheerfulness, "indeed, it had rendered him unable for a time to eat or drink more than a little coffee now and then, and a piece of bread."

In this noble modesty, in this beautiful simplicity, in this serene avoidance of the least attempt to "improve" an occasion which might be supposed to have sunk of its own weight into my heart, I seemed to have happily come, in a few steps, from the churchyard with its open grave, which was the type of Death, to the Christian dwelling side by side with it, which was the type of Resurrection. I never shall think of the former, without the latter. The two will always rest side by side in my memory. If I had lost any one dear to me in this unfortunate ship, if I had made a voyage from Australia to look at the grave in the churchyard, I should go away, thankful to GOD that that house was so close to it, and that its shadow by day and its domestic lights by night fell upon the earth in which its Master had so tenderly laid my dear one's head.

The references that naturally arose out of our conversation, to the descriptions sent down of shipwrecked persons, and to the gratitude of relations and friends, made me very anxious to see some of those letters. I was presently seated before a shipwreck of papers, all bordered with black, and from them I made the following few extracts.

A mother writes:

REVEREND SIR. Amongst the many who perished on your shore was numbered my beloved son. I was only just recovering from a severe illness, and this fearful affliction has caused a relapse, so that I am unable at present to go to identify the remains of the loved and lost. My darling son would have been sixteen on Christmas-day next.

He was a most amiable and obedient child, early taught the way of salvation. We fondly hoped that as a British seaman he might be an ornament to his profession, but, "it is well;" I feel assured my dear boy is now with the redeemed. Oh, he did not wish to go this last voyage! On the fifteenth of October, I received a letter from him from Melbourne, date August twelfth; he wrote in high spirits, and in conclusion he says: "Pray for a fair breeze, dear mamma, and I'll not forget to whistle for it! and, God permitting, I shall see you and all my little pets again. Good-bye, dear mother—good-bye, dearest parents. Good-bye, dear brother." Oh, it was indeed an eternal farewell. I do not apologise for thus writing you, for oh, my heart is so very sorrowful.

A husband writes:

MY DEAR KIND SIR. Will you kindly inform me whether there are any initials upon the ring and guard you have in possession, found, as the Standard says, last Tuesday? Believe me, my dear sir, when I say that I cannot express my deep gratitude in words sufficiently for your kindness to me on that fearful and appalling day. Will you tell me what I can do for you, and will you write me a consoling letter to prevent my mind from going astray?

A widow writes:

Left in such a state as I am, my friends and I thought it best that my dear husband should be buried where he lies, and, much as I should have liked to have had it otherwise, I must submit. I feel, from all I have heard of you, that you will see it done decently and in order. Little does it signify to us, when the soul has departed, where this poor body lies, but we who are left behind would do all we can to show how we loved them. This is denied me, but it is God's hand that afflicts us, and I try to submit. Some day I may be able to visit the spot, and see where he lies, and erect a simple stone to his memory. Oh! it will be long, long before I forget that dreadful night! Is there such a thing in the vicinity, or any shop in Bangor, to which I could send for a small picture of Moelfra or Llanallgo church, a spot now sacred to me?

Another widow writes:

I have received your letter this morning, and do thank you most kindly for the interest you have taken about my dear husband, as well for the sentiments yours contains, evincing the spirit of a Christian who can sympathise with those who, like myself, are broken down with grief.

May God bless and sustain you, and all in connection with you, in this great trial. Time may roll on and bear all its sons away, but your name as a disinterested person will stand in history, and, as successive years pass, many a widow will think of your noble conduct, and the tears of gratitude flow down many a cheek, the tribute of a thankful heart, when other things are forgotten for ever.

A father writes:

I am at a loss to find words to sufficiently express my gratitude to you for your kindness to my son Richard upon the melancholy occasion of his visit to his dear brother's body, and also for your ready attention in pronouncing our beautiful burial service over my poor unfortunate son's remains. God grant that your prayers over him may reach the Mercy Seat, and that his soul may be received (through Christ's intercession) into heaven!

His dear mother begs me to convey to you her heartfelt thanks.

Those who were received at the clergyman's house, write thus, after leaving it:

DEAR AND NEVER-TO-BE-FORGOTTEN FRIENDS. I arrived here yesterday morning without accident, and am about to proceed to my home by railway.

I am overpowered when I think of you and your hospitable home. No words could speak language suited to my heart. I refrain. God reward you with the same measure you have meted with!

I enumerate no names, but embrace you all.

MY BELOVED FRIENDS. This is the first day that I have been able to leave my bedroom since I returned, which will explain the reason of my not writing sooner.

If I could only have had my last melancholy hope realised in recovering the body of my beloved and lamented son, I should have returned home somewhat comforted, and I think I could then have been comparatively resigned.

I fear now there is but little prospect, and I mourn as one without hope.

The only consolation to my distressed mind is in having been so feelingly allowed by you to leave the matter in your hands, by whom I well know that everything will be done that can be, according to arrangements made before I left the scene of the awful catastrophe, both as to the identification of my dear son, and also his interment.

I feel most anxious to hear whether anything fresh has transpired since I left you; will you add another to the many deep obligations I am under to you by writing to me? And should the body of my dear and unfortunate son be identified, let me hear from you immediately, and I will come again.

Words cannot express the gratitude I feel I owe to you all for your benevolent aid, your kindness, and your sympathy.

MY DEARLY BELOVED FRIENDS. I arrived in safety at my house yesterday, and a night's rest has restored and tranquillised me. I must again repeat, that language has no words by which I can express my sense of obligation to you. You are enshrined in my heart of hearts.

I have seen him! and can now realise my misfortune more than I have hitherto been able to do. Oh, the bitterness of the cup I drink!

But I bow submissive. God *must* have done right. I do not want to feel less, but to acquiesce more simply.

There were some Jewish passengers on board the Royal Charter, and the gratitude of the Jewish people is feelingly expressed in the following letter bearing date from "the office of the Chief Rabbi:"

REVEREND SIR. I cannot refrain from expressing to you my heart-felt thanks on behalf of those of my flock whose relatives have unfortunately been among those who perished at the late wreck of the Royal Charter. You have, indeed, like Boaz, "not left off your kindness to the living and the dead."

You have not alone acted kindly towards the living by receiving them hospitably at your house, and energetically assisting them in their mournful duty, but also towards the dead, by exerting yourself to have our co-religionists buried in our ground, and according to our rites. May our heavenly Father reward you for your acts of humanity and true philanthropy!

The "Old Hebrew congregation of Liverpool" thus express themselves through their secretary:

REVEREND SIR. The wardens of this congregation have learned with great pleasure that, in addition to those indefatigable exertions, at the scene of the late disaster to the Royal Charter, which have received universal recognition, you have very benevolently employed your valuable efforts to assist such members of our faith as have sought the bodies of lost friends to give them burial in our consecrated grounds, with the observances and rites prescribed by the ordinances of our religion.

The wardens desire me to take the earliest available opportunity to offer to you, on behalf of our community, the expression of their warm acknowledgments and grateful thanks, and their sincere wishes for your continued welfare and prosperity.

A Jewish gentleman writes:

REVEREND AND DEAR SIR. I take the opportunity of thanking you right earnestly for the promptness you displayed in answering my note with full particulars concerning my much lamented brother, and I also herein beg to express my sincere regard for the willingness you displayed and for the facility you afforded for getting the remains of my poor brother exhumed. It has been to us a most sorrowful and painful event, but when we meet with such friends as yourself, it in a measure, somehow or other, abates that mental anguish, and makes the suffering so much easier to be borne. Considering the circumstances connected with my poor brother's fate, it does, indeed, appear a hard one. He had been away in all seven years; he returned four years ago to see his family. He was then engaged to a very amiable young lady. He had been very successful abroad, and was now returning to fulfil his sacred vow; he brought all his property with him in gold uninsured. We heard from him when the ship stopped at

Queenstown, when he was in the highest of hope, and in a few short hours afterwards all was washed away.

Mournful in the deepest degree, but too sacred for quotation here, were the numerous references to those miniatures of women worn round the necks of rough men (and found there after death), those locks of hair, those scraps of letters, those many many slight memorials of hidden tenderness. One man cast up by the sea bore about him, printed on a perforated lace card, the following singular (and unavailing) charm:

A BLESSING.

May the blessing of God await thee. May the sun of glory shine around thy bed; and may the gates of plenty, honour, and happiness be ever open to thee. May no sorrow distress thy days; may no grief disturb thy nights. May the pillow of peace kiss thy cheek, and the pleasures of imagination attend thy dreams; and when length of years makes thee tired of earthly joys, and the curtain of death gently closes around thy last sleep of human existence, may the Angel of God attend thy bed, and take care that the expiring lamp of life shall not receive one rude blast to hasten on its extinction.

A sailor had these devices on his right arm. "Our Saviour on the Cross, the forehead of the Crucifix and the vesture stained red; on the lower part of the arm, a man and woman; on one side of the Cross, the appearance of a half moon, with a face; on the other side, the sun; on the top of the Cross, the letters I.H.S.; on the left arm, a man and woman dancing, with an effort to delineate the female's dress; under which, initials." Another seaman "had, on the lower part of the right arm, the device of a sailor and a female; the man holding the Union Jack with a streamer, the folds of which waved over her head, and the end of it was held in her hand. On the upper part of the arm, a device of Our Lord on the Cross, with stars surrounding the head of the Cross, and one large star on the side in Indian ink. On the left arm, a flag, a true lover's knot, a face, and initials." This tattooing was found still plain, below the discoloured outer surface of a mutilated arm, when such surface was carefully scraped away with a knife. It is not improbable that the perpetuation of this marking custom among seamen, may be referred back to their desire to be identified, if drowned and flung ashore.

It was some time before I could sever myself from the many interesting papers on the table, and then I broke bread and drank wine with the kind family before I left them. As I brought the Coast-guard down, so I took the Postman back, with his leathern wallet, walking-stick, bugle, and terrier dog. Many a heart-broken letter had he brought to the Rectory House within two months; many a benignantly painstaking answer had he carried back.

As I rode along, I thought of the many people, inhabitants of this mother country, who would make pilgrimages to the little church-yard in the years to come; I thought of the many people in Australia, who would have an interest in such a shipwreck, and would find their way here when they visit the Old World; I thought of the writers of all the wreck of letters I had left upon the table; and I resolved to place this little record where it stands. Convocations, Conferences, Diocesan Epistles, and the like, will do a great deal for Religion, I dare say, and Heaven send they may! but I doubt if they will ever do their Master's service half so well, in all the time they last, as the Heavens have seen it done in this bleak spot upon the rugged coast of Wales.

Had I lost the friend of my life, in the wreck of the Royal Charter; had I lost my betrothed, the more than friend of my life; had I lost my maiden daughter, had I lost my hopeful boy, had I lost my little child; I would kiss the hands that worked so busily and gently in the church, and say, "None better could have touched the form, though it had lain at home." I could be sure of it, I could be thankful for it: I could be content to leave the grave near the house the good family pass in and out of every day, undisturbed, in the little churchyard where so many are so strangely brought together.

Without the name of the clergyman to whom—I hope, not without carrying comfort to some heart at some time—I have referred, my reference would be as nothing. He is the Reverend Stephen Roose Hughes, of Llanallgo, near Moelfra, Anglesey. His brother is the Reverend Hugh Robert Hughes, of Penrhos, Alligwy.

III

WAPPING WORKHOUSE

My day's no-business beckoning me to the East-end of London, I had turned my face to that point of the metropolitan compass on leaving Covent-garden, and had got past the India House, thinking in my idle manner of Tippoo-Sahib and Charles Lamb, and had got past my little wooden midshipman, after affectionately patting him on one leg of his knee-shorts for old acquaintance' sake, and had got past Aldgate Pump, and had got past the Saracen's Head (with an ignominious rash of posting bills disfiguring his swarthy countenance), and had strolled up the empty yard of his ancient neighbour the Black or Blue Boar, or Bull, who departed this life I don't know when, and whose coaches are all gone I don't know where; and I had come out again into the age of railways, and I had got past Whitechapel Church, and was—rather inappropriately for an Uncommercial Traveller—in the Commerical Road. Pleasantly wallowing in the abundant mud of that thoroughfare, and greatly enjoying the huge piles of building belonging to the sugar refiners, the little masts and vanes in small back gardens in back streets, the neighbouring canals and docks, the India vans lumbering along their stone tramway, and the pawnbrokers' shops where hard-up Mates had pawned so many sextants and quadrants, that I should have bought a few cheap if I had the least notion how to use them, I at last began to file off to the right, towards Wapping.

Not that I intended to take boat at Wapping Old Stairs, or that I was going to look at the locality, because I believe (for I don't) in the constancy of the young woman who told her sea-going lover, to such a beautiful old tune, that she had ever continued the same, since she gave him the baccer-box marked with his name; I am afraid he usually got the worst of those transactions, and was frightfully taken in. No, I was going to Wapping, because an Eastern police magistrate has said, through the morning papers, that there was no classification at the Wapping workhouse for women, and that it was a disgrace and a shame, and divers other hard names, and because I wished to see how the fact really stood. For, that Eastern police magistrates are not always the wisest men of the East, may be inferred from their course of procedure respecting the fancy-dressing and pantomime-posturing at St George's in that quarter: which is usually, to discuss the matter at issue, in a state of mind betokening the weakest perplexity, with all parties concerned and unconcerned, and, for a final expedient, to consult the complainant as to what he thinks ought to be done with the defendant, and take the defendant's opinion as to what he would recommend to be done with himself.

Long before I reached Wapping, I gave myself up as having lost my way, and, abandoning myself to the narrow streets in a Turkish frame of mind, relied on predestination to bring me somehow or other to the place I wanted if I were ever to get there. When I had ceased for an hour or so to take any trouble about the matter, I found myself on a swing-bridge looking down at some dark locks in some dirty water. Over against me, stood a creature remotely in the likeness of a young man, with a puffed sallow face, and a figure all dirty and shiny and slimy, who may have been the youngest son of his filthy old father, Thames, or the drowned man about whom there was a placard on the granite post like a large thimble, that stood between us.

I asked this apparition what it called the place? Unto which it replied, with a ghastly grin and a sound like gurgling water in its throat:

"Mr. Baker's trap."

As it is a point of great sensitiveness with me on such occasions to be equal to the intellectual pressure of the conversation, I deeply considered the meaning of this speech, while I eyed the apparition—then engaged in hugging and sucking a horizontal iron bar at the top of the locks. Inspiration suggested to me that Mr. Baker was the acting coroner of that neighbourhood.

"A common place for suicide," said I, looking down at the locks.

"Sue?" returned the ghost, with a stare. "Yes! And Poll. Likewise Emily. And Nancy, and Jane;" he rucked the iron between each name; "and all the bileing. Ketches off their bonnets or shorls, takes a run, and headers down here, they doos. Always a headerin' down here, they is. Like one o'clock."

"And at about that hour of the morning, I suppose?"

"Ah!" said the apparition. "*They* an't partickler. Two 'ull do for *them*. Three. All times o' night. On'y mind you!" Here the apparition rested his profile on the bar, and gurgled in a sarcastic manner. "There must be somebody comin'. They don't go a headerin' down here, wen there an't no Bobby nor gen'ral Cove, fur to hear the splash."

According to my interpretation of these words, I was myself a General Cove, or member of the miscellaneous public. In which modest character I remarked:

"They are often taken out, are they, and restored?"

"I dunno about restored," said the apparition, who, for some occult reason, very much objected to that word; "they're carried into the werkiss and put into a 'ot bath, and brought round. But I dunno about restored," said the apparition; "blow *that!*"—and vanished.

As it had shown a desire to become offensive, I was not sorry to find myself alone, especially as the "werkiss" it had indicated with a twist of its matted head, was close at hand. So I left Mr. Baker's terrible trap (baited with a scum that was like the soapy rinsing of sooty chimneys), and made bold to ring at the workhouse gate, where I was wholly unexpected and quite unknown.

A very bright and nimble little matron, with a bunch of keys in her hand, responded to my request to see the House. I began to doubt whether the police magistrate was quite right in his facts, when I noticed her quick, active little figure and her intelligent eyes.

The Traveller (the matron intimated) should see the worst first. He was welcome to see everything. Such as it was, there it all was.

This was the only preparation for our entering "the Foul wards." They were in an old building squeezed away in a corner of a paved yard, quite detached from the more modern and spacious main body of the workhouse. They were in a building most monstrously behind the time—a mere series of garrets or lofts, with every inconvenient and objectionable circumstance in their construction, and only accessible by steep and narrow staircases, infamously ill-adapted for the passage up-stairs of the sick or down-stairs of the dead.

A-bed in these miserable rooms, here on bedsteads, there (for a change, as I understood it) on the floor, were women in every stage of distress and disease. None but those who have attentively observed such scenes, can conceive the extraordinary variety of expression still latent under the general monotony and uniformity of colour, attitude, and condition. The form a little coiled up and turned away, as though it had turned its back on this world for ever; the uninterested face at once lead-coloured and yellow, looking passively upward from the pillow; the haggard mouth a little dropped, the hand outside the coverlet, so dull and indifferent, so light, and yet so heavy, these were on every pallet; but when I stopped beside a bed, and said ever so slight a word to the figure lying there, the ghost of the old character came into the face, and made the Foul ward as various as the fair world. No one appeared to care to live, but no one complained; all who could speak, said that as much was done for them as could be done there, that the attendance was kind and patient, that their suffering was very heavy, but they had nothing to ask for. The wretched rooms were as clean and sweet as it is possible for such rooms to be; they would become a pest-house in a single week, if they were ill-kept.

I accompanied the brisk matron up another barbarous staircase, into a better kind of loft devoted to the idiotic and imbecile. There was at least Light in it, whereas the windows in the former wards had been like sides of schoolboys' bird cages. There was a strong grating over the fire here, and, holding a kind of state on either side of the hearth, separated by the breadth of this grating, were two old ladies in a condition of feeble dignity, which was surely the very last and lowest reduction of self complacency to be found in this wonderful humanity of ours. They were evidently jealous of each other, and passed their whole time (as some people do, whose fires are not grated) in mentally disparaging each other, and contemptuously watching their neighbours. One of these parodies on provincial gentlewomen was extremely talkative, and expressed a strong desire to attend the service on Sundays, from which she represented herself to have derived the greatest interest and consolation when allowed that privilege. She gossiped so well, and looked altogether so cheery and harmless, that I began to think this a case for the Eastern magistrate, until I found that on the last occasion of her attending chapel she had secreted a small stick, and had caused some confusion in the responses by suddenly producing it and belabouring the congregation.

So, these two old ladies, separated by the breadth of the grating—otherwise they would fly at one another's caps—sat all day long, suspecting one another, and contemplating a world of fits. For, everybody else in the room had fits, except the wards-woman; an elderly, able-bodied pauperess, with a large upper lip, and an air of repressing and saving her strength, as she stood with hands folded before her, and her eyes slowly rolling, biding her time for catching or holding somebody. This civil personage (in whom I regretted to identify a reduced member of my honourable friend Mrs. Gamp's family) said, "They has 'em continiwal, sir. They drops without no more notice than if they was coach-horses dropped from the moon, sir. And when one drops, another drops, and sometimes there'll be as many as four or five on 'em at once, dear me, a rolling and a tearin', bless you!—this young woman, now, has 'em dreadful bad."

She turned up this young woman's face with her hand as she said it. This young woman was seated on the floor, pondering in the foreground of the afflicted. There was nothing repellant either in her face or her head. Many, apparently worse, varieties of epilepsy and hysteria were about her, but she was said to be the worst here. When I had spoken to her a little, she still sat with her face turned up, pondering, and a gleam of the mid-day sun shone in upon her.

—Whether this young woman, and the rest of these so sorely troubled, as they sit or lie pondering in their confused dull way, ever get mental glimpses among the motes in the sunlight, of healthy people and healthy things? Whether this young woman, brooding like this in the summer season, ever thinks that somewhere there are trees and flowers, even mountains and the great sea? Whether, not to go so far, this young woman ever has any dim revelation of that young woman—that young woman who is not here and never will come here; who is courted, and caressed, and loved, and has a husband, and bears children, and lives in a home, and who never knows what it is to have this lashing and tearing coming upon her? And whether this young woman, God help her, gives herself up then and drops like a coach-horse from the moon?

I hardly knew whether the voices of infant children, penetrating into so hopeless a place, made a sound that was pleasant or painful to me. It was something to be reminded that the weary world was not all aweary, and was ever renewing itself; but, this young woman was a child not long ago, and a child not long hence might be such as she. Howbeit, the active step and eye of the vigilant matron conducted me past the two provincial gentlewomen (whose dignity was ruffled by the children), and into the adjacent nursery.

There were many babies here, and more than one handsome young mother. There were ugly young mothers also, and sullen young mothers, and callous young mothers. But the babies had not appropriated to themselves any bad expression yet, and might have been, for anything that appeared to the contrary in their soft faces, Princes Imperial, and Princesses Royal. I had the pleasure of giving a poetical commission to the baker's man to make a cake with all despatch and toss it into the oven for one red-headed young pauper and myself, and felt much the better for it. Without that refreshment, I doubt if I should have been in a condition for "the Refractories," towards whom my quick little matron—for whose adaptation to her office I had by this time conceived a genuine respect—drew me next, and marshalled me the way that I was going.

The Refractories were picking oakum, in a small room giving on a yard. They sat in line on a form, with their backs to a window; before them, a table, and their work. The oldest Refractory was, say twenty; youngest Refractory, say sixteen. I have never yet ascertained in the course of my uncommercial travels, why a Refractory habit should affect the tonsils and uvula; but, I have always observed that Refractories of both sexes and every grade, between a Ragged School and the Old Bailey, have one voice, in which the tonsils and uvula gain a diseased ascendency.

"Five pound indeed! I hain't a going fur to pick five pound," said the Chief of the Refractories, keeping time to herself with her head and chin. "More than enough to pick what we picks now, in sich a place as this, and on wot we gets here!"

(This was in acknowledgment of a delicate intimation that the amount of work was likely to be increased. It certainly was not heavy then, for one Refractory had already done her day's task—it was barely two o'clock—and was sitting behind it, with a head exactly matching it.)

"A pretty Ouse this is, matron, ain't it?" said Refractory Two, "where a pleeseman's called in, if a gal says a word!"

"And wen you're sent to prison for nothink or less!" said the Chief, tugging at her oakum as if it were the matron's hair. "But any place is better than this; that's one thing, and be thankful!"

A laugh of Refractories led by Oakum Head with folded arms—who originated nothing, but who was in command of the skirmishers outside the conversation.

"If any place is better than this," said my brisk guide, in the calmest manner, "it is a pity you left a good place when you had one."

"Ho, no, I didn't, matron," returned the Chief, with another pull at her oakum, and a very expressive look at the enemy's forehead. "Don't say that, matron, cos it's lies!"

Oakum Head brought up the skirmishers again, skirmished, and retired.

"And *I* warn't a going," exclaimed Refractory Two, "though I was in one place for as long as four year—*I* warn't a going fur to stop in a place that warn't fit for me—there! And where the family warn't 'spectable characters—there! And where I fort'nately or hunfort'nately, found that the people warn't what they pretended to make theirselves out to be—there! And where it wasn't their faults, by chalks, if I warn't made bad and ruinated—Hah!"

During this speech, Oakum Head had again made a diversion with the skirmishers, and had again withdrawn.

The Uncommercial Traveller ventured to remark that he supposed Chief Refractory and Number One, to be the two young women who had been taken before the magistrate?

"Yes!" said the Chief, "we har! and the wonder is, that a pleeseman an't 'ad in now, and we took off agen. You can't open your lips here, without a pleeseman."

Number Two laughed (very uvularly), and the skirmishers followed suit.

"I'm sure I'd be thankful," protested the Chief, looking sideways at the Uncommercial, "if I could be got into a place, or got abroad. I'm sick and tired of this precious Ouse, I am, with reason."

So would be, and so was, Number Two. So would be, and so was, Oakum Head. So would be, and so were, Skirmishers.

The Uncommercial took the liberty of hinting that he hardly thought it probable that any lady or gentleman in want of a likely young domestic of retiring manners, would be tempted into the engagement of either of the two leading Refractories, on her own presentation of herself as per sample.

"It ain't no good being nothink else here," said the Chief.

The Uncommercial thought it might be worth trying.

"Oh no it ain't," said the Chief.

"Not a bit of good," said Number Two.

"And I'm sure I'd be very thankful to be got into a place, or got abroad," said the Chief.

"And so should I," said Number Two. "Truly thankful, I should."

Oakum Head then rose, and announced as an entirely new idea, the mention of which profound novelty might be naturally expected to startle her unprepared hearers, that she would be very thankful to be got into a place, or got abroad. And, as if she had then said, "Chorus, ladies!" all the Skirmishers struck up to the same purpose. We left them, thereupon, and began a long walk among the women who were simply old and infirm; but whenever, in the course of this same walk, I looked out of any high window that commanded the yard, I saw Oakum Head and all the other Refractories looking out at their low window for me, and never failing to catch me, the moment I showed my head.

In ten minutes I had ceased to believe in such fables of a golden time as youth, the prime of life, or a hale old age. In ten minutes, all the lights of womankind seemed to have been blown out, and nothing in that way to be left this vault to brag of, but the flickering and expiring snuffs.

And what was very curious, was, that these dim old women had one company notion which was the fashion of the place. Every old woman who became aware of a visitor and was not in bed hobbled over a form into her accustomed seat, and became one of a line of dim old women confronting another line of dim old women across a narrow table. There was no obligation whatever upon them to range themselves in this way; it was their manner of "receiving." As a rule, they made no attempt to talk to one another, or to look at the visitor, or to look at anything, but sat silently working their mouths, like a sort of poor old Cows. In some of these wards; it was good to see a few green plants; in others, an isolated Refractory acting as nurse, who did well enough in that capacity, when separated from her compeers; every one of these wards, day room, night room, or both combined, was scrupulously clean and fresh. I have seen as many such places as most travellers in my line, and I never saw one such, better kept.

Among the bedridden there was a great patience, great reliance on the books under the pillow, great faith in GOD. All cared for sympathy, but none much cared to be encouraged with hope of recovery; on the whole, I should say, it was considered rather a distinction to have a complication of disorders, and to be in a worse way than the rest. From some of the windows, the river could be seen with all its life and movement; the day was bright, but I came upon no one who was looking out.

In one large ward, sitting by the fire in arm-chairs of distinction, like the President and Vice of the good company, were two old women, upwards of ninety years of age. The younger of the two, just turned ninety, was deaf, but not very, and could easily be made to hear. In her early time she had nursed a child, who was now another old woman, more infirm than herself inhabiting the very same chamber. She perfectly understood this when the matron told it, and, with sundry nods and motions of her forefinger, pointed out the woman in question. The elder of this pair, ninety-three, seated before an illustrated newspaper (but not reading it), was a bright-eyed old soul, really not deaf, wonderfully preserved, and amazingly conversational. She had not long lost her husband, and had been in that

place little more than a year. At Boston, in the State of Massachu-
setts, this poor creature would have been individually addressed,
would have been tended in her own room, and would have had her
life gently assimilated to a comfortable life out of doors. Would that
be much to do in England for a woman who has kept herself out of
a workhouse more than ninety rough long years? When Britain first,
at Heaven's command, arose, with a great deal of allegorical confusion, from out the azure main, did her guardian angels positively
forbid it in the Charter which has been so much besung?

The object of my journey was accomplished when the nimble
matron had no more to show me. As I shook hands with her at the
gate, I told her that I thought Justice had not used her very well,
and that the wise men of the East were not infallible.

Now, I reasoned with myself, as I made my journey home again,
concerning those Foul wards. They ought not to exist; no person of
common decency and humanity can see them and doubt it. But what
is this Union to do? The necessary alteration would cost several
thousands of pounds; it has already to support three workhouses; its
inhabitants work hard for their bare lives, and are already rated for
the relief of the Poor to the utmost extent of reasonable endurance.
One poor parish in this very Union is rated to the amount of FIVE
AND SIXPENCE in the pound, at the very same time when the rich
parish of Saint George's, Hanover-square, is rated at about SEVEN-
PENCE in the pound, Paddington at about FOURPENCE, Saint James's,
Westminster, at about TENPENCE! It is only through the equalisa-
tion of Poor Rates that what is left undone in this wise, can be done.
Much more is left undone, or is ill-done, than I have space to suggest
in these notes of a single uncommercial journey; but, the wise men
of the East, before they can reasonably hold forth about it, must
look to the North and South and West; let them also, any morning
before taking the seat of Solomon, look into the shops and dwellings
all around the Temple, and first ask themselves "how much more
can these poor people—many of whom keep themselves with difficulty enough out of the workhouse—bear?"

I had yet other matter for reflection as I journeyed home, inasmuch as, before I altogether departed from the neighbourhood of
Mr. Baker's trap, I had knocked at the gate of the workhouse of St.
George's-in-the-East, and had found it to be an establishment highly
creditable to those parts, and thoroughly well administered by a
most intelligent master. I remarked in it, an instance of the collateral
harm that obstinate vanity and folly can do. "This was the Hall
where those old paupers, male and female, whom I had just seen,
met for the Church service, was it?"—"Yes."—"Did they sing the
Psalms to any instrument?"—"They would like to, very much; they
would have an extraordinary interest in doing so."—"And could none
be got?"—"Well, a piano could even have been got for nothing, but
these unfortunate dissensions——" Ah! better, far better, my
Christian friend in the beautiful garment, to have let the singing
boys alone, and left the multitude to sing for themselves. You

should know better than I, but I think I have read that they did so, once upon a time, and that "when they had sung an hymn," Some one (not in a beautiful garment) went up unto the Mount of Olives.

It made my heart ache to think of this miserable trifling, in the streets of a city where every stone seemed to call to me, as I walked along, "Turn this way, man, and see what waits to be done!" So I decoyed myself into another train of thought to ease my heart. But, I don't know that I did it, for I was so full of paupers, that it was, after all, only a change to a single pauper, who took possession of my remembrance instead of a thousand.

"I beg your pardon, sir," he had said in a confidential manner, on another occasion, taking me aside; "but I have seen better days."

"I am very sorry to hear it."

"Sir, I have a complaint to make against the master."

"I have no power here, I assure you. And if I had——"

"But allow me, sir, to mention it, as between yourself and a man who has seen better days, sir. The master and myself are both masons, sir, and I make him the sign continually; but, because I am in this unfortunate position, sir, he won't give me the countersign!"

IV

TWO VIEWS OF A CHEAP THEATRE

As I shut the door of my lodging behind me, and came out into the streets at six on a drizzling Saturday evening in the last past month of January, all that neighbourhood of Covent-garden looked very desolate. It is so essentially a neighbourhood which has seen better days, that bad weather affects it sooner than another place which has not come down in the world. In its present reduced condition it bears a thaw almost worse than any place I know. It gets so dreadfully low-spirited when damp breaks forth. Those wonderful houses about Drury-lane Theatre, which in the palmy days of theatres were prosperous and long-settled places of business, and which now change hands every week, but never change their character of being divided and sub-divided on the ground floor into mouldy dens of shops where an orange and half-a-dozen nuts, or a pomatum-pot, one cake of fancy soap, and a cigar box, are offered for sale and never sold, were most ruefully contemplated that evening, by the statue of Shakespeare, with the rain-drops coursing one another down its innocent nose. Those inscrutable pigeon-hole offices, with nothing in them (not so much as an inkstand) but a model of a theatre before the curtain, where, in the Italian Opera season, tickets at reduced prices are kept on sale by nomadic gentlemen in smeary hats too tall for them, whom one occasionally seems to have seen on race-courses, not wholly unconnected with strips of cloth of various colours and a rolling ball—those Bedouin establishments, deserted by the tribe, and tenantless, except when sheltering in one corner an irregular row of ginger-beer bottles, which would have made one shudder on such a night, but for its being plain that they had nothing in them, shrunk from the shrill cries of the newsboys at their Exchange in the kennel of Catherine-street, like guilty things upon a fearful summons. At the pipe-shop in Great Russell-street, the Death's-head pipes were like theatrical memento mori, admonishing beholders of the decline of the playhouse as an Institution. I walked up Bow-street, disposed to be angry with the shops there, that were letting out theatrical secrets by exhibiting to work-a-day humanity the stuff of which diadems and robes of kings are made. I noticed that some shops which had once been in the dramatic line, and had struggled out of it, were not getting on prosperously—like some actors I have known, who took to business and failed to make it answer. In a word, those streets looked so dull, and, considered as theatrical streets, so broken and bankrupt, that the FOUND DEAD on the black board at the police station might have announced the decease of the Drama, and the pools of water outside the fire-engine maker's at the corner of Long-acre might have been occasioned by his having brought out the whole of his stock to play upon its last smouldering ashes.

And yet, on such a night in so degenerate a time, the object of my journey was theatrical. And yet within half an hour I was in an immense theatre, capable of holding nearly five thousand people.

What Theatre? Her Majesty's? Far better. Royal Italian Opera? Far better. Infinitely superior to the latter for hearing in; infinitely superior to both, for seeing in. To every part of this Theatre, spacious fire-proof ways of ingress and egress. For every part of it, convenient places of refreshment and retiring rooms. Everything to eat and drink carefully supervised as to quality, and sold at an appointed price; respectable female attendants ready for the commonest women in the audience; a general air of consideration, decorum and, supervision, most commendable; an unquestionably humanising influence in all the social arrangements of the place.

Surely a dear Theatre, then? Because there were in London (not very long ago) Theatres with entrance-prices up to half-a-guinea a head, whose arrangements were not half so civilised. Surely, therefore, a dear Theatre? Not very dear. A gallery at three pence, another gallery at fourpence, a pit at sixpence, boxes and pit-stalls at a shilling, and a few private boxes at half-a-crown.

My uncommercial curiosity induced me to go into every nook of this great place, and among every class of the audience assembled in it—amounting that evening, as I calculated, to about two thousand and odd hundreds. Magnificently lighted by a firmament of sparkling chandeliers, the building was ventilated to perfection. My sense of smell, without being particularly delicate, has been so offended in some of the commoner places of public resort, that I have often been obliged to leave them when I have made an uncommercial journey expressly to look on. The air of this Theatre was fresh, cool, and wholesome. To help towards this end, very sensible precautions had been used, ingeniously combining the experience of hospitals and railway stations. Asphalt pavements substituted for wooden floors, honest bare walls of glazed brick and tile—even at the back of the boxes—for plaster and paper, no benches stuffed, and no carpeting or baize used; a cool material with a light glazed surface, being the covering of the seats.

These various contrivances are as well considered in the place in question as if it were a Fever Hospital; the result is, that it is sweet and healthful. It has been constructed from the ground to the roof, with a careful reference to sight and sound in every corner; the result is, that its form is beautiful, and that the appearance of the audience, as seen from the proscenium—with every face in it commanding the stage, and the whole so admirably raked and turned to that centre, that a hand can scarcely move in the great assemblage without the movement being seen from thence—is highly remarkable in its union of vastness with compactness. The stage itself, and all its appurtenances of machinery, cellarage, height and breadth, are on a scale more like the Scala at Milan, or the San Carlo at Naples, or the Grand Opera at Paris, than any notion a stranger would be likely to form of the Britannia Theatre at Hoxton, a mile north of St. Luke's Hospital in the Old-street-road, London. The Forty Thieves might be played here, and every thief ride his real horse, and the disguised captain bring in his oil jars on a train of real camels, and nobody be put out of the way. This really extraordinary place is the achievement of one man's enterprise, and was erected on the ruins of an inconvenient old building in less than five months, at a round cost of five-and-twenty thousand pounds. To dismiss this part of my subject, and still to render to the proprietor the credit that is strictly his due, I must add that his sense of the responsibility upon him to make the best of his audience, and to do his best for them, is a highly agreeable sign of these times.

As the spectators at this theatre, for a reason I will presently show, were the object of my journey, I entered on the play of the night as one of the two thousand and odd hundreds, by looking about me at my neighbours. We were a motley assemblage of people, and we had a good many boys and young men among us; we had also many girls and young women. To represent, however, that we did not include a a very great number, and a very fair proportion of family groups, would be to make a gross mis-statement. Such groups were to be seen in all parts of the house; in the boxes and stalls particularly, they were composed of persons of very decent appearance, who had many children with them. Among our dresses there were most kinds of shabby and greasy wear, and much fustian and corduroy that was neither sound nor fragrant. The caps of our young men were mostly of a limp character, and we who wore them, slouched, high-shouldered into our places with our hands in our pockets, and occasionally twisted our cravats about our necks like eels, and occasionally tied them down our breasts like links of sausages, and occasionally had a screw in our hair over each cheek-bone with a slight Thief-flavour in it. Besides prowlers and idlers, we were mechanics, dock-labourers, costermongers, petty tradesmen, small clerks, milliners, stay-makers, shoe-binders, slop-workers, poor workers in a hundred highways and byways. Many of us—on the whole, the majority—were not at all clean, and not at all choice in our lives or conversation. But we had all come together in a place where our convenience was well consulted, and where we were well looked after, to enjoy an evening's entertainment in common. We were not going to lose any part of what we had paid for through anybody's caprice, and as a community we had a character to lose. So, we were closely attentive, and kept excellent order; and let the man or boy who did otherwise instantly get out from this place, or we would put him out with the greatest expedition.

We began at half-past six with a pantomime—with a pantomime so long, that before it was over I felt as if I had been travelling for six weeks—going to India, say, by the Overland Mail. The Spirit of Liberty was the principal personage in the Introduction, and the Four Quarters of the World came out of the globe, glittering, and discoursed with the Spirit, who sang charmingly. We were delighted to understand that there was no liberty anywhere but among ourselves, and we highly applauded the agreeable fact. In an allegorical way, which did as well as any other way, we and the Spirit of Liberty got into a kingdom of Needles and Pins, and found them at war with a potentate who called in to his aid their old arch enemy Rust, and who would have got the better of them if the Spirit of Liberty had not in the nick of time transformed the leaders into Clown, Pantaloon, Harlequin, Columbine, Harlequina, and a whole family of Sprites, consisting of a remarkably stout father and three spineless sons. We all knew what was coming when the Spirit of Liberty addressed the king with a big face, and His Majesty backed to the side-scenes and began untying himself behind, with his big face all on one side. Our excitement at that crisis was great, and our delight unbounded. After this era in our existence, we went through all the incidents of a pantomime; it was not by any means a savage pantomime, in the way of burning or boiling people, or throwing them out of window, or cutting them up; was often very droll; was always liberally got up, and cleverly presented. I noticed that the people who kept the shops, and who represented the passengers in the thoroughfares, and so forth, had no conventionality in them, but were unusually like the real thing—from which I infer that you may take that audience in (if you wish to) concerning Knights and Ladies, Fairies, Angels, or such like, but they are not to be done as to anything in the streets. I noticed, also, that when two young men, dressed in exact imitation of the eel-and-sausage-cravated portion of the audience, were chased by policemen, and, finding themselves in danger of being caught, dropped so suddenly as to oblige the policemen to tumble over them, there was great rejoicing among the caps—as though it were a delicate reference to something they had heard of before.

The Pantomime was succeeded by a Melo-Drama. Throughout the evening I was pleased to observe Virtue quite as triumphant as she usually is out of doors, and indeed I thought rather more so. We all agreed (for the time) that honesty was the best policy, and we were as hard as iron upon Vice, and we wouldn't hear of Villainy getting on in the world—no, not on any consideration whatever.

Between the pieces, we almost all of us went out and refreshed. Many of us went to the length of drinking beer at the bar of the neighbouring public-house, some of us drank spirits, crowds of us had sandwiches and ginger-beer at the refreshment-bars established for us in the Theatre. The sandwich—as substantial as was consistent with portability, and as cheap as possible—we hailed as one of our greatest institutions. It forced its way among us at all stages of the entertainment, and we were always delighted to see it; its adapt-ability, to the varying moods of our nature was surprising; we could never weep so comfortably as when our tears fell on our sandwich; we could never laugh so heartily as when we choked with sandwich; Virtue never looked so beautiful or Vice so deformed as when we paused, sandwich in hand, to consider what would come of that resolution of Wickedness in boots, to sever Innocence in flowered chintz from Honest Industry in striped stockings. When the curtain fell for the night, we still fell back upon sandwich, to help us through the rain and mire, and home to bed.

This, as I have mentioned, was Saturday night. Being Saturday night, I had accomplished but the half of my uncommercial journey; for, its object was to compare the play on Saturday evening with the preaching in the same Theatre on Sunday evening.

Therefore, at the same hour of half-past six on the similarly damp and muddy Sunday evening, I returned to this Theatre. I drove up to the entrance (fearful of being late, or I should have come on foot), and found myself in a large crowd of people who, I am happy to state, were put into excellent spirits by my arrival. Having nothing to look at but the mud and the closed doors, they looked at me, and highly enjoyed the comic spectacle. My modesty inducing me to draw off, some hundreds of yards, into a dark corner, they at once forgot me and applied themselves to their former occupation of looking at the mud and looking in at the closed doors: which, being of grated iron-work, allowed the lighted passage within to be seen. They were chiefly people of respectable appearance, odd and impulsive as most crowds are, and making a joke of being there as most crowds do.

In the dark corner I might have sat a long while, but that a very obliging passer-by informed me that the Theatre was already full, and that the people whom I saw in the street were all shut out for want of room. After that, I lost no time in worming myself into the building, and creeping to a place in a Proscenium box that had been kept for me.

There must have been full four thousand people present. Carefully estimating the pit alone, I could bring it out as holding little less than fourteen hundred. Every part of the house was well filled, and I had not found it easy to make my way along the back of the boxes to where I sat. The chandeliers in the ceiling were lighted; there was no light on the stage; the orchestra was empty. The green curtain was down, and, packed pretty closely on chairs on the small space of stage before it, were some thirty gentlemen, and two or three ladies. In the centre of these, in a desk or pulpit covered with red baize, was the presiding minister. The kind of rostrum he occupied will be very well understood, if I liken it to a boarded-up fireplace turned towards the audience, with a gentleman in a black surtout standing in the stove and leaning forward over the mantelpiece.

A portion of Scripture was being read when I went in. It was followed by a discourse, to which the congregation listened with most exemplary attention and uninterrupted silence and decorum. My own attention comprehended both the auditory and the speaker, and shall turn to both in this recalling of the scene, exactly as it did at the time.

"A very difficult thing," I thought, when the discourse began, "to speak appropriately to so large an audience, and to speak with tact. Without it, better not to speak at all. Infinitely better, to read the New Testament well, and to let *that* speak. In this congregation there is indubitably one pulse; but I doubt if any power short of genius can touch it as one, and make it answer as one."

I could not possibly say to myself as the discourse proceeded, that the minister was a good speaker. I could not possibly say to myself that he expressed an understanding of the general mind and character of his audience. There was a supposititious working-man introduced into the homily, to make supposititious objections to our Christian religion and be reasoned down, who was not only a very disagreeable person, but remarkably unlike life—very much more unlike it than anything I had seen in the pantomime. The native independence of character this artisan was supposed to possess, was represented by a suggestion of a dialect that I certainly never heard in my uncommercial travels, and with a coarse swing of voice and manner anything but agreeable to his feelings, I should conceive, considered in the light of a portrait, and as far away from the fact as a Chinese Tartar. There was a model pauper introduced in like manner, who appeared to me to be the most intolerably arrogant pauper ever relieved, and to show himself in absolute want and dire necessity of a course of Stone Yard. For, how did this pauper testify to his having received the gospel of humility? A gentleman met him in the workhouse, and said (which I myself really thought good-natured of him), "Ah, John? I am sorry to see you here. I am sorry to see you so poor." "Poor, sir!" replied that man, drawing himself up, "I am the son of a Prince! *My* father is the King of Kings. *My* father is the Lord of Lords. *My* father is the ruler of all the Princes of the Earth!" &c. And this was what all the preacher's fellow-sinners might come to, if they would embrace this blessed book—which I must say it did some violence to my own feelings of reverence, to see held out at arm's length at frequent intervals and soundingly slapped, like a slow lot at a sale. Now, could I help asking myself the question, whether the mechanic before me, who must detect the preacher as being wrong about the visible manner of himself and the like of himself, and about such a noisy lip-server as that pauper, might not, most unhappily for the usefulness of the occasion, doubt that preacher's being right about things not visible to human senses?

Again. Is it necessary or advisable to address such an audience continually as "fellow-sinners"? Is it not enough to be fellow-crea-tures, born yesterday, suffering and striving to-day, dying to-morrow? By our common humanity, my brothers and sisters, by our common capacities for pain and pleasure, by our common laughter and our common tears, by our common aspiration to reach something better than ourselves, by our common tendency to believe in something good, and to invest whatever we love or whatever we lose with some qualities that are superior to our own failings and weaknesses as we know them in our own poor hearts—by these, Hear me!—Surely, it is enough to be fellow-creatures. Surely, it includes the other designa-tion, and some touching meanings over and above.

Again. There was a personage introduced into the discourse (not an absolute novelty, to the best of my remembrance of my reading), who had been personally known to the preacher, and had been quite a Crichton in all the ways of philosophy, but had been an infidel. Many a time had the preacher talked with him on that subject, and many a time had he failed to convince that intelligent man. But he fell ill, and died, and before he died he recorded his conversion—in words which the preacher had taken down, my fellow-sinners, and would read to you from this piece of paper. I must confess that to me, as one of an uninstructed audience, they did not appear particularly edifying. I thought their tone extremely selfish, and I thought they had a spiritual vanity in them which was of the before-mentioned refractory pauper's family.

All slangs and twangs are objectionable everywhere, but the slang and twang of the conventicle—as bad in its way as that of the House of Commons, and nothing worse can be said of it—should be studi-ously avoided under such circumstances as I describe. The avoidance was not complete on this occasion. Nor was it quite agreeable to see the preacher addressing his pet "points" to his backers on the stage as if appealing to those disciples to show him up, and testify to the multitude that each of these points was a clincher.

But, in respect of the large Christianity of his general tone; of his renunciation of all priestly authority; of his earnest and reiterated assurance to the people that the commonest among them could work out their own salvation if they would, by simply, lovingly, and duti-fully following Our Saviour, and that they needed the mediation of no erring man; in these particulars, this gentleman deserved all praise. Nothing could be better than the spirit, or the plain emphatic words of his discourse in these respects. And it was a most significant and encouraging circumstance that whenever he struck that chord, or whenever he described anything which Christ himself had done, the array of faces before him was very much more earnest, and very much more expressive of emotion, than at any other time.

And now, I am brought to the fact, that the lowest part of the audience of the previous night, *was not there*. There is no doubt about

it. There was no such thing in that building, that Sunday evening.
I have been told since, that the lowest part of the audience of the
Victoria Theatre has been attracted to its Sunday services. I have
been very glad to hear it, but on this occasion of which I write, the
lowest part of the usual audience of the Britannia Theatre, decidedly
and unquestionably stayed away. When I first took my seat and
looked at the house, my surprise at the change in its occupants was
as great as my disappointment. To the most respectable class of the
previous evening, was added a great number of respectable strangers
attracted by curiosity, and drafts from the regular congregations of
various chapels. It was impossible to fail in identifying the character
of these last, and they were very numerous. I came out in a strong,
slow tide of them setting from the boxes. Indeed, while the discourse
was in progress, the respectable character of the auditory was so
manifest in their appearance, that when the minister addressed a
supposititious " outcast," one really felt a little impatient of it, as a
figure of speech not justified by anything the eye could discover.

The time appointed for the conclusion of the proceedings was
eight o'clock. The address having lasted until full that time, and it
being the custom to conclude with a hymn, the preacher intimated in
a few sensible words that the clock had struck the hour, and that those
who desired to go before the hymn was sung, could go now, without
giving offence. No one stirred. The hymn was then sung, in good time
and tune and unison, and its effect was very striking. A comprehensive benevolent prayer dismissed the throng, and in seven or eight
minutes there was nothing left in the Theatre but a light cloud of
dust.

That these Sunday meetings in Theatres are good things, I do not
doubt. Nor do I doubt that they will work lower and lower down in
the social scale, if those who preside over them will be very careful
on two heads: firstly, not to disparage the places in which they speak,
or the intelligence of their hearers; secondly, not to set themselves in
antagonism to the natural inborn desire of the mass of mankind to
recreate themselves and to be amused.

There is a third head, taking precedence of all others, to which
my remarks on the discourse I heard, have tended. In the New
Testament there is the most beautiful and affecting history conceivable by man, and there are the terse models for all prayer and for
all preaching. As to the models, imitate them, Sunday preachers—
else why are they there, consider? As to the history, tell it. Some
people cannot read, some people will not read, many people (this
especially holds among the young and ignorant) find it hard to pursue
the verse-form in which the book is presented to them, and imagine
that those breaks imply gaps and want of continuity. Help them over
that first stumbling-block, by setting forth the history in narrative,
with no fear of exhausting it. You will never preach so well, you will
never move them so profoundly, you will never send them away with
half so much to think of. Which is the better interest: Christ's choice
of twelve poor men to help in those merciful wonders among the poor

and rejected; or the pious bullying of a whole Union-full of paupers? What is your changed philosopher to wretched me, peeping in at the door out of the mud of the streets and of my life, when you have the widow's son to tell me about, the ruler's daughter, the other figure at the door when the brother of the two sisters was dead, and one of the two ran to the mourner, crying, "The Master is come and calleth for thee"?—Let the preacher who will thoroughly forget himself and remember no individuality but one, and no eloquence but one, stand up before four thousand men and women at the Britannia Theatre any Sunday night, recounting that narrative to them as fellow creatures, and he shall see a sight!

V

POOR MERCANTILE JACK

Is the sweet little cherub who sits smiling aloft and keeps watch on the life of poor Jack, commissioned to take charge of Mercantile Jack, as well as Jack of the national navy? If not, who is? What is the cherub about, and what are we all about, when poor Mercantile Jack is having his brains slowly knocked out by pennyweights, aboard the brig Beelzebub, or the barque Bowie-knife—when he looks his last at that infernal craft, with the first officer's iron boot-heel in his remaining eye, or with his dying body towed overboard in the ship's wake, while the cruel wounds in it do "the multitudinous seas incarnadine"?

Is it unreasonable to entertain a belief that if, aboard the brig Beelzebub or the barque Bowie-knife, the first officer did half the damage to cotton that he does to men, there would presently arise from both sides of the Atlantic so vociferous an invocation of the sweet little cherub who sits calculating aloft, keeping watch on the markets that pay, that such vigilant cherub would, with a winged sword, have that gallant officer's organ of destructiveness out of his head in the space of a flash of lightning?

If it be unreasonable, then am I the most unreasonable of men, for I believe it with all my soul.

This was my thought as I walked the dock-quays at Liverpool, keeping watch on poor Mercantile Jack. Alas for me! I have long outgrown the state of sweet little cherub; but there I was, and there Mercantile Jack was, and very busy he was, and very cold he was: the snow yet lying in the frozen furrows of the land, and the north-east winds snipping off the tops of the little waves in the Mersey, and rolling them into hailstones to pelt him with. Mercantile Jack was hard at it, in the hard weather: as he mostly is in all weathers, poor Jack. He was girded to ships' masts and funnels of steamers, like a forester to a great oak, scraping and painting; he was lying out on yards, furling sails that tried to beat him off; he was dimly discernible up in a world of giant cobwebs, reefing and splicing; he was faintly audible down in holds, stowing and unshipping cargo; he was winding round and round at capstans melodious, monotonous, and drunk; he was of a diabolical aspect, with coaling for the Antipodes; he was washing decks barefoot, with the breast of his red shirt open to the blast, though it was sharper than the knife in his leather girdle; he was looking over bulwarks, all eyes and hair; he was standing by at the shoot of the Cunard steamer: off to-morrow, as the stocks in trade of several butchers, poulterers, and fishmongers, poured down into the icehouse; he was coming aboard of other vessels, with his kit in a tarpaulin bag, attended by plunderers to the very last moment of his shore-going existence. As though his senses, when released from the uproar of the elements, were under obligation to be confused by other turmoil, there was a rattling of wheels, a clattering of hoofs, a clashing of iron, a jolting of cotton and hides and casks and timber, an incessant deafening disturbance on the quays, that was the very madness of sound. And as, in the midst of it, he stood sway-ing about, with his hair blown all manner of wild ways, rather crazedly taking leave of his plunderers, all the rigging in the docks was shrill in the wind, and every little steamer coming and going across the Mersey was sharp in its blowing off, and every buoy in the river bobbed spitefully up and down, as if there were a general taunting chorus of "Come along, Mercantile Jack! Ill-lodged, ill-fed, ill-used, hocussed, entrapped, anticipated, cleaned out. Come along, Poor Mercantile Jack, and be tempest-tossed till you are drowned!"

The uncommercial transaction which had brought me and Jack together, was this:—I had entered the Liverpool police force, that I might have a look at the various unlawful traps which are every night set for Jack. As my term of service in that distinguished corps was short, and as my personal bias in the capacity of one of its members has ceased, no suspicion will attach to my evidence that it is an admirable force. Besides that it is composed, without favour, of the best men that can be picked, it is directed by an unusual intelli-gence. Its organisation against Fires, I take to be much better than the metropolitan system, and in all respects it tempers its remarkable vigilance with a still more remarkable discretion.

Jack had knocked off work in the docks some hours, and I had taken, for purposes of identification, a photograph-likeness of a thief, in the portrait-room at our head police office (on the whole, he seemed rather complimented by the proceeding), and I had been on police parade, and the small hand of the clock was moving on to ten, when I took up my lantern to follow Mr. Superintendent to the traps that were set for Jack. In Mr. Superintendent I saw, as anybody might, a tall, well-looking, well-set-up man of a soldierly bearing with a cavalry air, a good chest, and a resolute but not by any means ungentle face. He carried in his hand a plain black walking-stick of hard wood; and whenever and wherever, at any after-time of the night, he struck it on the pavement with a ringing sound, it instantly produced a whistle out of the darkness, and a policeman. To this remarkable stick, I refer an air of mystery and magic which pervaded the whole of my perquisition among the traps that were set for Jack.

We began by diving into the obscurest streets and lanes of the port. Suddenly pausing in a flow of cheerful discourse, before a dead wall, apparently some ten miles long, Mr. Superintendent struck upon the ground, and the wall opened and shot out, with military salute of hand to temple, two policemen—not in the least surprised themselves, not in the least surprising Mr. Superintendent.

"All right, Sharpeye?"

"All right, sir."

"All right, Trampfoot?"

"All right, sir."

"Is Quickear there?"

"Here am I, sir."

"Come with us."

"Yes, sir."

So, Sharpeye went before, and Mr. Superintendent and I went next, and Trampfoot and Quickear marched as rear-guard. Sharpeye, I soon had occasion to remark, had a skilful and quite professional way of opening doors—touched latches delicately, as if they were keys of musical instruments—opened every door he touched, as if he were perfectly confident that there was stolen property behind it—instantly insinuated himself, to prevent its being shut.

Sharpeye opened several doors of traps that were set for Jack, but Jack did not happen to be in any of them. They were all such miserable places that really, Jack, if I were you, I would give them a wider berth. In every trap, somebody was sitting over a fire, waiting for Jack. Now, it was a crouching old woman, like the picture of the Norwood Gipsy in the old sixpenny dream-books; now, it was a crimp of the male sex, in a checked shirt and without a coat, reading a newspaper; now, it was a man crimp and a woman crimp, who always introduced themselves as united in holy matrimony; now, it was Jack's delight, his (un)lovely Nan; but they were all waiting for Jack, and were all frightfully disappointed to see us.

"Who have you got up-stairs here?" says Sharpeye, generally. (In the Move-on tone.)

"Nobody, surr; sure not a blessed sowl!" (Irish feminine reply.)

"What do you mean by nobody? Didn't I hear a woman's step go up-stairs when my hand was on the latch?"

"Ah! sure thin you're right, surr, I forgot her! 'Tis on'y Betsy White, surr. Ah! you know Betsy, surr. Come down, Betsy darlin', and say the gentlemin."

Generally, Betsy looks over the banisters (the steep staircase is in the room) with a forcible expression in her protesting face, of an intention to compensate herself for the present trial by grinding Jack finer than usual when he does come. Generally, Sharpeye turns to Mr. Superintendent, and says, as if the subjects of his remarks were wax-work:

"One of the worst, sir, this house is. This woman has been indicted three times. This man's a regular bad one likewise. His real name is Pegg. Gives himself out as Waterhouse."

"Never had sitch a name as Pegg near me back, thin, since I was in this house, bee the good Lard!" says the woman.

Generally, the man says nothing at all, but becomes exceedingly round-shouldered, and pretends to read his paper with rapt attention. Generally, Sharpeye directs our observation with a look, to the prints and pictures that are invariably numerous on the walls. Always, Trampfoot and Quickear are taking notice on the doorstep. In default of Sharpeye being acquainted with the exact individuality of any gentleman encountered, one of these two is sure to proclaim from the outer air, like a gruff spectre, that Jackson is not Jackson, but knows himself to be Fogle; or that Canlon is Walker's brother, against whom there was not sufficient evidence; or that the man who says he never was at sea since he was a boy, came ashore from a voyage last Thursday, or sails to-morrow morning. "And that is a bad class of man, you see," says Mr. Superintendent, when he got out into the dark again, "and very difficult to deal with, who, when he has made this place too hot to hold him, enters himself for a voyage as steward or cook, and is out of knowledge for months, and then turns up again worse than ever."

When we had gone into many such houses, and had come out (always leaving everybody relapsing into waiting for Jack), we started off to a singing-house where Jack was expected to muster strong.

The vocalisation was taking place in a long low room up-stairs; at one end, an orchestra of two performers, and a small platform; across the room, a series of open pews for Jack, with an aisle down the middle; at the other end a larger pew than the rest, entitled SNUG, and reserved for mates and similar good company. About the room, some amazing coffee-coloured pictures varnished an inch deep, and some stuffed creatures in cases; dotted among the audience, in Snug and out of Snug, the "Professionals;" among them, the celebrated comic favourite Mr. Banjo Bones, looking very hideous with his blackened face and limp sugar-loaf hat; beside him, sipping rum-and-water, Mrs. Banjo Bones, in her natural colours—a little heightened.

It was a Friday night, and Friday night was considered not a good night for Jack. At any rate, Jack did not show in very great force even here, though the house was one to which he much resorts, and where a good deal of money is taken. There was British Jack, a little maudlin and sleepy, lolling over his empty glass, as if he were trying to read his fortune at the bottom; there was Loafing Jack of the Stars and Stripes, rather an unpromising customer, with his long nose, lank cheek, high cheek-bones, and nothing soft about him but his cabbage-leaf hat; there was Spanish Jack, with curls of black hair, rings in his ears, and a knife not far from his hand, if you got into trouble with him; there were Maltese Jack, and Jack of Sweden, and Jack the Finn, looming through the smoke of their pipes, and turning faces that looked as if they were carved out of dark wood, towards the young lady dancing the hornpipe: who found the platform so exceedingly small for it, that I had a nervous expectation of seeing her, in the backward steps, disappear through the window. Still, if all hands had been got together, they would not have more than half-filled the room. Observe, however, said Mr. Licensed Victualler, the host, that it was Friday night, and, besides, it was getting on for twelve, and Jack had gone aboard. A sharp and watchful man, Mr. Licensed Victualler, the host, with tight lips and a complete edition of Cocker's arithmetic in each eye. Attended to his business himself, he said. Always on the spot. When he heard of talent, trusted nobody's account of it, but went off by rail to see it. If true talent, engaged it. Pounds a week for talent—four pound—five pound. Banjo Bones was undoubted talent. Hear this instrument that was going to play—it was real talent! In truth it was very good; a kind of piano-accordion, played by a young girl of a delicate prettiness of face, figure, and dress that made the audience look coarser. She sang to the instrument, too; first a song about village bells, and how they chimed; then a song about how I went to sea; winding up with an imitation of the bagpipes, which Mercantile Jack seemed to understand much the best. A good girl, said Mr. Licensed Victualler. Kept herself select. Sat in Snug, not listening to the blandishments of Mates. Lived with mother. Father dead. Once a merchant well to do, but over-speculated himself. On delicate inquiry as to salary paid for item of talent under consideration, Mr. Victualler's pounds dropped suddenly to shillings —still it was a very comfortable thing for a young person like that, you know; she only went on six times a night, and was only required to be there from six at night to twelve. What was more conclusive was, Mr. Victualler's assurance that he "never allowed any language, and never suffered any disturbance." Sharpeye confirmed the statement, and the order that prevailed was the best proof of it that could have been cited. So, I came to the conclusion that poor Mercantile Jack might do (as I am afraid he does) much worse than trust himself to Mr. Victualler, and pass his evenings here.

But we had not yet looked, Mr. Superintendent—said Trampfoot, receiving us in the street again with military salute—for Dark Jack. True, Trampfoot. Ring the wonderful stick, rub the wonderful lantern, and cause the spirits of the stick and lantern to convey us to the Darkies.

There was no disappointment in the matter of Dark Jack; *he* was producible. The Genii set us down in the little first floor of a little public-house, and there, in a stiflingly close atmosphere, were Dark Jack, and Dark Jack's delight, his *white* unlovely Nan, sitting against the wall all round the room. More than that: Dark Jack's delight was the least unlovely Nan, both morally and physically, that I saw that night.

As a fiddle and tambourine band were sitting among the company, Quickear suggested why not strike up? "Ah, la'ads!" said a negro sitting by the door, "gib the jebblem a darnse. Tak' yah pardlers, jebblem, for 'um QUAD-rill."

This was the landlord, in a Greek cap, and a dress half Greek and half English. As master of the ceremonies, he called all the figures, and occasionally addressed himself parenthetically—after this manner. When he was very loud, I use capitals.

"Now den! Hoy! ONE. Right and left. (Put a steam on, gib 'um powder.) LA-dies' chail. BAL-loon say. Lemonade! Two. AD-warnse and go back (gib 'ell a breakdown, shake it out o' yerselbs, keep a movil). SWING-corners, BAL-loon say, and Lemonade! (Hoy!) THREE. GENT come for'ard with a lady and go back, hoppersite come for'ard and do what yer can. (Aeiohoy!) BAL-loon say, and leetle lemonade (Dat hair nigger by 'um fireplace 'hind a' time, shake it out o' yerselbs, gib 'ell a breakdown.) Now den! Hoy! FOUR! Lemonade. BAL-loon say, and swing. FOUR ladies meets in 'um middle, FOUR gents goes round 'um ladies, FOUR gents passes out under 'um ladies' arms, SWING—and Lemonade till 'a moosic can't play no more! (Hoy, Hoy!)"

The male dancers were all blacks, and one was an unusually power-ful man of six feet three or four. The sound of their flat feet on the floor was as unlike the sound of white feet as their faces were unlike white faces. They toed and heeled, shuffled, double-shuffled, double-double-shuffled, covered the buckle, and beat the time out, rarely, dancing with a great show of teeth, and with a childish good-humoured enjoyment that was very prepossessing. They generally kept together, these poor fellows, said Mr. Superintendent, because they were at a disadvantage singly, and liable to slights in the neigh-bouring streets. But, if I were Light Jack, I should be very slow to interfere oppressively with Dark Jack, for, whenever I have had to do with him I have found him a simple and a gentle fellow. Bearing this in mind, I asked his friendly permission to leave him restoration of beer, in wishing him good night, and thus it fell out that the last words I heard him say as I blundered down the worn stairs, were, "Jebblem's elth! Ladies drinks fust!"

The night was now well on into the morning, but, for miles and hours we explored a strange world, where nobody ever goes to bed, but everybody is eternally sitting up, waiting for Jack. This explora-tion was among a labyrinth of dismal courts and blind alleys, called Entries, kept in wonderful order by the police, and in much better order than by the corporation: the want of gaslight in the most dangerous and infamous of these places being quite unworthy of so spirited a town. I need describe but two or three of the houses in which Jack was waited for as specimens of the rest. Many we attained by noisome passages so profoundly dark that we felt our way with our hands. Not one of the whole number we visited, was without its show of prints and ornamental crockery; the quantity of the latter set forth on little shelves and in little cases, in otherwise wretched rooms, indicating that Mercantile Jack, must have an extraordinary fond-ness for crockery, to necessitate so much of that bait in his traps.

Among such garniture, in one front parlour in the dead of the night, four women were sitting by a fire. One of them had a male child in her arms. On a stool among them was a swarthy youth with a guitar, who had evidently stopped playing when our footsteps were heard.

"Well! how do *you* do?" says Mr. Superintendent, looking about him.

"Pretty well, sir, and hope you gentlemen are going to treat us ladies, now you have come to see us."

"Order there!" says Sharpeye.

"None of that!" says Quickear.

Trampfoot, outside, is heard to confide to himself, "Meggisson's lot this is. And a bad 'un."

"Well!" says Mr. Superintendent, laying his hand on the shoulder of the swarthy youth, "and who's this?"

"Antonio, sir."

"And what does *he* do here?"

"Come to give us a bit of music. No harm in that, I suppose?"

"A young foreign sailor?"

"Yes. He's a Spaniard. You're a Spaniard, ain't you, Antonio?"

"Me Spanish."

"And he don't know a word you say, not he; not if you was to talk to him till doomsday." (Triumphantly, as if it redounded to the credit of the house.)

"Will he play something?"

"Oh, yes, if you like. Play something, Antonio. *You* ain't ashamed to play something; are you?"

The cracked guitar raises the feeblest ghost of a tune, and three of the women keep time to it with their heads, and the fourth with the child. If Antonio has brought any money in with him, I am afraid he will never take it out, and it even strikes me that his jacket and guitar may be in a bad way. But, the look of the young man and the tinkling of the instrument so change the place in a moment to a leaf out of Don Quixote, that I wonder where his mule is stabled, until he leaves off.

I am bound to acknowledge (as it tends rather to my uncommercial confusion), that I occasioned a difficulty in this establishment, by having taken the child in my arms. For, on my offering to restore it to a ferocious joker not unstimulated by rum, who claimed to be its mother, that unnatural parent put her hands behind her, and declined to accept it; backing into the fireplace, and very shrilly declaring, regardless of remonstrance from her friends, that she knowed it to be Law, that whoever took a child from its mother of his own will, was bound to stick to it. The uncommercial sense of being in a rather ridiculous position with the poor little child beginning to be frightened, was relieved by my worthy friend and fellow-constable, Trampfoot; who, laying his hands on the article as if it were a Bottle, passed it on to the nearest woman, and bade her "take hold of that." As we came out the Bottle was passed to the ferocious joker, and they all sat down as before, including Antonio and the guitar. It was clear that there was no such thing as a nightcap to this baby's head, and that even he never went to bed, but was always kept up—and would grow up, kept up—waiting for Jack.

Later still in the night, we came (by the court "where the man was murdered," and by the other court across the street, into which his body was dragged) to another parlour in another Entry, where several people were sitting round a fire in just the same way. It was a dirty and offensive place, with some ragged clothes drying in it; but there was a high shelf over the entrance-door (to be out of the reach of marauding hands, possibly) with two large white loaves on it, and a great piece of Cheshire cheese.

"Well!" says Mr. Superintendent, with a comprehensive look all round. "How do *you* do?"

"Not much to boast of, sir." From the curtseying woman of the house. "This is my good man, sir."

"You are not registered as a common Lodging House?"

"No, sir."

Sharpeye (in the Move-on tone) puts in the pertinent inquiry, "Then why ain't you?"

"Ain't got no one here, Mr. Sharpeye," rejoin the woman and my good man together, "but our own family."

"How many are you in family?"

The woman takes time to count, under pretence of coughing, and adds, as one scant of breath, "Seven, sir."

But she has missed one, so Sharpeye, who knows all about it, says: "Here's a young man here makes eight, who ain't of your family?"

"No, Mr. Sharpeye, he's a weekly lodger."

"What does he do for a living?"

The young man here, takes the reply upon himself, and shortly answers, "Ain't got nothing to do."

The young man here, is modestly brooding behind a damp apron pendent from a clothes-line. As I glance at him I become—but I don't know why—vaguely reminded of Woolwich, Chatham, Portsmouth, and Dover. When we get out, my respected fellow-constable Sharpeye, addressing Mr. Superintendent, says:

"You noticed that young man, sir, in at Darby's?"

"Yes. What is he?"

"Deserter, sir."

Mr. Sharpeye further intimates that when we have done with his services, he will step back and take that young man. Which in course of time he does: feeling at perfect ease about finding him, and knowing for a moral certainty that nobody in that region will be gone to bed.

Later still in the night, we came to another parlour up a step or two from the street, which was very cleanly, neatly, even tastefully, kept, and in which, set forth on a draped chest of drawers masking the staircase, was such a profusion of ornamental crockery, that it would have furnished forth a handsome sale-booth at a fair. It backed up a stout old lady—HOGARTH drew her exact likeness more than once—and a boy who was carefully writing a copy in a copy-book.

"Well, ma'am, how do *you* do?"

Sweetly, she can assure the dear gentleman, sweetly. Charmingly,

charmingly. And overjoyed to see us!

"Why, this is a strange time for this boy to be writing his copy. In the middle of the night!"

"So it is, dear gentlemen, Heaven bless your welcome faces and send ye prosperous, but he has been to the Play with a young friend for his diversion, and he combinates his improvement with entertainment, by doing his school-writing afterwards, God be good to ye!"

The copy admonished human nature to subjugate the fire of every fierce desire. One might have thought it recommended stirring the fire, the old lady so approved it. There she sat, rosily beaming at the copy-book and the boy, and invoking showers of blessings on our heads, when we left her in the middle of the night, waiting for Jack.

Later still in the night, we came to a nauseous room with an earth floor, into which the refuse scum of an alley trickled. The stench of this habitation was abominable; the seeming poverty of it, diseased and dire. Yet, here again, was visitor or lodger—a man sitting before the fire, like the rest of them elsewhere, and apparently not distasteful to the mistress's niece, who was also before the fire. The mistress herself had the misfortune of being in jail.

Three weird old women of transcendent ghastliness, were at needlework at a table in this room. Says Trampfoot to First Witch, "What are you making?" Says she, "Money-bags."

"*What* are you making?" retorts Trampfoot, a little off his balance.

"Bags to hold your money," says the witch, shaking her head, and setting her teeth; "you as has got it."

She holds up a common cash-bag, and on the table is a heap of such bags. Witch Two laughs at us. Witch Three scowls at us. Witch sisterhood all, stitch, stitch. First Witch has a circle round each eye. I fancy it like the beginning of the development of a perverted diabolical halo, and that when it spreads all round her head, she will die in the odour of devilry.

Trampfoot wishes to be informed what First Witch has got behind the table, down by the side of her, there? Witches Two and Three croak angrily, "Show him the child!"

She drags out a skinny little arm from a brown dustheap on the ground. Adjured not at disturb the child, she lets it drop again. Thus we find at last that there is one child in the world of Entries who goes to bed—if this be bed.

Mr. Superintendent asks how long are they going to work at those bags?

How long? First Witch repeats. Going to have supper presently. See the cups and saucers, and the plates.

"Late? Ay! But we has to 'arn our supper afore we eats it!" Both the other witches repeat this after First Witch, and take the Uncommercial measurement with their eyes, as for a charmed winding-sheet. Some grim discourse ensues, referring to the mistress of the cave, who will be released from jail to-morrow. Witches pronounce Trampfoot "right there," when he deems it a trying distance for the old lady to walk; she shall be fetched by niece in a spring-cart.

As I took a parting look at First Witch in turning away, the red marks round her eyes seemed to have already grown larger, and she hungrily and thirstily looked out beyond me into the dark doorway, to see if Jack was there. For, Jack came even here, and the mistress had got into jail through deluding Jack.

When I at last ended this night of travel and got to bed, I failed to keep my mind on comfortable thoughts of Seaman's Homes (not overdone with strictness), and improved dock regulations giving Jack greater benefit of fire and candle aboard ship, through my mind's wandering among the vermin I had seen. Afterwards the same vermin ran all over my sleep. Evermore, when on a breezy day I see Poor Mercantile Jack running into port with a fair wind under all sail, I shall think of the unsleeping host of devourers who never go to bed, and are always in their set traps waiting for him.

VI

REFRESHMENTS FOR TRAVELLERS

In the late high winds I was blown to a great many places—and indeed, wind or no wind, I generally have extensive transactions on hand in the article of Air—but I have not been blown to any English place lately, and I very seldom have blown to any English place in my life, where I could get anything good to eat and drink in five minutes, or where, if I sought it, I was received with a welcome.

This is a curious thing to consider. But before (stimulated by my own experiences and the representations of many fellow-travellers of every uncommercial and commercial degree) I consider it further, I must utter a passing word of wonder concerning high winds.

I wonder why metropolitan gales always blow so hard at Walworth. I cannot imagine what Walworth has done, to bring such windy punishment upon itself, as I never fail to find recorded in the newspapers when the wind has blown at all hard. Brixton seems to have something on its conscience; Peckham suffers more than a virtuous Peckham might be supposed to deserve; the howling neighbourhood of Deptford figures largely in the accounts of the ingenious gentlemen who are out in every wind that blows, and to whom it is an ill high wind that blows no good; but, there can hardly be any Walworth left by this time. It must surely be blown away. I have read of more chimney-stacks and house-copings coming down with terrific smashes at Walworth, and of more sacred edifices being nearly (not quite) blown out to sea from the same accursed locality, than I have read of practised thieves with the appearance and manners of gentlemen— a popular phenomenon which never existed on earth out of fiction and a police report. Again, I wonder why people are always blown into the Surrey Canal, and into no other piece of water! Why do people get up early and go out in groups, to be blown into the Surrey Canal? Do they say to one another, "Welcome death, so that we get into the newspapers?" Even that would be an insufficient explanation, because even then they might sometimes put themselves in the way of being blown into the Regent's Canal, instead of always saddling Surrey for the field. Some nameless policeman, too, is constantly, on the slightest provocation, getting himself blown into this same Surrey Canal. Will SIR RICHARD MAYNE see to it, and restrain that weak-minded and feeble-bodied constable?

To resume the consideration of the curious question of Refreshment. I am a Briton, and, as such, I am aware that I never will be a slave—and yet I have latent suspicion that there must be some slavery of wrong custom in this matter.

I travel by railroad. I start from home at seven or eight in the morning, after breakfasting hurriedly. What with skimming over the open landscape, what with mining in the damp bowels of the earth, what with banging, booming and shrieking the scores of miles a way, I am hungry when I arrive at the "Refreshment" station where I am expected. Please to observe, expected. I have said, I am hungry; perhaps I might say, with greater point and force, that I am to some extent exhausted, and that I need—in the expressive French sense of the word—to be restored. What is provided for my restoration? The apartment that is to restore me is a windtrap, cunningly set to inveigle all the draughts in that country-side, and to communicate a special intensity and velocity to them as they rotate in two hurricanes: one, about my wretched head: one, about my wretched legs. The training of the young ladies behind the counter who are to restore me, has been from their infancy directed to the assumption of a defiant dramatic show that I am *not* expected. It is in vain for me to represent to them by my humble and conciliatory manners, that I wish to be liberal. It is in vain for me to represent to myself, for the encouragement of my sinking soul, that the young ladies have a pecuniary interest in my arrival. Neither my reason nor my feelings can make head against the cold glazed glare of eye with which I am assured that I am not expected, and not wanted. The solitary man among the bottles would sometimes take pity on me, if he dared, but he is powerless against the rights and mights of Woman. (Of the page I make no account, for, he is a boy, and therefore the natural enemy of Creation.) Chilling fast, in the deadly tornadoes to which my upper and lower extremities are exposed, and subdued by the moral disadvantage at which I stand, I turn my disconsolate eyes on the refreshments that are to restore me. I find that I must either scale my throat by insanely ladling into it, against time and for no wager, brown hot water stiffened with flour; or I must make myself flaky and sick with Banbury cake; or, I must stuff into my delicate organisation, a currant pincushion which I know will swell into immeasurable dimensions when it has got there; or, I must extort from an iron-bound quarry, with a fork, as if I were farming an inhospitable soil, some glutinous lumps of gristle and grease, called pork-pie. While thus forlornly occupied, I find that the depressing banquet on the table is, in every phase of its profoundly unsatisfactory character, so like the banquet at the meanest and shabbiest of evening parties, that I begin to think I must have "brought down" to supper, the old lady unknown, blue with cold, who is setting her teeth on edge with a cool orange at my elbow—that the pastrycook who has compounded for the company on the lowest terms per head, is a fraudulent bankrupt, redeeming his contract with the stale stock from his window—that, for some unexplained reason, the family giving the party have become my mortal foes, and have given it on purpose to affront me. Or, I fancy that I am "breaking up" again, at the evening conversazione at school, charged two-and-sixpence in the half-year's bill; or breaking down again at that celebrated evening party given at Mrs. Bogles's boarding-house when I was a boarder there, on which occasion Mrs. Bogles was taken in execution by a branch of the legal profession who got in as the harp, and was removed (with the keys and subscribed capital) to a place of durance, half an hour prior to the commencement of the festivities.

Take another case.

Mr. Grazinglands, of the Midland Counties, came to London by railroad one morning last week, accompanied by the amiable and fascinating Mrs. Grazinglands. Mr. G. is a gentleman of a comfortable property, and had a little business to transact at the Bank of England, which required the concurrence and signature of Mrs. G. Their business disposed of, Mr. and Mrs. Grazinglands viewed the Royal Exchange, and the exterior of St. Paul's Cathedral. The spirits of Mrs. Grazinglands then gradually beginning to flag, Mr. Grazinglands (who is the tenderest of husbands) remarked with sympathy, "Arabella, my dear, I fear you are faint." Mrs. Grazinglands replied, "Alexander, I am rather faint; but don't mind me, I shall be better presently." Touched by the feminine meekness of this answer, Mr. Grazinglands looked in at a pastrycook's window, hesitating as to the expediency of lunching at that establishment. He beheld nothing to eat, but butter in various forms, slightly charged with jam, and languidly frizzling over tepid water. Two ancient turtle-shells, on which was inscribed the legend, "SOUPS," decorated a glass partition within, enclosing a stuffy alcove, from which a ghastly mockery of a marriage-breakfast spread on a rickety table, warned the terrified traveller. An oblong box of stale and broken pastry at reduced prices, mounted on a stool, ornamented the doorway; and two high chairs that looked as if they were performing on stilts, embellished the counter. Over the whole, a young lady presided, whose gloomy haughtiness as she surveyed the street, announced a deep-seated grievance against society, and an implacable determination to be avenged. From a beetle-haunted kitchen below this institution, fumes arose, suggestive of a class of soup which Mr. Grazinglands knew, from painful experience, enfeebles the mind, distends the stomach, forces itself into the complexion, and tries to ooze out at the eyes. As he decided against entering, and turned away, Mrs. Grazinglands becoming perceptibly weaker, repeated, "I am rather faint, Alexander, but don't mind me." Urged to new efforts by these words of resignation, Mr. Grazinglands looked in at a cold and floury baker's shop, where utilitarian buns unrelieved by a currant, consorted with hard biscuits, a stone filter of cold water, a hard pale clock, and a hard little old woman with flaxen hair, of an undeveloped-farinaceous aspect, as if she had been fed upon seeds. He might have entered even here, but for the timely remembrance coming upon him that Jairing's was but round the corner.

Now, Jairing's being an hotel for families and gentlemen, in high repute among the midland counties, Mr. Grazinglands plucked up a great spirit when he told Mrs. Grazinglands she should have a chop there. That lady, likewise felt that she was going to see Life. Arriving on that gay and festive scene, they found the second waiter, in a flabby undress, cleaning the windows of the empty coffee-room; and the first waiter, denuded of his white tie, making up his cruets behind the Post-Office Directory. The latter (who took them in hand) was greatly put out by their patronage, and showed his mind to be troubled by a sense of the pressing necessity of instantly smuggling Mrs. Grazinglands into the obscurest corner of the building. This slighted lady (who is the pride of her division of the county) was immediately conveyed, by several dark passages, and up and down several steps, into a penitential apartment at the back of the house, where five invalided old plate-warmers leaned up against one another under a discarded old melancholy sideboard, and where the wintry leaves of all the dining-tables in the house lay thick. Also, a sofa, of incomprehensible form regarded from any sofane point of view, murmured "Bed;" while an air of mingled fluffiness and heeltaps, added, "Second Waiter's." Secreted in this dismal hold, objects of a mysterious distrust and suspicion, Mr. Grazinglands and his charming partner waited twenty minutes for the smoke (for it never came to a fire), twenty-five minutes for the sherry, half an hour for the tablecloth, forty minutes for the knives and forks, three-quarters of an hour for the chops, and an hour for the potatoes. On settling the little bill—which was not much more than the day's pay of a Lieutenant in the navy—Mr. Grazinglands took heart to remonstrate against the general quality and cost of his reception. To whom the waiter replied, substantially, that Jairing's made it a merit to have accepted him on any terms: "for," added the waiter (unmistakably coughing at Mrs. Grazinglands, the pride of her division of the county), "when indiwiduals is not staying in the 'Ouse, their favours is not as a rule looked upon as making it worth Mr. Jairing's while; nor is it, indeed, a style of business Mr. Jairing wishes." Finally, Mr. and Mrs. Grazinglands passed out of Jairing's hotel for Families and Gentlemen, in a state of the greatest depression, scorned by the bar; and did not recover their self-respect for several days.

Or take another case. Take your own case.

You are going off by railway, from any Terminus. You have twenty minutes for dinner, before you go. You want your dinner, and like Dr. Johnson, Sir, you like to dine. You present to your mind, a picture of the refreshment-table at that terminus. The conventional shabby evening-party supper—accepted as the model for all termini and all refreshment stations, because it is the last repast known to this state of existence of which any human creature would partake, but in the direst extremity—sickens your contemplation, and your words are these: "I cannot dine on stale sponge-cakes that turn to sand in the mouth. I cannot dine on shining brown patties, composed of unknown animals within, and offering to my view the device of an indigestible star-fish in leaden pie-crust without. I cannot dine on a sandwich that has long been pining under an exhausted receiver. I cannot dine on barley-sugar. I cannot dine on Toffee." You repair to the nearest hotel, and arrive, agitated, in the coffee-room.

It is a most astonishing fact that the waiter is very cold to you. Account for it how you may, smooth it over how you will, you cannot deny that he is cold to you. He is not glad to see you, he does not want you, he would much rather you hadn't come. He opposes to your flushed condition, an immovable composure. As if this were not enough, another waiter, born, as it would seem, expressly to look at you in this passage of your life, stands at a little distance, with his napkin under his arm and his hands folded, looking at you with all his might. You impress on your waiter that you have ten minutes for dinner, and he proposes that you shall begin with a bit of fish which will be ready in twenty. That proposal declined, he suggests—as a neat originality—"a weal or mutton cutlet." You close with either cutlet, any cutlet, anything. He goes, leisurely, behind a door and calls down some unseen shaft. A ventriloquial dialogue ensues, tending finally to the effect that weal only, is available on the spur of the moment. You anxiously call out, "Veal, then!" Your waiter having settled that point, returns to array your tablecloth, with a table napkin folded cocked-hat-wise (slowly, for something out of window engages his eye), a white wine-glass, a green wine-glass, a blue finger-glass, a tumbler, and a powerful field battery of fourteen casters with nothing in them; or at all events—which is enough for your purpose—with nothing in them that will come out. All this time, the other waiter looks at you—with an air of mental comparison and curiosity, now, as if it had occurred to him that you are rather like his brother. Half your time gone, and nothing come but the jug of ale and the bread, you implore your waiter to "see after that cutlet, waiter; pray do!" He cannot go at once, for he is carrying in seventeen pounds of American cheese for you to finish with, and a small Landed Estate of celery and water-cresses. The other waiter changes his leg, and takes a new view of you, doubtfully, now, as if he had rejected the resemblance to his brother, and had begun to think you more like his aunt or his grandmother. Again you beseech your waiter with pathetic indignation, to "see after that cutlet!" He steps out to see after it, and by-and-by, when you are going away without it, comes back with it. Even then, he will not take the sham silver cover off, without a pause for a flourish, and a look at the musty cutlet as if he were surprised to see it—which cannot possibly be the case, he must have seen it so often before. A sort of fur has been produced upon its surface by the cook's art, and in a sham silver vessel staggering on two feet instead of three, is a cutaneous kind of sauce, of brown pimples and pickled cucumber. You order the bill, but your waiter cannot bring your bill yet, because he is bringing, instead, three flinty-hearted potatoes and two grim head of broccoli, like the occasional ornaments on area railings, badly boiled. You know that you will never come to this pass, any more than to the cheese and celery, and you imperatively demand your bill; but, it takes time to get, even when gone for, because your waiter has to communicate with a lady who lives behind a sash-window in a corner, and who appears to have to refer to several Ledgers before she can make it out—as if you had been staying there a year. You become distracted to get away, and the other waiter, once more changing his leg, still looks at you—but suspiciously, now, as if you had begun to remind him of the party who took the great-coats last winter. Your bill at last brought and paid, at the rate of sixpence a mouthful, your waiter reproachfully reminds you that "attendance is not charged for a single meal," and you have to search in all your pockets for sixpence more. He has a worse opinion of you than ever, when you have given it to him, and lets you out into the street with the air of one saying to himself, as you cannot doubt he is, "I hope we shall never see *you* here again!"

Or, take any other of the numerous travelling instances in which, with more time at your disposal, you are, have been, or may be, equally ill served. Take the old-established Bull's Head with its old-established knife-boxes on its old-established sideboards, its old-established flue under its old-established four-post bedsteads in its old-established airless rooms, its old-established frouziness up-stairs and down-stairs, its old-established cookery, and its old-established principles of plunder. Count up your injuries, in its side-dishes of ailing sweetbreads in white poultices, of apothecaries' powders in rice for curry, of pale stewed bits of calf ineffectually relying for an adventitious interest on forcemeat balls. You have had experience of the old-established Bull's Head stringy fowls, with lower extremities like wooden legs, sticking up out of the dish; of its cannibalic boiled mutton, gushing horribly among its capers, when carved; of its little dishes of pastry—roofs of spermaceti ointment, erected over half an apple or four gooseberries. Well for you if you have yet forgotten the old-established Bull's Head fruity port: whose reputation was gained solely by the old-established price the Bull's Head put upon it, and by the old-established air with which the Bull's Head set the glasses and D'Oyleys on, and held that Liquid Gout to the three-and-sixpenny wax-candle, as if its old-established colour hadn't come from the dyer's.

Or lastly, take to finish with, two cases that we all know, every day.

We all know the new hotel near the station, where it is always gusty, going up the lane which is always muddy, where we are sure to arrive at night, and where we make the gas start awfully when we open the front door. We all know the flooring of the passages and staircases that is too new, and the walls that are too new, and the house that is haunted by the ghost of mortar. We all know the doors that have cracked, and the cracked shutters through which we get a glimpse of the disconsolate moon. We all know the new people, who have come to keep the new hotel, and who wish they had never come, and who (inevitable result) wish *we* had never come. We all know how much too scant and smooth and bright the new furniture is, and how it has never settled down, and cannot fit itself into right places, and will get into wrong places. We all know how the gas, being lighted, shows maps of Damp upon the walls. We all know how the ghost of mortar passes into our sandwich, stirs our negus, goes up to bed with us, ascends the pale bedroom chimney, and prevents the smoke from following. We all know how a leg of our chair comes off at breakfast in the morning, and how the dejected waiter attributes the accident to a general greenness pervading the establishment, and informs us, in reply to a local inquiry, that he is thankful to say he is an entire stranger in that part of the country, and is going back to his own connexion on Saturday.

We all know, on the other hand, the great station hotel belonging to the company of proprietors, which has suddenly sprung up in the back outskirts of any place we like to name, and where we look out of our palatial windows at little back yards and gardens, old summer-houses, fowl-houses, pigeon-traps, and pigsties. We all know this hotel in which we can get anything we want, after its kind, for money; but where nobody is glad to see us, or sorry to see us, or minds (our bill paid) whether we come or go, or how, or when, or why, or cares about us. We all know this hotel, where we have no individuality, but put ourselves into the general post, as it were, and are sorted and disposed of according to our division. We all know that we can get on very well indeed at such a place, but still not perfectly well; and this may be, because the place is largely wholesale, and there is a lingering personal retail interest within us that asks to be satisfied.

To sum up. My uncommercial travelling has not yet brought me to the conclusion that we are close to perfection in these matters. And just as I do not believe that the end of the world will ever be near at hand, so long as any of the very tiresome and arrogant people who constantly predict that catastrophe are left in it, so, I shall have small faith in the Hotel Millennium, while any of the uncomfortable superstitions I have glanced at remain in existence.

VII

TRAVELLING ABROAD

I GOT into the travelling chariot—it was of German make, roomy, heavy, and unvarnished—I got into the travelling chariot, pulled up the steps after me, shut myself in with a smart bang of the door, and gave the word, "Go on!",

Immediately, all that W. and S.W. division of London began to slide away at a pace so lively, that I was over the river, and past the Old Kent Road, and out on Blackheath, and even ascending Shooter's Hill, before I had had time to look about me in the carriage, like a collected traveller.

I had two ample Imperials on the roof, other fitted storage for luggage in front, and other up behind; I had a net for books overhead, great pockets to all the windows, a leathern pouch or two hung up for odds and ends, and a reading lamp fixed in the back of the chariot, in case I should be benighted. I was amply provided in all respects, and had no idea where I was going (which was delightful), except that I was going abroad.

So smooth was the old high road, and so fresh were the horses, and so fast went I, that it was midway between Gravesend and Rochester, and the widening river was bearing the ships, white-sailed or black-smoked, out to sea, when I noticed by the wayside a very queer small boy.

"Holloa!" said I, to the very queer small boy, "where do you live?"

"At Chatham," says he.

"What do you do there?" says I.

"I go to school," says he.

I took him up in a moment, and we went on. Presently, the very queer small boy says, "This is Gads-hill we are coming to, where Falstaff went out to rob those travellers, and ran away."

"You know something about Falstaff, eh?" said I.

"All about him," said the very queer small boy. "I am old (I am nine), and I read all sorts of books. But *do* let us stop at the top of the hill, and look at the house there, if you please!"

"You admire that house?" said I.

"Bless you, sir," said the very queer small boy, "when I was not more than half as old as nine, it used to be a treat for me to be brought to look at it. And now, I am nine, I come by myself to look at it. And ever since I can recollect, my father, seeing me so fond of it, has often said to me, 'If you were to be very persevering and were to work hard, you might some day come to live in it.' Though that's impossible!" said the very queer small boy, drawing a low breath, and now staring at the house out of window with all his might.

I was rather amazed to be told this by the very queer small boy; for that house happens to be *my* house, and I have reason to believe that what he said was true.

Well! I made no halt there, and I soon dropped the very queer small boy and went on. Over the road where the old Romans used to march, over the road where the old Canterbury pilgrims used to go, over the road where the travelling trains of the old imperious priests and princes used to jingle on horseback between the continent and this Island through the mud and water, over the road where Shakespeare hummed to himself, "Blow, blow, thou winter wind," as he sat in the saddle at the gate of the inn yard noticing the carriers; all among the cherry orchards, apple orchards, corn-fields, and hop-gardens; so went I, by Canterbury to Dover. There, the sea was tumbling in, with deep sounds, after dark, and the revolving French light on Cape Grinez was seen regularly bursting out and becoming obscured, as if the head of a gigantic light-keeper in an anxious state of mind were interposed every half-minute, to look how it was burning.

Early in the morning I was on the deck of the steam-packet, and we were aiming at the bar in the usual intolerable manner, and the bar was aiming at us in the usual intolerable manner, and the bar got by far the best of it, and we got by far the worst—all in the usual intolerable manner.

But, when I was clear of the Custom House on the other side, and when I began to make the dust fly on the thirsty French roads, and when the twigsome trees by the wayside (which, I suppose, never will grow leafy, for they never did) guarded here and there a dusty soldier, or field labourer, baking on a heap of broken stones, sound asleep in a fiction of shade, I began to recover my travelling spirits. Coming upon the breaker of the broken stones, in a hard, hot, shining hat, on which the sun played at a distance as on a burning-glass, I felt that now, indeed, I was in the dear old France of my affections. I should have known it, without the well-remembered bottle of rough ordinary wine, the cold roast fowl, the loaf, and the pinch of salt, on which I lunched with unspeakable satisfaction, from one of the stuffed pockets of the chariot.

I must have fallen asleep after lunch, for when a bright face looked in at the window, I started, and said :

"Good God, Louis, I dreamed you were dead!"

My cheerful servant laughed, and answered:

" Me? Not at all, sir."

"How glad I am to wake! What are we doing, Louis?"

"We go to take relay of horses. Will you walk up the hill?"

"Certainly."

Welcome the old French hill, with the old French lunatic (not in the most distant degree related to Sterne's Maria) living in a thatched dog-kennel half-way up, and flying out with his crutch and his big head and extended nightcap, to be beforehand with the old men and women exhibiting crippled children, and with the children exhibiting old men and women, ugly and blind, who always seemed by resurrectionary process to be recalled out of the elements for the sudden peopling of the solitude!

"It is well," said I, scattering among them what small coin I had; "here comes Louis, and I am quite roused from my nap."

We journeyed on again, and I welcomed every new assurance that France stood where I had left it. There were the posting-houses, with their archways, dirty stable-yards, and clean postmasters' wives, bright women of business, looking on at the putting-to of the horses; there were the postilions counting what money they got, into their hats, and never making enough of it; there were the standard population of grey horses of Flanders descent, invariably biting one another when they got a chance; there were the fleecy sheepskins, looped on

over their uniforms by the postilions, like bibbed aprons when it
blew and rained; there were their jack-boots, and their cracking
whips; there were the cathedrals that I got out to see, as under some
cruel bondage, in no wise desiring to see them; there were the little
towns that appeared to have no reason for being towns, since most
of their houses were to let and nobody could be induced to look at
them, except the people who couldn't let them and had nothing else
to do but look at them all day. I lay a night upon the road and enjoyed delectable cookery of potatoes, and some other sensible things,
adoption of which at home would inevitably be shown to be fraught
with ruin, somehow or other, to that rickety national blessing, the
British farmer; and at last I was rattled, like a single pill in a box,
over leagues of stones, until—madly cracking, plunging, and flourishing two grey tails about—I made my triumphal entry into Paris.

At Paris, I took an upper apartment for a few days in one of
the hotels of the Rue de Rivoli; my front windows looking into
the garden of the Tuileries (where the principal difference between
the nursemaids and the flowers seemed to be that the former were
locomotive and the latter not): my back windows looking at all
the other back windows in the hotel, and deep down into a paved
yard, where my German chariot had retired under a tight-fitting
archway, to all appearance for life, and where bells rang all day without anybody's minding them but certain chamberlains with feather
brooms and green baize caps, who here and there leaned out of some
high window placidly looking down, and where neat waiters with
trays on their left shoulders passed and repassed from morning to
night.

Whenever I am at Paris, I am dragged by invisible force into the
Morgue. I never want to go there, but am always pulled there. One
Christmas Day, when I would rather have been anywhere else, I was
attracted in, to see an old grey man lying all alone on his cold bed,
with a tap of water turned on over his grey hair, and running, drip,
drip, drip, down his wretched face until it got to the corner of his
mouth, where it took a turn, and made him look sly. One New Year's
Morning (by the same token, the sun was shining outside, and there
was a mountebank balancing a feather on his nose, within a yard of
the gate), I was pulled in again to look at a flaxen-haired boy of
eighteen, with a heart hanging on his breast—"from his mother,"
was engraven on it—who had come into the net across the river, with
a bullet wound in his fair forehead and his hands cut with a knife, but
whence or how was a blank mystery. This time, I was forced into the
same dread place, to see a large dark man whose disfigurement by
water was in a frightful manner comic, and whose expression was that
of a prize-fighter who had closed his eyelids under a heavy blow, but
was going immediately to open them, shake his head, and "come up
smiling." Oh what this large dark man cost me in that bright city!

It was very hot weather, and he was none the better for that, and
I was much the worse. Indeed, a very neat and pleasant little woman
with the keys of her lodging on her forefinger, who had been showing

him to her little girl while she and the child ate sweetmeats, observed monsieur looking poorly as we came out together, and asked monsieur with her wondering little eyebrows prettily raised, if there were anything the matter? Faintly replying in the negative, monsieur crossed the road to a wine-shop, got some brandy, and resolved to freshen himself with a dip in the great floating bath on the river.

The bath was crowded in the usual airy manner, by a male population in striped drawers of various gay colours, who walked up and down arm in arm, drank coffee, smoked cigars, sat at little tables, conversed politely with the damsels who dispensed the towels, and every now and then pitched themselves into the river head foremost and came out again to repeat this social routine. I made haste to participate in the water part of the entertainments, and was in the full enjoyment of a delightful bath, when all in a moment I was seized with an unreasonable idea that the large dark body was floating straight at me.

I was out of the river, and dressing instantly. In the shock I had taken some water into my mouth, and it turned me sick, for I fancied that the contamination of the creature was in it. I had got back to my cool darkened room in the hotel, and was lying on a sofa there, before I began to reason with myself.

Of course, I knew perfectly well that the large dark creature was stone dead, and that I should no more come upon him out of the place where I had seen him dead, than I should come upon the cathedral of Notre-Dame in an entirely new situation. What troubled me was the picture of the creature; and that had so curiously and strongly painted itself upon my brain, that I could not get rid of it until it was worn out.

I noticed the peculiarities of this possession, while it was a real discomfort to me. That very day, at dinner, some morsel on my plate looked like a piece of him, and I was glad to get up and go out. Later in the evening, I was walking along the Rue St. Honoré, when I saw a bill at a public room there, announcing small-sword exercise, broadsword exercise, wrestling, and other such feats. I went in, and some of the sword-play being very skilful, remained. A specimen of our own national sport, The British Boaxe, was announced to be given at the close of the evening. In an evil hour, I determined to wait for this Boaxe, as became a Briton. It was a clumsy specimen (executed by two English grooms out of place), but one of the combatants, receiving a straight righthander with the glove between his eyes, did exactly what the large dark creature in the Morgue had seemed going to do—and finished me for that night.

There was rather a sickly smell (not at all an unusual fragrance in Paris) in the little ante-room of my apartment at the hotel. The large dark creature in the Morgue was by no direct experience associated with my sense of smell, because, when I came to the knowledge of him, he lay behind a wall of thick plate-glass as good as a wall of steel or marble for that matter. Yet the whiff of the room never failed to reproduce him. What was more curious, was the capriciousness with which his portrait seemed to light itself up in my mind, elsewhere. I might be walking in the Palais Royal, lazily enjoying the shop windows, and might be regaling myself with one of the ready-made clothes shops that are set out there. My eyes, wandering over impossible-waisted dressing-gowns and luminous waistcoats, would fall upon the master, or the shopman, or even the very dummy at the door, and would suggest to me, "Something like him!"—and instantly I was sickened again.

This would happen at the theatre, in the same manner. Often it would happen in the street, when I certainly was not looking for the likeness, and when probably there was no likeness there. It was not because the creature was dead that I was so haunted, because I know that I might have been (and I know it because I have been) equally attended by the image of a living aversion. This lasted about a week. The picture did not fade by degrees, in the sense that it became a whit less forcible and distinct, but in the sense that it obtruded itself less and less frequently. The experience may be worth considering by some who have the care of children. It would be difficult to overstate the intensity and accuracy of an intelligent child's observation. At that impressible time of life, it must sometimes produce a fixed impression. If the fixed impression be an object terrible to the child, it will be (for want of reasoning upon) inseparable from great fear. Force the child at such a time, be Spartan with it, send it into the dark against its will, leave it in a lonely bedroom against its will, and you had better murder it.

On a bright morning I rattled away from Paris, in the German chariot, and left the large dark creature behind me for good. I ought to confess, though, that I had been drawn back to the Morgue, after he was put underground, to look at his clothes, and that I found them frightfully like him—particularly his boots. However, I rattled away for Switzerland, looking forward and not backward, and so we parted company.

Welcome again, the long, long spell of France, with the queer country inns, full of vases of flowers and clocks, in the dull little town, and with the little population not at all dull on the little Boulevard in the evening, under the little trees! Welcome Monsieur the Curé, walking alone in the early morning a short way out of the town, reading that eternal Breviary of yours, which surely might be almost read, without the book, by this time! Welcome Monsieur the Curé, later in the day, jolting through the highway dust (as if you had already ascended to the cloudy region), in a very big-headed cabriolet, with the dried mud of a dozen winters on it. Welcome again Monsieur the Curé, as we exchange salutations; you, straightening your back to look at the German chariot, while picking in your little village garden a vegetable or two for the day's soup: I, looking out of the German chariot window in that delicious traveller's trance which knows no cares, no yesterdays, no to-morrows, nothing but the passing objects and the passing scents and sounds! And so I came, in due course of delight, to Strasbourg, where I passed a wet Sunday evening at a window, while an idle trifle of a vaudeville was played for me at the opposite house.

How such a large house came to have only three people living in it, was its own affair. There were at least a score of windows in its high roof alone; how many in its grotesque front, I soon gave up counting. The owner was a shopkeeper, by name Straudenheim; by trade—I couldn't make out what by trade, for he had forborne to write that up, and his shop was shut.

At first, as I looked at Straudenheim's, through the steadily falling rain, I set him up in business in the goose-liver line. But, inspection of Straudenheim, who became visible at a window on the second floor, convinced me that there was something more precious than liver in the case. He wore a black velvet skull-cap, and looked usurious and rich. A large-lipped, pear-nosed old man, with white hair, and keen eyes, though near-sighted. He was writing at a desk, was Straudenheim, and ever and again left off writing, put his pen in his mouth, and went through actions with his right hand, like a man steadying piles of cash. Five-franc pieces, Straudenheim, or golden Napoleons? A jeweller, Straudenheim, a dealer in money, a diamond merchant, or what?

Below Straudenheim, at a window on the first floor, sat his house-keeper—far from young, but of a comely presence, suggestive of a well-matured foot and ankle. She was cheerily dressed, had a fan in her hand, and wore large gold earrings and a large gold cross. She would have been out holiday-making (as I settled it) but for the pestilent rain. Strasbourg had given up holiday-making for that once, as a bad job, because the rain was jerking in gushes out of the old roof-spouts, and running in a brook down the middle of the street. The housekeeper, her arms folded on her bosom and her fan tapping her chin, was bright and smiling at her open window, but otherwise, Straudenheim's house front was very dreary. The housekeeper's was the only open window in it; Straudenheim kept himself close, though it was a sultry evening when air is pleasant, and though the rain had brought into the town that vague refreshing smell of grass which rain does bring in the summer time.

The dim appearance of a man at Straudenheim's shoulder, inspired me with a misgiving that somebody had come to murder that flourishing merchant for the wealth with which I had handsomely endowed him: the rather, as it was an excited man, lean and long of figure, and evidently stealthy of foot. But, he conferred with Straudenheim instead of doing him a mortal injury, and then they both softly opened the other window of that room—which was immediately over the housekeeper's—and tried to see her by looking down. And my opinion of Straudenheim was much lowered when I saw that eminent citizen spit out of window, clearly with the hope of spitting on the housekeeper.

The unconscious housekeeper fanned herself, tossed her head, and laughed. Though unconscious of Straudenheim, she was conscious of somebody else—of me?—there was nobody else.

After leaning so far out of the window, that I confidently expected to see their heels tilt up, Straudenheim and the lean man drew their heads in and shut the window. Presently, the house door secretly opened, and they slowly and spitefully crept forth into the pouring rain. They were coming over to me (I thought) to demand satisfaction for my looking at the housekeeper, when they plunged into a recess in the architecture under my window and dragged out the puniest of little soldiers, begirt with the most innocent of little swords. The tall glazed head-dress of this warrior, Straudenheim instantly knocked off, and out of it fell two sugar-sticks, and three or four large lumps of sugar.

The warrior made no effort to recover his property or to pick up his shako, but looked with an expression of attention at Straudenheim when he kicked him five times, and also at the lean man when *he* kicked him five times, and again at Straudenheim when he tore the breast of his (the warrior's) little coat open, and shook all his ten fingers in his face, as if they were ten thousand. When these outrages had been committed, Straudenheim and his man went into the house again and barred the door. A wonderful circumstance was, that the housekeeper who saw it all (and who could have taken six such warriors to her buxom bosom at once) only fanned herself and laughed, as she had laughed before, and seemed to have no opinion about it, one way or other.

But the chief effect of the drama was the remarkable vengeance taken by the little warrior. Left alone in the rain, he picked up his shako; put it on, all wet and dirty as it was; retired into a court, of which Straudenheim's house formed the corner; wheeled about, and bringing his two forefingers close to the top of his nose, rubbed them over one another, cross-wise, in derision, defiance and contempt of Straudenheim. Although Straudenheim could not possibly be supposed to be conscious of this strange proceeding, it so inflated and comforted the little warrior's soul, that twice he went away, and twice came back into the court to repeat it, as though it must goad his enemy to madness. Not only that, but he afterwards came back with two other small warriors, and they all three did it together. Not only that—as I live to tell the tale! but just as it was falling quite dark, the three came back, bringing with them a huge bearded Sapper, whom they moved, by recital of the original wrong, to go through the same performance, with the same complete absence of all possible knowledge of it on the part of Straudenheim. And then they all went away, arm in arm, singing.

I went away too, in the German chariot at sunrise, and rattled on, day after day, like one in a sweet dream; with so many clear little bells on the harness of the horses, that the nursery rhyme about Banbury Cross and the venerable lady who rode in state there, was always in my ears. And now I came to the land of wooden houses, innocent cakes, thin butter soup, and spotless little inn bedrooms with a family likeness to Dairies. And now the Swiss marksmen were for ever rifle-shooting at marks across gorges, so exceedingly near my ear, that I felt like a new Gesler in a Canton of Tells, and went in highly-deserved danger of my tyrannical life. The prizes at these shootings, were watches, smart handkerchiefs, hats, spoons, and (above all) tea-trays; and at these contests I came upon a more than usually accomplished and amiable countryman of my own, who had shot himself deaf in whole years of competition, and had won so many tea-trays that he went about the country with his carriage full of them, like a glorified Cheap-Jack.

In the mountain-country into which I had now travelled, a yoke of oxen were sometimes hooked on before the post-horses, and I went lumbering up, up, up, through mist and rain, with the roar of falling water for change of music. Of a sudden, mist and rain would clear away, and I would come down into picturesque little towns with gleaming spires and odd towers; and would stroll afoot into market-places in steep winding streets, where a hundred women in bodices, sold eggs and honey, butter and fruit, and suckled their children as they sat by their clean baskets, and had such enormous goîtres (or glandular swellings in the throat) that it became a science to know where the nurse ended and the child began. About this time, I deserted my German chariot for the back of a mule (in colour and consistency so very like a dusty old hair trunk I once had at school, that I half expected to see my initials in brass-headed nails on his backbone), and went up a thousand rugged ways, and looked down at a thousand woods of fir and pine, and would on the whole have preferred my mule's keeping a little nearer to the inside, and not usually travelling with a hoof or two over the precipice—though much consoled by explanation that this was to be attributed to his great sagacity, by reason of his carrying broad loads of wood at other times, and not being clear but that I myself belonged to that station of life, and required as much room as they. He brought me safely, in his own wise way, among the passes of the Alps, and here I enjoyed a dozen climates a day; being now (like Don Quixote on the back of the wooden horse) in the region of wind, now in the region of fire, now in the region of unmelting ice and snow. Here, I passed over trembling domes of ice, beneath which the cataract was roaring, and here was received under arches of icicles, of unspeakable beauty; and here the sweet air was so bracing and so light, that at halting-times I rolled in the snow when I saw my mule do it, thinking that he must know best. At this part of the journey we would come, at mid-day, into half an hour's thaw: when the rough mountain inn would be found on an island of deep mud in a sea of snow, while the baiting strings of mules, and the carts full of casks and bales, which had been in an Arctic condition a mile off, would steam again. By such ways and means, I would come to the cluster of châlets where I had to turn out of the track to see the waterfall; and then, uttering a howl like a young giant, on espying a traveller—in other words, something to eat—coming up the steep, the idiot lying on the wood-pile who sunned himself and nursed his goître, would rouse the woman-guide within the hut, who would stream out hastily, throwing her child over one of her

shoulders and her goître over the other, as she came along. I slept at
religious houses, and bleak refuges of many kinds, on this journey,
and by the stove at night heard stories of travellers who had perished
within call, in wreaths and drifts of snow. One night the stove within,
and the cold outside, awakened childish associations long forgotten,
and I dreamed I was in Russia—the identical serf out of a picture-
book I had, before I could read it for myself—and that I was going to
be knouted by a noble personage in a fur cap, boots, and earrings,
who, I think, must have come out of some melodrama.

Commend me to the beautiful waters among these mountains!
Though I was not of their mind: they, being inveterately bent on
getting down into the level country, and I ardently desiring to linger
where I was. What desperate leaps they took, what dark abysses they
plunged into, what rocks they wore away, what echoes they invoked!
In one part where I went, they were pressed into the service of carrying wood down, to be burnt next winter, as costly fuel, in Italy. But,
their fierce savage nature was not to be easily constrained, and they
fought with every limb of the wood; whirling it round and round,
stripping its bark away, dashing it against pointed corners, driving it
out of the course, and roaring and flying at the peasants who steered
it back again from the bank with long stout poles. Alas! concurrent
streams of time and water carried *me* down fast, and I came, on an
exquisitely clear day, to the Lausanne shore of the Lake of Geneva,
where I stood looking at the bright blue water, the flushed white
mountains opposite, and the boats at my feet with their furled
Mediterranean sails, showing like enormous magnifications of this
goose-quill pen that is now in my hand.

—The sky became overcast without any notice; a wind very like
the March east wind of England, blew across me; and a voice said,
"How do you like it? Will it do?"

I had merely shut myself, for half a minute, in a German travelling
chariot that stood for sale in the Carriage Department of the London
Pantechnicon. I had a commission to buy it, for a friend who was
going abroad; and the look and manner of the chariot, as I tried the
cushions and the springs, brought all these hints of travelling
remembrance before me.

"It will do very well," said I, rather sorrowfully, as I got out at the
other door, and shut the carriage up.

<h1 style="text-align:center">VIII</h1>

<h3 style="text-align:center">THE GREAT TASMANIA'S CARGO</h3>

I TRAVEL constantly, up and down a certain line of railway that has a
terminus in London. It is the railway for a large military depôt, and
for other large barracks. To the best of my serious belief, I have never
been on that railway by daylight, without seeing some handcuffed
deserters in the train.

It is in the nature of things that such an institution as our English army should have many bad and troublesome characters in it. But, this is a reason for, and not against, its being made as acceptable as possible to well-disposed men of decent behaviour. Such men are assuredly not tempted into the ranks, by the beastly inversion of natural laws, and the compulsion to live in worse than swinish foulness. Accordingly, when any such Circumlocutional embellishments of the soldier's condition have of late been brought to notice, we civilians, seated in outer darkness cheerfully meditating on an Income Tax, have considered the matter as being our business, and have shown a tendency to declare that we would rather not have it misregulated, if such declaration may, without violence to the Church Catechism, be hinted to those who are put in authority over us.

Any animated description of a modern battle, any private soldier's letter published in the newspapers, any page of the records of the Victoria Cross, will show that in the ranks of the army, there exists under all disadvantages as fine a sense of duty as is to be found in any station on earth. Who doubts that if we all did our duty as faithfully as the soldier does his, this world would be a better place? There may be greater difficulties in our way than in the soldier's. Not disputed. But, let us at least do our duty towards *him*.

I had got back again to that rich and beautiful port where I had looked after Mercantile Jack, and I was walking up a hill there, on a wild March morning. My conversation with my official friend Pangloss, by whom I was accidentally accompanied, took this direction as we took the up-hill direction, because the object of my uncommercial journey was to see some discharged soldiers who had recently come home from India. There were men of HAVELOCK'S among them; there were men who had been in many of the great battles of the great Indian campaign, among them; and I was curious to note what our discharged soldiers looked like, when they were done with.

I was not the less interested (as I mentioned to my official friend Pangloss) because these men had claimed to be discharged, when their right to be discharged was not admitted. They had behaved with unblemished fidelity and bravery; but, a change of circumstances had arisen, which, as they considered, put an end to their compact and entitled them to enter on a new one. Their demand had been blunderingly resisted by the authorities in India; but, it is to be presumed that the men were not far wrong, inasmuch as the bungle had ended in their being sent home discharged, in pursuance of orders from home. (There was an immense waste of money, of course.)

Under these circumstances—thought I, as I walked up the hill, on which I accidentally encountered my official friend—under these circumstances of the men having successfully opposed themselves to the Pagoda Department of that great Circumlocution Office on which the sun never sets and the light of reason never rises, the Pagoda Department will have been particularly careful of the national honour. It will have shown these men, in the scrupulous good faith, not to say the generosity, of its dealing with them, that great national authorities can have no small retaliations and revenges. It will have made every provision for their health on the passage home, and will have landed them, restored from their campaigning fatigues by a sea-voyage, pure air, sound food, and good medicines. And I pleased myself with dwelling beforehand, on the great accounts of their personal treatment which these men would carry into their various towns and villages, and on the increasing popularity of the service that would insensibly follow. I almost began to hope that the hitherto-never-failing deserters on my railroad would by-and-by become a phenomenon.

In this agreeable frame of mind I entered the workhouse of Liverpool.—For, the cultivation of laurels in a sandy soil, had brought the soldiers in question to *that* abode of Glory.

Before going into their wards to visit them, I inquired how they had made their triumphant entry there? They had been brought through the rain in carts, it seemed, from the landing-place to the gate, and had then been carried up-stairs on the backs of paupers. Their groans and pains during the performance of this glorious pageant, had been so distressing, as to bring tears into the eyes of spectators but too well accustomed to scenes of suffering. The men were so dreadfully cold, that those who could get near the fires were hard to be restrained from thrusting their feet in among the blazing coals. They were so horribly reduced, that they were awful to look upon. Racked with dysentery and blackened with scurvy, one hundred and forty wretched soldiers had been revived with brandy and laid in bed.

My official friend Pangloss is lineally descended from a learned doctor of that name, who was once tutor to Candide, an ingenious young gentleman of some celebrity. In his personal character, he is as humane and worthy a gentleman as any I know; in his official capacity, he unfortunately preaches the doctrines of his renowned ancestor, by demonstrating on all occasions that we live in the best of all possible official worlds.

"In the name of Hunanity," said I, "how did the men fall into this deplorable state? Was the ship well found in stores?"

"I am not here to asseverate that I know the fact, of my own knowledge," answered Pangloss, "but I have grounds for asserting that the stores were the best of all possible stores."

A medical officer laid before us, a handful of rotten biscuit, and a handful of split peas. The biscuit was a honeycombed heap of maggots, and the excrement of maggots. The peas were even harder than this filth. A similar handful had been experimentally boiled six hours, and had shown no signs of softening. These were the stores on which the soldiers had been fed.

"The beef——" I began, when Pangloss cut me short.

"Was the best of all possible beef," said he.

But, behold, there was laid before us certain evidence given at the Coroner's Inquest, holden on some of the men (who had obstinately died of their treatment), and from that evidence it appeared that the beef was the worst of possible beef!

"Then I lay my hand upon my heart, and take my stand," said Pangloss, "by the pork, which was the best of all possible pork."

"But look at this food before our eyes, if one may so misuse the word," said I. "Would any Inspector who did his duty, pass such abomination?"

"It ought not to have been passed," Pangloss admitted.

"Then the authorities out there——" I began, when Pangloss cut me short again.

"There would certainly seem to have been something wrong somewhere," said he; "but I am prepared to prove that the authorities out there, are the best of all possible authorities."

I never heard of any impeached public authority in my life, who was not the best public authority in existence.

"We are told of these unfortunate men being laid low by scurvy," said I. "Since lime-juice has been regularly stored and served out in our navy, surely that disease, which used to devastate it, has almost disappeared? Was there lime-juice aboard this transport?"

My official friend was beginning "the best of all possible——" when an inconvenient medical forefinger pointed out another passage in the evidence, from which it appeared that the lime-juice had been bad too. Not to mention that the vinegar had been bad too, the vegetables bad too, the cooking accommodation insufficient (if there had been anything worth mentioning to cook), the water supply exceedingly inadequate, and the beer sour.

"Then the men," said Pangloss, a little irritated, "were the worst of all possible men."

"In what respect?" I asked.

"Oh! Habitual drunkards," said Pangloss.

But, again the same incorrigible medical forefinger pointed out another passage in the evidence, showing that the dead men had been examined after death, and that they, at least, could not possibly have been habitual drunkards, because the organs within them which must have shown traces of that habit, were perfectly sound.

"And besides," said the three doctors present, one and all, "habitual drunkards brought as low as these men have been, could not recover under care and food, as the great majority of these men are recovering. They would not have strength of constitution to do it."

"Reckless and improvident dogs, then," said Pangloss. "Always are—nine times out of ten."

I turned to the master of the workhouse, and asked him whether the men had any money?

"Money?" said he. "I have in my iron safe, nearly four hundred pounds of theirs; the agents have nearly a hundred pounds more; and many of them have left money in Indian banks besides."

"Hah!" said I to myself, as we went up-stairs, "this is not the best of all possible stories, I doubt!"

We went into a large ward, containing some twenty or five-and-twenty beds. We went into several such wards, one after another. I find it very difficult to indicate what a shocking sight I saw in them, without frightening the reader from the perusal of these lines, and defeating my object of making it known.

O the sunken eyes that turned to me as I walked between the rows of beds, or—worse still—that glazedly looked at the white ceiling, and saw nothing and cared for nothing! Here, lay the skeleton of a man, so lightly covered with a thin unwholesome skin, that not a bone in the anatomy was clothed, and I could clasp the arm above the elbow, in my finger and thumb. Here, lay a man with the black scurvy eating his legs away, his gums gone, and his teeth all gaunt and bare. This bed was empty, because gangrene had set in, and the patient had died but yesterday. That bed was a hopeless one, because its occupant was sinking fast, and could only be roused to turn the poor pinched mask of face upon the pillow, with a feeble moan. The awful thinness of the fallen cheeks, the awful brightness of the deep set eyes, the lips of lead, the hands of ivory, the recumbent human images lying in the shadow of death with a kind of solemn twilight on them, like the sixty who had died aboard the ship and were lying at the bottom of the sea, O Pangloss, GOD forgive you!

In one bed, lay a man whose life had been saved (as it was hoped) by deep incisions in the feet and legs. While I was speaking to him, a nurse came up to change the poultices which this operation had rendered necessary, and I had an instinctive feeling that it was not well to turn away, merely to spare myself. He was sorely wasted and keenly susceptible, but the efforts he made to subdue any expression of impatience or suffering, were quite heroic. It was easy to see, in the shrinking of the figure, and the drawing of the bed-clothes over the head, how acute the endurance was, and it made me shrink too, as if *I* were in pain; but, when the new bandages were on, and the poor feet were composed again he made an apology for himself (though he had not uttered a word), and said plaintively, "I am so tender and weak, you see, sir!" Neither from him nor from any one sufferer of the whole ghastly number, did I hear a complaint. Of thankfulness for present solicitude and care, I heard much; of complaint, not a word.

I think I could have recognised in the dismalest skeleton there, the ghost of a soldier. Something of the old air was still latent in the palest shadow of life I talked to. One emaciated creature, in the strictest literality worn to the bone, lay stretched on his back, looking so like death that I asked one of the doctors if he were not dying, or dead? A few kind words from the doctor, in his ear, and he opened his eyes, and smiled—looked, in a moment, as if he would have made a salute, if he could. "We shall pull him through, please God," said the Doctor. "Plase God, surr, and thankye," said the patient. "You are much better to-day; are you not?" said the Doctor. "Plase God, surr; 'tis the slape I want, surr; 'tis my breathin' makes the nights so long." "He is a careful fellow this, you must know," said the Doctor, cheerfully; "it was raining hard when they put him in the open cart to bring him here, and he had the presence of mind to ask to have a sovereign taken out of his pocket that he had there, and a cab engaged. Probably it saved his life." The patient rattled out the skeleton of a laugh, and said, proud of the story, "'Deed, surr, an open cairt was a comical means o' bringin' a dyin' man here, and a clever way to kill him." You might have sworn to him for a soldier when he said it.

One thing had perplexed me very much in going from bed to bed. A very significant and cruel thing. I could find no young man but one. He had attracted my notice, by having got up and dressed himself in his soldier's jacket and trousers, with the intention of sitting by the fire; but he had found himself too weak, and had crept back to his bed and laid himself down on the outside of it. I could have pronounced him, alone, to be a young man aged by famine and sickness. As we were standing by the Irish soldier's bed, I mentioned my perplexity to the Doctor. He took a board with an inscription on it from the head of the Irishman's bed, and asked me what age I supposed that man to be? I had observed him with attention while talking to him, and answered, confidently, "Fifty." The Doctor, with a pitying glance at the patient, who had dropped into a stupor again, put the board back, and said, "Twenty-four."

All the arrangements of the wards were excellent. They could not have been more humane, sympathising, gentle, attentive, or wholesome. The owners of the ship, too, had done all they could, liberally. There were bright fires in every room, and the convalescent men were sitting round them, reading various papers and periodicals. I took the liberty of inviting my official friend Pangloss to look at those convalescent men, and to tell me whether their faces and bearing were or were not, generally, the faces and bearing of steady respectable soldiers? The master of the workhouse, overhearing me, said he had had a pretty large experience of troops, and that better conducted men than these, he had never had to do with. They were always (he added) as we saw them. And of us visitors (I add) they knew nothing whatever, except that we were there.

It was audacious in me, but I took another liberty with Pangloss. Prefacing it with the observation that, of course, I knew beforehand that there was not the faintest desire, anywhere, to hush up any part of this dreadful business, and that the Inquest was the fairest of all possible Inquests, I besought four things of Pangloss. Firstly, to observe that the Inquest *was not held in that place*, but at some distance off. Secondly, to look round upon those helpless spectres in their beds. Thirdly, to remember that the witnesses produced from among them before that Inquest, could not have been selected because they were the men who had the most to tell it, but because they happened to be in a state admitting of their safe removal. Fourthly, to say whether the coroner and Jury could have come there, to those pillows, and taken a little evidence? My official friend declined to commit himself to a reply.

There was a sergeant, reading, in one of the fireside groups. As he was a man of very intelligent countenance, and as I have a great respect for non-commissioned officers as a class, I sat down on the nearest bed, to have some talk with him. (It was the bed of one of the grisliest of the poor skeletons, and he died soon afterwards.)

"I was glad to see, in the evidence of an officer at the Inquest, sergeant, that he never saw men behave better on board ship than these men."

"They did behave very well, sir."

"I was glad to see, too, that every man had a hammock."

The sergeant gravely shook his head. "There must be some mistake, sir. The men of my own mess had no hammocks. There were not hammocks enough on board, and the men of the two next messes laid hold of hammocks for themselves as soon as they got on board, and squeezed my men out, as I may say."

"Had the squeezed-out men none then?"

"None, sir. As men died, their hammocks were used by other men, who wanted hammocks; but many men had none at all."

"Then you don't agree with the evidence on that point?"

"Certainly not, sir. A man can't, when he knows to the contrary."

"Did any of the men sell their bedding for drink?"

"There is some mistake on that point too, sir. Men were under the impression—I knew it for a fact at the time—that it was not allowed to take blankets or bedding on board, and so men who had things of that sort came to sell them purposely."

"Did any of the men sell their clothes for drink?"

"They did, sir." (I believe there never was a more truthful witness than the sergeant. He had no inclination to make out a case.)

"Many?"

"Some sir," (considering the question). "Soldier-like. They had been long marching in the rainy season, by bad roads—no roads at all, in short—and when they got to Calcutta, men turned to and drank, before taking a last look at it. Soldier-like."

"Do you see any men in this ward, for example, who sold clothes for drink at that time?"

The sergeant's wan eye, happily just beginning to rekindle with health, travelled round the place and came back to me. "Certainly, sir."

"The marching to Calcutta in the rainy season must have been severe?"

"It was very severe, sir."

"Yet what with the rest and the sea air, I should have thought that the men (even the men who got drunk) would have soon begun to recover on board ship?"

"So they might; but the bad food told upon them, and when we got into a cold latitude, it began to tell more, and the men dropped."

"The sick had a general disinclination for food, I am told, sergeant?"

"Have you seen the food, sir?"

"Some of it."

"Have you seen the state of their mouths, sir?"

If the sergeant, who was a man of a few orderly words, had spoken the amount of this volume, he could not have settled that question better. I believe the sick could as soon have eaten the ship, as the ship's provisions.

I took the additional liberty with my friend Pangloss, when I had left the sergeant with good wishes, of asking Pangloss whether he had ever heard of biscuit getting drunk and bartering its nutritious qualities for putrefaction and vermin; of peas becoming hardened in liquor; of hammocks drinking themselves off the face of the earth; of lime-juice, vegetables, vinegar, cooking accommodation, water supply, and beer, all taking to drinking together and going to ruin? "If not (I asked him), what did he say in defence of the officers condemned by the Coroner's Jury, who, by signing the General Inspection report relative to the ship Great Tasmania, chartered for these troops, had deliberately asserted all that bad and poisonous dunghill refuse, to be good and wholesome food?" My official friend replied that it was a remarkable fact, that whereas some officers were only positively good, and other officers only comparatively better, those particular officers were superlatively the very best of all possible officers.

My hand and my heart fail me, in writing my record of this journey. The spectacle of the soldiers in the hospital-beds of that Liverpool workhouse (a very good workhouse, indeed, be it understood), was so shocking and so shameful, that as an Englishman I blush to remember it. It would have been simply unbearable at the time, but for the consideration and pity with which they were soothed in their sufferings.

No punishment that our inefficient laws provide, is worthy of the name when set against the guilt of this transaction. But, if the memory of it die out unavenged, and if it do not result in the inexorable dismissal and disgrace of those who are responsible for it, their escape will be infamous to the Government (no matter of what party) that so neglects its duty, and infamous to the nation that tamely suffers such intolerable wrong to be done in its name.

IX

CITY OF LONDON CHURCHES

IF the confession that I have often travelled from this Covent Garden lodging of mine on Sundays, should give offence to those who never travel on Sundays, they will be satisfied (I hope) by my adding that the journeys in question were made to churches.

Not that I have any curiosity to hear powerful preachers. Time was, when I was dragged by the hair of my head, as one may say, to hear too many. On summer evenings, when every flower, and tree, and bird, might have better addressed my soft young heart, I have in my day been caught in the palm of a female hand by the crown, have been violently scrubbed from the neck to the roots of the hair as a purification for the Temple, and have then been carried off highly charged with saponaceous electricity, to be steamed like a potato in the unventilated breath of the powerful Boanerges Boiler and his congregation, until what small mind I had, was quite steamed out of me. In which pitiable plight I have been haled out of the place of meeting, at the conclusion of the exercises, and catechised respecting Boanerges Boiler, his fifthly, his sixthly, and his seventhly, until I have regarded that reverend person in the light of a most dismal and oppressive Charade. Time was, when I was carried off to platform assemblages at which no human child, whether of wrath or grace, could possibly keep its eyes open, and when I felt the fatal sleep stealing, stealing over me, and when I gradually heard the orator in possession, spinning and humming like a great top, until he rolled, collapsed, and tumbled over, and I discovered to my burning shame and fear, that as to that last stage it was not he, but I. I have sat under Boanerges when he has specifically addressed himself to us— us, the infants—and at this present writing I hear his lumbering jocularity (which never amused us, though we basely pretended that it did), and I behold his big round face, and I look up the inside of his outstretched coat-sleeve as if it were a telescope with the stopper on, and I hate him with an unwholesome hatred for two hours. Through such means did it come to pass that I knew the powerful preacher from beginning to end, all over and all through, while I was very young, and that I left him behind at an early period of life. Peace be with him! More peace than he brought to me!

Now, I have heard many preachers since that time—not powerful; merely christian, unaffected, and reverential—and I have had many such preachers on my roll of friends. But, it was not to hear these, any more than the powerful class, that I made my Sunday journeys. They were journeys of curiosity to the numerous churches in the City of London. It came into my head one day, here had I been cultivating a familiarity with all the churches of Rome, and I knew nothing of the insides of the old churches of London! This befell on a Sunday morning. I began my expeditions that very same day, and they lasted me a year.

I never wanted to know the names of the churches to which I went, and to this hour I am profoundly ignorant in that particular of at least nine-tenths of them. Indeed, saving that I know the church of old GOWER's tomb (he lies in effigy with his head upon his books) to be the church of Saint Saviour's, Southwark; and the church of MILTON's tomb to be the church of Cripplegate; and the church on Cornhill with the great golden keys to be the church of Saint Peter; I doubt if I could pass a competitive examination in any of the names. No question did I ever ask of living creature concerning these churches, and no answer to any antiquarian question on the subject that I ever put to books, shall harass the reader's soul. A full half of my pleasure in them arose out of their mystery; mysterious I found them; mysterious they shall remain for me.

Where shall I begin my round of hidden and forgotten old churches in the City of London?

It is twenty minutes short of eleven on a Sunday morning, when I stroll down one of the many narrow hilly streets in the City that tend

due south to the Thames. It is my first experiment, and I have come
to the region of Whittington in an omnibus, and we have put down a
fierce-eyed, spare old woman, whose slate-coloured gown smells of
herbs, and who walked up Aldersgate-street to some chapel where
she comforts herself with brimstone doctrine, I warrant. We have
also put down a stouter and sweeter old lady, with a pretty large
prayer-book in an unfolded pocket-handkerchief, who got out at a
corner of a court near Stationers' Hall, and who I think must go to
church there, because she is the widow of some deceased old Company's Beadle. The rest of our freight were mere chance pleasure-
seekers and rural walkers, and went on to the Blackwall railway. So
many bells are ringing, when I stand undecided at a street corner,
that every sheep in the ecclesiastical fold might be a bell-wether. The
discordance is fearful. My state of indecision is referable to, and
about equally divisible among, four great churches, which are all
within sight and sound, all within the space of a few square yards.

As I stand at the street corner, I don't see as many as four people
at once going to church, though I see as many as four churches with
their steeples clamouring for people. I choose my church, and go up
the flight of steps to the great entrance in the tower. A mouldy
tower within, and like a neglected washhouse. A rope comes through
the beamed roof, and a man in the corner pulls it and clashes the
bell—a whity-brown man, whose clothes were once black—a man
with flue on him, and cobweb. He stares at me, wondering how I
come there, and I stare at him, wondering how he comes there.
Through a screen of wood and glass, I peep into the dim church.
About twenty people are discernible, waiting to begin. Christening
would seem to have faded out of this church long ago, for the font
has the dust of desuetude thick upon it, and its wooden cover
(shaped like an old-fashioned tureen-cover) looks as if it wouldn't
come off, upon requirement. I perceive the altar to be rickety and the
Commandments damp. Entering after this survey, I jostle the clergyman in his canonicals, who is entering too from a dark lane behind a
pew of state with curtains, where nobody sits. The pew is ornamented
with four blue wands, once carried by four somebodys, I suppose,
before somebody else, but which there is nobody now to hold or
receive honour from. I open the door of a family pew, and shut
myself in; if I could occupy twenty family pews at once I might have
them. The clerk, a brisk young man (how does *he* come here?),
glances at me knowingly, as who should say, "You have done it now;
you must stop." Organ plays. Organ-loft is in a small gallery across
the church; gallery congregation, two girls. I wonder within myself
what will happen when we are required to sing.

There is a pale heap of books in the corner of my pew, and while
the organ, which is hoarse and sleepy, plays in such fashion that I
can hear more of the rusty working of the stops than of any music, I
look at the books, which are mostly bound in faded baize and stuff.
They belonged in 1754, to the Dowgate family; and who were they?
Jane Comport must have married Young Dowgate, and come into

the family that way; Young Dowgate was courting Jane Comport when he gave her her prayer-book, and recorded the presentation in the fly-leaf; if Jane were fond of Young Dowgate, why did she die and leave the book here? Perhaps at the rickety altar, and before the damp Commandments, she, Comport, had taken him, Dowgate, in a flush of youthful hope and joy, and perhaps it had not turned out in the long run as great a success as was expected?

The opening of the service recalls my wandering thoughts. I then find, to my astonishment, that I have been, and still am, taking a strong kind of invisible snuff, up my nose, into my eyes, and down my throat. I wink, sneeze, and cough. The clerk sneezes; the clergyman winks; the unseen organist sneezes and coughs (and probably winks); all our little party wink, sneeze, and cough. The snuff seems to be made of the decay of matting, wood, cloth, stone, iron, earth, and something else. Is the something else, the decay of dead citizens in the vaults below? As sure as Death it is! Not only in the cold damp, February day, do we cough and sneeze dead citizens, all through the service, but dead citizens have got into the very bellows of the organ, and half choked the same. We stamp our feet to warm them, and dead citizens arise in heavy clouds. Dead citizens stick upon the walls, and lie pulverised on the sounding-board over the clergyman's head, and, when a gust of air comes, tumble down upon him.

In this first experience I was so nauseated by too much snuff, made of the Dowgate family, the Comport branch, and other families and branches, that I gave but little heed to our dull manner of ambling through the service; to the brisk clerk's manner of encouraging us to try a note or two at psalm time; to the gallery-congregation's manner of enjoying a shrill duet, without a notion of time or tune; to the whity-brown man's manner of shutting the minister into the pulpit, and being very particular with the lock of the door, as if he were a dangerous animal. But, I tried again next Sunday, and soon accustomed myself to the dead citizens when I found that I could not possibly get on without them among the City churches.

Another Sunday.

After being again rung for by conflicting bells, like a leg of mutton or a laced hat a hundred years ago, I make selection of a church oddly put away in a corner among a number of lanes—a smaller church than the last, and an ugly: of about the date of Queen Anne. As a congregation, we are fourteen strong: not counting an exhausted charity school in a gallery, which has dwindled away to four boys, and two girls. In the porch, is a benefaction of loaves of bread, which there would seem to be nobody left in the exhausted congregation to claim, and which I saw an exhausted beadle, long faded out of uniform, eating with his eyes for self and family when I passed in. There is also an exhausted clerk in a brown wig, and two or three exhausted doors and windows have been bricked up, and the service books are musty, and the pulpit cushions are threadbare, and the whole of the church furniture is in a very advanced stage of exhaustion. We are three old women (habitual), two young lovers (accidental), two tradesmen, one with a wife and one alone, an aunt and nephew, again two girls (these two girls dressed out for church with everything about them limp that should be stiff, and *vice versa*, are an invariable experience), and three sniggering boys. The clergyman is, perhaps, the chaplain of a civic company; he has the moist and vinous look, and eke the bulbous boots, of one acquainted with 'Twenty port, and comet vintages.

We are so quiet in our dulness that the three sniggering boys, who have got away into a corner by the altar-railing, give us a start, like crackers, whenever they laugh. And this reminds me of my own village church where, during sermon-time on bright Sundays when the birds are very musical indeed, farmers' boys patter out over the stone pavement, and the clerk steps out from his desk after them, and is distinctly heard in the summer repose to pursue and punch them in the churchyard, and is seen to return with a meditative countenance, making believe that nothing of the sort has happened. The aunt and nephew in this City church are much disturbed by the sniggering boys. The nephew is himself a boy, and the sniggerers tempt him to secular thoughts of marbles and string, by secretly offering such commodities to his distant contemplation. This young Saint Anthony for a while resists, but presently becomes a backslider, and in dumb show defies the sniggerers to "heave" a marble or two in his direction. Herein he is detected by the aunt (a rigorous reduced gentlewoman who has the charge of offices), and I perceive that worthy relative to poke him in the side, with the corrugated hooked handle of an ancient umbrella. The nephew revenges himself for this, by holding his breath and terrifying his kinswoman with the dread belief that he has made up his mind to burst. Regardless of whispers and shakes, he swells and becomes discoloured, and yet again swells and becomes discoloured, until the aunt can bear it no longer, but leads him out, with no visible neck, and with his eyes going before him like a prawn's. This causes the sniggerers to regard flight as an eligible move, and I know which of them will go out first, because of the over-devout attention that he suddenly concentrates on the clergyman. In a little while, this hypocrite, with an elaborate demonstration of hushing his footsteps, and with a face generally expressive of having until now forgotten a religious appointment elsewhere, is gone. Number two gets out in the same way, but rather quicker. Number three getting safely to the door, there turns reckless, and banging it open, flies forth with a Whoop! that vibrates to the top of the tower above us.

The clergyman, who is of a prandial presence and a muffled voice, may be scant of hearing as well as of breath, but he only glances up, as having an idea that somebody has said Amen in a wrong place, and continues his steady jog-trot, like a farmer's wife going to market. He does all he has to do, in the same easy way, and gives us a concise sermon, still like the jog-trot of the farmer's wife on a level road. Its drowsy cadence soon lulls the three old women asleep, and the unmarried tradesman sits looking out at window, and the married tradesman sits looking at his wife's bonnet, and the lovers sit looking at one another, so superlatively happy, that I mind when I, turned of eighteen, went with my Angelica to a City church on account of a shower (by this special coincidence that it was in Huggin-lane), and when I said to my Angelica, "Let the blessed event, Angelica, occur at no altar but this!" and when my Angelica consented that it should occur at no other—which it certainly never did, for it never occurred anywhere. And O, Angelica, what has become of you, this present Sunday morning when I can't attend to the sermon; and, more difficult question than that, what has become of Me as I was when I sat by your side!

But, we receive the signal to make that unanimous dive which surely is a little conventional—like the strange rustlings and settlings and clearings of throats and noses, which are never dispensed with, at certain points of the Church service, and are never held to be necessary under any other circumstances. In a minute more it is all over, and the organ expresses itself to be as glad of it as it can be of anything in its rheumatic state, and in another minute we are all of us out of the church, and Whity-brown has locked it up. Another minute or little more, and, in the neighbouring churchyard—not the yard of that church, but of another—a churchyard like a great shabby old mignonette box, with two trees in it and one tomb—I meet Whity-brown, in his private capacity, fetching a pint of beer for his dinner from the public-house in the corner, where the keys of the rotting fire-ladders are kept and were never asked for, and where there is a ragged, white-seamed, out-at-elbowed bagatelle board on the first floor.

In one of these City churches, and only in one, I found an individual who might have been claimed as expressly a City personage. I remember the church, by the feature that the clergyman couldn't get to his own desk without going through the clerk's, or couldn't get to the pulpit without going through the reading-desk—I forget which, and it is no matter—and by the presence of this personage among the exceedingly sparse congregation. I doubt if we were a dozen, and we had no exhausted charity school to help us out. The personage was dressed in black of square cut, and was stricken in years, and wore a black velvet cap, and cloth shoes. He was of a staid, wealthy, and dissatisfied aspect. In his hand, he conducted to church a mysterious child: a child of the feminine gender. The child had a beaver hat, with a stiff drab plume that surely never belonged to any bird of the air. The child was further attired in a nankeen frock and spencer, brown boxing-gloves, and a veil. It had a blemish, in the nature of currant jelly, on its chin; and was a thirsty child. Insomuch that the personage carried in his pocket a green bottle, from which, when the first psalm was given out, the child was openly refreshed. At all other times throughout the service it was motionless, and stood on the seat of the large pew, closely fitted into the corner, like a rain-water pipe.

The personage never opened his book, and never looked at the clergyman. *He* never sat down either, but stood with his arms leaning on the top of the pew, and his forehead sometimes shaded with his right hand, always looking at the church door. It was a long church for a church of its size, and he was at the upper end, but he always looked at the door. That he was an old bookkeeper, or an old trader who had kept his own books, and that he might be seen at the Bank of England about Dividend times, no doubt. That he had lived in the City all his life and was disdainful of other localities, no doubt. Why he looked at the door, I never absolutely proved, but it is my belief that he lived in expectation of the time when the citizens would come back to live in the City, and its ancient glories would be renewed. He appeared to expect that this would occur on a Sunday, and that the wanderers would first appear, in the deserted churches, penitent and humbled. Hence, he looked at the door which they never darkened. Whose child the child was, whether the child of a disinherited daughter or some parish orphan whom the personage had adopted, there was nothing to lead up to. It never played, or skipped, or smiled. Once the idea occurred to me that it was an automaton, and that the personage had made it; but following the strange couple out one Sunday, I heard the personage say to it, "Thirteen thousand pounds;" to which it added in a weak human voice, "Seventeen and fourpence." Four Sundays I followed them out, and this is all I ever heard or saw them say. One Sunday, I followed them home. They lived behind a pump, and the personage opened their abode with an exceeding large key. The one solitary inscription on their house related to a fire-plug. The house was partly undermined by a deserted and closed gateway; its windows were blind with dirt; and it stood with its face disconsolately turned to a wall. Five great churches and two small ones rang their Sunday bells between this house and the church the couple frequented, so they must have had some special reason for going a quarter of a mile to it. The last time I saw them, was on this wise. I had been to explore another church at a distance, and happened to pass the church they frequented, at about two of the afternoon when that edifice was closed. But, a little side-door, which I had never observed before, stood open, and disclosed certain cellarous steps. Methought "They are airing the vaults to-day," when the personage and the child silently arrived at the steps and silently descended. Of course, I came to the conclusion that the personage had at last despaired of the looked-for return of the penitent citizens, and that he and the child went down to get themselves buried.

In the course of my pilgrimages I came upon one obscure church which had broken out in the melodramatic style, and was got up with various tawdry decorations, much after the manner of the extinct London may-poles. These attractions had induced several young priests or deacons in black bibs for waistcoats, and several young ladies interested in that holy order (the proportion being, as I estimated, seventeen young ladies to a deacon), to come into the City as a new and odd excitement. It was wonderful to see how these young people played out their little play in the heart of the City, all among them-

selves, without the deserted City's knowing anything about it. It
was as if you should take an empty counting-house on a Sunday, and
act one of the old Mysteries there. They had impressed a small school
(from what neighbourhood I don't know) to assist in the performances,
and it was pleasant to notice frantic garlands of inscription on the
walls, especially addressing those poor innocents in characters impossible for them to decipher. There was a remarkably agreeable smell
of pomatum in this congregation.

But, in other cases, rot and mildew and dead citizens formed the
uppermost scent, while, infused into it in a dreamy way not at all
displeasing, was the staple character of the neighbourhood. In the
churches about Mark-lane, for example, there was a dry whiff of
wheat; and I accidentally struck an airy sample of barley out of an
aged hassock in one of them. From Rood-lane to Tower-street, and
thereabouts, there was often a subtle flavour of wine: sometimes, of
tea. One church near Mincing-lane smelt like a druggist's drawer.
Behind the Monument the service had a flavour of damaged oranges,
which, a little further down towards the river, tempered into herrings,
and gradually toned into a cosmopolitan blast of fish. In one church,
the exact counterpart of the church in the Rake's Progress where the
hero is being married to the horrible old lady, there was no speciality
of atmosphere, until the organ shook a perfume of hides all over us
from some adjacent warehouse.

Be the scent what it would, however, there was no speciality in the
people. There were never enough of them to represent any calling or
neighbourhood. They had all gone elsewhere over-night, and the few
stragglers in the many churches languished there inexpressively.

Among the Uncommercial travels in which I have engaged, this
year of Sunday travel occupies its own place, apart from all the rest.
Whether I think of the church where the sails of the oyster-boats in
the river almost flapped against the windows, or of the church where
the railroad made the bells hum as the train rushed by above the
roof, I recall a curious experience. On summer Sundays, in the gentle
rain or the bright sunshine—either, deepening the idleness of the idle
City—I have sat, in that singular silence which belongs to resting-
places usually astir, in scores of buildings at the heart of the world's
metropolis, unknown to far greater numbers of people speaking the
English tongue, than the ancient edifices of the Eternal City, or the
Pyramids of Egypt. The dark vestries and registries into which I have
peeped, and the little hemmed-in churchyards that have echoed to my
feet have left impressions on my memory as distinct and quaint as
any it has in that way received. In all those dusty registers that the
worms are eating, there is not a line but made some hearts leap, or
some tears flow, in their day. Still and dry now, still and dry! and the
old tree at the window with no room for its branches, has seen them all
out. So with the tomb of the old Master of the old Company, on which
it drips. His son restored it and died, his daughter restored it and
died, and then he had been remembered long enough, and the tree
took possession of him, and his name cracked out.

There are few more striking indications of the changes of manners and customs that two or three hundred years have brought about, than these deserted churches. Many of them are handsome and costly structures, several of them were designed by WREN, many of them arose from the ashes of the great fire, others of them outlived the plague and the fire too, to die a slow death in these later days. No one can be sure of the coming time; but it is not too much to say of it that it has no sign in its outsetting tides, of the reflux to these churches of their congregations and uses. They remain like the tombs of the old citizens who lie beneath them and around them, Monuments of another age. They are worth a Sunday-exploration, now and then, for they yet echo, not unharmoniously, to the time when the City of London really was London; when the 'Prentices and Trained Bands were of mark in the state; when even the Lord Mayor himself was a Reality—not a Fiction conventionally be-puffed on one day in the year by illustrious friends, who no less conventionally laugh at him on the remaining three hundred and sixty-four days.

X

SHY NEIGHBOURHOODS

So much of my travelling is done on foot, that if I cherished betting propensities, I should probably be found registered in sporting newspapers under some such title as the Elastic Novice, challenging all eleven stone mankind to competition in walking. My last special feat was turning out of bed at two, after a hard day, pedestrian and otherwise, and walking thirty miles into the country to breakfast. The road was so lonely in the night, that I fell asleep to the monotonous sound of my own feet, doing their regular four miles an hour. Mile after mile I walked, without the slightest sense of exertion, dozing heavily and dreaming constantly. It was only when I made a stumble like a drunken man, or struck out into the road to avoid a horseman close upon me on the path—who had no existence—that I came to myself and looked about. The day broke mistily (it was autumn time), and I could not disembarrass myself of the idea that I had to climb those heights and banks of cloud, and that there was an Alpine Convent somewhere behind the sun, where I was going to breakfast. This sleepy notion was so much stronger than such substantial objects as villages and haystacks, that, after the sun was up and bright, and when I was sufficiently awake to have a sense of pleasure in the prospect, I still occasionally caught myself looking about for wooden arms to point the right track up the mountain, and wondering there was no snow yet. It is a curiosity of broken sleep that I made immense quantities of verses on that pedestrian occasion (of course I never make any when I am in my right senses), and that I spoke a certain language once pretty familiar to me, but which I have nearly forgotten from disuse, with fluency. Of both these phenomena I have such frequent experience in the state between sleeping and waking, that I sometimes argue with myself that I know I cannot be awake, for, if I were, I should not be half so ready. The readiness is not imaginary, because I often recall long strings of the verses, and many turns of the fluent speech, after I am broad awake.

My walking is of two kinds: one, straight on end to a definite goal at a round pace; one, objectless, loitering, and purely vagabond. In the latter state, no gypsy on earth is a greater vagabond than myself; it is so natural to me, and strong with me, that I think I must be the descendant, at no great distance, of some irreclaimable tramp.

One of the pleasantest things I have lately met with, in a vagabond course of shy metropolitan neighbourhoods and small shops, is the fancy of a humble artist, as exemplified in two portraits representing Mr. Thomas Sayers, of Great Britain, and Mr. John Heenan, of the United States of America. These illustrious men are highly coloured in fighting trim, and fighting attitude. To suggest the pastoral and meditative nature of their peaceful calling, Mr. Heenan is represented on emerald sward, with primroses and other modest flowers springing up under the heels of his half-boots; while Mr. Sayers is impelled to the administration of his favourite blow, the Auctioneer, by the silent eloquence of a village church. The humble homes of England, with their domestic virtues and honeysuckle porches, urge both heroes to go in and win; and the lark and other singing birds are observable in the upper air, ecstatically carolling their thanks to Heaven for a fight. On the whole, the associations entwined with the pugilistic art by this artist are much in the manner of Izaak Walton.

But, it is with the lower animals of back streets and byways that my present purpose rests. For human notes we may return to such neighbourhoods when leisure and opportunity serve.

Nothing in shy neighbourhoods perplexes my mind more, than the bad company birds keep. Foreign birds often get into good society, but British birds are inseparable from low associates. There is a whole street of them in St. Giles's; and I always find them in poor and immoral neighbourhoods, convenient to the public-house and the pawnbroker's. They seem to lead people into drinking, and even the man who makes their cages usually gets into a chronic state of black eye. Why is this? Also, they will do things for people in short-skirted velveteen coats with bone buttons, or in sleeved waistcoats and fur caps, which they cannot be persuaded by the respectable orders of society to undertake. In a dirty court in Spitalfields, once, I found a goldfinch drawing his own water, and drawing as much of it as if he were in a consuming fever. That goldfinch lived at a bird-shop, and offered, in writing, to barter himself against old clothes, empty bottles, or even kitchen stuff. Surely a low thing and a depraved taste in any finch! I bought that goldfinch for money. He was sent home, and hung upon a nail over against my table. He lived outside a counterfeit dwelling-house, supposed (as I argued) to be a dyer's; otherwise it would have been impossible to account for his perch sticking out of the garret window. From the time of his appearance in my room, either he left off being thirsty—which was not in the bond—or he could not make up his mind to hear his little bucket drop back into his well when he let it go: a shock which in the best of times had made him tremble. He drew no water but by stealth and under the cloak of night. After an interval of futile and at length hopeless expectation, the merchant who had educated him was appealed to. The merchant was a bow-legged character, with a flat and cushiony nose, like the last new strawberry. He wore a fur cap, and shorts, and was of the velveteen race, velveteeny. He sent word that he would "look round." He looked round, appeared in the doorway of the room and slightly cocked up his evil eye at the goldfinch. Instantly a raging thirst beset that bird; when it was appeased, he still drew several unnecessary buckets of water; and finally, leaped about his perch and sharpened his bill, as if he had been to the nearest wine vaults and got drunk.

Donkeys again. I know shy neighbourhoods where the Donkey goes in at the street door, and appears to live upstairs, for I have examined the back-yard from over the palings, and have been unable to make him out. Gentility, nobility, Royalty, would appeal to that donkey in vain to do what he does for a costermonger. Feed him with oats at the highest price, put an infant prince and princess in a pair of panniers on his back, adjust his delicate trappings to a nicety, take him to the softest slopes at Windsor, and try what pace you can get out of him. Then, starve him, harness him anyhow to a truck with a flat tray on it, and see him bowl from Whitechapel to Bayswater. There appears to be no particular private understanding between birds and donkeys, in a state of nature; but in the shy neighbourhood state, you shall see them always in the same hands and always developing their very best energies for the very worst company. I have known a donkey—by sight; we were not on speaking terms—who lived over on the Surrey side of London-bridge, among the fast-nesses of Jacob's Island and Dockhead. It was the habit of that animal, when his services were not in immediate requisition, to go out alone, idling. I have met him a mile from his place of residence, loitering about the streets; and the expression of his countenance at such times was most degraded. He was attached to the establishment of an elderly lady who sold periwinkles, and he used to stand on Saturday nights with a cartful of those delicacies outside a gin-shop, pricking up his ears when a customer came to the cart, and too evidently deriving satisfaction from the knowledge that they got bad measure. His mistress was sometimes overtaken by inebriety. The last time I ever saw him (about five years ago) he was in cir-cumstances of difficulty, caused by this failing. Having been left alone with the cart of periwinkles, and forgotten, he went off idling. He prowled among his usual low haunts for some time, gratifying his depraved tastes, until, not taking the cart into his calculations, he endeavoured to turn up a narrow alley, and became greatly involved. He was taken into custody by the police, and, the Green Yard of the district being near at hand, was backed into that place of durance. At that crisis, I encountered him; the stubborn sense he evinced of being—not to compromise the expression—a blackguard, I never saw exceeded in the human subject. A flaring candle in a paper shade, stuck in among his periwinkles, showed him, with his ragged harness broken and his cart extensively shattered, twitching his mouth and shaking his hanging head, a picture of disgrace and obduracy. I have seen boys being taken to station-houses, who were as like him as his own brother.

The dogs of shy neighbourhoods, I observe to avoid play, and to be conscious of poverty. They avoid work, too, if they can, of course; that is in the nature of all animals. I have the pleasure to know a dog in a back street in the neighbourhood of Walworth, who has greatly distinguished himself in the minor drama, and who takes his portrait with him when he makes an engagement, for the illustration of the play-bill. His portrait (which is not at all like him) represents him in the act of dragging to the earth a recreant Indian, who is supposed to have tomahawked, or essayed to tomahawk, a British officer. The design is pure poetry, for there is no such Indian in the piece, and no such incident. He is a dog of the Newfoundland breed, for whose honesty I would be bail to any amount; but whose intellectual qualities in association with dramatic fiction, I cannot rate high. Indeed, he is too honest for the profession he has entered. Being at a town in Yorkshire last summer, and seeing him posted in the bill of the night, I attended the performance. His first scene was eminently successful; but, as it occupied a second in its representation (and five lines in the bill), it scarcely afforded ground for a cool and deliberate judgment of his powers. He had merely to bark, run on, and jump through an inn window, after a comic fugitive. The next scene of importance to the fable was a little marred in its interest by his over-anxiety; forasmuch as while his master (a belated soldier in a den of robbers on a tempestuous night) was feelingly lamenting the absence of his faithful dog, and laying great stress on the fact that he was thirty leagues away, the faithful dog was barking furiously in the prompter's box, and clearly choking himself against his collar. But it was in his greatest scene of all, that his honesty got the better of him. He had to enter a dense and trackless forest, on the trail of the murderer, and there to fly at the murderer when he found him resting at the foot of a tree, with his victim bound ready for slaughter. It was a hot night, and he came into the forest from an altogether unexpected direction, in the sweetest temper, at a very deliberate trot, not in the least excited; trotted to the foot-lights with his tongue out; and there sat down, panting, and amiably surveying the audience, with his tail beating on the boards, like a Dutch clock. Meanwhile the murderer, impatient to receive his doom, was audibly calling to him "Co-o-ome here!" while the victim, struggling with his bonds, assailed him with the most injurious expressions. It happened through these means, that when he was in course of time persuaded to trot up and rend the murderer limb from limb, he made it (for dramatic purposes) a little too obvious that he worked out that awful retribution by licking butter off his blood-stained hands.

In a shy street, behind Long-acre, two honest dogs live, who perform in Punch's show. I may venture to say that I am on terms of intimacy with both, and that I never saw either guilty of the falsehood of failing to look down at the man inside the show, during the whole performance. The difficulty other dogs have in satisfying their minds about these dogs, appears to be never overcome by time. The same dogs must encounter them over and over again, as they trudge along in their off-minutes behind the legs of the show and beside the drum; but all dogs seem to suspect their frills and jackets, and to sniff at them as if they thought those articles of personal adornment, an eruption—a something in the nature of mange, perhaps. From this Covent-garden window of mine I noticed a country dog, only the other day, who had come up to Covent-garden Market under a cart, and had broken his cord, an end of which he still trailed along with him. He loitered about the corners of the four streets commanded by my window; and bad London dogs came up, and told him lies that he didn't believe; and worse London dogs came up, and made proposals to him to go and steal in the market, which his principles rejected; and the ways of the town confused him, and he crept aside and lay down in a doorway. He had scarcely got a wink of sleep, when up comes Punch with Toby. He was darting to Toby for consolation and advice, when he saw the frill, and stopped, in the middle of the street, appalled. The show was pitched, Toby retired behind the drapery, the audience formed, the drum and pipes struck up. My country dog remained immovable, intently staring at these strange appearances, until Toby opened the drama by appearing on his ledge, and to him entered Punch, who put a tobacco-pipe into Toby's mouth. At this spectacle, the country dog threw up his head, gave one terrible howl, and fled due west.

We talk of men keeping dogs, but we might often talk more expressively of dogs keeping men. I know a bull-dog in a shy corner of Hammersmith who keeps a man. He keeps him up a yard, and makes him go to public-houses and lay wagers on him, and obliges him to lean against posts and look at him, and forces him to neglect work for him, and keeps him under rigid coercion. I once knew a fancy terrier who kept a gentleman—a gentleman who had been brought up at Oxford, too. The dog kept the gentleman entirely for his glorification, and the gentleman never talked about anything but the terrier. This, however, was not in a shy neighbourhood, and is a digression consequently.

There are a great many dogs in shy neighbourhoods, who keep boys. I have my eye on a mongrel in Somerstown who keeps three boys. He feigns that he can bring down sparrows, and unburrow rats (he can do neither), and he takes the boys out on sporting pretences into all sorts of suburban fields. He has likewise made them believe that he possesses some mysterious knowledge of the art of fishing, and they consider themselves incompletely equipped for the Hampstead ponds, with a pickle-jar and wide-mouthed bottle, unless he is with them and barking tremendously. There is a dog residing in the

Borough of Southwark who keeps a blind man. He may be seen, most days, in Oxford-street, haling the blind man away on expeditions wholly uncontemplated by, and unintelligible to, the man: wholly of the dog's conception and execution. Contrariwise, when the man has projects, the dog will sit down in a crowded thoroughfare and meditate. I saw him yesterday, wearing the money-tray like an easy collar, instead of offering it to the public, taking the man against his will, on the invitation of a disreputable cur, apparently to visit a dog at Harrow—he was so intent on that direction. The north wall of Burlington House Gardens, between the Arcade and the Albany, offers a shy spot for appointments among blind men at about two or three o'clock in the afternoon. They sit (very uncomfortably) on a sloping stone there, and compare notes. Their dogs may always be observed at the same time, openly disparaging the men they keep, to one another, and settling where they shall respectively take their men when they begin to move again. At a small butcher's, in a shy neighbourhood (there is no reason for suppressing the name; it is by Notting-hill, and gives upon the district called the Potteries), I know a shaggy black and white dog who keeps a drover. He is a dog of an easy disposition, and too frequently allows this drover to get drunk. On these occasions, it is the dog's custom to sit outside the public-house, keeping his eye on a few sheep, and thinking. I have seen him with six sheep, plainly casting up in his mind how many he began with when he left the market, and at what places he has left the rest. I have seen him perplexed by not being able to account to himself for certain particular sheep. A light has gradually broken on him, he has remembered at what butcher's he left them, and in a burst of grave satisfaction has caught a fly off his nose, and shown himself much relieved. If I could at any time have doubted the fact that it was he who kept the drover, and not the drover who kept him, it would have been abundantly proved by his way of taking undivided charge of the six sheep, when the drover came out besmeared with red ochre and beer, and gave him wrong directions, which he calmly disregarded. He has taken the sheep entirely into his own hands, has merely remarked with respectful firmness, "That instruction would place them under an omnibus; you had better confine your attention to yourself—you will want it all;" and has driven his charge away, with an intelligence of ears and tails, and a knowledge of business, that has left his lout of a man very, very far behind.

As the dogs of shy neighbourhoods usually betray a slinking consciousness of being in poor circumstances—for the most part manifested in an aspect of anxiety, an awkwardness in their play, and a misgiving that somebody is going to harness them to something, to pick up a living—so the cats of shy neighbourhoods exhibit a strong tendency to relapse into barbarism. Not only are they made selfishly ferocious by ruminating on the surplus population around them, and on the densely crowded state of all the avenues to cat's meat; not only is there a moral and politico-economical haggardness in them, traceable to these reflections; but they evince a physical deterioration.

Their linen is not clean, and is wretchedly got up; their black turns rusty, like old mourning; they wear very indifferent fur; and take to the shabbiest cotton velvet, instead of silk velvet. I am on terms of recognition with several small streets of cats, about the Obelisk in Saint George's Fields, and also in the vicinity of Clerkenwell-green, and also in the back settlements of Drury-lane. In appearance, they are very like the women among whom they live. They seem to turn out of their unwholesome beds into the street, without any preparation. They leave their young families to stagger about the gutters, unassisted, while they frouzily quarrel and swear and scratch and spit, at street corners. In particular, I remark that when they are about to increase their families (an event of frequent recurrence) the resemblance is strongly expressed in a certain dusty dowdiness, down-at-heel self-neglect, and general giving up of things. I cannot honestly report that I have ever seen a feline matron of this class washing her face when in an interesting condition.

Not to prolong these notes of uncommercial travel among the lower animals of shy neighbourhoods, by dwelling at length upon the exasperated moodiness of the tom-cats, and their resemblance in many respects to a man and a brother, I will come to a close with a word on the fowls of the same localities.

That anything born of an egg and invested with wings, should have got to the pass that it hops contentedly down a ladder into a cellar, and calls *that* going home, is a circumstance so amazing as to leave one nothing more in this connexion to wonder at. Otherwise I might wonder at the completeness with which these fowls have become separated from all the birds of the air—have taken to grovelling in bricks and mortar and mud—have forgotten all about live trees, and make roosting-places of shop-boards, barrows, oysters-tubs, bulk-heads, and door-scrapers. I wonder at nothing concerning them, and take them as they are. I accept as products of Nature and things of course, a reduced Bantam family of my acquaintance in the Hackney road, who are incessantly at the pawnbroker's. I cannot say that they enjoy themselves, for they are of a melancholy temperament; but what enjoyment they are capable of, they derive from crowding together in the pawnbroker's side-entry. Here, they are always to be found in a feeble flutter, as if they were newly come down in the world, and were afraid of being identified. I know a low fellow, originally of a good family from Dorking, who takes his whole establishment of wives, in single file, in at the door of the Jug Department of a disorderly tavern near the Haymarket, manœuvres them among the company's legs, emerges with them at the Bottle Entrance and so passes his life: seldom, in the season, going to bed before two in the morning. Over Waterloo-bridge, there is a shabby old speckled couple (they belong to the wooden French-bedstead, washing-stand, and towel-horse-making trade), who are always trying to get in at the door of a chapel. Whether the old lady, under a delusion reminding one of Mrs. Southcott, has an idea of entrusting an egg to that particular denomination, or merely understands that she has no business in the building and is consequently frantic to enter it, I cannot determine; but she is constantly endeavouring to undermine the principal door: while her partner, who is infirm upon his legs, walks up and down, encouraging her and defying the Universe. But, the family I have been best acquainted with, since the removal from this trying sphere of a Chinese circle at Brentford, reside in the densest part of Bethnal-green. Their abstraction from the objects among which they live, or rather their conviction that those objects have all come into existence in express subservience to fowls, has so enchanted me, that I have made them the subject of many journeys at divers hours. After careful observation of the two lords and the ten ladies of whom this family consists, I have come to the conclusion that their opinions are represented by the leading lord and leading lady: the latter, as I judge, an aged personage, afflicted with a paucity of feather and visibility of quill, that gives her the appearance of a bundle of office pens. When a railway goods van that would crush an elephant comes round the corner, tearing over these fowls, they emerge unharmed from under the horses, perfectly satisfied that the whole rush was a passing property in the air, which may have left something to eat behind it. They look upon old shoes, wrecks of kettles and saucepans, and fragments of bonnets, as a kind of meteoric discharge, for fowls to peck at. Peg-tops and hoops they account, I think, as a sort of hail: shuttlecocks, as rain, or dew. Gaslight comes quite as natural to them as any other light; and I have more than a suspicion that, in the minds of the two lords, the early public-house at the corner has superseded the sun. I have established it as a certain fact, that they always begin to crow when the public-house shutters begin to be taken down, and that they salute the potboy, the instant he appears to perform that duty, as if he were Phœbus in person.

XI

TRAMPS

The chance use of the word "Tramp" in my last paper, brought that numerous fraternity so vividly before my mind's eye, that I had no sooner laid down my pen than a compulsion was upon me to take it up again, and make notes of the Tramps whom I perceived on all the summer roads in all directions.

Whenever a tramp sits down to rest by the wayside, he sits with his legs in a dry ditch; and whenever he goes to sleep (which is very often indeed), he goes to sleep on his back. Yonder, by the high road, glaring white in the bright sunshine, lies, on the dusty bit of turf under the bramble-bush that fences the coppice from the highway, the tramp of the order savage, fast asleep. He lies on the broad of his back, with his face turned up to the sky, and one of his ragged arms loosely thrown across his face. His bundle (what can be the contents of that mysterious bundle, to make it worth his while to carry it about?) is thrown down beside him, and the waking woman with him sits with her legs in the ditch, and her back to the road. She wears her bonnet rakishly perched on the front of her head, to shade her face from the sun in walking, and she ties her skirts round her in conventionally tight tramp-fashion with a sort of apron. You can seldom catch sight of her, resting thus, without seeing her in a despondently defiant manner doing something to her hair or her bonnet, and glancing at you between her fingers. She does not often go to sleep herself in the daytime, but will sit for any length of time beside the man. And his slumberous propensities would not seem to be referable to the fatigue of carrying the bundle, for she carries it much oftener and further than he. When they are afoot, you will mostly find him slouching on ahead, in a gruff temper, while she lags heavily behind with the burden. He is given to personally correcting her, too—which phase of his character develops itself oftenest, on benches outside alehouse doors—and she appears to become strongly attached to him for these reasons; it may usually be noticed that when the poor creature has a bruised face, she is the most affectionate. He has no occupation whatever, this order of tramp, and has no object whatever in going anywhere. He will sometimes call himself a brickmaker, or a sawyer, but only when he takes an imaginative flight. He generally represents himself, in a vague way, as looking out for a job of work; but he never did work, he never does, and he never will. It is a favourite fiction with him, however (as if he were the most industrious character on earth), that *you* never work; and as he goes past your garden and sees you looking at your flowers, you will overhear him growl with a strong sense of contrast, "*You* are a lucky hidle devil, *you* are!"

The slinking tramp is of the same hopeless order, and has the same injured conviction on him that you were born to whatever you possess, and never did anything to get it: but he is of a less audacious disposition. He will stop before your gate, and say to his female companion with an air of constitutional humility and propitiation—to edify any one who may be within hearing behind a blind or a bush— "This is a sweet spot, ain't it? A lovely spot! And I wonder if they'd give two poor footsore travellers like me and you, a drop of fresh water out of such a pretty gen-teel crib? We'd take it wery koind on 'em, wouldn't us? Wery koind, upon my word, us would?" He has a quick sense of a dog in the vicinity, and will extend his modestly-injured propitiation to the dog chained up in your yard; remarking, as he slinks at the yard gate, "Ah! You are a foine breed o' dog, too, and *you* ain't kep for nothink! I'd take it wery koind o' your master if he'd elp a traveller and his woife as envies no gentlefolk their good fortun, wi' a bit o' your broken wittles. He'd never know the want of it, nor more would you. Don't bark like that, at poor persons as never done you no arm; the poor is down-trodden and broke enough without that; O DON'T!" He generally heaves a prodigious sigh in moving away, and always looks up the lane and down the lane, and up the road and down the road, before going on.

Both of these orders of tramp are of a very robust habit; let the hard-working labourer at whose cottage-door they prowl and beg, have the ague never so badly, these tramps are sure to be in good health.

There is another kind of tramp, whom you encounter this bright summer day—say, on a road with the sea-breeze making its dust lively, and sails of ships in the blue distance beyond the slope of Down. As you walk enjoyingly on, you descry in the perspective at the bottom of a steep hill up which your way lies, a figure that appears to be sitting airily on a gate, whistling in a cheerful and disengaged manner. As you approach nearer to it, you observe the figure to slide down from the gate, to desist from whistling, to uncock its hat, to become tender of foot, to depress its head and elevate its shoulders, and to present all the characteristics of profound despondency. Arriving at the bottom of the hill and coming close to the figure, you observe it to be the figure of a shabby young man. He is moving painfully forward, in the direction in which you are going, and his mind is so preoccupied with his misfortunes that he is not aware of your approach until you are close upon him at the hill-foot. When he is aware of you, you discover him to be a remarkably well-behaved young man, and a remarkably well-spoken young man. You know him to be well-behaved, by his respectful manner of touching his hat; you know him to be well-spoken, by his smooth manner of expressing himself. He says in a flowing confidential voice, and without punctuation, "I ask your pardon sir but if you would excuse the liberty of being so addressed upon the public Iway by one who is almost reduced to rags though it as not always been so and by no fault of his own but through ill elth in his family and many unmerited sufferings it would be a great obligation sir to know the time." You give the well-spoken young man the time. The well-spoken young man, keeping well up with you, resumes: "I am aware sir that it is a liberty to intrude a further question on a gentleman walking for his entertainment but might I make so bold as ask the favour of the way to Dover sir and about the distance?" You inform the well-spoken young man that the way to Dover is straight on, and the distance some eighteen miles. The well-spoken young man becomes greatly agitated. "In the condition to which I am reduced," says he, "I could not ope to reach Dover before dark even if my shoes were in a state to take me there or my feet were in a state to old out over the flinty road and were not on the bare ground of which any gentleman has the means to satisfy himself by looking Sir may I take the liberty of speaking to you?" As the well-spoken young man keeps so well up with you that you can't prevent his taking the liberty of speaking to you, he goes on, with fluency: "Sir it is not begging that is my intention for I was brought up by the best of mothers and begging is not my trade I should not know sir how to follow it as a trade if such were my shameful wishes for the best of mothers long taught otherwise and in the best of omes though now reduced to take the present liberty on the Iway Sir my business was the law-stationering and I was favourably known to the Solicitor-General the Attorney-General the majority of the Judges and the ole of the legal profession but through ill elth in my family and the treachery of a friend for whom I became security and he no other than my own wife's brother the brother of my own wife I was cast forth with my tender partner and three young children not to beg for I will sooner die of deprivation but to make my way to the seaport town of Dover where I have a relative i in respect not only that will assist me but that would trust me with untold gold Sir in appier times and hare this calamity fell upon me I made for my amusement when I little thought that I should ever need it excepting for my air this"—here the well-spoken young man put his hand into his breast—"this comb! Sir I implore you in the name of charity to purchase a tortoiseshell comb which is a genuine article at any price that your humanity may put upon it and may the blessings of a ouseless family awaiting with beating arts the return of a husband and a father from Dover upon the cold stone seats of London-bridge ever attend you Sir may I take the liberty of speaking to you I implore you to buy this comb!" By this time, being a reasonably good walker, you will have been too much for the well-spoken young man, who will stop short and express his disgust and his want of breath, in a long expectoration, as you leave him behind.

Towards the end of the same walk, on the same bright summer day, at the corner of the next little town or village, you may find another kind of tramp, embodied in the persons of a most exemplary couple whose only improvidence appears to have been, that they spent the last of their little All on the soap. They are a man and woman, spotless to behold—John Anderson, with the frost on his short smock-frock instead of his "pow," attended by Mrs. Anderson. John is over ostentatious of the frost upon his raiment, and wears a curious and, you would say, an almost unnecessary demonstration of girdle of white linen wound about his waist—a girdle, snowy as Mrs. Anderson's apron. This cleanliness was the expiring effort of the respectable couple, and nothing then remained to Mr. Anderson but to get chalked upon his spade in snow-white copy-book characters, HUNGRY! and to sit down here. Yes; one thing more remained to Mr. Anderson—his character; Monarchs could not deprive him of his hard-earned character. Accordingly, as you come up with this spectacle of virtue in distress, Mrs. Anderson rises, and with a decent curtsey presents for your consideration a certificate from a Doctor of Divinity, the reverend the Vicar of Upper Dodgington, who informs his Christian friends and all whom it may concern that the bearers, John Anderson and lawful wife, are persons to whom you cannot be too liberal. This benevolent pastor omitted no work of his hands to fit the good couple out, for with half an eye you can recognise his autograph on the spade.

Another class of tramp is a man, the most valuable part of whose stock-in-trade is a highly perplexed demeanour. He is got up like a countryman, and you will often come upon the poor fellow, while he is endeavouring to decipher the inscription on the milestone—quite a fruitless endeavour, for he cannot read. He asks your pardon, he truly does (he is very slow of speech, this tramp, and he looks in a bewildered way all round the prospect while he talks to you), but all of us shold do as we wold be done by, and he'll take it kind, if you'll put a power man in the right road fur to jine his eldest son as has broke his leg bad in the masoning, and is in this heere Orspit'l as is wrote down by Squire Pouncerby's own hand as wold not tell a lie fur no man. He then produces from under his dark frock (being always very slow and perplexed) a neat but worn old leathern purse, from which he takes a scrap of paper. On this scrap of paper is written, by Squire Pouncerby, of The Grove, "Please to direct the Bearer, a poor but very worthy man, to the Sussex County Hospital, near Brighton"—a matter of some difficulty at the moment, seeing that the request comes suddenly upon you in the depths of Hertfordshire. The more you endeavour to indicate where Brighton is—when you have with the greatest difficulty remembered—the less the devoted father can be made to comprehend, and the more obtusely he stares at the prospect; whereby, being reduced to extremity, you recommend the faithful parent to begin by going to St. Albans, and present him with half-a-crown. It does him good, no doubt, but scarcely helps him forward, since you find him lying drunk that same evening in the wheel-wright's sawpit under the shed where the felled trees are, opposite the sign of the Three Jolly Hedgers.

But, the most vicious, by far, of all the idle tramps, is the tramp who pretends to have been a gentleman. "Educated," he writes, from the village beer-shop in pale ink of a ferruginous complexion; "educated at Trin. Coll. Cam.—nursed in the lap of affluence—once in my small way the pattron of the Muses," &c. &c. &c.—surely a sympathetic mind will not withhold a trifle, to help him on to the market-town where he thinks of giving a Lecture to the *fruges consumere nati*, on things in general? This shameful creature lolling about hedge tap-rooms in his ragged clothes, now so far from being black that they look as if they never can have been black, is more selfish and insolent than even the savage tramp. He would sponge on the poorest boy for a farthing, and spurn him when he had got it; he would interpose (if he could get anything by it) between the baby and the mother's breast. So much lower than the company he keeps, for his maudlin assumption of being higher, this pitiless rascal blights the summer road as he maunders on between the luxuriant hedges: where (to my thinking) even the wild convolvulus and rose and sweet-briar, are the worse for his going by, and need time to recover from the taint of him in the air.

The young fellows who trudge along barefoot, five or six together, their boots slung over their shoulders, their shabby bundles under their arms, their sticks newly cut from some roadside wood, are not eminently prepossessing, but are much less objectionable. There is a tramp-fellowship among them. They pick one another up at resting stations, and go on in companies. They always go at a fast swing— though they generally limp too—and there is invariably one of the company who has much ado to keep up with the rest. They generally talk about horses, and any other means of locomotion than walking; or, one of the company relates some recent experiences of the road— which are always disputes and difficulties. As for example. "So as I'm a standing at the pump in the market, blest if there don't come up a Beadle, and he ses, 'Must'nt stand here,' he ses. 'Why not?' I ses. 'No beggars allowed in this town,' he ses. 'Who's a beggar?' I ses. 'You are,' he ses. 'Who ever see *me* beg? Did *you?*' I ses. 'Then you're a tramp,' he ses. 'I'd rather be that than a Beadle,' I ses." (The company express great approval.) " 'Would you?' he ses to me. 'Yes I would,' I ses to him. 'Well,' he ses, 'anyhow, get out of this town.' 'Why, blow your little town!' I ses, 'who wants to be in it? Wot does your dirty little town mean by comin' and stickin' itself in the road to anywhere? Why don't you get a shovel and a barrer, and clear your town out of people's way?'" (The company expressing the highest approval and laughing aloud, they all go down the hill.)

Then, there are the tramp handicraft men. Are they not all over England, in the Midsummer time? Where does the lark sing, the corn grow, the mill turn, the river run, and they are not among the lights and shadows, tinkering, chair-mending, umbrella-mending, clock-mending, knife-grinding? Surely, a pleasant thing, if we were in that condition of life, to grind our way through Kent, Sussex, and Surrey. For the worst six weeks or so, we should see the sparks we ground off, fiery bright against a background of green wheat and green leaves. A little later, and the ripe harvest would pale our sparks from red to yellow, until we got the dark newly turned land for a background again, and they were red once more. By that time, we should have ground our way to the sea cliffs, and the whirr of our wheel would be lost in the breaking of the waves. Our next variety in sparks would be derived from contrast with the gorgeous medley of colours in the autumn woods, and, by the time we had ground our way round to the heathy lands between Reigate and Croydon, doing a prosperous stroke of business all along, we should show like a little firework in the light frosty air, and be the next best thing to the blacksmith's forge. Very agreeable, too, to go on a chair-mending tour. What judges we should be of rushes, and how knowingly (with a sheaf and a bottomless chair at our back) we should lounge on bridges, looking over at osier-beds! Among all the innumerable occupations that cannot possibly be transacted without the assist-ance of lookers-on, chair-mending may take a station in the first rank. When we sat down with our backs against the barn or the public-house, and began to mend, what a sense of popularity would grow upon us! When all the children came to look at us, and the tailor, and the general dealer, and the farmer who had been giving small order at the little saddler's, and the groom from the great house, and the publican, and even the two skittle-players (and here note that, howsoever busy all the rest of village human-kind may be, there will always be two people with leisure to play at skittles, wherever village skittles are), what encouragement would be on us to plait and weave!

No one looks at us while we plait and weave these words. Clock-mending again. Except for the slight inconvenience of carrying a clock under our arm, and the monotony of making the bell go, whenever we came to a human habitation, what a pleasant privilege to give a voice to the dumb cottage-clock, and set it talking to the cottage family again! Likewise we foresee great interest in going round by the park plantations, under the overhanging boughs (hares, rabbits, partridges, and pheasants, scudding like mad across and across the chequered ground before us), and so over the park ladder, and through the wood, until we came to the Keeper's lodge. Then, would the Keeper be discoverable at his door, in a deep nest of leaves, smoking his pipe. Then, on our accosting him in the way of our trade, would he call to Mrs. Keeper, respecting "t'ould clock" in the kitchen. Then, would Mrs. Keeper ask us into the lodge, and on due examination we should offer to make a good job of it for eighteenpence; which offer, being accepted, would set us tinkling and clinking among the chubby, awe-struck little Keepers for an hour and more. So completely to the family's satisfaction would we achieve our work, that the Keeper would mention how that there was something wrong with the bell of the turret stable-clock up at the Hall, and that if we thought good of going up to the housekeeper on the chance of that job too, why he would take us. Then, should we go, among the branching oaks and the deep fern, by silent ways of mystery known to the Keeper, seeing the herd glancing here and there as we went along, until we came to the old Hall, solemn and grand. Under the Terrace Flower Garden, and round by the stables, would the Keeper take us in, and as we passed we should observe how spacious and stately the stables, and how fine the painting of the horses' names over their stalls, and how solitary all: the family being in London. Then, should we find ourselves presented to the housekeeper, sitting, in hushed state, at needlework, in a bay-window looking out upon a mighty grim red-brick quadrangle, guarded by stone lions disrespectfully throwing somersaults over the escutcheons of the noble family. Then, our services accepted and we insinuated with a candle into the stable-turret, we should find it to be a mere question of pendulum, but one that would hold us until dark. Then, should we fall to work, with a general impression of Ghosts being about, and of pictures indoors that of a certainty came out of their frames and "walked," if the family would only own it. Then, should we work and work, until the day gradually turned to dusk, and even until the dusk gradually turned to dark. Our task at length accomplished, we should be taken into an enormous servant's hall, and there regaled with beef and bread, and powerful ale. Then, paid freely, we should be at liberty to go, and should be told by a pointing helper to keep round over yinder by the blasted ash, and so straight through the woods, till we should see the town lights right afore us. Then, feeling lonesome, should we desire upon the whole, that the ash had not been blasted, or that the helper had had the manners not to mention it. However, we should keep on, all right, till suddenly the stable bell would strike ten in the dolefullest way, quite chilling our blood, though we had so lately taught him how to acquit himself. Then, as we went on, should we recall old stories, and dimly consider what it would be most advisable to do, in the event of a tall figure, all in white, with saucer eyes, coming up and saying, "I want you to come to a churchyard and mend a church clock. Follow me!" Then, should we make a burst to get clear of the trees, and should soon find ourselves in the open, with the town-lights bright ahead of us. So should we lie that night at the ancient sign of the Crispin and Crispanus, and rise early next morning to be betimes on tramp again.

Bricklayers often tramp, in twos and threes, lying by night at their "lodges," which are scattered all over the country. Bricklaying is another of the occupations that can by no means be transacted in rural parts, without the assistance of spectators—of as many as can be convened. In thinly peopled spots, I have known bricklayers on tramp, coming up with bricklayers at work, to be so sensible of the indispensability of lookers-on, that they themselves have sat up in that capacity, and have been unable to subside into the acceptance of a proffered share in the job, for two or three days together. Sometimes, the "navvy," on tramp, with an extra pair of half-boots over his shoulder, a bag, a bottle, and a can, will take a similar part in a job of excavation, and will look at it without engaging in it, until all his money is gone. The current of my uncommercial pursuits caused me only last summer to want a little body of workmen for a certain spell of work in a pleasant part of the country; and I was at one time honoured with the attendance of as many as seven-and-twenty, who were looking at six.

Who can be familiar with any rustic highway in summer-time, without storing up knowledge of the many tramps who go from one oasis of town or village to another, to sell a stock in trade, apparently not worth a shilling when sold? Shrimps are a favourite commodity for this kind of speculation, and so are cakes of a soft and spongy character, coupled with Spanish nuts and brandy balls. The stock is carried on the head in a basket, and, between the head and the basket, are the trestles on which the stock is displayed at trading times. Fleet of foot, but a careworn class of tramp this, mostly; with a certain stiffness of neck, occasioned by much anxious balancing of baskets; and also with a long, Chinese sort of eye, which an over-weighted forehead would seem to have squeezed into that form.

On the hot dusty roads near seaport towns and great rivers, behold the tramping Soldier. And if you should happen never to have asked yourself whether his uniform is suited to his work, perhaps the poor fellow's appearance as he comes distressfully towards you, with his absurdly tight jacket unbuttoned, his neck-gear in his hand, and his legs well chafed by his trousers of baize, may suggest the personal inquiry, how you think *you* would like it. Much better the tramping Sailor, although his cloth is somewhat too thick for land service. But, why the tramping merchant-mate should put on a black velvet waistcoat, for a chalky country in the dog-days, is one of the great secrets of nature that will never be discovered.

I have my eye upon a piece of Kentish road, bordered on either side by a wood, and having on one hand, between the road-dust and the trees, a skirting patch of grass. Wild flowers grow in abundance on this spot, and it lies high and airy, with a distant river stealing steadily away to the ocean, like a man's life. To gain the milestone here, which the moss, primroses, violets, blue-bells, and wild roses, would soon render illegible but for peering travellers pushing them aside with their sticks, you must come up a steep hill, come which way you may. So, all the tramps with carts or caravans—the Gipsy-tramp, the Show-tramp, the Cheap Jack—find it impossible to resist the temptations of the place, and all turn the horse loose when they come to it, and boil the pot. Bless the place, I love the ashes of the vagabond fires that have scorched its grass! What tramp children do I see here, attired in a handful of rags, making a gymnasium of the shafts of the cart, making a feather-bed of the flints and brambles, making a toy of the hobbled old horse who is not much more like a horse than any cheap toy would be! Here, do I encounter the cart of mats and brooms and baskets—with all thoughts of business given to the evening wind—with the stew made and being served out—with Cheap Jack and Dear Jill striking soft music out of the plates that are rattled like warlike cymbals when put up for auction at fairs and markets—their minds so influenced (no doubt) by the melody of the nightingales as they begin to sing in the woods behind them, that if I were to propose to deal, they would sell me anything at cost price. On this hallowed ground has it been my happy privilege (let me whisper it), to behold the White-haired Lady with the pink eyes, eating meat-pie with the Giant: while, by the hedge-side, on the box of blankets which I knew contained the snakes, were set forth the cups and saucers and the teapot. It was on an evening in August, that I chanced upon this ravishing spectacle, and I noticed that, whereas the Giant reclined half concealed beneath the overhanging boughs and seemed indifferent to Nature, the white hair of the gracious Lady streamed free in the breath of evening, and her pink eyes found pleasure in the landscape. I heard only a single sentence of her uttering, yet it bespoke a talent for modest repartee. The ill-mannered Giant—accursed by his evil race!—had interrupted the Lady in some remark, and, as I passed that enchanted corner of the wood, she gently reproved him, with the words, "Now, Cobby;"—Cobby! so short a name!—"ain't one fool enough to talk at a time?"

Within appropriate distance of this magic ground, though not so near it as that the song trolled from tap or bench at door, can invade its woodland silence, is a little hostelry which no man possessed of a penny was ever known to pass in warm weather. Before its entrance, are certain pleasant, trimmed limes; likewise, a cool well, with so musical a bucket-handle that its fall upon the bucket rim will make a horse prick up his ears and neigh, upon the droughty road half a mile off. This is a house of great resort for haymaking tramps and harvest tramps, insomuch that as they sit within, drinking their mugs of beer, their relinquished scythes and reaping-hooks glare out of the open windows, as if the whole establishment were a family war-coach of Ancient Britons. Later in the season, the whole country-side, for miles and miles, will swarm with hopping tramps. They come in families, men, women, and children, every family provided with a bundle of bedding, an iron pot, a number of babies, and too often with some poor sick creature quite unfit for the rough life, for whom they suppose the smell of the fresh hop to be a sovereign remedy. Many of these hoppers are Irish, but many come from London. They crowd all the roads, and camp under all the hedges and on all the scraps of common-land, and live among and upon the hops until they are all picked, and the hop-gardens, so beautiful through the summer, look as if they had been laid waste by an invading army. Then, there is a vast exodus of tramps out of the country; and if you ride or drive round any turn of any road, at more than a foot pace, you will be bewildered to find that you have charged into the bosom of fifty families, and that there are splashing up all around you, in the utmost prodigality of confusion, bundles of bedding, babies, iron pots, and a good-humoured multitude of both sexes and all ages, equally divided between perspiration and intoxication.

XII

DULLBOROUGH TOWN

It lately happened that I found myself rambling about the scenes among which my earliest days were passed; scenes from which I departed when I was a child, and which I did not revisit until I was a man. This is no uncommon chance, but one that befalls some of us any day; perhaps it may not be quite uninteresting to compare notes with the reader respecting an experience so familiar and a journey so uncommercial.

I call my boyhood's home (and I feel like a Tenor in an English Opera when I mention it) Dullborough. Most of us come from Dull-borough who come from a country town.

As I left Dullborough in the days when there were no railroads in the land, I left it in a stage-coach. Through all the years that have since passed, have I ever lost the smell of the damp straw in which I was packed—like game—and forwarded, carriage paid, to the Cross Keys, Wood-street, Cheapside, London? There was no other inside passenger, and I consumed my sandwiches in solitude and dreariness, and it rained hard all the way, and I thought life sloppier than I had expected to find it.

With this tender remembrance upon me, I was cavalierly shunted back into Dullborough the other day, by train. My ticket had been previously collected, like my taxes, and my shining new portmanteau had had a great plaster stuck upon it, and I had been defied by Act of Parliament to offer an objection to anything that was done to it, or me, under a penalty of not less than forty shillings or more than five pounds, compoundable for a term of imprisonment. When I had sent my disfigured property on to the hotel, I began to look about me; and the first discovery I made, was, that the Station had swallowed up the playing-field.

It was gone. The two beautiful hawthorn-trees, the hedge, the turf, and all those buttercups and daisies, had given place to the stoniest of jolting roads: while, beyond the Station, an ugly dark monster of a tunnel kept its jaws open, as if it had swallowed them and were ravenous for more destruction. The coach that had carried me away, was melodiously called Timpson's Blue-Eyed Maid, and belonged to Timpson, at the coach-office up-street; the locomotive engine that had brought me back, was called severely No. 97, and belonged to S.E.R., and was spitting ashes and hot water over the blighted ground.

When I had been let out at the platform-door, like a prisoner whom his turnkey grudgingly released, I looked in again over the low wall, at the scene of departed glories. Here, in the haymaking time, had I been delivered from the dungeons of Seringapatam, an immense pile (of haycock), by my own countrymen, the victorious British (boy next door and his two cousins), and had been recognised with ecstasy by my affianced one (Miss Green), who had come all the way from England (second house in the terrace) to ransom me, and marry me. Here, had I first heard in confidence, from one whose father was greatly connected, being under Government, of the existence of a terrible banditti, called "The Radicals," whose principles were, that the Prince Regent wore stays, and that nobody had a right to any salary, and that the army and navy ought to be put down—horrors at which I trembled in my bed, after supplicating that the Radicals might be speedily taken and hanged. Here, too, had we, the small boys of Boles's, had that cricket match against the small boys of Coles's, when Boles and Coles had actually met upon the ground, and when, instead of instantly hitting out at one another with the utmost fury, as we had all hoped and expected, those sneaks had said respectively, "I hope Mrs. Boles is well," and "I hope Mrs. Coles and the baby are doing charmingly." Could it be that, after all this, and much more, the Playing-field was a Station, and No. 97 expectorated boiling water and redhot cinders on it, and the whole belonged by Act of Parliament to S.E.R.?

As it could be, and was, I left the place with a heavy heart for a walk all over the town. And first of Timpson's upstreet. When I departed from Dullborough in the strawy arms of Timpson's Blue-Eyed Maid, Timpson's was a moderate-sized coach-office (in fact, a little coach-office), with an oval transparency in the window, which looked beautiful by night, representing one of Timpson's coaches in the act of passing a milestone on the London road with great velocity, completely full inside and out, and all the passengers dressed in the first style of fashion, and enjoying themselves tremendously. I found no such place as Timpson's now—no such bricks and rafters, not to mention the name—no such edifice on the teeming earth. Pickford had come and knocked Timpson's down. Pickford had not only knocked Timpson's down, but had knocked two or three houses down on each side of Timpson's, and then had knocked the whole into one great establishment with a pair of big gates, in and out of which, his (Pickford's) waggons are, in these days, always rattling, with their drivers sitting up so high, that they look in at the second-floor windows of the old-fashioned houses in the High-street as they shake the town. I have not the honour of Pickford's acquaintance, but I felt that he had done me an injury, not to say committed an act of boyslaughter, in running over my childhood in this rough manner; and if ever I meet Pickford driving one of his own monsters, and smoking a pipe the while (which is the custom of his men), he shall know by the expression of my eye, if it catches his, that there is something wrong between us.

Moreover, I felt that Pickford had no right to come rushing into Dullborough and deprive the town of a public picture. He is not Napoleon Bonaparte. When he took down the transparent stage-coach, he ought to have given the town a transparent van. With a gloomy conviction that Pickford is wholly utilitarian and unimaginative, I proceeded on my way.

It is a mercy I have not a red and green lamp and a night-bell at my door, for in my very young days I was taken to so many lyings-in that I wonder I escaped becoming a professional martyr to them in after-life. I suppose I had a very sympathetic nurse, with a large circle of married acquaintance. However that was, as I continued my walk through Dullborough, I found many houses to be solely associated in my mind with this particular interest. At one little green-grocer's shop, down certain steps from the street, I remember to have waited on a lady who had had four children (I am afraid to write five, though I fully believe it was five) at a birth. This meritorious woman held quite a reception in her room on the morning when I was introduced there, and the sight of the house brought vividly to my mind how the four (five) deceased young people lay, side by side, on a clean cloth on a chest of drawers; reminding me by a homely association, which I suspect their complexion to have assisted, of pigs' feet as they are usually displayed at a neat tripe-shop. Hot caudle was handed round on the occasion, and I further remembered as I stood contemplating the greengrocer's, that a subscription was entered into among the company, which became extremely alarming to my consciousness of having pocket-money on my person. This fact being known to my conductress, whoever she was, I was earnestly exhorted to contribute, but resolutely declined: therein disgusting the company, who gave me to understand that I must dismiss all expectations of going to Heaven.

How does it happen that when all else is change wherever one goes, there yet seem, in every place, to be some few people who never alter? As the sight of the greengrocer's house recalled these trivial incidents of long age, the identical greengrocer appeared on the steps, with his hands in his pockets, and leaning his shoulder against the door-post, as my childish eyes had seen him many a time; indeed, there was his old mark on the door-post yet, as if his shadow had become a fixture there. It was he himself; he might formerly have been an old-looking young man, or he might now be a young-looking old man, but there he was. In walking along the street, I had as yet looked in vain for a familiar face, or even a transmitted face; here was the very greengrocer who had been weighing and handling baskets on the morning of the reception. As he brought with him a dawning remembrance that he had had no proprietary interest in those babies, I crossed the road, and accosted him on the subject. He was not in the least excited or gratified, or in any way roused, by the accuracy of my recollection, but said, Yes, summut out of the common—he didn't remember how many it was (as if half-a-dozen babes either way made no difference) —had happened to a Mrs. What's-her-name, as once lodged there— but he didn't call it to mind, particular. Nettled by this phlegmatic conduct, I informed him that I had left the town when I was a child. He slowly returned, quite unsoftened, and not without a sarcastic kind of complacency, *Had* I? Ah! And did I find it had got on tolerably well without me? Such is the difference (I thought, when I had left him a few hundred yards behind, and was by so much in a better temper) between going away from a place and remaining in it. I had no right, I reflected, to be angry with the greengrocer for his want of interest, I was nothing to him: whereas he was the town, the cathedral, the bridge, the river, my childhood, and a large slice of my life, to me.

Of course the town had shrunk fearfully, since I was a child there. I had entertained the impression that the High-street was at least as wide as Regent-street, London, or the Italian Boulevard at Paris. I found it little better than a lane. There was a public clock in it, which I had supposed to be the finest clock in the world: whereas it now turned out to be as inexpressive, moon-faced, and weak a clock as ever I saw. It belonged to a Town Hall, where I had seen an Indian (who I now suppose wasn't an Indian) swallow a sword (which I now suppose he didn't). The edifice had appeared to me in those days so glorious a structure, that I had set it up in my mind as the model on which the Genie of the Lamp built the palace for Aladdin. A mean little brick heap, like a demented chapel, with a few yawning persons in leather gaiters, and in the last extremity for something to do, lounging at the door with their hands in their pockets, and calling themselves a Corn Exchange!

The Theatre was in existence, I found, on asking the fish-monger, who had a compact show of stock in his window, consisting of a sole and a quart of shrimps—and I resolved to comfort my mind by going to look at it. Richard the Third, in a very uncomfortable cloak, had first appeared to me there, and had made my heart leap with terror by backing up against the stage-box in which I was posted, while struggling for life against the virtuous Richmond. It was within those walls that I had learnt as from a page of English history, how that wicked King slept in war-time on a sofa much too short for him, and how fearfully his conscience troubled his boots. There, too, had I first seen the funny countryman, but countryman of noble principles in a flowered waistcoat, crunch up his little hat and throw it on the ground, and pull off his coat, saying, "Dom thee, squire, coom on with thy fistes then!" At which the lovely young woman who kept company with him (and who went out gleaning, in a narrow white muslin apron with five beautiful bars of five different-coloured ribbons across it) was so frightened for his sake, that she fainted away. Many wondrous secrets of Nature had I come to the knowledge of in that sanctuary: of which not the least terrific were, that the witches in Macbeth bore an awful resemblance to the Thanes and other proper inhabitants of Scotland; and that the good King Duncan couldn't rest in his grave, but was constantly coming out of it and calling himself somebody else. To the Theatre, therefore, I repaired for consolation. But I found very little, for it was in a bad and declining way. A dealer in wine and bottled beer had already squeezed his trade into the box-office, and the theatrical money was taken—when it came—in a kind of meat-safe in the passage. The dealer in wine and bottled beer must have insinuated himself under the stage too; for he announced that he had various descriptions of alcoholic drinks "in the wood," and there was no possible stowage for the wood anywhere else. Evidently, he was by degrees eating the establishment away to the core, and would soon have sole possession of it. It was To Let, and hopelessly so, for its old purposes; and there had been no entertainment within its walls for a long time except a Panorama; and even that had been announced as "pleasingly instructive," and I know too well the fatal meaning and the leaden import of those terrible expressions. No, there was no comfort in the Theatre. It was mysteriously gone, like my own youth. Unlike my own youth, it might be coming back some day; but there was little promise of it.

As the town was placarded with references to the Dullborough Mechanics' Institution, I thought I would go and look at that establishment next. There had been no such thing in the town, in my young days, and it occurred to me that its extreme prosperity might have brought adversity upon the Drama. I found the Institution with some difficulty, and should scarcely have known that I had found it if I had judged from its external appearance only; but this was attributable to its never having been finished, and having no front: consequently, it led a modest and retired existence up a stable-yard. It was (as I learnt, on inquiry) a most flourishing Institution, and of the highest benefit to the town: two triumphs which I was glad to understand were not at all impaired by the seeming drawbacks that no mechanics belonged to it, and that it was steeped in debt to the chimney-pots. It had a large room, which was approached by an infirm step-ladder: the builder having declined to construct the intended staircase, without present payment in cash, which Dullborough (though profoundly appreciative of the Institution) seemed unaccountably bashful about subscribing. The large room had cost—or would, when paid for—five hundred pounds; and it had more mortar in it and more echoes, than one might have expected to get for the money. It was fitted up with a platform, and the usual lecturing tools, including a large black board of a menacing appearance. On referring to lists of the courses of lectures that had been given in this thriving Hall, I fancied I detected a shyness in admitting that human nature when at leisure has any desire whatever to be relieved and diverted; and a furtive sliding in of any poor make-weight piece of amusement, shamefacedly and edgewise. Thus, I observed that it was necessary for the members to be knocked on the head with Gas, Air, Water, Food, the Solar System, the Geological periods, Criticism on Milton, the Steam-engine, John Bunyan, and Arrow-Headed Inscriptions, before they might be tickled by those unaccountable choristers, the negro singers in the court costume of the reign of George the Second. Likewise, that they must be stunned by a weighty inquiry whether there was internal evidence in Shakespeare's works, to prove that his uncle by the mother's side lived for some years at Stoke Newington, before they were brought-to by a Miscellaneous Concert. But, indeed, the masking of entertainment, and pretending it was something else—as people mask bedsteads when they are obliged to have them in sitting-rooms, and make believe that they are book-cases, sofas, chests of drawers, anything rather than bedsteads—was manifest even in the pretence of dreariness that the unfortunate entertainers themselves felt obliged in decency to put forth when they came here. One very agreeable professional singer, who travelled with two professional ladies, knew better than to introduce either of those ladies to sing the ballad "Comin' through the Rye" without prefacing it himself, with some general remarks on wheat and clover; and even then, he dared not for his life call the song, a song, but disguised it in the bill as an "Illustration." In the library, also—fitted with shelves for three thousand books, and containing upwards of one hundred and seventy (presented copies mostly), seething their edges in damp plaster—there was such a painfully apologetic return of 62 offenders who had read Travels, Popular Biography, and mere Fiction descriptive of the aspirations of the hearts and souls of mere human creatures like themselves; and such an elaborate parade of 2 bright examples who had had down Euclid after the day's occupation and confinement; and 3 who had had down Metaphysics after ditto; and 1 who had had down Theology after ditto; and 4 who had worried Grammar, Political Economy, Botany, and Logarithms all at once after ditto; that I suspected the boasted class to be one man, who had been hired to do it.

Emerging from the Mechanics' Institution and continuing my walk about the town, I still noticed everywhere the prevalence, to an extraordinary degree, of this custom of putting the natural demand for amusement out of sight, as some untidy housekeepers put dust, and pretending that it was swept away. And yet it was ministered to, in a dull and abortive manner, by all who made this feint. Looking in at what is called in Dullborough "the serious bookseller's," where, in my childhood, I had studied the faces of numbers of gentlemen depicted in rostrums with a gaslight on each side of them, and casting my eyes over the open pages of certain printed discourses there, I found a vast deal of aiming at jocosity and dramatic effect, even in them—yes, verily, even on the part of one very wrathful expounder who bitterly anathematised a poor little Circus. Similarly, in the reading provided for the young people enrolled in the Lasso of Love, and other excellent unions, I found the writers generally under a distressing sense that they must start (at all events) like story-tellers, and delude the young persons into the belief that they were going to be interesting. As I looked in at this window for twenty minutes by the clock, I am in a position to offer a friendly remonstrance—not bearing on this particular point—to the designers and engravers of the pictures in those publications. Have they considered the awful consequences likely to flow from their representations of Virtue? Have they asked themselves the question, whether the terrific prospect of acquiring that fearful chubbiness of head, unwieldiness of arm, feeble dislocation of leg, crispiness of hair, and enormity of shirt-collar, which they represent as inseparable from Goodness, may not tend to confirm sensitive waverers, in Evil? A most impressive example (if I had believed it) of what a Dustman and a Sailor may come to, when they mend their ways, was represented to me in this same shop-window. When they were leaning (they were intimate friends) against a post, drunk and reckless, with surpassingly bad hats on, and their hair over their foreheads, they were rather picturesque, and looked as if they might be agreeable men, if they would not be beasts. But, when they had got over their bad propensities, and when, as a consequence, their heads had swelled alarmingly, their hair had got so curly that it lifted their blown-out cheeks up, their coat-cuffs were so long that they never could do any work, and their eyes were so wide open that they never could do any sleep, they presented a spectacle calculated to plunge a timid nature into the depths of Infamy.

But, the clock that had so degenerated since I saw it last, admonished me that I had stayed here long enough; and I resumed my walk.

I had not gone fifty paces along the street when I was suddenly brought up by the sight of a man who got out of a little phaeton at the doctor's door, and went into the doctor's house. Immediately, the air was filled with the scent of trodden grass, and the perspective of years opened, and at the end of it was a little likeness of this man keeping a wicket, and I said, "God bless my soul! Joe Specks!"

Through many changes and much work, I had preserved a tenderness for the memory of Joe, forasmuch as we had made the acquaintance of Roderick Random together, and had believed him to be no ruffian, but an ingenious and engaging hero. Scorning to ask the boy left in the phaeton whether it was really Joe, and scorning even to read the brass plate on the door—so sure was I—I rang the bell and informed the servant maid that a stranger sought audience of Mr. Specks. Into a room, half surgery, half study, I was shown to await his coming, and I found it, by a series of elaborate accidents, be-strewn with testimonies to Joe. Portrait of Mr. Specks, bust of Mr. Specks, silver cup from grateful patient to Mr. Specks, presentation sermon from local clergyman, dedication poem from local poet, dinner-card from local nobleman, tract on balance of power from local refugee, inscribed *Homage de l'auteur à Specks*.

When my old schoolfellow came in, and I informed him with a smile that I was not a patient, he seemed rather at a loss to perceive any reason for smiling in connexion with that fact, and inquired to what was he to attribute the honour? I asked him, with another smile, could he remember me at all? He had not (he said) that pleasure. I was beginning to have but a poor opinion of Mr. Specks, when he said reflectively, "And yet there's a something too." Upon that, I saw a boyish light in his eyes that looked well, and I asked him if he could inform me, as a stranger who desired to know and had not the means of reference at hand, what the name of the young lady was, who married Mr. Random? Upon that, he said "Narcissa," and, after staring for a moment, called me by my name, shook me by the hand, and melted into a roar of laughter. "Why, of course, you'll remember Lucy Green," he said, after we had talked a little. "Of course," said I. "Whom do you think she married?" said he. "You?" I hazarded. "Me," said Specks, "and you shall see her." So I saw her, and she was fat, and if all the hay in the world had been heaped upon her, it could scarcely have altered her face more than Time had altered it from my remembrance of the face that had once looked down upon me into the fragrant dungeons of Seringapatam. But when her youngest child came in after dinner (for I dined with them, and we had no other company than Specks, Junior, Barrister-at-law, who went away as soon as the cloth was removed, to look after the young lady to whom he was going to be married next week), I saw again, in that little daughter, the little face of the hayfield, unchanged, and it quite touched my foolish heart. We talked immensely, Specks and Mrs. Specks, and I, and we spoke of our old selves as though our old selves were dead and gone, and indeed, indeed they were—dead and gone as the playing-field that had become a wilderness of rusty iron, and the property of S.E.R.

Specks, however, illuminated Dullborough with the rays of interest that I wanted and should otherwise have missed in it, and linked its present to its past, with a highly agreeable chain. And in Speck's society I had new occasion to observe what I had before noticed in similar communications among other men. All the schoolfellows and others of old, whom I inquired about, had either done superlatively well or superlatively ill—had either become uncertificated bank-rupts, or been felonious and got themselves transported; or had made great hits in life, and done wonders. And this is so commonly the case, that I never can imagine what becomes of all the mediocre people of people's youth—especially considering that we find no lack of the species in our maturity. But, I did not propound this difficulty to Specks, for no pause in the conversation gave me an occasion. Nor, could I discover one single flaw in the good doctor—when he reads this, he will receive in a friendly spirit the pleasantly meant record—except that he had forgotten his Roderick Random, and that he confounded Strap with Lieutenant Hatchway; who never knew Random, howsoever intimate with Pickle.

When I went alone to the Railway to catch my train at night (Specks had meant to go with me, but was inopportunely called out), I was in a more charitable mood with Dullborough than I had been all day; and yet in my heart I had loved it all day too. Ah! who was I that I should quarrel with the town for being changed to me, when I myself had come back, so changed, to it! All my early readings and early imaginations dated from this place, and I took them away so full of innocent construction and guileless belief, and I brought them back so worn and torn, so much the wiser and so much the worse!

XIII

NIGHT WALKS

SOME years ago, a temporary inability to sleep, referable to a distressing impression, caused me to walk about the streets all night, for a series of several nights. The disorder might have taken a long time to conquer, if it had been faintly experimented on in bed; but, it was soon defeated by the brisk treatment of getting up directly after lying down, and going out, and coming home tired at sunrise.

In the course of those nights, I finished my education in a fair amateur experience of houselessness. My principal object being to get through the night, the pursuit of it brought me into sympathetic relations with people who have no other object every night in the year.

The month was March, and the weather damp, cloudy, and cold. The sun not rising before half-past five, the night perspective looked sufficiently long at half-past twelve: which was about my time for confronting it.

The restlessness of a great city, and the way in which it tumbles and tosses before it can get to sleep, formed one of the first entertainments offered to the contemplation of us houseless people. It lasted about two hours. We lost a great deal of companionship when the late public-houses turned their lamps out, and when the potmen thrust the last brawling drunkards into the street; but stray vehicles and stray people were left us, after that. If we were very lucky, a policeman's rattle sprang and a fray turned up; but, in general, surprisingly little of this diversion was provided. Except in the Haymarket, which is the worst kept part of London, and about Kent-street in the Borough, and along a portion of the line of the Old Kent-road, the peace was seldom violently broken. But, it was always the case that London, as if in imitation of individual citizens belonging to it, had expiring fits and starts of restlessness. After all seemed quiet, if one cab rattled, half-a-dozen would surely follow; and Houselessness even observed that intoxicated people appeared to be magnetically attracted towards each other; so that we knew when we saw one drunken object staggering against the shutters of a shop, that another drunken object would stagger up before five minutes were out, to fraternise or fight with it. When we made a divergence from the regular species of drunkard, the thin-armed, puff-faced, leaden-lipped gin-drinker, and encountered a rarer specimen of a more decent appearance, fifty to one but that specimen was dressed in soiled mourning. As the street experience in the night, so the street experience in the day; the common folk who come unexpectedly into a little property, come unexpectedly into a deal of liquor.

At length these flickering sparks would die away, worn out—the last veritable sparks of waking life trailed from some late pieman or hot-potato man—and London would sink to rest. And then the yearning of the houseless mind would be for any sign of company, any lighted place, any movement, anything suggestive of any one being up—nay, even so much as awake, for the houseless eye looked out for lights in windows.

Walking the streets under the pattering rain, Houselessness would walk and walk and walk, seeing nothing but the interminable tangle of streets, save at a corner, here and there, two policemen in conversation, or the sergeant or inspector looking after his men. Now and then in the night—but rarely—Houselessness would become aware of a furtive head peering out of a doorway a few yards before him, and, coming up with the head, would find a man standing bolt upright to keep within the doorway's shadow, and evidently intent upon no particular service to society. Under a kind of fascination, and in a ghostly silence suitable to the time, Houselessness and this gentleman would eye one another from head to foot, and so, without exchange of speech, part, mutually suspicious. Drip, drip, drip, from ledge and coping, splash from pipes and water-spouts, and by-and-by the houseless shadow would fall upon the stones that pave the way to Waterloo-bridge; it being in the houseless mind to have a halfpenny worth of excuse for saying "Good-night" to the toll-keeper, and catching a glimpse of his fire. A good fire and a good great-coat and a good woollen neck-shawl, were comfortable things to see in conjunction with the toll-keeper; also his brisk wakefulness and excellent company when he rattled the change of halfpence down upon that metal table of his, like a man who defied the night, with all its sorrowful thoughts, and didn't care for the coming dawn. There was need of encouragement on the threshold of the bridge, for the bridge was dreary. The chopped-up murdered man, had not been lowered with a rope over the parapet when those nights were: he was alive, and slept then quietly enough most likely, and undisturbed by any dream of where he was to come. But the river had an awful look, the buildings on the banks were muffled in black shrouds, and the reflected lights seemed to originate deep in the water, as if the spectres of suicides were holding them to show where they went down. The wild moon and clouds were as restless as an evil conscience in a tumbled bed, and the very shadow of the immensity of London seemed to lie oppressively upon the river.

Between the bridge and the two great theatres, there was but the distance of a few hundred paces, so the theatres came next. Grim and black within, at night, those great dry Wells, and lonesome to imagine, with the rows of faces faded out, the lights extinguished, and the seats all empty. One would think that nothing in them knew itself at such a time but Yorick's skull. In one of my night walks, as the church steeples were shaking the March winds and rain with the strokes of Four, I passed the outer boundary of one of these great deserts, and entered it. With a dim lantern in my hand, I groped my well-known way to the stage and looked over the orchestra—which was like a great grave dug for a time of pestilence—into the void beyond. A dismal cavern of an immense aspect, with the chandelier gone dead like everything else, and nothing visible through mist and fog and space, but tiers of winding-sheets. The ground at my feet where, when last there, I had seen the peasantry of Naples dancing among the vines, reckless of the burning mountain which threatened to overwhelm them, was now in possession of a strong serpent of engine-hose, watchfully lying in wait for the serpent Fire, and ready to fly at it if it showed its forked tongue. A ghost of a watchman, carrying a faint corpse candle, haunted the distant upper gallery and flitted away. Retiring within the proscenium, and holding my light above my head towards the rolled-up curtain—green no more, but black as ebony—my sight lost itself in a gloomy vault, showing faint indications in it of a shipwreck of canvas and cordage. Methought I felt much as a diver might, at the bottom of the sea.

In those small hours when there was no movement in the streets, it afforded matter for reflection to take Newgate in the way, and, touching its rough stone, to think of the prisoners in their sleep, and then to glance in at the lodge over the spiked wicket, and see the fire and light of the watching turnkeys, on the white wall. Not an inappropriate time either, to linger by that wicked little Debtors' Door—shutting tighter than any other door one ever saw—which has been Death's Door to so many. In the days of the uttering of forged one-pound notes by people tempted up from the country, how many hundreds of wretched creatures of both sexes—many quite innocent—swung out of a pitiless and inconsistent world, with the tower of yonder Christian church of Saint Sepulchre monstrously before their eyes! Is there any haunting of the Bank Parlour, by the remorseful souls of old directors, in the nights of these later days, I wonder, or is it as quiet as this degenerate Aceldama of an Old Bailey?

To walk on to the Bank, lamenting the good old times and bemoaning the present evil period, would be an easy next step, so I would take it, and would make my houseless circuit of the Bank, and give a thought to the treasure within; likewise to the guard of soldiers passing the night there, and nodding over the fire. Next, I went to Billingsgate, in some hope of market-people, but it proving as yet too early, crossed London-bridge and got down by the water-side on the Surrey shore among the buildings of the great brewery. There was plenty going on at the brewery; and the reek, and the smell of grains, and the rattling of the plump dray horses at their mangers, were capital company. Quite refreshed by having mingled with this good society, I made a new start with a new heart, setting the old King's Bench prison before me for my next object, and resolving, when I should come to the wall, to think of poor Horace Kinch, and the Dry Rot in men.

A very curious disease the Dry Rot in men, and difficult to detect the beginning of. It had carried Horace Kinch inside the wall of the old King's Bench prison, and it had carried him out with his feet foremost. He was a likely man to look at, in the prime of life, well to do, as clever as he needed to be, and popular among many friends. He was suitably married, and had healthy and pretty children. But, like some fair-looking houses or fair-looking ships, he took the Dry Rot. The first strong external revelation of the Dry Rot in men, is a tendency to lurk and lounge; to be at street-corners without intelligible reason; to be going anywhere when met; to be about many places rather than at any; to do nothing tangible, but to have an intention of performing a variety of intangible duties to-morrow or the day after. When this manifestation of the disease is observed, the observer will usually connect it with a vague impression once formed or received, that the patient was living a little too hard. He will scarcely have had leisure to turn it over in his mind and form the terrible suspicion "Dry Rot," when he will notice a change for the worse in the patient's appearance: a certain slovenliness and deterioration, which is not poverty, nor dirt, nor intoxication, nor ill-health, but simply Dry Rot. To this, succeeds a smell as of strong waters, in the morning; to that, a looseness respecting money; to that, a strong smell as of strong waters, at all times; to that, a looseness respecting everything; to that, a trembling of the limbs, somnolency, misery, and crumbling to pieces. As it is in wood, so it is in men. Dry Rot advances at a compound usury quite incalculable. A plank is found infected with it, and the whole structure is devoted. Thus it had been with the unhappy Horace Kinch, lately buried by a small subscription. Those who knew him had not nigh done saying, "So well off, so comfortably established, with such hope before him—and yet, it is feared, with a slight touch of Dry Rot!" when lo! the man was all Dry Rot and dust.

From the dead wall associated on those houseless nights with this too common story, I chose next to wander by Bethlehem Hospital; partly, because it lay on my road round to Westminster; partly, because I had a night fancy in my head which could be best pursued within sight of its walls and dome. And the fancy was this: Are not the sane and the insane equal at night as the sane lie a dreaming? Are not all of us outside this hospital, who dream, more or less in the condition of those inside it, every night of our lives? Are we not nightly persuaded, as they daily are, that we associate preposter-

ously with kings and queens, emperors and empresses, and notabilities of all sorts? Do we not nightly jumble events and personages
and times and places, as these do daily? Are we not sometimes
troubled by our own sleeping inconsistencies, and do we not vexedly
try to account for them or excuse them, just as these do sometimes
in respect of their waking delusions? Said an afflicted man to me,
when I was last in a hospital like this, "Sir, I can frequently fly." I
was half ashamed to reflect that so could I—by night. Said a woman
to me on the same occasion, "Queen Victoria frequently comes to
dine with me, and her Majesty and I dine off peaches and maccaroni
in our night-gowns, and his Royal Highness the Prince Consort does
us the honour to make a third on horseback in a Field-Marshal's
uniform." Could I refrain from reddening with consciousness when
I remembered the amazing royal parties I myself had given (at night),
the unaccountable viands I had put on table, and my extraordinary
manner of conducting myself on those distinguished occasions? I
wonder that the great master who knew everything, when he called
Sleep the death of each day's life, did not call Dreams the insanity
of each day's sanity.

By this time I had left the Hospital behind me, and was again
setting towards the river; and in a short breathing space I was on
Westminster-bridge, regaling my houseless eyes with the external
walls of the British Parliament—the perfection of a stupendous
institution, I know, and the admiration of all surrounding nations
and succeeding ages, I do not doubt, but perhaps a little the better
now and then for being pricked up to its work. Turning off into Old
Palace-yard, the Courts of Law kept me company for a quarter of an
hour; hinting in low whispers what numbers of people they were
keeping awake, and how intensely wretched and horrible they were
rendering the small hours to unfortunate suitors. Westminster Abbey
was fine gloomy society for another quarter of an hour; suggesting a
wonderful procession of its dead among the dark arches and pillars,
each century more amazed by the century following it than by all
the centuries going before. And indeed in those houseless night walks
—which even included cemeteries where watchmen went round
among the graves at stated times, and moved the tell-tale handle of
an index which recorded that they had touched it at such an hour—
it was a solemn consideration what enormous hosts of dead belong
to one old great city, and how, if they were raised while the living
slept, there would not be the space of a pin's point in all the streets
and ways for the living to come out into. Not only that, but the vast
armies of dead would overflow the hills and valleys beyond the city,
and would stretch away all round it, God knows how far.

When a church clock strikes, on houseless ears in the dead of the
night, it may be at first mistaken for company and hailed as such.
But, as the spreading circles of vibration, which you may perceive
at such a time with great clearness, go opening out, for ever and ever
afterwards widening perhaps (as the philosopher has suggested) in
eternal space, the mistake is rectified and the sense of loneliness is

profounder. Once—it was after leaving the Abbey and turning my face north—I came to the great steps of St. Martin's church as the clock was striking Three. Suddenly, a thing that in a moment more I should have trodden upon without seeing, rose up at my feet with a cry of loneliness and houselessness, struck out of it by the bell, the like of which I never heard. We then stood face to face looking at one another, frightened by one another. The creature was like a beetle-browed hair-lipped youth of twenty, and it had a loose bundle of rags on, which it held together with one of its hands. It shivered from head to foot, and its teeth chattered, and as it stared at me—persecutor, devil, ghost, whatever it thought me—it made with its whining mouth as if it were snapping at me, like a worried dog. Intending to give this ugly object money, I put out my hand to stay it—for it recoiled as it whined and snapped—and laid my hand upon its shoulder. Instantly, it twisted out of its garment, like the young man in the New Testament, and left me standing alone with its rags in my hands.

Covent-garden Market, when it was market morning, was wonderful company. The great waggons of cabbages, with growers: men and boys lying asleep under them, and with sharp dogs from market-garden neighbourhoods looking after the whole, were as good as a party. But one of the worst night sights I know in London, is to be found in the children who prowl about this place; who sleep in the baskets, fight for the offal, dart at any object they think they can lay their thieving hands on, dive under the carts and barrows, dodge the constables, and are perpetually making a blunt pattering on the pavement of the Piazza with the rain of their naked feet. A painful and unnatural result comes of the comparison one is forced to institute between the growth of corruption as displayed in the so much improved and cared for fruits of the earth, and the growth of corruption as displayed in these all uncared for (except inasmuch as ever-hunted) savages.

There was early coffee to be got about Covent-garden Market, and that was more company—warm company, too, which was better. Toast of a very substantial quality, was likewise procurable: though the towzled-headed man who made it, in an inner chamber within the coffee-room, hadn't got his coat on yet, and was so heavy with sleep that in every interval of toast and coffee he went off anew behind the partition into complicated cross-roads of choke and snore, and lost his way directly. Into one of these establishments (among the earliest) near Bow-street, there came one morning as I sat over my houseless cup, pondering where to go next, a man in a high and long snuff-coloured coat, and shoes, and, to the best of my belief, nothing else but a hat, who took out of his hat a large cold meat pudding; a meat pudding so large that it was a very tight fit, and brought the lining of the hat out with it. This mysterious man was known by his pudding, for on his entering, the man of sleep brought him a pint of hot tea, a small loaf, and a large knife and fork and plate. Left to himself in his box, he stood the pudding on the bare table, and, instead of cutting it, stabbed it, overhand, with the knife, like a mortal enemy; then took the knife out, wiped it on his sleeve, tore the pudding asunder with his fingers, and ate it all up. The remembrance of this man with the pudding remains with me as the remembrance of the most spectral person my houselessness encountered. Twice only was I in that establishment, and twice I saw him stalk in (as I should say, just out of bed, and presently going back to bed), take out his pudding, stab his pudding, wipe the dagger, and eat his pudding all up. He was a man whose figure promised cadaverousness, but who had an excessively red face, though shaped like a horse's. On the second occasion of my seeing him, he said huskily to the man of sleep, "Am I red to-night?" "You are," he uncompromisingly answered. "My mother," said the spectre, "was a red-faced woman that liked drink, and I looked at her hard when she laid in her coffin, and I took the complexion." Somehow, the pudding seemed an unwholesome pudding after that, and I put myself in its way no more.

When there was no market, or when I wanted variety, a railway terminus with the morning mails coming in, was remunerative company. But like most of the company to be had in this world, it lasted only a very short time. The station lamps would burst out ablaze, the porters would emerge from places of concealment, the cabs and trucks would rattle to their places (the post-office carts were already in theirs), and, finally, the bell would strike up, and the train would come banging in. But there were few passengers and little luggage, and everything scuttled away with the greatest expedition. The locomotive post-offices, with their great nets—as if they had been dragging the country for bodies—would fly open as to their doors, and would disgorge a smell of lamp, an exhausted clerk, a guard in a red coat, and their bags of letters; the engine would blow and heave and perspire, like an engine wiping its forehead and saying what a run it had had; and within ten minutes the lamps were out, and I was houseless and alone again.

But now, there were driven cattle on the high road near, wanting (as cattle always do) to turn into the midst of stone walls, and squeeze themselves through six inches' width of iron railing, and getting their heads down (also as cattle always do) for tossing-purchase at quite imaginary dogs, and giving themselves and every devoted creature associated with them a most extraordinary amount of unnecessary trouble. Now, too, the conscious gas began to grow pale with the knowledge that daylight was coming, and straggling work-people were already in the streets, and, as waking life had become extinguished with the last pieman's sparks, so it began to be rekindled with the fires of the first street-corner breakfast-sellers. And so by faster and faster degrees, until the last degrees were very fast, the day came, and I was tired and could sleep. And it is not, as I used to think, going home at such times, the least wonderful thing in London, that in the real desert region of the night, the houseless wanderer is alone there. I knew well enough where to find Vice and Misfortune of all kinds, if I had chosen; but they were put out of sight, and my houselessness had many miles upon miles of streets in which it could, and did, have its own solitary way.

XIV

CHAMBERS

HAVING occasion to transact some business with a solicitor who occupies a highly suicidal set of chambers in Gray's Inn, I afterwards took a turn in the large square of that stronghold of Melancholy, reviewing, with congenial surroundings, my experiences of Chambers.

I began, as was natural, with the Chambers I had just left. They were an upper set on a rotten staircase, with a mysterious bunk or bulkhead on the landing outside them, of a rather nautical and Screw Collier-like appearance than otherwise, and painted an intense black. Many dusty years have passed since the appropriation of this Davy Jones's locker to any purpose, and during the whole period within the memory of living man, it has been hasped and padlocked. I cannot quite satisfy my mind whether it was originally meant for the reception of coals, or bodies, or as a place of temporary security for the plunder "looted" by laundresses; but I incline to the last opinion. It is about breast high, and usually serves as a bulk for defendants in reduced circumstances to lean against and ponder at, when they come on the hopeful errand of trying to make an arrangement without money—under which auspicious circumstances it mostly happens that the legal gentleman they want to see, is much engaged, and they pervade the staircase for a considerable period. Against this opposing bulk, in the absurdest manner, the tomb-like outer door of the solicitor's chambers (which is also of an intense black) stands in dark ambush, half open, and half shut, all day. The solicitor's apartments are three in number; consisting of a slice, a cell, and a wedge. The slice is assigned to the two clerks, the cell is occupied by the principal, and the wedge is devoted to stray papers, old game baskets from the country, a washing-stand, and a model of a patent Ship's Caboose which was exhibited in Chancery at the commencement of the present century on an application for an injunction to restrain infringement. At about half-past nine on every week-day morning, the younger of the two clerks (who I have reason to believe, leads the fashion at Pentonville in the articles of pipes and shirts) may be found knocking the dust out of his official door-key on the bunk or locker before mentioned; and so exceedingly subject to dust is his key, and so very retentive of that superfluity, that in exceptional summer weather when a ray of sunlight has fallen on the locker in my presence, I have noticed its inexpressive countenance to be deeply marked by a kind of Bramah erysipelas or small-pox.

This set of chambers (as I have gradually discovered, when I have had restless occasion to make inquiries or leave messages, after office hours) is under the charge of a lady named Sweeney, in figure extremely like an old family-umbrella: whose dwelling confronts a dead wall in a court off Gray's Inn-lane, and who is usually fetched into the passage of that bower, when wanted, from some neighbouring home of industry, which has the curious property of imparting an inflammatory appearance to her visage. Mrs. Sweeney is one of the race of professed laundresses, and is the compiler of a remarkable manuscript volume entitled "Mrs. Sweeney's Book," from which much curious statistical information may be gathered respecting the high prices and small uses of soda, soap, sand, firewood, and other such articles. I have created a legend in my mind—and consequently I believe it with the utmost pertinacity—that the late Mr. Sweeney was a ticket-porter under the Honourable Society of Gray's Inn, and that, in consideration of his long and valuable services, Mrs. Sweeney was appointed to her present post. For, though devoid of personal charms, I have observed this lady to exercise a fascination over the elderly ticket-porter mind (particularly under the gateway, and in corners and entries), which I can only refer to her being one of the fraternity, yet not competing with it. All that need be said concerning this set of chambers, is said, when I have added that it is in a large double house in Gray's Inn-square, very much out of repair, and that the outer portal is ornamented in a hideous manner with certain stone remains, which have the appearance of the dismembered bust, torso, and limbs of a petrified bencher.

Indeed, I look upon Gray's Inn generally as one of the most depressing institutions in brick and mortar, known to the children of men. Can anything be more dreary than its arid Square, Sahara Desert of the law, with the ugly old tiled-topped tenements, the dirty windows, the bills To Let, To Let, the door-posts inscribed like gravestones, the crazy gateway giving upon the filthy Lane, the scowling, iron-barred prison-like passage into Verulam-buildings, the mouldy red-nosed ticket-porters with little coffin plates, and why with aprons, the dry, hard, atomy-like appearance of the whole dust-heap? When my uncommercial travels tend to this dismal spot, my comfort is its rickety state. Imagination gloats over the fulness of time when the staircases shall have quite tumbled down—they are daily wearing into an ill-savoured powder, but have not quite tumbled down yet—when the last old prolix bencher all of the olden time, shall have been got out of an upper window by means of a Fire Ladder, and carried off to the Holborn Union; when the last clerk shall have engrossed the last parchment behind the last splash on the last of the mud-stained windows, which, all through the miry year, are pilloried out of recognition in Gray's Inn-lane. Then, shall a squalid little trench, with rank grass and a pump in it, lying between the coffee-house and South-square, be wholly given up to cats and rats, and not, as now, have its empire divided between those animals and a few briefless bipeds—surely called to the Bar by voices of deceiving spirits, seeing that they are wanted there by no mortal—who glance down, with eyes better glazed than their casements, from their dreary and lack-lustre rooms. Then shall the way Nor' Westward, now lying under a short grim colonnade where in summer-time pounce flies from law-stationering windows into the eyes of laymen, be choked with rubbish and happily become impassable. Then shall the gardens where turf, trees, and gravel wear a legal livery of black, run rank, and pilgrims go to Gorhambury to see Bacon's effigy as he sat, and not come here (which in truth they seldom do) to see where he walked. Then, in a word, shall the old-established vendor of periodicals sit alone in his little crib of a shop behind the Holborn Gate, like that lumbering Marius among the ruins of Carthage, who has sat heavy on a thousand million of similes.

At one period of my uncommercial career I much frequented another set of chambers in Gray's Inn-square. They were what is familiarly called "a top set," and all the eatables and drinkables introduced into them acquired a flavour of Cockloft. I have known an unopened Strasbourg pâté fresh from Fortnum and Mason's, to draw in this cockloft tone through its crockery dish, and become penetrated with cockloft to the core of its inmost truffle in three-quarters of an hour. This, however, was not the most curious feature of those chambers; that, consisted in the profound conviction entertained by my esteemed friend Parkle (their tenant) that they were clean. Whether it was an inborn hallucination, or whether it was imparted to him by Mrs. Miggot the laundress, I never could ascertain. But, I believe he would have gone to the stake upon the question. Now, they were so dirty that I could take off the distinctest impression of my figure on any article of furniture by merely lounging upon it for a few moments; and it used to be a private amusement of mine to print myself off—if I may use the expression—all over the rooms. It was the first large circulation I had. At other times I have accidentally shaken a window curtain while in animated conversation with Parkle, and struggling insects which were certainly red, and were certainly not ladybirds, have dropped on the back of my hand. Yet Parkle lived in that top set years, bound body and soul to the superstition that they were clean. He used to say, when congratulated upon them, "Well, they are not like chambers in one respect, you know; they are clean." Concurrently, he had an idea which he could never explain, that Mrs. Miggot was in some way connected with the Church. When he was in particularly good spirits, he used to believe that a deceased uncle of hers had been a Dean; when he was poorly and low, he believed that her brother had been a Curate. I and Mrs. Miggot (she was a genteel woman) were on confidential terms, but I never knew her to commit herself to any distinct assertion on the subject; she merely claimed a proprietorship in the Church, by looking when it was mentioned, as if the reference awakened the slumbering Past, and were personal. It may have been his amiable confidence in Mrs. Miggot's better days that inspired my friend with his delusion respecting the chambers, but he never wavered in his fidelity to it for a moment, though he wallowed in dirt seven years.

Two of the windows of these chambers looked down into the garden; and we have sat up there together many a summer evening, saying how pleasant it was, and talking of many things. To my intimacy with that top set, I am indebted for three of my liveliest personal impressions of the loneliness of life in chambers. They shall follow here, in order; first, second, and third.

First. My Gray's Inn friend, on a time, hurt one of his legs, and it became seriously inflamed. Not knowing of his indisposition, I was on my way to visit him as usual, one summer evening, when I was much surprised by meeting a lively leech in Field-court, Gray's Inn, seemingly on his way to the West End of London. As the leech was alone, and was of course unable to explain his position, even if he had been inclined to do so (which he had not the appearance of being), I passed him and went on. Turning the corner of Gray's Inn-square, I was beyond expression amazed by meeting another leech—also entirely alone, and also proceeding in a westerly direction, though with less decision of purpose. Ruminating on this extraordinary circumstance, and endeavouring to remember whether I had ever read, in the Philosophical Transactions or any work on Natural History, of a migration of Leeches, I ascended to the top set, past the dreary series of closed outer doors of offices and an empty set or two, which intervened between that lofty region and the surface. Entering my friend's rooms, I found him stretched upon his back, like Prometheus Bound, with a perfectly demented ticket-porter in attendance on him instead of the Vulture: which helpless individual, who was feeble and frightened, and had (my friend explained to me, in great choler) been endeavouring for some hours to apply leeches to his leg, and as yet had only got on two out of twenty. To this Unfortunate's distraction between a damp cloth on which he had placed the leeches to freshen them, and the wrathful adjurations of my friend to "Stick 'em on, sir!" I referred the phenomenon I had encountered: the rather as two fine specimens were at that moment going out at the door, while a general insurrection of the rest was in progress on the table. After a while our united efforts prevailed, and, when the leeches came off and had recovered their spirits, we carefully tied them up in a decanter. But I never heard more of them than that they were all gone next morning, and that the Out-of-door young man of Bickle, Bush and Bodger, on the ground floor, had been bitten and blooded by some creature not identified. They never "took" on Mrs. Miggot, the laundress; but, I have always preserved fresh, the belief that she unconsciously carried several about her, until they gradually found openings in life.

Second. On the same staircase with my friend Parkle, and on the same floor, there lived a man of law who pursued his business elsewhere, and used those chambers as his place of residence. For three or four years, Parkle rather knew of him than knew him, but after that—for Englishmen—short pause of consideration, they began to speak. Parkle exchanged words with him in his private character only, and knew nothing of his business ways, or means. He was a man a good deal about town, but always alone. We used to remark to one another, that although we often encountered him in theatres, concert-rooms, and similar public places, he was always alone. Yet he was not a gloomy man, and was of a decidedly conversational turn; insomuch that he would sometimes of an evening lounge with a cigar in his mouth, half in and half out of Parkle's rooms, and discuss the topics of the day by the hour. He used to hint on these occasions that he had four faults to find with life; firstly, that it obliged a man to be always winding up his watch; secondly, that London was too small; thirdly, that it therefore wanted variety; fourthly, that there was too much dust in it. There was so much dust in his own faded chambers, certainly, that they reminded me of a sepulchre, furnished in prophetic anticipation of the present time, which had newly been brought to light, after having remained buried a few thousand years. One dry, hot autumn evening at twilight, this man, being then five years turned of fifty, looked in upon Parkle in his usual lounging way, with his cigar in his mouth as usual, and said, "I am going out of town." As he never went out of town, Parkle said, "Oh indeed! At last?" "Yes," says he, "at last. For what is a man to do? London is so small! If you go West, you come to Hounslow. If you go East, you come to Bow. If you go South, there's Brixton or Norwood. If you go North, you can't get rid of Barnet. Then, the monotony of all the streets, streets, streets—and of all the roads, roads, roads—and the dust dust, dust!" When he had said this, he wished Parkle a good evening, but came back again and said, with his watch in his hand, "Oh, I really cannot go on winding up this watch over and over again; I wish you would take care of it." So, Parkle laughed and consented, and the man went out of town. The man remained out of town so long, that his letter-box became choked, and no more letters could be got into it, and they began to be left at the lodge and to accumulate there. At last the head-porter decided, on conference with the steward, to use his master-key and look into the chambers, and give them the benefit of a whiff of air. Then, it was found that he had hanged himself to his bedstead, and had left this written memorandum: "I should prefer to be cut down by my neighbour and friend (if he will allow me to call him so), H. Parkle, Esq." This was an end of Parkle's occupancy of chambers. He went into lodgings immediately.

Third. While Parkle lived in Gray's Inn, and I myself was uncommercially preparing for the Bar—which is done, as everybody knows, by having a frayed old gown put on in a pantry by an old woman in a chronic state of Saint Anthony's fire and dropsy, and, so decorated, bolting a bad dinner in a party of four, whereof each individual mistrusts the other three—I say, while these things were, there was a certain elderly gentleman who lived in a court of the Temple, and was a great judge and lover of port wine. Every day he dined at his club and drank his bottle or two of port wine, and every night came home to the Temple and went to bed in his lonely chambers. This had gone on many years without variation, when one night he had a fit on coming home, and fell and cut his head deep, but partly recovered and groped about in the dark to find the door. When he was afterwards discovered, dead, it was clearly established by the marks of his

hands about the room that he must have done so. Now, this chanced
on the night of Christmas Eve, and over him lived a young fellow who
had sisters and young country friends, and who gave them a little
party that night, in the course of which they played at Blindman's
Buff. They played that game, for their greater sport, by the light of
the fire only; and once, when they were all quietly rustling and
stealing about, and the blindman was trying to pick out the prettiest
sister (for which I am far from blaming him), somebody cried, Hark!
The man below must be playing Blindman's Buff by himself to-night!
They listened, and they heard sounds of some one falling about and
stumbling against furniture, and they all laughed at the conceit, and
went on with their play, more light-hearted and merry than ever.
Thus, those two so different games of life and death were played out
together, blindfolded, in the two sets of chambers.

Such are the occurrences, which, coming to my knowledge, imbued
me long ago with a strong sense of the loneliness of chambers. There
was a fantastic illustration to much the same purpose implicitly
believed by a strange sort of man now dead, whom I knew when I had
not quite arrived at legal years of discretion, though I was already in
the uncommercial line.

This was a man who, though not more than thirty, had seen the
world in divers irreconcilable capacities—had been an officer in a
South American regiment among other odd things—but had not
achieved much in any way of life, and was in debt, and in hiding.
He occupied chambers of the dreariest nature in Lyons Inn; his name,
however, was not up on the door, or door-post, but in lieu of it stood
the name of a friend who had died in the chambers, and had given
him the furniture. The story arose out of the furniture, and was to
this effect:—Let the former holder of the chambers, whose name was
still upon the door and door-post, be Mr. Testator.

Mr. Testator took a set of chambers in Lyons Inn when he had but
very scanty furniture for his bedroom, and none for his sitting-room.
He had lived some wintry months in this condition, and had found it
very bare and cold. One night, past midnight, when he sat writing and
still had writing to do that must be done before he went to bed, he
found himself out of coals. He had coals down-stairs, but had never
been to his cellar; however the cellar-key was on his mantelshelf, and
if he went down and opened the cellar it fitted, he might fairly assume
the coals in that cellar to be his. As to his laundress, she lived among
the coal-waggons and Thames watermen—for there were Thames
watermen at that time in some unknown rat-hole by the river, down
lanes and alleys on the other side of the Strand. As to any other
person to meet him or obstruct him, Lyons Inn was dreaming, drunk,
maudlin, moody, betting, brooding over bill-discounting or renewing
—asleep or awake, minding its own affairs. Mr. Testator took his coal-
scuttle in one hand, his candle and key in the other, and descended to
the dismallest underground dens of Lyons Inn, where the late vehicles
in the streets became thunderous, and all the water-pipes in the
neighbourhood seemed to have Macbeth's Amen sticking in their

throats, and to be trying to get it out. After groping here and there among low doors to no purpose, Mr. Testator at length came to a door with a rusty padlock which his key fitted. Getting the door open with much trouble, and looking in, he found, no coals, but a confused pile of furniture. Alarmed by this intrusion on another man's property, he locked the door again, found his own cellar, filled his scuttle, and returned up-stairs.

But the furniture he had seen, ran on castors across and across Mr. Testator's mind incessantly, when, in the chill hour of five in the morning, he got to bed. He particularly wanted a table to write at, and a table expressly made to be written at, had been the piece of furniture in the foreground of the heap. When his laundress emerged from her burrow in the morning to make his kettle boil, he artfully led up to the subject of cellars and furniture; but the two ideas had evidently no connexion in her mind. When she left him, and he sat at his breakfast, thinking about the furniture, he recalled the rusty state of the padlock, and inferred that the furniture must have been stored in the cellars for a long time—was perhaps forgotten—owner dead, perhaps? After thinking it over, a few days, in the course of which he could pump nothing out of Lyons Inn about the furniture, he became desperate, and resolved to borrow that table. He did so, that night. He had not had the table long, when he determined to borrow an easy-chair; he had not had that long, when he made up his mind to borrow a bookcase; then, a couch; then a carpet and rug. By that time, he felt he was "in furniture stepped in so far," as that it could be no worse to borrow it all. Consequently, he borrowed it all, and locked up the cellar for good. He had always locked it, after every visit. He had carried up every separate article in the dead of the night, and, at the best, had felt as wicked as a Resurrection Man. Every article was blue and furry when brought into his rooms, and he had had, in a murderous and guilty sort of way, to polish it up while London slept.

Mr. Testator lived in his furnished chambers two or three years, or more, gradually lulled himself into the opinion that the furniture was his own. This was his convenient state of mind when, late one night, a step came up the stairs, and a hand passed over his door feeling for his knocker, and then one deep and solemn rap was rapped that might have been a spring in Mr. Testator's easy-chair to shoot him out of it; so promptly was it attended with that effect.

With a candle in his hand, Mr. Testator went to the door, and found there, a very pale and very tall man; a man who stooped; a man with very high shoulders, a very narrow chest, and a very red nose; a shabby-genteel man. He was wrapped in a long threadbare black coat, fastened up the front with more pins than buttons, and under his arm he squeezed an umbrella without handle, as if he were playing bagpipes. He said, "I ask your pardon, but can you tell me ——" and stopped; his eyes resting on some object within the chambers.

"Can I tell you what?" asked Mr. Testator, noting his stoppage with quick alarm.

"I ask your pardon," said the stranger, "but—this is not the inquiry I was going to make—*do* I see in there, any small article of property belonging to *me*?"

Mr. Testator was beginning to stammer that he was not aware— when the visitor slipped past him, into the chambers. There, in a goblin way which froze Mr. Testator to the marrow, he examined, first, the writing-table, and said, "Mine;" then, the easy-chair, and said "Mine;" then, the bookcase, and said, "Mine!" in a word, inspected every item of furniture from the cellar, in succession, and said, "Mine!" Towards the end of this investigation, Mr. Testator perceived that he was sodden with liquor, and that the liquor was gin. He was not unsteady with gin, either in his speech or carriage; but he was stiff with gin in both particulars.

Mr. Testator was in a dreadful state, for (according to his making out of the story) the possible consequences of what he had done in recklessness and hardihood, flashed upon him in their fulness for the first time. When they had stood gazing at one another for a little while, he tremulously began:

"Sir, I am conscious that the fullest explanation, compensation, and restitution, are your due. They shall be yours. Allow me to entreat that, without temper, without even natural irritation on your part, we may have a little——"

"Drop of something to drink," interposed the stranger. "I am agreeable."

Mr. Testator had intended to say, "a little quiet conversation," but with great relief of mind adopted the amendment. He produced a decanter of gin, and was bustling about for hot water and sugar, when he found that his visitor had already drunk half of the decanter's contents. With hot water and sugar the visitor drank the remainder before he had been an hour in the chambers by the chimes of the church of St. Mary in the Strand; and during the process he frequently whispered to himself, "Mine!"

The gin gone and Mr. Testator wondering what was to follow it, the visitor rose and said, with increased stiffness, "At what hour of the morning, sir, will it be convenient?" Mr. Testator hazarded, "At ten?" "Sir," said the visitor, "at ten, to the moment, I shall be here." He then contemplated Mr. Testator somewhat at leisure, and said, "God bless you! How is your wife?" Mr. Testator (who never had a wife) replied with much feeling, "Deeply anxious, poor soul, but otherwise well." The visitor thereupon turned and went away, and fell twice in going down-stairs. From that hour he was never heard of. Whether he was a ghost, or a spectral illusion of conscience, or a drunken man who had no business there, or the drunken rightful owner of the furniture, with a transitory gleam of memory; whether he got safe home, or had no home to get to; whether he died of liquor on the way, or lived in liquor ever afterwards; he never was heard of more. This was the story, received with the furniture and held to be as substantial, by its second possessor in an upper set of chambers in grim Lyons Inn.

It is to be remarked of chambers in general, that they must have been built for chambers, to have the right kind of loneliness. You may make a great dwelling-house very lonely, by isolating suites of rooms and calling them chambers, but you cannot make the true kind of loneliness. In dwelling-houses, there have been family festivals; children have grown in them, girls have bloomed into women in them, courtships and marriages have taken place in them. True chambers never were young, childish, maidenly; never had dolls in them, or rocking-horses, or christenings, or betrothals, or little coffins. Let Gray's Inn identify the child who first touched hands and hearts with Robinson Crusoe, in any one of its many "sets," and that child's little statue, in white marble with a golden inscription, shall be at its service, at my cost and charge, as a drinking fountain for the spirit, to freshen its thirsty square. Let Lincoln's produce from all its houses, a twentieth of the procession derivable from any dwelling-house one-twentieth of its age, of fair young brides who married for love and hope, not settlements, and all the Vice-Chancellors shall thence-forward be kept in nosegays for nothing, on application to the writer hereof. It is not denied that on the terrace of the Adelphi, or in any of the streets of that subterranean-stable-haunted spot, or about Bedford-row, or James-street of that ilk (a grewsome place), or anywhere among the neighbourhoods that have done flowering and have run to seed, you may find Chambers replete with the accom-modations of Solitude, Closeness, and Darkness, where you may be as low-spirited as in the genuine article, and might be as easily murdered with the placid reputation of having merely gone down to the sea-side. But, the many waters of life did run musical in those dry channels once;—among the Inns, never. The only popular legend known in relation to any one of the dull family of Inns, is a dark Old Bailey whisper concerning Clement's, and importing how the black creature who holds the sun-dial there, was a negro who slew his master and built the dismal pile out of the contents of his strong box —for which architectural offence alone he ought to have been con-demned to live in it. But, what populace would waste fancy upon such a place, or on New Inn, Staple Inn, Barnard's Inn, or any of the shabby crew?

The genuine laundress, too, is an institution not to be had in its entirety out of and away from the genuine Chambers. Again, it is not denied that you may be robbed elsewhere. Elsewhere you may have—for money—dishonesty, drunkenness, dirt, laziness, and profound incapacity. But the veritable shining-red-faced shameless laundress; the true Mrs. Sweeny—in figure, colour, texture, and smell, like the old damp family umbrella; the tip-top complicated abomin-ation of stockings, spirits, bonnet, limpness, looseness, and larceny; is only to be drawn at the fountain-head. Mrs. Sweeney is beyond the reach of individual art. It requires the united efforts of several men to ensure that great result, and it is only developed in perfection under an Honourable Society and in an Inn of Court.

NURSE'S STORIES

THERE are not many places that I find it more agreeable to revisit when I am in an idle mood, than some places to which I have never been. For, my acquaintance with those spots is of such long standing, and has ripened into an intimacy of so affectionate a nature, that I take a particular interest in assuring myself that they are unchanged.

I never was in Robinson Crusoe's Island, yet I frequently return there. The colony he established on it soon faded away, and it is uninhabited by any descendants of the grave and courteous Spaniards, or of Will Atkins and the other mutineers, and has relapsed into its original condition. Not a twig of its wicker houses remains, its goats have long run wild again, its screaming parrots would darken the sun with a cloud of many flaming colours if a gun were fired there, no face is ever reflected in the waters of the little creek which Friday swam across when pursued by his two brother cannibals with sharpened stomachs. After comparing notes with other travellers who have similarly revisited the Island and conscientiously inspected it, I have satisfied myself that it contains no vestige of Mr. Atkins's domesticity or theology, though his track on the memorable evening of his landing to set his captain ashore, when he was decoyed about and round about until it was dark, and his boat was stove, and his strength and spirits failed him, is yet plainly to be traced. So is the hill-top on which Robinson was struck dumb with joy when the reinstated captain pointed to the ship, riding within half a mile of the shore, that was to bear him away, in the nine-and-twentieth year of his seclusion in that lonely place. So is the sandy beach on which the memorable footstep was impressed, and where the savages hauled up their canoes when they came ashore for those dreadful public dinners, which led to a dancing worse than speech-making. So is the cave where the flaring eyes of the old goat made such a goblin appearance in the dark. So is the site of the hut where Robinson lived with the dog and the parrot and the cat, and where he endured those first agonies of solitude, which—strange to say—never involved any ghostly fancies; a circumstance so very remarkable, that perhaps he left out something in writing his record? Round hundreds of such objects, hidden in the dense tropical foliage, the tropical sea breaks evermore; and over them the tropical sky, saving in the short rainy season, shines bright and cloudless.

Neither, was I ever belated among wolves, on the borders of France and Spain; nor, did I ever, when night was closing in and the ground was covered with snow, draw up my little company among some felled trees which served as a breastwork, and there fire a train of gunpowder so dexterously that suddenly we had three or four blazing wolves illuminating the darkness around us. Nevertheless, I occasionally go back to that dismal region and perform the feat

again; when indeed to smell the singeing and the frying of the wolves
afire, and to see them setting one another alight as they rush and
tumble, and to behold them rolling in the snow vainly attempting to
put themselves out, and to hear their howlings taken up by all the
echoes as well as by all the unseen wolves within the woods, makes
me tremble.

I was never in the robbers' cave, where Gil Blas lived, but I often
go back there and find the trap-door just as heavy to raise as it used
to be, while that wicked old disabled Black lies everlastingly cursing
in bed. I was never in Don Quixote's study, where he read his books
of chivalry until he rose and hacked at imaginary giants, and then
refreshed himself with great draughts of water, yet you couldn't move
a book in it without my knowledge, or with my consent. I was never
(thank Heaven) in company with the little old woman who hobbled
out of the chest and told the merchant Abudah to go in search of the
Talisman of Oromanes, yet I make it my business to know that she is
well preserved and as intolerable as ever. I was never at the school
where the boy Horatio Nelson got out of bed to steal the pears: not
because he wanted any, but because every other boy was afraid: yet
I have several times been back to this Academy, to see him let down
out of window with a sheet. So with Damascus, and Bagdad, and
Brobingnag (which has the curious fate of being usually misspelt
when written), and Lilliput, and Laputa, and the Nile, and Abyssinia,
and the Ganges, and the North Pole, and many hundreds of places—I
was never at them, yet it is an affair of my life to keep them intact,
and I am always going back to them.

But, when I was in Dullborough one day, revisiting the associations of my childhood as recorded in previous pages of these notes, my
experience in this wise was made quite inconsiderable and of no
account, by the quantity of places and people—utterly impossible
places and people, but none the less alarmingly real—that I found I
had been introduced to by my nurse before I was six years old, and
used to be forced to go back to at night without at all wanting to go.
If we all knew our own minds (in a more enlarged sense than the
popular acceptation of that phrase), I suspect we should find our
nurses responsible for most of the dark corners we are forced to go
back to, against our wills.

The first diabolical character who intruded himself on my peaceful
youth (as I called to mind that day at Dullborough), was a certain
Captain Murderer. This wretch must have been an offshoot of the
Blue Beard family, but I had no suspicion of the consanguinity in
those times. His warning name would seem to have awakened no
general prejudice against him, for he was admitted into the best
society and possessed immense wealth. Captain Murderer's mission
was matrimony, and the gratification of a cannibal appetite with
tender brides. On his marriage morning, he always caused both sides
of the way to church to be planted with curious flowers; and when his
bride said, "Dear Captain Murderer, I never saw flowers like these
before: what are they called?" he answered, "They are called Garnish

for house-lamb," and laughed at his ferocious practical joke in a horrid manner, disquieting the minds of the noble bridal company, with a very sharp show of teeth, then displayed for the first time. He made love in a coach and six, and married in a coach and twelve, and all his horses were milk-white horses with one red spot on the back which he caused to be hidden by the harness. For, the spot *would* come there, though every horse was milk-white when Captain Murderer bought him. And the spot was young bride's blood. (To this terrific point I am indebted for my first personal experience of a shudder and cold beads on the forehead.) When Captain Murderer had made an end of feasting and revelry, and had dismissed the noble guests, and was alone with his wife on the day month after their marriage, it was his whimsical custom to produce a golden rolling-pin and a silver pie-board. Now, there was this special feature in the Captain's courtships, that he always asked if the young lady could make pie-crust; and if she couldn't by nature or education, she was taught. Well. When the bride saw Captain Murderer produce the golden rolling-pin and silver pie-board, she remembered this, and turned up her laced-silk sleeves to make a pie. The Captain brought out a silver pie-dish of immense capacity, and the Captain brought out flour and butter and eggs and all things needful, except the inside of the pie; of materials for the staple of the pie itself, the Captain brought out none. Then said the lovely bride, "Dear Captain Murderer, what pie is this to be?" He replied, "A meat pie." Then said the lovely bride, "Dear Captain Murderer, I see no meat." The Captain humorously retorted, "Look in the glass." She looked in the glass, but still she saw no meat, and then the Captain roared with laughter, and suddenly frowning and drawing his sword, bade her roll out the crust. So she rolled out the crust, dropping large tears upon it all the time because he was so cross, and when she had lined the dish with crust and had cut the crust all ready to fit the top, the Captain called out, "*I* see the meat in the glass!" And the bride looked up at the glass, just in time to see the Captain cutting her head off; and he chopped her in pieces, and peppered her, and salted her, and put her in the pie, and sent it to the baker's, and ate it all, and picked the bones.

Captain Murderer went on in this way, prospering exceedingly, until he came to choose a bride from two twin sisters, and at first didn't know which to choose. For, though one was fair and the other dark, they were both equally beautiful. But the fair twin loved him, and the dark twin hated him, so he chose the fair one. The dark twin would have prevented the marriage if she could, but she couldn't; however, on the night before it, much suspecting Captain Murderer, she stole out and climbed his garden wall, and looked in at his window through a chink in the shutter, and saw him having his teeth filed sharp. Next day she listened all day, and heard him make his joke about the house-lamb. And that day month, he had the paste rolled out, and cut the fair twin's head off, and chopped her in pieces, and peppered her, and salted her, and put her in the pie, and sent it to the baker's, and ate it all, and picked the bones.

Now, the dark twin had had her suspicions much increased by the filing of the Captain's teeth, and again by the house-lamb joke. Putting all things together when he gave out that her sister was dead, she divined the truth, and determined to be revenged. So, she went up to Captain Murderer's house, and knocked at the knocker and pulled at the bell, and when the Captain came to the door, said: "Dear Captain Murderer, marry me next, for I always loved you and was jealous of my sister." The Captain took it as a compliment, and made a polite answer, and the marriage was quickly arranged. On the night before it, the bride again climbed to his window, and again saw him having his teeth filed sharp. At this sight she laughed such a terrible laugh at the chink in the shutter, that the Captain's blood curdled, and he said: "I hope nothing has disagreed with me!" At that, she laughed again, a still more terrible laugh, and the shutter was opened and search made, but she was nimbly gone, and there was no one. Next day they went to church in a coach and twelve, and were married. And that day month, she rolled the pie-crust out, and Captain Murderer cut her head off, and chopped her in pieces, and peppered her, and salted her, and put her in the pie, and sent it to the baker's, and ate it all, and picked the bones.

But before she began to roll out the paste she had taken a deadly poison of a most awful character, distilled from toads' eyes and spiders' knees; and Captain Murderer had hardly picked her last bone, when he began to swell, and to turn blue, and to be all over spots, and to scream. And he went on swelling and turning bluer, and being more all over spots and screaming, until he reached from floor to ceiling and from wall to wall; and then, at one o'clock in the morning he blew up with a loud explosion. At the sound of it, all the milk-white horses in the stables broke their halters and went mad, and then they galloped over everybody in Captain Murderer's house (beginning with the family blacksmith who had filed his teeth) until the whole were dead, and then they galloped away.

Hundreds of times did I hear this legend of Captain Murderer, in my early youth, and added hundreds of times was there a mental compulsion upon me in bed, to peep in at his window as the dark twin peeped, and to revisit his horrible house, and look at him in his blue and spotty and screaming stage, as he reached from floor to ceiling and from wall to wall. The young woman who brought me acquainted with Captain Murderer had a fiendish enjoyment of my terrors, and used to begin, I remember—as a sort of introductory overture—by clawing the air with both hands, and uttering a long low hollow groan. So acutely did I suffer from this ceremony in combination with this infernal Captain, that I sometimes used to plead I thought I was hardly strong enough and old enough to hear the story again just yet. But, she never spared me one word of it, and indeed commended the awful chalice to my lips as the only preservative known to science against "The Black Cat"—a weird and glaring-eyed supernatural Tom who was reputed to prowl about the world by night, sucking the breath of infancy, and who was endowed with a special thirst (as I was given to understand) for mine.

This female bard—may she have been repaid my debt of obligation to her in the matter of nightmares and perspirations!—reappears in my memory as the daughter of a shipwright. Her name was Mercy, though she had none on me. There was something of a shipbuilding flavour in the following story. As it always recurs to me in a vague association with calomel pills, I believe it to have been reserved for dull nights when I was low with medicine.

There was once a shipwright, and he wrought in a Government Yard, and his name was Chips. And his father's name before him was Chips, and *his* father's name before *him* was Chips, and they were all Chipses. And Chips the father had sold himself to the Devil for an iron pot and a bushel of tenpenny nails and half a ton of copper and a rat that could speak; and Chips the grandfather had sold himself to the Devil for an iron pot and a bushel of tenpenny nails and half a ton of copper and a rat that could speak; and Chips the great-grandfather had disposed of himself in the same direction on the same terms; and the bargain had run in the family for a long, long time. So, one day, when young Chips was at work in the Dock Slip all alone, down in the dark hold of an old Seventy-four that was haled up for repairs, the Devil presented himself, and remarked:

> " A Lemon has pips,
> And a Yard has ships,
> And *I*'ll have Chips!"

(I don't know why, but this fact of the Devil's expressing himself in rhyme was peculiarly trying to me.) Chips looked up when he heard the words, and there he saw the Devil with saucer eyes that squinted on a terrible great scale, and that struck out sparks of blue fire continually, and whenever he winked his eyes, showers of blue sparks came out, and his eyelashes made a clattering like flints and steels striking lights. And hanging over one of his arms by the handle was an iron pot, and under that arm was a bushel of tenpenny nails, and under his other arm was half a ton of copper, and sitting on one of his shoulders was a rat that could speak. So, the Devil said again:

> " A Lemon has pips,
> And a Yard has ships,
> And *I*'ll have Chips!"

(The invariable effect of this alarming tautology on the part of the Evil Spirit was to deprive me of my senses for some moments.) So, Chips answered never a word, but went on with his work. "What are you doing, Chips?" said the rat that could speak. "I am putting in new planks where you and your gang have eaten old away," said Chips. "But we'll eat them too," said the rat that could speak; "and we'll let in the water and drown the crew, and we'll eat them too." Chips, being only a shipwright, and not a Man-of-war's man, said, "You are welcome to it." But he couldn't keep his eyes off the half a ton of copper or the bushel of tenpenny nails; for nails and copper

are a shipwright's sweethearts, and shipwrights will run away with
them whenever they can. So, the Devil said, "I see what you are
looking at, Chips, You had better strike the bargain. You know the
terms. Your father before you was well acquainted with them, and
so were your grandfather and great-grandfather before him." Says
Chips, "I like the copper, and I like the nails, and I don't mind the
pot, but I don't like the rat." Says the Devil, fiercely, "You can't
have the metal without him—and *he's* a curiosity. I'm going." Chips,
afraid of losing the half a ton of copper and the bushel of nails, then
said, "Give us hold!" So, he got the copper and the nails and the pot
and the rat that could speak, and the Devil vanished. Chips sold the
copper, and he sold the nails, and he would have sold the pot; but
whenever he offered it for sale, the rat was in it, and the dealers
dropped it, and would have nothing to say to the bargain. So, Chips
resolved to kill the rat, and, being at work in the Yard one day with
a great kettle of hot pitch on one side of him and the iron pot with the
rat in it on the other, he turned the scalding pitch into the pot, and
filled it full. Then, he kept his eye upon it till it cooled and hardened,
and then he let it stand for twenty days, and then he heated the
pitch again and turned it back into the kettle, and then he sank the
pot in water for twenty days more, and then he got the smelters to
put it in the furnace for twenty days more, and then they gave it him
out, red hot, and looking like red-hot glass instead of iron—yet there
was the rat in it, just the same as ever! And the moment it caught
his eye, it said with a jeer:

> " A Lemon has pips,
> And a Yard has ships,
> And *I'll* have Chips!"

(For this Refrain I had waited since its last appearance, with inexpressible horror, which now culminated.) Chips now felt certain in
his own mind that the rat would stick to him; the rat, answering his
thought, said, "I will—like pitch!"

Now as the rat leaped out of the pot when it had spoken, and made
off, Chips began to hope that it wouldn't keep its word. But, a terrible
thing happened next day. For, when dinner-time came, and the Dock-
bell rang to strike work, he put his rule into the long pocket at the
side of his trousers, and there he found a rat—not that rat, but another rat. And in his hat, he found another; and in his pocket handkerchief, another; and in the sleeves of his coat, when he pulled it on
to go to dinner, two more. And from that time he found himself so
frightfully intimate with all the rats in the Yard, that they climbed
up his legs when he was at work, and sat on his tools while he used
them. And they could all speak to one another, and he understood
what they said. And they got into his lodgings, and into his bed, and
into his teapot, and into his beer, and into his boots. And he was
going to be married to a corn-chandler's daughter; and when he gave
her a work-box he had himself made for her, a rat jumped out of it;
and when he put his arm round her waist, a rat clung about her; so

the marriage was broken off, though the banns were already twice
put up—which the parish clerk well remembers, for, as he handed the
book to the clergyman for the second time of asking, a large fat rat
ran over the leaf. (By this time a special cascade of rats was rolling
down my back, and the whole of my small listening person was over-
run with them. At intervals ever since, I have been morbidly afraid
of my own pocket, lest my exploring hand should find a specimen or
two of those vermin in it.)

You may believe that all this was very terrible to Chips; but even
all this was not the worst. He knew besides, what the rats were doing,
wherever they were. So, sometimes he would cry aloud, when he was
at his club at night, "Oh! Keep the rats out of the convicts' burying-
ground! Don't let them do that!" Or, "There's one of them at the
cheese down-stairs!" Or, "There's two of them smelling at the baby
in the garret!" Or, other things of that sort. At last, he was voted
mad, and lost his work in the Yard, and could get no other work.
But, King George wanted men, so before very long he got pressed
for a sailor. And so he was taken off in a boat one evening to his ship,
lying at Spithead, ready to sail. And so the first thing he made out
in her as he got near her, was the figure-head of the old Seventy-four,
where he had seen the Devil. She was called the Argonaut, and they
rowed right under the bowsprit where the figure-head of the Argonaut,
with a sheepskin in his hand and a blue gown on, was looking out to
sea; and sitting staring on his forehead was the rat who could speak,
and his exact words were these: "Chips ahoy! Old boy! We've pretty
well eat them too, and we'll drown the crew, and will eat them too!"
(Here I always became exceedingly faint, and would have asked for
water, but that I was speechless.)

The ship was bound for the Indies; and if you don't know where
that is, you ought to, and angels will never love you. (Here I felt
myself an outcast from a future state.) The ship set sail that very
night, and she sailed, and sailed, and sailed. Chip's feelings were
dreadful. Nothing ever equalled his terrors. No wonder. At last, one
day he asked leave to speak to the Admiral. The Admiral giv' leave.
Chips went down on his knees in the Great State Cabin. "Your
Honour, unless your Honour, without a moment's loss of time,
makes sail for the nearest shore, this is a doomed ship, and her name
is the Coffin!" "Young man, your words are a madman's words."
"Your Honour no; they are nibbling us away." "They?" "Your
Honour, them dreadful rats. Dust and hollowness where solid oak
ought to be! Rats nibbling a grave for every man on board! Oh!
Does your Honour love your Lady and your pretty children?" "Yes,
my man, to be sure." "Then, for God's sake, make for the nearest
shore, for at this present moment the rats are all stopping in their
work, and are all looking straight towards you with bare teeth, and
are all saying to one another that you shall never, never, never, never,
see your Lady and your children more." "My poor fellow, you are a
case for the doctor. Sentry, take care of this man!"

So, he was bled and he was blistered, and he was this and that, for six whole days and nights. So, then he again asked leave to speak to the Admiral. The Admiral giv' leave. He went down on his knees in the Great State Cabin. "Now, Admiral, you must die! You took no warning; you must die! The rats are never wrong in their calculations, and they make out that they'll be through, at twelve to-night. So, you must die!—With me and all the rest!" And so at twelve o'clock there was a great leak reported in the ship, and a torrent of water rushed in and nothing could stop it, and they all went down, every living soul. And what the rats—being water-rats—left of Chips, at last floated to shore, and sitting on him was an immense overgrown rat, laughing, that dived when the corpse touched the beach and never came up. And there was a deal of seaweed on the remains. And if you get thirteen bits of seaweed, and dry them and burn them in the fire, they will go off like in these thirteen words as plain as plain can be:

> "A Lemon has pips,
> And a Yard has ships,
> And *I*'ve got Chips!"

The same female bard—descended, possibly, from those terrible old Scalds who seem to have existed for the express purpose of addling the brains of mankind when they begin to investigate languages—made a standing pretence which greatly assisted in forcing me back to a number of hideous places that I would by all means have avoided. This pretence was, that all her ghost stories had occurred to her own relations. Politeness towards a meritorious family, therefore, forbade my doubting them, and they acquired an air of authentication that impaired my digestive powers for life. There was a narrative concerning an unearthly animal foreboding death, which appeared in the open street to a parlourmaid who "went to fetch the beer" for supper: first (as I now recall it) assuming the likeness of a black dog, and gradually rising on its hind-legs and swelling into the semblance of some quadruped greatly surpassing a hippopotamus: which apparition—not because I deemed it in the least improbable, but because I felt it to be really too large to bear—I feebly endeavoured to explain away. But, on Mercy's retorting with wounded dignity that the parlour-maid was her own sister-in-law, I perceived there was no hope, and resigned myself to this zoological phenomenon as one of my many pursuers. There was another narrative describing the apparition of a young woman who came out of a glass-case and haunted another young woman until the other young woman questioned it and elicited that its bones (Lord! To think of its being so particular about its bones!) were buried under the glass-case, whereas she required them to be interred, with every Undertaking solemnity up to twenty-four pound ten, in another particular place. This narrative I considered I had a personal interest in disproving, because we had glass-cases at home, and how, otherwise, was I to be guaranteed from the intrusion of young women requiring *me* to bury them up to twenty-four pound ten, when I had only twopence a week? But my remorseless nurse cut the ground from under my tender feet, by informing me that She was the other young woman; and I couldn't say "I don't believe you;" it was not possible.

Such are a few of the uncommercial journeys that I was forced to make, against my will, when I was very young and unreasoning. And really, as to the latter part of them, it is not so very long ago— now I come to think of it—that I was asked to undertake them once again, with a steady countenance.

XVI

ARCADIAN LONDON

BEING in a humour for complete solitude and uninterrupted meditation this autumn, I have taken a lodging for six weeks in the most unfrequented part of England—in a word, in London.

The retreat into which I have drawn myself, is Bond-street. From this lonely spot I make pilgrimages into the surrounding wilderness, and traverse extensive tracts of the Great Desert. The first solemn feeling of isolation overcome, the first oppressive consciousness of profound retirement conquered, I enjoy that sense of freedom, and feel reviving within me that latent wildness of the original savage, which has been (upon the whole somewhat frequently) noticed by Travellers.

My lodgings are at a hatter's—my own hatter's. After exhibiting no articles in his window for some weeks, but sea-side wide-awakes, shooting-caps, and a choice of rough water-proof head-gear for the moors and mountains, he has put upon the heads of his family as much of this stock as they could carry, and has taken them off to the Isle of Thanet. His young man alone remains—and remains alone— in the shop. The young man has let out the fire at which the irons are heated, and, saving his strong sense of duty, I see no reason why he should take the shutters down.

Happily for himself and his country, the young man is a Volunteer; most happily for himself, or I think he would become the prey of a settled melancholy. For, to live surrounded by human hats, and alienated from human heads to fit them on, is surely a great endurance. But, the young man, sustained by practising his exercise, and by constantly furbishing up his regulation plume (it is unnecessary to observe that, as a hatter, he is in a cock's-feather corps), is resigned, and uncomplaining. On a Saturday, when he closes early and gets his Knickerbockers on, he is even cheerful. I am gratefully particular in this reference to him, because he is my companion through many peaceful hours. My hatter has a desk up certain steps behind his counter, enclosed like the clerk's desk at Church. I shut myself into this place of seclusion, after breakfast, and meditate. At such times I observe the young man loading an imaginary rifle with the greatest precision, and maintaining a most galling and destructive fire upon the national enemy. I thank him publicly for his companionship and his patriotism.

The simple character of my life, and the calm nature of the scenes by which I am surrounded, occasion me to rise early. I go forth in my slippers, and promenade the pavement. It is pastoral to feel the freshness of the air in the uninhabited town, and to appreciate the shepherdess character of the few milkwomen who purvey so little milk that it would be worth nobody's while to adulterate it, if anybody were left to undertake the task. On the crowded sea-shore, the great demand for milk, combined with the strong local temptation of chalk, would betray itself in the lowered quality of the article. In Arcadian London I derive it from the cow.

The Arcadian simplicity of the metropolis altogether, and the primitive ways into which it has fallen in this autumnal Golden Age, make it entirely new to me. Within a few hundred yards of my retreat, is the house of a friend who maintains a most sumptuous butler. I never, until yesterday, saw that butler out of superfine black broad cloth. Until yesterday, I never saw him off duty, never saw him (he is the best of butlers) with the appearance of having any mind for anything but the glory of his master and his master's friends. Yesterday morning, walking in my slippers near the house of which he is the prop and ornament—a house now a waste of shutters—I encountered that butler, also in his slippers, and in a shooting suit of one colour, and in a low-crowned straw-hat, smoking an early cigar. He felt that we had formerly met in another state of existence, and that we were translated into a new sphere. Wisely and well, he passed me without recognition. Under his arm he carried the morning paper, and shortly afterwards I saw him sitting on a rail in the pleasant open landscape of Regent-street, perusing it at his ease under the ripening sun.

My landlord having taken his whole establishment to be salted down, I am waited on by an elderly woman labouring under a chronic sniff, who, at the shadowy hour of half-past nine o'clock of every evening, gives admittance at the street door to a meagre and mouldy old man whom I have never yet seen detached from a flat pint of beer in a pewter pot. The meagre and mouldy old man is her husband, and the pair have a dejected consciousness that they are not justified in appearing on the surface of the earth. They come out of some hole when London empties itself, and go in again when it fills. I saw them arrive on the evening when I myself took possession, and they arrived with the flat pint of beer, and their bed in a bundle. The old man is a weak old man, and appeared to me to get the bed down the kitchen stairs by tumbling down with and upon it. They make their bed in the lowest and remotest corner of the basement, and they smell of bed, and have no possession but bed: unless it be (which I rather infer from an under-current of flavour in them) cheese. I know their name, through the chance of having called the wife's attention, at half-past nine on the second evening of our acquaintance, to the circumstance of there being some one at the house door; when she apologetically explained, "It's only Mr. Klem." What becomes of Mr. Klem all day, or when he goes out, or why, is a mystery I cannot penetrate; but at half-past nine he never fails to turn up on the door-step with the flat pint of beer. And the pint of beer, flat as it is, is so much more important than himself, that it always seems to my fancy as if it had found him drivelling his way below, Mr. Klem never goes down the middle of the passage, like another Christian, but shuffles against the wall as if entreating me to take notice that he is occupying as little space as possible in the house; and whenever I come upon him face to face, he backs from me in fascinated confusion. The most extraordinary circumstance I have traced in connexion with this aged couple, is, that there is a Miss Klem, their daughter, apparently ten years older than either of them, who has also a bed and smells of it, and carries it about the earth at dusk and hides it in deserted houses. I came into this piece of knowledge through Mrs. Klem's beseeching me to sanction the sheltering of Miss Klem under that roof for a single night, "between her takin' care of the upper part in Pall Mall which the family of his back, and a 'ouse in Serjameses-street, which the family of leaves towng ter-morrer." I gave my gracious consent (having nothing that I know of to do with it), and in the shadowy hours Miss Klem became perceptible on the door-step, wrestling with a bed in a bundle. Where she made it up for the night I cannot positively state, but, I think, in a sink. I know that with the instinct of a reptile or an insect, she stowed it and herself away in deep obscurity. In the Klem family, I have noticed another remarkable gift of nature, and that is a power they possess of converting everything into flue. Such broken victuals as they take by stealth, appear (whatever the nature of the viands) invariably to generate flue; and even the nightly pint of beer, instead of assimilating naturally, strikes me as breaking out in that form, equally on the shabby gown of Mrs. Klem, and the threadbare coat of her husband.

Mrs. Klem has no idea of my name—as to Mr. Klem he has no idea of anything—and only knows me as her good gentleman. Thus, if doubtful whether I am in my room or no, Mrs. Klem taps at the door and says, "Is my good gentleman here?" Or, if a messenger desiring to see me were consistent with my solitude, she would show him in with "Here is my good gentleman." I find this to be a generic custom. For, I meant to have observed before now, that in its Arcadian time all my part of London is indistinctly pervaded by the Klem species. They creep about with beds, and go to bed in miles of deserted houses. They hold no companship except that sometimes, after dark, two of them will emerge from opposite houses, and meet in the middle of the road as on neutral ground, or will peep from adjoining houses over an interposing barrier of area railings, and compare a few reserved mistrustful notes respecting their good ladies or good gentlemen. This I have discovered in the course of various solitary rambles I have taken Northward from my retirement, along the awful perspectives of Wimpole-street, Harley-street, and similar frowning regions. Their effect would scarcely be distinguishable from that of the primeval forests, but for the Klem stragglers; these may be dimly observed, when the heavy shadows fall, flitting to and fro, putting up the door-chain, taking in the pint of beer, lowering like phantoms at the dark parlour windows, or secretly consorting underground with the dust-bin and the water-cistern.

In the Burlington Arcade, I observe, with peculiar pleasure, a primitive state of manners to have superseded the baneful influences of ultra civilisation. Nothing can surpass the innocence of the ladies' shoe-shops, the artificial-flower repositories, and the head-dress depôts. They are in strange hands at this time of year—hands of unaccustomed persons, who are imperfectly acquainted with the prices of the goods, and contemplate them with unsophisticated delight and wonder. The children of these virtuous people exchange familiarities in the Arcade, and temper the asperity of the two tall beadles. Their youthful prattle blends in an unwonted manner with the harmonious shade of the scene, and the general effect is, as of the voices of birds in a grove. In this happy restoration of the golden time, it has been my privilege even to see the bigger beadle's wife. She brought him his dinner in a basin, and he ate it in his arm-chair, and afterwards fell asleep like a satiated child. At Mr. Truefitt's, the excellent hairdresser's, they are learning French to beguile the time; and even the few solitaries left on guard at Mr. Atkinson's, the per-fumer's round the corner (generally the most inexorable gentleman in London, and the most scornful of three-and-sixpence), condescend a little, as they drowsily bide or recall their turn for chasing the ebbing Neptune on the ribbed sea-sand. From Messrs. Hunt and Roskell's, the jewellers, all things are absent but the precious stones, and the gold and silver, and the soldierly pensioner at the door with his decorated breast. I might stand night and day for a month to come, in Saville-row, with my tongue out, yet not find a doctor to look at it for love or money. The dentists' instruments are rusting in their drawers, and their horrible cool parlours, where people pretend to read the Every-Day Book and not to be afraid, are doing penance for their grimness in white sheets. The light-weight of shrewd appearance, with one eye always shut up, as if he were eating a sharp gooseberry in all seasons, who usually stands at the gateway of the livery stables on very little legs under a very large waistcoat, has gone to Doncaster. Of such undesigning aspect is his guileless yard now, with its gravel and scarlet beans, and the yellow Break housed under a glass roof in a corner, that I almost believe I could not be taken in there, if I tried. In the places of business of the great tailors, the cheval-glasses are dim and dusty for lack of being looked into. Ranges of brown paper coat and waistcoat bodies look as funereal as if they were the hatch-ments of the customers with whose names they are inscribed; the measuring tapes hang idle on the wall; the order-taker, left on the hopeless chance of some one looking in, yawns in the last extremity over the book of patterns, as if he were trying to read that enter-taining library. The hotels in Brook-street have no one in them, and the staffs of servants stare disconsolately for next season out of all the windows. The very man who goes about like an erect

Turtle, between two boards recommendatory of the Sixteen Shilling Trousers, is aware of himself as a hollow mockery, and eats filberts, while he leans his hinder shell against a wall.

Among these tranquillising objects, it is my delight to walk and meditate. Soothed by the repose around me, I wander insensibly to considerable distances, and guide myself back by the stars. Thus, I enjoy the contrast of a few still partially inhabited and busy spots where all the lights are not fled, where all the garlands are not dead, whence all but I have not departed. Then, does it appear to me that in this age three things are clamorously required of Man in the miscellaneous thoroughfares of the metropolis. Firstly, that he have his boots cleaned. Secondly, that he eat a penny ice. Thirdly, that he get himself photographed. Then do I speculate, What have those seam-worn artists been who stand at the photograph doors in Greek caps, sample in hand, and mysteriously salute the public—the female public with a pressing tenderness—to come in and be "took"? What did they do with their greasy blandishments, before the era of cheap photography? Of what class were their precious victims, and how victimised? And how did they get, and how did they pay for, that large collection of likenesses, all purporting to have been taken inside, with the taking of none of which had that establishment any more to do than with the taking of Delhi?

But, these are small oases, and I am soon back again in metropolitan Arcadia. It is my impression that much of its serene and peaceful character is attributable to the absence of customary Talk. How do I know but there may be subtle influences in Talk, to vex the souls of men who don't hear it? How do I know but that Talk, five, ten, twenty miles off, may get into the air and disagree with me? If I rise from my bed, vaguely troubled and wearied and sick of my life, in the session of Parliament, who shall say that my noble friend, my right reverend friend, my right honourable friend, my honourable friend, my honourable and learned friend, or my honourable and gallant friend, may not be responsible for that effect upon my nervous system? Too much Ozone in the air, I am informed and fully believe (though I have no idea what it is), would affect me in a marvellously disagreeable way; why may not too much Talk? I don't see or hear the Ozone; I don't see or hear the Talk. And there is so much Talk; so much too much; such loud cry, and such scant supply of wool ; such a deal of fleecing, and so little fleece. Hence! in the arcadian season, I find it a delicious triumph to walk down to deserted Westminster, and see the Courts shut up; to walk a little further and see the Two Houses shut up; to stand in the Abbey Yard, like the New Zealander of the grand English History (concerning which unfortunate man, a whole rookery of mares' nests is generally being discovered), and gloat upon the ruins of Talk. Returning to my primitive solitude and lying down to sleep, my grateful heart expands with the consciousness that there is no adjourned Debate, no ministerial explanation, nobody to give notice of intention to ask the noble Lord at the head of her Majesty's Government five-and-twenty bootless questions in one, no term time with legal argument, no Nisi Prius with eloquent appeal to British Jury; that the air will to-morrow, and to-morrow and to-morrow, remain untroubled by this superabundant generating of Talk. In a minor degree it is a delicious triumph to me to go into the club, and see the carpets up, and the Bores and the other dust dispersed to the four winds. Again New Zealander-like, I stand on the cold hearth, and say in the solitude, "Here I watched Bore A 1, with voice always mysteriously low and head always mysteriously drooped, whispering political secrets into the ears of Adam's confiding children. Accursed be his memory for ever and a day!"

But, I have all this time been coming to the point, that the happy nature of my retirement is most sweetly expressed in its being the abode of Love. It is, as it were, an inexpensive Agapemone: nobody's speculation: everybody's profit. The one great result of the resumption of primitive habits, and (convertible terms) the not having much to do, is, the abounding of Love.

The Klem species are incapable of the softer emotions; probably, in that low nomadic race, the softer emotions have all degenerated into flue. But, with this exception, all the sharers of my retreat make love.

I have mentioned Saville-row. We all know the Doctor's servant. We all know what a respectable man he is, what a hard dry man, what a firm man, what a confidential man: how he lets us into the waiting-room, like a man who knows minutely what is the matter with us, but from whom the rack should not wring the secret. In the prosaic "season," he has distinctly the appearance of a man conscious of money in the savings bank, and taking his stand on his respectability with both feet. At that time it is as impossible to associate him with relaxation, or any human weakness, as it is to meet his eye without feeling guilty of indisposition. In the blest Arcadian time, how changed! I have seen him, in a pepper-and-salt jacket—jacket—and, drab trousers, with his arm round the waist of a bootmaker's housemaid, smiling in open day. I have seen him at the pump by the Albany unsolicitedly pumping for two fair young creatures, whose figures as they bent over their cans, were—if I may be allowed an original expression—a model for the sculptor. I have seen him trying the piano in the Doctor's drawing-room with his forefinger, and have heard him humming tunes in praise of lovely woman. I have seen him seated on a fire-engine, and going (obviously in search of excitement) to a fire. I saw him, one moonlight evening when the peace and purity of our Arcadian west were at their height, polk with the lovely daughter of a cleaner of gloves, from the door-steps of his own residence, across Saville-row, round by Clifford-street and Old Burlington-street, back to Burlington-gardens. Is this the Golden Age revived, or Iron London?

The Dentist's servant. Is that man no mystery to us, no type of invisible power? The tremendous individual knows (who else does?) what is done with the extracted teeth; he knows what goes on in the little room where something is always being washed or filed; he knows what warm spicy infusion is put into the comfortable tumbler from which we rinse our wounded mouth, with a gap in it that feels a foot wide; he knows whether the thing we spit into is a fixture communicating with the Thames, or could be cleared away for a dance; he sees the horrible parlour when there are no patients in it, and he could reveal, if he would, what becomes of the Every-Day Book then. The conviction of my coward conscience when I see that man in a professional light, is, that he knows all the statistics of my teeth and gums, my double teeth, my single teeth, my stopped teeth, and my sound. In this Arcadian rest, I am fearless of him as of a harmless, powerless creature in a Scotch cap, who adores a young lady in a voluminous crinoline, at a neighbouring billiard-room, and whose passion would be uninfluenced if every one of her teeth were false. They may be. He takes them all on trust.

In secluded corners of the place of my seclusion, there are little shops withdrawn from public curiosity, and never two together, where servants' perquisites are bought. The cook may dispose of grease at these modest and convenient marts; the butler, of bottles; the valet and lady's maid, of clothes; most servants, indeed, of most things they may happen to lay hold of. I have been told that in sterner times loving correspondence, otherwise interdicted, may be maintained by letter through the agency of some of these useful establishments. In the Arcadian autumn, no such device is necessary. Everybody loves, and openly and blamelessly loves. My landlord's young man loves the whole of one side of the way of Old Bond-street, and is beloved several doors up New Bond-street besides. I never look out of window but I see kissing of hands going on all around me. It is the morning custom to glide from shop to shop and exchange tender sentiments; it is the evening custom for couples to stand hand in hand at house doors, or roam, linked in that flowery manner, through the unpeopled streets. There is nothing else to do but love; and what there is to do, is done.

In unison with this pursuit, a chaste simplicity obtains in the domestic habits of Arcadia. Its few scattered people dine early, live moderately, sup socially, and sleep soundly. It is rumoured that the Beadles of the Arcade, from being the mortal enemies of boys, have signed with tears an address to Lord Shaftesbury, and subscribed to a ragged school. No wonder! For, they might turn their heavy maces into crooks and tend sheep in the Arcade, to the purling of the water-carts as they give the thirsty streets much more to drink than they can carry.

A happy Golden Age, and a serene tranquillity. Charming picture, but it will fade. The iron age will return, London will come back to town, if I show my tongue then in Saville-row for half a minute I shall be prescribed for, the Doctor's man and the Dentist's man will then pretend that these days of unprofessional innocence never existed. Where Mr. and Mrs. Klem and their bed will be at that time, passes human knowledge; but my hatter hermitage will then know them no more, nor will it then know me. The desk at which I have written these meditations will retributively assist at the making out of my account, and the wheels of gorgeous carriages and the hoofs of high-stepping horses will crush the silence out of Bond-street—will grind Arcadia away, and give it to the elements in granite powder.

XVII

THE ITALIAN PRISONER

THE rising of the Italian people from under their unutterable wrongs, and the tardy burst of day upon them after the long long night of oppression that has darkened their beautiful country, have naturally caused my mind to dwell often of late on my own small wanderings in Italy. Connected with them, is a curious little drama, in which the character I myself sustained was so very subordinate that I may relate its story without any fear of being suspected of self-display. It is strictly a true story.

I am newly arrived one summer evening, in a certain small town on the Mediterranean. I have had my dinner at the inn, and I and the mosquitoes are coming out into the streets together. It is far from Naples; but a bright, brown, plump little woman-servant at the inn, is a Neapolitan, and is so vivaciously expert in pantomimic action, that in the single moment of answering my request to have a pair of shoes cleaned which I have left up-stairs, she plies imaginary brushes, and goes completely through the motions of polishing the shoes up, and laying them at my feet. I smile at the brisk little woman in perfect satisfaction with her briskness; and the brisk little woman, amiably pleased with me because I am pleased with her, claps her hands and laughs delightfully. We are in the inn yard. As the little woman's bright eyes sparkle on the cigarette I am smoking, I make bold to offer her one; she accepts it none the less merrily, because I touch a most charming little dimple in her fat cheek, with its light paper end. Glancing up at the many green lattices to assure herself that the mistress is not looking on, the little woman then puts her two little dimple arms a-kimbo, and stands on tiptoe to light her cigarette at mine. "And now, dear little sir," says she, puffing out smoke in a most innocent and cherubic manner, "keep quite straight on, take the first to the right, and probably you will see him standing at his door."

I have a commission to "him," and I have been inquiring about him. I have carried the commission about Italy several months. Before I left England, there came to me one night a certain generous and gentle English nobleman (he is dead in these days when I relate the story, and exiles have lost their best British friend), with this request: "Whenever you come to such a town, will you seek out one Giovanni Carlavero who keeps a little wine-shop there, mention my name to him suddenly, and observe how it affects him?" I accepted the trust, and am on my way to discharge it.

The sirocco has been blowing all day, and it is a hot unwholesome

evening with no cool sea-breeze. Mosquitoes and fire-flies are lively
enough, but most other creatures are faint. The coquettish airs of
pretty young women in the tiniest and wickedest of dolls' straw hats,
who lean out at opened lattice blinds, are almost the only airs stirring.
Very ugly and haggard old women with distaffs, and with a grey tow
upon them that looks as if they were spinning out their own hair (I
suppose they were once pretty, too, but it is very difficult to believe
so), sit on the footway leaning against house walls. Everybody who
has come for water to the fountain, stays there, and seems incapable
of any such energetic idea as going home. Vespers are over, though
not so long but that I can smell the heavy resinous incense as I pass
the church. No man seems to be at work, save the coppersmith. In an
Italian town he is always at work, and always thumping in the dead-
liest manner.

I keep straight on, and come in due time to the first on the right: a
narrow dull street, where I see a well-favoured man of good stature
and military bearing, in a great cloak, standing at a door. Drawing
nearer to this threshold, I see it is the threshold of a small wine-shop;
and I can just make out, in the dim light, the inscription that it is
kept by Giovanni Carlavero.

I touch my hat to the figure in the cloak, and pass in, and draw a
stool to a little table. The lamp (just such another as they dig out of
Pompeii) is lighted, but the place is empty. The figure in the cloak
has followed me in, and stands before me.

"The master?"

"At your service, sir."

"Please to give me a glass of the wine of the country."

He turns to a little counter, to get it. As his striking face is pale,
and his action is evidently that of an enfeebled man, I remark that I
fear he has been ill. It is not much, he courteously and gravely
answers, though bad while it lasts: the fever.

As he sets the wine on the little table, to his manifest surprise I lay
my hand on the back of his, look him in the face, and say in a low
voice: "I am an Englishman, and you are acquainted with a friend of
mine. Do you recollect——?" and I mentioned the name of my
generous countryman.

Instantly, he utters a loud cry, bursts into tears, and falls on his
knees at my feet, clasping my legs in both his arms and bowing his
head to the ground.

Some years ago, this man at my feet, whose over-fraught heart is
heaving as if it would burst from his breast, and whose tears are wet
upon the dress I wear, was a galley-slave in the North of Italy. He
was a political offender, having been concerned in the then last rising,
and was sentenced to imprisonment for life. That he would have died
in his chains, is certain, but for the circumstance that the Englishman happened to visit his prison.

It was one of the vile old prisons of Italy, and a part of it was below
the waters of the harbour. The place of his confinement was an
arched under-ground and under-water gallery, with a grill-gate at the

entrance, through which it received such light and air as it got. Its condition was insufferably foul, and a stranger could hardly breathe in it, or see in it with the aid of a torch. At the upper end of this dungeon, and consequently in the worst position, as being the furthest removed from light and air, the Englishman first beheld him, sitting on an iron bedstead to. which he was chained by a heavy chain. His countenance impressed the Englishman as having nothing in common with the faces of the malefactors with whom he was associated, and he talked with him, and learnt how he came to be there.

When the Englishman emerged from the dreadful den into the light of day, he asked his conductor, the governor of the jail, why Giovanni Carlavero was put into the worst place?

"Because he is particularly recommended," was the stringent answer.

"Recommended, that is to say, for death?"

"Excuse me; particularly recommended," was again the answer.

"He has a bad tumour in his neck, no doubt occasioned by the hardship of his miserable life. If he continues to be neglected, and he remains where he is, it will kill him."

"Excuse me, I can do nothing. He is particularly recommended."

The Englishman was staying in that town, and he went to his home there; but the figure of this man chained to the bedstead made it no home, and destroyed his rest and peace. He was an Englishman of an extraordinarily tender heart, and he could not bear the picture. He went back to the prison gate; went back again and again, and talked to the man and cheered him. He used his utmost influence to get the man unchained from the bedstead, were it only for ever so short a time in the day, and permitted to come to the grate. It took a long time, but the Englishman's station, personal character, and steadiness of purpose, wore out opposition so far, and that grace was at last accorded. Through the bars, when he could thus get light upon the tumour, the Englishman lanced it, and it did well, and healed. His strong interest in the prisoner had greatly increased by this time, and he formed the desperate resolution that he would exert his utmost self-devotion and use his utmost efforts, to get Carlavero pardoned.

If the prisoner had been a brigand and a murderer, if he had committed every non-political crime in the Newgate Calendar and out of it, nothing would have been easier than for a man of any court or priestly influence to obtain his release. As it was, nothing could have been more difficult. Italian authorities, and English authorities who had interest with them, alike assured the Englishman that his object was hopeless. He met with nothing but evasion, refusal, and ridicule. His political prisoner became a joke in the place. It was especially observable that English Circumlocution, and English Society on its travels, were as humorous on the subject as Circumlocution and Society may be on any subject without loss of caste. But, the Englishman possessed (and proved it well in his life) a courage very uncommon among us: he had not the least fear of being considered a bore, in a good humane cause. So he went on persistently trying, and trying, and trying, to get Giovanni Carlavero out. That prisoner had been rigorously re-chained, after the tumour operation, and it was not likely that his miserable life could last very long.

One day, when all the town knew about the Englishman and his political prisoner, there came to the Englishman, a certain sprightly Italian Advocate of whom he had some knowledge; and he made this strange proposal. "Give me a hundred pounds to obtain Carlavero's release. I think I can get him a pardon, with that money. But I cannot tell you what I am going to do with the money, nor must you ever ask me the question if I succeed, nor must you ever ask me for an account of the money if I fail." The Englishman decided to hazard the hundred pounds. He did so, and heard not another word of the matter. For half a year and more, the Advocate made no sign, and never once "took on" in any way, to have the subject on his mind. The Englishman was then obliged to change his residence to another and more famous town in the North of Italy. He parted from the poor prisoner with a sorrowful heart, as from a doomed man for whom there was no release but Death.

The Englishman lived in his new place of abode another half-year and more, and had no tidings of the wretched prisoner. At length, one day, he received from the Advocate a cool, concise, mysterious note, to this effect. "If you still wish to bestow that benefit upon the man in whom you were once interested, send me fifty pounds more and I think it can be ensured." Now, the Englishman had long settled in his mind that the Advocate was a heartless sharper, who had preyed upon his credulity and his interest in an unfortunate sufferer. So, he sat down and wrote a dry answer, giving the Advocate to understand that he was wiser now than he had been formerly, and that no more money was extractable from his pocket.

He lived outside the city gates, some mile or two from the post-office, and was accustomed to walk into the city with his letters and post them himself. On a lovely spring day, when the sky was exquisitely blue, and the sea Divinely beautiful, he took his usual walk, carrying this letter to the Advocate in his pocket. As he went along, his gentle heart was much moved by the loveliness of the prospect, and by the thought of the slowly dying prisoner chained to the bedstead, for whom the universe had no delights. As he drew nearer and nearer to the city where he was to post the letter, he became very uneasy in his mind. He debated with himself, was it remotely possible, after all, that this sum of fifty pounds could restore the fellow-creature whom he pitied so much, and for whom he had striven so hard, to liberty? He was not a conventionally rich Englishman—very far from that—but, he had a spare fifty pounds at the banker's. He resolved to risk it. Without doubt, GOD has recompensed him for the resolution.

He went to the banker's, and got a bill for the amount, and enclosed it in a letter to the Advocate that I wish I could have seen. He simply told the Advocate that he was quite a poor man, and that he was sensible it might be a great weakness in him to part with so much money on the faith of so vague a communication; but, that there it was, and that he prayed the Advocate to make a good use of it. If he did otherwise no good could ever come of it, and it would lie heavy on his soul one day.

Within a week, the Englishman was sitting at his breakfast, when he heard some suppressed sounds of agitation on the staircase, and Giovanni Carlavero leaped into the room and fell upon his breast, a free man!

Conscious of having wronged the Advocate in his own thoughts, the Englishman wrote him an earnest and grateful letter, avowing the fact, and entreating him to confide by what means and through what agency he had succeeded so well. The Advocate returned for answer through the post, "There are many things, as you know, in this Italy of ours, that are safest and best not even spoken of—far less written of. We may meet some day, and then I may tell you what you want to know; not here, and now." But, the two never did meet again. The Advocate was dead when the Englishman gave me my trust; and how the man had been set free, remained as great a mystery to the Englishman, and to the man himself, as it was to me.

But, I knew this:—here was the man, this sultry night, on his knees at my feet, because I was the Englishman's friend; here were his tears upon my dress; here were his sobs choking his utterance; here were his kisses on my hands, because they had touched the hands that had worked out his release. He had no need to tell me it would be happiness to him to die for his benefactor; I doubt if I ever saw real, sterling, fervent gratitude of soul, before or since.

He was much watched and suspected, he said, and had had enough to do to keep himself out of trouble. This, and his not having prospered in his worldly affairs, had led to his having failed in his usual communications to the Englishman for—as I now remember the period—some two or three years. But, his prospects were brighter, and his wife who had been very ill had recovered, and his fever had left him, and he had bought a little vineyard, and would I carry to his benefactor the first of its wine? Ay, that I would (I told him with enthusiasm), and not a drop of it should be spilled or lost!

He had cautiously closed the door before speaking of himself, and had talked with such excess of emotion, and in a provincial Italian so difficult to understand, that I had more than once been obliged to stop him, and beg him to have compassion on me and be slower and calmer. By degrees he became so, and tranquilly walked back with me to the hotel. There, I sat down before I went to bed and wrote a faithful account of him to the Englishman: which I concluded by saying that I would bring the wine home, against any difficulties, every drop.

Early next morning, when I came out at the hotel door to pursue my journey, I found my friend waiting with one of those immense bottles in which the Italian peasants store their wine—a bottle holding some half-dozen gallons—bound round with basket-work for greater safety on the journey. I see him now, in the bright sunlight, tears of gratitude in his eyes, proudly inviting my attention to this corpulent bottle. (At the street-corner hard by, two high-flavoured, able-bodied monks—pretending to talk together, but keeping their four evil eyes upon us.)

How the bottle had got there, did not appear; but the difficulty of getting it into the ramshackle vetturino carriage in which I was departing, was so great, and it took up so much room when it was got in, that I elected to sit outside. The last I saw of Giovanni Carlavero was his running through the town by the side of the jingling wheels, clasping my hand as I stretched it down from the box, charging me with a thousand last loving and dutiful messages to his dear patron, and finally looking in at the bottle as it reposed inside, with an admiration of its honourable way of travelling that was beyond measure delightful.

And now, what disquiet of mind this dearly-beloved and highly-treasured Bottle began to cost me, no man knows. It was my precious charge through a long tour, and, for hundreds of miles, I never had it off my mind by day or by night. Over bad roads—and they were many—I clung to it with affectionate desperation. Up mountains, I looked in at it and saw it helplessly tilting over on its back, with terror. At innumerable inn doors when the weather was bad, I was obliged to be put into my vehicle before the Bottle could be got in, and was obliged to have the Bottle lifted out before human aid could come near me. The Imp of the same name, except that his associations were all evil and these associations were all good, would have been a less troublesome travelling companion. I might have served Mr. Cruikshank as a subject for a new illustration of the miseries of the Bottle. The National Temperance Society might have made a powerful Tract of me.

The suspicions that attached to this innocent Bottle, greatly aggravated my difficulties. It was like the apple-pie in the child's book. Parma pouted at it, Modena mocked it, Tuscany tackled it, Naples nibbled it, Rome refused it, Austria accused it, Soldiers suspected it, Jesuits jobbed it. I composed a neat Oration, developing my inoffensive intentions in connexion with this Bottle, and delivered it in an infinity of guard-houses, at a multitude of town gates, and on every drawbridge, angle, and rampart, of a complete system of fortifications. Fifty times a day, I got down to harangue an infuriated soldiery about the Bottle. Through the filthy degradation of the abject and vile Roman States, I had as much difficulty in working my way with the Bottle, as if it had bottled up a complete system of heretical theology. In the Neapolitan country, where everybody was a spy, a soldier, a priest, or a lazzarone, the shameless beggars of all four denominations incessantly pounced on the Bottle and made it a pretext for extorting money from me. Quires—quires do I say? Reams—of forms illegibly printed on whity-brown paper were filled up about the Bottle, and it was the subject of more stamping and sanding than I had ever seen before. In consequence of which haze of sand, perhaps, it was always irregular, and always latent with dismal penalties of going back or not going forward, which were only to be abated by the silver crossing of a base hand, poked shirtless out of a ragged uniform sleeve. Under all discouragements, however, I stuck to my Bottle, and held firm to my resolution that every drop of its contents should reach the Bottle's destination.

The latter refinement cost me a separate heap of troubles on its own separate account. What corkscrews did I see the military power bring out against that Bottle; what gimlets, spikes, divining rods, gauges, and unknown tests and instruments! At some places, they persisted in declaring that the wine must not be passed, without being opened and tasted; I, pleading to the contrary, used then to argue the question seated on the Bottle lest they should open it in spite of me. In the southern parts of Italy more violent shrieking, face-making, and gesticulating, greater vehemence of speech and countenance and action, went on about that Bottle, than would attend fifty murders in a northern latitude. It raised important functionaries out of their beds, in the dead of night. I have known half-a-dozen military lanterns to disperse themselves at all points of a great sleeping Piazza, each lantern summoning some official creature to get up, put on his cocked-hat instantly, and come and stop the Bottle. It was characteristic that while this innocent Bottle had such immense difficulty in getting from little town to town, Signor Mazzini and the fiery cross were traversing Italy from end to end.

Still, I stuck to my Bottle, like any fine old English gentleman all of the olden time. The more the Bottle was interfered with, the stauncher I became (if possible) in my first determination that my countryman should have it delivered to him intact, as the man whom he had so nobly restored to life and liberty had delivered it to me. If ever I had been obstinate in my days—and I may have been, say, once or twice—I was obstinate about the Bottle. But, I made it a rule always to keep a pocket full of small coin at its service, and never to be out of temper in its cause. Thus, I and the Bottle made our way. Once we had a break-down; rather a bad break-down, on a steep high place with the sea below us, on a tempestuous evening when it blew great guns. We were driving four wild horses abreast, Southern fashion, and there was some little difficulty in stopping them. I was outside, and not thrown off; but no words can describe my feelings when I saw the Bottle—travelling inside, as usual—burst the door open, and roll obesely out into the road. A blessed Bottle with a charmed existence, he took no hurt, and we repaired damage, and went on triumphant.

A thousand representations were made to me that the Bottle must be left at this place, or that, and called for again. I never yielded to one of them, and never parted from the Bottle, on any pretence, consideration, threat, or entreaty. I had no faith in any official receipt for the Bottle, and nothing would induce me to accept one. These unmanageable politics at last brought me and the Bottle, still triumphant, to Genoa. There, I took a tender and reluctant leave of him for a few weeks, and consigned him to a trusty English captain, to be conveyed to the Port of London by sea.

While the Bottle was on his voyage to England, I read the Shipping Intelligence as anxiously as if I had been an underwriter. There was some stormy weather after I myself had got to England by way of Switzerland and France, and my mind greatly misgave me that the Bottle might be wrecked. At last to my great joy, I received notice of his safe arrival, and immediately went down to Saint Katherine's Docks, and found him in a state of honourable captivity in the Custom House.

The wine was mere vinegar when I set it down before the generous Englishman—probably it had been something like vinegar when I took it up from Giovanni Carlavero—but not a drop of it was spilled or gone. And the Englishman told me, with much emotion in his face and voice, that he had never tasted wine that seemed to him so sweet and sound. And long afterwards the Bottle graced his table. And the last time I saw him in this world that misses him, he took me aside in a crowd, to say, with his amiable smile: "We were talking of you only to-day at dinner, and I wished you had been there, for I had some Claret up in Carlavero's Bottle."

XVIII

THE CALAIS NIGHT MAIL

IT is an unsettled question with me whether I shall leave Calais something handsome in my will, or whether I shall leave it my malediction. I hate it so much, and yet I am always so very glad to see it, that I am in a state of constant indecision on this subject. When I first made acquaintance with Calais, it was as a maundering young wretch in a clammy perspiration and dripping saline particles, who was conscious of no extremities but the one great extremity, sea-sickness—who was a mere bilious torso, with a mislaid headache somewhere in its stomach—who had been put into a horrible swing in Dover Harbour, and had tumbled giddily out of it on the French coast, or the Isle of Man, or anywhere. Times have changed, and now I enter Calais self-reliant and rational. I know where it is beforehand, I keep a look out for it, I recognise its landmarks when I see any of them, I am acquainted with its ways, and I know—and I can bear—its worst behaviour.

Malignant Calais! Low-lying alligator, evading the eyesight and discouraging hope! Dodging flat streak, now on this bow, now on that, now anywhere, now everywhere, now nowhere! In vain Cape Grinez, coming frankly forth into the sea, exhorts the failing to be stout of heart and stomach: sneaking Calais, prone behind its bar, invites emetically to despair. Even when it can no longer quite conceal itself in its muddy dock, it has an evil way of falling off, has Calais, which is more hopeless than its invisibility. The pier is all but on the bowsprit, and you think you are there—roll, roar, wash!—Calais has retired miles inland, and Dover has burst out to look for it.

It has a last dip and slide in its character, has Calais, to be especially commended to the infernal gods. Thrice accursed be that garrison-town, when it dives under the boat's keel, and comes up a league or two to the right, with the packet shivering and spluttering and staring about for it!

Not but what I have my animosities towards Dover. I particularly detest Dover for the self-complacency with which it goes to bed. It always goes to bed (when I am going to Calais) with a more brilliant display of lamp and candle than any other town. Mr. and Mrs. Birmingham, host and hostess of the Lord Warden Hotel, are my much esteemed friends, but they are too conceited about the comforts of that establishment when the Night Mail is starting. I know it is a good house to stay at, and I don't want the fact insisted upon in all its warm bright windows at such an hour. I know the Warden is a stationary edifice that never rolls or pitches, and I object to its big outline seeming to insist upon that circumstance, and, as it were, to come over me with it, when I am reeling on the deck of the boat. Beshrew the Warden likewise, for obstructing that corner, and making the wind so angry as it rushes round. Shall I not know that it blows quite soon enough, without the officious Warden's interference?

As I wait here on board the night packet, for the South-Eastern Train to come down with the Mail, Dover appears to me to be illuminated for some intensely aggravating festivity in my personal dishonour. All its noises smack of taunting praises of the land, and dispraises of the gloomy sea, and of me for going on it. The drums upon the heights have gone to bed, or I know they would rattle taunts against me for having my unsteady footing on this slippery deck. The many gas eyes of the Marine Parade twinkle in an offensive manner, as if with derision. The distant dogs of Dover bark at me in my mis-shapen wrappers, as if I were Richard the Third.

A screech, a bell, and two red eyes come gliding down the Admiralty Pier with a smoothness of motion rendered more smooth by the heaving of the boat. The sea makes noises against the pier, as if several hippopotami were lapping at it, and were prevented by circumstances over which they had no control from drinking peaceably. We, the boat, become violently agitated—rumble, hum, scream, roar, and establish an immense family washing-day at each paddlebox. Bright patches break out in the train as the doors of the post-office vans are opened, and instantly stooping figures with sacks upon their backs begin to be beheld among the piles, descending as it would seem in ghostly procession to Davy Jones's Locker. The passengers come on board; a few shadowy Frenchmen, with hatboxes shaped like the stoppers of gigantic case-bottles; a few shadowy Germans in immense fur coats and boots; a few shadowy Englishmen prepared for the worst and pretending not to expect it. I cannot disguise from my uncommercial mind the miserable fact that we are a body of outcasts; that the attendants on us are as scant in number as may serve to get rid of us with the least possible delay; that there are no night-loungers interested in us; that the unwilling lamps shiver and shudder at us; that the sole object is to commit us to the deep and abandon us. Lo, the two red eyes glaring in increasing distance, and then the very train itself has gone to bed before we are off!

What is the moral support derived by some sea-going amateurs from an umbrella? Why do certain voyagers across the Channel always put up that article, and hold it up with a grim and fierce tenacity? A fellow-creature near me—whom I only know to *be* a fellow-creature, because of his umbrella: without which he might be a dark bit of cliff, pier, or bulkhead—clutches that instrument with a desperate grasp, that will not relax until he lands at Calais. Is there any analogy, in certain constitutions, between keeping an umbrella up, and keeping the spirits up? A hawser thrown on board with a flop replies "Stand by!" "Stand by, below!" "Half a turn a head!" "Half a turn a head!" "Half speed!" "Half speed!" "Port!" "Port!" "Steady!" "Steady!" "Go on!" "Go on!"

A stout wooden wedge driven in at my right temple and out at my left, a floating deposit of lukewarm oil in my throat and a compression of the bridge of my nose in a blunt pair of pincers,—these are the personal sensations by which I know we are off, and by which I shall continue to know it until I am on the soil of France. My symptoms have scarcely established themselves comfortably, when two or three skating shadows that have been trying to walk or stand, get flung together, and other two or three shadows in tarpaulin slide with them into corners and cover them up. Then the South Foreland lights begin to hiccup at us in a way that bodes no good.

It is at about this period that my detestation of Calais knows no bounds. Inwardly I resolve afresh that I never will forgive that hated town. I have done so before, many times, but that is past. Let me register a vow. Implacable animosity to Calais everm——that was an awkward sea, and the funnel seems of my opinion, for it gives a complaining roar.

The wind blows stiffly from the Nor'-East, the sea runs high, we ship a deal of water, the night is dark and cold, and the shapeless passengers lie about in melancholy bundles, as if they were sorted out for the laundress; but for my own uncommercial part I cannot pretend that I am much inconvenienced by any of these things. A general howling, whistling, flopping, gurgling, and scooping, I am aware of, and a general knocking about of Nature; but the impressions I receive are very vague. In a sweet faint temper, something like the smell of damaged oranges, I think I should feel languidly benevolent if I had time. I have not time, because I am under a curious compulsion to occupy myself with the Irish melodies. "Rich and rare were the gems she wore," is the particular melody to which I find myself devoted. I sing it to myself in the most charming manner and with the greatest expression. Now and then, I raise my head (I am sitting on the hardest of wet seats, in the most uncomfortable of wet attitudes, but I don't mind it,) and notice that I am a whirling shuttlecock between a fiery battledore of a lighthouse on the French coast and a fiery battledore of a lighthouse on the English coast; but I don't notice it particularly, except to feel envenomed in my hatred of Calais. Then I go on again, "Rich and rare were the ge-ems she-e-e-e wore, And a bright gold ring on her wa-and she bo-ore, But O her beauty was fa-a-a-a-r beyond"—I am particularly proud of my execution here, when I become aware of another awkward shock from the sea, and another protest from the funnel, and a fellow-creature at the paddle-box more audibly indisposed than I think he need be—"Her sparkling gems, or snow-white wand, But O her beauty was fa-a-a-a-r beyond"—another awkward one here, and the fellow-creature with the umbrella down and picked up—"Her spa-rkling ge-ems, or her Port! port! steady! steady! snow-white fellow-creature at the paddle-box very selfishly audible, bump, roar, wash, white wand."

As my execution of the Irish melodies partakes of my imperfect perceptions of what is going on around me, so what is going on around me becomes something else than what it is. The stokers open the furnace doors below, to feed the fires, and I am again on the box of the old Exeter Telegraph fast coach, and that is the light of the for ever extinguished coach-lamps, and the gleam on the hatches and paddle-boxes is *their* gleam on cottages and haystacks, and the monotonous noise of the engines is the steady jingle of the splendid team. Anon, the intermittent funnel roar of protest at every violent roll, becomes the regular blast of a high pressure engine, and I recognise the exceedingly explosive steamer in which I ascended the Mississippi when the American civil war was not, and when only its causes were. A fragment of mast on which the light of a lantern falls, an end of rope, and a jerking block or so, become suggestive of Franconi's Circus at Paris where I shall be this very night mayhap (for it must be morning now), and they dance to the self-same time and tune as the trained steed, Black Raven. What may be the speciality of these waves as they come rushing on, I cannot desert the pressing demands made upon me by the gems she wore, to inquire, but they are charged with something about Robinson Crusoe, and I think it was in Yarmouth Roads that he first went a seafaring and was near foundering (what a terrific sound that word had for me when I was a boy!) in his first gale of wind. Still, through all this, I must ask her (who *was* she I wonder!) for the fiftieth time, and without ever stopping, Does she not fear to stray, So lone and lovely through this bleak way, And are Erin's sons so good or so cold, As not to be tempted by more fellow-creatures at the paddle-box or gold? Sir Knight I feel not the least alarm, No son of Erin will offer me harm, For though they love fellow-creature with umbrella down again and golden store, Sir Knight they what a tremendous one love honour and virtue more: For though they love Stewards with a bull's eye bright, they'll trouble you for your ticket, sir—rough passage to-night!

I freely admit it to be a miserable piece of human weakness and inconsistency, but I no sooner become conscious of those last words from the steward than I begin to soften towards Calais. Whereas I have been vindictively wishing that those Calais burghers who came out of their town by a short cut into the History of England, with those fatal ropes round their necks by which they have since been towed into so many cartoons, had all been hanged on the spot, I now begin to regard them as highly respectable and virtuous tradesmen. Looking about me, I see the light of Cape Grinez well astern of the boat on the davits to leeward, and the light of Calais Harbour undeniably at its old tricks, but still ahead and shining. Sentiments of forgiveness of Calais, not to say of attachment to Calais, begin to expand my bosom. I have weak notions that I will stay there a day or two on my way back. A faded and recumbent stranger pausing in a profound reverie over the rim of a basin, asks me what kind of place Calais is? I tell him (Heaven forgive me!) a very agreeable place indeed—rather hilly than otherwise.

So strangely goes the time, and on the whole so quickly—though still I seem to have been on board a week—that I am bumped, rolled, gurgled, washed and pitched into Calais Harbour before her maiden smile has finally lighted her through the Green Isle, When blest for ever is she who relied, On entering Calais at the top of the tide. For we have not to land to-night down among those slimy timbers—covered with green hair as if it were the mermaids' favourite combing-place—where one crawls to the surface of the jetty, like a stranded shrimp, but we go steaming up the harbour to the Railway Station Quay. And as we go, the sea washes in and out among piles and planks, with dead heavy beats and in quite a furious manner (whereof we are proud), and the lamps shake in the wind, and the bells of Calais striking One seem to send their vibrations struggling against troubled air, as we have come struggling against troubled water. And now, in the sudden relief and wiping of faces, everybody on board seems to have had a prodigious double-tooth out, and to be this very instant free of the Dentist's hands. And now we all know for the first time how wet and cold we are, and how salt we are; and now I love Calais with my heart of hearts!

"Hôtel Dessin!" (but in this one case it is not a vocal cry; it is but a bright lustre in the eyes of the cheery representative of that best of inns). "Hôtel Meurice!" "Hôtel de France!" "Hôtel de Calais!" "The Royal Hôtel, Sir, Angaishe ouse!" "You going to Parry, Sir?" "Your baggage, registair froo, Sir?" Bless ye, my Touters, bless ye, my commissionaires, bless ye, my hungry-eyed mysteries in caps of a military form, who are always here, day or night, fair weather or foul, seeking inscrutable jobs which I never see you get! Bless ye, my Custom House officers in green and grey; permit me to grasp the welcome hands that descend into my travelling-bag, one on each side, and meet at the bottom to give my change of linen a peculiar shake up, as if it were a measure of chaff or grain! I have nothing to declare, Monsieur le Douanier, except that when I cease to breathe, Calais will be found written on my heart. No article liable to local duty have I with me, Monsieur l'Officier de l'Octroi, unless the overflowing of a breast devoted to your charming town should be in that wise chargeable. Ah! see at the gangway by the twinkling lantern, my dearest brother and friend, he once of the Passport Office, he who collects the names! May he be for ever changeless in his buttoned black surtout, with his note-book in his hand, and his tall black hat, surmounting his round, smiling, patient face! Let us embrace, my dearest brother. I am yours à tout jamais—for the whole of ever.

Calais up and doing at the railway station, and Calais down and dreaming in its bed; Calais with something of "an ancient and fish-like smell" about it, and Calais blown and sea-washed pure; Calais represented at the Buffet by savoury roast fowls, hot coffee, cognac, and Bordeaux; and Calais represented everywhere by flitting persons with a monomania for changing money—though I never shall be able to understand in my present state of existence how they live by it, but I suppose I should, if I understood the currency question— Calais en gros, and Calais en détail, forgive one who has deeply wronged you.—I was not fully aware of it on the other side, but I meant Dover.

Ding, ding! To the carriages, gentlemen the travellers. Ascend then, gentlemen the travellers, for Hazebroucke, Lille, Douai, Bruxelles, Arras, Amiens, and Paris! I, humble representative of the uncommercial interest, ascend with the rest. The train is light to-night, and I share my compartment with but two fellow-travellers; one, a compatriot in an obsolete cravat, who thinks it a quite unaccountable thing that they don't keep "London time" on a French railway, and who is made angry by my modestly suggesting the possibility of Paris time being more in their way; the other, a young priest, with a very small bird in a very small cage, who feeds the small bird with a quill and then puts him up in the network above his head, where he advances twittering, to his front wires, and seems to address me in an electioneering manner. The compatriot (who crossed in the boat, and whom I judge to be some person of distinction, as he was shut up, like a stately species of rabbit, in a private hutch on deck) and the young priest (who joined us at Calais) are soon asleep, and then the bird and I have it all to ourselves.

A stormy night still; a night that sweeps the wires of the electric telegraph with a wild and fitful hand; a night so very stormy, with the added storm of the train-progress through it, that when the Guard comes clambering round to mark the tickets while we are at full speed (a really horrible performance in an express train, though he holds on to the open window by his elbows in the most deliberate manner), he stands in such a whirlwind that I grip him fast by the collar, and feel it next to manslaughter to let him go. Still, when he is gone, the small, small bird remains at his front wires feebly twittering to me—twittering and twittering, until, leaning back in my place and looking at him in drowsy fascination, I find that he seems to jog my memory as we rush along.

Uncommercial travels (thus the small, small bird) have lain in their idle thriftless way through all this range of swamp and dyke, as through many other odd places; and about here, as you very well

know, are the queer old stone farmhouses, approached by drawbridges, and the windmills that you get at by boats. Here, are the
lands where the women hoe and dig, paddling canoe-wise from field
to field, and here are the cabarets and other peasant-houses where the
stone dove-cotes in the littered yards are as strong as warders' towers
in old castles. Here, are the long monotonous miles of canal, with the
great Dutch-built barges garishly painted, and the towing girls,
sometimes harnessed by the forehead, sometimes by the girdle and
the shoulders, not a pleasant sight to see. Scattered through this
country are mighty works of VAUBAN, whom you know about, and
regiments of such corporals as you heard of once upon a time, and
many a blue-eyed Bebelle. Through these flat districts, in the shining
summer days, walk those long, grotesque files of young novices in
enormous shovel-hats, whom you remember blackening the ground
checkered by the avenues of leafy trees. And now that Hazebroucke
slumbers certain kilometres ahead, recall the summer evening when
your dusty feet strolling up from the station tended hap-hazard to a
Fair there, where the oldest inhabitants were circling round and
round a barrel-organ on hobby-horses, with the greatest gravity, and
where the principal show in the Fair was a Religious Richardson's—
literally, on its own announcement in great letters, THEATRE
RELIGIEUX. In which improving Temple, the dramatic representation was of "all the interesting events in the life of our Lord, from
the Manger to the Tomb;" the principal female character, without
any reservation or exception, being at the moment of your arrival,
engaged in trimming the external Moderators (as it was growing
dusk), while the next principal female character took the money, and
the Young Saint John disported himself upside down on the platform.

Looking up at this point to confirm the small, small bird in every
particular he has mentioned, I find he has ceased to twitter, and has
put his head under his wing. Therefore, in my different way I follow
the good example.

XIX

SOME RECOLLECTIONS OF MORTALITY

I HAD parted from the small bird at somewhere about four o'clock in
the morning, when he had got out at Arras, and had been received by
two shovel-hats in waiting at the station, who presented an appropriately ornithological and crow-like appearance. My compatriot and
I had gone on to Paris; my compatriot enlightening me occasionally
with a long list of the enormous grievances of French railway travelling: every one of which, as I am a sinner, was perfectly new to me,
though I have as much experience of French railways as most un-
commercials. I had left him at the terminus (through his conviction,
against all explanation and remonstrance, that his baggage-ticket
was his passenger-ticket), insisting in a very high temper to the
functionary on duty, that in his own personal identity he was four

packages weighing so many kilogrammes—as if he had been Cassim Baba! I had bathed and breakfasted, and was strolling on the bright quays. The subject of my meditations was the question whether it is positively in the essence and nature of things, as a certain school of Britons would seem to think it, that a Capital must be ensnared and enslaved before it can be made beautiful: when I lifted up my eyes and found that my feet, straying like my mind, had brought me to Notre-Dame.

That is to say, Notre-Dame was before me, but there was a large open space between us. A very little while gone, I had left that space covered with buildings densely crowded; and now it was cleared for some new wonder in the way of public Street, Place, Garden, Fountain, or all four. Only the obscene little Morgue, slinking on the brink of the river and soon to come down, was left there, looking mortally ashamed of itself, and supremely wicked. I had but glanced at this old acquaintance, when I beheld an airy procession coming round in front of Notre-Dame, past the great hospital. It had something of a Masaniello look, with fluttering striped curtains in the midst of it, and it came dancing round the cathedral in the liveliest manner.

I was speculating on a marriage in Blouse-life, or a Christening, or some other domestic festivity which I would see out, when I found, from the talk of a quick rush of Blouses past me, that it was a Body coming to the Morgue. Having never before chanced upon this initiation, I constituted myself a Blouse likewise, and ran into the Morgue with the rest. It was a very muddy day, and we took in a quantity of mire with us, and the procession coming in upon our heels brought a quantity more. The procession was in the highest spirits, and consisted of idlers who had come with the curtained litter from its starting-place, and of all the reinforcements it had picked up by the way. It set the litter down in the midst of the Morgue, and then two Custodians proclaimed aloud that we were all "invited" to go out. This invitation was rendered the more pressing, if not the more flattering, by our being shoved out, and the folding-gates being barred upon us.

Those who never have seen the Morgue, may see it perfectly, by presenting to themselves an indifferently paved coach-house accessible from the street by a pair of folding-gates; on the left of the coach-house, occupying its width, any large London tailor's or linendraper's plate-glass window reaching to the ground; within the window, on two rows of inclined plane, what the coach-house has to show ; hanging above, like irregular stalactites from the roof of a cave, a quantity of clothes—the clothes of the dead and buried shows of the coach-house.

We had been excited in the highest degree by seeing the Custodians pull off their coats and tuck up their shirt-sleeves, as the procession came along. It looked so interestingly like business. Shut out in the muddy street, we now became quite ravenous to know all about it. Was it river, pistol, knife, love, gambling, robbery, hatred, how many stabs, how many bullets, fresh or decomposed, suicide or murder? All wedged together, and all staring at one another with our heads thrust forward, we propounded these inquiries and a hundred more such. Imperceptibly, it came to be known that Monsieur the tall and sallow mason yonder, was acquainted with the facts. Would Monsieur the tall and sallow mason, surged at by a new wave of us, have the goodness to impart? It was but a poor old man, passing along the street under one of the new buildings, on whom a stone had fallen, and who had tumbled dead. His age? Another wave surged up against the tall and sallow mason, and our wave swept on and broke, and he was any age from sixty-five to ninety.

An old man was not much: moreover, we could have wished he had been killed by human agency—his own, or somebody else's: the latter, preferable—but our comfort was, that he had nothing about him to lead to his identification, and that his people must seek him here. Perhaps they were waiting dinner for him even now? We liked that. Such of us as had pocket-handkerchiefs took a slow, intense, protracted wipe at our noses, and then crammed our handkerchiefs into the breast of our blouses. Others of us who had no handkerchiefs administered a similar relief to our overwrought minds, by means of prolonged smears or wipes of our mouths on our sleeves. One man with a gloomy malformation of brow—a homicidal worker in white-lead, to judge from his blue tone of colour, and a certain flavour of paralysis pervading him—got his coat-collar between his teeth, and bit at it with an appetite. Several decent women arrived upon the outskirts of the crowd, and prepared to launch themselves into the dismal coach-house when opportunity should come; among them, a pretty young mother, pretending to bite the forefinger of her baby-boy, kept it between her rosy lips that it might be handy for guiding to point at the show. Meantime, all faces were turned towards the building, and we men waited with a fixed and stern resolution:—for the most part with folded arms. Surely, it was the only public French sight these uncommercial eyes had seen, at which the expectant people did not form *en queue*. But there was no such order of arrangement here; nothing but a general determination to make a rush for it, and a disposition to object to some boys who had mounted on the two stone posts by the hinges of the gates, with the design of swooping in when the hinges should turn.

Now, they turned, and we rushed! Great pressure, and a scream or two from the front. Then a laugh or two, some expressions of disappointment, and a slackening of the pressure and subsidence of the struggle.—Old man not there.

"But what would you have?" the Custodian reasonably argues, as he looks out at his little door. "Patience, patience! We make his toilette, gentlemen. He will be exposed presently. It is necessary to proceed according to rule. His toilette is not made all at a blow. He will be exposed in good time, gentlemen, in good time." And so retires, smoking, with a wave of his sleeveless arm towards the window, importing, "Entertain yourselves in the meanwhile with the other curiosities. Fortunately the Museum is not empty to-day."

Who would have thought of public fickleness even at the Morgue? But there it was, on that occasion. Three lately popular articles that had been attracting greatly when the litter was first descried coming dancing round the corner by the great cathedral, were so completely deposed now, that nobody save two little girls (one showing them to a doll) would look at them. Yet the chief of the three, the article in the front row, had received jagged injury of the left temple; and the other two in the back row, the drowned two lying side by side with their heads very slightly turned towards each other, seemed to be comparing notes about it. Indeed, those two of the back row were so furtive of appearance, and so (in their puffed way) assassinatingly knowing as to the one of the front, that it was hard to think the three had never come together in their lives, and were only chance companions after death. Whether or no this was the general, as it was the uncommercial, fancy, it is not to be disputed that the group had drawn exceedingly within ten minutes. Yet now, the inconstant public turned its back upon them, and even leaned its elbows carelessly against the bar outside the window and shook off the mud from its shoes, and also lent and borrowed fire for pipes.

Custodian re-enters from his door. " Again once, gentlemen, you are invited——" No further invitation necessary. Ready dash into the street. Toilette finished. Old man coming out.

This time, the interest was grown too hot to admit of toleration of the boys on the stone posts. The homicidal white-lead worker made a pounce upon one boy who was hoisting himself up, and brought him to earth amidst general commendation. Closely stowed as we were, we yet formed into groups—groups of conversation, without separation from the mass—to discuss the old man. Rivals of the tall and sallow mason sprang into being, and here again was popular inconstancy. These rivals attracted audiences, and were greedily listened to; and whereas they had derived their information solely from the tall and sallow one, officious members of the crowd now sought to enlighten *him* on their authority. Changed by this social experience into an iron-visaged and inveterate misanthrope, the mason glared at mankind, and evidently cherished in his breast the wish that the whole of the present company could change places with the deceased old man. And now listeners became inattentive, and people made a start forward at a slight sound, and an unholy fire kindled in the public eye, and those next the gates beat at them impatiently, as if they were of the cannibal species and hungry.

Again the hinges creaked, and we rushed. Disorderly pressure for some time ensued before the uncommercial unit got figured into the front row of the sum. It was strange to see so much heat and uproar seething about one poor spare, white-haired old man, quiet for evermore. He was calm of feature and undisfigured, as he lay on his back —having been struck upon the hinder part of the head, and thrown forward—and something like a tear or two had started from the closed eyes, and lay wet upon the face. The uncommercial interest, sated at a glance, directed itself upon the striving crowd on either side and behind: wondering whether one might have guessed, from the expression of those faces merely, what kind of sight they were looking at. The differences of expression were not many. There was a little pity, but not much, and that mostly with a selfish touch in it—as who would say, "Shall I, poor I, look like that, when the time comes!" There was more of a secretly brooding contemplation and curiosity, as "That man I don't like, and have the grudge against; would such be his appearance, if some one—not to mention names—by any chance gave him an ugly knock?" There was a wolfish stare at the object, in which the homicidal white-lead worker shone conspicuous. And there was a much more general, purposeless, vacant staring at it—like looking at waxwork, without a catalogue, and not knowing what to make of it. But all these expressions concurred in possessing the one underlying expression of *looking at something that could not return a look.* The uncommercial notice had established this as very remarkable, when a new pressure all at once coming up from the street pinioned him ignominiously, and hurried him into the arms (now sleeved again) of the Custodian smoking at his door, and answering questions, between puffs, with a certain placid meritorious air of not being proud, though high in office. And mentioning pride, it may be observed, by the way, that one could not well help investing the original sole occupant of the front row with an air depreciatory of the legitimate attraction of the poor old man: while the two in the second row seemed to exult at this superseded popularity.

Pacing presently round the garden of the Tower of St. Jacques de la Boucherie, and presently again in front of the Hôtel de Ville, I called to mind a certain desolate open-air Morgue that I happened to light upon in London, one day in the hard winter of 1861, and which seemed as strange to me, at the time of seeing it, as if I had found it in China. Towards that hour of a winter's afternoon when the lamplighters are beginning to light the lamps in the streets a little before they are wanted, because the darkness thickens fast and soon, I was walking in from the country on the northern side of the Regent's Park—hard frozen and deserted—when I saw an empty Hansom cab drive up to the lodge at Gloucester-gate, and the driver with great agitation call to the man there: who quickly reached a long pole from a tree, and, deftly collared by the driver, jumped to the step of his little seat, and so the Hansom rattled out at the gate, galloping over the iron-bound road. I followed running, though not so fast but that when I came to the right-hand Canal Bridge, near the cross-path to Chalk Farm, the Hansom was stationary, the horse was smoking hot, the long pole was idle on the ground, and the driver and the park-keeper were looking over the bridge parapet. Looking over too, I saw, lying on the towing-path with her face turned up towards us, a woman, dead a day or two, and under thirty, as I guessed, poorly dressed in black. The feet were lightly crossed at the ankles, and the dark hair, all pushed back from the face, as though that had been the last action of her desperate hands, streamed over the ground.

Dabbled all about her, was the water and the broken ice that had dropped from her dress, and had splashed as she was got out. The policeman who had just got her out, and the passing costermonger who had helped him, were standing near the body; the latter with that stare at it which I have likened to being at a waxwork exhibition without a catalogue; the former, looking over his stock, with professional stiffness and coolness, in the direction in which the bearers he had sent for were expected. So dreadfully forlorn, so dreadfully sad, so dreadfully mysterious, this spectacle of our dear sister here departed! A barge came up, breaking the floating ice and the silence, and a woman steered it. The man with the horse that towed it, cared so little for the body, that the stumbling hoofs had been among the hair, and the tow-rope had caught and turned the head, before our cry of horror took him to the bridle. At which sound the steering woman looked up at us on the bridge, with contempt unutterable, and then looking down at the body with a similar expression—as if it were made in another likeness from herself, had been informed with other passions, had been lost by other chances, had had another nature dragged down to perdition—steered a spurning streak of mud at it, and passed on.

A better experience, but also of the Morgue kind, in which chance happily made me useful in a slight degree, arose to my remembrance as I took my way by the Boulevard de Sébastopol to the brighter scenes of Paris.

The thing happened, say five-and-twenty years ago. I was a modest young uncommercial then, and timid and inexperienced. Many suns and winds have browned me in the line, but those were my pale days. Having newly taken the lease of a house in a certain distinguished metropolitan parish—a house which then appeared to me to be a frightfully first-class Family Mansion, involving awful responsibilities—I became the prey of a Beadle. I think the Beadle must have seen me going in or coming out, and must have observed that I tottered under the weight of my grandeur. Or he may have been in hiding under straw when I bought my first horse (in the desirable stable-yard attached to the first-class Family Mansion), and when the vendor remarked to me, in an original manner, on bringing him for approval, taking his cloth off and smacking him, "There, Sir! *There's* a Orse!" And when I said gallantly, "How much do you want for him?" and when the vendor said, "No more than sixty guineas, from you," and when I said smartly, "Why not more than sixty from *me?*" And when he said crushingly, "Because upon my soul and body he'd be considered cheap at seventy, by one who understood the subject—but you don't."—I say, the Beadle may have been in hiding under straw, when this disgrace befell me, or he may have noted that I was too raw and young an Atlas to carry the first-class Family Mansion in a knowing manner. Be this as it may, the Beadle did what Melancholy did to the youth in Gray's Elegy—he marked me for his own. And the way in which the Beadle did it, was this: he summoned me as a Juryman on his Coroner's Inquests.

In my first feverish alarm I repaired "for safety and for succour" —like those sagacious Northern shepherds who, having had no previous reason whatever to believe in young Norval, very prudently did not originate the hazardous idea of believing in him—to a deep householder. This profound man informed me that the Beadle counted on my buying him off; on my bribing him not to summon me; and that if I would attend an Inquest with a cheerful countenance, and profess alacrity in that branch of my country's service, the Beadle would be disheartened, and would give up the game.

I roused my energies, and the next time the wily Beadle summoned me, I went. The Beadle was the blankest Beadle I have ever looked on when I answered to my name; and his discomfiture gave me courage to go through with it.

We were impanelled to inquire concerning the death of a very little mite of a child. It was the old miserable story. Whether the mother had committed the minor offence of concealing the birth, or whether she had committed the major offence of killing the child, was the question on which we were wanted. We must commit her on one of the two issues.

The Inquest came off in the parish workhouse, and I have yet a lively impression that I was unanimously received by my brother Jurymen as a brother of the utmost conceivable insignificance. Also, that before we began, a broker who had lately cheated me fearfully in the matter of a pair of card-tables, was for the utmost rigour of the law. I remember that we sat in a sort of board-room, on such very large square horse-hair chairs that I wondered what race of Patagonians they were made for; and further, that an undertaker gave me his card when we were in the full moral freshness of having just been sworn, as "an inhabitant that was newly come into the parish, and was likely to have a young family." The case was then stated to us by the Coroner, and then we went down-stairs—led by the plotting Beadle—to view the body. From that day to this, the poor little figure, on which that sounding legal appellation was bestowed, has lain in the same place and with the same surroundings, to my thinking. In a kind of crypt devoted to the warehousing of the parochial coffins, and in the midst of a perfect Panorama of coffins of all sizes, it was stretched on a box; the mother had put it in her box—this box —almost as soon as it was born, and it had been presently found there. It had been opened, and neatly sewn up, and regarded from that point of view, it looked like a stuffed creature. It rested on a clean white cloth, with a surgical instrument or so at hand, and regarded from that point of view, it looked as if the cloth were "laid," and the Giant were coming to dinner. There was nothing repellent about the poor piece of innocence, and it demanded a mere form of looking at. So, we looked at an old pauper who was going about among the coffins with a foot rule, as if he were a case of Self-Measurement; and we looked at one another; and we said the place was well whitewashed anyhow; and then our conversational powers as a British Jury flagged, and the foreman said, "All right, gentlemen? Back again, Mr. Beadle!"

The miserable young creature who had given birth to this child within a very few days, and who had cleaned the cold wet door-steps immediately afterwards, was brought before us when we resumed our horse-hair chairs, and was present during the proceedings. She had a horse-hair chair herself, being very weak and ill; and I remember how she turned to the unsympathetic nurse who attended her, and who might have been the figure-head of a pauper-ship, and how she hid her face and sobs and tears upon that wooden shoulder. I remember, too, how hard her mistress was upon her (she was a servant-of-all-work), and with what a cruel pertinacity that piece of Virtue spun her thread of evidence double, by intertwisting it with the sternest thread of construction. Smitten hard by the terrible low wail from the utterly friendless orphan girl, which never ceased during the whole inquiry, I took heart to ask this witness a question or two, which hopefully admitted of an answer that might give a favourable turn to the case. She made the turn as little favourable as it could be, but it did some good, and the Coroner, who was nobly patient and humane (he was the late Mr. Wakley), cast a look of strong encouragement in my direction. Then, we had the doctor who had made the examination, and the usual tests as to whether the child was born alive; but he was a timid, muddle-headed doctor, and got confused and contradictory, and wouldn't say this, and couldn't answer for that, and the immaculate broker was too much for him, and our side slid back again. However, I tried again, and the Coroner backed me again, for which I ever afterwards felt grateful to him as I do now to his memory; and we got another favourable turn, out of some other witness, some member of the family with a strong pre-possession against the sinner; and I think we had the doctor back again; and I know that the Coroner summed up for our side, and that I and my British brothers turned round to discuss our verdict, and get ourselves into great difficulties with our large chairs and the broker. At that stage of the case I tried hard again, being convinced that I had cause for it; and at last we found for the minor offence of only concealing the birth; and the poor desolate creature, who had been taken out during our deliberation, being brought in again to be told of the verdict, then dropped upon her knees before us, with pro-testations that we were right—protestations among the most affect-ing that I have ever heard in my life—and was carried away insensible.

(In private conversation after this was all over, the Coroner showed me his reasons as a trained surgeon, for perceiving it to be impossible that the child could, under the most favourable circumstances, have drawn many breaths, in the very doubtful case of its having ever breathed at all; this, owing to the discovery of some foreign matter in the wind-pipe, quite irreconcilable with many moments of life.)

When the agonised girl had made those final protestations, I had seen her face, and it was in unison with her distracted heartbroken voice, and it was very moving. It certainly did not impress me by any beauty that it had, and if I ever see it again in another world I shall only know it by the help of some new sense or intelligence. But it came to me in my sleep that night, and I selfishly dismissed it in the most efficient way I could think of. I caused some extra care to be taken of her in the prison, and counsel to be retained for her defence when she was tried at the Old Bailey; and her sentence was lenient, and her history and conduct proved that it was right. In doing the little I did for her, I remember to have had the kind help of some gentle-hearted functionary to whom I addressed myself—but what functionary I have long forgotten—who I suppose was officially present at the Inquest.

I regard this as a very notable uncommercial experience, because this good came of a Beadle. And to the best of my knowledge, information, and belief, it is the only good that ever did come of a Beadle since the first Beadle put on his cocked-hat.

XX

BIRTHDAY CELEBRATIONS

It came into my mind that I would recall in these notes a few of the many hostelries I have rested at in the course of my journeys; and, indeed, I had taken up my pen for the purpose, when I was baffled by an accidental circumstance. It was the having to leave off, to wish the owner of a certain bright face that looked in at my door, "many happy returns of the day." Thereupon a new thought came into my mind, driving its predecessor out, and I began to recall—instead of Inns—the birthdays that I have put up at, on my way to this present sheet of paper.

I can very well remember being taken out to visit some peach-faced creature in a blue sash, and shoes to correspond, whose life I supposed to consist entirely of birthdays. Upon seed-cake, sweet wine, and shining presents, that glorified young person seemed to me to be exclusively reared. At so early a stage of my travels did I assist at the anniversary of her nativity (and become enamoured of her) that I had not yet acquired the recondite knowledge that a birthday is the common property of all who are born, but supposed it to be a special gift bestowed by the favouring Heavens on that one distinguished infant. There was no other company, and we sat in a shady bower—under a table, as my better (or worse) knowledge leads me to believe—and were regaled with saccharine substances and liquids, until it was time to part. A bitter powder was administered to me next morning, and I was wretched. On the whole, a pretty accurate foreshadowing of my more mature experiences in such wise!

Then came the time when, inseparable from one's own birthday, was a certain sense of merit, a consciousness of well-earned distinction. When I regarded my birthday as a graceful achievement of my own, a monument of my perseverance, independence, and good sense, redounding greatly to my honour. This was at about the

period when Olympia Squires became involved in the anniversary.
Olympia was most beautiful (of course), and I loved her to that
degree, that I used to be obliged to get out of my little bed in the
night, expressly to exclaim to Solitude, "O, Olympia Squires!"
Visions of Olympia, clothed entirely in sage-green, from which I infer
a defectively educated taste on the part of her respected parents,
who were necessarily unacquainted with the South Kensington
Museum, still arise before me. Truth is sacred, and the visions are
crowned by a shining white beaver bonnet, impossibly suggestive of
a little feminine postboy. My memory presents a birthday when
Olympia and I were taken by an unfeeling relative—some cruel uncle,
or the like—to a slow torture called an Orrery. The terrible instrument was set up at the local Theatre, and I had expressed a profane
wish in the morning that it was a Play: for which a serious aunt
had probed my conscience deep, and my pocket deeper, by reclaim-
ing a bestowed half-crown. It was a venerable and a shabby Orrery,
at least one thousand stars and twenty-five comets behind the age.
Nevertheless, it was awful. When the low-spirited gentleman with a
wand said, "ladies and gentlemen" (meaning particularly Olympia
and me), "the lights are about to be put out, but there is not the
slightest cause for alarm," it was very alarming. Then the planets
and stars began. Sometimes they wouldn't come on, sometimes they
wouldn't go off, sometimes they had holes in them, and mostly they
didn't seem to be good likenesses. All this time the gentleman with
the wand was going on in the dark (tapping away at the heavenly
bodies between whiles, like a wearisome woodpecker), about a sphere
revolving on its own axis eight hundred and ninety-seven thousand
millions of times—or miles—in two hundred and sixty-three thousand five hundred and twenty-four millions of something elses, until
I thought if this was a birthday it were better never to have been
born. Olympia, also, became much depressed, and we both slumbered
and woke cross, and still the gentleman was going on in the dark—
whether up in the stars, or down on the stage, it would have been
hard to make out, if it had been worth trying—cyphering away about
planes of orbits, to such an infamous extent that Olympia, stung to
madness, actually kicked me. A pretty birthday spectacle, when the
lights were turned up again, and all the schools in the town (including
the National, who had come in for nothing, and serve them right, for
they were always throwing stones) were discovered with exhausted
countenances, screwing their knuckles into their eyes, or clutching
their heads of hair. A pretty birthday speech when Dr. Sleek of the
City-Free bobbed up his powdered head in the stage-box, and said
that before this assembly dispersed he really must beg to express his
entire approval of a lecture as improving, as informing, as devoid of
anything that could call a blush into the cheek of youth, as any it
had ever been his lot to hear delivered. A pretty birthday altogether,
when Astronomy couldn't leave poor Small Olympia Squires and me
alone, but must put an end to our loves! For, we never got over it;
the threadbare Orrery outwore our mutual tenderness; the man with

the wand was too much for the boy with the bow.

When shall I disconnect the combined smells of oranges, brown paper, and straw, from those other birthdays at school, when the coming hamper casts its shadow before, and when a week of social harmony—shall I add of admiring and affectionate popularity—led up to that Institution? What noble sentiments were expressed to me in the days before the hamper, what vows of friendship were sworn to me, what exceedingly old knives were given me, what generous avowals of having been in the wrong emanated from else obstinate spirits once enrolled among my enemies! The birthday of the potted game and guava jelly, is still made special to me by the noble conduct of Bully Globson. Letters from home had mysteriously inquired whether I should be much surprised and disappointed if among the treasures in the coming hamper I discovered potted game, and guava jelly from the Western Indies. I had mentioned those hints in confidence to a few friends, and had promised to give away, as I now see reason to believe, a handsome covey of partridges potted, and about a hundredweight of guava jelly. It was now that Globson, Bully no more, sought me out in the playground. He was a big fat boy, with a big fat head and a big fat fist, and at the beginning of that Half had raised such a bump on my forehead that I couldn't get my hat of state on, to go to church. He said that after an interval of cool reflection (four months) he now felt this blow to have been an error of judgment, and that he wished to apologise for the same. Not only that, but holding down his big head between his two big hands in order that I might reach it conveniently, he requested me, as an act of justice which would appease his awakened conscience, to raise a retributive bump upon it, in the presence of witnesses. This handsome proposal I modestly declined, and he then embraced me, and we walked away conversing. We conversed respecting the West India Islands, and, in the pursuit of knowledge he asked me with much interest whether in the course of my reading I had met with any reliable description of the mode of manufacturing guava jelly; or whether I had ever happened to taste that conserve, which he had been given to understand was of rare excellence.

Seventeen, eighteen, nineteen, twenty; and then with the waning months came an ever augmenting sense of the dignity of twenty-one. Heaven knows I had nothing to "come into," save the bare birthday, and yet I esteemed it as a great possession. I now and then paved the way to my state of dignity, by beginning a proposition with the casual words, "say that a man of twenty-one," or by the incidental assumption of a fact that could not sanely be disputed, as, "for when a fellow comes to be a man of twenty-one." I gave a party on the occasion. She was there. It is unnecessary to name Her more particularly; She was older than I, and had pervaded every chink and crevice of my mind for three or four years. I had held volumes of Imaginary Conversations with her mother on the subject of our union, and I had written letters more in number than Horace Walpole's, to that discreet woman, soliciting her daughter's hand in

marriage. I had never had the remotest intention of sending any of
those letters; but to write them, and after a few days tear them up,
had been a sublime occupation. Sometimes, I had begun "Honoured
Madam. I think that a lady gifted with those powers of observation
which I know you to possess, and endowed with those womanly sympathies with the young and ardent which it were more than heresy
to doubt, can scarcely have failed to discover that I love your
adorable daughter, deeply, devotedly." In less buoyant states of
mind I had begun, "Bear with me, Dear Madam, bear with a daring
wretch who is about to make a surprising confession to you, wholly
unanticipated by yourself, and which he beseeches you to commit to
the flames as soon as you have become aware to what a towering
height his mad ambition soars." At other times—periods of profound
mental depression, when She had gone out to balls where I was not—
the draft took the affecting form of a paper to be left on my table
after my departure to the confines of the globe. As thus: "For Mrs.
Onowenever, these lines when the hand that traces them shall be far
away. I could not bear the daily torture of hopelessly loving the dear
one whom I will not name. Broiling on the coast of Africa, or con-
gealing on the shores of Greenland, I am far far better there than
here." (In this sentiment my cooler judgment perceives that the
family of the beloved object would have most completely concurred.)
"If I ever emerge from obscurity, and my name is ever heralded by
Fame, it will be for her dear sake. If I ever amass Gold, it will be to
pour it at her feet. Should I on the other hand become the prey of
Ravens——" I doubt if I ever quite made up my mind what was to
be done in that affecting case; I tried "then it is better so"; but not
feeling convinced that it would be better so, I vacillated between
leaving all else blank, which looked expressive and bleak, or winding
up with "Farewell!"

This fictitious correspondence of mine is to blame for the foregoing
digression. I was about to pursue the statement that on my twenty-
first birthday I gave a party, and She was there. It was a beautiful
party. There was not a single animate or inanimate object connected
with it (except the company and myself) that I had ever seen before.
Everything was hired, and the mercenaries in attendance were profound strangers to me. Behind a door, in the crumby part of the night
when wine-glasses were to be found in unexpected spots, I spoke to
Her—spoke out to Her. What passed, I cannot as a man of honour
reveal. She was all angelical gentleness, but a word was mentioned—
a short and dreadful word of three letters, beginning with a B—
which, as I remarked at the moment, "scorched my brain." She
went away soon afterwards, and when the hollow throng (though
to be sure it was no fault of theirs) dispersed, I issued forth, with a
dissipated scorner, and, as I mentioned expressly to him, "sought
oblivion." It was found, with a dreadful headache in it, but it didn't
last; for, in the shaming light of next day's noon, I raised my heavy
head in bed, looking back to the birthdays behind me, and tracking
the circle by which I had got round, after all, to the bitter powder and

the wretchedness again.

This reactionary powder (taken so largely by the human race I am inclined to regard it as the Universal Medicine once sought for in Laboratories) is capable of being made up in another form for birthday use. Anybody's long-lost brother will do ill to turn up on a birthday. If I had a long-lost brother I should know beforehand that he would prove a tremendous fraternal failure if he appointed to rush into my arms on my birthday. The first Magic Lantern I ever saw was secretly and elaborately planned to be the great effect of a very juvenile birthday; but it wouldn't act, and its images were dim. My experience of adult birthday Magic Lanterns may possibly have been unfortunate, but has certainly been similar. I have an illustrative birthday in my eye: a birthday of my Friend Flipfield, whose birthdays had long been remarkable as social successes. There had been nothing set or formal about them; Flipfield having been accustomed merely to say, two or three days before, "Don't forget to come and dine, old boy, according to custom;"—I don't know what he said to the ladies he invited, but I may safely assume it *not* to have been "old girl." Those were delightful gatherings, and were enjoyed by all participators. In an evil hour, a long-lost brother of Flipfield's came to light in foreign parts. Where he had been hidden, or what he had been doing, I don't know, for Flipfield vaguely informed me that he had turned up "on the banks of the Ganges"—speaking of him as if he had been washed ashore. The Long-lost was coming home, and Flipfield made an unfortunate calculation, based on the well-known regularity of the P. and O. Steamers, that matters might be so contrived as that the Long-lost should appear in the nick of time on his (Flipfield's) birthday. Delicacy commanded that I should repress the gloomy anticipations with which my soul became fraught when I heard of this plan. The fatal day arrived, and we assembled in force. Mrs. Flipfield senior formed an interesting feature in the group, with a blue-veined miniature of the late Mr. Flipfield round her neck, in an oval, resembling a tart from the pastrycook's: his hair powdered, and the bright buttons on his coat, evidently very like. She was accompanied by Miss Flipfield, the eldest of her numerous family, who held her pocket-handkerchief to her bosom in a majestic manner, and spoke to all of us (none of us had ever seen her before), in pious and condoning tones, of all the quarrels that had taken place in the family, from her infancy—which must have been a long time ago—down to that hour. The Long-lost did not appear. Dinner, half an hour later than usual, was announced, and still no Long-lost. We sat down to table. The knife and fork of the Long-lost made a vacuum in Nature, and when the champagne came round for the first time, Flipfield gave him up for the day, and had them removed. It was then that the Long-lost gained the height of his popularity with the company; for my own part, I felt convinced that I loved him dearly. Flipfield's dinners are perfect, and he is the easiest and best of entertainers. Dinner went on brilliantly, and the more the Long-lost didn't come, the more comfortable we grew; and the more highly we thought of him. Flipfield's own man (who has a regard for me) was in the act of struggling with an ignorant stipendiary, to wrest from him the wooden leg of a Guinea-fowl which he was pressing on my acceptance, and to substitute a slice of the breast, when a ringing at the door-bell suspended the strife. I looked round me, and perceived the sudden pallor which I knew my own visage revealed, reflected in the faces of the company. Flipfield hurriedly excused himself, went out, was absent for about a minute or two, and then re-entered with the Long-lost.

I beg to say distinctly that if the stranger had brought Mont Blanc with him, or had come attended by a retinue of eternal snows, he could not have chilled the circle to the marrow in a more efficient manner. Embodied Failure sat enthroned upon the Long-lost's brow, and pervaded him to his Long-lost boots. In vain Mrs. Flipfield senior, opening her arms, exclaimed, "My Tom!" and pressed his nose against the counterfeit presentment of his other parent. In vain Miss Flipfield, in the first transports of this re-union, showed him a dint upon her maidenly cheek, and asked him if he remembered when he did that with the bellows? We, the bystanders, were overcome, but overcome by the palpable, undisguisable, utter, and total break-down of the Long-lost. Nothing he could have done would have set him right with us but his instant return to the Ganges. In the very same moments it became established that the feeling was reciprocal, and that the Long-lost detested us. When a friend of the family (not myself, upon my honour), wishing to set things going again, asked him, while he partook of soup—asked him with an amiability of intention beyond all praise, but with a weakness of execution open to defeat—what kind of river he considered the Ganges, the Long-lost, scowling at the friend of the family over his spoon as one of an abhorrent race, replied, "Why, a river of water, I suppose," and spooned his soup into himself with a malignancy of hand and eye that blighted the amiable questioner. Not an opinion could be elicited from the Long-lost, in unison with the sentiments of any individual present. He contradicted Flipfield dead, before he had eaten his salmon. He had no idea—or affected to have no idea—that it was his brother's birthday, and on the communication of that interesting fact to him, merely wanted to make him out four years older than he was. He was an antipathetical being, with a peculiar power and gift of treading on everybody's tenderest place. They talk in America of a man's "Platform." I should describe the Platform of the Long-lost as a Platform composed of other people's corns, on which he had stumped his way, with all his might and main, to his present position. It is needless to add that Flipfield's great birthday went by the board, and that he was a wreck when I pretended at parting to wish him many happy returns of it.

There is another class of birthdays at which I have so frequently assisted, that I may assume such birthdays to be pretty well known to the human race. My friend Mayday's birthday is an example. The guests have no knowledge of one another except on that one day in the year, and are annually terrified for a week by the prospect of meeting one another again. There is a fiction among us that we have uncommon reasons for being particularly lively and spirited on the occasion, whereas deep despondency is no phrase for the expression of our feelings. But the wonderful feature of the case is, that we are in tacit accordance to avoid the subject—to keep it as far off as possible, as long as possible—and to talk about anything else, rather than the joyful event. I may even go so far as to assert that there is a dumb compact among us that we will pretend that it is NOT Mayday's birthday. A mysterious and gloomy Being, who is said to have gone to school with Mayday, and who is so lank and lean that he seriously impugns the Dietary of the establishment at which they were jointly educated, always leads us, as I may say, to the block, by laying his grisly hand on a decanter and begging us to fill our glasses. The devices and pretences that I have seen put in practice to defer the fatal moment, and to interpose between this man and his purpose, are innumerable. I have known desperate guests, when they saw the grisly hand approaching the decanter, wildly to begin, without any antecedent whatsoever, "That reminds me——" and to plunge into long stories. When at last the hand and the decanter come together, a shudder, a palpable perceptible shudder, goes round the table. We receive the reminder that it is Mayday's birthday, as if it were the anniversary of some profound disgrace he had undergone, and we sought to comfort him. And when we have drunk Mayday's health, and wished him many happy returns, we are seized for some moments with a ghastly blitheness, an unnatural levity, as if we were in the first flushed reaction of having undergone a surgical operation.

Birthdays of this species have a public as well as a private phase. My "boyhood's home," Dullborough, presents a case in point. An Immortal Somebody was wanted in Dullborough, to dimple for a day the stagnant face of the waters; he was rather wanted by Dullborough generally, and much wanted by the principal hotel-keeper. The County history was looked up for a locally Immortal Somebody, but the registered Dullborough worthies were all Nobodies. In this state of things, it is hardly necessary to record that Dullborough did what every man does when he wants to write a book or deliver a lecture, and is provided with all the materials except a subject. It fell back upon Shakespeare.

No sooner was it resolved to celebrate Shakespeare's birthday in Dullborough, than the popularity of the immortal bard became surprising. You might have supposed the first edition of his works to have been published last week, and enthusiastic Dullborough to have got half through them. (I doubt, by the way, whether it had ever done half that, but this is a private opinion.) A young gentleman with a sonnet, the retention of which for two years had enfeebled his mind and undermined his knees, got the sonnet into the Dullborough Warden, and gained flesh. Portraits of Shakespeare broke out in the bookshop windows, and our principal artist painted a large original portrait in oils for the decoration of the dining-room. It was not in the least like any of the other portraits, and was exceedingly admired, the head being much swollen. At the Institution, the Debating Society discussed the new question, Was there sufficient ground for supposing that the Immortal Shakespeare ever stole deer? This was indignantly decided by an overwhelming majority in the negative; indeed, there was but one vote on the Poaching side, and that was the vote of the orator who had undertaken to advocate it, and who became quite an obnoxious character—particularly to the Dullborough "roughs," who were about as well informed on the matter as most other people. Distinguished speakers were invited down, and very nearly came (but not quite). Subscriptions were opened, and committees sat, and it would have been far from a popular measure in the height of the excitement, to have told Dullborough that it wasn't Stratford-upon-Avon. Yet, after all these preparations, when the great festivity took place, and the portrait, elevated aloft, surveyed the company as if it were in danger of springing a mine of intellect and blowing itself up, it did undoubtedly happen, according to the inscrutable mysteries of things, that nobody could be induced, not to say to touch upon Shakespeare, but to come within a mile of him, until the crack speaker of Dullborough rose to propose the immortal memory. Which he did with the perplexing and astonishing result that before he had repeated the great name half-a-dozen times, or had been upon his legs as many minutes, he was assailed with a general shout of "Question."

XXI

THE SHORT-TIMERS

"WITHIN so many yards of this Covent-garden lodging of mine, as within so many yards of Westminster Abbey, Saint Paul's Cathedral, the Houses of Parliament, the Prisons, the Courts of Justice, all the Institutions that govern the land, I can find—*must* find, whether I will or no—in the open streets, shameful instances of neglect of children, intolerable toleration of the engenderment of paupers, idlers, thieves, races of wretched and destructive cripples both in body and mind, a misery to themselves, a misery to the community, a disgrace to civilisation, and an outrage on Christianity. I know it to be a fact as easy of demonstration as any sum in any of the elementary rules of arithmetic, that if the State would begin its work and duty at the beginning, and would with the strong hand take those children out of the streets, while they are yet children, and wisely train them, it would make them a part of England's glory, not its shame—of England's strength, not its weakness—would raise good soldiers and sailors, and good citizens, and many great men, out of the seeds of its criminal population. Yet I go on bearing with the enormity as if it were nothing, and I go on reading the Parliamentary Debates as if they were something, and I concern myself far more about one railway-bridge across a public thoroughfare, than about a dozen generations of scrofula, ignorance, wickedness, prostitution, poverty, and felony. I can slip out at my door, in the small hours after any midnight, and, in one circuit of the purlieus of Covent-garden Market, can behold a state of infancy and youth, as vile as if a Bourbon sat upon the English throne; a great police force looking on with authority to do no more than worry and hunt the dreadful vermin into corners, and there leave them. Within the length of a few streets I can find a workhouse, mismanaged with that dull short-sighted obstinacy that its greatest opportunities as to the children it receives are lost, and yet not a farthing saved to any one. But the wheel goes round, and round, and round; and because it goes round —so I am told by the politest authorities—it goes well."

Thus I reflected, one day in the Whitsun week last past, as I floated down the Thames among the bridges, looking—not inappropriately—at the drags that were hanging up at certain dirty stairs to hook the drowned out, and at the numerous conveniences provided to facilitate their tumbling in. My object in that uncommercial journey called up another train of thought, and it ran as follows:

"When I was at school, one of seventy boys, I wonder by what secret understanding our attention began to wander when we had pored over our books for some hours. I wonder by what ingenuity we brought on that confused state of mind when sense became nonsense, when figures wouldn't work, when dead languages wouldn't construe, when live languages wouldn't be spoken, when memory wouldn't come, when dulness and vacancy wouldn't go. I cannot remember that we ever conspired to be sleepy after dinner, or that we ever particularly wanted to be stupid, and to have flushed faces and hot heating heads, or to find blank hopelessness and obscurity this after-noon in what would become perfectly clear and bright in the fresh-ness of to-morrow morning. We suffered for these things, and they made us miserable enough. Neither do I remember that we ever bound ourselves by any secret oath or other solemn obligation, to find the seats getting too hard to be sat upon after a certain time; or to have intolerable twitches in our legs, rendering us aggressive and malicious with those members; or to be troubled with a similar uneasiness in our elbows, attended with fistic consequences to our neighbours; or to carry two pounds of lead in the chest, four pounds in the head, and several active blue-bottles in each ear. Yet, for certain, we suffered under those distresses, and were always charged at for labouring under them, as if we had brought them on, of our own deliberate act and deed. As to the mental portion of them being my own fault in my own case—I should like to ask any well-trained and experienced teacher, not to say psychologist. And as to the physical portion—I should like to ask PROFESSOR OWEN."

It happened that I had a small bundle of papers with me, on what is called "The Half-Time System" in schools. Referring to one of those papers I found that the indefatigable MR. CHADWICK had been beforehand with me, and had already asked Professor Owen: who had handsomely replied that I was not to blame, but that, being troubled with a skeleton, and having been constituted according to certain natural laws, I and my skeleton were unfortunately bound by those laws—even in school—and had comported ourselves accordingly. Much comforted by the good Professor's being on my side, I read on to discover whether the indefatigable Mr. Chadwick had taken up the mental part of my afflictions. I found that he had, and that he had gained on my behalf, SIR BENJAMIN BRODIE, SIR DAVID WILKIE, SIR WALTER SCOTT, and the common sense of mankind. For which I beg Mr. Chadwick, if this should meet his eye, to accept my warm acknowledgments.

Up to that time I had retained a misgiving that the seventy unfortunates of whom I was one, must have been, without knowing it, leagued together by the spirit of evil in a sort of perpetual Guy Fawkes Plot, to grope about in vaults with dark lanterns after a certain period of continuous study. But now the misgiving vanished, and I floated on with a quieted mind to see the Half-Time System in action. For that was the purpose of my journey, both by steamboat on the Thames, and by very dirty railway on the shore. To which last institution, I beg to recommend the legal use of coke as engine fuel, rather than the illegal use of coal; the recommendation is quite disinterested, for I was most liberally supplied with small coal on the journey, for which no charge was made. I had not only my eyes, nose, and ears filled, but my hat, and all my pockets, and my pocket-book, and my watch.

The V.D.S.C.R.C. (or Very Dirty and Small Coal Railway Company) delivered me close to my destination, and I soon found the Half-Time System established in spacious premises, and freely placed at my convenience and disposal.

What would I see first of the Half-Time System? I chose Military Drill. "Atten-tion!" Instantly a hundred boys stood forth in the paved yard as one boy; bright, quick, eager, steady, watchful for the look of command, instant and ready for the word. Not only was there complete precision—complete accord to the eye and to the ear—but an alertness in the doing of the thing which deprived it, curiously, of its monotonous or mechanical character. There was perfect uniformity, and yet an individual spirit and emulation. No spectator could doubt that the boys liked it. With non-commissioned officers varying from a yard to a yard and a half high the result could not possibly have been attained otherwise. They marched, and counter-marched, and formed in line and square, and company, and single file and double file, and performed a variety of evolutions; all most admirably. In respect of an air of enjoyable understanding of what they were about, which seems to be forbidden to English soldiers, the boys might have been small French troops. When they were dismissed and the broadsword exercise, limited to a much smaller number, succeeded, the boys who had no part in that new drill, either looked on attentively, or disported themselves in a gymnasium hard by. The steadiness of the broadsword boys on their short legs, and the firmness with which they sustained the different positions, was truly remarkable.

The broadsword exercise over, suddenly there was great excitement and a rush. Naval Drill!

In the corner of the ground stood a decked mimic ship, with real masts, yards, and sails —mainmast seventy feet high. At the word of command from the Skipper of this ship —a mahogany-faced Old Salt, with the indispensable quid in his cheek, the true nautical roll, and all wonderfully complete—the rigging was covered with a swarm of boys: one, the first to spring into the shrouds, outstripping all the others, and resting on the truck of the main-topmast in no time.

And now we stood out to sea, in a most amazing manner; the Skipper himself, the whole crew, the Uncommercial, and all hands present, implicitly believing that there was not a moment to lose, that the wind had that instant chopped round and sprung up fair, and that we were away on a voyage round the world. Get all sail upon her! With a will, my lads! Lay out upon the main-yard there! Look alive at the weather earring! Cheery, my boys! Let go the sheet, now! Stand by at the braces, you! With a will, aloft there! Belay, starboard watch! Fifer! Come aft, fifer, and give 'em a tune! Forthwith, springs up fifer, fife in hand—smallest boy ever seen—big lump on temple, having lately fallen down on a paving-stone —gives 'em a tune with all his might and main. Hooroar, fifer! With a will, my lads! Tip 'em a livelier one, fifer! Fifer tips 'em a livelier one, and excitement increases. Shake 'em out, my lads! Well done! There you have her! Pretty, pretty! Every rag upon her she can carry, wind right astern, and ship cutting through the water fifteen knots an hour!

At this favourable moment of her voyage, I gave the alarm "A man overboard!" (on the gravel), but he was immediately recovered, none the worse. Presently, I observed the Skipper overboard, but forbore to mention it, as he seemed in no wise disconcerted by the accident. Indeed, I soon came to regard the Skipper as an amphibious creature, for he was so perpetually plunging overboard to look up at the hands aloft, that he was oftener in the bosom of the ocean than on deck. His pride in his crew on those occasions was delightful, and the conventional unintelligibility of his orders in the ears of uncommercial land-lubbers and loblolly boys, though they were always intelligible to the crew, was hardly less pleasant. But we couldn't expect to go on in this way for ever; dirty weather came on, and then worse weather, and when we least expected it we got into tremendous difficulties. Screw loose in the chart perhaps—something certainly wrong somewhere —but here we were with breakers ahead, my lads, driving head on, slap on a lee shore! The Skipper broached this terrific announcement in such great agitation, that the small fifer, not fifeing now, but standing looking on near the wheel with his fife under his arm, seemed for the moment quite unboyed, though he speedily recovered his presence of mind. In the trying circumstances that ensued, the Skipper and the crew proved worthy of one another. The Skipper got dreadfully hoarse, but otherwise was master of the

situation. The man at the wheel did wonders; all hands (except the
fifer) were turned up to wear ship; and I observed the fifer, when we
were at our greatest extremity, to refer to some document in his
waistcoat-pocket, which I conceived to be his will. I think she struck.
I was not myself conscious of any collision, but I saw the Skipper so
very often washed overboard and back again, that I could only
impute it to the beating of the ship. I am not enough of a seaman to
describe the manœuvres by which we were saved, but they made the
Skipper very hot (French polishing his mahogany face) and the crew
very nimble, and succeeded to a marvel; for within a few minutes
of the first alarm, we had wore ship and got her off, and were all
a-tauto—which I felt very grateful for: not that I knew what it was,
but that I perceived that we had not been all a-tauto lately. Land
now appeared on our weather-bow, and we shaped our course for it,
having the wind abeam, and frequently changing the man at the
helm, in order that every man might have his spell. We worked into
harbour under prosperous circumstances, and furled our sails, and
squared our yards, and made all ship-shape and handsome, and so
our voyage ended. When I complimented the Skipper at parting on
his exertions and those of his gallant crew, he informed me that the
latter were provided for the worst, all hands being taught to swim
and dive; and he added that the able seaman at the main-topmast
truck especially, could dive as deep as he could go high.

The next adventure that befell me in my visit to the Short-Timers,
was the sudden apparition of a military band. I had been inspecting
the hammocks of the crew of the good ship, when I saw with astonishment that several musical instruments, brazen and of great size,
appeared to have suddenly developed two legs each, and to be trotting about a yard. And my astonishment was heightened when I
observed a large drum, that had previously been leaning helpless
against a wall, taking up a stout position on four legs. Approaching
this drum and looking over it, I found two boys behind it (it was too
much for one), and then I found that each of the brazen instruments
had brought out a boy, and was going to discourse sweet sounds. The
boys—not omitting the fifer, now playing a new instrument—were
dressed in neat uniform, and stood up in a circle at their music-stands
like any other Military Band. They played a march or two, and then
we had Cheer boys, Cheer, and then we had Yankee Doodle, and we
finished, as in loyal duty bound, with God Save the Queen. The band's
proficiency was perfectly wonderful, and it was not at all wonderful
that the whole body corporate of Short-Timers listened with faces
of the liveliest interest and pleasure.

What happened next among the Short-Timers? As if the band had
blown me into a great class-room out of their brazen tubes, *in* a great
class-room I found myself now, with the whole choral force of Short-
Timers singing the praises of a summer's day to the harmonium, and
my small but highly respected friend the fifer blazing away vocally,
as if he had been saving up his wind for the last twelvemonth; also
the whole crew of the good ship Nameless swarming up and down the

scale as if they had never swarmed up and down the rigging. This
done, we threw our whole power into God bless the Prince of Wales,
and blessed his Royal Highness to such an extent that, for my own
Uncommercial part, I gasped again when it was over. The moment
this was done, we formed, with surpassing freshness, into hollow
squares, and fell to work at oral lessons, as if we never did, and had
never thought of doing, anything else.

Let a veil be drawn over the self-committals into which the Uncommercial Traveller would have been betrayed but for a discreet
reticence, coupled with an air of absolute wisdom on the part of that
artful personage. Take the square of five, multiply it by fifteen,
divide it by three, deduct eight from it, add four dozen to it, give me
the result in pence, and tell me how many eggs I could get for it at
three farthings apiece. The problem is hardly stated, when a dozen
small boys pour out answers. Some wide, some very nearly right,
some worked as far as they go with such accuracy, as at once to show
what link of the chain has been dropped in the hurry. For the moment, none are quite right; but behold a labouring spirit beating the
buttons on its corporeal waistcoat, in a process of internal calculation,
and knitting an accidental bump on its corporeal forehead in a con-
centration of mental arithmetic! It is my honourable friend (if he will
allow me to call him so) the fifer. With right arm eagerly extended in
token of being inspired with an answer, and with right leg foremost,
the fifer solves the mystery: then recalls both arm and leg, and with
bump in ambush awaits the next poser. Take the square of three,
multiply it by seven, divide it by four, add fifty to it, take thirteen
from it, multiply it by two, double it, give me the result in pence, and
say how many halfpence. Wise as the serpent is the four feet of performer on the nearest approach to that instrument, whose right arm
instantly appears, and quenches this arithmetical fire. Tell me something about Great Britain, tell me something about its principal pro-
ductions, tell me something about its ports, tell me something about
its seas and rivers, tell me something about coal, iron, cotton, timber,
tin, and turpentine. The hollow square bristles with extended right
arms; but ever faithful to fact is the fifer, ever wise as the serpent is
the performer on that instrument, ever prominently buoyant and
brilliant are all members of the band. I observe the player of the
cymbals to dash at a sounding answer now and then rather than not
cut in at all; but I take that to be in the way of his instrument. All
these questions, and many such, are put on the spur of the moment,
and by one who has never examined these boys. The Uncommercial
invited to add another, falteringly demands how many birthdays a
man born on the twenty-ninth of February will have had on completing his fiftieth year? A general perception of trap and pitfall instantly
arises, and the fifer is seen to retire behind the corduroys of his next
neighbours, as perceiving special necessity for collecting himself and
communing with his mind. Meanwhile, the wisdom of the serpent
suggests that the man will have had only one birthday in all that
time, for how can any man have more than one, seeing that he is born

once and dies once? The blushing Uncommercial stands corrected, and amends the formula. Pondering ensues, two or three wrong answers are offered, and Cymbals strikes up "Six!" but doesn't know why. Then modestly emerging from his Academic Grove of corduroys appears the fifer, right arm extended, right leg foremost, bump irradiated. "Twelve, and two over!"

The feminine Short-Timers passed a similar examination, and very creditably too. Would have done better perhaps, with a little more geniality on the part of their pupil-teacher; for a cold eye, my young friend, and a hard, abrupt manner, are not by any means the powerful engines that your innocence supposes them to be. Both girls and boys wrote excellently, from copy and dictation; both could cook; both could mend their own clothes; both could clean up everything about them in an orderly and skilful way, the girls having womanly household knowledge superadded. Order and method began in the songs of the Infant School which I visited likewise, and they were even in their dwarf degree to be found in the Nursery, where the Uncommercial walking stick was carried off with acclamations, and where "the Doctor"—a medical gentleman of two, who took his degree on the night when he was found at an apothecary's door—did the honours of the establishment with great urbanity and gaiety.

These have long been excellent schools; long before the days of the Short-Time. I first saw them, twelve or fifteen years ago. But since the introduction of the Short-Time system it has been proved here that eighteen hours a week of book-learning are more profitable than thirty-six, and that the pupils are far quicker and brighter than of yore. The good influences of music on the whole body of children have likewise been surprisingly proved. Obviously another of the immense advantages of the Short-Time system to the cause of good education is the great diminution of its cost, and of the period of time over which it extends. The last is a most important consideration, as poor parents are always impatient to profit by their children's labour.

It will be objected: Firstly, that this is all very well, but special local advantages and special selection of children must be necessary to such success. Secondly, that this is all very well, but must be very expensive. Thirdly, that this is all very well, but we have no proof of the results, sir, no proof.

On the first head of local advantages and special selection. Would Limehouse Hole be picked out for the site of a Children's Paradise? Or would the legitimate and illegitimate pauper children of the long-shore population of such a river-side district, be regarded as unusually favourable specimens to work with? Yet these schools are at Limehouse, and are the Pauper Schools of the Stepney Pauper Union.

On the second head of expense. Would sixpence a week be considered a very large cost for the education of each pupil, including all salaries of teachers and rations of teachers? But supposing the cost were not sixpence a week, not fivepence? It is FOURPENCE-HALFPENNY.

On the third head of no proof, sir, no proof. Is there any proof in the facts that Pupil Teachers more in number, and more highly qualified, have been produced here under the Short-Time system than under the Long-Time system? That the Short-Timers, in a writing competition, beat the Long-Timers of a first-class National School? That the sailor-boys are in such demand for merchant ships, that whereas, before they were trained, 10*l.* premium used to be given with each boy—too often to some greedy brute of a drunken skipper, who disappeared before the term of apprenticeship was out, if the ill-used boy didn't—captains of the best character now take these boys more than willingly, with no premium at all? That they are also much esteemed in the Royal Navy, which they prefer, "because everything is so neat and clean and orderly"? Or, is there any proof in Naval captains writing, "Your little fellows are all that I can desire"? Or, is there any proof in such testimony as this: "The owner of a vessel called at the school, and said that as his ship was going down Channel on her last voyage, with one of the boys from the school on board, the pilot said, 'It would be as well if the royal were lowered; I wish it were down.' Without waiting for any orders, and unobserved by the pilot, the lad, whom they had taken on board from the school, instantly mounted the mast and lowered the royal, and at the next glance of the pilot to the masthead, he perceived that the sail had been let down. He exclaimed, 'Who's done that job?' The owner, who was on board, said, 'That was the little fellow whom I put on board two days ago.' The pilot immediately said, 'Why, where could he have been brought up?' That boy had never seen the sea or been on a real ship before"? Or, is there any proof in these boys being in greater demand for Regimental Bands than the Union can meet? Or, in ninety-eight of them having gone into Regimental Bands in three years? Or, in twelve of them being in the band of one regiment? Or, in the colonel of that regiment writing, "We want six more boys; they are excellent lads"? Or, in one of the boys having risen to be band-corporal in the same regiment? Or, in employers of all kinds chorusing, "Give us drilled boys, for they are prompt, obedient, and punctual"? Other proofs I have myself beheld with these Uncommercial eyes, though I do not regard myself as having a right to relate in what social positions they have seen respected men and women who were once pauper children of the Stepney Union.

Into what admirable soldiers others of these boys have the capabilities for being turned, I need not point out. Many of them are always ambitious of military service; and once upon a time when an old boy came back to see the old place, a cavalry soldier all complete, *with his spurs on*, such a yearning broke out to get into cavalry regiments and wear those sublime appendages, that it was one of the greatest excitements ever known in the school. The girls make excellent domestic servants, and at certain periods come back, a score or two at a time, to see the old building, and to take tea with the old teachers, and to hear the old band, and to see the old ship with her masts towering up above the neighbouring roofs and chimneys. As to the physical health of these schools, it is so exceptionally remarkable (simply because the sanitary regulations are as

good as the other educational arrangements), that when Mr. Tuf-
nell, the Inspector, first stated it in a report, he was supposed, in
spite of his high character, to have been betrayed into some extraordinary mistake or exaggeration. In the moral health of these
schools—where corporal punishment is unknown—Truthfulness
stands high. When the ship was first erected, the boys were forbidden
to go aloft, until the nets, which are now always there, were stretched
as a precaution against accidents. Certain boys, in their eagerness,
disobeyed the injunction, got out of window in the early daylight,
and climbed to the masthead. One boy unfortunately fell, and was
killed. There was no clue to the others; but all the boys were assembled, and the chairman of the Board addressed them. "I promise
nothing; you see what a dreadful thing has happened; you know
what a grave offence it is that has led to such a consequence; I cannot
say what will be done with the offenders; but, boys, you have been
trained here, above all things, to respect the truth. I want the truth.
Who are the delinquents?" Instantly, the whole number of boys
concerned, separated from the rest, and stood out.

Now, the head and heart of that gentleman (it is needless to say, a
good head and a good heart) have been deeply interested in these
schools for many years, and are so still; and the establishment is very
fortunate in a most admirable master, and moreover the schools of
the Stepney Union cannot have got to be what they are, without the
Stepney Board of Guardians having been earnest and humane men
strongly imbued with a sense of their responsibility. But what one set
of men can do in this wise, another set of men can do; and this is a
noble example to all other Bodies and Unions, and a noble example
to the State. Followed, and enlarged upon by its enforcement on bad
parents, it would clear London streets of the most terrible objects
they smite the sight with—myriads of little children who awfully
reverse Our Saviour's words, and are not of the Kingdom of Heaven
but of the Kingdom of Hell.

Clear the public streets of such shame, and the public conscience of
such reproach? Ah! Almost prophetic, surely, the child's jingle:

When will that be,
Say the bells of Step-ney!

XXII

BOUND FOR THE GREAT SALT LAKE

Behold me on my way to an Emigrant Ship, on a hot morning early
in June. My road lies through that part of London generally known
to the initiated as "Down by the Docks." Down by the Docks, is
home to a good many people—to too many, if I may judge from the
overflow of local population in the streets—but my nose insinuates
that the number to whom it is Sweet Home might be easily counted.
Down by the Docks, is a region I would choose as my point of em-

barkation aboard ship if I were an emigrant. It would present my intention to me in such a sensible light; it would show me so many things to be run away from.

Down by the Docks, they eat the largest oysters and scatter the roughest oyster-shells, known to the descendants of Saint George and the Dragon. Down by the Docks, they consume the slimiest of shell-fish, which seem to have been scraped off the copper bottoms of ships. Down by the Docks, the vegetables at greengrocers' doors acquire a saline and a scaly look, as if they had been crossed with fish and seaweed. Down by the Docks, they "board seamen" at the eating houses, the public-houses, the slop-shops, the coffee-shops, the tally-shops, all kinds of shops mentionable and unmentionable—board them, as it were, in the piratical sense, making them bleed terribly, and giving no quarter. Down by the Docks, the seamen roam in mid-street and mid-day, their pockets inside out, and their heads no better. Down by the Docks, the daughters of wave-ruling Britannia also rove, clad in silken attire, with uncovered tresses streaming in the breeze, bandanna kerchiefs floating from their shoulders, and crinoline not wanting. Down by the Docks, you may hear the Incomparable Joe Jackson sing the Standard of England, with a hornpipe, any night; or any day may see at the waxwork, for a penny and no waiting, him as killed the policeman at Acton and suffered for it. Down by the Docks, you may buy polonies, saveloys, and sausage preparations various, if you are not particular what they are made of besides seasoning. Down by the Docks, the children of Israel creep into any gloomy cribs and entries they can hire, and hang slops there—pewter watches, sou'-wester hats, waterproof overalls— "firtht rate articleth, Thjack." Down by the Docks, such dealers exhibiting on a frame a complete nautical suit without the refinement of a waxen visage in the hat, present the imaginary wearer as droop-ing at the yard-arm, with his seafaring and earthfaring troubles over. Down by the Docks, the placards in the shops apostrophise the customer, knowing him familiarly beforehand, as, "Look here, Jack!" "Here's your sort, my lad!" "Try our seagoing mixed, at two and nine!" "The right kit for the British tar!" "Ship ahoy!" "Splice the main-brace, brother!" "Come, cheer up, my lads. We've the best liquors here, And you'll find something new In our wonderful Beer!" Down by the Docks, the pawnbroker lends money on Union-Jack pocket-handkerchiefs, on watches with little ships pitching fore and aft on the dial, on telescopes, nautical instruments in cases, and such-like. Down by the Docks, the apothecary sets up in business on the wretchedest scale—chiefly on lint and plaster for the strapping of wounds—and with no bright bottles, and with no little drawers. Down by the Docks, the shabby undertaker's shop will bury you for next to nothing, after the Malay or Chinaman has stabbed you for nothing at all: so you can hardly hope to make a cheaper end. Down by the Docks, anybody drunk will quarrel with anybody drunk or sober, and everybody else will have a hand in it, and on the shortest notice you may revolve in a whirlpool of red shirts, shaggy beards,

wild heads of hair, bare tattooed arms, Britannia's daughters, malice,
mud, maundering, and madness. Down by the Docks, scraping fiddles
go in the public-houses all day long, and, shrill above their din and all
the din, rises the screeching of innumerable parrots brought from
foreign parts, who appear to be very much astonished by what they
find on these native shores of ours. Possibly the parrots don't
know, possibly they do, that Down by the Docks is the road to the
Pacific Ocean, with its lovely islands, where the savage girls plait
flowers, and the savage boys carve cocoa-nut shells, and the grim
blind idols muse in their shady groves to exactly the same purpose as
the priests and chiefs. And possibly the parrots don't know, possibly
they do, that the noble savage is a wearisome impostor wherever he is,
and has five hundred thousand volumes of indifferent rhyme, and no
reason, to answer for.

Shadwell church! Pleasant whispers of there being a fresher air
down the river than down by the Docks, go pursuing one another,
playfully, in and out of the openings in its spire. Gigantic in the basin
just beyond the church, looms my Emigrant Ship: her name, the
Amazon. Her figure-head is not *dis*figured as those beauteous founders
of the race of strong-minded women are fabled to have been, for the
convenience of drawing the bow; but I sympathise with the carver:

> A flattering carver who made it his care
> To carve busts as they ought to be—not as they were.

My Emigrant Ship lies broadside-on to the wharf. Two great gangways made of spars and planks connect her with the wharf; and up
and down these gangways, perpetually crowding to and fro and in
and out, like ants, are the Emigrants who are going to sail in my
Emigrant Ship. Some with cabbages, some with loaves of bread,
some with cheese and butter, some with milk and beer, some with
boxes, beds, and bundles, some with babies—nearly all with children
—nearly all with bran-new tin cans for their daily allowance of water,
uncomfortably suggestive of a tin flavour in the drink. To and fro,
up and down, aboard and ashore, swarming here and there and
everywhere, my Emigrants. And still as the Dock-Gate swings upon
its hinges, cabs appear, and carts appear, and vans appear, bringing
more of my Emigrants, with more cabbages, more loaves, more
cheese and butter, more milk and beer, more boxes, beds, and
bundles, more tin cans, and on those shipping investments accumu-
lated compound interest of children.

I go aboard my Emigrant Ship. I go first to the great cabin, and
find it in the usual condition of a Cabin at that pass. Perspiring
landsmen, with loose papers, and with pens and inkstands, pervade
it; and the general appearance of things is as if the late Mr. Amazon's
funeral had just come home from the cemetery, and the disconsolate
Mrs. Amazon's trustees found the affairs in great disorder, and were
looking high and low for the will. I go out on the poop-deck, for air,
and surveying the emigrants on the deck below (indeed they are

crowded all about me, up there too), find more pens and inkstands in action, and more papers, and interminable complication respecting accounts with individuals for tin cans and what not. But nobody is in an ill-temper, nobody is the worse for drink, nobody swears an oath or uses a coarse word, nobody appears depressed, nobody is weeping, and down upon the deck in every corner where it is possible to find a few square feet to kneel, crouch, or lie in, people, in every unsuitable attitude for writing, are writing letters.

Now, I have seen emigrant ships before this day in June. And these people are so strikingly different from all other people in like circumstances whom I have ever seen, that I wonder aloud, "What *would* a stranger suppose these emigrants to be!"

The vigilant, bright face of the weather-browned captain of the Amazon is at my shoulder, and he says, "What, indeed! The most of these came aboard yesterday evening. They came from various parts of England in small parties that had never seen one another before. Yet they had not been a couple of hours on board, when they established their own police, made their own regulations, and set their own watches at all the hatchways. Before nine o'clock, the ship was as orderly and as quiet as a man-of-war."

I looked about me again, and saw the letter-writing going on with the most curious composure. Perfectly abstracted in the midst of the crowd; while great casks were swinging aloft, and being lowered into the hold; while hot agents were hurrying up and down, adjusting the interminable accounts; while two hundred strangers were searching everywhere for two hundred other strangers, and were asking questions about them of two hundred more; while the children played up and down all the steps, and in and out among all the people's legs, and were beheld, to the general dismay, toppling over all the dangerous places; the letter-writers wrote on calmly. On the starboard side of the ship, a grizzled man dictated a long letter to another grizzled man in an immense fur cap: which letter was of so profound a quality, that it became necessary for the amanuensis at intervals to take off his fur cap in both his hands, for the ventilation of his brain, and stare at him who dictated, as a man of many mysteries who was worth looking at. On the larboard side, a woman had covered a belaying-pin with a white cloth to make a neat desk of it, and was, sitting on a little box, writing with the deliberation of a bookkeeper. Down upon her breast on the planks of the deck at this woman's feet, with her head diving in under a beam of the bulwark on that side, as an eligible place of refuge for her sheet of paper, a neat and pretty girl wrote for a good hour (she fainted at last), only rising to the surface occasionally for a dip of ink. Alongside the boat, close to me on the poop-deck, another girl, a fresh, well-grown country girl, was writing another letter on the bare deck. Later in the day, when this self-same boat was filled with a choir who sang glees and catches for a long time, one of the singers, a girl, sang her part mechanically all the while, and wrote a letter in the bottom of the boat while doing so.

"A stranger would be puzzled to guess the right name for these people, Mr. Uncommercial," says the captain.

"Indeed he would."

"If you hadn't known, could you ever have supposed——?"

"How could I! I should have said they were in their degree, the pick of the flower of England."

"So should I," says the captain.

"How many are they?"

"Eight hundred in round numbers."

I went between-decks, where the families with children swarmed in the dark, where unavoidable confusion had been caused by the last arrivals, and where the confusion was increased by the little preparations for dinner that were going on in each group. A few women here and there, had got lost, and were laughing at it, and asking their way to their own people, or out on deck again. A few of the poor children were crying; but otherwise the universal cheerfulness was amazing. "We shall shake down by to-morrow." "We shall come all right in a day or so." "We shall have more light at sea." Such phrases I heard everywhere, as I groped my way among chests and barrels and beams and unstowed cargo and ring-bolts and Emigrants, down to the lower-deck, and thence up to the light of day again, and to my former station.

Surely, an extraordinary people in their power of self-abstraction! All the former letter-writers were still writing calmly, and many more letter-writers had broken out in my absence. A boy with a bag of books in his hand and a slate under his arm, emerged from below, concentrated himself in my neighbourhood (espying a convenient skylight for his purpose), and went to work at a sum as if he were stone deaf. A father and mother and several young children, on the main deck below me, had formed a family circle close to the foot of the crowded restless gangway, where the children made a nest for themselves in a coil of rope, and the father and mother, she suckling the youngest, discussing family affairs as peaceably as if they were in perfect retirement. I think the most noticeable characteristic in the eight hundred as a mass, was their exemption from hurry.

Eight hundred what? "Geese, villain?" EIGHT HUNDRED MORMONS. I, Uncommercial Traveller for the firm of Human Interest Brothers, had come aboard this Emigrant Ship to see what Eight hundred Latter-day Saints were like, and I found them (to the rout and over-throw of all my expectations), like what I now describe with scrupulous exactness.

The Mormon Agent who had been active in getting them together, and in making the contract with my friends the owners of the ship to take them as far as New York on their way to the Great Salt Lake, was pointed out to me. A compactly-made handsome man in black, rather short, with rich-brown hair and beard, and clear bright eyes. From his speech, I should set him down as American. Probably, a man who had "knocked about the world" pretty much. A man with a frank open manner, and unshrinking look; withal a man of great quickness. I believe he was wholly ignorant of my Uncommercial individuality, and consequently of my immense Uncommercial importance.

UNCOMMERCIAL. These are a very fine set of people you have brought together here.

MORMON AGENT. Yes, sir, they are a *very* fine set of people.

UNCOMMERCIAL (looking about). Indeed, I think it would be difficult to find Eight hundred people together anywhere else, and find so much beauty and so much strength and capacity for work among them.

MORMON AGENT (not looking about, but looking steadily at Uncommercial). I think so.—We sent out about a thousand more, yes'day, from Liverpool.

UNCOMMERCIAL. You are not going with these emigrants?

MORMON AGENT. No, sir. I remain.

UNCOMMERCIAL. But you have been in the Mormon Territory?

MORMON AGENT. Yes; I left Utah about three years ago.

UNCOMMERCIAL. It is surprising to me that these people are all so cheery, and make so little of the immense distance before them.

MORMON AGENT. Well, you see; many of 'em have friends out at Utah, and many of 'em look forward to meeting friends on the way.

UNCOMMERCIAL. On the way?

MORMON AGENT. This way 'tis. This ship lands 'em in New York City. Then they go on by rail right away beyond St. Louis, to that part of the Banks of the Missouri where they strike the Plains. There, waggons from the settlement meet 'em to bear 'em company on their journey 'cross—twelve hundred miles about. Industrious people who come out to the settlement soon get waggons of their own, and so the friends of some of these will come down in their own waggons to meet 'em. They look forward to that, greatly.

UNCOMMERCIAL. On their long journey across the Desert, do you arm them?

MORMON AGENT. Mostly you would find they have arms of some kind or another already with them. Such as had not arms we should arm across the Plains, for the general protection and defence.

UNCOMMERCIAL. Will these waggons bring down any produce to the Missouri?

MORMON AGENT. Well, since the war broke out, we've taken to growing cotton, and they'll likely bring down cotton to be exchanged for machinery. We want machinery. Also we have taken to growing indigo, which is a fine commodity for profit. It has been found that the climate on the further side of the Great Salt Lake suits well for raising indigo.

UNCOMMERCIAL. I am told that these people now on board are principally from the South of England?

MORMON AGENT. And from Wales. That's true.

UNCOMMERCIAL. Do you get many Scotch?

MORMON AGENT. Not many.

UNCOMMERCIAL. Highlanders, for instance?

MORMON AGENT. No, not Highlanders. They ain't interested

enough in universal brotherhood and peace and good will.

UNCOMMERCIAL. The old fighting blood is strong in them?

MORMON AGENT. Well, yes. And besides; they've no faith.

UNCOMMERCIAL (who has been burning to get at the Prophet Joe Smith, and seems to discover an opening). Faith in——!

MORMON AGENT (far too many for Uncommercial). Well.—In anything!

Similarly on this same head, the Uncommercial underwent discomfiture from a Wiltshire labourer: a simple, fresh-coloured farm-labourer, of eight-and-thirty, who at one time stood beside him looking on at new arrivals, and with whom he held this dialogue:

UNCOMMERCIAL. Would you mind my asking you what part of the country you come from?

WILTSHIRE. Not a bit. Theer! (exultingly) I've worked all my life o' Salisbury Plain, right under the shadder o' Stonehenge. You mightn't think it, but I haive.

UNCOMMERCIAL. And a pleasant country too.

WILTSHIRE. Ah! 'Tis a pleasant country.

UNCOMMERCIAL. Have you any family on board?

WILTSHIRE. Two children, boy and gal. I am a widderer, *I* am, and I'm going out alonger my boy and gal. That's my gal, and she's a fine gal o' sixteen (pointing out the girl who is writing by the boat). I'll go and fetch my boy. I'd like to show you my boy. (Here Wiltshire disappears, and presently comes back with a big, shy boy of twelve, in a superabundance of boots, who is not at all glad to be presented.) He is a fine boy too, and a boy fur to work! (Boy having undutifully bolted, Wiltshire drops him.)

UNCOMMERCIAL. It must cost you a great deal of money to go so far, three strong.

WILTSHIRE. A power of money. Theer! Eight shillen a week, eight shillen a week, eight shillen a week, put by out of the week's wages for ever so long.

UNCOMMERCIAL. I wonder how you did it.

WILTSHIRE (recognising in this a kindred spirit). See theer now! *I* wonder how I done it! But what with a bit o' subscription heer, and what with a bit o' help theer, it were done at last, though I don't hardly know how. Then it were unfort'net for us, you see, as we got kep' in Bristol so long—nigh a fortnight, it were—on accounts of a mistake wi' Brother Halliday. Swaller'd up money, it did, when we might have come straight on.

UNCOMMERCIAL (delicately approaching Joe Smith). You are of the Mormon religion, of course?

WILTSHIRE (confidently). O yes, *I*'m a Mormon. (Then reflectively.) I'm a Mormon. (Then, looking round the ship, feigns to descry a particular friend in an empty spot, and evades the Uncommercial for evermore.)

After a noontide pause for dinner, during which my Emigrants were nearly all between-decks, and the Amazon looked deserted, a general muster took place. The muster was for the ceremony of passing the Government Inspector and the Doctor. Those authorities held their temporary state amidships, by a cask or two; and, knowing that the whole Eight hundred emigrants must come face to face with them, I took my station behind the two. They knew nothing whatever of me, I believe, and my testimony to the unpretending gentleness and good nature with which they discharged their duty, may be of the greater worth. There was not the slightest flavour of the Circumlocution Office about their proceedings.

The emigrants were now all on deck. They were densely crowded aft, and swarmed upon the poop-deck like bees. Two or three Mormon agents stood ready to hand them on to the Inspector, and to hand them forward when they had passed. By what successful means, a special aptitude for organisation had been infused into these people, I am, of course, unable to report. But I know that, even now, there was no disorder, hurry, or difficulty.

All being ready, the first group are handed on. That member of the party who is entrusted with the passenger-ticket for the whole, has been warned by one of the agents to have it ready, and here it is in his hand. In every instance through the whole eight hundred, without an exception, this paper is always ready.

Inspector (reading the ticket). Jessie Jobson, Sophronia Jobson, Jessie Jobson again, Matilda Jobson, William Jobson, Jane Jobson, Matilda Jobson again, Brigham Jobson, Leonardo Jobson, and Orson Jobson. Are you all here? (glancing at the party, over his spectacles).

Jessie Jobson Number Two. All here, sir.

This group is composed of an old grandfather and grandmother, their married son and his wife, and *their* family of children. Orson Jobson is a little child asleep in his mother's arms. The Doctor, with a kind word or so, lifts up the corner of the mother's shawl, looks at the child's face, and touches the little clenched hand. If we were all as well as Orson Jobson, doctoring would be a poor profession.

Inspector. Quite right, Jessie Jobson. Take your ticket, Jessie, and pass on.

And away they go. Mormon agent, skilful and quiet, hands them on. Mormon agent, skilful and quiet, hands next party up.

Inspector (reading ticket again). Susannah Cleverly and William Cleverly. Brother and sister, eh?

Sister (young woman of business, hustling slow brother). Yes, sir.

Inspector. Very good, Susannah Cleverly. Take your ticket, Susannah, and take care of it.

And away they go.

Inspector (taking ticket again). Sampson Dibble and Dorothy Dibble (surveying a very old couple over his spectacles, with some surprise). Your husband quite blind, Mrs. Dibble?

Mrs. Dibble. Yes, sir, he be stone-blind.

Mr. Dibble (addressing the mast). Yes, sir, I be stone-blind.

Inspector. That's a bad job. Take your ticket, Mrs. Dibble, and don't lose it, and pass on.

Doctor taps Mr. Dibble on the eyebrow with his forefinger, and away they go.

INSPECTOR (taking ticket again). Anastatia Weedle.

ANASTATIA (a pretty girl, in a bright Garibaldi, this morning elected by universal suffrage the Beauty of the Ship). That is me, sir.

INSPECTOR. Going alone, Anastatia?

ANASTATIA (shaking her curls). I am with Mrs. Jobson, sir, but I've got separated for the moment.

INSPECTOR. Oh! You are with the Jobsons? Quite right. That'll do, Miss Weedle. Don't lose your ticket.

Away she goes, and joins the Jobsons who are waiting for her, and stoops and kisses Brigham Jobson—who appears to be considered too young for the purpose, by several Mormons rising twenty, who are looking on. Before her extensive skirts have departed from the casks, a decent widow stands there with four children, and so the roll goes.

The faces of some of the Welsh people, among whom there were many old persons, were certainly the least intelligent. Some of these emigrants would have bungled sorely, but for the directing hand that was always ready. The intelligence here was unquestionably of a low order, and the heads were of a poor type. Generally the case was the reverse. There were many worn faces bearing traces of patient poverty and hard work, and there was great steadiness of purpose and much undemonstrative self-respect among this class. A few young men were going singly. Several girls were going, two or three together. These latter I found it very difficult to refer back, in my mind, to their relinquished homes and pursuits. Perhaps they were more like country milliners, and pupil teachers rather tawdrily dressed, than any other classes of young women. I noticed, among many little ornaments worn, more than one photograph-brooch of the Princess of Wales, and also of the late Prince Consort. Some single women of from thirty to forty, whom one might suppose to be embroiderers, or straw-bonnet-makers, were obviously going out in quest of husbands, as finer ladies go to India. That they had any distinct notions of a plurality of husbands or wives, I do not believe. To suppose the family groups of whom the majority of emigrants were composed, polygamically possessed, would be to suppose an absurdity, manifest to any one who saw the fathers and mothers.

I should say (I had no means of ascertaining the fact) that most familiar kinds of handicraft trades were represented here. Farm-labourers, shepherds, and the like, had their full share of representation, but I doubt if they preponderated. It was interesting to see how the leading spirit in the family circle never failed to show itself, even in the simple process of answering to the names as they were called, and checking off the owners of the names. Sometimes it was the father, much oftener the mother, sometimes a quick little girl second or third in order of seniority. It seemed to occur for the first time to some heavy fathers, what large families they had ; and their eyes rolled about, during the calling of the list, as if they half misdoubted

some other family to have been smuggled into their own. Among all
the fine handsome children, I observed but two with marks upon
their necks that were probably scrofulous. Out of the whole number of
emigrants, but one old woman was temporarily set aside by the
doctor, on suspicion of fever ; but even she afterwards obtained a
clean bill of health.

When all had "passed," and the afternoon began to wear on, a
black box became visible on deck, which box was in charge of
certain personages also in black, of whom only one had the conventional air of an itinerant preacher. This box contained a supply of
hymn-books, neatly printed and got up, published at Liverpool, and
also in London at the "Latter-Day Saints' Book Depôt, 30, Florence-
street." Some copies were handsomely bound; the plainer were the
more in request, and many were bought. The title ran: "Sacred
Hymns and Spiritual Songs for the Church of Jesus Church of Latter-
Day Saints." The Preface, dated Manchester, 1840, ran thus:—"The
Saints in this country have been very desirous for a Hymn Book
adapted to their faith and worship, that they might sing the truth
with an understanding heart, and express their praise, joy and
gratitude in songs adapted to the New and Everlasting Covenant.
In accordance with their wishes, we have selected the following
volume, which we hope will prove acceptable until a greater variety
can be added. With sentiments of high consideration and esteem,
we subscribe ourselves your brethren in the New and Everlasting
Covenant, BRIGHAM YOUNG, PARLEY P. PRATT, JOHN TAYLOR."
From this book—by no means explanatory to myself of the New and
Everlasting Covenant, and not at all making my heart an understanding one on the subject of that mystery—a hymn was sung, which did
not attract any great amount of attention, and was supported by a
rather select circle. But the choir in the boat was very popular and
pleasant; and there was to have been a Band, only the Cornet was
late in coming on board. In the course of the afternoon, a mother
appeared from shore, in search of her daughter, "who had run away
with the Mormons." She received every assistance from the Inspector,
but her daughter was not found to be on board. The saints did not
seem to me, particularly interested in finding her.

Towards five o'clock, the galley became full of tea-kettles, and an
agreeable fragrance of tea pervaded the ship. There was no scrambling
or jostling for the hot water, no ill humour, no quarrelling. As the
Amazon was to sail with the next tide, and as it would not be high
water before two o'clock in the morning, I left her with her tea in full
action, and her idle Steam Tug lying by, deputing steam and smoke
for the time being to the Tea-kettles.

I afterwards learned that a Despatch was sent home by the
captain before he struck out into the wide Atlantic, highly extolling
the behaviour of these Emigrants, and the perfect order and propriety
of all their social arrangements. What is in store for the poor people
on the shores of the Great Salt Lake, what happy delusions they are
labouring under now, on what miserable blindness their eyes may be

opened then, I do not pretend to say. But I went on board their ship to bear testimony against them if they deserved it, as I fully believed they would; to my great astonishment they did not deserve it; and my predispositions and tendencies must not affect me as an honest witness. I went over the Amazon's side, feeling it impossible to deny that, so far, some remarkable influence had produced a remarkable result, which better known influences have often missed.*

XXIII

THE CITY OF THE ABSENT

WHEN I think I deserve particularly well of myself, and have earned the right to enjoy a little treat, I stroll from Covent-garden into the City of London, after business-hours there, on a Saturday, or—better yet—on a Sunday, and roam about its deserted nooks and corners. It is necessary to the full enjoyment of these journeys that they should be made in summer-time, for then the retired spots that I love to haunt, are at their idlest and dullest. A gentle fall of rain is not objectionable, and a warm mist sets off my favourite retreats to decided advantage.

Among these, City Churchyards hold a high place. Such strange churchyards hide in the City of London; churchyards sometimes so entirely detached from churches, always so pressed upon by houses; so small, so rank, so silent, so forgotten, except by the few people who ever look down into them from their smoky windows. As I stand peeping in through the iron gates and rails, I can peel the rusty metal off, like bark from an old tree. The illegible tombstones are all lop-sided, the grave-mounds lost their shape in the rains of a hundred years ago, the Lombardy Poplar or Plane-Tree that was once a drysalter's daughter and several common-councilmen, has withered like those worthies, and its departed leaves are dust beneath it. Contagion of slow ruin overhangs the place. The discoloured tiled roofs of the environing buildings stand so awry, that they can hardly be proof against any stress of weather. Old crazy stacks of chimneys seem to look down as they overhang, dubiously calculating how far they will have to fall. In an angle of the walls, what was once the tool-house of the grave-digger rots away, encrusted with toadstools. Pipes and spouts for carrying off the rain from the encompassing gables, broken or feloniously cut for old lead long ago,

* After this Uncommercial Journey was printed, I happened to mention the experience it describes to Lord Houghton. That gentleman then showed me an article of his writing, in *The Edinburgh Review* for January, 1862, which is highly remarkable for its philosophical and literary research concerning these Latter-Day Saints. I find in it the following sentences :—"The Select Committee of the House of Commons on emigrant ships for 1854 summoned the Mormon agent and passenger-broker before it, and came to the conclusion that no ships under the provisions of the 'Passengers' Act' could be depended upon for comfort and security in the same degree as those under his administration. The Mormon ship is a Family under strong and accepted discipline, with every provision for comfort, decorum, and internal peace."

now let the rain drip and splash as it list, upon the weedy earth. Sometimes there is a rusty pump somewhere near, and, as I look in at the rails and meditate, I hear it working under an unknown hand with a creaking protest: as though the departed in the churchyard urged, "Let us lie here in peace; don't suck us up and drink us!"

One of my best beloved churchyards, I call the churchyard of Saint Ghastly Grim; touching what men in general call it, I have no information. It lies at the heart of the City, and the Blackwall Railway shrieks at it daily. It is a small small churchyard, with a ferocious, strong, spiked iron gate, like a jail. This gate is ornamented with skulls and cross-bones, larger than the life, wrought in stone; but it likewise came into the mind of Saint Ghastly Grim, that to stick iron spikes a-top of the stone skulls, as though they were impaled, would be a pleasant device. Therefore the skulls grin aloft horribly, thrust through and through with iron spears. Hence, there is attraction of repulsion for me in Saint Ghastly Grim, and, having often contemplated it in the daylight and the dark, I once felt drawn towards it in a thunderstorm at midnight. "Why not?" I said, in self-excuse. "I have been to see the Colosseum by the light of the moon; is it worse to go to see Saint Ghastly Grim by the light of the lightning?" I repaired to the Saint in a hackney cab, and found the skulls most effective, having the air of a public execution, and seeming, as the lightning flashed, to wink and grin with the pain of the spikes. Having no other person to whom to impart my satisfaction, I communicated it to the driver. So far from being responsive, he surveyed me—he was naturally a bottled-nosed, red-faced man—with a blanched countenance, And as he drove me back, he ever and again glanced in over his shoulder through the little front window of his carriage, as mistrusting that I was a fare originally from a grave in the churchyard of Saint Ghastly Grim, who might have flitted home again without paying.

Sometimes, the queer Hall of some queer Company gives upon a churchyard such as this, and, when the Livery dine, you may hear them (if you are looking in through the iron rails, which you never are when I am) toasting their own Worshipful prosperity. Sometimes, a wholesale house of business, requiring much room for stowage, will occupy one or two or even all three sides of the enclosing space, and the backs of bales of goods will lumber up the windows, as if they were holding some crowded trade-meeting of themselves within. Sometimes, the commanding windows are all blank, and show no more sign of life than the graves below—not so much, for *they* tell of what once upon a time was life undoubtedly. Such was the surrounding of one City churchyard that I saw last summer, on a Volunteering Saturday evening towards eight of the clock, when with astonishment I beheld an old old man and an old old woman in it, making hay. Yes, of all occupations in this world, making hay! It was a very confined patch of churchyard lying between Gracechurch-street and the Tower, capable of yielding, say an apronful of hay. By what means the old old man and woman had got into it, with an almost toothless hay-making rake, I could not fathom. No open window was within view; no window at all was within view, sufficiently near the ground to have enabled their old legs to descend from it; the rusty churchyard-gate was locked, the mouldy church was locked. Gravely among the graves, they made hay, all alone by themselves. They looked like Time and his wife. There was but the one rake between them, and they both had hold of it in a pastorally-loving manner, and there was hay on the old woman's black bonnet, as if the old man had recently been playful. The old man was quite an obsolete old man, in knee-breeches and coarse grey stockings, and the old woman wore mittens like unto his stockings in texture and in colour. They took no heed of me as I looked on, unable to account for them. The old woman was much too bright for a pew-opener, the old man much too meek for a beadle. On an old tombstone in the foreground between me and them, were two cherubim; but for those celestial embellishments being represented as having no possible use for knee-breeches, stockings, or mittens, I should have compared them with the hay-makers, and sought a likeness. I coughed and awoke the echoes, but the hay-makers never looked at me. They used the rake with a measured action, drawing the scanty crop towards them; and so I was fain to leave them under three yards and a half of darkening sky, gravely making hay among the graves, all alone by themselves. Perhaps they were Spectres, and I wanted a Medium.

In another City churchyard of similar cramped dimensions, I saw, that selfsame summer, two comfortable charity children. They were making love—tremendous proof of the vigour of that immortal article, for they were in the graceful uniform under which English Charity delights to hide herself—and they were overgrown, and their legs (his legs at least, for I am modestly incompetent to speak of hers) were as much in the wrong as mere passive weakness of character can render legs. O it was a leaden churchyard, but no doubt a golden ground to those young persons! I first saw them on a Saturday evening, and, perceiving from their occupation that Saturday evening was their trysting-time, I returned that evening se'nnight, and renewed the contemplation of them. They came there to shake the bits of matting which were spread in the church aisles, and they afterwards rolled them up, he rolling his end, she rolling hers, until they met, and over the two once divided now united rolls—sweet emblem!—gave and received a chaste salute. It was so refreshing to find one of my faded churchyards blooming into flower thus, that I returned a second time, and a third, and ultimately this befell:— They had left the church door open, in their dusting and arranging. Walking in to look at the church, I became aware, by the dim light, of him in the pulpit, of her in the reading-desk, of him looking down, of her looking up, exchanging tender discourse. Immediately both dived, and became as it were non-existent on this sphere. With an assumption of innocence I turned to leave the sacred edifice, when an obese form stood in the portal, puffily demanding Joseph, or in default of Joseph, Celia. Taking this monster by the sleeve, and luring him forth on pretence of showing him whom he sought, I gave time for the emergence of Joseph and Celia, who presently came towards us in the churchyard, bending under dusty matting, a picture of thriving and unconscious industry. It would be superfluous to hint that I have ever since deemed this the proudest passage in my life.

But such instances, or any tokens of vitality, are rare indeed in my City churchyards. A few sparrows occasionally try to raise a lively chirrup in their solitary tree—perhaps, as taking a different view of worms from that entertained by humanity—but they are flat and hoarse of voice, like the clerk, the organ, the bell, the clergyman, and all the rest of the Church-works when they are wound up for Sunday. Caged larks, thrushes, or blackbirds, hanging in neighbouring courts, pour forth their strains passionately, as scenting the tree, trying to break out, and see leaves again before they die, but their song is Willow, Willow—of a churchyard cast. So little light lives inside the churches of my churchyards, when the two are co-existent, that it is often only by an accident and after long acquaintance that I discover their having stained glass in some odd window. The westering sun slants into the churchyard by some unwonted entry, a few prismatic tears drop on an old tombstone, and a window that I thought was only dirty, is for the moment all bejewelled. Then the light passes and the colours die. Though even then, if there be room enough for me to fall back so far as that I can gaze up to the top of the Church Tower, I see the rusty vane new burnished, and seeming to look out with a joyful flash over the sea of smoke at the distant shore of country.

Blinking old men who are let out of workhouses by the hour, have a tendency to sit on bits of coping stone in these churchyards, leaning with both hands on their sticks and asthmatically gasping. The more depressed class of beggars too, bring hither broken meats, and munch. I am on nodding terms with a meditative turncock who lingers in one of them, and whom I suspect of a turn for poetry; the rather, as he looks out of temper when he gives the fire-plug a disparaging wrench with that large tuning-fork of his which would wear out the shoulder of his coat, but for a precautionary piece of inlaid leather. Fire-ladders, which I am satisfied nobody knows anything about, and the keys of which were lost in ancient times, moulder away in the larger churchyards, under eaves like wooden eyebrows; and so removed are those corners from the haunts of men and boys, that once on a fifth of November I found a "Guy" trusted to take care of himself there, while his proprietors had gone to dinner. Of the expression of his face I cannot report, because it was turned to the wall; but his rugged shoulders and his ten extended fingers, appeared to denote that he had moralised in his little straw chair on the mystery of mortality until he gave it up as a bad job.

You do not come upon these churchyards violently; there are shades of transition in the neighbourhood. An antiquated news shop, or barber's shop, apparently bereft of customers in the earlier days of George the Third, would warn me to look out for one, if any discoveries in this respect were left for me to make. A very quiet court, in combination with an unaccountable dyer's and scourer's, would prepare me for a churchyard. An exceedingly retiring public-house, with a bagatelle-board shadily visible in a sawdusty parlour shaped like an omnibus, and with a shelf of punch-bowls in the bar, would apprise me that I stood near consecrated ground. A "Dairy," exhibiting in its modest window one very little milk-can and three eggs, would suggest to me the certainty of finding the poultry hard by, pecking at my forefathers. I first inferred the vicinity of Saint Ghastly Grim, from a certain air of extra repose and gloom pervading a vast stack of warehouses.

From the hush of these places, it is congenial to pass into the hushed resorts of business. Down the lanes I like to see the carts and waggons huddled together in repose, the cranes idle, and the warehouses shut. Pausing in the alleys behind the closed Banks of mighty Lombard-street, it gives one as good as a rich feeling to think of the broad counters with a rim along the edge, made for telling money out on, the scales for weighing precious metals, the ponderous ledgers, and, above all, the bright copper shovels for shovelling gold. When I draw money, it never seems so much money as when it is shovelled at me out of a bright copper shovel. I like to say, "In gold," and to see seven pounds musically pouring out of the shovel, like seventy; the Bank appearing to remark to me—I italicise *appearing*—"if you want more of this yellow earth, we keep it in barrows at your service." To think of the banker's clerk with his deft finger turning the crisp edges of the Hundred-Pound Notes he has taken in a fat roll out of a drawer, is again to hear the rustling of that delicious south-cash wind. "How will you have it?" I once heard this usual question asked at a Bank Counter of an elderly female, habited in mourning and steeped in simplicity, who answered, open-eyed, crook-fingered, laughing with expectation, "Anyhow!" Calling these things to mind as I stroll among the Banks, I wonder whether the other solitary Sunday man I pass, has designs upon the Banks. For the interest and mystery of the matter, I almost hope he may have, and that his confederate may be at this moment taking impressions of the keys of the iron closets in wax, and that a delightful robbery may be in course of transaction. About College-hill, Mark-lane, and so on towards the Tower, and Dockward, the deserted wine-merchants' cellars are fine subjects for consideration; but the deserted money-cellars of the Bankers, and their plate-cellars, and their jewel-cellars, what subterranean regions of the Wonderful Lamp are these! And again: possibly some shoeless boy in rags, passed through this street yesterday, for whom it is reserved to be a Banker in the fulness of time, and to be surpassing rich. Such reverses have been, since the days of Whittington; and were, long before. I want to know whether the boy has any foreglittering of that glittering fortune now, when he treads these stones, hungry. Much as I also want to know whether the next man to be hanged at Newgate yonder, had any suspicion upon him that he was moving steadily towards that fate, when he talked so much about the last man who paid the same great debt at the same small Debtors' Door.

Where are all the people who on busy working-days pervade these scenes? The locomotive banker's clerk, who carries a black portfolio chained to him by a chain of steel, where is he? Does he go to bed with his chain on—to church with his chain on—or does he lay it by? And if he lays it by, what becomes of his portfolio when he is unchained for a holiday? The wastepaper baskets of these closed counting-houses would let me into many hints of business matters if I had the exploration of them; and what secrets of the heart should I discover on the "pads" of the young clerks—the sheets of cartridge-paper and blotting-paper interposed between their writing and their desks! Pads are taken into confidence on the tenderest occasions, and oftentimes when I have made a business visit, and have sent in my name from the outer office, have I had it forced on my discursive notice that the officiating young gentleman has over and over again inscribed AMELIA, in ink of various dates, on corners of his pad. Indeed, the pad may be regarded as the legitimate modern successor of the old forest-tree: whereon these young knights (having no attainable forest nearer than Epping) engrave the names of their mistresses. After all, it is a more satisfactory process than carving, and can be oftener repeated. So these courts in their Sunday rest are courts of Love Omnipotent (I rejoice to bethink myself), dry as they look. And here is Garraway's, bolted and shuttered hard and fast! It is possible to imagine the man who cuts the sandwiches, on his back in a hayfield; it is possible to imagine his desk, like the desk of a clerk at church, without him; but imagination is unable to pursue the men who wait at Garraway's all the week for the men who never come. When they are forcibly put out of Garraway's on Saturday night—which they must be, for they never would go out of their own accord—where do they vanish until Monday morning? On the first Sunday that I ever strayed here, I expected to find them hovering about these lanes, like restless ghosts, and trying to peep into Garraway's through chinks in the shutters, if not endeavouring to turn the lock of the door with false keys, picks, and screw-drivers. But the wonder is, that they go clean away! And now I think of it, the wonder is, that every working-day pervader of these scenes goes clean away. The man who sells the dogs' collars and the little toy coal-scuttles, feels under as great an obligation to go afar off, as Glyn and Co., or Smith, Payne, and Smith. There is an old monastery-crypt under Garraway's (I have been in it among the port wine), and perhaps Garraway's, taking pity on the mouldy men who wait in its public-room all their lives, gives them cool house-room down there over Sundays; but the catacombs of Paris would not be large enough to hold the rest of the missing. This characteristic of London City greatly helps its being the quaint place it is in the weekly pause of business, and greatly helps my Sunday sensation in it of being the Last Man. In my solitude, the ticket-porters being all gone with the rest, I venture to breathe to the quiet bricks and stones my confi-

dential wonderment why a ticket-porter, who never does any work
with his hands, is bound to wear a white apron, and why a great
Ecclesiastical Dignitary, who never does any work with his hands
either, is equally bound to wear a black one.

XXIV

AN OLD STAGE-COACHING HOUSE

BEFORE the waitress had shut the door, I had forgotten how many
stage-coaches she said used to change horses in the town every day.
But it was of little moment; any high number would do as well as
another. It had been a great stage-coaching town in the great stage-
coaching times, and the ruthless railways had killed and buried it.

The sign of the house was the Dolphin's Head. Why only head, I
don't know; for the Dolphin's effigy at full length, and upside down—
as a Dolphin is always bound to be when artistically treated, though
I suppose he is sometimes right side upward in his natural condition
—graced the sign-board. The sign-board chafed its rusty hooks outside the bow-window of my room, and was a shabby work. No visitor
could have denied that the Dolphin was dying by inches, but he
showed no bright colours. He had once served another master; there
was a newer streak of paint below him, displaying with inconsistent
freshness the legend, By J. MELLOWS.

My door opened again, and J. Mellows's representative came back.
I had asked her what I could have for dinner, and she now returned
with the counter question, what would I like? As the Dolphin stood
possessed of nothing that I do like, I was fain to yield to the suggestion of a duck, which I don't like. J. Mellows's representative was a
mournful young woman, with one eye susceptible of guidance, and
one uncontrollable eye; which latter, seeming to wander in quest of
stage-coaches, deepened the melancholy in which the Dolphin was
steeped.

This young woman had but shut the door on retiring again when
I bethought me of adding to my order, the words, "with nice vegetables." Looking out at the door to give them emphatic utterance, I
found her already in a state of pensive catalepsy in the deserted
gallery, picking her teeth with a pin.

At the Railway Station seven miles off, I had been the subject of
wonder when I ordered a fly in which to come here. And when I gave
the direction "To the Dolphin's Head," I had observed an ominous
stare on the countenance of the strong young man in velveteen who
was the platform servant of the Company. He had also called to my
driver at parting, "All ri-ight! Don't hang yourself when you get
there, Geo-o-rge!" in a sarcastic tone, for which I had entertained
some transitory thoughts of reporting him to the General Manager.

I had no business in the town—I never have any business in any
town—but I had been caught by the fancy that I would come and
look at it in its degeneracy. My purpose was fitly inaugurated by the

Dolphin's Head, which everywhere expressed past coachfulness and present coachlessness. Coloured prints of coaches, starting, arriving, changing horses, coaches in the sunshine, coaches in the snow, coaches in the wind, coaches in the mist and rain, coaches on the King's birthday, coaches in all circumstances compatible with their triumph and victory, but never in the act of breaking down or overturning, pervaded the house. Of these works of art, some, framed and not glazed, had holes in them; the varnish of others had become so brown and cracked, that they looked like overdone pie-crust; the designs of others were almost obliterated by the flies of many summers. Broken glasses, damaged frames, lop-sided hanging, and consignment of incurable cripples to places of refuge in dark corners, attested the desolation of the rest. The old room on the ground floor where the passengers of the Highflyer used to dine, had nothing in it but a wretched show of twigs and flower-pots in the broad window to hide the nakedness of the land, and in a corner little Mellows's perambulator, with even its parasol-head turned despondently to the wall. The other room, where post-horse company used to wait while relays were getting ready down the yard, still held its ground, but was as airless as I conceive a hearse to be: insomuch that Mr. Pitt, hanging high against the partition (with spots on him like port wine, though it is mysterious how port wine ever got squirted up there), had good reason for perking his nose and sniffing. The stopperless cruets on the spindle-shanked sideboard were in a miserably dejected state: the anchovy sauce having turned blue some years ago, and the cayenne pepper (with a scoop in it like a small model of a wooden leg) having turned solid. The old fraudulent candles which were always being paid for and never used, were burnt out at last; but their tall stilts of candlesticks still lingered, and still outraged the human intellect by pretending to be silver. The mouldy old unreformed Borough Member, with his right hand buttoned up in the breast of his coat, and his back characteristically turned on bales of petitions from his constituents, was there too; and the poker which never had been among the fire-irons, lest post-horse company should overstir the fire, was *not* there, as of old.

Pursuing my researches in the Dolphin's Head, I found it sorely shrunken. When J. Mellows came into possession, he had walled off half the bar, which was now a tobacco-shop with its own entrance in the yard—the once glorious yard where the postboys, whip in hand and always buttoning their waistcoats at the last moment, used to come running forth to mount and away. A "Scientific Shoeing-Smith and Veterinary Surgeon," had further encroached upon the yard; and a grimly satirical Jobber, who announced himself as having to Let "A neat one-horse fly, and a one-horse cart," had established his business, himself, and his family, in a part of the extensive stables. Another part was lopped clean off from the Dolphin's Head, and now comprised a chapel, a wheelwright's, and a Young Men's Mutual Improvement and Discussion Society (in a loft): the whole forming a back lane. No audacious hand had plucked down the vane from the central cupola of the stables, but it had grown rusty and stuck at N— Nil: while the score or two of pigeons that remained true to their ancestral traditions and the place, had collected in a row on the roof-ridge of the only outhouse retained by the Dolphin, where all the inside pigeons tried to push the outside pigeon off. This I accepted as emblematical of the struggle for post and place in railway times.

Sauntering forth into the town, by way of the covered and pillared entrance to the Dolphin's Yard, once redolent of soup and stable-litter, now redolent of musty disuse, I paced the street. It was a hot day, and the little sun-blinds of the shops were all drawn down, and the more enterprising tradesmen had caused their 'Prentices to trickle water on the pavement appertaining to their frontage. It looked as if they had been shedding tears for the stage-coaches, and drying their ineffectual pocket-handkerchiefs. Such weakness would have been excusable; for business was—as one dejected porkman who kept a shop which refused to reciprocate the compliment by keeping him, informed me—"bitter bad." Most of the harness-makers and corn-dealers were gone the way of the coaches, but it was a pleasant recognition of the eternal procession of Children down that old original steep Incline, the Valley of the Shadow, that those trades-men were mostly succeeded by vendors of sweetmeats and cheap toys. The opposition house to the Dolphin, once famous as the New White Hart, had long collapsed. In a fit of abject depression, it had cast whitewash on its windows, and boarded up its front door, and reduced itself to a side entrance; but even that had proved a world too wide for the Literary Institution which had been its last phase; for the Institution had collapsed too, and of the ambitious letters of its inscription on the White Hart's front, all had fallen off but these:

L   Y   INS   T

—suggestive of Lamentably Insolvent. As to the neighbouring mar-ket-place, it seemed to have wholly relinquished marketing, to the dealer in crockery whose pots and pans straggled half across it, and to the Cheap Jack who sat with folded arms on the shafts of his cart, superciliously gazing around: his velveteen waistcoat, evidently harbouring grave doubts whether it was worth his while to stay a night in such a place.

The church bells began to ring as I left this spot, but they by no means improved the case, for they said, in a petulant way, and speak-ing with some difficulty in their irritation, WHAT's-be-come-of-THE-coach-ES!" Nor would they (I found on listening) ever vary their emphasis, save in respect of growing more sharp and vexed, but invariably went on, "WHAT's-be-come-of-THE-coach-ES!"—always beginning the inquiry with an unpolite abruptness. Perhaps from their elevation they saw the railway, and it aggravated them.

Coming upon a coachmaker's workshop, I began to look about me with a revived spirit, thinking that perchance I might behold there some remains of the old times of the town's greatness. There was only one man at work—a dry man, grizzled, and far advanced in years,

but tall and upright, who, becoming aware of me looking on, straight-
ened his back, pushed up his spectacles against his brown-paper cap,
and appeared inclined to defy me. To whom I pacifically said:

"Good day, sir!"

"What?" said he.

"Good day, sir."

He seemed to consider about that, and not to agree with me.—
"Was you a looking for anything?" he then asked, in a pointed manner.

"I was wondering whether there happened to be any fragment of
an old stage-coach here."

"Is that all?"

"That's all."

"No, there ain't."

It was now my turn to say "Oh!" and I said it. Not another word
did the dry and grizzled man say, but bent to his work again. In the
coach-making days, the coach-painters had tried their brushes on a
post beside him; and quite a Calendar of departed glories was to be
read upon it, in blue and yellow and red and green, some inches thick.
Presently he looked up again.

"You seem to have a deal of time on your hands," was his queru-
lous remark.

I admitted the fact.

"I think it's a pity you was not brought up to something," said he.

I said I thought so too.

Appearing to be informed with an idea, he laid down his plane (for
it was a plane he was at work with), pushed up his spectacles again,
and came to the door.

"Would a po-shay do for you?" he asked.

"I am not sure that I understand what you mean."

"Would a po-shay," said the coachmaker, standing close before
me, and folding his arms in the manner of a cross-examining counsel
—"would a po-shay meet the views you have expressed? Yes, or
no?"

"Yes."

"Then you keep straight along down there till you see one. *You'll*
see one if you go fur enough."

With that, he turned me by the shoulder in the direction I was to
take, and went in and resumed his work against a background of
leaves and grapes. For, although he was a soured man and a discontented, his workshop was that agreeable mixture of town and country,
street and garden, which is often to be seen in a small English town.

I went the way he had turned me, and I came to the Beershop with
the sign of The First and Last, and was out of the town on the old
London road. I came to the Turnpike, and I found it, in its silent
way, eloquent respecting the change that had fallen on the road. The
Turnpike-house was all overgrown with ivy; and the Turnpike-
keeper, unable to get a living out of the tolls, plied the trade of a
cobbler. Not only that, but his wife sold ginger-beer, and, in the
very window of espial through which the Toll-takers of old times

used with awe to behold the grand London coaches coming on at a gallop, exhibited for sale little barber's-poles of sweetstuff in a sticky lantern.

The political economy of the master of the turnpike thus expressed itself.

"How goes turnpike business, master?" said I to him, as he sat in his little porch, repairing a shoe.

"It don't go at all, master," said he to me. "It's stopped."

"That's bad," said I.

"Bad?" he repeated. And he pointed to one of his sunburnt dusty children who was climbing the turnpike-gate, and said, extending his open right hand in remonstrance with Universal Nature. "Five on 'em!"

"But how to improve Turnpike business?" said I.

"There's a way, master," said he, with the air of one who had thought deeply on the subject.

"I should like to know it."

"Lay a toll on everything as comes through; lay a toll on walkers. Lay another toll on everything as don't come through; lay a toll on them as stops at home."

"Would the last remedy be fair?"

"Fair? Them as stops at home, could come through if they liked; couldn't they?"

"Say they could."

"Toll 'em. If they don't come through, it's *their* look out. Anyways, —Toll 'em!"

Finding it was as impossible to argue with this financial genius as if he had been Chancellor of the Exchequer, and consequently the right man in the right place, I passed on meekly.

My mind now began to misgive me that the disappointed coach-maker had sent me on a wild-goose errand, and that there was no post-chaise in those parts. But coming within view of certain allotment-gardens by the roadside, I retracted the suspicion, and confessed that I had done him an injustice. For, there I saw, surely, the poorest superannuated post-chaise left on earth.

It was a post-chaise taken off its axletree and wheels, and plumped down on the clayey soil among a ragged growth of vegetables. It was a post-chaise not even set straight upon the ground, but tilted over, as if it had fallen out of a balloon. It was a post-chaise that had been a long time in those decayed circumstances, and against which scarlet beans were trained. It was a post-chaise patched and mended with old tea-trays, or with scraps of iron that looked like them, and boarded up as to the windows, but having A KNOCKER on the off-side door. Whether it was a post-chaise used as tool-house, summer-house, or dwelling-house, I could not discover, for there was nobody at home at the post-chaise when I knocked; but it was certainly used for something, and locked up. In the wonder of this discovery, I walked round and round the post-chaise many times, and sat down by the post-chaise, waiting for further elucidation. None came. At last, I made my way back to the old London road by the further end of the allotment-gardens, and consequently at a point beyond that from which I had diverged. I had to scramble through a hedge and down a steep bank, and I nearly came down a-top of a little spare man who sat breaking stones by the roadside.

He stayed his hammer, and said, regarding me mysteriously though his dark goggles of wire:

"Are you aware, sir, that you've been trespassing?"

"I turned out of the way," said I, in explanation, "to look at that odd post-chaise. Do you happen to know anything about it?"

"I know it was many a year upon the road," said he.

"So I supposed. Do you know to whom it belongs?"

The stone-breaker bent his brows and goggles over his heap of stones, as if he were considering whether he should answer the question or not. Then, raising his barred eyes to my features as before, he said:

"To me."

Being quite unprepared for the reply, I received it with a sufficiently awkward "Indeed! Dear me!" Presently I added, "Do you——" I was going to say "live there," but it seemed so absurd a question, that I substituted "live near here?"

The stone-breaker, who had not broken a fragment since we began to converse, then did as follows. He raised himself by poising his finger on his hammer, and took his coat, on which he had been seated, over his arm. He then backed to an easier part of the bank than that by which I had come down, keeping his dark goggles silently upon me all the time, and then shouldered his hammer, suddenly turned, ascended, and was gone. His face was so small, and his goggles were so large, that he left me wholly uninformed as to his countenance; but he left me a profound impression that the curved legs I had seen from behind as he vanished, were the legs of an old postboy. It was not until then that I noticed he had been working by a grass-grown milestone, which looked like a tombstone erected over the grave of the London road.

My dinner-hour being close at hand, I had no leisure to pursue the goggles or the subject then, but made my way back to the Dolphin's Head. In the gateway I found J. Mellows, looking at nothing, and apparently experiencing that it failed to raise his spirits.

"*I* don't care for the town," said J. Mellows, when I complimented him on the sanitary advantages it may or may not possess; "I wish I had never seen the town!"

"You don't belong to it, Mr. Mellows?"

"Belong to it!" repeated Mellows. "If I didn't belong to a better style of town than this, I'd take and drown myself in a pail." It then occurred to me that Mellows, having so little to do, was habitually thrown back on his internal resources—by which I mean the Dolphin's cellar.

"What we want," said Mellows, pulling off his hat, and making as if he emptied it of the last load of Disgust that had exuded from his brain, before he put it on again for another load; "what we want, is a Branch. The Petition for the Branch Bill is in the coffee-room. Would you put your name to it? Every little helps."

I found the document in question stretched out flat on the coffee-room table by the aid of certain weights from the kitchen, and I gave it the additional weight of my uncommercial signature. To the best of my belief, I bound myself to the modest statement that universal traffic, happiness, prosperity, and civilisation, together with unbounded national triumph in competition with the foreigner, would infallibly flow from the Branch.

Having achieved this constitutional feat, I asked Mr. Mellows if he could grace my dinner with a pint of good wine? Mr. Mellows thus replied:

"If I couldn't give you a pint of good wine, I'd—there!—I'd take and drown myself in a pail. But I was deceived when I bought this business, and the stock was higgledy-piggledy, and I haven't yet tasted my way quite through it with a view to sorting it. Therefore, if you order one kind and get another, change till it comes right. For what," said Mellows, unloading his hat as before, "what would you or any gentleman do, if you ordered one kind of wine and was required to drink another? Why, you'd (and naturally and properly, having the feelings of a gentleman), you'd take and drown yourself in a pail!"

XXV

THE BOILED BEEF OF NEW ENGLAND

THE shabbiness of our English capital, as compared with Paris, Bordeaux, Frankfort, Milan, Geneva—almost any important town on the continent of Europe—I find very striking after an absence of any duration in foreign parts. London is shabby in contrast with Edinburgh, with Aberdeen, with Exeter, with Liverpool, with a bright little town like Bury St. Edmunds. London is shabby in contrast with New York, with Boston, with Philadelphia. In detail, one would say it can rarely fail to be a disappointing piece of shabbiness, to a stranger from any of those places. There is nothing shabbier than Drury-lane, in Rome itself. The meanness of Regent-street, set against the great line of Boulevards in Paris, is as striking as the abortive ugliness of Trafalgar-square, set against the gallant beauty of the Place de la Concorde. London is shabby by daylight, and shabbier by gaslight. No Englishman knows what gaslight is, until he sees the Rue de Rivoli and the Palais Royal after dark.

The mass of London people are shabby. The absence of distinctive dress has, no doubt, something to do with it. The porters of the Vintners' Company, the draymen, and the butchers, are about the only people who wear distinctive dresses; and even these do not wear them on holidays. We have nothing which for cheapness, cleanliness, convenience, or picturesqueness, can compare with the belted blouse. As to our women;—next Easter or Whitsuntide, look at the bonnets at the British Museum or the National Gallery, and think of the pretty white French cap, the Spanish mantilla, or the Genoese mezzero.

Probably there are not more second-hand clothes sold in London than in Paris, and yet the mass of the London population have a second-hand look which is not to be detected on the mass of the Parisian population. I think this is mainly because a Parisian workman does not in the least trouble himself about what is worn by a Parisian idler, but dresses in the way of his own class, and for his own comfort. In London, on the contrary, the fashions descend; and you never fully know how inconvenient or ridiculous a fashion is, until you see it in its last descent. It was but the other day, on a race-course, that I observed four people in a barouche deriving great entertainment from the contemplation of four people on foot. The four people on foot were two young men and two young women; the four people in the barouche were two young men and two young women. The four young women were dressed in exactly the same style; the four young men were dressed in exactly the same style. Yet the two couples on wheels were as much amused by the two couples on foot, as if they were quite unconscious of having themselves set those fashions, or of being at that very moment engaged in the display of them.

Is it only in the matter of clothes that fashion descends here in London—and consequently in England—and thence shabbiness arises? Let us think a little, and be just. The "Black Country" round about Birmingham, is a very black country; but is it quite as black as it has been lately painted? An appalling accident happened at the People's Park near Birmingham, this last July, when it was crowded with people from the Black Country—an appalling accident consequent on a shamefully dangerous exhibition. Did the shamefully dangerous exhibition originate in the moral blackness of the Black Country, and in the Black People's peculiar love of the excitement attendant on great personal hazard, which they looked on at, but in which they did not participate? Light is much wanted in the Black Country. O we are all agreed on that. But, we must not quite forget the crowds of gentlefolks who set the shamefully dangerous fashion, either. We must not quite forget the enterprising Directors of an Institution vaunting mighty educational pretences, who made the low sensation as strong as they possibly could make it, by hanging the Blondin rope as high as they possibly could hang it. All this must not be eclipsed in the Blackness of the Black Country. The reserved seats high up by the rope, the cleared space below it, so that no one should be smashed but the performer, the pretence of slipping and falling off, the baskets for the feet and the sack for the head, the photographs everywhere, and the virtuous indignation nowhere—all this must not be wholly swallowed up in the blackness of the jet-black country.

Whatsoever fashion is set in England, is certain to descend. This is a text for a perpetual sermon on care in setting fashions. When you find a fashion low down, look back for the time (it will never be far off) when it was the fashion high up. This is the text for a perpetual sermon on social justice. From imitations of Ethiopian Serenaders, to imitations of Prince's coats and waistcoats, you will find the original model in St. James's Parish. When the Serenaders become tiresome, trace them beyond the Black Country; when the coats and waistcoats become insupportable, refer them to their source in the Upper Toady Regions.

Gentlemen's clubs were once maintained for purposes of savage party warfare; working men's clubs of the same day assumed the same character. Gentlemen's clubs became places of quiet inoffensive recreation; working men's clubs began to follow suit. If working men have seemed rather slow to appreciate advantages of combination which have saved the pockets of gentlemen, and enhanced their comforts, it is because working men could scarcely, for want of capital, originate such combinations without help; and because help has not been separable from that great impertinence, Patronage. The instinctive revolt of his spirit against patronage, is a quality much to be respected in the English working man. It is the base of the base of his best qualities. Nor is it surprising that he should be unduly suspicious of patronage, and sometimes resentful of it even where it is not, seeing what a flood of washy talk has been let loose on his devoted head, or with what complacent condescension the same devoted head has been smoothed and patted. It is a proof to me of his self-control that he never strikes out pugilistically, right and left, when addressed as one of "My friends," or "My assembled friends;" that he does not become inappeasable, and run amuck like a Malay, whenever he sees a biped in broadcloth getting on a platform to talk to him; that any pretence of improving his mind, does not instantly drive him out of his mind, and cause him to toss his obliging patron like a mad bull.

For, how often have I heard the unfortunate working man lectured, as if he were a little charity-child, humid as to his nasal development, strictly literal as to his Catechism, and called by Providence to walk all his days in a station in life represented on festive occasions by a mug of warm milk-and-water and a bun! What popguns of jokes have these ears tingled to hear let off at him, what asinine sentiments, what impotent conclusions, what spelling-book moralities, what adaptations of the orator's insufferable tediousness to the assumed level of his understanding! If his sledge-hammers, his spades and pick-axes, his saws and chisels, his paint-pots and brushes, his forges, furnaces, and engines, the horses that he drove at his work, and the machines that drove him at his work, were all toys in one little paper box, and he the baby who played with them, he could not have been discoursed to, more impertinently and absurdly than I have heard him discoursed to times innumerable. Consequently, not being a fool or a fawner, he has come to acknowledge his patronage by virtually saying: "Let me alone. If you understand me no better than *that*, sir and madam, let me alone. You mean very well, I dare say, but I don't like it, and I won't come here again to have any more of it."

Whatever is done for the comfort and advancement of the working man must be so far done by himself as that it is maintained by himself. And there must be in it no touch of condescension, no shadow of patronage. In the great working districts, this truth is studied and understood. When the American civil war rendered it necessary, first in Glasgow, and afterwards in Manchester, that the working people should be shown how to avail themselves of the advantages derivable from system, and from the combination of numbers, in the purchase and the cooking of their food, this truth was above all things borne in mind. The quick consequence was, that suspicion and reluctance were vanquished, and that the effort resulted in an astonishing and a complete success.

Such thoughts passed through my mind on a July morning of this summer, as I walked towards Commercial Street (not Uncommercial Street), Whitechapel. The Glasgow and Manchester system had been lately set a-going there, by certain gentlemen who felt an interest in its diffusion, and I had been attracted by the following hand-bill printed on rose-coloured paper:

SELF-SUPPORTING
COOKING DEPÔT
FOR THE WORKING CLASSES
Commercial-street, Whitechapel,

Where Accommodation is provided for Dining comfortably

300 Persons at a time.

Open from 7 A.M. till 7 P.M.

PRICES.

All Articles of the BEST QUALITY.

Cup of Tea or Coffee	. . . .	One Penny
Bread and Butter	. . . .	One Penny
Bread and Cheese	. . . .	One Penny
Slice of Bread . . One half-penny or		One Penny
Boiled Egg	. . . . .	One Penny
Ginger Beer	. . . .	One Penny

The above Articles always ready.

Besides the above may be had, from 12 to 3 o'clock,

Bowl of Scotch Broth	. . . .	One Penny
Bowl of Soup	. . . .	One Penny
Plate of Potatoes	. . . .	One Penny
Plate of Minced Beef	. . . .	Twopence
Plate of Cold Beef	. . . .	Twopence
Plate of Cold Ham	. . . .	Twopence
Plate of Plum Pudding or Rice	. . .	One Penny

As the Economy of Cooking depends greatly upon the simplicity of the arrangements with which a great number of persons can be served at one time, the Upper Room of this Establishment will be especially set apart for a

PUBLIC DINNER EVERY DAY

From 12 till 3 o'clock,

Consisting of the following Dishes:

Bowl of Broth, or Soup.
Plate of Cold Beef or Ham.
Plate of Potatoes.
Plum Pudding, or Rice.

FIXED CHARGE 4½d.

THE DAILY PAPERS PROVIDED.

N.B.—This Establishment is conducted on the strictest business principles, with the full intention of making it self-supporting, so that every one may frequent it with a feeling of perfect independence.

The assistance of all frequenting the Depôt is confidently expected in checking anything interfering with the comfort, quiet, and regularity of the establishment.

Please do not destroy this Hand Bill, but hand it to some other person whom it may interest.

The Self-Supporting Cooking Depôt (not a very good name, and one would rather give it an English one) had hired a newly-built warehouse that it found to let; therefore it was not established in premises specially designed for the purpose. But, at a small cost they were exceedingly well adapted to the purpose: being light, well ventilated, clean, and cheerful. They consisted of three large rooms. That on the basement story was the kitchen; that on the ground floor was the general dining-room; that on the floor above was the Upper Room referred to in the hand-bill, where the Public Dinner at fourpence-halfpenny a head was provided every day. The cooking was done, with much economy of space and fuel, by American cooking-stoves, and by young women not previously brought up as cooks; the walls and pillars of the two dining-rooms were agreeably brightened with ornamental colours; the tables were capable of accommodating six or eight persons each; the attendants were all young women, becomingly and neatly dressed, and dressed alike. I think the whole staff was female, with the exception of the steward or manager.

My first inquiries were directed to the wages of this staff; because, if any establishment claiming to be self-supporting, live upon the spoliation of anybody or anything, or eke out a feeble existence by poor mouths and beggarly resources (as too many so-called Mechanics' Institutions do), I make bold to express my Uncommercial opinion

that it has no business to live, and had better die. It was made clear
to me by the account books, that every person employed was properly
paid. My next inquiries were directed to the quality of the provisions
purchased, and to the terms on which they were bought. It was made
equally clear to me that the quality was the very best, and that all
bills were paid weekly. My next inquiries were directed to the balance-
sheet for the last two weeks—only the third and fourth of the
establishment's career. It was made equally clear to me, that after
everything bought was paid for, and after each week was charged
with its full share of wages, rent and taxes, depreciation of plant in
use, and interest on capital at the rate of four per cent. per annum,
the last week had yielded a profit of (in round numbers) one pound
ten; and the previous week a profit of six pounds ten. By this time I
felt that I had a healthy appetite for the dinners.

It had just struck twelve, and a quick succession of faces had
already begun to appear at a little window in the wall of the parti-
tioned space where I sat looking over the books. Within this little
window, like a pay-box at a theatre, a neat and brisk young woman
presided to take money and issue tickets. Every one coming in must
take a ticket. Either the fourpence-halfpenny ticket for the upper
room (the most popular ticket, I think), or a penny ticket for a bowl
of soup, or as many penny tickets as he or she choose to buy. For
three penny tickets one had quite a wide range of choice. A plate of
cold boiled beef and potatoes; or a plate of cold ham and potatoes; or
a plate of hot minced beef and potatoes; or a bowl of soup, bread and
cheese, and a plate of plum-pudding. Touching what they should have,
some customers on taking their seats fell into a reverie—became
mildly distracted—postponed decision, and said in bewilderment,
they would think of it. One old man I noticed when I sat among the
tables in the lower room, who was startled by the bill of fare, and sat
contemplating it as if it were something of a ghostly nature. The
decision of the boys was as rapid as their execution, and always
included pudding.

There were several women among the diners, and several clerks
and shopmen. There were carpenters and painters from the neighbouring buildings under repair, and there were nautical men, and
there were, as one diner observed to me, "some of most sorts." Some
were solitary, some came two together, some dined in parties of
three or four, or six. The latter talked together, but assuredly no one
was louder than at my club in Pall-Mall. One young fellow whistled
in rather a shrill manner while he waited for his dinner, but I was
gratified to observe that he did so in evident defiance of my Uncommercial individuality. Quite agreeing with him, on consideration,
that I had no business to be there, unless I dined like the rest, I
"went in," as the phrase is, for fourpence-halfpenny.

The room of the fourpence-halfpenny banquet had, like the lower
room, a counter in it, on which were ranged a great number of cold
portions ready for distribution. Behind this counter, the fragrant
soup was steaming in deep cans, and the best-cooked of potatoes were

fished out of similar receptacles. Nothing to eat was touched with the hand. Every waitress had her own tables to attend to. As soon as she saw a new customer seat himself at one of her tables, she took from the counter all his dinner—his soup, potatoes, meat, and pudding—piled it up dexterously in her two hands, set it before him, and took his ticket. This serving of the whole dinner at once, had been found greatly to simplify the business of attendance, and was also popular with the customers: who were thus enabled to vary the meal by varying the routine of dishes; beginning with soup to-day, putting soup in the middle to-morrow, putting soup at the end the day after to-morrow, and ringing similar changes on meat and pudding. The rapidity with which every newcomer got served, was remarkable; and the dexterity with which the waitresses (quite new to the art a month before) discharged their duty, was as agreeable to see, as the neat smartness with which they wore their dress and had dressed their hair.

If I seldom saw better waiting, so I certainly never ate better meat, potatoes, or pudding. And the soup was an honest and stout soup, with rice and barley in it, and "little matters for the teeth to touch," as had been observed to me by my friend below stairs already quoted. The dinner-service, too, was neither conspicuously hideous for High Art nor for Low Art, but was of a pleasant and pure appearance. Concerning the viands and their cookery, one last remark. I dined at my club in Pall-Mall aforesaid, a few days afterwards, for exactly twelve times the money, and not half as well.

The company thickened after one o'clock struck, and changed pretty quickly. Although experience of the place had been so recently attainable, and although there was still considerable curiosity out in the street and about the entrance, the general tone was as good as could be, and the customers fell easily into the ways of the place. It was clear to me, however, that they were there to have what they paid for, and to be on an independent footing. To the best of my judgment, they might be patronised out of the building in a month. With judicious visiting, and by dint of being questioned, read to, and talked at, they might even be got rid of (for the next quarter of a century) in half the time.

This disinterested and wise movement was fraught with so many wholesome changes in the lives of the working people, and with so much good in the way of overcoming that suspicion which our own unconscious impertinence has engendered, that it is scarcely gracious to criticise details as yet; the rather, because it is indisputable that the managers of the Whitechapel establishment most thoroughly feel that they are upon their honour with the customers, as to the minutest points of administration. But, although the American stoves cannot roast, they can surely boil one kind of meat as well as another, and need not always circumscribe their boiling talents within the limits of ham and beef. The most enthusiastic admirer of those substantials, would probably not object to occasional inconstancy in respect of pork and mutton: or, especially in cold weather, to a little innocent trifling with Irish stews, meat pies, and toads in holes. Another drawback on the Whitechapel establishment, is the absence of beer. Regarded merely as a question of policy, it is very impolitic, as having a tendency to send the working men to the public-house, where gin is reported to be sold. But, there is a much higher ground on which this absence of beer is objectionable. It expresses distrust of the working man. It is a fragment of that old mantle of patronage in which so many estimable Thugs, so darkly wandering up and down the moral world, are sworn to muffle him. Good beer is a good thing for him, he says, and he likes it; the Depôt could give it him good, and he now gets it bad. Why does the Depôt not give it him good? Because he would get drunk. Why does the Depôt not let him have a pint with his dinner, which would not make him drunk? Because he might have had another pint, or another two pints, before he came. Now, this distrust is an affront, is exceedingly inconsistent with the confidence the managers express in their hand-bills, and is a timid stopping-short upon the straight highway. It is unjust and unreasonable, also. It is unjust, because it punishes the sober man for the vice of the drunken man. It is unreasonable, because any one at all experienced in such things knows that the drunken workman does not get drunk where he goes to eat and drink, but where he goes to drink—expressly to drink. To suppose that the working man cannot state this question to himself quite as plainly as I state it here, is to suppose that he is a baby, and is again to tell him in the old wearisome, condescending, patronising way that he must be goody-poody, and do as he is toldy-poldy, and not be a manny-panny or a voter-poter, but fold his handy-pandys, and be a childy-pildy.

I found from the accounts of the Whitechapel Self-Supporting Cooking Depôt, that every article sold in it, even at the prices I have quoted, yields a certain small profit! Individual speculators are of course already in the field, and are of course already appropriating the name. The classes for whose benefit the real depôts are designed, will distinguish between the two kinds of enterprise.

XXVI

CHATHAM DOCKYARD

THERE are some small out-of-the-way landing-places on the Thames and the Medway, where I do much of my summer idling. Running water is favourable to day-dreams, and a strong tidal river is the best of running water for mine. I like to watch the great ships standing out to sea or coming home richly laden, the active little steam-tugs confidently puffing with them to and from the sea-horizon, the fleet of barges that seem to have plucked their brown and russet sails from the ripe trees in the landscape, the heavy old colliers, light in ballast, floundering down before the tide, the light screw barks and schooners imperiously holding a straight course while the others patiently tack and go about, the yachts with their tiny hulls and great white sheets of canvas, the little sailing-boats bobbing to and fro on their errands of pleasure or business, and—as it is the nature of little people to do—making a prodigious fuss about their small affairs. Watching these objects, I still am under no obligation to think about them, or even so much as to see them, unless it perfectly suits my humour. As little am I obliged to hear the plash and flop of the tide, the ripple at my feet, the clinking windlass afar off, or the humming steam-ship paddles further away yet. These, with the creaking little jetty on which I sit, and the gaunt high-water marks and low-water marks in the mud, and the broken causeway, and the broken bank, and the broken stakes and piles leaning forward as if they were vain of their personal appearance and looking for their reflection in the water, will melt into any train of fancy. Equally adaptable to any purpose or to none, are the pasturing sheep and kine upon the marshes, the gulls that wheel and dip around me, the crows (well out of gunshot) going home from the rich harvest-fields, the heron that has been out a-fishing and looks as melancholy, up there in the sky, as if it hadn't agreed with him. Everything within the range of the senses will, by the aid of the running water, lend itself to everything beyond that range, and work into a drowsy whole, not unlike a kind of tune, but for which there is no exact definition.

One of these landing-places is near an old fort (I can see the Nore Light from it with my pocket-glass), from which fort mysteriously emerges a boy, to whom I am much indebted for additions to my scanty stock of knowledge. He is a young boy, with an intelligent face burnt to a dust colour by the summer sun, and with crisp hair of the same hue. He is a boy in whom I have perceived nothing incompatible with habits of studious inquiry and meditation, unless an evanescent black eye (I was delicate of inquiring how occasioned) should be so considered. To him am I indebted for ability to identify a Custom-house boat at any distance, and for acquaintance with all the forms and ceremonies observed by a homeward-bound Indiaman coming up the river, when the Custom-house officers go aboard her. But for him, I might never have heard of "the dumb-ague," respecting which malady I am now learned. Had I never sat at his feet, I might have finished my mortal career and never known that when I see a white horse on a barge's sail, that barge is a lime barge. For precious secrets in reference to beer, am I likewise beholden to him, involving warning against the beer of a certain establishment, by reason of its having turned sour through failure in point of demand; though my young sage is not of opinion that similar deterioration has befallen the ale. He has also enlightened me touching the mushrooms of the marshes, and has gently reproved my ignorance in having supposed them to be impregnated with salt. His manner of imparting information, is thoughtful, and appropriate to the scene. As he reclines beside me, he pitches into the river, a little stone or piece of grit, and then delivers himself oracularly, as though he spoke out of the centre of the spreading circle that it makes in the water. He never improves my mind without observing this formula.

With the wise boy—whom I know by no name other than the

Spirit of the Fort—I recently consorted on a breezy day when the
river leaped about us and was full of life. I had seen the sheaved corn
carrying in the golden fields as I came down to the river; and the rosy
farmer, watching his labouring-men in the saddle on his cob, had
told me how he had reaped his two hundred and sixty acres of long-
strawed corn last week, and how a better week's work he had never
done in all his days. Peace and abundance were on the countryside in
beautiful forms and beautiful colours, and the harvest seemed even to
be sailing out to grace the never-reaped sea in the yellow-laden barges
that mellowed the distance.

It was on this occasion that the Spirit of the Fort, directing his
remarks to a certain floating iron battery lately lying in that reach of
the river, enriched my mind with his opinions on naval architecture,
and informed me that he would like to be an engineer. I found him up
to everything that is done in the contracting line by Messrs. Peto and
Brassey—cunning in the article of concrete—mellow in the matter of
iron—great on the subject of gunnery. When he spoke of pile-driving
and sluice-making, he left me not a leg to stand on, and I can never
sufficiently acknowledge his forbearance with me in my disabled
state. While he thus discoursed, he several times directed his eyes to
one distant quarter of the landscape, and spoke with vague mysterious
awe of "the Yard." Pondering his lessons after we had parted, I
bethought me that the Yard was one of our large public Dockyards,
and that it lay hidden among the crops down in the dip behind the
windmills, as if it modestly kept itself out of view in peaceful times,
and sought to trouble no man. Taken with this modesty on the part
of the Yard, I resolved to improve the Yard's acquaintance.

My good opinion of the Yard's retiring character was not dashed
by nearer approach. It resounded with the noise of hammers beating
upon iron; and the great sheds or slips under which the mighty men-
of-war are built, loomed businesslike when contemplated from the
opposite side of the river. For all that, however, the Yard made no
display, but kept itself snug under hill-sides of corn-fields, hop-gardens, and orchards; its great chimneys smoking with a quiet—almost
a lazy—air, like giants smoking tobacco; and the great Shears
moored off it, looking meekly and inoffensively out of proportion,
like the Giraffe of the machinery creation. The store of cannon on the
neighbouring gun-wharf, had an innocent toy-like appearance, and
the one red-coated sentry on duty over them was a mere toy figure,
with a clock-work movement. As the hot sunlight sparkled on him he
might have passed for the identical little man who had the little gun,
and whose bullets they were made of lead, lead, lead.

Crossing the river and landing at the Stairs, where a drift of chips
and weed had been trying to land before me and had not succeeded,
but had got into a corner instead, I found the very street posts to be
cannon, and the architectural ornaments to be shells. And so I came
to the Yard, which was shut up tight and strong with great folded
gates, like an enormous patent safe. These gates devouring me, I
became digested into the Yard; and it had, at first, a clean-swept

holiday air, as if it had given over work until next war-time. Though indeed a quantity of hemp for rope was tumbling out of store-houses, even there, which would hardly be lying like so much hay on the white stones if the Yard were as placid as it pretended.

Ding, Clash, Dong, BANG, Boom, Rattle, Clash, BANG, Clink, BANG, Dong, BANG, Clatter, BANG BANG BANG! What on earth is this! This is, or soon will be, the Achilles, iron armour-plated ship. Twelve hundred men are working at her now; twelve hundred men working on stages over her sides, over her bows, over her stern, under her keel, between her decks, down in her hold, within her and without, crawling and creeping into the finest curves of her lines wherever it is possible for men to twist. Twelve hundred hammerers, measurers, caulkers, armourers, forgers, smiths, shipwrights; twelve hundred dingers, clashers, dongers, rattlers, clinkers, bangers bangers bangers! Yet all this stupendous uproar around the rising Achilles is as nothing to the reverberations with which the perfected Achilles shall resound upon the dreadful day when the full work is in hand for which this is but note of preparation—the day when the scuppers that are now fitting like great, dry, thirsty conduit pipes, shall run red. All these busy figures between decks, dimly seen bending at their work in smoke and fire, are as nothing to the figures that shall do work here of another kind in smoke and fire, that day. These steam-worked engines alongside, helping the ship by travelling to and fro, and wafting tons of iron plates about, as though they were so many leaves of trees, would be rent limb from limb if they stood by her for a minute then. To think that this Achilles, monstrous compound of iron tank and oaken chest, can ever swim or roll! To think that any force of wind and wave could ever break her! To think that wherever I see a glowing red-hot iron point thrust out of her side from within—as I do now, there, and there, and there!—and two watching men on a stage without, with bared arms and sledgehammers, strike at it fiercely, and repeat their blows until it is black and flat, I see a rivet being driven home, of which there are many in every iron plate, and thousands upon thousands in the ship! To think that the difficulty I experience in appreciating the ship's size when I am on board, arises from her being a series of iron tanks and oaken chests, so that internally she is ever finishing and ever beginning, and half of her might be smashed, and yet the remaining half suffice and be sound. Then, to go over the side again and down among the ooze and wet to the bottom of the dock, in the depths of the subterranean forest of dog-shores and stays that hold her up, and to see the immense mass bulging out against the upper light, and tapering down towards me, is, with great pains and much clambering, to arrive at an impossibility of realising that this is a ship at all, and to become possessed by the fancy that it is an enormous immovable edifice set up in an ancient amphitheatre (say, that at Verona), and almost filling it! Yet what would even these things be, without the tributary workshops and the mechanical powers for piercing the iron plates—four inches and a half thick—for rivets, shaping them under hydraulic pressure to the finest tapering turns of the ship's lines, and paring them away, with knives shaped like the beaks of strong and cruel birds, to the nicest requirements of the design! These machines of tremendous force, so easily directed by one attentive face and presiding hand, seem to me to have in them something of the retiring character of the Yard. "Obedient monster, please to bite this mass of iron through and through, at equal distances, where these regular chalk-marks are, all round." Monster looks at its work, and lifting its ponderous head, replies, "I don't particularly want to do it; but if it must be done——!" The solid metal wriggles out, hot from the monster's crunching tooth, and it *is* done. "Dutiful monster, observe this other mass of iron. It is required to be pared away, according to this delicately lessening and arbitrary line, which please to look at." Monster (who has been in a reverie) brings down its blunt head, and, much in the manner of Doctor Johnson, closely looks along the line—very closely, being somewhat near-sighted. "I don't particularly want to do it; but if it must be done——!" Monster takes another near-sighted look, takes aim, and the tortured piece writhes off, and falls, a hot, tight-twisted snake, among the ashes. The making of the rivets is merely a pretty round game, played by a man and a boy, who put red-hot barley sugar in a Pope Joan board, and immediately rivets fall out of window; but the tone of the great machines is the tone of the great Yard and the great country: "We don't particularly want to do it; but if it must be done——!"

How such a prodigious mass as the Achilles can ever be held by such comparatively little anchors as those intended for her and lying near her here, is a mystery of seamanship which I will refer to the wise boy. For my own part, I should as soon have thought of tethering an elephant to a tent-peg, or the larger hippopotamus in the Zoological Gardens to my shirt-pin. Yonder in the river, alongside a hulk, lie two of this ship's hollow iron masts. *They* are large enough for the eye, I find, and so are all her other appliances. I wonder why only her anchors look small.

I have no present time to think about it, for I am going to see the workshops where they make all the oars used in the British Navy. A pretty large pile of building, I opine, and a pretty long job! As to the building, I am soon disappointed, because the work is all done in one loft. And as to a long job—what is this? Two rather large mangles with a swarm of butterflies hovering over them? What can there be in the mangles that attracts butterflies?

Drawing nearer, I discern that these are not mangles, but intricate machines, set with knives and saws and planes, which cut smooth and straight here, and slantwise there, and now cut such a depth, and now miss cutting altogether, according to the predestined requirements of the pieces of wood that are pushed on below them: each of which pieces is to be an oar, and is roughly adapted to that purpose before it takes its final leave of far-off forests, and sails for England. Likewise I discern that the butterflies are not true butterflies, but wooden shavings, which, being spirted up from the wood by the violence of the machinery, and kept in rapid and not equal movement by the impulse of its rotation on the air, flutter and play, and rise and fall, and conduct themselves as like butterflies as heart could wish. Suddenly the noise and motion cease, and the butterflies drop dead. An oar has been made since I came in, wanting the shaped handle. As quickly as I can follow it with my eye and thought, the same oar is carried to a turning lathe. A whirl and a Nick! Handle made. Oar finished.

The exquisite beauty and efficiency of this machinery need no illustration, but happen to have a pointed illustration to-day. A pair of oars of unusual size chance to be wanted for a special purpose, and they have to be made by hand. Side by side with the subtle and facile machine, and side by side with the fast-growing pile of oars on the floor, a man shapes out these special oars with an axe. Attended by no butterflies, and chipping and dinting, by comparison as leisurely as if he were a labouring Pagan getting them ready against his decease at threescore and ten, to take with him as a present to Charon for his boat, the man (aged about thirty) plies his task. The machine would make a regulation oar while the man wipes his forehead. The man might be buried in a mound made of the strips of thin, broad, wooden ribbon torn from the wood whirled into oars as the minutes fall from the clock, before he had done a forenoon's work with his axe.

Passing from this wonderful sight to the Ships again—for my heart, as to the Yard, is where the ships are—I notice certain unfinished wooden walls left seasoning on the stocks, pending the solution of the merits of the wood and iron question, and having an air of biding their time with surly confidence. The names of these worthies are set up beside them, together with their capacity in guns —a custom highly conducive to ease and satisfaction in social intercourse, if it could be adapted to mankind. By a plank more gracefully pendulous than substantial, I make bold to go aboard a transport ship (iron screw) just sent in from the contractor's yard to be inspected and passed. She is a very gratifying experience, in the simplicity and humanity of her arrangements for troops, in her provision for light and air and cleanliness, and in her care for women and children. It occurs to me, as I explore her, that I would require a handsome sum of money to go aboard her, at midnight by the Dockyard bell, and stay aboard alone till morning; for surely she must be haunted by a crowd of ghosts of obstinate old martinets, mournfully flapping their cherubic epaulettes over the changed times. Though still we may learn from the astounding ways and means in our Yards now, more highly than ever to respect the forefathers who got to sea, and fought the sea, and held the sea, without them. This remembrance putting me in the best of tempers with an old hulk, very green as to her copper, and generally dim and patched, I pull off my hat to her. Which salutation a callow and downy-faced young officer of Engineers, going by at the moment, perceiving, appropriates —and to which he is most heartily welcome, I am sure.

Having been torn to pieces (in imagination) by the steam circular saws, perpendicular saws, horizontal saws, and saws of eccentric action, I come to the sauntering part of my expedition, and consequently to the core of my Uncommercial pursuits.

Everywhere, as I saunter up and down the Yard, I meet with tokens of its quiet and retiring character. There is a gravity upon its red brick offices and houses, a staid pretence of having nothing worth mentioning to do, an avoidance of display, which I never saw out of England. The white stones of the pavement present no other trace of Achilles and his twelve hundred banging men (not one of whom strikes an attitude) than a few occasional echoes. But for a whisper in the air suggestive of sawdust and shavings, the oar-making and the saws of many movements might be miles away. Down below here, is the great reservoir of water where timber is steeped in various temperatures, as a part of its seasoning process. Above it, on a tram-road supported by pillars, is a Chinese Enchanter's Car, which fishes the logs up, when sufficiently steeped, and rolls smoothly away with them to stack them. When I was a child (the Yard being then familiar to me) I used to think that I should like to play at Chinese Enchanter, and to have that apparatus placed at my disposal for the purpose by a beneficent country. I still think that I should rather like to try the effect of writing a book in it. Its retirement is complete, and to go gliding to and fro among the stacks of timber would be a convenient kind of travelling in foreign countries—among the forests of North America, the sodden Honduras swamps, the dark pine woods, the Norwegian frosts, and the tropical heats, rainy seasons, and thunderstorms. The costly store of timber is stacked and stowed away in sequestered places, with the pervading avoidance of flourish or effect. It makes as little of itself as possible, and calls to no one "Come and look at me!" And yet it is picked out from the trees of the world; picked out for length, picked out for breadth, picked out for straightness, picked out for crookedness, chosen with an eye to every need of ship and boat. Strangely twisted pieces lie about, precious in the sight of shipwrights. Sauntering through these groves, I come upon an open glade where workmen are examining some timber recently delivered. Quite a pastoral scene, with a background of river and windmill! and no more like War than the American States are at present like an Union.

Sauntering among the ropemaking, I am spun into a state of blissful indolence, wherein my rope of life seems to be so untwisted by the process as that I can see back to very early days indeed, when my bad dreams—they were frightful, though my more mature understanding has never made out why—were of an interminable sort of ropemaking, with long minute filaments for strands, which, when they were spun home together close to my eyes, occasioned screaming. Next, I walk among the quiet lofts of stores—of sails, spars, rigging, ships' boats—determined to believe that somebody in authority wears a girdle and bends beneath the weight of a massive bunch of keys, and that, when such a thing is wanted, he comes telling his keys like Blue Beard, and opens such a door. Impassive as the long lofts look, let the electric battery send down the word, and the shutters and doors shall fly open, and such a fleet of armed ships, under steam and under sail, shall burst forth as will charge the old Medway—where the merry Stuart let the Dutch come, while his not so merry sailors starved in the streets—with something worth looking at to carry to the sea. Thus I idle round to the Medway again, where it is now flood tide; and I find the river evincing a strong solicitude to force a way into the dry dock where Achilles is waited on by the twelve hundred bangers, with intent to bear the whole away before they are ready.

To the last, the Yard puts a quiet face upon it; for I make my way to the gates through a little quiet grove of trees, shading the quaintest of Dutch landing-places, where the leaf-speckled shadow of a shipwright just passing away at the further end might be the shadow of Russian Peter himself. So, the doors of the great patent safe at last close upon me, and I take boat again: somehow, thinking as the oars dip, of braggart Pistol and his brood, and of the quiet monsters of the Yard, with their "We don't particularly want to do it; but if it must be done——!" Scrunch.

XXVII

IN THE FRENCH-FLEMISH COUNTRY

"It is neither a bold nor a diversified country," said I to myself, "this country which is three-quarters Flemish, and a quarter French; yet it has its attractions too. Though great lines of railway traverse it, the trains leave it behind, and go puffing off to Paris and the South, to Belgium and Germany, to the Northern Sea-Coast of France, and to England, and merely smoke it a little in passing. Then I don't know it, and that is a good reason for being here; and I can't pronounce half the long queer names I see inscribed over the shops, and that is another good reason for being here, since I surely ought to learn how." In short, I was "here," and I wanted an excuse for not going away from here, and I made it to my satisfaction, and stayed here.

What part in my decision was borne by Monsieur P. Salcy, is of no moment, though I own to encountering that gentleman's name on a red bill on the wall, before I made up my mind. Monsieur P. Salcy, "par permission de M. le Maire," had established his theatre in the whitewashed Hôtel de Ville, on the steps of which illustrious edifice I stood. And Monsieur P. Salcy, privileged director of such theatre, situate in "the first theatrical arrondissement of the department of the North," invited French-Flemish mankind to come and partake of the intellectual banquet provided by his family of dramatic artists, fifteen subjects in number. "La Famille P. Salcy, composée d'artistes dramatiques, au nombre de 15 sujets."

Neither a bold nor a diversified country, I say again, and withal an untidy country, but pleasant enough to ride in, when the paved roads over the flats and through the hollows, are not too deep in black mud. A country so sparely inhabited, that I wonder where the peasants who till and sow and reap the ground, can possibly dwell, and also by what invisible balloons they are conveyed from their distant homes into the fields at sunrise and back again at sunset. The occasional few poor cottages and farms in this region, surely cannot afford shelter to the numbers necessary to the cultivation, albeit the work is done so very deliberately, that on one long harvest day I have seen, in twelve miles, about twice as many men and women (all told) reaping and binding. Yet have I seen more cattle, more sheep, more pigs, and all in better case, than where there is purer French spoken, and also better ricks—round swelling peg-top ricks, well thatched: not a shapeless brown heap, like the toast of a Giant's toast-and-water, pinned to the earth with one of the skewers out of his kitchen. A good custom they have about here, likewise, of pro- longing the sloping tiled roof of farm or cottage, so that it over- hangs three or four feet, carrying off the wet, and making a good drying-place wherein to hang up herbs, or implements, or what not. A better custom than the popular one of keeping the refuse-heap and puddle close before the house door: which, although I paint my dwelling never so brightly blue (and it cannot be too blue for me, hereabouts), will bring fever inside my door. Wonderful poultry of the French-Flemish country, why take the trouble to *be* poultry? Why not stop short at eggs in the rising generation, and die out and have done with it? Parents of chickens have I seen this day, followed by their wretched young families, scratching nothing out of the mud with an air—tottering about on legs so scraggy and weak, that the valiant word drumsticks becomes a mockery when applied to them, and the crow of the lord and master has been a mere dejected case of croup. Carts have I seen, and other agricultural instruments, un- wieldy, dislocated, monstrous. Poplar-trees by the thousand fringe the fields and fringe the end of the flat landscape, so that I feel, looking straight on before me, as if, when I pass the extremest fringe on the low horizon, I shall tumble over into space. Little white- washed black holes of chapels, with barred doors and Flemish inscriptions, abound at roadside corners, and often they are gar- nished with a sheaf of wooden crosses, like children's swords; or, in their default, some hollow old tree with a saint roosting in it, is similarly decorated, or a pole with a very diminutive saint enshrined aloft in a sort of sacred pigeon-house. Not that we are deficient in such decoration in the town here, for, over at the church yonder, outside the building, is a scenic representation of the Crucifixion, built up with old bricks and stones, and made out with painted canvas and wooden figures: the whole surmounting the dusty skull of some holy person- age (perhaps), shut up behind a little ashy iron grate, as if it were originally put there to be cooked, and the fire had long gone out. A windmilly country this, though the windmills are so damp and rickety, that they nearly knock themselves off their legs at every turn of their sails, and creak in loud complaint. A weaving country, too, for in the wayside cottages the loom goes wearily—rattle and click, rattle and click—and, looking in, I see the poor weaving peasant, man or woman, bending at the work, while the child, working too, turns a little handwheel put upon the ground to suit its height. An unconscionable monster, the loom in a small dwelling, asserting himself ungenerously as the bread-winner, straddling over the children's straw beds, cramping the family in space and air, and making himself generally objectionable and tyrannical. He is tributary, too, to ugly mills and factories and bleaching-grounds, rising out of the sluiced fields in an abrupt bare way, disdaining, like himself, to be ornamental or accommodating. Surrounded by these things, here I stood on the steps of the Hôtel de Ville, persuaded to remain by the P. Salcy family, fifteen dramatic subjects strong.

There was a Fair besides. The double persuasion being irresistible, and my sponge being left behind at the last Hotel, I made the tour of the little town to buy another. In the small sunny shops—mercers, opticians, and druggist-grocers, with here and there an emporium of religious images—the gravest of old spectacled Flemish husbands and wives sat contemplating one another across bare counters, while the wasps, who seemed to have taken military possession of the town, and to have placed it under wasp-martial law, executed warlike manœuvres in the windows. Other shops the wasps had entirely to themselves, and nobody cared and nobody came when I beat with a five-franc piece upon the board of custom. What I sought was no more to be found than if I had sought a nugget of Californian gold: so I went, spongeless, to pass the evening with the Family P. Salcy.

The members of the Family P. Salcy were so fat and so like one another—fathers, mothers, sisters, brothers, uncles, and aunts—that I think the local audience were much confused about the plot of the piece under representation, and to the last expected that everybody must turn out to be the long-lost relative of everybody else. The Theatre was established on the top story of the Hôtel de Ville, and was approached by a long bare staircase, whereon, in an airy situation, one of the P. Salcy Family—a stout gentleman imperfectly repressed by a belt—took the money. This occasioned the greatest excitement of the evening; for, no sooner did the curtain rise on the introductory Vaudeville, and reveal in the person of the young lover (singing a very short song with his eyebrows) apparently the very same identical stout gentleman imperfectly repressed by a belt, than everybody rushed out to the paying-place, to ascertain whether he could possibly have put on that dress-coat, that clear complexion, and those arched black vocal eyebrows, in so short a space of time. It then became manifest that this was another stout gentleman imperfectly repressed by a belt: to whom, before the spectators had recovered their presence of mind, entered a third stout gentleman imperfectly repressed by a belt, exactly like him. These two "subjects," making with the money-taker three of the announced fifteen, fell into conversation touching a charming young widow: who, presently appearing, proved to be a stout lady altogether irrepressible by any means—quite a parallel case to the American Negro—

fourth of the fifteen subjects, and sister of the fifth who presided over the check-department. In good time the whole of the fifteen subjects were dramatically presented, and we had the inevitable Ma Mère, Ma Mère! and also the inevitable malédiction d'un père, and likewise the inevitable Marquis, and also the inevitable provincial young man, weak-minded but faithful, who followed Julie to Paris, and cried and laughed and choked all at once. The story was wrought out with the help of a virtuous spinning-wheel in the beginning, a vicious set of diamonds in the middle, and a rheumatic blessing (which arrived by post) from Ma Mère towards the end; the whole resulting in a small sword in the body of one of the stout gentlemen imperfectly repressed by a belt, fifty thousand francs per annum and a decoration to the other stout gentleman imperfectly repressed by a belt, and an assurance from everybody to the provincial young man that if he were not supremely happy—which he seemed to have no reason whatever for being—he ought to be. This afforded him a final opportunity of crying and laughing and choking all at once, and sent the audience home sentimentally delighted. Audience more attentive or better behaved there could not possibly be, though the places of second rank in the Theatre of the Family P. Salcy were sixpence each in English money, and the places of first rank a shilling. How the fifteen subjects ever got so fat upon it, the kind Heavens know.

What gorgeous china figures of knights and ladies, gilded till they gleamed again, I might have bought at the Fair for the garniture of my home, if I had been a French-Flemish peasant, and had had the money! What shining coffee-cups and saucers I might have won at the turntables, if I had had the luck! Ravishing perfumery also, and sweetmeats, I might have speculated in, or I might have fired for prizes at a multitude of little dolls in niches, and might have hit the doll of dolls, and won francs and fame. Or, being a French-Flemish youth, I might have been drawn in a hand-cart by my compeers, to tilt for municipal rewards at the water-quintain; which, unless I sent my lance clean through the ring, emptied a full bucket over me; to fend off which, the competitors wore grotesque old scarecrow hats. Or, being French-Flemish man or woman, boy or girl, I might have circled all night on my hobby-horse in a stately cavalcade of hobby-horses four abreast, interspersed with triumphal cars, going round and round and round and round, we the goodly company singing a ceaseless chorus to the music of the barrel-organ, drum, and cymbals. On the whole, not more monotonous than the Ring in Hyde Park, London, and much merrier; for when do the circling company sing chorus, *there*, to the barrel-organ, when do the ladies embrace their horses round the neck with both arms, when do the gentlemen fan the ladies with the tails of their gallant steeds? On all these revolving delights, and on their own especial lamps and Chinese lanterns revolving with them, the thoughtful weaver-face brightens, and the Hôtel de Ville sheds an illuminated line of gaslight: while above it, the Eagle of France, gas-outlined and apparently afflicted with the prevailing infirmities that have lighted on the poultry, is in a very undecided state of policy, and as a bird moulting. Flags flutter all around. Such is the prevailing gaiety that the keeper of the prison sits on the stone steps outside the prison-door, to have a look at the world that is not locked up, while that agreeable retreat, the wine-shop opposite to the prison in the prison-alley (its sign La Tranquillité, because of its charming situation), resounds with the voices of the shepherds and shepherdesses who resort there this festive night. And it reminds me that only this afternoon, I saw a shepherd in trouble, tending this way, over the jagged stones of a neighbouring street. A magnificient sight it was, to behold him in his blouse, a feeble little jog-trot rustic, swept along by the wind of two immense gendarmes, in cocked hats for which the street was hardly wide enough, each carrying a bundle of stolen property that would not have held his shoulder-knot, and clanking a sabre that dwarfed the prisoner.

"Messieurs et Mesdames, I present to you at this Fair, as a mark of my confidence in the people of this so-renowned town, and as an act of homage to their good sense and fine taste, the Ventriloquist, the Ventriloquist! Further, Messieurs et Mesdames, I present to you the Face-Maker, the Physiognomist, the great Changer of Counten-ances, who transforms the features that Heaven has bestowed upon him into an endless succession of surprising and extraordinary visages, comprehending, Messieurs et Mesdames, all the contortions, energetic and expressive, of which the human face is capable, and all the passions of the human heart, as Love, Jealousy, Revenge, Hatred, Avarice, Despair! Hi hi! Ho ho! Lu lu! Come in!" To this effect, with an occasional smite upon a sonorous kind of tambourine —bestowed with a will, as if it represented the people who won't come in—holds forth a man of lofty and severe demeanour; a man in stately uniform, gloomy with the knowledge he possesses of the inner secrets of the booth. "Come in, come in! Your opportunity presents itself to-night; to-morrow it will be gone for ever. To-morrow morning by the Express Train the railroad will reclaim the Ventriloquist and the Face-Maker! Algeria will reclaim the Ventrilo-quist and the Face-Maker! Yes! For the honour of their country they have accepted propositions of a magnitude incredible, to appear in Algeria. See them for the last time before their departure! We go to commence on the instant. Hi hi! Ho ho! Lu lu! Come in! Take the money that now ascends, Madame; but after that, no more, for we commence! Come in!"

Nevertheless, the eyes both of the gloomy Speaker and of Madame receiving sous in a muslin bower, survey the crowd pretty sharply after the ascending money has ascended, to detect any lingering sous at the turning-point. "Come in, come in! Is there any more money, Madame, on the point of ascending? If so, we wait for it. If not, we commence!" The orator looks back over his shoulder to say it, lash-ing the spectators with the conviction that he beholds through the folds of the drapery into which he is about to plunge, the Ventrilo-quist and the Face-Maker. Several sous burst out of pockets, and ascend. "Come up, then, Messieurs!" exclaims Madame in a shrill voice, and beckoning with a bejewelled finger. "Come up! This presses. Monsieur had commanded that they commence!" Monsieur dives into his Interior, and the last half-dozen of us follow. His Interior is comparatively severe, his Exterior also. A true Temple of Art needs nothing but seats, drapery, a small table with two moderator lamps hanging over it, and an ornamental looking-glass let into the wall. Monsieur in uniform gets behind the table and surveys us with disdain, his forehead becoming diabolically intellectual under the moderators. "Messieurs et Mesdames! I present to you the Ventriloquist. He will commence with the celebrated Experience of the bee in the window. The bee, apparently the veritable bee of Nature, will hover in the window, and about the room. He will be with difficulty caught in the hand of Monsieur the Ventriloquist—he will escape—he will again hover—at length he will be recaptured by Monsieur the Ventriloquist, and will be with difficulty put into a bottle. Achieve then, Monsieur!" Here the proprietor is replaced behind the table by the Ventriloquist, who is thin and sallow, and of a weakly aspect. While the bee is in progress, Monsieur the Proprietor sits apart on a stool, immersed in dark and remote thought. The moment the bee is bottled, he stalks forward, eyes us gloomily as we applaud, and then announces, sternly waving his hand "The magnificent Experience of the child with the whooping-cough!" The child disposed of, he starts up as before. "The superb and extraordinary Experience of the dialogue between Monsieur Tatambour in his dining-room, and his domestic, Jerome, in the cellar, concluding with the songsters of the grove, and the Concert of domestic Farmyard animals." All this done, and well done, Monsieur the Ventriloquist withdraws, and Monsieur the Face-Maker bursts in, as if his retiring-room were a mile long instead of a yard. A corpulent little man in a large white waistcoat, with a comic countenance, and with a wig in his hand. Irreverent disposition to laugh, instantly checked by the tremendous gravity of the Face-Maker, who intimates in his bow that if we expect that sort of thing we are mistaken. A very little shaving-glass with a leg behind it is handed in, and placed on the table before the Face-Maker. "Messieurs et Mesdames, with no other assistance than this mirror and this wig, I shall have the honour of showing you a thousand characters." As a preparation, the Face-Maker with both hands gouges himself, and turns his mouth inside out. He then becomes frightfully grave again, and says to the Proprietor, "I am ready!" Proprietor stalks forth from baleful reverie, and announces "The Young Conscript!" Face-Maker claps his wig on, hind side before, looks in the glass, and appears above it as a conscript so very imbecile, and squinting so extremely hard, that I should think the State would never get any good of him. Thunders of applause. Face-Maker dips behind the looking-glass, brings his own hair forward, is himself again, is awfully grave. "A distinguished inhabitant of the Faubourg St. Germain." Face-Maker dips, rises, is supposed to be aged, blear-eyed, toothless, slightly palsied, supernaturally polite, evidently of noble birth. "The oldest member

of the Corps of Invalides on the fête-day of his master." Face-Maker
dips, rises, wears the wig on one side, has become the feeblest
military bore in existence, and (it is clear) would lie frightfully about
his past achievements, if he were not confined to pantomime. "The
Miser!" Face-Maker dips, rises, clutches a bag, and every hair of the
wig is on end to express that he lives in continual dread of thieves.
"The Genius of France!" Face-Maker dips, rises, wig pushed back and
smoothed flat, little cocked hat (artfully concealed till now) put a-top
of it, Face-Maker's white waistcoat much advanced, Face-Maker's left
hand in bosom of white waistcoat, Face-Maker's right hand behind
his back. Thunders. This is the first of three positions of the Genius
of France. In the second position, the Face-Maker takes snuff; in
the third, rolls up his right hand, and surveys illimitable armies
through that pocket-glass. The Face-Maker then, by putting out his
tongue, and wearing the wig nohow in particular, becomes the Village
Idiot. The most remarkable feature in the whole of his ingenious
performance, is, that whatever he does to disguise himself, has the
effect of rendering him rather more like himself than he was at first.

There were peep-shows in this Fair, and I had the pleasure of
recognising several fields of glory with which I became well acquainted a year or two ago as Crimean battles, now doing duty as
Mexican victories. The change was neatly effected by some extra
smoking of the Russians, and by permitting the camp followers free
range in the foreground to despoil the enemy of their uniforms. As no
British troops had ever happened to be within sight when the artist
took his original sketches, it followed fortunately that none were in
the way now.

The Fair wound up with a ball. Respecting the particular night of
the week on which the ball took place, I decline to commit myself;
merely mentioning that it was held in a stable-yard so very close to
the railway, that it is a mercy the locomotive did not set fire to it.
(In Scotland, I suppose it would have done so.) There, in a tent
prettily decorated with looking-glasses and a myriad of toy flags, the
people danced all night. It was not an expensive recreation, the price
of a double ticket for a cavalier and lady being one and threepence in
English money, and even of that small sum fivepence was reclaimable
for "consommation:" which word I venture to translate into refreshments of no greater strength, at the strongest, than ordinary wine
made hot, with sugar and lemon in it. It was a ball of great good
humour and of great enjoyment, though very many of the dancers
must have been as poor as the fifteen subjects of the P. Salcy Family.

In short, not having taken my own pet national pint pot with me to
this Fair, I was very well satisfied with the measure of simple enjoyment that it poured into the dull French-Flemish country life. How
dull that is, I had an opportunity of considering when the Fair was
over—when the tri-coloured flags were withdrawn from the windows
of the houses on the Place where the Fair was held—when the windows were close shut, apparently until next Fair-time—when the
Hôtel de Ville had cut off its gas and put away its eagle—when the

two paviours, whom I take to form the entire paving population of
the town, were ramming down the stones which had been pulled up
for the erection of decorative poles—when the jailer had slammed his
gate, and sulkily locked himself in with his charges. But then, as I
paced the ring which marked the track of the departed hobby-horses
on the market-place, pondering in my mind how long some hobby-
horses do leave their tracks in public ways, and how difficult they are
to erase, my eyes were greeted with a goodly sight. I beheld four
male personages thoughtfully pacing the Place together, in the sunlight, evidently not belonging to the town, and having upon them a
certain loose cosmopolitan air of not belonging to any town. One was
clad in a suit of white canvas, another in a cap and blouse, the third
in an old military frock, the fourth in a shapeless dress that looked as
if it had been made out of old umbrellas. All wore dust-coloured
shoes. My heart beat high; for, in those four male personages,
although complexionless and eyebrowless, I beheld four subjects of
the Family P. Salcy. Blue-bearded though they were, and bereft of the
youthful smoothness of cheek which is imparted by what is termed in
Albion a "Whitechapel shave" (and which is, in fact, whitening,
judiciously applied to the jaws with the palm of the hand), I recognised them. As I stood admiring, there emerged from the yard of a
lowly Cabaret, the excellent Ma Mère, Ma Mère, with the words, "The
soup is served;" words which so elated the subject in the canvas suit,
that when they all ran in to partake, he went last, dancing with his
hands stuck angularly into the pockets of his canvas trousers, after
the Pierrot manner. Glancing down the Yard, the last I saw of him
was, that he looked in through a window (at the soup, no doubt) on
one leg.

Full of this pleasure, I shortly afterwards departed from the town,
little dreaming of an addition to my good fortune. But more was in
reserve. I went by a train which was heavy with third-class carriages,
full of young fellows (well guarded) who had drawn unlucky numbers
in the last conscription, and were on their way to a famous French
garrison town where much of the raw military material is worked up
into soldiery. At the station they had been sitting about, in their
threadbare homespun blue garments, with their poor little bundles
under their arms, covered with dust and clay, and the various soils of
France; sad enough at heart, most of them, but putting a good face
upon it, and slapping their breasts and singing choruses on the
smallest provocation; the gayer spirits shouldering half loaves of
black bread speared upon their walking-sticks. As we went along,
they were audible at every station, chorusing wildly out of tune, and
feigning the highest hilarity. After a while, however, they began to
leave off singing, and to laugh naturally, while at intervals there
mingled with their laughter the barking of a dog. Now, I had to
alight short of their destination, and, as that stoppage of the train
was attended with a quantity of horn blowing, bell ringing, and
proclamation of what Messieurs les Voyageurs were to do, and were
not to do, in order to reach their respective destinations, I had ample

leisure to go forward on the platform to take a parting look at my
recruits, whose heads were all out at window, and who were laughing
like delighted children. Then I perceived that a large poodle with a
pink nose, who had been their travelling companion and the cause of
their mirth, stood on his hind-legs presenting arms on the extreme
verge of the platform, ready to salute them as the train went off.
This poodle wore a military shako (it is unnecessary to add, very
much on one side over one eye), a little military coat, and the
regulation white gaiters. He was armed with a little musket and a
little sword-bayonet, and he stood presenting arms in perfect
attitude, with his unobscured eye on his master or superior officer,
who stood by him. So admirable was his discipline, that, when the
train moved, and he was greeted with the parting cheers of the
recruits, and also with a shower of centimes, several of which struck
his shako, and had a tendency to discompose him, he remained
staunch on his post, until the train was gone. He then resigned his
arms to his officer, took off his shako by rubbing his paw over it,
dropped on four legs, bringing his uniform coat into the absurdest
relations with the overarching skies, and ran about the platform in
his white gaiters, wagging his tail to an exceeding great extent. It
struck me that there was more waggery than this in the poodle, and
that he knew that the recruits would neither get through their
exercises, not get rid of their uniforms, as easily as he; revolving
which in my thoughts, and seeking in my pockets some small money
to bestow upon him, I casually directed my eyes to the face of his
superior officer, and in him beheld the Face-Maker! Though it was
not the way to Algeria, but quite the reverse, the military poodle's
Colonel was the Face-Maker in a dark blouse, with a small bundle
dangling over his shoulder at the end of an umbrella, and taking a
pipe from his breast to smoke as he and the poodle went their mysterious way.

XXVIII

MEDICINE MEN OF CIVILISATION

My voyages (in paper boats) among savages often yield me matter
for reflection at home. It is curious to trace the savage in the civilised
man, and to detect the hold of some savage customs on conditions of
society rather boastful of being high above them.

I wonder, is the Medicine Man of the North American Indians
never to be got rid of, out of the North American country? He comes
into my Wigwam on all manner of occasions, and with the absurdest
"Medicine." I always find it extremely difficult, and I often find it
simply impossible, to keep him out of my Wigwam. For his legal
"Medicine" he sticks upon his head the hair of quadrupeds, and
plasters the same with fat, and dirty white powder, and talks a
gibberish quite unknown to the men and squaws of his tribe. For his
religious "Medicine" he puts on puffy white sleeves, little black

aprons, large black waistcoats of a peculiar cut, collarless coats with Medicine button-holes, Medicine stockings and gaiters and shoes, and tops the whole with a highly grotesque Medicinal hat. In one respect, to be sure, I am quite free from him. On occasions when the Medicine Men in general, together with a large number of the miscellaneous inhabitants of his village, both male and female, are presented to the principal Chief, his native "Medicine" is a comical mixture of old odds and ends (hired of traders) and new things in antiquated shapes, and pieces of red cloth (of which he is particularly fond), and white and red and blue paint for the face. The irrationality of this particular Medicine culminates in a mock battle-rush, from which many of the squaws are borne out, much dilapidated. I need not observe how unlike this is to a Drawing Room at St. James's Palace.

The African magician I find it very difficult to exclude from my Wigwam too. This creature takes cases of death and mourning under his supervision, and will frequently impoverish a whole family by his preposterous enchantments. He is a great eater and drinker, and always conceals a rejoicing stomach under a grieving exterior. His charms consist of an infinite quantity of worthless scraps, for which he charges very high. He impresses on the poor bereaved natives, that the more of his followers they pay to exhibit such scraps on their persons for an hour or two (though they never saw the deceased in their lives, and are put in high spirits by his decease), the more honourably and piously they grieve for the dead. The poor people submitting themselves to this conjurer, an expensive procession is formed, in which bits of stick, feathers of birds, and a quantity of other unmeaning objects besmeared with black paint, are carried in a certain ghastly order of which no one understands the meaning, if it ever had any, to the brink of the grave, and are then brought back again.

In the Tonga Islands everything is supposed to have a soul, so that when a hatchet is irreparably broken, they say, "His immortal part has departed; he is gone to the happy hunting-plains." This belief leads to the logical sequence that when a man is buried, some of his eating and drinking vessels, and some of his warlike implements, must be broken and buried with him. Superstitious and wrong, but surely a more respectable superstition than the hire of antic scraps for a show that has no meaning based on any sincere belief.

Let me halt on my Uncommercial road, to throw a passing glance on some funeral solemnities that I have seen where North American Indians, African Magicians, and Tonga Islanders, are supposed not to be.

Once, I dwelt in an Italian city, where there dwelt with me for a while, an Englishman of an amiable nature, great enthusiasm, and no discretion. This friend discovered a desolate stranger, mourning over the unexpected death of one very dear to him, in a solitary cottage among the vineyards of an outlying village. The circumstances of the bereavement were unusually distressing; and the survivor, new to the peasants and the country, sorely needed help, being alone with the remains. With some difficulty, but with the strong influence of a purpose at once gentle, disinterested, and determined, my friend—Mr. Kindheart—obtained access to the mourner, and undertook to arrange the burial.

There was a small Protestant cemetery near the city walls, and as Mr. Kindheart came back to me, he turned into it and chose the spot. He was always highly flushed when rendering a service unaided, and I knew that to make him happy I must keep aloof from his ministration. But when at dinner he warmed with the good action of the day, and conceived the brilliant idea of comforting the mourner with "an English funeral," I ventured to intimate that I thought that institution, which was not absolutely sublime at home, might prove a failure in Italian hands. However, Mr. Kindheart was so enraptured with his conception, that he presently wrote down into the town requesting the attendance with to-morrow's earliest light of a certain little upholsterer. This upholsterer was famous for speaking the unintelligible local dialect (his own) in a far more unintelligible manner than any other man alive.

When from my bath next morning I overheard Mr. Kindheart and the upholsterer in conference on the top of an echoing staircase; and when I overheard Mr. Kindheart rendering English Undertaking phrases into very choice Italian, and the upholsterer replying in the unknown Tongues; and when I furthermore remembered that the local funerals had no resemblance to English funerals; I became in my secret bosom apprehensive. But Mr. Kindheart informed me at breakfast that measures had been taken to ensure a signal success.

As the funeral was to take place at sunset, and as I knew to which of the city gates it must tend, I went out at that gate as the sun descended, and walked along the dusty, dusty road. I had not walked far, when I encountered this procession:

1. Mr. Kindheart, much abashed, on an immense grey horse.

2. A bright yellow coach and pair, driven by a coachman in bright red velvet knee-breeches and waistcoat. (This was the established local idea of State.) Both coach doors kept open by the coffin, which was on its side within, and sticking out at each.

3. Behind the coach, the mourner, for whom the coach was intended, walking in the dust.

4. Concealed behind a roadside well for the irrigation of a garden, the unintelligible Upholsterer, admiring.

It matters little now. Coaches of all colours are alike to poor Kindheart, and he rests far North of the little cemetery with the cypress-trees, by the city walls where the Mediterranean is so beautiful.

My first funeral, a fair representative funeral after its kind, was that of the husband of a married servant, once my nurse. She married for money. Sally Flanders, after a year or two of matrimony, became the relict of Flanders, a small master builder; and either she or Flanders had done me the honour to express a desire that I should "follow." I may have been seven or eight years old;—young enough, certainly, to feel rather alarmed by the expression, as not knowing where the invitation was held to terminate, and how far I was expected to follow the deceased Flanders. Consent being given by the heads of houses, I was jobbed up into what was pronounced at home decent mourning (comprehending somebody else's shirt, unless my memory deceives me), and was admonished that if, when the funeral was in action, I put my hands in my pockets, or took my eyes out of my pocket-handkerchief, I was personally lost, and my family disgraced. On the eventful day, having tried to get myself into a disastrous frame of mind, and having formed a very poor opinion of myself because I couldn't cry, I repaired to Sally's. Sally was an excellent creature, and had been a good wife to old Flanders, but the moment I saw her I knew that she was not in her own real natural state. She formed a sort of Coat of Arms, grouped with a smelling-bottle, a handkerchief, an orange, a bottle of vinegar, Flanders's sister, her own sister, Flanders's brother's wife, and two neighbouring gossips—all in mourning, and all ready to hold her whenever she fainted. At sight of poor little me she became much agitated (agitating me much more), and having exclaimed, "O here's dear Master Uncommercial!" became hysterical, and swooned as if I had been the death of her. An affecting scene followed, during which I was handed about and poked at her by various people, as if I were the bottle of salts. Reviving a little, she embraced me, said, "You knew him well, dear Master Uncommercial, and he knew you!" and fainted again: which, as the rest of the Coat of Arms soothingly said, "done her credit." Now, I knew that she needn't have fainted unless she liked, and that she wouldn't have fainted unless it had been expected of her, quite as well as I know it at this day. It made me feel uncomfortable and hypocritical besides. I was not sure but that it might be manners in *me* to faint next, and I resolved to keep my eye on Flanders's uncle, and if I saw any signs of his going in that direction, to go too, politely. But Flanders's uncle (who was a weak little old retail grocer) had only one idea, which was that we all wanted tea; and he handed us cups of tea all round, incessantly, whether we refused or not. There was a young nephew of Flanders's present, to whom Flanders, it was rumoured, had left nineteen guineas. He drank all the tea that was offered him, this nephew—amounting, I should say, to several quarts—and ate as much plum-cake as he could possibly come by; but he felt it to be decent mourning that he should now and then stop in the midst of a lump of cake, and appear to forget that his mouth was full, in the contemplation of his uncle's memory. I felt all this to be the fault of the undertaker, who was handing us gloves on a tea-tray as if they were muffins, and tying us into cloaks (mine had to be pinned up all round, it was so long for me), because I knew that he was making game. So, when we got out into the streets, and I constantly disarranged the procession by tumbling on the people before me because my handkerchief blinded my eyes, and tripping up the people behind me because my cloak was so long, I felt that we were all making game. I was truly sorry for Flanders, but I knew that it was no reason why we should be trying (the women with their heads in hoods like coal-scuttles with the black side outward) to keep step with a man in a scarf, carrying a thing like a mourning spy-glass, which he was going to open presently and sweep the horizon with. I knew that we should not all have been speaking in one particular key-note struck by the undertaker, if we had not been making game. Even in our faces we were every one of us as like the undertaker as if we had been his own family, and I perceived that this could not have happened unless we had been making game. When we returned to Sally's, it was all of a piece. The continued impossibility of getting on without plum-cake; the ceremonious apparition of a pair of decanters containing port and sherry and cork; Sally's sister at the tea-table, clinking the best crockery and shaking her head mournfully every time she looked into the teapot, as if it were the tomb; the Coat of Arms again, and Sally as before; lastly, the words of consolation administered to Sally when it was considered right that she should "come round nicely:" which were, that the deceased had had "as com-for-ta-ble a fu-ne-ral as comfortable could be!"

Other funerals have I seen with grown-up eyes, since that day, of which the burden has been the same childish burden. Making game. Real affliction, real grief and solemnity, have been outraged, and the funeral has been "performed." The waste for which the funeral customs of many tribes of savages are conspicuous, has attended these civilised obsequies; and once, and twice, have I wished in my soul that if the waste must be, they would let the undertaker bury the money, and let me bury the friend.

In France, upon the whole, these ceremonies are more sensibly regulated, because they are upon the whole less expensively regulated. I cannot say that I have ever been much edified by the custom of tying a bib and apron on the front of the house of mourning, or that I would myself particularly care to be driven to my grave in a nodding and bobbing car, like an infirm four-post bedstead, by an inky fellow-creature in a cocked-hat. But it may be that I am constitutionally insensible to the virtues of a cocked-hat. In provincial France, the solemnities are sufficiently hideous, but are few and cheap. The friends and townsmen of the departed, in their own dresses and not masquerading under the auspices of the African Conjurer, surround the hand-bier, and often carry it. It is not considered indispensable to stifle the bearers, or even to elevate the burden on their shoulders; consequently it is easily taken up, and easily set down, and is carried through the streets without the distressing floundering and shuffling that we see at home. A dirty priest or two, and a dirtier acolyte or two, do not lend any especial grace to the proceedings; and I regard with personal animosity the bassoon, which is blown at intervals by the big-legged priest (it is always a big-legged priest who blows the bassoon), when his fellows combine in a lugubrious stalwart drawl. But there is far less of the Conjurer and the Medicine Man in the business than under like circumstances here.

The grim coaches that we reserve expressly for such shows, are non-existent: if the cemetery be far out of the town, the coaches that are hired for other purposes of life are hired for this purpose; and although the honest vehicles make no pretence of being overcome, I have never noticed that the people in them were the worse for it. In Italy, the hooded Members of Confraternities who attend on funerals, are dismal and ugly to look upon; but the services they render are at least voluntarily rendered, and impoverish no one, and cost nothing. Why should high civilisation and low savagery ever come together on the point of making them a wantonly wasteful and contemptible set of forms?

Once I lost a friend by death, who had been troubled in his time by the Medicine Man and the Conjurer, and upon whose limited resources there were abundant claims. The Conjurer assured me that I must positively "follow," and both he and the Medicine Man entertained no doubt that I must go in a black carriage, and must wear "fittings." I objected to fittings as having nothing to do with my friendship, and I objected to the black carriage as being in more senses than one a job. So, it came into my mind to try what would happen if I quietly walked, in my own way, from my own house to my friend's burial-place, and stood beside his open grave in my own dress and person, reverently listening to the best of Services. It satisfied my mind, I found, quite as well as if I had been disguised in a hired hatband and scarf both trailing to my very heels, and as if I had cost the orphan children, in their greatest need, ten guineas.

Can any one who ever beheld the stupendous absurdities attendant on "A message from the Lords" in the House of Commons, turn upon the Medicine Man of the poor Indians? Has he any "Medicine" in that dried skin pouch of his, so supremely ludicrous as the two Masters in Chancery holding up their black petticoats and butting their ridiculous wigs at Mr. Speaker? Yet there are authorities innumerable to tell me—as there are authorities innumerable among the Indians to tell them—that the nonsense is indispensable, and that its abrogation would involve most awful consequences. What would any rational creature who had never heard of judicial and forensic "fittings," think of the Court of Common Pleas on the first day of Term? Or with what an awakened sense of humour would LIVINGSTONE's account of a similar scene be perused, if the fur and red cloth and goats' hair and horse hair and powdered chalk and black patches on the top of the head, were all at Tala Mungongo instead of Westminster? That model missionary and good brave man found at least one tribe of blacks with a very strong sense of the ridiculous, insomuch that although an amiable and docile people, they never could see the Missionaries dispose of their legs in the attitude of kneeling, or hear them begin a hymn in chorus, without bursting into roars of irrepressible laughter. It is much to be hoped that no member of this facetious tribe may ever find his way to England and get committed for contempt of Court.

In the Tonga Island already mentioned, there are a set of personages called Mataboos—or some such name—who are the masters of all the public ceremonies, and who know the exact place in which every chief must sit down when a solemn public meeting takes place: a meeting which bears a family resemblance to our own Public Dinner, in respect of it being a main part of the proceedings that every gentleman present is required to drink something nasty. These Mataboos are a privileged order, so important is their avocation, and they make the most of their high functions. A long way out of the Tonga Islands, indeed, rather near the British Islands, was there no calling in of the Mataboos the other day to settle an earth-convulsing question of precedence; and was there no weighty opinion delivered on the part of the Mataboos which, being interpreted to that unlucky tribe of blacks with the sense of the ridiculous, would infallibly set the whole population screaming with laughter?

My sense of justice demands the admission, however, that this is not quite a one-sided question. If we submit ourselves meekly to the Medicine Man and the Conjurer, and are not exalted by it, the savage may retort upon us that we act more unwisely than they in other matters wherein we fail to imitate them. It is a widely diffused custom among savage tribes, when they meet to discuss any affair of public importance, to sit up all night making a horrible noise, dancing, blowing shells, and (in cases where they are familiar with fire-arms) flying out into open places and letting off guns. It is questionable whether our legislative assemblies might not take a hint from this. A shell is not a melodious wind-instrument, and it is monotonous; but it is as musical as, and not more monotonous than, my Honourable friend's own trumpet, or the trumpet that he blows so hard for the Minister. The uselessness of arguing with any supporter of a Government or of an Opposition, is well known. Try dancing. It is a better exercise, and has the unspeakable recommendation that it couldn't be reported. The honourable and savage member who has a loaded gun, and has grown impatient of debate, plunges out of doors, fires in the air, and returns calm and silent to the Palaver. Let the honourable and civilised member similarly charged with a speech, dart into the cloisters of Westminster Abbey in the silence of night, let his speech off, and come back harmless. It is not at first sight a very rational custom to paint a broad blue strips across one's nose and both cheeks, and a broad red stripe from the forehead to the chin, to attach a few pounds of wood to one's under lip, to stick fish-bones in one's ears and a brass curtain-ring in one's nose, and to rub one's body all over with rancid oil, as a preliminary to entering on business. But this is a question of taste and ceremony, and so is the Windsor Uniform. The manner of entering on the business itself is another question. A council of six hundred savage gentlemen entirely independent of tailors, sitting on their hams in a ring, smoking, and occasionally grunting, seem to me, according to the experience I have gathered in my voyages and travels, somehow to do what they come together for; whereas that is not at all the general experience of a council of six hundred civilised gentlemen very dependent on tailors and sitting on mechanical contrivances. It is better that an Assembly should do its utmost to envelop itself in smoke, than that it should direct its endeavours to enveloping the public in smoke; and I would rather it buried half a hundred hatchets than buried one subject demanding attention.

XXIX

TITBULL'S ALMS-HOUSES

BY the side of most railways out of London, one may see Alms-Houses and Retreats (generally with a Wing or a Centre wanting, and ambitious of being much bigger than they are), some of which are newly-founded Institutions, and some old establishments transplanted. There is a tendency in these pieces of architecture to shoot upward unexpectedly, like Jack's bean-stalk, and to be ornate in spires of Chapels and lanterns of Halls, which might lead to the embellishment of the air with many castles of questionable beauty but for the restraining consideration of expense. However, the managers, being always of a sanguine temperament, comfort them-selves with plans and elevations of Loomings in the future, and are influenced in the present by philanthropy towards the railway passengers. For, the question how prosperous and promising the buildings can be made to look in their eyes, usually supersedes the lesser question how they can be turned to the best account for the inmates.

Why none of the people who reside in these places ever look out of window, or take an airing in the piece of ground which is going to be a garden by-and-by, is one of the wonders I have added to my always-lengthening list of the wonders of the world. I have got it into my mind that they live in a state of chronic injury and resentment, and on that account refuse to decorate the building with a human interest. As I have known legatees deeply injured by a bequest of five hundred pounds because it was not five thousand, and as I was once acquainted with a pensioner on the Public to the extent of two hundred a year, who perpetually anathematised his Country because he was not in the receipt of four, having no claim whatever to sixpence: so perhaps it usually happens, within certain limits, that to get a little help is to get a notion of being defrauded of more. "How do they pass their lives in this beautiful and peaceful place!" was the subject of my specula-tion with a visitor who once accompanied me to a charming rustic retreat for old men and women: a quaint ancient foundation in a pleasant English county, behind a picturesque church and among rich old convent gardens. There were but some dozen or so of houses, and we agreed that we would talk with the inhabitants, as they sat in their groined rooms between the light of their fires and the light shining in at their latticed windows, and would find out. They passed their lives in considering themselves mulcted of certain ounces of tea by a deaf old steward who lived among them in the quadrangle.

There was no reason to suppose that any such ounces of tea had ever been in existence, or that the old steward so much as knew what was the matter;—he passed *his* life in considering himself periodically defrauded of a birch-broom by the beadle.

But it is neither to old Alms-Houses in the country, nor to new Alms-Houses by the railroad, that these present Uncommercial notes relate. They refer back to journeys made among those common-place smoky-fronted London Alms-Houses, with a little paved court-yard in front enclosed by iron railings, which have got snowed up, as it were, by bricks and mortar; which were once in a suburb, but are now in the densely populated town; gaps in the busy life around them, parentheses in the close and blotted texts of the streets.

Sometimes, these Alms-Houses belong to a Company or Society. Sometimes, they were established by individuals, and are maintained out of private funds bequeathed in perpetuity long ago. My favourite among them is Titbull's, which establishment is a picture of many. Of Titbull I know no more than that he deceased in 1723, that his Christian name was Sampson, and his social designation Esquire, and that he founded these Alms-Houses as Dwellings for Nine Poor Women and Six Poor Men by his Will and Testament. I should not know even this much, but for its being inscribed on a grim stone very difficult to read, let into the front of the centre house of Titbull's Alms-Houses, and which stone is ornamented a-top with a piece of sculptured drapery resembling the effigy of Titbull's bath-towel.

Titbull's Alms-Houses are in the east of London, in a great highway, in a poor, busy, and thronged neighbourhood. Old iron and fried fish, cough drops and artificial flowers, boiled pigs'-feet and household furniture that looks as if it were polished up with lip-salve, umbrellas full of vocal literature and saucers full of shell-fish in a green juice which I hope is natural to them when their health is good, garnish the paved sideways as you go to Titbull's. I take the ground to have risen in those parts since Titbull's time, and you drop into his domain by three stone steps. So did I first drop into it, very nearly striking my brows against Titbull's pump, which stands with its back to the thoroughfare just inside the gate, and has a conceited air of reviewing Titbull's pensioners.

"And a worse one," said a virulent old man with a pitcher, "there isn't nowhere. A harder one to work, nor a grudginer one to yield, there isn't nowhere!" This old man wore a long coat, such as we see Hogarth's Chairmen represented with, and it was of that peculiar green-pea hue without the green, which seems to come of poverty. It had also that peculiar smell of cupboard which seems to come of poverty.

"The pump is rusty, perhaps," said I.

"Not *it*," said the old man, regarding it with undiluted virulence in his watery eye. "It never were fit to be termed a pump. That's what's the matter with *it*."

"Whose fault is that?" said I.

The old man, who had a working mouth which seemed to be trying to masticate his anger and to find that it was too hard and there was too much of it, replied, "Them gentlemen."

"What gentlemen?"

"Maybe you're one of 'em?" said the old man, suspiciously.

"The trustees?"

"I wouldn't trust 'em myself," said the virulent old man.

"If you mean the gentlemen who administer this place, no, I am not one of them; nor have I ever so much as heard of them."

"I wish *I* never heard of them," gasped the old man: "at my time of life—with the rheumatics—drawing water—from that thing!" Not to be deluded into calling it a Pump, the old man gave it another virulent look, took up his pitcher, and carried it into a corner dwelling-house, shutting the door after him.

Looking around and seeing that each little house was a house of two little rooms; and seeing that the little oblong court-yard in front was like a graveyard for the inhabitants, saving that no word was engraven on its flat dry stones; and seeing that the currents of life and noise ran to and fro outside, having no more to do with the place than if it were a sort of low-water mark on a lively beach; I say, seeing this and nothing else, I was going out at the gate when one of the doors opened.

"Was you looking for anything, sir?" asked a tidy, well-favoured woman.

Really, no; I couldn't say I was.

"Not wanting any one, sir?"

"No—at least I—pray what is the name of the elderly gentleman who lives in the corner there?"

The tidy woman stepped out to be sure of the door I indicated, and she and the pump and I stood all three in a row with our backs to the thoroughfare.

"Oh! *His* name is Mr. Battens," said the tidy woman, dropping her voice.

"I have just been talking with him."

"Indeed?" said the tidy woman. "Ho! I wonder Mr. Battens talked!"

"Is he usually so silent?"

"Well, Mr. Battens is the oldest here—that is to say, the oldest of the old gentlemen—in point of residence."

She had a way of passing her hands over and under one another as she spoke, that was not only tidy but propitiatory; so I asked her if I might look at her little sitting-room? She willingly replied Yes, and we went into it together: she leaving the door open, with an eye as I understood to the social proprieties. The door opening at once into the room without any intervening entry, even scandal must have been silenced by the precaution.

It was a gloomy little chamber, but clean, and with a mug of wallflower in the window. On the chimney-piece were two peacock's feathers, a carved ship, a few shells, and a black profile with one eyelash; whether this portrait purported to be male or female passed my comprehension, until my hostess informed me that it was her only son, and "quite a speaking one."

"He is alive, I hope?"

"No, sir," said the widow, "he were cast away in China." This was said with a modest sense of its reflecting a certain geographical distinction on his mother.

"If the old gentlemen here are not given to talking," said I, "I hope the old ladies are?—not that you are one."

She shook her head. "You see they get so cross."

"How is that?"

"Well, whether the gentlemen really do deprive us of any little matters which ought to be ours by rights, I cannot say for certain; but the opinion of the old ones is they do. And Mr. Battens he do even go so far as to doubt whether credit is due to the Founder. For Mr. Battens he do say, anyhow he got his name up by it and he done it cheap."

"I am afraid the pump has soured Mr. Battens."

"It may be so," returned the tidy widow, "but the handle does go very hard. Still, what I say to myself is, the gentlemen *may* not pocket the difference between a good pump and a bad one, and I would wish to think well of them. And the dwellings," said my hostess, glancing round her room; "perhaps they were convenient dwellings in the Founder's time, considered *as* his time, and therefore he should not be blamed. But Mrs. Saggers is very hard upon them."

"Mrs. Saggers is the oldest here?"

"The oldest but one. Mrs. Quinch being the oldest, and have totally lost her head."

"And you?"

"I am the youngest in residence, and consequently am not looked up to. But when Mrs. Quinch makes a happy release, there will be one below me. Nor is it to be expected that Mrs. Saggers will prove herself immortal."

"True. Nor Mr. Battens."

"Regarding the old gentlemen," said my widow slightingly, "they count among themselves. They do not count among us. Mr. Battens is that exceptional that he have written to the gentlemen many times and have worked the case against them. Therefore he have took a higher ground. But we do not, as a rule, greatly reckon the old gentlemen."

Pursuing the subject, I found it to be traditionally settled among the poor ladies that the poor gentlemen, whatever their ages, were all very old indeed, and in a state of dotage. I also discovered that the juniors and new-comers preserved, for a time, a waning disposition to believe in Titbull and his trustees, but that as they gained social standing they lost this faith, and disparaged Titbull and all his works.

Improving my acquaintance subsequently with this respected lady, whose name was Mrs. Mitts, and occasionally dropping in upon her with a little offering of sound Family Hyson in my pocket, I gradually became familiar with the inner politics and ways of Titbull's

Alms-Houses. But I never could find out who the trustees were, or where they were: it being one of the fixed ideas of the place that those authorities must be vaguely and mysteriously mentioned as "the gentlemen" only. The secretary of "the gentlemen" was once pointed out to me, evidently engaged in championing the obnoxious pump against the attacks of the discontented Mr. Battens; but I am not in a condition to report further of him than that he had the sprightly bearing of a lawyer's clerk. I had it from Mrs. Mitt's lips in a very confidential moment, that Mr. Battens was once "had up before the gentlemen" to stand or fall by his accusations, and that an old shoe was thrown after him on his departure from the building on this dread errand;—not ineffectually, for, the interview resulting in a plumber, was considered to have encircled the temples of Mr. Battens with the wreath of victory.

In Titbull's Alms-Houses, the local society is not regarded as good society. A gentleman or lady receiving visitors from without, or going out to tea, counts, as it were, accordingly; but visitings or tea-drinkings interchanged among Titbullians do not score. Such interchanges, however, are rare, in consequence of internal dissensions occasioned by Mrs. Saggers's pail: which household article has split Titbull's into almost as many parties as there are dwellings in that precinct. The extremely complicated nature of the conflicting articles of belief on the subject prevents my stating them here with my usual perspicuity, but I think they have all branched off from the root-and-trunk question, Has Mrs. Saggers any right to stand her pail outside her dwelling? The question has been much refined upon, but roughly stated may be stated in those terms.

There are two old men in Titbull's Alms-Houses who, I have been given to understand, knew each other in the world beyond its pump and iron railings, when they were both "in trade." They make the best of their reverses, and are looked upon with great contempt. They are little stooping, blear-eyed old men of cheerful countenance, and they hobble up and down the court-yard wagging their chins and talking together quite gaily. This has given offence, and has, moreover, raised the question whether they are justified in passing any other windows than their own. Mr. Battens, however, permitting them to pass *his* windows, on the disdainful ground that their imbecility almost amounts to irresponsibility, they are allowed to take their walk in peace. They live next door to one another, and take it by turns to read the newspaper aloud (that is to say, the newest newspaper they can get), and they play cribbage at night. On warm and sunny days they have been known to go so far as to bring out chairs and sit by the iron railings, looking forth; but this low conduct, being much remarked upon throughout Titbull's, they were deterred by an outraged public opinion from repeating it. There is a rumour—but it may be malicious—that they hold the memory of Titbull in some weak sort of veneration, and that they once set off together on a pilgrimage to the parish churchyard to find his tomb. To this, perhaps, might be traced a general suspicion that they are spies of "the gentlemen:"

to which they were supposed to have given colour in my own presence on the occasion of the weak attempt at justification of the pump by the gentlemen's clerk; when they emerged bare-headed from the doors of their dwellings, as if their dwellings and themselves constituted an old-fashioned weather-glass of double action with two figures of old ladies inside, and deferentially bowed to him at intervals until he took his departure. They are understood to be perfectly friendless and relationless. Unquestionably the two poor fellows make the very best of their lives in Titbull's Alms-Houses, and unquestionably they are (as before mentioned) the subjects of unmitigated contempt there.

On Saturday nights, when there is a greater stir than usual outside, and when itinerant vendors of miscellaneous wares even take their stations and light up their smoky lamps before the iron railings, Titbull's becomes flurried. Mrs. Saggers has her celebrated palpitations of the heart, for the most part, on Saturday nights. But Titbull's is unfit to strive with the uproar of the streets in any of its phases. It is religiously believed at Titbull's that people push more than they used, and likewise that the foremost object of the population of England and Wales is to get you down and trample on you. Even of railroads they know, at Titbull's, little more than the shriek (which Mrs. Saggers says goes through her, and ought to be taken up by Government); and the penny postage may even yet be unknown there for I have never seen a letter delivered to any inhabitant. But there is a tall, straight lady resident in Number Seven, Titbull's, who never speaks to anybody, who is surrounded by a superstitious halo of lost wealth, who does her household work in housemaids gloves, and who is secretly much deferred to, though openly cavilled at; and it has obscurely leaked out that this old lady has a son, grandson, nephew, or other relative, who is "a contractor." and who would think it nothing of a job to knock down Titbull's, pack it off into Cornwall, and knock it together again. An immense sensation was made by a gipsy-party calling in a spring-van, to take this old lady up to go for a day's pleasure into Epping Forest, and notes were prepared as to which of the company was the son, grandson, nephew, or other relative, the Contractor. A thick-set personage with a white hat and a cigar in his mouth, was the favourite: though as Titbull's had no other reason to believe that the Contractor was there at all, than that this man was supposed to eye the chimney stacks as if he would like to knock them down and cart them off, the general mind was much unsettled in arriving at a conclusion. As a way out of this difficulty, it concentrated itself on the acknowledged Beauty of the party, every stitch in whose dress was verbally unripped by the old ladies then and there, and whose "goings on" with another and a thinner personage in a white hat might have suffused the pump (where they were principally discussed) with blushes, for months afterwards. Herein Titbull's was to Titbull's true, for it has a constitutional dislike of all strangers. As concerning innovations and improvements, it is always of opinion that what it doesn't want itself, nobody ought to want. But I think I have met with this opinion outside Titbull's.

Of the humble treasures of furniture brought into Titbull's by the inmates when they establish themselves in that place of contemplation for the rest of their days, by far the greater and more valuable part belongs to the ladies. I may claim the honour of having either crossed the threshold, or looked in at the door, of every one of the nine ladies, and I have noticed that they are all particular in the article of bedsteads, and maintain favourite and long-established bedsteads and bedding as a regular part of their rest. Generally an antiquated chest of drawers is among their cherished possessions; a tea-tray always is. I know of at least two rooms in which a little tea-kettle of genuine burnished copper, vies with the cat in winking at the fire; and one old lady has a tea-urn set forth in state on the top of her chest of drawers, which urn is used as her library, and contains four duodecimo volumes, and a black-bordered newspaper giving an account of the funeral of Her Royal Highness the Princess Charlotte. Among the poor old gentlemen there are no such niceties. Their furniture has the air of being contributed, like some obsolete Literary Miscellany, "by several hands;" their few chairs never match; old patchwork coverlets linger among them; and they have an untidy habit of keeping their wardrobes in hatboxes. When I recall one old gentleman who is rather choice in his shoe-brushes and blacking-bottle, I have summed up the domestic elegances of that side of the building.

On the occurrence of a death in Titbull's it is invariably agreed among the survivors—and it is the only subject on which they do agree—that the departed did something "to bring it on." Judging by Titbull's, I should say the human race need never die, if they took care. But they don't take care, and they do die, and when they die in Titbull's they are buried at the cost of the Foundation. Some provision has been made for the purpose, in virtue of which (I record this on the strength of having seen the funeral of Mrs. Quinch) a lively neighbouring undertaker dresses up four of the old men, and four of the old women, hustles them into a procession of four couples, and leads off with a large black bow at the back of his hat, looking over his shoulder at them airily from time to time to see that no member of the party has got lost, or has tumbled down: as if they were a company of dim old dolls.

Resignation of a dwelling is of very rare occurrence in Titbull's. A story does obtain there, how an old lady's son once drew a prize of Thirty Thousand Pounds in the Lottery, and presently drove to the gate in his own carriage, with French Horns playing up behind, and whisked his mother away, and left ten guineas for a Feast. But I have been unable to substantiate it by any evidence, and regard it as an Alms-House Fairy Tale. It is curious that the only proved case of resignation happened within my knowledge.

It happened on this wise. There is a sharp competition among the ladies respecting the gentility of their visitors, and I have so often observed visitors to be dressed as for a holiday occasion, that I suppose the ladies to have besought them to make all possible display when they come. In these circumstances much excitement was one day occasioned by Mrs. Mitts receiving a visit from a Greenwich Pensioner. He was a Pensioner of a bluff and warlike appearance, with an empty coat-sleeve, and he was got up with unusual care; his coat-buttons were extremely bright, he wore his empty coat-sleeve in a graceful festoon, and he had a walking-stick in his hand that must have cost money. When, with the head of his walking-stick, he knocked at Mrs. Mitt's door—there are no knockers in Titbull's—Mrs. Mitts was overheard by a next-door neighbour to utter a cry of surprise expressing much agitation; and the same neighbour did afterwards solemnly affirm that when he was admitted into Mrs. Mitts's room, she heard a smack. Heard a smack which was not a blow.

There was an air about this Greenwich Pensioner when he took his departure, which imbued all Titbull's with the conviction that he was coming again. He was eagerly looked for, and Mrs. Mitts was closely watched. In the meantime, if anything could have placed the unfortunate six old gentlemen at a greater disadvantage than that at which they chronically stood, it would have been the apparition of this Greenwich Pensioner. They were well shrunken already, but they shrunk to nothing in comparison with the Pensioner. Even the poor old gentlemen themselves seemed conscious of their inferiority, and to know submissively that they could never hope to hold their own against the Pensioner with his warlike and maritime experience in the past, and his tobacco money in the present: his chequered career of blue water, black gunpowder, and red bloodshed for England, home, and beauty.

Before three weeks were out, the Pensioner reappeared. Again he knocked at Mrs. Mitts's door with the handle of his stick, and again was he admitted. But not again did he depart alone; for Mrs. Mitts, in a bonnet identified as having been re-embellished, went out walking with him, and stayed out till the ten o'clock beer, Greenwich time.

There was now a truce, even as to the troubled waters of Mrs. Saggers's pail; nothing was spoken of among the ladies but the conduct of Mrs. Miggs and its blighting influence on the reputation of Titbull's. It was agreed that Mr. Battens "ought to take it up," and Mr. Battens was communicated with on the subject. That unsatisfactory individual replied "that he didn't see his way yet," and it was unanimously voted by the ladies that aggravation was in his nature.

How it came to pass, with some appearance of inconsistency, that Mrs. Mitts was cut by all the ladies and the Pensioner admired by all the ladies, matters not. Before another week was out, Titbull's was startled by another phenomenon. At ten o'clock in the forenoon appeared a cab, containing not only the Greenwich Pensioner with one arm, but, to boot, a Chelsea Pensioner with one leg. Both dismounting to assist Mrs. Mitts into the cab, the Greenwich Pensioner bore her company inside, and the Chelsea Pensioner mounted the box by the driver: his wooden leg sticking out after the manner of a bowsprit, as if in jocular homage to his friend's sea-going career. Thus the equipage drove away. No Mrs. Mitts returned that night.

What Mr. Battens might have done in the matter of taking it up, goaded by the infuriated state of public feeling next morning, was anticipated by another phenomenon. A Truck, propelled by the Greenwich Pensioner and the Chelsea Pensioner, each placidly smoking a pipe, and pushing his warrior breast against the handle.

The display on the part of the Greenwich Pensioner of his "marriage lines," and his announcement that himself and friend had looked in for the furniture of Mrs. G. Pensioner, late Mitts, by no means reconciled the ladies to the conduct of their sister; on the contrary, it is said that they appeared more than ever exasperated. Nevertheless, my stray visits to Titbull's since the date of this occurrence, have confirmed me in an impression that it was a wholesome fillip. The nine ladies are smarter, both in mind and dress, than they used to be, though it must be admitted that they despise the six gentlemen to the last extent. They have a much greater interest in the external thoroughfare too, than they had when I first knew Titbull's. And whenever I chance to be leaning my back against the pump or the iron railings, and to be talking to one of the junior ladies, and to see that a flush has passed over her face, I immediately know without looking round that a Greenwich Pensioner has gone past.

XXX

THE RUFFIAN

I ENTERTAIN so strong an objection to the euphonious softening of Ruffian into Rough, which has lately become popular, that I restore the right word to the heading of this paper; the rather, as my object is to dwell upon the fact that the Ruffian is tolerated among us to an extent that goes beyond all unruffianly endurance. I take the liberty to believe that if the Ruffian besets my life, a professional Ruffian at large in the open streets of a great city, notoriously having no other calling than that of Ruffian, and of disquieting and despoiling me as I go peacefully about my lawful business, interfering with no one, then the Government under which I have the great constitutional privilege, supreme honour and happiness, and all the rest of it, to exist, breaks down in the discharge of any Government's most simple elementary duty.

What did I read in the London daily papers, in the early days of last September? That the Police had "AT LENGTH SUCCEEDED IN CAPTURING TWO OF THE NOTORIOUS GANG THAT HAVE SO LONG INFESTED THE WATERLOO ROAD." Is it possible? What a wonderful Police! Here is a straight, broad, public thoroughfare of immense resort; half a mile long; gas-lighted by night; with a great gas-lighted railway station in it, extra the street-lamps; full of shops; traversed by two popular cross thoroughfares of considerable traffic; itself the main road to the south of London; and the admirable Police have, after long infestment of this dark and lonely spot by a gang of Ruffians, actually got hold of two of them. Why, can it be doubted that any man of fair

London knowledge and common resolution, armed with the powers of the Law, could have captured the whole confederacy in a week?

It is to the saving up of the Ruffian class by the Magistracy and Police—to the conventional preserving of them, as if they were Partridges—that their number and audacity must be in great part referred Why is a notorious Thief and Ruffian ever left at large? He never turns his liberty to any account by violence and plunder, he never did a day's work out of gaol he never will do a day's work out of gaol. As a proved notorious Thief he is always consignable to prison for three months. When he comes out, he is surely as notorious a Thief as he was when he went in. Then send him back again. "Just Heaven!" cries the Society for the protection of remonstrant Ruffians. "This is equivalent to a sentence of perpetual imprisonment!" Precisely for that reason it has my advocacy. I demand to have the Ruffian kept out of my way, and out of the way of all decent people. I demand to have the Ruffian employed, perforce, in hewing wood and drawing water somewhere for the general service, instead of hewing at her Majesty's subjects and drawing their watches out of their pockets. If this be termed an unreasonable demand, then the tax-gatherer's demand on me must be far more unreasonable, and cannot be otherwise than extortionate and unjust.

It will be seen that I treat of the Thief and Ruffian as one. I do so, because I know the two characters to be one, in the vast majority of cases, just as well as the Police know it. (As to the Magistracy, with a few exceptions, they know nothing about it but what the Police choose to tell them.) There are disorderly classes of men who are not thieves ; as railway-navigators, brickmakers, wood-sawyers, coster-mongers. These classes are often disorderly and troublesome; but it is mostly among themselves, and at any rate they have their industrious avocations, they work early and late, and work hard. The generic Ruffian—honourable member for what is tenderly called the Rough Element—is either a Thief, or the companion of Thieves. When he infamously molests women coming out of chapel on Sunday evenings (for which I would have his back scarified often and deep) it is not only for the gratification of his pleasant instincts, but that there may be a confusion raised by which either he or his friends may profit, in the commission of highway robberies or in picking pockets. When he gets a police constable down and kicks him helpless for life, it is because that constable once did his duty in bringing him to justice. When he rushes into the bar of a public-house and scoops an eye out of one of the company there, or bites his ear off, it is because the man he maims gave evidence against him When he and a line of comrades extending across the footway—say of that solitary mountain-spur of the Abruzzi, the Waterloo Road—advance towards me "skylarking" among themselves, my purse or shirt-pin is in pre-destined peril from his playfulness. Always a Ruffian, always a Thief. Always a Thief, always a Ruffian.

Now, when I, who am not paid to know these things, know them daily on the evidence of my senses and experience; when I know that the Ruffian never jostles a lady in the streets, or knocks a hat off, but in order that the Thief may profit, is it surprising that I should require from those who *are* paid to know these things, prevention of them?

Look at this group at a street corner. Number one is a shirking fellow of five-and-twenty, in an ill-favoured and ill-savoured suit, his trousers of corduroy, his coat of some indiscernible groundwork for the deposition of grease, his neckerchief like an eel, his complexion like dirty dough, his mangy fur cap pulled low upon his beetle brows to hide the prison cut of his hair. His hands are in his pockets. He puts them there when they are idle, as naturally as in other people's pockets when they are busy, for he knows that they are not roughened by work, and that they tell a tale. Hence, whenever he takes one out to draw a sleeve across his nose—which is often, for he has weak eyes and a constitutional cold in his head—he restores it to its pocket immediately afterwards. Number two is a burly brute of five-and-thirty, in a tall stiff hat; is a composite as to his clothes of betting-man and fighting-man; is whiskered; has a staring pin in his breast, along with his right hand; has insolent and cruel eyes; large shoulders; strong legs, booted and tipped for kicking. Number three is forty years of age; is short, thick-set, strong, and bow-legged; wears knee cords and white stockings, a very long-sleeved waistcoat, a very large neckerchief doubled or trebled round his throat, and a crumpled white hat crowns his ghastly parchment face. This fellow looks like an executed postboy of other days, cut down from the gallows too soon, and restored and preserved by express diabolical agency. Numbers five, six, and seven, are hulking, idle, slouching young men, patched and shabby, too short in the sleeves and too tight in the legs, slimily clothed, foul-spoken, repulsive wretches inside and out. In all the party there obtains a certain twitching character of mouth and furtiveness of eye, that hint how the coward is lurking under the bully. The hint is quite correct, for they are a slinking sneaking set, far more prone to lie down on their backs and kick out, when in difficulty, than to make a stand for it. (This may account for the street mud on the backs of Numbers five, six, and seven, being much fresher than the stale splashes on their legs.)

These engaging gentry a Police-constable stands contemplating. His Station, with a Reserve of assistance, is very near at hand. They cannot pretend to any trade, not even to be porters or messengers. It would be idle if they did, for he knows them, and they know that he knows them, to be nothing but professed Thieves and Ruffians. He knows where they resort, knows by what slang names they call one another, knows how often they have been in prison, and how long, and for what. All this is known at his Station, too, and is (or ought to be) known at Scotland Yard, too. But does he know, or does his Station know, or does Scotland Yard know, or does anybody know, why these fellows should be here at liberty, when, as reputed Thieves to whom a whole Division of Police could swear, they might all be under lock and key at hard labour? Not he; truly he would be a wise man if he did! He only knows that these are members of the "notorious gang," which, according to the newspaper Police-office reports of this last past September, "have so long infested" the awful solitudes of the Waterloo Road, and out of which almost impregnable fastnesses the Police have at length dragged Two, to the unspeakable admiration of all good civilians.

The consequences of this contemplative habit on the part of the Executive—a habit to be looked for in a hermit, but not in a Police System—are familiar to us all. The Ruffian becomes one of the established orders of the body politic. Under the playful name of Rough (as if he were merely a practical joker) his movements and successes are recorded on public occasions. Whether he mustered in large numbers, or small; whether he was in good spirits, or depressed; whether he turned his generous exertions to very prosperous account, or Fortune was against him; whether he was in a sanguinary mood, or robbed with amiable horse-play and a gracious consideration for life and limb; all this is chronicled as if he were an Institution. Is there any city in Europe, out of England, in which these terms are held with the pests of Society? Or in which, at this day, such violent robberies from the person are constantly committed as in London?

The Preparatory Schools of Ruffianism are similarly borne with. The young Ruffians of London—not Thieves yet, but training for scholarships and fellowships in the Criminal Court Universities—molest quiet people and their property, to an extent that is hardly credible. The throwing of stones in the streets has become a dangerous and destructive offence, which surely could have got to no greater height though we had had no Police but our own riding-whips and walking-sticks—the Police to which I myself appeal on these occasions. The throwing of stones at the windows of railway carriages in motion—an act of wanton wickedness with the very Arch-Fiend's hand in it—had become a crying evil, when the railway companies forced it on Police notice. Constabular contemplation had until then been the order of the day.

Within these twelve months, there arose among the young gentlemen of London aspiring to Ruffianism, and cultivating that much-encouraged social art, a facetious cry of "I'll have this!" accompanied with a clutch at some article of a passing lady's dress. I have known a lady's veil to be thus humorously torn from her face and carried off in the open streets at noon; and I have had the honour of myself giving chase, on Westminster Bridge, to another young Ruffian, who, in full daylight early on a summer evening, had nearly thrown a modest young woman into a swoon of indignation and confusion, by his shameful manner of attacking her with this cry as she harmlessly passed along before me. Mr. CARLYLE, some time since, awakened a little pleasantry by writing of his own experience of the Ruffian of the streets. I have seen the Ruffian act in exact accordance with Mr. Carlyle's description, innumerable times, and I never saw him checked.

The blaring use of the very worst language possible, in our public thoroughfares—especially in those set apart for recreation—is another disgrace to us, and another result of constabular contemplation, the like of which I have never heard in any other country to which my uncommercial travels have extended. Years ago, when I had a near interest in certain children who were sent with their nurses, for air and exercise, into the Regent's Park, I found this evil to be so abhorrent and horrible there, that I called public attention to it, and also to its contemplative reception by the Police. Looking afterwards into the newest Police Act, and finding that the offence was punishable under it, I resolved, when striking occasion should arise, to try my hand as prosecutor. The occasion arose soon enough, and I ran the following gauntlet.

The utterer of the base coin in question was a girl of seventeen or eighteen, who, with a suitable attendance of blackguards, youths, and boys, was flaunting along the streets, returning from an Irish funeral, in a Progress interspersed with singing and dancing. She had turned round to me and expressed herself in the most audible manner, to the great delight of that select circle. I attended the party, on the opposite side of the way, for a mile further, and then encountered a Police-constable. The party had made themselves merry at my expense until now, but seeing me speak to the constable, its male members instantly took to their heels, leaving the girl alone. I asked the constable did he know my name? Yes, he did. "Take that girl into custody, on my charge, for using bad language in the streets." He had never heard of such a charge. I had. Would he take my word that he should get into no trouble? Yes, sir, he would do that. So he took the girl and I went home for my Police Act.

With this potent instrument in my pocket, I literally as well as figuratively "returned to the charge," and presented myself at the Police Station of the district. There, I found on duty a very intelligent Inspector (they are all intelligent men), who, likewise, had never heard of such a charge. I showed him my clause, and we went over it together twice or thrice. It was plain, and I engaged to wait upon the suburban Magistrate to-morrow morning at ten o'clock.

In the morning I put my Police Act in my pocket again, and waited on the suburban Magistrate. I was not quite so courteously received by him as I should have been by The Lord Chancellor or The Lord Chief Justice, but that was a question of good breeding on the suburban Magistrate's part, and I had my clause ready with its leaf turned down. Which was enough for *me*.

Conference took place between the Magistrate and clerk respecting the charge. During conference I was evidently regarded as a much more objectionable person than the prisoner;—one giving trouble by coming there voluntarily, which the prisoner could not be accused of doing. The prisoner had been got up, since I last had the pleasure of seeing her, with a great effect of white apron and straw bonnet. She reminded me of an elder sister of Red Riding Hood, and I seemed to remind the sympathising Chimney Sweep by whom she was attended, of the Wolf.

The Magistrate was doubtful, Mr. Uncommercial Traveller, whether this charge could be entertained. It was not known. Mr. Uncommercial Traveller replied that he wished it were better known, and that, if he could afford the leisure, he would use his endeavours to make it so. There was no question about it, however, he contended. Here was the clause.

The clause was handed in, and more conference resulted. After which I was asked the extraordinary question: "Mr. Uncommercial, do you really wish this girl to be sent to prison?" To which I grimly answered, staring: "If I didn't, why should I take the trouble to come here?" Finally, I was sworn, and gave my agreeable evidence in detail, and White Riding Hood was fined ten shillings, under the clause, or sent to prison for so many days. "Why, Lord bless you, sir," said the Police-officer, who showed me out, with a great enjoyment of the jest of her having been got up so effectively, and caused so much hesitation: "if she goes to prison, that will be nothing new to *her*. She comes from Charles Street, Drury Lane!"

The Police, all things considered, are an excellent force, and I have borne my small testimony to their merits. Constabular contemplation is the result of a bad system; a system which is administered, not invented, by the man in constable's uniform, employed at twenty shillings a week. He has his orders, and would be marked for discouragement if he overstepped them. That the system is bad, there needs no lengthened argument to prove, because the fact is self-evident. If it were anything else, the results that have attended it could not possibly have come to pass. Who will say that under a good system, our streets could have got into their present state?

The objection to the whole Police system, as concerning the Ruffian, may be stated, and its failure exemplified, as follows. It is well known that on all great occasions, when they come together in numbers, the mass of the English people are their own trustworthy Police. It is well known that wheresoever there is collected together any fair general representation of the people, a respect for law and order, and a determination to discountenance lawlessness and disorder, may be relied upon. As to one another, the people are a very good Police, and yet are quite willing in their good-nature that the stipendiary Police should have the credit of the people's moderation. But we are all of us powerless against the Ruffian, because we submit to the law, and it is his only trade, by superior force and by violence, to defy it. Moreover, we are constantly admonished from high places (like so many Sunday-school children out for a holiday of buns and milk-and-water) that we are not to take the law into our own hands, but are to hand our defence over to it. It is clear that the common enemy to be punished and exterminated first of all is the Ruffian. It is clear that he is, of all others, *the* offender for whose repressal we maintain a costly system of Police. Him, therefore, we expressly present to the Police to deal with, conscious that, on the whole, we can, and do, deal reasonably well with one another. Him the Police deal with so inefficiently and absurdly that he flourishes, and multiplies, and, with all his evil deeds upon his head as notoriously as his hat is, pervades the streets with no more let or hindrance than ourselves.

<h1 style="text-align:center">XXXI</h1>

<h3 style="text-align:center">ABOARD SHIP</h3>

MY journeys as Uncommercial Traveller for the firm of Human-Interest Brothers have not slackened since I last reported of them, but have kept me continually on the move. I remain in the same idle employment. I never solicit an order, I never get any commission, I am the rolling stone that gathers no moss,—unless any should by chance be found among these samples.

Some half a year ago, I found myself in my idlest, dreamiest, and least accountable condition altogether, on board ship, in the harbour of the city of New York, in the United States of America. Of all the good ships afloat, mine was the good steamship "Russia," CAPT. COOK, Cunard Line, bound for Liverpool. What more could I wish for?

I had nothing to wish for but a prosperous passage. My salad-days, when I was green of visage and sea-sick, being gone with better things (and no worse), no coming event cast its shadow before.

I might but a few moments previously have imitated Sterne, and said, "'And yet, methinks, Eugenius,'—laying my forefinger wistfully on his coat-sleeve, thus,—'and yet, methinks, Eugenius, 'tis but sorry work to part with thee, for what fresh fields, . . . my dear Eugenius, . . . can be fresher than thou art, and in what pastures new shall I find Eliza, or call her, Eugenius, if thou wilt, Annie?' "—I say I might have done this; but Eugenius was gone, and I hadn't done it.

I was resting on a skylight on the hurricane-deck, watching the working of the ship very slowly about, that she might head for England. It was high noon on a most brilliant day in April, and the beautiful bay was glorious and glowing. Full many a time, on shore there, had I seen the snow come down, down, down (itself like down), until it lay deep in all the ways of men, and particularly, as it seemed in my way, for I had not gone dry-shod many hours for months. Within two or three days last past had I watched the feathery fall setting in with the ardour of a new idea, instead of dragging at the skirts of a worn-out winter, and permitting glimpses of a fresh young spring. But a bright sun and a clear sky had melted the snow in the great crucible of nature; and it had been poured out again that morning over sea and land, transformed into myriads of gold and silver sparkles.

The ship was fragrant with flowers. Something of the old Mexican passion for flowers may have gradually passed into North America, where flowers are luxuriously grown, and tastefully combined in the richest profusion; but, be that as it may, such gorgeous farewells in flowers had come on board, that the small officer's cabin on deck,

which I tenanted, bloomed over into the adjacent scuppers, and
banks of other flowers that it couldn't hold made a garden of the
unoccupied tables in the passengers' saloon. These delicious scents
of the shore, mingling with the fresh airs of the sea, made the atmosphere a dreamy, an enchanting one. And so, with the watch aloft
setting all the sails, and with the screw below revolving at a mighty
rate, and occasionally giving the ship an angry shake for resisting,
I fell into my idlest ways, and lost myself.

As, for instance, whether it was I lying there, or some other entity
even more mysterious, was a matter I was far too lazy to look into.
What did it signify to me if it were I? or to the more mysterious entity,
if it were he? Equally as to the remembrances that drowsily floated
by me, or by him, why ask when or where the things happened? Was
it not enough that they befell at some time, somewhere?

There was that assisting at the church service on board another
steamship, one Sunday, in a stiff breeze. Perhaps on the passage out.
No matter. Pleasant to hear the ship's bells go as like church-bells
as they could; pleasant to see the watch off duty mustered and come
in: best hats, best Guernseys, washed hands and faces, smoothed
heads. But then arose a set of circumstances so rampantly comical,
that no check which the gravest intentions could put upon them
would hold them in hand. Thus the scene. Some seventy passengers
assembled at the saloon tables. Prayer-books on tables. Ship rolling
heavily. Pause. No minister. Rumour has related that a modest
young clergyman on board has responded to the captain's request
that he will officiate. Pause again, and very heavy rolling.

Closed double doors suddenly burst open and two strong stewards
skate in, supporting minister between them. General appearance as
of somebody picked up drunk and incapable, and under conveyance
to station-house. Stoppage, pause, and particularly heavy rolling.
Stewards watch their opportunity, and balance themselves, but
cannot balance minister; who, struggling with a drooping head and
a backward tendency, seems determined to return below, while they
are as determined that he shall be got to the reading-desk in mid-
saloon. Desk portable, sliding away down a long table, and aiming
itself at the breasts of various members of the congregation. Here
the double doors, which have been carefully closed by other stewards,
fly open again, and worldly passenger tumbles in, seemingly with
pale-ale designs: who, seeking friend, says "Joe!" Perceiving incon-
gruity, says, "Hullo! Beg yer pardon!" and tumbles out again. All
this time the congregation have been breaking up into sects,—as the
manner of congregations often is,—each sect sliding away by itself,
and all pounding the weakest sect which slid first into the corner.
Utmost point of dissent soon attained in every corner, and violent
rolling. Stewards at length make a dash; conduct minister to the
mast in the centre of the saloon, which he embraces with both arms;
skate out; and leave him in that condition to arrange affairs with
flock.

There was another Sunday, when an officer of the ship read the service. It was quiet and impressive, until we fell upon the dangerous and perfectly unnecessary experiment of striking up a hymn. After it was given out, we all rose, but everybody left it to somebody else to begin. Silence resulting, the officer (no singer himself) rather reproachfully gave us the first line again, upon which a rosy pippin of an old gentleman, remarkable throughout the passage for his cheerful politeness, gave a little stamp with his boot (as if he were leading off a country dance), and blithely warbled us into a show of joining. At the end of the first verse we became, through these tactics, so much refreshed and encouraged, that none of us, howsoever unmelodious, would submit to be left out of the second verse; while as to the third we lifted up our voices in a sacred howl that left it doubtful whether we were the more boastful of the sentiments we united in professing, or of professing them with a most discordant defiance of time and tune.

"Lord bless us!" thought I, when the fresh remembrance of these things made me laugh heartily alone in the dead water-gurgling waste of the night, what time I was wedged into my berth by a wooden bar, or I must have rolled out of it, "what errand was I then upon, and to what Abyssinian point had public events then marched? No matter as to me. And as to them, if the wonderful popular rage for a plaything (utterly confounding in its inscrutable unreason) had not then lighted on a poor young savage boy, and a poor old screw of a horse, and hauled the first off by the hair of his princely head to 'inspect' British volunteers, and hauled the second off by the hair of his equine tail to the Crystal Palace, why so much the better for all of us outside Bedlam!"

So, sticking to the ship, I was at the trouble of asking myself would I like to show the grog distribution in "the fiddle" at noon to the Grand United Amalgamated Total Abstinence Society? Yes, I think I should. I think it would do them good to smell the rum, under the circumstances. Over the grog, mixed in a bucket, presides the boatswain's mate, small tin can in hand. Enter the crew, the guilty consumers, the grown-up brood of Giant Despair, in contradistinction to the band of youthful angel Hope. Some in boots, some in leggings, some in tarpaulin overalls, some in frocks, some in pea-coats, a very few in jackets, most with sou'wester hats, all with something rough and rugged round the throat; all, dripping salt water where they stand; all pelted by weather, besmeared with grease, and blackened by the sooty rigging.

Each man's knife in its sheath in his girdle, loosened for dinner. As the first man, with a knowingly kindled eye, watches the filling of the poisoned chalice (truly but a very small tin mug, to be prosaic), and, tossing back his head, tosses the contents into himself, and passes the empty chalice and passes on, so the second man with an anticipatory wipe of his mouth on sleeve or handkerchief, bides his turn, and drinks and hands and passes on, in whom, and in each as his turn approaches, beams a knowingly kindled eye, a brighter temper, and a suddenly awakened tendency to be jocose with some

shipmate. Nor do I even observe that the man in charge of the ship's
lamps, who in right of his office has a double allowance of poisoned
chalices, seems thereby vastly degraded, even though he empties
the chalices into himself, one after the other, much as if he were
delivering their contents at some absorbent establishment in which
he had no personal interest. But vastly comforted, I note them all
to be, on deck presently, even to the circulation of redder blood in
their cold blue knuckles, and when I look up at them lying out on the
yards, and holding on to life among the beating sails, I cannot for
my life see the justice of visiting on them—or on me—the drunken
crimes of any number of criminals arraigned at the heaviest of assizes.

Abetting myself in my idle humour, I closed my eyes, and recalled
life on board of one of those mail-packets, as I lay, part of that day,
in the Bay of New York. O! The regular life began—mine always
did, for I never got to sleep afterwards—with the rigging of the pump
while it was yet dark, and washing down of decks. Any enormous
giant at a prodigious hydropathic establishment, conscientiously
undergoing the water-cure in all its departments, and extremely
particular about cleaning his teeth, would make those noises. Swash,
splash, scrub, rub toothbrush, bubble, swash, splash, bubble, toothbrush, splash splash bubble, rub. Then the day would break, and,
descending from my berth by a graceful ladder composed of half-
opened drawers beneath it, I would reopen my outer dead-light and
my inner sliding window (closed by a watchman during the water-
cure), and would look out at the long-rolling, lead-coloured, white-
topped waves over which the dawn, on a cold winter morning, cast
a level, lonely glance, and through which the ship fought her melancholy way at a terrific rate. And now, lying down again, awaiting the
season for broiled ham and tea, I would be compelled to listen to the
voice of conscience,—the screw.

It might be, in some cases, no more than the voice of stomach; but
I called it in my fancy by the higher name. Because it seemed to me
that we were all of us, all day long, endeavouring to stifle the voice.
Because it was under everybody's pillow, everybody's plate, everybody's camp-stool, everybody's book, everybody's occupation. Because we pretended not to hear it, especially at meal-times, evening
whist, and morning conversation on deck, but it was always among
us in an under monotone, not to be drowned in pea-soup, not to be
shuffled with cards, not to be diverted by books, not to be knitted
into any pattern, not to be walked away from. It was smoked in the
weediest cigar, and drunk in the strongest cocktail; it was conveyed
on deck at noon with limp ladies, who lay there in their wrappers
until the stars shone; it waited at table with the stewards; nobody
could put it out with the lights. It was considered (as on shore) ill-
bred to acknowledge the voice of conscience. It was not polite to
mention it. One squally day an amiable gentleman in love gave much
offence to a surrounding circle, including the object of his attachment, by saying of it, after it had goaded him over two easy-chairs
and a skylight, "Screw!"

Sometimes it would appear subdued In fleeting moments, when bubbles of champagne pervaded the nose, or when there was "hot pot" in the bill of fare, or when an old dish we had had regularly every day was described in that official document by a new name,—under such excitements, one would almost believe it hushed. The ceremony of washing plates on deck, performed after every meal by a circle as of ringers of crockery triple-bob majors for a prize, would keep it down. Hauling the reel, taking the sun at noon, posting the twenty-four hours' run, altering the ship's time by the meridian, casting the waste food overboard, and attracting the eager gulls that followed in our wake,—these events would suppress it for a while. But the instant any break or pause took place in any such diversion, the voice would be at it again, importuning us to the last extent. A newly married young pair, who walked the deck affectionately some twenty miles per day, would, in the full flush of their exercise, suddenly become stricken by it, and stand trembling, but otherwise immovable, under its reproaches.

When this terrible monitor was most severe with us was when the time approached for our retiring to our dens for the night; when the lighted candles in the saloon grew fewer and fewer; when the deserted glasses with spoons in them grew more and more numerous; when waifs of toasted cheese and strays of sardines fried in batter slid languidly to and fro in the table-racks; when the man who always read had shut up his book, and blown out his candle; when the man who always talked had ceased from troubling; when the man who was always medically reported as going to have delirium tremens had put it off till to-morrow; when the man who every night devoted himself to a midnight smoke on deck two hours in length, and who every night was in bed within ten minutes afterwards, was buttoning himself up in his third coat for his hardy vigil: for then, as we fell off one by one, and, entering our several hutches, came into a peculiar atmosphere of bilge-water and Windsor soap, the voice would shake us to the centre. Woe to us when we sat down on our sofa, watching the swinging candle for ever trying and retrying to stand upon his head! or our coat upon its peg, imitating us as we appeared in our gymnastic days by sustaining itself horizontally from the wall, in emulation of the lighter and more facile towels! Then would the voice expecially claim us for its prey, and rend us all to pieces.

Lights out, we in our berths, and the wind rising, the voice grows angrier and deeper. Under the mattress and under the pillow, under the sofa and under the washing-stand, under the ship and under the sea, seeming to rise from the foundations under the earth with every scoop of the great Atlantic (and oh! why scoop so?), always the voice. Vain to deny its existence in the night season; impossible to be hard of hearing; screw, screw, screw! Sometimes it lifts out of the water, and revolves with a whirr, like a ferocious firework,—except that it never expends itself, but is always ready to go off again, sometimes it seems to be in anguish, and shivers; sometimes it seems to be terrified by its last plunge, and has a fit which causes it to struggle, quiver, and for an instant stop. And now the ship sets in rolling, as only ships so fiercely screwed through time and space, day and night, fair weather and foul, *can* roll.

Did she ever take a roll before like that last? Did she ever take a roll before like this worse one that is coming now? Here is the partition at my ear down in the deep on the lee side. Are we ever coming up again together? I think not; the partition and I are so long about it that I really do believe we have overdone it this time. Heavens, what a scoop! What a deep scoop, what a hollow scoop, what a long scoop! Will it ever end, and can we bear the heavy mass of water we have taken on board, and which has let loose all the table furniture in the officers' mess, and has beaten open the door of the little passage between the purser and me, and is swashing about, even there and even here? The purser snores reassuringly, and the ship's bells striking, I hear the cheerful "All's well!" of the watch musically given back the length of the deck, as the lately diving partition, now high in air, tries (unsoftened by what we have gone through together) to force me out of bed and berth.

"All's well!" Comforting to know, though surely all might be better. Put aside the rolling and the rush of water, and think of darting through such darkness with such velocity. Think of any other similar object coming in the opposite direction!

Whether there may be an attraction in two such moving bodies out at sea, which may help accident to bring them into collision? Thoughts, too, arise (the voice never silent all the while, but marvellously suggestive) of the gulf below; of the strange, unfruitful mountain ranges and deep valleys over which we are passing; of monstrous fish midway; of the ship's suddenly altering her course on her own account, and with a wild plunge settling down, and making *that* voyage with a crew of dead discoverers. Now, too, one recalls an almost universal tendency on the part of passengers to stumble, at some time or other in the day, on the topic of a certain large steamer making this same run, which was lost at sea, and never heard of more. Everybody has seemed under a spell, compelling approach to the threshold of the grim subject, stoppage, discomfiture, and pretence of never having been near it. The boatswain's whistle sounds! A change in the wind, hoarse orders issuing, and the watch very busy. Sails come crashing home overhead, ropes (that seem all knot) ditto; every man engaged appears to have twenty feet, with twenty times the average amount of stamping power in each. Gradually the noise slackens, the hoarse cries die away, the boatswain's whistle softens into the soothing and contented notes, which rather reluctantly admit that the job is done for the time, and the voice sets in again.

Thus come unintelligible dreams of up hill and down, and swinging and swaying, until consciousness revives of atmospherical Windsor soap and bilge-water, and the voice announces that the giant has come for the water-cure again.

Such were my fanciful reminiscences as I lay, part of that day, in the Bay of New York, O! Also as we passed clear of the Narrows, and got out to sea; also in many an idle hour at sea in sunny weather? At length the observations and computations showed that we should make the coast of Ireland to-night. So I stood watch on deck all night to-night, to see how we made the coast of Ireland.

Very dark, and the sea most brilliantly phosphorescent. Great way on the ship, and double look-out kept. Vigilant captain on the bridge, vigilant first officer looking over the port side, vigilant second officer standing by the quarter-master at the compass, vigilant third officer posted at the stern rail with a lantern. No passengers on the quiet decks, but expectation everywhere nevertheless. The two men at the wheel very steady, very serious, and very prompt to answer orders. An order issued sharply now and then, and echoed back; otherwise the night drags slowly, silently, with no change.

All of a sudden, at the blank hour of two in the morning, a vague movement of relief from a long strain expresses itself in all hands; the third officer's lantern tinkles, and he fires a rocket, and another rocket. A sullen solitary light is pointed out to me in the black sky yonder. A change is expected in the light, but none takes place. "Give them two more rockets, Mr. Vigilant." Two more, and a blue-light burnt. All eyes watch the light again. At last a little toy sky-rocket is flashed up from it; and, even as that small streak in the darkness dies away, we are telegraphed to Queenstown, Liverpool, and London, and back again under the ocean to America.

Then up come the half-dozen passengers who are going ashore at Queenstown, and up comes the mail-agent in charge of the bags, and up come the men who are to carry the bags into the mail-tender that will come off for them out of the harbour. Lamps and lanterns gleam here and there about the decks, and impeding bulks are knocked away with handspikes; and the port-side bulwark, barren but a moment ago, bursts into a crop of heads of seamen, stewards, and engineers.

The light begins to be gained upon, begins to be alongside, begins to be left astern. More rockets, and, between us and the land, streams beautifully the Inman steamship City of Paris, for New York, outward bound. We observe with complacency that the wind is dead against her (it being *with* us), and that she rolls and pitches. (The sickest passenger on board is the most delighted by this circumstance.) Time rushes by as we rush on; and now we see the light in Queenstown Harbour, and now the lights of the mail-tender coming out to us. What vagaries the mail-tender performs on the way, in every point of the compass, especially in those where she has no business, and why she performs them, Heaven only knows! At length she is seen plunging within a cable's length of our port broadside, and is being roared at through our speaking-trumpets to do this thing, and not to do that, and to stand by the other, as if she were a very demented tender indeed. Then, we slackening amidst a deafening roar of steam, this much-abused tender is made fast to us by hawsers, and the men in readiness carry the bags aboard, and return for more, bending under their burdens, and looking just like the pasteboard figures of the miller and his men in the theatre of our boyhood, and comporting themselves almost as unsteadily. All the while the unfortunate tender plunges high and low, and is roared at. Then the Queenstown passengers are put on board of her, with infinite plunging and roaring, and the tender gets heaved up on the sea to that surprising extent that she looks within an ace of washing aboard of us, high and dry. Roared at with contumely to the last, this wretched tender is at length let go, with a final plunge of great ignominy, and falls spinning into our wake.

The voice of conscience resumed its dominion as the day climbed up the sky, and kept by all of us passengers into port; kept by us as we passed other lighthouses, and dangerous islands off the coast, where some of the officers, with whom I stood my watch, had gone ashore in sailing-ships in fogs (and of which by that token they seemed to have quite an affectionate remembrance), and past the Welsh coast, and past the Cheshire coast, and past everything and everywhere lying between our ship and her own special dock in the Mersey. Off which, at last, at nine of the clock, on a fair evening early in May, we stopped, and the voice ceased. A very curious sensation, not unlike having my own ears stopped, ensued upon that silence; and it was with a no less curious sensation that I went over the side of the good Cunard ship "Russia" (whom prosperity attend through all her voyages!) and surveyed the outer hull of the gracious monster that the voice had inhabited. So, perhaps, shall we all, in the spirit, one day survey the frame that held the busier voice from which my vagrant fancy derived this similitude.

XXXII

A SMALL STAR IN THE EAST

I HAD been looking, yesternight, through the famous "Dance of Death," and to-day the grim old woodcuts arose in my mind with the new significance of a ghastly monotony not to be found in the original. The weird skeleton rattled along the streets before me, and struck fiercely; but it was never at the pains of assuming a disguise. It played on no dulcimer here, was crowned with no flowers, waved no plume, minced in no flowing robe or train, lifted no wine-cup, sat at no feast, cast no dice, counted no gold. It was simply a bare, gaunt, famished skeleton, slaying his way along.

The borders of Ratcliff and Stepney, eastward of London, and giving on the impure river, were the scene of this uncompromising dance of death, upon a drizzling November day. A squalid maze of streets, courts, and alleys of miserable houses let out in single rooms. A wilderness of dirt, rags, and hunger. A mud-desert, chiefly inhabited by a tribe from whom employment has departed, or to whom it comes but fitfully and rarely. They are not skilled mechanics in any wise. They are but labourers,—dock-labourers, water-side labourers, coal-porters, ballast-heavers, such-like hewers of wood and drawers of water. But they have come into existence, and they propagate their wretched race.

One grisly joke alone, methought, the skeleton seemed to play off here. It had stuck election-bills on the walls, which the wind and rain had deteriorated into suitable rags. It had even summed up the state of the poll, in chalk, on the shutters of one ruined house. It adjured the free and independent starvers to vote for Thisman and vote for Thatman; not to plump, as they valued the state of parties and the national prosperity (both of great importance to them, I think); but, by returning Thisman and Thatman, each naught without the other, to compound a glorious and immortal whole. Surely the skeleton is nowhere more cruelly ironical in the original monkish idea!

Pondering in my mind the far-seeing schemes of Thisman and Thatman, and of the public blessing called Party, for staying the degeneracy, physical and moral, of many thousands (who shall say how many?) of the English race; for devising employment useful to the community for those who want but to work and live; for equalising rates, cultivating waste lands, facilitating emigration, and, above all things, saving and utilising the oncoming generations, and thereby changing ever-growing national weakness into strength: pondering in my mind, I say, these hopeful exertions, I turned down a narrow street to look into a house or two.

It was a dark street with a dead wall on one side. Nearly all the outer doors of the houses stood open. I took the first entry, and knocked at a parlour-door. Might I come in? I might, if I plased, sur.

The woman of the room (Irish) had picked up some long strips of wood, about some wharf or barge; and they had just now been thrust into the otherwise empty grate to make two iron pots boil. There was some fish in one, and there were some potatoes in the other. The flare of the burning wood enabled me to see a table, and a broken chair or so, and some old cheap crockery ornaments about the chimney-piece. It was not until I had spoken with the woman a few minutes, that I saw a horrible brown heap on the floor in a corner, which, but for previous experience in this dismal wise, I might not have suspected to be "the bed." There was something thrown upon it; and I asked what that was.

"'Tis the poor craythur that stays here, sur; and 'tis very bad she is, and 'tis very bad she's been this long time, and 'tis better she'll never be, and 'tis slape she does all day, and 'tis wake she does all night, and 'tis the lead, sur."

"The what?"

"The lead, sur. Sure 'tis the lead-mills, where the women gets took on at eighteen-pence a day, sur, when they makes application early enough, and is lucky and wanted; and 'tis lead-pisoned she is, sur, and some of them gets lead-pisoned soon, and some of them gets lead-pisoned later, and some, but not many, niver; and 'tis all according to the constitooshun, sur, and some constitooshuns is strong, and some is weak; and her constitooshun is lead-pisoned, bad as can be, sur; and her brain is coming out at her ear, and it hurts her dreadful; and that's what it is, and niver no more, and niver no less, sur."

The sick young woman moaning here, the speaker bent over her, took a bandage from her head, and threw open a back door to let in the daylight upon it, from the smallest and most miserable backyard I ever saw.

"That's what cooms from her, sur, being lead-pisoned; and it cooms from her night and day, the poor, sick craythur; and the pain of it is dreadful; and God he knows that my husband has walked the sthreets these four days, being a labourer, and is walking them now, and is ready to work, and no work for him, and no fire and no food but the bit in the pot, and no more than ten shillings in a fortnight; God be good to us! and it is poor we are, and dark it is and could it is indeed."

Knowing that I could compensate myself thereafter for my self-denial, if I saw fit, I had resolved that I would give nothing in the course of these visits. I did this to try the people. I may state at once that my closest observation could not detect any indication whatever of an expectation that I would give money: they were grateful to be talked to about their miserable affairs, and sympathy was plainly a comfort to them; but they neither asked for money in any case, nor showed the least trace of surprise or disappointment or resentment at my giving none.

The woman's married daughter had by this time come down from her room on the floor above, to join in the conversation. She herself had been to the lead-mills very early that morning to be "took on," but had not succeeded. She had four children; and her husband, also a water-side labourer, and then out seeking work, seemed in no better case as to finding it than her father. She was English, and by nature, of a buxom figure and cheerful. Both in her poor dress and in her mother's there was an effort to keep up some appearance of neatness. She knew all about the sufferings of the unfortunate invalid, and all about the lead-poisoning, and how the symptoms came on, and how they grew,—having often seen them. The very smell when you stood inside the door of the works was enough to knock you down, she said: yet she was going back again to get "took on." What could she do? Better be ulcerated and paralyzed for eighteen-pence a day, while it lasted, than see the children starve.

A dark and squalid cupboard in this room, touching the back door and all manner of offence, had been for some time the sleeping-place of the sick young woman. But the nights being now wintry, and the blankets and coverlets "gone to the leaving shop," she lay all night where she lay all day, and was lying then. The woman of the room, her husband, this most miserable patient, and two others, lay on the one brown heap together for warmth.

"God bless you, sir, and thank you!" were the parting words from these people,—gratefully spoken too,—with which I left this place.

Some streets away, I tapped at another parlour-door on another ground-floor. Looking in, I found a man, his wife, and four children, sitting at a washing-stool by way of table, at their dinner of bread and infused tea-leaves. There was a very scanty cinderous fire in the grate by which they sat; and there was a tent bedstead in the room with a bed upon it and a coverlet. The man did not rise when I went in, nor during my stay, but civilly inclined his head on my pulling off my hat, and, in answer to my inquiry whether I might ask him a question or two, said, "Certainly." There being a window at each end of this room, back and front, it might have been ventilated; but it was shut up tight, to keep the cold out, and was very sickening.

The wife, an intelligent, quick woman, rose and stood at her husband's elbow; and he glanced up at her as if for help. It soon appeared that he was rather deaf. He was a slow, simple fellow of about thirty.

"What was he by trade?"

"Gentleman asks what are you by trade, John?"

"I am a boilermaker;" looking about him with an exceedingly perplexed air, as if for a boiler that had unaccountably vanished.

"He ain't a mechanic, you understand, sir," the wife put in: "he's only a labourer."

"Are you in work?"

He looked up at his wife again. "Gentleman says are you in work, John?"

"In work!" cried this forlorn boilermaker, staring aghast at his wife, and then working his vision's way very slowly round to me: "Lord, no!"

"Ah, he ain't indeed!" said the poor woman, shaking her head, as she looked at the four children in succession, and then at him.

"Work!" said the boilermaker, still seeking that evaporated boiler, first in my countenance, then in the air, and then in the features of his second son at his knee: "I wish I *was* in work! I haven't had more than a day's work to do this three weeks."

"How have you lived?"

A faint gleam of admiration lighted up the face of the would-be boilermaker, as he stretched out the short sleeve of his threadbare canvas jacket, and replied, pointing her out, "On the work of the wife."

I forget where boilermaking had gone to, or where he supposed it had gone to; but he added some resigned information on that head, coupled with an expression of his belief that it was never coming back.

The cheery helpfulness of the wife was very remarkable. She did slop-work; made pea-jackets. She produced the pea-jacket then in hand, and spread it out upon the bed,—the only piece of furniture in the room on which to spread it. She showed how much of it she made, and how much was afterwards finished off by the machine. According to her calculation at the moment, deducting what her trimming cost her, she got for making a pea-jacket tenpence half-penny, and she could make one in something less than two days.

But, you see, it come to her through two hands, and of course it didn't come through the second hand for nothing. Why did it come through the second hand at all? Why, this way. The second hand took the risk of the given-out work, you see. If she had money enough to pay the security deposit,—call it two pound,—she could get the work from the first hand, and so the second would not have to be deducted for. But, having no money at all, the second hand come in and took its profit, and so the whole worked down to tenpence half-penny. Having explained all this with great intelligence, even with some little pride, and without a whine or murmur, she folded her work again, sat down by her husband's side at the washing-stool, and resumed her dinner of dry bread. Mean as the meal was, on the bare board, with its old gallipots for cups, and what not other sordid make-shifts; shabby as the woman was in dress, and toning done towards the Bosjesman colour, with want of nutriment and washing,—there was positively a dignity in her, as the family anchor just holding the poor shipwrecked boilermaker's bark. When I left the room, the boilermaker's eyes were slowly turned towards her, as if his last hope of ever again seeing that vanished boiler lay in her direction.

These people had never applied for parish relief but once; and that was when the husband met with a disabling accident at his work.

Not many doors from here, I went into a room on the first floor. The woman apologised for its being in "an untidy mess." The day was Saturday, and she was boiling the children's clothes in a sauce-pan on the hearth. There was nothing else into which she could have put them. There was no crockery, or tinware, or tub, or bucket. There was an old gallipot or two, and there was a broken bottle or so, and there were some broken boxes for seats. The last small scraping of coals left was raked together in a corner of the floor. There were some rags in an open cupboard, also on the floor. In a corner of the room was a crazy old French bedstead, with a man lying on his back upon it in a ragged pilot jacket, and rough oil-skin fantail hat. The room was perfectly black. It was difficult to believe, at first, that it was not purposely coloured black, the walls were so begrimed.

As I stood opposite the woman boiling the children's clothes,—she had not even a piece of soap to wash them with,—and apologising for her occupation, I could take in all these things without appearing to notice them, and could even correct my inventory. I had missed, at the first glance, some half a pound of bread in the otherwise empty safe, an old red ragged crinoline hanging on the handle of the door by which I had entered, and certain fragments of rusty iron scattered on the floor, which looked like broken tools and a piece of stove-pipe. A child stood looking on. On the box nearest to the fire sat two younger children; one a delicate and pretty little creature, whom the other sometimes kissed.

This woman, like the last, was wofully shabby, and was degener-ating to the Bosjesman complexion. But her figure and the ghost of a certain vivacity about her, and the spectre of a dimple in her cheek, carried my memory strangely back to the old days of the Adelphi Theatre, London, when Mrs. Fitzwilliam was the friend of Victorine.

"May I ask you what your husband is?"

"He's a coal-porter, sir,"—with a glance and a sigh towards the bed.

"Is he out of work?"

"Oh, yes, sir! and work's at all times very, very scanty with him; and now he's laid up."

"It's my legs," said the man upon the bed. "I'll unroll 'em." And immediately began.

"Have you any older children?"

"I have a daughter that does the needle-work, and I have a son that does what he can. She's at her work now, and he's trying for work."

"Do they live here?"

"They sleep here?" They can't afford to pay more rent, and so they come here at night. The rent is very hard upon us. It's rose upon us too, now,—sixpence a week,—on account of these new changes in the law, about the rates. We are a week behind; the landlord's been shaking and rattling at that door frightfully; he says he'll turn us out. I don't know what's to come of it."

The man upon the bed ruefully interposed, "Here's my legs. The skin's broke, besides the swelling. I have had a many kicks, working, one way and another."

He looked at his legs (which were much discoloured and misshapen) for a while, and then appearing to remember that they were not popular with his family, rolled them up again, as if they were something in the nature of maps or plans that were not wanted to be referred to, lay hopelessly down on his back once more with his fantail hat over his face, and stirred not.

"Do your eldest son and daughter sleep in that cupboard?"

"Yes," replied the woman.

"With the children?"

"Yes. We have to get together for warmth. We have little to cover us."

"Have you nothing by you to eat but the piece of bread I see there?"

"Nothing. And we had the rest of the loaf for our breakfast, with water. I don't know what's to come of it."

"Have you no prospect of improvement?"

"If my eldest son earns anything to-day, he'll bring it home. Then we shall have something to eat to-night, and may be able to do something towards the rent. If not, I don't know what's to come of it."

"This is a sad state of things."

"Yes, sir; it's a hard, hard life. Take care of the stairs as you go, sir, —they're broken,—and good day, sir!"

These people had a mortal dread of entering the workhouse, and received no out-of-door relief.

In another room, in still another tenement, I found a very decent woman with five children,—the last a baby, and she herself a patient of the parish doctor,—to whom, her husband being in the hospital, the Union allowed for the support of herself and family, four shillings a week and five loaves. I suppose when Thisman, M.P., and Thatman, M.P., and the Public-blessing Party, lay their heads together in course of time, and come to an equalization of rating, she may go down to the dance of death to the tune of sixpence more.

I could enter no other houses for that one while, for I could not bear the contemplation of the children. Such heart as I had summoned to sustain me against the miseries of the adults failed me when I looked at the children. I saw how young they were, how hungry, how serious and still. I thought of them, sick and dying in those lairs. I think of them dead without anguish; but to think of them so suffering and so dying quite unmanned me.

Down by the river's bank in Ratcliff, I was turning upward by a side-street, therefore, to regain the railway, when my eyes rested on the inscription across the road, "East London Children's Hospital." I could scarcely have seen an inscription better suited to my frame of mind; and I went across and went straight in.

I found the children's hospital established in an old sail-loft or storehouse, of the roughest nature, and on the simplest means. There were trap-doors in the floors, where goods had been hoisted up and down; heavy feet and heavy weights had started every knot in the well-trodden planking: inconvenient bulks and beams and awkward staircases perplexed my passage through the wards. But I found it airy, sweet, and clean. In its seven and thirty beds I saw but little beauty; for starvation in the second or third generation takes a pinched look: but I saw the sufferings both of infancy and childhood tenderly assuaged; I heard the little patients answering to pet playful names, the light touch of a delicate lady laid bare the wasted sticks of arms for me to pity; and the claw-like little hands, as she did so, twined themselves lovingly around her wedding-ring.

One baby mite there was as pretty as any of Raphael's angels. The tiny head was bandaged for water on the brain; and it was suffering with acute bronchitis too, and made from time to time a plaintive, though not impatient or complaining, little sound. The smooth curve of the cheeks and of the chin was faultless in its condensation of infantine beauty, and the large bright eyes were most lovely. It happened as I stopped at the foot of the bed, that these eyes rested upon mine with that wistful expression of wondering thoughtfulness which we all know sometimes in very little children. They remained fixed on mine, and never turned from me while I stood there. When the utterance of that plaintive sound shook the little form, the gaze still remained unchanged. I felt as though the child implored me to tell the story of the little hospital in which it was sheltered to any gentle heart I could address. Laying my world-worn hand upon the little unmarked clasped hand at the chin, I gave it a silent promise that I would do so.

A gentleman and lady, a young husband and wife, have bought and fitted up this building for its present noble use, and have quietly settled themselves in it as its medical officers and directors. Both have had considerable practical experience of medicine and surgery; he as house-surgeon of a great London hospital; and she as a very earnest student, tested by severe examination, and also as a nurse of the sick poor during the prevalence of cholera.

With every qualification to lure them away, with youth and accomplishments and tastes and habits that can have no response in any breast near them, close begirt by every repulsive circumstance inseparable from such a neighbourhood, there they dwell. They live in the hospital itself, and their rooms are on its first floor. Sitting at their dinner-table, they could hear the cry of one of the children in pain. The lady's piano, drawing-materials, books, and other such evidences of refinement are as much a part of the rough place as the iron bedsteads of the little patients. They are put to shifts for room, like passengers on board ship. The dispenser of medicines (attracted to them not by self-interest, but by their own magnetism and that of their cause) sleeps in a recess in the dining-room, and has his washing apparatus in the sideboard.

Their contented manner of making the best of the things around them, I found so pleasantly inseparable from their usefulness! Their pride in this partition that we put up ourselves, or that partition that we took down, or in that other partition that we moved, or in the stove that was given us for the waiting-room, or in our nightly conversion of the little consulting-room into a smoking-room! Their admiration of the situation, if we could only get rid of its one objectionable incident, the coal-yard at the back! "Our hospital carriage, presented by a friend, and very useful." That was my presentation to a perambulator, for which a coach-house had been discovered in a corner down-stairs, just large enough to hold it. Coloured prints, in all stages of preparation for being added to those already decorating the wards, were plentiful; a charming wooden phenomenon of a bird, with an impossible top-knot, who ducked his head when you set a counter weight going, had been inaugurated as a public statue that very morning; and trotting about among the beds, on familiar terms with all the patients, was a comical mongrel dog, called Poodles. This comical dog (quite a tonic in himself) was found characteristically starving at the door of the institution, and was taken in and fed, and has lived here ever since. An admirer of his mental endowments has presented him with a collar bearing the legend, "Judge not Poodles by external appearances." He was merrily wagging his tail on a boy's pillow when he made this modest appeal to me.

When this hospital was first opened, in January of the present year, the people could not possibly conceive but that somebody paid for the services rendered there; and were disposed to claim them as a right, and to find fault if out of temper. They soon came to understand the case better, and have much increased in gratitude. The mothers of the patients avail themselves very freely of the visiting rules; the fathers often on Sundays. There is an unreasonable (but still, I think, touching and intelligible) tendency in the parents to take a child away to its wretched home, if on the point of death. One boy who had been thus carried off on a rainy night, when in a violent state of inflammation, and who had been afterwards brought back, had been recovered with exceeding difficulty; but he was a jolly boy, with a specially strong interest in his dinner, when I saw him.

Insufficient food and unwholesome living are the main causes of disease among these small patients. So nourishment, cleanliness, and ventilation are the main remedies. Discharged patients are looked after, and invited to come and dine now and then; so are certain famishing creatures who were never patients. Both the lady and the gentleman are well acquainted, not only with the histories of the patients and their families, but with the characters and circumstances of great numbers of their neighbours: of these they keep a register. It is their common experience, that people, sinking down by inches into deeper and deeper poverty, will conceal it, even from them, if possible, unto the very last extremity.

The nurses of this hospital are all young,—ranging, say, from nineteen to four and twenty. They have even within these narrow limits, what many well-endowed hospitals would not give them, a comfortable room of their own in which to take their meals. It is a beautiful truth, that interest in the children and sympathy with their sorrows bind these young women to their places far more strongly than any other consideration could. The best skilled of the nurses came originally from a kindred neighbourhood, almost as poor; and she knew how much the work was needed. She is a fair dressmaker. The hospital cannot pay her as many pounds in the year as there are months in it; and one day the lady regarded it as a duty to speak to her about her improving her prospects and following her trade. "No," she said: she could never be so useful or so happy elsewhere any more; she must stay among the children. And she stays. One of the nurses, as I passed her, was washing a baby-boy. Liking her pleasant face, I stopped to speak to her charge,—a common, bullet-headed, frowning charge enough, laying hold of his own nose with a slippery grasp, and staring very solemnly out of a blanket. The melting of the pleasant face into delighted smiles, as this young gentleman gave an unexpected kick, and laughed at me, was almost worth my previous pain.

An affecting play was acted in Paris years ago, called "The Children's Doctor." As I parted from my children's doctor, now in question, I saw in his easy black necktie, in his loose buttoned black frockcoat, in his pensive face, in the flow of his dark hair, in his eyelashes, in the very turn of his moustache, the exact realisation of the Paris artist's ideal as it was presented on the stage. But no romancer that I know of has had the boldness to prefigure the life and home of this young husband and young wife in the Children's Hospital in the east of London.

I came away from Ratcliff by the Stepney railway station to the terminus at Fenchurch Street. Any one who will reverse that route may retrace my steps.

XXXIII

A LITTLE DINNER IN AN HOUR

IT fell out on a day in this last autumn, that I had to go down from London to a place of seaside resort, on an hour's business, accompanied by my esteemed friend Bullfinch. Let the place of seaside resort be, for the nonce, called Namelesston.

I had been loitering about Paris in very hot weather, pleasantly breakfasting in the open air in the garden of the Palais Royal or the Tuileries, pleasantly dining in the open air in the Elysian Fields, pleasantly taking my cigar and lemonade in the open air on the Italian Boulevard towards the small hours after midnight. Bullfinch —an excellent man of business—had summoned me back across the Channel, to transact this said hour's business at Namelesston; and thus it fell out that Bullfinch and I were in a railway carriage together on our way to Namelesston, each with his return-ticket in his waistcoat-pocket.

Says Bullfinch, "I have a proposal to make. Let us dine at the Temeraire."

I asked Bullfinch, did he recommend the Temeraire? inasmuch as I had not been rated on the books of the Temeraire for many years.

Bullfinch declined to accept the responsibility of recommending the Temeraire, but on the whole was rather sanguine about it. He "seemed to remember," Bullfinch said, that he had dined well there. A plain dinner, but good. Certainly not like a Parisian dinner (here Bullfinch obviously became the prey of want of confidence), but of its kind very fair.

I appeal to Bullfinch's intimate knowledge of my wants and ways to decide whether I was usually ready to be pleased with any dinner, or—for the matter of that—with anything that was fair of its kind and really what it claimed to be. Bullfinch doing me the honour to respond in the affirmative, I agreed to ship myself as an able trencherman on board the Temeraire.

"Now, our plan shall be this," says Bullfinch, with his forefinger at his nose. "As soon as we get to Namelesston, we'll drive straight to the Temeraire, and order a little dinner in an hour. And as we shall not have more than enough time in which to dispose of it comfortably, what do you say to giving the house the best opportunities of serving it hot and quickly by dining in the coffee-room?"

What I had to say was, Certainly. Bullfinch (who is by nature of a hopeful constitution) then began to babble of green geese. But I checked him in that Falstaffian vein, urging considerations of time and cookery.

In due sequence of events we drove up to the Temeraire, and alighted. A youth in livery received us on the door-step. "Looks well," said Bullfinch confidentially. And then aloud, "Coffee-room!"

The youth in livery (now perceived to be mouldy) conducted us to the desired haven, and was enjoined by Bullfinch to send the waiter at once, as we wished to order a little dinner in an hour. Then Bullfinch and I waited for the waiter, until, the waiter continuing to wait in some unknown and invisible sphere of action, we rang for the waiter; which ring produced the waiter, who announced himself as not the waiter who ought to wait upon us, and who didn't wait a moment longer.

So Bullfinch approached the coffee-room door, and melodiously pitching his voice into a bar where two young ladies were keeping the books of the Temeraire, apologetically explained that we wished to order a little dinner in an hour, and that we were debarred from the execution of our inoffensive purpose by consignment to solitude.

Hereupon one of the young ladies rang a bell, which reproduced—at the bar this time—the waiter who was not the waiter who ought to wait upon us; that extraordinary man, whose life seemed consumed in waiting upon people to say that he wouldn't wait upon them, repeated his former protest with great indignation, and retired.

Bullfinch, with a fallen countenance, was about to say to me, "This won't do," when the waiter who ought to wait upon us left off keeping us waiting at last. "Waiter," said Bullfinch piteously, "we have been a long time waiting." The waiter who ought to wait upon us laid the blame upon the waiter who ought not to wait upon us, and said it was all that waiter's fault.

"We wish," said Bullfinch, much depressed, "to order a little dinner in an hour. What can we have?"

"What would you like to have, gentlemen?"

Bullfinch, with extreme mournfulness of speech and action, and with a forlorn old fly-blown bill of fare in his hand which the waiter had given him, and which was a sort of general manuscript index to any cookery-book you please, moved the previous question.

We could have mock-turtle soup, a sole, curry, and roast duck. Agreed. At this table by this window. Punctually in an hour.

I had been feigning to look out of this window; but I had been taking note of the crumbs on all the tables, the dirty table-cloths, the stuffy, soupy, airless atmosphere, the stale leavings everywhere about, the deep gloom of the waiter who ought to wait upon us, and the stomach-ache with which a lonely traveller at a distant table in a corner was too evidently afflicted. I now pointed out to Bullfinch the alarming circumstance that this traveller had *dined*. We hurriedly debated whether, without infringement of good breeding, we could ask him to disclose if he had partaken of mock-turtle, sole, curry, or roast duck? We decided that the thing could not be politely done, and we had set our own stomachs on a cast, and they must stand the hazard of the die.

I hold phrenology, within certain limits, to be true; I am much of the same mind as to the subtler expressions of the hand; I hold physiognomy to be infallible; though all these sciences demand rare qualities in the student. But I also hold that there is no more certain index to personal character than the condition of a set of casters is to the character of any hotel. Knowing, and having often tested this theory of mine, Bullfinch resigned himself to the worst, when, laying aside any remaining veil of disguise, I held up before him in succession the cloudy oil and furry vinegar, the clogged cayenne, the dirty salt, the obscene dregs of soy, and the anchovy sauce in a flannel waistcoat of decomposition.

We went out to transact our business. So inspiriting was the relief of passing into the clean and windy streets of Namelesston from the heavy and vapid closeness of the coffee-room of the Temeraire, that hope began to revive within us. We began to consider that perhaps the lonely traveller had taken physic, or done something injudicious to bring his complaint on. Bullfinch remarked that he thought the waiter who ought to wait upon us had brightened a little when suggesting curry; and although I knew him to have been at that moment the express image of despair, I allowed myself to become elevated in spirits. As we walked by the softly-lapping sea, all the notabilities of Namelesston, who are for ever going up and down with the changelessness of the tides, passed to and fro in procession. Pretty girls on horseback, and with detested riding-masters; pretty girls on foot; mature ladies in hats,—spectacled, strong-minded, and glaring at the opposite or weaker sex. The Stock Exchange was strongly represented, Jerusalem was strongly represented, the bores of the prosier London clubs were strongly represented. Fortune-hunters of all denominations were there, from hirsute insolvency, in a curricle, to closely-buttoned swindlery in doubtful boots, on the sharp look-out for any likely young gentleman disposed to play a game of billiards round the corner. Masters of languages, their lessons finished for the day, were going to their homes out of sight of the sea; mistresses of accomplishments, carrying small portfolios, likewise tripped homeward; pairs of scholastic pupils, two and two, went languidly along the beach, surveying the face of the waters as if waiting for some Ark to come and take them off. Spectres of the George the Fourth days flitted unsteadily among the crowd, bearing the outward semblance of ancient dandies, of every one of whom it might be said, not that he had one leg in the grave, or both legs, but that he was steeped in grave to the summit of his high shirt-collar, and had nothing real about him but his bones. Alone stationary in the midst of all the movements, the Namelesston boatman leaned against the railings and yawned, and looked out to sea, or looked at the moored fishing-boats and at nothing. Such is the unchanging manner of life with this nursery of our hardy seamen; and very dry nurses they are, and always wanting something to drink. The only two nautical personages detached from the railing were the two fortunate possessors of the celebrated monstrous unknown barking-fish, just caught (frequently just caught off Namelesston), who carried him about in a hamper, and pressed the scientific to look in at the lid.

The sands of the hour had all run out when we got back to the Temeraire. Says Bullfinch, then, to the youth in livery, with boldness, "Lavatory!"

When we arrived at the family vault with a skylight, which the youth in livery presented as the institution sought, we had already whisked off our cravats and coats; but finding ourselves in the presence of an evil smell, and no linen but two crumpled towels newly damp from the countenances of two somebody elses, we put on our cravats and coats again, and fled unwashed to the coffee-room.

There the waiter who ought to wait upon us had set forth our knives and forks and glasses, on the cloth whose dirty acquaintance we had already had the pleasure of making, and which we were pleased to recognise by the familiar expression of its stains. And now there occurred the truly surprising phenomenon, that the waiter who ought not to wait upon us swooped down upon us, clutched our loaf of bread, and vanished with the same.

Bullfinch, with distracted eyes, was following this unaccountable figure "out at the portal," like the ghost in Hamlet, when the waiter who ought to wait upon us jostled against it, carrying a tureen.

"Waiter!" said a severe diner, lately finished, perusing his bill fiercely through his eye-glass.

The waiter put down our tureen on a remote side-table, and went to see what was amiss in this new direction.

"This is not right, you know, waiter. Look here! here's yesterday's sherry, one and eightpence, and here we are again, two shillings. And what does sixpence mean?"

So far from knowing what sixpence meant, the waiter protested that he didn't know what anything meant. He wiped the perspiration from his clammy brow, and said it was impossible to do it,—not particularising what,—and the kitchen was so far off.

"Take the bill to the bar, and get it altered," said Mr. Indignation Cocker, so to call him.

The waiter took it, looked intensely at it, didn't seem to like the idea of taking it to the bar, and submitted, as a new light upon the case, that perhaps sixpence meant sixpence.

"I tell you again," said Mr. Indignation Cocker, "here's yesterday's sherry—can't you see it?—one and eightpence, and here we are again, two shillings. What do you make of one and eightpence and two shillings?"

Totally unable to make anything of one and eightpence and two shillings, the waiter went out to try if anybody else could; merely casting a helpless backward glance at Bullfinch, in acknowledgment of his pathetic entreaties for our soup tureen. After a pause, during which Mr. Indignation Cocker read a newspaper and coughed defiant coughs, Bullfinch arose to get the tureen, when the waiter reappeared and brought it,—dropping Mr. Indignation Cocker's altered bill on Mr. Indignation Cocker's table as he came along.

"It's quite impossible to do it, gentlemen," murmured the waiter; "and the kitchen is so far off."

"Well, you don't keep the house; it's not your fault, we suppose. Bring some sherry."

"Waiter!" from Mr. Indignation Cocker, with a new and burning sense of injury upon him.

The waiter, arrested on his way to our sherry, stopped short, and came back to see what was wrong now.

"Will you look here? This is worse than before. *Do* you understand? Here's yesterday's sherry, one and eightpence, and here we are again two shillings. And what the devil does ninepence mean?"

This new portent utterly confounded the waiter. He wrung his napkin, and mutely appealed to the ceiling.

"Waiter, fetch that sherry," says Bullfinch, in open wrath and revolt.

"I want to know," persisted Mr. Indignation Cocker, "the meaning of ninepence. I want to know the meaning of sherry one and eightpence yesterday, and here we are again two shillings. Send somebody."

The distracted waiter got out of the room on pretext of sending somebody, and by that means got our wine. But the instant he appeared with our decanter, Mr. Indignation Cocker descended on him again.

"Waiter!"

"You will now have the goodness to attend to our dinner, waiter," said Bullfinch, sternly.

"I am very sorry, but it's quite impossible to do it, gentlemen," pleaded the waiter; "and the kitchen——"

"Waiter!" said Mr. Indignation Cocker.

"—Is," resumed the waiter, "so far off, that——"

"Waiter!" persisted Mr. Indignation Cocker, "send somebody."

We were not without our fears that the waiter rushed out to hang himself; and we were much relieved by his fetching somebody,—in graceful, flowing skirts and with a waist,—who very soon settled Mr. Indignation Cocker's business.

"Oh!" said Mr. Cocker, with his fire surprisingly quenched by this apparition; "I wished to ask about this bill of mine, because it appears to me that there's a little mistake here. Let me show you. Here's yesterday's sherry one and eightpence, and here we are again two shillings. And how do you explain ninepence?"

However it was explained, in tones too soft to be overheard. Mr. Cocker was heard to say nothing more than "Ah-h-h! Indeed; thank you! Yes," and shortly afterwards went out, a milder man.

The lonely traveller with the stomach-ache had all this time suffered severely, drawing up a leg now and then, and sipping hot brandy-and-water with grated ginger in it. When we tasted our (very) mock-turtle soup, and were instantly seized with symptoms of some disorder simulating apoplexy, and occasioned by the surcharge of nose and brain with lukewarm dish-water holding in solution sour flour, poisonous condiments, and (say) seventy-five per cent. of miscellaneous kitchen stuff rolled into balls, we were inclined to trace his disorder to that source. On the other hand, there was a silent anguish upon him too strongly resembling the results established within ourselves by the sherry, to be discarded from alarmed con-

sideration. Again, we observed him, with terror, to be much overcome by our sole's being aired in a temporary retreat close to him,
while the waiter went out (as we conceived) to see his friends. And
when the curry made its appearance he suddenly retired in great
disorder.

In fine, for the uneatable part of this little dinner (as contra-
distinguished from the undrinkable) we paid only seven shillings and
sixpence each. And Bullfinch and I agreed unanimously, that no
such ill-served, ill-appointed, ill-cooked, nasty little dinner could be
got for the money anywhere else under the sun. With that comfort to
our backs, we turned them on the dear old Temeraire, the charging
Temeraire, and resolved (in the Scotch dialect) to gang nae mair to
the flabby Temeraire.

XXXIV

MR. BARLOW

A GREAT reader of good fiction at an unusually early age, it seems to
me as though I had been born under the superintendence of the
estimable but terrific gentleman whose name stands at the head of
my present reflections. The instructive monomaniac, Mr. Barlow, will
be remembered as the tutor of Master Harry Sandford and Master
Tommy Merton. He knew everything, and didactically improved all
sorts of occasions, from the consumption of a plate of cherries to the
contemplation of a starlight night. What youth came to without Mr.
Barlow was displayed in the history of Sandford and Merton, by the
example of a certain awful Master Mash. This young wretch wore
buckles and powder, conducted himself with insupportable levity at
the theatre, had no idea of facing a mad bull single-handed (in which
I think him less reprehensible, as remotely reflecting my own
character), and was a frightful instance of the enervating effects of
luxury upon the human race.

Strange destiny on the part of Mr. Barlow, to go down to posterity
as childhood's experience of a bore! Immortal Mr. Barlow, boring his
way through the verdant freshness of ages!

My personal indictment against Mr. Barlow is one of many counts.
I will proceed to set forth a few of the injuries he has done me.

In the first place, he never made or took a joke. This insensibility
on Mr. Barlow's part not only cast its own gloom over my boyhood,
but blighted even the sixpenny jest-books of the time; for, groaning
under a moral spell constraining me to refer all things to Mr. Barlow,
I could not choose but ask myself in a whisper when tickled by a
printed jest, "What would *he* think of it? What would *he* see in it?"
The point of the jest immediately became a sting, and stung my
conscience. For my mind's eye saw him stolid, frigid, perchance
taking from its shelf some dreary Greek book and translating at full
length what some dismal sage said (and touched up afterwards,

perhaps, for publication), when he banished some unlucky joker from Athens.

The incompatibility of Mr. Barlow with all other portions of my young life but himself, the adamantine inadaptability of the man to my favourite fancies and amusements, is the thing for which I hate him most. What right had he to bore his way into my Arabian Nights? Yet he did. He was always hinting doubts of the veracity of Sindbad the Sailor. If he could have got hold of the Wonderful Lamp, I knew he would have trimmed it and lighted it, and delivered a lecture over it on the qualities of sperm-oil, with a glance at the whale fisheries. He would so soon have found out—on mechanical principles—the peg in the neck of the Enchanted Horse, and would have turned it the right way in so workmanlike a manner, that the horse could never have got any height into the air, and the story couldn't have been. He would have proved, by map and compass, that there was no such kingdom as the delightful kingdom of Casgar, on the frontiers of Tartary. He would have caused that hypocritical young prig Harry to make an experiment,—with the aid of a temporary building in the garden and a dummy,—demonstrating that you couldn't let a choked hunchback down an Eastern chimney with a cord, and leave him upright on the hearth to terrify the sultan's purveyor.

The golden sounds of the overture to the first metropolitan pantomime, I remember, were alloyed by Mr. Barlow. Click click, ting ting, bang bang, weedle weedle weedle, bang! I recall the chilling air that ran across my frame and cooled my hot delight, as the thought occurred to me, "This would never do for Mr. Barlow!" After the curtain drew up, dreadful doubts of Mr. Barlow's considering the costumes of the Nymphs of the Nebula as being sufficiently opaque, obtruded themselves on my enjoyment. In the clown I perceived two persons; one a fascinating unaccountable creature of a hectic complexion, joyous in spirits though feeble in intellect, with flashes of brilliancy; the other a pupil for Mr. Barlow. I thought how Mr. Barlow would secretly rise early in the morning, and butter the pavement for *him*, and, when he had brought him down, would look severely out of his study window and ask *him* how he enjoyed the fun.

I thought how Mr. Barlow would heat all the pokers in the house, and singe him with the whole collection, to bring him better acquainted with the properties of incandescent iron, on which he (Barlow) would fully expatiate. I pictured Mr. Barlow's instituting a comparison between the clown's conduct at his studies,—drinking up the ink, licking his copy-book, and using his head for blotting-paper—and that of the already mentioned young prig of prigs, Harry, sitting at the Barlovian feet, sneakingly pretending to be in a rapture of youthful knowledge. I thought how soon Mr. Barlow would smooth the clown's hair down, instead of letting it stand erect in three tall tufts; and how, after a couple of years or so with Mr. Barlow, he would keep his legs close together when he walked, and would take his hands out of his big loose pockets, and wouldn't have a jump left in him.

That I am particularly ignorant what most things in the universe are made of, and how they are made, is another of my charges against Mr. Barlow. With the dread upon me of developing into a Harry, and with a further dread upon me of being Barlowed if I made inquiries, by bringing down upon myself a cold shower-bath of explanations and experiments, I forebore enlightenment in my youth, and became, as they say in melodramas, "the wreck you now behold." That I consorted with idlers and dunces is another of the melancholy facts for which I hold Mr. Barlow responsible. That pragmatical prig, Harry, became so detestable in my sight, that, he being reported studious in the South, I would have fled idle to the extremest North. Better to learn misconduct from a Master Mash than science and statistics from a Sandford! So I took the path, which, but for Mr. Barlow, I might never have trodden. Thought I, with a shudder, "Mr. Barlow is a bore, with an immense constructive power of making bores. His prize specimen is a bore. He seeks to make a bore of me. That knowledge is power I am not prepared to gainsay; but, with Mr. Barlow, knowledge is power to bore." Therefore I took refuge in the caves of ignorance, wherein I have resided ever since, and which are still my private address.

But the weightiest charge of all my charges against Mr. Barlow is, that he still walks the earth in various disguises, seeking to make a Tommy of me, even in my maturity. Irrepressible, instructive monomaniac, Mr. Barlow fills my life with pitfalls, and lies hiding at the bottom to burst out upon me when I least expect him.

A few of these dismal experiences of mine shall suffice.

Knowing Mr. Barlow to have invested largely in the moving panorama trade, and having on various occasions identified him in the dark with a long wand in his hand, holding forth in his old way (made more appalling in this connection by his sometimes cracking a piece of Mr. Carlyle's own Dead-Sea fruit in mistake for a joke), I systematically shun pictorial entertainment on rollers. Similarly, I should demand responsible bail and guaranty against the appearance of Mr. Barlow, before committing myself to attendance at any assemblages of my fellow-creatures where a bottle of water and a note-book were conspicuous objects; for in either of those associations, I should expressly expect him. But such is the designing nature of the man, that he steals in where no reasoning precaution or prevision could expect him. As in the following case:—

Adjoining the Caves of Ignorance is a country town. In this country town the Mississippi Momuses, nine in number, were announced to appear in the town-hall, for the general delectation, this last Christmas week. Knowing Mr. Barlow to be unconnected with the Mississippi, though holding republican opinions, and deeming myself secure, I took a stall. My object was to hear and see the Mississippi Momuses in what the bills described as their "National ballads, plantation break-downs, nigger part-songs, choice conundrums, sparkling repartees, &c." I found the nine dressed alike, in the black coat and trousers, white waistcoat, very large shirt-front, very large shirt-collar, and very large white tie and wristbands, which constitute the dress of the mass of the African race, and which has been observed by travellers to prevail over a vast number of degrees of latitude. All the nine rolled their eyes exceedingly, and had very red lips. At the extremities of the curve they formed, seated in their chairs, were the performers on the tambourine and bones. The centre Momus, a black of melancholy aspect (who inspired me with a vague uneasiness for which I could not then account), performed on a Mississippi instrument closely resembling what was once called in this island a hurdy-gurdy. The Momuses on either side of him had each another instrument peculiar to the Father of Waters, which may be likened to a stringed weather-glass held upside down. There were likewise a little flute and a violin. All went well for awhile, and we had had several sparkling repartees exchanged between the performers on the tambourine and bones, when the black of melancholy aspect, turning to the latter, and addressing him in a deep and improving voice as "Bones, sir," delivered certain grave remarks to him concerning the juveniles present, and the season of the year; whereon I perceived that I was in the presence of Mr. Barlow—corked!

Another night—and this was in London—I attended the representation of a little comedy. As the characters were life-like (and consequently not improving), and as they went upon their several ways and designs without personally addressing themselves to me, I felt rather confident of coming through it without being regarded as Tommy, the more so, as we were clearly getting close to the end. But I deceived myself. All of a sudden, àpropos of nothing, everybody concerned came to check and halt, advanced to the foot-lights in a general rally to take dead aim at me, and brought me down with a moral homily, in which I detected the dread hand of Barlow.

Nay, so intricate and subtle are the toils of this hunter, that on the very next night after that, I was again entrapped, where no vestige of a spring could have been apprehended by the timidest. It was a burlesque that I saw performed; an uncompromising burlesque, where everybody concerned, but especially the ladies, carried on at a very considerable rate indeed. Most prominent and active among the corps of performers was what I took to be (and she really gave me very fair opportunities of coming to a right conclusion) a young lady of a pretty figure. She was dressed as a picturesque young gentleman, whose pantaloons had been cut off in their infancy; and she had very neat knees and very neat satin boots. Immediately after singing a slang song and dancing a slang dance, this engaging figure approached the fatal lamps, and, bending over them, delivered in a thrilling voice a random eulogium on, and exhortation to pursue, the virtues. "Great Heaven!" was my exclamation; "Barlow!"

There is still another aspect in which Mr. Barlow perpetually insists on my sustaining the character of Tommy, which is more unendurable yet, on account of its extreme aggressiveness. For the purposes of a review or newspaper, he will get up an abstruse subject with infinite pains, will Barlow, utterly regardless of the price of midnight oil, and indeed of everything else, save cramming himself to the eyes.

But mark. When Mr. Barlow blows his information off, he is not contented with having rammed it home, and discharged it upon me, Tommy, his target, but he pretends that he was always in possession of it, and made nothing of it,—that he imbibed it with mother's milk, —and that I, the wretched Tommy, am most abjectly behindhand in not having done the same. I ask, why is Tommy to be always the foil of Mr. Barlow to this extent? What Mr. Barlow had not the slightest notion of himself, a week ago, it surely cannot be any very heavy backsliding in me not to have at my fingers' ends to-day! And yet Mr. Barlow systematically carries it over me with a high hand, and will tauntingly ask me, in his articles, whether it is possible that I am not aware that every school-boy knows that the fourteenth turning on the left in the steppes of Russia will conduct to such and such a wandering tribe? with other disparaging questions of like nature. So, when Mr. Barlow addresses a letter to any journal as a volunteer correspondent (which I frequently find him doing), he will previously have gotten somebody to tell him some tremendous technicality, and will write in the coolest manner, "Now, sir, I may assume that every reader of your columns, possessing average information and intelligence, knows as well as I do that"— say that the draught from the touch-hole of a cannon of such a calibre bears such a proportion in the nicest fractions to the draught from the muzzle; or some equally familiar little fact. But whatever it is, be certain that it always tends to the exaltation of Mr. Barlow, and the depression of his enforced and enslaved pupil.

Mr. Barlow's knowledge of my own pursuits I find to be so profound, that my own knowledge of them becomes as nothing. Mr. Barlow (disguised and bearing a feigned name, but detected by me) has occasionally taught me, in a sonorous voice, from end to end of a long dinner-table, trifles that I took the liberty of teaching him five-and-twenty years ago. My closing article of impeachment against Mr. Barlow is, that he goes out to breakfast, goes out to dinner, goes out everywhere, high and low, and that he WILL preach to me, and that I CAN'T get rid of him. He makes me a Promethean Tommy, bound; and he is the vulture that gorges itself upon the liver of my uninstructed mind.

XXXV

ON AN AMATEUR BEAT

IT is one of my fancies, that even my idlest walk must always have its appointed destination. I set myself a task before I leave my lodging in Covent-garden on a street expedition, and should no more think of altering my route by the way, or turning back and leaving a part of it unachieved, than I should think of fraudulently violating an agreement entered into with somebody else. The other day, finding myself under this kind of obligation to proceed to Limehouse, I started punctually at noon, in compliance with the terms of the con-tract with myself to which my good faith was pledged.

On such an occasion, it is my habit to regard my walk as my beat, and myself as a higher sort of police-constable doing duty on the same. There is many a ruffian in the streets whom I mentally collar and clear out of them, who would see mighty little of London, I can tell him, if I could deal with him physically.

Issuing forth upon this very beat, and following with my eyes three hulking garrotters on their way home,—which home I could con-fidently swear to be within so many yards of Drury-lane, in such a narrow and restricted direction (though they live in their lodging quite as undisturbed as I in mine),—I went on duty with a considera-tion which I respectfully offer to the new Chief Commissioner,—in whom I thoroughly confide as a tried and efficient public servant. How often (thought I) have I been forced to swallow, in police-reports, the intolerable stereotyped pill of nonsense, how that the police-constable informed the worthy magistrate how that the associates of the prisoner did, at that present speaking, dwell in a street or court which no man dared go down, and how that the worthy magistrate had heard of the dark reputation of such street or court, and how that our readers would doubtless remember that it was always the same street or court which was thus edifyingly discoursed about, say once a fortnight.

Now, suppose that a Chief Commissioner sent round a circular to every division of police employed in London, requiring instantly the names in all districts of all such much-puffed streets or courts which no man durst go down; and suppose that in such circular he gave plain warning, "If those places really exist, they are a proof of police inefficiency which I mean to punish; and if they do not exist, but are a conventional fiction, then they are a proof of lazy tacit police connivance with professional crime, which I also mean to punish"—what then? Fictions or realities, could they survive the touchstone of this atom of common sense? To tell us in open court, until it has become as trite a feature of news as the great gooseberry, that a costly police-system such as was never before heard of, has left in London, in the days of steam and gas and photographs of thieves and electric telegraphs, the sanctuaries and stews of the Stuarts! Why, a parity of practice, in all departments, would bring back the Plague in two summers, and the Druids in a century!

Walking faster under my share of this public injury, I overturned a wretched little creature, who, clutching at the rags of a pair of trousers with one of its claws, and at its ragged hair with the other, pattered with bare feet over the muddy stones. I stopped to raise and succour this poor weeping wretch, and fifty like it, but of both sexes, were about me in a moment, begging, tumbling, fighting, clamour-ing, yelling, shivering in their nakedness and hunger. The piece of money I had put into the claw of the child I had overturned was clawed out of it, and was again clawed out of that wolfish gripe, and again out of that, and soon I had no notion in what part of the obscene scuffle in the mud, of rags and legs and arms and dirt, the money might be. In raising the child, I had drawn it aside out of the main thoroughfare, and this took place among some wooden hoardings and barriers and ruins of demolished buildings, hard by Temple Bar.

Unexpectedly, from among them emerged a genuine police constable, before whom the dreadful brood dispersed in various directions, he making feints and darts in this direction and in that, and catching nothing. When all were frightened away, he took off his hat, pulled out a handkerchief from it, wiped his heated brow, and restored the handkerchief and hat to their places, with the air of a man who had discharged a great moral duty,—as indeed he had, in doing what was set down for him. I looked at him, and I looked about at the disorderly traces in the mud, and I thought of the drops of rain and the footprints of an extinct creature, hoary ages upon ages old, that geologists have identified on the face of a clift; and this speculation came over me: If this mud could petrify at this moment, and could lie concealed here for ten thousand years, I wonder whether the race of men then to be our successors on the earth could, from these or any marks, by the utmost force of the human intellect, unassisted by tradition, deduce such an astounding inference as the existence of a polished state of society that bore with the public savagery of neglected children in the streets of its capital city, and was proud of its power by sea and land, and never used its power to seize and save them!

After this, when I came to the Old Bailey and glanced up it towards Newgate, I found that the prison had an inconsistent look. There seemed to be some unlucky inconsistency in the atmosphere that day; for though the proportions of St. Paul's Cathedral are very beautiful, it had an air of being somewhat out of drawing, in my eyes. I felt as though the cross were too high up, and perched upon the intervening golden ball too far away.

Facing eastward, I left behind me Smithfield and Old Bailey,— fire and faggot, condemned hold, public hanging, whipping through the city at the cart-tail, pillory, branding-iron, and other beautiful ancestral landmarks, which rude hands have rooted up, without bringing the stars quite down upon us as yet,—and went my way upon my beat, noting how oddly characteristic neighbourhoods are divided from one another, hereabout, as though by an invisible line across the way. Here shall cease the bankers and the money-changers; here shall begin the shipping interest and the nautical-instrument shops; here shall follow a scarcely perceptible flavouring of groceries and drugs; here shall come a strong infusion of butchers; now, small hosiers shall be in the ascendant; henceforth, everything exposed for sale shall have its ticketed price attached. All this as if specially ordered and appointed.

A single stride at Houndsditch Church, no wider than sufficed to cross the kennel at the bottom of the Canon-gate, which the debtors in Holyrood sanctuary were wont to relieve their minds by skipping over, as Scott relates, and standing in delightful daring of catchpoles on the free side,—a single stride, and everything is entirely changed in grain and character. West of the stride, a table, or a chest of drawers on sale, shall be of mahogany and French-polished; east of the stride, it shall be of deal, smeared with a cheap counterfeit resembling lip-salve. West of the stride, a penny loaf or bun shall be compact and self-contained; east of the stride, it shall be of a sprawling and splay-footed character, as seeking to make more of itself for the money. My beat lying round by Whitechapel Church, and the adjacent sugar-refineries,—great buildings, tier upon tier, that have the appearance of being nearly related to the dock-warehouses at Liverpool,—I turned off to my right, and, passing round the awkward corner on my left, came suddenly on an apparition familiar to London streets afar off.

What London peripatetic of these times has not seen the woman who has fallen forward, double, through some affection of the spine, and whose head has of late taken a turn to one side, so that it now droops over the back of one of her arms at about the wrist? Who does not know her staff, and her shawl, and her basket, as she gropes her way along, capable of seeing nothing but the pavement, never begging, never stopping, for ever going somewhere on no business? How does she live, whence does she come, whither does she go, and why? I mind the time when her yellow arms were naught but bone and parchment. Slight changes steal over her; for there is a shadowy suggestion of human skin on them now. The strand may be taken as the central point about which she revolves in a half-mile orbit. How comes she so far east as this? And coming back too! Having been how much farther? She is a rare spectacle in this neighbourhood. I receive intelligent information to this effect from a dog—a lopsided mongrel with a foolish tail, plodding along with his tail up, and his ears pricked, and displaying an amiable interest in the ways of his fellow-men,—if I may be allowed the expression. After pausing at a pork-shop, he is jogging eastward like myself, with a benevolent countenance and a watery mouth, as though musing on the many excellences of pork, when he beholds this doubled-up bundle approaching. He is not so much astonished at the bundle (though amazed by that), as the circumstance that it has within itself the means of locomotion. He stops, pricks his ears higher, makes a slight point, stares, utters a short, low growl, and glistens at the nose,—as I conceive with terror. The bundle continuing to approach, he backs, turns tail, and is about to fly, when, arguing with himself that flight is not becoming in a dog, he turns, and once more faces the advancing heap of clothes. After much hesitation, it occurs to him that there may be a face in it somewhere. Desperately resolving to undertake the adventure, and pursue the inquiry, he goes slowly up to the bundle, goes slowly round it, and coming at length upon the human countenance down there where never human countenance should be, gives a yelp of horror, and flies for the East India Docks.

Being now in the Commercial Road district of my beat, and bethinking myself that Stepney Station is near, I quicken my pace that I may turn out of the road at that point, and see how my small eastern star is shining.

The Children's Hospital, to which I gave that name, is in full force. All its beds are occupied. There is a new face on the bed where my pretty baby lay, and that sweet little child is now at rest for ever. Much kind sympathy has been here since my former visit, and it is good to see the walls profusely garnished with dolls. I wonder what Poodles may think of them, as they stretch out their arms above the beds, and stare, and display their splendid dresses. Poodles has a greater interest in the patients. I find him making the round of the beds, like a house-surgeon, attended by another dog,—a friend,— who appears to trot about with him in the character of his pupil dresser. Poodles is anxious to make me known to a pretty little girl looking wonderfully healthy, who had had a leg taken off for cancer of the knee. A difficult operation, Poodles intimates, wagging his tail on the counterpane, but perfectly successful, as you see, dear sir! The patient, patting Poodles, adds with a smile, "The leg was so much trouble to me, that I am glad it's gone." I never saw anything in doggery finer than the deportment of Poodles, when another little girl opens her mouth to show a peculiar enlargement of the tongue. Poodles (at that time on a table, to be on a level with the occasion) looks at the tongue (with his own sympathetically out) so very gravely and knowingly, that I feel inclined to put my hand in my waistcoat-pocket, and give him a guinea, wrapped in paper.

On my beat again, and close to Limehouse Church, its termination, I found myself near to certain "Lead-Mills." Struck by the name, which was fresh in my memory, and finding, on inquiry, that these same lead-mills were identified with those same lead-mills of which I made mention when I first visited the East London Children's Hospital and its neighbourhood as Uncommercial Traveller, I resolved to have a look at them.

Received by two very intelligent gentlemen, brothers, and partners with their father in the concern, and who testified every desire to show their works to me freely, I went over the lead-mills. The purport of such works is the conversion of pig-lead into white-lead. This conversion is brought about by the slow and gradual effecting of certain successive chemical changes in the lead itself. The processes are picturesque and interesting,—the most so, being the burying of the lead, at a certain stage of preparation, in pots, each pot containing a certain quantity of acid besides, and all the pots being buried in vast numbers, in layers, under tan, for some ten weeks.

Hopping up ladders, and across planks, and on elevated perches, until I was uncertain whether to liken myself to a bird or a bricklayer, I became conscious of standing on nothing particular, looking down into one of a series of large cocklofts, with the outer day peeping in through the chinks in the tiled roof above. A number of women were ascending to, and descending from, this cockloft, each carrying on the upward journey a pot of prepared lead and acid, for deposition under the smoking tan. When one layer of pots was completely filled, it was carefully covered in with planks, and those were carefully covered with tan again, and then another layer of pots was begun above; sufficient means of ventilation being preserved through wooden tubes. Going down into the cockloft then filling, I found the heat of the tan to be surprisingly great, and also the odour of the lead and acid to be not absolutely exquisite, though I believe not noxious at that stage. In other cocklofts, where the pots were being exhumed, the heat of the steaming tan was much greater, and the smell was penetrating and peculiar. There were cocklofts in all stages; full and empty, half filled and half emptied; strong, active women were clambering about them busily; and the whole thing had rather the air of the upper part of the house of some immensely rich old Turk, whose faithful seraglio were hiding his money because the sultan or the pasha was coming.

As is the case with most pulps or pigments, so in the instance of this white-lead, processes of stirring, separating, washing, grinding, rolling, and pressing succeed. Some of these are unquestionably inimical to health, the danger arising from inhalation of particles of lead, or from contact between the lead and the touch, or both. Against these dangers, I found good respirators provided (simply made of flannel and muslin, so as to be inexpensively renewed, and in some instances washed with scented soap), and gauntlet gloves, and loose gowns. Everywhere, there was as much fresh air as windows, well placed and opened, could possibly admit. And it was explained that the precaution of frequently changing the women employed in the worst parts of the work (a precaution originating in their own experience or apprehension of its ill effects) was found salutary. They had a mysterious and singular appearance, with the mouth and nose covered, and the loose gown on, and yet bore out the simile of the old Turk and the seraglio all the better for the disguise.

At last this vexed white-lead, having been buried and resuscitated, and heated and cooled and stirred, and separated and washed and ground, and rolled and pressed, is subjected to the action of intense fiery heat. A row of women, dressed as above described, stood, let us say, in a large stone bakehouse, passing on the baking-dishes as they were given out by the cooks, from hand to hand, into the ovens. The oven, or stove, cold as yet, looked as high as an ordinary house, and was full of men and women on temporary footholds, briskly passing up and stowing away the dishes. The door of another oven, or stove, about to be cooled and emptied, was opened from above, for the uncommercial countenance to peer down into. The uncommercial countenance withdrew itself, with expedition and a sense of suffocation, from the dull-glowing heat and the overpowering smell. On the whole, perhaps the going into these stoves to work, when they are freshly opened, may be the worst part of the occupation.

But I made it out to be indubitable that the owners of these lead-mills honestly and sedulously try to reduce the dangers of the occupation to the lowest point.

A washing-place is provided for the women (I thought there might have been more towels), and a room in which they hang their clothes, and take their meals, and where they have a good fire-range and fire, and a female attendant to help them, and to watch that they do not neglect the cleansing of their hands before touching their food. An experienced medical attendant is provided for them, and any premonitory symptoms of lead-poisoning are carefully treated. Their teapots and such things were set out on tables ready for their afternoon meal, when I saw their room; and it had a homely look. It is found that they bear the work much better than men: some few of them have been at it for years, and the great majority of those I observed were strong and active. On the other hand, it should be remembered that most of them are very capricious and irregular in their attendance.

American inventiveness would seem to indicate that before very long white-lead may be made entirely by machinery. The sooner, the better. In the meantime, I parted from my two frank conductors over the mills, by telling them that they had nothing there to be concealed, and nothing to be blamed for. As to the rest, the philosophy of the matter of lead-poisoning and workpeople seems to me to have been pretty fairly summed up by the Irishwoman whom I quoted in my former paper: "Some of them gets lead-pisoned soon, and some of them gets lead-pisoned later, and some, but not many, niver; and 'tis all according to the constitooshun, sur; and some constitooshuns is strong and some is weak."

Retracing my footsteps over my beat, I went off duty.

XXXVI

A FLY-LEAF IN A LIFE

ONCE upon a time (no matter when), I was engaged in a pursuit (no matter what), which could be transacted by myself alone; in which I could have no help; which imposed a constant strain on the attention, memory, observation, and physical powers; and which involved an almost fabulous amount of change of place and rapid railway travelling. I had followed this pursuit through an exceptionally trying winter in an always trying climate, and had resumed it in England after but a brief repose. Thus it came to be prolonged until, at length—and, as it seemed, all of a sudden—it so wore me out that I could not rely, with my usual cheerful confidence, upon myself to achieve the constantly recurring task, and began to feel (for the first time in my life) giddy, jarred, shaken, faint, uncertain of voice and sight and tread and touch, and dull of spirit. The medical advice I sought within a few hours, was given in two words: "instant rest." Being accustomed to observe myself as curiously as if I were another

The Uncommercial Traveller 763

man, and knowing the advice to meet my only need, I instantly halted in the pursuit of which I speak, and rested.

My intention was, to interpose, as it were, a fly-leaf in the book of my life, in which nothing should be written from without for a brief season of a few weeks. But some very singular experiences recorded themselves on this same fly-leaf, and I am going to relate them literally. I repeat the word: literally.

My first odd experience was of the remarkable coincidence between my case, in the general mind, and one Mr. Merdle's as I find it recorded in a work of fiction called LITTLE DORRIT. To be sure, Mr. Merdle was a swindler, forger, and thief, and my calling had been of a less harmful (and less remunerative) nature; but it was all one for that.

Here is Mr. Merdle's case:

"At first, he was dead of all the diseases that ever were known, and of several bran-new maladies invented with the speed of Light to meet the demand of the occasion. He had concealed a dropsy from infancy, he had inherited a large estate of water on the chest from his grandfather, he had had an operation performed upon him every morning of his life for eighteen years, he had been subject to the explosion of important veins in his body after the manner of fire-works, he had had something the matter with his lungs, he had had something the matter with his heart, he had had something the matter with his brain. Five hundred people who sat down to break-fast entirely uninformed on the whole subject, believed before they had done breakfast, that they privately and personally knew Physician to have said to Mr. Merdle, 'You must expect to go out some day, like the snuff of a candle;' and that they knew Mr. Merdle to have said to Physician, 'A man can die but once.' By about eleven o'clock in the forenoon, something the matter with the brain, became the favourite theory against the field; and by twelve the something had been distinctly ascertained to be 'Pressure.'

"Pressure was so entirely satisfactory to the public mind, and seemed to make every one so comfortable, that it might have lasted all day but for Bar's having taken the real state of the case into Court at half-past nine. Pressure, however, so far from being over-thrown by the discovery, became a greater favourite than ever. There was a general moralising upon Pressure, in every street. All the people who had tried to make money and had not been able to do it, said, There you were! You no sooner began to devote yourself to the pursuit of wealth, than you got Pressure. The idle people improved the occasion in a similar manner. See, they said, what you brought yourself to by work, work, work! You persisted in working, you overdid it, Pressure came on, and you were done for! This con-sideration was very potent in many quarters, but nowhere more so than among the young clerks and partners who had never been in the slightest danger of overdoing it. These, one and all declared, quite piously, that they hoped they would never forget the warning as long as they lived, and that their conduct might be so regulated as to keep off Pressure, and preserve them, a comfort to their friends, for many years."

Just my case—if I had only known it—when I was quietly basking in the sunshine in my Kentish meadow!

But while I so rested, thankfully recovering every hour, I had experiences more odd than this. I had experiences of spiritual conceit, for which, as giving me a new warning against that curse of mankind, I shall always feel grateful to the supposition that I was too far gone to protest against playing sick lion to any stray donkey with an itching hoof. All sorts of people seemed to become vicariously religious at my expense. I received the most uncompromising warning that I was a Heathen: on the conclusive authority of a field preacher, who, like the most of his ignorant and vain and daring class, could not construct a tolerable sentence in his native tongue or pen a fair letter. This inspired individual called me to order roundly, and knew in the freest and easiest way where I was going to, and what would become of me if I failed to fashion myself on his bright example, and was on terms of blasphemous confidence with the Heavenly Host. He was in the secrets of my heart, and in the lowest soundings of my soul—he!—and could read the depths of my nature better than his A B C, and could turn me inside out, like his own clammy glove. But what is far more extraordinary than this—for such dirty water as this could alone be drawn from such a shallow and muddy source—I found from the information of a beneficed clergyman, of whom I never heard and whom I never saw, that I had not, as I rather supposed I had, lived a life of some reading, contemplation, and inquiry; that I had not studied, as I rather supposed I had, to inculcate some Christian lessons in books; that I had never tried, as I rather supposed I had, to turn a child or two tenderly towards the knowledge and love of our Saviour; that I had never had, as I rather supposed I had had, departed friends, or stood beside open graves; but that I had lived a life of "uninterrupted prosperity," and that I needed this "check, overmuch," and that the way to turn it to account was to read these sermons and these poems, enclosed, and written and issued by my correspondent! I beg it may be understood that I relate facts of my own uncommercial experience and no vain imaginings. The documents in proof lie near my hand.

Another odd entry on the fly-leaf of a more entertaining character, was the wonderful persistency with which kind sympathisers assumed that I had injuriously coupled with the so suddenly relinquished pursuit, those personal habits of mine most obviously incompatible with it, and most plainly impossible of being maintained, along with it. As, all that exercise, all that cold bathing, all that wind and weather, all that uphill training—all that everything else, say, which is usually carried about by express trains in a portmanteau and hat-box, and partaken of under a flaming row of gas-lights, in the company of two thousand people. This assuming of a whole case against all fact and likelihood, struck me as particularly droll, and was an oddity of which I certainly had had no adequate experience in life until I turned that curious fly-leaf.

My old acquaintances the begging-letter writers came out on the fly-leaf, very piously indeed. They were glad, at such a serious crisis, to afford me another opportunity of sending that Post-office order. I needn't make it a pound, as previously insisted on; ten shillings might ease my mind. And Heaven forbid that they should refuse, at such an insignificant figure, to take a weight off the memory of an erring fellow-creature! One gentleman, of an artistic turn (and copiously illustrating the books of the Mendicity Society), thought it might soothe my conscience, in the tender respect of gifts misused, if I would immediately cash up in aid of his lowly talent for original design—as a specimen of which he enclosed me a work of art which I recognized as a tracing from a woodcut originally published in the late Mrs. Trollope's book on America, forty or fifty years ago. The number of people who were prepared to live long years after me, untiring benefactors to their species, for fifty pounds apiece down, was astonishing. Also, of those who wanted bank-notes for stiff penitential amounts, to give away:—not to keep, on any account.

Divers wonderful medicines and machines insinuated recommendations of themselves into the fly-leaf that was to have been so blank. It was specially observable that every prescriber, whether in a moral or physical direction, knew me thoroughly—knew me from head to heel, in and out, through and through, upside down. I was a glass piece of general property, and everybody was on the most surprisingly intimate terms with me. A few public institutions and complimentary perceptions of corners in my mind, of which, after considerable self-examination, I have not discovered any indication. Neat little printed forms were addressed to those corners, beginning with the words: "I give and bequeath."

Will it seem exaggerative to state my belief that the most honest, the most modest, and the least vain-glorious of all the records upon this strange fly-leaf, was a letter from the self-deceived discoverer of the recondite secret "how to live four or five hundred years"? Doubtless it will seem so, yet the statement is not exaggerative by any means, but is made in my serious and sincere conviction. With this, and with a laugh at the rest that shall not be cynical, I turn the Fly-leaf, and go on again.

CHAPTER XXXVII

A PLEA FOR TOTAL ABSTINENCE

ONE day this last Whitsuntide, at precisely eleven o'clock in the forenoon, there suddenly rode into the field of view commanded by the windows of my lodging an equestrian phenomenon. It was a fellow-creature on horseback, dressed in the absurdest manner. The fellow-creature wore high boots; some other (and much larger) fellow-creature's breeches, of a slack-baked doughy colour and a baggy form; a blue shirt, whereof the skirt, or tail, was puffily tucked into the waistband of the said breeches; no coat; a red shoulder-belt; and a demi-semi-military scarlet hat, with a feathered ornament in front, which, to the uninstructed human vision, had the appearance of a moulting shuttlecock. I laid down the newspaper with which I had been occupied, and surveyed the fellow-man in question with astonishment. Whether he had been sitting to any painter as a frontispiece for a new edition of " Sartor Resartus;" whether "the husk or shell of him," as the esteemed Herr Teufelsdroch might put it, were founded on a jockey, on a circus, on General Garibaldi, on cheap porcelain, on a toy shop, on Guy Fawkes, on waxwork, on gold-digging, on Bedlam, or on all,—were doubts that greatly exercised my mind. Meanwhile, my fellow-man stumbled and slided, excessively against his will, on the slippery stones of my Covent-garden street, and elicited shrieks from several sympathetic females, by convulsively restraining himself from pitching over his horse's head. In the very crisis of these evolutions, and indeed at the trying moment when his charger's tail was in a tobacconist's shop, and his head anywhere about town, this cavalier was joined by two similar portents, who, likewise stumbling and sliding, caused him to stumble and slide the more distressingly. At length this Gilpinian triumvirate effected a halt, and, looking northward, waved their three right hands as commanding unseen troops, to "Up, guards! and at 'em." Hereupon a brazen band burst forth, which caused them to be instantly bolted with to some remote spot of earth in the direction of the Surrey Hills.

Judging from these appearances that a procession was under way, I threw up my window, and, craning out, had the satisfaction of beholding it advancing along the streets. It was a Teetotal procession, as I learnt from its banners, and was long enough to consume twenty minutes in passing. There were a great number of children in it, some of them so very young in their mothers' arms as to be in the act of practically exemplifying their abstinence from fermented liquors, and attachment to an unintoxicating drink, while the procession defiled. The display was, on the whole, pleasant to see, as any good-humoured holiday assemblage of clean, cheerful, and well-conducted people should be. It was bright with ribbons, tinsel, and shoulder-belts, and abounded in flowers, as if those latter trophies had come up in profusion under much watering. The day being breezy, the insubordination of the large banners was very reprehensible. Each of these being borne aloft on two poles and stayed with some half-dozen lines, was carried, as polite books in the last century used to be written, by "various hands," and the anxiety expressed in the upturned faces of those officers,—something between the anxiety attendant on the balancing art, and that inseparable from the pastime of kite-flying, with a touch of the angler's quality in landing his scaly prey,—much impressed me. Suddenly, too, a banner would shiver in the wind, and go about in the most inconvenient manner. This always happened oftenest with such gorgeous standards as those representing a gentleman in black, corpulent with tea and water, in the laudable act of summarily reforming a family, feeble and pinched with beer. The gentleman in black distended by wind would then conduct himself with the most unbecoming levity, while the beery family, growing beerier, would frantically try to tear themselves away from his ministration. Some of the inscriptions accompanying the banners were of a highly determined character, as " We never, never will give up the temperance cause," with similar sound resolutions rather suggestive to the profane mind of Mrs. Micawber's "I never will desert Mr. Micawber," and of Mr. Micawber's retort, "Really, my dear, I am not aware that you were ever required by any human being to do anything of the sort."

At intervals, a gloom would fall on the passing members of the procession, for which I was at first unable to account. But this I discovered, after a little observation, to be occasioned by the coming on of the executioners,—the terrible official beings who were to make the speeches, by-and-by,—who were distributed in open carriages at various points of the cavalcade. A dark cloud and a sensation of dampness, as from many wet blankets, invariably preceded the rolling on of the dreadful cars containing these headsmen; and I noticed that the wretched people who closely followed them, and who were in a manner forced to contemplate their folded arms, complacent countenances, and threatening lips, were more overshadowed by the cloud and damp than those in front. Indeed, I perceived in some of these so moody an implacability towards the magnates of the scaffold, and so plain a desire to tear them limb from limb, that I would respectfully suggest to the managers the expediency of conveying the executioners to the scene of their dismal labours by unfrequented ways, and in closely-tilted carts, next Whitsuntide.

The procession was composed of a series of smaller processions, which had come together, each from its own metropolitan district. An infusion of allegory became perceptible when patriotic Peckham advanced. So I judged, from the circumstance of Peckham's unfurling a silken banner that fanned heaven and earth with the words, "The Peckham Lifeboat." No boat being in attendance, through life, in the likeness of "a gallant, gallant crew," in nautical uniform, followed the flag, I was led to meditate on the fact that Peckham is described by geographers as an inland settlement, with no larger or nearer shore-line than the towing-path of the Surrey Canal, on which stormy station I had been given to understand no lifeboat exists. Thus I deduced an allegorical meaning, and came to the conclusion, that if patriotic Peckham picked a peck of pickled poetry, this *was* the peck of pickled poetry which patriotic Peckham picked.

I have observed that the aggregate procession was on the whole pleasant to see. I made use of that qualified expression with a direct meaning, which I will now explain. It involves the title of this paper, and a little fair trying of teetotalism by its own tests. There were many people on foot, and many people in vehicles of various kinds. The former were pleasant to see, and the latter were not pleasant to see; for the reason that I never, on any occasion or under any circumstances, have beheld heavier overloading of horses than in this public show. Unless the imposition of a great van laden with from ten to twenty people on a single horse be a moderate tasking of the poor creature, then the temperate use of horses was immoderate and cruel. From the smallest and lightest horse to the largest and heaviest, there were many instances in which the beast of burden was so shamefully overladen, that the Society for the Prevention of Cruelty to Animals have frequently interposed in less gross cases.

Now, I have always held that there may be, and that there unquestionably is, such a thing as use without abuse, and that therefore the total abolitionists are irrational and wrong-headed. But the procession completely converted me. For so large a number of the people using draught-horses in it were so clearly unable to use them without abusing them, that I perceived total abstinence from horseflesh to be the only remedy of which the case admitted. As it is all one to teetotalers whether you take half a pint of beer or half a gallon, so it was all one here whether the beast of burden were a pony or a cart-horse. Indeed, my case had the special strength that the half-pint quadruped underwent as much suffering as the half-gallon quadruped. Moral: total abstinence from horseflesh through the whole length and breadth of the scale. This pledge will be in course of administration to all teetotal processionists, not pedestrians, at the publishing office of "All the Year Round," on the 1st day of April, 1870.

Observe a point for consideration. This procession comprised many persons in their gigs, broughams, tax-carts, barouches, chaises, and what not, who were merciful to the dumb beasts that drew them, and did not overcharge their strength. What is to be done with those unoffending persons? I will not run amuck and vilify and defame them, as teetotal tracts and platforms would most assuredly do, if the question were one of drinking instead of driving: I merely ask what is to be done with them! The reply admits of no dispute whatever. Manifestly, in strict accordance with teetotal doctrines, THEY must come in too, and take the total abstinence from horseflesh pledge. It is not pretended that those members of the procession misused certain auxiliaries which in most countries and all ages have been bestowed upon man for his use, but it is undeniable that other members of the procession did. Teetotal mathematics demonstrate that the less includes the greater; that the guilty include the innocent, the blind the seeing, the deaf the hearing, the dumb the speaking, the drunken the sober. If any of the moderate users of draught-cattle in question should deem that there is any gentle violence done to their reason by these elements of logic, they are invited to come out of the procession next Whitsuntide, and look at it from my window.

Made and Printed in Great Britain by
Hazell, Watson & Viney Ltd. London and Aylesbury